THREE COMPLETE NOVELS

DOMINICK DUNNE

THREE COMPLETE NOVELS

DOMINICK DUNNE

The Two Mrs. Grenvilles

People Like Us

An Inconvenient Woman

WINGS BOOKS
New York · Avenel, New Jersey

This omnibus was originally published in separate volumes under the titles:

The Two Mrs. Grenvilles, copyright © 1985 by Dominick Dunne.
People Like Us, copyright © 1988 by Dominick Dunne.
An Inconvenient Woman, copyright © 1990 by Dominick Dunne.

This 1994 edition is published by Wings Books,
distributed by Random House Value Publishing, Inc.,
40 Engelhard Avenue, Avenel, New Jersey 07001,
by arrangement with Crown Publishers, Inc.

Random House
New York • Toronto • London • Sydney • Auckland

Printed and bound in the United States of America

Library of Congress Cataloging-in-Publication Data

Dunne, Dominick.
    [Novels. Selections]
    Three complete novels / Dominick Dunne.
      p.   cm.
    Contents: The two Mrs. Grenvilles—People like us—An inconvenient woman.
    ISBN 0-517-11916-1
    1. City and town life—New York (N.Y.)—Fiction.   2. Upper class—New York
(N.Y.)—Fiction. I. Title.
PS3554.U492A6 1994
813'.54—dc20
                                     94-18339
                                     CIP

8   7   6   5   4   3   2   1

CONTENTS

THE TWO MRS. GRENVILLES

PEOPLE LIKE US

AN INCONVENIENT WOMAN

THE TWO
MRS.
GRENVILLES

For my son
Alexander Dunne

PART ONE

THE ROOM WAS filled with the heady scent of roses past their prime. Pink petals fell from swollen blossoms in a Chinese bowl onto the polished surface of an ormolu escritoire. Although it was day, rose-shaded lamps were lit, and curtains of the same hue, drawn for the night in voluminous folds, remained closed. The bed had been rested upon, but not slept in, its rose-colored linens still pristine and uncreased. A vermeil clock, unwound too long, had ceased to tick; a radio, left on too long, had lost its tonal focus.

Lying on the floor, face down on the rose border of an Aubusson rug, was a golden-haired woman in a satin-and-lace nightgown. She was dead. More than a day dead. Perhaps even two.

Had she been alive, she would have told you, whether you asked her or not, that the Chinese bowl had once belonged to Magda Lupescu; that the escritoire had once belonged to Marie Antoinette; that the vermeil clock had been given to the Empress Elizabeth of Austria by the mad King Ludwig of Bavaria; that the Aubusson rug was a gift of the Belgian court to the Empress Carlotta of Mexico. That they were ill-fated women was of less consequence to the deceased than the sense of luster she acquired when repeating the history of her possessions.

The dead woman's name was Ann Grenville. Leaning against a wall of her bedroom was the infamous portrait by Salvador Dali that had so deeply offended her on its completion years before. Long gone from sight, surprisingly present now, it stared out from its canvas at the rose-hued tableau, its knife-slash repaired, its prophecy fulfilled. Carnage had it promised. Carnage had it delivered.

HER OBITUARY, when it appeared, was not impressive. If you had not been reading about the defeat of the German Chancellor on page one of Section A of the *New York Times* that continued over on the next-to-last page of Section D, after the business news and stock market quotations, you might have missed it, for that was where it appeared. There was her name, Ann Grenville, with the word "Dead" after it, and then a few paragraphs, all easily missable.

On second thought, of course, the placement of Ann Grenville's obituary was probably exactly where Old Alice Grenville wanted it to be, and if she had called whatever Sulzberger was in charge of the *Times* and requested exactly that remote a placement in the paper for her daughter-in-law's obituary, no one who knew her would have been surprised. It would not have been her first call asking for considerations from the newspaper on behalf of her family. Exceedingly old, in her nineties, Alice Grenville, born one of the Pleydell triplets, was still running things in her family, and one thing she felt, and felt strongly about, was that her family had been far, far too much in the news.

The obituary said Ann Grenville had been found dead in her apartment on Fifth Avenue. It said she was the widow of sportsman William Grenville, Junior, the mother of Diantha Grenville, the daughter-in-law of Alice Grenville, the philanthropist and social figure. It said she had a history of heart ailments. It said she was fifty-seven years old. It said she had been cleared in 1955 of slaying her husband.

She wasn't fifty-seven at all, and hadn't been for three years, but her lie, if lie it could be called, was closer by far to the truth than the age she had given twenty years earlier, at the peak of her notoriety, when, at forty, she had claimed to be thirty-two.

"MRS. GRENVILLE. Mrs. Ann Grenville," called out a ship's steward, hitting the gong that he was carrying as he walked along the decks and through the public rooms. "Telephone for Mrs. Ann Grenville." Not a head turned at her paged name. Too many years had gone by. Not a soul on the ship remembered what *Life* magazine had called the shooting of the century.

A few years before her death I encountered her, for the first time in many years, aboard a steamship heading to Alaska. Long vanished from the social scene, she was, even on shipboard, a reclusive voyager. Unlike the Ann Grenville of yore, she was no longer the life of the party; rather she had resigned herself to the sidelines, not just of the party, but of life. I was transfixed. Her once beautiful face was ravaged a bit, perhaps by drink, and had acquired the similarity of surgically treated faces of women after middle age. Her slender splendid figure had widened some. Her golden hair seemed less lustrous.

And yet there was magic still. Perhaps it was magic for the memory of her, for the weeks of my youth when she had held center stage. Her clothes were expensive and simple. Her perfume filled the air around her. Her jewelry was mostly gold, except for a sapphire-and-diamond ring of a size and cut that looked as if it had been handed down for several generations in the same family. She read. She did needlepoint. She looked for hours at the coastline of Oregon and Washington, smoking cigarettes, inhaling deeply, dropping the butts into the sea. She spoke to no one.

"Not bad news, I hope," I said later, passing her deck chair.

"What's that?" she asked, as if she were being intruded upon.

Of course, I knew who she was, right from the beginning, even though I only said that she looked familiar, nothing more, when the man in the next deck chair, a Mr. Shortell from Tacoma, asked me if I knew anything about her. It is one of my traits that I least care for that I am very often a bundle of pertinent information about people I don't know, especially important people I don't know. But Ann Grenville I did know, although not as a friend. In the years when she was riding high as Mrs. William Grenville, Junior, and her name constantly appeared in Fydor Cassati's column in the *New York Journal American* and her pictures, photographed by Louise Dahl-Wolf and Horst, appeared in all the glossy magazines, our paths sometimes crossed in the dining rooms of New York. She resisted me. In fact, she never trusted me. I felt she thought I could see right through the performance that her life was, in the same way that Salvador Dali had seen right through her when he painted her picture.

"Your telephone call. I hope it wasn't bad news," I said.

She had developed a way of looking at you without connecting with you, the way film stars sometimes do to protect themselves from the curious, as if deciding whether to get into a conversation or not. It took the tragedy to give Ann and Billy Grenville the prominence accorded them in the social history of New York. During that time, the autumn of 1955, all of New York, and much of the country, and world, rocked with horrified impatience at each day's revelations in the Grenville case. What is so enticing as the rich and powerful in a criminal circumstance? Even the stately *New York Times* and the conservative *Herald Tribune* read like lurid scandal sheets. Except for it, Ann and Billy Grenville would have been nothing more than a rich and fashionable couple, both endowed with great looks, who dazzled for a time in the society of New York.

"It was, rather," she said finally. "Bad news, that is." Her voice was deep and rich and matched the look of her.

"I'm sorry," I said.

"My dog died in New York. That probably doesn't seem a bit serious to you, but I was incredibly devoted to her."

"I'm sorry."

She smiled faintly and went back to her book, indicating that the conversation was at an end. I returned to my deck chair.

Please do not think that I stalked her through the years, gathering information on her. I did not. But I did, even then, before it happened, occasionally make entries about her, and Billy too, in my journal.

From the festivities elsewhere aboard the ship, dance music was heard in our lonely corner of the deck. I noticed that her elegantly shod foot tapped to the beat. In that instant it was still possible to conceive of this middle-aged woman as young and beautiful, a show girl in headdress and feathers slithering across a nightclub stage, the mistress of rich men, the wife of a handsome American aristocrat, the hostess and social figure of an earlier decade, and, alas, the killer.

"Good legs," I said admiringly, omitting the word "still" that occurred to me.

She laughed a low throaty chuckle and raised her leg in the air to look at it, turning her foot one way and then the other. "Not bad," she agreed, admiring her limb, "for the golden years."

"The golden years," I repeated, laughing.

"Fuck the golden years," she said, bursting into laughter, letting me know in her tone that the highly praised charm of the golden years had escaped her completely.

It was how we started to talk. She didn't register surprise that I was there. She didn't mention the last time we had met, in St. Moritz, when I had affixed the nickname Bang-Bang to her, a nickname that stuck as a permanent appellation. She just accepted the situation. She hadn't talked to anyone for the whole trip and was ready to talk, and I hadn't talked to anyone for the whole trip, except Mr. Shortell from Tacoma, and I was ready to listen. We talked about books we were reading, plays we had seen, places we had been. We talked about people on the ship.

"What do you suppose he does, in the yellow T-shirt, pretending he's reading Proust?" she asked.

"How do you know he's pretending?"

"It's the sort of thing I used to do," she replied and laughed. She had beautiful teeth and a lovely mouth. "When I first married my husband, during the war, my mother-in-law tried to groom me into being a Grenville and gave me a list of fifty books to read, but I could never read Proust then, so I pretended to."

"The man in the yellow T-shirt is a Mr. Shortell from Tacoma. Not bad. He finds you fascinating. Would you like to meet him?"

"Oh, no. I tend to avoid new people."

"Why?"

"Everything works out well at first, and then, somehow, they find out my story. 'She's the woman who killed her husband,' someone tells them. And then they look at me differently and wonder about me. Alone is better." Then she changed the subject. "What's at the movies?"

"An oldie."

"Which one?"

Le Rouge et le Noir."

"Gérard Philipe. I never saw that," she said.

"Neither did I," I replied.

"Let's go."

It is a fact of my life that coincidences happen to me or things with thousand-to-one odds against happening happen. I didn't know, never having seen it before, that there was a scene in *Le Rouge et le Noir* in which a husband enters his wife's bedroom in the middle of the night, and the wife, mistaking him for someone else, shoots him. Imagine, with the devious plan I had up my sleeve, that I should be sitting with Ann Grenville in the ship's theater watching this scene.

Ann, with a hand on each arm of the theater seat, raised herself to almost standing height and, mesmerized, watched the scene. Then she lowered herself back into her seat when the scene was over. I did not know what to say, and said nothing, continuing to look straight ahead at the screen.

On the way back to our staterooms after the film, neither of us said anything for a bit, but I could not let the moment that had been provided for me pass without speaking.

"Would you ever talk about it, Ann?" I asked.

"Never," she replied.

"It might help if—"

"Never."

"But no one has ever heard your side."

"My husband's death was an accident, but no one believed me except for the grand jury. I know that people refer to me as 'the murderess.' I know that my children suffered."

"Sit here," I said, leading her to a bench on the deck.

"I made a deal with my mother-in-law that I would never discuss it, ever, ever. And I lived by that deal. Several times a year I was trotted out by the family, my sisters-in-law and my mother-in-law, and shown off at their parties. It beatified them in the eyes of New York for being so blessed to the tart who had married their brother and son and then killed him. There are people, I know, who say I was a hooker. I wasn't a hooker. Oh, yes, I took the occasional lizard bag from one of those dress manufacturers I used to go out with before I married Billy Grenville, with the implicit understanding, never stated, that there would be a hundred-dollar bill inside, way back in the forties when a hundred dollars was still a lot of money, but that was part of life in those days. What's so goddam wrong about wanting to do better for yourself in life? Would you want to live on that farm where I was born?"

"Do you want a drink?" I asked.

"Listen, Basil," she said, standing up and walking to the rail. "It's a mistake to try to get friendly with me."

"Oh?"

"I seem to have acquired the capacity to drive everyone away from me. Even my children." She made the motions of retreat, looking about for her bag and scarf and book. Those things found, she gave me her hand. "Well," she said, "so ends our night."

I didn't want her to go, but I didn't know how to keep her, other than not to release her hand. "You're a different person, Ann, from the Ann Grenville who—"

"—who necked with a Kraut in the bar of the Palace Hotel in St. Moritz a year after I killed my husband?" she asked, finishing my sentence for me in a way I had not intended to finish it. In the darkness I blushed and let go of her hand.

"You can't spend as much time alone as I have in the last few years and not arrive at some conclusions about yourself," she said, turning to leave, terminating our intimacy.

IT IS A FACT that even today, years after it happened, there are people you meet at New York dinner parties who can tell you, in vivid detail, the whole story of that October night in 1955, or at least the whole story as far as they know it, because no one knew the whole story except the two principal players, and one of those was shot dead and the other went to her grave without ever, not once, talking about it. Except to me.

Yes, I know that people say I killed Ann Grenville. Oh, not literally kill, as in "Bang Bang you're dead," but that I am responsible for the twenty-two Seconals and the pint and a half of vodka that she gulped them down with after reading a chapter from my novel that appeared in the magazine *Monsieur*. But I feel absolutely no responsibility whatsoever. I didn't call her Ann Grenville in my story. I called her Ann Hapgood. If she chose to think I was writing about her, that was her problem.

In the years when I was as famed in the media for my intimate, if platonic, friendships with some of the great ladies of New York, like Jeanne Twombley and Petal Wilson, neither of whom speak to me now, as I was for my exquisite little books, they told me things about Ann and Billy and the Grenville family that I would have had no way of knowing. Jeanne Twombley was the only one of the whole North Shore crowd who made any attempt to see Ann after it happened. She feels now that I betrayed her, but what did those ladies think when they whispered into my ear all the secrets of their world? After all, they knew I was a writer. You see, I have this ability to get people to talk to me. I don't even have to maneuver, very much, to make it happen. I listen beautifully. I laugh appreciatively. I never register shock or dismay at shocking or dismaying revelations, for that will invariably inhibit the teller of the tale.

On that damn ship, where I wish now I'd never seen her again, my own life was in a precarious state. It could even be said that I feared for it. Not that my life was in danger. It wasn't. At least not from criminal elements or terminal illness. What I feared was that the totality of it amounted to naught. Oh, the blazing moment here, the blazing moment there, of course, but too many wrong turns and different tacks along the way for it to be seriously considered by those concerned with such matters, and serious consideration was what I had always aspired to.

It was whispered more and more about me that drink and drugs and debauchery were interfering with my work, that I was throwing away my talent in drawing rooms playing the court jester, and in discotheques. The people who said these things let it be known that I was unable to complete what I had immodestly referred to as my masterwork when I appeared on television talk shows. Sometimes I called it a mosaic. Other times a collage. Or even a pastiche. In fiction, of course, depicting the thousand facets of my life that, when placed together, would present the whole of myself—mind, body, heart, and soul.

I was stung by their criticism. Trying to pick up the pieces of my wrecked life, I took to the sea to rethink my unfinished work. Ideas did not come. And then I saw her, Ann Grenville. A name from the past trying to pick up the pieces of *her* wrecked life. The idea began to form. So much had been written about her all those years ago. Was now not the time to tell her side of the story, to set the record straight? She, so much maligned, had never spoken in her own defense. We were there, on the same ship, and conversation would have to take place if a situation was manipulated. Yes, yes, yes, I admit that what I did was wrong, but I was helpless to resist the opportunity. I knew, I simply knew, that with time she would tell me, Basil Plant, what she had never told a living soul. I am the kind of person to whom people confess their secrets. It has always been so with me.

I, who can remember the commas in people's sentences, began to think back on Ann Grenville's story as I had heard it and read about it.

WHEN YOU LOOK at old photographs of Ann Grenville, at the yearling sales in Saratoga, for instance, sitting between the Ali Khan, with whom she was said to be having an affair, and Mrs. Whitney, of racing fame, or on safari in India, wearing huntress array from London, or at the de Cuevas ball in Biarritz, jeweled and haute-coutured, what you see is a woman at one with her world. Her world, however, was her husband's world. When she married Billy Grenville, during the war, she forsook any prior existence of her own and stepped, with sure foot, into her husband's exquisite existence.

Look for yourself at Mr. Malcolm Forbes's list of the richest people in America, and you will see how the wealth in our country has changed hands over the last thirty years. There isn't a Vanderbilt on the list. Even Babette Van Degan is not, nor are any of the people who appear in this tale. While those still alive continue to linger in the Social Register, except for poor Esme Bland in the loony bin, and Neddie Pavenstedt, who left Petal, and the bank, to run off with a television actor whom he later adopted, they are no longer considered rich by the rich today. But at the time of which I write, the Grenvilles were considered to be among the richest families in the land.

William Grenville, Junior, was used to many things, not the least of which was adoration. From his father. From his mother. And from the four sisters who preceded him into this world. It was never a spoken thing, but had he arrived earlier in the lineup of children, it is safe to say that there would have been fewer daughters. In a family like the Grenvilles, sons were the thing.

When he was born, he received a note from President Wilson welcoming him to the world, and, framed, it hung over all the beds of his life. The Grenvilles lived in a Stanford White French Renaissance mansion just off Fifth Avenue, across the street from old Mrs. Vanderbilt, next door to the Stuyvesant family home. Weekends were spent on a five-hundred-acre estate in Brookville, Long Island, summers in a cottage in Newport, following the annual sojourn to Europe.

It was a splendid life, and he emerged from it splendidly. His nanny, Templeton, and his tutor, Simon Fleet, and his dancing teacher, Mr. Dodsworth, were all enchanted with his sweetness, his shyness, and his exceedingly good manners. It was through Templeton, who had been nanny to his four sisters before him, that he acquired the precise manner of speaking that would distinguish his voice, for the rest of his life, from the voices of nearly everyone he encountered, except the few who were brought up in the exact manner that he was.

In time his father began to feel that he was too much adored and that the constant companionship of four sisters who could not get enough of holding him and passing him about among themselves might lead to a softness of character. He was sent to the same early school that his father had attended before him, expensive and spartan, in preparation for the great life and responsibilities that were to be passed on to him in time.

Indeed, there was a melancholy streak. He was fascinated reading about the two English princes who were beheaded in the Tower of London. It was a moment of history that he read over and over, and was always moved, often to tears. On an early trip to England, he was taken to the Tower on a guided tour, and a chill ran through him when he saw the room where they were held captive. He told his sister Cordelia, closest to him in age and spirit, that he felt he would die young.

In later years his most vivid memory of the New York house, where the family spent most of its time, was of the vast chandelier in the main hall. He was always to pass beneath it with trepidation and repeat the story to newcomers about what had happened on the eve of Rosamond's coming-out ball. Rosamond was his eldest sister, already fourteen when he was born, a distant and glamorous figure of his childhood who married an English lord at nineteen, a year after her ball, and moved away to London. The chandelier, quite inexplicably, crashed to the floor, killing the man who was cleaning it. Funeral expenses and generous recompense were provided rapidly and quietly, and it was agreed, among the household, that it be unmentioned so as not to cast a pall on the ball. It was his first experience of death; it was also his first experience of closing ranks. Much was to be expected of him. There was the bank, the Cambridge Bank of New York, founded by his grandfather, of which his father was president. There were the directorships of half a dozen big corporations. There were the Grenville racing stables, and the Grenville stud farm, twenty-five hundred acres in Kentucky, a vastly successful commercial enterprise, having produced three Kentucky Derby winners. It was for all these things, and more, that the young boy was being groomed.

At some point doubt began to stir within him. There was a quality beneath his elegant shyness that eluded happiness, a consciousness of his own limitations. When he thought about such things, which was not often, the fear was deep that he would have been a failure in the world if he were not an inheritor of such magnitude.

His father sensed his secret fears and dealt with them contemptuously so as to shame weakness out of him. At one point his father said about him, in front of him, and his sisters, and his mother, that he should have been a girl. It was not a thing his father meant. It was said, like a lot of things he said, in careless dismissal without thought of the psychic consequences. The wound to the young boy was devastating, made worse when his mother, whom he worshiped, failed to swoop him up, comfort him, and defend his gender. Nor did his sisters. None of them dared to contradict the head of the family.

"I don't like my father," said Junior one day.

"It's not so. It's not so," cried Alice. "You don't mean that."

"But I do," persisted the boy.

"No, you don't," insisted his mother.

He was never sure what he felt, because he was taught by the person he loved most, his mother, that what he felt wasn't so, that what she told him he felt or didn't feel was so. Her interpretation of his feelings conformed to the proprieties of their way of life.

Only Cordelia, the fourth daughter, the one closest in age to Junior, understood. And Bratsie; he understood.

IT IS OF NO significance to this story but of great significance to his character that Jellico Bleeker, or Bratsie, as he was known to one and all, except his mother, the partygiver Edith Bleeker, who loathed the nickname, that he had only four fingers on his right hand. He lost his index finger during a Fourth of July accident, when he was ten years old, holding on too long to a lit cherry bomb that he had been expressly forbidden to play with. On another occasion, a year or so later, he took one of the family sailboats from the house on Long Island, without supervision, or any real knowledge of sailing, and set sail for he knew not where. He was not missed until after darkness, and it was twelve hours before the Coast Guard, having nearly given up hope, spotted the small craft bobbing about aimlessly in Long Island Sound with the nearly frozen Bratsie safe and totally unconcerned about the drama he had caused. His smiling photographs in all the newspapers made him somewhat of a hero to his contemporaries, among them Junior Grenville, whose best friend he was.

The incident further confirmed Edith Bleeker's strong feeling that her untamed colt needed to be tamed, and she was going to do it. Life thereafter became for him a game of getting even with her. He accompanied his mother to a relation's society wedding and escorted her down the aisle wearing, unbeknownst to her, a yarmulke atop his head. He swung from a chandelier at Mr. Dodsworth's dancing class and was asked to leave and not return. He listed his mother's Pekinese, Rose, in the New York Social Register as Miss Rose Bleeker. He could imitate any limp or speech impediment with unerring accuracy, and did. He memorized the ritual of confession, although he was not a Catholic, and confessed elaborate sins to a shocked priest. He was the first of the boys in the group to smoke cigarettes, to sneak drinks, to masturbate, to get kicked out of school, to have sex with a prostitute, and to wreck the family car.

Bratsie Bleeker's accounts of his escapades kept the less adventuresome Junior Grenville rolling on the floor in uncontrolled laughter. Junior Grenville adored his friend. They were chauffeured back and forth between the Grenville house and the Bleeker house in the city and the Grenville estate in Brookville and the Bleeker estate in Glen Cove in the country.

In contrast to the tall and handsome Junior Grenville, Bratsie Bleeker was small and compact, fair-haired and always tanned. Five generations of Long Island Bleekers gave him a natural look of haughtiness and superiority, which he interrupted repeatedly with the beguiling and mischievous smile that was his own contribution to his looks. He contradicted his upper-class accent with lower-class words, and he had a way of snapping Junior Grenville out of his melancholy moods as no one else could do.

"You didn't have to explain that the fart on the elevator wasn't yours," said Bratsie one day after school. "No one said it was."

"I felt guilty," said Junior.

"Sometimes I think you don't know who you are," replied Bratsie.
"I don't," said Junior.

EXCEPT FOR BRATSIE, with whom he was at ease, the boys at Buckley found Junior Grenville aloof and uncommunicative and often joshed him for the elegant ways his family's life-style was manifested through him. It embarrassed Junior that he was driven the thirteen blocks to and from school each day in the family's Packard limousine, but it was a thing his father insisted upon. Junior would have preferred to be left on the corner of Seventy-third Street and Park Avenue and to walk to the entrance of the school, because he dreaded the razzing of the other boys, many of whom were allowed to walk, or even take the bus. He appealed to his mother in heartfelt tones to decrease the grandeur of his arrivals and departures, and the compromise that was reached was that his nanny, Templeton, not ride in the car with him, and that the chauffeur, Gibbs, not open the door for him so that he could scoot in and out of the limousine by himself.

On a Friday afternoon, when he was being picked up to go to the country for the weekend, he bade farewell to Bratsie Bleeker and hopped into the Packard. A man wearing a wide-brimmed hat that partially concealed his face appeared out of nowhere in the crowd of boys mingling on the street and followed Junior into the backseat of the car. For a moment the boy thought the man was a friend of the chauffeur's, and the chauffeur thought the man was a friend of the boy's. It was a well-planned maneuver.

The man pulled a gun and took hold of the terrified boy and directed the equally terrified Gibbs, whose name he knew, to proceed across Seventy-third Street to First Avenue and turn uptown, where, at a given point, there would be a rendezvous with the car of an accomplice. So expertly was it carried off that no one standing outside the school realized what had happened, even Bratsie, who had been standing there with Junior, and who would be jealous for years that the kidnapping had not happened to him.

At the corner of Seventy-fifth Street and First Avenue, Gibbs, old and nervous, ran a red light while reaching for the already-prepared ransom note that the kidnapper handed him, missing by inches a Gristede's truck crossing First Avenue. Amid shrieking brakes and angry horns, a police car took off in hot pursuit, red lights flashing and siren screaming, and flagged the limousine to the side of the avenue.

Maintaining his calm, the kidnapper stepped out of the limousine as unobtrusively as he had entered it, hailed a passing cab, stepped into it, and was gone, never to be seen again, before the police officer arrived at the chauffeur's door to deal with the privileged occupant who felt, the officer assumed, above the law in traffic matters. The only evidence of the six-minute drama, other than the weeping boy and frightened chauffeur, was the dropped ransom note.

"I hated it most when he touched me," said Junior.
"Touched you? How did he touch you?" asked his father.

"He held me by grabbing my blazer in the back."

"How did you feel?"

"I wanted to kill him."

A call was made by Alice Grenville to Mrs. Sulzberger, whose family owned the *New York Times*, asking that the newsworthy story not be used, and it was not. Bars were put on the windows of all the bedrooms in the Grenville house. For the rest of the school year, Junior was driven to school in the Chevrolet that was otherwise used for family shopping and transporting the servants to the country on weekends. The following fall he was sent off to Groton.

As a precautionary measure, so as not to waste time in a future emergency, packets of money, thousands and thousands of dollars in hundred-dollar bills, were placed in manila envelopes beneath the leather jewel cases in a wall safe behind a Constable painting of Salisbury Cathedral in Alice Grenville's bedroom. The money would sit there, untouched, for twenty-three years.

JUNIOR GRADUATED from Groton in 1938. All the family attended. His sisters thought he was the handsomest boy in his class, and he was. He would have graduated from Groton even if his father had not donated the new dormitory called Grenville House, but it did assure the certainty, as well as entrance to Harvard. Knowing that so much was expected of him, sometimes he froze in examinations, even when he knew the answers. His masters, which was what his teachers were called, and even Endicott Peabody, the headmaster, praised the young man's beautiful manners. He won no prizes, either academic or athletic, but he sang in the chapel choir, which pleased his mother, and acquired a passion for guns, which pleased his father. He said that in time he would like to shoot big game, tigers in India, and the exoticism of the desire appealed to the entire family's perception of son, brother, and heir to the name Grenville.

Europe was on the verge of war. A cross-country trip in Bratsie Bleeker's new car, a Cadillac convertible, planned with meticulous care by the two friends, was deemed inappropriate by William Grenville for his son. It was decided instead that Junior would spend the summer in New York with his father, training at the Cambridge Bank, and in Saratoga, attending the yearling sales. He complied, as he always complied. He confessed to Bratsie and to Cordelia that he was not seriously interested in banking, but he applied himself diligently to the work that was expected of him. Unlike his sister Grace, who could quote the pedigrees of a thousand horses off the top of her head and who knew the stallion register backward, he was not much interested in the business of racing either.

"Every time I look at my father, all that I ever see in his eyes is his disappointment with me," said Junior to Bratsie.

"That's the problem with being an only son," answered Bratsie. "Your life was mapped out for you the minute you were born. Buckley. Groton. Harvard. The bank. The horses. Marriage to a friend of one of your sisters in St. James'

Church with ten ushers in morning coats. An apartment on the Upper East Side. A house on the North Shore. And then another little Grenville for you to send to the same schools you went to, and it starts all over again."

"You too," said Junior.

"Oh, no, not me," said Bratsie. "They'll never get me."

"Me either," said Junior, but he didn't mean it.

"Balls, my friend," retorted Bratsie. "In a very few years every mother in New York with a marriageable daughter will be out to trap you."

What William Grenville wanted to do was to avoid for his son the inevitable pitfalls of a young man pampered from birth who would one day inherit a great fortune. For his daughters he would say, "Learn golf and learn bridge, or you'll have a very lonely old age," and leave the rest of their upbringing to Alice, but for his son his counsel was more exacting.

"Out there in this world," he told Junior, as Gibbs drove them uptown from Wall Street, "no one is going to feel sorry for your problems. They will say about you, no matter what befalls you, 'I wish I had his problems.' They will think that because you are rich the kind of problems you have are of little consequence."

"Do you remember Brenda Frazier?"

It was what Ann Grenville asked me, when finally we spoke, aboard the ship on the way to Alaska. Do I remember Brenda Frazier indeed! Who could forget Brenda Frazier? Poor sad Brenda. She had been, Ann told me, Billy Grenville's first girl friend, but I already knew that. At Edith Bleeker's party, on the night of the shooting, when Jeanne Twombley brought me along at the last minute when Alfred couldn't go, I was seated next to Brenda Frazier at dinner, and Billy Grenville was on her other side, so I heard about it straight from the horse's mouth.

In 1938 there probably wasn't a more famous woman in America than Brenda Frazier, and she was only seventeen years old and had accomplished absolutely nothing except being the most beautiful debutante of her time. Her picture appeared on the cover of *Life* magazine and people read more about her than any movie star in Hollywood. Her every step was chronicled in the society columns, and even the news pages, of every paper in the city.

In those days Billy Grenville was still called Junior. It was Ann who changed his name to Billy when she said she didn't want to be married to a man called Junior. Well, Junior met Brenda going through the receiving line at her coming-out party in the old Ritz-Carlton Hotel on Madison Avenue, which has long since been demolished. She was a beauty, and he was a knockout, and when he asked her to dance, people stepped back to watch, and all the photographers took their picture, and Maury Paul, the society columnist then called Cholly Knickerbocker, wrote that Brenda Frazier and Junior Grenville were the most beautiful young couple in New York.

Needless to say, Alice Grenville was not pleased. She had those four daughters, but Junior was the apple of her eye, and she had big marital plans for him when that time came. She felt that Brenda Frazier got much too much publicity and not nearly enough parental supervision. Alice Grenville was of the old school who believed that a lady's name appeared in the papers only three times—when she was born, when she married, and when she died—and Brenda Frazier, at least in New York, was a household word.

One day Brenda went to tea at that big gray pile of stone the Grenvilles used to live in, in the Eighties just off Fifth Avenue. It was Junior who asked his mother to invite her. All the sisters came too, just to stare at her. The sisters all had had their coming-out parties at home, in the family ballroom, with no press invited, and no outsiders on the list. They were all prepared to dislike her, but they couldn't. She was too nice, and they found her absolutely charming. Even Alice, who called her Miss Frazier throughout, liked her and could see the possibilities of her.

They saw each other for a while, but Junior was starting Harvard and not ready to think about anything serious. Along came a football player called Shipwreck Kelly and swept Brenda off her feet and into Catholic marriage in the Lady Chapel of St. Patrick's cathedral. Alice breathed a sigh of relief.

The thing about Brenda was, she and Billy stayed friends right up until the last day of his life. She was probably the last person he spoke to that night at Edith Bleeker's before he got into the fight with Ann.

"DO YOU REMEMBER Kay Kay Somerset?"

Ann Grenville asked me that too on the ship. She was Billy's second crush. Her life didn't turn out well, but in those days, she was pretty hot stuff, before all those marriages and the drink and the drugs took their toll. I once read in the columns about Kay Kay Somerset that she played tennis in white gloves so as not to coarsen her lovely hands, and she never played until after five when the rays of the sun ceased to burn. That was also about the time she was getting up.

Kay Kay was a very different cup of tea from Brenda and the Grenville sisters. She was very very rich; even rich people called her rich. The money came from spark plugs on her mother's side and a hydraulic drill used in the production of oil on her father's. Her kind of out-of-town money, no matter how much of it there was, never seemed the same to people like the Grenvilles as their kind of New York money. Remember, too, in those days, people were still concerned about family, as in bloodlines.

Kay Kay went to the very best schools, and came out at a party even more lavish than the lavish party of Brenda Frazier, under a tent lined with ice-blue satin at an estate in Southampton, marred only by Bratsie Bleeker's swinging from a chandelier while drinking champagne out of a bottle.

Kay Kay was not asked to join the Junior Assembly, as all the Grenville sisters were, and the flaw of it heightened her glamour in the eyes of Junior Grenville, on whom she had cast her eyes. "It would be a wonderful first marriage for you," said her mother, the spark-plug heiress, a remark unheard by Alice Grenville but nonetheless sensed by her.

William Grenville was disinclined to interfere in Junior's affairs of the heart, being secretly pleased that his early fears of other inclinations were unfounded. However, when Junior announced to his astonished family that he would leave the day after Christmas for a cruise in Caribbean waters on a hundred-and-eighty-foot yacht made available to Kay Kay by her indulgent father, it was felt that the time was at hand to break off the incipient romance.

His father forbade him to go. Junior, accommodating always, did not accommodate. Suppressed wrath surfaced instead; a litany of remembered disappointments poured out. Shocked by the unexpected outburst, William Grenville remained implacable. Bratsie Bleeker, in a similar outburst with his mother, ran off and joined the Royal Canadian Air Force. Junior Grenville threatened to do the same. On the day following Christmas, he left for Palm Beach, where he joined Kay Kay Somerset and her party on the yacht called *Kay Kay.* He did not feel triumphant in his victory.

Shortly thereafter, certainly unrelatedly, William Grenville suffered an aneurism of the aorta, a bursting of the main blood vessel to the heart. The Packard, with Gibbs at the wheel, awaited him at the front of the house to drive him downtown and to the business day. When he had not appeared at nine minutes after eight, Gibbs went to the front door and informed Cahill, the butler. He was found by Cahill in his bathroom, to which he had repaired, as was his habit, with the *Times* and the *Wall Street Journal,* after his breakfast.

Alice Grenville, who would achieve personal fulfillment in widowhood, telephoned the home of the Somersets in Palm Beach and asked Arthur Somerset to contact the yacht, wherever it was, and have Junior call his home in New York. Within several hours a call came from Junior in Barbados. "He is dying," said his mother. "You must come right away, to speak to him." She understood the never-reconciled chasm between son and father.

But it was not to happen. He stood in the hospital room of Bleeker Pavilion at New York Hospital, with his weeping mother and weeping sisters, and watched the expiration of a man who did not want to expire. When he felt nothing but relief that his days of disappointing were over, he simulated grief, for appearance's sake, for grief was the order of the day.

The casket was open and set up in the reception room off the main hall. Over the mantelpiece was a large portrait of three young ladies in long white dresses poised in elegant comfort among the cushions of an immense green sofa. They were the Pleydell triplets, painted by John Singer Sargent nearly forty years before. Alice Pleydell was on the right. The legend was that William Grenville had fallen in love with the face in the picture, pursued her, and won her.

Alice, and Junior, and the four sisters stood in front of the mantelpiece and received the hundreds of mourners who passed through their house: the banking world, the racing world, the membership of his nine clubs, the part of New York society in which they moved, and the friends of Alice, and Rosamond, and Felicity, and Grace, and Cordelia, and Junior. The smell of flowers was oppressive. Outside it was raining.

And then Bratsie Bleeker arrived, unexpectedly, in his Royal Canadian Air Force uniform, waiting his turn in line, behind Archie Suydem, the family doctor, ahead of Edith Bleeker, his own mother. "Let's get out of here," he said to Junior after making his amenities to the family. "Where?" asked Junior. "Wherever," said Bratsie.

Outside was Bratsie's Cadillac convertible, its bright-yellow color glaringly inappropriate for the circumstance, between limousines with umbrella-carrying chauffeurs helping elderly people in and out of the huge Grenville house. They entered Central Park at Seventy-second Street and sped across in silence. Junior was lost in thought, believing, even in death, that the disapproving eyes of his father were upon him.

At a red light on Central Park West, three toughs eyeing the young swells raised their thumbs in the hitchhiking position. "We're only kids and we have a Cadillac," screamed Bratsie at them, gunning the car and speeding off, breaking the gloom within. As always, Junior was Bratsie's best audience and screamed with shocked laughter.

"Let me ask you something, Junior," said Bratsie.

"What's that?" asked Junior.

"The truth," stipulated Bratsie.

"The truth," agreed Junior.

"Have you ever been laid?"

"Bratsie!"

"The truth."

"No."

"That's what I thought."

"What's this all about?"

"I am about to introduce you to the establishment of Miss Winifred Plegg, also known as Bootsie, on West End Avenue and Ninety-first Street."

"Tonight?"

"It's the perfect time."

THE GRENVILLES were not the kind of people who cried at funerals. To remain stoic in adversity was, like honesty, a trait learned early. At William Grenville's funeral at St. James' Church and the burial in the family plot at Woodlawn Cemetery, with Dr. Kinsolving in attendance, William Grenville, Junior, stood, stalwart, by his mother's side, his long elegant hands holding her arm, guiding her through the rituals of the long day with nothing in his demeanor to divulge the debauchery of the night before at the establishment of Miss Winifred Plegg on West End Avenue.

Junior Grenville was much admired, and it was whispered from pew to pew that he would be, after Harvard and the war, a worthy successor to the positions and responsibilities of his father. When, at the graveside, his eyes fell on the Caribbean-tanned Kay Kay Somerset, he felt a deep disinclination toward her, as if his single act of disobedience, over her, might have caused the burst blood vessel that ended his father's life.

William Grenville left his large estate in perfect order, so there would be no lessening of grandeur in scale of living for any of his descendants during their lifetimes. His daughters, already married rich, became independently rich. His widow, Alice, received all the houses outright to do with as she wanted, with the fervent hope expressed that the vast structure off Fifth Avenue, which he had built, would continue to be lived in by her for her lifetime and then, dynastically, be passed on to Junior so that he could raise his own family, when that time came, in the house in which he had been raised. Alice, who understood money, got the main bulk of the fortune, with it, in turn, to be passed on to Junior when she died. Junior himself received ten million dollars, a vast sum in that preinflationary decade, making him one of the wealthiest young men in the country.

Life resumed, after the mourning period, in the Grenville houses in New York and Long Island and Newport. Alice's children would have been surprised to know that their mother felt released by her widowhood. Slowly the strictures imposed on all their lives by William Grenville abated, and, despite the impending war, laughter was heard again in the huge houses where they lived. Alice, freed from the constant entertaining of bankers and horse breeders that had made up her husband's life, enjoyed more and more the companionship of her children and her friends, and parties and concerts filled the houses.

It was inevitable that when the war actually came Bratsie Bleeker would be the first to enlist, transferring from the Royal Canadian Air Force, and the first to distinguish himself in combat, where his natural bent for recklessness was often mistaken for bravery.

Junior Grenville could not wait to follow suit, but he promised his mother that he would finish Harvard first. He did, spending most weekends in New York enjoying the renewed adoration of his four sisters. Immediately upon graduation he enlisted in the Navy and entered Officers Training School, from which he graduated as an ensign.

On February 19, 1943, Ann Grenville, who was then called Ann Arden, and before that had been called Urse Mertens, walked into the life of Ensign William Grenville, Junior.

"GLAMOROUS" was more the word than "beautiful" that applied to her. She had a bright glow about her, and there was an interplay between her lovely blue eyes and glossy red mouth that captured you with its seductiveness. From the age of twelve she knew, even before she really knew, that she could wrap men around her little finger, an expression her mother was fond of using.

She was at this time a show girl by night and a radio actress by day. Although she was voted the most beautiful girl in radio, it was as a show girl that she was magnificent. Elaborately costumed in sequins and feathers and giant headdress, she held her arms aloft and beautifully presented her beautiful body as she glided across the stage of a Broadway musical behind the star, Miss Ethel Merman. Her most ardent admirer would not have called her talented, as either a singer or a dancer, but she possessed something that called attention to herself—there was amusement in her eyes and a private smile on her lips—and men followed her every movement across the stage, ignoring the other girls in the line. And of all the girls in the line, she was the most sought-after, and her nights, after the show, were spent with the kind of men who took chorus girls to nightclubs, and whose names occasionally appeared in Broadway columns. There was always the hope of being discovered by a talent scout from Hollywood, and the possibility of movie stardom was a dream that she cherished.

Sometimes it terrified her that her life was advancing, had advanced, in fact, and she had not achieved her potential. Young still, she had already begun to lie about her age to make herself younger. It was when she was looking into a mirror, applying powder and colors to her face, that she confronted herself. She was not a star; she was not going to be a star. Adele Jurgins, with whom she had danced in the line at Fefe's Monte Carlo, had gone on to Hollywood and was starring in films at Republic, and Babette Lesniak, with whom she had danced in the line at the Copacabana, well, everyone knew what had happened to Babette, or, at least, everyone who read the tabloids knew what wonders had come to Babette. Perhaps, she thought, this is not what I am supposed to be doing. Perhaps this is not it, after all.

Overdrawn at the bank again, rent looming, fighting off feelings of despair, she dressed and went to El Morocco. You never know what's going to happen, she thought to herself. Tonight I might meet the man who is going to change my life.

She was with the Argentinian playboy Arturo de Castro. She thought he was the best dancer in New York, and she told her best friend, Babette Van Degan, that the Latin beat was in his blood. She loved to dance and knew that people looked at her when she and Arturo took to the floor, but she realized, before he told her, that he was about to kiss her off. She had read in Cholly Knickerbocker's column that he was seeing a Standard Oil heiress, and she knew that the affair would be winding down and that her days were numbered. She fought down the rage of rejection that was within her, determined that she would not make a scene at El Morocco. She concentrated instead on a white fox jacket he had seen her admire in the window of Saks and hoped he would at least give her that when the end came.

She loved El Morocco, with its white palm trees and blue-and-white zebra-striped banquettes, and could never stop looking around her at the other tables and the other people on the dance floor.

She had a habit of singing into the ear of the man she was dancing with in her deep throaty voice:

> *"Dear, when you smiled at me,*
> *I heard a melody*
> *that haunted me from the start.*
> *Something inside of me*
> *started a symphony.*
> *Zing went the strings of my heart!"*

At that instant zing went the strings of her heart.

"Who's that?" asked Ann.

"Who's who?" asked Arturo back.

She had spotted him over Arturo's shoulder when he entered. She didn't know who he was, but she knew right away that he was more than just a handsome naval officer on leave. Johnny Perona himself was on the door that night, and Johnny Perona greeted Junior Grenville with the deference he usually reserved for Alfred Vanderbilt and Gary Cooper and the Rockefeller brothers.

"That ensign saying hello to Brenda Frazier," answered Ann, refraining from saying the one with the beautiful teeth and the beautiful smile.

"Where's Brenda? I don't see Brenda," answered Arturo.

She had an instinct for quality. It went beyond looks and clothes; she could spot it even in nakedness. When she squeezed past the ensign on her way to the ladies' room and said, "Excuse me," in a teasing but somehow intimate tone, he noticed her for the first time. She was wearing a black satin dress cut low. Her looks brought pleasure to his eyes, and he feasted on them for the moment of passage. The thing that he noticed about her, that he would always notice about her, even when he was long used to her, was her breasts. He was alone, having come from one of his mother's parties, having slipped out during Madam Novotna's musicale. He was standing in the same place when she came back from the ladies' room.

"We have to stop meeting like this," she said to him as she squeezed past him the second time. She laughed at her own joke, and he joined in the laughter, and the contact was made.

"I'm Junior Grenville," he said.

"I'm Ann Arden," she replied.

"Hello, Ann."

"Hi, Junior."

There was a moment of stillness amid the racket of the packed nightclub as they looked at each other.

"Junior, are you going to join us?" called out Brenda Frazier.

"In a minute, Brenda," he called back.

Ann's heart was beating very fast. It astonished her that anyone would not leap at the chance to sit at the table of the beautiful Brenda Frazier.

"I should be getting back," said Ann.

Later, when she was dancing with Arturo again, not singing into his ear this time, Ensign Grenville cut in on the dance floor, tapping Arturo heavily on the shoulder. Arturo turned around to the tapper.

"May I?" asked Junior, holding out his hands.

"See here, Lieutenant," said Arturo, annoyed.

"Ensign," corrected Junior.

"This sort of thing is just not done here at El Morocco. Save it for the proms back at the base." He turned back to Ann to resume his fox-trot.

"Oh," said Ann, gleeful at the possibility of a scene. "Get into a fight over me, why don't you? Let's have pictures in all the papers! Finally I'll get a screen test."

Arturo, furious, walked off the dance floor. "I'll be at the table," he said, not pleasantly, over his shoulder.

Ann and Junior stood on the dance floor looking at each other for a moment, and smiled.

"It was just one of those things," she started to sing. She held her arms out and he stepped in to dance with her.

> *"Just one of those fabulous things,*
> *A trip to the moon on gossamer wings,*
> *Just one of those things."*

He told her he liked her voice more than Libby Holman's, and Libby Holman had been his favorite singer. She moved in closer to him.

"I suppose it would be impossible for you to extricate yourself from whoever that is you're with?" he stated as a question.

"And do what?" she asked.

"Leave here with me," he answered.

She liked his precise manner of speaking. It was a voice peculiar to a tiny portion of the Upper East Side of New York City and the North Shore of Long Island.

"No," she replied. "That wouldn't be impossible at all. Meet me at the front door."

HER BEDROOM was in morning disarray. Her fastidiousness did not begin until later in the day. Stockings and underwear were strewn where they fell, and chairs were smothered with clothes and towels. From the bathroom came the sound of the shower stopping; it awakened her, although she was not used to awakening until noon.

Through mostly closed eyes she watched him dress. She liked the look of him in undershorts and shirtsleeves—shaved, bathed, combed—tying his tie in front of her mirror, completely concentrated. She wished she hadn't sat on his face on the first date, but she always got carried away with the rich boys, the old-money boys, not the new-rich ones you met around the stage door, but the ones who had that look that comes from generations of breeding, and that speaking voice that identified them all to each other. On top of that, Ensign Grenville was without doubt the handsomest boy she had ever seen. She longed to know who he was.

All of a sudden Arturo de Castro, who she had thought was so divine for so long, looked like a greaseball to her, even if he was, as Babette Van Degan had told her, from one of the oldest families in Argentina. She felt, suddenly, patriotic that the good old U.S.A. had produced a specimen of aristocracy that was right up there with the best that England had to offer with all their dukes and earls, and, of course, their king, or, rather, their ex-king. Her mother, lately departed, always called him the catch of catches, and the lady who landed him, Mrs. Simpson, now the Duchess of Windsor, was the woman she, and her mother, admired more than any woman alive.

She supposed she shouldn't pray for such things, but she prayed that Ensign Grenville wouldn't think that she sat on the face of every man she went out with, especially the first time. It was just that he was so beautiful, and young, and well-built, but also so totally inexperienced that she had inadvertently assumed the role of teacher, and her passions, which were abundant, had simply run away with her. Even at the moment of climax, he had retained his wonderful accent, and that, more than anything else, brought her to new heights of desire.

She stared at his profile as he finished his tie and went looking for his shoes. She surprised herself as she heard herself say, in her first words of the day, "I like to see a man's shoes in my closet."

She saw his shirttail stand out in excitement at what she had said. He blushed; she liked his shyness. Watching him, she lit a Camel. She lipsticked the tip, inhaled deeply, and held it, and when she exhaled allowed some of the smoke to escape up her nose.

"Come over here," she said, "and let me get a good look at that in the daylight." She remembered from last night that her rough talk thrilled him. He walked over to her, and she reached into the opening of his shorts. "It's really lovely," she said. "I could be awfully happy with this for a while. How long's your leave?"

She didn't wait for an answer. Her mind was on other things. As he lunged for her hungrily, she said, "No. No, stand back. This one's on me." She pulled his shorts down his legs and knelt on the floor in front of him. She didn't know if she should let him see how good at it she really was.

Looking down, he was mesmerized watching her, still holding her Camel. He thought he had never seen such a beautiful woman. He knew he had never seen such beautiful breasts.

"You're much too quick, you know," she said afterward. "Speed is *not* of the essence. I'm going to enjoy teaching you. How long did you say your leave was?"

ENSIGN GRENVILLE could not get enough of Ann Arden. Everything about her fascinated him. The ashtrays in her apartment were from the Stork Club, and her refrigerator was filled with splits of champagne, wilted gardenias, and doggie bags from El Morocco. V-letters from captains and lieutenants in far-off places vanished from her desk top after his first night with her, and 8-by-10 glossy pictures taken in nightclubs with a variety of men disappeared from the walls of her bathroom. She had records of all the show tunes and knew every lyric to every song.

Each noon he met her in the lobby of the Plaza Hotel, or the St. Regis Hotel, or the old Ritz-Carlton Hotel, and they ordered martinis, and ate lobster salad, and stared into each other's eyes. Each night, to the consternation of his mother and sisters, who wanted to show him off so splendidly uniformed, he sat, transfixed, in the Music Box Theater and watched Ann descend a silver stairway and sidle across the stage, as if there were not another person on it. He was consumed with curiosity about her radio career and listened avidly to each daily episode of "Marge Minturn, Girl Intern," in which she played Marge's best friend, thrilling him with the sound of her deep actressy voice. She talked of Chet Marx, her agent, and her hopes of a screen test, and the possibility of a meeting with Humphrey Bogart.

He did not withhold information about himself, but he did not thrust his suitability at her either. Of the two of them, he found her to be the stellar attraction; everything about her was new to him. Once aware of the possibilities of him, beyond his good looks and beautiful manners, she asked the pertinent questions impertinently, and bits and pieces of his story came out.

"Where did you go to school?" she asked him.

"Just the usual places," he answered, and when she looked at him, he went on, "Buckley, Groton, and Harvard."

"Oh," she answered over her rush of pleasure.

"Not exactly expanded horizons, is that what you mean?" he asked, fearing she thought it was too conventional.

"No, that wasn't what I meant at all," she replied.

She knew he was someone very swell, but as with all very swell people, there were no hints forthcoming. Finding out would be up to her. It was after he told her about the near kidnapping that she decided to pay a visit to her old friend Babette Van Degan, and check out, as Babette would say, the lay of the land. She took a Madison Avenue bus from Murray Hill, where she lived in a tiny penthouse, to Sixty-seventh Street, and walked over to the Park Avenue apartment where Babette lived. Babette was everything that Ann wanted to be.

She had started out life as Barbara, then Baby, then Babette Lesniak, somewhere in the middle of a large Lithuanian family in Willimantic, Connecticut, where her father was a milkman. She left home early and made for New York, where she somehow ended up as a show girl at the Copacabana nightclub. She had no theatrical ambitions whatsoever and no real aim; she simply waited for life to happen to her and rolled with whatever did, all with life-of-the-party good humor. Her luck was astonishing. Dickie Van Degan, the stupidest of the very rich Van Degan brothers, swooped her up in a whirlwind romance and eloped with her to Elkton, Maryland, a marriage that captivated readers of the tabloid press for its Cinderella theme. With no guile on her part, simply forgetfulness, she became instantly pregnant. By the time the marriage ended a year and a half after it began, to the intense relief of all the Van Degans, she was the possessor of not only the first Van Degan heir but the largest divorce settlement in the history of New York. Since her great good fortune, she became a meticulous reader of all things financial and read the stock market quotations with the same enthusiasm that she had once read the gossip columns. In time her divorce settlement would double, treble, and, perhaps, quadruple under her uncanny ministrations.

Babette claimed that she knew Ann before anyone else in New York knew Ann, and she was very nearly correct. She was one of the very few in Ann's life who overlapped from one phase to another, and she was probably the only one in New York who ever knew Ann's mother. Unlike Ann, who never looked back, or remembered back, Babette was a great one for reminiscence. "There was a guy around New York in those days called Chet Marx," she once said. "He called me up one day and said, 'Babette, I need a black dress and a pair of size six shoes,' and I said, 'Chet, what the hell do you need with a black dress and a pair of size six shoes? You're not going nelly on me, are you?' And Chet says, 'You of all people ought to know me better than that, Babette.' We had a good laugh over that one. He told me there was a new girl in town, and he got her an audition for the Copa, and she didn't have a thing to wear. So I took the dress and shoes over to Chet's place, where she was staying, and that's how I met Ann."

Babette's Park Avenue apartment was big and sloppy; the few pieces of Van Degan furniture were lost amid the more florid examples of her own imperfect taste, and the rooms were littered with her son's toys. Her poodle, Phydeaux, had untidy habits, and her maids sometimes didn't wear uniforms, but there was about the place a pleasant and relaxed atmosphere.

When Ann entered Babette's bedroom, she found her friend sitting up in bed, breakfast tray in front of her, grumbling over the *Wall Street Journal.* "Ann," she said, looking up, "what brings you out at this hour of the morning?"

"Are those sheets yellow satin?" asked Ann.

"Yes," said Babette, caressing the satin against her. "I bet you don't know who said yellow satin can console one for all the miseries of life." She buttered her corn muffin, using her index finger as a knife and then licking the finger.

"Some queen," asked Ann, not interested in literary talk, impatient to get on with the business at hand.

"It was Oscar Wilde," said Babette grandly.

"That's what I said, some queen," replied Ann. Their conversations were bawdy and their language blue, and they always laughed at each other's vulgarities. "Now listen, Babette. I'm here on important business. I need some information on somebody I've met."

"What do you want to know?"

"If he's the real turtle soup, or merely the mock."

"Look him up in the Social Register."

"Do you have one?"

"My husband got kicked out of the Social Register when he married me and was promptly reinstated when he divorced me, so it's not a book I happen to have lying around."

"How, then?"

"Who is it?"

"His name is Junior Grenville."

"William Grenville?"

"Junior."

"Oh, my God! Millions."

"What?"

"You heard me. Millions."

"Do you know him?"

"No, but the Grenvilles are right up there with the Van Degans. The old boy was quite dashing. I saw him at the track once. He cut quite a figure in racing circles, flower-in-the-buttonhole, that kind of look. Courtly manners, but only with his own crowd. Terrible snob otherwise. Mrs. Grenville has the same table at the Colony every day for lunch. What's he like, this Junior? Is he good-looking?"

"Very."

"Are you in love?" asked Babette.

"I'm in physical attraction," replied Ann.

"What is it you notice first about a man?" asked Babette. It was the sort of conversation she liked best, and she settled in for a long chat with her friend.

Babette was several years senior to Ann, but they were not women who discussed their age, even with each other; they simply allowed the older woman/younger woman relationship to occur.

"His hands," replied Ann.

"Hands!" exclaimed Babette. "What an odd thing to notice first."

"I can't *bear* small hands on a man."

"Why even think about them?" asked Babette.

"You know what they say, don't you?"

"What do they say?"

"Small hands, small dick."

"I never heard that," said Babette, screaming with laughter.

"And by the same token, large hands, large, uh, need I go on?"

"Dickie Van Degan had small hands," said Babette, captivated by the conversation. "As a matter of fact, Dickie Van Degan had a small dick too, now that I think about it. What kind of hands does Junior Grenville have?"

"Large, darling," replied Ann, stretching luxuriously.

"Have you, uh—"

"Yes."

"Is he a good lover, then?"

"Not yet."

"Those swell families, you know. Prep-school sex. Slam, bam, thank you, ma'am."

"When I kissed him the first time, he held his lips together, and I could feel his teeth pressing against my mouth."

"Not one of the great feelings."

"No. But you know, he's just waiting to be taught."

"Knowing you, you probably sat on his face on the first date, and he probably thought he'd died and gone to heaven." They screamed with laughter again. "Am I right?"

"Something like that," conceded Ann.

Babette told her to look up the Grenvilles in the Social Register at the Rhinelander Florist on the corner of Madison Avenue and Seventy-second Street. She saw that Junior's mother's name was Alice Pleydell Grenville, and that he had four sisters named Rosamond, and Felicity, and Grace, and Cordelia. There were other abbreviated things that she could not understand, and the addresses and telephone numbers of the house in New York, and the house on Long Island, and the summer residence in Newport. Her heart began to beat faster. She felt that the florist was watching her, which he was not, and ordered flowers, a half-dozen roses, to be sent to Mrs. Babette Van Degan.

She walked fourteen blocks up Madison Avenue until she came to the street where the address was that she had memorized and turned left toward Fifth Avenue until she came abreast of number 9. It was a châteaulike gray stone mansion. In front of it was parked a Packard limousine. From inside the house a butler opened an iron-grilled door, and a tall woman past middle age, beautifully attired, emerged from it and entered the rear of the limousine, helped and then covered with a blanket by a chauffeur, to whom she spoke warmly.

Standing opposite, Ann watched. She did not know if she felt elated or depressed. She retraced her steps back to Madison Avenue deep in thought.

When people asked her when it was that she fell in love with Junior Grenville, she did not tell them that it was then.

He called her later in the afternoon to make arrangements for meeting that night after her show. Already she had given him keys to her apartment, and she asked him to meet her there, as he had to dine with his family.

"And Junior?" she said in closing.

"Yes?"

"When you open the door to let me in?"

"Yes?"

"Be naked."

If, indeed, a man could swoon, she knew, over the telephone, that William Grenville, Junior, had just swooned.

He was astonished by the magnitude of her passion for him. "Hold it!" she had ordered him the night before as she felt his excitement building to a too early conclusion. "Not yet, for God sake! We're just getting started." It thrilled him when she barked out her sexual orders to him.

He slipped away from his mother's dinner when Horowitz began to play and let himself into her tiny penthouse in Murray Hill. It worried him that there was not a doorman or an elevator man in the building where she lived. Since his near kidnapping ten years before, he was always conscious of personal safety for himself and his friends. Throughout dinner at his mother's, he had talked to plain and pretty Esme Bland about the importance of having a gun for her own protection. He did not notice her stricken look when he told her he was going to slip out.

He lit Ann's rooms by candlelight. He moved the two dozen long-stemmed roses to a more pictorial spot. He arranged champagne and ice and glasses. When he heard the gentle and excited taps of her gloved hand on the doorway of her own apartment, he undid the belt of his silk foulard dressing gown and let it slide off his shoulders and drop to the floor. He walked naked toward the door in his loose casual stride, elongating in front as he moved, in anticipation. He opened the door.

There she stood, looking more ravishing than ever: that smile, that look in her eye. Her eyes traveled down his splendid body.

"Oh, my darling," she said, entering the room, closing the door behind her, reaching out for him. It excited Billy that she liked to have her throat kissed before her mouth. She, in turn, found areas of his body to explore that he had not known were part of the sexual experience. It was not, she explained to him, with the patience of a teacher to her favorite pupil, an act simply to be gotten through. It was an experience to be savored and prolonged. There would be plenty of time for champagne and conversation later.

JUNIOR WAS bewildered by the contents of her dressing table; it could have been a makeup counter at Saks. He was further bewildered by the enormous amount of time she spent there, and he watched her, fascinated by her expertise and concentration.

"I want you to meet my friend Jellico Bleeker," he said.

"How could anyone name a child Jellico Bleeker?" asked Ann, continuing to do her face.

"Mrs. Jellico Bleeker could," answered Junior.

"His mother?"

"His mother."

"Don't any of you guys have names like Joe or Jim?"

Junior laughed.

"I hope you don't call him Jelly," said Ann.

"No, he hates that. We call him Bratsie."

"And he likes that?"

Junior laughed again. "It suits him," he answered. "You'll see."

"When will I see?"

"I'm bringing him to the show tonight," answered Junior.

There was a silence. "To look me over, I suppose," said Ann. "Check me out. Case me."

Junior Grenville was not in the habit of having to clarify his reasons. "He's my best friend," he said. "He always has been. I want you to know him and I want him to know you. That's all. No big deal."

"Okay," she said, turning from her dressing table, her beautiful face perfectly attended to, and smiling at him in the chair where he sat watching her.

Miss Ethel Merman, performing rambunctiously, did not exist for the two young officers that night. Their eyes were riveted on the near-nude show girl gliding magnificently behind the star. Ensign Grenville looked proprietary. Captain Bleeker looked dazzled. Their applause was fervent, exceeding by far the extent of the show girl's accomplishment.

Amid a great deal of laughter the trio had supper in the Cub Room of the Stork Club, and Sherman Billingsley greeted the two young officers affectionately and sent them champagne. Ann, thrilled to be there, gazed at the two old friends, fascinated by their lifelong friendship, and listened to stories of Bratsie's antics at bygone deb parties. Their faces shared the look of easy living and freedom from financial stress; it was a look she liked. Her bare shoulders moved to the Latin beat from the orchestra in the main room.

"Junior, I want to dance with this beautiful lady," said Bratsie, rising to do an elaborate mime of the rumba.

"He may be little, Ann, but he's some dancer," said Junior about his friend.

"Did you know the only part of your body that shouldn't move when you do the rumba is your bowels?" asked Bratsie.

"Bratsie!" shouted Junior, screaming with laughter. "You'll have to excuse him, Ann. He's just back from the front."

Ann was delirious when, dancing with Bratsie and following his dips, she caught a lucky balloon and was rewarded with a giant bottle of perfume. It seemed to her that life had never been so lovely, and she wanted to prolong the night with these young men for whom favors happened for no other reason than that they were who they were.

"Bratsie's a bona fide war hero," explained Junior, building him up. "He's downed all kinds of planes. Tell Ann, Brats. Explain your decorations to her. He's the bravest man I know."

The merry young man, drunk now, looked sad suddenly. "It doesn't have a damn thing to do with bravery," he said. "I just don't care, Junior. I never did."

They sat silent as more wine was poured.

"I care, Bratsie," said Junior finally. "I need you in my life."

"You'll be a hero pretty soon yourself," said Bratsie. "It's swell, but it doesn't change what's wrong. We still have our father's banks to come back to after the war and those proper marriages. My mother would die happy if I married Junior's sister and Junior's mother would die happy if he married one of the English princesses."

Junior, embarrassed, blushed. "That's only a family joke, Bratsie."

"A thick fog of gloom is surrounding this table all of a sudden," said Ann. "I think we should dance again or go to El Morocco and sit at John Perona's Round Table or think up something festive to do."

"Right you are," cried Bratsie. "Let's hit the road. You lucked out with this lady, Junior."

"It means more to me than anything that you two like each other," said Junior.

They got into Bratsie's Cadillac convertible and began touring the night-clubs of the city. Bratsie, buoyant again, regaled them with tales of mad adventures and drunken behavior.

"You ought to write a book, Bratsie," said Ann.

"What would I call it?" asked Bratsie.

"Remembrance of Things Pissed," she volunteered.

"Ah, a rare literary allusion from Miss Arden," said Junior, delighted with her, and the three screamed with laughter, and the festivities continued, finally winding down at an all-night diner on Second Avenue with the implicit but unspoken understanding between them that Ann had passed the test of Bratsie's approval with flying colors.

"My mother would like you to come to tea," said Junior abruptly, catching Ann unaware.

"How does your mother know about me?" asked Ann.

"I've told her. She knows I've been seeing someone every night of my leave."

Bratsie watched the interchange.

"Did your mother ask to meet me or did you ask her to?"

"Somewhere in between, I suppose," answered Junior. He smiled at her.

"This I'd like to see," said Bratsie.

"You come too, Brats," said Junior.

"I'll be gone the day after tomorrow," said Bratsie.

The waitress, tired, pounced on them with orders of scrambled eggs on thick chipped plates and noisily distributed them. Pouring coffee, she slopped it over into the saucers, an irritation for Ann, for whom it had associations. She did not allow herself to remember that she had once, briefly, been a waitress in a coffee shop herself. Now she concentrated on applying paper napkins to the soaked saucers as Bratsie, who took advantage of every situation, loudly slurped his coffee directly from the saucer, to Junior's delight. Ann's heart was beating rapidly. She did not understand what her feelings were exactly, somewhere between triumph and fear, and she did not wish either emotion to register on her face.

"Will you come with me?" she asked finally, her chore completed, bringing the conversation back to where it had been before the interruption.

"I'll be there already. It's where I live."

"Will there be others?"

"Perhaps a sister or two. They usually drop in at that time to see Mère."

"Is that what you call your mother? Mère?"

"We always have, yes."

The French word seemed to make him more remote from her, another thing to accentuate their differences. "What will I wear?" she asked.

"I think this white fox jacket you have on and an orchid corsage," said Bratsie, holding up the fur that Arturo de Castro had given her. It was not lost on Ann that it was her wrongness that made her so eminently suitable in Bratsie's eyes as a companion for his rigid friend.

"And high-heeled shoes and socks," he went on.

Junior put his hand over Ann's and leaned over and kissed her gently. "You'll be fine," he said, and she felt reassured by his tone and his protectiveness, and the tension in her body abated. He enjoyed holding her hand and calming her in moments of nervousness. Protected always himself, he felt strong in his role of protector. She understood his kiss and his role. By now, she loved him, but what she understood was that he loved her even more.

AFTER SENDING little Dickie and his nanny off to Central Park for the afternoon, Babette Van Degan lay on her sofa in a relaxed manner hearing the latest developments in her friend's story. On Ann's finger was Babette's nearly flawless emerald-cut pink diamond, a Van Degan treasure, over which Ann never did not exclaim and which she often tried on.

"I want all the colors someday," said Ann matter-of-factly, handing back the ring. "Red and green and blue."

"And the pastels, too," added Babette. "Some of the pastels are nice."

"No, no, I don't care about the pastels," said Ann. "Just the ems and the saffs and the rubes, thank you very much."

"Has Junior given you anything yet?" asked Babette.

"No," answered Ann. "Except roses and champagne and lunch at the Plaza and supper at the Stork Club, first cabin all the way, that sort of thing, but no gifts, no."

"Even that tango dancer gave you a white fox jacket," said Babette.

"But Arturo's so ugly. He's the only man I ever met that I'd rather go down on than kiss." They laughed. "Wait until you see Junior. He's beautiful."

"They're all tight, though, those rich kids," said Babette. "Mama probably controls the purse strings."

"Mère," corrected Ann.

"What?"

"They call her Mère, not Mama."

"Jesus." They laughed again. Babette helped herself to another chocolate from the huge box on her faux-malachite coffee table.

"You're going to get fat, Babette, if you keep eating that candy all the time," said Ann.

"No, I've got some great diet pills," she answered, shrugging off the suggestion of fat. "Have I told you about Dr. Skinner?"

"I don't know what to wear. I was thinking of that green suit I got at Bergdorf's, and white gloves, and a hat. I thought I might buy a new hat at Hattie Carnegie, and I thought maybe you'd lend me your lizard bag."

"Sure thing."

"I feel like Kitty Foyle," said Ann nervously.

"Kitty Foyle was a typist, honey. You're a show girl," answered Babette.

"Which is better? Or worse?"

"Neither one is what Alice Grenville has in mind for Junior. Let's put it that way," said Babette, reaching for another chocolate.

As SHE TOOK A five-dollar bill from the lizard bag she had borrowed from Babette Van Degan, Ann looked up at the Grenville house from the interior of the cab. A six-storied limestone château with balconies, it appeared larger than she remembered from her previous expedition.

"That's some mansion," said the driver, leaning over to look up himself. "That must be one of the Vanderbilts' houses, I think."

"Grenville," Ann corrected him.

"Who?"

"It's the William Grenville house," she repeated, while making the transaction for change and tip.

"Probably related to the Vanderbilts," insisted the driver. "I wonder what it's like to live in a pile like that."

She wondered if he was talking to her as if he assumed that she didn't know any more about it than he did, and she terminated the momentary cordiality. For reassurance she opened her compact and appraised herself favorably. She got out of the taxi, breathed deeply the February air, and walked across the street to the iron-grated front doors that opened into the entranceway. Up a half-dozen stone stairs were the glossy black double doors that opened into the front hall. Almost immediately after her ring, the door was opened by a butler. They eyed each other. He was almost elderly, and there was a quiet elegance about the dark uniform he wore, less formal, she noticed, than those of stage or screen butlers.

"I'm expected," she said, acting expected. She thought Junior would be there to greet her. "I'm Miss Arden."

"Good afternoon, Miss Arden," the butler said, widening the opening as she passed into the hallway. Where was he? She saw, while experiencing his absence, that the floor was black-and-white marble in a geometric pattern, that the hallway was circular, that a stairway of vast proportions ascended upward flight after flight. Above her was an enormous chandelier with hundreds of prisms tinkling from the momentary blast of cold air. Her heart beat with excitement for being where she was and concurrently beat with fear at the possibility of abandonment. Unexpectedly self-conscious, she felt suddenly stiff and clumsy.

"What?" she replied, aware of having been asked something.

"Your coat," repeated the butler.

"Yes," she said, allowing herself to be helped in its removal. At least she was not being turned away. Where was he? She needed, she knew, a mirror to look into to check the extent of her flush. She would know in an instant if it reflected high color or panic.

"I wanted to be here when you arrived!" came his blessed voice from above. She looked up. Dressed in his uniform, he ran down the stairway several steps at a time to greet her. "You look"—he paused before completing his sentence, taking her in—"ravishing." She liked the word at once.

He could tell by the look on her face that she was nervous. Except for Bratsie and a few others like Bratsie, it was a look he had seen on the face of everyone he had ever brought into this vast house for the first time.

"Did you meet Cahill?" he asked, turning to include the butler in the conversation. "This is Miss Arden, Cahill."

"Miss Arden," acknowledged Cahill.

"Cahill knows all the family secrets," said Junior charmingly. "At least all mine."

"I've known Mister William since he was this high," said Cahill, holding his hand to a very low level over the marble squares. Ann smiled.

"Let me put your coat in here," said Junior, leading Ann to a sitting room off the hall that looked out on the street.

"Is this the living room?" she asked, looking around.

"They call it the reception room," said Junior. "The living room's upstairs. That's where Mère is."

"What is this room used for?"

"It's where people wait before they go upstairs, or sometimes Mère meets people here who come on business."

"I see."

"It's where my father's casket was. I suppose it will be where mine is as well."

"What a curious thing to say."

"I don't know what made me say it."

She looked up at the portrait of the three young ladies in long white dresses.

"That's by Sargent," he said.

"My word," she answered. "Is one of them your mother?"

"On the right."

"And the other two are her sisters?"

"My mother was a triplet. Did I tell you that?"

"No."

Suddenly she felt unprepared for the event at hand. "Junior," she said in an uncertain voice.

"Yes?"

"I've never been in a mansion like this before."

"Listen."

"What?"

"Just say 'house.' Don't say 'mansion.' It's a silly thing, I know, but it's just not a word we use."

"You don't say 'mansion'? It's one of my favorite words."

"Not in this mansion," he answered, and they both laughed. He pressed up against her, kissing her on the cheek. "I hope you don't mind my correcting you."

"Not at all," replied Ann quickly. "I don't want to make mistakes. You'll find I'm a quick learn. You won't ever have to tell me twice."

He smiled. "I like you better and better."

They moved back out into the hall, and she looked around her again.

"How many servants does it take to run a place like this?" she asked, lowering her voice.

"Fourteen, I think it is," answered Junior.

"Imagine."

"Used to be twenty-one when my father was still alive."

"Cutting corners, huh?"

"The war."

"Oh, yes, the war."

She knew she was delaying going up.

"Where do they all sleep?" she asked.

"The top floor. There's seven or ten rooms up there. The chauffeur, Gibbs, sleeps in his own apartment over where the cars are kept a few blocks away in the old carriage house."

"My." They looked at each other.

"We'd better go up," he said. "The elevator's over here." He started leading the way.

"Oh, no, no," she replied. "I want to walk up those stairs."

"This house had the first private elevator in New York," he said, as if that way up were preferable.

"I still want to walk up those stairs," she said, heading for them. As he always did when passing beneath it, Junior glanced up at the great chandelier, remembering.

"What a beautiful chandelier," said Ann, looking up at it as she ascended the stairs, a hand on the banister. She could imagine Marie Antoinette having danced beneath it.

"It fell once when I was a little boy, and a man was killed," said Junior. "Did I tell you that?"

"No," she answered.

On the landing they stood outside the glossy white panels of the drawing-room doors and looked at each other.

"What a lot you have to tell me," she said, and he heard a whole future in her sentence.

"You're swell," he said, turning to open the door. As he did so, voices from behind were heard in relaxed conversation.

"Guess who's getting married?"

"Who?"

"Cheever Chadwick. It's in the *Times.*"

"To whom?"

"A Miss Green. Rhoda Green. From Brooklyn."

"Oh, dear."

"His poor mother."

"Jewish, do you suppose?"

"Only on her mother's and father's sides."

"Felicity! Really!"

"When I was growing up, we all knew each other."

Ann was always to remember that room as she first saw it in the fading winter sunlight with her own senses heightened by the impression she hoped to make and the conversation that came to her in snatches from the group seated far distant in front of a fire. The pale-green drawing room was dominated by white-and-gilt furniture, great gold consoles, and a chinoiserie mirror. The upholstery picked up the colors of the Aubusson rug. Everywhere was a profusion of books, paintings, and flowers massed in Meissen bowls. She tried not to let it show that she was speechless.

Alice Grenville was an exceedingly observant woman. What she saw, in the moments it took for Junior and the beautiful woman who accompanied him to enter the room and walk the considerable distance to the fireplace where she was seated with her daughters and where the tea table had been set, was that her son was madly in love for the first time in his life. She knew that the other girls who had come before this woman were no more than crushes. She sensed instantly that her son and this woman were involved in an already consummated love affair. She felt a pang of distress that she had too quickly dismissed the lovely Brenda Frazier as a publicity-mad adventuress. This, coming toward her, was the adventuress.

Alice set aside her needlework on a bench overflowing with magazines and rose from her chair to extend her hand to Ann, peering at her through the dark glasses she always wore as if she recognized a person with whom she was meant to interact in life. Elegantly, but not modishly, dressed in plain black silk, with pearls and a small diamond brooch, her reddish-brown hair simply arranged, Alice looked just as she had looked for a number of years and would continue to look for a number of years more.

"Mère, this is Ann Arden," said Junior proudly. He looked absurdly handsome to his mother in his smartly cut naval uniform, his eyes barely leaving the face of the woman, as if he could not get enough of looking at her.

"I am so pleased you could come, Miss Arden," said Alice. Her smile was warm. Her handshake was firm. "We are all alone, you see. Just family. We have asked no one else," she continued, as if Ann might be expecting a cocktail party. She introduced her daughters: Rosamond, Felicity, Grace, and Cordelia. Felicity, still reading the *Times,* gave Ann her hand without looking at her. Ann seated herself carefully so that her skirt would fall gracefully about her. She pulled at the fingers of her gloves, removing them.

Alice asked if people wanted India tea or China and went about the business of pouring, with assistance from Cordelia, whom the sisters called Cookie. She said there were cucumber sandwiches, and also watercress. She said she had been to the new production of *La Bohème* at the Metropolitan

Opera the night before and that Jarmila Novotna was glorious. She said she had lunched across the street at Grace Vanderbilt's and a general had told her the invasion would be in April. She said she adored the new musical *Oklahoma,* and had Ann seen it? She said she was in the midst of a new novel by John P. Marquand and was enthralled. She said she never missed Edward R. Murrow's broadcasts from London, no matter what. She said her English grandchildren were coming to the country for the weekend.

If Ann thought she would be quizzed about herself, she was wrong. Not a single personal question was asked. Alice Grenville was extremely friendly, as was Cordelia, but the conversation was of the general sort.

"I'm off, Mère," said Felicity, putting down her cup and gathering up her things. "I have a million things to do still. I'm going to the Soldiers and Sailors Ball tonight, and I have to get my hair done. Goodbye, dear Mère. Kiss kiss. Goodbye, Miss Eden."

"Arden," corrected Junior.

"Arden. Excuse me. Walk out with me, Junior." When they got to the door of the room, she whispered to him, "I liked your blonde."

"Her name is Ann."

"Marvelous figure." She was off.

"Would you like another cup of tea, Miss Arden?" asked Alice. "This cake, by the way, is the cook's specialty."

"No, thank you," replied Ann, handing her empty cup to Junior to replace on the tea table.

"Perhaps a sherry, or a drink even?"

"No, thank you, but I would like to use your ladies' room," said Ann.

Cordelia and Junior both leaped to their feet to show her in which direction to go.

"I'll take Miss Arden up to my room," said Alice. "Stay here and talk to your sister. You never see enough of her."

AS THEY ASCENDED the stairs, Ann looked up at the topmost floor, where twelve male heads were painted, friezelike, into the wall just below the ceiling, looking down on the house.

"One, two, three, four . . ." she started to count.

"There're twelve," said Alice.

"The twelve apostles?" asked Ann.

"The twelve Caesars," replied Alice. "My husband was a student of Roman history when he was a young man, and he had them designed into the plans of the house when he built it in 1918. I've become quite fond of them over the years."

"This is a very beautiful house, Mrs. Grenville."

"It's not beautiful really. It's just big."

"It could be a palace."

"One day I'm sure it will be an embassy, or a school, but I like it and I'm going to stay here until the end of my life. Junior was born in this house, and one day I would love to see him take it over."

The two women looked at each other. Ann wondered if the remark was meant to exclude the possibility of her in their lives. She had smiled sweetly in the face of Felicity's rudeness, and she would continue to smile sweetly, no matter what.

"This is my room," said Alice when they reached the third landing. "Those are guest rooms over there, and all the children's rooms are on the next flight up. Junior still has the same room he always had, except he has his own sitting room as well, and the other rooms that used to belong to the girls are always filled with Junior's friends. I expect you've met Bratsie."

"Yes, I have. How lovely this room is," Ann said, walking to the bed with its great pale-green canopy cascading down from the ceiling. "Green again."

"What?"

"You like green, I said."

"Yes, I do. You notice things, don't you?"

"Is that wrong?"

"No, no, it's not wrong. I was a triplet. Did you know that?"

"Junior told me."

"We were identical. No one could tell us apart, sometimes not even our parents, so we wore different color ribbons always. Amelia wore red, and Antoinette blue, and I wore green, and it stayed my favorite color. The bathroom's over there."

Ann wondered why she had been brought up here rather than sent downstairs to the bathroom off the reception room. In the lavender-scented dressing room she leaned to look at the dozens of framed family photographs: childhood pictures on the decks of ocean liners and foreign beaches, the sisters in coming-out dresses and wedding gowns, Junior on a football team, Junior an usher in a wedding, Junior in a nightclub picture with Brenda Frazier. She realized how little she knew about his life, or his family. Apart from the others was a photograph of Junior's father taken at a racetrack, a forbidding figure, but dashing: a cigar in his mouth, held arrogantly; a carnation in his buttonhole; a hard glint in his eyes behind glasses; an expression of how-dare-you-take-my-picture on his face. She felt instinctively that they had all feared him in the family; she would rather have had him to contend with than the mother and the four sisters. Men she understood.

She made up her mouth with scarlet lipstick, combed her hair, appraised herself favorably. She had, she felt, behaved demurely. Around here were the personal effects of Alice Grenville—her swansdown powder puff, her Floris soap, her gold-backed brushes and mirrors. She noticed her clothes had been laid out for the evening ahead: a black evening dress on a cushioned hanger, shoes, stockings, purse, gloves, and an ermine coat. She wondered what kind of party or ball Alice was going to. She ran her hands in a backward motion down the pelts of the ermine coat and longed to try it on. She thrilled at the kind of arranged and prepared life it was that this woman led.

In the bedroom Alice sat back on her chaise. Behind her was a large marquetry table covered with expensive photographs of elegant people in silver frames. A photograph of Queen Mary was signed simply "Mary," with the letter R following.

"Tell me about yourself, Miss Arden," she said in her distinctive manner of speaking.

Alice Grenville was a woman to be reckoned with, and Ann recognized her instantly for the adversary she was going to be. She decided that truth, or at least proximity to truth, in her own background story was the route to take.

"Is that Queen Mary?" asked Ann, pointing to the photograph while sorting out her tale in her mind.

"Yes," answered Alice simply, not turning to look at the picture, understanding the diversionary tactic, waiting for an answer to her question.

"I was born in Kansas," began Ann.

"Ah, yes, Kansas," said Alice. "Mr. Grenville and I were there some years ago, for a wedding. Lottie Holmes of Kansas City married my husband's second cousin, Eustice Coffin. Do you know the Holmeses? They live in that area, what do you call it, just outside Kansas City, like Greenwich, or Grosse Point, what do you call that part?"

"We were from Pittsburg, Kansas, in the southwest corner of the state, about a hundred and twenty miles from Kansas City," said Ann rapidly, almost all as one word. All her life she had hated the name of the town she was from; always she had to explain she was not from the Pittsburgh in Pennsylvania but the Pittsburg in Kansas that no one had ever heard of, and inevitably a joke was made.

"What do your people do?" asked Alice.

"I'm an orphan, Mrs. Grenville," she said. She felt a momentary pang of guilt that she was glad her mother was no longer alive so that she would not have to explain her to this tall and formidable woman. Early the previous spring her mother had died, and she had taken her back to the place where she was from and about which she never spoke, buried her in the Mertens plot, contacted no one, and returned to New York—contacted no one, that is, except her father's cousin, who owned the pharmacy, and that had been by accident.

"You're not staying on?" he had asked.

"No, no, I'm up for a part in Hollywood," she had answered, dazzling him. She hadn't told him that she was no longer called Urse, or Mertens, or that this was the last time she would ever be there.

"Sad," said Alice Grenville.

"Sad?"

"Being an orphan." She rose. The interview was over. "I'm tired, Miss Arden. I think I shall rest before this evening. Will you send whichever of my daughters are left up? I've so enjoyed meeting you. If you're dining with Junior, tell him not to stay out late. We're leaving for the country early tomorrow. His nephews are coming, and I have a large party on Saturday who particularly want to see him before he leaves."

Ann felt dismissed, as if her visit were a onetime thing with no follow-up to be expected. It was a feeling she remembered from an earlier time. Rarely did she think back—her life seemed always to begin at the period in which she was living—but an old rejection consumed her as, dispirited, she descended the stairs of the house that one day Alice Grenville hoped her son would take over. She fought down feelings of rage at having been asked to give an account of herself, and having inadequately accounted.

*   *   *

Below, the sisters' verdict, after the departure of their brother and his blonde, was unanimous, but not favorable.

"The cheapest woman I ever saw."

"Reeks of scent."

"Eye shadow in the afternoon, my dear."

"Those blood-red nails."

"Poor Mère."

"You go up, Cordelia. You're the favorite."

Above, Alice Grenville lay back on the chaise longue by her fireplace. The point of the afternoon had been to accommodate a sailor's crush, but she felt a sense of unease about the power of the woman who had walked into her home. As a mother, she had seen to it that her children were exposed only to the eligible from the world in which her family played a dominant role. Her daughters, well married into the kind of families of high social standing that she and her late husband approved of, used to tease their mother that no one would be good enough for Junior but one or the other of the English princesses. She had watched every moment of the meeting while she poured tea and carried on the middle-of-the-road conversation that had ensued. She saw that Junior was solicitous of including Ann in the conversation and listened avidly to the few remarks she had made, as if they were more clever than they were. "It's this damn war," she said to herself. If it weren't for the war, he wouldn't have met a girl like that.

Cordelia entered the room. She handed her mother the needlework that she had discarded below. She picked up a magazine and turned the pages.

"Have they gone?"

"Yes. To the theater. She's an actress. Did you know that?"

"No."

"Well?" asked Cordelia finally.

"The look on my face is disappointment, in case you need to have it translated," said her mother.

"All of a sudden Brenda Frazier's looking awfully good," said Cordelia.

"I wish you hadn't felt it necessary to say that, but, yes, I would welcome Brenda to my bosom at this moment," said Alice.

"But she has become Mrs. Kelly," said Cordelia.

"Alas."

"Did you think Miss Arden was beautiful?"

"Yes, but too conspicuous," replied Alice. "She is a conspicuous character."

"I thought that was a good-looking bag."

"I hate lizard."

"Actually, so do I. Are you interested in the consensus of the sisters?"

"Tell me."

"Rosamond says gold digger. Grace says trash. You saw Felicity's performance—"

"I wasn't proud of Felicity."

"Junior said Felicity was a bitch and why hadn't he ever noticed it before."

"And you, Cordelia? What did you think?"

"I say, 'Poor Junior.' On top of which he wants me to take her to lunch. He's mad about her."

"Besotted."

"Do you suppose they're having an affair?" asked Cordelia.

"Absolutely," said Alice. "That's her secret weapon."

"The thing is, Mère, I've never seen Junior so happy."

"If only your father were alive. He would put the fear of God into him. He loathed stage people."

"It would be absurd for him to even consider marrying anyone so far beneath him."

"If you want to *make* him marry the girl, tell him that."

"Of course, you're right."

"She conceals her past. She gave me vague answers."

They sat together in silence. Cordelia switched on a rose-shaded lamp. On the table were Ann's gloves.

"Look, Mère, she's left her gloves."

"I saw them."

"Shouldn't we have the chauffeur deliver them to her doorman? That way she won't have to come back."

"Women like her don't have doormen," answered Alice Grenville. Her meaning was clear to her daughter. "Junior hasn't told us anything at all about Miss Ann Arden," she continued, placing a scornful stress on each syllable. "For all we know, that's not even her name. How old do you think she is?"

"Older than he is."

"I think so too. Why is it I don't like her?"

Alice's question was a statement and didn't demand an answer. There was another long silence in the room. They listened to the logs crackling in the fireplace. Alice took pains that the shudder that ran through her body not be evident to Cordelia.

"Are you all right?" asked Cordelia.

"Yes, of course. Just thinking," replied her mother.

"About her?"

"It's odd, isn't it, how someone like that waltzes into your house one day, from out of nowhere, and some deep inner instinct tells you to beware."

"YOU CAME ALONG from out of nowhere" went the lyrics to the song. She was wearing his ensign's hat, cocked on one side of her head, her lovely blonde hair cascading from under it. There were strands of hair in her mouth and a dark-brown Scotch in her hand. She sat on the floor of her tiny living room with her back against the sofa, moodily crooning the words to the song.

"You get mean when you're drunk," said Junior.

"Your sister gets mean over tea," answered Ann.

"I've apologized for Felicity," he said helplessly.

"One of my least attractive traits is that I always get even," she said. "It's the outsider in me reacting. It may take a long time, but the moment will present itself, it always does, and I will take advantage of that moment."

"You're scaring me," he said, alternately meaning it and feeling aroused by her emotion. The Grenvilles did not show emotion.

His leave was drawing to a close. He did not wish it to end on a discordant note. Neither had declared love for the other, only passion and mutual admiration of bodies. ("I'm mad for this hair below your belly button," she would say, kissing his stomach. "I adore the color of your nipples," he would say, his face buried.) She waited for him to declare his love for her before she declared her love for him. She never rushed it. Like sex, it was a thing she understood. She never talked marriage, or even a permanent liaison, and when the subject came up, obliquely, she not only did not leap on it, she let it pass by. Every debutante he had ever known would have leaped at the oblique suggestion.

"I have a present for you," he said quietly.

"You do?" she asked, her mood brightening, her heart beginning to beat fast.

He disappeared into the kitchen and reappeared with a white cardboard box, which he handed her. It was not the kind of box she had in mind.

"Ah, orchids!" she exclaimed delightedly, as though they were what she most longed for. She wondered why she couldn't act onstage the way she could in life, concealing her disappointment with delight, as she was doing. She stared at them, white with yellow centers, and brushed her face against the scentless blossoms, collecting herself for the next moment.

"You like them then?" he asked.

"So much," she said. She was reminded of what Babette had said about rich boys being tight.

"Good," he replied, settling himself in a chair contentedly; for an instant she thought of Percy V. Jordan, the way he sat, contentedly, with pipe and slippers. She shuddered. Since her interview with Alice Grenville, images of her long-ago past kept recurring to her.

"Aren't you going to put them in something?" he asked.

"Oh, yes," she said, remaining sitting where she was on the floor. "I will in a bit."

"There's more," he said.

"What?"

"You heard me." They looked at each other. "Dig deeper."

She lifted the bouquet from the heavy cardboard box. There, hidden among the flowers, was a small red leather box from Cartier's. Junior was to discover in that moment that her joy in receiving gifts was wondrous to behold, sweeping away any dark moments that preceded it, restarting the evening in rapturous mood. The memory of Christmases past, giftless, entered and exited her mind.

It was a pin, a circle of diamonds, such as his sisters wore on the collars of their suits, a gift for a lady, not a gift for a show girl, and she felt tenderness for him, and love. That mother, those sisters, she thought. She understood him better, having met them. Although they had pointed out to her, in their own secretive ways, the vastness of the chasm between them, she was not deterred.

Later—sated, satisfied—she said to him, "Do you never discuss your feelings?"

"What have we been doing for the last hour?" he asked.

"Worshiping bodies. It's not the same."

"But I told you."

"When you were coming. I don't count that. It doesn't commit you, you know. It's a love affair, and you're leaving soon, and who knows what will happen then? Let's go to the moon for however long we have. Are you waiting for me to go first, is that it?"

Enraptured, he stared at her but said nothing.

"I love you," she said.

He felt unleashed. Torrents of blocked feelings flowed from him, a lifetime of withheld emotion. "I love you," he whispered to her, and repeated and repeated and repeated the words. He could not stop saying them.

When he asked her to fly with him out to Tacoma, Washington, where he was to be stationed, she refused. She had to earn her living, she said. She had been voted the most beautiful girl in radio, and she thought there might be interest in her at the movie studios. At least that was what Chet Marx told her, she told him. Chet Marx wanted her to dine with Humphrey Bogart; he thought she ought to get to know some of the Hollywood crowd. There was talk of a screen test, she told him.

WHEN JUNIOR'S favorite sister, Cordelia, called and asked her to lunch, Ann knew it was only as a favor to her soon departing brother, but, of course, she went, wearing her new diamond circle pin. When she walked into the Colony Restaurant, ten minutes past the appointed time, to make sure Cordelia was there ahead of her, even Gene Cavallero, who owned the fashionable restaurant and snubbed impostors at the door, could not tell that she had never been there before, so assured was her gait.

When Cordelia admired her pin, she did not say it was from her brother. She did not call Cordelia Cookie. She did not talk excessively about Junior. Nor did she ask questions about the family. She did talk about her radio career and her hoped-for film career. She asked who various people were who waved at Cordelia and was delighted that she could wave at her friend Babette Van Degan across the room.

She watched as people she read about in society columns passed by on their way to their tables. She studied the look of them. Catching sight of herself in the mirror, she realized her look was wrong, more show business than social, and that the time had come to do something about it.

At two o'clock she looked at her watch and said that she had an appointment with her agent about a screen test and must depart. She shook hands charmingly in farewell and did not attempt to make a return lunch date.

Cordelia reported to her mother that she definitely did not think that Miss Arden had marital designs on Junior. "She seems very keen on her career. Didn't even stay for coffee. Rushed off about a screen test or something. She's not at all designing, Mère. She's terribly amusing, as a matter of fact. She told me the funniest story about that Lithuanian girl Dickie Van Degan was married to for about ten minutes."

"You relieve my mind," said Alice Grenville.

"It's Junior sowing his wild oats, Mère, nothing more. She's the wild oats. It's probably a very good arrangement. He'd never marry her."

"How can you be so sure?"

"She pronounces the 't' in 'often.' "

HE WAS possessed with love. He didn't want her to know how much for fear it would not be returned; at the same time he wanted her to know the full and total extent of it. His moods were up; his moods were down. His skin was sallow, and there were dark circles from sleeplessness under his eyes; he was more handsome than he had ever been.

"Will you marry me?" he asked. Less than a week was left of his leave. He could not bear to think of being apart from her.

"You must let me think it over," she replied. "It's such a big step. It would be mad to hurry. I don't believe in divorce, you see. I've seen firsthand what it does."

"Nor do I!" he agreed. "There's never been a divorce in our family. Except my Aunt Amelia, one of the triplets, and that's only because Uncle Binkie was a fairy, something he neglected to tell poor Aunt Amelia."

"Let's not talk about Aunt Amelia and Uncle Binkie now," said Ann. "Let's talk about us."

"I want to marry you, Ann," he said again. The hesitancy of the first offer was gone. Having said it, he knew it was the thing he desired most.

"I need a little time."

"For what?"

"To make sure it's the right thing."

He felt deflated. He had thought she would jump at the chance. Like Brenda Frazier, or Kay Kay Somerset, or Esme Bland, or any of a dozen ladies in society who had their eye on him.

"I thought you loved me," he stated.

"I do," she replied.

"When will you let me know? My leave is up on Friday."

"I'll let you know before then."

"When?"

"Please, Junior."

"When?"

"I'll let you know this Thursday."

"For sure?"

"For sure."

"It will be a wonderful life, I promise you that. After the war, I mean."

"Thursday."

There was never any doubt as to what her answer would be, except to

Junior, and he shared with no one, not even Cordelia, that the very thread of his life was in abeyance, waiting for Thursday to arrive. He had moments of elation; he had moments of despair. He was bad-tempered and spoiled; he was loving and generous. The eyes of his mother and sisters would meet as his moods fluctuated. Except for her immediate present, he did not know a single thing about Ann, other than that she was an orphan from the Midwest. She never discussed her origins, and there was not a single picture in her small penthouse that suggested a past life.

They were at tea, just the family, and Beth Leary, his mother's closest friend, who was practically family, never having married, when the letter arrived. They had all heard the doorbell, and thought it must be one of the husbands come to join one of the sisters, but no one appeared, and they resumed their conversation about the war, which was all anybody talked about.

Cahill entered, too early to clear away the tea things, but bearing a letter on a silver tray.

"Yes, Cahill?" asked Alice.

"It's a letter, madam, for Mr. William, delivered by messenger," said Cahill.

Junior leaped to his feet, aroused from his lethargy, and his Scotch and soda, which he had preferred to tea, went flying all over his mother's half-finished needlepoint rug. If he had not been in uniform, and with but a few days left of his leave, she might have expressed annoyance, but she merely lifted the rug to her lap and wiped off the liquid with a tea napkin, all the time watching her son as he reached out to take the letter off the tray proffered by Cahill.

Junior's heart sank. There, in Palmer penmanship, round and right-leaning, the i's dotted with circles, was written "Ensign William Grenville, Junior, U.S.N." Lower, on the left side of the envelope, was written "By Hand." He felt with certainty that she had deserted him; why else would she have written to him instead of waiting to see him that evening? He could not bear to open the letter in front of his family, knowing all eyes were on him. He put the envelope in his pocket as if it were of no importance and returned to his place.

"I'm sorry, Mère, about spilling my drink on your needlework. It was awfully clumsy of me," said Junior.

"Doesn't matter," she answered. "Lyd will know how to take out the stain."

"Soda water, I think, is how you do it," said Beth Leary. "Simply soak it in soda water, and when it dries, the stain will have gone."

"Lyd will know," said Alice, who wasn't interested in that kind of conversation.

"What's in the letter?" asked Felicity.

"I haven't read it," answered Junior.

"Why not?"

"None of your business."

"You've gotten so secretive, Junior."

"You've gotten so nosy, Felicity."

"I bet it's from your blonde."

"You don't have to call her that all the time in that bitchy way. Her name is Ann. You're a real bitch, Felicity. I never knew that before."

"Junior!" cried Alice.

He wanted the conversation to move off him onto other things: the opera, the theater, the war, he didn't care which. His heart was beating ferociously, and he was trying not to let the feeling of loss that was lurking around him move in and envelop him. When Beth Leary started to tell a story about Grace Vanderbilt across the street, whom they all loved to discuss, Junior walked out of the room.

Up two flights of stairs he charged and down the long thickly carpeted corridor paneled with bedroom doors to his own door. He entered his room and closed the door behind him, escaping into the white-tiled refuge of his bathroom, where he watered his face with cold water and dried it while looking at himself in the mirror and recognizing the fear in his eyes.

He reentered his bedroom. It was the room that he had grown up in and was now in its fourth stage of decoration. Gone was the memorabilia of childhood, of teen-age, of college. Now it was decorated for a young man, tailored and dark-blue, with horse paintings by John Frederick Herring that had belonged to his father and drawings of prize horses from the Grenville racing stables. The handsome desk had also belonged to his father, and the wingback chairs. He stood there surveying it, as if for the first time, undecided which place to gravitate to that was not dominated by his father. He moved to the window seat in the large dormer window overlooking the park and the street five stories below. It was where he had sat most often as a child and seemed the least-changed part of the room. He peered out the window for several minutes and then reached into his pocket and took out the letter, which seemed to heat against his body. He looked at the envelope again, filled with trepidation, sat down and tore it open.

It read:

> *Miss Ann Arden*
> *accepts with pleasure*
> *the kind invitation of*
> *Ensign William Grenville, Junior, U.S.N.*
> *to become his lawful wedded wife.*

War whoops, cheers, screams of joy, and stamping of feet altered the mood of the room.

WHEN ANN ARDEN was eight years old, and her name was Ursula Mertens, and she was called Urse, her father, whose name was Claud, and whom she adored, took her for supper, just the two of them, to the counter at Crowell's Pharmacy on Broadway in Pittsburg, Kansas. They exchanged pleasantries with Paul Crowell, her father's first cousin, who owned the pharmacy. Paul told Urse she was the prettiest young thing who'd been into his store all that day. Urse looked up at him, startled into a brilliant flush by the compliment, and beamed with pleasure.

"You're going to turn her head," said Claud to Paul, looking affectionately at his daughter, although his mind seemed to be occupied by other matters.

"What are you going to be when you grow up?" asked Paul.

"I'm going to be an actress in the movies," answered the lovely child without a moment's hesitation. Paul chuckled, and her father, preoccupied, looked off into space.

They ordered cheese delights, which Paul said were the *specialité de la maison,* melted cheese and bacon sandwiches served open-faced and eaten with a knife and fork, and chocolate milkshakes so thick and plentiful that each canister filled up the milkshake glass nearly twice. It was a rare treat in the young life of Urse Mertens, and she rose to the occasion by keeping her taciturn father entertained with an endless stream of chatter about the dancing lessons and music lessons she wanted to take, and the birthday present she was making for Grandma Smiley.

Her social vivacity deflected totally the purpose of the meal. Claud Mertens had things to tell Urse, important things, about leaving Pittsburg, which was growing into such a big town, nearly fifteen thousand people now, not a place for farming anymore, and moving on to Hugoton to homestead. He was losing his farm on the outskirts of Pittsburg.

"What's 'homestead' mean?" she asked finally.

"It means you live on the land for a year, make improvements on it, you know, fences and barns, like that, and then it becomes yours," answered Claud, more at home in that kind of conversation than about dancing and music lessons that he could not afford to give her.

Urse could feel her lovely evening on the town with her father beginning to crumble in front of her. "Is that where you were when you were out of town last month?" she asked.

"That's right, Urse," answered Claud. "Beautiful country, good soil, you'll love it."

She sat silently, absorbed completely in wiping up spilled milkshake from the marble counter with a paper napkin, frightened by the portent of the conversation.

"Say something, Urse," said her father.

"Mama said there was a big black snake on the front porch up there in Hugoton. Mama said you have to go to the bathroom in a little house outside. Mama said there's only a one-room schoolhouse, and the kids there don't even speak good English. Oh, Daddy, please, please, don't make me leave here and move to Hugoton," pleaded Urse.

"You're your mother's daughter, honey," said Claud, nodding his head slowly and looking at her, holding back his tears. Ethel Mertens had come to Hugoton to look at the new life her husband envisioned for his family there, stayed one night, and returned to Pittsburg, vowing that she would never move there. When they were young and in love a dozen years before, it hadn't mattered that he was just a farm boy with an eighth-grade education and that Ethel had attended normal school and was qualified to teach. But that was before Urse, and Ethel had great plans for Urse.

Claud couldn't bear to tell Urse what he had planned to tell her if his last-ditch hope of interesting her in a life that her mother had rejected failed. He was leaving her mother, allowing her mother to divorce him, moving out of her life.

"I better get you home," he said. "It's almost nine o'clock. If you weren't such a big girl, I'd carry you out to the truck." He wanted to hold her and hug her and tell her that he loved her and always would, but he couldn't.

The next day her mother told her that her father had moved away. Ethel Mertens consoled the weeping child.

"Does a divorce mean he'll never come back?" sobbed Urse.

"Sure, he'll come back and visit you, honey," soothed her mother.

"But why didn't he even say goodbye, Mama?"

"You know how hard it is for your daddy to say things. I know he wanted to, Urse, but he probably couldn't find the words. Even when he gets mad it's hard for him to say what it is he's mad about."

"Is that why he took me out to Crowell's Pharmacy for supper last night, to tell me he was going to leave us?" She wondered if Paul Crowell knew. She remembered herself prattling on about dancing and music lessons. She felt betrayed.

"He wanted to tell you by himself, Urse, and explain to you what he wanted out of life, and that it wasn't here in Pittsburg anymore."

"He did start to tell me that."

"You see?"

"About homesteading in Hugoton and making improvements on the land."

"All that."

"But I didn't know he was going to move out there and leave us if we didn't want to go."

"It's not the kind of life out there I want for you, Urse," said Ethel Mertens.

"What's going to happen to us, Mama?" She shivered in fear as she looked around her at the holes in the linoleum floor of the kitchen and the broken steps out the kitchen door that you had to jump over. Their little frame house had not been painted in years, and tar paper covered holes in the shingled roof.

"We're going to be all right. Don't you worry about that," answered her mother, but neither of them knew whether to believe that.

"When I grow up, Mama . . ."

"Yes, honey?"

"I'm never going to get a divorce, never, no matter what."

URSE MERTENS always looked ahead to the time when her life would start. Her childhood and adolescence were years to be gotten through, in preparation for the time ahead when her life would really begin. She longed to be center stage in life, to have her world focused on her. When her celebrity finally came, in a manner radically different from her youthful dreams, reporters sought out her roots for early clues. It astonished them that so few people remembered her. She left no mark; she erased all traces of her deprived youth by remaining unmemorable.

"Now hold still, Urse, or one of these pins is going to stick in you," said Ethel Mertens, intent on her work.

"I can't understand you when you talk with pins in your mouth, Mama," said the little girl, straining around to look at the fitting in the mirror over the bureau.

"Turn around to the mirror and let me look at the length of this skirt."

"I love this color blue, Mama. It's my favorite color."

"Do you know what people are going to say about you?" asked her mother, satisfied with her nearly completed chore.

"They're going to say, 'Urse Mertens has the prettiest dresses of any girl in Pittsburg, Kansas,'" said Urse, and they both laughed, knowing people wouldn't say that at all, but it was a line they often used.

"I've been thinking, Urse," said her mother.

"Oh-oh," said Urse.

"What's that supposed to mean?"

"When you say 'I've-been-thinking-Urse,' that means changes."

"Well, just listen to me. With your daddy gone, there's no reason for the two of us to stay way out here on the outside of town. How about if we sold this farm and moved into Pittsburg?"

"Who would buy it, Mama? It's all falling down."

"Well, somebody would. The other day I saw a real nice house on West Quincy Street that Mr. and Mrs. Cremer want to sell. It'd be perfect, Urse. You'd be able to walk to Lakeside School and have friends right on the street. That Fredda Cunningham lives only two houses away, and you said yourself she's the most popular girl in the school."

"But she's so stuck-up, Mama. She never says hello."

"She will, honey. You'll be best friends in no time."

"Won't you miss the farm, Mama?"

"I don't think either of us is the farm-girl type, Urse. Do you?"

"No, but I thought maybe Daddy might decide to come back if things didn't work out in Hugoton." She pulled the new dress over her head so that she wouldn't have to meet her mother's eyes in the mirror and avoid a finality she was still not ready to accept.

"It'll be easier for us to figure out a way for you to take your music lessons," said Ethel, helping her out of the dress.

"We don't have enough money for music lessons."

"Well, there's something else I've been thinking."

"Oh-oh. More changes."

"I've been thinking of going back to teaching. I went to normal school before I married your father, and I was always planning to teach, but when we got married we moved out here, and I never got around to it."

"What would you teach?"

"Social studies."

"A lot of changes, Mama."

"But exciting, huh?"

"And we'll be able to afford the lessons?"

"That's the whole point. Wouldn't you like that?"

"Oh, yes, Mama," she said, hugging her mother. "I always said I wanted to be an actress in the movies."

HURT, SHE WAILED, "Sometimes I wish my father was dead!" It was Christmas.

"Ursula Mertens!" cried her mother, in the tone of voice she used to let her daughter know she didn't mean what she was saying.

"I mean it, Mama," persisted Urse, not allowing herself to give in to the tears that were welling in her sad eyes.

"No, you don't," her mother insisted.

"Every birthday, every Christmas, is a disappointment. If he was dead, you wouldn't wonder if he was going to remember or not."

"Now listen, you," said Ethel, putting her arm around her daughter. "We didn't have such a bad Christmas, did we? Look at all those nice things you got under the tree. Grandma Smiley knitted you that scarf herself, and Aunt Edna and Aunt Lucy are going to pay for your dancing lessons for a whole year, and Paul Crowell sent you that bath powder from his drugstore, and don't forget the five dollars."

"But I didn't hear from my daddy, not even a Christmas card, and not on my birthday either. It's like he forgot me already, and I know that he loved me."

"You know, there's still one special thing I haven't even told you about yet," said Ethel, her voice filled with enticement, a sound that Urse could never resist.

"What's that?" asked Urse slowly.

"It's from Mr. Percy V. Jordan."

"Who's Mr. Percy V. Jordan, Mama?"

"He's the manager of the telephone company, Urse, not just for Pittsburg, but for the whole region," said Ethel expansively.

"Why would, uh, what's his name again?"

"Percy V. Jordan."

"Why would Mr. Percy V. Jordan give me a Christmas present when I don't even know him?"

"He's coming over after Christmas dinner, and you will get a chance to know him."

"Is he your boyfriend or something?"

"Oh, Urse, I only just met him, over at the high school when they put in the new phone system."

"What's the present?"

"He wants to drive you and me over to Kansas City next week—"

"Kansas City!"

"—and we're going to have lunch in a hotel, and go to the pictures, and, more to come—"

"More?" cried Urse.

"He's going to have your picture taken at Swanson's Department Store. Three poses."

"I'm going to have my picture taken? At Swanson's Department Store? Three poses?"

"That's right!"

"Wait until that stuck-up Fredda Cunningham hears about this," said Urse, delighted with the way the day had turned out after all.

"MRS. PERCY V. JORDAN. How do you think it sounds, Urse?" asked Ethel Mertens.

"Kind of ritzy," said Urse.

"That's what I think, too. I like the sound of it."

"Is it going to change things, Mama?"

"Only for the better, honey. There'll be more money, and we'll be able to do more things, and I'm sure we'll start getting invited to some of the nice houses. Some of the ladies in this town don't take kindly to a divorced woman. You know that."

"Mrs. Cunningham, for instance," said Urse.

"Mrs. Cunningham, for instance," agreed her mother, and they both laughed.

"You don't love him, do you, Mama?"

"I think he's a very good man. A nice man."

"That's not an answer to my question."

"I'm thirty-one years old. It's different now than when I was married the first time. I'm looking for different things out of life. I want to be able to educate you and give you all the lessons and things you want, and have a nice house, and parties on your birthday, and friends for you, and when it comes time for you to get married, the nicest boys in town to come and call on you, and maybe even some of the swells from Kansas City."

"Is the manager of the telephone company such a good job as all that? He only has two suits as far as I can see, and he doesn't even live in as good a house as this one. Paul Crowell says he rents the apartment over his drugstore on Broadway."

"Don't you listen to that Paul Crowell, what he has to say," said Ethel, sensitive to the implied criticism from her former husband's cousin. "If that's the way Paul Crowell talks, I don't want you stopping in his drugstore on your way home from school anymore."

"Mama, Paul's my friend. He charges Fredda Cunningham for her sarsaparilla, but he always says that mine's on the house, and anyway, if you want to marry Percy V. Jordan, that's all right with me," said Urse, her eyes filling with tears.

"Oh, Urse," said Ethel, pulling her child toward her, hugging her, no longer holding back her own tears. "It's going to work out fine. I know it. You'll see."

"And at least we'll have our own telephone, not a party line anymore," said Urse.

"If I decide to say yes, he's going to paint the house all white, with green shutters, just like the Cunninghams', and he said he'd put up new wallpaper in the front room and in the two bedrooms, and he wants to buy us a Frigidaire, and maybe even a new range. And he has a *car!*"

"He has funny hair," said Urse.

"I think it's a wig," said Ethel.

"DON'T TALK TO Ma until after she's had her coffee," Urse warned Percy V. Jordan, as if that were the explanation for her mother's peculiar behavior. Ethel's behavior in her new marriage was difficult for even her daughter to understand. When the excitement of acquisition had diminished—the newly papered rooms; the telephone; the Frigidaire; and the automobile, a Diana Moon—there was the man himself to contend with. Ethel was as sickened when his soft-boiled eggs dripped on his mustache as she was revolted by his bathroom smells. She could not bear to bathe in the tub when his pubic hairs were caught in the drain and refused to wash it herself.

She continuously nagged and found fault with him, and used scurrilous and defamatory language toward him. She accused him of killing his first wife; accused him of being infected with a venereal disease; and accused him of associating with women of questionable character. One quarrel was so violent that Urse Mertens called the police.

For her birthday Percy V. Jordan had promised Urse to take her to Kansas City to see the touring Marilyn Miller in *Sunny*. It was the thing she wanted to do more than anything else. She knew the words to all the songs, and, for once, Fredda Cunningham was jealous of her when she bragged about her forthcoming birthday trip.

On the birthday morning Percy V. Jordan announced that he had had enough annoyance and abusive treatment from his new wife, that the trip to Kansas City was off, and that he was leaving the premises permanently. Urse Mertens was disconsolate and embarrassed by what she expected Fredda's reaction would be. When Ethel realized that Percy was in fact leaving her, she flew into a rage and followed him for blocks through the streets of Pittsburg, screaming abuse at him and attempting to tear his clothes.

Ethel Mertens was hauled into the police station, fired from the faculty of the high school, and divorced by Percy V. Jordan, whereupon her peculiar behavior ceased.

Urse, shamed, remained more and more a solitary figure. She knew that the marriage of her mother and Percy was over almost before it started, and that it was only a matter of time before readjustments in their lives and life-styles were to occur again, that another starting-over was to take place.

She hated the feelings of uncertainty about how they would live, where they would live, if they would be able to manage. She wondered if ever there would be security in her life. She thought of Fredda Cunningham and her seventy-five cents allowance every week, come rain or shine, who always had money to go to the pictures on Saturday afternoons, or buy *Photoplay*, or even a cheese delight, if she wanted one, at Crowell's Pharmacy, and she directed the anger she felt over her own lot in life into jealousies toward Fredda.

The following September she entered high school, and her mother got a new job as the dispatcher at the local taxi service. With the defection of Percy from the scene, both were determined that Urse not give up her dancing and music lessons. She got herself after-school jobs to pay for them herself, first as a check-out girl at the Cash and Carry and then as a counter waitress at Crowell's Pharmacy, serving milkshakes and cheese delights and pouring coffee into thick white chipped cups. Most of all she hated serving Fredda Cunningham.

One night, just before closing, in walked Billy Bob Veblen, the captain of the football team, the handsomest boy at Pittsburg High. Up to that time Billy Bob Veblem, whom all the girls were mad for, had never even noticed Urse Mertens.

Her hand was shaking when she poured him his cup of coffee, but not a drop of it slopped over into the saucer. She was experiencing feelings inside of her that she had never experienced before.

"Where have you been all my life, beautiful?" he asked her, and she felt like she was in a scene in the movies.

MOROSE, THE TWO old friends sat in the dining room of the Brook Club, safe from the world, out of uniform.

"She won't do, you know," said Bratsie. "She won't do at all, as far as they're concerned. Here, let me pour you some more of this wine. It's the most expensive on the menu."

Junior stared at the glass as Bratsie poured the burgundy too close to the top of the glass. Cahill would have frowned, thought Junior, trying to assimilate what his friend was saying, trying not to feel let down.

"Mind you, that's not how I feel. I'm simply doing what you're not doing, which is anticipating what Alice and the sisters are going to have to say on the matter."

"But they adored her," protested Junior. "Except Felicity."

"You're in uniform, home on leave, and in a few days you go off, possibly never to return; they are humoring you until this little affair is over. They think you are sowing your wild oats. Talk marriage to them, and you will see their attitudes change very quickly."

"I love her," said Junior hopelessly.

"I know you do."

"I have never had sex like this before, Bratsie. It's not like at Miss Winifred Plegg's on West End Avenue. I didn't know what sex was all about," confided Junior in a rare moment of intimacy. "What am I going to do?"

"Mistress her for now. And when the war's over, see how you feel then."

He drank some of the burgundy. "I'm not sure I'm going to come back from the war," he said quietly.

"You've always thought that, haven't you?"

"Thought what?"

"That you were going to die young."

"Why do you say that?"

"You've said things like that before."

"I don't remember."

"Would you care?"

"I would now that I've met Ann."

"She'll wait for you."

"That's where you're wrong, Brats. She won't."

"You're pissed off at me, aren't you?" asked Bratsie.

"I thought you would have supported me more, Brats, you of all people. None of all this," he said, looking around the paneled dining room, indicating with his hand the world it represented and the men at nearby tables who had been friends of their fathers', "ever meant anything to you."

"You know, Junior, people always joke and say that Alice wants you to marry Princess Margaret. You see, I think she's serious, only I think she wants you to marry Princess Elizabeth and become the next King of England, or whatever her husband will become."

"That's a nice shirt, Brats," said Junior, not wanting to talk about it anymore, now that his exuberance was spent.

"Had it made," answered Bratsie, glad for a reprieve, looking down at the maroon-and-white-striped monogrammed shirt with white collar and cuffs.

"Expensive?"

"Not for us."

They laughed. They were talking about a shirt, but they were thinking about other things. As Bratsie went on talking, he removed his cuff links, then his tie, then his jacket. Then he unbuttoned the buttons, pulled out the tails, and took the shirt off in the crowded quiet dining room. For a moment he sat there, bare-chested, as men at every table turned to gape at the spectacle of the half-naked man continuing his conversation with great enthusiasm.

"For God's sake, Bratsie, what are you doing?" gasped Junior.

"I'd give you the shirt off my back," said Bratsie, rising, hairy-chested, hairy-armpitted, and handing the shirt across the table to his friend.

"Bratsie!" cried Junior, trying not to look at the other tables and the horrified look of the captain bearing down on them. Bratsie sat down again, oblivious completely to the scene he was causing, and put the jacket of his suit on over his nudity.

"Mr. Bleeker," said the captain. "I'm afraid, sir, I must ask you to—"

"Ah, Casper," said Bratsie. "My mother asked that I send you her best regards. She said my father was fonder of you than almost anyone he knew. What we'd like to order is a marvelous bottle of your best champagne. My friend, Ensign Grenville, and I are celebrating his forthcoming marriage—"

"Bratsie!"

"But it's a great secret, Casper, and you must tell *no* one."

*   *   *

HE TAPPED on the glossy white paneled door of his mother's bedroom the way he used to when he was sixteen years old to tell her he was home from a dance.

"Come in," she said, and he entered. She was sitting up in her enormous canopied bed, reading.

"Mère, I have the most wonderful news," said Junior.

She looked at her son's love-besotted face. "No," she said, lifting her hand and waving it negatively between them, answering his news before he could tell it to her.

"Mère, please."

"No, no, no, no, no, no, no, no. That's all there is to it. Go to bed, Junior."

"Try to remember what it was like when you first met Father, all those stories you have always told us."

"What I felt for your father does not apply to this situation," she answered him, angrily dismissing the comparison of his lust-filled love with her marriage. Her marriage was so totally appropriate. A more perfect match could not have been imagined, from either family, and out of its appropriateness had grown respect, harmony, understanding, and love. Passion had never played a part. At that moment she missed her husband, because he would have known how to deal with this out-of-hand situation.

Angered, he turned about and left his mother's room, slamming the door behind him.

THE ROOM was hot. Candles dripped wax on the table, but Madame Sophia did not seem to notice. The card table between them was wobbly, and the leatherette on the seat of his chair was ripped and felt uncomfortable against his leg. Yellow and red wax roses were covered with dust, and a statuette of the Virgin Mary had been broken and pasted together again. Junior noticed that Madame Sophia's fingernail polish was chipped. Her eyes were heavily made up, and her hair was hidden beneath a magenta chiffon scarf; he felt she might not be sufficiently bathed. A small girl with pierced ears slept on a sofa. He wondered why, if she knew all the answers to the future, she lived in such squalor.

The sign in her window said two dollars for the reading, but she suggested that for five her work would be more detailed, and he agreed. He was confused and lonely in Tacoma, Washington; the strenuous routine of his training at the naval station did not erase from his mind his unpleasant departure from New York, estranged from both Ann and his mother. When, to soothe his troubled mother, he asked Ann to wait for him until after the war, she refused. It pained him to hear that the very next night she was dancing at El Morocco with Arturo de Castro. For the first time in his life he fought bitterly with his mother when she pointed out to him that Miss Arden's instant defection to a former beau showed, more than any words of hers ever could, exactly what kind of person Miss Arden was. Except for Cahill and Gibbs, only Cordelia saw him off.

"There is beautiful lady I see," said Madame Sophia, laying out her soiled cards on the table.

"Yes, yes," cried Junior eagerly.

"Her hair yellow."

"Golden," said Junior only the briefest second before Madame Sophia said "yellow."

"Blue eyes," she went on as if there in her shabby card she had conjured up his glorious lady and feasted on her beauty in agreement with him. From his attitudes she read his story. From his despair she told him they had fought and parted (Yes, yes.) From his longing she told him that the beautiful lady longed for him also. (Are you sure?) From his worry she told him that the obstacles in their way (Were there not obstacles? Yes, yes) were only there as a test to prove their love. From his ecstasy at her revelations she told him that happiness was his.

"Is there anything else you would like to ask me?" she asked, warming to him for his enthusiasm for her powers, noticing in his transformation from despair to ecstasy how extraordinarily handsome he was.

"Yes," he answered. "There is."

She looked at him and waited for him to ask.

"This will seem awfully stupid to you. . . ."

"Just ask," she said, shaking her head.

"Will I be killed in the war?"

She laughed, quite kindly, and shook her head again, and a feeling of relief began to flood his body.

"No," she said, moving her cards.

"When?" he asked quietly.

"When what?" She looked at him.

"You see, I've always had this feeling that I would die young."

"Not in the war," she repeated.

"But when?" he persisted. Their eyes met. From his pocket he took a twenty-dollar bill and placed it on the table. She looked down at the cards in front of her. Then, unexpectedly, she pushed the twenty-dollar bill back at him across the table.

"Please," he said, pushing it back toward her. "It's very important that I know."

"Five, five, five, five," she said finally, wanting to be done with what she was doing.

"I don't understand," he said.

"The fifth day, the fifth month, 1955," she said.

The date she gave him, twelve years in his future, seemed, at that moment of his youth, so far distant that he was filled with exuberance over the postponement of the inevitability of his early demise. It was a date to be filed away for years to come. Then, there, in that shabby room in Tacoma, Washington, the vise of anxiety that the war would finish him was unwound.

*   *   *

BABETTE VAN DEGAN, her hands behind her head, lay back against the leopard-skin pillows on the sofa of her mirrored living room and commiserated with the miserable Ann.

"That mother. Those sisters," she said, acknowledging the root of the problem. They, daughters of adversity, had been through the story over and over.

For Ann, her sense of loss over the departed Junior Grenville was overwhelming. She had gone from the heights of ecstasy to the depths of despair in a twenty-four-hour period and remained in the latter. There was a perception of missed opportunity that might not ever come her way again, at least in the elegant packaging that Junior Grenville presented. She was sure she would have loved him if he were less affluent, she thought, but the sight of his life had aroused in her a passion for him that she had not expected in herself.

Even with her natural acceptance of hard facts, the thing she most feared in life was poverty; she had experienced it. She knew, nearly always, that she had within her the means to go beyond, by far, the life into which she had been born, and she merely passed through the first eighteen years of it in anticipation of moving out of it, leaving no traces. Although it was Fredda Cunningham as Cecily Cardew and not Urse Mertens as Gwendolen Fairfax who was remembered in the Pittsburg High School senior class production of *The Importance of Being Earnest,* it was then she had decided for sure that the stage, when she got to it, would be the means for her to experience the kind of life she knew was waiting. In the meantime, after high school, she and her mother had moved to Kansas City where, in due time, she had modeled for several years at Swanson's Department Store. She enjoyed being looked at and had a natural ability for walking down a runway, turning this way, turning that, removing gloves, removing coats and jackets, with what Miss Rose, in Couture, called real class. In no time, half the eligible men in Kansas City, and a few ineligible married ones, had heard about and were in pursuit of Miss Urse Mertens. Ethel Mertens was delighted with her daughter's popularity, and she and Urse, always close, spent many an hour discussing the relative merits of Mr. Barney, or Mr. Hasseltine, or Mr. Stackpole. The only bad fight the two ever had was when Billy Bob Veblen, from Pittsburg, appeared on the scene, and Billy Bob Veblen (Ethel Mertens was the first one to say), was headed exactly nowhere in life. His finest moment, she claimed, had already been played four years earlier in his celebrated eighty-yard run against Hugoton. So Urse continued to see Mr. Barney, and Mr. Hasseltine, and Mr. Stackpole, to please her mother, but, in secret, she sometimes saw Billy Bob Veblen too when he drove up to Kansas City.

After five years in New York, Ann—renamed by Chet Marx, who told her the name Urse Mertens had to go, honey—knew that she had striking good looks, but that her talents as a dancer and an actress were modest. The stage was for her a means to an end. She danced away the nights of her life in the nightclubs of the city with rich South Americans, dress manufacturers, and some second-string producers from Hollywood. She bestowed and received, waiting for fame or marriage, whichever came first, but all previous perceptions of her unfocused dream paled when Junior Grenville came into her life.

"Did I ever tell you what my father, the milkman, used to say?" asked Babette of her grieving friend.

"No," replied Ann.

" 'If he's got the cow's milk, why buy the cow?' " quoted Babette.

"That sounds like Willimantic, Connecticut," said Ann.

"That's probably what Alice Grenville said to Junior. Some Social Register version of that," said Babette.

Ann wondered if she had given too much.

WHEN HIS ORDERS came to be shipped out, Junior called Ann in New York and pleaded with her to fly out to Tacoma and marry him. Joyously she agreed. She knew for sure that she loved him and wanted to be his wife. The contract for the film with Humphrey Bogart had come to naught—a couple of evenings at El Morocco, one of them culminating in a drunken fight over a stuffed panda bear; her name narrowly escaped being mentioned in Walter Winchell's column, a thing she had once craved.

"Yes, yes, yes, yes, yes, yes, yes," she cried.

"I am so happy, my darling," he said.

"When do you want me?"

"As soon as you can get here."

"Listen, Junior," she said.

"I'm listening," he answered.

"I don't want to be married to a man called Junior."

"But I've always been called Junior."

"That doesn't mean you always have to be."

"What's wrong with Junior?"

"It's a boy's name. I want to marry a man."

"They called my father William."

"I don't want to call you William either."

"Bill?" he asked.

"Billy," she answered.

She suspected she might be pregnant, although she did not go to see a doctor about it, once she agreed to marry Billy, because, if it was true, she wanted to get the news at the same time he got the news so that it would not be a condition of the marriage.

"No one is ever going to claim I trapped him with the old pregnancy routine," said Ann to Babette when she related the news to her.

"I think you really love this guy," said Babette.

Ann did not call, or call on, Alice Grenville before she left New York to tell her of the plans, leaving that for Billy to do.

Somehow he was able to book a suite in the finest hotel in the city for an indefinite period of time, and it was there that she lived during the week before the marriage. He left all the wedding plans to her, as he was mostly confined to the base, and was delighted that she chose to be married in a religious ceremony in the Episcopal church instead of by a justice of the peace. Each, independently, was thinking of Alice and her beloved St. James'. "North, East, South, West," thought Ann, "Episcopalian is the best."

She went to St. Andrew's Church rectory and asked to speak to the minister. As always, she was carefully dressed, wearing the same green suit meant to impress Alice Grenville, and gloves, and hat. The ancient housekeeper informed her that the Reverend Dr. Tiffany was in the church. She was invited to wait in the rectory but decided instead to go into the church so as to see what it looked like. The minister stood on the altar performing a service for himself alone. Ann slipped into a pew to wait. After a few minutes the minister became aware that there was someone in the church and turned and saw her in the front pew watching him.

"May I help you?" he asked.

"I would like to speak with you, Reverend Tiffany," replied Ann.

"Can't you see that I am in the middle of a service?"

"I meant when you have finished," said Ann.

"What is it concerning?"

"A marriage."

"Are you a member of this church?"

"No."

"Is it a military marriage?"

"Naval. My fiancé is stationed at the base."

"There are chaplains at the base," he answered and turned back to the altar to complete his service. He was unobliging and ungracious, but she was determined not to be dismissed by him as if she were a gob's girl friend. She continued to sit there, fingering her pearls, as if they were real, in the manner she had seen Alice Grenville finger hers when she was vexed, until Dr. Tiffany completed the service.

"Are you still here?" he asked when he had finished and was about to go around and turn out the few lights that were on.

"The family of my husband-to-be are long-standing members of St. James' Episcopal Church in New York City, and Dr. Kinsolving of that church suggested to us that we come here to this church to marry," said Ann, having prepared her sentence and her exact tone of voice, firm but courteous, to achieve the utmost effect.

"Come along, come along," he said, his manner changing. "Let's go back to the rectory and talk a bit. Tell me, how is Dr. Kinsolving? I'm sorry if I appeared brusque before, but there are so many people from the bases who come here wanting a church wedding when they have no interest whatsoever in the church, do you see what I mean? What is the name of your fiancé's family?"

The fluttery white curtains in the rectory reminded her of Fredda Cunningham's living room in Pittsburg, Kansas. He asked her if she would like a glass of sherry. She declined, but he took one and then another. He talked on and on. She realized that he was considerably older than she had at first thought him to be in the darkened church. He asked her questions and then did not wait for answers, although he seemed considerably impressed with Dr. Kinsolving and the grand church on Madison Avenue that he oversaw.

Ann discussed flowers and talked over music that she wanted played, asking specifically for a hymn that Billy had told her had been his favorite hymn at Groton. The service was set for eleven o'clock the following Saturday at the side altar. He took another sherry, and she wondered if he was getting senile or perhaps drank a bit, but decided that it was the war. He was long past retirement age and all the younger ministers were away being chaplains. He had a confused look in his eyes; she was not sure if he had the plans straight and thought she would call him again the next day and double-check them. To ensure that nothing would go awry, she opened her purse and took from it several large bills, which she handed him as a contribution to the church, telling him that her husband-to-be would be making a further contribution to the church at the time of the wedding. She asked him if he would join them later at their wedding celebration at the hotel where she was staying. When she departed, he called her Miss Grenville instead of Miss Arden.

IN ANOTHER PART of the city, in the area known as the country-club district, a murder occurred. A young girl of good family had been strangled by a former suitor, a soldier, with whom she had broken off a romance. For several days the story remained on the front pages of the Tacoma newspapers while the soldier was apprehended and arraigned. Pictures of the lovely-looking girl appeared in the papers with accounts of her family background, her education, her accomplishments.

Ann, with little else to do during the days, became avidly interested in the story, shuddering at the thought of a young life ending in so violent a manner. She took a taxi out to the address given in the papers to look at the home of the parents of the victim and felt even sorrier for her when she saw the impressive house and grounds where the girl had lived.

When Ann returned to the hotel, she saw that Billy's bags for their three-day honeymoon and a case of liquor from the PX for the wedding reception had been dropped off at the suite by a friend of Billy's from the naval base. She could not bear to have things out of place, and the sight of the bags and case in the center of her sitting room disturbed her sense of symmetry. When she moved the bags into a closet, she noticed for the first time that there was a manila envelope containing unopened mail that the friend had dropped off as well.

She was drawn to one particular letter like a moth to a flame. Although she had never seen Alice Grenville's handwriting, she would have known it was hers—tall, slender, strong, privileged—even if the address of the house in New York had not been thickly engraved on the rear of the pale-blue envelope. She felt snubbed by it, just as she knew its contents concerned her. Long before she did what she did, she knew what she was going to do. She stared at it as if it were an enemy. She wished that the suite had a kitchenette so that she could boil water and steam open the envelope. Instead, she bolted the door of her room and locked the door of her bathroom. Breathing heavily, standing in front of the mirror, she ripped open the envelope and read Alice Grenville's letter to her son. She read slowly. Had she been observed, her slowness would have been exasperating, but it was dread that slowed her.

"My darling son," the letter read. "I am heartsick that we have parted on such dreadful terms. I cannot bear that you go off to war like this, and I beg you to call me once you have received this letter. I know you think you are in love with Miss Arden, but it is an infatuation. I beg you not to marry her. If your father were alive, he could explain things to you that it is difficult for me to say. Yes, yes, she is lovely, vivacious, witty, all the things you say she is, but she has a past, Junior, other men, older men, many men, all rich. Perhaps she is what you need for this moment in your life. Perhaps your life, as we have brought you up, has stifled you a bit, and you need to flap your wings. Flap them, my darling, but do not marry her! Through Mr. Mendenhall at the bank, I have engaged a private detective. She is older than you think, and Ann Arden is not her real name. There was a party several years ago given by Earl Jones and Freddie Strawbridge, at the Waldorf, in a private suite, for Teddy Mander's bachelor dinner, and Miss Arden was drunken and disorderly and nude—"

The telephone rang in the outer room. She realized it might have rung before she became aware of its ringing. The sound startled her from her furtive work. She felt it must be Billy. Her armpits felt moist. Her face looked bloodless. In an instant, without finishing reading, she savagely tore the pale-blue pages into small pieces and flushed them down the toilet.

By the time she got to the telephone, it had rung four more times. By the next ring the person on the other end would have hung up.

"Hello?" She was out of breath.

"Miss Arden," the voice said with relief. "I was afraid you were not there."

"Who is it?"

"Dr. Tiffany." A pause. "From St. Andrew's Church."

"Yes, yes, Reverend Tiffany. Forgive me. I have been distracted. So much to do still, before tomorrow."

"I have made a terrible error, Miss Arden."

"Error?"

"I have booked a funeral at the same time that I booked your wedding, and I must ask you to postpone your wedding for an hour or two."

"No, no, no, no," she cried. "Eleven o'clock. That is when my wedding is going to be. I will not change it."

"But you see, it is the funeral of the unfortunate young Wentworth girl."

"It doesn't matter."

"She is the girl who was murdered by the soldier. Her family are regular members of my church. The error is mine. I ask you to bear with me. It is to be an enormous funeral, and the hour has been sent to the papers and cannot be changed."

"It would be bad luck for me to change. I will not," said Ann. "They must change."

She could not, would not, back down. Her vehemence astonished the befuddled minister. She knew that if Billy had read his mother's letter, he would not have married her. She felt if her wedding was postponed, even for an hour, it would not take place.

* * *

FOR PROPRIETY's sake, Ann insisted that Billy spend the night before the wedding at his barracks at the base; they were not to meet until they saw each other at the altar of St. Andrew's. This maidenly retreat pleased the sensibilities of Ann, who wanted to be sure that any word of her wedding that made its way back to New York would be well received.

Eruptions of thunder preceded daylight on the morning of the wedding, and rain beat angrily on the windows of Ann's room. Alone, she refused to acknowledge the gloom she felt. She thought of her mother, who would have cherished this day, marrying as she was beyond the wildest dreams of either of them in the days back in Kansas, when they planned ahead what her wedding would be like. Her mother would have said about Billy Grenville that he was a gentleman to his fingertips, a favorite expression of hers that she had once applied to Mr. Percy V. Jordan. She wondered what Billy would have thought of her mother, whether the indications of snobbery she occasionally glimpsed in him would have surfaced. She felt twinges of guilt about her mother whenever she thought about her in relation to the Grenville family.

As she arranged flowers in the sitting room of the suite for the small reception that was to follow the ceremony, she regretted the furtive aspects of this day and wished she had someone from her own life to witness the occasion. She could only think of Fredda Cunningham from Pittsburg, but that friendship was long abandoned, and Babette Van Degan. She missed Babette terribly and wished that Billy had not dissuaded her from asking Babette to come out to be her matron of honor. She knew that the matron of honor she was to have, Gail Bumpers, the wife of an officer from the base, would never overlap to the new life she envisioned for herself and Billy after the war.

Late morning brought an uneasy dark-skied truce with the weather. When Bratsie Bleeker arrived, magically, the day seemed not to be lost. Ann's delight in the unexpected arrival of Billy's best friend was boundless, and the cheerless day brightened.

She dressed in white, bridelike, her face covered with virginal veils. Carrying a bouquet of stephanotis, she walked up the aisle of the nearly empty church on the arm of an officer, in the role of father, whom she had met only the night before, to be delivered to her groom. He, nervous as she, for the secretiveness of their act, lit up with pleasure when his bride appeared. He could not imagine a time when the sight of her would not erase whatever misgivings there were. He seemed not to notice the coldness of the minister, Dr. Tiffany, who performed the ceremony, or the noise of crowds of people outside the church waiting for the funeral to start.

It was too late for the press to print the change of time for the funeral of the slain Wentworth girl, and hundreds of people showed up only to be told they had to wait until the wedding inside was over. As the bridal party emerged from the church, for pictures to be taken and confetti and rice to be thrown, the mourners for the funeral lined up and somberly watched them.

By the curb in front of the church the flower-filled hearse and limousines carrying members of the heartbroken family waited until the wedding party had moved on its way. As the chauffeur opened the door of the car bearing the parents and two brothers of the dead girl, a gust of wind blew multicolored confetti into their car.

Bratsie, when not being irrepressible, observed his old friend's new wife, and wondered. It had all happened so quickly from the night of their boisterous romp through the nightclubs of New York to this subdued wedding reception in a flower-filled but dour hotel suite in Tacoma, Washington, without family on either side. What sort of ambition was it, he wondered, that brought about this conclusion—and conclusion it was—against so many odds?

He wondered if, behind Ann's squeals of delight, he did not sense disappointment in the proportions of her just-arrived engagement ring, from Cartier's, impressive but no match for Babette Van Degan's. He wondered if the matron of honor, Gail Bumpers, officiating in a fairy-tale performance, sensed she was being condescended to by the Cinderella of the piece. He wondered why, hours later, the Reverend Dr. Tiffany of St. Andrew's Episcopal Church had not made his obligatory minister's appearance, his church hundreds of dollars richer through the bridegroom's largess. He wondered about that funeral and those mourners waiting their turn to mourn while eyeing the bold wedding festivities, and shuddered.

"Surely this glum figure is not the infamous Bratsie Bleeker?" It was the bride speaking. A nascent hostess, she felt her party dragging and wanted the playboy to be a playboy and breathe life into it.

"But you haven't provided me with a chandelier to swing from," he replied, adjusting his mood to the role expected of him. Champagne was poured. Livelier music was suggested to the piano player. The rug was rolled back. Dancing began. With more officers than ladies present, the bride was cut in on incessantly, and the appropriate mood of mirth restored to the room.

"Where is the groom?" asked Bratsie, during one of his turns.

"Calling Mère," answered Ann. She moved her cheek against his to avoid eye contact.

"To break the news," he said as both a question and a statement. They dipped elaborately, and amusingly, he shorter than she, and would-be dancing partners held back from cutting in.

"Your career?" he asked.

"My career will be to be Mrs. William Grenville, Junior," she replied.

"Theatrical aspirations abandoned, then?" he asked.

"What is it you are saying to me, Bratsie? You led me to believe you approved of me for Billy." He liked her directness, and told her that, as he turned her, fox-trotting all the while.

"What I'm saying is, don't try to become one of them, like Alice or the sisters, or any of the girls like that he might have married. Be your own self among them, and stay special," said Bratsie.

"The unknown serious side of Bratsie," said Ann, matching his steps expertly: Mr. Dodsworth's classes and Broadway melding on the dance floor.

"Hark," he said. It was a favorite word of his.

"Hark?" she asked. "Isn't that what the herald angels sing?"

"It means, listen to what I'm saying," said Bratsie.

The moment was ended by Billy, about whom Bratsie was speaking all the time.

"It's Mère on the telephone," said Billy. "She wants to talk to you."

"Have you told her?"

"Yes."

"And?"

"Well, more surprised than anything else, I suppose," he said, obviously relieved that the dreaded task was over.

In the bedroom, the door closed against the music, Ann answered the telephone.

"Hello, my dear," said Alice Grenville. Her voice, aristocratic in tone, had resignation added to it, and disappointment. It was a voice that Ann would always fear. "This is, of course, a surprise, but I assure you I will have recovered from it by the time you return to New York. I look forward to getting to know you."

"And I you," answered Ann.

"Have you telephoned your parents?" asked Alice.

"What?" asked Ann.

"Your parents, my dear—have you telephoned them with the news?" persisted Alice.

"I don't have a family," said Ann.

"Oh, yes, yes. You told me that, didn't you?"

"SHE'S BAD NEWS, that one," said Alice Grenville to her daughters. She had minutes before hung up the telephone and presented her family with the disheartening news.

"But your letter, Mère," said Cordelia.

"My letter was never mentioned," replied Alice.

"Did he ignore it, do you suppose, or not get it?" asked Grace.

"My God!" said Felicity.

"What?"

"Suppose it comes now, when he's married to her, about all those men."

"We must act now as if it never happened," said Alice.

"Will you announce it to the papers, Mère?" asked Cordelia.

"I must."

"What about the Copacabana? Will you mention that?"

"What about the Copacabana?" asked Felicity.

"She danced there," said Cordelia.

"Growing up, I accepted the fact that no stage person would ever be asked to our house as a friend. And now look. We have a show girl in our midst," said Alice.

They sat in the late twilight, each in private thoughts of explaining Junior's extraordinary marriage to their relations, friends, and the press.

"In my day people like us knew who everyone's parents were and where they came from," Alice continued. "We were insulated from people outside of us. There was never any question of disobedience. If one of my parents said, 'This is not a suitable person,' that was it; there was nothing more to discuss."

"What about her parents?" asked Felicity.

"She said she's an orphan," replied her mother. "No family whatever."

"That could be a blessing, Mère," said Grace. "At least you won't have to invite her mother and father here or to the country."

"It's this damn war," said Alice. "He would never have met her if it weren't for the war. Going overseas, maybe not coming back. All those things are what she banked on, and she won. I knew the first time she walked into this house what was on her mind."

"What will we do about her?" asked Cordelia.

"I won't speak to her," said Felicity.

"Nor will I," said Grace.

"She is now Mrs. William Grenville, Junior," said Alice quietly, reminding them of whom they were speaking. "We must make the best of this bargain."

"She's not the kind of girl a person like Billy Grenville marries. She's the kind of girl you set up in an apartment on the West Side for however long it lasts, and when it's over, as it certainly will be, you pay her ten thousand dollars and buy her something nice. And marry someone we've all heard of. Like Esme Bland."

Jeanne Twombley, who heard it from Alfred, of course, told me that was the kind of thing that was said at the time at all those clubs where Billy Grenville belonged and where his father belonged before him. What they meant was that that sort of marriage, to a show girl with a dubious reputation, was all right for someone like Tommy Manville, but not for Billy Grenville. They felt, those members, mostly friends of his late father's, that Billy had let them down, and that he had certainly let his mother down.

"What's she look like?" asked Alfred Twombley.

"Bratsie says she has great tits," said Piggy French.

It was not thought ill-mannered in the Grenvilles' circle to ask, about a bride, "Who is she?" or "Who was she?" The new Mrs. Grenville fit into none of the categories of identification to which families like theirs surrendered their heirs: schools, summer resorts, clubs, and Social Register. It could not be said about Ann Grenville that she was a relation of someone they knew, or that she had been at Foxcroft with one of the sisters, or that Billy had met her when she visited with friends in Newport or Southampton. The name of the town she was from in Kansas required explanations—"No, no, it's not Pittsburgh, Pennsylvania, it's Pittsburg, *Kansas*"—and her career as a show girl onstage and in nightclubs was an embarrassment. As was her reputation.

The brief announcement of the marriage in the *New York Times,* strategically placed, without a bridal picture, made by Mrs. William Grenville, Senior, said that the wedding of her son, Ensign William Grenville, Junior, to Miss Ann Arden had taken place at St. Andrew's Episcopal Church in Tacoma, Washington. It said that Miss Arden was from Kansas City and had attended schools in that city as well as Kansas City Junior College. It said that Ensign Grenville had attended Groton and Harvard and was the son of the late William Grenville, former president of the Cambridge Bank in New York and owner of the Grenville racing stables and breeding farm in Kentucky. It listed Ensign Grenville's homes as being in New York, Newport, and Upper Brookville, Long Island.

Only Walter Winchell, the Broadway columnist, reported that the new Mrs. Grenville, of, as he put it, "the veddy social Grenvilles," had "showgirled" behind Ethel Merman in *Anything Goes* and, before that, in the line at the Copacabana nightclub. If any of Alice Grenville's friends read Walter Winchell's column, they did not mention it to her. It was whispered, among themselves, that she was heartbroken over the match, although both she and her daughters professed to be delighted with the originality of her son's choice.

Shortly after the wedding, when Billy was shipped to the Pacific, Ann returned to New York. Tacoma, as a waiting place, was not for her. Pregnant now, for sure, she kept her discovery a secret. She wanted her marriage to be dealt with before her motherhood. She lived, until other arrangements could be made, in her own apartment in Murray Hill. It occurred to her that she might be asked to stay in the huge Grenville house, even to occupy the same rooms in which Billy had lived all his life.

The first interview between the two Mrs. Grenvilles was not auspicious. When she arrived at her mother-in-law's house, a lunch party was still in progress. Afterward she remembered maids in aprons and caps and the sound of heels on marble and parquet floors as she waited in the hallway beneath the giant chandelier. Cahill, in greeting her, assumed the attitude of the house in which he had been employed for so many years. Madam would be delayed due to the lateness of an admiral who was, at that moment, delivering a toast to his gracious hostess. Affectionate laughter and applause were heard from the dining room as Cahill led the new Mrs. Grenville across the marble hall to the elevator and up to the third floor, where she was taken to her mother-in-law's sitting room off her bedroom to wait.

It was the first small room Ann had seen in the house, and she found it warm and cozy. Chairs were slipcovered in glazed chintz, and a biography of Lady Asquith had been left open on one of them. A portrait of a handsome young Alice Pleydell, sisterless here, by Boldini, looked down on the room. A needlepoint bell cord, for maids to be summoned, struck Ann's eye, the first one she had ever seen, and she longed to pull it and issue commands. Engraved invitations, piled one upon the other, were propped against the mantelpiece. She wanted to look at them, but did not. The writing desk was littered with sheets of paper, the same pale-blue stationery Ann knew so well, as if Alice had been disturbed in her writing to greet her luncheon guests. Ann shuddered with the remembrance of the purloined and destroyed letter meant to expose her shabby history to her husband. Suddenly she saw that a Pekinese dog, nestled into a chair, followed her every movement. Their eyes met. She was glad she had not looked at the invitations.

She wondered if she would always feel like an outsider in this house. She had not been welcomed as a bride by Cahill, nor had she been asked to meet the luncheon guests downstairs, nor did the Pekinese staring haughtily at her seem to recognize her right to be there. She began to worry about her reception. Uncomfortable, undecided where to sit, she lit a Camel cigarette and inhaled deeply while walking around the small room. Looking for somewhere to drop her match, she saw there were no ashtrays in the room and placed the match beneath the luxuriant leaves of a cyclamen plant in full bloom. She cupped her hand and deposited, nervously, an ash in it. How, then, could she shake hands, she wondered, with ashes in her palm, when Mrs. Grenville came in? Finally, she took a Chinese plate from a teakwood stand on the mantelpiece, placed it on a table, and put out her cigarette on it.

It was the first thing Alice Grenville noticed when she entered the room fifteen minutes later, her luncheon guests having finally departed. Her nostrils flared as though offended by the disagreeable odor. Without comment, she emptied the cigarette butt and ashes into a wastebasket, wiped off the Chinese plate with a piece of her pale-blue stationery, and replaced it on the teakwood stand.

"I cannot bear cigarette smoke in this room" were her first words to her new daughter-in-law. "It is where I tend to my affairs."

"I'm sorry," said Ann simply. She was determined not to be thrown. It was, after all, only a cigarette.

"But you had no way of knowing," said Alice, relenting, willing to let the moment pass. It had made any sort of greeting—a handshake, an embrace—unnecessary.

It was said of Alice Grenville, by her triplet sisters, and her friends of old, that as a young girl she was superbly handsome, and the various paintings of her, particularly the Boldini, in her presentation dress and feathers, attested to this. As a young girl she would rather have been thought beautiful than handsome, but the beauties of her youth, whom she had envied, had not, for the most part, weathered the storm of the years in the way her handsomeness had. Ann was struck by her looks in a way she had not been at their first meeting.

"Have you met Winston?" asked Alice, displacing the Pekinese from her chair and sitting down. "We think he looks so much like Mr. Churchill. Here, Winston, I've brought you something lovely from the table." The Pekinese went mad with delight at the attention he was receiving. Alice broke a cookie in two and threw first one and then the other half of it in the air, and watched in complete concentration as the dog scurried for his favors, yipping and yapping. Ann, forgotten, stared at the interplay between dog and mistress.

"What a good doggie you are, yes, yes, what a good doggie you are, and how your mummy loves you, yes she does, yes she does," cried Alice, swooping the Pekinese up in her arms and holding him aloft. She pulled the needlepoint bell cord, and when her maid, Lyd, appeared, kissed her dog between his eyes and handed him to her maid. Lyd, in the family for years, took in the scene, understood, and departed wordlessly. That accomplished, Alice turned back to the business at hand. The two Mrs. Grenvilles looked at each other once again.

"You must tell me about your wedding," said Alice. "Edith Bleeker, who heard from Bratsie, tells me you wore white. This was your first marriage?"

"Yes."

"Have you brought pictures? I hope so. The girls will want copies. Their only brother, you know. Ah, your ring, do let me look at it."

Ann, barraged, moved forward and held out her hand. For the first time she was glad her pear-shaped diamond was not as big as Babette Van Degan's.

"Lovely," said Alice, looking at it but not taking her daughter-in-law's hand. "Mr. Glaenzer, I suppose."

"No, Cartier's," corrected Ann.

"Mr. Glaenzer is our man at Cartier's," said Alice.

"Oh." She felt she could say nothing right. She turned toward the mantelpiece. "Is that what you do with invitations?" she asked, grasping.

"What?"

"Pile them up like that on the mantelpiece?" It did not seem to demand an answer, and none was given, but she continued to pursue an inane topic. "It looks very smart. You get invited to an enormous number of things."

"I've noticed this about you before," said Alice.

"What?" asked Ann.

"You talk about props to avoid talking about issues," answered Alice.

"Props?"

"But you are theatrical, Ann. Surely you know what that means. The last time we met you talked about my ermine coat and a photograph of Queen Mary. Today you talk about the placement of invitations on a mantelpiece. Then you had designs on my son. Now you are married to him. Shall we begin this conversation?"

Ann Grenville tried to look straight into Alice Grenville's eyes, but she found them impenetrable and unwelcoming.

"I know you don't think I'm good enough for your son, Mrs. Grenville," she said. Alice Grenville did not deny the allegation. She simply did not answer.

"Your parents are dead?" she asked instead.

"Yes."

"They were what?"

Unsure what she meant, Ann answered, "Poor."

"I meant what occupation."

"My father was a farmer. My mother was sometimes a teacher."

"Were they divorced?"

"Yes. When I was eight. My mother married again and divorced again."

"Good heavens."

"Why is it you don't like me?"

Alice, taken aback by Ann's directness, replied, "You are ambitious."

"I *am* ambitious," conceded Ann. "I didn't know it was a bad thing to be."

"*Too* ambitious, which is very different."

"Teach me how to be." She said it simply, without guile. "I love your son. I have never loved a man as I love him. I intend to be an excellent wife. My career on the stage is behind me. Are these the issues you wish to deal with?"

"You needn't be belligerent, Ann," chastised Alice. Her brown velvet eyes assessed anew the woman in front of her. "After all, you are already Mrs. William Grenville, Junior."

"I know I am," said Ann. "I only feel tolerated by you because I am married to Billy Grenville. I feel you are waiting for my marriage to be over, as if it were a wartime thing. It isn't, you know. Till death do us part."

For a while Alice did not answer. She reached out and twisted off a brown leaf from the cyclamen plant. "You call my son Billy?" she asked finally.

"Yes. I didn't want to marry a man called Junior."

"You're right. I suppose he has outgrown that name. Where will you live?"

It was a conversation full of starts, stops, and stumbles. Each, in her different way, was used to controlling, but each knew she had met her match. Until Billy Grenville returned from the war, a state of unspoken truce would be observed.

THE SISTERS, with the exception of Billy's favorite, Cordelia, remained aloof. What they thought of their sister-in-law, that she had trapped their brother, was never expressed, except among themselves, since their code would permit no outside criticism of their brother's wife. But what they felt was sufficiently plain for their friends to form an opinion.

Esme Bland, for one, rolling bandages one afternoon in the Grenville library for the war effort, watched Billy Grenville's glamorous new wife, fascinated. Poor plain Esme Bland had always nurtured the secret hope that one day she would become Billy's wife. She watched the sisters talk about people Ann did not know and parties she had not been to, using nicknames and private allusions, familiar to them, incomprehensible to her.

Ann began appearing at family lunches and dinners without being accepted by the family itself. It soon became apparent that Alice, resigned, had taken her daughter-in-law in hand to show her the ropes of the life she had married into. She suggested books for her to read, which Ann read, and made subtle suggestions about the way her hair was done and the kind of clothes she wore, and Ann listened and acted upon the suggestions.

"I very much hope you won't mind if I make a suggestion," said Alice, determined to make the suggestion whether it was minded or not.

"No," replied Ann, who said about herself that she never had to be told a thing twice.

"When you're in conversation, Ann, your eyes should not dart around the room to see who else is there. Give your undivided attention to the person with whom you are talking."

"Right," said Ann.

"And just pass your hand over the top of your wineglass before the butler pours if you don't want any wine. Never turn your glass upside down."

"All right."

"Don't cut your roll with a knife. Break it always."

"Yes."

And on and on.

Ann sat among them, a stranger in their midst. When she realized that no amount of friendliness would change their impression of her, she stopped extending herself. She watched, listened, and learned, improving herself in small ways not at first apparent to them. Although she was aware of the importance of her new position almost immediately, from the attitude of sales-people in shops she began to frequent, she was content to wait before she began to make her presence felt in her new family.

WHEN LIVING accommodations at the Grenville house were not offered Ann, Babette Van Degan found her a sunny apartment on Park Avenue that she moved into and began to fix up. Babette remained in her life, but she did not try to bring Babette into her new family, not wanting Babette to see her cold-shouldered by Billy's sisters, nor wanting Billy's sisters to size them up as a pair of Cinderellas. In a very short time she began to see her old friend through Grenville eyes.

"With freesia, you know, if you crush the end of the stem, they live longer," said Cordelia when she and Felicity came to see Ann's new apartment. Ann, who did not see the point of crushing stems to make blossoms last longer when you could simply buy fresh blossoms, wondered how they knew all the things they knew, these people, that had so little to do with survival. She wondered if she would ever settle into their kind of life.

"I think you're using the wrong brocade," said Felicity. She will never get it right, Felicity thought: candles at lunch, chrysanthemums in summer, gold brocade.

"You don't like it?" asked Ann, crestfallen.

"Gold, you know, it's not quite the thing. It's so . . ." She stopped before she said "Babette Van Degan," of whom they all made fun.

" 'Show girl'?" asked Ann, bristling. "Is that what you were going to say?" One day, she thought, she would get even with Felicity.

"Pas avant les domestiques," said Felicity to Ann, knowing the Irish maids did not understand, knowing Ann didn't either.

She changed the brocade. She softened the color of her hair. Even her handwriting changed: the round letters of the Palmer method taught in the Pittsburg, Kansas, school system gave way to the fashionable backhand printing of the Farmington–Foxcroft–St. Timothy's school system. In everything the sisters were her models. She had an eye for the aristocratic gesture, and she acquired that. She had an ear for the aristocratic voice, and she acquired that, with the help of a teacher, found for her by Count Rasponi, whom she paid handsomely for social guidance.

"But you are Mrs. Grenville," he said to her the first time they met, reassuring her.

"They sense that I am different," said Ann.

"But that's what makes you special," he insisted.

"I want to talk like them, dress like them, handwrite like them, think like them. *Then* I'll add my special thing on top of that."

Count Rasponi laughed with delight.

ONE MORNING, in the seconds before awakening, Ann saw Billy's face clearly, brightly. Awake, she was sure he was dead. She examined her feelings. She missed terribly the handsome young man she barely knew, who had defied his family for her, and realized how deeply she needed him. She wondered what would become of her. She knew she would be dropped by the family that had only tolerated her. She knew that even in so brief a time she was beyond returning to the chorus line. The stage had been no more than the means to an end, and the end was where she now was. Later, to her joy, she discovered that Billy Grenville was not dead at all. Rather he had distinguished himself in battle in the Pacific.

The news of Billy's heroism in the Pacific, saving the life of an enlisted man, for which he was awarded a Silver Star, coincided with Ann's announcement to the family that she was going to have his baby. Providence, again, was on her side. It was a miracle of timing, and even Felicity rose to the occasion.

"SHE DON'T get up until noon," Ann heard her maid say on the telephone to whoever was calling. Certainly it was true what the woman said, she didn't get up until noon, but the sound of it, at least in Mary's brogue, was wrong to her ear, and she began her day by firing Mary for insubordination, although it might have been for bad grammar. Later, she told Babette Van Degan, who called to remind her of their lunch date, that she couldn't possibly have lunch because the baby was kicking and her goddam maid had walked out on her, leaving her high and dry.

"Hello, is that you, Ann?" said the voice on the other end of the telephone, in a gravelly kind of way that Ann recognized immediately as the voice of Kay Kay Somerset.

"Yes, it is," she answered brightly.

"It's Kay Kay Somerset." No matter who Kay Kay Somerset married, and she married quite often, three times before she was thirty, she was always called Kay Kay Somerset. Ann read every word about her in the society columns, where her name constantly appeared, and listened avidly to the stories Cordelia told her about Kay Kay's early pursuit of Billy. "She came out, of course, but she wasn't taken into the Junior Assembly," explained Cordelia. "Pots of money, though."

"Oh, hello," said Ann, hoping the thrill she felt at being called by Kay Kay Somerset was not too apparent in her voice.

"I thought you looked so pretty at the Eburys' last night."

"Thank you." She hadn't known she had been noticed. "I feel so enormous these days."

"When will it be?"

"Not for three more months."

"I wondered if you'd like to have lunch today."

"Well, I'm, uh . . . ." She thought of Babette, just abandoned.

"I'm driving back to the country at three, but I thought it would be fun to get together. You know, we've never talked."

"I think that sounds marvelous."

"I'll meet you at the Colony at one. In the bar. Away from all the old ladies."

Ann was ecstatic. She bounded from her bed, ran her tub, picked out her most becoming maternity outfit, and wished she had not fired her maid. She walked into the Colony at fifteen minutes past one in splendid good looks and high good humor and was escorted by Mr. Cavallero himself to Kay Kay Somerset's table. It was the beginning of her first friendship in her new life.

"Weren't you on the stage?" asked Kay Kay.

"Oh, only very briefly," answered Ann quickly. "My family really didn't approve at all. And then I met Billy."

"Oh," said Kay Kay. It seemed quite a disappointing answer to Kay Kay, who would have preferred her new friend to flaunt her theatrical past, especially as it was well known that the Grenville family considered her a totally unsuitable choice for Billy to have made. Ann, on the other hand, thought she had answered Kay Kay's inquiry marvelously. She felt no qualms in the least about letting go of any of her past story before becoming Mrs. Grenville. She was more interested in hearing about Kay Kay's life than in revealing to Kay Kay anything about her own life, and she drew out Kay Kay, who loved talking about herself, into hilarious stories of her marital failures.

"It was our usual conversation," she said about her most recent ex-husband. " 'Where's the check?' 'It's in the mail.' 'Fuck you.' Slam."

The happy occasion was marred somewhat by the appearance in the same restaurant of Babette Van Degan and her luncheon replacement for Ann, another former show girl. Babette, through indignant looks, made no secret of the fact that she was offended by her friend's defection. Ann realized that the time had come to lessen her attachment to Babette, whose loyalty to her former show-girl friends now seemed excessive to Ann.

Kay Kay fascinated Ann, and she treasured her new friendship as she once had treasured her friendship with Babette. She began going places on her own, away from the grudging sponsorship of her Grenville relations.

"Who painted that?" asked Ann, pointing to a large pastoral scene hung over a console table in Kay Kay's apartment. She was ever alert in the learning process.

"I don't know, some Italian," answered Kay Kay, not even bothering to turn around to look at it. She was constantly moving, a new apartment to begin a marriage, a new apartment when the marriage ended. Wherever she was was in the process of being done up or dismantled. Disarray prevailed; she entertained in restaurants, arriving late to her own dinners, face flushed, eyes glazed, *placement* left behind. "Oh dear, you go there, and you go there, by

Binkie," she would say, trying to remember her seating plan. Beneath the madcap air, Ann began to sense the deep insecurities of the very rich heirs and heiresses of this group she was beginning to meet.

After several meetings, Ann's awe of Kay Kay began to diminish, and she started to take charge of the friendship, using Kay Kay to meet people she read about in the papers. "I sat between Vere Cecil and Bluey Chisholm," she would say to her sisters-in-law, hoping to impress them with the excellence of her *placement.* More often than not, they did not reply, and she went on, recounting the guest list, at least the illustrious names.

"Let me look them up in the old S.R. here," said Felicity, picking up the Social Register. The Grenvilles thought of themselves as old New York, and therefore superior to Kay Kay's flashy friends. "Surprise, surprise, here they are." She was disappointed to find them.

ANN HOPED and prayed that the child she carried would be a son. Pregnancy was for her a long and tiring period that impeded the progress of the great new life that awaited her. Even Billy, in his letters from the Pacific, referred to the unborn child as "he" and "him." It was, however, more for Alice Grenville than her husband that she wished to deliver the Grenville heir, as if by preserving the name and continuing the tradition she would cement her place in the family and win the affection she yearned for from this woman rather than merely the politeness she received.

All the Grenvilles went to Archie Suydem, and, it seemed, had forever. He'd been in attendance when all the Grenville children were born, and he'd been at the girls' weddings. Archie Suydem was the best doctor in New York, everyone knew that, they told Ann, and furthermore he belonged to the Union Club and the New York Yacht Club, and that said a lot.

Ann, who longed to do the right thing, to conform to all things Grenville, at least until she was sufficiently established in their midst to develop into the self she foresaw, could not bear the thought of such an old man as Dr. Archie Suydem placing his brown-spotted hands on and in her body, Union Club or no Union Club. As there was no one in the family to whom she could speak of her revulsion, she was determined, as her mother would have said, had she been alive, to grin and bear it.

"I have such trouble sleeping, Dr. Suydem," she said during an examination in her final weeks.

"Hot milk and honey before bedtime," replied Dr. Suydem.

"You suggested that last time, doctor, and it hasn't worked. I would like a prescription for some sleeping pills."

"No, no, that's not a good thing," he said, shaking his head. "In all my years of practice, forty-odd, I've never heard of anyone dying from lack of sleep." He chuckled his old doctor's chuckle. "Hot milk and honey and walks in the afternoon. Exercise is very important."

From Babette Van Degan and Kay Kay Somerset, Ann heard about Dr.

Skinner. Sidney Silkwood Skinner was fifty, with luxuriant hair, gray turning white, and wavy. Both his hair, of which he was inordinately proud, and his pencil-line mustache appeared always to have been freshly trimmed, and his nails were manicured and polished to a sheen. He was not a member of the Union Club or the New York Yacht Club, and people like the Grenvilles referred to him, snobbishly, as a Park Avenue doctor. He was thrilled when the beautiful Mrs. William Grenville, Junior, forsook the doctors recommended by her husband's family and sought out his services. He was putty in her hands, made house calls day or night, and prescribed a potpourri of refillable prescriptions for the tensions and stress of New York life.

From Dr. Skinner, she heard about Dr. Virgil Stewart, then very much in fashion with the young matrons of New York, and, much to the disapproval of the Grenville family, switched from Dr. Suydem to Dr. Stewart to deliver her baby. When her time was at hand, she picked the fashionable Doctors Hospital, overlooking the East River, with Dr. Skinner's and Dr. Stewart's blessing, rather than Columbia Presbyterian Hospital, where all the Grenvilles were born, and ordered her meals to be sent in from the Colony Restaurant.

Following an easy birth at an inconvenient hour, Dr. Stewart, who arrived at the hospital in evening clothes to deliver the Grenville heir, informed Ann that she was the mother of a bouncing baby girl. Her disappointment in the sex of her child was apparent to both the doctor and the nurses present in the room, and she tried not to let show the resentment she felt toward the baby when it was placed in her arms. While she was reflecting that she would have to go through the nine-month ordeal again, the thought of Alice Grenville's four daughters before the son flashed through her mind, not for the first time. Rather than dwell on a subject so disagreeable to her, she inquired of Dr. Stewart what party her inconveniently timed birth-giving had dragged him away from.

In secrecy Ann would have liked to name her daughter Wallis, after the Duchess of Windsor, or Brenda, after Brenda Frazier, who were the kind of women she admired, as had her mother before her, but she knew better than to risk the derision of her sisters-in-law at these suggestions. She rejected all the names of the Grenville women. She didn't want an Alice, she said to Babette, or a Rosamond, nor a Grace, nor a Cordelia, and most certainly not a Felicity. She decided on Diantha, a name she had read in a novel, and agreed to call her Dolly when Alice said she thought Billy would find the name contrived and theatrical. Dolly Grenville. She began to like the sound of it. It was a name that would read well in social columns, she thought, when that time came.

The Reverend Dr. Kinsolving performed the baptismal service of Diantha Grenville in the chapel of St. James' Church on a cold afternoon in March. Observing every family tradition, she wore the Pleydell christening dress that had been worn by Alice and all of her four daughters. Cordelia was the godmother. Bratsie, in absentia, fighting in North Africa, was the godfather.

A small party followed at Alice's great house off Fifth Avenue. Ann, looking exceedingly smart in dark blue, sat on a sofa in an elegant and relaxed pose, made loving references to Billy, and allowed herself to remain a sideline figure. Outside, the St. Patrick's Day parade passed by—marching bands, baton twirlers, waving politicians, Irish songs, and a cheering populace. Inside, where the christening party assembled for cocktails, only the maids, passing canapés, bothered to look out, and their glances were stolen.

Finished with the photographs and a lengthy discourse on the heirloom baptismal dress, Alice Grenville did not linger in grandmotherly attitudes. "Find the nanny, will you?" she said to her butler, handing him the baby.

PART TWO

I LIKE IT WHEN you whisper all the filth in my ear," Billy confessed to Ann, holding her tightly, his face in her hair. Jealous by nature, she liked to drain him of desire before leaving in the evenings for the constant round of dinner parties that had begun to make up their life. They were in their bed, where they were good together; there they satisfied and understood each other. Elsewhere it was not always so.

For all her years it seemed to Ann she had been waiting for her life to begin. When Billy returned home from the war, she felt that finally that beginning had come. The apartment, finished, was not satisfactory. Billy, used to large houses, felt constricted by the proximity of the child's nurse and nursery sounds that began too early in the morning. It was felt, by Billy and his mother, that a house would better serve their needs, and a house was found in the East Seventies between Park Avenue and Lexington Avenue, less grand by far than the grand Grenville house but grander by far than the abodes of nearly every other young couple in the city.

Ann was attracted to her young husband's spoiledness. She realized how little she knew him out of uniform. She realized also that the battle of winning him having been won, the heightened and heady drama of their courtship and wedding had now settled into real life. She was anxious for him to see and approve of her advancements in the years that he had been gone, but she found instead that she merely bewildered him.

"Sometimes I don't recognize you anymore," said Billy. "You're like a different person."

"I thought you'd be proud of me," said Ann.

"If that was what I wanted, I could have married the real thing," he answered. Her eyelids flickered, and her eyes, moistening slightly, widened. She had been hurt. He had not meant the remark to sting her, but it did.

Billy suggested a sojourn to his mother's country house in Brookville, Long Island, as a kind of honeymoon to reacquaint themselves with each other and to introduce Ann to the friends of his childhood with whom he had grown up. The house, called Fairfields, was to be theirs for the several weeks they stayed, without Alice, without the sisters, without Diantha and the nurse. It was Ann's first encounter with the North Shore. Days were filled with sport, at which Ann proved herself to be surprisingly proficient. Nights were filled with parties at neighboring estates.

That night Ann observed the group at Alfred and Jeanne Twombley's: the Chesters; the Dudleys; the Webbs; the Chisholms; Teddy Plum; Bratsie Bleeker; the McBeans; Sass Buffington; Tucky Bainbridge; the Eburys; Petal Wilson. No stray noblemen here, no late-blooming millionaires. This was the core: friends from childhood they were, and their parents before them. Sixty percent of the land of the North Shore of Long Island could be traced to the ownership of those present. In advance she knew their histories: past stories of suicided parents; kidnapped brothers; institutionalized children; divorce; depravity; drink; depression; death in crashed planes, on sunken yachts, off fallen horses. But how elegantly they behaved. She was transfixed by the aristocracy of them.

She noticed how very alike the young women all were. They talked the same way, in the same accent, as if they had shared the same nanny. Their hair was done in the same pageboy style, held back with gold bar pins, and their long skirts, blouses, and cashmere cardigan sweaters over their shoulders were interchangeable. She realized that for country life she was overdressed, overcoiffeured, overjeweled, a mistake she would not make again.

Ann, entering Jeanne Twombley's bedroom after dinner, knew instinctively the women were talking about her. She shrank back against the yellow-distempered wall, undetected by the others, as if to lose herself in it, and heard her background or lack of it discussed.

"She's the cheapest thing I've ever seen," said Sass Buffington, combing her hair.

"Felicity said you must go to one of her parties before she finds out it's the wrong way to do it," said Tucky Bainbridge, and the other ladies laughed.

"Piggy said she went through two polo teams on Gardiners Island before the war," said Petal Wilson.

"N.O.C.D., darling."

Smarting, she turned and left the room, walking down the curved stairway to rejoin the men left behind in the dining room with cigars and brandy. On her entrance, the men rose as one to greet her into their womanless turf. She was pleased to see that Billy felt a glow of proprietorship over her, and she smiled charmingly at him as she sidled next to him.

Later, when the party reassembled in the chintz-slipcovered drawing room, Ann asked Billy, "What's N.O.C.D. mean?"

" 'Not our class, darling,' Why?" he replied.

"No reason."

To herself she vowed that someday these ladies would eat their words, and, silently, she dedicated herself to achieving the social acceptance her husband's family and friends denied her. Ignored by the women, she ignored being ignored, and plunged herself amid them, wanting to be accepted by people who did not want to accept her, prepared to play the waiting game. She looked over at the handsome, rich, socially impeccable young man who had married her and would enable her to open any door, and smiled at him affectionately.

"Bratsie likes you," said Billy, back home.

"But not for the right reasons," replied Ann.

"What does that mean?"

"He likes me because I'm wrong."

"Wrong?"

"Wrong side of the tracks."

"He didn't say that."

"He didn't have to. I can read the look."

IT FILLED ANN with inordinate pleasure when her name appeared for the first time in the New York Social Register. "Grenville, Mr. and Mrs. William, Jr. (Ann Arden)," it read, and then a list of incomprehensible abbreviations that turned out to be the many clubs that Billy belonged to. When she arranged her sitting room, she liked having the black-and-terra-cotta book in a prominent place on her desk, visible to the eyes of visitors and readily available to her touch. She remembered the time when she had looked up the address of the Grenville family in the same pages of an earlier edition in a florist shop. Now, listed herself, it provided proof positive of who she was.

Ann did not understand Bratsie Bleeker's early admonition to her not to try to become one of them but to remain her own self among them and therefore be special. What she wanted most *was* to become one of them, and on the occasions when she was asked, by a new acquaintance, if she had gone to Farmington or if she had been there on the night Bratsie Bleeker swung on the chandelier at Kay Kay Somerset's coming-out party, she felt that she was succeeding in her performance.

She bought her books at Wakefield's, was photographed by Dorothy Wilding, had Dr. Stewart as her gynecologist, and ordered her flowers at Constance Spry. She worshiped at St. James', when she worshiped, which was not often, and lunched at the Colony, which was very often. Caruso did her hair, Blanchette her nails, and she was massaged by Gerd. Hattie Carnegie dressed her for day, and Mainbocher for evening. Jules Glaenzer jeweled her. She was attended to by a cook, two maids, a chauffeur, and a nanny for her daughter. It did not appear that she was unused to this way of life.

As time went on, Ann feared sometimes that there was less to Billy than had at first appeared. He seemed like a second son in a first-son role. When he arrived late at his office, after a night of parties and nightclubs, Ann knew that it did not matter. There was no one to chastise him for unseriousness of purpose. He spent a number of hours there each day, involving himself in unimportant business, reading newspapers and magazines, checking with his stockbroker on conservative investments, making dates for squash or backgammon. He lunched at one of his clubs with friends and stopped for a drink at another on the way home, and his men friends would say about him, after he was gone, what a perfectly lovely fellow he was. Sometimes it surprised Ann that he had seen films that she had not seen, and she discovered that he often went alone, or with Bratsie, during the afternoons. He did not think much about advancing in life, because where he already was, financially and socially, was where most ambitious men he knew wanted to be.

Billy's feelings for Ann were ambivalent. He loved her. She gratified his sexual desires. She made him laugh. She stood up to his sisters. For a long time she even made him happy.

At the same time he disapproved of her. It was an ongoing fact of her life that she could not keep help. Servants, in their various capacities, came and went in varying degrees of haste, stung by her suspicions and imperious tones. Mostly, her social ambition was too apparent for him. She did not give parties to enjoy herself but to advance herself.

"Tell her she doesn't have to climb so hard. Tell her she's already there," Bratsie said to him one night, observing her work the room, as Bratsie called it, at one of Edith Bleeker's parties, collecting future invitations, and Billy, though honor-bound to support his wife, agreed with his friend.

He accepted, without curiosity, the minimal facts of her history that she gave him. References to her past were sparse. If pressed, she presented the life of Fredda Cunningham as her own. When she showed no longing to return to Kansas to present him to relations or friends, he felt relieved of that obligation. When he discovered, applying for a passport, that she was a different age than she had told him, he wondered about other things.

Having provided her with so much that she had never had before, he expected that her gratitude would continue and become the basis of their relationship. Instead, he watched her not only settle into her role too quickly but become the dominant member of their match. Where once he had ruled the relationship, because the world into which he had brought her was his and he had acted as her interpreter and guide, she was now overtaking the reins. He felt anger, and the anger that he felt persisted, but he did nothing to rid himself of it.

As IF SENSING the rumblings of his disaffection, Ann invariably would accomplish something that would make Billy proud, and harmony would be restored. Preferring men's pastimes to women's, she took up backgammon and then skeet shooting, and became proficient in both, winning skeet tournaments at Piping Rock. She loved the feel of a gun in her arms and longed, as Billy longed, for big game. But it was the son she produced and the home she created that cemented her marriage in seeming permanence.

Loathing pregnancy, for the time it took away from her life, and the distention of her lovely body and breasts, she undertook it and the doing of her new home concurrently. She knew her bridal apartment had not been a success, but she found herself unable to get along with the series of fashionable decorators suggested by her mother-in-law to help her: Rose Cummings came and went, as did Mrs. Brown, Mrs. McMillan, and Mrs. Parrish. To a lady they pronounced the young Mrs. Grenville impossible. Then, at a party of Babette Van Degan's, Ann met Bertie Lightfoot. Bertie Lightfoot was the director for her life she had been longing for without realizing it. Under his tutelage she began to give the performance she had been waiting all her life to play.

Ann never firmly committed herself to one of Babette Van Degan's invitations in case something more social should turn up. She said she thought she might have to dine that evening at "the family's," as she referred to evenings at Alice's, or that Billy might be working that night. Babette had become the kind of woman greatly admired by men who would never marry. Decorators and designers filled her rooms, and merriment prevailed. Junior said No, Absolutely Not, he would *never* go there again. Uninterested herself in that kind of appreciation, Ann, on the occasions she did attend, took to dropping in briefly, on her way to somewhere else, where she would be meeting Billy. On what she vowed would be her last time *ever* at a Babette Van Degan party, she met Bertie Lightfoot. He was at the time helpless with laughter at one of Babette's stories of her chorus-line days. His eyes, vividly Alice-blue, matched his shirt exactly and looked, to Ann, sad beneath his merriment.

"You're not leaving, darling?" asked Babette, breaking in on her own story. "You just got here."

"I must," answered Ann. "I'm meeting Billy." She was evening-dressed, carrying a fur, refastening a bracelet.

"What smart place are you off to tonight?" asked Babette. Bertie Lightfoot watched the exchange with fascination. So *this* was Mrs. Grenville of the society columns.

"Kay Kay Somerset's having a dinner for Lady Starborough," answered Ann. She had learned to neither flaunt grand names, as she once did, nor minimize them.

"She's gone swell on us," explained Babette to Bertie and turned away to take several cheese puffs from a tray passed by her young son, Dickie Junior, and to yell out a request to Edie and Rack, who were playing at twin pianos, to play "Spring Will Be a Little Late This Year."

"*Printemps* is in the air," said Bertie.

Ann nodded farewell to Blue Eyes.

"Linger awhile, so fair thou art," he said.

"Gallantry in Mrs. Van Degan's drawing room," replied Ann. She liked him instantly. He made her laugh.

Not one to let an opportune moment pass, Bertie admired Ann extravagantly: praised her clothes, her hair, her style. Unused to compliments, other than sexual, from her husband, Ann responded to Bertie's flow.

"Tell me again what your name is," she said.

"Lightfoot. Bertie Lightfoot."

"And what do you do?"

"Decorate."

"Decorate what?"

"Whatever."

She hesitated leaving.

"Cigarette?" he asked, snapping open a smart leather cigarette case.

"Leather? In town?" she asked, in mock social horror.

Again he collapsed with laughter. She enjoyed having her humor appreciated.

"I have a new house I'd like to show you," she said.

The house which Billy Grenville had purchased for his family was on a quiet street lined with leafy trees in the East Seventies between Park Avenue and Lexington Avenue. On each side of the street were elegant brick and brownstone houses in which still lived, in those days, but one family apiece and the servants who administered to their needs. The stucco exterior of the Grenville house, at number 113, was freshly painted a cream color, and its doors and shutters were lacquered black, as were its geranium-filled window boxes. Exceedingly smart, like its new occupants, it was a house meant to be noticed and commented upon.

Within, Bertie Lightfoot, making his name in New York, decorated the rooms in muted luxury. The furniture Billy's family handed over to Ann, in English and French shapes, she realized they did not value highly, assuming that she would not know the difference. It was Bertie Lightfoot, turning the pieces upside down, who, contemptuously, pronounced them reproductions. They were discarded or put aside for country-house guest rooms, when a country house of her own became a reality, which, she knew, it would, and fine furniture was sought in its stead. With Bertie she began to attend auctions, and visit collections, and develop an eye for only the best.

"You have a faggot's eye," he said to her admiringly, "for being able to spot exactly what's right." Bertie was good at intimacy with women but devoid of passion for them.

"I think I'll refrain from repeating that compliment to my mother-in-law," she answered. They enjoyed being together and maintaining absolute secrecy about the interior of the house until it was completed and could be presented as her creation.

Bertie of the light blue eyes was a merry man with a fund of camp wit, a knowledge of eighteenth-century French furniture, and a passion for rough trade. After his evenings in society, or at the opera, especially if he had been drinking, Bertie often changed from black tie and patent-leather pumps into less distinctive gear and took to the streets.

On his way out again after a dinner with Billy and Ann, a young man spoke to him on the street in an easy friendly way. "Hi," he said. "How's it going?" When he smiled, he had a dimple and good teeth, and there was a directness in his eyes. Bertie, who was more than a little drunk, thought for a moment that perhaps he knew him, from a party, or somewhere, and said, "Hi," back, in a matching easy friendly way, and asked him back to his apartment, blessing his luck for the easiness of the conquest.

Bertie had another drink, and a marijuana cigarette that the young man offered him, and a line or two of cocaine, all of which Bertie took without noticing that the young man took none.

The first punch was to the Adam's apple, rendering Bertie speechless. It was a full minute more before he realized what was happening to him: the sound of the switchblade knife opening, its cold blade being pulled across his cheek and neck, its point scratching the skin of his chest and stomach; the thirty-foot telephone wire tying his hands behind his back and attaching his feet and his hands; the pleasant young man of the street turning into a schizo-phrenic monster, destroying the antique-filled apartment, kicking the inert body, taunting, snarling, hating. He put a brown grocer's bag over Bertie's head and dropped lit kitchen matches on the paper.

Death was in the air. The end of his life was at hand, but his thoughts were not yet with God. Instead they were on the tabloid papers, and what they would say, after he was dead. He heard another match being struck and knew that his face would burn if that match dropped on the bag.

"God, help this man who is killing me," whispered Bertie. "God, help this man who is killing me." Again and again he whispered it, as in a litany. For a long time there was silence, and then he heard the click of a closing door. Amid the carnage of smashed antiques he lay there in shame long after his near-murderer had departed. The most he could do to extricate himself was to shake the brown grocer's bag off his head. There was no way he could untie the cord that bound his hands and feet behind him.

In time he crawled parameciumlike across the floor to the telephone and removed the receiver by knocking it off with his head. It did not surprise him that the telephone was out of commission; his night caller had removed the diaphragm from the earpiece to ensure that it would not be used after his departure.

He struggled more with the cord but did no more than tighten the knots. Had he been able to see his hands and feet behind him, he would have seen that they were turning white from blocked circulation.

He thought of the morning, and the maid coming and finding him in the deplorable state that he was in. Gerta, the maid, a German woman, came to him several mornings a week. The shame of being so discovered by Gerta was overwhelming, naked and bound as he was, and the subsequent story from maid to other clients, including Basil Plant, the writer, to whom she went on Fridays, was a kind of hell that further paralyzed him in its contemplation.

There was another telephone, hidden away in a linen closet, with a different number entirely, for his business calls. Again he crawled across the floor, proceeding by inches, down the hall, across the bedroom, and into the bathroom where the linen closet was.

Again he removed the receiver by knocking it off with his head, and the dial tone to a world outside sounded precious to him. Holding a pencil stub in his teeth, he slowly began to dial.

The number he dialed rang, and rang, and rang again, and then it was answered.

"Hello?"

"Oh, thank God, I thought your telephone was off."

"It is, but I could hear it ringing downstairs. Who is this?"

"Bertie."

"Are you crying?"

"I need help, Ann."

"Where are you?"

"My apartment."

"What's the matter?"

"I'm in a jam."

"Isn't there anyone else you can call?"

"No."

"I'll leave right away."

Ann Grenville rose from her bed and dressed quietly while her husband slept. Arriving at his apartment after three, she let herself in with a key he had given her. She untied him, covered him, poured him a brandy, massaged circulation into his whitened wrists, picked up broken things, and helped him into bed.

"Do you want to talk about it?" she asked.

"I was on my way out to meet some friends from California at the

Westbury, but I forgot my money, so I came back here to the apartment, and I must have interrupted the guy in the middle of a robbery, and he . . ."

"Save that story for the maid, Bertie," said Ann quietly, as she picked up the vial of cocaine and the plastic bag of marijuana. "Where do you want me to put this stuff?"

"I don't care."

"Talk about it, Bertie."

"Every year in the *Daily Mirror* I read about some decorator on the Upper East Side they find garroted and murdered, and that's all I could think of, how it was going to look in the papers," he said, crying.

"Why did he stop?" she asked him.

"I suppose I gave up."

"Bertie?"

"Yes?"

"While you thought you were dying . . ."

"Yes?"

"Is that all you thought about? The papers? What people would say about you after you were gone?"

"Yes."

"Not about God, and all that?" She waved her hand vaguely heavenward. He looked away from her. Tears filled his eyes again.

"I'm not criticizing you, Bertie. I'm afraid that's how I'd be thinking, too, how it would look, if something terrible ever happened to me." She breathed deeply. There was a long silence. "I'd better go. My husband will think I'm at Doctors Hospital having the baby."

"Ann, I want to explain to you how it happened."

"Oh, Bertie, it's not necessary for you to explain the particulars to me. I get the overall picture."

"I'll never forget this, Ann."

WHEN HER CHILD was born three weeks later, it was the much-needed son. Amid family joy for the name preserved and the tradition of Grenvilles carried on into a new generation of New York, Ann vowed, privately, that her childbearing days were over. *Now* was the time for her much-postponed life to begin. They named the child, of course, William Grenville III, and when Alice and the sisters began cooing the name Willy to him in his Grenville family cradle, Ann said she wanted her son called Third, and Billy was delighted with her inventiveness and agreed.

SHE WAS, FRANKLY, disappointed with the size of the sapphire in the ring he gave her when the baby was born. She placed it on her finger, looked and looked at it, and looked again, holding her hand at one angle and then another.

"It's just not me," she said, taking it off.

He was crestfallen, she could see that, and she sought quickly to make up. "But the flowers, my darling, the orchids are so lovely, and we have our wonderful son."

"Yes," he said. "There was another sapphire there that I could exchange this for, perhaps."

"Billy."

"Yes?"

"I'd like to go with you when you buy me jewelry."

"LOOK AT THIS, isn't it marvelous, what Billy bought me when Third was born," said Ann, showing her sapphire ring at the christening party in her splendid new house, finished finally. Over the mantelpiece in the living room was a Monet of irises, which Bertie said was the final touch in the beautiful and greatly admired room. In the thrill of acquisition, there was a resumption of warm feelings between Billy and Ann, and their guests, including his mother and sisters, were struck by the appearance of harmony between them.

SO AS NOT TO seem completely without antecedents, Ann began to mention her mother, although the mother she mentioned bore little resemblance to the mother that had been. Her mother was the one person who had understood her completely. She had been the first to perceive her inner longings and help to mold them into ambitions which she encouraged her to pursue. "Things happen to you, and they always will," said her mother. That she had become who she had become surpassed even her mother's wildest dreams for her, and she sometimes wished for that look of admiration she had grown to expect in her mother's eyes when she began to make her ascensions.

Ethel Mertens had not minded that she was left alone each night when Ann was at the Copacabana performing; nor did she expect her back after the final show, knowing and glowing in the fact that her daughter regularly attended the nightclubs of the city with eligible men who sent her gifts, one of whom might, she hoped, marry her one day. Ethel was quite content with her tabloid papers and gossip columns, over which she pored in the hopes of finding Ann's name; she became as well versed as Elsa Maxwell or Maury Paul in the comings and goings of such prominent social figures as Wallis Simpson and Barbara Hutton and Brenda Frazier.

Sad as it was, Ann knew that her mother's death the spring before she met Billy had been timely. It was not a thought she cared to formulate, but her ascent into the Grenville family, difficult as it was, would have been more difficult, perhaps impossible, with Ethel Mertens to explain. It was a threshold her mother would not have dared to cross. Once uprooted from the Kansas plain she had longed to flee, she invariably did the wrong thing in social situations, knew it, and suffered remorse when she embarrassed her daughter. Eventually she was content to stay behind, root for her daughter, and listen to her stories of life in the great world. Ann, to assuage her guilt from the unformed but lurking thoughts about her mother, began to bring her into conversations, referring to her not as Ma, but as Mother, the way Kay Kay Somerset talked about her mother, as if she were some elegant creature, now gone, whose silver it was, or whose tureen, that was being admired. "Oh, that was Mother's," Ann would say.

Then there appeared the portrait, not prominently placed, to call too much attention to it, but in the hallway of the second-floor landing, over a Regency bamboo settee that was never sat upon. It was Bertie Lightfoot who pointed out the picture to her in the back room of an antiques shop they were scouring through. It was turned against the wall because the frame was broken and the glass cracked, a forgotten lady of gentle birth painted in pastels in a style favored by society painters in the years preceding the First World War.

"She looks like you, Ann," said Bertie in great excitement. "I think maybe it's a Brocklehurst."

Later, when Bertie had gone to see about other matters, Ann returned to the antiques shop and purchased the picture, which did indeed resemble her. "That was Mother," she would say sometimes about the picture, in passing, to new friends not familiar with her history, and she came to believe it was so.

The picture, however, nearly ruptured the remnants of her friendship with Babette Van Degan, who came to call to see the celebrated house. Ann greeted her and led the way back for a tour room by room of the five-story house.

"Look," she said, at the door of her splendid drawing room, looking at it herself, yet again, with a pride of ownership. She moved a needlepoint pillow imperceptibly to the left and surveyed its symmetry with its matching pillow. Each day she secretly reexperienced the beauty of her home. Babette, always enthusiastic at her friend's progress in the world, responded accordingly to each fashionable room.

"Oh, how swank this all is," she said.

Upstairs, on the second-floor landing, on the way to Ann's bedroom, Ann said, in the offhand manner she had acquired about the portrait, waving her hand at it in passing, "You remember Mother, don't you?"

"Of course I remember your mother," replied Babette, "but who's the broad in the picture?"

"How was Babette?" asked Billy later.

"Oh, fine," answered Ann listlessly.

"Not much conviction in your voice."

"She's so cheap, Babette."

"But rich."

"And getting richer by the minute."

"Is Hyman Wunch still in the picture?"

"On and off."

"Think she'll marry him?"

"Darling, you don't change your name from Van Degan to Wunch," said Ann. "I mean, you just don't. A name like Van Degan makes life easier. That's all there is to it. It's a name people like to say, like Vanderbilt, or Rockefeller, or Astor. All over the world it's a name people recognize."

"Is that what Babette said?"

"That's what I said, but it's what she feels."

"You two have a falling-out?"

"Oh, let's not talk about Babette. I'm not going to see her for a while. You'd better get dressed. We're due at Eve Soby's."

SHE WORKED as hard as an office girl on the daily advancements of her insatiable ambition. Next it mattered exceedingly to her that she be named as one of the best-dressed women in New York. When she achieved that distinction, she pretended to consider it an inconsequential thing.

Bratsie Bleeker, her early champion, began to dislike her. Sensing this, she withdrew from him, not wanting to be what he wanted her to be, the single act of defiance in Billy's life. Neither spoke of their disenchantment to Billy; he would have had to side with one, and neither wanted to risk banishment.

Reluctantly in some quarters, it had to be acknowledged that Ann Grenville had made it. She was not the only maiden of modest social and financial pretensions to marry into a fine old family of wealth and position, but she was the first of the Cinderella girls, as Babette Van Degan called them, to conquer the highest brackets of New York.

Wherever one went, one heard her name. As a new word, once learned, suddenly appears constantly in conversation and print, so her name was spoken in every social gathering. Everyone seemed to know her, or to have heard of her, and to have opinions about her. People who had not intended to take her up took her up. She was seen in the best seat at the best table at the best parties. Men liked her exceedingly; she danced every dance, sang lyrics in their ear, and her conversation was ribald and spicy. Women liked her less but could not deny she was an asset at their parties and on their committees for their charities. Her husband's family, once so reluctant to accept her completely, in hopes the alliance would be brief, were astonished that she so rapidly penetrated an impenetrable world. An intruder in the family, she had become its most highly visible member, eclipsing her husband's sisters in social life.

There was no doubt in anyone's mind that she intended to make a go of her marriage and avoid becoming a former wife with a great last name, like Babette Van Degan, relegated to the sidelines of the social world. She understood that her power lay in remaining Mrs. William Grenville, Junior, no matter what. Despite the mismatch that they may have been as a couple, she knew that she still exercised a fascination over her husband that was stronger than the doubts he sometimes felt about their union.

Fydor Cassati, the society columnist, wrote constantly about the young Grenvilles in his column, far too often for Billy's taste, not often enough for Ann's, whose thirst for prominence was unquenchable. He said they were one of the most glamorous couples in New York and that no party was complete without them. Ann purred in silent pleasure at the superiority she now felt as she read every word about herself, and clipped the clippings, and pasted them in scrapbooks, along with photographs and telegrams and invitations, as if to prove that what was happening to her was, in fact, happening, but also, as if she knew, at some deep level of herself she was not in contact with, that it could not possibly last and should be recorded. If she created in her scrapbooks a perfect picture of a perfect life, then that was how it was.

Their pace of living became more and more frantic. Be here. Be there. Be everywhere. Know this person. Know that person. She could take in a room at a glance with a skilled and rapid eye and understand perfectly the circles within circles of the overlapping groups that composed the fashionable life of New York. Alice Grenville, always sensible, knew that a young couple who went out every night of the week were a couple who didn't have much to say to each other at home. The times of being alone together, just them, became less and less frequent, and their conversational moments, about family, about children, and nannies and nursery school, occurred only at parties, giving them the appearance of togetherness.

Her dinners were noted as much for the careful selection and placement of those invited as for the style shown in the decoration of her tables with their marvelous arrangements of exotic flowers, and embroidered clothes, and antique porcelain, which she had begun to collect with a passion. The very latest novels, which you were going to read the reviews of in next Sunday's *New York Times*, were already on her tables, artfully arranged. People came on time and stayed late. Billy, standoffish all his life, found himself, not unwillingly, at the center of a pleasure-bent society.

"I don't see Felicity," said Billy to Ann, looking around their crowded living room.

"The point of the party," answered Ann. Her eyes wandered around the room as her husband talked to her, looking over shoulders, glancing sideways, in case there might be a more interesting conversation in progress.

"You mean you didn't invite her?" asked Billy about his sister.

"That's exactly what I mean."

"There'll be hell to pay for this."

"Worth it. Go talk to Wallis. Bertie's hogging her."

By THE TIME Bratsie Bleeker eloped with a Mexican movie star, several inches taller than himself, who spoke no English, his friends, with the exception of Billy Grenville, had become less tolerant of his antics. They were raising children and beginning careers in banks and brokerage houses and settling down in small houses on their parents' estates on Long Island. It was Billy, rather than Ann, who went to Cartier's and ordered from Jules Glaenzer the silver box on which was engraved, in Billy's handwriting, "To Bratsie and Maria Theresa with love from Billy and Ann," because Ann said it seemed ridiculous to spend four hundred dollars on a gift for a marriage that wouldn't last six months.

It didn't last six months, but that was not the point as far as Billy was concerned. Bratsie was his friend, and not to have honored his marriage would have been an affront to the friendship. Billy remembered, even if Ann didn't, that Bratsie had made his way to Tacoma, in wartime, to attend their shunned wedding ceremony, and it troubled him that Ann had put a distance between him and Bratsie, without any conflict ever having taken place.

There were stories in the gossip columns about Bratsie from time to time, chumming around with Errol Flynn and Bruce Cabot in Hollywood, or sailing with Freddy McEvoy in the South of France, always in the company of starlets and playgirls. Very often he was drunk, and in time he was prevailed upon to enter a sanitarium in South Carolina near his mother's plantation for the purpose of drying out.

He invited Billy and Ann to the plantation for a shooting weekend of quail and turkey after he left the sanitarium, but Ann chose not to go when she heard from Edith Bleeker who the other guests would be—"Jellico's cast of characters," Edith called them, in that tone of voice that told, without a single word of reproach being spoken, that the cast of characters were *not*, by any stretch of the imagination, the right sort.

Ann prevailed upon Billy to go on safari in India instead, a longtime dream that appealed to Billy as well as herself, and they were there, with a maharaja and a maharanee, shooting tigers, when they heard, days after he had been buried, that Bratsie was dead, shot mysteriously while racing his jeep at two o'clock in the morning on the grounds of his mother's plantation.

Ann was quite unprepared for the depths of Billy's grief, and she suspected again, as she had before, that there was something in the rigidity of Billy's character that cried out for the devil-may-care attitude that Bratsie had always expressed toward their upbringing, as if he knew there was more to him than what he was getting out of himself, but he didn't know what it was or how to seek it.

When they returned to New York, Billy and Ann paid a condolence call on Edith Bleeker at her red brick townhouse on upper Park Avenue. They were shown into the library by her butler, Dudley.

"Oh, Edith," cried Billy, embracing his best friend's mother.

"Sit here by me, Billy," she said, patting a place next to her on the red damask sofa. For half an hour they talked and reminisced and laughed about Bratsie. Edith Bleeker had always wished that her son were more like Billy Grenville, with his unfailing good manners and obedience to his family, except in the matter of his marriage, and without the wild streak that had always been a part of Bratsie's makeup.

"I'm glad he had you for a friend, Billy," said Edith.

"I hope they hang the guy who did it," said Billy.

For a moment there was a silence in the room, and Ann, who saw nothing wrong in what Billy had said, felt that an awkward moment was in progress.

"The case has been closed," said Edith Bleeker. She changed her position on the sofa and reached over to push a button to summon Dudley to bring fresh drinks.'

"Closed?" asked Billy, shocked.

"Yes," she said quickly, rising, wanting an end to the conversation.

"How could that be?" persisted Billy, and Ann watched the interchange between them.

"It was an accident," said Edith, and added, "an unexplained accident."

"But surely you're not satisfied with that?" asked Billy, wanting to see his friend's death avenged. "What they have is nothing but inconclusive evidence."

"Oh, Dudley," said Edith to her butler, who had entered the room. "Will you bring the drink tray in here."

Later, at dinner at Alice Grenville's house a few blocks away, Billy related the conversation to his mother. "So much better this way," answered his mother, serving herself asparagus from the tray that Cahill held out for her.

"Why?" asked Ann from her end of the table.

"Poor Edith doesn't need all that dirty laundry brought out," answered Alice, and, like her friend Edith Bleeker ordering the drink tray, signaled an end to the conversation.

Later still, at El Morocco, where they stopped for drinks on the way home, Ann related the story to Babette Van Degan, whom she encountered in the ladies' room. "It was odd, Babette," she said, adjusting her makeup and combing her hair. "It was as if Edith Bleeker didn't want to know how Bratsie was killed."

"You understand that, don't you?" asked Babette.

"No, I don't," answered Ann, wanting to know.

"It's those old families. They don't want outsiders getting near them. They'd rather let whoever did it get away with it than have their family secrets all over the newspapers. Their theory is, it's not going to bring him back."

"My word," said Ann, evening her lipstick with her little finger.

"You can be sure Bratsie was up to something unsavory," Babette continued, "like screwing the foreman's wife."

"That's what he was doing, apparently," said Ann. "Edith's maid told that to my mother-in-law's maid."

"You see?"

ANN NEEDED constant proof that she was who she had become. She wanted a signet ring with the Grenville seal. She wanted a guest book on her hall table for signatures of the fashionable people who attended her parties. She wanted scrapbooks and photograph albums. It wasn't enough for her to write "Harry Kingswood" in her diary, for having been at her house for dinner, or beneath a photograph. The point hadn't been made, for either herself or others, unless she wrote "Viscount Kingswood" or "Lord Kingswood" at the very least.

She wanted her portrait painted. From the day she had first walked into Alice Grenville's house and seen the Sargent and the Boldini and the Lazlo, she wanted to have her picture done. She knew where in her drawing room she would hang it and could imagine herself lounging elegantly beneath it on her damask sofa surrounded by needlepoint pillows.

It was Bertie Lightfoot who suggested that Salvador Dali paint her, and the instant she heard his suggestion she knew how right it was, how unpredictable, how original, how like her. "That was my mother," she could imagine Diantha saying in years to come, regaling her friends with passed-down stories of the amusing and bizarre sittings that had taken place in the late afternoons in the painter's suite at the St. Regis Hotel.

Ann reveled in the exoticism of the court of the famed Spanish surrealist. The ends of his black waxed mustache turned roguishly upward to almost the corners of his eyes. She liked the scented candles, leopard-skin pillows, and bowls full of birds of paradise. An entourage, led by his red-haired wife, Gala, eyebrows plucked out and painted on in black arches of perpetual surprise, and handsome young men and pretty young women, convinced him daily of his genius.

"Let me peek. Let me peek," Ann would say playfully, about the easel that faced away from her, but Dali would not, and her enticements, which bordered on the flirtatious, were of no avail. He was not interested in the opinions of his expensive sitters, only in his interpretations of them. If they were thrilled with the results, he was pleased. If they were not, he was indifferent.

On the day of the unveiling, Ann brought Billy with her, check in pocket. She passed in front of the picture and turned toward it. When her eyes met her image, she drew back, and her cheeks flushed for a moment. An outsider might have thought it was a flush of modesty. Someone who knew her, like Billy, knew it was a flush of displeasure. A look of hostility came into her eyes, as if she sensed that the artist recognized some hidden depths of herself that she preferred to keep hidden.

"I want everybody out of this room except Mr. Dali and my husband," she said to his wife and the assembled court, and the rage in her voice and the anger in her face made them retreat quickly and quietly to other rooms of the suite, where they listened in fascination through the doors to the screams of the disenchanted sitter. It was Billy's first encounter with the enormity of his wife's temper. He was startled by her crudeness. Her words were not used by women of his class. He blew out his lower lip, as he did when she did things that embarrassed him; it replaced the reprimand that he did not give.

Billy would have paid for the portrait and left it behind, treating it as a bad investment. Not Ann. She grabbed the check from her husband and tore it and threw the pieces at the bemused artist. "Never!" she cried. When she grabbed her mink coat off the chair where she had dropped it, she knocked over a vase of flowers but made no attempt to pick it up.

She thought, and Billy thought, the matter was at an end until she read in the papers a few days later that the artist was suing her and her husband for immediate payment. Billy was shocked to find themselves in a story in the tabloids.

"I'm going to pay it, Ann," he said. "I can't have this sort of publicity. It makes Dali more famous, and it makes us look ridiculous. You should have heard the razzing I got at the Brook Club this noon."

"You are not going to pay it," she said. It was a trait of hers that she would not back down, ever.

When the newspapers reached Billy at his office for a statement, he backed his wife's position.

"I looked at the picture," he said, "and walked away scared. It was like walking away from a monster. It was ugly and grim, and I feel Mr. Dali just sort of slapped it together. It is a heck of an unpleasant picture."

"Are you going to pay up, Mr. Grenville?" asked a reporter.

"No," answered Billy.

Dali, clever about publicity, kept the story alive in the papers. "The personal opinion of Mrs. Grenville is not for me so interesting. From an artistic point of view, it is not interesting at all."

The Grenvilles did not attend the court hearing and were shocked to be informed that they had lost the case and were ordered to pay the artist in full for the portrait. Billy, without consulting Ann, paid the money.

The picture was delivered to their house by the lawyer who represented them, never to hang over the damask sofa in the drawing room. One night, when Ann had been drinking, she slashed it, and it vanished to the rear of a closet in her bedroom.

"WHAT ARE all those pills?" Billy asked her one evening.

"Sidney," she answered, meaning Dr. Sidney Silkwood Skinner, as if the mysteries of medicine were beyond her, and the answer sufficed. Her daily intake of appetite suppressant spantules increased, and she began eating almost nothing. Obsessed with slimness, she allowed waiters and maids to remove her plates, the food fashionably untouched. You can't be too rich or too thin, Bertie told her the Duchess said, and she agreed.

At Voisin one afternoon for lunch, she looked across the crowded restaurant and saw, in a far corner, in deep conversation, Billy and a woman whose hat masked her face. She wondered why Billy never engaged her in intense conversation. Jealousy began to squirt its poison into her system. She gulped her second martini, and, combined with her pills, it prompted her to reckless action. Abruptly excusing herself from her luncheon companions, she charged across the restaurant, prepared for a public scene with the woman who was usurping her husband.

"Why, *hello*, what a surprise!" she said loudly as she approached his table, heavy irony in her voice. She was surprised that Billy did not blanch when he saw her. Then she saw that the expensively dressed woman was Cordelia, his own sister, with whom he was lunching. She realized, from the look on Cordelia's face, that they had been discussing her, and blushed. She would rather have come upon him with a mistress.

* * *

HER DATE BOOK was filled for weeks in advance. She liked to know that on two weeks from Thursday they would be dining with Eve Soby, black tie, and that a month from Friday they would be sailing on the *Queen Mary* for Europe. Tonight was Bertie Lightfoot's dinner to show off his brand-new apartment.

Ann took in the room at a glance. Like an art connoisseur having an instant and total reaction to a painting, she could reel off in her mind the entire guest list of a crowded room. The Chesters. The Dudleys. Billy Baldwin. Lady Starborough. George Saybrook. Thelma Foy. The Webbs. The Chisholms. Cole Porter. Elsa Maxwell. Barbara Hutton. Nicky de Guinzberg. Lanfranco Rasponi. Dear, dear, dear, so much disinclination toward women, she thought. Basil someone or other. Plant, maybe. She could never remember his name and didn't care much. He was petit, pale, unprepossessing, and poor, the type who could be counted upon to appear in a dinner jacket at the last moment when someone else dropped out. Ah ha, the handsome Viscount Kingswood, mercifully without Kay Kay Somerset. Things were looking up. She smiled her dazzling smile as she entered the room, aware, as she always was aware, that she understood how to enter a room better than anyone she knew.

"Bertie!" she cried out in greeting. Her voice was less a society woman's voice than the voice of an actress playing, and playing very well, the role of a society woman in a drawing-room comedy. Or drama. Early regional traces had long been obliterated, and a glossy patina of international partying had given her a sound so distinctive as to make people remark on what a lovely speaking voice she had. "It's heavenly! I'm mad about the color!" she said about the new apartment.

They were each other's favorite person, Ann and Bertie, and they kissed elaborately on both cheeks.

"Billy," said Bertie in greeting.

"Bertie," said Billy in greeting.

"Isn't this the apartment where Hillary Burden jumped out the window?" asked Ann.

"Mrs. Grenville chills the room again," said Billy.

"Come in. Come in. Who don't you know?"

When Harry Kingswood bowed to kiss her hand, in the Continental manner, Ann was astonished and thrilled to feel the wetness of his tongue on the back of her hand. As he raised his head, their eyes met, for an instant only, before she moved on to greet the other guests, but both sets were eyes of experience and recognition, and a sexual encounter was agreed upon without a word being exchanged. If he had been of less lengthy lineage, she would have resented his understanding of her availability, but it was, of course, the very thing that made her available.

"Hello, Elsa," she said to Elsa Maxwell.

Later, near the conclusion of the evening, she brought out a small Fabergé box and swallowed two pills she took from it.

"What are those?" asked Harry Kingswood.

"For sleep," Ann replied. "If I take them here, they will have started to work by the time we get home."

"Why not a brisk walk with the dogs to tire you out?"

"Not for me."

"Or warm milk with honey."

"You sound like the Grenvilles' doctor."

Billy appeared with her mink coat. Without knowing why, he resented Harry Kingswood. "Come along, mother of two," he nagged.

"Coming, father of one," she replied. "Goodnight," she said to Lord Kingswood.

"You must ring me when you come to London," he said. He knew she would. So did she.

"And how many heartbeats did you quicken this evening, my dear?" said Billy, in a sort of mock-caressing tone he sometimes adopted toward her, as they waited in front of the apartment building for their chauffeur to bring the car.

"You know I adore Bertie," said Ann irritably. "No one makes me laugh more, but I do think it's tiresome of him to palm off his arty friends on us at dinner. I mean, I was dying to talk with Harry Kingswood—he's supposed to have the best shoot in England—but I got stuck next to that Basil Plant with the tiny hands."

"The writer?"

"They say."

"What does he write?"

"Slender volumes no one reads."

"Overly shy, wasn't he?"

"I think shy people should stay home."

"Let's go to the country tomorrow."

"I told Elsa we'd go to the opening of Cole's show."

"Christ," Billy muttered.

"Didn't you have a good time?" she asked when they were settled into the back seat of their car.

"No, I had a terrible time," he answered.

"But it was a marvelous party! Why didn't you have a good time?"

"I feel uncomfortable with all those people. They all do things. They accomplish. After all, who are we? We're the couple with all the money whose name is in the papers too much for going out every night to too many parties."

"I wish there were eight nights in the week. I'd be out every one of them," said Ann.

"Look at Neddie Pavenstedt, my old Groton roommate. He's number-two man at the bank where my grandfather was president, and then my father, and where I was supposed to be after him. As for Basil Plant, with the tiny hands, his slender volumes get printed. I've never done anything. I feel like a failure, Ann."

"Oh, really," she said. It was a conversation she had heard before and was sick of before it began.

"Do you know what's happening to me, Ann? I only feel safe with people just like myself, out on the North Shore. I've become just who I swore I'd never be, one of those fourth-generation blank-faced men with sad eyes who laugh all the time. When I married you, I wanted you to save me from all that, and all that I did was get in deeper."

"How can you be a failure, Billy, when you have ten million dollars, and God knows how many more millions to come, *après* Mère? This is the most ridiculous conversation I've ever heard in my life."

"That's just the outsider in you talking. You don't understand."

"Oh, so I'm an outsider, am I?" she asked indignantly, readying herself for a fight.

"Let's not turn this conversation around to be about you, Ann. It's so rarely I get a chance to talk about myself, and how I feel, and what I think."

"Oh, poor Billy, poor, poor Billy. Let's all feel sorry for Billy."

"God, I miss Bratsie. He's the only person who ever understood. Why did you have to die, Bratsie?"

"Because he fucked the foreman's wife, darling, and the foreman shot him dead, that's why."

"Ah, the meaning of life, as explained by the fashionable Mrs. Grenville."

"What's the new chauffeur's name?"

"Why?"

"What's his name, Billy?"

"Lee."

"Lee," she called out to the front seat. "We're not going home. We're going to El Morocco."

"No, we're not."

"Yes, we are. I'm not going home with you in this mood. And, Billy?"

"What?"

"Tomorrow tell what's-his-name to take his rosary beads off the rearview mirror. I can't stand that look."

WAY OVER EAST on Seventy-second Street, near the river but not on the river, in a block of fancified tenements occupied mostly by poor friends of the Astor family, who owned the block, as they owned a great many blocks in the city, my light burned late that night in the fifth-floor walk-up friends of friends of an Astor connection had arranged for me to call my home. My name, Basil Plant, appeared in the vestibule next to the buzzer system. The apartment, called a railroad flat, was tiny and somewhat squalid. A typewriter, reams of paper, a bulletin board with pink and blue and white file cards thumbtacked to it, and a wastebasket too full of discarded pages announced my writer's life.

In those days, as now, I never went to bed, no matter how late, or how drunken, or how drugged the evening had been without recording first my impressions of the people I had met in my multifaceted existence, seeing it all as bits and pieces of a giant mosaic that one day would fit together in a literary Byzantine pattern that would explain my life.

My bathroom cabinet was filled with the small bottles of Listerine, guest-sized tubes of toothpaste, and unused bars of Floris soap I took each weekend from the guest-room baths in the rich houses I was beginning to visit. I was always looking for economies. Ann Grenville was right when she said I wrote slender volumes no one read. The bitch. Even my aspirin bottles were purloined, and from one of them I took the four aspirins I invariably took before retiring after an evening of too much drink.

I was still smarting from Mrs. Grenville's snub, because I would have liked to become her friend. I like social climbers. They interest me. But she resisted me, right from the beginning. Neither my inquisitiveness nor my wit appealed to her. I looked at myself in my bathroom mirror. What I saw was a slender, fragile-looking, almost androgynous young man with a shy manner and a sweet smile. The loss was hers, I decided.

"Dinner at Bertie Lightfoot's," I wrote in soft pencil on a lined yellow tablet in my small, neat, and precise handwriting. "A last-minute replacement. Bertie gave me instructions to be interesting, and witty, and earn my bread and butter. It was his usual crowd of high-society people, the type who go out every night. On one side Natasha Paley, a Russian princess who works for Mainbocher. On the other the beautiful Mrs. Grenville of the social columns, who helped make Bertie Lightfoot the great success he is today. Brightly painted, she looked into her compact seven times during dinner, readjusting her face. She seemed to be engaged in secret smiles and looks with an Englishman called Harry Kingswood at the next table. My presence mattered very little to her. She picked up my place card, so as to read my name, and said, 'Bertie tells me you're a writer, and quite interesting,' and then sat back as if waiting for me to entertain her.

"I said to her, trying to hold up my end of the conversation, 'Weren't you in show business once?' I knew for a fact she danced in the line at the Copa. 'Briefly,' she answered, redoing her lips at the same time. 'But my family was furious, and then I married Billy Grenville,' conveying the impression she had been a rebellious deb. Then she snapped shut her compact, signaling the end of that conversation. I felt about her that her life began when she became Mrs. Grenville. She made no effort to conceal her boredom with me. So I got drunk. All that marvelous wine of Bertie's, Lafite-Rothschild.

"There is something about Mrs. Grenville, beneath her Mainbocher dress and perfect pearls, that made me think of a tigress in heat. I feel wantonness beneath her social perfection. I think she is bored, at least sexually, with her husband. Billy Grenville is very handsome. He doesn't have that overbred look so many of those North Shore people have, as if their mother and father were first cousins. Mrs. Grenville is a very silly girl."

BILLY FELT, in time, like a hostage, imprisoned in the relationship, and, like a hostage, he befriended his captor, but merely for the sake of survival. There were plans, furtive to be sure, for escape.

It was Ann who suggested to him that horses, the Grenville stables, Jacaranda Farm, twenty-five hundred acres in the Blue Grass country, the producer of three Kentucky Derby winners, would be his salvation.

"But I've never been seriously interested in horses," he protested. "That was always Grace's domain."

"Well, *become* seriously interested in horses. You own the farm, not Grace. Your father left it to you. I'll take care of Grace. It would be madness to just let the reins slip through your fingers, as you let the bank slip through your fingers."

It bothered Billy when she enumerated his failures to him. He looked off, away from her, out the window, thinking back to the days of his youth when his father made him, Saturday after Saturday, walk through the stables and paddocks, greeting people, talking horses, looking at horses, and the queasiness in his stomach returned to him that always returned to him when he thought of his greatly admired father.

"Look at Alfred Twombley," said Ann, citing the example of one of Billy's lifelong friends to prove her point. "He's made the most marvelous life for himself in racing. He works hard. He makes money. Everyone respects him. Why can't you do the same thing?"

GRACE GRENVILLE GRAINGER was in well-cared-for early middle age. Horses and dogs had always interested her more than people and society, and she lived a country life, happy that the business of the Grenville stables had fallen to her when her brother was indifferent to the management of his inheritance. "The thrill is in breeding rather than racing," she was fond of saying.

Grace made no preparations for visitors; they could take her as she was, or leave her, she didn't care. Not bothering to check her appearance in a mirror, or pick up fallen newspapers off the carpet, or puff up crushed cushions, she was on the floor cleaning up after her new puppy when Billy and Ann entered her living room.

"Grace, how could you?" cried Ann.

"How could I what?" replied Grace.

"Be down on your hands and knees like that, cleaning up."

"I'm cleaning up dog shit."

"Even so. Get someone to do it for you," said Ann.

The implication was quite clear. People like them, Grenvilles, did not do servants' work. It was not lost on either Grace or Billy that Ann had become more Grenville than the Grenvilles.

"I like this room, Grace," said Billy.

He was making conversation, Ann knew, dreading having to tell her that he was here to reclaim his inheritance. They were seated at opposite ends of a long sofa, slipcovered in well-worn chintz, facing a fire. All the bookshelves were untidily filled with horse books, dog books, and detective novels, some horizontally atop the vertical ones, and other books filled tabletops. The fireplace bench was heaped with magazines and newspapers, rendering it useless for sitting. A cracked Lowestoft plate, which they were using for an ashtray, on the cushion between them, was glued together rather messily. The glasses on the drink table, where Ann went to mix herself a Bloody Mary, were a mis-matched lot, from a jelly glass to a chipped Baccarat goblet. The room annoyed her; only someone as rich as Grace could get away with a room like this. She knew that Billy was next going to say that it looked lived in.

"It looks lived in," he said.

Ann lit another cigarette and kept silent. She concentrated on how she would redecorate the room if it were her house. Her bracelet dropped off her wrist and fell on the floor by the fireplace. Grace picked up the fire tongs, retrieved the bracelet, and handed it to Ann on the end of her tongs. Grace sensed, before the conversation began, that there was a motive in the unex-pected visit.

"There's a marvelous man on Second Avenue in the Eighties, Mr. Some-thing, I have it written down, who could repair this plate for you so the crack wouldn't show," said Ann.

"What a lot of bother," said Grace, who didn't care about the crack. Among themselves the sisters laughed at the grandeur of their sister-in-law.

Ann felt slighted, as she always did by her husband's sisters. Her makeup suddenly felt stale and caked on her face after the long drive. She was no longer in a good humor.

"Billy, why don't you go outside and look at the horses. I want to talk to Grace," said Ann.

Later Grace, who heard the language of the stables, and used it occasion-ally, to the hysterical dismay of her sisters, called their sister-in-law a cunt. What she actually said was that Ann gave new meaning to the word.

So it was that Billy Grenville began his new career in racing and breeding as the head of the Grenville stables.

ANN GRENVILLE stood outside the Colony Restaurant, under the green awning, and kissed the cheek of her mother-in-law and then the cheek of her sister-in-law Cordelia, with whom she had just lunched. As Alice Grenville's car drew up, Ann pulled back slightly the sleeve of her mink coat and quickly glanced at her watch.

"Wherever are you going, Ann?" asked Alice. "That's the third time in the last half hour I've seen you glance at your watch, and you made us gulp down our coffee."

"Doctor's appointment, Mère," Ann answered.

"You're awfully eager to get there," grumbled Alice, allowing Charles, her chauffeur, to assist her into the car. "Are you coming with me, Cordelia?"

"Yes, Mère. Goodbye, Ann."

As Alice Grenville's car headed for Madison Avenue, Ann took off in the direction of Park Avenue. Halfway to the corner, she looked back and saw that the car had turned uptown. She reversed her steps and headed back toward Madison Avenue, crossed, and walked swiftly toward Fifth Avenue. From her handbag she took out a pair of dark glasses and put them on, although there was no sun in the sky that day.

The Hotel Fourteen was her idea. She knew, from experience, that they asked no questions and catered to a clientele that was unlikely to have heard of her or any of the people in her group. It was next door to the Copacabana, and it had served, on more than one occasion, during her show-girl days, as a locale for a between-shows tryst with one of the garment manufacturers she sometimes saw when she was in financial distress.

She walked straight through the small lobby to the elevator as if she were registered as a guest. In an earlier period of her life, she had found the hotel elegant, but, with an eye grown familiar with elegance, she saw now that it was too gold, too red, too vulgar, but exactly right for the purpose at hand.

She stepped out of the elevator at the sixth floor and knocked at the door of Room 612 with a gloved knuckle. In an instant the door opened; its occupant had been waiting for her knock.

"Don't tell me I'm late," she said, walking in, dropping her mink coat off her, and dragging it along the carpeted floor. "Just ask me what I feel like."

"What do you feel like?"

"I feel like a call girl."

He laughed, bowed courteously, and kissed her hand. She felt the wetness of his tongue on the back of it. "Mrs. Grenville," he said.

"Lord Kingswood," she replied.

"A drink?"

"Let's not waste time on drinks."

"Good."

He wrapped his arms around her.

"Oh, I have been waiting for this," she said.

"And I."

"Oh, Harry, how did you know I like to be kissed on my throat, just like that," she said, her head back, her hands on his head, as he kissed up and down her lovely neck. "Oh, yes, handsome Harry, that is so nice. I do love the sound of kissing."

"Get undressed," he whispered.

"Unzip me," she answered, turning her back to him. With knowing fingers, he undid the hook and eye of her Mainbocher dress and slowly unzipped the back of her down past the hooks of her brassiere. "No, no, darling, I'll take off my own brassiere, thank you very much. You just sit down over there and watch. Oh, and Harry?"

"Yes?"

"You get undressed too. And I mean really undressed. None of that socks-on, shirt-on English stuff. Take off everything."

"Unbutton my fly for me," he answered.

"You English ought to learn about zippers," she replied, kissing him, as her expert fingers undid the seven buttons. "Oh, my God."

"What?"

"An uncoaxed erection."

Nothing excited Ann Grenville more than to watch a man see her breasts for the first time. They were, she knew, perfect, and the look of lust that came over Harry Kingswood's face at the sight of them and the expectation of touching them filled her with passion that matched his own.

"Harry?"

Harry Kingswood's face was buried between her breasts, too occupied to reply, but his bare shoulders made an answering gesture.

"You're not in any great hurry, are you?"

He shook his head, his tongue traveling from the bottom of one breast to her large excited beige nipple.

"Oh, good. I hate wham, bam, thank you, ma'am."

She lay back in the center of the double bed in Room 612 of the Hotel Fourteen and watched as this direct descendant of the fifth wife of Henry VIII entered her with the precision of an expert and for an hour held back his own arrival until she had been thrice satisfied.

"My God," she whispered when they had concluded. "And the missionary position! It's nice getting back to the basics."

Harry Kingswood laughed, at the same time fondling her breast.

"Let's hear it for love in the afternoon!" said Ann. "Do I look beautiful?"

"You do."

"I feel beautiful. What are you doing tomorrow afternoon, and the next, and the next?"

"I hope I'm going to be meeting you in Room 612 of the Hotel Fourteen."

She lifted his hand from her breast to kiss it and noticed the time on his wristwatch. "I have to dress, Harry. I still have to have my hair done. Billy and I are going to Eve Soby's party tonight, and Billy gets furious if I'm late."

"I'm going to Eve Soby's, too," said Harry.

"If you feel a hand between your legs under Eve's tablecloth, it'll be me," said Ann, dressing.

Harry Kingswood looked at Ann in delight. Each understood they were embarking on a love affair, without commitment or any thought of upsetting either of their marriages.

"The shooting season starts next month. Have you told Billy about coming to England yet?"

"I will tonight."

"I WISH YOU wouldn't sit on the bed. It's been fixed for the party, and you're wrinkling the coverlet," said Ann irritably.

"Too bad you're not fixed for your party," answered Billy, turning on the satin-and-lace coverlet, wrinkling it more.

"I'm not well," she replied, in self-defense.

"You stayed out all night dancing and drinking, and then you took a handful of sleeping pills at dawn."

"I did not."

"Do you ever think about this ridiculous marriage we have?"

"Billy," she said. Her voice was now placating. "There are people arriving any minute for cocktails. There's the bell now. Please go down and greet them. It'll take me twenty minutes at least. My eyes are all puffed."

"You're full of sleeping pills."

"Please, Billy. Our friends are arriving."

"Your friends. I think I'm going to walk out the front door as they're walking in and go to the Brook Club."

But he didn't. "How very pleasant this is," he said, entering his living room, to greet the already arrived Harry Kingswood. They were to have drinks there and dine at Maud Chez Elle, a restaurant then much in fashion, and go on to dance at El Morocco. Billy and Harry had the outward camaraderie of two members of the same class who recognized each other's equality, but there remained, nonetheless, an unease between them.

When finally Ann entered the room, fastening a bracelet—late, sure, unhurried, beautiful—for the evening of revelry ahead, Billy was astonished, as he always was astonished, at how she was able to pull herself together. Later, after midnight, he disengaged himself from the celebrants at El Morocco, waving goodbye to Ann and Harry Kingswood on the dance floor, and went home. He was, those days, up early and out at the track at Belmont for the morning workouts.

Billy often said that some of his best ideas came to him at breakfast. It was for that reason that he liked to breakfast alone, very often staring off into space while sipping his coffee or munching his toast. It was at such a moment that his troubled feelings connected the fact of Harry Kingswood's visit and his wife's duplicity. With the taste of strawberry preserve still in his mouth, he bolted from the room.

Upstairs, in their darkened bedroom, all signs of daylight were shut out, and would be for hours to come. He watched his wife in restless sleep, her arms embracing a pillow, one strap of her satin-and-lace nightgown fallen from her shoulder. On her bedside table were no clues of duplicity, if that was what he expected to find, only an apothecary of prescriptions, and lists and notes of things to be done, for her relentless pursuit of social life, when her day would finally begin.

"Why are you staring at me?" she asked, without opening her eyes, or changing her position, which was faced away from him.

"I'm not staring at you," he answered, backing away from their wide bed as if he had been caught stealing.

"Yes, you are," she said, from her sleep.

"I forgot something," he mumbled with a note of apology in his voice and withdrew from the room, not having spoken what he intended to speak. A new maid, observing the morning rules of silence, nodded to him as he left the room but did not speak either.

Outside the house the chauffeur, Lee, waited with the car and all the morning papers for Billy to read on his way out to the track.

"I'm going to walk for a bit before we start out," Billy said to his driver and proceeded toward Park Avenue. At the corner he stood through two light changes before crossing and failed to notice an acquaintance who greeted him. He was unused to examining his feelings and could not tell if the deep distress he was experiencing was because he loved his wife so much, or because his wife had not valued sufficiently the name and position that he had bestowed upon her. He wondered how many of their group knew of the liaison. He wondered if he had been made to look a fool.

That night, back at El Morocco, after another cocktail party, and another dinner party, Billy, drunk, finally said what it had been on his mind all day to say, but, out of sheer weakness, he ascribed his accusation to others. "Someone came to me with a s-s-story about you," he said.

"Who?" she instantly demanded.

"D-d-don't you want to know w-w-what was said before w-w-who said it?" he asked. His speech was interrupted by an occasional stammer, a slight impediment of childhood, long since overcome, that reappeared only during intoxication.

"What, then?" she asked, knowing in advance what he was going to say. She had meant to tell him of her plan to visit Harry Kingswood, to shoot, but the moment had not presented itself.

"A-d-d-dultery," he replied.

"Really, Billy," she laughed. "How drunk are you?"

"Who said I was d-d-drunk?"

"You begin no stutter."

"I d-d-do not."

"Yes, you d-d-do."

During scenes she focused on things. She looked at the candlelit flowers, leaned forward and moved a rose, surveyed it with satisfaction, as if it made a difference. But there was no scene. They sat on interminably, nearly never speaking, watching, like a movie, the drama of nightclub life. Once they had thought there would never be enough time for them to say all the things to each other they had to say. She placed her hand over his finally and squeezed it. She wanted his feelings for her to remain constant, even while hers expanded to include others.

"I love you," she said.

"You don't love me, Ann," he replied, no longer drunk. "You just love the life that happens around me."

What he said frightened her. She lipsticked her mouth crimson, using the blade of her table knife as a mirror. Billy found her gesture vulgar and exciting. It was when he liked her best. At home later, enticing him to sexual frenzy, she erased his suspicions of infidelity. With the outpouring of her lover still within her, she received the fresher outpouring of her husband. And peace prevailed again.

A few nights later they went to a ball on the North Shore. A Hutton heiress was being presented to society in an indoor tennis court attached to a guesthouse on one of the great estates still in full swing. Young couples wandered about in the formal gardens. Ann took in the scene at a glance. The Eburys. The Phippses. The Hitchcocks. The Schiffs. The lot of them. The cream of the North Shore. She felt she had never seen anything so beautiful, and she valued her life and her marriage. Hello, Sass, she said. Hello, Titi. Hello, Molly. Marvelous dress, Brenda. Kiss-kiss, Lita.

She wandered about with Billy in tow. In the guest house—nicknamed the Playhouse—were a living room, a dining room, many bedrooms, and a vast music room with acoustics so perfect that combinations from the New York Philharmonic often came to play for the musically inclined hostess. Billy told her that the family used the Playhouse mostly as a guesthouse and a place to relax after tennis. Its courtyard, he said, had been brought from Fotheringay Castle in Scotland, and its cobblestones were the very ones Mary Queen of Scots had walked over on her way to the guillotine.

"Enjoy it," Billy said about the ball and the estate. "It's the end of an era. No one will be able to afford to give parties like this or live on places like this for long."

The orchestra played "Full Moon and Empty Arms." She sang into his ear as they danced, "Full moon and empty legs." He laughed with delight and remembered their first meeting in El Morocco.

"This is where I want to live, darling," whispered Ann into Billy's ear.

He laughed again.

"I don't mean this whole vast place," she said. "I mean the Playhouse, and the grounds around it."

"What about old lady McGamble? Don't you think she'd have a thing or two to say about that?" asked Billy, who never quite understood her sudden passions for having to have things instantly, not always with the best results. He still smarted over her squabble with Salvador Dali.

"I had a feeling about this house the minute we drove up the drive," she said. "It was meant for us. I can feel us living here. It would be perfect for the children. We can't go on staying at your mother's house every weekend. I think we've worn out our welcome there. I know her servants all complain about me, not that I care one damn bit about that, but it's time for us, Billy, to have a weekend place of our own."

THE WALKING ring outside the Saratoga sales pavilion was dark except for the orange glow of a hanging lantern on a stable door. The bidding was over on the yearling Thoroughbreds that had been walked around the ring on the last night of the sale. About a hundred yards away in the garden of the Spuyten Duyvil bar, horse breeders and buyers from around the world were drinking whiskey and talking horses. The main topic of conversation was the record price paid by the neophyte breeder Billy Grenville for a yearling colt he had already named Tailspin.

"You've got an eye like your father's," said Sunny Jim O'Brien, the old horse trainer from the Grenville stables who had known Billy since he was a child and had been brought reluctantly to Saratoga by his dashing father.

"Do you think so, Jim?" asked Billy. "Really?"

"A chip off the old block," replied Sunny Jim, knocking back the only whiskey he allowed himself. "This Tailspin of yours is a winner, and you spotted it the instant you saw him. Your father had that instinct with Ishmael."

"This Tailspin of *ours*, you mean. We're going to do the same things, you and I, that you and my father did. Come on now, Jim, break your rule and have another drink. This is a night to celebrate."

Alfred Twombley and Piggy French, the two biggest names in racing, joined in the celebration. It thrilled Billy that old Sunny Jim thought he approximated his father. All his life he only remembered disappointment in his father's eye. He wished his father had lived longer.

ANN COULD NOT believe that she was in the company, for the weekend, of one of the English princesses. Sometimes she marveled at her life, to herself only, for she would not have admitted, even to her husband, that she did not take in stride whatever happened to her. It was times like this that she missed her mother. Her mother would have understood, her mother would have been overjoyed. She felt, alternately, thrilled and disappointed: thrilled with the event, disappointed with the person. She wanted the princess to be slimmer. She wanted her country tweeds to be less country, and her diamond pin to be more country. The perfection of royalty interested her. She was determined to buy herself an amber cigarette holder when she got to London, at Asprey's, like the one the princess had, and she stared and stared at her until she was able to memorize exactly the way the princess held the holder, in an elegant way she had not seen before, and the way she inhaled and the way she exhaled.

She took up her camera and, almost surreptitiously, snapped a photograph of the princess, who was in conversation with Harry Kingswood, listening to him explain the history of Kingswood Castle. Ann liked the way it looked, the informality of it, the princess in a tweed skirt and a silk blouse and walking shoes for the tour of the gardens and the grounds that was about to come. It was not a way many people saw her, and Ann could see the picture of the two of them, Harry and the princess, sitting on the chintz-covered sofa, in conversation, on one of the pages of her scrapbook. She took another picture, feeling braver, and then another. She wished the camera did not click so loudly. What a marvelous gift this will be for Harry, she thought to herself, as if she were a historian preserving an important moment of history, unconscious, in her zeal, of the looks the other guests were giving her to desist from her mission. There was silence in the room, but the clicking of the camera persisted. Looks of royal displeasure were to be evermore preserved in the scrapbooks of Ann Grenville. She was by this time aware of her faux pas, but she could not stop herself until the roll ran out, and the roll, alas, was of thirty-six exposures.

"I feel, Harry," came the royal voice of the royal princess, in ice-water tones, "that I am on duty at a charity bazaar being click-click-clicked away at instead of being a guest in your house. *When* is she going to stop taking my picture?"

Ann blushed in embarrassment, knowing that all eyes were upon her. From the sofa where the princess remained seated, she heard muffled excuses from Harry for her. "American, you know. She didn't know, ma'am."

Her love affair with Harry, so successful in New York, had, like some wines, not traveled well. "I say, Ann," said Harry, bearing down on her, in a hissing whisper, "this sort of thing is just not done. For God's sake, put that camera away!"

That evening Ann pleaded a headache and did not come down to join the house party for dinner. The telephone was located, for facts only, not confidences, in an upstairs hall of the castle, with not even a chair by it, lest one linger. By now Ann was familiar with Harry Kingswood's frugality. The next morning, before the other guests arose, she left by car for London, reliving the scene all the way, wondering if they were laughing at her, hoping the story would not get back to New York, knowing she would never see Harry Kingswood again. She understood instinctively that when one was married, love affairs had a natural termination. She flew to Rome and looked forward to a reunion with Billy.

Thereafter her passion for the English abated. Later, in another city, introduced to the same princess again, she gave no recognition of ever having met her before as she bowed her head and bobbed her curtsy.

"HIS ROBES, my dear, are made for him in Paris by a couturier. They shimmer and sparkle and are said to outdo in grandeur the robes of the Pontiff. Don't you love it? Fulco told me." Lipsticked already, Ann took a comb from her bag and ran it through her hair, automatically.

"He's a priest?" asked Billy.

"No, no, a monsignor, and a great wit and diner-outer. I mean, everyone knows him."

"He's American, you say?" Billy did not share his wife's passion for European society, and the endless stream of gossip that she brought back with her each day from her forays into the palazzos of Rome went, for the most part, in one ear and out the other.

"Yes. He married Tyrone Power and Linda Christian. I told you that. But, now, listen to this!"

"I'm listening."

"He has arranged an audience for us with the Pope, and I have bought a black lace mantilla that is so divine, and I thought I'd wear that black dress that I wore to your sister's party in London."

"But we're not Catholic."

"You don't have to be a Catholic to have an audience with the Pope, for God's sake."

"When?"

"May fifth."

"May fifth?" Five, five, five, five. The fifth day, the fifth month, 1955.

"That's what I said. May fifth. Ten A.M."

"I can't go."

"Why can't you go?"

He turned away from her, embarrassed to tell her what day it was. "That's the day that . . ."

"What day? Oh, for God's sake, Billy, do you mean the day you're supposed to die?"

"I know it sounds insane, but I've never forgotten what that fortune-teller in Tacoma said. Five, five, five five. It seemed so far off then, and now here it is upon us."

"You don't believe that?"

"No, of course I don't, but I do, too."

"Well, if you're going to die, what better way to do it than to see the Pope first? It'll pave the way *right* to heaven for you."

"What will we talk to the Pope about? The latest parties?"

"It won't be just *us,* for God's sake, there'll be others, and afterward the monsignor is giving a lunch for us at the Palazzo Doria."

IT RAINED steadily on the morning of the papal audience. Eruptions of thunder preceded daylight, and rain beat angrily on the windows of the Grenvilles' suite at the Grand Hotel in Rome. Awakening late, after a night of too much drink, each was reminded of the morning of their wedding day in Tacoma twelve years earlier. Both bad-tempered, they dressed and drank coffee in silence. Why, Billy wondered, had they sat up until four drinking brandy at Bricktop's with a strange trio from Pasadena whom they had never seen before and would, probably, never see again? Why was it they always were out, out, out?

Below, in the downpour, there were at least thirty people ahead of them waiting for taxis in the drive-through of the hotel, and the hour of the audience was fast approaching.

"Whatever will I tell the monsignor?" wailed Ann.

"That we sat up until four drinking brandy at Bricktop's with a *ménage à trois* from Pasadena that you picked up. The Pope will understand. So will the monsignor in his couturier robes," said Billy.

"Sometimes I hate you," she said to him. Their eyes met in mutual discord.

"It looks hopeless," said Billy, about the taxi situation.

"I can't understand why you didn't hire a car and driver when you knew perfectly that we had to be at the Vatican by ten." She, feeling mocked, was ready for a fight.

At that moment a car and driver went by and then stopped abruptly. A woman called out the window, "Is that really you, Billy Grenville?"

"Esme!" cried Billy. "I simply don't believe it! Could you drop us at the Vatican? We're late for an audience, and there's not a taxi in sight, and we're soaked."

Esme Bland, who had always loved Billy Grenville from afar, had never voiced her opinion on the subject, even to her great friend Cordelia, but she thought Billy had wasted himself on Ann.

"You have met Ann, haven't you, Esme?" asked Billy when they were settled in the back seat.

"Yes," replied Esme.

"At Cordelia's," said Ann.

There was a silence.

"It's raining cats and dogs," said Billy finally.

"My mantilla will be ruined," said Ann.

"Here, take my umbrella, Ann," said Esme.

WHEN THEY LEFT the Vatican, the sun was shining brightly on St. Peter's Square.

"He was adorable, just as cute as he could be," said Ann about the Pope.

"His flock will be touched by your description," replied Billy.

"Now I'm stuck with this damned umbrella of Esme's," said Ann.

"Why don't we wander around the cathedral a bit," said Billy.

"We haven't time," said Ann, looking at her wrist.

"I can't imagine having to report to Mère that we've been here and haven't looked at the *Pietà.*"

"Billy, we're due for lunch at Monsignor Herrick's at the Palazzo Doria," said Ann.

"I'm not going to lunch at Monsignor Herrick's at the Palazzo Doria," replied Billy, repeating her words exactly, diminishing them in importance.

"Of course you are."

"I'm not," he said. He was quiet, and his face did not have the stubborn look it assumed when he took a stand on something. She looked at him in the May sunlight, crowds of tourists jostling them, and realized she did not understand his withdrawn mood.

"What are you going to do?" she asked.

"I'm going to look at the *Pietà,* and then I'm going back to the Grand Hotel and order a chicken sandwich in the room, and then I'm going to lie on my bed and look off into space."

"Simonetta d'Este's going to be there for lunch, and the Crespis, and Princess Ruspoli," went on Ann enticingly, as if he, like her, would have his mind changed by titles.

"You should be in hog heaven."

"Does this have anything to do with that damn fortune-teller?" she asked in a mocking voice.

"I'll put you in a taxi, Ann."

LATER, AFTER the lunch, Ann returned to the hotel, bubbling with gossip about what he had missed and thrilled that she had gotten them invited that evening to a ball at the Pecci-Blunts. Billy said he didn't want to go. His refusal exasperated and infuriated her.

"Let's not get into a fight over this, Ann."

"I did not come all the way to Rome to sit here in this room because in 1943 some fortune-teller in Tacoma, Washington, told you you were going to die today. It's the most ridiculous thing I've ever heard of. If fortune-tellers know so damn much, why do they always live in some filthy hovel?"

"You don't have to sit here. Go to the ball. Enjoy yourself. I'm quite content here."

"I may be quite late."

"That's all right."

"It gives me the creeps, all this silence and gloom."

HE WORE A MAROON polka-dotted dressing gown over his undershorts and shirt. The only light on in the room was the lamp between the double beds. Lying on one of the beds, he read the international edition of the *Herald Tribune* and the *Rome American.* He listened to the radio. He napped. He thought about his children. He thought about his father. He wondered why, with so much, he felt so dissatisfied with his life. He wondered, as he always wondered, in his rare moments of introspection, if he would have amounted to anything if he had not inherited so much money. He felt that the deference he received from people, for the name and fortune he possessed, was unearned and undeserved, and he wondered if others thought this about him.

He started to say the Lord's Prayer, but he felt embarrassed, as he always felt embarrassed, when he prayed outside of St. James' Episcopal Church, which he attended only for weddings and funerals. He felt the urge to get off the bed and get down on his knees to say the prayer, but he thought how extremely foolish he would feel if Ann should happen to walk in the door at that moment, even though he knew it was highly unlikely that Ann would ever leave her ball for any reason. He wondered if he minded dying, and it surprised him that, yes, he did mind, although only yesterday it had not seemed such a terrible loss to him.

Then he heard the bells from the Campanile begin to sound across the city, ringing the hour of midnight. The day was over. He had lived. The gypsy fortune-teller from Tacoma was wrong. He leaped up from the bed, joyous again with his life, and picked up the telephone and asked the operator to connect him with another hotel in the city. He asked the operator in that hotel to connect him with the room of one of its guests. He could hear the telephone ring several times, and then it was answered by a sleepy voice.

"Esme?" he boomed. "It's Billy. Get up. Get dressed. Let me come and pick you up and let's go out somewhere for a drink!"

"SHE'S NOT AFRAID to lose control, you know. I am," said Billy to Esme about Ann. They sat in the spring night in the bar on the roof of Esme's hotel.

"Why do you stay with her?" asked Esme.

"There was a time when I loved her, and during that time I was the happiest that I ever have been," he replied.

"That was then. This is now."

"You will not admire me if I tell you why."

"Don't worry about that."

"I'm afraid of her. There is something reckless about her."

"Reckless?"

"Once, when I was courting her, I went to the apartment she was living in, in the thirties somewhere, Murray Hill. She was a dancer in those days. For some reason the street door was open, and I went right through without ringing her buzzer, and ran up the flights of stairs to her apartment, and rang her bell. I was carrying flowers. She opened the door and she was holding a gun pointed at me, and there was on her face a truly horrible look, like a woman who had lost control completely, slack and loose and ready to kill. And then she recognized that it was me, and in an instant she pulled herself together and tried to turn the whole thing into an enormous joke, saying that the gun was not really a gun at all, but a starter's pistol for races. I never knew who it was she was expecting, probably some boyfriend she was trying to break off with now that I had come into her life, but I have never forgotten the look on her face."

"Did you ever talk about it with her?"

"She always made light of it. I think it embarrassed her that she had shown me her dark side so blatantly, but I was madly in love with her then, and she almost made me believe that I had imagined the moment."

"Could she kill, do you think?"

"Dear God, Esme, we're talking about my wife."

"Could she?"

"On safari, none of the natives wanted to be with her. She shot first and looked later, they said. Nothing ever happened, of course, but she appeared dangerous to them, and I understood their feelings."

"Is she a good shot?"

"She has an itchy trigger finger."

"That's not the same thing."

"She doesn't wait. There is a recklessness about her."

"You must leave her, Billy."

"She never forgets an injury, Esme. She would eventually find her revenge."

"But what kind of a marriage is it you have?"

"She enjoys being Mrs. William Grenville, Junior, and will never give up being that unless an Italian prince or an English lord or the Ali Khan asks her to marry him."

Esme looked away from Billy and sighed deeply.

"Is that a sigh?" asked Billy.

"I suppose it is," she answered.

"Will you translate it?"

"I would have enjoyed being Mrs. William Grenville, Junior, too, you know, but I would have been a very different one."

"Oh, Esme."

* * *

"IT'S TIME FOR us to go back home, Ann," said Billy. They were on the
Riviera staying at Chateau de l'Horizon as the guests of Ali Khan.

"No, no, not yet, Billy," pleaded Ann.

"Well, I'm going back to New York."

"Please, Billy, just stay for the Marquis de Cuevas's ball in Biarritz, and
then, after that, I promise you I'll go back."

"Every time I want to go home, you tell me of another party that's bigger
and better than the last party. There's always going to be another party."

"Just this one, Billy, and then we'll go. It's costume, and they want us to be
in the Dante's *Inferno* tableau. It's going to be such fun. I'm going to be a devil
all in red and carry a pitchfork. Ali's part of the tableau. And they want you to
be dressed as—"

"Listen to me, Ann."

"Don't you remember how much you used to like me in my little cat
costume?" She sensed a difference in his ardor toward her and applied herself
to attracting him.

"YOU DON'T LIKE costume parties, Mr. Grenville?" asked Simonetta
d'Este. Billy had withdrawn from the spectacle, watching the ballroom below
from the splendid isolation of a rococo balcony. She was an elegant Madame
Du Barry in court finery, powdered wig, and magnificent pearls.

"Why do you say that?" asked Billy.

"Your white tie, your tails, your red sash across your chest. It's what all
men wear who hate costume parties but go to please their wives."

Billy laughed. "I suppose you're right."

"I'm Simonetta d'Este."

"I know."

"Do you hate to dance too, Mr. Grenville?"

"My name is Billy."

"I know. Do you hate to dance too, Billy?"

"I dance rather well, I think. Would you like to?"

"I've sought you out. Of course I would."

TO BE PART OF the Dante's *Inferno* tableau at the de Cuevas's ball in
Biarritz was of great importance to Ann Grenville. Among the dozen red-clad
participants of Hades were some of the oldest titles in Europe as well as the

kind of names that dazzled the readers of Fydor Cassati's column back in New York. For her it represented a triumph of social acceptance that she felt she had never achieved in the New York and Long Island circles of her husband's family. In the group of international partygoers and pleasure seekers that was then beginning to be called the Jet Set, people who got on airplanes and went to parties the world over, wherever the season was, she was accepted as the beautiful and witty Mrs. Grenville of the famous New York family, and who she was before she became who she had become was of no consequence, as it was on the North Shore. She was on this night at the peak of her beauty and fame.

For days preceding the ball, the merrymakers rehearsed their entrance with the dedication of courtiers, as if winning a prize for best tableau were a thing that mattered.

And win they did, the dozen devils of Dante's *Inferno,* amid hugs and kisses and toasts and congratulations. Ann, delirious with her success, looked among the celebrants for her husband, wanting his approval, needing his approval, knowing he would brag about her back in New York, to his mother, to his sisters, to his friends. She took a drink from a passing tray.

"Have you seen Billy?" she asked someone.

"He's dancing, I think," was the reply. She drank her drink and drank another.

"Have you seen Billy?" she asked someone else.

"He's dancing, I think," came the reply.

"Which room?"

"The nightclub." She drank another drink. He had, she realized, not seen the tableau, nor witnessed her moment. Her eyes flashed dangerously at the marital slight. The pills she had become used to taking—to wake, to sleep, to diet, to remain calm—and the liquor she drank combined to free the latent savagery within her.

IN ANOTHER room of the de Cuevas villa, fitted out for the evening as a nightclub, Billy Grenville danced with Simonetta d'Este, oblivious to the pageantlike festivities of the ballroom. It was a romance, but the romance of a party, without sex, without kisses even. Champagne, banter, laughter, dancing.

". . . and *I* thought that when the audience with the Pope was scheduled on the very day that the fortune-teller told me was going to be my last, it was a sure sign that she was right."

"What a marvelous story this is," said Simonetta. "No wonder you didn't come to that silly lunch at that silly monsignor's. I would have done the same thing. You were preparing yourself, in case."

"Exactly. And at midnight the Campanile rang. You can't imagine the relief. I never believed it, but at the same time I did, and it'd been hanging over me."

"And now you have a new life ahead of you."

"That's what I've been thinking. You're a wonderful dancer."

"So are you."

Eyes closed, abandoning herself to the music, Simonetta d'Este was unprepared for the force with which Ann Grenville grabbed her from behind by the shoulder and yanked her away from her husband.

"Bitch!" screamed Ann.

"Ann!" cried Billy.

Not satisfied, Ann grabbed Simonetta again, tearing the front of her Madame Du Barry costume and breaking the strands of precious pearls that were around her neck. Pearls fell all over the floor of the darkened room.

"Ann, for God's sake," said Billy.

"You stay away from my husband!" screamed Ann.

The orchestra stopped playing. The room was in silence as people crowded around to witness the melee, stepping on the scattering pearls. Billy grabbed Ann, but she pulled herself away from him, then turned on him, scratched his face, and tore his tie away.

"Please, Mrs. Grenville," pleaded Simonetta d'Este.

"I know your tricks," screamed Ann, attacking the woman again. She was out of control, and people stepped away from her.

"Someone, call the police!" It was the outraged voice of the Marquis de Cuevas, who, dressed as Cardinal Richelieu, pushed his way into the crowd surrounding the fight. "Get these people out of my house!"

Drunk and shamed for the scandal she had created, but convinced of her rightness in the matter, Ann retreated to the Hotel de Palais, where they were staying. Her purse lost, still in her red devil costume, she made her way across the white-and-gold lobby, aware, by the looks she was receiving, that word of her social debacle had preceded her return in the early-morning hours. Her face assumed the look of hauteur as she demanded the key to the Grenville suite.

"If my husband should return," she said to the hall porter, in the measured words of drunkenness, "please inform him he is to seek accommodations elsewhere."

Once inside, she locked the several doors of her suite, after hanging Do Not Disturb signs on the exterior handles. In a standing gold-framed three-way mirror, she caught sight of herself. What she saw was not the elegant lady of international society that she had become, but who she once was—a chorus girl in a chorus-girl costume looking like a chorus girl. In addition, her stockings were ripped, her makeup was smeared, her hair was in disarray. To her own snobbish eye she looked common and aging, and it reawakened her terrible rage toward her husband. She pulled his suitcases from closets and piled his clothes inside. She opened the door of the suite and pushed his luggage into the hall, bags half closed, sleeves hanging out, his brushes and shoes thrown after them.

Mollified somewhat, she sat on the edge of the tall, deep, old-fashioned bathtub and took several pills. Sleep, she knew, would obliterate the night for her, and she would deal with tomorrow when it came.

Billy, unable to get another room in the crowded hotel, too embarrassed at that hour to telephone friends with villas to get a bed for the night, used his key and entered the suite, bringing in his luggage, shoes, and brushes from the hall outside. He made up a bed for himself on a sofa in the sitting room. When he went into the bathroom, he found his wife passed out in the tub, still dressed in her costume of the evening.

The tub was too deep for him to lift her out and carry her to her bed without awakening her. He took her shoes off and went into the bedroom to get a pillow to place under her head in the tub and a sheet to cover her.

Ann awakened to see Billy coming down on her with a pillow in his hands. Drunk and drugged, she thought he meant to kill her, and a piercing scream was heard up and down the corridors of the staid Hotel de Palais.

Police were called for the second time. "My husband tried to kill me," said the hysterical Ann to the prefect. "You must believe me, he tried to kill me. He was going to smother me, but I awoke, just in time, to see him coming down on me with a pillow in both hands. He was going to put it over my mouth."

"I found my wife passed out in the bathtub," said Billy to the prefect. "If you ask any of the people who were at the ball this evening, they will tell you that she had too much to drink. What I was doing was trying to make her comfortable in the tub, as it was apparent she was going to spend the night there."

By morning the Grenvilles had departed Biarritz by separate cars.

PART THREE

PART THREE

A DULTERY WAS NOT the straw that broke the camel's back. The marriage survived their mutual infidelities, as did the marriages of most of the couples in the circles in which they traveled, in both New York and Europe. However, Ann's public displays of jealousy and erratic behavior caused much speculation that she was either mad or taking too many diet pills, and his friends wondered for just how long poor Billy Grenville was going to put up with his beautiful wife's unfortunate scenes. Even the most casual observer of their lives knew that the marriage was in poor straits. The fact that Fydor Cassati, the society columnist, had not reported on it was attributable to his deep affection for Billy, who had always treated him as a fellow gentleman and not as a newspaper writer, playing golf and tennis with him and inviting him to lunch at the Beach Club in the summer. There was hardly a person in café society who had not heard that Ann had thrown a drink in Rita Sinclair's face at El Morocco over an imagined flirtation with Billy, and that Billy, shamefaced for his wife, had taken her home. The debacle in Biarritz had stunned the international assemblage, and the resulting gossip and publicity on both sides of the Atlantic were agonizing for Billy, who worried always about what his mother would think.

Walter Winchell, who had written items about Ann Grenville when she was a show girl, reported in his column that "the veddy social Grenvilles of sassiety and racing circles have Reno on the beano." Finally they separated. Billy's friends breathed a sigh of relief. He moved out of the house into the Brook Club, where according to Doddsie, the night porter, he spent long and sullen evenings alone in the bar. He returned to the house only to see the children, at a specified time in the late afternoons, and it was a condition of his visits that Ann not be in the house at the time, because she created embarrassing scenes in front of the servants. Whatever his family said among themselves was not known, but they remained noncommittal to people who questioned them about the separation. When Billy asked Ann for a divorce, she became hysterical and told him she would never grant him one.

To the surprise of all, themselves included, apartness diminished rather than enhanced them. They did not stand up singly as they had as a couple. With all his social perfection, and good looks, and excellent manners, there was a blandness of personality about Billy that made him less interesting alone than as a partner to the firebrand he had married. He missed, he discovered, the relentless social life that Ann was expert at arranging for him. He missed also, he discovered, the comforts of the beautiful house that Ann had put together for him. He liked comfort, but he liked comfort arranged for him; he did not know, nor want to cope with, the intricacies of arranging it himself. The Brook Club was fine for the moment, but its bylaws forbade him to stay on there indefinitely.

Ann appeared on the scene with great fanfare as the latest companion of the notorious womanizer, Ali Khan. They were photographed in nightclubs and at the yearling sales in Saratoga, on her husband's home turf, but her stature as his companion was lessened by his continued attachment to the film star Rita Hayworth. There followed an Italian prince, with whom she had dallied in Rome, but he found her less exciting, and more demanding, now that she was available, and he returned to Italy.

All their friends expected a divorce, but to everyone's surprise they appeared together smiling and lovey-dovey at a large party at Alice Grenville's house a few weeks later attended by all the members of Billy's family. They did not so much reconcile as go back together. The marriage was over but endured with decreasing ties. Each recognized the other's signals of conclusion. She began to smoke in bed again, a habit that enraged him. He no longer lifted the toilet seat to pee, a habit that enraged her. First she wanted separate newspapers. Then she wanted separate bathrooms. Eventually she wanted separate bedrooms. After they stopped loving each other, or even liking each other, they continued, on occasion, to be attracted to each other, although rarely at the same time, so that lovemaking, on those occasions, was often unsatisfying and unpleasant.

BILLY SAID HE was having lunch at the Brook Club with Teddy Vermont, but when Ann called the club she found that he was not there and had not been there, and Teddy Vermont was in Lyford Key with Alfred and Jeanne Twombley. A look of displeasure passed over her face. Distracted, she knotted and unknotted the sleeves of the sweater that hung fashionably over her shoulders. She thought back on the conversation of the morning.

"The Haverstrikes are here from California, and I said we'd meet them for lunch at '21,' " she had said.

"Can't," he had replied, brushing his hair with two brushes.

"About the safari."

"Still can't."

"Why?"

"I'm having lunch at the Brook Club with Teddy Vermont."

"Teddy Vermont?" She did not know Teddy Vermont.

"Groton," he had replied, explaining him, removing him from her sphere.

"What does Teddy Vermont own? The state?"

"You should be on television with your wit—*Leave It to the Girls,*" he answered, walking out the door.

She suspected him of infidelity. Jealousy flooded her insides with its vile juices. It was Simonetta d'Este, she suspected, a princess, tall and dominant, as she was, strong, as she was, pedigreed, as she was not. She felt the insecurity of her position, unloved by both his family and his friends.

"IT'S NOT A good idea for us to go out anywhere alone, Billy. It would be misinterpreted, and I'm not keen about having a public encounter with the terrible-tempered Mrs. Grenville."

"Please, Esme."

"No, Billy."

"How about Hamburger Heaven, then? Isn't that innocent enough? We could have met there by chance."

"All right."

"IT'S HARD, YOU know, when you've done something as unpopular as what I did, marry someone no one approved of, not a single person, not even Bratsie, to say, 'Yes, everybody, you were right, all of you, and I was wrong.' It takes a bigger person than I am for that."

"What is your alternative, Billy?"

"The horses, I suppose. I have that. The farm is making money. And Tailspin, you've heard about Tailspin. He'll be a champion."

"Mr. Grenville?" They were being interrupted.

"Yes?"

"I'm Ashton Grimes."

"Hello." Billy could not remember who Ashton Grimes was.

"From Buckley School. I'm Third's teacher."

"Of course. How are you?"

"I don't mean to interrupt."

"Quite all right."

"I had hoped to see you at Parents' Day, and I thought we could talk then."

"Yes, I was in Europe." He was, he remembered, in Biarritz on the day. "This is, uh, Miss Bland. Ashton Grimes."

"Hello."

"He's not doing well, Third, is he?" asked Billy.

"He's not."

"What shall we do about it?"

"I think we must meet, Mr. Grenville. Something must be done. He is, uh, disturbed."

"May I call you tomorrow?"

"Yes, of course. Goodbye, Miss Bland. Goodbye, sir."

"He is disturbed, I suppose, about his mother and father," said Billy. "I've often wondered if they hear us, the fights, the screaming. I guess they do, and the servants, too."

"What are you going to do?"

"I never did well in school either, in my time. And then my father would give a gymnasium or a dormitory, and everything would work out all right."

"It's not the same."

"No, it's not the same."

"That teacher is telling you your son needs help, Billy," said Esme Bland, who, if asked, would know what to do.

"I have to go," said Billy. "The adulteress is expecting me for dinner."

"GET YOURSELF a smart lawyer, just in case," advised Babette Van Degan, who had received the largest divorce settlement in the history of New York, and Sam Rosenthal was the smart lawyer Babette Van Degan advised her to get. There was something about Babette, despite her appearance that never outgrew her brassy show-girl look, that made you take her advice in matters of finance and legalities.

"Tell me about him," said Ann.

"He is a snake, a liar, completely dishonest. He will be perfect for you."

"Where is he from?"

"Oh, Minsk. Or Pinsk. One of those places."

"I meant what firm."

"His own."

Ann didn't really have to be told who Sam Rosenthal was. Every wife in New York in a precarious marriage to a rich man knew who Sam Rosenthal was. She went to his office in Rockefeller Center. His intense black eyes showed white between the bottom of the iris and the lower lid, giving a hypnotic effect. His black eyebrows met in the center.

Sam Rosenthal knew who the Grenvilles were and how much they were worth. "A lotta simoleons," he said. He told her the name of a private detective who would be able to find out for her whether Billy was having an affair with Simonetta d'Este. She told him she wanted to keep their marriage together, not divorce. He advised her, when that moment came, to ask so much money that Billy would prefer to keep the marriage going. "Those old New York families like the Grenvilles would do anything rather than break up the fortunes," he told her. She liked Sam Rosenthal and felt she had made a friend.

"This is my private telephone number," he said to her, handing her a card. "They will always know where to reach me, day or night. Put it in your book in case you ever need me."

"MRS. GRENVILLE will be down directly, sir," said the maid.

"Thank you," replied the man, whose name was McCarthy. He liked to guess people's names from their looks, and very often he was right. He guessed the maid's name was either Mary or Margaret. He knew she was Irish, like himself. He knew she had been to Mass that morning; the ashes of Ash Wednesday thumbed into her forehead by some Catholic priest paid tribute to that. He guessed that she was new in this grand household where he found himself, by invitation, and he guessed correctly. He guessed also, correctly again, that the word "directly" in Mrs. Grenville-will-be-down-directly had been taught her to say, like a line in a play concerned with gracious living. He would have lingered with her in conversation until Mrs. Grenville appeared, but she did not and so he did not. Pretty little thing, he thought when she left the room. She closed the door to the hallway, leaving him free to prowl the room. He wondered if these people called it a living room or a drawing room. His eye, unschooled in art, nevertheless recognized value, and he judged the pictures on the wall to be "museum-quality," as he would later describe them to his partner, although this estimation, which was correct, was arrived at more from the elaborate gilt frames than from the pictures themselves.

In a corner was a discreetly placed drink tray bulging with the right liquors, wines, and brandies. In an instant he lifted a decanter, cut-glass with a silver necklace identifying it as Scotch, gulped from it, and replaced it in a movement so swift that an observer, had there been one, which there was not, might have missed it. He heard voices on the stairs outside and seated himself on a *bergère* chair covered in gray silk, obscuring its delicate lines with the extra weight that he carried and always meant to rid himself of. He placed his left ankle over his right knee, and then shifted to his right ankle over his left knee, and then placed both feet on the floor, tapping the sole of his Thom McAn shoe on the Portuguese carpet. Finally he reached over and picked up a magazine that had been left open to a particular page. If it appeared incongruous that this red-faced, white-haired, stout man in an inexpensive three-piece suit should be reading *Harper's Bazaar,* the incongruity was soon dispelled by his very real interest in the page he happened upon. There, elegantly seated in the very *bergère* chair in which he was now seated, was Mrs. William Grenville, Junior, photographed by Louise Dahl-Wolf in a setting of such high fashion and high style as to remove it almost from reality. He wondered if it had been placed there for him to see.

From outside the room he heard:

"We'll be four for lunch, Mary."

"Yes, ma'am."

"You'll have to help cook serve."

"Yes, ma'am."

"What's-her-name left."

"Yes, ma'am."

"Just walked off the job."

"Yes, ma'am."

"What's that smudge on your forehead?"

"Ashes."

"What?"

"You know, Ash Wednesday."

"Wipe it off before the duchess comes."

"Yes, ma'am."

Mr. McCarthy guessed, correctly, that the next time he was in this house, Mary would have left, like what's-her-name. The door to the room—living room? drawing room?—opened, and Mrs. William Grenville, Junior, entered, her expensive perfume preceding her. Tall, striking, blonde, lipsticked, exquisitely bosomed, she observed him observing her.

"I'm sorry to have kept you waiting, Mr. McCormick," she said, advancing toward him, offering her hand, "but we have had a crisis in the kitchen."

"McCarthy," he corrected her.

"I beg your pardon. Mr. McCarthy. I have guests for lunch, and the little waitress has simply walked out." Her gaze came distracted by a misplaced iris in a flower arrangement, and she repositioned it to her satisfaction.

"Do please sit down," she said. "I see you've seen my picture. Do you think it's good? I'm terribly pleased with it, although my mother-in-law thinks I am too much in the papers and magazines. She is of that school that thinks a lady's name appears in the papers only three times in her life."

Mr. McCarthy sensed that she was having difficulty getting around to the purpose of the meeting between them.

"Are you interested in protection for your home, ma'am?" he asked, helping her out.

"Do you mean like guards? Heavens, no! Is that what you thought?"

"We do that sort of work."

"I heard of you through Mr. Sam Rosenthal."

"Ah, yes, Mr. Rosenthal. We do a great deal of work for Mr. Rosenthal. It's that sort of thing?"

She walked away from him toward the window. Seeing her from behind was as nearly pleasurable an experience as looking at her face-on for Mr. McCarthy. Every proportion was perfect. Her legs. Her back. Her well-exercised buttocks beneath her smart wool dress. She looked around at him from the window. The part of herself that she totally understood was her physical presence, and she was never displeased, during any circumstance, to know that it was being admired. She was not seductive to him, had no wish to be, but she warmed toward him when she realized he had responded to her.

"I have reason to believe that my husband is being unfaithful to me," she said. If it had been a play, and she had been its author, she would have assigned to the private detective the line "He must be mad," referring to the deceiving husband, but it was not a play, and he did not say that line, but he thought it, or at least his own version of it.

"I would like to have him followed—discreetly, of course. You see, I love my husband. There is no thought of divorce, but I am most anxious to protect my marriage. I trust this is all confidential, what we are discussing?"

"Completely."

"I do not want him to be aware that I suspect him."

"No problem there."

"His office is on Wall Street, but he lunches most days uptown at the Brook Club, or the Racquet Club, or the Knickerbocker Club. The thing is, of late he has not been returning to his office in the afternoons, and I would like to find out where he is spending his time."

"Do you have a suspicion of a particular person?"

"I do."

"Good."

"What do you mean, good?"

"I don't mean good in that sense. I mean if it's a case of general philandering, it's a more difficult thing to pinpoint."

"I would prefer philandering. There is no threat in philandering," she added softly. She looked down at her vast ring, which he would later describe to his partner as a skating rink, as if it were a symbol of her marriage. When she looked up at him, she smiled sadly and blinked a tear away from her eye. Mr. McCarthy was absurdly touched, even though he realized he was witnessing a performance rather than a true emotion. He sensed, and quite rightly, that it was fear of loss of status and position that concerned her.

"Her name?" he asked.

She turned her back to him again and looked past the elaborate gray silk curtains to the street outside. Her slightly flushed face and stiffened back belied her serenity.

"She is called Simonetta d'Este."

He reached for his pad and pen.

"*Princess* Simonetta d'Este," she continued.

The correct spelling would come later. He did not interrupt her for that. He sensed that she felt rage toward this woman who threatened her marriage but at the same time was impressing him with the caliber of woman who was capable of unseating her. He realized she liked to have credentials established.

"What aroused your suspicions?"

"As to adultery or to the particular person?"

"As to adultery, ma'am."

"That's very embarrassing."

"Lipstick on a handkerchief, that sort of thing?"

"I smelled another woman on his fingers."

The detective turned scarlet.

They exchanged particulars: the address and marital status of the princess; the rates of his private detective agency, which she already knew from Sam Rosenthal, she said, anxious not to be overcharged. From below a doorbell rang.

"My God, she's early," said Ann Grenville, glancing at a clock on the mantelpiece. Her assurance seemed to leave her, as if figuring out how to get rid of one element of her life before another entered. "You see," she said to the private detective, who suddenly looked to her exactly like a private detective, as if he were wearing a badge proclaiming himself to be just that, so that explanations would have to be made, "it's the Duchess of Windsor coming to lunch, and, uh . . ."

"And you would like me to make a hasty exit down the back stairs, so as not to be seen, is that it?"

As she shook his hand in hasty farewell, she said, "I would like photographs."

* * *

IT WAS A RARE family outing: Alice Grenville, Billy and Ann, Diantha and
Third. They were sitting in the Grenville box at the Belmont track watching
Tailspin. Alice detected, but did not address, the strain she felt between her
son and his wife. After the race, and photographs, and congratulations to the
jockey and trainer, Ann wandered off to greet friends in the bar, and the
children were taken by their nanny to buy hot dogs.

"What's the matter with Ann?" asked Alice.

"Nothing," replied her son, waving to the reporters and photographers in a
gesture concurrently friendly and dismissive.

"Don't say 'nothing' to me, Billy. I'm your mother."

"She's jealous."

"Of whom?"

"Simonetta."

"With reason?"

"No."

The closeness that had once existed between them had never been the
same since the night she had refused to sanction his marriage. She sensed his
unhappiness now and wanted to reach out to him, but dared not. For an instant
their eyes met.

"Marvelous about the race," she said rather than what she wanted to say,
raising her field glasses and watching the track.

"Wasn't it?" he replied, hollow-voiced.

"I think Tailspin's going to win the Triple Crown next year."

"Wouldn't it be marvelous."

"I'm proud of you, darling."

"Thanks, Mère."

"Your father would have been, too."

"Do you think?"

"Oh, yes."

He sounded better. She felt better.

INSIDE, AT THE members' bar, Ann ran into Babette Van Degan. They sat
down at a table together and ordered daiquiris. Babette munched peanuts as
she watched her old friend.

"Why the morose silence?" she asked.

"Oh, I don't know. *La vie*," answered Ann.

"What did you think of Sam Rosenthal?"

"His eyebrows meet in the middle."

"You're not seriously thinking of divorce, are you?"

"Murder, yes. Divorce, no," Ann answered.

They roared with laughter.

"I won a bundle on your horse," said Babette.

"Good," said Ann. "I know you need the money."

They laughed again. Ann felt better.

"How's your son?" she asked, lighting a cigarette.

"Just got kicked out of another school," replied Babette. "How are your kids?"

"Oh, fine, I guess," said Ann.

THE COFFEE SHOP of the Astor Hotel on Times Square was jammed with a jostling crowd of conventioneers. Perfect, Ann thought to herself as she inched her way through to the booth where private detective Danny McCarthy waved to her. Better to meet here, she reasoned, near his office, than to risk meeting again in her home, especially as there were photographs to be viewed.

She wore a raincoat, a last-minute decision, leaving behind her mink coat, and she was glad not to stand out. She turned her ring around on her finger, stone inward.

"Coffee?" asked the waitress, pouring and spilling it over into the saucer.

"Bring me a clean saucer," Ann said to the waitress. It was a thing that always annoyed her exceedingly. She never allowed herself to remember that she had once, briefly, been a waitress in a coffee shop herself, at Crowell's Pharmacy in Pittsburg, Kansas. Greetings with Mr. McCarthy completed, her favorite kind of sandwich ordered, she settled back for the business at hand. The photographs were handed to her in an eight-by-ten manila envelope.

"Urse Mertens! Is that you? Urse?"

Before she raised her eyes from the six black-and-white photographs of Billy and Simonetta d'Este sitting on a bench in Central Park, at opposite ends of the bench, turning to face each other, talking only, not provocative in the least, near the children's playground, where her children were probably playing, Ann knew that the voice that addressed her belonged to Fredda Cunningham of West Quincy Street in Pittsburg, Kansas. At first she pretended not to hear as she perused the enlargements handed to her by Mr. McCarthy. She regretted her decision to dress down for the occasion. Her mink coat would have made her less approachable. Beneath the table she turned around to the outside the flawless emerald-cut pink diamond that she had turned inside for the meeting with Mr. McCarthy. It was too confusing a situation to cope with, explaining to Mr. McCarthy who Fredda Cunningham was, explaining to Fredda Cunningham that Mr. McCarthy was not her husband.

"Urse?"

"Are you speaking to me?" she asked, looking up at the childhood acquaintance she had once longed to be accepted by. There was grandeur in her voice. She brought her left hand up to her face, and the huge diamond, the skating rink, as Mr. McCarthy had described it to his partner, dazzled brilliantly in the fluorescent light of the coffee shop. Fredda, embarrassed, crimsoned.

"I beg your pardon," said the flustered Fredda. "You reminded me of someone I once knew."

Ann smiled pleasantly, acknowledging the woman's error. Standing behind Fredda was a man. Every instinct within her told her not to look at him, but she did. It was Billy Bob Veblen, the best-looking boy in Pittsburg High, with whom she had once "gone steady," with whom she had made plans and promises, to whom she had . . .

Again she smiled pleasantly at the two staring people as if they were strangers. The cheese-and-bacon sandwich she had ordered arrived, unexpectedly open-faced, like the cheese delight from Crowell's Pharmacy in Pittsburg, Kansas. Ann, beneath her makeup, flushed and dared not raise her eyes, lest the same thought occur to them.

"Sorry to have bothered you," said Fredda Cunningham.

"Not at all," answered Ann. They moved on past her and went to the cashier, where they paid their check.

"That was her," said Billy Bob Veblen to Fredda Cunningham, and his voice carried back to the table where Ann sat with the private detective she had hired to follow her husband.

Although he was impassive throughout the encounter, the moment was not lost on Mr. McCarthy, whose dress and girth belied his sensibilities. How does it feel, he wondered, to snub old friends? He made a mental note of the name Urse Mertens, and of the name tag of the conventioneer, William R. (Billy Bob) Veblen, Mathieson Aircraft, Pittsburg, Kansas.

"Is this it?" asked Ann about the photographs. She didn't know if she was pleased or disappointed that they were so nonincriminating.

"He's clean as a whistle," replied Mr. McCarthy about the husband Ann Grenville thought was deceiving her.

IF IT HAD BEEN Fredda Cunningham alone, Ann would have run after her, through the lobby of the Astor Hotel, to set things straight. She possessed a vivid imagination and could have thought of something that would have explained, in a reasonable way, her rude behavior to her childhood friend. She would, she thought at that moment, even enjoy bringing Fredda up to her house and watching the richest girl in Pittsburg, Kansas, react to the magnificence of her life.

But Billy Bob Veblen. That was something else again. What could she say to him that would not upset, irretrievably, both their lives, and other people's as well? That he should reappear like that, in a coffee shop she had never entered before and would never enter again! She wondered if her life was closing in on her. She had simply ceased to remember that Billy Bob Veblen had played a part in her life.

* * *

"WHAT'S A SAFARI, Daddy?"

"It's a hunting expedition."

"Hunting what?"

"In this case, Bengal tigers."

"Here on Long Island?"

"No, no, no, India. Now run along, Third. Nanny's calling you."

"Night, Mummy."

"Goodnight, Third."

"Hug him," said Billy to Ann.

"I can't wait for my son to grow up so he can take me out dancing," said Ann, embracing her child. It was a thing she often said when moments of affection were required. It implied that then, in his young adulthood, would her motherhood come into flower.

At the last minute Billy backed out of going on the safari. Tailspin was running at Santa Anita, and old Sunny Jim O'Brien, the trainer, thought he should be there, he said. Ann didn't believe him. She wanted to back out too, but she knew she would never be asked again if she backed out at the last minute after all the elaborate arrangements had been made. The Haverstrikes had already left, and the Maharajas of Patiala and Alwar were expecting them in India on the eleventh. Besides, she loathed California; too many people in the film business remembered her from her chorus-girl days. By this time she had settled into her success. It was part of her. She didn't like people who remembered her from earlier periods.

In London, en route to New Delhi, she picked up a twelve-gauge double-barreled shotgun at Churchill's. Billy had ordered it for her after last year's safari, made up to her specific measurements, to decrease the kickback on her shoulder. Engraved on it was "To Ann from Billy, with love." She felt very touched by his thoughtfulness and wired him thanks in Pasadena.

Dressed in exceedingly smart huntress attire, she managed to be the dominant figure of the safari, admired greatly by the men but disliked by the women, including the maharanee, whose servants she thought nothing of ordering about.

"Open the safe and get me my jewels," she said.

"I cannot open the safe unless the maharanee is present, madam," said the steward.

"I said, open the safe."

"I cannot, madam."

"I order you to open the safe."

Mrs. Haverstrike suspected her husband of having an affair with Mrs. Grenville. Heretofore Mrs. Oswald Haverstrike, of Hillsborough, California, had not begrudged Ozzie the occasional dalliance. He knew the rules and played by them; that part of his life was kept far afield from their life together. However, Ozzie's dalliance with Ann Grenville was more than she was willing to put up with, happening under her nose as it did. It terminated with an emerald-and-ruby-necklace that Ozzie purchased for Ann in New Delhi.

Ozzie Haverstrike said she became excited and rattled when a tiger was in the neighborhood, but she shot the biggest tiger of the safari, a ten-foot Bengal, the first woman ever to shoot a tiger of that size in the territory. Her reputation as an excellent shot, accompanied by the photograph of her and her prey that became so famous after the tragedy, preceded her back to America.

IT WAS NOT that she was lunching with Ali Khan that was incriminating. They had picked a public place frequented by people they knew, and, it could be reasoned, if they had anything to hide, they would have sought an out-of-the-way bistro. It was an attitude of passion toward the Moslem prince that she knew Felicity had seen. She felt herself crimsoning. Always a clever strategist, she knew she could outargue Felicity in a showdown with Billy, but she knew that Felicity had not misread what she had witnessed.

"When she saw me, she blushed," said Felicity. "You can't even say she blushed. She turned beet-red. She looked frightfully common, actually."

"You've never liked her," said Billy.

"You're quite right, I never have, not from the first day," replied Felicity. "But I do like you, little brother."

TAILSPIN WAS the coming three-year-old that season, his earnings just under a million dollars, a record for that time. He was setting record after record and was spoken of as a Triple Crown contender. The public took to the horse with the same affection they had taken to Man o' War, and Billy Grenville, after years of nonaccomplishment, was considered, along with Alfred Twombley and Piggy French, one of the most successful breeders in American racing.

Alice Grenville felt that he was living up to the high expectations of his father, and Billy basked in her approval, as well as the approval of his sisters.

Ann felt it was she who had reawakened Billy's interest in the family sport and was proud of his success at the same time that she was frightened of his newfound independence. More and more she was at the track for the big races, and the photographs of Billy and Ann that appeared on the sports pages and the newsreels after the big wins, hugging and laughing, made them look like one of the most glamorous and in-love couples in the country.

DIANTHA AND Third preceded Billy and Ann to the country that Halloween weekend. The chauffeur, Lee, picked them up at their schools in New York and drove them and the new cook, Anna Gorman, out to the house in Oyster Bay. Billy and Ann came down later, after a cocktail party she had wanted to attend and he didn't. For him the party had not been amusing. He was sick to death of the International Set, the titled Europeans that Ann found so irresistible; more and more he preferred the company of the people he had grown up with on Long Island. He was angry when he heard her invite Dougie DeLesseps to lunch on Sunday when she knew that he did not enjoy having guests on the weekends.

"I'm not going to be there," he said.

"Fine," she answered.

They drove in Billy's specially designed car, a Studelac, which combined the sleek design of a Studebaker body with the powerful force of a Cadillac engine. Driving it was one of the things he most enjoyed doing, and part of each weekend in the country was spent in solitary journeys to the farther reaches of Long Island, enjoying the stares of passersby. A few days before, he had returned from Kansas, where he had treated himself handsomely, from Tailspin's million-dollar earnings, to a gleaming silver four-seater airplane, for further solitary pursuits. If it occurred to Ann that Billy was spending more and more time away from her with his cars and plane and, of course, the horses, which had become a sort of obsession with him, she did not mention it.

They were arguing, as they often did when they drove. It was either that or silence. Billy was distressed to have heard at the cocktail party that a photograph of Ann, and Ali Khan, and Mrs. Whitney, taken at the yearling sales in Saratoga, had come out that day in a new issue of *Town and Country.* It was certain, he said, to pour fuel on the much-circulated story in racing circles that Ann was having an affair with the Moslem playboy. A few weeks earlier Billy had enraged Ann by ordering the caretaker at the country house to drain and clean the swimming pool after Ali Khan had swum in it.

Ahead of them, in the center lane of the Long Island Expressway, an old couple in an old car, unsure of their exit, had simply stopped in the road to consult a map. Billy, traveling too fast and directing his attention toward Ann rather than the expressway, did not see them.

"Billy!" screamed Ann.

At the last second before crashing into the rear of the old people's car, he swerved out of the way, narrowly missing a truck. The Studelac screamed to a stop at the side of the expressway, and they looked at each other, ashen-faced and breathing heavily, knowing they had come very close to death. He thought of the fortune-teller in Tacoma and wondered if she had been off in her dates by a few months. Do people who are about to encounter catastrophe meet warning signals along the way?

Resting his head on the steering wheel, Billy said, "Let's go to Rothman's and have a few drinks and dinner."

"But I told the new cook we'd have dinner in," said Ann.

"The hell with the new cook. We just almost died."

The owner of Rothman's knew the Grenvilles and instantly found them a choice table in the bar, even though it was Friday night and people were lined up waiting for their reservations. He liked it when the social crowd from the North Shore stopped in on their way to and from their country houses, and he made room for them ahead of his regular customers. Neither the cold and perfect martinis that were speedily produced nor their brush with disaster made conversation easy for them. It distressed Ann to be observed dining in silence, even by servants or waiters. She had heard that the Duchess of Windsor recited the alphabet to the duke, in various conversational attitudes, when they had nothing to say to each other in public, but she dared not try that on Billy, especially in the mood he was in. Instead she kept a running commentary on the other diners.

"Dear God, look at that woman with high-heeled shoes and socks," she said.

"Hmmm," replied Billy.

The piano player played "Full Moon and Empty Arms." Once it had been a favorite of theirs. "Full moon and empty legs," she sang to him, but he did not laugh, as he used to when she sang that lyric.

The waiter served.

"What is this?" she asked. "Whitebait?"

"Whitebait."

They ate in silence.

"Oh, look," she said, thinking finally to engage him. "There's Eve Soby. Drunk. Again. Hello, Eve."

"If all else fails for you, Ann, you could always write a column," he said unkindly. *"Urse Mertens's New York."*

A flash of anger passed over her face at his mockery. She hated that name and regretted having once told Billy that she had been born with it. Her appetite ruined, the food followed. An eggplant soufflé dwindled cold on her plate. The Camembert hardened. The lemon ice melted. Only the wine was touched, but its excellence went unheeded. An error in the bill was ignored, and they left the restaurant in silence.

WHEN THE house the Grenvilles lived in on Long Island had been part of the vast Helena Worth McGamble estate, it was always called the Playhouse, and the name remained even after Billy Grenville bought it as a weekend house for himself, Ann, and their children.

A curious condition of the sale was that Billy Grenville honor an agreement Helena McGamble had made with the New York Philharmonic allowing them to use the indoor tennis court as a recording studio for seven years. Billy, always honorable, adhered to the agreement, but Ann Grenville, who had pressured Billy into buying the house in order to break away from the restrictive weekends at Alice Grenville's house in Brookville, found the sounds and presence of the members of the orchestra, on the rare occasions they were there, annoying and tiresome. She quarreled constantly with Ralph Wiggins, the guard hired by the Philharmonic, who lived in the caretaker's room on the far side of the tennis court, for refusing to undertake chores she asked him to do on behalf of the Grenville family and was always urging Billy to abrogate the agreement.

THE COBBLESTONES in the courtyard of the Playhouse had been packed and brought over from Fotheringay Castle by Helena Worth McGamble's father, Frank Worth, when he had dreams of creating a dynasty through his favorite daughter. What she noticed as the headlights of Billy's Studelac flashed over the cobblestones when the car pulled up to the front door was that the gardeners had not been doing their job sufficiently; the late-fall leaves were blowing messily around the courtyard, and if there was one thing Ann Grenville could not stand, it was for things not to be looking their best.

She was startled also to see Ralph Wiggins enter the courtyard as if he had been waiting for the sound of the car. He went straight to Billy's side of the car, opened the door for him, and greeted him. Ralph Wiggins never came around to this side of the house, and both Billy and Ann looked at him as if something might be the matter.

"I'm sure there's nothing to worry about, Mr. Grenville," he said, "but there's been a break-in at the cabana by the pool, and I wanted to tell you without the children or the new cook hearing about it."

"That's very kind of you, Ralph," said Billy, getting out of the car. Neither of them ever brought luggage for the weekend, as they kept their country clothes here. This weekend, however, because of Edith Bleeker's dinner for the duchess the next night, Ann had brought an elaborate evening dress as well as her jewel case, and Billy went around to the trunk to get her things out.

"But there's nothing to take in the cabana," said Ann.

"I don't think anything was taken, except perhaps some food from the refrigerator, and the window was broken," Ralph answered.

"I'm cold," said Ann.

"Go on in," said Billy. "How did you happen to notice it, Ralph?"

"The Oyster Bay police came by this afternoon before the children arrived, and I was the only one about. The Eburys across Berry Hill Road have had an intruder, and so have the Twombleys, so we took a look around, but that was all we could find."

"Perhaps I should drop in on the police tomorrow," said Billy, not allowing his deep fear of intruders to show. Since he had been briefly kidnapped at ten, the fear was always with him.

"I don't think it's anything to worry about, Mr. Grenville, but I wanted you to know."

"Thank you, Ralph."

"If you'd like, I'll put your car in the garage for you, and I'll leave the keys in the kitchen with the new cook."

"Thank you."

*   *   *

THE NEXT morning, Ann Grenville, who usually slept until noon, in troubled Seconal slumber, arose early and appeared in the dining room, to the amazement of her husband and two children. Her beauty, which was considerable, was not yet in evidence, her eyes still puffed from the early rising and her expert ministrations at her makeup table not yet attended to.

"Do, please, remove the milk bottle from the table," she called into the kitchen to her new cook. A milk bottle on a dining table, or catsup bottle, or mustard, reactivated an erased memory of an earlier life and filled her with irritation.

Billy returned to his newspapers while coffee was poured for her. With no columns, Saturday papers bored her.

"Daddy's going to take me flying in the new plane tomorrow," said Third.

"Nice," replied Ann, drinking her coffee. "Do not feed the dog toast, Diantha."

"Why are you up so early, Mommy?" asked Diantha.

"Hairdresser in the village for the party tonight."

"Are we having a party?"

"Mrs. Bleeker's having a party." She loathed morning conversation.

"Is it a costume party?"

"Why would Mrs. Bleeker be having a costume party?"

"It's Halloween."

"Oh." She had forgotten it was Halloween. Pumpkins and candy and trick or treat had all slipped her mind. Damn that nanny for leaving.

Billy's words, when he spoke, were inappropriate to the situation, but his words, and hers, when they spoke to each other, had been inappropriate to the situation for a long time.

"I don't suppose there's anything in that pharmacy by the side of your bed so simple as an aspirin?"

"I told you not to drink those two brandies."

"Is there?"

"Is there what?"

"An aspirin."

"Of course there's an aspirin."

"Where?"

"Look for it. You don't think I'm going to look for it for you, do you?"

"No, that's one thing that never crossed my mind."

When the telephone rang, Billy thought it would be the mechanic from the hangar to tell him if the new plane was ready to fly. The children thought it would be the riding teacher about the trials for the horse show. Ann thought it would be the hairdresser in the village calling to confirm her appointment.

"Hello?" she answered as if she knew who it was going to be. "Oh," she said, surprised. "Mère." When she married into the family, Ann had picked up the habit of calling her mother-in-law what Billy and his sisters called her, although there was never a bit of affection shared between the two Mrs. Grenvilles, only carefully observed amenities. Ann relinquished the telephone to her husband and went about the day's business.

"What did your mother want?" she asked Billy later.

"She's canceled out of Edith's party tonight. She's not coming to the country this weekend. She's decided to stay in New York."

Ann was delighted, although she didn't say so. She always felt inhibited at parties when her mother-in-law was there. Later, looking for signposts along the way, people wondered whether if Alice Grenville had *not* canceled out of Edith Bleeker's party, the tragic event that followed it might not have happened. Certainly, Ann would not have made the scene she made with her mother-in-law present. She was known to be frightened of her. And the scene she made, everyone who was there agreed, no matter what they said to the police afterward, must have led up to what happened.

HER GARDEN was closing down for winter. There were early chrysanthemums, late dahlias, and a few surviving roses. Ann leaned over and plucked off two dead dahlias and lay them on the edge of the bed for the gardener to find. "I can't bear them when they turn brown like that," she said. Ann was proud of her garden, and liked nothing more on a weekend than to walk guests through it and point out this flower and that bed, and talk about annuals and perennials in the way she had observed English ladies doing it.

"I am talking to you," said Billy, measuring his words in quiet fury.

"I'm listening. I'm listening," she replied. "Go on."

The situation did not warrant his stalking off in a state of agitation, but she knew it was what he was considering.

"About the car," she helped him. "The Studelac, wasn't it? The prowler broke into the Studelac, you were saying. He'd probably never seen one before. That's all. What was taken?"

"Nothing, actually," he said finally. "After all, what is there to take in a car? Maps. Gloves. Dark glasses. I mean, that's not the point, what was taken. The point is, there was someone here, several times, in our garage, and in the cabana by the pool."

"Kids, probably. The caddies from that Jewish golf club through the trees."

"I wish you'd take me seriously."

"Look at that marvelous rose still blooming this late in October. I'm going to cut some flowers for the table."

"I'm going out to look at the new plane."

"No, not now, Billy. I told the new cook we'd have lunch at one with the children, and it's lamb chops, so don't go off now."

She looked after him as he walked toward the house. The prowler, real or imaginary, did not seem to her the problem with Billy. What, after all, was a prowler to them? A call to the Oyster Bay police station to report it, or, at most, the hiring of a guard to patrol the grounds, as the Twombleys had done, and the matter of the prowler would be at rest. People who lived behind gates and high walls must expect to be preyed upon. It was in the natural order of things. Did not Alice Grenville keep an unheard-of amount of money in the wall safe behind the Constable painting in her bedroom ever since the attempted kidnapping of Billy over twenty years earlier, simply to be prepared in the case of an emergency? The trouble with Billy had more to do than with prowlers, she knew. It had to do with their marriage. Uncourageous, except for his single incident of bravery in wartime, he could not bring himself to keep after her about the divorce he wanted, and, in frustration, seized upon the prowler as something to brood about.

With her blunt garden scissors she clipped the October rose, and another, open to full lushness, and searched for more. She could, she knew, cajole Billy through this period of marital unrest. Settled now, even complacent, in her own success, she was, to her very marrow, Mrs. William Grenville, Junior, and nothing was going to disrupt that fact of her life, even if it meant giving up her lover. She would miss Ali Khan, but she could do without him.

"Mommy."

"Mommy."

From the house Diantha and Third called her for lunch, excited to be sharing a meal with their parents.

"WHAT'S THE new cook's name?" Billy was leaning against the door to Ann's room, still in his maroon polka-dot dressing gown.

"Anna, I think. Or Annie." She was seated at her dressing table, putting on her makeup.

"Which?"

"What difference does it make?"

"It makes a good deal of difference. It's one of the reasons we have a new cook every two weeks." There was a tone of annoyance in his voice. "In my mother's house—"

"Oh, for God's sake, spare me that old chestnut about your mother having her cook for thirty-two years, and her butler for twenty-eight, and her maid for seventeen."

"My mother knows how to treat them properly, and that's why they stay with her."

"Do you want to move back home?"

"You are a pain in the ass, Ann."

"You're always disagreeable after you come. Does your wop princess ever tell you that?"

She leaned toward the mirror and rubbed her finger back and forth across her lip, evening her lipstick. Her eyes met his in the mirror. She watched him turn sulkily and walk across the hall to his own room and regretted she had mentioned Simonetta d'Este.

"Billy," she called after him.

He didn't answer.

"It's Anna," she called again.

"What's Anna?" He appeared again in her sightline in the mirror.

"The cook's name. It's Anna. Anna Gorman. Fifty-six years old. From the Creedon Domestic Agency. Good references. Last worked for a Mrs. Slater of 563 Park Avenue, *not* the Mrs. Slater we know. Why this great interest in the cook's name?"

"I want to show her how to lock the doors after we leave."

"You'd better get dressed. We can't drift in late tonight. Edith wants everyone there at eight sharp, before the duchess comes down."

"I still want to talk to the cook about locking the front door. It's tricky."

"How do I look?" She stood up and turned around toward him.

" 'Mrs. William Grenville, Junior, was in powder-blue satin by Mainbocher,' your friend Elsa Maxwell will write."

"Balenciaga. I'm branching out. And Elsa Maxwell was not invited."

"No rocks tonight?"

"If there is this prowler around, as you insist, I'm not going to put on my jewels until I'm in the car."

"ANNA!" SHE called out. "Anna!"

"What's the matter?" asked Billy, crossing over from his room, adjusting his black tie.

"Where the hell is she?"

"She's in the kitchen eating her dinner. What's the trouble?"

"There're some things I want her to do after we go out."

"That's no reason to yell for her like that. I thought something was wrong."

"Oh, go tie your tie," said Ann.

"Did you want me, Mrs. Grenville?" asked Anna Gorman, opening the door into the small hallway that separated their two bedrooms.

"Mr. Grenville said I was interrupting your dinner. I am sorry," said Ann in exaggerated friendliness.

"That's all right, missus," said Anna. Anna Gorman had heard a thing or two about Mrs. William Grenville, Junior, at the employment agency.

"We'll be leaving in a few minutes, Anna, and there are a few things I wanted to go over with you. You see, we can't be late, because we're going to a dinner for the Duchess of Windsor, and all the guests must arrive before the duchess comes down."

Behind the cook's back, Billy Grenville shook his head slowly in disapproval of his wife's name-dropping in front of a servant, a thing he would never have done himself, and returned to his own room to finish dressing. His head-shaking was not lost on Ann, and it added to her annoyance that the cook did not seem impressed with her social disclosure.

"The chauffeur's bringing the children home from the riding instructor's Halloween party at about eight-thirty."

"Mr. Grenville told me."

"Tell the children to go right to bed, no television. Mr. Grenville's going to take Third flying in the new plane in the morning, and he won't if he stays up late. Also, would you telephone this number in the city and say that Third is in the country with his parents for the weekend and cannot come to Bobby Strauss's birthday party tomorrow. If the nurse hadn't left, she'd be doing this."

"Yes, Mrs. Grenville."

"I bought a lot of cosmetics in the village this afternoon. I wonder if you'd unwrap all those packages for me and throw away all the papers and strings."

"Yes, Mrs. Grenville."

"When you pick up my clothes and straighten up the bathroom, I wonder if you'd do me the most enormous favor, Anna?"

"What's that, Mrs. Grenville?"

"The laundress—what's her name?"

"Lil."

"Lil, yes. She creased my sheets when she ironed them, and I simply cannot bear to have my sheets creased. She's supposed to fold them over her arm and carry them to the bed to change. Do you think you could run the iron over them, just this once, and I'll explain it again to Lil when I see her on Monday."

"I'm just the cook, Mrs. Grenville."

"Yes, of course, but I just thought if you had a few minutes to spare after we leave and before the children get home, you might, uh, you know, run the iron over the creases, and also, about the lights, leave all the lights on in the house, don't be worried about the electric bill, the people who rent the indoor tennis court pay all the electricity bills, and if there's a prowler in the area, as Mr. Grenville seems to think, he won't come near a house that's all lit up."

"I'll light it up like the Catholic church," said Anna.

"What?"

"Just an expression, missus."

"Now, the telephone number where we'll be having dinner at Mrs. Baker's is—"

"Mr. Grenville gave me the number, missus, in case he received a call."

Ann let this fact register but said nothing. Instead she picked up her brush and brushed hard her already brushed hair. She wondered from whom he was expecting a call.

"Is there a guard on the place, Mrs. Grenville?"

"No, there's not, but the Oyster Bay police patrol the grounds every hour or so, and there is a guard that the people who rent the indoor tennis court have, called Ralph, or something. We're going to be late. Billy, are you ready? Hand me that bag with my jewels, would you, Anna?"

"Here, missus," said Anna, handing Ann her bag.

"And you won't forget about the sheets, will you?" she said, finishing the conversation and sweeping out of the room.

Anna Gorman looked after her, shaking her head slowly in the same way Billy Grenville had. She turned toward the unmade bed with its upholstered headboard and creased linen sheets, and resignedly stripped them from the bed. On Monday, she decided, she would call the Creedon Employment Agency in Manhattan.

* * *

THE CAR was parked in the cobblestone courtyard, and Billy Grenville was seated behind the wheel smoking a cigarette. Beside him on the seat was a revolver.

"What in the name of God are you carrying a gun for?" asked Ann as she opened the door of the car and got in.

"The garage has been broken into. The cabana has been broken into. I'm not taking any chances," said Billy.

"But nothing was taken, except some food in the cabana," said Ann. "It's probably kids."

"I think it's someone who's living in the woods there," said Billy, pointing in the direction beyond the garden and the swimming pool. "I'm going to set a trap for him."

"Oh, Billy, for God's sake, if you're so concerned, you should have hired a guard," said Ann. She did not press her point and suggest that if he was so concerned about the prowler, they should remain with the children and stay home from the party instead of leaving them alone in the house with a brand-new cook. She particularly wanted to go to this party to show all the North Shore families that the Grenville marriage, despite all the rumors to the contrary, remained on a firm footing. "What are you stopping for?"

"I'm going to turn on all the driveway lights down to the road."

The lights shone on the rhododendron bushes that lined the long driveway. Ann shivered, wondering if anyone was standing behind one watching them drive away. From her gold minaudier she took a cigarette and matches. Ignoring Billy's outstretched lighter, she lit her own cigarette with a match. The matchbook, she saw in the flash of flame, was from an obscure French restaurant where she had lunched the day before with Ali Khan. Billy, meanwhile, withdrew his gold Zippo.

"Those lights are so bright."

"That's the point."

"Anna will say it's lit up like a Catholic church."

"What?"

"Just an expression, missus."

"I don't know what the hell you're talking about."

"It's quicker to go 25A than Berry Hill Road," said Ann as the car turned out from the driveway.

"You don't have to tell me how to get to Edith Bleeker's house. I've been going there since I was ten years old."

"Right," said Ann, twisting the rearview mirror around to watch herself put on her earrings. "Just don't tell me that story again of Bratsie's tenth birthday party."

"I wish you wouldn't twist the rearview mirror around like that when I'm driving," said Billy. "It's very dangerous."

"If you'd put a mirror on the back of the visor as I've asked you to, I wouldn't need to use your damn rearview mirror."

"Poor Bratsie," said Billy quietly, as he always did when Jellico Bleeker's name came into the conversation.

"Necklace, earrings, ring, bracelet, brooch," Ann said, checking off her jewelry in the rearview mirror. "I hate this damn clasp Jules Glaenzer talked me into. It pinches my earlobe."

"Did I tell you I drove by your old house in Pittsburg, Kansas, last week when I was picking up the new plane?" asked Billy. "West Quincy Street, I think it was."

Ann's face reddened in the dark car. She had, even before meeting the family she married into, disengaged herself from her past. She disliked being from a place for which apologies had to be made. "And just what is that supposed to mean?"

"Nothing, really," said Billy. "It just seemed like a natural segue from your sapphires pinching your earlobes."

"You're a shit, Billy," she said, lighting another Camel.

"I want a divorce, Ann." The words held no threat for her, as they once had. Too often spoken and never acted upon, they had become part of their conversational discord.

They arrived at the gates of Edith Bleeker's estate on Viking's Cove. "Look," said Ann quietly. "I don't want to be the first one there. Let's drive around for a few minutes before we turn in at Edith's."

Billy dutifully backed the Studelac out of the drive and took off in the direction of Locust Valley.

"Did you hear what I said?" he persisted.

"Do I feel the presence of Princess Simonetta d'Este in this domestic crisis?" asked Ann.

"You keep Simonetta out of this," he said.

She did not want to let him know that she had been having him followed by private detectives and wished she had not introduced Simonetta d'Este's name into the conversation.

"I want a divorce, Ann," he repeated. The calmness of his request began to unnerve her.

"His own kind. That's what they'll say about Simonetta d'Este. So much more suitable than the show girl. What his mother always wanted for him."

"I am waiting for an answer," said Billy.

"You know my price and my conditions," said Ann nervously, taking a gold-and-diamond compact from her gold-and-diamond minaudier. She opened it, looked at herself in the mirror, and began powdering her face.

"I haven't seen that before," said Billy.

"Seen what?"

"That compact."

"Of course you have."

"Who bought you that, Ann? My old roommate Neddie Pavenstedt? Or that greaseball Ali Khan?"

He wound down the window of the car.

"What are you doing that for?" she asked. "I'm cold, and it will blow my hair."

"To do this," he answered. He reached over, pulled the compact out of her hands, and threw it out of the window as he sped on. Again her face reddened in the dark car, this time with rage.

"The duchess will say what lovely color you have tonight, Ann," taunted Billy.

"I'm going to get even with you for this," said Ann, stabbing her cigarette butt into the ashtray where, unextinguished, it continued to emit smoke. She lit another.

"And do me a favor, will you? Don't curtsy to the duchess. It's so tacky."

THEY TURNED through Edith Bleeker's massive wrought-iron gates, each supported by a red brick column surmounted by a stone griffin on a ball of stone, and drove silently up the long white-pebble driveway to the porte cochere extending from the entrance of the enormous red brick house over the adjacent driveway. The air of the Studelac was clouded with the smoke of Ann's Camel. The outdoor staff, dressed for the occasion in black mess jackets and ties, lined up to park the arriving cars. Ann drew deeply on her cigarette one last time, as if she wanted more out of it than it could give her.

Billy, lugubrious no longer, sprang from the car when his door was opened. Edith Bleeker's was a house he always enjoyed coming to, and he never was not filled with childhood memories when he reached up to push the bell that hung from a cord in the ceiling of the porte cochere. "Bratsie and I used to stick pins in this bell on Halloween when we were kids, and the bell rang inside interminably, and Edith would have a fit, but Brats and I would run like hell, and . . ."

But Ann was never interested in Billy's endless reminiscences of dead Bratsie Bleeker and was not listening. Instead she was mourning for her gold-and-diamond compact given to her only the day before by Ali Khan.

"Good evening, Mrs. Grenville," said the old and distinguished butler, Dudley, who bowed formally at the entrance. It was a mark of distinction on the North Shore to be personally greeted by Edith Bleeker's celebrated butler. He was an indispensable contributor to the success of Mrs. Bleeker's frequent entertainments, so highly thought of that the late George Bleeker's will provided generous bonuses for every five years that Dudley remained in his widow's service. He knew all the connections and cross-connections of the North Shore, but of no one was he more fond than Billy Grenville.

"Good evening," answered Ann, not looking at him as she passed him and entered the hall. She walked straight to a gilt Chippendale mirror over a console table and eyed her wind-blown hair critically in it.

"Good evening, Junior," said the butler.

"You know, Dudley, you're the only person who can get away with calling me Junior still," said Billy affectionately.

"I've known your husband since he was ten years old, Mrs. Grenville, when he used to come here for poor Jelly's birthday parties," said Dudley.

"Don't tell me we're the first ones here?" asked Ann in reply.

"Mr. Freeman's already in the drawing room," replied Dudley.

"The piano player, you mean?" asked Ann.

"Yes," said Dudley. "Mrs. Bleeker has had him learn all the new tunes from *The Boy Friend.*"

"We're the first ones here," said Ann, looking at Billy.

"You wanted to be on time," replied Billy.

"I stupidly have come off without my compact, Dudley," said Ann. "Do you suppose I could go upstairs?"

"Of course," said Dudley.

"You go on, Billy. I'll join you," said Ann, walking up the sweeping staircase.

"Say, Dudley?" said Billy in a confidential voice when Ann had disappeared from sight.

"Yes, Junior," answered the butler, moving closer.

"I may be receiving a call later."

The doorbell rang. Other guests were arriving.

"I'll find you, sir," said Dudley.

"Long distance," said Billy.

OUTSIDE THE drawing-room windows the grounds and gardens were floodlit, and beyond, ships bearing freight sailed silently by on Long Island Sound. Only the piano player, hired for the evening, found the breathtaking sight more compelling than the guests.

"Everyone's been to the vault, I see," observed Ann, surveying the jewels in the room, knowing her own stacked up. She was, she knew, madly chic, just as Fydor Cassati often described her in his column. She heard the sound of her satin and smelled the scent of her perfume and caught the gleam of her diamonds. She looked down the front of her strapless dress at her lovely breasts, and pleasure filled her. She breathed in deeply. She was ready to make her entrance.

"Who is that marvelous-looking creature?" asked Lord Cowdray, pointing his whiskey glass toward the entrance doors of the room where Edith Bleeker stood to receive her arriving guests.

"Which?" asked Tucky Bainbridge, following his gaze toward the gathering assemblage of the proudest peacocks of the North Shore of Long Island—the Phippses, the Hitchcocks, the Schiffs, the Guests—spilling in one upon another, the nobility of North America, or so they thought, honoring their hostess's request for promptness in arriving before the Duchess of Windsor.

"Brightly painted. Blazing jewels. Sweeping in," said Lord Cowdray. "Ravishing."

"Oh, her," said Tucky, putting withering scorn into the two words. "That's Ann Grenville."

"Now that's the way a woman should enter a room," he went on, not taking his eyes from her.

"Her Copa training, no doubt," said Tucky sourly, losing interest in her assigned task of pointing people out to the visiting Englishman.

"Her what?"

"She used to dance at the Copacabana. We call them the prince and the show girl out here. Hello, Brenda," she called to Brenda Frazier.

"I do hope Edith has seated me next to her."

"To Brenda?"

"I meant Mrs. Grenville."

"If not, don't fret, Lord Cowdray. When she hears your title, she'll seek you out."

"Not one of your favorites, I take it?"

"The life and death of every party. How Billy Grenville could have thrown himself away on her is something I'll never understand," said Tucky.

"Billy Grenville who owns Tailspin?"

"The very one."

"The best horse in America. Is that Billy Grenville next to her?"

"Yes. He's got the class, and she's got the brass."

"They appear ideally suited."

"Just an act. Lord Cowdray. Just an act."

I WAS ALWAYS reading in the social columns of the brilliant conversations that took place at Edith Bleeker's dinner parties, but what I heard was nothing more than desultory chatter, where they had been, where they were going, that sort of thing. "Were you at Cornelia's?" "Ghastly." "Who was there?" "Taytsie and Winkie and the Delissers, and old Mrs. Altemus with all the white powder and bright red cheeks."

But I can tell you this much about that night: Ann Grenville was surprised to see me in that grand house at that august gathering. From across the room I could see the wheels working in her social climber's mind. What in the world is Basil Plant doing *here* at Edith Bleeker's? she was thinking. Edith Bleeker's parties, like Alice Grenville's, were closed to newcomers and outsiders. Even the recent successes of my slender volumes, particularly *Candles at Lunch*, thirteen weeks on the *New York Times* best-seller list and soon to be a major motion picture, did not qualify me for social entrance to Viking's Cove. However, my success had made me a favorite of certain of the North Shore ladies with literary leanings, particularly Jeanne Twombley and Petal Wilson, and I was spending that weekend with the Twombleys when Alfred was felled by the flu at the last minute and Jeanne pressed me into service as her escort. That's how I got there and bore witness to Ann Grenville's performance.

Once, urged on by Bertie Lightfoot, who was intent on launching me, Ann had traipsed up flight after flight of dark stairs that she complained smelled of cat urine to the tenement flat way over east on Seventy-second Street where I then lived and worked. Once there, the style of it surprised her; she had hardly expected to see a gesso console table in a fifth-floor walk-up. It was, I told her, a gift from Kay Kay Somerset, who was redecorating and getting rid of things. We drank red wine and gossiped about Salvador Dali and her portrait, and Bertie, and people in society, and laughed a great deal. She could see the possibility of me as a witty addition to her dinner parties, but something about me made her cautious. I think she felt that I saw through her the way Dali had, past the soda fountain waitress, into her self. She never did invite me.

"Ah, the beautiful Mrs. Grenville," I said when our eyes met, and I crossed the room to greet her, whiskey spilling over a bit from my glass onto Edith Bleeker's Aubusson carpet.

"Hellohowyou," she answered, all in one word, in that chi-chi voice of hers, the way she had heard Billy's sisters do when people spoke to them they didn't want to talk to. She moved on away from me to greet Neddie Pavenstedt, leaving me with egg on my face. I looked after her, my eyes boring into her splendid back, and made a mental note for my journal.

IT WAS THE duchess only; the duke was not there. She said business in Paris had delayed him from making the trip in time. His absence in no way diminished the splendor of the occasion; she had eclipsed her royal husband as a social curiosity. It was not yet fashionable to decry the Duchess of Windsor. That would come later, after the duke died, and the sum total of his wasted life was laid bare. At the time of which we speak, the duke and duchess were considered to be exquisite still, and those who basked in their light acquired a patina of exquisiteness themselves in the upper echelons of New York society.

"Wallis," said Edith Bleeker, taking her guest of honor around her drawing room, "you know this attractive couple, I know. Ann and Billy Grenville. Billy Grenville was my son Jellico's best friend." In death Bratsie Bleeker had taken on a nobility he had not possessed in life, and the shabby circumstances of his unsolved murder had passed from memory.

"Hello, Billy," said the duchess, extending her hand. "How's your divine mother?"

"She's well, Your Grace," said Billy, inclining his head.

"Do give her my love." She moved and spoke as if she were a royal presence, which is what she believed her marriage had made her. Ann watched her, glowing in her reflected glory. She was in green. Ann knew that her dress was from Dior, and that the emeralds at her neck, on her ears, and at her shoulder were Queen Alexandra's emeralds, left to the duke for his future queen when he was the Prince of Wales. She also knew they had been reset in Paris at Cartier's, secretly, so that they could not be reclaimed by the English royal family as part of the Crown Jewels. The man from Cartier's who had made the ear clip that pinched her lobe had told her that. It was the sort of information that Ann always knew.

"Good evening, Ann," said the duchess. "What marvelous color you have this evening."

Ann Grenville had never looked so lovely as now. It thrilled her that the Duchess of Windsor should call her by her first name, and the mixture of excitement and success of the moment enhanced her already striking appearance. She bobbed a curtsy, somewhat less deep than she would have liked to give, and the duchess beamed at her for this recognition. "It's lovely to see you again, ma'am," said Ann. She wondered what her mother would have thought if she had witnessed this familiarity with the famed romantic figure she had admired so extravagantly.

She longed to prolong the conversation. She knew that the duchess found her more entertaining than the Long Island ladies, and she enjoyed the feeling that it gave her. Although it was not a thing she discussed, even with Billy, she was aware that the ladies of the North Shore, like Tucky Bainbridge for instance, did not care for her and tolerated her only because she was married to William Grenville, Junior, whose position in the society of New York and Long Island was as inviolate as any of theirs. With the men, it was another thing. It was only to Babette Van Degan, who was never asked anywhere anymore, that she confessed she saw a parallel between her marriage to Billy and Wallis Simpson's marriage to the Prince of Wales.

"I'm so sorry you missed the race at Belmont, ma'am," said Ann, placing her hand on Billy's arm with wifely pride. "It was thrilling."

"We read all about Tailspin in Paris," said the duchess. "It's so exciting for you, Billy."

Billy Grenville was constantly astonished by the performance of marital bliss his wife was able to enact in the presence of others, always managing to confuse the skeptics who were certain that the stormy union had run its course. As always he fell into step with her performance, and the conversation between the duchess and the attractive Grenvilles became animated and filled with laughter, prompting the duchess to say about them, to Edith Bleeker, that they were an ideally suited couple.

"IT'S NOT FUNNY, darling. Poor Ann is terribly worried about the prowler. He broke into Billy's car last night."

"She's not so worried she'd miss a party. After all, who's home with the kids if she's so damn worried? Some new cook who just arrived."

"She was never going to get mother-of-the-year award."

"I don't believe that prowler story anyway. I bet it's Ann. Ann always has to create a drama with herself at the center of it."

"But of course there're prowlers, darling. It's the North Shore. People like us are fair game."

"It's only food he's after. He's probably just a vagrant."

"I have the most marvelous idea," said Kay Kay Somerset.

"What's that?"

"Why not set a trap for him?"

"What kind of trap?"

"If all he's after is food, make him a sandwich and leave it in the fridge of your pool house, and sprinkle some sleeping pills on it, in the mayonnaise or something, and he'll fall asleep, darling, right there on the chaise by your pool, and the police can catch him, snoring away, and take him off to the slammer *toute suite*. Now how's that for the idea of the evening?"

"Did you hear Kay Kay's idea for the Grenvilles' prowler?" asked Tucky

Bainbridge, screaming with laughter. "Kay Kay said to put sleeping pills in a sandwich. Don't you think it's divine?"

"God knows, and so does everyone else, that Ann has enough sleeping pills around to fell an army of prowlers."

AFTER ELEVEN the telephone rang in the house in Oyster Bay. Upstairs Anna Gorman put aside reading *The Messenger of the Sacred Heart* and wondered about people who called that late. There was no telephone in the room where she was sleeping, and she felt quite sure that by the time she rose and put on her robe and went downstairs to the telephone in the hall, whoever was calling would have hung up. The night outside was dark and wet, and the house was strange to her, and she decided not to answer it. Instead she switched off her bed light.

LATER IN THE evening, after dinner, Dudley, the butler, whispered in Billy's ear that there was a telephone call for him.

"Is it the cook from the house?" Billy asked Dudley, knowing it wasn't, for the benefit of his companion.

Dudley, who was used to the complicated affairs of the people he served, met Billy's eyes and mouthed the words "long distance."

"Excuse me, Brenda," Billy said to Brenda Frazier. "There's been this damn prowler."

Across the room Ann talked to Lord Cowdray about Princess Margaret and Peter Townsend, her equerry, if she would marry him or if she wouldn't. It was a conversation that Ann could carry on in great detail without giving her full attention to it. She watched the butler whisper in her husband's ear, and she kept on talking. She saw her husband nod his head, and she kept on talking. She met her husband's eye as he glanced furtively at her and looked away again, and she kept on talking. She followed with her eyes as her husband left Edith Bleeker's drawing room, and she kept on talking. She listened to an illicit proposition being made to her, and she let the Englishman know it might be a future possibility.

"You will ring me when you are in London next?" he asked her.

She smiled at him. "Excuse me, will you?" she said and rose and walked out of Edith Bleeker's drawing room.

WHATEVER the conversation had been, it was brief. By the time Ann quietly opened the doors of the library, she saw her husband across the room standing by the desk with his back to the door. He was speaking into the telephone in an extremely low voice, but she was able to hear him say, "Goodnight, my darling, sleep well," make a kissing sound, and end the conversation with "I love you, too."

Ann threw the Baccarat glass containing Scotch and soda that she had carried with her from the drawing room. It narrowly missed Billy and crashed into a Lowestoft platter on a teakwood stand that separated the leather-bound copies of Melville from the leather-bound copies of Dickens on the shelves of Edith Bleeker's library, smashing the armorial platter into worthless fragments.

Within an instant she was across the room and pulled the telephone receiver out of his hand. "Listen to me, you wop whore!" she screamed into the instrument. "You leave my husband alone!" If it was Simonetta d'Este, she heard no more, as Billy broke the connection.

"Are you out of your mind?" he said to her.

"How dare you embarrass me like this?" she screamed at him, at the same time slapping his face.

"You understand, don't you," he said to her, grabbing her hand from his face and holding it hard, "that if you make one of your scenes in Edith Bleeker's house, it will be the end of you on the North Shore. Not of me, mind you. Just you."

She knew what he said was true.

"All that Jet Set trash at de Cuevas's ball may have forgiven you for the scene you made there, but you won't get away with it here."

Behind them the doors to the library opened, and Edith Bleeker, the grande dame of Long Island, walked into her room. In the hallway outside stood Basil Plant and Kay Kay Somerset and Jeanne Twombley staring into the room as more guests arrived to look in.

"Edith, my darling, I am sorry. This is totally my fault," said Billy Grenville. "My elbow must have hit this beautiful platter, and I knocked it off the stand. We seem to have caused quite a spectacle at your lovely party, and I would very much appreciate it if you would excuse us and allow us to leave through the kitchen, and I will be in touch with you tomorrow to make amends and restitution for the damage I have caused."

Edith knew, as did everyone else, that Billy Grenville was covering for his wife. Tucky Bainbridge was sent upstairs to fetch Ann Grenville's fur jacket, and Dudley retrieved Billy's coat from the hall closet. Stan Freeman, accompanied now by a bass and drums, stuck up some of the tunes from *The Boy Friend*, and Mrs. Sanford grabbed Lord Cowdray to dance with her, and other guests followed suit, anxious to keep Edith Bleeker's party from being destroyed by the disgraceful fight of the Grenvilles. Long after their flight into the cold October night, the Grenvilles were discussed in various corners of Edith Bleeker's drawing room. Many of the conversations ended with the words "Poor Alice," meaning Billy's beloved mother, Alice Grenville, who had never from the beginning approved of her son's misalliance with the Broadway show girl who wanted so terribly to be part of the Grenvilles' world.

*   *   *

THEY DROVE over the Long Island roads from Viking's Cove in Locust Valley to Oyster Bay in murderous silence. Ann stared out as the windshield wipers made a swish sound, back and forth, back and forth. She dared not tell him he was driving too fast. She feared he might stop the car and strike her if she cautioned him about his speed. She pulled her sable fur around her and sat as far away from him as she could.

She knew she had gone too far. Inwardly she always suffered from remorse when she lost control and created scenes in public. For someone who cared so much about belonging, she could not understand about herself why she continually sabotaged herself socially. She wondered if there was a connection between it and her menstrual period, which she could feel was beginning.

The speedometer on the dashboard hovered at seventy-five. The dark roads were wet, and she closed her eyes and tried to remember exactly how much she had had to drink. Usually she nursed a single drink for the entire evening when she was out with the North Shore group, but the talk about divorce in the car on the way to the party had unsettled her. There were two Scotches before dinner, she counted, and white wine with the fish, and red wine with the beef, and champagne with the sweet, while most of the food was left fashionably uneaten. No brandy, she had turned down the brandy, but there had been another Scotch, or maybe two, not counting the one she had hurled across the library that had broken Edith Bleeker's Lowestoft platter. She shuddered at the thought and forced it out of her mind. She wondered if the pills she took that Dr. Sidney Skinner prescribed for her—for diet, and nerves, and sleep—could have had an adverse effect on her system combined with all the liquor she had had.

He turned off 25A onto Berry Hill Road without looking left or right, but the wet roads were empty. As they pulled into the driveway, she could see that they had made the trip in only sixteen minutes. The lights were brightly lit along the long driveway, reminding them both of the prowler. In her corner of the front seat, Ann removed her earrings, her rings, her bracelet, her brooch, and her necklace, placed her jewels in the leather bag she had put into the glove compartment, and put the bag in the pocket of her fur coat. The car pulled into the courtyard and around to the side door of the Playhouse.

For a few seconds they both sat in the car and surveyed their house. The bare branches of the large oak tree to the left of the side door scratched the roof of the house over Ann's room, and dead brown leaves, soaked by the rain, covered the cobblestones of the courtyard.

"Who were you talking to on the telephone, Billy?" she asked.

"None of your business," he answered.

"Are you going to put the car in the garage?"

"No."

"Are you going to turn off the driveway lights?"

"No."

They opened the doors of the car and got out. Billy walked up to the side door, put his hand on the knob, and found it locked. She saw for the first time that he was holding his revolver.

"Shit," he said.

"What?"

"It's locked."

"Of course it's locked. You gave what's-her-name locking instructions for fifteen minutes before we left."

"I forgot to bring a key."

"Great."

"You didn't bring one?"

"Of course I didn't bring one."

"How the hell are we going to get in?"

"Wake up cookie."

He ignored her and walked over to the window of his bedroom and peered in. The curtains had been drawn, but the window was unlocked, and he pushed it up and crawled in. Ann stood outside in the wet courtyard, uncertain if she was supposed to enter the house in the same fashion or if Billy would return and open the door for her. A chill went through her, and she felt frightened, as if someone were watching her. Then the front door opened.

"Lock all the doors and leave the windows open!" said Ann sarcastically, to hide her fright. "Guaranteed to fool all the burglars in the neighborhood."

"Why don't you shut your big fucking mouth," said Billy at the door. "Don't you think you've had enough to say for one night?"

She walked into the narrow hall past Billy. Her bedroom was to the right and Billy's was to the left. She went into her room and took off her fur jacket, removing the bag of jewels from the pocket. She placed it on her dressing table. She switched on a lamp in the room and saw that Anna had unpacked her cosmetics, as she had asked her to, and had repressed her sheets so that the offending creases had been removed.

"I don't suppose your motherly instincts would include going upstairs to check on the children?" asked Billy.

"You go upstairs and check on the children," she replied. "You're the one with the gun."

"I wonder if I always thought this was a creepy house," he said, "or if it just seems creepy to me tonight."

"Billy."

"What?"

"Bring me back a beer, will you?"

"Funny."

"What?"

"I thought you were going to say bring you back a gun."

They looked at each other for a minute. He turned away from her and opened the door of the bedroom hallway that led into the front hall of the house. To the right was the dining room and kitchen. He switched on the lights. Across the hall was the paneled living room that looked down on the indoor tennis court. He entered the living room and switched on the lights. He crossed the length of the living room. Beyond it was another hallway. He switched on the lights in the hallway. To the right were the double doors that led to the vast music room. To the left was a stairway that led upstairs to where the children and the cook were sleeping. He switched on the stair light and walked upstairs. At the top of the stairs he turned on the upstairs hall light and entered Diantha's room. He pulled her blanket up over her and kissed her on the cheek. She sighed in her sleep and hugged the dog that slept next to her. Then he walked into Third's room and looked down at his son. He turned back to the hall and then walked over to Third's bed and leaned down and kissed him.

"Goodnight, little boy," he whispered.

"Night, Daddy," whispered Third.

"Why aren't you asleep?" he asked.

"Are you going to take me flying tomorrow?"

"Yes, yes. Now go to sleep."

He retraced his steps through the house, turning out all the lights he had turned on. Passing through the living room, he walked to one of the windows and peered out at the grounds as if he expected to see someone out there.

"What was that called?" she asked.

"The final fuck," he answered.

He was different to her. She did not understand why he seemed to be in control, but she did not change her performance.

"Good, I won't have to fake it anymore," she said, preparing herself for bed, putting on the black brassiere that she always wore beneath her nightgown, for the support of her beautiful breasts.

"I'll say this much for you, Ann—you've still got great tits."

"Such gallantry," she replied.

"Let's talk divorce."

"You want a divorce, Billy? Fine. Shall I go over the figures? I want five million dollars. Plus this house. Plus the house in New York. Plus full custody of the children. When you're ready to talk my language about divorce, then we'll talk divorce. Now go to bed. We have people coming for lunch."

"Those aren't the kind of figures I have in mind, Ann."

"What do you think this has been like for me, this marriage? How do you think it feels to know that your mother and sisters loathe me, have always loathed me, will always loathe me, even if we should happen to stay married fifty years?"

"All the more reason to divorce."

"I don't want a divorce."

He picked up his revolver, which he had placed on her bedside table, and started for the door.

"Did I tell you I saw your old house on West Quincy Street in Pittsburg last week?" he asked.

"Yes, you did," she replied. She was sitting at her dressing table. She swallowed a few sleeping pills with some beer, which she drank from the bottle.

"I went to the cemetery, too," he said, "and looked up the Mertens plot. I didn't know that, uh . . ."

She watched him in the mirror as she applied cold cream to her face.

There was something about his voice and manner that gave her a feeling of warning and apprehension.

"You don't look as well nude as you used to," she interrupted him, hoping to deflect the conversation away from her past, that part of her life that she no longer considered part of herself.

". . . that you had a little brother. Odd you never mentioned him," continued Billy, not feeling uncomfortable in his nudity.

"He was only three when he died," said Ann, relieved. "I never think of him."

"Claud his name was, in case you forgot."

"I didn't forget. Why this great interest in my family all of a sudden? You haven't evinced much curiosity about my background all the years we've been married."

"Curious," he said, reflecting on the word as he spoke it.

"What's curious?"

"Life."

"What are you babbling about, Billy? You'd better go to bed. It's very late. Aren't you taking Third flying in the morning?" She lifted the bottle of beer to her lips and took several deep swallows, all the time not taking her eyes off him in the mirror. She knew there was more he had to say; her curiosity was intense but her desire not to hear any more of it was equally intense.

"Don't you think it's odd, in the overall scheme of things, I mean, that the particular airplane that I wanted to own should be manufactured in the very tiny little town in the southwestern corner of the state of Kansas where my wife was born?"

"Are we getting mystical at one o'clock in the morning? Fate? Is that going to be next?" She got up from her dressing table and went into the bathroom, wanting to get away from him, and began brushing her hair in the bathroom mirror away from his gaze.

"I said to them, at the aircraft plant, that my wife was from that town, I believed." He walked across her room and leaned against the bathroom door, again watching her in the mirror.

"I wish you'd go to bed, Billy," she said. "I want to put in my Tampax."

"I said her name was Urse Mertens, but no one seemed to remember you."

"I left there years ago, Billy."

"Except one fella. He remembered. He didn't speak up at the time, though. He was an accountant with the firm, not one of the big honchos, as he referred to them later when he called me at the Vel-Fre Motel. We had dinner in a Chinese restaurant on South Broadway, new since your time, right next to Crowell's Pharmacy. He said you used to be a waitress at Crowell's when you were in high school."

"I'm going to close this door."

"Four pens in his breast pocket, that kind of person. He's the one who took me out to the cemetery. Nicely attended, your mother's grave, and little Claud's. He called you Urse. Urse Mertens, he said. Funny. You don't look like an Urse Mertens."

"If you're just deciding that you married beneath you, Mr. Grenville, that's something your mother and sisters tried to tell you years ago," she answered.

"Aren't you curious to know what his name was? Billy Bob Veblen! He said he went to high school with you."

Ann stared at her husband. She could begin to feel panic rising within her.

"He said he was in *Lady Windermere's Fan* with you."

She continued to stare.

"HE SAID HE WAS MARRIED TO YOU!"

Hatred and wrath, which had been accumulating within her for the whole evening, suddenly boiled over. "THAT IS NOT TRUE!" she screamed.

He grabbed her by her arm, pulled her across the room to her bed, pushed her down on it by her shoulders and leaned over her, breathing heavily, poised to enter her or kill her. He was what he thought he would never be, out of control. Saliva dripped from his loose mouth onto her. The thought of striking her, and worse, went through his mind.

"He said he joined the Marines and when he came back, you had vanished from the earth, as far as he knew. He didn't know you had changed your name to Ann Arden. He said he never got a divorce from you."

"No," she screamed.

"You know what this means, don't you? This is not a moment that either of us should be deceived by. We're not even married! You're still Mrs. Billy Bob Veblen, the bigamist, from Pittsburg, Kansas!"

Pushing down on her, he heaved himself upward, off her and off the bed, terrified by the thoughts of violence that had entered his head, that he knew she had read. She snaked her body away from him while they continued to stare at each other.

"What has happened to us?" he asked, aghast.

"You're drunk," she said.

"No, I'm not," he replied.

She was not listening. Why had she not paid more attention to him when he told her he was going to Kansas to buy his airplane? She dreaded to think of Alice Grenville's reaction to her earlier marriage. She wondered if even Sam Rosenthal, the divorce lawyer who had been so sympathetic to her marital plight, would have the same regard for her when he heard there had been an earlier marriage that she had never dissolved.

Billy walked to the window and peered out at the cobblestone courtyard. He thought he heard footsteps outside.

"You know my motto, don't you?"

"What?"

"Shoot first and ask questions later."

"What are you talking about?"

"The prowler."

UPSTAIRS, at the other end of the house, Anna Gorman, the new cook, whose duties this night included keeping an eye on the sleeping children, heard voices below. They were not the voices of conversation; they were the voices of combat. She picked up her ticking clock from the bedside table and saw that it was half past two in the morning, then remembered that she had forgotten to reset her clock from Daylight Savings Time to Eastern Standard Time. Spring forward, fall back, she remembered, as she turned the hands back an hour, all the time listening to the sounds below.

The door to her room was ajar, as were the doors across the hall to the rooms of Diantha and Third. Anna Gorman rose, shivered in the cold, pulled her heavy wool comforter around her, and knotted its braided cord. She slipped her feet into fleece-lined slippers and padded to the door.

A flight of stairs and the length of a long living room and hall below separated her from the bedrooms, across the hall from one another, of Mr. and Mrs. Grenville, but through some quirk of construction in this house that was conceived to be a playhouse and not a domicile, with its indoor tennis court and music room, the sounds of anger and reproach traveled eerily across rooms and up the stairs. Anna Gorman, who believed in God and family, felt that it was her duty to close the doors of the children's rooms, not only to assure their sleep but to shield them from the ugliness below should either of them awake.

Diantha, she saw when she peered into the dark room, was already awake. With her in the bed, listening to the fight below, was Third. Between them was Diantha's dog, Sloppy.

As SHE OFTEN did in moments of panic and despair, Ann missed her mother, the only person who had ever understood her completely, the only person with whom she had never had to pretend to be anything other than what she was. That Billy Bob Veblen, long since forgotten, should reenter her life twelve years into her marriage and bring her enviable existence crashing down was inconceivable to her. Her mother had discovered her all those years back engaged in sexual intercourse with Billy Bob Veblen, the captain of the Pittsburg High football team, the handsomest boy in the school, on the davenport of the front room of the house on West Quincy Street. To her surprise there was no reprimand. Or punishment. What her mother said she had never forgotten. "Don't waste it here," said Ethel Mertens, meaning Pittsburg, Kansas. "That's the mistake I made." Her elopement several years later from Kansas City across the state line to Oklahoma, before Billy Bob Veblen enlisted in the Marines, was the event that precipitated her mother to move her to New York.

"As they say in the movies, 'My lawyers will be in touch with you,'" said Billy to his ominously silent wife. He began to whistle as he turned to walk back to his room.

Her lips curled back from her teeth. Her eyes flashed dangerously and Billy saw the fiery gleam that he had come to dread in them, like a flash of lightning in the sky preceding terrifying thunder. She made an inarticulate, almost animal sound in her throat. "I'm glad you're leaving," she snarled at him. Her voice was low and guttural. All traces of tonal culture evaporated.

"I'm glad you're leaving." She repeated the words, her crescendo building. Nothing could stop the savage force of her rage. *"I'm glad you're leaving!"*

Billy watched her distorted face as she screamed up at him from her bed, like a caged animal.

"I hope you don't think you're being impressive," he said quietly as he turned and walked back to his room, unaware that his earlier words to her about the prowler had set in motion a lethal train of thought. His bed had been turned down. His pajamas and dressing gown had been laid at the foot of the bed. His slippers, velvet with embroidered initials, from Lobb in London, were on the floor by the side of the bed. He walked to the window and opened it to the cold night, looking across the cobblestone courtyard as he did so. For an instant he thought he saw a shadow moving toward the house, but decided that it was the branches of the large trees that surrounded the courtyard, still lit by the bright exterior lights that he had not turned off.

His armpits felt moist, even in the cold; the result, no doubt, of the triumph of his disclosure to Ann, the secret that he had nurtured within himself for over a week now, sharing it with no one, not even his lawyer, saving it for just the right moment. He felt exultation within himself for the freedom that was at hand for his life. He walked into his bathroom, turned on both taps full blast, and stepped into the shower.

She walked to the door of her bedroom when she heard the sounds of his shower. The room was chilly, and her shoulders were cold in the diaphanous silk-and-lace nightgown she wore. At the foot of her bed Anna Gorman had laid out a matching bedjacket and slippers. She put on the bedjacket and noticed in the mirror, even in the calm of her resolution to act, that the jacket concealed the black brassiere that she always wore to sleep. She slipped her feet into the satin slippers and walked out into the narrow hallway that separated their two bedrooms. The door to Billy's room was closed. Beyond it the sounds of the shower continued. She opened the door of the bedroom hallway that led into the front hall of the house.

Immediately to the left of where she was standing in the hall was a narrow curved stairway that went down to the basement area and the tennis court. At the top of the stairway she turned on a light and went down the stairs to another hall off which there were several closed doors. One led to a wine cellar. Another led to a fur vault. The third led to the gun room, where guns and ammunition were stored in glass-fronted gun cabinets. There were guns for skeet, and guns for duck and pheasant shooting, and guns for big-game hunting.

From a hidden drawer in one of the cabinets she took a ring of keys, then opened the gun cabinet. The third gun in on the rack was the expensive double-barreled weapon that Billy had purchased from Churchill's in London as a gift for her.

She took it out of the case. From a drawer beneath she took out a box of ammunition and loaded both chambers. Shoot first and ask questions later. Those were Billy's very own instructions about the prowler. She took several extra rounds of ammunition and stuffed them into her black brassiere. She turned off the lights and shut the door behind her and walked up the narrow stairs. At the top she turned off the light, reentered the hallway that separated her bedroom from Billy's, listened at his door to the continuing shower sounds.

She walked into her bedroom and placed the heavy gun on a slipper chair next to her bed. Her finger, ringed and manicured, brushed past the cold metal of the engraved inscription, "To Ann from Billy, with love," as on a wedding band.

Billy walked into his bedroom from the shower, naked still. He intended to put on his pajamas and drop into bed and go to sleep. He was planning to take Third up in the new plane for the first time in the morning, and it was getting late.

From across the hall he heard Ann scream. "Help!" she shouted. "Don't! Please! Please don't!"

He remembered the feelings of being grabbed by a kidnapper when he was ten years old. He moved with speed but felt as if he were moving in slow motion and opened the door to his bedroom. In hazy darkness his eyes locked with the eyes of his wife holding her double-barreled shotgun aimed at him. Their throats tightened. The roofs of their mouths went dry. In their brains was a screaming silence. Never were they more as one. Only then did it occur to him that the message in his fortune cookie at the Chinese restaurant in Pittsburg, Kansas, had been blank. He turned away from her.

A massive reverberating roar filled the room, followed almost instantly by a second massive reverberating roar. Rockets' red glare. Bombs bursting in air. The nude body was knocked backward and fell with a resounding thud onto the carpeted floor. Blood soaked the carpet.

Yet death was not instantaneous for William Grenville, Junior, merely painless, and, for the fifteen minutes left to him before expiration, thoughts of the dying variety passed through whatever thought process was left to him. He saw himself as a son, a brother, a lover, a husband, a father, and a man. With total clarity he recognized himself as a passive figure of fate whose death would catapult him into a notoriety he had, mercifully, never achieved in life.

ON THE OTHER side of the indoor tennis court, Ralph Wiggins, the guard hired by the New York Philharmonic, was awakened by the double blast. He sat straight up in the narrow single bed in the bedroom of what had once been a caretaker's apartment. He knew for a fact that he felt fear and did not want to get up and investigate. His thoughts were on the prowler. The Oyster Bay police had said to call at any time of day or night if there was any sign of him. He waited. He listened. There was only silence. He was nearing retirement age, and there was a pension to be considered. He decided to wait and do nothing until he was sure.

UPSTAIRS, at the far end of the house, Anna Gorman, the new cook, heard the shots. First one, then another. There was no scream. There were no sounds

after the shots. She did not know these people. She did not want to be involved
with them. She knew only that on Monday morning she would be back at the
Creedon Employment Agency on East Thirty-sixth Street. She wondered only
about the little children across the hall. If she heard them get up from their
beds, she would get up. Otherwise she would stay where she was. Whatever
happened, it was not her responsibility.

"I'M SCARED," said Third.
"Don't talk," whispered Diantha.
They listened. They heard nothing.
"I have to go to the bathroom," said Third.
"You can't."
"Do you think the new cook heard it?"
"If she did, she would have been in here."
"Do you think it's the prowler?"
"Stop talking, Third. Just listen."
"Where's the dog, Diantha?"

HE WONDERED if his children would be scarred by growing up in the
shadow of a disgrace and scandal in which he had been an active participant.
He thought of his mother. He thought of the fortune-teller in Tacoma, who had
known what she was talking about even if her dates were off by a few months.
He thought of poor Esme Bland whose telephone call at Edith Bleeker's party
had set this evening in motion.

"Dear God," he heard his wife say. "Dear God." And then he heard her
repeat it again. "Dear God." He heard her shotgun fall to the floor. He heard
her go to the telephone and ask, not for the police, not for an ambulance, not
for a doctor, but for a lawyer called Sam Rosenthal.

SHE HAD PUT the telephone number in her address book under L for lawyer
instead of under R for Rosenthal in case Billy should ever go through her book
to look for a number and come upon it. She found his initials, S.R., between
the Lafayette Cleaners and Lord and Taylor. She picked up the telephone by
the side of her bed and gave the number in New York City to the operator in a
voice of complete calm. He had told her it was his private number, and whoever answered would always know where to reach him day or night. She heard
the number ring once, twice, three times.

"Mr. Rosenthal's residence," came a voice that she knew was an answering service.

"I must speak to Mr. Rosenthal."

"I'm sorry. Mr. Rosenthal is away from the city for the weekend."

"Can you tell me where he is."

"Mr. Rosenthal is in Westhampton."

"Will you give me the number please."

"May I ask who is speaking?"

"This is—." She didn't know what to call herself. If she did not give her right name, he would not know it was she. On the other hand, she did not want to call herself Mrs. William Grenville, Junior. She heard Diantha's dog, Sloppy, scratching at the hall door. She looked through her open door across the narrow hallway into Billy's room and saw his naked body lying face down on the floor. She knew that she had to act quickly. "This is Ann Grenville."

"Will Mr. Rosenthal know who you are?"

"Yes."

"I am not at liberty to give out Mr. Rosenthal's number, but I will call him in the morning and give him your number if you will give it to me."

"I must talk to Mr. Rosenthal *now!*"

"It is almost two o'clock in the morning."

"I don't care."

The answering service operator paused. "Give me your number, Ann, and I will call him."

As HIS EYEBALLS receded upward into his head, he thought of his friend Bratsie Bleeker, also shot dead, also in ignominious circumstances, and he knew that once more vengeance would not be sought. And then he died.

SHE STEPPED into the front hallway and listened. There was silence in the house except for the dog. She picked it up, took it in the kitchen, and closed the door. She moved to the left and went down the narrow curved stairway that led to the basement area and the tennis court. She walked past the wine cellar, past the fur vault, and entered the small room where the guns and ammunition were stored. She reached into her black brassiere and took out the extra rounds of ammunition that she had stuffed there. Some of the rounds fell on the cement floor, others on the shelf of the gun rack. Upstairs she heard a telephone ring. She raced back to the stairs, ran up them, crossed the front hall, opened the door that led into the narrow hall that separated the two bedrooms. To the right of her was Billy's body. She went into her bedroom and picked up the receiver before it rang a third time.

"Yes?"

"Ann?"

"Sam?"

"Yes. What's the matter?"

"Oh, Sam." The tears, the panic, the hysteria that she had held in abeyance since she blew off her husband's head came to the fore.

"I can't understand you, Ann."

"It was an accident, Sam. I swear it was an accident."

"You must pull yourself together, Ann, or I cannot be of any help to you."

"I'm trying."

"First . . ."

"Yes?"

"Does anyone else know?"

"No."

"All right, now tell me exactly what has happened."

"Billy's dead. I shot him."

"Start from the beginning, Ann."

RALPH WIGGINS had not heard a sound for over fifteen minutes, and he was beginning to believe that it had been the backfire of a car or truck that he had heard and not gunshots. He had pulled on his trousers and flannel shirt and boots and placed the loaded .38 revolver on the bureau of his bedroom. He had never fired a gun, although he had kept that information to himself when he applied for the job of watchman in the sylvan surroundings of the McGamble estate. He sat down on a wooden chair and began to untie the laces of his boots, ready to return to his bed for the rest of the night. From the other side of the indoor tennis court came the sounds of screams, hysterical screams. Again he froze. This time he knew there was no doubt. He rose from the wooden chair, picked up the revolver, and held it in his hand as he walked to the telephone. He picked up the receiver and dialed 0.

"Operator," replied a harassed voice.

"This is the night watchman at the Grenville house on Berry Hill Road," he said in a low voice. "I need the police."

"There is a hysterical woman on the other line, and I cannot understand a word she is saying, except the Grenville name," said the operator.

"Get the police. There is trouble here."

SHE REMEMBERED the instructions Sam Rosenthal repeated and repeated in her ear over the telephone, with complete calmness, as if death by gunshot were a thing he was used to dealing with.

"If there are any lamps or hall lights on, turn them off. You must be in darkness when the police arrive. . . .

"Listen, carefully. Tell them you heard the dog bark. It woke you. Then you heard a sound. Outside. Maybe in the tree. Maybe on the roof. It doesn't matter. You heard a sound. And Billy must have heard the same sound in his room. You both must have gotten up to investigate the sound at the same time. . . .

"Remember this, Ann. About the gun. Your husband insisted you go to bed with a gun by your side because of the prowler. Having a gun was his idea. . . .

"Now, you must both have opened your bedroom doors at the same time. You saw the shadow of a man standing there. You fired. Once. Twice. And then you realized it was your husband that you shot. . . .

"Be by your husband's body when they find you. And don't forget about the lights."

"No," she answered. "Turn out the lights."

"Now, Ann, listen."

"Yes?"

"Are you going to call the old lady, or am I?" he asked.

"I can't. I can't," she said, hysteria beginning to break through her forced calm.

"I'll do it. We're going to need some blank checks. Some signed blank checks."

"Oh, my God," said Ann.

"Who else from the family should I call, Ann? There should be someone to arrive at the house shortly after the police. The sister, Felicity. Doesn't she have some sons? Doesn't she have a house out there near you? I'll call Felicity. Now hang up, Ann. And pick up the telephone and get the operator. Tell the operator there has been a terrible accident and you need the police. Answer no questions when the police arrive. Just keep repeating over and over again that you thought Billy was the prowler. I'll take care of everything else."

THE PRISMS on the great chandelier in the main hall of Alice Grenville's house sounded—coldly, not musically—as if a wind passed through them. Alice Grenville, waking, opened her eyes an instant before the telephone rang in her darkened bedroom. She remembered for the first time in years when the chandelier had fallen on a workman and killed him. Instantly alert, she did not take the time to turn on her bedside lamp before picking up the receiver.

"Hello?"

"Mère." It was Cordelia. It was trouble.

"What time is it?"

"Late. Early. Mère—"

"What's happened? Are you crying?"

"You must wake up completely."

"I am awake."

"Turn on your light."

"Tell me what's happened, Cordelia."

"Something terrible. I can't even say it. Something so terrible. I'm driving into town to be with you, but I was afraid someone might call to tell you before I got there."

"It's Billy, isn't it?"

"She shot him, Mère. She killed him!"

The blood drained from Alice Grenville's face. She felt as if she were going to faint. "Oh, my darling Billy. Oh, no. No. No. It is not possible."

"SHE WAS SAYING, 'Please help me, please help me, something terrible has happened,'" said Ralph Wiggins to the detective in the courtyard of the house. "You can see her through the window on the floor, but I can't open the door."

"See if you can climb in that window that's open to the left of the front door," said Detective Kramer to one of the policemen. "Then come around and open the door. You and you," he called to two other policemen who had just driven up, "search the grounds."

When the police entered the house, they found Ann Grenville lying over the naked body of her dead husband. She was screaming his name over and over. So covered with his blood was she that at first Detective Kramer thought she had been shot as well. They tried to pull the hysterical woman away from her husband's body, but she would not let go. It was as if she were trying to breathe life back into him.

"Who shot your husband?" asked Detective Kramer.

Ann Grenville screamed.

"Wipe the blood off her face," said Kramer to a policeman. "Mrs. Grenville, please, tell us who shot your husband."

Hysterical and screaming, she was incoherent.

"Search the house," said Kramer. "See if there's anyone here."

He began to rise, then saw the woman reach out to him from the floor where she was lying.

"I shot him," she whispered. "I thought he was the prowler."

Detective Kramer stared at Ann Grenville as if he had not heard her correctly. "You shot your husband, Mrs. Grenville?"

She nodded through her sobbing.

"This is your gun?" he asked.

"I thought he was the prowler," she repeated.

"Why did you think he was the prowler?"

"I heard a sound, and it woke me."

"What kind of sound?"

"The dog barked."

"The dog? What dog?"

"There's a dog tied to a kitchen chair," said one of the policemen.

"I mean, I heard a sound outside or on the roof," she said.

"You were in bed asleep when you heard the sound?" asked Detective Kramer.

"Yes."

"And when you got up, you grabbed your gun?"

"Yes."

"Are you in the habit of going to bed with a gun, Mrs. Grenville?"

She feared that the man who was questioning her did not believe her. "My husband insisted. There was a prowler in the area. Our cabana had been broken into, and my husband insisted when we got home from Mrs. Bleeker's party that we both arm ourselves. He got the guns out of the gun room in the basement when we came home from the party."

Detective Kramer nodded to one of the policemen to check the gun room in the basement. "When did you put on your negligee, Mrs. Grenville—before or after you grabbed your gun?"

"What?"

"You are dressed in a negligee. I was curious at what point in your fear of the prowler you remembered to put it on."

"I sleep in my negligee."

"Oh?"

"Yes, my shoulders get cold on these October nights, and I sleep in a negligee."

"I see," said Detective Kramer, staring at her, disbelieving her story.

Ann Grenville was breathing heavily. She looked at the detective as if he were an enemy.

"One other thing, Mrs. Grenville."

"Yes?"

"I notice that under your nightgown you are wearing a black brassiere. Do you sleep in your brassiere too?"

"Yes, always. I have always slept in a brassiere."

A policeman interrupted the detective.

"Detective Kramer?"

"What is it?"

"There's children upstairs, and the cook."

"Put Mrs. Grenville in her bedroom," said Kramer. "Get Inspector Pennell on the telephone. I'll talk to the children and be right back."

FELICITY'S SON, Tommy Ashcomb, age nineteen, drove up the driveway of his Uncle Billy's house in Oyster Bay. He had never seen the long driveway so lit up. He knew that his young cousins, Diantha and Third, were asleep in the house and that he must get them out and back to his mother's house in Glen Cove before they were told what had happened. He was to wait until the local doctor, Dr. Curry, came to sign the death certificate and make sure the doctor gave his Aunt Ann, the sexpot, who had once tried to seduce him, or so he claimed, a shot to calm her hysteria.

Ahead of him he saw that the entire courtyard was filled with police cars, at least twenty of them. His heart began to beat rapidly. He pulled his car over to the side of the driveway. As he turned off the ignition, a policeman approached his car and shone a bright flashlight in his face.

"Who are you?" asked the policeman.

"My name is Tom Ashcomb. I am the nephew of Mr. Grenville."

"What are you doing here?"

"I have been asked to identify my uncle's body and to remove the children from the house."

ALICE GRENVILLE sat on the side of her bed and picked up the telephone again.

"I would like to talk to Sands Point, Long Island," she said to the operator. "The number is 555-8121."

She waited for what seemed an eternity.

"Please, God, let him be there," she whispered to herself. "Please, God, don't let a servant answer the telephone."

"Governor Milbank's residence," said the sleepy voice of the butler. At the same time, on another extension, a woman's voice said, "Hello? What is it?"

"Marie! Oh, thank God, you're there. It's Alice Grenville. I am sorry to call you at this disgraceful hour, but it is a matter of the utmost urgency that I speak with Payson."

"THE WOMAN IS utterly hysterical," said the police officer over the telephone to Inspector Stanley Pennell. "When we entered the house, we thought she had been shot as well as Mr. Grenville. We had to pry her away from his body. She was clinging to him, saying she loved him, and she was covered with his blood. She is a possible suicide, and we think that there should be a nurse sent out from the village to sit with her while the investigation is going on."

ALICE GRENVILLE dialed the telephone again, looking up the number in an address book that she kept by her bed. When she spoke, she spoke very rapidly.

"Charles? Charles, you must wake up. It's Mrs. Grenville. I need your full attention, Charles. Do you need to put water on your face? . . . It's two-thirty in the morning, Charles. That's what time it is. I want you to go to the garage and bring one of the cars here to the house. It is not necessary that you get into your uniform. It is preferable if you do not, in fact. Don't bring the limousine. Or the convertible. The Ford, or Chevrolet, whichever it is that you market in, bring it. Come to the front door of the house, but don't ring the bell. I will be there waiting for you. There will be an envelope that I want you to take out to Mr. Billy's house in Oyster Bay, and I want you to give that envelope to

Felicity's boy, Tommy Ashcomb, and no one else. There has been a terrible tragedy, Charles, and I am counting on you."

She hung up the telephone. She locked the door of her bedroom. She moved behind the marquetry table covered with photographs in silver frames and pulled away from the wall a Constable painting of Salisbury Cathedral that hung on hinges and concealed a safe. Quickly she worked the combination, and the door sprang open. She lifted out her jewel box and placed it on the table. Then she reached inside again and began taking out packets of money that had been sitting in the safe for more than twenty years, since the kidnapping scare. She placed the money in a large manila envelope, ten packets of five thousand dollars each. She went into the bathroom and moistened a washcloth, which she then wiped over the glue portion of the envelope and stuck it. She dressed herself in a warm robe and walked down the stairway three flights below to wait for her chauffeur to take the money out to the house on Long Island.

"ON WHOSE ORDERS did you give her a shot?"

"She was hysterical."

"I repeat, on whose orders did you give her a shot?"

"No one's orders. She was hysterical."

"You are aware, are you not, that a death by shooting has taken place in this house?"

"What is it that you are saying, officer?"

"I am saying that in a homicide, when a person is hysterical, that is when we get the information that we most need."

"I don't know anything about that."

"How long will she be out, doctor?"

"Several hours."

"Swell, doctor."

"THERE'S ENOUGH bottles of pills in this room to fill a couple of bags," said Mary Lou Danniher, the nurse from Oyster Bay.

"Then fill a couple of bags, nurse. Just don't let Mrs. Grenville near a pill when she comes to."

"Oh, my God," said Mary Lou Danniher, looking for the first time at the body on the floor. "Is that Mr. Grenville?"

"That was Mr. Grenville." The only thing alive about him was the ticking watch on his left wrist.

"Don't you think you could cover him up? At least his private parts."

"They're still taking pictures."

"They don't have to take a picture of his private parts. You can't expect me to walk back and forth by a naked man for the rest of the night. I mean, it's not proper."

"Say a rosary, Nurse Danniher."

"WHAT IS THE name of that doctor of hers with the slim mustache? The one she went to when Archie Suydem wouldn't give her the sleeping pills she was always asking for?" asked Alice.

"Oh, yes, the Park Avenue one. They all go to him. Babette Van Degan. All of them. Oh, what is his name? Skinner! That's it. Dr. Sidney Skinner. Why?"

"Get him for me on the telephone."

"Mère, it's three o'clock in the morning."

"Tell him it's Mrs. William Grenville, the mother-in-law of Mrs. William Grenville, Junior. Tell him it's an emergency. I guarantee you he will be here in twenty minutes."

"When do you want to see him?"

"In twenty minutes."

"Why?"

"I am going to send him out to the house in Oyster Bay and put him in charge of her. She cannot, must not, be put into the hospital in Mineola, where she would be under the jurisdiction of the Nassau County police. Mr. Rosenthal and Payson Milbank both feel it will be better all the way around if she is put into Doctors Hospital here in the city."

"Why are you doing all this for her, Mère?"

"Make the call, Cordelia."

"Yes, Mère. Did you know they fought terribly at Edith Bleeker's party? Did you know she threw a drink at him and smashed one of Edith's Lowestoft platters? We're in a scandal, Mère. A terrible, terrible scandal."

"Make the call, Cordelia. I'll deal with Edith Bleeker in a few hours when she wakes up, and I'll guarantee you there won't be one word about that fight."

IT SEEMED TO Ann that Edith Bleeker's party had been long, long ago, not yesterday, and that her present agony had lasted longer than her childhood, her career, and her marriage, and would go on forever. Stripped for once of artifice and social veneer, she had, in her fragility and stillness, a pathetic quality, like an abandoned foundling. She looked as if she belonged nowhere, frightened and homeless, grandiosity behind her, uncertainty ahead.

"Please," she whispered.

"What is it?" asked the nurse.

"Why is there a siren?"

"It's the ambulance, Mrs. Grenville."

"For my husband?"

"No, Mrs. Grenville. They already took Mr. Grenville's bod—They already took Mr. Grenville."

"Is it for me?"

"Yes, ma'am. They're going to take you to the hospital."

"Where's Dr. Skinner?"

"He's in the living room talking with the police, ma'am."

"What's all that noise outside?"

"What noise?"

"All those people talking in the courtyard."

"The media," said the nurse, pleased with herself for knowing the new word that was coming into the language.

"The what?"

"The press. The photographers. The television cameras."

"Will I have to go past them when they put me in the ambulance?"

"It'll just be for a few seconds."

"There is something I want."

"What's that, Mrs. Grenville?"

"Cover my face with a towel."

"But—"

"Please." There was a begging tone in her voice. "I don't want them to take my picture."

"She wants her face covered with a towel," said Anna Gorman to the nurse in an ordering tone, from the corner of the room where she had been standing.

"Then you cover it for her."

"Anna? Is that you?" asked Ann.

"I'll cover it for you, missus."

"Where are my jewels?"

"Your what?"

"My jewels that I wore to Mrs. Bleeker's party last night."

"I don't know, missus."

"They should be in a bag on my dressing table."

"Here they are."

"Give them to me, Anna. I want to take them with me."

What Anna Gorman thought, but did not say, then or ever, was that Mrs. Grenville had asked for her jewels but had not asked for her children.

Those wounded creatures watched from above. Covered and carried, their mother did not have to meet their eyes peering from an upstairs window. Lying still as death beneath her linen towel, she listened to the thousand clicks of camera shutters and heard the sounds of the press jostling each other inches from her stretcher to view her inert form.

The task of telling her children that their father was dead had not been hers. Nor had it been their cousin Tommy Ashcomb's, though he had come to the house to take them away. Nor their Aunt Felicity's, to whose house they were eventually taken. Detective Kramer of the Oyster Bay police assumed that difficult duty.

From the moment he entered the house of death, Kramer began to have the feeling that other forces were taking over an investigation that was his. Lawyers, doctors, and snobbish relations of the deceased addressed themselves to decisions and plans that were not of his making. Smarting still with anger that Dr. Curry, acting on unknown orders, had administered a shot to Mrs. Grenville that rendered her insensate for six hours, incapable of being questioned during her period of hysteria, when inconsistencies in her story might have led somewhere, Detective Kramer was not to be thwarted in his questioning of Mrs. Grenville's children. He did not believe her story that she had mistaken her husband for a prowler.

WHEN KATHLEEN MCBRIDE was preparing to go to the seven-o'clock Mass at St. Patrick's Church in Glen Cove, she listened to the early news on the small radio that her employer, Edith Bleeker, had given her for Christmas. "A gunshot early this morning," said the newscaster, "took the life of William Grenville, Junior, thirty-five-year-old financier, sportsman, and owner of the great racehorse Tailspin." Kathleen McBride gasped. "District Attorney Sal Scoppettone of Nassau County said the gun was fired by the victim's wife, Ann Arden Grenville, thirty-two, who told investigators she thought she had aimed it at a prowler."

Kathleen saw out the window that the chauffeur had parked the station wagon to take all the maids into the village for Mass, and she was torn between her desire to receive communion and her strong feelings of obligation toward Mrs. Bleeker, for whom she had worked for twenty-three years. Kathleen knew all about the young Grenvilles; there wasn't a servant in the house who hadn't heard about the fight Mr. and Mrs. Grenville had had in the library last night, humiliating poor Mrs. Bleeker in front of the Duchess of Windsor, for whom she wanted everything to be so perfect, not to mention breaking Mrs. Bleeker's beautiful platter.

"Healy's waitin' with the car, Kathleen," came Mary Whelan's voice through the door.

"You go ahead without me, Mary," replied Kathleen, removing the pin from her hat.

"You gonna miss Mass?" asked Mary's shocked voice through the door, implying that mortal sin was about to be committed.

"You go ahead, Mary. I'll go to the eleven."

Kathleen knew she was within her rights to go into the darkened bedroom of Mrs. Bleeker and awaken her with the news of Mr. Grenville's death, even though Mrs. Bleeker had not planned to arise until eleven, in time to attend Mrs. Slater's luncheon for the duchess. Kathleen remembered another time five years earlier at the plantation in South Carolina when she had had to awaken Mrs. Bleeker to tell her that Bratsie was dead. Funny, she thought, as she made her way through the halls to Mrs. Bleeker's room, the duchess was there that weekend, too.

Standing outside the bedroom when she arrived there was Dudley, the butler.

"Did you hear?" asked Dudley.

"Terrible thing," answered Kathleen.

"The police have requested a copy of the guest list from last night's party,"
said Dudley.

"Whatever for?"

"They intend to question each guest."

"What about?"

"The fight."

"Dear God."

"What is it? What's the matter?" came the sound of Edith Bleeker's sleep-
filled voice.

"There's been a tragedy, ma'am," said Kathleen as she entered the room.

"THAT LITTLE incident that happened in my library last night between
them, with the glass and the platter and so forth, we must forget that ever
happened," said Edith Bleeker to Jeanne Twombley over the telephone from
her bed. "Kathleen, this coffee is cold. Excuse me, Jeanne. I talked to Alice,
the poor darling. She called me an hour ago, and she had talked to the governor and a Mr. Sam Rosenthal, and they both advised her, separately, to ask us
not to mention the fight when the police question us. You know what it will be
like if something like that gets in the papers. Will you tell Petal? And Tucky?
I've already called Neddie Pavenstedt, and he's going to play golf with Lord
Cowdray at Piping Rock and will tell him. Just say they were an ideally suited
couple. Fine. You're going to be at Elsie Slater's for lunch, aren't you? I'll see
you there. Oh, and Jeanne?"

"Yes, Edith?"

"That Basil Plant you brought to my house, the writer. He won't talk, will
he?"

"Basil? Never, darling. He's one of my best friends. I trust him implicitly."

Jeanne Twombley was right about me. I wouldn't talk to the police about
the fight I had witnessed between Ann and Billy Grenville. I wouldn't waste
what I had seen and heard on the police. I had a book to write.

DURING THE DAYS that followed, all of New York, and much of the country,
waited with fascinated impatience for each day's newspaper, radio, and television revelations in what quickly became known as the Grenville case. As far
afield as London, Paris, and Rome, men and women who had known the
couple discussed the tragedy in shocked tones, avid for more details. They read
the coroner's reports on the body of William Grenville, Junior, describing
minutely the terrible wound that he had suffered, and gasped that he had still
lived for fifteen minutes. They pored over diagrams of the Playhouse, saw the
narrowness of the hall that separated the bedrooms of the ill-fated couple,
and wondered among themselves how it was possible that the celebrated

markswoman, who had so recently bagged a ten-foot Bengal tiger, could have mistaken her nude husband for a prowler at such close range. Might it not, they asked each other, have been one of her children she fired at without calling out, "Who goes there?"

Fydor Cassati, the society columnist, who had been Billy's friend, re-counted, on the front page of the Hearst paper, the insane jealousy of Ann Grenville. Her fits of temper, he wrote, were enough to put the fear of God in a platoon of British grenadiers. Stories that hitherto had not been published, because of his great affection for Billy, were now there for all the world to read.

"People believe she is guilty, and they want to see her tried like any other criminal," said Kay Kay Somerset to Petal Wilson.

AT SIX O'CLOCK Monday morning Dr. Sidney Silkwood Skinner walked into Room 1010 of Doctors Hospital in New York City, tapping on the door slightly as he entered to announce himself. He saw that during the night bars had been placed on the windows of the room but made no comment.

Ann Grenville, who usually slept until noon, was up from her bed, sitting on a visitor's chair, dressed for the street. She was wearing a wide-brimmed black hat under which her hair had been totally concealed. On her lap was a black broadtail coat, a black alligator bag, and black gloves. In her hands was a pair of black-lensed dark glasses of the style favored by film stars incognito. An empty coffee cup was on a table by her side.

"Do they think I'm going to jump?" asked Ann.

"What?" said Sidney Skinner, although he knew what she meant.

"The bars on the window."

"Orders from the police," he said. "It was hard getting you out of Nassau County, you know."

"Have you seen any newspapers?"

"No," he lied. "Are you ready?"

"Yes," replied Ann.

"Did you sleep?"

"No."

As if she sensed that he thought she looked bad, she reached into her bag and pulled out her compact. She opened it and stared at herself in the mirror. Her skin was sallow and liverish. Even when she made her mirror face, which she felt presented her at her best, she could see that even in so brief a time she had aged considerably. A shudder went through her. The sight of herself in the mirror, looking as old as her mother had looked at the end of her life, was at that moment more terrifying to Ann than the widowhood that stretched before her.

"Don't put on any makeup, Ann," said Dr. Skinner sharply.

"I'm not going to put on any makeup, Sidney," replied Ann just as sharply.

"What I've told them at the desk is that I am taking you to an interview with Inspector Pennell of Nassau County at your mother-in-law's house."

"Will there be press outside?"

"I am taking you in a wheelchair down the freight elevator to the basement and then out a side door to Eighty-eighth Street. My car and driver are there. Ready?"

The streets were wet and dark. Ann and Sidney drove in silence for the most part. She looked out the window of the Lincoln as the streetlights turned off and the first rustlings of morning began. A girl in an evening dress got out of a taxi and raced past her doorman before daylight came. White-aproned men unloaded crates of oranges in front of Gristede's market. A young couple unloaded weekend luggage from the rear of a station wagon. She wondered if she had valued life enough when it was there at her disposal.

"The front door of the shop will be open," said Sidney, "so you can walk straight in without having to wait on the street for someone to answer."

"You think of everything, Sidney," said Ann.

"Caruso will be ready for you. I've asked him not to talk with you, just to do what has to be done as quickly as possible. He said it will take an hour. There is a possibility that a few other customers will come in at seven-thirty, some women executives from the department stores who have regular appointments at that time that he was not able to change, but he will take you in a private room. The only time that you might encounter anyone is when you leave. Wear your hat and dark glasses then. The car will be parked right at the front door of the shop."

"You understand why I'm doing this, don't you, Sidney? I mean, you know, don't you, that it has nothing to do with vanity?"

"It's an awful risk, Ann, when the police haven't even questioned you yet."

"I don't want it known that my hair turned white overnight, Sidney. I don't want Alice, or Cordelia, or any of those sisters, or, God knows, the police, to know that my hair turned white overnight."

"It could be interpreted as grief," he said.

"They would interpret it as guilt," she corrected him.

Dr. Skinner looked at her sideways and wondered if that was her interpretation.

"AND CALL BERGDORF'S, Cordelia," said Alice Grenville. "Get Jo Hughes. We'll need black hats, veils, dresses. She'll know exactly what to get. Ask her to bring them up to the house this afternoon."

"Yes, Mère."

"And Grace."

"Yes, Mère."

"The maids want to go to the funeral. They should be seated behind all the family but in the side aisle."

"Yes, Mère."

"Make sure they all have black hats. If they don't, call Altman's and order what they need."

"Yes, Mère."

"Felicity!"

"Yes, Mère."

"Please don't look out the window like that. One of those reporters will photograph you with a telephoto lens."

"I'm sorry, Mère," said Felicity, closing the curtain. "I heard commotion outside."

"More flowers, probably. Or those awful press," said Alice.

"It's Governor Milbank arriving, Mère," said Felicity.

"Oh, Payson, thank God," said Alice.

"Did you know Governor Milbank was coming?" asked Felicity.

Alice did not answer her daughter.

The governor entered the reception room off the front hall, where Billy's casket had been placed against the wall opposite the fireplace in the same spot where his father's casket had been placed. Floral arrangements were behind and on either side of it. The main hallway beyond under the chandelier was also filled with great profusions of flowers. The governor went directly to the kneeler in front of the closed casket, knelt, and bowed his head in prayer. Rising, he turned toward the fireplace, where Alice Grenville stood with her daughters and her triplet sisters.

"My dear Alice," he said. "I am so terribly sorry. I remember so well when he was born, and Woodrow Wilson wrote him a letter welcoming him to this world. Do you remember?"

"We must find that letter and give it to Third," said Alice to her daughters.

The governor greeted Alice's sisters and daughters. He looked above the fireplace to the large portrait of the triplets that had been painted more than half a century before. Alice followed his gaze.

"I'm the one with the green ribbon," she said.

"Sargent, isn't it?" asked the governor. "Marvelous."

His mission was not to admire the paintings, however, and his gubernatorial time was precious. He looked at Alice, and she understood his look, and took him by the arm and led him out of the reception room into the main hall, knowing that he wanted to talk to her privately.

"There are people everywhere," she said. "Every room is full. Relations are arriving by the hour from everywhere. Perhaps up to my room. There won't be anyone there."

"Fine," said the governor.

"Cahill," Alice called to her butler.

"Yes, ma'am."

"See to it that the secretaries write on each card exactly what the flower arrangement is, and then enter it into that book I've left on the hall table."

"Yes, ma'am."

"This house has the first private elevator in New York, Payson," said Alice Grenville.

"Let's walk up the three flights, Alice."

"We're getting old, Payson."

"We've got thirty years more in us, you and I, Alice. Maybe more," answered the governor.

They sat in her room, away from the green-canopied bed, on two chintz-covered chairs beneath the Constable painting of Salisbury Cathedral.

THE TWO MRS. GRENVILLES

"You never know what to do when your children bring home these second-rate people and say they're in love with them. You want to scream out, at the top of your lungs, no, no, no, no, no, it must not be! There was nowhere for this to end but in disaster."

"You must understand, Alice," said the governor, "a case like this is a criminal lawyer's dream. A national reputation will be made. What is more fascinating to the American public than the rich and powerful in a criminal circumstance? Look at the newspapers. Listen to the radio. Watch the television. The country is consumed with curiosity."

"She took my only son's life, Payson."

"And in order to save hers, they will take his again," replied the governor, taking her hand in his to give her comfort.

"How so?"

"They will put your son on trial. All the dirty laundry of their marriage will be brought out. They will dig up every perverse aspect of his character, every marital infidelity, his drinking habits, his bedroom habits, his bathroom habits, for all I know."

"Oh, my God."

"Yes."

"What are you suggesting?"

"Stand behind her."

"You must be mad!"

"Believe her story about the prowler."

"She killed my Billy."

"Embrace her for the world to see."

"But she is guilty."

"There will be a shift in sympathy. You will see. In a few months, when the shock of this terrible tragedy wears off, they will begin to forget Billy, and it will be Ann's tragedy that will take its place."

"The chorus girl from Kansas and the millionaire's son."

"That's it exactly. In time they will root for her, not for you."

"It's so unfair."

"The healing process can't begin with the trial looming ahead like a dark and evil cloud, and either way, whatever happens, there is no winning. If Ann goes to prison, it will only scar the children more than they have been scarred already."

"You know what this will do, Payson? It will bind us to that woman more closely than if she had been born one of us."

SIDNEY SKINNER burst into Room 1010, radiating good news. From her bed, the aged Ann Grenville turned slowly to look at him. In her hands was a newspaper she had bribed a nurse to bring her, with graphic details of the killing. All her life she had wanted to be famous, and now she was, but the fame that had found her at last was not the variety she had craved.

"There is good news, Ann," exclaimed the doctor, at the same time seeing the forbidden newspaper on the bed. "I have just had a call from Sam Rosenthal."

"What has happened?" she asked.

"They have found the prowler!"

Ann stared at him unable to believe what she was hearing.

"It is as you said. There *was* a prowler, and they have found him," said Sidney.

She wanted to know and was afraid to know what the prowler had said. She wanted him to go on. He, in turn, wondered if she was too sedated to absorb the glad tidings he was bringing her.

"I cannot believe the terrible stories that Fydor Cassati has written about me in his column," she said.

"It doesn't matter about Fydor Cassati," said Sidney Skinner. "What matters is that the prowler has been caught."

WHEN ALICE GRENVILLE hung up the telephone from Iphigene Sulzberger, whose family owned the *New York Times,* and Betsy Whitney, whose husband owned the *New York Herald Tribune,* she next called Millicent Hearst, the long-estranged wife of William Randolph Hearst, the newspaper baron, for whom Fydor Cassati was such a star, selling more papers than any other with his daily coverage of the Grenville case.

"Millicent," she said.

"Oh, Alice, my dear, I am so terribly sorry about your tragedy," replied Millicent Hearst. A onetime show girl and beauty, she was captivated with society in New York. While her husband romped and built castles in the West for the actress Marion Davies, she, the mother of his five Hearst sons, enjoyed the homage paid to her by the society columns of her husband's papers. "I saw dear Billy only weeks ago at the Belmont Ball, and he was in such marvelous form with all the great success he was having in racing. I can't bear it that you are suffering so much."

"Yes," replied the mother of the slain Billy Grenville. "Thank you, Millicent." Wanting to rush through the condolence, she allowed it its full course for the favor she was about to ask. She had never had Millicent Hearst to any of her parties, nor had she ever contributed to the Milk Fund, which was the charity dear to Millicent's heart, but she resolved then and there to do both if she got what she wanted.

"What I'm calling you about, Millicent, is Fydor Cassati," said Alice, getting straight to the heart of the matter. "My son was so fond of him, and he is indeed such a charming fellow, but we feel that his columns these past few afternoons, since Billy's death, have been excessive and unfair."

"But Fydor adored Billy," protested Millicent.

"Apparently he did not adore Ann," replied Alice.

"But I have no say over what he writes in his column," said Millicent.

"Nonsense," said Alice firmly. "Your husband owns the paper. Please, Millicent, make him stop. What happened in Osyter Bay on Saturday night was an accident, and his columns are suggesting that my daughter-in-law shot my son on purpose."

"Willie owns the papers, Alice. I have no say," she said again.

"That's not so," perservered Alice Grenville. "You got Fydor the job, after all that nasty business in Washington, with the tar and feathering, just as you got Elsa Maxwell her job. And Cobina Wright. They will do anything for you, those people. Make him stop! Oh, and Millicent, when the mourning period is over, my daughters and I will attend your next benefit for the Milk Fund and contribute handsomely to it."

"SHE DIDN'T know it was loaded," said Kay Kay Somerset, screaming with laughter.

"Kay Kay!" said Petal Wilson, adjusting her makeup in the mirror of the ladies' room at El Morocco.

"It could have been worse, I suppose," Kay Kay went on, reapplying lipstick in the same mirror.

"What do you mean?" asked Petal.

"She could have killed Tailspin," answered Kay Kay, screaming with laughter again.

"Kay Kay!"

"Billy told Brenda he had changed his will."

"No!"

"And—"

"Go on. I'm riveted."

"Not a word of this to anyone. Promise?"

"On my life, darling."

"He said the children would get it all, leaving Ann out completely."

"How could he do that? With widow's share, and all that."

"He had the goods on her, finally. He was going to divorce her."

"How much should I tip her?" whispered Petal, indicating the ladies'-room attendant.

"A quarter's plenty," said Kay Kay.

"Are you going to the funeral?"

"Of course, darling. It's the funeral of the decade."

STILL DAZED in sedated slumber, Ann Grenville planned her husband's funeral. She wanted to wear black veils and her Mainbocher black dress from last season with only a single strand of pearls and the diamond circle pin that Billy had given her before they were married. She wanted to have her nails done, plain, no color; Blanchette could come here to the hospital to do them. She would wear only her wedding ring, she decided; her engagement ring was too big. She would sit in the reception room off the main hall of her mother-in-law's house off Fifth Avenue for the prayers before the pallbearers put the casket into the hearse to take it to St. James' Church for the service. Names went through her head of the men she wanted to be her husband's pallbearers.

"The hymn!" she cried out suddenly.

"What?" asked Miss Toomey, the nurse, who had been snoozing in her chair in a corner of the darkened room.

"What was the name of that hymn?"

"What hymn, Mrs. Grenville?"

"From Groton, that hymn. The one Billy liked so much."

"I don't know, Mrs. Grenville."

"About God and honor, that kind of thing."

"Oh."

"I want that sung at the service."

"Yes, ma'am."

"THE DUCHESS will be in directly," said Cecil, her butler, to Inspector Stanley Pennell and Detective Kramer in the living room of the Duchess of Windsor's ornate suite on the twenty-eighth floor of the Waldorf Towers. There were flowers everywhere of different varieties and heights but uniform color, as if Constance Spry, her florist, had advised her gift-givers that this season the duchess favored yellow and white. Invitation cards leaned against a mirror over the fireplace.

"What do we call her?" whispered Detective Kramer to Inspector Pennell, eyeing the elaborate gold furniture.

"I should have asked that Cecil," whispered back Inspector Pennell.

Three English pug dogs yapped and snapped at the intruders.

"I hate these fucking little dogs," whispered Detective Kramer.

"Shhhh," said Inspector Pennell.

Two of the dogs, exhausted, retired to their bamboo baskets and curled up on needlepoint cushions that bore their names. The third continued to be unpleasant to the inspector and his assistant, letting him know that their call on his mistress, official though it might be, was inappropriate.

"Disraeli, you naughty boy!" cried the Duchess of Windsor to her dog as she entered the room. "You must forgive this naughty beast, Inspector Pennell. He is just protecting his mummy. Aren't you, you naughty thing? Yes, you are. Kiss, kiss, kiss. Yes. Now you go over there to your basket and lie down. Oh, please, do sit down, Detective Kramer. Would you like to smoke?" she asked, opening a gold box with a royal seal and offering it to them. "Or a drink?"

The sheer social power of her overwhelmed the room. Wafts of expensive perfume surrounded her. Earrings, bracelet, pin, and rings matched. She sat perfectly and with a gesture turned the meeting over to them, as if she were in their power, but they knew, as she did, that they were in hers.

"We are here, uh, Duchess, because of the, uh, sad—"

"Yes, yes, I know," she said. "What a sad occasion this is. Poor Alice

Grenville, his mother. Such an old friend. I talked to her today. She is bereft with the tragedy."

"You talked with Mr. and Mrs. Grenville on the night of the party, I understand?" asked Inspector Pennell.

"Yes, I did, and he was in such good spirits. You know about his horse, Tailspin, don't you? Well, he was so excited."

"There is a telephone call, your grace," said the butler.

"No, no, I can't, Cecil. You see, I have the inspector."

"It is Mrs. Bleeker, Your Grace."

"Would you excuse me, Inspector? I must take this call. Would you ask these gentlemen again, Cecil, if they would like something to drink. Hello, Edith. Yes, darling. Of course. They're here now. Yes. Uh-huh. Fine. Now about tonight. That nice Jimmy Donahue is picking me up. We're going to Thelma Foy's for cocktails, for an instant only. She has the Stamirskys, whom I long to see. I don't think long dress, do you? Under the circumstances? Right. Then we'll drop by poor Alice's. And then meet up with Serge Obolensky for dinner. Maud Chez Elle, Serge thought. Somewhere quiet. I told Kay Kay Somerset no El Morocco until after the funeral. Strict orders from David. Now about the funeral. Do you want to go together? Fine. I'll be ready. And after, there's lunch at Kitty Miller's. Yes, yes, I won't forget. Say it once more. Fine. Fine. Goodbye, Edith. . . . I am sorry, Inspector. Forgive me. Oh, look at the time it's getting to be. Has the hairdresser arrived, Cecil? It's such a tragedy, the whole thing. They were an ideally suited couple, Inspector."

Detective Kramer wrote in his notebook the words "an ideally suited couple" and nodded his head quietly.

"What is your impression of Mrs. Grenville, Duchess?" asked the inspector.

"Alice Grenville?" asked the Duchess.

"No, I meant Ann Grenville," replied Inspector Pennell.

"Oh, Ann." She had an urge to say that Billy Grenville had told Brenda Frazier on the night of the shooting that he had changed his will, cutting out Ann, but she did not. "For bringing together all kinds of people in a gay, airy, but flawless setting, I have never known anyone to equal Ann Grenville," she said instead to the bewildered detectives. "She mixes people like a cocktail, and the result is sheer genius."

"Yes, ma'am. Thank you, ma'am," said Inspector Pennell.

The afternoon editions quoted Inspector Pennell quoting the Duchess of Windsor as saying that the Grenvilles were an ideally suited couple. Elsa Maxwell, smarting still because she hadn't been asked to Edith Bleeker's party and had missed out on what might have been the newspaper scoop of her career, belittled the duchess's statement in her society column as "extremely odd," since, as she wrote, "everybody who is anybody knew that Billy and Ann Grenville both had detectives spying on each other for months."

"ONE OF US MUST go to the hospital before the funeral, or it will appear to the press that we do not believe her story," said Alice Grenville, at the same time going over the list of pallbearers with her daughters. She crossed off one of the names on the list. "I don't want Neddie Pavenstedt to be a pallbearer."

"Mère, he was Billy's roommate at Groton, and at Harvard, and he's number-two man at Father's bank," said Cordelia.

"And he had an affair with Billy's wife," answered Alice. The daughters, stunned, looked at their mother.

"How do you know that, Mère?" asked Cordelia.

"I know," said Alice. "Which one of you is going to the hospital?"

"I won't go," said Felicity. "I don't like her. I never did like her. And I was the only one in the family, except you, Mère, who made my position perfectly clear to Billy."

"Grace?"

"I won't go either. I hated the manner in which she did me out of the breeding farm. Billy was so embarrassed that day."

"Rosamond?"

"I don't live in this country. I scarcely know her, Mère."

"I suppose it's me, Mère," said Cordelia.

"Do you mind?"

"She'll ask about you. She was always afraid of you. What will I tell her?" asked Cordelia.

"Perhaps we should think about having some of these flowers sent to the children's wards at the hospitals," replied Alice. "They are now going up the stairs, there are so many. The scent is overpowering. I hate stock. Why do they always put stock in funeral bouquets?"

"MÈRE HEARD FROM the President and Mrs. Eisenhower," said Cordelia, making conversation, aghast at the haggard sight of her sister-in-law in the hospital bed. "And Governor Milbank came to call. And the letters, and telegrams, and flowers are arriving by the hundreds each day. Billy's secretary is there at Mère's house, trying to keep track of everything, and the bank has been marvelous sending secretaries to help. There is simply no room for any more flowers, and Mère has sent them over to the children's wards at New York Hospital. The staff is devastated. Poor Cahill has had to take to his bed. He's old, you know."

"Where is my mail?" asked Ann.

"What mail?" replied Cordelia.

"My condolence notes. I am, after all, his widow, and all that I am hearing is about the hundreds of messages arriving each day at his mother's house, for his mother. What about me? It was an accident. They have caught the prowler. Is no one sorry for me?"

Cordelia, embarrassed, crimsoned.

"Are there any telephone messages for me?" asked Ann.

"A Mr. Claud Mertens called from Detroit," replied Cordelia.

Ann lay motionless in the bed. No muscle moved to indicate that she had heard the name that Cordelia told her.

"He said he was your father," Cordelia went on.

"My father is dead," said Ann, shaking her head in a dismissive way.

"A Mr. Billy Bob Veblen, from Pittsburg, Kansas."

"I never heard of him," said Ann.

"He said that—"

"Kooks," interrupted Ann, and then repeated the word again, although it was a word she had never used before. "Kooks. There's a certain kind of person who's attracted to the negative glamour of, uh"—she paused for the word—"this kind of tragic situation. Did Bertie Lightfoot call?"

"No, Babette Van Degan did," said Cordelia.

"Oh, Babette," said Ann. It was the first name that interested her. She thought of Babette warmly and remembered the friendship they had once shared. "I would like to see Babette."

"I will call and tell her," said Cordelia, getting up from a chair, ready to leave.

"Is there a policeman outside my door?" asked Ann.

"Yes," replied Cordelia.

"Are there press outside the hospital?"

"Yes."

"What will you say to them?"

"I don't know."

"Tell me about your mother."

"Mère? What do you want to know?"

"I have not heard from her."

"There are the preparations for the funeral. She is involved in those. It will be enormous, they say."

"Will she and I be in the same car at the funeral?" asked Ann.

Cordelia, stunned, stared at the woman on the bed. "You certainly don't plan on attending the funeral, Ann?"

"Why not?"

"My mother has gone all the way to the President of the United States to get the police to back off questioning you, Ann, until a suitable story is worked out. She has your Dr. Skinner telling the police that you are so hysterical with grief he has had to put you under sedation, so that they cannot question you. If you are well enough to attend the funeral, they will say you are certainly well enough to face the police."

Ann covered her face with her hands and started to weep uncontrollably, great heaving sobs. Miss Toomey, who had vacated the room on Cordelia's arrival, instantly returned. Cordelia quietly picked up her bag and gloves and walked out.

Charles, her mother's chauffeur, held open the rear door of her mother's Packard limousine, as Cordelia made her way through the reporters who waited outside the hospital.

"She's been having a terrible time, poor thing," said Cordelia to the reporters who questioned her. Inside the closed door, she looked out at them staring in at her, flashing pictures of her. What, she wondered, has this woman done to our lives? We have become the kind of people you read about in tabloids. And then the thought came to Cordelia that she dared not speak aloud, even to her sisters: If only Ann would commit suicide. It would make everything so much better. It would be over.

ANN WAS distressed to find that the pallbearers who would be carrying Billy's casket had already been picked without her approval. She felt the feeling that she most hated, that she was being left out by not being allowed to attend the funeral. But she insisted on playing a part, and her instructions were relayed to the family by Dr. Skinner. She wanted a particular hymn sung that she said had been Billy's favorite hymn from his days at Groton, and she wanted the flowers that covered the casket to be flowers from her. A great blanket of red and orange carnations, the colors of the Grenville stables, arrived at Alice Grenville's house on the morning of the funeral to displace the spray of white orchids provided by Alice and her daughters. In gold paper letters pasted on a cut ribbon and bow was the message: "To Fad, I love you always, Mud." Dr. Skinner explained to the family that Fad and Mud were nicknames for Father and Mother that Billy and Ann gave to each other after they became parents. Alice Grenville looked straight ahead. The sisters looked at each other but said nothing. Not one of them could ever remember having heard Ann call Billy Fad or Billy call Ann Mud.

The flags of the Brook Club, the Union Club, the Knickerbocker Club, and the Racquet Club flew at half-mast on the day of Billy Grenville's funeral. As the long black cars of the funeral cortege pulled up to the doors of St. James' Church, where the Grenville family had worshiped for fifty years, the occupants were astonished to see that thousands of people lined Madison Avenue to stare at the procession.

"Look, there's Edith Bleeker's entire staff," said Felicity to her sisters, looking out the window of her limousine.

"They say every servant on the Upper East Side got the morning off," said Felicity's husband.

"One of the policemen outside the house said it's the biggest funeral in New York since Babe Ruth's," said Grace.

"Poor Billy, wouldn't he have hated it," said Cordelia.

"Listen to this from this morning's *Times,*" said Felicity's husband, reading. " 'Not in this century have circumstances combined to produce so sensational a shooting—a tragedy involving people of great wealth, the meteoric career of a poor girl carried to the heights of fame, and elements of mystery that will persist until a grand jury weighs all explanations.' "

"Put that paper away, Dexter," said Felicity.

"Look at Mère," said Cordelia.

A hush fell over the crowd as Alice Grenville, erect and dignified in black mourning veils, emerged from the first limousine, assisted by her chauffeur. She stopped to speak to Billy's great friend Alfred Twombley, who was a pallbearer, and then ascended the steps of the church with her granddaughter, Diantha, on one side of her and her grandson, William Grenville, on the other.

In a pew behind the family—bereft, forlorn, only she knowing the extent of her grief—sat Esme Bland, just returned from vacation, tanned still amid the white faces of November.

Later, after the Reverend Dr. Kinsolving's eulogy, after the hymns and prayers, after the filing-out while the organ played "The Battle Hymn of the Republic," in the Grenville family plot in Woodlawn Cemetery, close by the graves of Vanderbilts and Whitneys and other great families of the city of New York, the body of William Grenville, Junior, was laid to rest in a grave marked by chrysanthemums and carnations.

EVEN SEDATED, Ann noticed things. She noticed that the paper around the yellow roses Babette Van Degan brought her had been squeezed tight from nervous fingers. She noticed, beneath Babette's Sen-Sen–scented breath, the whiff of gulped gin and knew it had been downed for courage in this encounter. Is this how people are going to react to me from now on? she wondered, observing the only visitor outside of Cordelia and Dr. Skinner and Sam Rosenthal allowed to visit her closely watched room.

Babette occupied herself filling a vase with water in the bathroom and then jammed the dozen and a half roses into the vase in an untidy arrangement, cutting her finger on a thorn in the process.

"Shit," she cried out in exaggerated pain and wrapped toilet paper around the bleeding finger. The moment relaxed the two old friends, and Babette dropped her huge mink coat on a chair and dragged another chair up to the side of the bed, and they began to talk. Other than what she had read in the few newspapers she was allowed to see, Ann had heard nothing about the funeral the day before.

"There wasn't an empty seat. Even the choir loft was full, and there were so many flowers there wasn't enough room on the main altar."

"What flowers were on the casket?" asked Ann, fearful that hers might not have been used.

"Awful. Red and orange carnations. Like something you'd put on a horse after a race," answered Babette. "Afterward everyone who wasn't going to Kitty Miller's lunch for the Duchess of Windsor made a beeline for the bars at the Westbury and the Carlyle. Only the family went to the cemetery."

"Was Simonetta d'Este there?"

"Simonetta d'Este's in Italy."

"Italy? How long has she been in Italy?"

"A couple of weeks. Fydor Cassati told me."

If Simonetta d'Este had been in Italy on Saturday night, who had Billy been talking to on the telephone during Edith Bleeker's party? Ann wondered. If she hadn't flared out, as she had, she might not have set in motion the terrible events that followed.

"Babette, tell me something."

"If I can."

"What are people saying about me?"

"They're saying you fought with Billy at Edith Bleeker's."

"Anything else?"

"They're saying at El Morocco that Billy cut you out of his will," said Babette.

"Who's saying that?" snapped Ann.

"They."

"Who's they?"

"The ladies'-room attendant."

"You believe me, don't you, Babette, about the prowler?"

Babette looked at Ann. "Sure, kid," she answered.

"I don't know which I'm more afraid of, Babette, the police or my mother-in-law."

"CAN YOUR life bear close scrutiny, Ann?" asked Sam Rosenthal.

"What do you mean?" asked Ann from her hospital bed, knowing full well what he meant.

"Just what you think I mean," said Sam. She was beginning to see the rough side of him that she had heard about. "Are there infidelities?"

"I don't think I need to answer that," she said with indignation, as if she were in a situation in which she was in charge.

"Please know I am undeterred by your arrogance and haughtiness, Mrs. Grenville." His assumption of her full name was not lost on her. "Nor will the district attorney be, should he put you on the stand."

She turned her head away, terrified. Tears sprang into her eyes. She was overwhelmed with fear at the thought of the police or a trial.

When Sam Rosenthal continued, his voice was more gentle. "You must remember that I am on your side, and it is my job to prepare you for the worst, Mrs. Grenville."

She nodded her head. "Call me Ann again," she said.

"Can your life bear close scrutiny, Ann?" he repeated.

"Whose life can bear close scrutiny?" she answered in a conciliatory tone.

"I'm only interested in yours at the moment."

"Have you, uh, have you heard things about me?"

"Yes."

"From whom?"

"From several of Mrs. Bleeker's guests."

"That's not true. Mrs. Bleeker's guests were unanimous in describing my husband and me as an ideally suited couple. I read that in the paper."

"That's so."

"Then what are you talking about?"

"That is what they said to Inspector Pennell and Detective Kramer, who questioned them. However, several of those same people, anonymously to be sure, wrote letters to Inspector Pennell, saying they had been pressured to make the statements that they had made."

It occurred to Ann as she looked around the flowerless room that she should ask to have pictures of her children brought to her. She poured herself a glass of water from a carafe on the hospital bed table and sipped it as she watched a barge on the East River outside her window. She speculated who had written the anonymous letters. Kay Kay Somerset, she imagined. Basil Plant. Names went through her mind.

Finally she spoke. "Did you say the letters were anonymous?"

"Yes. They won't hold up in court, but there is information in those letters that could be tracked down."

"What sort of information?"

"Names of men who have been your lovers."

"What men?"

"Ali Khan. Viscount Kingswood. Edward Pavenstedt."

Ann continued to look out the window. She was relieved that Billy Bob Veblen's name did not mar the magnificence of the list.

"Imagine the headlines," she said simply, still not looking at him.

"Is that all you have to say?"

"Are we talking adultery, Sam?"

"We are."

"What about Simonetta d'Este? Or that little mouse Esme Bland? Or a certain Miss Winifred Plegg, also known as Bootsie, who runs an establishment catering to bizarre tastes on West End Avenue and Ninety-first Street?"

"Have you been there, Ann?"

"I only go to the West Side on my way to Europe," she answered.

Sam Rosenthal picked up his hat and put on his overcoat.

"Sam," she said. "It's very silly for the police to investigate the marital lives of my husband and myself. In the marital lives of anyone we know on the North Shore, they would find reasons for murder."

"Don't try to impress me with how swell you are. I'm interested in the other part of your life, the part you outgrew, the part people say you never talk about. You got any dark secrets there, Ann?"

"No," she answered.

WITH THE unexpected entrance of Alice Grenville, all activity ceased. Tall, erect, her hat covered with veils of mourning, she stood in command of the room, an in-person reminder of the tragedy that still absorbed the city. Miss Toomey, wordlessly, abandoned her task of changing pillowcases and retreated to the hallway outside.

Ann, unprepared, looked like a ghost. She was thin and drawn, even plain in her appearance, and her hair, often described as her crowning glory, looked, to Alice Grenville, lank and even dyed. Alice wondered, as she often had, what her daughter-in-law's age was. Older certainly than Billy, although she claimed to be younger. Of that Alice was certain, but this was not the time for age speculation.

"How are you feeling, Ann?" Alice asked finally. She made no attempt to sit down. It was to be a standing visit.

"Oh, Mère," said Ann. Her eyes, which looked as if she had wept for a week, filled with tears. More than any person, Ann Grenville feared her mother-in-law. "Oh, Mère, I am so sorry. I have dreaded this moment, having to face up to you. I know how you loved him, your only son, and you must believe me that I loved him, too. It was an accident, Mère, I swear to you, what happened was an accident. It's true what they said, we had argued at Edith's, but every couple argues. There was a prowler, Mère. And we had guns. It was Billy who insisted we go to bed with guns in our rooms. He even said to me, 'If you hear anything, shoot first and ask questions later.' Let me tell you exactly what happened."

Alice Grenville raised the veils from her face, unpinned and removed her hat, and placed it and her bag at the foot of Ann's bed.

"I know how it happened," she said, "but I have chosen to believe your story. I will stand behind you from this day until the day I die, as will my daughters. You will be welcome in my home and theirs. We are prepared to accept this tragedy as the accident you say it is."

Ann, speechless, stared at Alice.

"Why? Are you wondering why, Ann? I do not want you to go on trial for murdering my son. I do not want the filthy laundry of your marriage to come out in public. I want the headlines of this scandal to stop. And most of all, I do not want my already deeply scarred grandchildren to bear the further shame of growing up with a mother in prison."

"Mère," Ann whispered.

"My son's will has not been read yet, but there is speculation at every party in the city, and I believe it to be true, from Mr. Mendenhall at the bank, that my son cut you out of his will before he died. If this is true, I am prepared, from my own money, to settle on you what you would have received from him before he cut you out."

"I don't care about the money," said Ann.

"Of course you care about the money," replied Alice impatiently. "If there's one thing you've always been eminently practical about, Ann, it's money. I always felt your love for my son began on the moment you walked into my house the first time and saw the kind of life your handsome ensign came from."

Receiving absolution, Ann was in no position to reply to the taunt. Remembering back, she knew it was true.

"There are conditions to all this," said Alice.

"Conditions?"

"Things I want in return."

"Like what?"

"That you never, ever, for as long as you live, talk to a reporter, or a writer, or even a friend about what happened in Oyster Bay last Saturday night."

"I agree to that," whispered Ann.

"You must go to the grave with your story."

"I wish you believed my story, Mère."

"I do."

"No, I mean in your heart."

"I am trying."

"Have I ever lied to you?" asked Ann.

"Yes, you have," replied Alice, calmly meeting her gaze, without challenge in it, so certain was she of her position.

"When?" asked Ann. "Give me an instance."

"You told me your father was dead. There's an instance. You told me that on the first day we met, and you repeated it to me on your wedding day, and you have said it again several times over the years."

"My father is dead."

"According to this morning's papers," said Alice, opening her black bag and taking from it an envelope full of newspaper clippings, which she handed to Ann, "your father is very much alive and is a streetcar conductor in Detroit."

A deep hot flush of crimson burst through the pasty paleness of Ann's face. She dreaded exposure of her shabby origins, and there it was, for all to see, in every edition of every tabloid: the ramshackle farmhouse; the idiosyncrasies of her mother's curious personality; her father identified as a streetcar conductor.

"Is it for his occupation or his existence that you blush, Ann?" asked Alice.

Outside, on the East River, a tugboat passed, the same as any of a dozen tugboats that had passed in the last few hours. Ann watched it with a complete absorption that suggested a fear of dealing with the moment she was living.

"I don't like speaking to the back of your head," snapped Alice.

"Will you take your bag and hat off the foot of my bed? I don't like things on the foot of my bed," replied Ann.

Alice moved them to the window ledge.

"Would you like to sit down?" asked Ann.

"No, thank you."

"How are the children?"

"They're fine."

"Are they in school?"

"I haven't sent them back yet, no," replied Alice.

"They can't miss school."

"Surely you read the papers, Ann."

"I'm talking about my children."

"So am I," said Alice quietly. "The situation is all over the newspapers still and probably will be until you appear before the grand jury. It is the principal subject of conversation in every house on the Upper East Side. I have talked with the headmaster of Buckley and the headmistress at Spence, and they both agree that it would be terribly difficult at school for the children at this time. I have hired a tutor, who is working in conjunction with their teachers, and they are studying at home until after things die down."

"Don't you think I should have been consulted about these decisions?" asked Ann. A mild form of panic made itself felt beneath her worn-off sedation. She wondered if Alice was thinking of taking her children away from her.

Alice chose not to continue the conversation, although it occurred to her to say that this difficult woman might have thought of that before she killed her children's father.

"Cordelia and I took them to a film yesterday," she said instead.

"I want to see them," said Ann.

"But you will, when this is over," replied Alice.

"That's not what I mean. I want to see them here. I want them to come and visit me. I want them to hear from their mother what happened."

"I don't think that's wise, Ann," said Alice. "There are reporters camped out downstairs."

"I want my children brought here tomorrow," said Ann in the chilling tone Alice had often heard Ann use to Billy.

"Do you not wonder why it is you are here in this hospital overlooking the East River in Manhattan rather than in the Nassau County Hospital in Mineola, where you would have been in the jurisdiction of the police who are investigating your husband's killing? Or do you just accept this as your due?"

Ann's heart began to beat very fast. Feelings of fear rushed through her as she remembered the police questioning her on the night of the shooting before the doctor mercifully gave her the shot that sedated her for so many hours.

"Yes, of course, I will have the children brought here tomorrow," said Alice. She picked up her hat again and put it on, pinning it with two pearl-topped pins, noticing as she did so there were no mirrors in the room. As she let the black mourning veil fall over her face, as a reminder of the circumstance in which they found themselves, she said, in a duplication of her daughter-in-law's chilling tone, "And, please, don't ever again, ever, and I repeat the word once more, ever, speak to me in that tone of voice. You need me more than I need you, Ann, although I wouldn't have thought I needed to point that out to you."

"Mère, I'm sorry," said Ann in a voice filled with alarm. She reached out and touched her mother-in-law's arm, but Alice moved past her bed to the door, opened it without looking back, and left the room.

AN ARRANGEMENT of birds of paradise in a clear glass bowl, left behind by a departed patient, filled the center of the round maple coffee table in the tenth-floor waiting room.

"Don't you loathe birds of paradise?" asked Cordelia when her mother, walking slowly, joined her. Alice Grenville glanced at the flamboyant flowers, which were just past their prime. They reminded her of the woman she had just left.

Alice looked down at her shoes and didn't answer. Her left hand brushed off the right sleeve of her black coat, which had just touched Ann. "I hate her," she said in a voice so low that only her daughter could hear.

"Are you all right, Mère?"

"Yes," she answered. "Let's go."

When the doors of the elevator opened, Cordelia and her mother entered and rode down to the street floor in silence, aware that the elevator operator and a nurse and two visitors were looking at them. When the doors opened on the ground floor, the other occupants of the car stood back in deference, or curiosity, and allowed them to exit first.

Cordelia took her mother's arm and steered her toward the entrance, where the car would be waiting. Outside the hospital on East End Avenue a crowd of reporters and photographers awaiting them became instantly alert. Cordelia held her hand in front of her mother's face to shield her from the flashbulbs popping and the reporters who started shouting questions at her, the pack moving in closer on the two women.

Charles, the chauffeur, made his way through the crowd to assist Cordelia in getting Alice into the car. Suddenly Alice Grenville stopped and brushed away her daughter's protective hand. She turned at the door of the car and faced directly the onslaught that was pressing in on her. She lifted her veil and did not flinch as the flashbulbs and newsreel cameras recorded the scene. There was about her presence a grace of carriage and aristocratic bearing that kept the crowd from jostling her and moving in any closer.

"How is she, Mrs. Grenville?" shouted one of the reporters.

"I grieve for my son," she said, "but I also grieve for my daughter-in-law. I am very fond of her. My son's death was an unfortunate accident. I have never thought otherwise. I am fed up with the scandalous rumors and innuendos that have plagued his death. It is time that you knew the truth. The police were convinced from the beginning that it was an accident, and they still believe that, because there is no reason for them to believe otherwise."

Alice Grenville appeared very old as she dropped the veil over her face again, signaling the completion of her statement. With the help of Cordelia and Charles, she entered her car.

"You understand the consequences of this, Mère?" said Cordelia.

"Certainly I do. We are bound to her forever."

"And how do you feel about that?"

"It is a very steep price to pay."

The limousine turned right on Eighty-sixth Street and made its way toward Fifth Avenue as the two women sat in silence in the darkening November afternoon.

FELICITY WAS less compliant than her sisters concerning their mother's decision. "We are more than bound to her; we are chained to her. A divorce would have been too scandalous, so she remained married to Billy. Now a murder trial would be too scandalous, so we remain sistered to her for all time. I am sick of that woman in our lives. I hate her."

No one answered Felicity. They allowed her to rant and rave. She voiced what the rest of them thought but did not speak. Then her mother spoke what were to be the last words on the subject.

"We must behave as if we believe her. All of us. That goes for you too, Felicity. To whoever speaks to us about it. Even our best friends. What happened to Billy was an accident, and our heart grieves for his widow."

"You are asking too much of us, Mère," said Felicity.

"I am not doing this for her, Felicity. I am doing it for Billy's children. My grandchildren. They will already have enough to grow up with, having a slain father. We cannot allow that their mother be in prison as well. Remember the children."

"Yes, Mère."

"If your father were alive, he would have arrived at this same conclusion."

"Yes, Mère."

WHEN INSPECTOR Pennell and Detective Kramer left Alice Grenville's house just off Fifth Avenue, the same group of reporters that had dogged their footsteps since the night of the shooting converged on them before they could get to the police car that was parked in front of the house. Among themselves the reporters made no secret of the fact that they felt Inspector Pennell behaved with obsequious deference to the powerful people connected with the Grenville case.

"What about this report that Mrs. Grenville made a mysterious telephone call after her husband was shot but before the police were notified?" asked the Hearst reporter.

"I don't know where you guys pick up all this stuff," replied Detective Kramer.

The reporters ignored Detective Kramer. "What about it, Inspector Pennell?"

Reporters made Inspector Pennell nervous. Out on the North Shore, when he said, "No comment," they would back off. In the city, where he was not on his home ground, they persisted when he ignored them.

"It seems to me ridiculous on the face of it," replied Inspector Pennell, trying to push his way through to the car.

"Check the telephone records and it won't look so ridiculous," said the Hearst reporter.

"Naturally, we'll check it," said Pennell.

"How about the telephone call that was made to Mr. Grenville during Mrs. Bleeker's party? Would you care to comment on that? Who was that from?"

"I have no information on that," said the inspector.

"When do you plan to question Mrs. Grenville?"

"We would prefer that the questioning take place either at headquarters or in some other suitable place rather than at the hospital, where there are so many people around. It's cold, gentlemen, and I would like to get into my car."

"The night watchman says Mrs. Grenville didn't scream for help until twenty minutes after the shots."

"I don't think that is significant," answered Pennell.

"Oh, no? Wouldn't that be when she was making the mysterious telephone call?"

"No one knows exactly what time the shooting took place. The watchman is probably very confused as to details now. It will be up to the grand jury to attack the watchman's statement, if they want to. Now please, enough. I have an appointment to get to."

Looking straight ahead, they drove off while the reporters continued to shout questions at them. At Fifth Avenue, they turned left and drove on in silence for a block.

"Jesus Christ," said Inspector Pennell.

"THERE ARE rumors everywhere that my son disinherited his wife," said Alice Grenville.

"She will not be destitute, Mrs. Grenville," said Mr. Mendenhall from the bank. The tone of his voice told her that he, and the bank, felt very little sympathy for the killer of her son.

"Why did Billy cut her out of his will?" asked Alice.

"He did not, in fact, cut her out. What he did was decrease her portion of his estate. He built up the children's shares and cut down hers. He was planning to divorce her."

"Still . . ."

"But the house in Oyster Bay is in her name. She insisted on that when he bought it, and Billy gave it to her. The same with the house in New York. That's in her name, too."

"She was always clever, Ann."

"Don't forget her jewels. She's supposed to have one of the best jewel collections in the city. And paintings."

Alice nodded, aware of the jewels and paintings.

"And her portfolio," added Mr. Mendenhall.

"What portfolio?"

"From time to time Billy gave her money, rather sizable amounts, and she has an aptitude for investment."

"I knew none of this."

"She has a friend called Babette Van Degan."

"Yes, yes, Mrs. Van Degan. Used to be married to Dickie Van Degan." Cut from the same piece of cloth, those two, she thought.

"Babette Van Degan is one of the shrewdest investors on the stock market," said Mr. Mendenhall, removing his pince-nez and massaging their resting place on either side of his nose. "She received a five-million-dollar divorce settlement from Dickie Van Degan when they divorced, and she has been able to turn that into about thirty million."

"My word."

"And Babette Van Degan has been helping your daughter-in-law invest."

Alice stood up and walked around the little sitting room off her bedroom where she dealt with her correspondence and business affairs. She was deep in thought. She looked for a moment into the fireplace, where a small fire laid by Cahill to take the chill off the late-fall day was burning down. She walked over to the window, lifted back the glazed-chintz curtain, and looked down on her bare garden below, her terrace stripped of furniture, her shrubs wrapped in burlap for the coming winter. Finally she turned back to the financial adviser who had acted in her behalf, and her children's, since her husband's death.

"I'm going to take care of her. I want her to have what she would have gotten from Billy if he hadn't changed his will."

"That is overly generous, Mrs. Grenville," said Mr. Mendenhall, who did not approve of remuneration for a woman who had brought so much grief to a family he had known for thirty years.

"I don't want her going to the newspapers, or around New York, saying that her husband's rich family refuses to take care of her. There has been enough about this family in the newspapers."

"I see your point."

"However, there will be conditions. She will have only the income from what she would have inherited, and that income will come monthly from me, signed by me, and is subject to stop at any time that certain requests I have made of her are not met."

IN THE GERMAN consulate on East Forty-second Street a hastily called meeting was taking place. The prowler arrested by the Oyster Bay police had been discovered to be a German.

"What information do you have on him?" asked Dolf von Hoffman, the German consul.

"His name is Horst Berger. Twenty-two years old. An immigrant from Berlin. Entered the United States two years ago. Has been in and out of trouble ever since. His father is a bricklayer, which is also his profession, although he does not work at it. He was arrested a year ago for robbing a market in Mineola. According to his sister, he is a bad sort." The undersecretary looked up from his clipboard.

"That is all you have?"

"Yes, sir."

"What I want to know is, was he on the grounds of the Grenville estate at the time of the killing?"

"He claims not to have been, although he admits to having been there on another occasion, the night before, when he broke into the cabana of the pool house."

"He took what?"

"Food, nothing of consequence."

"Was he armed?"

"He had a shotgun he had stolen from a house in Mineola."

"Is he represented by a lawyer?" asked the consul.

"No, sir."

"We must get a lawyer for him."

"Why would we want to be drawn into this thing?"

"These Grenvilles are rich and powerful people. I have seen them at the track and the opera. Whatever they think of their daughter-in-law, which is not much, I understand, they are not going to let her go to jail. She said she heard a prowler. They might force Horst Berger to say he was there, even if he wasn't, in order to make her story believable. I know people like this. They are not above handing money around to the police to work things out in their favor."

"There is an attorney called Strasser who represented him when he broke into the market in Mineola."

"Engage him. Pay him whatever he asks."

"WHO'S HE?" asked Third.

"Is he a detective?" asked Diantha.

"No, no, he's not a detective, children," said Ann. She had not known her children would walk into her hospital room unannounced. She had always been successful in keeping the separate elements of her complicated life compartmentalized, and when one converged upon another, unexpectedly, she was thrown into confusion. "This is, uh, Mr. Mertens, from Kansas. These are my children, Diantha and Third." She did not say to the children that Mr. Mertens from Kansas was their grandfather.

Claud Mertens had a hard weathered face and the stance of a person uncomfortable with his surroundings. Shaving with nervous fingers in strange surroundings had left several unsightly nicks on his chin, and his round silver-rimmed glasses magnified the confusion in his eyes over his role in his daughter's drama. Instinctively he knew, in front of these aristocratic little children, that his peaked baseball cap was wrong; he pulled it off and stuffed it into the pocket of the suit he had bought the day before.

"Third?" asked Claud Mertens, covering the awkward moment, as if it were a name he had never heard of before, which he had not.

"He's named after his father, who was a junior, you see. His name is William Grenville the Third, but we call him Third, you know, as a nickname."

"Pleased to make your acquaintance, Third, Diantha," said their grandfather.

"How do you do?" each child replied, perfectly mannered.

"We saw the detective," said Diantha.

"He asked us lots of questions," said Third. "He wanted to know if you and Daddy had fights, but we said no."

"Grand'mère told us to say no," said Diantha.

"Children, Mr. Mertens is going to have to leave in just a minute. I'd like you to wait outside, and as soon as he goes, you can come in, and the three of us will have a lovely visit."

"We brought you flowers," said Third, holding up a basket of carefully arranged carnations he carried on his arm. It looked to Ann as if their grandmother had sent them off with a basket someone had sent to her.

"She's a real Mertens all right, that Diantha," said Claud Mertens, after the children left the hospital room. His eyes were brimming over with tears.

It was true what he said, she realized, but Ann Grenville had long since forgotten that *she* was a Mertens. "She resembles her grandmother Grenville," she corrected her father. "Her height. The dark-brown velvet color of her eyes."

"I always think of that last time, Urse, when you were eight, when we had supper that night at Crowell's in Pittsburg, and you had the cheese delight and a chocolate milkshake, and—"

"I was as old that night as my son is today," she said, interrupting him. "Too much time has gone by. Too much has happened. It's too late for us. You've got to understand that. I've lived a lifetime without you. I can't take you back into my life now. I can't cope with any more than I already have to cope with."

"There's something I've got to tell you, Urse. It's important to me that you know. I didn't abandon you. I didn't. It was your mother who told you that. I swear to God I didn't. I tried to find you."

"All those Christmases. All those birthdays. Never a word," said Ann, looking out the window at the East River.

"But I sent you five dollars every birthday, every Christmas, even when I couldn't afford it," Claud Mertens said, standing by her bed in the same position Alice Grenville had stood the day before. Ann turned and looked at him. She remembered the five dollars. She had always assumed it was something her mother had managed to eke out of her small wages. "You must have gotten it, Urse, but I never heard back, and then you were gone from Pittsburg, and then you were gone from Kansas City, and I didn't know where to send it anymore."

"I'm sorry," said Ann.

"You know something, Urse? Somebody told me you'd changed your name to Arden and gone into the show business, like you always wanted to when you was a little girl. You know what I thought? I thought that actress Eve Arden, I thought that was you, and I was proud of you that you done so good."

"Oh, Daddy," she whispered, crying softly now.

"When I first read about it in the papers, Urse, I didn't even know it was you. Then Ken Simons from Pittsburg called me. Do you remember Ken? From the paper? He's the one who told me that Mrs. William Grenville was you. Pretty soon the phone started ringing off the hook, and all these reporters from everywhere were trying to question me to find out about you. That's how I got your number and your mother-in-law's number."

"Listen," she said.

"I'm sorry if I told them you was forty instead of thirty-two, Urse, but I was confused."

"Listen," she said. "It's okay. When this is all over, after the grand jury, if everything goes okay, I'll look you up. I'll find you, and we'll try to catch up, but not now. Please, please, Daddy. Not now. I can't handle any more."

HORST BERGER hoped Mr. Strasser would not make him go through the story again. He had spent most of the day with three detectives walking over the grounds of the Grenville estate in Oyster Bay, climbing the tree, walking across the roof of the house. He knew Mr. Strasser, who had been sent by the German consulate to represent him, did not believe his story.

"Let me understand you, Horst," said Mr. Strasser, speaking patiently. He noticed that the thin shifty young man rarely looked at him in the eye, fixing his stare instead on a color photograph of President Eisenhower in Western attire on the cover of the most recent copy of *Life* magazine that Inspector Pennell had left behind when he allowed his office to be used for this interview. In the magazine, both knew, was a ten-page article entitled "The Shooting of the Century" about the case that was the subject of this visit.

"Is my picture in there?" asked Horst.

"No," replied Mr. Strasser.

"They took my picture today, many times," said Horst.

"I want to get back to the night of the shooting, Horst," said Strasser, the first tone of impatience in his voice. "You said you waited for hours outside the Grenville house when you believed it was unoccupied, when they were at the party."

"I didn't know the cook and the kids were in there," said Horst.

"And you only tried to break into the house after Mr. and Mrs. Grenville returned home? That doesn't make sense, Horst."

"I saw the lights go on and off in the different rooms after they got back, and then waited about half an hour when it was quiet in the house before climbing up the tree and onto the roof," answered Horst.

"Now, you say that you climbed the tree with a loaded shotgun in one hand?" asked the lawyer.

"Yes, sir."

"And you were on the roof when you heard the shots from within the house?"

"Yes, sir."

"After you heard the shots, how did you get off the roof?"

"I jumped to the ground."

"Still carrying the shotgun?"

"Yes, sir."

"Are you aware, Horst, that it is twenty feet from the roof to the ground?"

"No, sir."

"You jumped, carrying a loaded shotgun, in the dark, from the roof to the ground twenty feet below?"

"Yes, sir."

"Why is it I don't believe you, Horst?"

"The truth."

"Horst."

"*Ja?*"

"Why did you say when you were first caught that you were not anywhere near the Grenville house that night?"

"I thought they would think I killed the man."

"Did they force you to change your story, Horst?"

"No, it is like I say."

"I want you to look at me straight in the eye, Horst, and answer a question," said Strasser.

Horst Berger looked at the lawyer and looked away again.

"In my eye, Horst."

"*Ja.*"

"Is someone from the Grenville family paying you to say you were on the roof of the house on Saturday night?"

The young German immigrant concurrently shook his head in denial and reddened.

"YOU SEE, I knew he was unhappy. He didn't have to tell me in those words, but I am his mother. I know. I have always been able to understand more from the tone of someone's voice than from the words that are spoken, because we are trained from birth to say words that camouflage our feelings, but there is no way to hide the secrets of the tone of voice."

"Yes, ma'am."

"It haunts me now that I did not say to him, 'Come to me, talk to me, whatever it is, it's all right.' I would never have said to him, 'I told you so,' never, it wasn't in my nature to do that, but I understood his terrible pride. I understood that he didn't want me to know that the marriage had failed because he had gone so far out on a limb on a marriage that he knew was such a source of unhappiness for us."

"Yes, ma'am."

More and more pictures of Billy Grenville began to appear in his mother's room. When Alice wasn't meeting with Sam Rosenthal or Dr. Skinner or Mr. Mendenhall or Inspector Pennell, she poured through old scrapbooks and photograph albums and found pictures from the many stages of his life that reminded her of pleasant events and happy times and had them put in silver frames, on her bedside table and her writing table and her dressing table and the table by her chaise where she lay to rest each afternoon. Wherever she looked there were pictures of Billy.

"Look how handsome he was there," she said to Lyd, her personal maid. "That was the day of the Groton–St. Mark's game when he made a field goal. He said it was the happiest day of his life, and, oh, Lyd, if you could have seen Mr. Grenville, he was bursting, absolutely bursting, with fatherly pride. I know he wanted to hug Billy, and I think Billy even wanted to be hugged by his father, but you know how they were, all the Grenville men, they just shook hands instead, and Mr. Grenville said, 'I'm so proud of you, son,' and Billy answered, 'Thank you, Father,' and I think it was the closest moment they ever had together. Oh, Lyd, why did this have to happen? Why? Why?"

She was crying now, the sobs coming out of her in great heaving gasps. "I have led a good life," she said. "I believe in God. I honor Him in my prayers every day. I attend church regularly. I attend to my duties as a mother, and to my obligations as a woman of wealth. Why? Why has this happened to me?"

* * *

IN SECRET Alice wished Ann had the decency to commit suicide, to swallow the pills or slit the wrists that would end her existence. She saw her daughter-in-law as a lowly cockroach, scurrying here, scurrying there, fighting for her existence, as if she mattered. At first she could not understand the feelings that were overwhelming her. She dared not confess them to anyone, not even Cordelia. They were all-consuming within her, hot and unpleasant, rage and anger and hate, all directed at Ann, for taking away the life of the son she loved so much. She hated this chorus girl who had undulated her way into Billy's existence. She wished that in the beginning she had acted on her instincts about the woman, instead of going against her feelings, and capitulating, because she could not bear to disappoint Billy. Oh, how she regretted that. Cut off from his family, and his money, the marriage would not have outlasted the war, and the wretched girl could have been paid off and gone her way. Instead she usurped Billy, took over his life, ran it, used it, all to advance herself. Alice understood that it was a marriage cemented only by sexual pleasure.

Awakening, she looked at the clock on her bedside table. She felt a longing for her son and a sense of the great void his loss was in her life. It was five-thirty in the morning. Soon there would be stirring in the kitchen and servants' quarters in the house, and she knew that she would have to act quickly to do what she had to do before anyone ran into her. She got up from her bed, put on her slippers and her wrapper, and quietly opened the door to her bedroom and peered out into the hall. There was no one about. She walked out to the third-floor landing and looked down the several flights of stairs to the marble-floored main hallway below. No one. Quickly and quietly, pulling her wrapper around her for warmth, she walked down the three flights of red-carpeted stairway. Above, the twelve Caesars looked down upon her. She would meet their eyes on the way back up and think they were nodding in approval at what she was doing. The Caesars knew a thing or two about retribution.

It seemed odd to her to be operating in stealth in her own home where she had lived for forty years. At the bottom of the stairs she walked across the hall beneath the chandelier and opened a door to a secondary hall leading to the back rooms and the garden. Stored there in open disarray was sporting gear for all seasons: walking sticks, velvet riding hats, umbrellas, ice skates, raincoats, gloves, and dog leashes. Chinese export bowls held car keys and spare house keys and dark glasses. On a marble-topped table, where she knew it would be, was a riding crop. It was been William's. Then it had been Billy's. Various grandchildren now used it when they came into the city and wanted to ride in Central Park. She picked it up and felt the leather strength of it. Below her on the kitchen floor she heard the first sound of stirring. Quickly she returned up the three flights of stairs, one hand on the banister, the other holding the leather riding crop close to her side to escape detection if old Lyd should make an early appearance.

The activity heightened the adrenaline within her, but the rage she felt had not abated. She locked the door of the bedroom behind her. She stripped back the blankets and blanket cover on her bed. She placed in vertical position a long pillow. In her mind's eye, she conjured up the image of her daughter-in-law, Ann.

"Murderess!" she hissed at the pillow, repeating the word over and over. She raised the riding crop and began to beat the pillow. She beat it and beat it and beat it until exhaustion overtook her. The linen pillowcase was in tatters. Feathers from the down pillow rose in fright into the air, making Alice think of life leaving a body.

After several minutes of resting on her chaise to collect herself and calm her racing heartbeat, she rallied again, feeling tired but strangely tranquil for the exertion she had put herself through. She hid away the mutilated pillow in the back of a closet and the riding crop in the back of her lingerie drawer, ready for another day, unlocked her door, and returned to her bed, pulling the covers up over her. It was thus that Lydia found her when she arrived with her tray of hot water and quartered lemons a few minutes later.

"Good morning, Mrs. Grenville," said Lyd. "Did you rest well? You look better this morning."

Sipping her hot lemon juice, Alice Grenville watched the woman who had waited on her for a quarter of a century perform the tasks of morning: draw back the curtains, pick up the clothes of the night before, arrange the newspapers, draw the bath. She felt overcome with affection for her.

"Are you comfortable up there where you are, Lyd?" she suddenly asked.

"I'm comfortable, ma'am," replied Lyd.

"It's been years since I've been up on that floor. I can't remember which room you have."

"All the way at the end of the hall."

"Does it look out on the park?"

"The other end of the hall. I look out on Mrs. Vanderbilt's house."

"Do you share it?"

"Not since Mae died, ma'am. I have it alone."

"And the bathroom. It's right next to you, isn't it?"

"Yes, ma'am."

"And whom do you share it with?"

"Kathleen and Mary and Bridgit and Maeve."

"Do you know what I think?"

"No, ma'am."

"I think you ought to move down to the fifth floor, where the children's bedrooms used to be. Take one of those and have your own bath. Would you like that?"

"Oh, yes, ma'am."

"I'll have a television set put in there if there isn't one already."

"Thank you, ma'am."

"Mr. Grenville always wanted this house to go to Billy when I died. Now I don't know what will happen."

"You don't have to worry about it now, Mrs. Grenville."

"I wonder what they must think upstairs."

"Who, ma'am?"

"Fourteen of them up on that floor with only two bathrooms, and only me living in the rest of this enormous house."

"Your bath is ready, Mrs. Grenville."

"I'M HERE TO see my client," said the lawyer to the desk sergeant in the Mineola jail.

"Your client?"

"Horst Berger."

"Oh, yes, you are Mr. Strasser," said the sergeant, going through some papers on his desk.

"That's correct."

"I have a message here for you, Mr. Strasser."

"Is it from the German consulate?"

"No, sir."

"From whom?"

"From Horst Berger."

"That's who I've driven out from the city to see."

"He says to tell you he don't want a lawyer."

"This is ridiculous."

"I'm just readin' you the message as it was given to me."

"I would like to see Mr. Berger."

"It says here he don't wish to see you."

"Do you know what I think, Sergeant?"

"No."

"I think someone's paying this kid to say he was where he wasn't in order to back up this Mrs. Grenville's story."

THIS TIME Chief of Detectives Stanley Pennell was not caught unaware when stopped by the reporters in front of the television news cameras. He was, in fact, prepared and almost rehearsed.

"Our most searching investigation into the married life of this couple has revealed what is apparently a well-balanced marriage between two well-balanced people," he said. "They had their minor disagreements, as all married couples do, but they were well adjusted and happy despite all rumors, published and otherwise, to the contrary."

The reporters were disgruntled with his answer. Between them they thought of Inspector Pennell as a toady to the rich of the North Shore.

"Why did she make a telephone call to some unknown person after the shooting before she called the police?" asked the Hearst reporter, not for the first time.

"There was no call made by Mrs. Grenville after the shooting to anyone except the operator to ask for the police," replied Pennell. "I would like to set that rumor to rest. Oyster Bay does not have the dial system, and therefore every call must be placed with the operator on duty. The telephone company has no record of any such call."

"We've all heard of telephone records being suppressed before, Inspector Pennell," said O'Brien from the *Daily Mirror*.

Stanley Pennell ignored the reporter and continued with his statement. "I have found nothing in all of this investigation to indicate that the shooting of William Grenville was other than purely accidental."

THE STRAIN had told upon her. She needed no mirror to remind her that youth had left her forever. That she was not three years younger than her late husband, as had always been supposed, by her own admission, but five years older had been made much of in the press, because of her father's unfortunate interview with a reporter who had managed to track him down in a suburb of Detroit. The eight forgotten years, and more, had found themselves on her face in the twenty-two days since the night of the killing.

She dressed in silence in the black of widowhood, stopping only to gulp black coffee and inhale deeply on a Camel cigarette that rested in the saucer. She brushed her hair and powdered her face without meeting her own eye in the mirror provided by Miss Toomey. Finally she put on her black broadtail coat and wide-brimmed black hat, to which a black veil had been attached, to drop when the time came. She was ready for the ordeal ahead.

"I've put your tranquilizers in your gold pillbox inside your bag, Mrs. Grenville," said Miss Toomey.

"Thank you."

"Here's your black gloves. It's bitter cold out there today."

"Thank you."

"And your black glasses."

"Thank you."

"Dr. Skinner's going to wheel you down in the wheelchair, and Mr. Rosenthal is already downstairs, and the two gentlemen will take you from the wheelchair to the car at the hospital entrance."

"Did my mother-in-law send her car?"

"No, ma'am, it's Lee, your own chauffeur, in your Rover. I heard Mr. Rosenthal say that would look better to the reporters than a great limousine."

"Thank you for everything, Miss Toomey. I would like you to take this," said Ann, opening the black bag and taking out an envelope.

"It's not necessary, Mrs. Grenville."

"Please."

"I'll pack up all your things, and the pictures of the children, and have them sent over to your house."

"Thank you." Ann wanted to tell this good woman that she was frightened to go to Mineola to face the grand jury, but Sam Rosenthal, who knew about such things, had told her not to confide in other people about anything because they might sell her story to the press.

"Good luck, Mrs. Grenville."

"MRS. GRENVILLE was greatly concerned with the prowler that night," said Kay Kay Somerset on the stand. "As was Mr. Grenville. They talked of nothing else."

"You know of no argument that took place between Mr. and Mrs. Grenville at Mrs. Bleeker's house?" asked the district attorney.

"Argument? There was no argument that I know of," said Kay Kay.

"Are you aware that Mr. Grenville received a telephone call that night?"

"I'm not aware of that."

"Did Mrs. Grenville throw a drink at Mr. Grenville and break some of Mrs. Bleeker's china?"

"Goodness, no. I certainly would have known about *that* if it had happened. I don't know how these stories get started. Billy and Ann, Mr. and Mrs. Grenville rather, were as they always were that night, divine."

"Thank you, Miss Somerset. That will be all. Will you call the telephone operator, Mrs. Gaedgens, please. And have the cook, Anna Gorman, standing by."

Sam Rosenthal walked back and forth between the courtroom and an office that had been made available for Ann to wait in away from the reporters and photographers.

"There's a discrepancy between the time the guard said he heard the shots and the time the telephone operator said she got your call for help," reported Rosenthal.

Ann, pale, sat there knitting with a madness of speed, like a contestant in a knitting race. Both she and Sam knew they were talking about the time during which she had called Sam that night, but neither of them said it.

"It was the night Daylight Savings ended, did you know that?" asked Sam. "So everyone's fucked up about the time."

"Spring forward. Fall back," mumbled Ann to herself.

"What?"

"Nothing."

The door to the hallway was ajar. Ann looked up from her knitting as Horst Berger, the prowler of the North Shore, walked past accompanied by two uniformed guards. For an instant their eyes met. Each recognized the other from photographs in the newspapers. He, she knew, was her salvation. One of the guards roughly pulled him on.

She heard the clang of a cell door swinging closed, and the sound of the key in the lock, loud and metallic. Her body stiffened as a shiver ran through it. When she raised her eyes, she saw that Sam Rosenthal was looking at her, as if testing her reaction to the sound of what might have been her own fate. A blush flushed her cheeks.

"It's warm in here," she said, opening her broadtail coat.

"Steam heat," answered Sam in agreement.

"They're ready for you, Mrs. Grenville," said a police officer.

HER APPEARANCE before the grand jury was brief. Escorted to the stand by Sam Rosenthal, who stayed by her while she swore on a Bible to tell the truth, the whole truth, and nothing but the truth, she spoke barely above a whisper throughout the proceedings. Both the judge and the district attorney deferred to her importance with unfailing courtesy.

"I am sorry to have to put you through this, Mrs. Grenville," said the district attorney, "but would you recount for us, to the best of your ability, step by step, exactly what took place on the night of October thirty-first at your estate in Oyster Bay."

It was a story from which Ann Grenville had never veered, from the night of the shooting, and was never to veer, not for the rest of her life. She recounted her devotion to her husband. She told of her deep fear of the prowler and the decision of her husband to take guns to bed that night for protection of themselves and their children. She was awakened, she said, by a sound. She rose from her bed. She picked up her gun, a double-barreled shotgun that her husband had had specially made for her. She opened the door of her bedroom. There she saw the figure of a man in the dark hallway that separated the bedrooms of her husband and herself. She fired her gun twice. Almost instantly, she said, crying hysterically now on the stand, she realized the man she had mistaken for the prowler was her husband. At that point she collapsed in grief.

The eighteen-man jury hung on every word, completely fascinated by the former show girl turned society woman. Several of the jurors wept with her. Their verdict was swift. Ann Grenville was found blameless in the shooting death of her husband. It was termed a tragic accident. There were to be no criminal proceedings brought against her. There was to be no trial. Her ordeal was over.

Driving back from Mineola to New York City that night, Ann returned to her house for the first time since the shooting.

"MRS. GRENVILLE BLAMELESS!" screamed the headlines.

Sighs of relief were audible from Maine to Southampton. The sighs were not for the good fortune of Mrs. Grenville. The sighs were for the private, privileged, Protestant existences which Mrs. Grenville's damnable deed had almost laid open for the world to see. They had closed ranks and protected her, an outsider in their midst, but what they were protecting really was themselves. Now they could return to governing, to banking, to business, to sport, and to pleasure knowing that their superiority, although cracked a bit, remained undaunted.

"Thank God for Alice Grenville," men said at the Brook Club, the Knickerbocker Club, the Union Club, and the Racquet Club. "She did the right thing." They were gentlemen in high places, and they looked after one another like the old schoolmates they once were.

PART FOUR

I F THE DUCHESS of Windsor should come," she said to her maid, "or Mrs. Bleeker, be sure to let me know, and I'll see them right away ahead of the others."

It was the day Ann Grenville had decreed she would accept her condolences. Declared blameless by the grand jury, she believed her acquittal and felt the suspicions of others would be allayed by it. The speculation of the press as to her culpability in the tragedy was at an end, and she was ready to begin her life again. She saw herself as a tragic figure, a participant in a ghastly accident, and she saw no reason why others would not accept the court's validation of her situation. Through Cordelia she let it be known that she would like to see her friends on an early December afternoon. It had distressed her, during her hospitalization, to hear of the many condolence messages that had been sent to her mother-in-law and sisters-in-law, messages she felt should have been sent to her.

She examined her house, from which she had been absent a month. She puffed up needlepoint cushions and arranged them in exact positions. She filled jade boxes with cigarettes. She lessened flower arrangements so as to diminish any appearance of festivity or party-giving. It was her intention to receive her callers upstairs in her bedroom one or two at a time while the others mingled in the living room with tea or drinks waiting their turn.

Sheets from Paris, sprayed with flowers and butterflies, scalloped and monogrammed, adorned her bed. Dressed in a satin-and-lace nightgown with matching negligee, she arranged herself on a chaise longue by the window so that when her guests entered they would find her reclining gracefully against the velvet cushions.

Her doorbell rang below. She speculated who it would be. The duchess, she thought. Or Edith Bleeker. Or both together probably. It rang again. Petal Wilson, she thought. Jeanne Twombley. Even Kay Kay Somerset. Or Eve Soby, if she wasn't tight already. From beneath her counterpane she produced her compact and applied powder again to her face and expressed satisfaction with her choice of a pale lipstick. There was a tap on her door.

"Come in," she said in a quiet voice.

"You have a visitor, ma'am," said the maid.

"Thank you, Mary," said Ann. "Send her in."

In came Babette Van Degan.

"Oh, Babette," said Ann. It was not who she was expecting. "Who else is here?"

"Honey, there's nobody here but us Cinderellas," said Babette.

Later, after Babette, she lay motionless on her chaise longue, beginning to realize that she had been ignored. Partially smoked cigarettes were ground into a Lowestoft plate by her side. Her eyes were red from crying. On a table next to her was a bowl of ice and half a dozen linen napkins, four of them soaked, that she used to keep her lids from swelling. Even Bertie Lightfoot, she thought bitterly, had not come.

At a sound in the street she peered out through her drawn curtains. Outside gold chairs and round tables were being delivered to a neighbor's house for a large party. She stared. A florist's truck pulled up. From behind her curtains she counted the number of pink-and-red rose centerpieces and estimated there would be forty-eight for dinner. Feeling rejected, although she did not know her neighbors, she wondered if she would ever again be asked anywhere.

In the shock of the happening, and the aftermath in the hospital and the court, she had buried deep within her all feelings of loss, grief, responsibility—perhaps, or perhaps not, to be dealt with at a later time. Now she experienced the sense of the void of his presence in her life. It was the hour that Billy usually came home after having stopped at one of his clubs to have a drink or play backgammon or talk horses with Alfred Twombley or Piggy French. He would open the door and call out, "I'm home," and the children would scream, "Daddy, Daddy, Daddy," and madly running footsteps would be heard racing down the several flights of stairs from the nursery to the living room. At that moment her longing for the man she had killed was overwhelming.

HER VERMEIL clock, which had once been given to the Empress Elizabeth of Austria by the mad King Ludwig of Bavaria, struck three. She was exhausted, but sleep eluded her again. She twisted and turned, trapped by her own thoughts, her vitality ebbing away in the darkness of the room she had once shared with her husband.

She could summon up no other picture of him than how he had looked dead, his face still so handsome, his head partially blown away. When that face crept into her dreams, as it began to do, she awakened from her pill-induced sleep, her satin-and-lace nightgown drenched with wet sweat, her moist hair clinging soggily to her face and forehead. She lay there in a state of near paralysis for several minutes until her heart calmed. Then she reached for the Porthault towel that she now took to bed with her each night, dried her face and armpits in the darkness, and took two more of the turquoise-and-scarlet capsules that were always at hand.

"Everybody dropped her like a hot potato. Most people wouldn't have her in the house."

                                                                Kay Kay Somerset

"Was there any mail, Myrna?" Ann asked her secretary.

"Only bills, which I have taken up to the office, a letter from the headmistress of Spence, which I did not open and left on your desk, an invitation to—"

"To what?" asked Ann, too quickly, she realized.

"To the showing of the Mainbocher collection."

"Oh."

"And the new edition of the Social Register, which I put on the telephone table in the sitting room."

"Thank you." She had forgotten about the Social Register. She wondered if they had dropped her name. Poor Babette made it for the two years she was married to Dickie Van Degan and then was never listed again. And Patsy French was dropped when Piggy named the groom at their stable as correspondent in their divorce. And Bratsie Bleeker's Mexican movie star disappeared from the pages in the edition following his demise. She did not want it to be apparent to her secretary that the matter was of any consequence to her, so she continued to read the lastest issue of *Harper's Bazaar* until Myrna left the room to attend to a household matter.

When she was alone, she leaped to her feet and darted to the telephone table in her sitting room, where the latest edition of the Social Register had been placed next to her Louis Vuitton address book. She positioned herself in such a way that if Myrna English appeared in the doorway she would not be able to see what Ann was reading.

From years of practice she opened the book instantly to the G's, even to the Gr's. She turned two pages to the correct page. There, of course, was Alice, Mrs. William Grenville, Senior, in all her social perfection. Ann hardly dared to lower her eyes to the next name, fearing in her heart that it would be Diantha and Third, without her.

But it was there. Mrs. William Grenville, Junior, her address, her telephone number, her clubs, her children, all in their proper place. An immense feeling of relief passed through her. She felt that her own position in New York was inviolate, that she was not simply an appendage to her deceased husband.

She looked at a photograph of Billy in a silver frame on her desk, looked away, looked back again. She did not care to meet its eye. Abruptly she placed it face down on the table. It remained so for several days. The maid dared not move it. One day it was gone.

THE VELVET ropes were not put up to bar her way into the smart clubs and restaurants where she had become a fixture in the decade of her social success, but the attitudes of the proprietors and captains and maître d's who bowed her in were different. They remained courteous as always, but were less effusive in their welcomes. There were those, they knew, who did not wish to dine in proximity to the woman who had killed one of their own. For the first time Ann Grenville sometimes reached into her purse and rewarded her greeters with cash, in the manner of rich out-of-towners trying to establish credentials in fashionable watering holes.

She walked into "21" at the height of the lunch hour, without a reservation, in the company of a Spanish couple who were visiting New York. For a moment there was silence throughout the chattering crowd; not a person did not turn to look at her. On her face she fixed an expression of nonchalance as Mac Kriendler led her across the first section of the room to the table where members of the Grenville family were used to being seated. All her life she had craved to be the center of attention, and, in disgrace, she had succeeded.

Piggy French watched her entrance and turned quickly back to engage himself in conversation with his luncheon companions, hunching himself over his martini as if to make himself invisible.

"Hello, Piggy," cried out Ann, passing his table, in her exaggerated society-woman voice, as if the circumstances of their friendship were unchanged.

Piggy French looked up as if he had not been aware of her and only half rose from his chair, saying as he did, "Oh, hello," not calling her by name.

Ann stopped and kissed him, first on one cheek and then on the other, in the fashion of their group, giving the impression of great friendship and the continuation of her husband's lifelong affection. She looked him in the eye and held his gaze with almost a defiance. She had learned to tell what the other person felt about her by reading the look in their eyes. Piggy mumbled something in reply and did not introduce her to his guests. Ann walked on to her table and reseated the Spaniards, who had already seated themselves.

"I wasn't a bit pleased to be kissed by her," said Piggy to his guests when conversation resumed.

"She was found to be blameless, though, wasn't she?" asked Taytsie Davis.

"Thanks to Billy's mother," said Piggy. "Alice Grenville is a saint. She loathed Ann and stood by her."

"Who are those people with her?" asked Taytsie.

"Foreigners. They're the only ones who see her."

"However you look at it, she's ruined," said the fascinated Taytsie, unable to take her eyes off Ann's table.

Ann remembered every slight, every averted eye, and stored this away in the recesses of her mind, to be dealt with later, when her life began again. This was not life that she was in. This was an interim period, a limbo, between what was and what would be.

"She was a woman who took advantage of every opportunity that life offered her, and the prowler offered her the opportunity of widowhood."

Tucky Bainbridge

Key figures in Alice Grenville's life let it be known to friends, who passed it on to acquaintances, that she wished not to have the tragedy mentioned to her. True to her word, she stood behind her daughter-in-law, appearing with her in public on occasion to give the show of unity in her family. Although people in their world were tolerant of Ann in the presence of the beloved Alice, they remained hostile to her when Ann, alone, tried to brazen out her situation in New York.

Leaving the opera with her one night, Alice told Charles that she had decided to go straight home rather than on to dinner in a restaurant, as had been planned. When he had closed the window that separated the chauffeur from the passengers, she sat in silence for a while looking out at the New York night while Ann talked on about someone she had seen in the box next to theirs.

"Yes, yes, you saw her, Mère, wearing that same dress Cordelia wore to the Pells last week. She's married to a Cypriot violinist and lives in Paris. The story is that she once—"

"I think you must give some thought to leaving the city, Ann," interrupted Alice, who had not been listening.

"What do you mean, leave the city?" asked Ann.

"Just that," replied Alice. "Move away."

As she always did when she felt trapped or nervous, Ann concentrated on a different activity. She opened her gold-and-diamond minaudier and took out her compact. Staring at herself in the compact mirror, she applied scarlet lipstick over and over to her lower lip.

"Your makeup is absolutely fine, Ann," said Alice.

"I was thinking of going to Palm Beach for a few weeks," said Ann, continuing her application.

"When you have completed your ministrations, I will continue this conversation," said Alice, looking out the window at Park Avenue.

The word "ministrations," pronounced in four syllables, signaled to Ann that her mother-in-law was not to be deterred. She put her compact back in her minaudier, clicked it shut, breathed deeply, and stared straight ahead. The two women sat in silence for a block.

"I think you should move to a different place," Alice began. "And I don't mean going to Palm Beach for two weeks. I think you should consider leaving the city, perhaps even leaving the country."

"Never," answered Ann, aghast at the suggestion.

"You must be aware that things have changed for you here."

"What about Newport?"

"I've decided against opening the house in Newport this year."

"I sense a beat missing in this story," said Ann.

"They have turned you down for membership at Bailey's Beach, Ann. Not your children. Just you. It would be an impossible situation there."

Ann, stung, wanted to retreat to her compact again, but dared not.

"Let us overlook sensibilities for a moment," said Alice, "and deal in realities. You are being dropped, right and left. Can't you feel it yourself?"

"I suppose you've heard from Felicity that Edith Bleeker cut me dead at Piping Rock last weekend. She must have loved running to you with that one."

Alice Grenville did not answer. The Packard drew up in front of Ann's house. Ann looked out at her black front door, expensively glossed, and saw the ending of her life in that perfect house that she had created and where she had reigned.

"Have you seen the new edition of the Social Register?" she asked, as if she were playing a trump card. "I have not been dropped by it."

"That's so."

"You've seen it?"

Alice Grenville smiled sadly. "If you were not listed, Ann, I would have withdrawn my name and the names of my four daughters."

"It was a deal then?" asked Ann.

"It was a deal."

Ann's heart sank. She knew it was true. Charles stood outside in the cold night waiting to open the door. She motioned out the window that she was ready.

"One more thing, Ann," said Alice, putting her hand on the sleeve of Ann's fur. "I would like to bring up my grandchildren."

Ann turned to her mother-in-law, flushed with anger. "I knew this was what was on your mind. I knew it from the day you came to visit me at Doctors Hospital. Never will you take my children from me. Never!"

Outside the car Charles heard the raised harsh voice and did not open the car door.

"I will send them to spend vacations with you. You may visit them anytime when you return to this country, but I would like to take over their education and upbringing."

"I repeat, never."

"Wherever you go, for the rest of your life, people are going to point at you and say, 'That's the woman who shot her husband.' Do you think that's fair to your children?"

"I think I know what's best for my children," snapped Ann.

"Diantha and Third have been deeply wounded by this terrible tragedy. Can't you see yourself how silent they've become? It is a wound that cannot begin to heal until the notoriety dies down."

"I will hire lawyers and go to the press before I allow you to take my children, Alice," said Ann, leaning forward to her mother-in-law. She had never called her by her first name before. It was not spoken with affection, and the time for calling her Mère was at an end.

"Let me remind you that we made a deal in the hospital that you would never talk to the press as long as you lived," said Alice.

"And let me remind you," said Ann, pointing her finger toward her mother-in-law's face, "that the deal we made referred to my not talking to the press, or anyone else, about the night of the accident in Oyster Bay. It had nothing to do about not talking to the press about your taking my children away from me."

"Don't point your finger at me."

"Have you picked a place for me?"

"The sneer in your voice is not necessary."

Ann tapped on the window for Charles to open the door. As she left the car, she turned back to Alice Grenville. "If Billy had accidentally shot me, everything would have gone on as normal."

"Billy Grenville would be alive today if he hadn't married that actress."
                                                              Sass Buffington

More than ten years in their midst had not made her one of them. The doors that counted on the Upper East Side, the North Shore, Newport, and Southampton were slammed in her face. The kind of people who were willing to see her were not the kind of people she was willing to see. In that world, once you were mixed up in a scandal that knocked the lid off their kind of life, it was inevitable that you would be dropped.

She felt rage at the lot that life had dealt her and refused to reason that it was she, not life, who had fired the shots that blew off her husband's head. There were those who believed that it was an accident, as she steadfastly maintained, but even those knew that she was capable of doing what the others believed she had done.

With no other options than what her mother-in-law suggested, she sold her house in New York and left the country. The house in Oyster Bay, with no buyers interested, was closed up. At the end of their school term, her children followed her to Switzerland.

ALTHOUGH THE Europeans were more tolerant of the position Ann Grenville found herself in than the Americans she knew, everyone felt she returned far too quickly to her old life in the International Set playgrounds. As if frightened she would be forgotten, she did not retire for a year or two of obligatory mourning and reflection, or even motherhood, in a quiet country atmosphere, but plunged back into the set that got on airplanes to go to parties. Wherever she went, it was at the height of the season. She told new acquaintances she felt banished, dramatizing her plight. They, mostly Europeans, accepted that what had happened was an accident, or else that it was passion, and, for them, a crime of passion was an excusable act.

Kay Kay Somerset, who no longer spoke to her, saw her at the Givenchy collection in Paris, sitting on a gilt chair in the front row checking off numbers on her program as models in evening dress paraded in front of her, as if she were anticipating a gala season ahead. Worse, under the circumstances, she continued to shoot and traveled with four gun cases to shooting weekends at country estates in Austria, France, and Spain.

It was in the bar of the Palace Hotel in St. Moritz, at the height of the season, that I heard her, in quite a loud voice, cast aspersions on my nature. I won't say the word she used. It pains me. Not that it's not true; it is. Of course, she was drunk at the time, or well on her way to being.

Outside it was nearly dark. The bar was mobbed. Late diners were still in après-ski dress, preparatory to going to their rooms to dress for dinner. Early diners were already in evening clothes. Every seat was taken. I, a celebrity now and in great social demand after the enormous international success of my book Candles at Lunch, made into an equally successful film with Audrey Hepburn and Cary Grant, was seated on a bar stool in conversation with the always entertaining Madame Badrutt, the then wife of the fashionable innkeeper who owned the Palace Hotel and kept the riffraff out. A Europeanized American who spoke English with a foreigner's intonations, Madame Badrutt, formerly of the San Fernando Valley, gave me a short précis of each guest whose looks interested me and brought many of them forward to meet me. "This is Mr. Basil Plant," she said to a very old woman emblazoned with diamonds. She was a countess, or a viscountess, or a duchess, or something, but she, an admirer of mine, told me to call her Kitty.

"Kitty knew Proust," said Madame Badrutt.

"Why, Kitty!" I cried, clapping my hands in delight. "How simply marvelous. Tell me everything. What was he like?"

"Ghastly!" exclaimed the old lady.

There were shrieks of laughter. The bar was in full cocktail swing.

"Of course, even in this swell group, the American murderess stands out in the pecking order," said Madame Badrutt.

"Who?" I asked.

"Mrs. Grenville," she said.

"Where?" I asked, fascinated, pushing my mimosa to the bartender to be refilled.

When the crowd broke, I saw her across the room in a corner. Her shoulder caressed the arm of the man with whom she was seated.

"Let's have another one of these," said Ann, pushing her empty glass ahead of her. He pushed his glass forward and signaled to the waiter.

"Who's the man?" I asked Madame Badrutt.

"Count Zeilern," she said. "No money. Fair title. Likes rich women."

Mrs. Grenville whipped out her lipstick and gave herself bright new lips. Her companion turned his attention back to her and whispered something in her ear. She looked at him. Her lovely mouth, long unkissed, yearned, not for love, but for promiscuity. When he, reading her signal, leaned forward to kiss her, she joined in the kiss. His whiskeyed tongue intoxicated her, and her eyes closed in public passion. Rarely am I shocked. In my mind I was figuring the time difference to New York and wondering if Jeanne Twombley or Petal Wilson would be at home, knowing it was the sort of story they would love and a pay-back, to boot, for all the juicy tales they had whispered in my willing ears.

As she opened her eyes from her lovemaking, she caught sight of me across the room staring at her. We had not seen each other since she had snubbed me, once again, at Edith Bleeker's party on the night of the tragedy. Her back became intimidatingly rigid. She was thinking, I knew, that Basil Plant was a bearer of tales.

That is when I heard her, in quite a loud voice, cast aspersions on my nature. Others heard it too and turned to me for my reaction. The dynamics of our acquaintance had changed. I excused myself from the woman who had found Proust ghastly, and from Madame Badrutt, rose from my bar stool, and walked across the crowded room to where Ann Grenville sat with her German. His mouth, I noticed, bore the stains of her lipstick. Ignoring him, I stared down at Ann Grenville, who had always resisted my attempts at friendship, and she, knowing she had made a mistake, gazed back insolently at me.

Suddenly I raised my hands, as if I were positioning a shotgun, one hand on the imaginary barrel and the other on the imaginary trigger, and aimed the imaginary shotgun straight at her head.

"Billy, is that you?" I called out. My high-trebled voice reverberated through the Palace bar. Silence screamed. Waiting for my moment, like the actor I always wanted to be, I then cried out the word, *"Bang!"* and pulled the imaginary trigger, allowing my body to react to the imaginary force of the imaginary shot. And then I repeated again, *"Bang!"* as if firing for the second time, again allowing my body to react to the imaginary force of the imaginary shot. Then I lowered the imaginary shotgun, my eyes never leaving hers. I watched a look of shame and humiliation replace the look of arrogance and insolence that had adorned her beautiful face only a moment before.

"When I write this up in my mosaic, Bang-Bang, I'll send you an advance copy."

Then I turned and walked out of the bar, secure in the feeling that I had done the right thing. Within minutes the story spread throughout the hotel. That night the dinner parties at the Palace Grill, or at the Chesa Viglia, talked of nothing else. The next day the skiers and the group who arrived by funicular to lunch at the Corviglia Club at the top of the mountain had embellishments on the story. "Is that you, Billy?" people were saying over and over, followed by a reenactment of my bang-bang performance, followed by helpless laughter. People claimed to have been eyewitnesses to the event who had not witnessed it at all but could not bear to be left out.

Next morning Mrs. Grenville left for Paris with instructions that her luggage, twenty-eight pieces and four gun cases, be packed for her and sent on to the Ritz Hotel. Count Zeilern did not accompany her. The name Bang-Bang did.

"DON'T YOU FIND this odd?"

"What?"

"I mean, look here." I was sitting in an upstairs office of the Mineola Police Station, after hours, reading the statements of the guests at Edith Bleeker's party on the night that Ann Grenville shot and killed her husband. "The Duchess of Windsor, from her suite in the Waldorf Towers, described the Grenvilles to Inspector Pennell as an ideally suited couple."

"What's odd about that?" asked Detective Meehan, looking toward the door, nervous that he had allowed himself to be conned by me into opening what was supposed to be a closed file on the Grenville shooting. In the old you-scratch-my-back-I'll-scratch-yours theory, I had agreed to read the short stories of Margaret Mary Meehan, the detective's daughter, a sophomore at New Rochelle, and tell her, honestly, whether or not I thought she should pursue a literary career or go into nursing as her father wanted.

"Nothing, in itself. But look, on this page Brenda Frazier, in her New York apartment, described the Grenvilles to the inspector as an ideally suited couple. And here Mrs. Phipps, at her house in Westbury, described the Grenvilles as an ideally suited couple. And so did old Edith Bleeker. In fact, thirty-three of the fifty-eight people who attended the same party the Grenvilles attended on the night of the shooting described the Grenvilles to the police as an ideally suited couple. That's what strikes me as odd."

"I'm not following you." Detective Meehan was being, I felt, deliberately obtuse, but I chose to treat him as a confrere.

"Those words, 'an ideally suited couple,' are not four words that spring to the forefront of your mind, at least most people's minds, when asked to describe a couple, especially a couple who were most definitely *not* ideally suited."

"Are you building to a point?" asked Detective Meehan, gathering up the report and returning it to the file.

"I am. Yes. Closing the ranks, it's called. Bringing the stagecoaches in closer. Keeping the outsiders out. There must have been behind-the-scenes phone calls. Tell them, somebody must have said, when they question you, that Billy and Ann were an ideally suited couple, and the guests were, at least thirty-three out of fifty-eight of them, sufficiently uncreative as to repeat the exact words. That's the point I'm building to."

"You better clear out of here now."

"About that prowler."

"Another time. You better get out of here now."

"She traveled from country to country, made a gaffe, and moved on."
                                                                    Eve Soby

She was a good traveler, kept track of an enormous quantity of luggage, gun cases, and fur coats, and intimidated customs officials into speeding her through. People thought it odd that she continued to shoot, after she had shot and killed, but she enjoyed her reputation as a huntress, and continue to shoot she did at shooting parties across the Continent.

In Austria she insisted that her host, Prince Windisch-Graetz, dismiss his gamekeeper for making improper advances toward her, when the truth of the matter was, as old Prince Windisch-Graetz and every other guest at the shooting party knew, that it was Mrs. Grenville who had made the improper advances toward the gameskeeper. Mrs. Grenville left. The gameskeeper remained.

In Spain the Duke of Lerma introduced her to the Marquis de Fuego as America's most famous instant widow, and she did not take offense. When, a few weeks later, their affair having expired, the Marquis de Fuego walked out on her, down the stairs of his hunting lodge, she toppled over a marble bust, narrowly missing him.

In Marrakesh she was asked to leave the Villa Naylor by the Countess de Guigne for luring young Moroccan boys over the wall at night.

During her brief friendship with Chiquita McFadden, before she slept with Chiquita's husband and ruined it, Ann and Chiquita traveled together in India, on safari, visiting various maharajas and maharanees along the way. Dressed in a pink mohair coat, a chiffon scarf over her head, pearls at her neck and wrist, she was not an inconspicuous figure when she rendezvoused with her lover at the gates of the pink palace in Jaipur.

"Who *are* all these people?" she asked the wife of an American film star at a cocktail party in Gstaad. She knew perfectly well who they all were. They were the second echelon of society in the resort and climbers from the third. She realized she had been recategorized in the social structure.

"Why doesn't she marry again?" she heard someone say about her at one of her own parties.

"Who would want her?" was the reply. "She gives it away so freely."

"Please remember that this is my party and I'm paying for it," said Ann, flushing with anger, pointing her finger.

"How could I forget, Mrs. Grenville?" said Count Stamirsky. "If you weren't paying, you wouldn't have been invited."

"She made herself available to too many men for the kind of man she wanted to marry to feel he had to marry her. And the shooting was always with her."
                                                                    Alfred Twombley

"That woman is in town. Will you be a darling, Bertie, and come to dinner?" said Alice Grenville to Bertie Lightfoot.

Every time Ann returned to the country, whether by ship or air, Alice Grenville sent the car to meet her. There were always flowers waiting for her at the apartment on upper Fifth Avenue that she took after she sold her house, and an invitation to dinner. It was part of a ritual that was to continue always. At least once a year, never more than twice, each of Billy's sisters had Ann to a party. One often heard, in the drawing rooms of the city, "Yes, I saw Ann last night at Cordelia and Jack's" or "Ann was at Felicity and Dexter's anniversary dance last week." Her inclusion was often noted in the society columns, and the impression was given, as it was meant to be given, that the Grenville family, in all its various branches, remained on friendly terms with their widowed in-law.

Behind the scenes it was different. Disapprovingly, Alice Grenville saw her daughter-in-law going about with too many men, flaunting the independence of widowhood.

"I thought you would take a house somewhere and start a new life. I never imagined you would live in hotels and wander from resort to resort with the seasons. What kind of way is that to bring up your children?"

They were more comfortable with each other on the telephone. When they met in person, there was always another person there, usually one of the sisters, and they talked of inconsequential things—clothes, parties, plays they had seen, books they had read. On the telephone, however, Alice said what was on her mind.

" 'Unseemly' is such an old-fashioned word, but unseemly is exactly what it is."

"It suits you, however."

"They say you are often drunk or drugged."

"Who are 'they'?"

"What difference does that make, Ann? It is what is being said about you."

"And where there is smoke, there is fire. Is that what you're going to say next?"

"You are not a beloved figure, Ann, or a tragic one either. You are a mess. An embarrassing mess. Dinner is at eight promptly."

Ann would have liked not to go, but she did. Alice would have liked not to have her, but she did. "Do you know my daughter-in-law?" she asked new friends, taking Ann about her drawing room, and the friends marveled at the solidarity of the family and the goodness of Alice.

Ann was not pleased to see that her mother-in-law had seated her next to Bertie Lightfoot at the table. If it had been in any other dining room in New York, she would have switched her place card, not to improve her position, as she had in the past, but to remove herself from Bertie, for whom she felt bitterness for not having rallied to her side in the months following the tragedy.

"You're looking marvelous, Ann," said Bertie, knowing her to be unembarrassed by praise of her looks and appearance. He took the tactic of compliments to override the awkwardness between them.

She chose not to answer him. She could tell that he was nervous and as displeased as herself to be so seated at Alice's table. On the other side of her was the Spanish Ambassador to the United Nations, and she conversed with him in Spanish, about Madrid, the Prado, Horcher's restaurant, and the marvelous towels at the Ritz Hotel. After two courses, the lady on the other side of him, Alice's old friend Beth Leary, usurped the ambassador, with a withering look at Ann, and when he turned his head toward her, to answer her questions about the possible restoration of the monarchy after the death of Franco, she found herself excluded.

"Are you planning on keeping the house in Oyster Bay?" asked Bertie, making a second attempt at conversation.

"It is not a house in great demand on the real estate market," she replied coldly, without looking at him.

"You are living in Switzerland?" he asked.

"I will be taking a house in Sardinia for the summer and will probably go to Ireland in the fall." She looked straight ahead. She wondered if he had heard from Basil Plant about what had happened in Switzerland.

"Why did I think you were in Switzerland?" he asked.

"The children are in school there. I go there several times a year to be with them."

"How is Dolly?"

"She prefers to be called Diantha," said Ann, spacing her words, letting him know that he was intruding.

"Look here, Ann," he said. "I don't know why you're taking this position with me. Alice thought that—"

"Oh, Alice thought, did she?" interrupted Ann. "You've moved up in the world to become Alice's confidant now, have you? It's called 'taking advantage of a situation.' "

"Please, Ann."

"You should have written me, Bertie, or telephoned me, at the time of the accident, or come to see me," she said. Her words were very precise and she was very angry, although she kept her voice down and did not call attention to herself.

"I wanted to write, but I didn't know what to say," said Bertie. "It was so awful."

"Bullshit, Bertie. You've never been at a loss for words about anything. If you think I'm not going to remind you that I came to your aid when you were in trouble and had no one else in New York to turn to, you're quite wrong, because I am going to remind you of exactly that."

"I know, Ann. I know you did," he replied quickly, panicked that others would pick up on the conversation.

"I was eight months pregnant at the time, Bertie."

"I know."

THE TWO MRS. GRENVILLES

"I could have made you the laughingstock of New York if I had told that story," she said, her fury building quietly.

"Please, Ann."

"All tied up and fat and naked, amid the carnage of smashed antiquities. You don't think that would have gotten a laugh in these very circles and dining rooms where you take your position as the number-one escort of New York so seriously?"

"Please, Ann."

"I never told one soul that story, not even my husband, and you couldn't find the time or take the trouble to write me or call me because you didn't know what to say? You, who have something to say about everything?"

"I'm sorry, Ann," he said, crushed by the scene. "I'm deeply sorry for you, for Billy, for the children, for the terrible tragedy that's happened."

"Too late, Miss Lightfoot," she said, meeting his gaze, knowing she had gone too far once more, mocking him at a gender level, finishing forevermore the possibility of resurrecting a friendship that she had once cared about.

THE DOGWOOD was fading and the daffodils already withered. I forgot to look at spring this year, thought Ann.

She was alone in the house in Oyster Bay, without servants, without children. There was no one to observe her. She walked through the rooms of her house deciding if she could be there, or if the terrible event had darkened the premises for habitation. The furniture was covered with cretonne. Rugs were rolled up. She felt no ghostly reverberations. There, on that slipper chair, she thought, had been the gun. She walked toward her bedroom door, melding into an image of herself in her blue nightgown, black brassiere, and blue bedjacket. She opened the door, expecting him to be there to relive the scene with her so that she could know and quiet her demons.

"Who's there?" cried Ralph Wiggins. "Oh, my God, it's you, Mrs. Grenville."

She walked past him, out to the courtyard, and got into the Rover. When she reached New York, she made plans to return to Europe. Her publicized past lingered with her, as much a part of her as a hump on her back.

"There are some people they widen the ranks for; she was not one of them."
                                                            Kay Kay Somerset

Ann had always liked Rosie Fairholm. She was one of the few, she used to say, out of that inner-circle group, who was nice to her, not because she was Billy's wife, but because she was Ann. But Rosie Fairholm cut her dead at Harry's Bar in Venice. She heard Rosie say, to one of the Van Degan brothers, "You simply have to draw the line somewhere. I mean, she did kill him."

Slowly Ann began to pass from the center of things. She was heard of as being in Marbella with a handsome French boy, but out of season. Someone saw her in Ireland at the rented castle of a Hollywood film director. There was a story about a problem in Tahiti on somebody's yacht, and the threat of lawsuits for damages done. Brookie Herbert said she was at the *feria* in Seville with her two children quietly following her with brand-new cameras. But she no longer belonged anywhere. She was no longer a part of a group. She was at a side table watching the dinner party in the center of the room. She was a rich nomad, wandering from place to place, creating incidents and moving on. Banished from her land, the heights that had been her aspiration had crashed down on her like an avalanche.

There were always young men in tow, but she clung to her distinguished name as if it were a title.

PACO CAME and went. Pablo came and went. Each complained Ann was ungenerous with him on his departure. And then there was Paul. Paul was English, twenty-two years old, handsome, like all of them, but, as Ann was the first to say about him, different from all of them. He worked. He was the bartender at the Gringo Club in Sardinia, outside of Porto Cervo, where, that season, late-nighters ended up their late nights, after the dinners and dances on the Costa Esmeralda. He spent his days, when he wasn't at the beach, where he turned very brown, and swam very well, writing a screenplay on a battered Olivetti about a Cambridge drop-out who worked as a bartender at the Gringo Club in Sardinia at the height of the season.

It was, for Ann Grenville, lust at first sight. The group she arrived with, some second-rate titles she had met at a second-rate party on the same night the Aga Khan was entertaining the first-rate titles at a first-rate party, became bored and tired and cranky that the first-rate crowd hadn't shown up at the Gringo and wanted not to mix with the third-rate crowd who were already there.

"Let's go, Ann," said Jaime Carrera, whose well-trimmed goatee did not totally disguise his unfortunate chin. She had seated herself at the bar, on a stool, and pushed her glass toward the handsome bartender for a refill.

"But we just got here," she answered.

"It's a dog's dinner tonight," Jaime said, contemptuously, about the crowd. Ann, once so particular about being in the right place at the right time with the right people, yearned less those days about social perfection, knowing it had escaped from her grasp forever that night in Oyster Bay.

"I'm staying," she replied.

"Lucille's got a crowd at her house. We thought we'd go there," he insisted.

"You go on," said Ann.

"How will you get back to Cervo?" he asked.

The bartender handed Ann a freshened drink. For the first time he met the eyes of the beautiful woman who had been staring at him for the last fifteen minutes.

"Do you have a car, bartender?" she asked him.

"I do," he answered. She liked the sound of his voice. It was not too eager.

"That's how I'll get back to Cervo, Jaime," she said to her escort, gesturing her blonde head toward the bartender. "Anyway, I can't stand Lucille."

"Don't mix with the help, Ann," said Jaime.

"*Buenas noches,* Jaime," she replied, dismissing him.

She did not look after him as he left. Instead she lit a cigarette and further examined the face and figure of the young man behind the bar.

"You don't look like a bartender," she said.

"So they tell me," he answered.

"Let me guess. You're really a painter."

"Guess again."

"A writer. You're here writing the great English novel."

"The great English screenplay," he corrected her.

"Ah, movies. You see, I wasn't that far off. You be good to me, and I'll introduce you to my friend David Ladera. You know who that is, don't you?"

"Of course. He directed *Candles at Lunch.*"

"By that little shit Basil Plant."

"You don't like Basil, I take it."

"Don't tell me you know Basil?"

"Everyone knows Basil."

She opened her purse and took out some cash. "Turn this into pesos, will you, and put it all in that jukebox, and let's you and me dance for a bit."

"It's a hot night to dance in here."

"Take off your shirt if you're hot," she answered.

"You don't mean that," he said, smiling at her.

"Oh, yes, I do," she replied. "Here, I'll unbutton it for you."

"Let me get somebody to take over back here," he said, stripped to the waist. "José."

"You know who that is, don't you?" whispered José to him when he asked José to take over the bar duties.

"No."

"She's the rich American lady who shot her husband."

"I HAVE TO GO," he whispered. Although shades and curtains and draperies kept the bedroom of this rented villa in darkness from outside, he knew that dawn must be breaking.

"No, no, don't go," she whispered back, looking down on his young and handsome face. The bed they shared was lit by a lamp covered with the head scarf she had worn when he drove her home from the Gringo Club several hours earlier. He reminded her of Billy, not the Billy she had killed, but the Billy of the beginning, the beautiful Billy, when life seemed so full of love and hope.

"I have to. I have to work."

"You just got home from work."

"My other work. I write for three hours every morning."

"Just put your head down there again," she whispered. "I love the way you do that. It looks so nice, watching the top of your head do that. Oh, my darling bartender, you have what is known as a magical tongue. Now, swing around here, the rest of you, but don't stop what you're doing. I want to return the favor."

"I can't come another time."

"At your age, of course you can."

"I can't."

"Try."

In the building frenzy of rekindled passion, neither heard the door of the bedroom open, nor noticed the child, Third, who stood there.

"I don't even know your name," she said, lifting her head from its sexual duties and then returning to them when she finished speaking.

"Paul," he answered, lifting his head from her.

"Paul what?"

"Cooper."

"As in Duff and Diana?"

"I can't talk and fuck at the same time, and you're getting me very close to blast-off time."

"My darling bartender."

Later, finished, he pulled on his trousers, put his feet into loafers without socks, and stuck his shirt into his belt. Dressed, ready to leave, he stood at the foot of her bed and looked down on her.

"Was this a one-night stand, or did you have something more affairlike in mind?" he asked.

No, she thought to herself, he isn't a bit like Billy Grenville. Beneath his youth and beauty, there was a wantonness, without refinement, that matched her own. Lying nude, she looked back at him; her magnificent breasts, she knew, were at their most appealing angle. She smiled.

"How much do you earn at the Gringo Club?" she asked.

"Why?"

"I'll triple it, whatever it is. You move in here, write your movies, teach my kids how to swim and sail, and spend your nights doing what we just did all night."

"Will I get to meet David Ladera?"

"He's in Ireland."

"When I finish my screenplay, can we go to Ireland and show it to him?"

"Yes."

"You're quite a lady, Mrs. Grenville."

"How did you know my name?"

"You're pretty famous, Mrs. Grenville."

"It's Ann."

"Ann."

"Write well."

"Did you know your bedroom door was open all the time?" he asked.

PAUL WAS unlike Paco and unlike Pablo. He seemed to want nothing from her. In Milan she had some suits made for him, and shoes, and shirts, but they were not things that he had asked for. They were things that she wanted him to have. When the season was over in Sardinia, and they went on to the next place, after the children returned to school in Switzerland, she wanted him to look presentable, so that their situation, which was obvious to most of the people in their set in Porto Cervo, would not be so obvious when they checked into the Ritz in Paris in the fall.

Diantha and Third had reluctantly come to accept him in their lives, although at first they were resistant to him in a way that Ann could not understand. Diantha was now fourteen. Third twelve. Sometimes she wondered about the open bedroom door and wondered if one or the other had come in that night and seen what was going on, but she did not pursue the subject with them. She was, she knew, afraid of her children in a way. When they looked at her sometimes, they looked with the look of Grenvilles, not the look of Mertenses, and she reexperienced each time the feelings of her first visit with Billy's family when he had brought her to the great New York house to meet his mother and sisters for tea. She had always meant to sit down with her children and explain to them the circumstances of the night of the shooting, but she never had, other than repeating to them over and over in the hospital that it had been an accident. She would have been satisfied with that if she had not made the discovery that the acoustics of the house in Oyster Bay made everything that was said in her bedroom audible to the bedroom upstairs at the far end of the house where her children slept.

Within a week of moving into the villa, Paul had won over Diantha and Third. He loved to swim and sail and water-ski, and he had infinite patience in teaching them sports. They seemed to him like wounded birds, spending most of their time together, and not mixing with the other English-speaking young people on the island that their mother would round up for them to befriend. Paul came to realize that other children, hearing from their parents of the shooting, invariably brought up the story, and each time Diantha and Third suffered and did not wish to see the child again. When Paul was around, the children got along with their mother, and the strained silences that often existed between Ann and her children disappeared. He possessed an almost childlike understanding of children, and the weeks passed in a vacation atmosphere.

One day, returning from a sailing trip, Paul rushed up the steps to the house with the children to discover that his Olivetti typewriter and reams of paper had been moved from the place on the terrace where he had left them before going to the beach. Seated on the terrace next to Ann, who was dressed in a silk dress and pearls, rather than her customary trousers or shorts and shirt, was a distinguished older woman, also dressed in silk and wearing pearls, as well as a younger woman, similarly attired.

"Grand'mère!" shrieked the children, who ran up the steps and threw themselves into the arms of their grandmother and their Aunt Felicity.

"Isn't this a surprise?" said Alice Grenville to the children. "Felicity and I have been staying in the South of France with friends, and, on a whim, we decided to fly over and spend a few days at the hotel so we could see you."

Ann, as surprised by the visit as her children, looked on at the affection displayed between Alice and Diantha and Third. Never did her children run to her in that way.

When Paul reached the top of the steps to the terrace, wearing only a pair of cut-off shorts, the conversation stopped. He looked to Ann almost young enough to be her son, and she cringed that she had told him only a few hours before, during a sexual climax, that she loved him. Felicity, with a trace of a smile on her face, took in the sight of the nearly naked young man who had joined the group and looked from him to her sister-in-law and back again. Alice, who noticed everything, saw a look on her daughter-in-law's face that signaled a warning to the young man.

"Oh, Mère, and Felicity, this is the children's tutor," she said after a moment of silence. "Mr. Paul Cooper. This is my mother-in-law, Mrs. Grenville, and my sister-in-law, Mrs. Ashcomb."

"Tutor? I didn't know you children had a tutor," said Alice. "What are you studying?"

"Mostly sports," answered Ann, before her children could reply. "Mr. Cooper has been teaching them how to sail and water-ski. Mr. Cooper went to Cambridge and is going to be a writer." She knew she was talking too quickly. She could never cope when her worlds overlapped. "Paul," she said, in the voice she used when she talked to her help, "would you get ice and some white wine. Then you may have the evening off. We'll be dining with Mrs. Grenville at her hotel."

"Yes, Mrs. Grenville," answered Paul.

IN SEPTEMBER Diantha and Third went back to school. Ann took them to Switzerland. Paul stayed behind to close up the rented house in Porto Cervo. By that time he had finished the screenplay and it was time for Ann to deliver on her promise to introduce him to David Ladera and ask him to read his screenplay. Ann spent several days in Paris ordering clothes for the winter and then went on to Ireland, where she arrived at David Ladera's Georgian house several days ahead of Paul. He was due to arrive in time for dinner, and a car had been dispatched to the airport in Dublin to bring him back to Roscommon.

There had been a change in their relationship since the visit of Alice and Felicity. For the first time since they had been together, he felt like a hustler. There had been no fight afterward. He had not called her on the way she had treated him. He wanted so much to meet and possibly work for the famous director that he put aside his feelings and went along as if nothing had changed.

But it had. The sexual part of their lives, so fulfilling in the beginning, had become strained. She, fearing to lose him, put more and more demands on him, barking out sexual orders. Often she could not reach her satisfaction, as he could, and she blamed him for selfishness in the sexual act.

She looked forward to the sojourn in Ireland with mixed feelings. She had read his screenplay and thought it was good. It occurred to her that if Ladera liked his work and hired him, Paul might leave her, not needing her anymore.

On the other hand, she thought that his gratitude to her for arranging the meeting might be so overwhelming that they could return to the bliss of the first weeks of their meeting.

Sardinia was shrouded with fog on the morning that Paul was to leave, and the plane for Milan was hours late in taking off. When finally he arrived in Milan, he had missed the plane for London, and when he finally got to London, he had missed the plane for Dublin. When he got to Dublin, the driver who was sent to meet him had returned to Roscommon, and he had to hire a car to make the hour-and-a-half drive through a strange countryside. He drove through the gates of the Ladera house at two in the morning.

David Ladera, who had started in Hollywood and had achieved an international reputation, both as a film director and as a womanizer, was going up the stairs to bed as Paul entered the front door. "There are sandwiches out in the dining room, and several bottles of wine," he called down. "I'm sorry I can't stay down to greet you, but I've had too much to drink. You and I will talk in the morning."

"Thank you, sir," replied Paul at the bottom of the stairs.

"Your room is next to Ann's down that corridor and to the left, and the bathroom that you will use is outside your door, turn left, turn right, and it's the second door. 'Night."

Paul had not eaten for hours and went into the dining room. He poured himself a glass of red wine and drank it down and ate several chicken sandwiches and drank another glass of wine. He was weary from the long day. Carrying the bottle of red wine with him, he took his bag upstairs. A butler, in a robe and slippers, appeared to show him the way and help him and told him again the directions to the bathroom.

"Would you like me to unpack for you, sir?" asked the butler.

"Oh, no, thank you very much," he replied. "I'm going straight to sleep. I'm exhausted. I'll unpack in the morning." He pulled off his clothes down to his shirt and shorts and flopped on the bed. Within seconds he was asleep.

The door to the adjoining bedroom opened, and Ann entered, dressed in a satin-and-lace nightgown and matching negligee. Her perfume preceded her. She was dressed for reunion and seduction. It surprised her to see that he was asleep. She went to his bed and sat down on the mattress beside him and began to shake him.

"Paulie, Paulie, wake up," she said. Paul hated to be called Paulie. "Wake up."

"Hi," he answered sleepily.

"You were just going to go to sleep and not bother to say hello to me?" she asked.

"It was a terrible day, Annie. The plane was late leaving Sardinia, and I missed my connection in Milan, and then I missed my connection in London, and the driver left before I got to Dublin, and I had to find my own way here in the dark in a rented car, and I caved in."

"You weren't going to come in and say hello to me?" she asked again.

"I thought you'd be asleep," he answered.

"You knew I wouldn't be asleep. You knew I'd be waiting for you."

"I saw Ladera. He said we'd talk in the morning."

"Mr. Ladera," she corrected him.

"Mr. Ladera, I mean."

Her hands began to rub the inside of his thighs, starting at his knees and working upward. Eyes closed still in near sleep, he shifted position. She slid her fingers under his shorts and began to massage his flaccid penis.

"Come on, Annie. I don't feel like it. It's been a terrible day. I'm tired and dirty and I need a bath and I need some sleep. Let's wait till tomorrow."

"I like the smell of a man's sweat," she answered, oblivious of his protestations. She unbuttoned his shirt and began to kiss his chest, at the same time pulling down his undershorts.

"How about that I don't feel like doing this?" he asked angrily.

"Well, start to feel like it," she answered in the same tone of voice. She could hear herself speak as she had sometimes spoken to Billy Grenville.

"What the hell am I? Your wind-up dildo?" He sat up in the bed and picked up the red wine from the bedside table and drank it from the bottle, gulp after gulp.

"You drink too much," she said.

He looked at her. She saw in his eyes the look of Billy Grenville in the final months of their marriage. He placed the bottle back on the table, turned away from her, and started to go back to sleep, lying on his stomach.

He could hear her get off the bed. He assumed that she was returning to her adjoining room. He could not see that she was removing the belt from the trousers that he had dropped on the floor. With all her strength she whipped the leather belt, straplike, across his exposed buttocks.

Paul leaped from the bed. He saw on her face the look of a woman who could kill.

"You want to get fucked that bad, cunt?" he lashed out at her, hate in his voice. He grabbed her, forced her against the side of the bed, and pushed his now erect penis into her, ripping her nightgown. In four brutal thrusts, the act was complete. Shamed, he withdrew from her. In silence, they retreated to their separate beds.

PAUL AWAKENED earlier than he had intended, considering the lateness of the hour that he had finally closed his eyes for rest. He had, furthermore, a red-wine hangover. His tongue was dry. His breath was foul, even to him. His head throbbed. His stomach, he knew, was about to erupt. He remembered being told on his arrival the night before that the bathroom for this room was down the hall to the left, and then turn down a corridor to the left, or maybe the right, and it was the first door, or maybe the second.

He knew he was going to be sick. He sat up in the bed. The Irish linens were wet and wrinkled from sweat and angry sleep. Goose feathers rose from the pillows. Around him, he was aware, were bits and pieces of paper, ripped or cut, like large confetti, but he did not linger to examine them. His eye spied a basin and pitcher for morning ablutions, and he bolted from the bed toward them. Naked, he vomited, poured cold water over his head, and vomited again, sometimes missing the flowered basin. He pulled on a robe. He now had to get down the hall to the bathroom for further relief.

At the door, when he opened it, was the butler from the night before, holding a cup of tea on a small silver tray. The cord from his robe was missing, and he held the robe together with one hand, while covering his mouth with the other.

"Which way is the bathroom?" he asked.

The butler directed him to the left and then to the right and to the second door.

"I'm afraid I've made rather a mess in there," Paul said as he retreated down the hall to the bathroom. When he returned some minutes later, the offending basin had been removed, and in the center of the room was his traveling bag, with his clothes in it, neatly packed. Laid out for him was a clean shirt, tie, undershorts, socks, flannels, and jacket.

"The car is ready, sir," said the butler.

"For what?" asked Paul.

"Mrs. Grenville has informed me that your plans have changed and that you will be leaving," he answered.

"Oh," said Paul.

"The train for Dublin leaves at nine-oh-five from Roscommon, which is about a twenty-five-minute drive from here," continued the butler, carrying out his orders in the domestic drama without wishing to play a part in it.

"Where is Mrs. Grenville?" he asked.

"She is sleeping, sir, and asked not to be disturbed."

"And Mr. Ladera? He was to meet with me this morning to discuss my screenplay."

"Mr. Ladera has gone hunting, sir."

"And will be back when?"

"For tea."

The realization came to Paul Cooper that he had been dismissed, like one of the maids that Ann hired and fired in such quick succession.

"I'll carry your bag down, sir, and cook will pack some biscuits for you to eat in the car."

"Thank you," said Paul. He sat back on the edge of the bed to pull on his socks. Around him he became aware again of pieces of paper strewn on the bed, thousands of pieces. He picked up a handful of them. It was a moment before he realized that they were his screenplay, ripped in spite for services not satisfactorily performed.

WHEN DIANTHA and Third returned to the United States, during vacations, they always stayed with their grandmother if their mother remained behind in Europe. They looked like Grenvilles; Alice was pleased about that. They spoke French as well as they spoke English, but they had become strangers in the land of their birth, and the friends they had left behind had found new friends to replace them. Nearly everyone remarked on how quiet they were. Their grandmother and their aunts, with cousins in tow, took them to films and plays, and arranged for them to attend dances and parties in New York and Newport for teen-agers home from boarding schools for the holidays.

They felt, in New York and on the North Shore, that people, outside the family, meeting them, always reacted to their name and the turbulent history of their parents. "Yes, yes, I'm the one who was in the house on the night my mother killed my father," screamed Third at a young girl who had asked him if he was related to the Grenvilles who used to live in Oyster Bay, and pink cheeks of embarrassment followed.

He did not do well in school and had to repeat a year. He said he had no wish to go to college. Asked what he wanted to do in life, he invariably replied that he wanted to become a carpenter. Ann scoffed at the notion, but his grandmother, as a gift, put in a woodworking shop in the basement of her house, and Third spent more and more time there, working on boxes and miniature furniture.

Throughout their adolescence both Diantha and Third saw doctors, in Switzerland when they were there, in New York when they were there. The person with whom they never discussed what they were feeling was their mother. As they grew older and more independent, they spent less and less time where she was. She wondered often what they had heard that night their father died. Anna Gorman, the cook, who had been with them on the night their father died, had sworn to the police and the grand jury that she had heard nothing. Ann did not allow herself to think that Anna Gorman had been paid off for her silence. She knew only that Anna was no longer in her employ when she returned from the hospital. Once she tried to find her. Anna Gorman had retired at an early age and lived in a sunny apartment in Queens, but Ann could not bring herself to enter the apartment when she got there.

Third did not live to take his mother dancing, as she always promised him he would. People said about Third Grenville that his leap was incredibly considerate. He landed on no one. He damaged nothing. In the early morning he walked out the window of the room his father had grown up in on the fifth floor of his grandmother's house off Fifth Avenue.

"I INTEND TO sell the house, and I intend to sell everything in it, right down to the glasses in the cupboards," said Alice Grenville to Cordelia.

"But why?"

"I want to move to a hotel. I want to entertain in restaurants. I want to change my entire way of life."

NO LONGER attractive, Ann avoided her reflection in shop windows to keep the knowledge from herself. Her skin was pulled tightly on her thin face, the tiny scars visible where her earlobes had been made smaller, and other scars below where the skin had been tightened. The harsh lights of her dressing-table mirror were changed to pink, and in her boudoir she saw herself as she once was. She imagined herself still a seductress. Man-hungry, she prowled parties for prey. Boys came, boys went. Terminating before she was terminated, she imagined herself in charge of her romantic life.

"I HATE THAT COAT," said Ann. "You look like Ann Sheridan in *They Drive by Night.*"

"All your references are before my time," replied Diantha.

"It's the belt that's so awful, and the way you have the collar turned up in the back," Ann went on.

"I'll take it off," said Diantha, unbelting the coat, letting it slide off her shoulders, placing it on the foot of her mother's bed.

"Please don't place it on the foot of my bed. I can't bear to have anything on the foot of my bed."

"Aren't we off to a nice start," said Diantha. She sat awkwardly whenever she was with her mother, which was not often, her feet circled around the rungs of the French chair.

"You look mussed. Those ink-stained fingers. When did you wash your hair last?"

"Stop it! I'm only here because you called me and said that you were in trouble. This is not a social call. Now what's the matter? I have a date, and I can't stay long."

"Please God, not that assistant political science professor from NYU, with the hairy hands. I thought you were over your despising-the-rich period."

"No, Mother. I'm going to Grand'mère's for dinner," replied Diantha.

"Oh." Outside, on Fifth Avenue, a siren screamed. Ann disguised the shiver that passed through her. She had never told anyone that every time she heard a siren she shivered with fear that they—the police, the law—were coming to take her away.

Diantha watched her mother. "Why were you so hysterical on the telephone?"

"The maid's gone."

"So what else is new? Did she quit, or did you fire her?"

"Quit."

"What did you do this time? Accuse her of stealing? Or did she iron creases into your sheets, and you told her how stupid she was? I don't even know their names anymore, Mother, they come and go so quick in this house."

"Will you call the agency tomorrow and get me someone else?"

"Will *I* call the agency and get you someone else? No. Did it ever occur to you that it's *you,* not the maids, and the cooks, and the chauffeurs, and the nannies?"

"I'm sick."

"I won't do it. Get that Prince Tchelitchew you're always talking about. Let him hire you a new maid."

"His great-grandfather killed Rasputin."

"At least you have something in common."

Diantha stood up. "I'm sorry I said that, Mother. It was uncalled for. It just came out."

Her mother turned her head away.

"I don't suppose there's anything in that pharmacy by the side of your bed so simple as an aspirin?" asked Diantha. A memory of times past struck both of them at the same time, and they looked at each other.

"There's a Percodan, but it seems a shame to waste that on pain."

"I don't want a Percodan."

"Your hair's too short."

"I like it like that."

"Are you a dyke?"

"I might have known I could count on you to reduce my life to a four-letter word, Mother," said Diantha, letting contempt pour over the word "Mother."

"You are, aren't you?" asked Ann. "It's what I always suspected. Back at Château Brillantmont, that Greek girl in your class, what was her name, the one who didn't shave her armpits in Sardinia that summer. Oh, I know all about her. I asked Ari and Stavros who she was. Not even one of the good Greeks. Salad oil, or something like that. I mean, they roared with laughter about her family."

"The next time you have one of your emergencies, don't call me. I don't want to hear from you again. I like living in Seattle. I like running a bookstore. I like never having anyone say to me, 'Aren't you the one whose mother killed your father?' No one ever heard of us out in Seattle, and if people mispronounce my name and call me Granville, I never even correct them, because I know it's me they're responding to, not the name of my illustrious family."

"You can't go back."

"Oh, yes I can. That's why I'm having my farewell dinner with Grand'mère."

"I won't leave you my money if you go. It won't be easy for you."

"That's what it's all about with you, isn't it, Mother, the money? You know, I don't care about your money, but one of the things Grand'mère had me do while I was here was see old Mr. Mendenhall down at the bank, and you don't have any say over your money. It's only on loan to you for as long as you live. It's not yours to give. My father saw to that. He was willing to have it taxed doubly and triply in order not to give you any rights over the disposition of it."

"Is that what Mr. Mendenhall told you?"

"I'm going to be the richest one of anybody. I'm going to have your money, and Third's money, and Granny's money, when she dies. I'm going to be worth millions. I'm going to be one of the richest girls of my generation."

"I never saw this side to you before, Diantha."

"I may have my father's looks, but I'm as tough as my mother when pushed to the edge, and you have pushed me to the edge. Don't you think at some point in our lives, you owed us an explanation, Third and me, about what happened? Not your story, your famous story from which you never veered, not for your whole life, but what happened, what really happened that night? I was eleven years old, remember. I wasn't any babe in arms. We heard you fighting with Daddy that night. Do you ever think about it? Do you ever dream about it? Do you ever run it over in your mind and relive those minutes when you picked up the shotgun and killed him?"

"Is that what you've always thought about me?"

"Always."

"And Third, too?"

"And Third, too."

"Why didn't Third ever say anything to me?"

"He did. He jumped out a window. That was his statement to you. He sent you a Mother's Day card. It was Mother's Day, you know, the day he jumped. I often wondered if you had noticed."

"Dear God."

"You never talked to us about anything. You had a mother and a father and aunts and a life in Kansas, and you never told us a word about that part of your life, and we were your children. We wouldn't have snubbed you. You never talked about your past for all the years we lived in your houses and hotel suites as your children. All we ever heard about was Jaime, and Pablo, and Paul, and Vere, and Gianni, and Gunther, and—"

"Don't leave me, Diantha. I'm afraid to be alone. Jaime's gone. Jaime left me. He opened up my purse and took all the money out and called me some terrible names and left. He said I was old."

"I have to go. I can't be late for my grandmother. Goodbye, Mother."

PART FIVE

FOR SEVERAL LONG moments I stood there staring after the retreating figure of Ann Grenville. Was this, I wondered, the point of my trip? Nowadays, with all the legal technicalities available to criminal offenders, the guilty walk among us, exonerated, and a few I could mention are lionized as social catches by some of the same people who slammed their doors in the face of Ann Grenville nearly three decades ago.

My story began to form. I am the receptacle of other people's secrets and have long understood there is no point in having a secret if you make a secret of it. Yes, she warned me off her, but I sensed that in time, the next day, or the next, she would return to her post by the ship's rail to stare at the coastline. She had started to talk, and then withdrew, but she would come again, and I would be there.

IT WAS HER Fracas perfume I smelled before I realized she was standing beside me, her elbows leaning on the rail. She made no sign of greeting.

"Do you suppose that's Seattle we're passing?" she asked.

"Yes," I replied.

"My daughter, Diantha, lives there. She runs a bookshop, of all things. I once longed for her to be a figure in social life, but she, wise girl, wanted no part of it. We are—what is the right word to use?—estranged."

"How many children do you have?" I asked, knowing perfectly well how many children she had.

She hesitated a moment, eyeing me deeply. "Why is it I never trusted you, Basil?"

"Too much alike, maybe," I offered for an explanation.

"I think I recognize in you the things I dislike about myself," she said.

"That's what I mean," I answered.

"I had two children, and one of them is dead, as you probably know."

"Yes, yes, I had heard."

"It's hard when people ask how many children I have. I never know whether to say 'Two, and one is dead,' or just 'One.' If I say 'One,' I feel guilty about poor Third, but when I say 'Two, and one is dead,' I have to explain."

"I'm sorry."

"I am, too. I was a lousy mother. In many ways I was frightened of my kids when they were little. They were so incredibly upper class. They were Grenvilles, and I was always an outsider with the Grenvilles."

"I'm sure your kids didn't feel that."

"That's what my daughter told me the last time I saw her."

"Was it an illness?"

"No."

"An accident?"

"No. It was a suicide. I spent several years saying it was an accident, that his jump out the fifth-floor window of his grandmother's house was a fall. But it wasn't. Heirs to ten million dollars don't wash their own windows, especially at five o'clock in the morning, in a house filled with servants. But that is what I insisted happened, and if I was able to convince people of that, then I believed it was so."

"Perhaps it was so," I said.

She shook her head slowly. "There was a note, written on a Mother's Day card. Did I tell you it was Mother's Day when he jumped?"

I was moved by her admission. "Terrible things have happened to you," I said.

"Sometimes I think I make terrible things happen," she replied quietly.

"Ann," I said, matching her quietness, my business unfinished. "Esme Bland told Jeanne Twombley you were married before Billy married you, and you'd never gotten a divorce."

What was it I read on her face at that moment? Shock? Fear? Or relief? "Perhaps that's why Esme Bland is in the loony bin today," she answered, as if it were an answer.

"Is it true, Ann?" I persisted, but she had turned away.

I longed for a drink. Cruise festivities were in high gear in the public rooms of the old ship. I pretended I did not see Mr. Shortell from Tacoma waving to me to join his table of merrymakers in party hats. In my stateroom were dozens of the miniature bottles of Scotch whiskey that I had taken to stuffing my pockets with in recent years, for bathroom gulps during editorial meetings, and I repaired there. One. Two. Three. I gulped them down and reached for one of the lined yellow tablets by my bunk and took a sharpened soft-lead pencil from a drawer and began to write in my neat precise hand.

The telephone rang. It was long after midnight. I knew before I picked up the telephone that it was going to be her. "Hello?"

"Basil?"

"Hi."

"It's Ann Grenville."

"I know."

"There's something that's bothering me that I've got to get off my chest," she said.

"What's that?"

"Are you writing down everything I was saying to you?"

"Of course not," I replied, rising from my bunk, letting go of both tablet and pencil.

"This is my life. These are my secrets. It would be very painful for me," she said, discounting my reply. "I'll sue you if you betray me."

"I'm not," I repeated.

"Basil?"

"Yes?"

"I don't want to walk into that bar alone with all those people in funny hats," she said.

"Want me to walk in with you?" I asked.

"Yes."

"Five minutes?"

"Yes."

You see, at some subliminal level of her, she was setting it up for me to do what she said she did not want me to do. That was the night I decided to write her story.

She did not want the solitude of the deck. She wanted to be where the crowd was, but not part of the crowd. There was but one table left in the noisy bar, and we made our way to it. I ordered a bottle of wine, and for a moment or two we watched the revelers on the dance floor.

"I always wanted to dance with you," I confessed to her.

"Now's not your chance," she replied, but she was pleased to have been asked.

"Once I saw you dancing at the Stork Club, and you sang the lyrics of the song into the ear of the man you were dancing with, and I thought to myself, 'This is the reason I came to New York, to see people like this.' "

"That was probably Billy," she answered, smiling. "He used to love it when I did that."

The wine came. I poured for us both. She drank a glass in a few swallows, and I poured her another.

"I couldn't sleep," she said finally. She did not raise her voice to combat the din of the room. Instead she turned her head and leaned toward me, her chin on her hand, so that she talked directly into my ear. "You're the first person who ever said that to me, what you said about Esme Bland."

"Was it true?"

"Do many people know that? Is it a thing that's said about me, that I was married before Billy Grenville and not divorced?"

"I don't think so. No one believed Esme," I said.

"She's in the bins, Esme," said Ann.

"So you said."

"Funny that she would have known."

"Is it true?"

"Billy bought an airplane a week before he died. The plant where they built the plane was in the very same little town in southwest Kansas where I was born and where I fled from when I was seventeen and had returned to only once, when I went home to bury my mother. It was just a coincidence. I didn't know until the night he died that that was where he'd gone to buy the plane."

"And that's where Billy found out?"

"He said at the factory that he thought his wife was from that town, but no one remembered me, which is the way I always wanted it. But one of the men at the aircraft plant called Billy later at the motel where he was staying and they went out for dinner in a Chinese restaurant, and he told Billy that if his wife's name was Urse Mertens, he was married to me."

I reached for the bottle of wine. She placed her fingers over the glass to tell me that she cared for no more, but I poured anyway, over her fingers, between her fingers, filling her glass again, and all the time she went on talking, so absorbed was she in releasing her secrets, even licking her wine-coated fingers before drying them on a cocktail napkin, as if she had not noticed.

"His name was Veblen. Billy Bob Veblen. I was only married to him for two days, and he went off to join the Marines. Then I left Kansas City for New York to do an audition for George White's Scandals, which I didn't get, but I never went back. I changed my name and started a career in clubs. I always intended to get a divorce one day, but I didn't do anything about it, and then I met Billy Grenville, and everything happened so quickly."

"I always heard you met and married in ten days," I said, but she seemed not to have heard me and proceeded with her story at her own pace as the noise level in the ship's bar grew louder and louder.

"There's no way to describe to you what it was like, the romance, the glamour of it, being pursued by a young man like Billy Grenville. It was like being in the midst of a drama, and nothing, absolutely nothing, was going to mar that chance for me, to make a marriage like that. The reason he fell so madly in love with me—and make no mistake about that, he did fall madly in love with me, in a way that he could never have fallen madly in love with any of the ladies of his own circle—was that I saved him from what he most deeply feared about himself."

"What was that?" I asked.

"You of all people ought to be able to figure that one out, Basil. It happened in a lot of those families. And he wasn't going to let me go. His family hated me. Oh, they were polite and courteous, as they always are, even to this day, but I was not what they had in mind for their darling Junior, which is what they called him in those days. When they saw he was determined, his mother tried to talk him into waiting until after the war, but if we had done that, it never would have happened. I knew I could only marry him if it happened quickly. One more obstacle besides the fact that I was a show girl, like having to get a divorce first, or even being divorced, and I would have lost him, and I took the chance."

"Go on," I urged quietly, as she seemed to falter.

"I used to live in horror that what happened would happen, that Billy would someday find out, but when it didn't, I gradually forgot about it, that first marriage, and as the years went by it became to me like a thing that never happened. And then about six months before the acc—before Billy was killed, I saw my first husband in the coffee shop of the Astor Hotel and pretended I didn't know who he was. It was like an omen of what was going to happen."

"What was he doing there?"

"He was on a convention for the aircraft plant where Billy later bought his plane," she said. "It was all in the works, I guess. I'll say this for Billy. He was always a gentleman. He asked me for a divorce on the way to Edith Bleeker's party that night, and I turned him down flat, saying he knew my price, which was exactly half of all his money, knowing he'd never agree to that. I still thought I had the upper hand. It wasn't until we got home from Edith's party, where I had made an ass out of myself over a phone call Billy got, that he told me he'd met my first husband and that I was still married to him when we were married. He called me Mrs. Veblen. It was like the bottom fell out of my life. It meant that he didn't even have to leave me with sufficient financial provision. I panicked, you see. I totally panicked. The only thing I could think of was the newspapers saying that I was a bigamist. He went in to take a shower, and I went down to the gun room and got the gun. There was that prowler, you remember. Fortuituous, that prowler. Billy had said, about the prowler, that we would shoot first and ask questions later. I screamed, as if the prowler were in the house, and Billy came charging in and I fired twice and killed him. I didn't know what I'd done until after I'd done it, and then it was too late."

She pulled back from me, reached in her bag, and got out a cigarette. While I reached for a match, she lit her own cigarette, inhaled deeply, and exhaled as she quietly said, "People say I got away with it. Ha. Do you call this getting away with it? Sometimes I wonder if prison wouldn't have been better."

I didn't answer, nor did she expect me to. "It was madness what I did," she went on. "I thought his family would turn on me, publicly disavow me. I thought the shooting would be proof positive to them that I was everything they ever thought I was, and worse.

"But no. They publicly embraced me, for all the world to see. They stood by me. They said they believed me. They said they grieved for me.

"And they did. Publicly. Privately was something else. But you see, Basil, Alice Grenville didn't do it for me. She did it for my children. For the Grenville name.

"And what I have come to realize over the years is that Billy would have done the same thing. He would never have denounced me as a bigamist at the time of our marriage. Whatever else he was, he was a gentleman, and he wouldn't have done that to his children. He would have let me divorce him on ordinary grounds and probably have taken good care of me. It's what I think about."

She began to look about for her bag and cigarettes and made preparations for leaving. "I used to fear my past coming out, the secrets of my humble origins, about which I was then ashamed, but am no longer. Then all my secrets came out, after the shooting, and it didn't matter anymore." She stood up. "Be kind to me, Basil," she said and walked out.

When I awakened the next morning, late and hungover, I noticed a note had been slipped under my door. It said simply, "Dear Basil: By the time you receive this, I will have disembarked. I am flying from Fairbanks directly back to New York. Love, Ann Grenville."

INSIDE THE house in Oyster Bay, the real estate woman, Mrs. Pratt, was showing the house to one of the new buyers, a priest named Father Kiley. "It is no more than a meter," she said. She meant the distance between what had once been the bedrooms of Billy and Ann Grenville. She meant that however long a meter was, it was too short a distance not to be able to distinguish that the figure one shot at was one's husband. She meant that it was unlikely, at such a short distance, to mistake one's naked husband for a prowler. But she said none of these things, only that it was no more than a meter between their two rooms. To this small group of priests who would soon be occupying the country home that had once been called the Playhouse, its murderous history that had frightened off potential purchasers for years was the thing that had made it financially feasible for them.

Outside, Ann Grenville, there for a last look at the closed-up structure, said to the young priest, Father Hodiac, who walked about the untended grounds with her, "I've always had a passion for this house. I've always felt about it as a lover feels." Tears welled up in her eyes but did not fall. "I came here one night to a dance, and I said to Billy Grenville, 'This is the house where we must live.' It wasn't even for sale, but we bought it anyway, as if it were meant for us to have it. A pity you never saw my garden. We loved it here, all of us. Odd that it should have been the scene where everything ended."

She walked away from him. Her hands were in the pockets of her coat. She was having, Father Hodiac supposed, a private moment about her smashed life, and he did not follow her. Instead he sat on a wooden garden bench in the chilled comfort of the October sun and surveyed the overgrown flower beds of the Grenvilles' Playhouse. In time she sat beside him on the bench.

"Nice," he said.

"What?"

"These garden benches."

"I bought those in England. They used to be at Kingswood Castle, near Salisbury. You can have them."

"Oh, no, no, Mrs. Grenville."

"What in the world am I going to do with them?"

"They're beautiful."

"I'd like you to have them."

"It's odd about you, Mrs. Grenville," said Father Hodiac.

"What's odd?"

"You're much nicer than people say you are. If I had only hearsay to go on, I wouldn't have thought much of you."

"Perhaps you've caught me in a rare tender moment, Father Hodiac."

"Perhaps not."

"I tend to wear out my welcomes."

Through the woods came the sound of horses' hooves and laughter. They turned to look as two riders in tweed jackets, jodhpurs, and velvet riding hats cantered along a bridle path onto the grounds of the Grenville property.

"Those people are coming on your land," said Father Hodiac.

"People on horseback are allowed to ride across all the estates," she answered. "Some kind of North Shore communal courtesy borrowed from the English." She turned back, faced away from them. They, unaware they were being observed, rode closer to the house than they would have if it had been occupied.

"Oh, God, it's the Twombleys," said Ann.

"Who?" asked the priest.

"Alfred and Jeanne Twombley."

"Horseracing?"

She seemed to draw herself into her coat and sink down in the wooden bench as if she wanted them to ride by without seeing her.

"Ann," cried the woman, reining in her horse. "Is that you? Alfred, look, it's Ann Grenville."

"Ann," said Alfred Twombley.

Ann rose from the bench and walked across the lawn toward them. As she did, her stance and gait changed, and in a few steps across the hard ground her enormous style returned to her.

"Hello," she said to them.

"It's been years," said Jeanne.

"Forever," she answered.

"We were so sorry about Third."

"He was lovely, Third," answered Ann.

"Are you going to open the house again?" asked Alfred.

"I've sold it. I've just come to look at it for the last time," she answered.

"Not developers, I hope."

"Priests," she answered.

"Priests?"

"They're turning the music room into a chapel. Now your maids can walk through the woods to Mass, Alfred, and you won't have to get up and drive them into St. Gertrude's in Bayville every Sunday. It used to drive Billy mad, having to get up on Sundays and drive them over to St. Gertrude's, especially after a late night."

The mention of Billy's name in the conversation seemed to remind them of their relationship to each other, and a moment of silence ensued. Alfred turned back to his horse and got on.

"We're riding over to the Ebury's for tea," he said.

"Ann," said Jeanne Twombley suddenly. "Why don't you come with us? Neddie and Petal are going to be there, and then we're going to have dinner on trays back at our house. It's been so long, Ann. Come."

"Yes, do, Ann," said Alfred.

"I can't," Ann answered.

"Why?"

"I have to get back to the city. I have an engagement for dinner. Prince Tchelitchew. In fact, I should go. There's a four fifty-nine from Syosset."

They said their goodbyes.

"Could you drive me into the station, Father Hodiac?" she asked the young priest. "Or, if it's inconvenient, I could call a cab." She seemed in a hurry to be gone.

IN SYOSSET she sat in the front seat of the young priest's old Oldsmobile. When her train pulled into the station, she watched it from the car but made no attempt to get out to catch it.

"You're going to miss your train," he said to her.

"It doesn't matter," she answered. "I don't have any place to go, Father. I haven't had any place to go in a long time."

"What you said to the Twombleys. About a dinner engagement, with the prince."

"I didn't want them to think I was up for grabs on a Saturday night."

"Oh, Mrs. Grenville."

"Don't feel sorry for me. Tell me I'm a silly ass with a lot of false pride, but don't feel sorry for me."

"Okay. You're a silly ass with a lot of false pride."

"And don't get too familiar either," she said and smiled at the same time. In the dark October afternoon he thought he saw the trace of a tear in her eye. "There's not another train for fifty-five minutes," she said.

"I'll wait with you."

"Are you hungry?"

"Sure."

"There's a coffee shop over on Main Street. I'll buy you the blue plate special."

THE WAITRESS spilled the coffee into Ann Grenville's saucer. From a dispenser on the vinyl table Ann took a handful of paper napkins and dried out her saucer and the bottom of her cup and went on talking to the priest. "I acquired the look of belonging, and the manner of belonging, but I always felt like an outsider here on the North Shore. My life was a life of appearance. If I could make you believe what I was acting out, then I would have succeeded. No matter how many diamonds I put on my fingers or wrists, no matter how many Balenciaga dresses I hung in my closet, no matter how many signed French pieces I had in my various drawing rooms, no matter how many Impressionist paintings I had on my walls, I still felt I was going through life on a scholarship. Do you know anything about photography, Father?"

"A bit. Why?"

"I used to be pretty good at taking pictures. Someday I'll show you all my scrapbooks. I'm thinking of going into the business."

"What business?"

"Photography. Taking pictures professionally. There's a course they give in the extension program at NYU, and I signed up for that."

"You did?"

"Something to do. Not under my own name, of course. Ann Arden, I'm going to call myself. That's what I used to call myself before I married Billy Grenville. I've got a man coming to see me about turning Diantha's room—Diantha is my daughter—into a darkroom."

"I'd like to see that."

"If you come to town on priestly duties, give me a ring."

"I will."

"What kind of Catholic do you think I'd be, Father?"

"Are you thinking about that, too?"

"I don't know."

"We should talk. How's your week?"

"Wednesday afternoon there's an auction of French furniture from Madam Balsan's estate at Parke-Bernet. That's my week."

She began to gather up her things from the orange Naugahyde booth where they were sitting. "I think I hear my train."

"Are you going to be all right, Mrs. Grenville?"

"Yes, I'm going to be fine."

"I'll call you when I'm in town."

"Yes, do, Father. I'll take you to the Côte Basque for lunch. You'll like that. And don't forget about that outdoor furniture. It's yours. Goodbye."

She was gone.

MRS. GRENVILLE rarely missed an afternoon at the auctions. Although shunned by people she once knew, she found herself always welcome at Parke-Bernet, where, on even the most crowded days, a seat was found for her. Mrs. Grenville was a bidder and a buyer, and her knowledge of French furniture of the eighteenth century was respected by the authorities of the auction house. She enjoyed the afternoons there more than sitting in a movie house because she liked to watch the people and feel a part of the excitement. She understood how to bid. While less experienced buyers held up paddles with numbers on them, she simply nodded her head, almost imperceptibly, when the auctioneer looked at her.

"Sold to Mrs. Grenville," said the auctioneer.

People turned around to look at her. She rose to leave.

"Nicely priced, that pair of *bergères,*" said Mr. Crocus of Parke-Bernet, catching up with her at the entrance of the room. Mr. Crocus admired Mrs. Grenville.

"I need another gilt *bergère* chair like I need a hole in the head," replied Ann. They looked at each other quickly, in embarrassment, at her using the expression "hole in the head." "I'll have to do a bit of rearranging of furniture at home to make room. Perhaps you'd let me keep all this here for a bit until I decide where to put everything."

"Of course," said Mr. Crocus.

At the entrance on Madison Avenue she ran into Prince Tchelitchew, who was coming in as she was leaving. He kissed her hand.

"I'd hoped to get here," he said, "but I was detained at Petal Wilson's lunch."

"It's all right," replied Ann. She seemed muted, and he had expected anger.

"How was the auction?"

"Another auction."

"What did you buy?"

"Some things I don't need and don't have room for."

"You seem down."

"No, I'm fine."

"Shall I put you in a taxi?"

"I think I'll walk."

"Awfully cold."

"I don't mind."

"Shall I walk with you?"

"If you like."

She pulled her sable coat around her and started up Madison Avenue. After nine blocks they turned west toward Fifth Avenue.

"Isn't that the house where you used to live?" he asked suddenly.

"No," she said. "I never lived in that house."

"Why did I think that?"

"My mother-in-law lived in that house for fifty years. My husband grew up in that house. My son jumped out the window of that house. But, no, I never lived there."

"What is it now?"

"Something religious, I believe. If Billy hadn't died, we were supposed to have moved in there after his mother died. It was what his father wanted. It's a bad-luck house."

"Beautiful chandelier," he said, looking up into the windows of the vast gray stone house.

"Once that chandelier fell on the day before a ball and killed the man who was cleaning it, and the ball went on the next night, and no one mentioned that a man was killed."

"Dear."

"People say I'm tough, I know. But my mother-in-law's tougher. I don't get away with it, though, and she does. People think of her as a saint."

"Do you still see her?"

"Sometimes. Rarely now. For years, when I was living abroad, she would give a dinner for me every time I came back to visit New York, but that petered out."

"Here you are home."

"Thank you, Alexis. I'd ask you in, but I'm tired."

"Are you all right, Ann?"

"Yes, yes, I'm fine."

Inside she went through her mail on the hall table. In a manila envelope delivered by messenger was an advance copy of *Monsieur,* an elegant magazine with a literary following, containing a chapter from Basil Plant's long-awaited novel, intended to prove to his detractors that his writing career was neither blocked nor finished. An interior warning let her know that the contents of the magazine pertained to her. She could see Basil Plant's face on the ship to Alaska listening to her, studying her, writing in his mind as she knew he had been writing. Without removing her heavy sable coat, she walked into her overcrowded drawing room that she would have to rearrange to accommodate her afternoon's acquisitions, switched on a lamp, sat down in the center of a white damask sofa, and began to read the chapter called "Annie Get Your Gun."

*   *   *

SHE WAS STILL in her sable coat when she finished reading Basil Plant's story an hour later. For a long time she simply sat on her white damask sofa in her overcrowded drawing room, lit by a single lamp, and looked off into space. She had for years given the impression that she was impervious to the slights and barbs of others, because she thought that one day it would end, that her atonement would be recognized. But that was not to be. Basil's piece brought up the old story again, for a new generation to gloat over, like a wound that would never heal. Basil Plant had called her what no one had ever called her in print before. He had called her a murderess.

An immense weariness came over her. Rising, she looked at herself in a gilt mirror over the mantelpiece. In the semi-darkened room, she saw herself as she had once looked in her glamorous heyday as Mrs. William Grenville, Junior, and, face to face with herself, made her decision. For weeks she had been only going through the motions of life; death had been lingering in the outskirts of her mind. She was tired of running away and had run out of places to run away to. She took a bottle of vodka from her long-unused liquor cabinet. In the kitchen she put ice in a glass and more ice in a silver bowl.

Upstairs, she drew a bath and filled her tub with scented oil. She bathed with purpose and did not linger in the warm comforts of her sunken tub. She put fresh linen sheets on her bed. She wound her vermeil clock. From a drawer she took a satin-and-lace nightgown made for her in Paris, and a negligee to match, and put them on. She sat at her makeup table and made up her face and perfumed her body. She was glad that she had had her hair and nails done that day. She took off her sapphire and diamond rings and watched them reflected doubly in the mirrored top of her dressing table. She wanted those to be for Diantha.

A longing for her daughter overcame her. They had not spoken, nor been in contact, for several years. She worried how Basil Plant's story would affect Diantha, even in the faraway life she had picked for herself. She picked up the receiver and dialed her daughter in Seattle. The telephone rang and rang without a reply. She wondered if it was still the right number that she had. Then it was picked up.

"Miss Grenville's residence."

"Is she there?"

"This is the answering service. She's not here."

"Do you know where I can reach her?"

"No."

"Is she in Seattle, or is she traveling?"

"I don't know. Would you like to leave a message?"

"Tell her her mother called."

"Does she have a number where she can reach you?"

"Just give her the message. Thank you."

She hung up the telephone and then picked it up again and dialed the private number of her mother-in-law. On the day Alice Grenville realized people were deferring to her in bridge, because she was old, she had ceased to play except with her nurses, although it was one of the few things left that she enjoyed. Shortly thereafter, she had withdrawn to her apartment high in the Waldorf Towers and did not venture forth again. In time she stopped receiving and maintained contact only on the telephone. Only nurses, maids, daughters, and an occasional grandchild glimpsed her in her decline. Bertie Lightfoot, encountering old friends in restaurants or at parties, always said, "Phone Alice, and tell her about the party. She loves to hear everything. She's sharp as a tack still. It's just physically she's so unwell."

"Hello?" It was the voice of a very old woman.

"Alice?"

"Yes, who is it? Speak up."

"It's Ann."

"Oh, Ann. What is it?"

"I'm trying to locate Diantha. I wondered if you knew where she was."

"She lives in Seattle."

"I know, but she's not there, and I thought she might have been in touch with you. You see, I haven't seen her in quite a while, and I would like to talk to her."

"Is something the matter?"

"I need to talk to her."

"I'm playing bridge, Ann. Couldn't you call tomorrow?"

"Goodbye, Mère."

She had not called her mother-in-law Mère for many years, and Alice listened.

"I'm sorry," said Ann, very quietly.

"About what?" asked Alice.

Ann's answer could scarcely be heard. "About Billy," she said.

"You'll have to talk louder, Ann. You know I have trouble hearing. What are you sorry about?"

"I'm sorry that I disturbed your bridge game."

She sat down at her ormolu escritoire and began to write a letter to her daughter. "I want to set the record straight," she wrote, offering her estranged child the explanation she had never given her. From the bathroom cabinet she took a vial of Seconal pills and began, slowly, to swallow them with the iced vodka as she wrote.

She remembered that in her closet, hidden behind racks of clothes and furs, was the Salvador Dali portrait, and she wanted to look at it. The pills were starting to work, and she knew that she had to act quickly. She pulled the picture out and looked at it. The slash where she had once attacked it with a knife had been repaired, she could not remember how. She looked at the face of the beautiful young woman in whom the artist had seen evil. She wondered why she had not destroyed the picture. Weakened by her intake of pills, she had to return to her bed before she could replace the picture in its hiding place.

On her bed she picked up her telephone once more and dialed the number of her house in Oyster Bay. The telephone was immediately answered.

"Hello?"

"May I speak with Father Hodiac, please."

"This is Father Hodiac."

"This is Ann Grenville, Father."

"Oh, Mrs. Grenville." His voice sounded glad to hear her. "Has the man come to see you about your darkroom yet?"

"The darkroom? I don't understand."

"For your photography."

"Oh, no, not yet."

"Are you all right, Mrs. Grenville?"

"Yes." Her voice was weak. "Father?"

"Yes?"

"I'm not a Catholic."

"I know."

"Can you pray for someone who's not a Catholic?"

"Of course."

"Pray for me, Father."

"Of course."

"Do you like the house?"

"Oh, yes."

"Once I went upstairs in that house, after my husband's death, and I was standing in the bedroom where my children had slept when they were little. From downstairs, way on the other side of the house, in the rooms where my husband and I slept, I could hear people talking as clearly as if they were in the room next to me. Through some acoustical fluke in the architecture, their voices carried up through the walls. That was how I realized that my children had heard their father and me fight on the night that he was killed. It has always haunted me. If you should ever meet my daughter, Diantha, will you tell her that, Father? Will you tell her I'm sorry? Will you tell her I love her."

"Mrs. Grenville, are you all right?"

"Promise, Father."

"I promise."

"I have to go, Father."

As she lay there dying, her hair, makeup, dress, nails, all perfectly attended to, she wondered if anyone would come to her funeral. She wondered if Alice Grenville would bury her next to Billy and Third in the family plot. She even wondered about God, if there really was more afterward, if you really did meet up with those who had gone before. She looked forward to the possibility of encountering Billy Grenville.

THE OBITUARY said Ann Grenville had been found dead in her duplex apartment on upper Fifth Avenue. It said she was the widow of sportsman William Grenville, Junior, the mother of Diantha Grenville, the daughter-in-law of Alice Grenville, the philanthropist. It said she had a history of heart ailments. It said she was fifty-two years old. It said she had been cleared in 1955 of slaying her husband.

*   *   *

A LOT OF PEOPLE didn't see the obituary, and by the time the word was out, most of the ones who might have come had gone to the country for the weekend. The service took place at St. James' Episcopal Church, on Madison Avenue and Seventy-first Street, with not a single photographer or reporter in sight and barely thirty people in attendance. The thing that was on each person's mind was the other funeral of twenty years before, the companion piece to this, when one thousand people had crowded into the same church, with thousands more lined up outside to watch, and the flags of the Brook Club, the Union Club, the Knickerbocker Club, and the Racquet Club had flown at half-mast, in tribute. No flags flew today.

One who did see the obituary was Babette Van Degan. She became aware of the slow thump of her heartbeat against her ample breast. Tears welled in her eyes. If Ann Grenville had been hovering about, as some think the dead do, watching the reactions to her demise, she would have been surprised to see that Babette Van Degan, who had not figured importantly in the events of her life for many years, exhibited a remorse, in the privacy of her boudoir, greater than that of any of the principal players in her story. But then, for someone who created the role she played in life, as Ann Grenville had created her role, she very often misjudged the effects of her spectacular performance.

"They could have held this at the side altar," whispered Babette to the man beside her, Bertie Lightfoot, as they waited in a pew midway in the nearly empty church for the service to begin. "Surprised to see you here, Bertie," she added when he did not reply.

"I'm only here because of dear Alice," whispered Bertie Lightfoot in his precise and slightly sibilant voice, feeling it necessary to declare what branch of the grand Grenville family he was allied with. "Alice is my friend."

Babette looked sideways at Bertie Lightfoot and decided not to say what it was on her mind to say. Instead she took in his exquisitely groomed self and leaned closer toward him, squinting her eyes, knowing how uncomfortable it made him, and decided his eyes had been "done" and his reddish-tinged hair touched up.

"I didn't know Ann had a history of heart ailments," whispered Bertie in a conciliatory manner, anxious to have Babette's scrutiny of him terminated.

"She wasn't fifty-two either, darling, as you perfectly well know," answered Babette, pulling the voluminous folds of her mink coat around her. She was glad the weather had turned autumnal and brisk. She was sick to death of Indian summer. She felt less obese when she could lose herself in her furs.

"You mean she didn't have a history of heart ailments?" whispered Bertie again, a bit of excitement in his whisper, as it began to dawn on him what might have happened.

"Shhhh," said Babette, tapping the forefinger of her gloved hand against her lips, smearing it with lipstick the way she smeared her coffee cups with lipstick. "Your eyebrows are hitting what used to be your hairline."

"You don't mean . . . ?"

"There's your friend Alice coming in."

"She's such a wonderful woman," said Bertie. Whenever people mentioned Alice Grenville's name, they invariably said about her that she was a wonderful woman. Everyone knew what she had done for her daughter-in-law.

"Did you ever stop to think how many caskets she's followed down this aisle?" asked Babette.

Bertie Lightfoot looked back to where the eight pallbearers were lining up, four to a side, by the rose-covered casket in the rear of the church, and then back at Babette Van Degan again, questions churning within him.

Alice Grenville moved slowly down the aisle to the front pew of the church where she had worshiped most of her life. Tall, slender, erect of carriage, her only concession to her advanced years was the ivory-handled ebony cane that she carried. Black-veiled, formidable still, she evoked feelings of awe from the scattered assemblage. She stared straight ahead, but it was not lost on her how few were there, or even that Babette Van Degan, a name from the past, had grown enormously fat.

Beside Alice, but not assisting her as one assists the elderly, walked and sat her granddaughter Diantha Grenville. Hatless, plainly dressed, only just returned to New York for the occasion at hand, she was unmistakably her parents' daughter, although she possessed neither the beauty of Ann Grenville nor the aristocratic elegance of Billy Grenville. Like her grandmother, she was there to do her duty.

Old Dr. Kinsolving, who had performed at Grenville baptisms, weddings, and funerals for nearly forty years, was gone, of course, long since dead, and a new minister, without connections to the family, went about the religious duties: a few psalms; a hymn, some prayers for the dead; no personal words of farewell; the amenities observed, nothing more.

Alice Grenville looked up at the rose window that she had given in memory of the three William Grenvilles who had gone before her, her husband William, her son Billy, and her grandson Third. The late-morning sun shone through its stained glass, and rose and violet rays fell on her and Diantha, missing the casket of Ann Grenville.

Her doctor had forbidden her to make the long journey to Woodlawn Cemetery, but Alice overruled his decision, as she knew she was going to when she agreed to comply with it, and accompanied the small cortege to watch her daughter-in-law be buried in the Grenville plot, between her husband and her son. Never could it be said of Alice Grenville that she had failed to honor her beloved son's widow.

AFTERWARD, for the reception, the receiving of the loyal who had attended the service and journeyed to Woodlawn Cemetery, Diantha volunteered to take over the hostess obligations at her mother's apartment on Fifth Avenue, freeing her grandmother to return to her own home, her duties completed. Ann Grenville's apartment was shortly to be sold and its contents to be auctioned. James Crocus, of the Parke-Bernet auctioneer firm, was already at work—sorting, cataloguing, appraising—but he remained upstairs throughout.

Some of the guests knew each other. Some of them didn't. A few came out of curiosity, attracted by the negative glamour of Ann Grenville's story. There was Babette Van Degan, of course, and Bertie Lightfoot, and Kay Kay Somerset, and Prince Tchelitchew, who had been friends of Ann's at different points in her life. There was a Brazilian woman whose name none of them seemed to know. There was a crisp and tweedy Miss Petrie, who had once been a social secretary for Ann. And a few others. And me, Basil Plant, who looked and felt awkward, as if I should not have been there.

The entrance hall had a black-and-white marble floor and a graceful winding stairway. To the right was the drawing room where they gathered. It was a high-ceilinged gilt-and-white room, but dark. Antique furniture, in far too great abundance, filled it in multiple groupings in the French manner. She always had far too much furniture, far too many dresses, far too many fur coats, far too many pairs of shoes. It was one of the things about her that gave her away. Of course, there were very good pictures in gilt frames lit from above, and collections of jade and porcelain and Fabergé eggs. A cheerless fire beneath an elaborate mantelpiece did not draw the group to it. Among the disparate company there was a low-spirited intimacy, for the common bond of the occasion, that would evaporate at the completion of the rite.

"It was good of you to come," said Diantha, repeating the same words to each, but she remained a hostess on the outskirts of the gathering. Bottles and glasses crowded an ornate table, and she indicated self-service, with a wave of her hand, when the single servant, a butler from a catering agency, was hard pressed in pouring and passing and replenishing. No frou-frou about her, I noticed. She picked up a bellows and began to puff at the dying fire, coaxing it back, until the firelight danced on her face.

"Hello, Mrs. Van Degan," she said.

"Oh, Dolly, it's been so many years," said Babette.

"I'm not called Dolly anymore. It's Diantha. I always hated the name Dolly. I think my mother used to think that Dolly Grenville would look good in the society columns when I was a debutante, but I never became a debutante and my name never appears in columns."

"Where is it you live?" asked Babette.

"Seattle," replied Diantha.

"And what's that like?"

"Quite nice."

"Far from the madding crowd, I suppose?"

"The very point." She smiled for the first time. Her looks grew on you as she talked, I noticed, watching the exchange. There was a shyness about her that was appealing.

"You sounded like your mother when you said that," said Babette. Diantha rose from her kneeling position by the fire, placed her fingertips on the mantelpiece between delicate pieces of china on teakwood stands, and stared into the renewed fire. It occurred to me that she was not, perhaps, pleased with the comparison to her mother.

The Brazilian lady approached to speak to Diantha. Turning too abruptly to acknowledge her, she knocked over a piece of china, and it crashed to the hearth, smashing. People rushed forward to assist. "It doesn't matter," said Diantha, meaning it, waving away their concern for smashed porcelain. She is nothing like her mother, I thought. For her mother it would have been a tragic experience.

Some of the people she remembered, like Bertie Lightfoot, who had decorated all their houses. Others she didn't, like Kay Kay Somerset, except by name. A few she had never known, like Prince Tchelitchew, who had entered her mother's life after her own defection from it.

"You're meant to take anything you want to take," said Diantha, waving around the room, indicating other rooms, and upstairs, with her expressive hands. "As a memento, if you desire, of Mother. It is what she would have wanted."

"Except the Balenciaga dresses," piped in the crisp and tweedy Miss Petrie, a model of efficiency. She put her clipboard bearing lists and check marks and Polaroid photographs of paintings on one of a pair of glass-topped tables skirted in heavy velvet and covered with small objects of great value, each with its individual history. "The Balenciaga dresses are earmarked for the Fashion Institute."

"Except the Balenciaga dresses," repeated Diantha, not caring, but remembering other instructions. "And, oh yes, certain of the paintings. The Modigliani, the two Vuillards, the Fantan La Tour, the Manet of the prunes, the Cézanne drawings, and the Bonnard of the two women. They are going to the Metropolitan Museum. Other than that." She shrugged, or shuddered faintly, as she indicated her mother's possessions.

Racks of dresses and shoes and furs were out on display in the dining room, and the table was laden with pieces of silver. Babette Van Degan, the richest by far of the assembled group, took a sable coat. Bertie Lightfoot could not decide between two Fabergé eggs and was told he could take both. Kay Kay Somerset, who loathed Ann Grenville but liked to go to funerals, took the small vermeil clock that King Ludwig had given to the Empress Elizabeth. The Brazilian lady picked a pair of Georgian candlesticks, and Prince Tchelitchew decided upon, of all things, the Salvador Dali portrait of Ann that had so enraged her she had gone to court over it.

During the rummage-sale atmosphere, I sought out Miss Petrie. "There's that lovely little jade Chinese clock. Would you like that?" she asked, trying to be helpful.

"No, no, thank you," I said.

"There's the Allejo Vidal-Quadras drawings of her. And the René Bouché portrait's lovely, in the white evening dress."

"There's something I must know, Miss Petrie," I said.

"Luggage!" she cried, clapping her hands as if the solution had been found. "She had all the good kind of Vuitton, before the wrong sort of people took it up. Masses of it."

"Do you happen to know if she received a manila envelope I mailed her?"

"A manila envelope?"

"With a magazine inside."

"What magazine?"

"*Monsieur.*"

"I don't recall seeing it. Why?"

"Would you tell me something, Miss Petrie?" I looked around to make sure no one was listening.

"If I can."

"Did Mrs. Grenville commit suicide?"

"No." She clipped the word and closed her eyes, signifying a termination to the way the conversation had turned.

"It's vital that I know."

"The medical examiner's report isn't in yet."

"Did she leave a note?"

"Mrs. Grenville had a history of heart ailments."

"So I read."

A burst of thunder and the sound of rain against the curtained windows ended our conversation. People started to leave. When the door opened, fat round raindrops plopped on the sidewalk noisily.

"How about that photograph of Mrs. Grenville on safari in India, with the ten-foot tiger she shot?" suggested Miss Petrie, wanting to be rid of me. "She was so proud of that."

"No, thank you."

"There must be something, Mr. Plant."

"An umbrella," I answered.

"An umbrella?" repeated Miss Petrie.

"Yes," I said. "That's all I want."

My choice resulted in a single moment of intimacy, only a look, between myself and Diantha, as if she understood that, like her, I didn't want anything either in this stage set of props and dressing.

"Goodbye," I said to her.

She, not knowing me, made a vague gesture of farewell.

Upstairs, in a drawer of the escritoire that had once belonged to Marie Antoinette, James Crocus, the man from Parke-Bernet, found an advance copy of *Monsieur*. In the magazine was an unsealed envelope containing a letter on pale-blue stationery written in the hand he had come to recognize as Ann Grenville's. "Dear Diantha," the letter began. "I would like to set the record straight."

Propriety did not allow James Crocus to peer further, but, in replacing the pale-blue pages with shaking fingers in their matching envelope, he could not help but read these words: "When last we met, you said to me, 'Don't you think at some point in our lives you owed us an explanation, Third and me, about what happened, what really happened, that night?' Now Mr. Basil Plant has taken it upon himself to tell, not only you, but anyone with the price of a magazine what I promised your grandmother I would never tell. . . ."

YESTERDAY EVENING, dining at Le Cirque, at a less good table than I used to receive, I looked up from the desultory chatter of my companion, the former wife of a television personality, whom, in truth, I would not have had time for in the days when I was riding high, and peered straight into the relentless stare of Diantha Grenville. My face, already flushed from red wine, pinkened in distress, and our eyes locked for what seemed an eternity, every eon of which I hated. It was she, finally, who broke the look, and when her eyes discharged mine I saw in them the disdain of the two Mrs. Grenvilles, her grandmother Alice and her mother Ann.

Don't you think it's odd how, in death, people beatify for sainthood the most unlikely prospects? Bratsie Bleeker, for instance. Everyone knows that Bratsie was shot because he was screwing the wife of the foreman on his mother's plantation, but to have listened to Edith Bleeker, in the years after Bratsie's elimination, you would have thought that Bratsie died helping the Boat People. Such is the strange commanding power of death. It's the same thing with Diantha Grenville. She couldn't stand her mother. Everyone knows that. They didn't even speak for the last two years. But once her mother died, that all changed. She lives, they say, in rooms as overcrowded as her mother's, with all that French furniture that once belonged to famous ladies that her mother collected for so many years, and that Diantha always laughed at. Diantha tried to see me several times, but there was no point to that. Once I did see her, face to face, on Ninth Street, in the Village. I screamed at her, "Stop following me!" How was I to know her psychiatrist was in the same building that my psychiatrist was in?

No. No. No. I am not responsible for what happened to Ann Grenville. I don't care what that priest said that she telephoned at the last minute. Imagine Ann Grenville asking someone to pray for her! So likely. That's the trouble with those Catholic priests. They always think everyone wants to convert. Her trouble was that she had all those face lifts, and the wrinkles were still coming, and there were no longer men in attendance as there had been all her life, and without a man around, she couldn't function. "I always like to see a man's shoes in my closet." That was one of her lines.

There was nothing in my story that she had not told me herself, or that I had not heard firsthand from someone in her life. At least, almost all of it. I wanted not to let go of my theory. I didn't want it to turn out to be an accident, like she said, in that story she stuck to, like Bette Davis in *The Letter.*

Last night I dreamed of Alice Grenville. Her face was covered with mourning veils, but I was able to see through them to her. She was trying to tell me something, but I could not understand what it was that she was trying to tell me, except that she was, slowly, shaking her head, as if telling me that I had intruded into places where I did not belong. She was, I suppose, still protecting her daughter-in-law, from outsiders, like me, as if, finally, she, and the rest of them, had accepted Ann as one of them.

PEOPLE LIKE US

To Virginia Dunne Finley
with love

═══ PROLOGUE ═══

I T WAS HALF after one, as Ezzie Fenwick always called it, in his rococo
manner of speaking, on the Tuesday noon following Black Monday, and the
midday social frenzy at Clarence's was at its peak, with every table filled to
capacity, as if a financial catastrophe had not taken place. The bar, where those
who couldn't get tables waited patiently until after the personal friends of
Chick Jacoby, who owned Clarence's and ruled Clarence's with an iron hand,
lunched and lingered over decaffeinated espresso for as long as they wanted,
no matter how many people were waiting for tables, was three deep. Black
Monday. Black Monday. Black Monday. It was the topic of conversation everywhere that noon.

Ezzie Fenwick was securely seated in the window table, the very smart
restaurant's very best table, except on the rare occasions when the First Lady
came to lunch, or the King of Spain, and the Secret Service advised Chick
Jacoby that the window table was far too visible from the street, in times like
this, with mad people about, and insisted on moving them into the unfashion-
able second room, where Ezzie Fenwick would never be caught dead sitting.

The previous day the stock market had fallen five hundred and eight
points, and there was panic in the city, especially among the speculators and
the nouveau riche. There was also a smug satisfaction, only covertly expressed,
that the new billionaires of New York, whom no one had ever heard of six or
seven years ago, and who now seemed to control the financial, charitable, and
social life of the city, were publicly hurting. Herkie Saybrook reported to
Justine Altemus that one of the Zobel brothers, of Zobel Brothers, had been
seen weeping uncontrollably at his desk over his enormous losses, ha ha ha,
and might have to apply for a federal bail-out. Sims Lord reported that Milton
Sofiar, whose personal fortune had been depleted by between three hundred
and five hundred million dollars in a single day, had attempted suicide, although not seriously, and had been admitted to Harcourt Pavilion at Manhattan Hospital under an assumed name. The joke of the day was that the only
winner on Wall Street the day before was Elias Renthal, who was in prison and
barred from trading on the stock market forever, ha ha ha.

Ezzie Fenwick, who knew everything about everyone, was, as always, surrounded by adoring ladies in the very latest of fashion who laughed and
laughed each noon at his witty accounts of what had happened the night before
at whatever party he had attended. Ezzie reported to Lil Altemus, who was
born a Van Degan, and Matilda Clarke, who was the widow of Sweetzer
Clarke, and old Cora Mandell, who was society's favorite decorator, that he

had dined the night before at the billionaire Bulbenkians, and that Reza Bulbenkian gave an ultimatum to his new wife, Yvonne, that her spending spree simply had to stop. Yvonne Bulbenkian, he explained to Lil Altemus, who sometimes pretended she didn't know who people were, when she knew perfectly well who they were, used to be Yvonne Lupescu, when she was the constant companion of Constantine de Rham.

Reza Bulbenkian, who was the richest of all the New People, as the Old Guard called them, now that Elias Renthal was in prison, was smarting already from the bad publicity engendered by Yvonne's allowing their new limestone mansion on Park Avenue to be photographed by the *Times Sunday Magazine* in the same issue that featured a cover story on the homeless of New York. He begged Yvonne, even before the officers of his company begged him to beg her, to desist from her extravagant spending habits. How could he, he reasoned with her, fire a thousand of his employees, in an economic cutback, when Dolly De Longpre, the society columnist, was reporting in her column that Yvonne had spent a hundred and fifteen thousand dollars for a lynx coat and was planning to fly to Paris, on the company jet, for a private view of the new Lacroix collection, not to mention her noisy bidding at the auction of the Van Gogh irises, which had raised eyebrows, even before the crash.

"She's so frightfully common," said Matilda Clarke.

"The stories I could tell you about her," said Ezzie, his hand to his heart.

"Oh, tell, tell," said old Cora Mandell, who knew that Ezzie only needed to be urged a bit.

"Laurance knew all this was going to happen," said Lil Altemus, getting back to the crash, because it did not interest her to discuss people like the Bulbenkians. "Laurance has been saying for some time that the market was at an unsustainably high level." Lil Altemus quoted her brother, Laurance Van Degan, more than any other person in her life. She spoke with the ease of someone whose fortune had remained intact throughout the recent financial panic. "Laurance got out of the market a week ago, and, of course, I did too, and so did Justine."

Although they all liked to say that they had gotten out of the market in time, or that their losses were only on paper, as if they didn't matter, Rochelle Prud'homme, of Prud'homme Products, makers of cordless hairdryers, pulled Chick Jacoby aside to tell him that she was canceling her dinner dance for one hundred and forty people that she had booked the restaurant for several weeks earlier, and Chick Jacoby, who had already ordered fourteen pink moiré tablecloths and a hundred and forty pink moiré table napkins cut and hemmed by the seamstress around the corner, looked crestfallen. Jamesey Crocus, the specialist in fine French furniture, arrived at Clarence's for lunch with the distressing news that the auction of fine French furniture that morning at Sackville's had been a major bust, with most of the ormolu-encrusted pieces not meeting their reserve prices. And Maisie Verdurin, the art dealer, looked particularly peaked behind her smile, although she had as yet told no one that two of her most important clients had reneged that morning on Post-Impressionist pictures that they had agreed to buy.

On the very rare occasions that Ezzie Fenwick removed the dark glasses he invariably wore, you could see that he had one peculiar eye, rather like a poached egg in appearance, that looked off in a different direction entirely from his other eye, and it made you believe him when he said, as he often did, in his nasal voice that all his friends could imitate, "I never miss a trick. When I'm walking on Fifth Avenue, I can tell you what's happening on Madison and Park." So none of them was surprised when Ezzie interrupted Lil Altemus, who thought she had his full attention with all her inside information about the crash, to say, "My dears, you will not *believe* who just walked into this restaurant."

No one appreciated social drama the way Ezzie Fenwick did, and he was beside himself with joy when the reclusive Ruby Renthal, so long out of sight, and the just-released-from-prison Augustus Bailey walked into Clarence's at that moment, without a reservation. Ezzie's companions, and everyone else in the front part of Clarence's, where all the good people, as Ezzie called them, sat, turned to look at the curious duet who stood quietly just inside the door waiting for Chick Jacoby to hurry forward to greet them, albeit with furrowed brow. Chick Jacoby spent the latter part of each morning seating his luncheon tables with the artistic precision of a stage director, as aware as Ezzie of the ever-changing marital, financial, and social statuses of his regular customers, and last-minute changes, such as this one now, upset his sense of divine order. But it was, after all, Ruby Renthal who was upsetting the divine order, and the businessman behind the perfectionist in him knew that Dolly De Longpre would surely print that the unusual couple had lunched at Clarence's in her column the next morning if he seated them prominently and then got to the telephone in time to beat Dolly's deadline.

"For heaven's sake," said Chick, who could scowl and smile at the same time, pushing his round-rimmed glasses up on the bridge of his nose with his long forefinger.

"I'm a country lady these days, Chick," said Ruby. She spoke in the deep throaty voice that people used to remark on in the days when she was the most discussed woman in New York.

"She looks beautiful," said Cora Mandell, who had decorated the Renthals' famous apartment.

"Good-looking suit she has on," said Matilda Clarke.

Lil Altemus did not look at her. She could neither forget nor forgive that Elias Renthal's despicable financial manipulations had sullied the name of her brother, Laurance Van Degan, causing him to have to resign as the president of the Butterfield, which broke his heart, and she was sure caused the slight stroke that had moved his mouth to the side of his face.

"You watch," said Ezzie, in his nasal voice, to Lil and Matilda and Cora. "Chick will move Lord Biedermeier and Constantine de Rham over to his own table, as if he's giving them a big treat, and put Ruby and the jailbird there."

"What possessed us to come here?" asked Ruby.

"I haven't a clue," said Gus.

"Did you see Loelia?" asked Ruby. Ruby didn't have to tell Gus that Loelia Manchester used to be her best friend.

"And Matilda, and Lil, and Ezzie, and Cora," replied Gus. "And Lord Biedermeier and Constantine de Rham. Nothing seems to change."

"There was a time when I found all this very attractive," said Ruby, looking around, as she put her napkin in her lap, but not meeting anyone's eye. "There's Maisie Verdurin over there. I bet she's not selling many Post-Impressionist paintings today," said Ruby. Maisie Verdurin had probably never had a client who had made her as rich as Elias and Ruby Renthal had, with the accumulation of art they had collected.

"The first time I ever met you was at one of Maisie Verdurin's parties," said Gus.

"Oh, I remember. I was a nervous wreck that night. Dressed all wrong. Bright blue sequins. I bought it in Cleveland. Said *cunt* by mistake to Maisie, and she looked at me like she was thinking, Where did this girl come from? Then I ate the artichoke with a knife and fork."

Gus roared with laughter. "You sure changed quick."

Ruby smiled. She was the most elegant lady in the room.

"Was it awful in prison?" she asked.

Gus shrugged. "I knew when I did what I did I was going to go to prison. For me, it was just part of what my life was supposed to be. And I wrote a book there."

"Ezzie Fenwick always said you were going to write a book. He said you were always listening."

"For once Ezzie Fenwick was right."

1

EXCEPT FOR July and August, when everyone was away from the city, Maisie Verdurin, the art dealer, entertained in her Park Avenue apartment at large monthly dinner parties that had become so significant a part of the social life of New York that even people in the subways, at least those people in the subways who read the social columns, knew her name. In her interviews, as a hostess of repute, Maisie Verdurin often talked about society today being made up of people of accomplishment—the doers, she called them —and she had only words of contempt for the highly pedigreed few who rode through life on inherited wealth and social perfection. What she could not, simply could not, stand, ever, was to be bored, she often said, and the kind of people who came each month to sit on her sixty gilded ballroom chairs placed around eight tables—six tables of eight, two tables of six—set up in her drawing room, dining room, and library, were guaranteed to provide the kind of conversation that could never, ever, bore.

All the Cézannes, Van Goghs, Picassos, and Monets on her green moiré walls were for sale, and her dinners, which her detractors claimed she used as tax deductions, were a way of doing business and bringing together the political, financial, media, and literary figures of New York into her Rigaud-scented rooms.

Maisie infinitely preferred her own dinners to other people's dinners, but on the occasions she was asked back by the people she had invited, she sometimes called Augustus Bailey to escort her. Gus Bailey, a perennial spare man, obliged if he was free, and their conversations, in taxicabs on their way to and from the dinners, were always monopolized by Maisie, who rarely expressed any curiosity about Gus's life. She knew that he had a California past; she knew he had been something or other in films at one time; but neither California nor films interested her, in the way that Wall Street financiers did, or arbitrage traders, or real-estate entrepreneurs, whose first step on the road to riches was the acquisition of art, and she simply assumed Gus's agreement when she sometimes asked, "Aren't you glad to be away from California?" Gus was glad to be away from California, but not for the reasons Maisie supposed, which had mostly to do with what she called a singleness of theme, the movies, in dinner-table conversations "out there." Maisie also knew that Gus had a wife in California, with money, called, improbably, Peach, whom a lot of people knew, but that sort of information was of less interest to Maisie than the facts that Gus Bailey had a good dinner jacket, could keep up his end of the conversation, and didn't have to be whispered to by the butler to remove the finger bowl and doily before the *crème brûlée* could be served.

Maisie took Gus to Rochelle Prud'homme's party at Clarence's to launch her new line of cordless hairdryers, which Gus hadn't wanted to go to, but there he ran into his old friend Nestor Calder, a Brooklyn-born novelist of note, whose latest book, *Judas Was a Redhead,* was on the best-seller list.

"I liked your new book, Nestor," said Gus. "It'll make a terrific movie."

"They don't make movies of books anymore, Gus. They make mini-series of books. One of the studios is interested in making a mini-series of it," answered Nestor. "But they don't want me to write the screenplay, and I'll only sell it if I do write the screenplay."

"It seems to me I've heard that song before," said Gus.

Nestor laughed.

"How's it going, Gus?" asked Nestor Calder. They had once worked on a film together.

"Oh, okay," replied Gus. When anyone became personal with Gus Bailey, he replied in as few words as possible.

"How's Peach?" he asked.

"She's okay."

"Do you hear from her?"

"Sure."

"Give her my love, will you?"

"Sure."

"I'm going to be in L.A. next week to meet with the studio," said Nestor.

"Peach will want to hear from you," replied Gus.

Even after they were divorced, people who had been their friends still thought of Gus and Peach Bailey as a couple. Gus and Peach, people would say. "Do you remember that night at Gus and Peach's house in Malibu?" Or, "I still think that Gus and Peach's black-and-white dance was the prettiest party I've ever been to." When friends would meet Peach in California, they'd say to her, "How's Gus?" Or, if they ran into Gus in New York, they'd say, "How's Peach?" as if they were still one when they hadn't been one for nearly as many years as they had been.

"Are you involved with anyone, Gus?" asked Nestor.

"No."

"I'm not being snoopy, you know."

"I know."

"It's just that you never talk about yourself."

"I talked nonstop all through dinner."

"You talked nonstop all through dinner about all those people you write articles about."

Gus's friends, like Edwina and Nestor Calder, teased Gus because he went out to dinner every night. Some nights he went out with writers, like the Calders. Some nights he went out with movie people he knew from his Hollywood days. Some nights he went out with people in society, who called him up after they read the articles he wrote, or had their social secretaries call him up. "Mrs. Harcourt wondered if you could dine on Wednesday the twenty-first, black tie," they would say, in voices every bit as grand as those of the people for whom they telephoned. Mostly he listened to what his dinner partners had to say, for he was an excellent listener, giving them his full attention, whether they were witty or dull, intriguing or boring. It seemed to make no difference to him.

"What do you see in all those people you're always having dinner with?" asked Nestor.

"I like to listen to them talk," answered Gus.

"When does that guy get out of prison?" asked Nestor, changing the subject and lowering his voice.

Gus didn't have to say, "What guy?"

"Two years from now," he answered, quietly, wanting to withdraw from the direction the conversation was taking. There was a part of Gus's life that he did not discuss with the people with whom he spent his time, even a friend like Nestor Calder, who spanned both his old life and his new life.

Nestor whistled. "So soon, huh?"

"So soon."

"What was his name?"

Gus hesitated, as he always hesitated when the name came up. "Lefty Flint," he answered.

"Does it worry you?" asked Nestor.

"Yes," said Gus. "It worries Peach too."

"The *nerve* of that Edwina Calder," Maisie Verdurin said indignantly in the taxi on the way home. "She said she didn't like her seat at my last party, for the Vice President and his wife. Can you imagine?"

Gus, who liked Edwina Calder, didn't reply, but Maisie didn't expect a reply.

"She said that I never seat her at what she called one of the *good* tables, but that I always seated Nestor at one of the good tables. So I said to her, 'After all, Edwina, Nestor is a first-rate writer, and people want to talk to him.' "

"But Edwina is so beautiful," said Gus.

"Beautiful girls are not what my dinners are about," Maisie answered haughtily. "My dinners are about conversation. I think it's a waste of time at one of my dinners when a man flirts with a pretty girl, like Bernie Slatkin does for instance, when there are such marvelous things being said at every table. It's called missing the point of the evening."

Maisie always spoke possessively about her dinner parties, as creative output, in the way that a poet might speak about "my poems," or an author might speak about "my novels," and woe to anyone who displeased Maisie, for banishment from her list was the consequence. After each of her evenings, she dissected her guest list: who had pulled his weight in conversation, who hadn't, whom she had given too good a seat to, whom she had not given a good enough seat to, and who would never be invited back, no matter what.

One of the things about escorting Maisie Verdurin anywhere, Gus discovered, was that the end of the evening came at exactly the point where she was delivered back to the canopy in front of her apartment building and into the safekeeping of her doorman. There were no invitations upstairs for a nightcap, and all the things that implied. It was not ever necessary to follow her out of the taxi to her doorstep. With her sables wrapped tightly around her, she dashed for her own door with only an over-the-shoulder reminder of her next dinner.

"You're coming to me on the twenty-fourth, remember."

"Okay."

"You didn't write a thank-you note after my last dinner," she added.

"I sent you flowers instead," said Gus. "I felt I was beginning to repeat myself with my notes."

"Don't send me flowers," said Maisie. "I never go into my living room except on the nights I have parties. Just send me a note. I save them all and put them in a scrapbook."

Since Gus Bailey had moved to New York from Los Angeles and begun writing articles about famous people for a fashionable magazine, Maisie Verdurin, who had an eye for new people, had begun inviting him to her dinners and, through Maisie's dinners, he met other people who began inviting him to their dinners, and soon he was what is known as on-the-circuit in that group of New Yorkers who went out to dinners every night.

However, as Gus's literary reputation was not commensurate with that of Nestor Calder's, for instance, who was year after year on the best-seller lists, he was more often than not assigned to a table in Maisie's library, which was generally conceded to be a less desirable location for seating than her adjoining drawing and dining rooms. When confronted, Maisie stoutly denied that this was so, but the less celebrated wives, husbands, lovers, and escorts of the celebrated were usually placed there, seated beneath a Tissot or a Bombois, while their mates of the evening dined in the drawing or dining room beneath a Monet or a Manet.

"I'm on my best behavior tonight," said Edwina Calder to Gus, kissing him on both cheeks, when he walked into Maisie's drawing room for the cocktail hour. "I'm in Dutch with our hostess, have you heard? She'll probably seat me in the kitchen tonight."

Gus laughed. "Where's Nestor?"

"He's out in Hollywood," said Edwina.

"He told me he was going to write the mini-series of *Judas Was a Redhead,*" said Gus.

"He went to see Peach," said Edwina.

"Peach never tells me anything."

"What are you writing about now, Gus?"

"Oh, some gigolo who got all the money off a rich old lady," replied Gus, shrugging, dismissing the story as not important. "And then I'm going to do a story on a society walker who got murdered after taking a rich lady home from a party."

"I liked your article on Faye Converse," said Edwina. "She was always my favorite movie star growing up. Do you think she's really off the sauce for good?"

Rochelle Prud'homme, who made her fortune in hairdryers and was sponsored in her social rise by Matilda Clarke, advanced into the room in tiny little running steps, her left hand beneath her pearls, clutching a panel of her couturier dress. Known in New York as the Petite Dynamo, Rochelle stood barely

five feet tall, and was known to be one of the best bridge players in the city, a
passion she indulged in when she wasn't running her industrial empire or going
to parties. She waved little waves to acquaintances, held her cheek to be kissed
by friends, and smiled perfectly for the flashing strobe light of a reporter doing
a feature story for a new magazine on the world of Maisie Verdurin. "Otherwise, you know, I *never* have reporters at my parties," said Maisie to each
guest, "except Dolly, of course, but Dolly is a friend." Dolly De Longpre,
beloved by all, never missed one of Maisie Verdurin's dinners, no matter what,
and filled whole columns with Maisie's guest lists, who was there and what they
wore and all the sparkling things they said at Maisie's tables, even though
Maisie was not, by her own admission, in society at all, at least in the sense of
old family and old money.

"Biarritz was a disaster," Rochelle said to Maisie. "Rain, rain, rain, and the
worst people you ever saw. Not a soul one knew."

"Ain't she grand? Listen to her. Nestor swears her real name was Roxy
Persky, and she was three classes ahead of him at Erasmus High," said Edwina
Calder to Gus.

"Whose real name?" asked Gus.

"Rochelle Prud'homme."

But Gus Bailey's attention had been drawn to someone else entering
Maisie's drawing room. He heard Rochelle Prud'homme conclude to Maisie,
"You're coming to me on Thursday the nineteenth. I'll send you a *pour
mémoire*. Princess Murat is coming to town." *Pour mémoire* was French for
reminder, and Rochelle had taken up French, along with bridge, with a passion.

"Oh, I'll remember," said Maisie.

It was the appearance in the room of the tall and bearded Constantine de
Rham that occupied Gus's attention. De Rham made a gesture of kissing
Maisie's hand by raising it toward his lips and then dropping it. Maisie dressed
for her parties with expensive care, and de Rham, who noticed such things,
complimented her on the handsomeness of her pearl-encrusted bodice. Maisie,
more used to business tycoons than French aristocrats, was charmed by his
courtly manners. Whether entering a party, or a restaurant, or a theater, there
was always someone present who whispered to someone else, "There's Constantine de Rham." In years past, when playboys were still in fashion, his
escapades and exploits had filled the international gossip columns, but a fatal
car crash outside of Paris a half dozen years earlier had ended his days as a
romantic figure; his beautiful young companion, the daughter of a French
duke, had gone through his car's windshield when he was speeding home in the
early hours of the morning from a ball at a country estate. It was a part of his
story and always took precedence over the other dramatic circumstance of his
life, the death of his wife, the immensely rich Consuelo Harcourt de Rham,
Adele Harcourt's daughter, who had died falling down the marble stairway of
their house on Sutton Place, after returning home from a party she had not
wanted to attend.

"There's Constantine de Rham," said Edwina.

"I know all about Constantine de Rham," replied Gus.

At Constantine de Rham's side was a young woman dressed far too elaborately for a Maisie Verdurin dinner in a revealing gown of gold lamé, with

diamonds in great quantity on her wrists, ears, neck, and bosom. Her blond hair was combed straight back and coiled silkily in a bun at the nape of her neck, giving her the look of the wife of a South American dictator.

Maisie's drawing room was now filled with guests. Waiters carried trays of drinks and hors d'oeuvres, and passage from one side of the room to the other, which seemed to be Constantine de Rham's intention, necessitated a circuitous routing. Followed by his young companion, he edged his way sideways between Maisie's white brocade sofa and the coffee table in front of it, murmuring charming apologies to Dolly De Longpre and a quartet of seated guests, like a person taking a seat in a theater after the curtain has gone up.

Dolly De Longpre, glamorous and voluptuous, dimpled and pink-skinned, barely acknowledged Constantine de Rham and went on with her own conversation. "Seating can make or break a party," she said. "And Maisie Verdurin has a genius for seating. She agonizes over her *placement.*"

A painting by Monet of water lilies had been hung over Maisie's fireplace only that afternoon, in anticipation of the arrival of the immensely rich art collector Elias Renthal, whom no one in New York yet knew, except Constantine de Rham, who had brought him to Maisie to start his collection. Reaching his goal, Constantine de Rham held his black-rimmed spectacles like a lorgnette and leaned toward the pink in the center of a water lily, as if it possessed scent. "Ah, ravishing," he pronounced admiringly to Maisie about the painting, and she smiled modestly about her acquisition.

"Isn't the pink marvelous?" asked Maisie.

"Like the inside of a seashell," agreed de Rham.

"It's the pink that has so intrigued Elias Renthal's new wife, you know. If he decides to buy it, it's to be the color of the walls in the drawing room of the Renthals' new apartment that they just bought from Matilda Clarke."

Constantine smiled a superior smile, including Maisie in on this joint superiority, over people like the Elias Renthals of the world, who looked on art as an extension of interior decoration. "What an impressive group you have gathered, Maisie," he said, looking around the room.

"Your friends the Renthals have still not appeared, and I don't intend to wait for them when the butler announces dinner," she replied, taking his arm and leading him around the crowded room to introduce him, knowing that, as hostess, paths would be cleared. Maisie always gave a thumbnail sketch of each guest's accomplishments when she introduced him or her. "You'll be at my table, Constantine, between me and Rochelle Prud'homme. You know Rochelle, don't you? Prud'homme Products? Cordless hairdryers? Home permanents? One of America's most outstanding women. Plays such good bridge. And I'm counting on you to draw Elias Renthal into the conversation. He's hopeless at parties, I understand."

They walked past a group of laughing men whom Maisie always called "my bachelors," although they were the same group of bachelors who sat nightly on gilded chairs in the dining rooms of Lil Altemus, or Loelia Manchester, or Matilda Clarke, when she was still giving parties, or any of the other hostesses of the city, balancing out tables where widows or divorced ladies of quality sat. There was owlish-looking Jamesey Crocus, who knew more about eighteenth-century French furniture than anyone in New York, people said, and always pushed his round black-rimmed spectacles up on his nose with his forefinger as he talked excitedly about collectors and collecting, his favorite topic of conversation. And Nevel, just Nevel, which was Leven spelled backwards, who designed dresses for most of the ladies in society, and always counted how many ladies in the room were wearing his elegant gowns. And Freddy Winslow, about whom people said such terrible things, who bought and sold estate jewelry. And Count Motulsky, whose mother was one of the de Brown sisters from San Francisco, who taught French to Rochelle Prud'homme and sold porcelain at Sackville's.

"I always expect the lights to dim when Constantine de Rham walks into a room," said Gus.

"He doesn't seem like Maisie's kind of guest," said Edwina.

"Who's the Evita Perón look-alike trailing behind de Rham?" asked Gus.

"That is Mrs. Lupescu, or Baroness Lupescu, as she sometimes calls herself, but it's a bogus title. Constantine de Rham calls her Yvonne," replied Edwina.

"Are they lovers?"

"So it would seem."

"She's showing a lot of tit for a Maisie Verdurin party," said Gus.

"I don't know where to look first, at her tits or her diamonds," answered Edwina.

"Why doesn't anyone speak to her?"

"She has what's called a dicey reputation."

"Ah, the plot thickens."

"May I present Constantine de Rham," said Maisie, when she got to where Gus Bailey and Edwina Calder were standing.

De Rham held out his hand to be shaken, but Gus did not take it. Instead, he nodded at the tall man but still did not take his hand. De Rham, overlooking the slight, turned away, as Maisie led him on to the next group.

Gus wondered that Maisie, so obsessed with people who "do things," could treat in such a special manner a man who had done absolutely nothing with his life, except marry an heiress who had died before she even came into her inheritance. After her daughter's death, Adele Harcourt cut her son-in-law in public, and thereafter he was no longer invited to the sort of parties he had been used to attending. He continued to live in the house he had inherited from Consuelo, and there were rumors he sometimes used it for nefarious purposes to make ends meet.

Maisie's efficient secretary marshaled the guests to their various tables. "Senator Marx, you're over there, next to Justine Altemus, in the short blue strapless dress, beneath the little Renoir. You know, don't you, Justine Altemus is Laurance Van Degan's niece?" And, "Oh, Mr. Fenwick, you're next to Mrs. Renthal, who doesn't know a soul, but her husband is the richest man in Cleveland, and Maisie's counting on you to make her feel at home, if she ever shows up, that is."

It was just at this point that Elias Renthal and his young wife, Ruby, entered Maisie's apartment, flustered by their lateness. Elias was stout and not tall, with broad hands and broad chest, suggesting physical strength, and his presence was such that people turned to look at him. His glance, which was described as terrifying by the people who worked for him, was open and expectant in Maisie's drawing room, where he was unsure of himself. Social life was as yet an unknown quantity for him, but he had been told that casual talk at New York dinner parties could be an important source of business information for him. His third wife, Ruby, years younger, with whom he was besotted, was pretty but not smartly dressed in a gown of bright blue sequins, and her hair was arranged in an unbecoming fashion.

Except for Constantine de Rham, to whom Elias nodded, and Rochelle Prud'homme, the Renthals seemed to know no one in Maisie's rooms, although all the businessmen present, like Emil Jorst and the Zobel brothers, knew who the very rich Elias Renthal from Cleveland was. His purchase of the ailing conglomerate known as Miranda Industries for six billion dollars, using relatively little of his own money, and then liquidating it, had netted him a profit of three billion dollars in only sixteen months, a widely heralded transaction that was thought to be the most lucrative leveraged buyout ever, making the heretofore unknown Elias Renthal a financial celebrity.

"I'd almost given up on you," said Maisie, rushing to greet the latecomers. If the Renthals had not been the possible purchasers of the Monet water lilies, asking price six million, but negotiable, Maisie, who insisted on promptness in her guests, would certainly have been less charming.

"I'm sorry we're so late," said Elias. Loyalty to his new wife forbade him telling Maisie that Ruby had changed her dress and hairstyle three times in the previous hour. "I don't think you've met my wife. Ruby, this is Maisie Verdurin."

"I'm so pleased," said Maisie. "The painting is over there, and I'm mad to have you look at it. Constantine de Rham *raved* about it. But the waiters are about to serve."

"Plenty of time to look at pictures," said Elias.

"That *is* the color pink I like, Elias," said Ruby, looking across the room at the Monet.

"I hear Elias bought you the Palumbo pearl," said Maisie to Ruby, as she took her to a table in the library, after directing Elias to her own table in the drawing room.

"Yes," said Ruby, holding out the pearl, which hung from a chain around her neck.

"How marvelous."

"It's very, uh, useful," answered Ruby, unable to think of a more appropriate word.

"I've put you next to Ezzie Fenwick, who's the best friend of all the famous ladies in New York, but be careful what you say to him, because he repeats *everything*. And Gus Bailey on the other side. He writes all those magazine pieces on famous people. I hope you'll enjoy yourself."

"Augustus Bailey?" asked Ruby.

"Yes. Everyone calls him Gus. Do you know him?" asked Maisie.

"No," replied Ruby, quickly. Maisie could tell that Ruby was nervous and wished that she were sitting with her husband.

"Is this your first New York party, Mrs. Renthal?"

"Yes."

"I so admire your husband, the few times I've met him," said Maisie, who always admired financiers, especially financiers who were starting collections.

"He knows what he wants in art and goes after it, although, I must admit, sometimes he scares me to death if things don't work out. He does swear a bit, doesn't he?"

"Oh, honey, he doesn't mean anything by that," said Ruby, waving her hand dismissively at the thought. "If I hadn't understood that *cunt* meant *sweetheart,* this marriage wouldn't have lasted out the first year."

Maisie, startled, looked at Ruby with an astonished smile that plainly said, "Where was this woman brought up?" Depositing her at her table, she said, "Your seat's here," and returned to her own table.

"Your husband's shorter than I thought he would be, Mrs. Renthal," said Ezzie Fenwick.

"My husband is very tall when he stands on his wallet, Mr. Fenwick," replied Ruby.

"Hmm," said Ezzie. *"Touché."*

Gus Bailey, seated on Ruby Renthal's other side, smiled at her and introduced himself. For an instant, Ruby looked at Gus, as if she might have known him.

"Where'd you get that dress?" asked Ezzie, squinting his good eye at Ruby's bright blue sequins.

"Cleveland," replied Ruby.

"I thought so," said Ezzie.

In the library, where she was also placed, beneath a tiny Tissot, young Mrs. Lupescu was displeased that she had not been seated at Maisie's table in the drawing room where Constantine de Rham and Rochelle Prud'homme and Elias Renthal and Justine Altemus had been seated, and said audibly to her dinner partner, Bernard Slatkin, an anchorman on the television news, whom she had never met before, that Mrs. Verdurin had seated her at the C table in the C room. Thereafter she maintained a haughty silence, and lit cigarettes throughout the meal, to the distress of Matilda Clarke, who loathed smoking and constantly waved her napkin in the air to clear away the smoke.

Gus Bailey observed Mrs. Lupescu through the white anthuriums of the centerpiece, while his dinner partner on the other side, Matilda Clarke, the widow of Sweetzer Clarke, who died when he fell off his horse fox hunting, drunk, and left her in bad financial straits, talked into Gus's ear about their mutual friend Evangeline Simpson, while patting the back of her pageboy hairdo with both hands.

"Evangeline's drunk all the time, Gus. Hiding Jack Daniel's in her Lazlo bottles, that sort of thing. I took her to Smithers to detox and dry out. No one has to tell me anything about Smithers, God knows. I took poor Sweetzer there enough times, but Evangeline wouldn't stay, or they wouldn't have her, I don't know which, and I don't care anymore, for that matter. If you could have seen the way she behaved, to *me,* her oldest friend."

Gus listened, as he always listened when people told him things at dinner parties, which they always did. He planned someday to write a book about these people who went out to dinner every night, and talked and talked and talked about each other, who was rich, who was broke, who took drugs, who drank, who had cancer, who was having an affair with whom, who was getting a divorce, who was straight, who was gay. There was very little they didn't know about each other, and very little they didn't discuss about each other.

"Odd, don't you think, Maisie having Constantine de Rham to dinner?" replied Gus.

Matilda Clarke, used to conversational shifts at dinner parties, abandoned Evangeline Simpson as a subject. "He's a new acquisition of Maisie's. I think he introduced her to this ghastly common Renthal man who bought my apartment and is trying to assemble an art collection in ten minutes. Maisie probably pays Constantine a finder's fee for digging up these new billionaires."

"Hmm," said Gus, signaling to Matilda that Mrs. Renthal was on his other side.

"Constantine's very cultured, you know," Matilda continued. "And he's awfully amusing to sit next to at dinner, Gus. I bet you don't know the name of Talleyrand's chef at the Congress of Vienna, but Constantine does. Or the name of Sebastian Flyte's teddy bear in *Brideshead Revisited.* Constantine does."

Across the table Yvonne Lupescu, who had already pronounced Maisie's veal "mystery meat," now declined the cheese. "I hate brie breath," she said to no one in particular, although Matilda Clarke kicked Gus under the table to listen and signaled Ezzie Fenwick by pointing to Yvonne with her eyes.

"She just won't do. She just won't do at all," said Matilda, holding her hand in front of her mouth, as if she expected Mrs. Lupescu to read lips. "Constantine must be out of his mind."

"Hmm," said Gus.

"Will you look at the way she's overdressed," said Matilda, tying and untying and then tying again the sleeves of a cashmere sweater she had tossed over her shoulders to protect herself from the icy blast of Maisie's air conditioner, even though it was nearly winter outside. "When I was giving parties, when darling Sweetzer was still alive, and we still had the big apartment, I always had my secretary call my guests on the morning of the party and say, 'Mrs. Clarke is wearing a long dress tonight,' or, 'Mrs. Clarke is wearing a short dress,' so that all the women would be dressed alike. I mean, look at this woman. She looks like she's going to the opening night of the opera in Istanbul."

"Rather hard to pinpoint her nationality," said Gus, studying Mrs. Lupescu's ample mouth and wide-apart eyes.

"Oh, Peruvian, maybe," said Matilda, giving it some thought. "Or Corsican, possibly, and maybe more than a tinge of Albanian tossed in. What Sweetzer used to call a mongrel."

"Pretty, though."

"Shows too much gum when she smiles. Ask Ezzie Fenwick about Mrs. Lupescu sometime. Ask Ezzie what she did at the airport in Tangier when she didn't have enough money to pay for her excess baggage." Matilda rolled her eyes. "Nice china Maisie Verdurin has," she continued, picking up the dessert plate that had been placed in front of her and turning it over. "You don't often see the Fitz Hugh border like this. Do you suppose it's for sale? Like all her pictures?" A waiter passing the dessert interrupted her. "Oh, look at this *crème brûlée,* will you! It's far too pretty to break into, but I will. A million calories, that's all."

Across the table, Yvonne Lupescu, unrushed, stared down at Maisie's *crème brûlée* for half a minute before tasting it and then, with a shake of her head, dropped her spoon loudly on her plate. "That's not worth getting fat over," she said to Bernie Slatkin.

As a rule toasts were not given at Maisie Verdurin's dinners, except when a former President was present, or a cabinet minister, so it was unexpected when Constantine de Rham rose to his feet, after the champagne was poured, and tapped his fork against the side of his champagne glass until there was silence in the three rooms where Maisie's guests were seated.

"I would like to propose a toast to our hostess," said Constantine, and, encouraged by several "Hear, hears," in the rooms, he spoke charmingly about Maisie as a formidable force in the art world of New York as well as a hostess of such note that her monthly fêtes would one day be recorded as part of the social history of the city. Maisie flushed prettily. "She has given her talent to her work," Constantine concluded, "but she has given her genius to her life."

No one applauded more enthusiastically than Mrs. Lupescu, as if approval of Constantine de Rham was the thing she most ardently desired, reflecting, as it did, on herself.

"Marvelous, wasn't it, what Constantine said about Mrs. Verdurin?" said Yvonne Lupescu to her table. "That she gives her talent to her work but her genius to her life. Marvelous."

"It was even more marvelous when Oscar Wilde said it originally, about himself," said Gus to Matilda Clarke.

Throughout dinner, Ruby Renthal, terrified of the sophisticated society-wit Ezzie Fenwick, sat in silence and watched, declining to participate for fear of making another mistake. She understood from his remark that her dress was all wrong, as well as her hairstyle, just from the look he gave it with his one good eye, which she figured out was not the one that went off in another direction. And worse, her table manners, once she realized she was the only one who ate her artichoke with a knife and fork, were wrong. On the several occasions she tried to speak to Gus Bailey, she saw that his ear was monopolized by Matilda Clarke, whose apartment the Renthals had bought, but his eyes were focused on Yvonne Lupescu.

When Gus went down the long hallway to the bedrooms to find his coat, Ruby Renthal followed him. "Mr. Bailey," she said.

Gus turned. "I think the ladies' coats are in Maisie's bedroom on that side, Mrs. Renthal," said Gus.

"Mr. Bailey," she said again.

"It's Gus," said Gus.

"Gus," she said. She looked both ways in the hall, as if to see if anyone was coming, and Gus realized that she wanted to say something to him. He remembered then that she had looked at him strangely when they had been introduced. "Didn't you use to live in Los Angeles?" she asked.

"Yes," he replied.

"My name before I was married was Ruby Nolte. Does that name mean anything to you?"

Gus looked at her, as if the name struck a note, although her face did not look familiar to him. "Help me," he said.

"Does the name Lefty Flint mean anything to you?"

"Oh, yes," said Gus, quietly. The name Lefty Flint, whenever he heard it, caused a violent reaction within him. He walked into the bedroom where the coats were hanging on a rack and turned to look back at Ruby Renthal, who followed him into the room.

"It was in your family that it happened, wasn't it?" she asked.

Gus nodded. Something stopped him from pulling away from her.

"I used to be a redhead. I used to be an airline stewardess too, at least at the time. I went out with Lefty Flint for a while. Then I grew scared of him. When I tried to break off with him, he beat me up. He broke my nose. He knocked out two of my teeth. He blacked my eyes. He fractured my jaw. I thought I would never again have a face I could look at in the mirror."

"Dear God," said Gus. He sat down on the edge of the bed.

"I was in the hospital for ten days, thanks to Mr. Lefty Flint," said Ruby.

"Dear God," Gus repeated.

"Did you ever hear of a lawyer called Marv Pink?" she asked.

"Oh, yes, I know Marv Pink," said Gus.

"Some of Lefty's friends came to visit me in the hospital. They told me if I testified against Lefty, Marv Pink would nail me to the cross. My background is not of the Virgin Mary variety, if you get my point. It would all end up looking like I got what I deserved. Do you know what I mean?"

"Yes, I know what you mean," said Gus. "It's the fashion in the courts these days, blame the victim."

"They paid my hospital bill, and I disappeared. It's something I've always regretted," she said.

"And Flint walked away, scot free."

"I know."

"How come you told me all this? I wouldn't have known Mrs. Elias Renthal was Ruby Nolte if you hadn't told me," said Gus.

"I couldn't believe it when we sat next to each other tonight. You see, I read about what happened in your family a few years later, and I always felt guilty. I felt that if I'd gone to the police at the time, what happened to you might not have happened."

Gus nodded.

Ruby sat down on the bed next to Gus and took his hand. "I'm sorry for what happened to you," she said.

"I'm sorry for what happened to you," replied Gus.

"When does he get out of prison?"

"He only got three years."

"Three years?" she said in disbelief.

"He was a jury pleaser. He wore a coat and tie, and he always carried a Bible. They fell for it."

Ruby shook her head.

In the hallway there were voices as other people began to look for their coats. Ruby jumped off the bed and went to the mirror and started to brush her hair.

"Listen, Gus, my husband doesn't know," said Ruby. "I never told him. A guy doesn't want to marry a girl who's been beaten up like I was. Elias would have thought I was damaged goods, and Elias Renthal is the best thing that ever happened to me."

"It's not a thing I'd ever talk about," said Gus.

"Ruby?" called out Elias in the hallway.

"In here, Elias," she called back.

"What the hell's going on in here?" asked Elias, staring at Gus sitting on the bed and Ruby brushing her hair in the mirror.

"Just getting my coat, Elias," said Ruby.

"Maisie wants us to look at the picture," said Elias.

"Elias, this is Augustus Bailey. My husband, Elias Renthal. Mr. Bailey wrote that article you liked on Laurance Van Degan."

"Pleased to meetcha, Mr. Dailey," said Elias. He shook hands without looking at Gus.

"Same," said Gus, taking his coat. "Nice meeting you, Mrs. Renthal," he added. Their eyes met in the mirror, and Gus walked out.

"That guy's old enough to be your father," said Elias.

"So are you," replied Ruby, still adjusting her makeup at the mirror.

"So am I what?"

"Old enough to be my father."

"What the hell is this? We go to our first New York party, and you end up in the bedroom with some guy."

"Oh, calm down, Elias. I end up in the bedroom with the coats, talking to Mr. Bailey. He's a writer. He writes about rich people. One of these days, you and I are going to have to get to know guys like that, when we start moving in this town. And, listen, this dress of mine is a disaster. There's a guy here tonight called Nevel who—"

"A guy called Nevel?"

"Leven spelled backwards. He designed Maisie Verdurin's dress, and the young Altemus girl who's Laurance Van Degan's niece. I'm going there tomorrow, so get out your checkbook, big boy, because he costs an arm and a leg, and I'm going to buy him out."

"Okay, okay. How'd you know this Dailey?"

"Bailey, not Dailey, Elias. If he was from Wall Street, you'd remember his name."

"Bailey then."

"I sat next to him tonight at dinner, and I met him once before in L.A. I met a lot of people before I met you, Elias, and if you're going to start getting jealous every time I run into someone you don't know, we're going to have a boring few years in front of us. Okay?"

"Okay," said Elias.

"Now smile." She put her finger under his chin.

"I'm smiling."

"Love me?"

"Love you." He kissed her shoulder.

"Same here. Now let's go look at that six-million-dollar Monet and see if it's the right color pink."

No one lingered after dinner at Maisie Verdurin's parties; the evenings always ended with the liquored coffee, after which there was a mass exit for the elevator. That night the consensus was that Mr. and Mrs. Elias Renthal were never going to make it in New York, no matter how much money they brought with them from Cleveland.

"How was Mrs. Renthal?" asked Matilda Clarke in the crowded elevator.

"She called her evening dress a formal," said Ezzie. "And she ate her artichoke with a knife and fork."

"Imagine people like that in my apartment. Sweetzer must be turning over in his grave. He grew up in that apartment," said Matilda.

Gus closed his eyes. He felt protective about Ruby Renthal. "I thought she was very pretty," he said, "and very nice."

"Hmm," said Ezzie.

"Gus, come out to the country for the weekend," said Matilda Clarke, when they got out on the first floor. "Rochelle's coming, and maybe the Calders, if Nestor gets back from Hollywood."

"Thank you, but I can't."

"Where are you off to?" insisted Matilda.

"I'm going in the other direction this weekend," replied Gus, smiling at Matilda.

"You're always going off some place mysterious, Gus," said Matilda.

Outside Maisie's building several homeless people slept on the sidewalk, with packing cases beneath them and over them. On the street limousines were lined up waiting for the departing guests. "They shouldn't allow this," said Ezzie Fenwick, as he gathered Matilda Clarke and Violet Bastedo into the back of Violet's limousine, careful that the long skirts of their dresses would not be caught in the door.

"Can you help me out? I don't have anything to eat," said a beggar, holding his hand out to Ezzie Fenwick as he was about to step into the car.

Ezzie, frightened by the proximity of the young man, put his hand in his pocket and handed him some silver without looking at him and then hopped into the limousine with a litheness that belied his age and girth.

"Did you give him anything?" asked Matilda.

"It's hard to say you have no money when you're getting into a limousine wearing a coat with a fur collar and black patent-leather pumps with grosgrain ribbons on them," answered Ezzie.

The three sat in silence for a moment, while the chauffeur pulled his car out in front of the other cars.

"Let's go hear Bobby Short," said Violet Bastedo.

2

B ERNARD SLATKIN knew Justine Altemus by sight for several months before he actually spoke to her. Justine, the daughter of the famous Lil
Altemus, and the niece of Laurance Van Degan, was a regular figure at
most of the fashionable parties in New York that Bernard Slatkin, in the first
flush of his professional success, had started being invited to in the last year.

"We've met before," he said to her in the elevator leaving Maisie
Verdurin's party.

"Where?" Justine replied.

"Here at Maisie's."

"I've just attended my last party at Maisie's," said Justine. "Too crowded,
and I don't like having to sit at a table with Constantine de Rham's mistress.
Consuelo de Rham was my mother's best friend."

"It was the party where one of the Zobel brothers bought the Toulouse-
Lautrec," said Bernie.

"Tonight Elias Renthal was buying a Monet," said Justine. She looked at
him. "Oh, yes, I do remember you. You were talking to Violet Bastedo about
corruption in city government. Oh, so serious you were. And Violet was pretending she was understanding the conversation, which she wasn't."

"Would you like a ride home?" he asked quietly.

"One of the advantages of being a Van Degan, even by indirection, is that I
have a car and driver. Not a limousine, mind you. That's for the Mr. Renthals
of the world. Just your average station wagon, but it relieves my mother's mind
to know I'm not standing out in the street waving for a cab at ungodly hours,"
replied Justine. She spoke in a breezy manner, friendly but distant, with the
assumption that great heiresses possess that the young man knew exactly who
she was.

"I thought your name was Altemus," he said.

"It is, but my mother was a Van Degan."

Bernie Slatkin looked at this youngish woman who had now mentioned her
mother three times. Her eyebrows were dark and gracefully arched. Her face
was unmistakably the face of a well-born woman, but, somehow, beauty escaped it. "Do you live with your mother?" he asked.

"Same building. Different apartments. Different elevators too," she answered.

The elevator stopped with a jolt. When she accidentally bumped against
him, she could feel his erection, even through their coats.

"How about giving me a ride then?" asked Bernie, meeting her eyes.

"As long as you don't live in the outer boroughs," she replied. Then she remembered what she knew about this man. It was the very same Violet Bastedo who told her. Violet, who discussed such things, said he was more than amply endowed, referring to his male member. Violet said it right in front of the waiter at Clarence's while he was serving them their chicken paillard. Of course, Violet had said it in French, but, even so, Justine had been shocked and screeched, "Violet!"

"Just Central Park West," said Bernie.

"Just don't get fresh with me in the backseat," said Justine, wagging her finger at him, in a joking way that covered her shyness. "My driver doubles as a bodyguard."

Bernie Slatkin laughed. "Only my thoughts will be impure," he said.

"Now I know who you are," said Justine. "It's the dimple. I recognized the dimple. You're on the television news."

"And all the time I thought you knew that."

"You see?"

In the car he held her hand and told her about being an anchorman on the local New York news. She made appropriate comments, saying "Fascinating" from time to time, but her mind was on other things. Sleeping with men, or "sleeping around," as her friends like Violet Bastedo called it, was not a thing that Justine Altemus did. She had had the occasional affair—with Toby Walters, for instance, when she was thinking of marrying Toby, and Jean-Claude St. Cloud, one summer in France—but those carnal events were rare, widely spaced in time, and only occurred after careful deliberation on her part. To sleep with a man within the first hour of meeting him was altogether unthinkable, but, at this moment, in the backseat of her mother's car, with a man she had just met in an elevator, whose erection she had accidentally bumped into, it was the thing she most desired in the world and intended to consummate, with no thought of consequence, if he made the request.

It had been a dozen years since her presentation, a small dinner dance at Grandfather Van Degan's house in Syosset, for family and close friends, and then a ball under a pink tent for six hundred, with a list carefully honed by her mother to eliminate all the arrivistes, outsiders, and "New People," as her mother called them, who were being invited everywhere in New York. The hope was, of course, that she would have a year of dancing and parties, and then a year of traveling, meeting all the most eligible young men, and after that would take her pick of the many suitors her mother envisioned would be lined up for the tall, pretty heiress, but it hadn't worked out that way, and Justine Altemus, at thirty, had still not wed.

"Drink?" asked Bernie, when the car stopped.

"Where?"

"My place. Great view."

"Great view right across the park at my mother's apartment."

"Yours, too."

"I'm on the other side of the building."

"Well?"

"I'm going to be having a drink at Mr. Slatkin's, Joe," said Justine to the driver. At thirty she still behaved as if she were twenty.

She was nervous when she entered Bernie's apartment. She looked around at the stark black-and-white room with its floor-to-ceiling windows. "Is this what they call the minimal look?" she asked.

"Like it?" asked Bernie.

"Actually, no," replied Justine. "Now don't look crestfallen. It's just that I've been brought up in rooms of cabbage-rose chintz, as dictated by old Cora Mandell."

"Who's Cora Mandell?"

"Oh, well, now's not the time for chintz lessons," said Justine. "At least, that's not what I thought you had in mind when you asked me to your West Side aerie."

"No, no, it wasn't," said Bernie.

"Drinks, wasn't it?"

"It wasn't drinks either." By this time Bernie had had enough repartee. He took off his overcoat and dropped it on a chair, untied his black tie, and unbuttoned the top button of his dinner shirt. When he kissed her the first time, he put his hand under her short evening dress and between her legs.

"Oh, the finesse of it all," she whispered. Justine, unused to passion in her few refined forays into physical love, thrilled to his blunt approach. In less than a minute, his trousers and undershorts were off and flung far afield, and he was guiding her hands to his hairy regions. "That's awfully nice, what you're doing," she whispered.

"That feels pretty good, what you're doing, too," said Bernie.

"I feel quite content."

"This is only the pregame warmup, Miss Altemus," said Bernie, taking his tongue out of her mouth only long enough to answer.

"Do you prefer to be called Bernie or Bernard?" she asked, between kisses.

"Whatever turns you on, honey," he answered, unzipping her dress and helping her step out of it. The consummation of their lust was swift and violent. It was only in repetition that the beauty of the act of love became apparent to Justine. She liked looking at his body, every inch of it, and she allowed him to look at hers, every inch of it. With Toby Walters, who later married her friend Marie Harcourt, it was over each time almost before it started. With Jean-Claude St. Cloud, that summer in France, it was romantic but unsatisfying, each too aware of the perfection of the match. With Bernard Slatkin, it was passion and carnality.

"I never heard a man talk so dirty," she said afterward.

"Too low for you?"

"Quite the contrary," she astonished herself by saying.

"I knew we were going to hit it off," he said, smoothing her forehead with his hand. "Why the worried brow?"

"I was thinking of my mother's chauffeur downstairs," replied Justine.

Bernie chuckled and shook his head in disbelief. "How old are you, Justine?" he asked.

She blushed. Her age was for her a sensitive subject, as it was one her mother never let her forget.

"Thirty?" he asked when he saw her hesitate.

"Thirty," she conceded.

Bernie got up, making no attempt to cover his nakedness, and walked over to the intercom by the front door and buzzed. "Jose, it's Mr. Slatkin in Twenty-two C. Miss Altemus's chauffeur is in a dark blue Buick station wagon outside. His name is Joe. Would you tell him that Miss Altemus said for him to go home?"

"What am I going to say to my mother tomorrow?" she asked.

"Take this in your mouth while you're thinking about it," he answered, pushing her head down on him. Justine Altemus was not offended. She had fallen madly in love with Bernard Slatkin.

3

INVITATIONS TO DINNERS, dances, screenings of new films, and publication parties to launch new books crowded the chipped gilt frame of a nineteenth-century reproduction of an eighteenth-century mirror. Gus Bailey, bathed, shaved, but not yet dressed, was wearing a white terrycloth robe he had once stolen from the Ritz Hotel in Paris. As he brushed his hair with two brushes, a blizzard raged outside his window, and for an instant he regretted his decision to make the bus trip into New England that he had promised to make.

The doorbell rang, as it always rang, at ten minutes past seven each morning. Gus opened the door. It was, as he knew it would be, Innocento, the delivery boy from the coffee shop on the corner, bringing him his standing order of three dark coffees with artificial sweetener in cardboard containers. Innocento always handed Gus his morning papers, which had already been dropped outside the door by the elevator man, always gave him a weather report, and always received a dollar tip.

"Cold as a nun's cunt out there," reported Innocento.

"Cold as a witch's tit has a better ring to it at this hour of the morning, Innocento," said Gus.

"Hey, I like that, Mr. Bailey."

The interstate bus carrying Gus Bailey traveled between the Port Authority Terminal in New York and Brattleboro, Vermont, with stops along the way. Gus tried to read and could not. He tried to sleep and could not. He wished the man in the next seat would stop smoking, but an attitude of unfriendliness on that person's part made Gus disinclined to make such a request, and there were no empty seats to move to. He wondered again why he had agreed to make the trip that he was making.

People said about Gus Bailey, on occasion, "Isn't it marvelous the way he got over it so well and put the whole terrible thing behind him?" Because he never mentioned it, or rarely, and seemed to have progressed on to a full productive life. He was seen about, asked places, and considered an addition. But none of them could know that his last thought before sleep and his first thought on awakening dealt with his torment. Nor did they notice those moments, sometimes even in the midst of frivolity, when his mind blanked to the topic at hand and dwelled in private thoughts.

He looked out the window of the bus. Near here, somewhere, there was an aunt in a nursing home, an aunt who had brought him up. Tante, they called her in the family. It had started as a joke, calling her Tante. His sister Eliza, dead now, cancer, claimed it was she who had given Aunt Mary the name Tante, but Gus knew it was he. He could even remember exactly when, on the day in French class he had first learned the phrase *la plume de ma tante.* It became the name the whole family called her. Unmarried, by choice, she had always been called Aunt Mary until then, and there were stories that she had once wanted to be a nun but her father had discouraged her from that calling. Even she grew to enjoy the name and signed postcards to them from her endless travels, "Love, Tante." Old now, ninety, she no longer knew him when he visited her, and each day he expected the call that would tell him she was dead.

Three and a half hours out of New York the bus pulled to the side of the road near the Connecticut-Massachusetts border, and Gus descended onto the icy highway. A car, described to him in advance as a six-year-old Oldsmobile, was parked near the sheltered bus stop. From behind the wheel he saw the driver make a gesture toward him, and he stepped toward and entered the car.

"Mrs. Haber?" he asked.

"Mr. Bailey," she replied.

She was Chinese. It had not occurred to him that she would be Chinese. Her handwriting, in the letter she had written to him, asking him to come, reminded him of Peach's handwriting, suggesting good schools and thrifty wealth. Her voice, when he had responded to her letter by telephone, was unaccented and American, and her name, Faith Haber, certainly gave no indication of an Oriental background. In the car, driving to where they were going, for the reason he had come, he was able to postpone the subject at hand by eliciting from her that she was from a Chinese banking family in Honolulu, had gone to a school there where Peach had gone during the year her parents almost divorced but didn't, and then to college in New England where she had married the brother of her roommate and later divorced him. Gus liked vital statistics and had an ability to draw them out without direct questioning.

"That was a terrible story you told me on the phone about your daughter's death, Mrs. Haber," said Gus, when the car pulled into the parking lot.

"That was a terrible story you wrote about your daughter's death, Mr. Bailey," said Faith Haber.

"Listen, call me Gus."

"Call me Faith."

"Did they catch the guy?"

"No." For an instant their eyes met in the darkened car. Gus reached over and touched Faith's hand, which still gripped the steering wheel.

"He stabbed her twenty-six times," said Faith Haber. "I have never been able to walk into her room again."

Inside the hired room of a church hall where Faith Haber led him, he met the other parents who had suffered the same grievous assault on their lives that he and Peach had suffered. Folding chairs had been arranged in a circle, and the room smelled of the coffee brewing in a small urn plugged into the wall. He wondered, as he always wondered, what he could do to help them, what it was these groups expected from him when they asked him to come, ever since he had written about Lefty Flint, who killed his daughter, Becky.

Faith Haber sat next to him and told about her daughter's murder, and the parents next to her told about their son's, and the single father next to them about his son, and the couple next to him about their daughter. On the other side of Gus sat a woman too numb with grief to tell her story, so recently had it happened, and Faith Haber told the tale for her as the woman sobbed uncontrollably. Gus held her hand.

"No one really understands," said Gus. "All our friends are helpful and loving during the time of the tragedy, but then they withdraw into their own lives, which is only natural, and soon you can see a glaze in their eyes when you bring it up because they don't want to talk about it anymore, and it is the only thing that's on your mind. That's why these groups are so helpful. No one really knows what you are going through like someone else who has been through it."

There were murmurs of assent in the room.

"The thing that makes me most angry is when people say to me, 'At least you have another child,'" said Faith Haber. "What do you say to these people?"

"I have no answers. I know of no secrets to assuage your pain. I can only tell you that you go on. You carry on somehow. You live your life. You work hard. In time you'll go to films and parties again. You'll see your friends and start to talk about other things than this. You'll even learn to laugh again, as strange as that may seem now, if you allow it to happen. My wife and I—"

He stopped. He never said "my ex-wife and I." "Don't call me your ex-wife," Peach had once said to him. It was too complicated to explain about himself and Peach, what it was like between them. Only he and Peach understood that, and, anyway, that was not what he was here to talk about. Dealing with loss. That was the theme tonight.

"But it is always there, what happened to us. It becomes a part of you. It has become as much a part of me as my left-handedness."

He talked on, but he knew that what he said was not reaching them. They wanted an answer.

"Out there, in Vacaville, California," he said, finally, "there is a man called Lefty Flint. Lefty Flint held his hands around my daughter's neck for five minutes, choking her until she was dead. Lefty Flint read the Bible all during the trial. Lefty Flint was sentenced to only three years in prison. In two years he will be out, having atoned, he thinks, for the murder of our daughter."

Gus stopped, withdrawing into his thoughts. He remembered the trial. He remembered her friend, Wendy, who said, on the stand, "It was when she opened the door and saw Lefty Flint standing there that Becky knew, before he even raised a hand to grab hold of her body, that the end of her life was at hand."

"Objection, your honor," Marv Pink, the defense attorney, had screamed at the judge. "The witness cannot state what was in Miss Bailey's mind."

"Sustained," said the judge.

"What would you do if you ever saw him?"

There was a silence before Gus realized that someone in the group had asked him a question.

"What?" he asked.

"What would you do if you ever saw Lefty Flint, after he gets out?" It was the single father whose sixteen-year-old son had been beaten to death with a baseball bat in a racial encounter.

Gus looked at the man. "The thought haunts me, because I feel almost certain it will happen, as if some higher power is directing such an encounter."

"What would you do?" asked the man again.

"I may appear to be a calm man," answered Gus, "but there is within me a rage that knows no limits."

"What would you do?" persisted the man.

"What I want to do is kill him. Does that shock you? It shocks me. But it is what I feel."

He did not add, "It is what I am going to do."

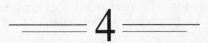

O N THURSDAY Justine Altemus canceled out of a benefit performance of the Manhattan Ballet Company, for which she was on the committee, to have dinner with Bernard Slatkin at a little restaurant on Bleecker Street in Greenwich Village. On Friday she backed out of a family dinner at Uncle Laurance and Aunt Janet Van Degan's to celebrate their thirtieth wedding anniversary to go to the television studio and watch Bernie's newscast and have dinner with him afterward at a restaurant on Columbus Avenue frequented by theatrical people. On Saturday morning she called Ceil Somerset and said she couldn't possibly go to the country for the weekend because she had such a terrible cold and spent the entire weekend in bed with Bernie at his apartment on Central Park West. On Monday she told her mother she wouldn't be sitting in her box at the opera that night for the new production of *Tosca*, which the Van Degan Foundation had partially financed, and took Bernie to Clarence's, where he was curious to go, as it was the hangout, as he called it, for all the people he read about in Dolly De Longpre's column.

"I'm not crazy about the way they cooked this fish," said Bernie.

"Oh, people don't come to Clarence's for the food. People come to Clarence's to look at each other. Almost everybody here knows each other. We call it the club, although it isn't a club at all. Of course, Mother says she won't come anymore because her sable coat was stolen when she went to the ladies' room, but she'll be back. Just wait."

"Point out Clarence to me," said Bernie.

"Oh, there is no Clarence. That's just a name. It's Chick Jacoby who owns Clarence's, and unless Chick likes you, or knows who you are, you'll never get a table at Clarence's," said Justine.

Bernie looked around him. "Looks like we have the best table."

"We do," laughed Justine.

"I guess Chick Jacoby likes you."

"He does."

"Tell me about your father," said Bernie. "You never talk about him."

"Oh, Daddy," said Justine. "He's so sweet. Drinks a bit. More than a bit, if you want the truth. He married badly after he divorced my mother, and no one in the family sees him. He lives up in Bedford with his new wife in a house she got in her divorce settlement from one of her previous marriages. Belinda, she's called, and she looks like a Belinda. Mother calls her a strumpet, but Mother would have called anyone a strumpet whom Daddy married. She never got over the fact that Daddy left her."

"She loved him then?"

"It's not that she loved him that much. They used to fight all the time, and my brother and I were glad they got a divorce at the time. Mother thought she was calling the shots in the marriage because she was a Van Degan and had so much money. The Altemuses are what's called good goods. Marvelous family. Goes way back, but no money to speak of, at least no money in the way the Van Degans have money. Look, there's Violet Bastedo over there. Your old girl-friend."

"She's not my old girlfriend," said Bernie.

"You went to bed with her."

"She told you that?"

"Oh, she told me a lot more than that," said Justine, her cheeks turning pink with embarrassment.

"What else did she tell you about me?" asked Bernie, amused that this shy girl was embarrassed.

"Oh, nothing."

"Don't give me 'oh-nothing,'" he persisted.

"She said you had a huge you-know-what." Justine covered her face with her hands.

"At least she's not a liar."

Justine laughed. "No, she's not a liar."

"I didn't know proper young ladies like you and Violet Bastedo talked about the size of men's dicks."

Justine blushed. "She said it in French."

Bernie roared with laughter.

"Were you serious about Violet?"

"It was a one-night stand, for God's sake. I never saw her again."

"I wonder if Maisie Verdurin knows that you are the terror of her parties. She thinks her parties are all about conversation, you know, and all the time it's a launch pad for Bernard Slatkin's assignations."

"We're having a conversation right now. Maisie would be proud of us."

"Violet Bastedo is getting another divorce. That's her new lawyer she's having dinner with."

"I want to talk about Justine Altemus, not Violet Bastedo," said Bernie. He put out his hand across the table and took hers. Whereas Violet Bastedo was flighty and silly, Justine, Bernie could see, was more serious. Although she was no less interested in the parties, travels, comings and goings of the people she knew than Violet was, she was also a great reader, of both books and newspapers, and could converse on issues of the day, which Violet couldn't. Justine not only watched Bernie interview news figures on his daily newscast, but could remember specific details of the interviews, and this delighted Bernie. "I didn't believe Assemblyman Walsh for a single moment when you asked him about kickbacks." Or, "That poor little Missie Everett girl. I wept for her when she told you about her sister. I hope that man gets life."

"Did you ever think of having a career?" Bernie asked her.

Justine looked at him. He thought he detected a defensive look in her face. "I do a great deal of charity work," she answered evenly. "Committees and things, and one day a week I work at the hospital as a nurses' aide. And, of course, there's Adele Harcourt's book club. There's an enormous amount to be read for that. I am, at the moment, deep in Dostoyevski."

At that time Bernie had never heard of Adele Harcourt's book club, but, like all New Yorkers, he knew who Adele Harcourt was, and, in time, he became impressed that Justine was a member of it, and had to have, no matter what, *The Idiot* read in its entirety by the following Monday evening when they would meet to discuss it in Adele Harcourt's apartment.

"I suppose never having to worry about food or rent money must make it less urgent for you to compete," he said.

"You're not going to put me on guilt trip because I was born into a rich family, are you?" she asked.

"No," he said, smiling at her.

She smiled back at him. "I still have a brother you haven't asked me about."

"Hubie. Right. Mysterious Hubie. I've got my theories about Hubie."

"Oh, poor Hubie. The apple of me mum's eye. Blind to all his faults, she is. He's always getting beaten up by all those hustlers he picks up. I mean, my mother would die if she knew. She thinks all the girls are just mad about Hubie and that Hubie's just mad about all the girls. Half the time he's got a black eye or a broken nose."

"Does he drink too?"

"He has an occasional lapse into insobriety, of course, but nothing compared to the way he used to be," said Justine. "Ever since Juanito came into his life."

"Who's Juanito?"

"Don't ask."

Bernie laughed. "We're real square in my family compared to you," he said.

Across the room at Clarence's, Violet Bastedo told Herkie Saybrook, her lawyer for her second divorce, that she didn't want anything for herself from Pony Bastedo except, as she put it, "Out. Out. Out," of the marriage, but she did want a trust set up for little Violet, as well as all the usual things like Nanny's salary, school fees through college, medical care, and "whatever else you can think of."

"I can't believe my eyes," said Violet.

"What?" asked Herkie.

"There's Justine Altemus over there, with Bernard Slatkin of all people."

"Who's Bernard Slatkin?"

"On TV, that one."

"What's so strange about that?"

"He'd fuck an umbrella," said Violet.

Herkie Saybrook blushed.

"Sorry, Herkie. I should have said it in French."

Voices became reserved at the mention of Hubie Altemus's name, but his mother, Lil Altemus, doted on him completely and knew, simply knew, that the new art gallery in SoHo that she had financed for him, against the advice of her brother, Laurance Van Degan, who handled her money for her, was exactly the place for Hubie to be. All that Van Degan pressure at the bank, being one of the family and all, was what caused the problems there, she was sure.

"I know there's something wrong, Hubie," said Lil, replacing her cup and saucer on the tea table that her butler had set up in her library. She took a moment, before the unpleasant scene that she knew was at hand, to admire the tangerine-colored border of her Nymphenburg tea set. "I can just tell by the way you're standing there that there's something wrong. I can always tell."

"Let up, will you?" said Hubie. Hubie was not as tall as Justine, his sister, but the aristocratic Altemus forehead and the aquiline Van Degan nose made him unmistakably her brother. There was, however, an unsureness of self about Hubie that showed in his eyes and facial expressions. His Altemus father, and his Van Degan grandfather, uncle, and cousin had all gone to St. Swithin's and Harvard, but Hubie had been asked to leave St. Swithin's, under embarrassing circumstances, and then went to several other schools of lesser stature. He was kicked out of Harvard in his first year for cheating in a Spanish examination and called before his Uncle Laurance, who was the head of the family. "Cheating in *Spanish?* The language of maids," Uncle Laurance had said contemptuously, as if it would have been a lesser offense to have cheated in economics or trigonometry.

"Just tell me one thing, Hubie," said Lil.

"What?"

"Is it murder?"

"Good God, no. How could you ask me that, Mother?"

"Drugs, then?"

"No."

"You haven't embezzled, or stolen, or anything like that?"

"Of course not."

"I just wanted to get rid of all the serious things first. So, you see, whatever it is, it doesn't really matter. You're not overdrawn again, Hubie? Oh, please don't tell me that."

"I'm not overdrawn."

"Don't make me play guessing games, for God's sake, Hubie."

Hubie breathed in deeply. "Lewd conduct," he said.

"What does that mean?"

"What it sounds like."

"Well, explain it to me."

"I was caught—" He stopped, unable to finish his sentence. He turned away from his mother before he finished his confession. "I was caught, doing it, in Central Park, with a man."

For a moment Lil was tempted to say, "Doing what?" for innocence was her trademark in the family, but she knew what he meant, and she knew, too, that her son would answer her question with the sort of words she could not bear to have repeated in her presence. Instead she said, quietly, "I don't want to hear." Her copy of *Vogue* slipped from her lap and fell to the floor. She turned her forlorn face toward the fireplace. Hubie, scarlet now, looked down on his mother as she stared at the fire. Her King Charles spaniels, Bosie and Oscar, awakened by the sound of the magazine hitting the carpet, jumped on the side of Lil's chaise, trying to get her attention. Without looking at them, she reached over to a damask-draped end table and took two cookies from a plate and threw them in the air for the dogs to leap at. Hubie watched for a minute and then turned and moved quickly toward the door of his mother's room. "Isn't this what happened at St. Swithin's?" she asked.

"Yes."

"And in Newport that summer with the lifeguard?"

"Yes."

"You promised me when Uncle Laurance got you into Simsbury that it wouldn't happen again."

"It did. At Simsbury, and at college too." Hubie opened the door.

"Don't go, Hubie," said Lil. "Look, we'll figure this out. Come over here. Sit down. Uncle Laurance will know how to get this fixed without any publicity, or fine, or anything. You'll have to go and see Uncle Laurance, Hubie."

"I can't."

"It will be just as important to Uncle Laurance as it is to you, Hubie, that this thing is handled with dispatch."

"I can't go to see him, Mother. I can't. He hates me. He makes me feel like I'm nothing. He's always comparing me to young Laurance. I can't go to see him. I'd rather go to jail," said Hubie, whose body was twisted in anguish. For a minute Lil was afraid Hubie was going to start to cry.

"Don't cry, Hubie. Please don't cry."

"I'm not crying, Mother."

"I'll go to see him."

"I'm sorry."

"If you knew, simply knew, how I hate to have to go to see your Uncle Laurance."

"I'm really sorry. I don't know what else to say."

"I'll tell you what. After this is all over, you and I will go away for a little vacation together. We could go to Venice, and stay at the Gritti, and swim at the Cipriani, and have lunch at Harry's. It'll be divine. Alessandro will be there, in that heavenly old palace of his, and I tell you, Hubie, you have never seen ceilings like the Tiepolo ceilings in Alessandro's palace. To die. It'll be such fun. You'll see. By the time we get back all this will be over. We can count on Uncle Laurance to straighten all this out."

In Justine's mind, marriage was the logical sequel to love.

"Didn't you ever hear of an affair?" asked Bernie, for whom marriage held no allure.

"Isn't that what we're having?" asked Justine.

"I was never one to believe that every romance had to end up in marriage," said Bernie.

"But this isn't just any old romance, my darling. Can't you tell? Can't you feel it? This is incredible, what we have."

Justine was fastidious about herself, not only in her neatness of grooming, but in the care of her body, which always carried the expensive scents of deodorants, and bath oils, and powder, and perfume. After they had made love several times, Bernie asked Justine not to mute her natural woman's scents with sprays and atomizers. He told her a woman's scent was like her fingerprints, hers alone, and it aroused him to know her as she really was.

Bernie rubbed his finger up and down Justine's rib cage. Too thin, she wished her ribs did not protrude so much, but she was proud of her breasts, not too big, not too small, just right, perfectly formed. She watched Bernie lean down to kiss them. She liked to watch the total absorption of his eyes on her nipples, and the look of desire on his face.

"I'm glad your nipples are pink," he said. "I like pink nipples better than beige." As his hand traveled down her body to between her legs, he brushed his face back and forth over her breasts, moaning with pleasure, and then his lips began the slow descent downward to where his moist fingers were preparing for his tongue's reception.

"Oh, Bernie," whispered Justine, her hands now in his hair. She had never known there could be such bliss as Bernie Slatkin had brought into her life. She did not know it was possible to love the way she loved him.

"My Aunt Hester asked me if you were pretty," he said, without lifting his head from his carnal task.

"What did you tell her?" Justine asked.

"I said you were as tall as me."

"That wasn't an answer to her question."

"I said you were refined looking."

Justine, enthralled with her lover's lovemaking, replied, "Did you tell her I'm going to marry her nephew?"

5

You COULD PICK out Constantine de Rham from a block away when he walked up or down Madison Avenue. His enormous head with its black beard and hooded eyes had a kind of reptilian magnificence. He was taller by far than most people and walked with such great strides that strollers on the avenue stepped aside as he passed and turned to stare after him at his aristocratic swagger. In fall and spring he wore his topcoat over his shoulders like a cape.

He had that day, in what was for him a rare burst of generosity, given a dollar to a beggar on the street, and, then, not ten minutes later, returning the same way, was offended and irritated that the same beggar held up his hand for more, having already forgotten him, rather than rewarding him with a smile of recognition and gratitude that he felt his previous contribution to the fellow's welfare deserved.

Augustus Bailey and Constantine de Rham sighted each other from a block away and passed each other without speaking, each aware of the other and each aware that the other was aware of him. An unpleasant feeling stirred within Gus Bailey, as he turned to peer into the window of the Wilton House Bookshop, pretending to concentrate on the display of copies of Nestor Calder's latest novel, *Judas Was a Redhead,* until Constantine de Rham had passed. Sometimes Gus felt prescient, and he felt in that moment of passage that he was sometime going to have to play a scene, as he used to call it in Hollywood, with Constantine de Rham. Concentrating on Nestor Calder's book, Gus did not see Elias Renthal pass behind him and enter a coffee shop, carrying a briefcase.

Inside the bookshop he could see Matilda Clarke, looking at the latest books with Arthur Harburg, the proprietor. He walked in.

"I'm sick, sick, sick to death of reading about the Mitfords," said Matilda.

"There's *Judas Was a Redhead,*" suggested Arthur.

"I've read that. I even went to Nestor Calder's publication party at Clarence's."

"Have you read *Inspired by Iago*?"

"Heavens, no!"

"It's not what you think. It opens in a trailer park."

"Right away you've lost me. A little trailer park goes a long way with me."

"What do you like?" asked Arthur Harburg, patiently. He was used to dealing with his spoiled clients.

"I like a book with short chapters," said Matilda. "I love to be able to say, 'I just want to finish this chapter,' and do it. Such a feeling of accomplishment. What have you got with short chapters, about rich people?"

"There's always Trollope," said Gus, breaking in. "He writes short chapters."

"Gus Bailey," said Matilda, with a laugh. "Trollope indeed. You missed such a good weekend in the country."

"Sorry about that."

"How was your mystery weekend in the other direction?"

"Oh, okay."

"This man leads a mystery life, Arthur."

In Gus's bathroom, Matilda went through his medicine chest. It interested her to know what men kept in their medicine chests. To her surprise, behind the boxes of his English soap and talcum powder, she found a package of Ramses, a prelubricated prophylactic, according to the copy on the box. She had not thought of Gus Bailey in terms of sexual pursuits. There was always that wife somewhere in his past whose photographs were in his apartment, and the tragedy people talked about, whatever it was. Opening the package of three, she saw that two were missing and was consumed with curiosity to know the kind of women who came to his apartment. She placed the remaining prophylactic in her evening bag and returned to Gus's living room.

There was classical music on the stereo, and Gus was settled into the chintz-covered chair that was obviously his regular chair, leafing through a copy of *Judas Was a Redhead.* For the first time she noticed him in a different way and wondered what he was like as a lover.

"Did you find everything?" he asked.

"Yes," she replied, not taking her eyes off him. With both hands she patted the back of her hair. Nearing fifty, she still wore her hair in the same pageboy style that she had worn as a debutante of eighteen. "Find your style and stick with it," she was often quoted as saying, when the fashion pages of the papers were still quoting her, before Sweetzer died.

"Drink?" Gus asked, sensing a change in the atmosphere. He rose.

"I'll have a whiskey, with a splash of water," she said. She looked around the sitting room. "Well, how nice this is, your little apartment. It's so chic."

"Hardly chic," said Gus.

"Well, cozy. I meant this run-down look you have. It's so English-second-son sort of thing."

Gus laughed. In the kitchen he made her a scotch with a splash of water. Gus was precise in all things. He refilled the ice tray, put it back in the freezer, and sponged the wet off the kitchen counter before returning to his sitting room.

"It's my first drink since New Year's Eve," she said, taking it from him. "Spirits, that is. Only wine since then, but I don't count wine. What are you having?"

"Oh, bottled water, I suppose. I keep a variety to choose from."

"Bottled water? That's all?"

"Yes."

"You don't drink?"

"No."

"Ever?"

"No."

"Did you ever?"

"Yes, but I stopped."

"Why?"

"I just did."

"By yourself, or with help?"

"With help."

"Oh, so you're a drunk!" she chortled, feeling better about herself.

"No more. Cured in Minnesota," said Gus, smiling. He returned to his chair. "There are several options for the evening," he said. "I called Chick Jacoby, and we can get a table at Clarence's. Or we can go around the corner and see the new Woody Allen movie. Or we can go to the Marty Leskys' who are having a party with a lot of movie stars."

"A veritable olio," she replied.

"Do you have a preference?"

"Yes."

"What?"

"Let me see how you look with this on," she said, opening her bag and tossing the rubber across the room to him.

"You are surprising, Gus," she said thirty minutes later.

"How so?"

"I mean, you look like and act like you have no interest in this sort of thing whatsoever, and, actually, you're terribly good at it."

"Well, so are you."

"But everybody knows about me, so I'm no surprise. Do you always wait for the lady to make the first move?"

"I suppose."

"Are you, as they say, involved at the moment?"

"I'm more for the quick encounter than for romance," said Gus. "I have been a failure at romance."

"Is that a nice way of telling me no repeats?"

"No, no. It just means, let's wait until we bump into each other at the bookshop again."

She lay back against the pillows, opened her bag, took out a gold mirror, and examined herself. "Look, my color's marvelous. I always feel so much better after a good fuck."

He laughed.

"You should laugh more, Gus," said Matilda. "You sound nice laughing. Sometimes I think that beneath that very calm veneer of yours, you are exploding with thoughts that none of us know anything about."

Dressed, they moved from the bedroom back into the living room. Matilda looked at the photographs on one of Gus's tables.

"May I suggest something to you?" she asked.

"Of course."

"Why don't you remove those pictures of your dead child from your apartment? It's just a constant reminder."

There was a silence before he replied. "May I suggest something to you?" he asked.

"Of course," she answered, unaware of the steel in his voice.

"Mind your own fucking business."

Matilda, scarlet, replied, "But I just meant—"

"I understand what you meant." He breathed deeply. "Now, about tonight. What will it be?"

"You're livid with me," she said.

"I'll get over it."

"I think I should just go back to the country."

"No, you shouldn't just go back to the country. We have had a misunderstanding. There is a part of my life I do not share, that's all, just as I'm sure there is a part of your life that you do not share. We are people of a certain age. We should be able to deal with a crisis. Right?"

"I suppose."

"Now, about tonight, what will it be?"

"You're not just being polite because we had a sort of date?"

"Of course not."

"Let's go to Marty Lesky's movie-star party. I'm so glad you know all those Hollywood people, Gus. I read in Mavis Jones's column that Faye Converse is going to be there."

"Perfect."

"You know Faye Converse, don't you?"

"Yes."

"I read the story you wrote about her."

"I like her."

"You're strange, Gus."

"How?"

"You listen to all of us talk, but you never say anything about yourself."

Gus looked at Matilda but did not reply.

"I better keep my mouth shut and quit when I'm ahead," she said, and they both laughed.

6

VERY FEW PEOPLE would have guessed that Loelia Manchester was one of the unhappiest women in New York. For twenty years the dazzling blond society figure was known as the girl who never missed a party, no matter where. She had once been reported, in the same fortnight, to have danced at balls at a maharanee's palace in Jaipur, and a German prince's castle in Regensburg, and an industrialist's villa in Palm Beach, and it was true. She flew to Paris thrice a year for her clothes, and was so often photographed in the fashion and society press, for no other reason than her social perfection and perfect taste, that her face had become as familiar in New York as a film star's.

Loelia was the youngest of Fernanda Somerset's four children, the only daughter after three sons, and the child the Somersets called their reconciliation gift to each other following an estrangement that had mercifully not ended in divorce. Arthur Somerset adored his beautiful child and, when he was killed in a plane crash in the Bahamas, left her a fortune equal to the fortunes he left to the three Somerset sons who had preceded her.

When, at twenty-two, Loelia told her mother that Edward Potter Manchester had asked her to be his wife, Fernanda Somerset was beside herself with joy. Ned Manchester was known to have no inclination for social life. He detested dinner parties and charity balls, often refusing even to go. So it was a surprise to one and all when he fell in love with the excessively social Loelia.

The Somerset fortune dwarfed the Manchester fortune, but the Manchester family superseded the Somersets in social standing, going back in American history to Gerald Manchester, who signed the Declaration of Independence, and in American society to Honoria Manchester, whose gold-and-white paneled ballroom in her Fifth Avenue house, now demolished, had been brought over from Castleberry House in London when that great pile of gray stones had been pulled down early in the century.

On each side the families were delighted with the match, from both a family and financial point of view, and the Manchesters felt certain that Loelia would grow to enjoy country life and sport while the Somersets felt that Loelia would be able to persuade Ned to take more of an interest in social life. Thereafter Loelia, following a brilliant wedding, moved into a world of New York society where she was asked everywhere, even by people who disliked her, and Ned, for years, trailed dutifully behind.

So it was that the rumored divorce of the Edward Potter Manchesters, after twenty-two years of marriage and two children, would put every other dinner-table conversation into oblivion for at least three months that season, or, at least, put every other dinner-table conversation into oblivion in the fashionable world in which Loelia and Ned Manchester moved. Whenever Dolly De Longpre wrote about the Edward Potter Manchesters in her column, which was often—for the Manchesters, particularly Loelia, were not only involved in charitable fundraising at the highest level but entertained privately in a manner that very few social aspirants could hope to emulate—she always used all three of the Manchester names and then added, in case the point was not already made, "of the New York *Social Register*." Furthermore, to add to their cachet, there was, as the saying goes in society, money on both sides.

Cora Mandell, who had decorated the Manchesters' Fifth Avenue apartment, as well as their house on Long Island, and their house in Bermuda, and all the houses of Loelia's mother, Fernanda Somerset, was rarely at a loss for words, but when Ezzie Fenwick, who knew all the news ahead of everyone else, told her about what he called "the Manchester splituation" when they were having lunch at Clarence's, she was so overwhelmed that she was speechless. Cora Mandell always wore black, no matter what the season, always wore three strands of perfect pearls, always wore her white hair parted in the middle, and worked harder than most people half her age. Ezzie often said about Cora that if she'd only let Bobo touch up her hair a bit and give her a more up-to-date coiffure, you'd think she was sixty rather than seventy-eight.

"But it can't be true," cried Cora, putting down her iced-tea glass on the table with such force that Lil Altemus and her daughter, Justine, sitting at the next table, interrupted their argument to turn and stare. "I'm making new summer slipcovers for the dining-room chairs in Locust Valley. Loelia would hardly be ordering new slipcovers if she were getting a divorce. I mean, would she?"

"Take my word for it, honey," said Ezzie, full of himself as he always was when he was the first one with the latest news. "Have I ever been wrong?"

"Who told you?" asked Cora, who knew that Ezzie, even if he was an old gossip, usually had his facts straight.

Ezzie drew himself up archly and announced, "I'm not telling."

"But why? After twenty-one years?"

"Twenty-two years," Ezzie corrected her.

"Twenty-two," Cora conceded. "Don't you think couples should just put up with each other after all that time?"

Ezzie Fenwick, whose restless eyes roamed everywhere, even during the most intimate conversation, followed with undisguised interest the entrance into the restaurant of Constantine de Rham and Yvonne Lupescu and then barely acknowledged de Rham's courtly bow and looked right through Mrs. Lupescu as the couple passed his table on the way to their own. At times, with lesser mortals or upstarts, a favorite word of his, Ezzie's face assumed attitudes of aristocratic hauteur, although they were attitudes studied and memorized but not inherited. Cora liked Ezzie. His snobbery amused her. She could remember many years ago when Ezzie had been considered an upstart himself in New York and people claimed that his father, who bought up all the foreign-car franchises that Ezzie's considerable income was derived from, had anglicized his more exotic name to the Episcopal-sounding Fenwick.

"The things I could tell you about that one," said Ezzie to Cora about Mrs. Lupescu, but Cora had no interest whatever in either Constantine de Rham or Yvonne Lupescu, or any of the other "trash Europeans," as she called them, who were overcrowding New York and driving up the price of real estate.

"Pretty cuff links," she replied, tapping a long red fingernail against one of the tiny green enamel frogs with ruby eyes that Ezzie wore on each wrist.

"Blanche Abdy gave me these when Hector died," said Ezzie, glancing down to admire how perfectly they went with his green-and-white striped shirt and green paisley tie.

Ezzie Fenwick had never had to make a living, and never had, nor had he ever gone in for any of the artistic pursuits of rich men with time on their hands, like founding magazines, or producing plays, or running art galleries or antique shops, offering, as credentials, their perfect taste, as well as their bankrolls. Ezzie was always considered close, meaning, as Laurance Van Degan often put it, that he was tight with a buck, although he was known to be extremely generous, in gifts of flowers and restaurant dinners, to certain hostesses and fashionable ladies of the city whom he particularly admired.

Early on he was known as a good seat, meaning that he was amusing to sit next to at dinner, and ladies vied for his attention, although he was quite capable of wounding any one of those same ladies who were kindest to him if he didn't care for her choice of dress for the evening ("That color yellow is *all wrong* for you!" he once said to Loelia Manchester), or if he thought she had seated a table badly ("Imagine, wasting *me* next to Maude Hoare!" he had complained to Lil Altemus), or if he felt she had redecorated her library incorrectly ("Never, ever, quilt chintz! So tacky!" he once said to Baba Timson).

Although Ezzie was now a stalwart figure in the most fashionable groups in society, it had not always been so. Cora Mandell could remember forty years ago when Ezzie was often asked to leave parties he hadn't been invited to, not only because he was a crasher, but because he dared to criticize the flower arrangements as puny, as he had at Sibila Monroe's coming-out dance, or complain that the chicken hash was all cream and no chicken, as he had at Blanche Abdy's supper party. But that was all long ago and no one else remembered.

"Back to the Manchesters," Cora redirected Ezzie, with a rap on the tabletop to get his attention away from Mrs. Lupescu.

"There's someone else involved," said Ezzie.

"There can't be," replied Cora, with disbelief in her voice.

"There has to be," said Ezzie, knowingly. "Why get a divorce after all that time unless there is someone else in the picture?"

"But Ned doesn't seem like a player-arounder," mused Cora.

"How do you know it's Ned? It might be Loelia," answered Ezzie.

"Never," said Cora affirmatively. "Loelia loves all the parties, and dresses, but she's not the type to have affairs. I mean, I've known Loelia all her life. I decorated all her mother's houses, and I've watched her grow up."

"We'll see," replied Ezzie, raising his eyebrows mysteriously, to let her know he knew something he was not telling her. "Let's have some of that grapefruit sorbet. It's delish and practically no calories. Old big ears Lil Altemus at the next table has been trying to listen to every word we've said. Now, why do you suppose Justine never married, with all that money?"

"Young people are marrying later these days," replied Cora.

"That's not Justine's problem. Justine's problem is that no one has asked her."

When Loelia Manchester's private line rang, on the telephone number that not a living soul had, except Lil Altemus, and Matilda Clarke, and her mother, and Bobo, her hairdresser, and, of course, Dimitri Minardos, she was surprised that her caller, when she answered the ring, was Dolly De Longpre. For an instant, her heart sank.

"Listen, Loelia," said Dolly. "The story's all over town that you and Ned are separating."

"There's not a word of truth to it, Dolly," replied Loelia. There was panic in her voice. She had still not told her children, which did not frighten her, and she had still not told her mother, which did frighten her.

"Come on, Loelia, it's me, Dolly. We've known each other twenty-five years," said Dolly. Dolly De Longpre was not to be brushed off.

"I can't think how these stories get started, Dolly," said Loelia.

"Loelia," said Dolly, with great patience in her voice, pronouncing the name Loelia in three syllables rather than two, for greater emphasis.

"Yes?"

"If I don't print it, someone else will," said Dolly, in her direct and plain-spoken manner. There were at this time many social chroniclers in the city, reporting on the comings and goings of the rich and super rich, but everyone agreed, in the opulent and much-photographed circle in which Loelia Manchester moved, that no one approached Dolly De Longpre's supremacy in the field. It was to her column that they all turned first thing each day, after the headlines and before the obituaries, to read about themselves, where they had been the night before, and what they wore, ate, and said.

"Oh, my word," said Loelia, understanding at once that the "someone" Dolly was referring to was Florian Gray, who was young and just starting out in Dolly's line of work, but would never, ever, she and her friends all believed, be able to understand people like them the way Dolly did.

"My word," Loelia repeated, thinking hard.

Dear, darling Dolly De Longpre, she would know how to handle it, thought Loelia. Dolly always knew how to do things just right when unpleasantness of this nature had to be dealt with. It was almost as if she were one of them, she had been writing about them all for so long, and dining with them, and staying with them in the country, and attending their weddings and christenings and memorial services. Even if Dolly didn't have her column, everyone would still invite her, they always said. Yes, Dolly De Longpre would know how to handle the divorce announcement and counteract all the perfectly awful things people were saying about Loelia and Dimitri Minardos.

"Listen, Dolly, why don't you come up and have a cup of tea with me, and that way we can talk, really talk," said Loelia.

And Dolly handled it beautifully, just as Loelia had known Dolly would, with a discreet announcement that the Edward Potter Manchesters, of the New York *Social Register,* had agreed to disagree, much to the dismay of their family and friends. But it was young Florian Gray, just making a name for himself as a commentator in the world of high society, who called a great deal of attention to the hitherto undisclosed romance of Mrs. Manchester and the shoe designer Dimitri Minardos, known as Mickie, as well as a great deal of attention to himself.

Hidden in Paris, incognito, on an outing of love, Loelia and Mickie instructed the telephone operator at the Ritz Hotel to take messages from everyone who called from America, and then decided between them which calls to return. Loelia found it irresistible that Dom Belcanto, the Hollywood ballad singer, who had promised to entertain at her benefit for the stroke center, called to wish her well, leaving a call-back number in New York.

"So sweet of Dom to call, Mickie," said Loelia, lying back in her chaise. "People say the worst sort of things about him, that he's Mafia, or mob, or whatever you call people like that, but I don't believe a word of it. When there's good work to be done, like my benefit, Dom Belcanto is there every time."

When she returned the call, the voice that answered the telephone turned out to be that of Florian Gray, who was stealing a bit of Dolly De Longpre's thunder in the New York press.

"I just wanted to know, Mrs. Manchester, if you and Mr. Minardos are planning to marry after your divorce," said Florian quickly, in the event that Loelia might hang up on him. All that he wanted was a single quote from her that would titillate his readers. Loelia, who had still not been able to bring herself to tell her children there was a new man in her life, turned ashen and mouthed to Mickie that it was Florian Gray and not Dom Belcanto on the telephone.

"What a cheap trick this is, you little piece of shit," screamed Mickie, who always became volatile in anger, into the receiver that he had pulled out of Loelia's hand. His voice, beneath the glossy patina of its New York society sound, reverted to the accent of the Greek province where he was born.

The dressing down that Mickie gave the upstart columnist was thought by both Loelia and Mickie to have been brilliant, as if their outrage would quell any thoughts Florian Gray might have had in printing their story before they could get a chance to tell Loelia's family and a few close friends of their intentions.

How wrong they were.

HEIRESS LOELIA SOMERSET MANCHESTER ELOPES TO PARIS WITH HER COBBLER, read the headline in Florian Gray's column the next morning. Florian Gray could have had no way of knowing how wounding to Mickie Minardos that headline was going to be.

7

"WHO'S THAT HANDSOME young man I keep seeing with your daughter?" asked Baba Timson, during bridge.

"A handsome young man with Justine?" replied Lil Altemus, surprised, but delighted. "You don't mean Herkie Saybrook, do you?"

"Oh, no, not Herkie," said Baba. "Everyone knows Herkie."

"Not Thayer Good, I hope?" said Lil.

"Heavens, no. Handsome, I said. Thayer Good looks like a premature baby at thirty-five."

"I don't know," said Lil, who intended to find out. "It's your bid, Loelia."

Late at night, after Bernie took Justine home, or early in the morning, when they both woke up, Justine telephoned Bernie, or Bernie telephoned Justine. They seemed never to run out of things to talk about.

"I haven't the vaguest idea how much money I'm going to inherit," said Justine. "I come from the kind of family that never fills the women in on things like that. My brother and I each have a trust, rather ample, and we live on that until Grandfather Van Degan dies, when we'll come into something, and then the rest, I suppose, when Mother dies."

"You don't have to tell me all this, you know, Justine. I can pay the bills. I intend to pay the bills," said Bernie.

"Music to my ears," said Justine. She laughed at her joke. "I've heard since I was five years old to beware of everyone, even the girls I went to school with, because they were only interested in the money. It's an awful way to grow up, you know, distrusting everyone."

"I'm never really gonna understand people like you," said Bernie.

"You know something, Bernie? You're my least suitable suitor, in terms of family and that kind of thing, but you're also the only suitor I've ever had who really didn't give a damn about the money. The things I could tell you about Jean-Claude St. Cloud, for instance, whom my mother had all picked out for me."

"I guess I'm just filled with middle-class values," said Bernie.

"More music to my ears," answered Justine.

"A couple of things I want to talk about, speaking of middle-class values," said Bernie.

"Yes?"

"I don't want to live in the same building your mother lives in, and, I have to tell you right now, I hate cabbage-rose chintz."

Justine laughed again. "Okay," she said. "Good-bye to Fifth Avenue, and good-bye to Cora Mandell and cabbage-rose chintz. But I don't want to live in your building either, and I don't want the minimal look."

"A deal," said Bernie.

"One other thing, so everything's out in the open."

"What's that?"

"I'm a spoiled girl, Bernie," Justine said. "I adore you, worship you, in fact, can't get enough of you, love to look at you, every part of you, but I'm not going to get up every morning to fry your eggs, over easy, when I have a perfectly good cook who can do that sort of thing far better than I can."

"Good. I hate to talk when I'm reading the *Times.*"

"We're going to get along great, Bernie."

"Here's to us, kid."

"Want me to come over?" she asked.

"It's two o'clock in the morning."

"I know."

"I'm not shaved, and I stink," he said.

"All the better," she answered.

"I need a fourth for bridge," said Lil Altemus, over the telephone. "I've got Matilda, and Nonie, but Loelia has backed out on me. Loelia's always backing out on me these days, and that boring Baba Timson has an appointment with her daughter's analyst that she won't break. Be here at two, will you, or earlier if you want lunch. Matilda's coming for lunch."

"I can't, Mother," said Justine.

"Why?"

"Just because I can't."

"What am I going to do?"

"I hear Rochelle Prud'homme has taken up bridge with a vengeance."

"That's what Matilda said, but I don't think Rochelle Prud'homme is quite right for our little group. You can't talk freely in front of people like that."

"I thought you liked Rochelle Prud'homme."

"She does do wonderful things for charity, but this is just old friends playing bridge."

"It's Matilda who got Rochelle to learn bridge."

"And why would Matilda do that, for heaven's sake?"

"Because Rochelle Prud'homme wants to play bridge with Lil Altemus and Loelia Manchester."

Lil listened, but as a matter of principle, she refused to show undue interest in anything Justine related, preferring to receive her information from other sources. "And why can't you play?" she asked.

"Because I am otherwise engaged."

"People are talking about you and that television announcer."

"I think we should talk about it, Mother."

"This is not at all right, you know, Justine. I'm sure he's very nice and all that, but, darling, listen to your old mother, these things have a way of just not working."

"Oh, please, Mother. Don't say listen-to-your-old-mother to me. You don't know how hilarious that sounds coming from you."

"You're just asking for trouble, Justine, with people like that."

"Have lunch with me tomorrow at Clarence's, and we'll talk."

"Christ, I hate sex with condoms," said Bernie Slatkin, removing his and flushing it down the toilet.

"Oh, God, another intellectual conversation," said Brenda Primrose, as she pulled on her pantyhose.

"It just never feels as good," said Bernie.

"The way you cat around, Bernie, it's that or nothing with me," said Brenda. They had been on-and-off lovers for several years, with never a thought of love. Brenda Primrose did the research for Bernie's newscasts. She was smart. She was flip. She was sexy. They both understood their relationship perfectly.

"I don't cat around anymore," said Bernie, defensively. "I've reformed." It was a sensitive point with him. He had been warned by a senior executive at the network, who admired his work, that a promiscuous reputation was not the best one for a successful newscaster with political ambitions.

"Since when?" asked Brenda. "Three minutes ago?"

Bernie paused. It was the reason he had asked her over, to tell her about Justine, but then, sex happened, as it always seemed to happen when they were alone, in his office, in his apartment, wherever, even in an elevator once, always quick, always lustful, never romantic. Then they went back to work, as if nothing had happened, and in her off hours, she had dates with other men, and he had dates with other women, with no need for explanation on either side.

"Since I, uh, became, uh, engaged to be married," he said. The words *engaged to be married* came out as one word, *engagedtobemarried.* He quickly turned to look in a mirror to button his shirt and tie his tie so that he could face away from her for that moment.

"Since you *what?*" she asked.

"Became engaged to be married."

"Who did you become engaged to?"

"She's called Justine Altemus."

"Laurance Van Degan's niece?"

"Yes."

Brenda walked over to the mirror, took hold of Bernie's arm, and pulled him around to face her. For an instant, they looked at each other. He smiled at her his little-boy smile, as if expecting her congratulations. Then she slapped his face, very hard. "You bastard, Bernie," she said.

"Hey, that hurt," he said, surprised, putting his hand up to the spot where she slapped him.

"That was the point of the slap, Bernie," said Brenda, angrily. "To hurt. So like you." Bernie had never seen her angry before, or at least angry with him before.

"What the hell are you talking about, Brenda?"

"You had to wait until after you came *twice* before you told me you were going to get married?"

Bernie, embarrassed, winced. Then he walked to the bar. "Want a drink?" he asked her.

"Sure," she said. She finished dressing and went over to the same mirror he had just used and readjusted her lipstick and started brushing her hair. Watching Brenda from behind, Bernie was struck, as always, by how perfect her legs were. She was the first of all the girls he knew to start wearing the new short short skirts, even before the fashion leaders let the world know it was the right look for the right girl with the right legs.

"Here," Bernie said, handing her a glass of wine.

Brenda took a sip. "You're going to have to get better wine than this, Bernie, if you're going to marry the Van Degan heiress."

"I didn't even know who she was when I met her," he said.

"You don't read Dolly De Longpre's column."

"I didn't then. I do now."

"Where'd you meet her?"

"In an elevator."

"That sounds familiar."

"No, no, no, not like that. We were both leaving a party at Maisie Verdurin's, and she gave me a ride home."

Brenda nodded. "I'm not hurt, Bernie, but I do feel a bit used. I realize I'm just the office fuck, but us office fucks have feelings too."

"Office fuck, indeed," said Bernie. He hugged her.

"Congratulations," she said, finally.

"Thanks, Brenda. I'm really going to make this marriage work."

Brenda didn't believe him, but she nodded. She knew he was an alley cat. She knew that six months after his marriage he would be on the prowl again.

"Have you told Sol and Hester yet?" she asked. Brenda Primrose had once met Bernie Slatkin's aunt and uncle, who brought him up, when they came to the studio to watch him broadcast, and she always called them Sol and Hester when she mentioned them to Bernie.

"Not yet."

"I don't think they're going to be thrilled with a *shiksa* for a niece-in-law, do you?"

"When they meet Justine, they'll like her," said Bernie.

"Sure, Bernie. Probably about as much as Mrs. Altemus and Laurance Van Degan are going to like you."

Lil Altemus looked up and watched her daughter enter the restaurant. Lil resented Justine's height and often blamed her single status, although she was only thirty, on the fact that she had towered over most of the boys in Mrs. Godfrey's dancing classes at the Colony Club when her age group was growing up in New York. Mostly, however, Lil Altemus resented Justine's height because she felt it would have far better suited her son. Still stubbornly mistaken about Hubie, Lil insisted that he would eventually find a woman, even encouraging him to pursue this one or that one, and she once gave him her discarded engagement ring, a rather large diamond from her own failed marriage, when she thought, incorrectly, that he might have found his life choice in the unlikely person of Violet Bastedo.

Lil watched as Justine, on her way to the table, stopped to speak to a trio of young married women whom she had come out with who were lunching together. Justine had never, like the Millingtons' daughter, taken to dope. Nor had she ever, like Emerald de Grey's daughter, become radical and slept with NYU associate professors with ponytails. And, thank God, she hadn't become a dyke, like poor Baba Timson's Nan, whom Baba never spoke about anymore. Lil could find nothing to fault in Justine's perfect appearance, but, used to faulting her, she stared and then squinted at her daughter's hair in such a way that Justine's hands went immediately to her coiffure, as if the wind outside had mussed it, although there had been no wind outside.

"Who's that great fat man with the foot-long cigar?" asked Lil, after her daughter was seated. Lil Altemus often pretended she didn't know things she knew very well, and she knew perfectly well who the great fat man with the cigar was.

"He's called Elias Renthal," answered Justine, who knew that her mother knew.

"The one who bought Matilda's apartment? Looks horrid. Brown shoes with a blue suit. His wife is the pushiest woman ever. Ruby, she's called. She asked me to have lunch. I mean, I know her about as well as I know this waiter." She waved her hand in the direction of the waiter who was placing a glass of white wine in front of her. "First she served a cheese soufflé, and then a chocolate soufflé for dessert. Can you imagine? Even her Rigaud candles were the wrong color. Get Matilda going on the Renthals sometime." She sipped her wine.

"Why did you go if you feel like that?" asked Justine.

"I was raising money for the new stroke center for the hospital, and all my friends said they simply couldn't give another cent, and Mrs. Renthal couldn't get her checkbook out fast enough so, of course, I had to go. It's what's called a once-only. Chick Jacoby really shouldn't allow him to smoke cigars in here."

Lil waved her napkin back and forth in the air, as if to clear it of the offending cigar smoke.

"Chick Jacoby wouldn't have the nerve to tell Elias Renthal to put it out," said Justine.

"I wonder how he got such a good table," said Lil.

"Rich, rich, rich, Mother. Or, Big Bucks, as Bernard Slatkin would say. Richer even than the Van Degans, I hear."

Lil Altemus had a horror of what she referred to as the New People, and her own immense fortune had always protected her from having to fraternize socially with any of them, except when she asked them for money for one of her charities. Recently, however, with the publication of Mr. Forbes's annual list of the four hundred richest people in America, she was aware that her still immense fortune was less immense than the fortunes of such New People as Elias Renthal "and his ilk," meaning the Bulbenkians, and the Zobel brothers, and the Jorsts. The feeling was unsettling.

"Imagine anyone wearing a pale blue gabardine suit," said Lil, still staring over at Elias Renthal. Then she added, "Who's Bernard Slatkin?"

"He's the man I'm going to marry," answered Justine.

"Goodness," said Lil.

Justine expected a great furor of protestations from her mother, and possibly a scene. Bernard Slatkin possessed none of the requisites that Lil Altemus, who never let anyone forget that she was born a Van Degan, adhered to in past suitors for her daughter's hand. Surprisingly, Lil was, if not exactly enthusiastic, at least not defiant in her opposition to Justine's choice. Justine was, after all, thirty, or, to be precise, practically thirty-one. The kind of boys she had grown up with, gone to dancing school with, spent weekends with at Yale or Princeton, and who now worked downtown, in banks or brokerage houses, almost never married girls as rich as Justine Altemus was going to be. As one after another of them had drifted into solid if less spectacular marriages, Lil's greatest fear was that Justine would fall into the clutches of one of the fortune-hunting foreigners who preyed on American heiresses. Every time she thought of her childhood friend, Consuelo Harcourt de Rham, she shuddered at her sad fate. The sight of Consuelo's widower, Constantine de Rham, several tables away, spending Consuelo's money on a blond strumpet half his age, wearing far too many jewels for daytime, may have softened Lil's opposition to Bernard Slatkin.

"Slatkin," said Lil. "I don't know that name."

"It's not in the *Social Register,* Mother," answered Justine.

"That's not what I meant, and you know it."

"He earns a great deal of money, Mother."

"A television announcer, someone told me."

"No, he is a broadcaster. On the evening news."

"Not the little Chinese?"

"No, Mother, that's the weatherman, and he's Korean, not Chinese. Bernie is one of the anchormen."

"Oh, yes, of course. Is he the one with the dimple or the one with the toupee?"

"The dimple. He's very handsome, Mother."

"Of course he is, darling. Where in the world did you meet such a person?"

"At Maisie Verdurin's."

"Mrs. Verdurin has all those celebrities to dinner, doesn't she? I'm forever reading about her in Dolly's column. What were you doing at Mrs. Verdurin's?"

"We're here to talk about the man I'm going to marry, not about Maisie Verdurin."

"What do you suppose old Cora Mandell and Ezzie Fenwick are being so intense about at the next table?" asked Lil.

"Mother!"

"I'm listening, Justine," said her mother, sharply. "Forgive me if I can't absorb it all in a flash. This is quite important news, and, after all, we don't know anything about Mr. Bernard Slatkin, now, do we?"

Justine knew, before her mother even said it, that she was going to say, "Who is he?" She also knew that her mother meant, "Who is his family? What are his schools?"

"Who is he?" asked her mother.

"His parents are dead. He was raised by an aunt and uncle, Sol and Hester Slatkin. Sol is in the printing business. They live in New Jersey. Weehawken."

"Hmm," said Lil.

"Bernie went to Rutgers on a scholarship," said Justine. She loved saying, "He went to Rutgers on a scholarship," as if it added to the worth of him, a romantic asset to his history. In all her life she had never known anyone who had gone to school on a scholarship, and she found the idea glamorous. Even the names Sol and Hester evoked images in her mind of Ellis Island, and the Statue of Liberty, and huddled masses, although Sol and Hester Slatkin were several generations removed from Ellis Island and lived comfortable lives in comfortable circumstances. "He waited on tables in a fraternity house," Justine continued, her voice filled with excitement. "And then he went to law school for a year, I forget where, but he dropped out, because he was mad-keen to be in television news. First he was an on-the-air reporter covering City Hall, and then he filled in for a week as anchorman when Charlie Walsh broke his leg, and there was such a favorable reaction to him, I mean, people wrote in about him, he's so good-looking, wait till you see him, and then they made him a coanchorman full time after Charlie went to Los Angeles."

"Hmm," said Lil.

"He's not after my money, if that's what you're worried about, because he earns a fortune, an absolute fortune."

"They all earn a lot of money, those announcers, don't they?"

"He's an anchorman, Mother, not an announcer, and he writes all his own copy. He's very successful."

"I meant an anchorman," said Lil.

"I want a big wedding, Mother, with bridesmaids, and a reception at the Colony Club, and, you know, the works," said Justine.

"This is so nice, Justine," said Lil. She shaped her lips into an obligatory smile, but Lil's lips were very little involved in her smiles. Instead she raised her eyebrows and blinked her eyes shut several times in rapid succession in a manner that suggested, somehow, mirth. "You know, of course, there will be things to discuss with Uncle Laurance down at the bank."

"Yes."

"When will I meet Mr. Slatkin?"

"As soon as you say. You won't be difficult, will you, Mother, if Daddy gives me away?"

"Of course not, darling, as long as that tramp he's married to doesn't come within my sight lines and is seated somewhere at the back of the church," said Lil.

"Oh, Mother, I'm so thrilled. And you're going to love Bernie. He knows everything about Libya and nuclear disarmament and all those things. He's fascinating."

"Justine."

"Yes, Mother?"

"Mr. Slatkin, uh—"

"Please call him Bernie."

"Yes, of course, Bernie."

"What about him?"

"He doesn't wear one of those little beanie hats, does he?"

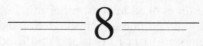

P EOPLE WHO WORKED for Elias Renthal accused him, behind his back, of course, as having a vile nature, as he had no patience whatever for people who were not as consumed with the desire to make money as he was. The accusation would not have offended him if he had been confronted with it. Elias looked on his unpopularity as a natural consequence of wealth and power. Maxwell Luby, Elias's head trader, was a second-echelon executive, knew it, accepted it, and aspired only to be the best second-echelon executive, an indispensable acolyte to Elias Renthal. Only Max Luby, who had known Elias from the beginning, in Cleveland, did not fear his wrath, which could be extreme, and dared to sometime caution him on the enormity of his wealth, although he refrained from voicing disapproval of the manner of Elias's rapid acquisition of his fortune.

"You're like a heroin addict, Elias," he said, "only about money."

"What the hell are you talking about?" asked Elias impatiently. Introspection was not a thing that Elias had any time for, especially during business hours, when he liked to devote his full attention to the fifty computers in his office, beaming fiscal information.

"I remember when you used to think everything would be all right with your life if you had a million dollars. And then I remember when you set ten million as your goal, and then fifty, and then a hundred. You thought the world was going to be your oyster with a hundred million, do you remember?"

"C'mon, c'mon, we got work to do. What is this? Psych One at Cleveland University?"

"But it still wasn't enough," Max went on, unperturbed by Elias's impatience. "Then it was five hundred million. And then you had a billion, even though Mr. Malcolm Forbes said you only had eight hundred million. And now you got three billion. Where does it stop, Elias? How much more do you need?"

Elias looked at Max. "I can't stop, Max. It's just too fucking easy. You know what it's like? It's like placing red meat in front of a lion."

Even Max Luby, who knew everything about Elias Renthal, did not know about his several secret bank accounts in Swiss banks with branch offices in Nassau in the Bahamas. He thought that when Elias went to Nassau, it was in connection with a new vacation house he was building in Lyford Key. He didn't know that one of the accounts was in his name, Max Luby, or that another was in Ruby's maiden name, R. Nolte. He didn't know that when Elias got a tip, from a variety of young lawyers in firms that dealt with mergers, or young stockbrokers with access to information not available to everyone, he made collect calls to his Swiss banks in Nassau, who did his buying for him, with no one the wiser.

Lord Biedermeier surveyed the lunch crowd from his favorite table at Clarence's with a proprietary air. It was he, he was fond of telling all his friends and acquaintances, who had come up with the name for the popular restaurant, when Chick Jacoby was searching for a name that would have an English flavor. "Call it Clarence House," Lord Biedermeier had proposed, with the speed that he was able to give authors better titles for their books than they had been able to think up themselves. Lord Biedermeier was a great admirer of the Queen Mother, to whom he owed the knighthood that had preceded his title, and had been in the past a frequent visitor at her London residence known as Clarence House. Like all things concerned with Lord Biedermeier, snobbery played a great part. When Clarence House became fondly referred to as Clarence's, by the people who were regularly seated there by the very fussy Chick Jacoby, Lord Biedermeier, who lunched there most days when he was in New York, was delighted.

He waved his hand in greeting to Charlie Dashwood as Charlie passed his table to join Teddy Vermont and wondered what it was the two men were meeting about. Curiosity, both business and social, always consumed Lord Biedermeier, even about people he scarcely knew. Staring, he removed his pince-nez and, with his thumb and forefinger, massaged the reddened bridge of his nose before returning to a photocopy of an article from the front page of that morning's *New York Times* business section about the imminent collapse of Oswald Slingerland's hotel empire.

He pushed back the cuffs of his custom-made dark gray pin-stripe suit and custom-made Turnbull and Asser shirt and looked at the time on his Cartier watch. It was usually he who kept his guests waiting, but he did not want to risk arriving after Elias Renthal, who did not feel comfortable at Clarence's, and came ten minutes before the appointed time. As Rochelle Prud'homme passed his table he rose and kissed her hand.

"Such a nice party that was, Rochelle," he said to her.

"Your flowers were lovely, Lucien," said Rochelle.

"Who are you joining?" asked Lord Biedermeier.

"My sales staff. I'm bringing out a new line of liquid vitamins, made from the live cells of sheep embryos," she said.

"My word," said Lord Biedermeier.

"Longer life, Lucien," said Rochelle.

"I'm serious about doing your autobiography," said Lord Biedermeier. "Ah, here is Mr. Renthal." He eyed Elias Renthal's pale blue gabardine suit critically. "Do you know each other? Rochelle Prud'homme. Elias Renthal."

"Hello, Eli," said Rochelle.

"Hello, Roxy," said Elias.

"Rochelle," she corrected him, meeting his eye, about her name.

"Elias," he corrected her, about his.

"Ta, Lucien," said Rochelle, moving off to her table. The unfriendly exchange between Rochelle Prud'homme and Elias Renthal was not lost on Lord Biedermeier.

"Old friends, I take it," he said, commenting on the scene he had just witnessed.

"Old acquaintances would be a better description," said Elias.

"Business fallout?" asked Lord Biedermeier.

"A corporate raid on Prud'homme Hairdryers. One of my few failures," said Elias, smiling. "A tough cookie, Roxy Persky, for such a tiny little lady."

"It's all this sort of thing, your takeovers, that I think the public will find so fascinating, Elias. Rags to riches is irresistible stuff for your American audiences. What you have done is the American dream," said Lucien Biedermeier. He halted the conversation while he ordered the wine and the main course, asking Elias to defer to his culinary decisions because the chef, a Hungarian he had known in Budapest who later worked at the Ritz Hotel in London, knew how best to make a dish that was prepared especially for him every time he called ahead.

"Have you ever written?" Lord Biedermeier asked.

"Just checks for Ruby," replied Elias, laughing, as if he had made a *bon mot.*

Lord Biedermeier smiled appreciatively and then said, "No, seriously."

"I don't have time to do all the things I'm doing," said Elias. "How the hell am I ever to get the time to write my autobiography, Lord Biedermeier?"

"It's Lucien, Elias," said Biedermeier. "You won't have to write a word of your autobiography. I'll make all the arrangements. All that you'll have to do is give two hours a week to the writer I'll hire for you. You just tell him or her your stories, and all the writing will be done for you. It's that simple."

"As soon as I get back from London, I'll meet the writer," said Elias. He was beginning to warm to the idea of an autobiography.

"How long will you be gone?"

"Just a few days. We'll be staying at the Claridge's Hotel."

"No, no, no," said Lord Biedermeier. "Simply say Claridge's. Not *the* Claridge's. Nor Claridge's Hotel either. Oh, dear me, no. Just say Claridge's."

"What difference does it make?" asked Elias.

"These are the little signals by which people like us recognize each other," said Lord Biedermeier.

"Do you think I'll ever learn all these ins and outs?"

"Oh, certainly, Elias. Certainly."

"I had this idea, Lucien," said Elias, taking out a comb from his pocket and combing his hair as he talked.

"No, no, no, you mustn't do that, Elias," said Lucien.

"Do what?"

"Comb your hair at Clarence's, I mean, it's just not done."

"God, you sound like Ruby. She's always telling me I don't do things the right way. Except make money, of course. That's what I wanted to talk to you about. The profits from this book. There will be profits, I assume," said Elias.

"That is always the hope in publishing, Elias, and there is a great interest in tycoon biographies at the moment, especially self-made tycoons. We have every reason at Biedermeier and Lothian to think that there will be a major audience for the story of Elias Renthal, especially since your recent marriage. All that running around you did after your last divorce might not have gone over in middle America, especially for a man your age, but now, with Ruby, you will start to build a place for yourself here in New York. How is the divine Ruby?"

With all his heart Elias Renthal wished he hadn't once told Lord Biedermeier, in a moment of fraternal camaraderie aboard the Concorde from London to New York, that Ruby could take, as he put it at the time, both his nuts in her mouth at the same time. And with all his heart he wished he hadn't added, "And I got big nuts," when he shared that confidence with Lord Biedermeier. He hadn't known at that point that he was going to marry Ruby Nolte. He knew it was what was on Lord Biedermeier's mind every time Lord Biedermeier saw Ruby. He wondered if Lord Biedermeier had told other people what he had said, because he knew he would have told if Lord Biedermeier had said the same thing to him about some girl he was involved with.

"What Ruby and I thought was that I would donate the profits from the book and the paperback sale to the homeless of New York, or to the families of victims of violent crime, or something we think up, as a sort of public-relations pitch."

"What a good idea, Elias. There's that young police officer who was paralyzed by the drug dealer. You could give him something. The public eats up that sort of thing."

"Oh, shit," said Elias.

"What?" asked Lord Biedermeier.

"I dropped some of this goulash you ordered on my new suit."

"Quite dashing haberdashery you are wearing," said Lord Biedermeier.

"Don't you like my new suit?" asked Elias.

"Pale blue gabardine was never one of my favorites."

"Oh."

"But I prefer it by far to the rust-colored gabardine you had on at the office yesterday."

"I'm all wrong. Is that what you're trying to tell me?"

"I think with your growing position in the city, you should give more thought to your clothes. Dark grays. Dark blues. And the subtlest pin stripes. You must let me take you to my tailor," said Lord Biedermeier. "While we're on the subject, what manicurist do you use?"

"Blanchette, at my office," said Elias.

"You must tell Blanchette at your office to buff your nails. That glossy polish is frightfully common."

Elias, bewildered, stared at his fingers. He wondered if he would ever learn all that he was supposed to learn.

"I don't get it," said Elias, looking over at the entrance of the restaurant, where Chick Jacoby was turning away some customers whose look did not appeal to him.

"What don't you get, Elias?" asked Lord Biedermeier.

"This place. Clarence's. Why do people fight to come here?"

"It's cheap. That is Chick Jacoby's secret."

"That's what I don't get."

"My dear Elias. It's something you will learn. There is nothing the rich enjoy more than a bargain, especially a bargain that is reserved exclusively for them."

"Why can't Ruby learn that? She only likes it if it costs the most."

"Oh, look who's coming in," said Lord Biedermeier, whose eyes were riveted on the door where Chick Jacoby was welcoming some arriving guests, with flourishes, to signal their importance.

"The man with Jamesey Crocus is Dimitri Minardos. Some people call him Mickie Minardos."

"Who the hell is Dimitri Minardos, for Christ's sake? Ruby knows who all these people are, but I never do," said Elias, buttering a roll.

"He designs shoes."

"Shoes? That's a big deal? Shoes?" asked Elias, unimpressed.

"Dimitri Minardos is the name on every lip this week," said Lord Biedermeier.

"What did Dimitri Minardos do?"

"The fascinating Loelia Manchester has fallen madly in love with him, and be assured that Ruby knows who Loelia Manchester is."

"Damn, I wish Ruby was here," said Elias.

Ruby at that time was occupied with Cora Mandell on the redecoration of the vast apartment that she and Elias had recently purchased from Matilda Clarke, who, even before the death of Sweetzer Clarke, had not been able to afford to live there any longer.

"Those drapes must have been pretty in their day," said Ruby, "but I bet they haven't been changed since the nineteen fifties."

"Those curtains were hung in nineteen fifty-eight," said Cora Mandell.

"How do you know?" asked Ruby.

"I did this room in nineteen fifty-eight for Sweetzer Clarke's mother, before Sweetzer and Matilda were married."

"I'm glad I said the drapes were pretty," said Ruby.

"I had those curtains made up from some antique damask that Sweetzer's mother found in the Fortuny factory in Venice," said Cora.

Each time Ruby said the word *drapes,* Cora Mandell repeated the word *curtains* in the following sentence, as a way of letting her know that *drapes* was a word that was simply not used, an offense even to her ear, without actually correcting the newly rich woman who wanted so much for Cora Mandell to decorate her apartment. By the third time, the point had been made, and Ruby Renthal never used the word *drapes* again.

"The price, of course, is quite different for a window treatment today than it was in nineteen fifty-eight," said Cora.

Ruby Renthal seemed indifferent to cost, but Cora Mandell pursued the topic nonetheless, so that there would be no misunderstandings later.

"You have to figure on not less than seven thousand dollars a window for curtains. That, of course, includes the fringe," said Cora.

Ruby did not react adversely.

"It's how long it takes, not how much it costs, that I am interested in," answered Ruby.

"How many windows are there?"

"Ninety, perhaps, on the three floors, but I shouldn't think the curtains in the servants' rooms need be anything more than something pretty on a rod," said Ruby.

"Exactly," said Cora.

"We have a new painting, a Monet, with water lilies, and I was thinking that the walls of this room should be the same color pink as the inside of the water lilies in the painting," said Ruby. "Pink happens to be my favorite color."

"Persimmon, I think, would be a prettier color than pink. In lacquer, nineteen or twenty coats of lacquer," said Cora.

"Sounds nice," said Ruby.

"Is there furniture you would like me to see, Mrs. Renthal?" asked Cora.

"We have to get everything new," answered Ruby.

"For all three floors? My word," said Cora. "Do you mean there is nothing to recover?"

"We're starting from scratch," said Ruby, "but I want everything first rate."

"I see. There is an auction coming up in London in a few weeks."

"I love auctions," said Ruby.

"The Orromeo family has come on hard times and are selling their priceless collection of furniture."

"My word," said Ruby, using the phrase Cora Mandell had just used.

"There is a pair of eighteenth-century console tables, with inlaid rams' heads, which are too beautiful for words. They would be marvelous right there, on either side of the fireplace, with the Monet over the fireplace," said Cora. It wasn't often, even with the opulence of the decade, and the abundance of the new rich, that she was given carte blanche to start from scratch in an apartment of forty-one rooms. She realized she would have, finally, enough of a nest egg to retire.

"We can fly over in my husband's jet," said Ruby.

"My word, how grand," said Cora.

"We're going to get along great, Mrs. Mandell," said Ruby.

"Yes, Mrs. Renthal," said Cora.

Lil Altemus sat in the back of her car next to her daughter and stared out at Central Park, while she organized her plans for the day in her head. "Tap on the glass, will you, Justine, and tell Joe to take me straight down to the Van Degan Building first."

"Yes, Mother," said Justine. She removed her glove and tapped on the glass with her ring. "Joe, Mother wants you to stop first at the Van Degan Building."

"Okay, Miss Justine," said Joe, closing the glass between them again.

"Is that your engagement ring?" asked Lil.

"Isn't it perfect?" Justine replied, defensively.

"Let me see it," said Lil.

Justine held out her hand to her mother.

Lil picked up Justine's hand and peered at her daughter's engagement ring without comment. She opened her bag, took out her reading spectacles, put them on, and picked up Justine's hand again. "That's not even a ruby," said Lil. "I thought you said he was going to give you a ruby. That's a garnet, for God's sake. He gave you a garnet with a lot of poky little diamonds around it. Now, don't pretend to me you think that's a big deal, because it's not. One thing I can't stand, it's a cheapskate. Either you tell Mr. Slatkin, or I tell him, that this just won't do. A man who earns four hundred thousand dollars a year can do better than a garnet."

"How do you know how much Bernie earns?" asked Justine. "I don't even know how much he earns."

"Uncle Laurance checked him out."

"Mother, I can't tell Bernie that. The ring belonged to his mother."

"Yes, I'm sure it did." Lil turned to look out the window again. "Look, my God, there's Loelia Manchester holding hands on Fifth Avenue with Mickie Minardos. I can't believe my eyes. Look! He's kissing her, right there on the street!"

"And Loelia's kissing him right back. Don't leave out that part of the story, Mother," said Justine.

"I don't know what the world's coming to," said Lil. She sat back in her seat and stared straight ahead. "I'll get out here, Joe," she called to the chauffeur when he pulled up in front of the Van Degan Building. She turned to Justine. "I have to see Uncle Laurance, Justine. There's no need for you to come in. Why don't you take my hair appointment at Bobo's? Then if you'd pick up my shoes at Delman's and then go to Tiffany's and see if the invitations are in for the engagement party. Nevel wants you to look at some preliminary sketches for the wedding dress, but you can always do that tomorrow. I'm meeting Matilda Clarke for lunch at Clarence's, and I'm sure Matilda would love to see you, so join us, but, for God's sake, don't show Matilda that ring."

"Jesus Christ, Lil," said Laurance Van Degan. He stood and walked to the window of his office, shaking his head slowly in disgust as he gazed down on the street forty stories below, while Lil told him, in the roundabout fashion she always used when speaking to her brother of Hubie, the son she adored, about Hubie's latest transgression. "I always thought people like that shot themselves."

"Laurance, how could you say such a dreadful thing about Hubie?" screamed Lil, like a tigress protecting her young. Lil, of course, didn't want Hubie to shoot himself, because she loved him in a way that she had never been able to love Justine, but she had always thought, when she and Laurance were growing up, that there was something noble when "people like that" did commit suicide, like Warkie Taylor, who hanged himself at Yale, and poor sweet Mungo Fitz Alyn, Dodo Fitz Alyn's uncle, who quietly slipped over the side of the *Queen Elizabeth* one midnight somewhere between New York and Southampton and wasn't missed for two days, after that terrible situation on board with the sailor who lied so at the inquiry.

"Now, calm down, Lil," said Laurance.

"Once the right girl comes along, Hubie will settle down and be just fine, Laurance. I guarantee it. Look how marvelously he's doing with his art gallery."

"Okay, Lil," said Laurance. "I'll make a couple of calls. Tell Hubie he's got to come in and see me."

"He won't, Laurance."

"If he wants to keep his name out of the newspapers, you tell him to come in."

"Yes, Laurance. Thank you, Laurance."

"Oh, and one thing, Lil. I want a little something in return."

"Of course, darling, anything," said Lil, gathering her bag and gloves and holding up her mink coat for her brother to help her put on.

"When the invitations go out for Justine's wedding, I want you to invite Mr. and Mrs. Elias Renthal. They live in Matilda's old apartment."

"You can't be serious, Laurance."

"I am serious, Lil."

"You mean that fat man with the powder-blue gabardine suits, and the big smelly cigars, and the wife who's trying to push herself onto every committee in New York? Not on your life. Justine's wedding is just for family and friends."

"Family, friends, and the Elias Renthals, Lil."

"But why?"

"Because I asked you to."

9

IT WAS AT THE opening night of *Carmen* at the Metropolitan Opera, the new *Carmen,* straight from Paris, that everyone said was to be "too divine for words" and "full of surprises," that Loelia Manchester and Mickie Minardos made their first public appearance together since the word of their romance began to titillate New York society. Even then, observing propriety, they were not together as a couple, merely seated in the same box as members of an extremely fashionable group. Loelia arrived with Ezzie Fenwick, the society wit, who had often in the past few years served as her approved escort when Ned Manchester, tired after squash at the Racquet Club, began to beg off going out every night of the week with the artistic people that Loelia found so fascinating and Ned found so boring.

"Mickie Minardos?" gasped Lil Altemus, in her box, keeping her eyes averted from Loelia's box. "I don't believe it. It can't be true. I mean, Mickie's divine. Such a sense of fantasy. So amusing. And *such* a good dancer. Have you ever tangoed with Mickie, Matilda? To die. And the best possible fun on a weekend, or on someone's boat. But marriage? Loelia can't be thinking of marrying him. I mean, she just can't."

All eyes were riveted on Mickie's box. They called it Mickie's box, and Mickie played host, but they knew, those in the know, that it was Loelia who paid.

"Do stop staring up at their box, and, for God's sake, don't stare with your opera glasses," whispered Ruby Renthal to her husband Elias from their orchestra seats, although her fascination with the romance of Loelia Manchester and Mickie Minardos, if anything, exceeded her husband's.

"She's standing with her back to the audience, so she can't see me," said Elias.

"You sure?" asked Ruby.

"Unless she's got eyes in the back of her head," answered Elias.

"What's she wearing?"

"Pink."

"Long sleeves? High neck?"

"Yeah."

"That's a Nevel. I almost ordered that dress," said Ruby, wishing she had, imagining the furor it would cause if she and Loelia Manchester, whom everybody considered to be the best-dressed woman in New York society, turned up at the opera in the same Nevel dress.

"Who's that fat man staring up at us with his opera glasses?" asked Mickie Minardos, looking down from his box. Mickie Minardos had found fame and fortune as a designer of women's shoes, although his artistic talents, he and his acolytes believed, and none more fervently than Loelia Manchester, were scarcely tapped by his occupation. He could have been, they said about him, a stage designer, or a ballet designer, or, even, an opera designer, and his comments on the opera designs of that evening had been scathing, but amusing.

"He's called Elias Renthal," replied Ezzie Fenwick. "Worth a billion, I understand, at last count, and made it all in the last eight or nine years."

"Oh, and his wife is so pushy," said Loelia, not turning around to look. "Ruby she's called. They bought Matilda Clarke's apartment, and Cora Mandell's doing it up for them, and you should hear Cora's stories about them. Too funny."

"What's he like?" asked Mickie.

"He calls a dinner jacket a monkey suit," replied Ezzie.

"Oh, dear," said Loelia.

"But everything he touches turns to gold. He can't seem to get enough money. And they learn very quickly, those people," said Ezzie, who knew all there was to know about everybody.

"He's supposed to be a great art collector, courtesy of Maisie Verdurin, who guides his every move, and they're doing the apartment around the pictures, according to Cora," said Loelia.

"Elias Renthal has a great collection, but I most certainly don't think of him as a great collector," said Jamesey Crocus from his corner of the box, and they all turned to listen because Jamesey Crocus knew more about fine French furniture and art collecting than any man in New York. Although Jamesey was originally from Seattle, he spoke with an upper class British accent acquired during a year's training course at an auction house in London, and he claimed to have studied as the last pupil of Bernard Berenson at I Tatti in Florence. "He has probably thirty true masterpieces, and many fine lesser pictures, but you have to realize that he acquired the entire collection in a couple of years, and only buys pictures for specific locations in his apartment. A great collector never stops buying. And, besides, you can't take anyone seriously as a collector, no matter what masterpieces he has, if he also collects all those Steuben animals Elias has."

"How do you make so much money in such a short time?" asked Mickie Minardos.

"Airplane wheels first, somewhere out in Ohio. Then a hamburger franchise. The real money came from the takeover of Miranda Industries, where he is supposed to have cleared three billion in under two years," said Ezzie.

"Heavens!" said Loelia, and they all gasped at the amount of money. "But can that possibly be legal?"

"Anyone who acquires that much money in that short a time can't have done it legally. It's simply not possible, but that, whether we approve or not, is not our concern," said Jamesey Crocus, who was involved with fundraising. "Look what he's doing for the museum. What I like about Elias is that you can call him up and ask for six hundred thousand or seven hundred and fifty thousand dollars, or whatever it is you need, for an exhibit, or a purchase, and he simply gives it to you, or he doesn't. There's no board of directors that has to vote on it. He makes all his own decisions, and, of course, he's very generous. But, there's only X number of times you can do that with someone like Elias Renthal before he expects something in return."

"The problem with people like that is before long they want to come to dinner," said Loelia.

"And more," said Jamesey.

"Like what?"

"Like a position on our board at the museum."

"Oh, no. No, no, no," said Loelia. "That would never do. Too rough around the edges."

"Exactly," agreed Jamesey Crocus, nodding his head gravely.

"I play a certain amount of men's doubles," said Laurance Van Degan, from the back of the box, "but I've never played with anyone like Elias Renthal. The way that man plays tennis. To kill. I never saw anything like it."

"I'm told that's the way he conducts his business as well," said Jamesey.

"I'm dying to turn around and look at Mr. Renthal," said Loelia. "Give me your opera glasses, Mickie. His wife stares at me at the hairdresser, and Bobo says however I wear my hair she wants the same thing."

"She looks pretty," said Mickie.

"She might be if only her nose were her own," said Loelia, staring back through her glasses at the Renthals. "Dr. Apted."

"Who?"

"Dr. Apted does those little turned-up noses where you can see right up the nostrils."

When the photographers from the social and fashion press began to descend on the closed doors of Dimitri Minardos's box during the intermission between the first and second acts, hoping to get a picture of Loelia Manchester and Mickie together, Loelia, always cooperative with the press because of her numerous charitable activities, came out and posed in animated conversation with Ezzie Fenwick, who loved to be photographed, but who was not the one they wanted to photograph, while Mickie remained inaccessible in his box.

Ezzie Fenwick was critical of everything. With so much free time on his hands, he was always the first to see the new films, new plays, new art shows, new musical events, new fashion collections, both in Paris and New York, and he could amuse at lunch and dinner parties with his witty critiques, because, quite frankly, he enjoyed watching failure.

"Simply ghastly!" he said, rolling his eyes in mock horror, about the *Carmen* that was being sung in front of them, and declared out loud that the role of Carmen was beyond, simply beyond, the vocal capabilities of the soprano at hand. During the second act, after the photographers had returned to the bar until the next intermission, Ezzie rallied the inhabitants of Loelia's box to sneak out, giggling, on tiptoe, to a marvelous party he knew about at the Rhinelander.

After the opera, Ruby Renthal, disconsolate, sat at her ten-thousand-dollar table on the promenade of the opera house and surveyed the empty table next to hers. With a promise to Janet Van Degan of a large donation by her husband to the Opera Guild, Ruby had secured a table strategically placed next to the table that was supposed to be occupied by Loelia Manchester and Dimitri Minardos and their friends, but they, alas, had fled.

"Elias, you're not supposed to wipe the plate clean with your dinner roll," whispered Ruby, irritably. "You're supposed to waste some of the food."

"I get hungry, Ruby," said Elias.

"I tell you what we're going to do. I'm going to have the cook feed you before we go out to these functions, and then you can pick at your food, like all these people do, when we sit down to dinner."

"I'll buy that," said Elias, reaching out to hold his wife's hand. Elias's bow tie was black on one side and red on the reverse, and, in the tying, the left half was black and the right half red. He seemed inordinately proud of it, as if he were dictating a new fashion.

"Honey, that bow tie has got to go," said Ruby.

"I just bought this tie," said Elias. "What's wrong with it?"

"It's the only two-tone bow tie here; that's what's wrong with it," she said.

"It's the latest thing, the guy in the shop told me," insisted Elias.

"The latest thing somewhere else, not here."

"But—"

"The invitation said black tie. It did not say half black, half red tie. If there's going to be a new fashion, we aren't in any position to be the ones setting it."

"Yet," said Elias.

"Yet," agreed Ruby, smiling at him. She looked back at the empty table next to her. "I wonder what happened to Mickie and Loelia."

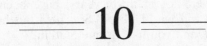

10

"I THOUGHT I MIGHT get a little drunk if you don't mind. Or even if you do mind," said Hubie Altemus. "All this terribly good champagne just sitting here."

"Why did I think you weren't drinking?" asked Lil, looking at her son through the mirror of her dressing table. He looked back at her as he picked up a bottle of champagne from a silver tray and poured himself a glass. Lil bent her head and concentrated on fastening the clasp of a diamond and sapphire bracelet on her wrist.

"I really don't know why you thought that, Mother," answered Hubie.

"What's he called, that friend of yours from the gallery, with the Spanish name?"

"Juanito?"

"Yes, Juanito. I thought Juanito got you to stop drinking."

"He did. I'm on what's called a slip in some circles, in honor of the bride- and groom-to-be."

"You will behave in front of the family, won't you, Hubie?"

Hubie poured another glass of champagne, all the time looking at his mother.

"I really wish you'd worn a suit, Hubie. Not those damn jeans. And you're going to have to borrow a tie. With the whole family here, you simply can't dress like that. You know how Uncle Laurance gets."

Hubie laughed.

"What did Uncle Laurance say, Hubie?" asked Lil. "You did see Uncle Laurance today, didn't you?"

"He said I was a disgrace to the family. He said I had no consideration for you whatsoever. Stuff like that. He said that he always thought people like me shot themselves."

"He didn't say that!" said Lil.

"He said it was the last time, the very last, that he was going to get me out of trouble. He said from here on in he didn't give a flying fuck what I did."

"Really, Hubie. You know I can't bear that kind of talk."

"He's your brother, Mother. You asked me what he said, and I told you."

"You won't get in trouble again, will you, Hubie?" Lil looked up at her son. For an instant their eyes met, and then they both looked away. "Look, darling, let's just get through this damn party, and then we'll sit down and have a real talk."

"I'm not staying for the party, Mother," said Hubie.

"Of course you're staying for the party. We'll find you a tie. It's your own sister's engagement party. And your old mother needs all the moral support she can get."

"I can't stay."

"Fulco made this bracelet for me years ago with the stones from Granny B.B.'s tiara, but I never, not in thirty years, have been able to work this goddamn clasp. Fix it, will you, Hubie?" She held out her wrist to her son. "Why can't you stay? Don't you like Bernie Slatkin?"

"I like Bernie Slatkin fine. I just wish he was as gung-ho on this wedding as Justine is," said Hubie.

"What are you *talking* about?" asked Lil, waving her wrist in the air, waiting for Hubie to take it.

"Just what I said."

"Oh, don't be silly. He's *mad* about Justine."

"No, Justine's mad about him. It ain't the same thing."

"Push that bell for Lourdes, will you, Hubie? She'll find you a tie. There must be some in your old room. Or in the present drawer."

"Mother, I said I'm not staying for the party."

"But why?"

"I can't face all those fucking Van Degans," said Hubie. He picked up his mother's wrist and fastened the clasp for her.

"Even your grandfather is coming."

"That's what I mean. Grandfather Van Degan. Uncle Laurance. Aunt Janet. Young shitface Laurance and his dreary wife with her homemade dresses. I can't stand any of them. Except poor Dodo."

"There's the doorbell. People are beginning to arrive. Answer it, will you, Hubie?"

"That's what you keep a butler for, Mother. I'm going out the back way."

"Justine will be so disappointed."

"If anybody will understand, Justine will understand."

"You look tired, Hubie."

"I'm not sleeping well."

"You stay out too late. That's your problem."

"Not anymore."

"Don't you think you're getting too thin, Hubie?"

"Yeah, I do," he answered.

"We all love to be thin. 'You can't be too rich or too thin,' as the Duchess used to say to Mother, but there's a limit."

"Good-bye, Mother."

"You should understand something, Bernie," said Justine.

"What's that?" asked Bernie. They were standing in Lil's drawing room waiting for the guests to arrive, while Hubie was in with his mother.

"Sometimes my mother can be dreadful. Polite and charming, you know, but dreadful."

Bernie laughed. "I read my Edith Wharton. I know all about people like your mother."

Justine kissed Bernie on the cheek. It fascinated her that he was not intimidated by her family or her life. Bernie, with Lil or the other Van Degans, was always polite and charming, but he never backed down when disagreeable subjects, like politics and religion, came into the conversation. Once he even mocked the President and First Lady, fully aware that Lil and her friends revered and sometimes even entertained them, and, after the silence that followed, did not disagree when Uncle Laurance explained to the family that people in the media more often than not held liberal views.

"It's just one of my boring old migraines," said Lil Altemus to her father, Ormonde Van Degan, who, after his eightieth birthday almost four years ago, rarely ventured forth to any social event, much less a cocktail party. Lil lounged elegantly on a deep tufted red damask sofa at the far end of her massive drawing room overlooking Fifth Avenue during the whole of her cocktail party to announce Justine's engagement to Bernard Slatkin.

Once Ormonde Van Degan had commanded as much respect in banking, political, and social circles as his son Laurance presently commanded, but age had diminished his capabilities, and pity among Lil's and Laurance's friends and suppressed smiles among the next generation had taken the place of the awe he inspired in earlier times. As he shuffled through his daughter's drawing room, forgetful now, only Dodo Fitz Alyn seemed able to communicate with him. Dodo Fitz Alyn, a Van Degan poor relation and the object of family jokes, had the job of leading Ormonde Van Degan around the room in his walker to greet all the family members. Poor Dodo, as she was referred to behind her back, had long since abandoned hopes of marriage and ceased to care about weight or appearance. Her wispy hair was parted in the middle and pulled together behind her ears with a rubber band, or, on party occasions, like today, with a black ribbon.

"Dodo, dear, take Father around the room, will you?" said Lil, with effusive cordiality, as if she was speaking to a beloved nanny who had long served the family well, instead of a relation.

"I have taken him around the room, Lil," said Dodo.

"Tell him Matilda's coming," said Lil to Dodo, in front of her father, as if he were deaf and blind, rather than merely old. "He's always been so fond of Matilda, and he adored Sweetzer." With that instruction taken care of, Lil went back to her guests. It was not lost on any of them that it was Lil and not Justine who was the center of attention at Justine's engagement party. She held a glass of champagne, which was constantly replenished by her maid Lourdes, and lifted her cheek to be kissed by her old friends like Matilda Clarke and Mary Finch and Cora Mandell, and practically the whole of the Van Degan family.

"Dodo Fitz Alyn always leaves the chair seats warm when she gets up. Have you noticed?" asked Cora Mandell, when she lowered herself into a black Regency chair next to Lil's sofa that Dodo had just vacated.

"Poor Dodo," said Lil, rolling her eyes.

"Bernie's *so* attractive," said Mary Finch to Lil. "Lucky, lucky Justine. I was always *mad* about men with dimples in their chin. Who was that movie star who had the dimple? You know the one, in the picture about Africa, that one."

Bernard Slatkin watched the spectacle of the Van Degan family and their friends with an amused and remote smile. He stood near the piano, on the other side of the long room from Lil, talking and joking with Justine, often with his arm around her waist, and fulfilling his social obligations by chatting charmingly with each person that Justine introduced him to.

Loelia Manchester entered the party in a whirl of raspberry satin, on her way to another party. Mickie Minardos was not with her, as Lil Altemus's drawing room was practically home ground for Loelia and her estranged husband Ned. As always, people turned to look at Loelia, because of her clothes and because of her scandal. Thin beyond thin, fashionable beyond fashion, Loelia had taken to wearing her now very blond hair pulled back into a tiny knot, a style favored, people said, by Mickie Minardos, but a style deplored by the popular hairdressers of the city who feared, because of Loelia's influence in matters of taste and style, that it might become a rage. Loelia's eyes moved rapidly around the room, even as she was kissing relations and old friends on first one cheek and then the other, or greeting Justine, or being introduced to Bernie, not wanting, if possible, to have to come into contact with Ned Manchester, who would certainly be there.

"When you set the date, Justine, let me know immediately, and Mickie and I will give a little dinner for you and Bernie at the Rhinelander," said Loelia. "I'm so pleased to meet you, Bernie. I always watch you, and Mickie thinks you're the best, absolutely the best, of all the anchormen."

Every time Bernie received a compliment, on his work as an anchorman, or on his good looks, or both, Justine beamed with pride and moved even closer to her fiancé.

"Thank you, Mrs. Manchester," said Bernie, who seemed to be enjoying all the attention he was getting. "I'd like you to meet some of the gang from the news staff," and he pulled over his coanchorman and his weatherman to meet the glamorous Mrs. Manchester, whom they had all read about in the newspapers and magazines.

"Who's the little Chinese eating all the cheese puffs and talking to Dodo Fitz Alyn?" asked Cora Mandell, surveying the scene.

"Oh, Charlie *quelque chose,*" answered Lil, rearranging the pillows behind her. "And don't say 'Chinese.' They get so upset. He's Korean, or Vietnamese, one of those. He's the weatherman on Bernie's show, and the other one, with the salt-and-pepper toupee and the drink in each hand, is Bernie's cohost, or coanchor, or whatever they call them."

"I've never seen poor Dodo so animated," said Cora.

Lil screened her lips with her left hand and said to Cora Mandell, "Whisper to Loelia that I told Ned not to come until after eight, so she can relax for an hour. Ned was thrilled to come late because it won't interfere with his squash game."

"Do you think it's true that Ned won't agree to give Loelia a divorce? It was in Dolly's column," said Cora.

"I know it's true," answered Lil, "but Ned is my cousin on the Altemus side, and I'm godmother to Charlotte, and I just can't take sides. I mean, what's happening to everyone these days? I suppose it'll be poor Dodo and the weatherman next."

"Lil, how sad you're not feeling well," said Loelia Manchester.

"Hello, Loelia. Kiss kiss."

"How exciting this must be for you, Lil," said Loelia. "Mickie thinks Bernie is just about the best of all the newscasters. When's the wedding going to be?"

"Too soon for this old mother to make all the proper arrangements," said Lil. "You look different, Loelia."

"How do you like my new face?" asked Loelia.

"I liked your old face, and I'm sure I'll get to like your new one," answered Lil. Loelia looked at Lil Altemus and decided to let the jibe pass.

"I want to say hello to Uncle Ormonde," she said, indicating with a little half wave to Lil that she would slip out without saying good-bye, like an experienced leavetaker who had another party to attend.

"I don't think she liked what you said," said Cora.

"Well, you know, since Mickie Minardos came into her life, Loelia's seeing all the New People in New York. She's moved on from us."

The elevator door opened. "Big hug," said Loelia to Matilda Clarke in farewell and turned to get on the elevator. Getting out of it at the same time as Loelia was about to get on were Ned Manchester with Charlotte and Bozzie, Ned and Loelia's children. Ned and Loelia stared at each other. As always Ned's hair was wet, as if he had just showered after his afternoon game of squash. Loelia noticed that hardness had come into Ned's face and that his look showed cold dislike for her.

"Oh, hello, Ned," she said to her husband.

Ned, who had loved her so much for so long, nodded, shifted his eyes, and replied, "Hello." Loelia remembered once when his mother, Honoria, long dead, had replied to someone she disliked who had greeted her in a public place. "Hello," she replied. Nothing more. It was exactly the way her husband had greeted her.

Loelia turned away quickly, aware that her color was rising, as Ned passed by her into the entrance of Lil's apartment.

"You look lovely, Charlotte," she said to her daughter. She had forgotten her children would be invited to this family party. Charlotte passed her mother without speaking and hurried after her father.

"Bozzie," said Loelia.

"Hello, Mother," said Bozzie.

"How grown up you look," said Loelia. "And handsome, too." They looked at each other and smiled.

"Thank you for my birthday present, Mother," said Bozzie.

"I thought it would be perfect for Bermuda."

"It is."

"I hope the size was right."

"It was."

"I'm sorry I couldn't get to your party, but, you know, I was on the committee for the Opera Guild benefit that night, and—"

"It's all right."

"Charlotte didn't speak to me."

"Charlotte was afraid you might be here with Mr. Minardos, and she didn't want to see you with him," said Bozzie.

Loelia blushed.

Charlotte reappeared in the entry. "Bozzie, Daddy wants you to meet Uncle Ormonde Van Degan."

"Good-bye, Mother."

"Good-bye, Bozzie. Good-bye, Charlotte." Loelia stepped into the elevator and turned to look back to face her children.

"You look beautiful, Mother," said Bozzie. As the elevator door was closing, Loelia looked at Charlotte, who stared back at her mother without replying. Alone in the elevator, Loelia sank back against the mahogany-paneled wall and closed her eyes. Then she opened her eyes and turned around to face the elevator mirror, but there was no mirror.

"If I lived in this building, I would insist that there be a mirror in the elevator instead of all these wood walls," said Loelia to the elevator man.

"Yes, ma'am," said the elevator man.

Loelia opened her gold minaudier and took out a mirror and looked at herself. She wiped away a tear at the corner of her eye and pinched some color into her cheeks.

"Shall I ring for a taxi, ma'am?" asked the elevator man.

"What?"

"A taxi. Do you want me to ring for a taxi?"

"No, thank you. I have a car."

When the elevator door opened, Loelia pulled her raspberry satin coat with the sable collar and cuffs around her and walked through the lobby to the door. The doorman opened the door for her and she walked out under the canopy onto Fifth Avenue. A limousine that had been double parked pulled up to the entrance of the building. Before the driver could get out, the back door was opened by someone inside, and Loelia stepped quickly into the car. Mickie Minardos, in evening clothes, was seated there.

"Are you all right?" asked Mickie.

"Why do you ask that?" Loelia replied.

"I saw Ned and the children get out of a taxi and go in."

"Did they see you?"

"I don't know. I ducked down in the seat."

"It was awful. Ned didn't speak to me. Neither did Charlotte. Only Bozzie. It was awful."

"Do you want to skip the party and go back to the hotel?"

"No. I want to be occupied. I don't want to have to think. I'm desperate to get a bit inebriated."

"Are you sorry?"

"Sorry?"

"Sorry this has happened, between you and me?"

"No, I'm not sorry. I'm madly in love with you, Mickie Minardos."

"Even if you can't include me in your family gatherings?"

"Even if I can't include you in my family gatherings."

* * *

The next morning Bernie Slatkin read of his engagement to Justine Altemus in the *New York Times*. It said that the Van Degan family had been prominent in the affairs of the city—socially, politically, and in business—since the beginning of the century. It was the first time he knew that Justine was descended, not just from the Van Degans, but from the Rhinelanders and the Republican branch of the Whitbecks as well. He thought he'd better call his Aunt Hester and Uncle Sol Slatkin, in Weehawken, New Jersey, to tell them of his engagement before someone else told them first.

11

"MAISIE, WILL you explain to me why this horror I am looking at is a work of art?" asked Ruby Renthal, perplexed, as she stared up at the huge canvas. She had asked Maisie Verdurin to take her on a tour of the SoHo galleries on a Saturday afternoon.

"A horror! How can you say it's a horror?" asked Maisie Verdurin, aghast.

"All those broken cups and saucers stuck into that canvas. I don't understand why that is great art. I'm perfectly willing to learn, but you must explain it to me."

It interested Maisie that Ruby never pretended to like something that she didn't like, even if it was enjoying a great success. "I think perhaps Julian Schnabel is not your cup of tea," answered Maisie.

"Tell me what is then."

"Elias has developed a great fondness for Rubens and El Greco," said Maisie.

"I can't bear all those martyrs with blood coming out of their wounds hanging on my living room walls," said Ruby.

"I think the Impressionists, or the Post-Impressionists will be more to your liking," said Maisie. She was used to dealing with wives of rich men who needed pictures to hang on their walls. "You liked the Monet, remember."

"I liked the pink in the Monet. I'd rather put the money into jewelry myself," said Ruby.

"But people don't come to your house for dinner to see your jewelry. They see your jewelry when you go out. People come to your house for dinner to see your pictures, though," said Maisie. It was an argument she often used to explain to the wives of great financiers the social advantages of collecting art.

"Ah ha," answered Ruby, understanding immediately. More than anything, Elias wanted to be made a member of the board of directors of the museum and was anxious to develop a great collection as soon as possible. "No wonder everyone says you're the best at what you do, Maisie. Let's give some more thought to the Impressionists, or the Post-Impressionists."

$$12$$

C ORA MANDELL, the fashionable decorator, knew everything about everyone in society and gossiped on to Ruby Renthal, who never got sick of hearing her stories, especially her stories about Loelia Manchester, whom Ruby admired more than any other woman, and whose friend she yearned to be. Ruby now knew, from Cora, that Loelia Manchester's brothers and their wives had sided with Ned Manchester and not Loelia in the approaching divorce, and that Fernanda Somerset, Loelia's mother, did not speak to Matilda Clarke, and had not for years, although Ruby did not yet know the reason. She felt a connection to the last bit of news, as Ruby was herself now the owner of Matilda Clarke's apartment, although she wished fervently that people would stop referring to it as the old Sweetzer Clarke apartment and begin to refer to it as the Elias Renthal apartment.

Ruby and Cora were seated facing each other in Elias Renthal's company jet. Between them the stewardess had set up a table for them to go over the revised floor plans for the new apartment. In tote bags on the floor beside Ruby were four Fabergé eggs that she had just bought at an estate sale in New Orleans, and a gold tea service that had once been given to the Empress Josephine as a wedding gift by the island of Martinique. Cora had said it was much too expensive when they saw it at an antiques shop on Bourbon Street, but Ruby had insisted it would be a perfect wedding present for Justine Altemus.

"Oh, are you going to the Altemus wedding?" asked Cora, hoping that the surprise she felt did not show in her voice.

"Yes," said Ruby.

"I didn't know you knew Lil Altemus."

"I don't."

"Justine, then."

"Not even Justine. I sat next to Bernie Slatkin at my first New York party, at Maisie Verdurin's."

"Oh, I see," said Cora, as if the problem was solved. "You're a friend of Bernie Slatkin's." That made more sense to Cora, who knew that Lil Altemus abhorred all the New People, and the Renthals could not be classified as anything other than New People.

"No, I'm not," answered Ruby. "I never saw him again after that night."

"Oh," said Cora, dying of curiosity, but she couldn't bring herself to ask Ruby how she had received an invitation.

"Elias and Laurance Van Degan do a great deal of business together," said Ruby, understanding what Cora was thinking.

"I see," said Cora. She did not say that Laurance Van Degan did business with a lot of people who would certainly not be getting an invitation.

"Go on with your story, Cora," said Ruby.

"Where was I?" asked Cora.

"Bitsy and Brassy," prompted Ruby.

"Oh, yes. Bitsy inherited all the money," said Cora. "She's gone off somewhere, I don't remember where. Antibes, I think. Someplace like that. The other sister is called Brassy. Actually she's a half-sister. She married Harry Kingswood, but they were divorced years ago. Her son by Harry died of a heroin overdose. Did I tell you that story? Awful. Brassy didn't marry again. They say she's a lesbian with one of the English duchesses, but I don't believe it. They both love horses. That's all. People are so quick these days to say that women are lesbians when they're just great friends."

Bitsy, Brassy, Harry, dykes. Ruby closed her eyes to store all this information. She always wanted to take notes when Cora told her stories, so she could repeat them all to Elias, who was as interested as she was, although he sometimes missed the point, the way he did when she told him about the marriage of Justine Altemus's aunt, Grace Gardiner, who had had, according to Cora, *"a mariage blanc,* and a very happy *mariage blanc,"* until the death of Winkie Gardiner.

"What the hell is a *mariage blanc?"* Elias had asked Ruby, giving the words the exaggerated pronunciation he always gave to foreign words, which embarrassed him to speak.

"A marriage of companionship, friendship, that sort of thing," Ruby had answered, in her explaining voice, giving Elias the same explanation Cora had given her when she asked the same question.

"You mean, no fucking? Is that what you're trying to say?" Elias had said.

"Oh, Elias," Ruby had replied in an exasperated voice.

All this time Ruby had been perusing the revised floor plans of her apartment on the table between them. She knew that if her apartment ever got finished, it would be the most discussed apartment in New York, but it drove her mad that everything took so long to complete, especially when she was willing to spend any amount of money to speed things along. She could never say to Cora, who had just told her that a fringe she had ordered from Paris for the window hangings in her persimmon drawing room would not arrive for another six weeks, that she felt her New York life could not begin until she was in her grand apartment, receiving all the people she was only hearing about and reading about and watching from afar.

"Where's my bidet in this bathroom?" asked Ruby Renthal, changing the subject, as something caught her eye on the floor plans.

"Oh, there's not going to be a bidet in that bathroom," answered Cora Mandell.

"Who said there's not going to be a bidet in that bathroom?" asked Ruby.

"Elias said he only wanted to spend thirty thousand doing over that bathroom, and it would cost an additional ten to remove the tiles to put the bidet in, so we decided to dispense with the bidet," said Cora.

"Let me get this straight," said Ruby, slowly and carefully, drumming her long red fingernails on the floor plan. "You made the decision that I wasn't going to have a bidet. Is that correct?"

"No, Ruby, I didn't make the decision," replied Cora evenly. "It was Elias who said he didn't want to spend—"

"Never mind about Elias," snapped Ruby, who was really annoyed about the six-week delay of the French fringe. "The bottom line is that you made the decision that I wasn't to have a bidet. Is that it?"

Cora Mandell began to finger her three strands of pearls as she stared back at the beautiful young woman with the beautiful jewelry who was behaving in a manner Cora would have described as ungracious. "It was not a decision I made by myself, Mrs. Renthal," Cora said, aware that her shift from first name to formal address was not lost on Ruby. "It was after I showed the plans to your husband at his office that the decision was arrived at."

"Fine," said Ruby. She began folding the floor plans and then pushed them away from her to Cora for Cora to fold. "I don't care how much it costs to remove the tiles, Mrs. Mandell. I want a bidet in that bathroom. I'm going to have a bidet in that bathroom, and don't bring up the matter to me again."

If Ruby Renthal could have read the thoughts of the distinguished older woman, who had decorated all the Van Degan, Manchester, and Altemus houses, she would have read, "I've seen these people come, and I've seen these people go," but she could not read Cora Mandell's thoughts, and Cora Mandell was not the type to make known such thoughts.

"Of course, Mrs. Renthal," said Cora, folding the plans and putting them in the bag where she carried her needlework.

"One other thing," said Ruby.

"No, there's no one-other-thing, Mrs. Renthal," said Cora, rising from her place and moving toward another seat in the back of the empty plane.

"And what is that supposed to mean?" asked Ruby. Looking after the retreating figure, she was instantly aware that she had offended her one precarious link to the world of Loelia Manchester and Lil Altemus.

"Your next decorator can deal with whatever your one-other-thing is," said Cora, seating herself. She reached into her bag and brought forth a copy of Nestor Calder's book, *Judas Was a Redhead,* and proceeded to read.

"I don't want another decorator, Cora. I want you. After all these months, we can't stop now. Think of the delays, just trying to get to know someone else. And there's the Orromeo auction coming up in Paris. You promised you'd go with me. Besides, you're the best. The very best. Everyone says so. Forgive me if I appeared rude. I have the curse, you know, and every time I get my period, I don't behave well. Just ask Elias. He'll tell you. Please don't go, Cora. Please. There's the big party that Elias and I are giving, and we have to have the apartment finished by the party. Please."

"You know, poor Ruby hates me to smoke cigars," said Elias. "So she's fixing up this room for me to smoke in to my heart's content. I think it's called a fumary, or some goddamn fancy name like that."

Ruby had made a rule that no one would get in to see the new apartment until Cora Mandell had finished all the decorating, but Elias took advantage of Ruby's being out of town on a shopping trip with Cora to bring a young man called Byron Macumber from the law firm of Weldon & Stinchfield up to the new place and give him a tour. It was, he thought, a safer place for a first meeting than a restaurant, or even a coffee shop, where he might run into someone he knew.

Byron Macumber, thirty-four, was dressed in a bankers' gray suit, with a blue shirt and dark red tie. Looking around at the unfinished rooms, he was dazzled by the magnificence of the Renthal apartment.

"I'd love to bring my wife here sometime, after you all get moved in," he said, showing the trace of a Georgia accent.

"I'm sure in time that could be arranged, Byron," said Elias.

"She would drop dead seeing a place like this."

"Do you have children?"

"Two little girls. Kimberly, three, and Sharon, one."

"Where do you live, Byron?"

"We have a condominium in Bronxville, but one day, if I ever strike it rich, I'd like to build a house on the water in Fairfield, or Darien, or someplace like this," said Byron.

"And have a tennis court and a swimming pool. Right?"

"Something like that," said Byron, laughing.

"For the arrangement I have in mind, Byron, there would be nothing risky. All that you would have to do is identify certain companies that retain Weldon and Stinchfield for protection from the predators, not to mention guys like me."

Byron Macumber, nervous at being in such an intimate conversation with a man of Elias Renthal's wealth, took out a handkerchief from his pocket and wiped his forehead, at the same time nodding an acknowledgment that he understood Elias's request.

"Timing is everything, you see," continued Elias, as if he were giving a lecture in finance. "I want to get into situations so early that my activities couldn't possibly attract attention from," he paused, and shrugged, and then finished his sentence, "whomever."

In the room that would be Elias's smoking room when the apartment was finished was an antique pool table that had recently arrived from England. Byron Macumber rubbed his hand across the mahogany of the table and the faded green felt.

"This is beautiful," he said.

"Used to belong to Edward the Seventh," said Elias. "That's the original felt."

"Beautiful," repeated Byron.

"It'll happen to you too," said Elias, meaning possessions. "Whatever profit I make on a tip you give me, I will pay you five percent. Five percent, paid in cash, on, say, eighty thousand shares of Tennessee Natural Gas, is a very handsome amount of money. Enough to have a nanny for your kids and pay her for a year, and to take your wife on a nice vacation to Mustique, and maybe even buy her a mink coat for Christmas. And that's only one tip."

"Holy smoke," said Byron Macumber.

13

A S THE WEDDING day approached, with the heightened activity that surrounded the coming event, Lil Altemus's enthusiasm for Justine's marriage increased, or, to be more exact, her enthusiasm for the wedding
increased, while her enthusiasm for the marriage remained tepid, as she was of
the school that firmly believed in what her own mother used to call marrying
your own kind.

The nuptials were frequently mentioned in the social columns of Dolly De
Longpre and Florian Gray, when friends of Justine's gave dinners and cocktail
parties, most of which, but not all, Lil attended. She chose to have a headache
on the night of Violet Bastedo's dinner, and did have a "nasty cold" on the
night Bernie's Aunt Hester and Uncle Sol entertained a small group of
Bernie's relations and friends from the television station in a favorite steak
house of Bernie's. She attended all the Van Degan family celebrations and
most of the parties given by her friends, like Loelia Manchester's dinner at the
Rhinelander, and the old friends of Justine from school and debutante days.

She took a particular interest in the wedding gifts as they began to pour in,
judging each one accordingly. Grandfather Van Degan sent gold candlesticks,
and Uncle Laurance and Aunt Janet Van Degan personally dropped off a tiny
Renoir, "marvelously framed," as Lil was the first to point out, from their own
collection. Pearls came from Aunt Minnie Willoughby, who said she saw no
point in waiting until she died to leave them to Justine, and Lil's great friends
the Todescos, with whom she always stayed in Rome, sent a Chinese export
vase that Lil explained to Bernie was of museum quality. Pieces of silver in vast
quantity, old and new, large and small, ornate and plain, came from cousins
and friends, as well as from business associates of Bernie's. From Justine's
father, whom Lil never saw again after her divorce and his unfortunate second
marriage, came a vermeil clock that Lil recognized as having belonged to his
mother. Hubie sent something frightfully modern, as Lil described it, from his
art gallery in SoHo, which Lil asked Justine to pretend to like, and Lil herself,
after much deliberation, decided to give Justine an Aubusson carpet that had
been in storage since she gave up the house in Newport, after Hubie's unfortunate incident with the lifeguard at Bailey's Beach, as well as the diamond-and-
sapphire bracelet with the clasp that never worked that Fulco de Verdura had
made for her from her Granny B.B.'s old tiara.

Bridesmaids were something of a problem for a girl of Justine's age. The
friends of her school and debutante years were all long married and having

their second and even third child by this time. The thought of all married bridesmaids only pointed out the lateness of Justine's journey to the altar, and the notion of pregnant bridesmaids was abhorrent to Lil. On one thing both mother and daughter, who rarely agreed, agreed totally. No matter what pressure was brought by the family, Dodo Fitz Alyn, poor Dodo, the poor relation, would not, absolutely would not, waddle up the aisle in the bridal party. Of all people, Lourdes, Lil's maid Lourdes, came up with the idea of having only children as attendants, and the idea thrilled Lil. There were several Van Degan nieces, she pointed out to Justine, and little Nina Willoughby, and Violet Bastedo's daughter, and the Trefusis twins. "It will be divine, and so chic, little taffeta dresses, like shepherdesses," said Lil. "They could even carry crooks, and Lorenza could do something marvelous with trailing ivy and rosebuds." Lil, who loved to organize, was in heaven.

"Justine," she said, in a voice that Justine recognized as a prelude to a request.

"Yes, Mother," replied Justine, who seemed to lose all the wedding decisions.

"I think Herkie Saybrook should be an usher," said Lil.

"Herkie Saybrook, Mother? Bernie doesn't even know Herkie Saybrook. A groom can't have an usher he doesn't even know."

"There has to be someone from our side who knows who all our friends are. You can't expect that Chinese weatherman, excuse me, Korean, to know where to seat Aunt Minnie Willoughby and the Todescos."

"Hubie knows who all the family are, Mother," said Justine.

"Hubie is not an usher. Hubie is going to take me down the aisle and sit with me. I am most certainly not going to sit with your father."

"Hubie can take you down the aisle, sit with you, and still be an usher, Mother."

"Will you please just talk to Bernie about Herkie? For me? For your mother, Justine?" asked Lil.

The tension between mother and daughter was broken when Lourdes walked into the room carrying another wedding present.

"Oh, heaven," cried Lil, clapping her hands, which she did each time a new present arrived.

"Look how beautifully wrapped this box is, Mrs. Altemus," said Lourdes. "Save me the paper and ribbons."

"Who's it from?" asked Lil, still in bed with a breakfast tray.

"Young Laurance and Laura Van Degan," said Justine, reading the card.

"Good wrapping, cheap gift, wait and see," said Lil, sipping her hot water and lemon juice.

"Oh, Mother," said Justine, tearing apart the white satin ribbons and gold and white paper.

"They're so tight. They sent Baba Timson a lucite paperweight, after Baba had lent them her house in Barbados for their honeymoon. Save all those ribbons and wrappings for Lourdes. God knows what she does with them. Where's it from?"

"Scully and Scully," said Justine.

"Don't tell me, let me guess," said Lil, holding her hand over her eyes. "A wastebasket with a horse print by Stubbs."

"Wrong," said Justine.

"A white bamboo breakfast tray with a place for the *New York Times.*"

"Wrong again," said Justine.

"Five dinner plates from your Morning Glory pattern."

"A cut-glass vase," said Justine, holding it up.

"I knew it. I knew they wouldn't spend over sixty dollars," said Lil. "The Van Degans are all the same. Let me see it."

Justine handed the vase to her mother.

"Not bad," said Lil, handing it to Lourdes.

"It'll be marvelous for anemones," said Justine.

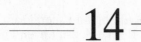

G US BAILEY, working at his computer, heard the telephone ring several times before he remembered he had forgotten to put on his message machine.

"Hello?"

"Is that Gus Bailey?"

"Yes."

"It's Ceil Somerset. Do you remember me?"

"Yes," he answered, but he didn't actually remember. She had the fashionable voice of someone he had probably been introduced to at a fashionable party, and he knew before the conversation began that she was going to invite him to another fashionable party, probably as a last minute fill-in.

"We met at Justine Altemus's engagement party," said Ceil Somerset.

"Oh, yes," replied Gus. He still didn't remember, but it didn't matter. If he was free, he would go. It interested him to see how the various groups of New York overlapped.

"I was the one who loved your article about the movie star who gave up booze."

"Oh, yes." Gus was fifty by the time people started to recognize him by name, and even face, and it never ceased to amaze him.

"Are you still writing about that ghastly gigolo who took all that old lady's money?"

"Yes, I am. I thought this call might be he. He hasn't shown up for the last two appointments I had with him."

"You can't trust people like that, Gus. You should know that by now."

Gus laughed. "What can I do for you?"

"I'm Loelia Manchester's sister-in-law. My husband's her brother."

"Yes."

"You're not by any chance free for dinner tonight, are you? I know this is terribly last minute, but, you see, someone's dropped out, and I'm having a dinner before Mary Finch's dance for Justine Altemus and Bernie Slatkin, and Justine said you were coming to the dance, so I wondered if maybe you'd like to come to dinner." She talked very fast, as if she thought he would be offended at being asked so late.

"Sure," said Gus.

"You would?" She sounded amazed that he had accepted. "Oh, you are divine. Eight o'clock. Our apartment's too small, so we're giving it at my mother-in-law's. Do you know where she lives?"

"No."

"The same building as Lil Altemus."

"You're over here, Gus, next to me," called out Lil Altemus, patting the needlepoint seat of a Chippendale chair, when she saw Gus make a late entrance into the dining room, after being shown through the apartment by Ceil Somerset's mother-in-law, Fernanda Somerset. Gus was overwhelmed by the art on the walls, and Fernanda Somerset, who was also the mother of Loelia Manchester, was always keen on showing off to an interested guest the masterpieces that her late husband, who had a taste for art and a lust for the gentlemanly sport of collecting, had amassed and that her own children and their friends simply took for granted. Fernanda Somerset was known to be dismayed and distressed over her daughter's liaison with Dimitri Minardos, the shoe designer, whom she considered totally inappropriate for her daughter, but she kept her opinions on the matter to herself. When Gus excused himself to go into dinner, Fernanda retired to her room, as she was not a member of the party going on that evening.

"I hear you've been getting the grand tour from Fernanda," said Lil, when Gus was seated.

"And grand is the right word," said Gus, sitting down, after giving Lil a kiss on the cheek. "That's what's called a collection."

"All going to the museum when Fernanda dies," said Lil.

"She told me that."

"Did she tell you about Mr. Renthal's offer?" asked Lil.

"Elias Renthal? No."

"He offered to buy the entire collection, can you imagine? 'Name your price,' he said. Or had Mrs. Verdurin say for him. To furnish his new apartment," said Lil.

She gave a sharp little laugh, her Lil laugh, her children called it, a sort of intake of breath that sounded a bit like a cultured snort, although, according to Janet Van Degan, it would have been better named her Van Degan laugh, for both Lil's mother and her grandmother had had the same laugh when they were amused by the pretensions of the New People. "Too funny, really," she finished by saying. Lil looked around her at the dining room and the people in it. This was her kind of life. These were her kind of people.

"I didn't see Justine and Bernie."

"Bernie had to work at the last minute, and Justine wouldn't come without him. We'll meet up with them later at Mary's dance."

"Congratulations on Justine's engagement."

No words of disapproval for her daughter's choice of partner passed Lil Altemus's lips, but her wry smile, her weary shrug, and her look of forebearance conveyed her feelings more than any expressed thoughts ever would.

"He's charming," said Lil cautiously. "Not one of us, of course, but charming."

Gus laughed. It amused him when she said *not one of us* to him, as if he were. "Neither am I," he said.

"Neither are you what?"

"One of you."

"But you're not going to marry my daughter," she replied.

"I know Bernie," said Gus. "I like him."

"On TV, you mean?"

"On TV, yes, but in life too. I see him at Maisie Verdurin's parties."

"Awfully good looking. I'll say that for him," conceded Lil.

"Far more than good looking, Lil," said Gus. "He's a very successful young man. He earns a fortune. He's working. That's more than most of the guys do whom Justine could have married. People say he'll get the top spot one of these days."

"You sound just like Justine. That's what she keeps saying." Lil gave a little dismissive laugh. Earned money, no matter how abundant, never impressed Lil Altemus the way inherited money did. Then, not unexpectedly, she mouthed but did not speak the word *Jewish*.

In the several years Gus Bailey had known Lil Altemus, he had seen her, in other circumstances, about other people, mouth but not speak other words in explanation of their identities: *Cancer,* she once mouthed about Honoria Manchester. Or, *Adopted,* about Dodo Fitz Alyn. Or, *Alcoholic,* about Sweetzer Clarke. Or, *Lesbian,* about Nan Timson.

A young man on the other side of Lil cleared his throat to get Lil's attention, in order to resume a story he had been telling her when Gus came to the table.

"Laurance has been telling us the most fascinating story," said Lil. "Do you know my nephew, Laurance Van Degan? Gus Bailey. And Maude, you know, don't you? Maude Hoare?"

Sure of himself, bespectacled, balding too early, Laurance Van Degan, whom everyone in the family called young Laurance, acknowledged Lil's introduction of Gus without absorbing his name, eager to continue with his story. Lil often wished that her son Hubie was more like her nephew, who fit in, who continued on in the things that had made the family famous, or even that her son and her nephew were friends, which they never had been. "There's a man called Elias Renthal," said Laurance Van Degan, in explanation to Gus about the subject of his story, as if Gus would have no idea who Elias Renthal was. Young Van Degan, like a lot of the group at Ceil Somerset's who thought of themselves, without actually putting it into words, as old New York, had strong feelings about Elias Renthal and his manner of conducting business.

"You see the Renthals everywhere these days," he continued. "They were at the opera the other night, with Constantine de Rham, and that woman he is

always seen with, Mrs. Lupescu, who was wearing wh
diamonds."

"She's ghastly, that woman," said Lil.

"Renthal is apparently an old friend of Constantine
Van Degan.

"Doesn't that tell you a lot?" said Lil, who still had
herself to tell anyone that the Renthals were coming to
ding.

"Hear me out, Aunt Lil," said her nephew, who didn't like to be interrupted. "Mrs. Renthal, however, who's on the make, as everyone knows, didn't
enjoy being seen in public with de Rham and his girl-friend, and she and Elias
had a few words during the first act, and the people around them kept shushing
them up."

A waiter from the catering service brought in to supplement the Somerset
staff nodded a greeting to Gus over Lil Altemus's head while she took asparagus from a silver platter he held for her.

"Oh, hi," said Gus in return to the waiter.

"But that was nothing," continued Laurance Van Degan with his story.
"You won't believe what happened. During the second act, when Montserrat
Caballé was singing her *Vissi d'Arte*, more beautifully than I've ever heard it
sung, incidentally, one of Mrs. Lupescu's diamond earrings fell with a great
clunk to the floor of the Metropolitan."

"No," cried Lil.

"Oh, yes, and both she and de Rham got right down on the floor to look
for it, first things first, right in the middle of the aria, and even lit a match to aid
their search."

"Extraordinary," said Lil.

"Laura and I were there with Mother. You can imagine Mother's reaction,
Aunt Lil. She insisted they halt their search until the end of the act when the
house lights came on."

"Good for Janet," said Lil.

"Mrs. Renthal is trying to get on Mother's opera committee, and she was
so embarrassed that Mother saw her with de Rham and Mrs. Lupescu that she
took off, and, of course, Elias had to follow her. He's a bad apple, de Rham."

"Consuelo was one of my best friends," said Lil, shaking her head.

"Bad apple, how?" asked Gus, entering the conversation for the first time.

"Owes money everywhere. Rents out that house he inherited from Consuelo for all sorts of purposes, they say. Herkie Saybrook says if he ever wanted
to have someone taken care of, he'd go to Constantine de Rham."

"No," said Lil, in disbelief.

"I don't mean to imply he'd do anything himself, but he would know
exactly the person to go to to have it done."

"What exactly do you mean?" persisted Gus.

"Just what I said," replied young Laurance Van Degan, who then turned to
speak to Maude Hoare on his other side.

On the other side of Gus sat a young woman who did not seem to know
anyone at the party but acted perfectly content to watch it without participating. When Gus turned to speak to her, he found that she was staring at him. He
picked up her place card and saw that her name was Inez Peretti.

u a friend of Justine's?" asked Gus, trying to find an opening for
tion.

ve never met Justine," replied Inez Peretti.

"Bernie then. Are you a friend of Bernie's from the television station?"
asked Gus again.

"I've never met Bernie either. I don't even know his last name, just that
he's going to marry Justine Altemus," said Inez.

Gus, curious, framed his next question.

"I'm Ceil Somerset's psychic," she said in explanation to Gus, who had
been about to ask her what her connection was to all these people, and Gus
laughed that she had anticipated his question.

"Ah, a psychic. How interesting."

"Have you ever been to one?"

"In California. Not here. Do you make house calls?" asked Gus, making
conversation.

"I prefer not to."

"Where do you live?"

"Sullivan Street. Do you know where that is?"

"Off Houston. Right?"

"Right. Most of these friends of Ceil's think it's in Tasmania, or someplace
equally remote. That Mrs. Lupescu, Mr. Van Degan was just talking about. She
got my name from someone and called for an appointment, but when she
heard where I lived, she canceled, saying she never went below Fiftieth Street.
She said Saks Fifth Avenue was her downtown limit."

Gus laughed. "That sounds like the sort of thing Mrs. Lupescu would say,
from what I gather about Mrs. Lupescu," he said.

"You're going somewhere tonight, aren't you?" asked Inez Peretti.

Gus looked at her. "Mary Finch's dance for Justine and Bernie," replied
Gus, cautiously.

Inez Peretti ignored his evasive answer. "Before that, I mean."

Gus continued to stare at her.

"Whatever it is you're planning on doing, don't," she said. Their eyes met
for an instant. Gus picked up Inez's place card again.

"Next you're going to ask me for my telephone number," said Inez, smiling.

"Right," replied Gus, and he wrote it down on the place card when she
gave it to him, then put the card in the pocket of his dinner jacket.

Laura Van Degan appeared behind young Laurance and put her hand on
his shoulder. He looked up at Laura and smiled. She wore no makeup, a plain
evening dress, and her uncoiffured hair, straight with bangs, hung like a schoolgirl's to her shoulders. Ruby Renthal would have said, had she been present to
make the comment, that you had to be as rich and as entrenched as the Van
Degans to appear at a party dressed like that. Laurance, however, seemed
delighted with her. "Time?" he asked.

"Yes, darling," she replied.

"Laura's still breastfeeding the new baby," explained Laurance to Lil.
"We're going on home, and we'll meet up with you later at Mary's."

"Little Janet is so excited about being a bridesmaid for Justine, Lil. You
just can't imagine," said Laura.

"You're missing all this delicious coconut ice cream," said Lil, spooning out some from the silver bowl the waiter held.

"My favorite thing," said Gus, when the waiter held the bowl for him to take some.

"There's rum in the coconut ice cream, Gus," whispered the same waiter who had spoken to Gus earlier. Gus looked longingly at his favorite dessert and declined with a shake of his head.

"Who's your friend the waiter?" asked Lil.

"Someone I know from A.A.," said Gus.

"That reminds me, Evangeline Simpson's drinking again," said Lil.

"Do you suppose Constantine de Rham will be at Mary Finch's dance tonight?" asked Gus.

"Not likely," answered Lil.

"But they're the couple of the season, it seems," said Gus.

"Maybe at Maisie Verdurin's, and at Clarence's, and all those places you frequent, Gus, but not in this crowd," answered Lil, waving her hand to indicate the thirty-two guests in the Somerset dining room. "I think everyone's moving on to Mary's. Do you want a ride? My car's downstairs."

"No, thank you, Lil. I'll meet you there. I have to make another stop first."

"That's what Matilda always says about you."

"What does Matilda always say about me?"

"That you're always going somewhere mysterious."

If Constantine de Rham thought it strange that he should be receiving a call at ten o'clock at night from a man who had refused to speak to him at Maisie Verdurin's parties, he gave no such indication. Gus Bailey was surprised that he answered his own door, although a butler of advanced age hovered disagreeably in the background, as if his duties of door opener had been usurped. Later, Gus remembered that de Rham wore velvet slippers with the initials *C de R* elaborately intertwined in gold and a smoking jacket of dark green velvet, but at that moment, standing outside in the rain on Sutton Place, looking into what had once been Consuelo Harcourt de Rham's house, he was aware only of the marble stairway behind Constantine, down which Consuelo had fallen two years earlier, and the black-and-white marble floor on which she had landed.

"My name is Augustus Bailey," began Gus.

"Yes, I know who you are," answered Constantine. "You refused to shake my hand at Maisie Verdurin's party."

Gus, having come as a supplicant, blushed.

"I remember slights. Even averted eyes are recorded in my computer up here," Constantine said, pointing to his head. He stared at Gus, cold and wet, standing in the street under an umbrella, as if he enjoyed the feeling of power he possessed by not immediately giving him entrance. "My inclination is to slam the door in your face, but curiosity overrides that desire. Come in."

Gus passed him and walked into the house.

"Give your wet things to Ramon," he said, as Gus took off his coat. The butler gathered up Gus's umbrella and coat, soaking the front of his white jacket in the process.

"The Filipinos, they say, are an intelligent race, but my butler is an exception to the rule," said de Rham, in front of the butler. "Don't put those wet things on the upholstered bench, Ramon. Take them into the kitchen."

Gus turned to a mirror and readjusted his black tie, which had become crushed under his coat.

"You are either coming from or on your way to Mary Finch's dance for Justine Altemus and Mr. Slatkin," said de Rham, observing Gus's dinner jacket and black patent-leather pumps.

"On my way to," replied Gus.

"Wouldn't you love to have been a fly on the wall when Justine told Lil she was going to marry Mr. Slatkin? Or perhaps you were, Mr. Bailey. A fly on the wall, that is."

"No, I wasn't, Mr. de Rham."

"With one of your magazine articles?"

"No."

"I'm sure Mr. Slatkin wasn't quite what Lil had in mind for Justine. I rather think her hopes were higher."

It had not occurred to Gus, in his anticipatory thoughts about his night visit, that Constantine de Rham would gossip with him about an approaching society wedding. From another room, the sounds of a television drama could be heard.

"Yvonne is watching *Dynasty*," explained Constantine, with a tolerant smile. He pronounced *dynasty* "dinasty" in the British manner and indicated with a head gesture that Gus should follow him. They walked down a hallway into Constantine's den, and Constantine closed the door behind them.

On one dark red wall, over a deep tufted sofa piled high with damask and tapestry pillows, was a large painting of a stag being torn apart by hounds. On another Gus's eye was drawn to a bookcase full of tall slender volumes, bound in red Moroccan leather with gold lettering, that appeared to be privately printed: aristocratic biographies of aristocratic de Rhams: Casimir, Stanislaus, Edouard, and Thierry, the revered ancestors that Constantine claimed as his own. "The guillotine played havoc with my family during the Terror," de Rham said, watching Gus look at the books, "but enough members survived to perpetuate the name and reclaim the estates."

Gus turned from the books and looked up into the eyes of the tall man whose gaze was boring into him, daring him to disbelieve his ancestral claims. In the close quarters of the den a scent of not-quite-fresh perspiration clouded the air. It occurred to Gus that perhaps Constantine de Rham was not an everyday bather. Inwardly Gus asked himself why he was in this man's house, on this rainy night, and for an instant he considered flight. Instead, needing him, he fought his distaste and admired the elegant French desk behind which de Rham seated himself. The desk was, de Rham explained, signed by Boulle. He passed his long fingers lovingly over its highly polished ormolu-encrusted surface.

"But surely you have not delayed going to Mary Finch's dance to come crosstown on a rainy night to discuss a Boulle desk," said de Rham.

"No."

De Rham rose and pulled the velvet curtains closed on the two windows behind his desk. When he turned around, he made a show of surprise, by raising his eyebrows, that Gus had already seated himself, as if he had expected him to remain standing until he had been invited to sit.

"No, not there. Sit in the Regency chair," Constantine said, pointing to a black lacquer chair with a cane seat that looked considerably less comfortable than the club chair that Gus had chosen. "I can see you better there."

Gus complied, understanding that Constantine needed to be in charge.

"Now, how can I help you, Mr. Bailey?" asked de Rham.

"There is a man who will be coming up for release from prison," began Gus, cautiously.

Constantine de Rham again raised his eyebrows, in an exaggerated grimace of amazement. "Yes?"

"I would like to have this man followed."

"I find it utterly extraordinary that you should come to see me on such a matter."

"I was told that you knew people who could lead one to other people who performed such services."

"Am I supposed to feel flattered by such a reputation?"

"Please let me finish."

De Rham shrugged, as if the matter were of complete indifference to him.

"I want this man followed," Gus repeated.

"You've already said that."

Gus, sweating a bit, wished he had not come.

"Starting when?" asked Constantine, surprisingly.

"From the day of his release."

"Where is the prison?"

"California."

"Where in California?"

"Vacaville."

"How long will you want him followed?"

"Indefinitely."

"That sort of thing can prove very expensive."

"I don't care."

"Have you thought of the police?"

"I don't want the police."

"Perhaps a private detective would be more what you wanted."

"I don't want a private detective either."

"Is it possible you have something more in mind than merely following him?"

"Perhaps."

"That sort of thing can be arranged from within."

"I don't want it to be arranged from within," said Gus.

"What is the name of this man who haunts you, Mr. Bailey?"

"I didn't say he haunted me, Mr. de Rham."

"You didn't have to, Mr. Bailey. I know an obsession when I see one."

Gus laughed. "Hardly an obsession."

"Hmm." Constantine de Rham folded his arms and waited for Gus to answer.

"Flint. Francis Flint. He is called Lefty Flint," said Gus, quietly, but a movement of his shoulders belied the sound of his voice.

"Even the sound of Mr. Flint's name seems to upset you, Mr. Bailey."

Gus looked at Constantine for a moment.

"What has this man done to you?"

Gus shook his head and waved his hands to indicate that he did not wish to discuss the matter.

Constantine watched him and then rose and walked toward the window. He pushed back the red velvet curtain he had just closed and looked out at the rain coming down on Sutton Place.

"I think I know someone who might be able to lead you to someone, as you put it."

Constantine de Rham unlocked a drawer of the Boulle desk and withdrew a worn leather address book that he carried to the sofa, settling himself. As he slowly looked through the pages, he seemed interested only in a piece of skin on his thumb, which he tried first to twist off and then to bite off.

Yvonne Lupescu opened the door and entered without knocking. Her satin-and-lace negligee revealed the cleavage between her breasts.

"Finally Alexis Carrington has gotten her come-uppance!" she said, referring to the television series she had been watching. Both men turned to look at her, and she turned from Constantine to Gus, as if she had been unaware of his presence. "But, Constantine, I didn't know you had a guest," she cried, crossing her hands modestly over her breasts.

Gus rose to his feet. It was the first time that he had seen Yvonne Lupescu with her blond hair hanging loosely about her shoulders. They looked at each other.

"An unexpected visit, my dear, at this late hour. Mr. Bailey. Baroness Lupescu," he said, making an introduction. "You remember, Yvonne. Mr. Bailey was not friendly toward us at Maisie's parties."

"Yes, yes, I remember. He and Matilda Clarke were speculating about me across the table," said Yvonne.

Again Gus blushed.

"Ah, look at him, Constantine. He blushes. How smart you look, Mr. Bailey. Now let me guess: you're going on to Mary Finch's dance," said Yvonne playfully.

"Correct."

"Of course, we weren't invited."

"I've explained that to Mr. Bailey."

"I don't know Mr. Bailey's first name, Constantine."

"It's Augustus," said Gus.

"And, of course, they call you Gus. Or is it Gussy?"

"Gus."

"That's what I'm going to call you. Now, Gus, before you go off to Mrs. Finch's, come into the library and drink a glass of champagne with Constantine and me."

"No, no, thank you. I don't drink, and I must be off, Mrs. Lupescu."

"Leave your address," said Constantine.

Gus leaned over and wrote it on a pad on the desk.

"I'll see Mr. Bailey to the door, Constantine," said Yvonne.

Mrs. Lupescu preceded Gus down the corridor.

"Tigers' whiskers," she said.

"Tigers' whiskers?" repeated Gus, not understanding.

"Chopped very fine and mixed with food. The victim dies a few days later, and nobody can detect the cause." She turned to him and smiled.

Gus realized she had listened to the conversation.

"Ah, but where does one find tigers' whiskers?" he asked, as if they were sharing a joke.

"That, of course, is the problem," said Yvonne Lupescu. "Once, in Albania, my grandmother, who was the mistress of King Zog—"

Gus's coat and umbrella, dried, had been left in the hallway. He again turned to the mirror and straightened the bow of his black tie.

"That's not the way to tie a black tie," said Yvonne, interrupting her story.

"What's the matter with it?" asked Gus, fingering it on both sides.

"It's entirely too lopsided. See? Too much tie on the left. Not enough on the right. Here, let me do it for you," Yvonne said, untying his tie and standing close to him while she held each end, looking him squarely in the eye. "You start this way, with both sides even, and then you make a half bow on the right side, like this, and then you wrap the left side around the half bow, like this, and then you pull it through this hole, like this. *Voilà.*"

She moved even closer to him. Her breasts had become more exposed in the tying of his tie. Gus, embarrassed, blushed again.

"Do you want me to take care of that hard-on for you?" she whispered, smiling at him.

"No," whispered Gus, looking back toward the door of Constantine's den.

"Danger's half the fun, Gus," she said.

"I'm late."

"What I have in mind won't take a minute and a half."

"That's incredibly kind of you, but no, thank you," said Gus, heading for the door.

"What do you want, Mr. Bailey?"

"I'd like to hear about King Zog and your grandmother some time," said Gus. He opened the front door and left.

15

IT WAS THE same conversation that was going on everywhere for the few weeks that people were discussing the breakup of the Edward Potter Manchester marriage and the romance of Loelia Manchester and Mickie Minardos. It did not rivet Gus Bailey the way it riveted those who knew the principals better than Gus knew them, but by now Gus understood that these people were more interested in talking about themselves than any other topic.

"You see, it was all so well disguised, Gus. No one suspected a thing," said Lil Altemus, settling back into her chair at Clarence's. "*I* certainly didn't and I, after all, am one of Loelia's very best friends."

Michael, the waiter with the ponytail, who was everyone's favorite waiter at Clarence's, came up to them and told them the specials. Lil never spoke directly to a waiter if she was dining with a man. "Tell him I'll have the chicken paillard with some sort of green vegetable. Nothing first, and perhaps some of that marvelous Chilean wine, whatever-it's-called, that they have here. Tell, him to ask Chick Jacoby the name. Look, there's Ezzie Fenwick.

"Anyway, Mickie Minardos made Loelia laugh. Mickie was a marvelous dancer, all that sort of thing, and we all know how Loelia loves to dance, and Ned, Ned always had two left feet when it came to dancing. But no one suspected for an *instant* that a romance was involved. Least of all poor Ned. Did you know that Ned was a cousin of mine on the Altemus side?

"But then, in Egypt, in Luxor, where they went to hear *Aida* sung at the pyramids, with people from everywhere who knew them, it was obvious to anyone with half a brain that they had progressed from giggling best friends to romantic lovers. It was my friend Gertie Todesco, poor Gertie, never could keep a secret, who spread the word, and what Loelia did, to make matters worse, was call Ned from Cairo, with a bad connection, and ask him for a divorce, after twenty-two years. Can you imagine? Is it any wonder that Ned is put out?"

Although Loelia Manchester was a rich woman in her own right, the bulk of the Somerset fortune, which was considerable, was controlled with an iron hand by Fernanda Somerset, Loelia's mother, and Fernanda Somerset was fond of saying about herself that she understood money management like a man.

Loelia and Fernanda had always enjoyed the closest of mother-daughter relationships, and it was no secret that Fernanda took great pride in Loelia's social accomplishments. She was, furthermore, greatly attached to her son-in-law, Edward Potter Manchester. Even though she found his constant talk of sport dull at times, she admired his country ways, especially as she spent more and more of her own time in the country, so she could be near Ned and Loelia's children, on whom she doted, especially Bozzie, their teenage son.

Fernanda and her daughter lunched that day at a table set up in a corner of the room Fernanda called her garden room, with its antique bamboo furniture, orchid plants, and blue-and-white porcelain garden benches. A René Bouché portrait of Fernanda arranging flowers, wearing trousers and a straw hat, that had been painted thirty years before in this same room, dominated the wall behind her, reminding Loelia of how beautiful her mother had been. The topic that was the purpose of this country lunch had not been broached, although Loelia knew when she was summoned from the Rhinelander, where she now lived, by a note from her mother delivered by her chauffeur that the conversation she dreaded was at hand.

"Have you had another facelift?" Fernanda asked her daughter.

"Don't you think it's a good one?" Loelia replied.

"You didn't need it."

"Oh, but I did. It's a new way Dr. James does it. He cuts up here on the scalp and then pulls it all back, and your hair covers all the scars. Too marvelous."

"Your eyes look like they're popping out of your head."

"They do not!"

"They do. And your hair is much too blond."

Loelia's hands went to her hair, defensively. "Mickie likes it this color," she said.

"I'm sure," said Fernanda. "Stop taking food off my plate."

"I'm not taking food off your plate."

"You've taken two shrimp, half my roll, and now you've scooped up a spoonful of my cheese soufflé."

Loelia, nervous, pushed back her bamboo chair from the table, and it made an unpleasant screeching sound on the terrazzo floor of the garden room. "Mother, why are you being so cranky with me?" she asked. For an instant she thought she was going to cry.

"Let's get down to brass tacks, Loelia. What is going on in your life?" asked Fernanda.

"I'm going to marry Mickie Minardos," said Loelia.

"What a grotesque announcement," said her mother.

"I didn't think I'd hear that from you, Mother!"

"Yes, you did. You knew perfectly well that was what you were going to hear from me. Isn't this man younger than you?"

"Yes."

"How many years?"

"Ten."

"He's a gigolo."

"He is the most successful shoe designer in the world."

Fernanda shook her head impatiently. A shoe designer was not a person who was going to impress Fernanda Somerset, no matter how successful he was.

"Someday he is going to design for the theater and the ballet," insisted Loelia.

"A lady can take her chauffeur to bed, but she can't take him out to dinner, Loelia," said Fernanda. "I'm surprised you of all people don't understand that."

"How incredibly unkind that is, Mother."

"You're going to be kicked out of the *Social Register* if you marry this man."

"You know that means nothing to me."

Fernanda looked at her daughter, whose greatest achievement had been as a figure in society, and disbelieved her.

"What do you know about his family?"

"His father is a banker," said Loelia proudly, playing her trump card, to prove that her fiancé was not a fortune hunter.

The flowered uniform on the maid who came in carrying demitasse cups matched the flowered tablecloth and the flowered napkins of the luncheon table. "Just leave the coffee there, Adoración, and don't bother to clear," said Fernanda to the maid, waving her off.

"You know, Loelia. There are Greeks and Greeks, and none of the Greeks we know, like Stavros and Christina and Alecco, have ever heard of the family of Mickie Minardos."

"I don't care," said Loelia quietly.

"I do," replied her mother, just as quietly.

Fernanda Somerset was not an impractical woman. She understood the callings of sexual desire and recognized it as that in her daughter's attachment to Mickie Minardos. She had herself briefly enjoyed a discreet indiscretion during the time her husband had engaged in his affair with Matilda Clarke. When the affair ended, after Sweetzer came out of the alcoholic institution in Minnesota where he had lingered for six months, both marriages resumed into the companionship that all successful marriages become, with neither the children having to suffer the trauma of divorce, nor the Somerset fortune having been dissipated as it would have been by divorce.

"Take a trip with your Greek," said Fernanda. "And when it's over, as it will be over, come back to your husband and children. Ned will wait for you. He loves you."

"I'm going to marry Mickie Minardos."

"You have crushed your family."

"Help me, Mother."

"No, I won't help you, Loelia. And there is something else I have to remind you of, though I had hoped that I would not have to."

"Money, I suppose," said Loelia, picking up her things, as an indication of leaving.

"Yes, money. What you have is all you're ever going to have, if you go through with this, Loelia."

Loelia Manchester was horrified when she learned from her lawyer a week later that Ned had asked for half her fortune before he would agree to the divorce she wanted so much, so that she could be free to marry Dimitri Minardos. Ned Manchester was already rich, although not as rich as Loelia, and it was uncharacteristic of him to ask for money from a woman. In the years of their marriage, he had never shown any sign of avarice. Loelia knew immediately that her mother had joined forces with Ned to block the divorce, as neither he nor her mother wanted Loelia to leave him.

Loelia had countered with an offer of half as much as he had asked, but Ned, again through the lawyers, had turned down her offer and declared that he was sticking to his guns. All her friends told Loelia that Ned was acting the way he was because he was so hurt and didn't want a divorce at all and certainly didn't want her money, but none of that information was of any comfort to Loelia. She had given herself up to a passion she had never experienced before and wanted to marry Dimitri Minardos more than anything else in the world. Of course her children had to be considered and proprieties to be observed. She had moved out of the beautiful Manchester apartment, leaving behind everything but her clothes, and moved into a large suite in the Rhinelander Hotel, where everyone they knew who was getting a divorce moved. Her friends consoled her with lovely baskets of flowers, and needlepoint pillows, and scented candles, and pieces of china to use for ashtrays to make the suite more homelike, and Lil Altemus, who didn't even approve of the romance with Mickie, lent her pictures to hang on her walls after she confessed to Lil that she found the hotel pictures too dreary for words.

One afternoon Loelia was on her way to meet her realtor, Helene Whitbeck, to look at an apartment on Fifth Avenue that had just come on the market. Helene said it might be the ideal place for Loelia and Mickie to live after they were married. When she stepped into the Rhinelander elevator, Elias Renthal was standing there. She was impressed that he took off his hat when he spoke to her.

"I'm Elias Renthal, Mrs. Manchester," he said, making a slight but courtly bow.

"Yes, of course," Loelia replied. "Howareyou?"

Elias could see right away that Loelia was unhappy and, when the elevator came to the lobby, he asked her if she wanted to have a drink in the bar, which was always quiet at that time of the afternoon. Loelia was amazed to hear herself say that she wouldn't have a drink but she would have a cup of tea. She hoped that Elias didn't know that it was she who had blackballed him from being elected to the board of directors of the New York Art Museum, even though he had been a generous contributor. Since then, she had heard from Jamesey Crocus and others that he had become very polished in the interim. "That wife of his, Ruby, is sandpapering the edges," Jamesey had said.

In no time at all Loelia and Elias were talking as if they were old friends, and Loelia poured out her heart to the famous financier about her troubles with Ned and the divorce. Loelia became so engrossed in her conversation that she forgot all about her appointment with Helene Whitbeck, who was waiting for her in the lobby of the Fifth Avenue apartment building.

"I can't believe he'd hold me up for money," Loelia confided to Elias about her husband. "Ned really never had any interest in possessions. I told him he can have the house in the country, and the house in Bermuda, and he wants them, but he also wants I-don't-know-how-many million on top of that. Imagine Ned acting like that after all these years. It's not as if Ned doesn't have any money of his own."

"His pride's hurt, and he's being vindictive," said Elias.

"I'm deeply sick of hearing about Ned's pride being hurt," replied Loelia. "After all, we are not the first couple in the world to get a divorce."

"Why not call his bluff? Why not offer him more than he's asking? It's not how much you pay them," Elias said, "it's how you pay it out to them."

"I don't understand what that means, Mr. Renthal," said Loelia.

"Let's say, for instance, you offer Ned twenty million in alimony," Elias began.

"Twenty million!" exclaimed Loelia. "Please, Mr. Renthal!"

"A ballpark figure. Now hear this through," said Elias patiently, taking a cigar from a case. Elias enjoyed talking about money. It was the one area of conversation in which he bowed to no man in his opinions. He opened the button of his gray pin-striped suit and made himself comfortable. Loelia noticed, while he was lighting his cigar, how much better dressed Elias had become than when she first met him. His suit was beautifully cut, and his pale pink shirt with white collar and cuffs and discreet rose monogram on his chest, and his enamel-and-gold cuff links could all have been things Mickie Minardos might have worn.

"However much money it is, you have no choice in the matter if that's the only way Ned's going to divorce you so that you can marry Mickie. You don't give him the five million or the ten million bucks all at once. You spread it out. You work it out so you pay him a million a year for ten years, or even half a million a year for twenty years, but you can afford a million a year with your kind of money."

She wondered how he knew how much money she had, but she felt sure that he did know. In time she would discover about Elias Renthal that he knew exactly how much money everyone had.

"Understand?"

She did understand. She could afford a million a year. Suddenly it was all beginning to fall into place. She wondered why her expensive lawyers had not come up with so simple a solution as Elias Renthal had come up with in ten minutes.

"And then," Elias continued.

"Yes," said Loelia.

"In a year or so, Ned will meet someone and probably remarry, and then, when he's happy again, he won't hold you to this agreement. After all, everyone says Ned's a gent."

"Yes, of course," said Loelia. It had not occurred to her until that moment that Ned would fall in love again and even marry again. She had only imagined him alone, or with the children. "Do you live here in the Rhinelander, Mr. Renthal?" Loelia asked when she was gathering up her gloves and bag.

"No, no, Ruby and I are just camping out here while Cora Mandell is doing over the new apartment we bought from Matilda Clarke. We thought we'd be in in time for Easter, but you know what a perfectionist Cora is. She's got nineteen coats of persimmon lacquer on the living-room walls, and the rugs are being woven in Portugal, and things like that take time. Not to mention all the faux marble," Elias added with a grin that charmed Loelia. "She's got some guy she brought over from Rome just to paint all the faux marble. The truth of the matter is, Loelia, I never heard of any of these absolutely essential refinements like persimmon lacquer and faux marble six years ago, and now they're dictating our lives."

Loelia laughed. "And Mrs. Renthal? How is she?"

"Her name is Ruby. And I'm Elias, Loelia."

"Yes, of course, Elias."

"Ruby's over in London bidding on a pair of eighteenth-century console tables at the Orromeo auction."

"Oh, yes, I heard about those tables from Jamesey Crocus. Inlaid, aren't they, with ram's heads on the legs?"

"I dunno."

"Sad about the Orromeos, isn't it?"

"I dunno."

"They've lost everything."

Elias shuddered. There were very few things in life that could make Elias Renthal shudder, but the thought of losing his fortune, as the Orromeos, whoever the Orromeos were, had lost theirs, was one of the things that could make him shudder.

"How?" he asked.

"How what?"

"How did the Orromeos lose all their money?"

"The usual thing that happens several generations down the line," replied Loelia.

"Spoiled brats that don't work? Like that?" asked Elias.

"I suppose. Too many divorces. Nothing depletes a fortune like divorce these days."

"As we were just saying," agreed Elias.

"When is Mrs. Renthal, I mean Ruby, coming back?" asked Loelia.

"She'll be back in time for Justine Altemus's wedding. Ruby wouldn't miss that event for all the tea in China," said Elias, stubbing out his cigar.

"Oh, I didn't know Ruby was a friend of Justine's," said Loelia, trying to keep the surprise out of her voice.

"She's not. Never met her."

"Oh, Bernard, then, of course. You're friends of Bernard Slatkin's."

"No, don't know Bernie Slatkin either, except on TV, of course."

"You're not a friend of Lil's, are you? I've never seen you at Lil's, have I?"

Elias laughed. "We're not planning on crashing, Loelia, if that's what you're thinking."

"Of course that's not what I'm thinking, Elias!"

"I'm involved in a couple of business deals with Laurance Van Degan, and he arranged for Ruby and me to get invited."

"Oh," said Loelia, again keeping the surprise out of her voice. "I'm staying here at the Rhinelander too, at least until I find a new apartment. Perhaps when Ruby gets back from London, the four of us can have dinner here in the hotel one night."

"That would be just swell, Loelia," said Elias. "Give my best to Mickie." Elias couldn't wait to get to the telephone so that he could call Ruby in London to tell her to get her ass home so that they could have dinner right out in public with Loelia Manchester and Mickie Minardos.

"You paid *how much* for those fucking tables?" shouted Elias Renthal over the telephone to his wife in London.

"You can't lose money on eighteenth-century French furniture, Elias. I swear to God," shouted Ruby back over the telephone.

"How much?"

"You heard what I said the first time."

"I couldn't have heard right."

"You'll love them, Elias. I swear to God. On either side of the fireplace, with the Monet with the water lilies overhead. Wait till you see them."

"Inlaid, aren't they, with ram's heads on the legs?"

"What do you know about ram's heads?" asked Ruby, surprised.

"Only what Loelia Manchester told me when I had tea with her this afternoon," replied Elias.

"What? You had tea with Loelia Manchester? Tell me everything."

"I'll tell you all about it when you get home."

"Are you sending the plane for me, or am I taking the Concorde?"

"Whichever's fastest."

"Elias. Is it okay about the consoles?"

"I don't even know what the fuck a console table is, Ruby."

"Is it okay?"

"Yeah, it's okay."

"You know what I'm going to do to you, Elias, when I get home, don't you?"

"I know, but I want to hear you say it."

"Your favorite. Both of them in my mouth. At the same time. Just the way you like it."

Mickie Minardos was in a quiet rage. He threw down the newspaper and leaped to his feet, pulling the belt of his green silk polka-dot dressing gown tighter around his slender waist. Loelia, seated at her dressing table, watched him in the mirror and noticed that his face was pink and his lips were pursed tightly together.

Since Florian Gray, in revenge for Mickie's verbal attack on him, had referred to Mickie in his column as a cobbler rather than a shoe designer, the word *cobbler* had caught on. He was told from time to time, always causing him great pain, that many of Loelia's friends, including her husband, now referred to him, behind his back, as the cobbler.

What Florian Gray had no way of knowing was that Mickie Minardos's father, back in his provincial town in Greece, was the village cobbler for all of Mickie's youth. Then Demetreus Minardos, who knew nothing of society and the grand life, achieved a certain local fame by designing a sandal popular with the working classes that utilized the rubber from discarded tires as soles and sold for less than the equivalent of a dollar. With the windfall, or what seemed like a windfall to old Demetreus Minardos, he was able to send his son, named Dimitri, but called Mickie, to a better school in Athens than any that existed in the place where they lived, and later, to Paris to study. Mickie's aim was to "do something" in the theater, but the something was undefined.

In Paris, attractive Greeks had always enjoyed a popularity, because, as Bijou McCord Thomopolous, the great hostess, who had married several Greeks, said, "They are such wonderful dancers, and they know how to treat their women." Mickie Minardos, who was a wonderful dancer, and an admirer of beautiful feet, began his career as a shoe designer, until the time came when he could "do something" in the theater. Before New York and Loelia Manchester, he had enjoyed the companionship of several fashionable ladies, among them Bijou McCord Thomopolous.

It was a curious aspect of Mickie's makeup that, although he felt shame about his father's profession, he had achieved great success in a more glamorous version of it. When interviewed by the fashion press, Mickie Minardos always described his father as a banker, which he did become, in a small branch of a small bank in the provincial town where his sandal factory was, giving the impression to the interviewer that banking, rather than the unmentioned cobbler business, was the source of the family fortune. A misprint in the fashion pages of the *Times* called his father a baker rather than a banker, and the mistake sent him into paroxysms of grief, as a baker was to him even lower on the social scale than a cobbler. He demanded a retraction from the *Times* and got one.

"What's the matter, darling?" asked Loelia finally, knowing that her beloved was upset.

"Nothing," Mickie replied. Already, in the months they had been living together, she had discovered that Mickie was inclined to sulk when he became angry and tended to deny anger when questioned about it.

"Darling, I can see that you're upset over something. What is it?"

"Florian Gray."

"Him again," said Loelia. "Now what has he said?"

"Don't read it."

"Of course, I'll read it. What difference does it make what people like that say? The only one of those people who matters is Dolly, and Dolly has been lovely to everyone."

"He calls me a cobbler again and says my father was a baker, instead of a banker, when he had to have seen the retraction in the *Times*."

"So what?" said Loelia. It always amazed Mickie that Loelia was unaffected by criticism of him.

"He says your friends don't accept me."

"Oh, puleeze, Mickie. It's too ridiculous."

"He says your mother is saying she will disinherit you if you marry me."

"I assure you, Mickie, that if my mother were ever to make such a statement, which she would not, it would never be to a gossip columnist from a tabloid newspaper. So calm down. It's simply not true."

"It is true that your friends won't accept me."

"But it was you who said that my friends were very dull. Narrow-in-their-outlook is what you said. You said people like Lil Altemus and Matilda Clarke and all the Van Degan clan were the most boring people in the world."

Mickie Minardos turned away from Loelia. He had said what Loelia said he said about her friends and relations, but he hadn't meant it. He had also said that the New People were more interesting by far than the old families, but he hadn't meant that either. In his heart, the world of Loelia Manchester was the part of New York that he most wanted to enter.

"One of these days they'll see how talented I am, and they'll be fighting to have me," he said.

Loelia heard the petulance in his voice. She looked at Mickie intently in the way a woman looks at a man she loves, but in whom she discovers an unpleasant trait that she had not known he possessed.

"Darling, you are considered to be the most successful man in your field in New York. Tell me how many shoe designers there are who have your sense of style."

"I'm going to break his face, that little pipsqueak Florian Gray, the next time I run into him."

"I adore you when you act tough, Mickie." She stood up and turned to him. "How do I look?"

"Turn around," he said.

Loelia assumed a model's pose and whirled around. Mickie eyed her critically, as if she were his creation, and she watched his face for his approval.

"Almost perfect," he said. "Sit down a minute. Here, let me do your eyes again. You need a little more green shadow to go with the color of your shoes."

16

WHEN JORGIE SANCHEZ-JULIA failed to show up for two scheduled interviews with Gus Bailey, Gus decided to abandon the story he was planning to write, which dealt with the growing trend of rich and elderly widows and widowers to leave their entire fortunes to late-life mates. Or, at least, he decided to abandon that part of the story that dealt with Jorgie Sanchez-Julia, a thirty-year-old Spanish gigolo who had married a crippled Washington millionairess almost fifty years his senior and then inherited her entire fortune, down to family heirlooms, much to the consternation of her children.

"Tell Jorgie to shove it," Gus told the young lady who answered the telephone in Jorgie's suite at the Rhinelander, when he called to complain that he had been kept waiting over an hour for the second day in a row.

The next morning a large bouquet of roses from Lorenza's shop arrived at Gus's apartment in Turtle Bay, together with a contrite and charming note from Jorgie Sanchez-Julia, saying that he had been unexpectedly called to Washington the day before. Gus didn't believe that Jorgie had been called to Washington, but he did believe that Jorgie, who loved publicity, did not want to pass up the opportunity to be interviewed, so a third appointment was set.

It surprised Gus that Jorgie wanted to meet at Clarence's rather than in the privacy of Gus's apartment, or in his suite at the Rhinelander, or in a less conspicuous restaurant than Clarence's, as Jorgie Sanchez-Julia was involved in a court battle over the money that he had inherited. Gus, his back to the room, flicked through the pages of his looseleaf notebook and read some previously written notes, while Jorgie Sanchez-Julia watched with inner excitement but a sullen expression the passing parade that lunch at Clarence's always was. Gus noted that Jorgie had a spoiled, full-lipped, pouting mouth, sallow skin, curly blond hair, and wore a Spanish suit that showed to full advantage his slender hips, waist, and rump.

"Help me out here, Jorgie," said Gus. "How old were you when you married Mrs. Acton?"

"Countess Sanchez-Julia," corrected Jorgie. A cigarette hung from the corner of his mouth.

"But certainly she was Mrs. Acton when you married her?"

"I was twenty-six."

"And the countess was how old?"

"Oh, seventy something or other. Geraldine, you know, never talked about age. She was so young in heart," answered Jorgie, his eye on the door of the restaurant where fashionable people kept coming in.

"And the title of Countess came from where?"

"Papal," replied Jorgie. "Geraldine was rewarded by His Holiness for her philanthropic endeavors."

"Ah, yes, papal. Tell me about the Countess's limp," said Gus. "Did she always have a limp?"

"She was born with a clubfoot," answered Jorgie. "Look, there's Yvonne Lupescu coming in. Do you know her? Used to be one of Madam Myra's girls. Carried her whips in a custom-made Vuitton bag. Such a dominatrix she is. Oh, my dear, the things I could tell you about that one."

Gus, working now, looked up from his notes to register what Jorgie had just said.

"I didn't know Mrs. Lupescu was one of Madam Myra's girls," he said.

"Used to be," Jorgie corrected himself. "You know of Madam Myra then?"

"Yes," replied Gus. "Ms. Myra she's known as in New York."

"How very amusing," said Jorgie. "I must remember that."

Gus tapped his pencil on the tabletop to get the subject back to the point of the lunch. "But your wife, the Countess, the late Countess, danced so well for a woman with a clubfoot."

"I taught her how to dance," said Jorgie. "Geraldine loved to dance. You see, I brought joy into her life. Those twins of hers, those playboys, paid no attention to their mother at all. Wait for her to die, that's all they thought, so they could get the money. If I hadn't come along and swept her off her foot, they would have put her in an old ladies' home. I gave her a wonderful life. Now they say about me that I exerted undue influence on her to leave me all her money. It was Geraldine's choice. I was as surprised as everyone else when the will was read."

"Yes, yes, of course," said Gus, writing down Jorgie's words.

"She was a wonderful woman," said Jorgie.

"Is it true that the pair of Renoir paintings were copies and you sold off the originals during her last illness?" asked Gus.

"Heavens, no!" replied Jorgie, laughing merrily at the absurdity of Gus's questions. "How do these terrible stories start?"

"There's something I'd like to ask you. Rather personal."

"You ask me, Mr. Bailey."

"Gus."

"You ask me, Gus."

"Did you, uh, have to make love to the Countess?"

"Oh, yes, on a regular basis. Geraldine was very attracted to me."

"I see." Gus sipped his water, as if it were a drink. "Tell me, Jorgie. Isn't it difficult to make love to a septuagenarian lady with a limp?"

Jorgie Sanchez-Julia smiled and shook his head. "I have never met the person, woman or man, I couldn't get it up for, Gus," he said. He thought for a moment, and then added, with a slight wink, "if the price was right."

"This is on the record, I assume," said Gus.

"On the record means what?" asked Jorgie.

"Hello, Jorgie," said Yvonne Lupescu, coming up to the table. "I didn't know you were in New York."

"Hello, Yvonne," Jorgie said unenthusiastically, holding out his hand to her without rising.

"Up," said Yvonne, with a thumbs-up gesture for him to rise. "That's no way to greet a lady."

"I just arrived on the Concorde yesterday," said Jorgie, rising lazily and winking at Gus to cover his lie. He kissed Yvonne in a lackluster manner on both cheeks, at the same time looking around the restaurant. They were both young and attractive, but indifferent to each other physically. "And you?"

"I live here now," said Yvonne.

"Oh, yes, I heard something about that. Constantine de Rham, isn't it?"

"I read that Geraldine died," said Yvonne.

"I miss her dreadfully," replied Jorgie.

"I'm sure."

"Do you know Mr. Augustus Bailey? Baroness Lupescu," said Jorgie, introducing.

"Yes, we know each other," said Gus.

"Jorgie, Fritzi von Stauffenberg is in the other room and would like you to say hello," said Yvonne.

"Fritzi is here? How marvelous. This is why I wanted to come to Clarence's, Mr. Bailey. Everyone who is in New York comes here. Would you excuse me for a minute?"

When Jorgie Sanchez-Julia moved away from the table, Gus, not wanting to get into a conversation with Yvonne, went back to studying his notes.

"May I sit down, Gus?" asked Yvonne.

"Of course."

"Such a naughty boy, Jorgie Sanchez-Julia," she said. "The things I could tell you about that one. But he was so sweet to his poor sister, the nun. He inherited everything, I heard."

Gus put away his notebook.

"That makes him the most successful male hooker in the world, I suppose," said Yvonne.

"Did the old lady know, do you suppose?"

"Geraldine? She couldn't have cared less. Jorgie showered her with roses, dozens at a time, which, of course, her accountants would get the bills for eventually, but she loved the attention."

"Good God," said Gus.

"Better than a nursing home," answered Yvonne, with a shrug of practicality.

"Depends," said Gus.

"I was wondering about something, Gus," said Yvonne.

"What?"

"How about doing one of your articles on me? I could stand a little exposure in New York."

"You'd have to shoot someone first, Mrs. Lupescu. Or inherit someone's money. Those are the kind of people I write about."

"I'm too dull, is that it?" asked Yvonne, smiling at him. "I'm twenty-eight years old. I've never been divorced. I've never even been married!"

Gus smiled, wanting to, but refraining from, asking her about Ms. Myra. "How's Constantine?"

"Oh, the same as ever."

"What is the-same-as-ever with Constantine de Rham?"

"He is dismayed that he is no longer received in New York," said Yvonne. "It haunts him. After all, for him, what else is there to life but lunching out and dining out?"

"Mrs. Verdurin invites him," said Gus.

"That's only once a month. There are twenty-nine more nights with no place to go. He came here for dinner the other night, and Chick Jacoby made him wait an hour for a table. He blames me. He thinks he is not invited because I am an encumbrance. The time is coming, I know, I can feel it, when I am going to have to leave him."

"Then what happens to you? Where will you go?"

"I know, if I left him, he would be in despair," said Yvonne, as if Gus had not spoken. "In fact, just between us, Gus, I rather enjoy Constantine's despair. It's so utterly abject. I like it when he begs me not to leave him. All his grandiosity leaves him completely. It makes me feel, oh, what is the right word for the feeling? Imperious, I suppose. I feel filled with power that a man could love me so passionately."

"Like a dominatrix, you mean?" asked Gus.

Yvonne smiled. "Jorgie's been gossiping about me, has he?"

Gus, paying his check, looked at Yvonne.

"You look so disapproving, Gus. So proper. So aboveboard."

"I don't know. Am I so different from any of the rest of you?"

"This is my stepson," said Fritzi von Stauffenberg, introducing Jorgie Sanchez-Julia to his luncheon companion.

"Yes, I know Jorgie," answered Jamesey Crocus. "He used to be my stepson."

Gus had no instinct for the chase. He had no desire for love. He did not want an involvement that would complicate his life and deflect him from what he knew he was going to do when Lefty Flint was released from prison. It was his friend George Eardley who introduced him to Myra Wealth. In Europe, they called her Madam Myra. In New York, they called her Miss Wealth. She preferred to be called Ms. Myra, a name that amused her, once she favored you. Ms. Myra ran an establishment of utter discretion from her apartment in the once-grand Murray Hill section of New York, catering to what she herself described as some of the most successful men in the city, although, she was quick to point out, none of the political crowd—since they lowered the standards of a place and, invariably, brought down an establishment as their political opponents and enemies sought to undo them.

"On the turn," was the way she described herself. Closer to forty than thirty, perhaps even beyond, she was in a voluptuous period of life and felt not remotely threatened by the younger girls of her establishment who were in greater demand than she was. She could spot in an instant the sort of men who were attracted to her ripe charms. Ms. Myra, in time, grew fond of Gus, whom she liked to call Augustus, and their business arrangement settled into a weekly visit, at his apartment, on Saturday nights, when most people he knew were in the country. No whips. No chains. No aberrations. No cocaine. His sexual tastes were plebeian, rarely varying from the missionary position. She stayed for an hour and a half, but one hour of the time was always taken up with conversation, when she told him tales of more exotic behavior of the clients of her house, always careful never to name names.

"There is a man on Wall Street, very important, you would know his name in a minute, lives on Park Avenue, has a house in Southampton, and his wife is always written up in Dolly De Longpre's column. He likes to cross dress." Or, "There is a Hollywood producer. Very important. You must have known him from your time there, when he was at Colossus. Old now. He only wants me to sleep by his side. Nothing more. Nothing ever happens. So sweet." Or, "I've stopped seeing the rich Arabs entirely. Two of my girls have disappeared." In turn, she would ask him about people he had written about. "I read your article about Faye Converse. She was always my favorite movie star, when I was growing up in Paris. Some people say I look like her. Do you think so?"

Leaving, Gus never handed her her money outright. In advance he placed the several hundred dollars in an envelope and left it on the hall table. It was only after he helped Ms. Myra into her black mink coat that he discreetly placed the envelope into her pocket.

"So sweet," she said to him, touching his face. She reapplied her lipstick, using his chipped gilt mirror. Then she put on the evening hat she always wore and arranged a black veil over her face.

"Ravishing," said Gus, smiling at her.

"So sweet," she said again.

"Saturday," he said.

"Saturday," she repeated, acknowledging the date.

He opened the front door of the apartment to ring for the elevator.

"When does that man get out of prison?" she asked.

"Much too soon," Gus answered. He never minded when she asked him questions that he would have minded from someone else.

"Does it worry you?"

"Yes."

From below, he could hear the elevator.

"Did you ever hear of someone called Yvonne Lupescu?" he asked her.

She looked at him, and their eyes met. Then she lifted her hand to her face and assumed a pensive expression, as if she were searching her memory. "No," she answered.

The elevator came. She got in and turned back to him as the door closed in front of her. They smiled at each other.

17

W HEN EZZIE FENWICK looked in the mirror, he turned his head sideways
so that he would not have to confront his peculiar eye, the one that
looked off in a different direction entirely. If Ezzie could have had a
say in his own physical formation, he would not only have given himself eyes
that matched, but a pencil-slim silhouette as well, and higher eyebrows, and
more height, but, alas, weight problems also plagued his life, and, in retaliation, he long.ago discovered that solace for what God had denied him was to
be found in clothes, for which he had a limitless passion. Each day, dressing,
Ezzie Fenwick gave as much thought to combinations and compatible colors as
Elias Renthal gave to making money and Nestor Calder gave to plots and
characters.

On the day of Justine Altemus's wedding, Ezzie Fenwick was fit to be tied.
The lavender shirt with the violet monogram and the white collar and cuffs had
not arrived from London as his shirtmaker there had promised it would, along
with the eleven other shirts he had ordered weeks earlier, but the eleven other
shirts didn't matter, only the lavender shirt with the violet monogram and the
white collar and cuffs, because Ezzie had expressly explained to his shirtmaker
that he must have it finished and delivered in time to wear with his new pearl
gray flannel suit, with the gray-and-white striped silk lining, to Justine Altemus's wedding to the television announcer.

Constantine de Rham tapped his boiled egg with a knife and then, with a
clean thrust, like a beheading, cut off the top of it, and proceeded to eat the
egg from the shell in silence. Yvonne Lupescu, watching from her end of the
table, knew when not to talk to Constantine and returned her eyes to Dolly De
Longpre's column, about the excitement in society over Justine Altemus's
wedding that day. She knew that Constantine's anger was because he no longer
was invited to the sort of rarefied social events, like Justine Altemus's wedding,
that he had been invited to during the years of his marriage to Consuelo.

When he left the breakfast table, carrying the *Times,* there was a look of
hostility on his face that prevented her from telling him that there was egg on
his chin. He walked very slowly past her to the door of the dining room, but he
always moved slowly on the mornings after she had whipped him. She was
aware that he never responded to her on those days, although it was he, never
she, who instigated the arrangement and begged to be whipped. At the door,

before walking out, he said his first words of the day to her, without turning to look at her. "I would like you to pack your bags and get out."

"I never saw you in an outfit like that before," said Juanito, lying on the bed as he watched Hubie dress for Justine's wedding. Juanito was in one of his sullen moods, which always happened when Hubie had family obligations from which he was excluded.

"I don't often wear striped trousers, a cutaway, spats, and a top hat," said Hubie. "That's why you never saw me dressed like this before."

"I want to go to the wedding," said Juanito. It was not the first time that day or that week that Juanito had said, "I want to go to the wedding."

"You can't," said Hubie, patiently. It was not the first time that day or that week that Hubie had said, "You can't."

"Why?"

"You know why, Juanito. We've been through all this a hundred times."

"Tio Laurance, I suppose," said Juanito, doing a facial gesture of Uncle Laurance's Van Degan grandeur that always made Hubie laugh.

"Yeah, that's it. Tio Laurance. Not to mention Madre Lil. And Padre Hubert. And Hermana Justine. And *todos los* Van Degans."

"I thought you said your sister liked me," said Juanito, in his sulking voice.

"Well, she does, in her own way, but this is a situation she doesn't want to have to deal with on her wedding day at St. James's church. She's already walking on eggs with her TV announcer."

"You and your sister both go for the lower classes, it looks like."

"Bernie's not lower class. Just different from us."

"But I'm lower class, right?"

"Come on, Juanito. I'll make it up to you. I promise." He opened his wallet and took out some bills and handed them to Juanito. "Go buy yourself that leather jacket you said you liked."

"Don't blow my low," said Juanito.

"Sometimes you're a real pain in the ass, Juanito," said Hubie.

They both laughed. "You look classy, Hubie."

"Thanks, Juanito. How does this look?" he asked, patting his chin. He had applied a flesh-colored makeup base where the skin of his chin was blemished.

"You could never tell."

"Can you tell there's makeup on over it?"

"No. I told you, you look great."

"Listen."

"What?"

"A church is a public place, even St. James's. I can't keep you out of the church if you want to stand in the back and look."

"You mean it?"

"They let the homeless stand in the back and look."

"Oh, thanks."

"But no Colony Club." Hubie looked out the window of his loft. "My mother's car is here." He opened the window and called down, "I'll be right down, Joe."

"Joseph," corrected Juanito. "You're supposed to call your chauffeur Joseph, not Joe, for God's sake."

"Oh, is this something you know a lot about?" asked Hubie, amused.

"Sure, my family always had chauffeurs down in Puerto Rico."

Hubie put on his top hat.

"Let me see you in your top hat," said Juanito.

Hubie, shy, turned around.

"Give it a little angle," said Juanito.

Hubie gave his hat a little angle.

"You look just like a swell."

Hubie shrugged. "I *am* a swell."

"Will you give me a ride uptown?" asked Juanito. "I never rode in a limo."

"Let's go."

Juanito opened the door and, with a flourish, waved Hubie out the door.

"After you," said Hubie.

"No, after you. AIDS before beauty."

Hubie shook his head. "You're a class act, Juanito."

"I do wish you wouldn't pee in my new bidet, Elias," said Ruby. "It's disgusting. The new maid is going to think we don't know anything."

"Let's worry a lot what Candelaria with the harelip who can't speak a word of English thinks about us," said Elias.

"I'm not wearing too much jewelry, am I?" asked Ruby.

"You look great, Ruby. New dress?"

"Of course it's new. Pretty soon they're going to say about Ruby Renthal that she never wears the same dress twice. Do you think mink or sable?"

"Honey, I don't know."

"This is the first time we've been to one of these affairs where we haven't had to buy tickets to get in."

"Nervous?"

"Yeah."

"Me too."

"Don't leave my side the whole time, Elias."

"I won't."

"Elias, I just love my new ring."

"I hear you had the about-to-be bride and groom out to the country for the weekend, Matilda," said Maisie Verdurin, walking down Madison Avenue to St. James's church after Violet Bastedo's lunch at Clarence's.

"Just a little dinner for the Bedford crowd," said Matilda.

"Bernie and Justine met at one of my parties. Did you know that?" asked Maisie, pleased with her matchmaker role.

"I'm not sure the Van Degans are going to send you a thank-you note for that, Maisie," said Matilda.

"Don't you like Bernie?"

Matilda Clarke, who thought Bernard Slatkin was very attractive, hesitated for a moment before answering. "Tall, dark, handsome, clever. Too clever. Won all the word games as if his life depended on it. And he might, just might, have a bit of a roving eye. My God, look at the crowds outside the church."

* * *

Yvonne Lupescu pushed open the door of Constantine de Rham's den, entered, and closed the door behind her. The room was, in the absence of its occupant, dark, but she dared not pull back the red velvet curtains to let in light or turn on the wall lights. She knew exactly how much time she had. Constantine was in the lavatory off the entrance hall. She stood for several moments until her eyes became accustomed to the dark. Then she crossed and seated herself behind Constantine's ormolu-encrusted Boulle desk. She opened the long center drawer and felt around inside, under papers and leather address books. She closed the drawer quietly and opened the top drawer of the two drawers on the left and immediately she felt what she was looking for. At that instant the door opened and the lights went on.

"What are you doing here?" asked Constantine.

Yvonne Lupescu, frightened, rose.

"There is no money in that desk if that is what you are looking for, Yvonne," said Constantine.

"My passport, Constantine," she replied. One of her hands was behind her back. "I cannot leave without my passport."

"Your passport, Yvonne, is in your traveling case where you always keep it. What are you looking for in my desk?"

"Where's Ramon?" asked Yvonne.

"It is Ramon's day off."

Yvonne smiled.

"I asked what you were looking for in my desk," he repeated.

Constantine walked over to the desk where Yvonne was standing. Calmly she brought her hand around from behind her back and pointed a pistol at him.

"Oh, Yvonne, don't be ridiculous," said Constantine, dismissively, as he moved around the desk toward her.

"You can't think, Constantine, that I am going to walk out of here without any, shall we say, compensation," said Yvonne, thrilled by the excitement of such a scene, as she backed away from him.

"For the past six months I have given you a home such as you have never lived in," said Constantine.

"Am I supposed to consider that a generous act?"

"There are some who would think so."

"Without what I do to you, Constantine, you can't get erect, and you know it, and that's worth a lot more than a free bed with some of your dead wife's Porthault sheets on it."

"I will have the accountant send you a check for your services," said Constantine.

"You're in a vile mood because you weren't invited to Justine Altemus's wedding, and in an ugly mood because there are welts on your ass that you begged me to put there. Don't hold either of those things against me."

Constantine moved forward and held out his hand for Yvonne to give him the gun. She, defiant, continued to hold it on him. In an instant, Constantine leaned forward and grabbed Yvonne's wrist.

"What in the world do you want with that gun, you foolish girl?" he asked.

Instead of releasing the gun, Yvonne pulled it back toward her. Laughing at her, Constantine pulled it up toward him, as a shot rang out in the room. For an instant they held each other's eye, disbelief on his face, excitement on hers. She watched as the color drained from his face and he crumpled in front of her and fell to the floor.

"Oh, my God, Constantine," she said. She moved to his body, knelt by him, and listened to his heart. Sitting up, she leaned into his face. His eyes, glazed, stared back at hers.

"You pulled that trigger, you son of a bitch. I didn't pull that trigger," she hissed at his face.

Then she carefully erased her fingerprints from the trigger and handle of the gun with a handkerchief she took from Constantine's jacket and placed the gun in his hand, arranging his finger on the trigger. Slowly she rose from the floor, closed the drawers of the desk, and walked to the door of the room. In the hallway she listened for a minute to the silence of the mansion. Closing the door of the room behind her, she raced for the marble stairs and ran up them. In her bathroom, she turned on the taps of her shower to full blast, rushed to her closet, and began pulling out dresses, rejecting one after the other, until she found the yellow one that looked so right for the occasion at hand.

On the third ring, the message machine in Gus Bailey's apartment answered. "Hello, this is Augustus Bailey. I'm not able to come to the telephone right now. Leave your name and number and the time you called, and I will get back to you as soon as possible. Wait for the beep."

"Call me, Mr. Bailey. I have some information for you." The voice was Detective Johnston and Detective Johnston never called Gus unless there was a very good reason.

There were so many more people on the bride's side of the church than on the groom's side that the ushers ceased to ask the guests on which side they wanted to be and seated the later arrivals on the groom's side to correct the imbalance. Only the Elias Renthals, not wishing to be thought of as friends of the groom, insisted to the usher, whom they mistook for Chinese, that they be seated on the Altemus side rather than the Slatkin side, although they had barely met Lil Altemus and only knew Justine from seeing her across the rooms at Maisie Verdurin's parties or nodding to her at Clarence's. However, their credentials, coming as they had from Laurance Van Degan, were the best, and they were seated impressively toward the front of the church, only two rows behind Loelia Manchester and Matilda Clarke, who were practically family, and one row behind Ezzie Fenwick, the social arbiter, beneath the famous rose window given to the church by the late Alice Grenville in memory of her son.

Ezzie Fenwick knelt, head bowed in a devotional attitude for a minute, and then sat back in the pew and looked around to see who was there. He waved to the Todescos across the aisle and blew a kiss to old Aunt Minnie Willoughby and Cora Mandell. Ruby Renthal nudged Elias to watch Ezzie. Then both Elias and Ruby knelt, heads bowed in devotional attitudes for a minute, and then sat back in their pew and looked around to see who was there. Ruby waved and blew a kiss to Cora Mandell who was the only person present she knew well enough to wave and blow a kiss to.

Everyone was enchanted with the string quartet on the altar that Jamesey

Crocus, who knew more about Bach fugues than anyone, had found for Justine, who wanted Bach, and Bach alone. The flowers, fully opened peach and coral roses in great abundance, all arranged by Lorenza, were admired by everyone. There were nods of approval for old Ormonde Van Degan, as he inched his way up the aisle on his walker, helped along by a smiling and considerate Dodo Fitz Alyn.

"I think Ormonde must have had a stroke," said Aunt Minnie Willoughby to Cora Mandell. "Something about his mouth doesn't work very well. Droops a bit."

"Drips a bit too," said Cora.

Aunt Minnie Willoughby mouthed but did not speak the word *incontinent.*

"Poor Dodo. She looks happy though. Lil says she's been an angel to Ormonde," replied Cora.

"Nevel did Justine's dress and all the bridesmaid's dresses and Lil Altemus's too," whispered Ruby to Elias.

"Who's Nevel?" asked Elias.

"Leven spelled backwards," whispered Ruby.

After forty minutes, the guests became restless and began to wonder if the wedding was about to be canceled. Then, led by Ezzie Fenwick, who loved social drama, they began to speculate, pew by pew, to great guffaws, that the holdup was because Bernie Slatkin was refusing to sign the prenuptial agreement that Lil Altemus, as a last-minute precaution against fortune hunting, had insisted upon. It was not so. Bernie Slatkin, whose broadcasting income was far more impressive than any of Justine's Wall Street suitors' incomes had ever been, had willingly signed a prenuptial agreement several weeks earlier, but, waiting in the groom's room for the bride to show up, he told his best man, Fielder Black, the coanchor on the evening news, that he bet the people in the church were making jokes about his not wanting to sign a prenuptial agreement. He worried about his aunt and uncle, whom he could see sitting in the front row, and hoped they would not think that Justine was not going to show up.

Sol Slatkin, seated in the front row on the groom's side, patted his wife's hand. Hester, staring straight ahead, nodded her head in acknowledgment of Sol's pat.

"I hate to think what these flowers must have cost," said Hester.

"They can afford it," said Sol.

"Where do you suppose she is?"

"Aren't brides always late?" asked Sol.

"I wasn't," said Hester.

Sol smiled at his wife. "There's Bernie. Do you see Bernie? Peeking out the door of the groom's room."

"It's not Bernie I'm worried about, Sol. I know Bernie's here. It's Bernie's intended I'm worried about. Do you dare turn around?"

"Why?"

"Pretend you're looking for the Perelmans and see if there's any activity at the back of the church. You don't think she wouldn't show up, do you, Sol?"

Sol Slatkin turned discreetly in his place. He waved a half wave to the

Perelmans and then turned back. "Something's happening back there," he reported.

Lil Altemus, helped out of her car by her driver Joe, smiled at the photographers who took her picture. She was wearing a gray chiffon afternoon dress under her sable coat. Lest it be considered too somber in coloring, Nevel, who designed it, had added shades of coral and peach into the gray chiffon hat that he also designed. Lil wore, as always on great occasions, her famous pearls, inherited from her mother, and a sunburst of diamonds on her shoulder. Hubie Altemus, very thin, but sober, took his mother by the arm and led her up the steps into the church, but his presence was so overwhelmed by his mother's magnificence that the makeup he wore to cover the lesion on his face went unnoticed.

In the backseat of the Van Degan limousine on the way from Lil Altemus's apartment to St. James's church, a distance of only a few blocks, but a journey made slow by one-way streets and late afternoon traffic, Justine Altemus, her face veiled, sat next to her father.

"Are you happy with this guy, Justine?" he asked.

"Daddy, what a time to ask me such a question. You've had weeks to ask me that."

"But I never see you alone," he said, turning to look at her through her veil.

Justine smiled fondly at her father. She remembered the smell of his kisses when he used to stop by to kiss her good-night on his way to whatever dinner or party he was always going to: a romantic mélange of Floris shaving lotion, Camel cigarettes, and scotch from the scotch mist he always drank while he was dressing.

"I'm sorry about Belinda, Daddy, that Mother wouldn't let her sit up with the family."

"We're all used to your mother by now," said Hubert. From a small silver flask, he hastily swallowed a gulp of scotch whiskey.

"Here we are at the church," said Justine nervously. "Oh, look, an awning. I'd forgotten there was to be an awning. I adore awnings at weddings."

"This is where your mother and I were married," said Hubert Altemus.

"That's a very somber thought," said Justine. They both laughed. "Yes, Daddy, I am very happy with this guy."

"Good," he said and patted her hand. "An awful lot of photographers out there."

"That's not for the Van Degans, you know, or the Altemuses. That's for Bernie Slatkin. My guy's a star, Daddy."

"Good God."

In the vestibule, the small bridesmaids, nervous and tittering in the final moments before the processional, greeted the radiant bride on her arrival with her father. Lil Altemus and her former husband looked at each other.

"Hello, Lil," said Hubert.

"Hubert," replied Lil, in a return greeting.

"You're looking well, Lil," said her former husband.

Lil Altemus, who had never been able to deal with the fact that Hubert Altemus had left her, bent down, in a rare motherly gesture, to straighten out the cream satin folds of Justine's train.

"Your bouquet is lovely, Justine," said Lil, rising, eyes away from Hubert. "There's no one like Lorenza for flowers."

"Do I look all right, Mother?" asked Justine.

"Perfect. Nevel at his best."

"I meant me," said Justine.

"You look beautiful, Justine," said her father.

"I guess it's time for you to take me up, Hubie," said Lil to her son, who had been watching the family exchange from a corner of the small room.

"Good luck, Justine," said Hubie.

"Oh, Hubie," said Justine, leaning down to kiss her shorter brother on the cheek. She saw the makeup that covered the lesion on his chin. "What is that?" she whispered.

"Nothing," answered Hubie. "An astringent in my aftershave lotion caused an irritation."

Their eyes met, in a moment of silent understanding, like when they were children long ago.

"Come along, Hubie," said Lil.

When the strains of *Lohengrin* were finally heard, to everyone's relief, Justine Altemus, billowing in cream-colored satin and rosepoint lace, carrying cream-colored roses, fully opened, nearly ran up the aisle to her groom, restrained only by the careful walk of her slightly inebriated father. Preceded by ten little girls dressed as shepherdesses carrying crooks, Justine's eyes searched longingly ahead for the husband who was waiting for her. Not a person present, except possibly her mother, did not think that the match, although unusual, was not romantic.

The Bradleys' cook jumped out the window, "splash, splash, all over the corner of Park Avenue and Sixty-second Street," as Ezzie Fenwick was to report it later, just as the wedding party was entering the Colony Club for the reception, but, inside, it was a thing not to be mentioned, as no one wanted to cast a pall on the happy occasion of Justine Altemus's marriage to Bernard Slatkin. The Bradleys, whose cook had just jumped, stayed, for propriety's sake, only long enough to go through the line and greet the handsome couple.

"So marvelous, Lil. All the old families," said Mame Bradley. "None of those New People." Just then Elias and Ruby Renthal came into her line of vision. "Except, of course, the Renthals."

Lil Altemus mouthed but did not speak the word *business,* so there could be no misunderstanding as to the reason for the presence of the Elias Renthals at her daughter's wedding.

Justine, standing in the receiving line between Bernie and her mother, shielded her mouth with her bouquet and whispered into Lil Altemus's ear, "Mother, *please,* speak to Mrs. Slatkin. She's just standing there with no one to talk to."

"Come stand here by me, Hester," said Lil. "Have you met my great friend, Cora Mandell?"

"Hellohowareyou?" said Cora to Hester.

"Isn't this all lovely?" replied Hester, trying to make conversation with the septuagenarian decorator, whose work she read about in house magazines.

"So pretty, yes. I'm looking everywhere for Ezzie," said Cora, turning to Lil. "He's in such a snit about his shirtmaker. Really too funny."

"He's over there talking to Madge Tree's son," replied Lil.

"Excuse me, Mrs. Slatkin. I must see this friend of mine," said Cora Mandell, hurrying off. Hester, aware but unfazed, knew that she was the aunt of the handsomest young man in the room.

"Now, Hester," said Lil, "who don't you know?"

"Hello, Uncle Ormonde," said Matilda Clarke. Old Ormonde Van Degan, afflicted now with sporadic senility and an unreliable memory, smiled blankly at Matilda without recognizing her. Dodo Fitz Alyn opened her handbag, took out a handkerchief, and wiped the saliva off his chin.

"What is he becoming, Dodo? Blind or deaf?" asked Matilda. "I mean, should I talk louder or move closer?"

"It's Matilda Clarke, Ormonde," said Dodo in a loud voice directly into Ormonde's ear. "Sweetzer's widow, Matilda."

"Good God, he knows that, Dodo," said Matilda.

"I miss Sweetzer," said Ormonde Van Degan, finally placing Matilda. His voice was as frail as his body was fragile. "He was a keen sportsman. Marvelous fisherman. Good shot, too. I miss Sweetzer."

"Thank you, Uncle Ormonde," said Matilda, rushing on.

"That was your great aunt Grace Gardiner," said Laurance Van Degan, looking at a white marble bust on a stand in the entrance to the ballroom. "The New York Gardiners used the *i* in their name, but the Boston Gardners spelled it without the *i*. Your great aunt Grace was one of the founders of this club, and, from all reports, was a very interesting woman."

But Hubie Altemus didn't want to hear what made old great aunt Grace Gardiner, spelled with an *i*, a very interesting woman. For years he had heard his uncle expound on the various branches of the family, but it was a topic that never interested Hubie in the least. What interested Hubie was Juanito Perez. "Excuse me, Uncle Laurance, I have to make a call."

In the men's room, standing at the urinal, was Hubie's cousin, young Laurance Van Degan, who was everything in the family that Hubie was not. As Hubie approached the second urinal, Laurance, spotting his first cousin, turned his body away in a protective gesture.

"If you think I have any curiosity about your pecker, old man, give it another thought," said Hubie.

"You're disgusting, Hubie," said young Laurance Van Degan, his face acquiring the haughty Van Degan expression that Juanito could mimic so well.

Hubie, seeing it, laughed. "Asparagus for lunch, huh?" he asked.

"Have you become psychic in addition to your other worldly successes?" asked Laurance.

"No. Your piss stinks," said Hubie.

"You're disgusting, Hubie."

"You put those three inches of yours away so fast, Laurance, you forgot to shake it off, and now you've got a big wet urine stain all over your grays."

Laurance, red-faced, headed for the door.

"You better hurry back to Laura, Laurance. It must be time to breastfeed the baby again."

"I can remember the Depression only too well," said Cora Mandell. "We had to sell half the land in Bar Harbor. I couldn't go to school in Switzerland, and Uncle Joe Leyland had to pay for my debut dress."

"It's a terrible thing to have a great name and not enough money," said Ezzie Fenwick. Then he turned to Dodo Fitz Alyn and asked, "Don't you think so?"

Dodo, poor always, blushed.

"A perfect world for me would be where everyone I know and cared for had about forty million dollars," said Ezzie. "With forty million you can do everything you want to do and go everywhere you want to go, but you're not up there with Rochelle Prud'homme and Elias Renthal, thank the good lord. How do you suppose the Renthals got here? They made a big fuss about sitting on the bride's side, did you notice?"

"Mrs. Renthal fired me, then begged me to come back," said Cora, looking over at Elias and Ruby.

Ezzie Fenwick often used the word *frightfully* in conversation. "Frightfully funny," he'd say about an amusing story. "Frightfully nice," he'd say about some people. "Frightfully grand," about others. Or, "frightfully common." He said frightfully common more often than he said frightfully funny or frightfully nice or frightfully grand.

"Frightfully common," said Ezzie Fenwick.

"Who?" asked Cora Mandell.

"Mrs. Renthal, that's who. Look at the size of the ring on her finger. If that rock is fake, it's silly, and if it's real, it's ridiculous."

"It's real, all right," said Cora. "I can assure you of that."

"Bernie and Justine are dancing, Cora. Do you want to come and look?" asked Tucky Bainbridge.

"I'm perfectly content to sit right here and listen to Ezzie criticize everyone's clothes," said Cora.

"Talk to me, Elias. We can't stand here like we don't know anyone," said Ruby.

"Why do mice have such small balls?" asked Elias.

"So-few-of-them-dance-well. You already told me that one, Elias."

"I'm just trying to make it look like we're having a conversation, Ruby. Don't bite my head off because you already heard the fucking joke."

"My God, Elias, here comes Loelia Manchester to speak to us. Don't tell her any of your jokes, and don't say *fuck.*"

"I get along with Loelia Manchester just fine, Ruby," replied Elias.

Loelia, approaching them, was struck anew by the change in the appearance of Elias Renthal, a change far more profound than could be brought about by expensive tailoring and barbering. What she saw in the florid face that she had once considered vulgar was the unmistakable look of power, and she was drawn to it.

Whatever reservations most of the guests of Lil Altemus and the Van Degan family might have about people like Elias Renthal and his third wife, there was the beginning of a noticeable change in the whispered information about them whenever someone asked, "Who in the world is that?" or "How do you suppose they got here?" Elias Renthal, it was now said, was a wizard in business, and his comments about "interesting situations" in the stock market, with which he was selectively generous, were to be acted upon by all means if one was so favored. Indeed, it was said that Laurance Van Degan himself, that most conservative of bankers and investors, had made a killing on a stock tip from Elias Renthal. Then, of course, there was the much discussed Renthal apartment, as yet unseen, but tales of its splendors were constantly circulated. "The furniture, my dear, is priceless," said no less an authority than Jamesey Crocus. Dolly De Longpre had spread the word in her column that Elias Renthal had also purchased Merry Hill, the magnificent estate and horse-breeding farm that, years ago, had belonged to a family called Grenville, and already dozens of masons and carpenters were at work to enlarge and refront the mansion from Tudor to Georgian as a fitting residence for his beloved Ruby. There was also, one heard, a house in the tropics, and apartments in London and Paris, where Elias's business interests took him frequently, always on his own plane with its own computers and telephones and other equipment so that his work day need never be interrupted. Certainly there was money, seemingly limitless money, and no disinclination on the part of either Mr. or Mrs. Renthal to spend it. Mrs. Renthal wore the largest gems in New York and traveled to and from her hairdresser and to and from her other appointments in a pale blue limousine of foreign make that was the only one of its kind in New York. Her wedding gift to Justine Altemus and Bernie Slatkin was of such extravagance that Lil Altemus insisted it be returned, and only the intervention of Laurance, her brother, who suggested that it would be "unseemly" to return the gift, a gold tea service that had once belonged to the Empress Josephine, prevented Lil from carrying out her threat.

"Hello, Elias," said Loelia, and Ruby was thrilled with the proximity of her, as well as the vocal tones that announced her utter perfection of birth and breeding. Loelia Manchester's attire was simplicity itself, as Dolly De Longpre said the next day in her column, but she was by far the best-dressed woman in the room.

"Loelia, this is Ruby," said Elias.

"Your husband was so charming to me, Ruby, when you were away. I've looked forward to meeting you."

"Same here," said Ruby. "Love your outfit."

"Love your ring," said Loelia, and the two ladies laughed.

"We were wondering, Mickie and I, if you and Elias would dine with us on Monday and go on to the opera."

"Monday?" asked Ruby. She looked at Elias. Monday was the night of the birthday of Elias's daughter by his first marriage. Their eyes met. He nodded that it would be all right.

"We'd be delighted, Loelia," said Ruby in her smartest voice.

"Jaime's coming," said Loelia.

"Hymie?" answered Ruby.

"You'll adore Jaime."

"Hymie who?"

"The Honduran ambassador."

* * *

"Have some champagne, Gus," said Lil Altemus. "There's going to be toasts."

"I have my old faithful here," said Gus, clutching a glass of fizzy water. Gus always held his water glass as if it were a cocktail.

"Oh, I always forget," said Lil. "One glass can't hurt, surely?"

"I'm fine, thanks."

"Do me a favor, will you, Gus?" asked Lil. "Will you talk to those Renthals. They don't know anyone here, and Laurance is determined that they have a good time, God knows why."

"Loelia Manchester is dancing with Elias Renthal," said Gus.

"Loelia? Really? That's a new one. Be a love and go dance with what's-her-name, his wife," said Lil.

"Ruby," said Gus.

"Yes, of course, Ruby," said Lil, who had known her name was Ruby all along.

Ruby was thrilled to dance with Gus. Her conversation with Loelia Manchester had made her feel for the first time that she was going to be able to make it in New York.

"I'm just an old fox-trotter," said Gus. "I'm not up on all the new steps."

"You and Elias," said Ruby.

"You're looking great, Ruby. I read about you in the papers all the time."

Ruby laughed. "How's everything with you?" she asked.

"Okay."

"You feel tense to me."

"Our mutual friend, Lefty Flint, is up for a parole hearing on the thirteenth of next month," said Gus.

"I can't believe it," she said. The color drained from her face.

"It's true."

"Are you going out for the hearing?"

"No."

"Why?"

"He's got an automatic release. A perfect jail record. Everybody's little darling."

"You know he's going to do it again, don't you?" she said.

"I do."

"Where's the hearing?"

"The Men's Correctional Institute. Vacaville, California."

Ruby looked at Gus, as if she were going to say something.

"My husband's about to cut in on you," she said.

When the drummer from Peter Duchin's orchestra rolled the drums for silence, Lil Altemus went to the microphone with a glass of champagne in her hand and made a charming speech, even if she didn't believe what she was saying, which she didn't, saying how much she liked Bernie Slatkin and how perfect she thought he was for Justine, and how glad she was to have Bernie's aunt and uncle, Hester and Sol Slatkin, in the family. When Bernie got up to deliver his speech, he said he thought he was the luckiest man on earth to be married to Justine Altemus, and his dimple was admired by all of Justine's friends as he raised his glass to toast his beautiful new wife.

"You should be off, Justine," said Lil.

"After I throw the bouquet, Mother," replied Justine.

"Throw it to poor Dodo," said Lil.

"Isn't it sweet the way she takes care of Grandfather, wiping all the drool off his mouth all the time," said Justine.

"Where's Bernard?"

"Dancing with his aunt."

Lil Altemus and her daughter both looked toward the dance floor. Bernie, dancing with Hester, gave Justine a wink. At that moment a late arriving guest entered the ballroom. Wearing a turban, she had an exotic look about her. She appeared to be looking for someone.

"My God, there's that horrible woman," said Lil. "What's she doing here?"

"What horrible woman?"

"In the yellow dress, and the turban. Mrs. Lupescu. Did you invite her?"

"I certainly didn't invite her, Mother."

"She's surely not one of Uncle Laurence's business acquaintances, like Elias Renthal."

"Do you suppose Constantine de Rham is here too?"

"He'd better not be. Consuelo was one of my best friends. That woman crashed. I never heard of anyone crashing a wedding reception before. That's the tackiest thing I ever heard. Throw your bouquet, Justine. I want to wind up this party."

"Oh, hello, Gus. I'm sorry I'm so late," said Yvonne Lupescu.

"Late?" asked Gus, surprised to see her.

"I was so thrilled when you asked me to come. Poor Constantine wasn't feeling well. He's been so depressed, and he thought it would be marvelous for me to get out. So sweet of you, Gus," said Yvonne.

Gus looked at Yvonne. She smiled at him and linked her arm in his and looked at the dance floor. "Shall we dance?" she asked.

"No," said Gus. "I don't like to dance."

"I bet you're a marvelous dancer."

"I'm not."

"Oh, look, Gus, Justine's going to throw her bouquet. Let's go watch." She took Gus by the arm and led him into the room.

Justine, with Bernie by her side, stood on the stairway of the club, her train wrapped around her arm, and looked down at her friends. People pushed Dodo Fitz Alyn and Violet Bastedo to the front. There was a drumroll from Peter Duchin's band, and Justine raised her hand and threw the bouquet. Dodo, crimson with embarrassment, reached her hands up in the air. Violet, already twice-married, squealed with excitement as she held up her arms. In an instant, Yvonne Lupescu stepped in front of both ladies and grabbed the bouquet just as it was about to land in Dodo Fitz Alyn's hands.

"Oh, how marvelous," said Yvonne. "Wait till Constantine hears. Gus, isn't it exciting?"

Gus, speechless, stared at Yvonne Lupescu.

*   *   *

Meanwhile, Constantine de Rham's body, as yet undiscovered, lay in a pool of blood on the floor of the den in his house on Sutton Place.

18

T HE NEXT MORNING, Gus was rushing for the airport to go to Los Angeles, in response to a message Detective Johnston had left on his answering machine. At the same time Innocento was arriving in the lobby of his building with Gus's standing order of three containers of coffee and the morning papers. "I'll be gone for a few days, Innocento," said Gus, grabbing the papers and the coffee and heading for the car that he had ordered to take him to the airport. "I'll call you when I get back to start up the papers again."

"Have a good trip," called out Innocento, but by that time Gus was telling the driver not to put his bag in the trunk of the sedan but to keep it on the seat next to him, as he was late, so that he could just make a run for it when he got to JFK. The driver, who looked Hispanic, nodded as if he understood Gus's instructions, but he didn't understand Gus's instructions and put the bag in the trunk of the sedan anyway.

"Innocento," Gus called out. "Tell this guy I'm in a hurry. I've got an eight ten to catch."

If the plane hadn't been late, Gus would have missed it, but planes were always late these days, and he arrived at the airport in plenty of time, although not on speaking terms with his driver.

"When was the last time you were on a plane that wasn't late starting?" asked the pretty middle-aged advertising executive who was sitting next to Gus in the business section, looking up from some copy she was revising with a pink Hi-Liter. She was wearing a tailored suit and gold jewelry, and her nails were perfectly manicured. And she was ready for some cross-country conversation.

Gus smiled politely and said, "I can't remember." Then he picked up the newspapers that Innocento had brought him and buried his face in them, starting with the tabloids, saving the *Times,* because he didn't want to get into a conversation about late planes and the reason for their lateness, and because he knew, from instinct and experience, that by the time the plane had flown over the border of the state of New York, the woman would have told him about her impending divorce, her husband's girlfriend who used to be her best friend, her daughter's abortion, and her ideas for the new advertising campaign of a cigarette company her agency had just taken on.

It was then, aloft, that Gus read about the suicide attempt of Constantine de Rham. De Rham, dying, had been discovered by his Filipino butler, who had returned early to the house on Sutton Place from his day off, because he was feeling unwell. The butler, Ramon Enrile, 62, found de Rham when he began turning on lights in the darkened house, lying in a pool of blood on the floor of his den, beneath a painting of a stag being torn apart by hounds. In his left hand was a revolver. A single shot had been fired into his stomach. At first the butler thought he was dead. He went to look for Mrs. Yvonne Lupescu, Mr. de Rham's companion, who was a visitor in the house, but she was not there. He then called the police. De Rham was in the intensive care unit of New York Hospital under police watch. No note had been found near the body nor was any reason given as to why the 50-year-old de Rham should wish to take his life. When Mrs. Lupescu returned to the house, she was informed by police of the suicide attempt and became hysterical. She blamed herself, she said, because she had decided to leave him. It was later ascertained by police that at the time of the suicide attempt Mrs. Lupescu had been attending the society wedding reception of the Van Degan heiress, Justine Altemus, to the television anchorman Bernard Slatkin at the Colony Club.

Gus, stunned, put down the tabloid and stared out the window of the airplane. In his pocket, on a sheet of expensive but plain white paper, typewritten, was the name, address, and telephone number of a man in Los Angeles called Anthony Feliciano. It had arrived in the mail the day before in an unmarked envelope, with no accompanying letter, several hours before Detective Johnston's message had been left on his answering machine telling him the date Lefty Flint was to be released from prison. Gus knew that the sender was Constantine de Rham.

Gus approached Los Angeles with dread. He always approached Los Angeles with dread. Once he had lived there. Once he had worked there. Once he had raised a family there. Once he had been happy there. But that was long ago and far away.

There were several places Gus could have stayed. Peach, possibly, would have him. Peach no longer lived in the house where they had lived when they were married. Several years earlier she had moved to a smaller house in the part of Beverly Hills known as the flats. She did not enjoy guests, but the house had a guest room, which she called a spare room, to discourage guests, as well as a small apartment in the pool house that she let out to students from U.C.L.A. so that there would always be someone on the property, and Gus happened to know that the apartment was empty at the moment. But Gus didn't want Peach to know he was in town until after he had done what he had come to do.

He thought about staying at Cecilia Lesky's house in Bel-Air, but Cecilia, who was the daughter of the film mogul Marty Lesky, as well as an old friend of Gus's, was always giving parties, or going to parties, or having people drop in from noon until two in the morning. There were times when he enjoyed Cecilia Lesky's kind of pandemonium, but this was not one of them.

Then there were his friends Nestor and Edwina Calder, who had rented a house in Malibu while Nestor was writing the screenplay for the mini-series of *Judas Was a Redhead,* but being with Nestor and Edwina would have meant having to answer questions about his trip to Los Angeles, and he did not wish to either lie to them or be questioned by them.

In the end Gus decided to stay at a hotel on the Sunset Strip where it was unlikely he would run into anyone he knew, as he most certainly would have if he had stayed in any of the well-known hotels in Beverly Hills or Bel-Air, where even the waitresses in the coffee shops all called him by name. Checking in at the Sunset Marquis, he was pleased to find out it was within walking distance of the address that Constantine de Rham had given him for Anthony Feliciano.

"How did you get my name?" asked Anthony Feliciano.

"In New York, where I live," said Gus.

"New York, huh?" Anthony Feliciano seemed pleased that he had been discussed in New York. "Who told you about me in New York?"

"A man called Constantine de Rham."

"That's a name from the past. How is Constantine de Rham?"

"Almost dead, apparently, according to this morning's New York papers."

"How almost dead?"

"Shot in the stomach, by his own hand."

"He never struck me as a suicide type," said Feliciano.

"Nor me," replied Gus.

"Did you know him long?"

"No, and not well at that."

Anthony Feliciano sat behind a desk of fake mahogany in a small office in a second-class building on a street that looked down on the Sunset Strip. Behind him on a credenza that matched the desk was a huge fake orchid plant in full purple bloom. Next to it were several color photographs of the same woman, excessively blond and pretty, one of her in a bathing suit, arm in arm with Feliciano, stripped to the waist, on what appeared to be a Hawaiian beach.

"That's Wanda," said Feliciano, seeing Gus look at the photographs. "My wife Wanda."

"Very pretty," replied Gus.

"What is it you wanted to see me about?"

"There is someone I would like to have followed."

"And you went to Constantine de Rham?"

"I felt he would know."

"He did. Who is this person you want to have followed?"

"His name is Francis Flint. He is called Lefty Flint."

Anthony Feliciano jotted the name on a pad in front of him with a desk pen. "What is it you want to know about this man?"

"I want to know where he lives. I want to know what he does with his time."

"When will you want me to start?"

"October thirteenth. That is the day he is to be released from prison."

"Where is the prison?"

"Vacaville."

"What is he?"

"A strangler," replied Gus.

"A strangler?" repeated Feliciano, surprised.

"A strangler is someone who puts his hands around another person's neck and chokes the life out of that person," said Gus.

"I am aware of the definition of a strangler, Mr. Bailey. What I meant was, what is this man's profession."

"Oh," said Gus, shaking his head. "Jack of all trades."

"Like what?"

"A guitarist sometimes. Or a singer. Then again a sculptor."

"A nothing, you mean," said Feliciano.

"No, that's not what I mean. A charmer would be a better word to describe him. The ladies always liked him."

"What is this man's connection to you?"

"He has caused grievous harm to me and my wife."

"Grievous harm of a strangulation nature, I take it?" asked Feliciano.

Gus did not reply directly to the question. "He was also a jury pleaser, especially to the ladies on the jury. They all wanted to be his mother. He carried a Bible. He used to be an altar boy, his lawyer said. He wore preppy clothes. No, no, he could never be what they said he was, he convinced them. It was a one-time thing, a crime of passion, a boy who simply loved too much. That's what he made them think. Or, rather, that's what his lawyer made them think about Lefty Flint."

Feliciano nodded but did not press for a more specific answer. "That shouldn't come as a surprise to you, Mr. Bailey. Any smart defense lawyer's going to do that. He's only interested in one thing—getting his client off, guilty or not guilty. It don't matter to him."

"And slander the victim? That's okay too?"

"I didn't say it's okay. I said it was legal."

Gus shook his head.

"How long will you want him followed?" asked Feliciano.

"Indefinitely."

"You have credentials?"

"Constantine de Rham, if he lives, will back me up."

"What is it you have in mind, Mr. Bailey?"

"I've told you, Mr. Feliciano."

"You've only kind of told me. Do you want this guy thrown out a window?"

"No. I don't want anything like that."

"It will look like an accident. No one will ever know. You won't meet the person who is going to do it, and he will never have heard your name. Very easily arranged. Not cheap, but safe."

"No, that's not what I want," said Gus, shaking his head.

"I sense there's more that you want than what you're telling me."

Gus looked out the dirty window at the flat sunlight of the California afternoon beating down on the Sunset Strip. "How do you think I feel, knowing that Lefty Flint is going to be out there, living a free life, having dinner in restaurants, going to movies, moving in a world of people who probably don't know that he has killed someone, and served a joke sentence, and that he feels he has atoned and has a right to a normal life?"

Gus made no effort to raise his voice for Anthony Feliciano to hear him, as if he were voicing to himself for the first time what he felt and what he wanted to do. "I used to think how great it would be if he was murdered in prison. Or raped, by gangs of prisoners. He was an arrogant son of a bitch, and I prayed for something like that to happen to him, but, alas, he has proved to be a model prisoner."

"You don't go around expressing these thoughts to people, do you, Mr. Bailey?"

"No."

"Don't confide that sort of thing to anyone. It can all be used against you."

"Strangling, you know, requires a great deal of strength. It's not every killer's choice," said Gus.

"What is it you have in mind, Mr. Bailey?" asked Feliciano. He wondered for a moment if Gus was mad.

"I want his hands put in a giant vise and crushed," said Gus, calmly, without turning to face Anthony Feliciano.

Feliciano remained silent for a moment, staring at Gus. Then he chuckled. "He won't be able to strum a guitar anymore," he said.

"He won't be able to strangle anyone either," said Gus.

"La Señora," said Immaculata, the housekeeper, "is in the garden."

Gus walked toward the French doors at the back of the small house. To the right was the dining room. To the left was the living room. The furniture was furniture he had once lived with, in different arrangements and different coverings. On the piano were silver-framed photographs of a family that once was and now was no longer, a family demolished by divorce and disease, estrangement and murder. Gus did not stop to look, other than to notice that Immaculata had been sparing of late with the silver polish, a housekeeping shortcoming that would go unnoticed by Peach, who had long since ceased looking at the photographs, or who looked at them without seeing them. He went out the door and across the lawn to the white stucco wall that ran from the house to the pool house. He pushed open the wrought-iron gate that led into Peach's small garden. For a moment the wisteria bushes on each side of the gate, dripping in heavy lavender bloom, partially obscured his view of the rose bushes that were Peach's pride and joy.

"I'm over here," called Peach, when she heard the wrought-iron gate slam. She was sitting in her wheelchair next to a wooden bench. Gus walked toward her on a grass path between two rose beds with blossoms of every color mixed together, without thought of symmetry or balance. Symmetry was of no concern to Peach. Symmetry, when they were married, had been Gus's concern, which Peach resisted. Without Gus, it became inconsequential. Her garden flourished with a sort of wildness and lack of design.

Gus knew, even before he reached the place where Peach was sitting, that gardening was not what was occupying her thoughts. Her clippers, her gloves, her wicker basket filled with roses lay on the wooden bench. She was wearing, as always, a caftan, to cover her useless legs, and she had sheltered her skin from the sun with a wide-brimmed straw hat. Next to her, sleeping, was one of the several black cats that were always with her. Gus had not seen her for five months. The disease that ravaged her beauty and incapacitated her legs had taken five months' toll.

"Oh, hi," she said when she saw who it was. She never said more than,

"Oh, hi," to Gus when he came to visit her on his infrequent trips to Los Angeles. She did not register surprise, or delight, or displeasure.

"Hi," Gus answered, in the same manner. He looked at her for a minute. He used to think there was a natural conclusion to love. He had, after all, been in love before Peach, and after her he had been involved several times, but it was always to Peach that his thoughts and longings returned.

"What kind of a name is Peach?" he asked her the first time they met.

"It's what I'm called," she answered simply.

"Gus and Peach. How do you think that sounds?" he asked her.

"It doesn't really get me," she replied.

"Maybe Peach and Gus sounds better," he said.

Actually her name was Rebecca, but if there was ever anyone who was not a Rebecca type, it was she. Her father, whom she loved, called her Peach, and Peach became what she was called.

When Gus asked Peach Prindeville to marry him, he didn't really expect her to say yes. He thought that she had seen the deficiencies in him, recognized them inwardly, the way women were supposed to. The surprise was when, after thinking about it, she said yes, she would like to marry him. She said it by letter. He was thrilled. He was also terrified. He was in awe of her. Always was. Still was. Awe, of course, was never what Peach wanted.

If a day went by when he did not telephone her, on some pretext, often invented, he missed her. But she rarely telephoned him, and then only for an important reason. Peach would never call Gus to say, "You won't believe who's getting married," or divorced, or who's inherited a great deal of money, or gone broke. But he would call her with that kind of news, and he felt sure that although she often sounded indifferent, she enjoyed his calls. Since Peach, he had distanced himself from the possibility of love.

"I'm just in town for overnight," said Gus.

"Did you tell me you were coming?" she asked. Her question acknowledged that she sometimes forgot things.

"No."

"Is anything the matter?"

They were people who had known extreme grief and had become able, among themselves, to ask and answer questions pertaining to disaster in an impersonal way.

"I wanted to tell you that I have hired a private detective."

"Why did you do that?"

"Lefty Flint is getting out of prison."

"I know," said Peach.

"You know? Detective Johnston just called me in New York last night. He wanted me to be the one to tell you."

From a pocket in her caftan, Peach pulled out a cheap white envelope and handed it to Gus. The stamp, imperfectly cornered, said LOVE.

"It's from him," said Peach.

Gus blanched and felt the sick feeling he always felt when Lefty Flint's presence was sensed. He moved Peach's gardening equipment from the bench and sat down next to her. He looked at the envelope but didn't open it.

"What's he want?" he asked.

"He wants to come and see me."

"Jesus Christ."

"When he's out, that is."

Nearly three years earlier Gus and Peach Bailey, separated in marriage but brought together by adversity, had sat side by side in a courtroom for seven weeks, a kind-of couple again. She needed him then, as much as he needed her, and they became, in a way neither had tried to explain to the other, closer than they had been when they were close. Less than ten feet from them sat Lefty Flint, the killer of their child, holding a Bible in his hands and with a look of piety on his face, dressed with the black-and-white simplicity of a sacristan in a seminary, although he was previously known to be a mocker of God. Peach had shuddered, seeing through it all, the sham of justice they were witnessing, knowing how it was going to end, that poor sweet Becky was going to be forgotten and Lefty Flint was only going to get his wrist slapped, in the name of love.

"Do you have any statement to make?" a television reporter had asked Gus at the conclusion of the trial.

"I sometimes wonder why the prosecution does not have the same relentless passion to convict the guilty that the defense attorneys have to free them," Gus had answered.

"Get me a gun, will you, Gus?" said Peach, simply.

"Would you kill him if he came here?" asked Gus.

"Of course," she answered.

"You can't do that, Peach," said Gus.

"You don't think they'd send a crip like me to prison, do you?"

Gus hated it when Peach called herself a crip, but it wasn't the moment to get into that.

"He can't come to see you. It's in violation of his parole if he contacts us. Detective Johnston told me that. He can't go to visit her grave either," said Gus. "Let me take this letter and turn it over to the police."

"Who's the private detective you've hired?"

"Let me put it this way, 'private detective' is kind of a classy description of him."

"Dicey, huh?" she asked.

"Dicey, yeah," he replied.

"Where did you hear about him?"

"Constantine de Rham."

"Speaking of dicey," said Peach, shaking her head dismissively at the mention of Constantine de Rham's name. "You do know the swellest people, Gus."

"Lefty Flint's going to be followed. If he comes anywhere near this house, they're going to throw him right back in the can."

"Does Detective Johnston know you've hired this private detective?"

"No."

"Are you going to tell him?"

"No."

Peach nodded. "Wheel me inside, will you, Gus. I have to get back into bed."

Gus looked at his watch. It was time to leave for the plane to fly back to New York. Peach was lying in bed looking at a soap opera on television.

"Turn off the sound, will you?" said Gus.

Without replying, Peach felt around on her large bed between slumbering cats, mail, magazines, books, packages of cigarettes, and an assortment of Cricket lighters until she found the remote control for the television. Three times a day Immaculata came in to straighten out the jumble that the bed became. Peach adjusted the remote control but continued to stare at the set after the sound stopped.

"Time to go," he said.

"You just arrived."

"I'm going to Paris the day after tomorrow."

"What's in Paris?"

"I'm interviewing someone for my gigolo story."

"Is Paris safe? There're a lot of bombings in Paris these days."

"Just my luck to get killed on my way to interview the new ladyfriend of a bisexual gigolo who married an old lady millionairess and inherited all her money."

"Where do you dig up these awful people you always write about?" asked Peach.

"The gigolo told me he never met the person yet he couldn't get it up for, if the price was right."

"Those people might fascinate you, Gus, but they don't fascinate me," said Peach.

"Don't knock it, Peach," said Gus evenly. "It keeps my mind occupied. It keeps me from going nuts. It keeps me from dwelling on things I can't do anything about."

"I know, Gus. I'm not criticizing you. I might even envy you, now that I come to think of it."

"I have to go."

Peach continued to stare at the television set. People were yelling at each other, but the sound was still off. In bed, she was barricaded from him. What had once been a coffee table, now piled high with the accoutrements of an invalid's life, ran the length of her bed. Her wheelchair blocked the opening between the end of the table and her bed. Gus moved her wheelchair aside and bent down and kissed her on the cheek.

"I'm sorry I made you unhappy, Peach," he said.

Peach knew what he meant without his having to spell it out for her. She knew he was talking about back then, when they were married, not now.

"I'm not much for looking back, Gus," she said, staring at the set.

"I just wanted to tell you I'm sorry."

"Okay. You told me."

"Aren't you ever going to let up on me?"

"Oh, Gussie, come on. That was a long time ago."

He took hold of her foot and squeezed it. "So long, Peach," he said.

She understood there was affection in the gesture. "Good-bye, Gus," she answered.

Every time Gus drove out Wilshire Boulevard past the cemetery where Becky was buried, he beeped twice on his car horn in greeting to her, wherever she was.

19

"**T**HAT'S WHERE THE butler found poor Constantine," said Yvonne Lupescu, pointing to the dark spot on the Portuguese carpet.

In the week following Constantine de Rham's suicide attempt, Yvonne Lupescu knew happiness. "Yvonne," the tabloid papers called her, simply Yvonne, with no last name, signifying her newfound prominence as the "companion," which the papers always used with quotation marks, to the mysterious Constantine de Rham, who had, apparently, shot himself after he thought the Baroness Lupescu was going to leave him.

"No, no, I would never leave my darling Constantine," Yvonne was quoted as saying to Mavis Jones, the Broadway columnist, to whom she gave an exclusive interview, sitting in the very room where Constantine de Rham had been found bleeding. "It was all a terrible misunderstanding. We love each other."

"WE LOVE EACH OTHER," SAYS YVONNE, ran the headline in Mavis Jones's column.

"Where are you from, Baroness?" asked Mavis, trying to place Yvonne's accent.

"Paris," replied Yvonne.

For six days Yvonne gave daily bulletins from the hospital steps on Constantine's condition, dressed always in new suits that might have been from Chanel, but weren't, but she kept her pithy quotes for Mavis Jones, who was, after all, syndicated in sixty newspapers throughout the country. "He squeezed my hand," she said. Or, "Today he begged me not to leave him."

Yvonne wanted her prominence to last forever, but, alas, Faye Converse, the film star, was robbed of all her jewels by a masked gunman in the elevator of the Rhinelander Hotel, and Yvonne could only get Mavis's assistant, Claire, on the telephone, as Mavis was having an exclusive interview with Faye Converse. The story was moved to the back pages and then disappeared entirely, and Yvonne complained bitterly to Ramon, the butler, that the city had no heart.

During the weeks of Constantine's recuperation at New York Hospital, Yvonne could often be seen dining alone at Clarence's. Sometimes she brought a book to read, but mostly she sat quietly, exotically turbaned, and watched the ebb and flow of the restaurant, as if she were looking at a film. Occasionally she made notes in a notebook that she always had with her.

Sometimes Chick Jacoby would sit at her table for a few minutes, perched on the edge of a chair to indicate that his visit was merely transitory, and get the latest reports on Constantine's condition, which he would then pass on to anyone who happened to evince interest in the subject of Constantine de Rham's gunshot wound. If it hadn't been for Chick Jacoby, no one would have spoken to Mrs. Lupescu, but she gave no indication that that was a matter of concern to her.

20

FOR LIL ALTEMUS and her friends, there were only ten buildings in Manhattan where people like themselves could live, four on Fifth Avenue, three on Park Avenue, one on Gracie Square, one on Sutton Place, and, of course, River Place, but even River Place had begun to let in what Lil called "a certain element."

After their marriage, Justine and Bernie Slatkin moved to a new apartment in a new building on Park Avenue that Lil Altemus described as "one of those buildings on Park Avenue where no one we know lives," although that was a statement she made to her daughter, but not to her son-in-law. Bernie Slatkin, she soon found out, did not capitulate to her every wish, as Justine once did, nor was Justine available anymore to make up a fourth for bridge at the last minute or fill in at the opera if someone dropped out of her box.

"Poor Cora Mandell is very hurt that you didn't use her to decorate your new apartment," said Lil Altemus to her daughter. "After all, she's done every one of the Altemus houses."

"Bernie didn't like cabbage-rose chintz," replied Justine. "In fact, Bernie hates cabbage-rose chintz. And, lest you forget, Mother, I'm no longer an Altemus. I'm Mrs. Slatkin now."

"No, I haven't forgotten that, Justine," said Lil.

"Come and see how the living room looks. It's marvelous, really. A whole new look for me."

Lil Altemus, on her first visit to the new apartment, walked silently through Justine's just completed living room. Occasionally she nodded at things she recognized from before. "Sweet," she said finally in judgment, in a qualified tone. And then she repeated the word again. "Sweet."

"Sweet?" replied Justine.

Lil continued looking, without further comment.

"Sweet wasn't the effect I was striving for, Mother," said Justine.

"But it was meant as a compliment, Justine," said Lil.

"I find the word inadequate," said Justine.

"My dear, isn't marriage making us independent," said Lil. She sat down in a bergère chair and took off her gloves. "These lamp shades aren't quite first rate. They should be lined in pink."

"'Lined in pink,'" repeated Justine, as if she were making a list. "It so happens that my husband doesn't like lamp shades lined in pink."

"It makes women look so much prettier, tell him," said Lil, giving a gracious smile to her daughter. "You have far too many hyacinths in here, darling." She fanned herself with her gloves and pretended to reel from the heavy scent.

"Make the best of it," said Justine, impatiently.

Lil, who had expected Justine to remove the hyacinths, said, "Well, pardon me."

"I wouldn't, if I were you, Mother, make any of these comments in front of my husband," said Justine. "Hubie and I, we're used to you. We put up with you. But Bernie will let you have it."

"Ho, ho, ho. I'd like to see Bernie Slatkin let me have it," said Lil, chortling at the thought.

"Just be warned."

"Hmmm," said Lil. She continued to look around the room. "What do you call this color?"

"Green, mother."

"Well, of course, it's green. I know it's green. What I meant was, does the green have a name?"

"Oh, I don't know, Mother. Forest, I think it's called. Or evergreen. I can't remember. Do you like it, and, please, don't say it's sweet."

"Where's my Aubusson rug?" Lil cried, as she suddenly remembered that her wedding gift was not under her feet.

"Bernie didn't like it."

"Bernie Slatkin didn't like my Aubusson rug! That's the laugh of the week. If you don't like it, I'll take it back then, thank you very much," said Lil, indignant.

"We sold it," said Justine.

"You what?"

"Ruby Renthal bought it for her swell new apartment."

"That rug belonged to Grandmother Van Degan, from the house in Newport."

"That's why Ruby liked it so much. 'It has history,' she said."

"Really, Justine. That awful Mrs. Renthal."

"Bernie calls Ruby Renthal the talk of the town," said Justine. "Here, there, and everywhere, as Dolly says."

"I'm going to ask Cora to get it back from Mrs. Renthal," said Lil.

"Look, you gave it to us, Mother. You didn't say there were strings attached," said Justine.

Lil nodded, then rose, putting her gloves back on. "Well, I'm off."

"I thought you came for tea," said Justine. "Bonita's making tea."

"No, I must go. What's all that ladder equipment in the dining room?" asked Lil.

"I'm having the wall behind the buffet painted in *trompe l'oeil* to look like a coromandel screen. Don't you think that's a good idea?"

"Donina did that in her dining room," said Lil.

"You're a hard lady to get a compliment out of," said Justine. "I'm using the same painter that Donina used."

"He better paint quick, from what I hear."

"Why?"

"What's that disease they all have, those boys, where they're dropping like flies?" asked Lil. Justine turned quickly to look at her mother. "Bobo says there won't be a man left in New York to hang a curtain or hem a dress." Bobo was her hairdresser.

Justine continued to look at her mother.

"How's Hubie?" she asked.

"Hubie? Fine. Why?"

"Just asking," said Justine.

"D O YOU MIND if I light a cigar?" asked Elias Renthal.

"No, not at all," replied Ruby Nolte, who loathed cigars, especially in confined areas.

"Some women do," said Elias.

"Surely you can't think I am one of those women who would interfere with a man's pleasures, Mr. Renthal," said Ruby, smiling at him.

"It's Elias, please," replied Elias, smiling back at her.

"Elias," repeated Ruby, as if she were savoring the word. "Here, let me light it for you."

Ruby Nolte took Elias's gold lighter out of his hand and leaned forward toward him, holding the lighter in both hands. Elias, as if to steady her hands, took them both in his as he put his cigar into the flame.

"How come you took off your wedding ring?" asked Ruby.

"Well, you know." Elias, embarrassed, shrugged.

"Put it back on."

"Why?"

"What's the point of adultery if you pretend it's something else? Right? Besides, it adds to the charge."

Elias, only just satisfied minutes earlier, was ready to go again. They stared into each others' eyes for the several moments of the lighting process. Only then, her head surrounded by clouds of pearl-gray smoke, did Ruby allow her imagination to revel in the possibilities that the future held for her with this immensely rich man: the clothes, the jewels, the furs, the houses, and that which meant more to her than anything else, money of her own, in her own name.

All of this had happened four years ago. Or five. In Cleveland. It was not the first time Elias Renthal had removed his wedding ring for the purpose of extracurricular love, but, as things turned out, it was the last. Gladyce Renthal, the wife from that marriage, Elias's second, had been taken care of quite handsomely in the divorce settlement. She continued to live in her large suburban house in Shaker Heights, the smart part of Cleveland, and, until she began to read in the press of the splendors of the life-style of Elias and his new wife in New York, she had been reasonably contented. People from Cleveland, when they ran into Elias, told him that Gladyce had started to drink and, when drunk, talked badly about Elias, saying he had treated her shabbily. They didn't tell him that Gladyce called Ruby a whore, if she was feeling kind, or a cunt, if she wasn't.

Ruby Renthal's picture was everywhere. Photographers waited for her on the opening nights at the opera and ballet, at the library and the museum. She became known as a patroness of the arts but, in truth, she only attended the opera and the ballet on the nights of the gala performances when there were supper dances on the promenade afterward. Pieces on the life-style of the Renthals had begun to appear in all the fashionable magazines. The name Renthal was, in short order, becoming as well known in social circles as it already was in business circles. If Ruby Renthal's name was on the committee of a charity, followers of such matters knew that that was the event to be at that night.

Matilda Clarke said to Lil Altemus about Ruby Renthal, "She has someone," and Lil Altemus nodded in agreement. They didn't mean a lover. They meant a publicist, someone quietly behind the scenes orchestrating Ruby's rise to social prominence.

"They come, they go, these people," said Lil Altemus. "Last year everyone was talking about Constantine de Rham. Now you never hear his name, or you hear it and people shudder. This year Mr. Renthal's is the name on every lip, and his wife is here, there, and everywhere, and it seems like only yesterday that no one had ever heard of them."

"Loelia Manchester claims that Ruby Renthal is here to stay," said Matilda.

"We'll see," said Lil.

"That's Lorenza, isn't it?" asked Ruby, looking at an antique coffee pot crammed full with dozens of multicolored roses in various stages of rose life, from buds to swollen blossoms, the trademark of Lorenza, the most expensive florist in the city, that was only one of several on the tables in Loelia Manchester's temporary suite in the Rhinelander Hotel.

"What?" asked Loelia.

"The flowers? Aren't they Lorenza?"

"Lorenza, oh, yes. She comes here every Monday and Thursday to do the flowers."

Ruby was thrilled with this information. Imagine, she thought, having

Lorenza herself come to your house to arrange your flowers twice a week, even when there were no parties planned. It seemed to her yet another level of refinement what these people, who had begun to take her into their midst, understood and took for granted as normal living.

Loelia Manchester snuggled back against the pale yellow damask of a bergère chair, one arm resting on the gilt frame over her head. What an elegant pose, thought Ruby. I must practice that. Loelia dazzled Ruby with her glamour. Ruby was spellbound and, at first, tongue-tied in her presence. She had not imagined that such a thing as conversation could be so exhilarating, and she was always asking Loelia to speak louder so as not to miss anything she said in her husky, fashionable voice. Loelia, in turn, was flattered by Ruby's adoration, especially as her own friends, like Lil Altemus and Matilda Clarke, were being cool to her since she had abandoned Ned for Mickie, whom they all liked to dance with at charity balls but found totally inappropriate as a suitor for her. Loelia also found Ruby lacking in artifice and was herself spellbound by the truth of her tales.

"Go on," said Loelia to her new friend, prodding her to continue with her story.

"I began having my period when I was eight," confided Ruby.

"Eight?" cried Loelia, aghast.

"I was advanced for my age," explained Ruby.

"An understatement!" exclaimed Loelia.

"By the time I was ten, I was like a woman, full breasts, the works. By the time I was twelve, I was having sex. By the time I was fourteen, I was having affairs. By the time I was sixteen, I was married for the first time. By the time I was twenty-two, I was married three times."

"Heavens!" said Loelia, fascinated with such a story.

"I was twenty-eight when I met Elias and ready to settle down. By that time I'd seen a thing or three. I knew about people like you and how you live. I wanted to be one of you. And when I met Elias, I knew I could be, with his bucks and my brains."

"Riveting," was the only thing that Loelia could think to say about Ruby's life.

"Let me tell you one thing, Loelia. You see me do anything wrong, ever, you correct me. I guarantee you I won't take offense."

"Of course, Ruby," replied Loelia. "Tell me something."

"Shoot."

"Were you the cause of the breakup of Elias's marriage?" Loelia asked.

Ruby shrugged her shoulders. "They'd been together for fourteen years. That was long enough."

Loelia stared at Ruby. The directness of Ruby's answers to questions about herself always fascinated Loelia.

Ruby, mistaking Loelia's stare for disapproval, continued. "Look, Loelia, I wasn't the first little chickadee Elias Renthal had dallied with, believe me. If it hadn't been me, it would have been someone else. But I was the one who told him it was one thing to be the biggest fish in Cleveland, Ohio, where they wouldn't even let him in the country club, and quite another thing to be the biggest fish in New York City."

"Is it true you were a stewardess?"

"Among other callings."

"You met him on a flight?"

" 'Coffee, tea or me,' I said. He picked me."

Loelia laughed.

"I was also a hostess at Howard Johnson's, but, for God's sake, don't tell anyone that," said Ruby.

"Do you love Elias?"

"Sure, I love him, and of all the wives he's had, I'm the best one for him. It's a package deal when a young girl marries an older man. He has this talent for making money. I have this talent for spending it. We needed each other."

"And if he weren't so rich?"

"Would I still have fallen in love with him? Is that what you want to know?"

Loelia, embarrassed, blushed.

"Probably not," Ruby answered. "But he is so rich, and I love him very much. How's that for an answer?"

"Honest," said Loelia, smiling at her.

"Tell me something about Mickie, Loelia," said Ruby.

Loelia knew what Ruby was going to ask her about Mickie, but she was not prepared to be as forthright about her private life as Ruby was about hers. Ruby, studying Loelia, noticed the slight stiffening of her body and understood the reluctance it implied.

"Don't misunderstand me, Loelia," she said, as a new idea suggested itself to her. "What I meant was about Mickie's career at the moment. You see, Elias and I are planning to give a ball, to show off the new place, whenever Cora Mandell finishes it, for about four hundred guests. *Tout* New York, as Dolly De Longpre would say, and we were wondering if Mickie would be interested in designing it for us. I mean, you're always saying how Mickie really should have been a stage designer instead of a shoe designer. We want it to be something they write about for years to come. The Renthal ball. I've been thinking of butterflies for a theme. Do you think that would appeal to Mickie?"

"Oh, Ruby, darling Ruby, I can't think of anything more marvelous," exclaimed Loelia, hugging her new friend. "Wait till Mickie hears! He will be beside himself. Fantasy, Ruby. Mickie has such a sense of fantasy. And butterflies! If you knew how Mickie adores butterflies! It will be magical, whatever he does. I can guarantee you of that. And everyone will come. I can guarantee you of that too."

Ruby pushed back the sleeve of her perfect red suit and looked at her perfect gold watch, oval shaped with Roman numerals, that once belonged to the Duchess of Windsor. Ruby's watch, although beautiful and historic as a piece of jewelry, was often inaccurate as a timepiece, falling behind twenty minutes every twenty-four hours, with the result that she always arrived late to her hairdresser, or for her lingerie fittings, or her French lessons, to the consternation of those poor souls who serviced her, but she was so abject with apology for the inconveniences that she had caused, that she was instantly forgiven, and her tips and her gifts at Christmas were such as no other client in the city gave. "Holy cow, I gotta get my ass in gear," she said to Loelia. "I have a French lesson with Count Motulsky at two. I'm going to Jamesey Crocus's lecture on Sèvres china at the museum at four. I have to be at Madame

Orromeo's cocktail party at six thirty, and we're going to the opera with Laurance and Janet Van Degan at eight."

The following morning Ruby flew on her husband's plane to Vacaville, California. She told Elias she wanted to use the plane to attend an auction at a California ranch. She said some horse sculptures by Frederick Remington were being offered, and she thought she might add one or two to the collection that Elias had begun for their house in the country. Ruby promised Elias she would be back in New York in time for Loelia Manchester's dinner.

A car and driver waited for her at the small airport in Vacaville. A decorator friend of Cora Mandell's had purchased two Remington horse sculptures from a San Francisco collector and placed them in the car for Ruby to take back to New York. She told the pilot of the plane that she was attending an auction but would not be long. In the car was a lawyer from San Francisco.

"Hi, Mrs. Renthal, I'm Morrie Sable."

"Hello," she replied.

"All the arrangements have been made. The hearing is scheduled for eleven. It's about a fifteen-minute drive."

"Let's go," said Ruby.

As the car drove over the dusty roads to the prison, Morrie Sable several times tried to make conversation with Ruby, but she was preoccupied with her own thoughts.

"Shall I send the bill to your husband's office in New York, Mrs. Renthal?" he asked.

"Heavens, no," she replied. "I've brought a check with me."

"But I won't know how much the tally is until I've figured out the hours involved," he said.

"It's blank, and it's signed. You fill it in, Mr. Sable."

"Okay."

"Under no circumstances do I want my husband to know about this."

"Mind if I ask you why you're doing this?" he asked.

"Four years ago I sat in a car outside a church in Beverly Hills during Becky Bailey's funeral, feeling too guilty to go in, because I knew that if I had stepped forward when I should have stepped forward, what happened to that poor young girl might not have happened. This is my way of seeing that it doesn't happen again," she answered.

Morrie Sable looked at her.

In the hearing room, the session was already in progress. Lefty Flint sat at a table, with his lawyer, Marv Pink, at his side. He held a ballpoint pen in his hand and wrote notes on a yellow lined scratch pad. At another table sat the prison warden and two parole officers. Several guards from the prison sat in the spectators' section, as did Marguerite Hanrahan, Lefty's fiancée, who was waiting to testify on Lefty's behalf.

When the doors of the room opened, everyone turned to look at the beautiful and elegantly dressed woman who entered. She carried an alligator bag with a gold chain. Lefty Flint, seeing Ruby, blanched.

Ruby walked past the table where Lefty was seated without looking at him and took a chair that had been placed for her next to the presiding parole officer. After introductions had been made, the warden called on Mrs. Renthal to speak.

"My name is Ruby Nolte Renthal," she began. "I have come here today from my home in New York to plead with you not to grant Francis Flint an early release from his prison sentence."

"Warden, I object," said Marv Pink, rising from his seat.

"This is a hearing, not a trial, Mr. Pink. There are no objections recognized. Mrs. Renthal's lawyer called me and asked that his client be allowed to come here to speak," said the warden. "Go on, Mrs. Renthal."

"I had a two-year relationship with Francis Flint that ended several years before the murder of Becky Bailey. On four separate occasions Mr. Flint beat me. Once when I tried to escape from him, he threw me down a stairway. On two separate occasions I was hospitalized as a result of his beatings. The latter time, Mr. Flint, whom I called Lefty, broke my nose and teeth, blacked my eyes, and fractured my jaw."

"Did you press charges at the time?" asked the warden.

"No," replied Ruby. She opened her bag and took out a handkerchief.

"May I ask why, Mrs. Renthal?"

Ruby looked at Marv Pink and answered, "I was warned not to."

"By whom?"

"It doesn't matter now," she replied, wiping a tear away. "The jury at his trial for the murder of Becky Bailey was allowed to think that her strangulation was a single isolated incident on the part of Lefty Flint in an otherwise impeccable life. This is not true. Mr. Flint is a classic abuser of women, and his weapon is his hands."

The room was in silence.

"Are you finished, Mrs. Renthal?" asked the warden.

"Yes, sir, I am, except to say that I feel this man is a danger to women. I have seen him froth at the mouth in anger. I know how little it takes for him to lose control."

Lefty Flint, breathing heavily, pushed back his chair from the table. The ballpoint pen that he had been holding snapped in two in his hand. Marv Pink placed his hand on Lefty's arm in a cautionary gesture.

"Sit down, Lefty," whispered Marguerite from behind him.

"Thank you, Mrs. Renthal," said the warden.

"Am I excused?" she asked.

"Yes."

Ruby rose. Morrie Sable rose. As Ruby walked past Lefty Flint on her way to the door, their eyes met for an instant.

22

ROMANTIC LONGEVITY was never Bernie Slatkin's long suit. He was used to the adoration of five or six women at the same time, in the compartmentalized way he had always lived his life, with no part encroaching upon another. Women who watched him on television wrote him letters, or waited for him outside the studio in the hopes of meeting him. Even women he met at society parties looked at him across dinnertables in an inviting manner, sometimes even slipping their place cards into his pocket with their telephone numbers hastily scribbled on them. He liked the chase. He liked seduction. He liked the madness of ecstasy that came with new partners. He liked not having to answer to anyone for his time and affections. His affairs, when he had had them before his marriage, were brief, mostly culminating after week-long love-soaked sojourns to tropical islands, when the sameness began to pall.

Bernie could not deny that Justine's love had begun to bore him. He preferred the flippancy of Brenda Primrose, in the news room, with whom he had had an affair and with whom, from time to time, for old times' sake, if they had both been working late, he still sought quick satisfaction. He knew that during their affair she had been seeing two other men at the same time, and he liked her for it because it showed that she played the game the way he did, for sex, not love.

At the bal masqué following the opening of the ballet, Bernie and Justine Slatkin were the guests of Elias and Ruby Renthal. Ruby, the best dancer on the small dance floor, could feel Bernie Slatkin's erection boring into her. Looking up, she could see that his eyes had the look of a man in the throes of deep desire. "Uh, uh," she said, shaking her head in refusal, at the same time backing her pelvis away from him without missing a beat of the dance. "It feels good, Bernie, and I hear you're great in bed, but I already got myself a fella. And you've already got yourself a lady, and I do mean a lady, in case it slipped your mind." The music stopped. "Thanks for the dance, Bernie. I love to samba. Now I'm off to find my husband."

That year Justine gave Bernie many gifts: gold cuff links from Tiffany for day, sapphire-and-gold cuff links from Cartier for evening, silk pajamas with his monogram over the pocket, a maroon polka-dot dressing gown, and writing paper with his name engraved in all sizes and shapes. For a while Bernie loved her gifts and was amused by her extravagances. In return, on Justine's occasions, Bernie was never ungenerous, but often unimaginative, settling at the last minute for flowers, or a gold bracelet, when their apartment was already full of flowers arranged by Lorenza and Justine had more gold bracelets than she could ever wear. But Justine, madly in love, raved over his gifts as if they were precious and special, conceived only for her.

Bernie enjoyed Justine's kind of social life, up to a point, although it dismayed him that they went out almost every night. He also enjoyed the kind of sporting life that Justine's friends led on the weekends in the country: tennis, golf, shooting. He enjoyed the kind of powerful people he met through his marriage into the Van Degan family, like the Elias Renthals. He enjoyed the admiration he felt he received from Uncle Laurance Van Degan because of the kind of money he earned, and the recognition factor he possessed in public. He was quick to act on any tips in the stock market that Uncle Laurance offered him. If he were to go into politics sometime in the future, which people told him he could, with his sincerity and his dimple, the kind of people he was meeting and being accepted by were the kind of people to guide and finance him in his political schemes.

He could have been happy. But he couldn't be faithful.

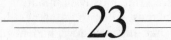

23

LAURANCE VAN DEGAN accepted the astonishing news without astonishment. It was not for him to register shock, or surprise, or fear, in front of a servant, although, strictly speaking, Miss Mae Toomey could not exactly be classified as a servant. Laurance Van Degan's consciousness of his superiority did not desert him during the fifteen-minute encounter with his father's nurse. However, when Laurance Van Degan imparted that same news to his sister later in the day, in his office, it was almost more than Lil could bear. Their father, Ormonde Van Degan, the head of the family—although stroked, incontinent, and possibly senile—had made it known to Miss Toomey that he intended to elope with Dodo Fitz Alyn.

Lil, weeping, said, "But, surely, Laurance, there can be nothing *intimate* in their relationship."

"Don't be too sure of that, Lil," said Laurance.

"What do you mean? The man is eighty-four."

"She runs dirty videos for him."

"Oh, Laurance, for God's sake. It's too ridiculous."

"It's also true."

"How do you know that?"

"Miss Toomey."

"Who's Miss Toomey?"

"The nurse."

"Oh, yes, of course, Miss Toomey. I always called her ~~

"And then she jerks him off."

"Miss Toomey jerks Father off?"

"No, Lil, for God's sake. Don't be so dense. Dodo jerks off Father whe~
looks at the dirty videos."

Lil shuddered. "After all we've done for Dodo Fitz Alyn, Laurance. No
one wanted her. Reared among all those peculiar people. Her father went to
prison for tax evasion. Her mother ran off with one of those awful Orromeo
brothers. Her uncle jumped off the *Queen Elizabeth* after doing whatever
unspeakable act he did with that Cockney sailor. And we, poor fools, took her
in and gave her a home and paid for her education."

"I know her history, Lil."

"Next thing I suppose she'll expect to figure in Father's will?"

"More than that."

Lil stiffened. In matters of inheritance and heirlooms, Lil Altemus always
became alert. "What do you mean?"

"Up front. Dodo wants money up front as well."

"How much money?"

"Twelve million."

She laughed at the absurdity. "I can't believe any of this, Laurance."

"Plus," he added.

"What do you mean *plus?*"

"She wants the house in Southampton to be put in her name."

"Mother's house?" asked Lil, aghast.

"And she wants the Romney picture of Lady Rushington to be hers. And
the Fabergé eggs to be put in her name as well."

"But those were Mother's things, Laurance," said Lil.

"Now they're going to be Dodo's," answered Laurance.

"But Mother always said they were to be mine. You know that. You heard
her say it a thousand times, Laurance."

"She didn't put it in writing, though. She just assumed Father would leave
them to you in his will."

"All this time we thought 'poor Dodo' was pushing around his wheelchair,
she's been taking inventory?"

"So it appears."

"And you're going to allow this, Laurance? You of all people? The
strength of the family. You're going to let this fat orphan dictate those terms to
us? Stand up to that sneaky bitch. Show her who's boss. What's she going to do
if you tell her no, absolutely no?"

"She's going to stop jerking off Father. That's what she's going to do. And,
apparently, Father likes to be jerked off."

Lil, crestfallen, began to gather up her things. "I always thought—" she
said and then stopped midsentence.

"Thought what, Lil?" asked her brother.

"I always thought Dodo was a dyke."

Laurance looked at her. "What's a dyke?" he asked.

"A Daughter of Bilitis," said Lil, in explanation.

I don't know what the hell you're talking about, Lil," said her brother. "Like Aunt Grace Gardiner."

"Oh," said Laurance, understanding at last. "A lezzie, you mean. Do you know something, Lil? I always thought Dodo was a lezzie too."

They looked at each other and started to laugh. Within seconds they became helpless with laughter. Laurance rested his forehead against the cool glass of the window looking down on the street below, and shook with uncontrollable laughter. Lil fell backward onto the sofa and stared upward, shrieking with laughter. Images of their octogenarian father being jerked off by fat Dodo Fitz Alyn brought fresh torrents of laughter.

Only the appearance of Miss Wentworth, Laurance's secretary, entering without knocking, quelled their near hysteria. Lil reached again for a handkerchief in her handbag and blew her nose and wiped her eyes. In charge of herself once more, she wondered why Miss Wentworth dyed her hair so very black. She considered offering Miss Wentworth a free appointment with Bobo, to have her hair colored and frosted correctly, and then abandoned the idea.

"Yes, Irene," said Laurance, collecting himself.

"I'm sorry, Mr. Van Degan, but I rang and you didn't hear me."

"What is it, Irene?"

"Elias Renthal is on the telephone. He says it's important."

"Oh, yes, thank you, Irene." Laurance Van Degan was back to business again, his momentary lapse into mirth already forgotten. He picked up the telephone. "Hello, Elias," he said, with the sort of cordiality he usually reserved for cabinet ministers. It was only later that Lil remembered that note of affability in her brother's voice as he spoke to a man she still considered the most vulgar man in New York.

24

"I'M THINKING OF writing a book," said Yvonne Lupescu.

"These days everyone's thinking of writing a book," replied Gus Bailey.

"Very few people know anything about Albania, as it was, before communism, of course, but it has a fascinating history. My grandmother was the mistress of King Zog."

Gus stared at her. "You once told me that, as I remember," he said.

"I wondered if you'd help me with it," she said. They were sitting at Clarence's, having lunch.

"Is that the urgent thing you wanted to discuss over lunch at Clarence's? Court life in Albania?" asked Gus.

"Yes."

"It is not a topic that enthralls me," said Gus.

"But it's fascinating. You know what Constantine always says, don't you?" she asked, smiling in advance at the quotation she was about to give.

"No, I don't know what Constantine always says," he replied.

"He always says, 'Life at court is rotten to the core, but it spoils you for everything else.'" She laughed. "Don't you think that's marvelous?"

"It was even more marvelous when Congreve wrote it," replied Gus.

Undeterred, she proceeded. "I'd tell you everything, and you would write it."

"I'm planning on writing my own book."

"You're not turning me down?"

"Yes."

"You turn me down a lot, Gus."

"You've noticed."

She stared at him.

"Why did you aim so badly?" asked Gus.

"What is that supposed to mean?"

"People say you shot Constantine," said Gus.

Yvonne smiled wearily and shook her head slowly, as if what Gus had said was a falsehood that she had grown accustomed to hearing. "It's not true," she said calmly. "Constantine shot himself. What is true is that I was going to leave him. My bags were packed. The police will tell you that. He couldn't bear it when I told him I was going to leave, and, poor darling, he tried to do away with himself."

"Where were you?"

"When?"

"When he shot himself."

"I was at Justine Altemus's wedding reception. You saw me."

"So did half New York."

"I hear Bernie Slatkin's playing around already," said Yvonne, her eyes sparkling with the latest gossip.

"I don't know anything about that," said Gus quickly, determined not to let her change the subject.

"Someone I know saw him at an out-of-the-way restaurant on the West Side with a young lady. Very beautiful," she said.

Gus ignored her. "You weren't invited to Justine's wedding, and you came."

"But I was meeting you."

"But I didn't ask you to meet me."

"Gus," she said, in a tone a mother would use to a favorite forgetful child.

"Yvonne, it's me," said Gus, pointing to himself. "Don't bullshit with me. You crashed the wedding. You pretended you were meeting me. You caught the bride's bouquet just to make sure everyone saw that you were there. The wedding reception was your alibi."

"You should take up fiction, Gus."

"Aren't you afraid Constantine will blow the whistle on you?"

"No."

"Why not?"

"Because Constantine needs me in a way you know nothing about," replied Yvonne, smiling mysteriously.

"He likes it when you whip him, is that it?"

"Wherever did you hear such a story?"

"One of your cohorts."

"That awful Jorgie Sanchez-Julia, I bet."

Gus did not reply.

"It was never an every-night sort of thing," said Yvonne, dismissively. "Nor remotely dangerous. Quite mild, in fact. I just whip him on his buttocks and sometimes on his back. A few welts, that's all, enough to feel pain, but nothing serious. I call him a failure, a flop, a nothing, while I whip him. It's his deepest fear, you see, under all that pomposity of his, that that is what people think of him. Curiously, it excites him. Otherwise he can't become erect."

Gus stared at her. He never knew if she was lying or not.

"The boredom, of course, is that he becomes so bad tempered on the mornings afterward, after begging me to do it," said Yvonne.

"Where did you first connect with Constantine de Rham?"

"I was in Paris on my way to Brazil to meet the grandmother of a man I was at the time engaged to marry," said Yvonne. Yvonne enjoyed telling Gus tales of her adventures. She saw herself as the basis for a character in a novel and could even imagine herself saying at some future dinner party, "Oh, that Gus Bailey. That awful man. He based that character on me, but he got it all wrong. I should sue. Really, I should," but all the time basking in the importance that the notoriety gave her.

"Rudi Guevara, he was called," she said, going on with her story. "Did you hear of him? His brother was the polo player, Carlos Guevara?"

"No," answered Gus. "I don't know any of those people."

"His grandmother had all the money, and Rudi insisted I meet her before we married so that we could be in her good graces. At the last minute the grandmother got sick, and the trip was canceled. At least I got canceled. Rudi went on to Brazil. I was all alone in Paris and didn't know many people there. There was a big party that night for an American financier, and they needed an extra girl, someone pretty, and a friend of a friend suggested that I go."

"Was the friend of the friend Madam Myra, by any chance?"

Yvonne looked at Gus and ignored his interruption. "I suppose I was meant to provide amusement for the rich American. I was asked to come in late, after dinner, something I wouldn't do now, come in after dinner—it's an insult to be asked to come in after dinner—but I was lonely and had nothing better to do. Are you listening?"

"Yes, I'm listening," said Gus.

"I was looking great that night. I even remember what I was wearing, a little number from Dior that Rudi bought me to knock them dead in Brazil, and I put his engagement ring on the other hand and went to the party. When I walked into the party, there was the financier sitting on a chair with his teenage daughter on his lap. When he saw me, he stood up, and the daughter went toppling over on the floor. The financier didn't ever notice her. He came right over to me and introduced himself. He had a big fat stomach, and he was drunk, but he was said to be one of the richest men in America, and everyone overlooked his drawbacks. He followed me around all night and kept whispering to me that he was going to marry me."

"How does Constantine de Rham fit into this story?"

"Constantine rescued me from the rich, fat, drunk American. He was so charming."

"I see. And it went on from there?"

"It went on from there," answered Yvonne.

"What about the Brazilian?"

"Oh, Rudi. He got lost along the way."

For a while they sat, saying nothing.

"I thought you were a good reporter, Gus?"

Gus shrugged.

"You didn't ask me who the rich, fat, drunk American was."

"You're right. I didn't."

"Elias Renthal."

Gus did not react to what she had said. He had long ago learned to look as if nothing startled him.

"That was just before he met the present Mrs. Renthal, of course, Ruby, and she classed him up," said Yvonne.

"You mean, if you'd played your cards right that night in Paris, you might be the immensely rich Mrs. Elias Renthal these days, instead of the companion, with quotation marks, as Mavis Jones refers to you in her column, to Constantine de Rham."

"Something like that," replied Yvonne, shaking her head, to indicate she had made a wrong choice.

"My feeling is that Constantine is not generous with you. Am I correct?" asked Gus.

"It's a myth that Constantine is so rich," answered Yvonne. "He's not. A few million, that's all, that he can't even touch the principal on."

"That's not rich, a few million?"

"Rich to him, perhaps," she answered, pointing her fork at the waiter, Michael, with the ponytail, who was removing the dishes from the table, as if he were blind and deaf. "But not rich like people are rich nowadays, like Elias Renthal is rich, for instance. Now that's rich."

"What's going to happen to you? Where are you going to live now?"

"In the house on Sutton Place. Where else? It's a divine house. You saw it. Whatever one thought about Consuelo, she had perfect taste. The house couldn't be more comfortable."

"But surely you can't continue to stay there when Constantine gets home from the hospital?"

"Of course. He'll need me then."

"How will he feel having you there after what happened?"

"Safe," said Yvonne simply. She smiled.

Gus shook his head and laughed. "What was really the purpose of this lunch?" he asked.

"Chick Jacoby has taken to seating me in the back room," she said. "And I wanted a better table."

Gus signaled for a check. When he was helping Yvonne into her coat, he said to her, from behind, "That's your book, Yvonne. The story you just told me. Big bucks in a book like that, and you like big bucks. *Ms. Myra's Girl,* you could call it. Forget about your grandmother giving head to King Zog of Albania."

25

B EHIND RUBY RENTHAL'S back, there was no snickering. Those who took it upon themselves to instruct her in fashion, in decoration, in French, in literature, and in life, their kind of life, became her champions. They were entertained by her wit. They were charmed by her honesty. They were struck by her determination to learn, and to learn fast.

Jamesey Crocus, who had been handed over to Ruby Renthal by Loelia Manchester, for assistance in her furniture-buying spree, gave a practiced eye to Ruby's console tables, finally arrived, from the Orromeo auction in London. When people spoke of Jamesey Crocus, they usually added "who knows his antiques." He was a connoisseur of objects of art who liked nothing better than to give advice, with an air of expert knowledge, on furniture, porcelain, carpets, and paintings.

"Marvelous, Ruby," he said, moving one of Lorenza's multicolored rose bouquets aside to touch the marble top and rub his hand over an inlaid ram's head. "Simply marvelous."

Ruby modestly preened a great collector's kind of preening, as if Jamesey's words were a compliment to her increasingly expert eye for French eighteenth-century furniture.

"Klaus van Rijn himself made these," Jamesey Crocus went on. "I recognize his work every time. A genius, van Rijn. Wasn't even French, you know. Lived in Antwerp, and he made these simply brilliant reproductions of eighteenth-century French furniture. I went to see him once, when I was studying with Bernard Berenson at I Tatti, but he was so old and doddering by then that he wasn't making sense."

Ruby's face went white. "Reproductions? Surely, Jamesey, you can't think my console tables are reproductions?" She almost, but did not, tell him that she had paid one million dollars for them.

"About nineteen thirty-six, I would think. The late thirties were his peak years. He didn't make much furniture during the war. I, for one, never believed those stories that he was a collaborator. It was simply that he was besotted with a German soldier, and all those stories started that ruined him. Mr. Berenson believed—"

But Ruby was not listening to the saga of Klaus van Rijn. "You must be wrong, Jamesey," she said, remembering not to lose her new cultured speaking voice that she had copied from Loelia Manchester, even in an urgent moment. "These console tables were from the Orromeos' house in Paris."

"Old Bolivio Orromeo had a lot of van Rijn pieces. He really foxed the auctioneers, you know, when he went broke and sold everything. The auctioneers were *furious* when they found out. But these are very good, Ruby. You could realize forty or fifty thousand for them any day. I guarantee you."

"Nineteen thirty-six?" she asked.

"Thereabouts."

"A lousy fifty years old? That's all?"

"More or less."

"Get rid of them," said Ruby.

"What? You can't be serious, Ruby."

"Get rid of them. I only want the best in this house. No repros. But, for God's sake, don't tell Elias they're fakes."

"Heavens, no," said Jamesey.

"He'd kill me."

"Nonsense," laughed Jamesey. "They say there are only two things in the world Elias Renthal loves: making money and Ruby Renthal."

"He'd still kill me. I haven't told you how much I paid for those lousy fakes."

Jamesey Crocus snapped his fingers as an idea came to his mind. "You know, Ruby, I have the most marvelous idea for these console tables," said Jamesey.

26

OTHER THAN Loelia Manchester, Jamesey Crocus, and Cora Mandell, Gus Bailey was the only person allowed to see the new residence of Elias and Ruby Renthal prior to the splendid ball that was being planned to launch it. His visit, which was professional, had been arranged for by Loelia Manchester and Jamesey Crocus, who felt that a Sunday piece in the *Times Magazine* would be an important way for the rich newcomers to talk about their many charitable interests, especially since Florian Gray had started referring to Ruby in his column as the Billionaire's Wife.

The fabulous Renthal Impressionist and Post-Impressionist art collection, ever growing, rested against the drawing-room walls, ready to be hung after the final of the nineteen coats of persimmon lacquer had been applied to the huge room. Ancestral portraits of other people's ancestors, grand ladies and patrician gentlemen, some in coronation robes, by Sargent and Boldini and Oswald Birley, leaned against the hall and dining-room walls.

"That's King Boris of Bulgaria, in hunting attire," explained Elias to Gus, in his role of art collector.

Drop cloths covered pieces of antique furniture, which Jamesey Crocus told Gus over and over again were of museum quality, ready to be arranged. Upholstered pieces, the trademark of Cora Mandell's look of cozy grandeur, were wrapped tight in brown paper and tied with ropes. All work was at a momentary standstill, waiting for the nineteenth coat of persimmon lacquer to dry before the twentieth and final coat could be applied.

"Elias adores collecting. He thinks nothing of getting on our plane and flying anywhere when Maisie Verdurin or our curator, Jamesey Crocus, tell him about any artwork that is coming on the market," said Ruby. She had become conversant in matters of art and furniture and porcelain and decoration and knew the history of each addition to her new collections.

Gus Bailey marveled at the transformation of Ruby Renthal since their first meeting at one of Maisie Verdurin's dinners, when she had been dressed in bright blue sequins and shared with Gus a deep secret of her life that bound the two of them together. Since then, almost no reference to that moment had ever been repeated on the several occasions they had met in New York, but there was an unspoken understanding between them. Dressed now in simple but stylish elegance in a black-and-white hounds-tooth skirt and black cashmere sweater that perfectly showed her splendid breasts that people said had been reduced to their present perfection by cosmetic surgery in Brazil, she lounged gracefully on the edge of a packing case. Her only jewelry was the massive diamond she wore on her engagement finger. She had removed the hounds-tooth jacket that matched her skirt, and it lay next to her, the label Nevel, Leven spelled backwards, visible on its satin lining. Her smart Minardos pump dangled elegantly on the tip of her toe as she described their life.

"As you can see, we're camping out, Mr. Bailey," she said, and they all chuckled, as if Mrs. Renthal had made a witticism. "But if we don't, you see, the work will never get finished."

"How many houses do you have, Mrs. Renthal?" asked Gus.

"Does that include apartments?" she asked. "We have apartments, you know, in both London and Paris."

"Yes, of course," said Gus, adjusting his notes. "Homes, I should have said, not houses."

Ruby, puzzled, turned to her husband. "Is it eight or nine, darling?" she asked.

"We sold Palm Beach," replied Elias, nervously.

"But bought in Nassau," answered Ruby, as if to remind him of something he had forgot. She thought she detected a signal to halt from her husband.

"Nine, Mr. Bailey," said Elias, answering the question put to Ruby by Gus. "But, you know, that don't sound so good in the papers and the magazines, if you see what I mean."

Ruby mouthed but did not speak the word *doesn't* to Elias, correcting his grammar, in the way she had watched Lil Altemus mouth but not speak words.

"What?" asked Elias.

"Nothing," said Ruby.

There had also been a transformation in Elias Renthal, Gus noticed, a kind of sureness of self that comes with the accumulation of great wealth and the public respect that wealth engenders. There were neighbors Elias encountered in the elevator of his own exclusive building who still did not speak to him and continued to refer to his apartment as Matilda Clarke's apartment, but the doormen and the elevator men in the building, who were recipients of his large tips, gave him precedence over all the old swells who had dwelled there for decades. That, coupled with his change of tailor, gave the stout financier an impressive and even friendly presence.

"I'll keep it at eight, if you think that will sound better," replied Gus. "Is that complicated? Eight houses?"

"Oh, puleeze," replied Ruby, in the same way that she had heard Loelia say *puleeze.* "Just to remember the names of the staff in each house is complicated. And I always find that the shoes I need for the dress I'm going to wear that night are in the apartment in Paris when I need them in London and then the plane has to go and pick them up. This is all off the record, Mr. Bailey. This is what Loelia calls the problems of the very, very rich."

Gus shrugged. "This is good stuff you're telling me I can't write."

"Do you see, Elias, how nice Mr. Bailey is? My husband is convinced, simply convinced, that the press is out to get us."

"I meant the financial press, Ruby," said Elias.

"And he thinks my picture is in the paper too much, too, Mr. Bailey," said Ruby.

"It is," said Elias.

" 'The Billionaire's Wife,' " said Gus. "How could it be otherwise?"

"I wish I could get my hands on whoever gave me that name," said Ruby. "It makes me sound like a lady who lunches, and I'm not, except occasionally. I want to do something meaningful. The problem is that there are so many causes after us, and I haven't sorted out yet what it is that we are going to concentrate on. I mean, of course, after the museum and the ballet."

"Do you always have bodyguards, Mr. Renthal?" he asked.

"Oh, yes, twenty-four hours a day. They work in shifts," said Elias, beginning to relax. "When I drive to and from our house in the country, or to and from my office, I don't like them in the car with me, not even up front with the chauffeur, because I do a great deal of work in my car, mostly on the telephone, and I don't like other people listening to me, so the guards always follow in a second car."

"I see," said Gus, making a note. "Have you ever been threatened or harmed?"

"No. But, you know, there are so many mad people out there who read about people like us."

"My husband is security mad, Mr. Bailey," said Ruby. "He built a ten-foot-high brick wall all around our place in the country, with electrified wire on top of the wall. And guards everywhere you look."

"Ruby," said Elias, in mock exasperation, as if to control her.

"It's true," she went on. "And even this. He wants me to carry a gun. Look at this little pearl-handled number he gave me as a stocking present last

Christmas. It used to belong to Queen Marie of Rumania. Elias bought it at auction in London and had Purdy's put it in working order."

"Ruby," repeated Elias.

"Fits right into my bag, it's so small. I wouldn't dream of using it, no matter what, but it makes Elias happy for me to carry it."

"How about if I take you on a tour of the apartment, Mr. Bailey," said Elias, standing up to terminate the interview.

Later, dressing for a party, Ruby said to Elias, "Who's Byron Macumber?"

Elias, who was putting studs in his evening shirt, paused, startled. "Why?" he asked.

"Why?" repeated Ruby. "What kind of an answer is why to your own wife?"

"Oh, he's just some kid who works for Weldon and Stinchfield," replied Elias.

"He's a lawyer then?"

"Yeah, a junior lawyer. Why this big interest in Byron what's-his-name?"

"Charming on the telephone. He called you when you were taking Gus Bailey for the tour of the apartment. He wants you to call him. He said you knew the number."

"He called *here?*" There was surprise in Elias's tone.

"Yes, Elias, Byron Macumber called here, and your wife answered the telephone, and he asked that you call him as soon as you were free. Where are you going?"

"I'm going downstairs. I left my briefcase down there."

"What the fuck are you calling me at my house for, you asshole?" said Elias, in whispered fury into the telephone.

"I'm sorry, Mr. Renthal, but you'd left your office, and I knew by morning that the word would be out, and I thought that you'd want to know."

"What word?"

"Omaha Natural Gas has hired Weldon and Stinchfield as adviser in connection with a proposal by Tri-World, Inc., to acquire ONG," said Byron Macumber.

"Holy shit," said Elias.

"I'm sorry I bothered you at home, Mr. Renthal."

"No, no, Byron. I'm sorry I blew my stack. You did the right thing. Now, listen, it's not a good idea to call me here at home, but if you have to, here's a different number, five-five-five, four-one-two-eight, my own private line. I'll put a message machine on it by tomorrow, and just leave a message, and I'll get back to you, and, listen, Byron, use a different name. You're Mr. Brown. Okay?"

When Elias hung up, he looked at his watch while lighting up a cigar. He picked up the telephone again and dialed some numbers. "Operator, this is a collect call to Mr. Rufus Courtauld, in Nassau, from Mr. Nolte."

Elias drummed his fingers on the table while waiting for the long-distance call to go through.

"Nolte here," said Elias, when Rufus Courtauld picked up the receiver on the other end. "Fine, fine," he went on impatiently, getting over with the pleasantries that his Swiss connection invariably engaged in at the beginning of every conversation. "Buy a hundred and eighty thousand shares of Omaha Natural Gas the instant the market opens in the morning." With that he hung up the telephone.

The door to the little room opened, and Ruby entered. She was dressed in evening clothes. "I can hardly see you through all this cigar smoke, Elias," she said.

"That's why you gave me this smoking room, Ruby, so that I could cloud up the air here and not in the swell rooms up front."

"I'm not complaining. I'm just commenting."

"You look beautiful, Ruby," answered Elias. "New dress?"

"Of course, it's new," she said, tweaking his chin. "You wanted a wife on the best-dressed list and you're going to get a wife on the best-dressed list. I need some help with this necklace, Elias. Can you do the clasp?"

"With pleasure," he said, standing behind her. When he finished, he leaned down and kissed Ruby's bare shoulder. "Did I ever tell you I was crazy about your shoulders?"

"Yeah, but it's not something I get sick of hearing," said Ruby, rubbing her shoulder against his lips.

"Where are we going tonight?" he asked.

"Adele Harcourt's, and we can't be late."

"Oh, Adele Harcourt?" he said, impressed. "Fancy-schmancy." He pulled himself out of further amatory pursuit.

"Don't say fancy-schmancy."

"Why?"

"It's tacky. We're past that."

AFTER SWEETZER CLARKE DIED, Matilda felt very lucky to be able to finally sell the great Fifth Avenue apartment Sweetzer had grown up in and later inherited after his mother's death. The building had been constructed on the site of what had once been the Clarke townhouse, and the apartment, forty-one rooms on the top three floors, had been built to the extravagant specifications of Sweetzer's father in the late 1920s as part of the transaction for selling the land and tearing down the Clarke house to make way for the building. Matilda and Sweetzer and their children lived there for nineteen years, first closing up rooms and then whole floors as the cost of

maintaining the vast establishment drained their steadily diminishing re-
sources.

When the lawyers handling Sweetzer's estate told Matilda that she would
have to give up either the apartment in town or the place in the country, she
said, without a second thought, that she would give up the apartment, as life
without Malvern, the Clarkes' place in Bedford, would have been absolutely
unthinkable for Matilda, who raised Norwich terriers and rode horses every
day of her life. Her two sons had married early and advantageously and retreated to other parts of the country, away from the sight of their mother in
decline.

At the time of Sweetzer's death, forty-one-room apartments were not in
great demand, and the apartment stood empty for several years. Finally, in
desperation, Matilda sold it for a negligible sum to someone whose name she
pretended she could never remember. The problem had been getting the purchaser, Elias Renthal, approved by the board of directors of the building, and it
was only the purchaser's guarantee, in writing, that he would not break up the
apartment into smaller apartments that finally assured his acceptance into a
building that otherwise was deeply selective about what Matilda called "the
sort of people" who lived there.

The first time Lil Altemus visited Matilda's new small flat, which she had
taken for the few nights a week she spent in the city, she pronounced it
charming, calling it Matilda's *pied à terre,* as if Matilda had done something
"frightfully clever," in abandoning such an enormous establishment for something so very manageable. But Matilda brushed aside all compliments on its
charm, or coziness, a word she despised, referring to it always as "my little
hovel," because it was, at least in her eyes, a little hovel compared to the
grandeur of her former home that was now being done up by the Renthals. She
was often heard to exclaim, "The things they've done to it!" about the new
owners, rolling her eyes and shaking her head, although she had not seen it, did
not know anyone who had, and knew, from personal experience, that Cora
Mandell was not only the best decorator in New York but had been her own
decorator when she still had money.

"Sweetzer left me high and dry," said Matilda. "And I was a very good wife
to Sweetzer, except for that one time. I had to auction off all the French
furniture and sell the apartment. I wasn't doing all that because I chose to live
a simpler life, as Dolly De Longpre, dear sweet Dolly, told her readers. I sold
everything to survive."

"But, darling Matilda," cried Lil. "We've been friends all our lives. You
could have come to me, and I would have seen that Laurance took care of
you."

"Oh, no. That sort of thing never works out," said Matilda. "I'm not a
charity case. And, besides, along came Rochelle Prud'homme, and she put me
on the board of directors of Prud'homme Products, and pays me a salary. Now,
I know you don't give Rochelle the right time, Lil, and won't have her to your
house, but she happens to be a damn nice woman, and a damn rich woman,
and a damn successful woman in the hairdryer business. They call her the
Petite Dynamo. All she wanted was to become a queen in society, and she
couldn't get to first base. She needed me to open some doors, and I needed
her, and everybody's happy. What Ezzie Fenwick calls tit for tit."

"But what in the world do you do on the board of directors?" asked Lil. "You've never worked a day in your life."

"I don't do anything," answered Matilda. "I just go to meetings several times a year and sit there, and Rochelle nods to me which way to vote."

"Then why does Mrs. Prud'homme want you on her board of directors?" asked Lil.

"Oh, Lil," answered Matilda, as if the answer were so apparent the question needn't have been asked.

"Why?" insisted Lil.

"For the same reason Elias Renthal has your brother and Loelia Manchester and Lord Biedermeier on the board of Miranda Industries. We add class."

"Heavens!" said Lil, clapping her hands, and the two old friends roared with laughter.

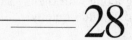

A MONG THE NEW PEOPLE, with whom Loelia now felt more comfortable, everyone that season called Mickie Minardos and Loelia Manchester the lovebirds. "We've just had lunch with Mickie and Loelia," people said, and it immediately identified them as intimates of the most in-love couple in the city. If, at dinners, they weren't seated together, which they preferred to be, they wrote notes to each other during the meal and passed them behind the backs of the intervening people, read them, and then shrieked with private laughter together, or simply met each other's eyes and stared deeply. Everyone in this group said, leaving them, "They're madly in love."

The altogether splendid invitation to the Elias Renthals' ball in honor of the Earl and Countess of Castoria was the talk of every table at Clarence's that day. Ezzie Fenwick, who usually waited until the very last minute to reply to invitations, in case a better one to a grander party should come along, accepted his invitation on the same day it arrived, because he knew, absolutely knew, that on that night, June 21, there would be no better place to be in the whole world.

The ladies who gave parties never invited Matilda Clarke and Fernanda Somerset to the same parties, because Matilda had once had an affair with Fernanda's husband, and Fernanda never spoke to Matilda again, but Ruby Renthal invited both of them, and everyone was curious to see how the two ladies in question would handle the problem. At the large charity dinners, when it was inevitable that both would attend, the ladies who seated the tables knew that they had to seat Fernanda and Matilda as far from each other as possible, in separate rooms even, if there were more than one, with Fernanda Somerset always getting the better seat in the better room because she was a benefactress, which Matilda Clarke, for economic reasons, could no longer be.

"You're not going to the Renthals', are you?" asked Lil Altemus.

"Of course, I'm going," said Matilda to Lil.

"I'm not," said Lil.

"You have to play along with these New People," said Matilda.

"Why do I have to play along with these New People?" asked Lil.

"People like us, WASPS in the *Social Register*, we're practically an extinct race. These New People are the ones who are taking charge."

"My brother Laurance is still in charge. The Van Degan bank is his. The Van Degan Foundation is his. The Van Degan Building is his," stated Lil. "You can't get more in charge than that."

"But Laurance is the exception to the rule. Most of the kind of people who were the heads of Wall Street and the banks when Laurance took over from his father have been sent out to pasture. All these New People are the people with the money nowadays. The kind of money we thought was money is nothing to the kind of money these New People have."

"I have no intention of playing along with them," said Lil emphatically.

"You're going to have to," said Matilda quietly.

"Have to what?"

"Go to the Renthals' ball."

"Why am I going to have to?"

"Because Laurance is going to insist you go."

Lil looked at Matilda. It was impossible for her to understand her brother's affinity for a lout like Elias Renthal, but she would never discuss her brother with anyone, even someone she had known all her life, like Matilda Clarke.

29

L IL ALTEMUS HAD Easter that year. It alternated each year between Laurance and Janet Van Degan's apartment and Lil's, and it was Lil's turn, although she felt a bit put upon by so much family so soon after Justine's wedding. Justine and Bernie were there, of course, although their roles as newlyweds had been superseded by Ormonde and Dodo Van Degan, recently returned from their Hobe Sound honeymoon. Hubie came, without Juanito, of course, who always caused a scene whenever Hubie was summoned to one of the family rites. Christmas he could understand, he said. Easter he couldn't, even after Hubie told him they had been having Easter lunch, at either Uncle Laurance's or his mother's, ever since he could remember, and the practice had been started long before that, at Grandfather Van Degan's when he and Grandmother, dead for years, still lived in the old Van Degan house on 79th Street. "If it's any consolation to you, Juanito, I hate going," said Hubie, leaving.

"I really wish you wouldn't dress like that, Hubie, especially with the whole family here," said Lil to her son, when he greeted her on his arrival.

"What's wrong with the way I dress?" asked Hubie.

"You know perfectly well what's wrong," said his mother. Although Hubie dressed in blue jeans and cowboy boots, he did not remotely resemble a denizen of Greenwich Village, which his mother insinuated, as his shirts, with their button-down collars, were so unmistakably from Brooks Brothers, and his tweed jackets, with their double vents, were made to order for him by Mr. Sills. Even during the period when he exasperated his mother even more by wearing his hair too long for her taste, and certainly too long for the taste of Uncle Laurance, he had it trimmed every two weeks by the barber at the Butterfield, his father's club, so that he ended up by being an outsider in the world he was born into as well as the world he aspired to be a part of.

Ned Manchester, Lil's cousin on the Altemus side, who, since the romance of Loelia Manchester and Mickie Minardos, had to be taken care of on family occasions, was present that Easter, as he had the two children who refused even to meet Mickie. "What a wonderful father Ned is," everybody always said. The lunch party was filled out by old friends like Matilda Clarke, whose sons lived in Santa Barbara and Santa Fe, and who always came. And then there were what Lil always called her strays, like Gus Bailey, who had no family that she knew of and no place to go. Ezzie Fenwick, who usually came, backed out at the last minute when he was asked to spend the weekend in the country with Elias and Ruby Renthal at Merry Hill, their new weekend retreat.

"Tell me about this marvelous picture," said Gus Bailey, admiring a large family painting over a sofa in the drawing room.

"That's the whole Van Degan family painted by Mr. Sargent in nineteen ten," said Lil, who loved to describe the picture to newcomers. "That was the drawing room in the original Van Degan house on lower Fifth Avenue, where the New York Public Library is now. You see, there's the Commodore, and his wife Annie. She was one of the Houghton sisters, meant to be ugly beyond belief, but look how beautiful Mr. Sargent made her look. And that little boy there, in the pale blue satin suit, playing with the collie, is my father, Ormonde, age six."

"My dear, look at your dogwood! Too beautiful!" cried Janet Van Degan, entering her sister-in-law's drawing room. "Lorenza's been here, I see."

"Only just left minutes ago. It's getting harder and harder to get Lorenza these days," said Lil. "Of course, her success pleases me, but, after all, it was *I* who discovered her." She spoke in the possessive way that she claimed also to have discovered Bobo, her hairdresser, and Nevel, her dress designer, meaning that she had been the first of the ladies in her group who had her flowers arranged each week by Lorenza. "Mrs. Renthal seems to be monopolizing all her time."

"Mrs. Renthal, Mrs. Renthal, that's all I ever hear these days," said Janet, throwing her hands up in the air in mock horror.

"And that damn ball. I can't believe the things Lorenza's been telling me about it," said Lil.

"Unbelievable," agreed Janet Van Degan.

"Imagine brand-new people like the Renthals giving this kind of party," continued Lil. "And inviting all of us. Two years ago no one ever heard of them. I wouldn't *dream* of going."

Laurance, overhearing, said to his sister, "We should talk about that, Lil."

Their conversation was interrupted by the arrival of the young Van Degans, Laurance and Laura, with little Janet, and the baby, Laurance III, whom everyone called Third. Little Janet, whom everyone said was a handful, made a dash for her grandmother.

"Who is this who is coming to see me? Who is it? Who?" cried Janet Van Degan, as her granddaughter ran to throw herself into her arms. Amid great screams of laughter, Janet picked up the child. "The preciousness of her! Look at this adorable creature, Lil. Edible, that's what she is. Edible."

Lil watched her sister-in-law and envied her her joy. If she had a grandchild, which she did not have and which she might never have, she suspected, she wondered if she would, and doubted if she would at the same time, feel the kind of joy that Janet felt every time she saw her granddaughter.

"I suppose I should ask Bernie to carve the lamb," Lil said to her daughter. "Does Bernie know anything about carving, Justine? Hubie is so hopeless at it, and you know how cross Uncle Laurance gets if the roast isn't carved right."

"You ask Bernie, Mother," replied Justine.

Bernie, as it turned out, carved very well. Bernie played games very well. Bernie danced very well. Bernie knew how to decant wine. Bernie knew how to give charming toasts. Lil always wished that Hubie took as naturally to these things that she thought so important in a man, or gentleman, as Bernie, whom she did not think of as a gentleman, did.

"No more peanuts, children. You won't believe the goodies Gertie has in store for us," said Lil to the Manchester children. "Laurance, help me with the seating. Where shall I put our new stepmother?" she asked, pointing ironically toward Dodo. "She's so used to sitting at the wrong end of the table, but I suppose I have to move her up this year."

When Lil's butler, Parker, told her that luncheon was served, he handed her a silver bell, and she rang it and rang it from room to room, to announce to her family and friends to move into the dining room. It was one of Lil's characteristic things to do at all her parties, and it was thought to increase the merriment of the occasion.

There were two tables at lunch, the long table with the Chippendale chairs, called the grownups' table on family occasions, and, in the window, the smaller round table, called the children's table. Looking down, Lil admired the vermilion-colored border of her fish plates. She loved her dozens of sets of dishes and took as much pleasure in their selection for each course as she did in the exquisite food that her cook prepared to go on them. Glancing down from her place at the head of the grownups' table, Lil was glad to see that Matilda Clarke, dear Matilda, her oldest friend, was making Ned Manchester laugh, the first time anyone had seen Ned laugh since Loelia ran off with Mickie.

Across from Matilda, she looked at her new stepmother, Dodo Fitz Alyn Van Degan, poor Dodo, no longer poor Dodo, rich Dodo, who would always remain poor Dodo to Lil. Dodo's appearance in the brief weeks of her marriage had improved, and Lil wondered if she were dieting strenuously or better corseted, and if her suit was a real Chanel. A curious alliance in the family was the friendship of Dodo and Hubie. Dodo, it developed, had bought several of Juanito's paintings at Hubie's gallery in SoHo and hung them in the hallway of Ormonde Van Degan's apartment on Fifth Avenue, a few buildings up from Lil's, that was now hers to do with as she saw fit. "I think they're charming," she said, about Juanito's work, the first time she saw them, and she did. She sent several other people to Hubie's gallery to buy Juanito's pictures too. In return, Juanito got her the dirty movies that she was too embarrassed to rent herself to show old Ormonde night after night.

"You will be sure, won't you, Parker, to tell Gertie how much we enjoyed the fish mousse," said Lil to her butler, as he cleared away the first course. Gertie was her cook, and Lil always interrupted her own conversation to send her compliments via her butler. "You used to be able to drive through Southampton and know who everyone was. Or, if you didn't actually know them, you knew who they were. Now you see all these new names on those same houses, and you don't know who any of them are, except they've all got about fifty million dollars. Who, pray tell, are the Reza Bulbenkians who just bought Evangeline's house?"

Lil, who had cases of champagne left over from the wedding, decided to dispense with red and white wines that day and serve only champagne throughout the meal, making the occasion more festive. She raised her glass and welcomed the new members of the family, meaning Bernie Slatkin and Dodo Fitz Alyn, although Dodo could not strictly be considered a new member of the family, having been a part of it, at a secondary level, since she was taken in by them as a teenager. Dodo, blushing, thanked Lil and raised her glass to Ormonde, who wore his napkin like a bib, whom she said had changed her life. Lil and Laurance exchanged glances, as if to say, "I should say so," but only applauded both Dodo and their father. Bernie sprang to his feet and made everyone laugh telling what it felt like for a person like him to suddenly find himself a member of a family like the Van Degans. Justine hopped to her feet and kissed Bernie, whom she had started to call dear heart when she addressed him, although it was a name that Bernie could not bear to be called. It was not lost on Matilda Clarke that Bernie Slatkin found Justine's excessive affection irritating. Old Ormonde, seated next to Matilda, told her three times how much he missed Sweetzer and what a keen sportsman he had been. The toasts ended with Uncle Laurance asking everyone to rise to thank Lil for the wonderful day she had provided for them.

The late spring afternoon had turned rainy and chilly, and Parker lit a fire as the group reentered the drawing room to settle in Lil's dark red damask sofas and chairs for coffee. Hubie and Justine stood together in front of one of the tall windows and looked out at the park, talking quietly. Laura Van Degan minded little Janet, who needed changing. Dodo minded Ormonde, who needed changing. Bernie Slatkin settled into a spirited game of backgammon with Matilda Clarke, who considered herself a champion, and was mildly put out that Bernie kept winning. Ned Manchester talked with Uncle Laurance and young Laurance about the state of the stock market and expressed concern about what he, too, called the New People, like Elias Renthal and Reza Bulbenkian, who seemed to be running the financial world, but Uncle Laurance assured Ned that Elias Renthal was the most fascinating man in the financial community in years, and necessary to it. Gus Bailey, quiet that day, as he always was on holidays, talked with Lil Altemus, who had placed him next to her at lunch, about Trollope, who was her favorite writer, as she fed cookies to her King Charles spaniels. Bozzie Manchester excused himself to go to the men's room but used the escape to telephone his mother, Loelia, at the Rhinelander Hotel to wish her a happy Easter; there was no answer and he did not leave a message.

Inevitably, during Van Degan gatherings, photograph albums were brought out and several people at a time pored over the pictures and captions. "Do you remember that time, Laurance, at Evangeline Simpson's wedding? Look how pretty Evangeline was way back then. Poor Evangeline. She was so drunk the other night at the Dashwoods'," said Lil.

"Look at Sonny Thomas. My God, Lil. Whatever happened to old Sonny?" asked Laurance.

"He married that woman with one leg, what'shername, with the son on heroin. Betsy Babcock. He married Betsy."

A sense of melancholy filled the air of Lil's large room, as if they all knew that this would be their last Van Degan Easter.

"Where's Juanito today?" asked Justine. She and Hubie were staring out the window at a bag lady establishing a beachhead for herself on a park bench across the street. Behind her a magnolia tree was in its first day of full blossom.

"Oh, lordie, I haven't a clue," replied Hubie, as if Juanito were no more than a casual acquaintance. It was not a truthful answer, but he did not wish to appear, even to his own sister, from whom he had no secrets, or very few, to be in the thrall of his Puerto Rican lover, even though he knew that she knew that he was. Juanito Perez had the power to make him miserably unhappy with his rampant promiscuity, as well as ecstatically happy on the occasions he focused his amatory attentions on Hubie.

"Hubie, when are you going to tell me?" asked Justine suddenly.

"Spring is bustin' out all over," replied Hubie, pointing to the magnolia tree.

"Hubie?" insisted Justine.

"Tell you what?"

"Hubie, it's me, remember, your sister."

"What's to tell? You already know. I knew you knew."

"How?"

"At your wedding. Just before you were going up the aisle. When you kissed me. I saw in your eyes then that you knew."

Her eyes filled with tears. "What's going to happen, Hubie?"

"I'm going to cool, I suppose."

"Don't be flippant about this, Hubie."

"I'm not being flippant, Justine. Believe me. I just haven't arrived at my attitude yet. I don't know how to play this scene."

"Are you afraid?"

"Yes."

"Do you think it was Juanito who gave it to you?" asked Justine.

Hubie smiled. "Could have been. He tested positive. On the other hand, it could have been about six hundred other guys too. I was never what you would call inactive. Does that shock you, Justine?"

"I'm trying not to be shocked, Hubie."

"Given my proclivities, there was a time not too long ago I even would have put the make on that hot number you got yourself married to."

"Bernie?" They both laughed. "He would have broken your nose."

"Wouldn't have been the first time somebody broke my nose."

"Oh, Hubie," said Justine, putting her hand on her brother's shoulder.

"Don't cry, Justine. Just don't cry. Not here. Not with all this family around."

"I won't, Hubie. What about Mother? When are you going to tell her?"

"After everyone leaves today."

"Do you want me to be with you?"

"I think this is something I have to do alone. But, thanks, Justine."

It rained the whole Easter weekend at Merry Hill, and the men of the house party, except for Ezzie Fenwick, were put out that the inclement weather thwarted their sporting plans.

The Renthals had bought a house where, years past, a shooting had taken place. It had belonged to a family called Grenville, a name long faded from day-to-day usage, but, still, a name that recalled past glories. "This was once the Grenvilles' house," people would say about it, traipsing through the woods to look at the structure, boarded up, unwanted for several decades, since the scandal that rendered it unlivable. "He was going to leave her, and she shot him. Something like that," they would say.

For the Renthals, however, who didn't know the Grenvilles, had never even heard of them, other than a faint recollection of grandeur associated with the name, there was not a moment's hesitation about buying the property when the only daughter of that sad family decided to sell. They liked owning things that had once belonged to grand people. At a Rothschild auction in Europe, Elias bought every bit of glass, china, silverware, and household linen with the letter R engraved or embroidered on it, more than enough to accommodate vast groups at both his enormous apartment in town and his new estate in the country.

Ruby was awakened early by the sounds of her maids arguing below with Lorenza, about vases. Temperamental and demanding Lorenza, in her mini-skirt, had arrived early from the city to arrange the peonies and delphinium, and the forsythia and lilac branches in the downstairs rooms, and she always argued with the maids about vases. Far from being cross, Ruby stretched luxuriously and nestled into her linen sheets, enjoying hearing the bustle of a life below that was preparing for her day. She never took her new status for granted and always, in moments like these, when she stopped to notice, she said, to whomever it was one thanked, a short and shy prayer of gratitude. Then, glancing at her gold vermeil traveling clock, which had once belonged to the Empress Elizabeth of Austria, she knew, in her perfectly run life, that in nine minutes Candelaria would knock on her door with her tray, her mail, and her morning papers.

It had taken but one weekend at Castle Castor, the Wiltshire seat of the Earl and Countess of Castoria, for Ruby to learn most of the amenities of grand country life: bags unpacked by the butler, clothes pressed by the maid, biscuits and fruit and bottles of Malvern water on the bed tables, breakfast on trays for the ladies, breakfast in the small dining room for the gentlemen, and separate newspapers for all.

Elias Renthal, his eggs finished, lit the first cigar of the day as he read the business section of the *Times*. He and the male members of the weekend party had gathered for breakfast in the smaller of the two dining rooms in the house, while the ladies took breakfast in their rooms. Elias relished the thought that important men, in dressing gowns, reading newspapers, were his weekend guests, at his country estate, while their wives and lady friends breakfasted above in their rooms. It was not until his marriage to Ruby, whose desire for social life was insatiable, that Elias began to understand the pleasures of popularity. It was Ruby who made Elias understand the advantages of social life for his business career, knowing the players at dinner, as she put it, instead of only at lunch. He found to his astonishment that people found him amusing, and he decided that he quite liked being liked. He even began to enjoy dinnertable conversation, as it was a way of spreading the word on his ever increasing art collection. "You must let me show you my new Caravaggio," he liked to say, or, "Personally, I prefer Picasso's blue period." His most fervent secret hope was that, in time, a place would be found for him on the board of directors of the museum.

"Journalism is not an exact science," Elias stated impatiently, hurling the newspaper to the floor, a gesture that caused the others to look up from their papers.

"Is something wrong?" asked Lord Biedermeier.

"I gave this fella from the *Times* an interview, and he misquotes me all the way through the article," said Elias.

"About what?" asked Mickie Minardos.

"My takeover of Miranda Industries. He says, in effect, that I took away the personality of the company. What he don't realize is I gave the company its identity. In the first place, I'm the one who renamed it Miranda. It had nine names and no corporate identity at all until I bought the company. These are things I understand. This article makes me sound like a predator, for Christ's sake, moving in for the kill. What I learned a long time ago is to sell a company, or a hotel, or a business as soon as I start to love it."

"I don't understand that," said Mickie Minardos.

"What's to understand?" asked Elias.

"If you love a company, why do you sell it?"

Elias looked at Mickie. "That's why you're not rich," he said.

Mickie, who thought of himself as rich, assumed a look of one whose worth has been underestimated.

Elias understood his look. "I mean really rich," he said. "What I am is a man who understands timing, the exact moment to make a move. That's my instinct. That's something I was born with. You either got it, or you don't. I deal with hundreds of millions of dollars a day in my business. I didn't fire more than five hundred people, and I brought in a whole new board of directors, responsible people like Laurance Van Degan, Loelia Manchester, Lord Biedermeier here, and my English friend the Earl of Castoria, high-profile people like that. Now we have a working operation. By the end of this year, I expect we'll do something like a billion two, a billion five, around there."

Elias's guests listened avidly. Elias Renthal talked a great deal about himself: his takeovers, his boards of directors, his profits, his acquisitions. And his guests listened, mesmerized, as if they, too, would get rich by sitting at the table of such a rich man.

"All right now," said Elias, clapping his hands, changing the subject. "Let's see what you've got, Winston."

Winston Bergerac, half French, half English, was famed for his paintings of horses. A modern Stubbs, they called him in the Sackville's catalogue. He had painted the horses of the Queen of England and had only just completed a painting of Elias Renthal's prize stud, Flash, which Elias had acquired from the Saratoga sales.

Winston Bergerac left the small dining room and returned in an instant with an easel, which he set up at the head of the table by the seat of Elias Renthal. He left the room again and returned in another instant with a painting under his arm, faced away from his audience, which he then turned around and placed on the easel. Murmurs of pleasure at the beauty of the elegant animal went around the table. Elias puffed at his cigar and stared at his latest commission, like a great collector collecting. He rose from his seat and went closer, bending in to look, stepping back to look, bending in to look again.

"I don't like it," he said finally, and a low gasp went around the table.

"But why?" asked the astonished Winston Bergerac.

"The prick's too big," said Elias. "I can't hang that in my dining room like that, with that big dork hanging down there. Ruby wouldn't approve."

"But, surely, Mr. Renthal," remonstrated Winston Bergerac, "that is the nature of the animal."

Elias scowled at what he sensed to be a superior tone in the voice of the painter. Lord Biedermeier, who knew that Elias could be formidable in displeasure, stepped in to make the suggestion that perhaps that part of the beautiful animal's anatomy could be repainted.

"All right. All right. Make the prick smaller, and I'll reconsider," said Elias, magnanimously. He gathered up the rest of his newspaper and walked out of the room to spend an hour on the telephone on business calls and to give some attention to the book on corporate takeovers that he was writing for Lord Biedermeier.

On a fireplace bench in the library lay newspapers and magazines from all over the world, rarely read, changed weekly by the butler, and available for any guest to take along to his room. Ezzie Fenwick, who disliked sport of any kind, excepting country walks, was the only member of the house party who enjoyed the bad weather. Long afternoons of bridge, or reading in front of the fire, or gossiping over drinks about parties and fashion and the upcoming Renthal ball, were to him infinitely preferable to swimming pools, or tennis courts, or golf links, or horseback riding, or, horrors, skeet shooting.

"Elias Renthal has taken to the grand life as if he's afraid it's not going to last," Ezzie said to Loelia Manchester.

"Shh," cautioned Loelia.

"These New People spend more for their houses than rich people in my day used to inherit," went on Ezzie.

"Shh," said Loelia.

"There's a Toulouse-Lautrec in the gentleman's loo. I've never seen that before," Ezzie continued, undaunted.

"Shh," said Loelia.

Like trophies, invitations to the best parties in town were lined up one next to the other on Ruby's elegant mantelpiece. Ezzie nosed through them. Mrs. Sims Lord's dinner. Mrs. Van Degan Altemus's dinner. Mrs. Laurance Van Degan's dinner. Mrs. Charles Bradley's dinner. Miss Maude Hoare's dinner. Mrs. Violet Bastedo's cocktail party. Mrs. Loelia Somerset Manchester's opera supper.

The door of the library opened, and Ruby Renthal entered, carrying her copy of the *The Memoirs of Madame de la Tour du Pin*, which Jamesey Crocus told her she simply must read if she wanted to understand about life at Versailles under Marie Antoinette in the final days before the Revolution.

"The flowers are beautiful, Ruby," said Ezzie Fenwick quickly, moving away from the invitations, as he nodded approvingly at the masses of blue delphinium and pink peonies that Lorenza had arranged on the console tables while they were all still at breakfast.

"Thank you, Ezzie," said Ruby, beaming. The ladies of the group always craved Ezzie's approval of their clothes, houses, flowers, and the seating of their tables. The men were less enthusiastic about Ezzie.

"I don't understand why you kowtow to that guy, Ruby," Elias had said to Ruby the evening before, in a loud whisper in the hallway, after Ezzie said that only waiters and bandleaders wore black tie on Sunday nights, when Ruby suggested they dress for dinner.

"Ezzie Fenwick's an arbiter," replied Ruby.

"Ezzie Fenwick's an asshole," answered Elias.

Ezzie pretended not to have heard. It was a way he had learned of ignoring the cruel taunts of his youth. Instead he went on chatting nonstop, over bridge, at which he excelled, about the terrible state of Aline Royceton's teeth, and why didn't she do something about them; about Evangeline Simpson throwing up in the powder room at Adele Harcourt's during one of her book-club meetings, and why didn't someone simply take poor Evangeline by the hand out to Minnesota where they do all those marvelous things about drunks; and about the vicious rumor that the Duchess of Windsor was really a man, and how can those terrible stories like that get started, when the truth of the matter was that not a soul in the room had heard the story before that moment.

Ruby took Mickie Minardos away with her, and they locked themselves behind closed doors to go over plans for the ball, which were being kept secret from even the closest of friends, except Loelia, of course, but Loelia wasn't telling. After she left, everyone remarked on the beauty of Ruby Renthal. She had recently returned from a trip to Brazil with a changed chin and smaller breasts. Her marvelous clothes, even in the country, her fabulous jewels, even for day, her newfound ability to enter a room so that everyone turned to look at her, and the allure of vast wealth that had become a part of her drew people into her orbit. Near, they were not disappointed. Her voice, changed too, so like the voice of Loelia Manchester, her greatest friend, enhanced the wit and charm that had been hers to begin with. Had she met people from the earlier parts of her life, before her prominence, she need not have worried, and didn't, for, most likely, they would not have recognized her. Ruby Renthal had become a great lady.

Lord Biedermeier removed his pince-nez and, with his thumb and forefinger, massaged the reddened bridge of his nose, all the time staring at the tropical fish in the aquarium that Elias Renthal had recently installed in the morning room of his new house.

"Are you shaking your head at those tropical fish, Lucien?" asked Loelia Manchester, looking up from her needlepoint.

"My first wife was Venezuelan. Do you remember her, Loelia?" Lord Biedermeier asked.

"Mother knew her," answered Loelia.

"Concepción de la Madrid she was called," continued Lord Biedermeier.

"Marvelous skin, I remember," said Loelia.

"Yes, she had beautiful skin, and her flesh was not quite firm. Just the way I like it."

"Really, Lucien! That's a conversation for the men's breakfast. Not here."

"The Latins, you know, are superstitious. Concepción always said that fish in bowls were bad luck."

"Oh, dear," said Loelia, staring at the fish tank. "I never heard that."

"Oh, yes, true," agreed Ezzie Fenwick, from his deep chair, laying aside a *Vogue*. "Fish in bowls are meant to be bad luck."

"Almost as bad luck as peacocks," chimed in Winston Bergerac, from his easel, where he was repainting Flash's prick.

Later, after tea, the sun came out. Ruby came into the room. "Outside, everyone. There's a rainbow."

For Ruby the beauty of the locale was secondary to the beauty that she created for the locale. The rainbow was less beautiful to her than the Edwardian gazebo she had built where she took her guests to watch the rainbow.

Lord Biedermeier, who was stout, said, "To the pool, finally. You really must not miss the opportunity to see me in a bathing suit." Everyone laughed.

"And you must see the new peacocks that Elias has bought for the place," said Ruby. "Too beautiful for words."

Entering the room that had been set aside as his weekend office, Elias closed the door behind him. At the console where his computers were placed, in a modified version of the switchboard with a hundred direct telephone lines to brokers and traders that he had in his Fifth Avenue offices, sat Maxwell Luby, dressed in lime-green country clothes of a different variety from the country clothes of the houseguests sitting in the smaller of the two dining rooms.

"Oh, Max, sorry if I have ruined your Sunday by asking you out here," said Elias. "There's a favor I'd like you to do me in the morning. I'm not going to be able to get back to town until after noon tomorrow. There's a new horse I have to see in the morning, and this simply has to be done at ten fifteen, no earlier, no later."

"What is it, Elias?" asked Max, used now to strange requests.

"Do you know the coffee shop called the Magnolia on Madison Avenue and Sixty-second Street?"

"No."

"Well, it's there. Just in from the corner. East side of the street. You've walked by it a hundred times without noticing."

"What about it?"

"I'd like you to go in there at exactly ten fifteen tomorrow morning. There will be a young man sitting at the counter on the second stool from the end. About thirty-two years old. Ivy League look. Dark hair, crew cut, just the beginning of going bald. He'll be wearing a gray flannel suit, blue shirt, dark red tie."

Max, used to such assignments, nodded.

"He will be reading the *Times.* On the empty stool next to him will be an old copy of *Forbes,* the one with the picture of me on the cover. You say to him, 'Do you mind if I move your *Forbes?*' That's all. No more. When he says, 'Excuse me, I'll move it,' you sit down next to him and order a cup of coffee."

"That's it?" asked Max, with a question in his voice to indicate there was an element missing.

"That's it," answered Elias. "Oh, yes, one more thing. You'll be carrying this briefcase. All you have to do when you sit down is leave the briefcase next to his leg. When he gets up, he'll take it with him. Okay?"

"Okay, Elias," said Max, lifting the briefcase and testing it for weight. "Why ten fifteen exact?"

"After the breakfast crowd. Before the lunch crowd. There'll be an empty stool."

"This is not Guy Howard again, is it?"

"No, no, not Guy," said Elias, shaking his head with displeasure at the name of Guy Howard. "He's called Byron Macumber, but no names are necessary." He looked for a moment at Max Luby's lime-green country clothes in the manner that Lord Biedermeier had once looked at Elias's clothes, although Elias had now forgotten that he had ever worn similar lime-green country clothes. "I'd ask you to stay, Max, but Ruby's got a house party going."

Max knew he didn't fit. "No problem, Elias. I've gotta get back to Pelham Manor anyway."

Later, in his car, when he stopped for gas, Max opened the briefcase. Beneath the newspapers on the top, there were, as he knew there were going to be, packets and packets of hundred-dollar bills for Byron Macumber.

"Isn't this nice, Hubie? Dinner on trays, just the two of us, in front of the fire? Oh, the deliciousness of an evening at home," said Lil Altemus, clapping her hands. "I get so tired of going out, out, out, all the time. You can't imagine how thrilled I was when you said you wanted to spend an evening alone together."

"There's something I wanted to tell you, Mother," said Hubie.

"I bet you didn't know your old mother could rustle up such a good meal, did you? I couldn't ask Gertie and Parker to stay on, after all those people all day long. And Lourdes is hopeless on days like Easter. Has been hopeless the whole of Holy Week! Church, church, church, she can't get enough church. On her knees every minute."

"Mother."

"Look at the doggies, Hubie? Aren't they precious? Worn out. Simply worn out. Those children ran them ragged all afternoon. Do you know that Bosie's going to be twelve?"

"Mother."

"The baby's adorable, isn't she? Hubie?"

"What?"

"The baby. Little Janet. Don't you think she's adorable?"

"Cute. Farts a lot. But cute."

"Hubie, you know how I hate words like that. What did you think of the newlyweds?"

"Which set?"

"Dodo and your grandfather."

"Good for Dodo is what I say," said Hubie.

"Oh, Hubie, you always say exactly the opposite of what you should say. Dodo's turned out to be just a little gold digger, and after all this family has done for her."

"You didn't want to change Grandfather's diapers, Mother."

"That's not the point. That's what nurses are for."

"Better he marries Dodo than Miss Toomey, Mother."

"Oh, Hubie, you are the limit. She's getting everything, you know. Laurance has seen Father's new will. All the paintings, all the furniture, all the bibelots on the tables even, all Mother's silver and china. Everything." There was such sadness in Lil's voice that Hubie turned to look at her.

"Mother, it would be hard in court for anyone to feel sorry for you, you know," said Hubie.

"What do you mean? Some of those things aren't even Van Degan things. Some are from Aunt Grace Gardiner's side of the family," insisted Lil.

"Mother," said Hubie, holding out his hands in exasperation. "There's not a spare inch in this huge apartment that is not crammed with valuable objects. What more do you need?"

"It's the principle of the thing," Lil said, rising and going over to the television set.

"Now, listen, Mother, we have to talk," said Hubie.

"Do you want to watch 'Sixty Minutes' or just talk? Diane Sawyer is interviewing the First Lady."

"Just talk."

"Good. Try some of this fig mousse. It's Gertie's specialty. I don't know how she manages to make it so light. Something about the egg whites, I think. I watched her once."

"You can see that I'm not well, can't you, Mother?" Hubie raised the level of his voice.

"The figs have to be very ripe," Lil continued. "And white figs only. That's very important."

"I have AIDS, Mother."

"It's just your color, darling. Your color's not good. And you need to fatten up a bit. You eat like a sparrow, you know. What you need is some good food and some good mountain air." Lil broke two cookies and threw them up in the air for Bosie and Oscar to catch. "There you are, you naughty doggies. I knew what you were waiting for. Yes, I did. Look at them, Hubie."

"I've got lymphoma, Mother. That means three or four months, the doctor said. Maybe no months," said Hubie, so quietly that he thought perhaps she had not heard him.

"I thought you and I might take a little trip to the mountains. They say Saint Moritz out of season is too beautiful for words, and so healthy. But when? That is the problem. There's that damn ball of the Renthals' that Laurance insists I not miss, and the Todesco wedding, and the final gala for the ballet where I'm the chairperson. After that, we'll go."

"By September I might very well have been dead for several weeks," said Hubie.

Lil had started to breathe heavily. "Oh, please, Hubie. This sort of talk is so morbid. I don't know how you could do this to your family."

"Thank you for your support, Mother."

"Does anyone know?" asked Lil.

"Juanito knows."

"Oh, I don't care about *Juanito,* for God's sake. I mean, does anyone we know or anyone in the family know?"

"Justine, only."

"Before me, you told Justine?"

"She guessed."

Lil put her hand to her heart and held it there, as if she were attempting to calm herself from considering the consequences of what her son had just told her.

"Paris!" she screamed.

"What?"

"Paris. That's where you should go. The Duchess, Wallis, Windsor, you know, my mother's great friend, she and the Duke used to stay with Mother and Father in Palm Beach every winter."

"I'm telling you I'm going to die, and you're talking to me about the fucking Duchess of Windsor?"

"No, no, there is a point to all this. She left all her money to the Pasteur Institute, and they do all those marvelous things for that particular disease. I'll send you to Paris."

"Do you want to get rid of me, is that it, Mother? So your friends don't have to know that your son is gay and has AIDS. That's why you want to send me to Paris, isn't it? Well, I'm not going to go to Paris." He got up from his chair, kicked the tray table with his foot, and the tray went flying to the floor. Bosie and Oscar began barking and tearing at the uneaten food on the plates. Hubie watched the manic scene for a moment and then started for the door.

"Please, please, Hubie, don't go," cried Lil. "Please don't leave me now. *Please.* I've heard all about that disease from Bobo, you know, my hairdresser Bobo. His salon has been decimated. Alfonso, Peregrine, Jose, they're all gone, and all those dancers in the musicals, and in the ballet, and, oh, my dear, in fashion, you wouldn't believe the numbers. Nevel told me. But I didn't think people like us got it, Hubie. I didn't. I didn't."

Even through her sobs, Lil could hear the door close and knew Hubie had gone. For a long time she sat in her chair without moving. When the telephone rang, she did not answer it. Then, slowly, she rose and carried her tray out to the butler's pantry and left it on the counter. Then she returned to the library and picked up Hubie's tray off the floor where he had kicked it, replaced the plates and glass on it and carried it back to the butler's pantry where she placed it on the counter next to her own. She turned off the lights and started to leave the pantry. Suddenly, she turned on the lights again and went back to the counter.

She picked up her mother's apple-green-bordered Meissen dinner plate that Hubie had used and looked at it, in a porcelain farewell. Then she dropped the plate on the pantry floor and watched it smash into irretrievable disrepair. Then she dropped the wine glass that her son had used and watched it smash. She picked up a fork and spoon off his tray, looked for an instant at the Montmorency pattern with her maiden monogram *L V D* engraved on the handles, and dropped them down the trash chute.

By the telephone on the counter was a pad and pencil where Gertie kept her notes. "Order Malvern water," it said, and under that, "Israeli melons." Under these reminders, Lil wrote:

"Gertie: Please forgive the ghastly mess I've made. I tripped. P.S. The fig mousse was yummy!"

30

LAURANCE VAN DEGAN rarely lunched in the fashionable restaurants of the city. Unlike his sister, Lil Altemus, who lunched out almost every day, and usually at Clarence's, Laurance preferred lunch in the private dining room of his offices in the Van Degan Building, or, on special occasions, at the Butterfield, where he felt almost as at home as he felt in his own home. The Butterfield on Fifth Avenue in the Sixties was the least known and most exclusive of the men's clubs in New York. Unlike the Knickerbocker Club, the Racquet Club, or the Union Club, the Butterfield was never called the Butterfield Club, simply the Butterfield, and membership was by invitation, never by application. Laurance had been invited to join by his father, Ormonde, the year after he graduated from Harvard, and Laurance had invited his son, young Laurance, on his graduation from Harvard.

The entrance to the Butterfield was sedate and identified only by a small brass plaque, so long embedded in the red brick of the building as to be virtually unnoticeable. Within, the austerity gave way to more noble trappings:

red carpets, paneled walls, crystal chandeliers, and what many considered to be the most graceful marble stairway in New York, winding elegantly upward for four stories. Large undraped windows looked out on Fifth Avenue and the park opposite, and in two tufted green leather chairs in front of one of these windows sat Laurance Van Degan and his luncheon guest, Elias Renthal.

"Another martini?" asked Laurance.

"No, no, Laurance," said Elias, raising his hand in mild protest. "I make it a point never to have more than one drink at lunch."

"A man after my own heart," said Laurance, who then signaled to old Doddsie, the waiter, who had been at the Butterfield as long as Laurance had been a member, to bring the menus. It had amused Laurance earlier in the day when Elias had suggested lunching at the Butterfield, saying he would like to see the famous staircase that Ruby had heard about from Jamesey Crocus since he and Ruby were planning to rip out the staircase at Merry Hill and build a new one there.

Old friends of Laurance's like Addison Cheney, Charlie Dashwood, and Sims Lord had nodded greetings when he and Elias had entered the bar shortly before one, but none made any effort to join them, and Laurance understood, as their behavior was consistent with what his own would have been under similar circumstances. Laurance watched Elias survey the scene.

"I think it might be a good idea for you to buy a couple of thousand shares of Sims Lord's company, Laurance," said Elias, as his eyes rested on Sims Lord. "It's a little high now, sixty-eight, and it'll take a dip in a couple of weeks down to about forty-two, but then it will begin to make a climb up, up, up, and go right through the roof. It's good to get in early and ride with the dip so as not to attract any undue attention, if you get what I mean."

"Sims Lord's company?" asked Laurance. He could feel himself beginning to redden. Laurance and Sims Lord had been in the same class at St. Swithin's and at Harvard and had been ushers in each other's weddings. Sims Lord was one of his oldest friends, and for years Ormonde Van Degan had sat on the board of Lord and Co. In the last year Elias Renthal's tips preceding his corporate raids had enriched Laurance Van Degan by millions. It was not that Laurance Van Degan, or any of the Van Degans, needed more money than they already had, but Laurance had found that the Van Degan Foundation, which benefited museums, opera companies, ballet companies, several hospitals, and other causes, equally worthy, was hard pressed to address the problem of the homeless of the city, and he had taken to supplementing the income of the foundation, for philanthropic purposes only.

"We don't talk business here at the Butterfield," cautioned Laurance Van Degan. "House rule."

"Got you," answered Elias. "Have any women members in the club?"

"No, no, goodness, no," answered Laurance. "And we won't have any, I assure you, despite those women's libbers always protesting at the Century. Twice a year we have ladies' nights here, and that's it."

"Nice chairs," said Elias, patting the arms of the green leather club chair. "I like a chair you can sink yourself into. English Regency, these chairs, aren't they?"

"Yes, they are," said Laurance, impressed. "You're becoming quite the authority on furniture."

"I'm spending enough dough on furniture, thanks to the very expensive advice Ruby's curator, Mr. Jamesey Crocus, is giving Ruby, so I figure I should get to know something about it."

"I hear your country house is charming. Loelia Manchester told Janet."

"Ruby and I want you to come out some weekend real soon."

"Delightful."

"It's English looking, like the Butterfield here. I said to Ruby, 'You got all the Louis the Terrible French furniture in New York. Let's have a little comfort in the country.'"

Laurance smiled appreciatively at Elias's little joke. "I know your house well. Billy Grenville was a few classes ahead of me at St. Swithin's."

"The wife shot him, I hear. Is that right?"

"It seemed."

"Where did that take place?"

"In your house."

"Merry Hill?"

"Yes."

"Christ, you'd think the realtor would have brought that up."

"Perhaps she didn't know. It all happened thirty-five years ago. People forget."

"This club all wasps?" asked Elias. Laurance noticed that Elias often shifted themes abruptly, as if his mind were on one thing while he was talking about another.

"Wasps?"

"Protestants, I mean. Are there just Protestants in this club?"

"Oh, goodness, no, Elias. That sort of thing went out years ago. Over there, at that table by the bar, for instance. The man playing backgammon with Herkie Saybrook is Quentin Sullivan, one of the outstanding Catholic laymen of the city, knighted by the Pope, all that sort of thing."

"Mother was a Morgan too. That don't hurt, I suppose."

"Mother was a Morgan. Yes, you're right. She was. I forgot about that."

"I'd like to become a member here, Laurance," said Elias.

Laurance, startled, picked up the menu and started to peruse the specialties of the day. Elias's request was not a thing that Laurance had expected. In the name of business, Laurance Van Degan could insist that his reluctant sister invite the Elias Renthals to the wedding of her daughter, or that his equally reluctant wife include the Elias Renthals as guests in her box on the fashionable nights at the opera, or that his wife, sister, son, and niece change whatever plans they had in order to attend the forthcoming ball of the Elias Renthals, but he did not have the same altruistic feeling about membership in the Butterfield, which his own grandfather had helped to found.

"Well, we must discuss this, Elias," he said, meaning at some time in the future.

"What's to discuss?" asked Elias.

"May I suggest to you either the cold poached salmon, which is marvelous, or the chicken hash, which is the best anywhere in New York."

"I'll try the hash."

"Marvelous choice." Laurance picked up the pad and small pencil that

Doddsie had left on the table and wrote the order down. He then tapped on a bell to signal the waiter.

"You write up your own order, huh?"

"No mistakes that way."

"Yes, sir, Mr. Van Degan," said Doddsie, arriving.

"Here you are, Doddsie," Laurance said, tearing off the page and handing it to him.

"Nothing first, sir?"

"I think not. Must watch our waistlines, Doddsie."

"You have nothing to worry about, Mr. Van Degan," said Doddsie, looking down at Laurance Van Degan's slender waist.

"Don't look over at my waistline, Doddsie," said Elias, patting his girth, and the three laughed. "And I will have something first. Like a salad."

"Yes, sir. House dressing?"

"Thousand Island."

"We'll go up to the dining room in a minute, Doddsie," said Laurance.

When the waiter left, there was silence for a moment. Herkie Saybrook, on his way up to the dining room, passed the table and greeted Laurance Van Degan.

"Playing squash later today with young Laurance, Mr. Van Degan," said Herkie.

Any mention of his son always brought a smile of pleasure to the face of Laurance Van Degan. "Mr. Saybrook, Mr. Renthal," he said, introducing them.

"What a pleasure, Mr. Renthal," said Herkie Saybrook. "May I present Quentin Sullivan. Elias Renthal."

"Pleasure, pleasure," said Elias. "I was just saying to Larry here what a nice club this is."

No one ever called Laurance Van Degan Larry. Even as a boy in school, no diminutive of the name Laurance was applied to him. For an instant Laurance assumed the look on his face of a person who had been called by a wrong name. Then, not wanting to correct Elias in front of other people, he smiled and winked at Herkie Saybrook, as if amused by the presumption of the billionaire.

"We'll see you upstairs," said Laurance.

"Nice fella, Herkie Saybrook," said Elias.

"Lovely," agreed Laurance. "A great friend of my son's."

"What about it?" asked Elias.

"About what?"

"Me joining the club."

"You see, Elias. It's not that easy. There would be opposition."

"What kind of opposition?"

"All the members of the Butterfield have to have been born in New York."

"Quentin Sullivan was born in Pittsburgh."

"There are occasional exceptions, and in the case of Quentin Sullivan, his grandfather on the Morgan side was a member, and his great grandfather as well."

"How would I go about joining?"

"You have to be invited to join by someone who has been a member for at least twenty years."

"That's you."

"You have to have letters of recommendation from six other members."

"That shouldn't be difficult."

"Ah, but it is, you see."

"I've been helpful to a few people I've seen around here today," said Elias.

"We should go upstairs to the dining room," said Laurance.

"I'm starved."

"One other thing, Elias."

"What's that?"

"If the person who has been proposed for membership is turned down, the member who proposed him must resign."

"That's the best news yet."

"How so?"

"Don't tell me anyone is going to ask Laurance Van Degan to resign from the Butterfield. No fucking way. Say, I'm dying to walk up that winding stairway."

The following Saturday afternoon, on the seventeenth hole of the golf course of the Maidstone Club in East Hampton, Long Island, Laurance Van Degan said to his son, young Laurance, "I would like you to write a letter for Elias Renthal."

"What sort of letter, Dad?" asked young Laurance.

"For membership in the Butterfield."

"You must be joking."

"I'm not joking."

"I can't believe what I'm hearing."

"It would mean a great deal to me, Laurance," said his father.

"Elias Renthal? Herkie Saybrook told me he called you Larry the other day. Herkie said he didn't know which way to look."

"He did, yes, he did call me Larry, but you see, he didn't know."

"There are so many clubs he could join, Dad, if he wants to join a club, but not the Butterfield. You can't mean the Butterfield."

"I do mean the Butterfield."

"But, Dad, only a year ago you blackballed—"

"I hate the word *blackballed*, Laurance," said his father, cutting in on his son's sentence. He leaned down to place his ball on the tee.

Young Laurance began again, rewording his sentence. "You kept Whelan O'Brian from joining, when Sonny Thomas, your old friend, proposed him. You called him a mick, don't you remember?"

"I would appreciate it if you would ask Herkie Saybrook to write a letter also, Laurance," said Laurance, as if his son had not spoken. "I need six letters."

= 31 =

G US WAS EXPECTING to hear from Peach in California and picked up the
telephone on the first ring, but it was not Peach, who had promised to
call after she spoke with Mr. Feliciano. Instead it was Matilda Clarke.

"Oh, Gus, good, you're home," said Matilda.

"Yes," answered Gus.

"I'd like to stop by."

"When?"

"Now."

"I'm going out to dinner at eight."

"I'll be there in ten minutes."

"Is there anything wrong?"

"Heavens, no. I just felt like seeing you for a drink."

Gus continued to dress, expecting the telephone to ring at any time. He
hoped Peach would call before Matilda arrived. When his black tie was tied
and his cummerbund in place, he picked up the telephone and called California. Peach answered on the first ring.

"It's Gus," he said.

"I was going to call you," Peach answered.

"I've been waiting."

"I was waiting until five our time before calling."

"Why?" But, of course, he knew the answer why. He had been married to
her for years.

"The rates go down at five."

"For God's sake, Peach," said Gus. It was a bone of contention between
them always. Peach was one of the thrifty rich, even in semi-emergency situations. "I would have been gone by then."

"Well, anyway," said Peach. "I talked to your private detective."

"What did he want?"

"He said he's going to get married."

"He's already married. To someone called Wanda. He's got pictures of her
all over his office."

"No, Gus, not Mr. Feliciano. He told me Lefty Flint is going to get married, as soon as he's released."

Gus was silent.

Peach continued. "Someone he's been corresponding with the whole time he's been in prison. You know those nuts who write to prisoners and fall in love with them. One of those."

"Who is she?"

"She's called Marguerite Somebody. She owns a bar in Studio City where he's going to work when he gets out."

"Is Marguerite Somebody out of her mind?"

"Perhaps she doesn't have a mind."

"Look. I have to go. There's someone ringing my bell."

"All right."

"Listen, Peach. I may be coming out for a day."

"I won't be going anywhere."

When he put down the telephone, he had the same disquieting feeling he always had when he talked with Peach, as well as the same feeling of anger he always got when anything about Lefty Flint was mentioned to him.

As he went to the front door of his apartment, he put on his dinner jacket. Opening the door, Matilda Clarke was standing there. Behind her was Ned Manchester.

"Don't you look smart, Gus," said Matilda. "Gus is one of the most popular men in New York," she said, turning to Ned. "You know each other, don't you? Ned Manchester. Gus Bailey."

"Easter at Lil Altemus's," said Gus, remembering where they had met.

"Exactly," said Ned. He seemed slightly ill at ease. "Charming, your flat," he said to Gus.

"Isn't it?" agreed Matilda. "Exactly the right amount of shabby."

Gus laughed. "Such compliments. How about if I make you drinks in some chipped glasses?"

"Scotch for me," said Ned.

"Wine for me," said Matilda.

When Gus went into the kitchen, Ned picked up some books on tables to look at the titles. "I wish I had time to read," he said.

"Play a few less hours of squash every day, and you'd have time to read," said Matilda.

"You sound just like someone I used to be married to," said Ned.

Matilda snapped her fingers quietly to get Ned's attention and pointed to the photograph of Gus's daughter on a tabletop and mouthed but did not say the word *dead*.

"I saw Constantine de Rham today at Clarence's," said Matilda, when Gus returned with the drinks.

"Out again, is he?" asked Gus.

"Looks about a hundred," said Matilda.

"Very aging, a gunshot wound in the stomach," offered Ned Manchester.

"Did you talk with him?" asked Gus.

"Heavens, no. He was with that young woman with the Eva Perón hairstyle," said Matilda.

"Yvonne Lupescu, her name is," said Gus.

"She was playing nursie, leading him to his table."

"A strange pair," said Ned.

"I'm sure she's the one who shot him," said Matilda.

"It's a theory," said Gus.

There was a pause in the conversation. Gus, curious, wondered what the purpose of the visit was.

"What time are you off, Gus?" asked Matilda.

"Almost immediately, in fact," said Gus. "I'm going to Maisie Verdurin's, and you can't be late at Maisie's. In at eight. Out at eleven. Like clockwork."

"Loelia and Mickie are going to Maisie's too," said Matilda to Ned.

"Lucky Maisie," said Ned. There was a note of bitterness in his voice.

"Listen, Gus," said Matilda. "My son's here from Santa Barbara. He's turned my little hovel upside down. Would you mind very much if we stayed on a bit after you left?"

Gus looked up and immediately understood the situation. Ned, turning away, went back to examining the books on Gus's coffee table. Gus smiled at Matilda.

"No problem," said Gus, taking his glass into the kitchen, and Matilda followed him.

"We're having dinner around the corner, at that little French place, whatever it's called, and we thought we could wait here until our reservation at nine," Matilda went on quickly. "I mean, it's so cozy here."

"No problem," repeated Gus.

Matilda turned on the tap in the sink and rinsed out Gus's glass. "Don't you *dare* say loose woman to me, Gus Bailey," she whispered.

"Who said loose woman?" asked Gus.

"You're thinking it."

"No, you are," said Gus, laughing.

"He's so forlorn since Loelia," said Matilda.

"You know where the rubbers are," said Gus.

"You are *awful!*" she said, pretending to pound him with her fists. "I could ask that nice elevator man of yours to lock up after we leave."

"Sure," said Gus.

"Would you like to come out to the country over the weekend?" asked Matilda, in a normal voice, returning to the living room.

"I'll be away," answered Gus.

"Another one of your mysterious trips? This man, Ned, I'm sure he's leading a double life. One of these days we're going to find out he's not a writer at all, but an assassin."

"Gus, I was thrilled with the piece you wrote about us for the *Times Magazine*," said Ruby Renthal, at Maisie Verdurin's dinner.

"Thanks," said Gus.

"You were a pal not to repeat some of those damn fool things I said," said Ruby.

"I told you I wouldn't."

"A lot of you guys say you won't and then you do," said Ruby. Gus noticed that people stared at Ruby Renthal the way they stared at film stars.

"If I had, I wouldn't have gotten invited to your ball, and I want to go to your ball," said Gus. They both laughed.

Lest anyone had not picked up on the change in status of Elias and Ruby Renthal, Maisie Verdurin, whose dinners were always a barometer of exactly who was successful in the mercurial world of big business, seated Elias Renthal on her right that night, the place of honor that she usually reserved for cabinet ministers and former presidents. As Ruby Renthal was every bit as important a social star as her husband was a business star, Maisie had been in a quandary all day at exactly how to seat Ruby at no less elevated a place than Elias's, especially as the invitations to their ball were out and they had become even greater objects of curiosity.

Finally Maisie had broken one of her own rules never to seat husbands and wives at the same table and placed Ruby across from her between the chief executive officers of an airline and a petroleum company.

"I have never seen Mrs. Renthal wear the same dress twice," said Rochelle Prud'homme to Maisie. Rochelle, who had resisted the Renthals' rapid rise, had now fallen into line, praising them on every occasion, especially as they were giving the grandest party of the decade. "I hear Ezzie Fenwick tells her what to wear."

"Isn't she beautiful?" Maisie had replied. "I think she's the chicest woman in New York." Maisie did not add that she had never had clients like Elias and Ruby Renthal for buying art, even though she could not bear Jamesey Crocus, who had now become their private curator. As Elias's walls, both in town and country, were now filled with works of art, his collecting spree had abated somewhat, except for the occasional swap, when a finer specimen of a painter's work came on the market. Maisie, ever on the lookout for new walls to fill, had taken an interest in Reza Bulbenkian, another of the New People whose wealth was incalculable, and invited him and his wife Babette to the same party that the Renthals were attending, but she seated them at less exalted tables than her own. The Bulbenkians were also rising in society, although in adjacent groups of lesser smartness than the group that had taken in the Renthals, and they were not often mentioned in social conversation, except in that month each year when Mr. Forbes brought out his list of the four hundred richest people in America, on which Reza Bulbenkian's name kept rising.

"Who in the world is this Reza Bulbenkian?" Loelia had asked Ruby, looking up from the magazine.

"You see him at benefits," answered Ruby. "He always buys several tables, or whole rows of seats, and fills them with people you never saw before."

"With the hair in his ears, that one?" asked Loelia.

"Exactly. And the wife who weighs about three hundred."

With that, the Bulbenkians were dismissed until the following year, except, of course, on Wall Street, where he was discussed almost as much as Elias Renthal.

Maisie placed Reza Bulbenkian at what she considered her third best table, next to Yvonne Lupescu, and she placed Babette, who had been married to Reza for thirty years, in the little room in the back, next to Constantine de Rham, who was responsible for introducing the Bulbenkians to Maisie, just as he had been responsible for introducing Elias Renthal to Maisie. Maisie knew that the dream of the Bulbenkians' life was to be asked to the Renthals' ball, but she had declined to intercede in their behalf, agreeing only to have them to the same party and let them take it from there.

"Marvelous, your toupee," said Yvonne Lupescu to Reza Bulbenkian, in an effusive tone, as if she were complimenting him on an exquisite article of clothing, and then continued, pretending not to notice the look of discomfort on his face, "No one would ever know."

Bulbenkian had heretofore paid no attention to his dinner companion, casting looks instead at the table where the Renthals were seated, in the hopes of catching Elias Renthal's eye to wave a greeting to him. Now, furious, he turned to Yvonne, picked up her place card to familiarize himself with her name, and saw that she was a baroness. Thereafter he gave her his full attention, not only to quiet her enthusiasm over his toupee, which he thought no one, not even his wife of thirty years, had ever detected, but because Baroness Lupescu proved to be an enchanting dinner companion, whose diamond-ringed fingers found their way to the bulge between his legs beneath Maisie's pristine white tablecloth at the same time that she was telling him stories of her grandmother in the court of King Zog of Albania.

At Maisie's table, Ruby Renthal held her dinner companions in her thrall. "At the White House the other night, the First Lady seated me next to the Vice President," she said to the table at large. "I said to him, 'You've got to change your glasses, sir. No one is ever going to be elected President of the United States who wears rimless glasses.' "

"You didn't say that to the Vice President?" asked Maisie Verdurin, aghast, as the rest of the table laughed at the audacity of the beautiful Mrs. Renthal.

"Oh, I did, and he's going to change them. You mark my words, Maisie. Just keep watching him on the news."

"How was the White House?" asked Maisie, wistfully. She longed to be invited there.

"So pretty, the whole thing," said Ruby. "The First Lady had rose geranium in the finger bowls, Maisie. We must all try that."

Looking across the table, Elias Renthal caught Ruby's eye and winked at his wife. She smiled back at him. What Elias knew, as surely as he knew that he was the fifth richest man in the United States, was that he had married the perfect wife. When he had been married to Gladyce, and before that, when he had been married to his first wife, Sylvia, his social life in Cleveland was confined to an occasional party for a special event, or dinners in restaurants with business associates and their wives. Being in society, as he now was, was a different thing altogether. He and Ruby were out every night, usually "dressed to the nines," as he put it, and, although he grumbled about never staying home, he liked being invited everywhere almost as much as Ruby did. Ruby, who was born for society, had taken on the airs of someone who had always been rich. She understood the intricacies of the overlapping groups in the two thousand people who went out to dinner every night. With neither Gladyce nor Sylvia could he have risen to the heights that he had risen to with Ruby by his side.

Ruby had not resisted earlier that day when Elias told her he had settled a portion of his fortune on her. That way, he told her, in the unlikely event of adversity, the money that was in her name would be secure.

"We are a team," he said to her.

"A great team," she agreed. At that moment in time, she was the happiest that she had ever been in her life, and no man could have attracted her in the way that her husband did.

Although Ruby claimed not to understand a thing about business, she had taken to reading the financial pages with the same relish with which only last year she had read the society columns. She would have been able to tell anyone, if anyone had thought to ask her, which they didn't, that Sims Lord & Co. had closed at thirty-seven and an eighth the day before the takeover, fallen immediately to twenty-four, and then risen to forty-six, and that Elias, even on that relatively small buyout, had profited by twenty-four million dollars.

Maisie Verdurin, the evening's hostess, had been struck dumb by the grandeur of Ruby Renthal's conversation about the White House. She waited an appropriate length of time while Elias Renthal, on her right, explained to the table the modus operandi of his takeover of Sims Lord & Co., the kind of conversation that usually took place at Maisie Verdurin's tables. When Justine Altemus Slatkin, who had been unusually silent throughout the evening, accidentally knocked over a glass of red wine and the waiters came scurrying to place napkins over the wet tablecloth, Maisie, unconcerned about Justine's accident, said casually to Elias, "I didn't realize Ruby was so friendly with the First Lady."

"Oh, yes," said Elias proudly. "The First Lady is very fond of Ruby, ever since Ruby's gift to the White House."

"Her gift?" asked Maisie.

"She gave her console tables, the ones she bought at the Orromeo auction in London, with the inlaid rams' heads, to the White House for the redecoration of the Green Room."

"My word," said Maisie.

"After the First Lady came to lunch at the apartment, Ruby just gave them to the White House. She said the country had been good to her and she wanted to give something back to the country."

"The First Lady went to Ruby's apartment for lunch?" asked Maisie.

"If I tell you a little secret, Maisie, you won't let on to anyone, will you?"

"Me? Never!" said Maisie.

"Because if this got out—"

"My lips are sealed. Talking to me is like talking to the dead," said Maisie.

"The First Lady might, just might, come to the ball, if she can readjust her schedule so that she can visit an orphanage in Harlem on the same day."

"My word," said Maisie.

Of all the news that went around Maisie Verdurin's tables that night, the death of Baron von Lippe in Brussels from AIDS, the divorce of the Herkie Saybrooks, the death by overdose of the Wagstaffs' daughter, and the rumored merger of the airline and the petroleum company, whose CEOs had graced Maisie's table, none was more repeated the next day than the news that the First Lady might, just might, be coming to the ball of the Elias Renthals.

32

IN THE AMBASSADORS' Club of the airline, Gus watched as the film star Faye Converse entered, causing excitement and stir, even among the corporate executives waiting for their planes. Faye Converse, a star for as long as most people could remember, still created a glamorous havoc in her wake, although her screen appearances had dwindled to the occasional mini-series on television. Finally, seated, a soft drink brought to her, she engaged in conversation with a young companion, probably a secretary, Gus thought, who nodded assents and occasionally wrote something down on a list.

"Is that you, Gus?" Faye called out, having caught his eye.

"Hello, Faye," said Gus, rising to go over to her.

"Leave it to you not to make a fuss over me," she said.

They both laughed.

"You look great, Faye," he said.

"That's better," she said. "You know how I like compliments. If I hadn't spotted you, I bet you wouldn't have gotten up to speak to me."

"Oh, yes, I would have. I was just waiting for your usual hubbub to quiet down."

"You going to L.A. or Europe?"

"L.A. For a day."

"I liked that piece you wrote about me."

"Thanks."

"Still off the sauce, you see," she said, holding up her soft drink.

"Same here," he said, holding up his.

"This is my secretary. Brucie Hastings. Gus Bailey."

"Oh, I read your piece on Faye," she said.

Gus shook hands with the young woman. Her handshake was gentle.

"Are you working?" asked Gus, turning back to Faye.

"I'm going to be in *Judas Was a Redhead*. Have you read it? Marvelous book."

"Nestor Calder's a friend of mine," said Gus.

"I'm playing Magdalena, the old hooker with the heart of gold," she said.

"Perfect," said Gus.

"How do you like that, Brucie? Did you hear what this son of a bitch said to me? I tell him I'm playing a hooker with a heart of gold, and he says 'perfect,' like in perfect casting."

Brucie laughed. She appeared fragile to Gus.

"Are you in first class, Gus, or are you still riding back in steerage?"

"Steerage."

"Here, give me your ticket. Brucie, take Mr. Bailey's ticket over to that nice lady at the desk, Robin I think her name was, the one I gave the autograph to, and ask her to upgrade Mr. Bailey to first class and seat him next to me, and you sit in his seat in steerage. There are a few things I want to talk to Gus about."

"I don't normally sign autographs in planes, but I'll make an exception this time," said Faye to the woman who interrupted her conversation with Gus when the plane was aloft.

"Oh, thank you, Miss Converse," said the woman. "Will you sign it to Darlene?"

"She looked like a Darlene, didn't she?" said Faye, when the woman had gone back to her seat. Gus laughed. "I bet you were an only child, Gus," said Faye. They were drinking Perrier water.

"No, I wasn't."

"You seem like you were an only child. That loner thing about you."

"One of four, as a matter of fact."

"New England, right?"

"Hartbrook. A little town on the Connecticut River that you'd have to be born in to know about."

"Where's the rest of the four of you?"

"Two dead. One suicide. One cancer."

"The other?"

"A brother."

"Where is he?"

"Boston, I think. We don't keep in touch."

"What does he do?" asked Faye.

"Designs condominiums in New England resorts, to the great displeasure of the Old Guard and the environmentalists," said Gus, shifting in his seat. "This isn't why you kicked Brucie out of her first-class seat to sit back in steerage, is it, so you could ask me about my background?"

"No. I was just vamping."

"That's what I thought."

They laughed again.

"You know someone called Elias Renthal, don't you?" she asked.

"I know him, kind of. I interviewed him and his wife."

"I read it," said Faye.

"I see him at parties. The last time I saw him, he said, 'Hi, Bus,' and I said, 'It's Gus, not Bus,' and he said, 'That's what I said.' That's how well I know him. Why?"

"He's rich, isn't he?"

"Oh, yes, he's rich."

"Very rich?"

"We're talking big bucks here."

"Generous?"

"What are you getting at, Faye? I don't think he'd finance a movie, if that's what you're interested in."

Faye shook her head no. She looked out the window of the plane. Then she said, "Brucie, my secretary."

"In steerage."

"She's dying."

"Oh, no."

"She's got the dread disease," said Faye.

"God almighty," said Gus.

"She's married to a dancer on the Larkin show. He has it too. Get the picture?"

"Got it," said Gus.

"I'm trying to raise money for the disease, a lot of money, big money. Do you think Mr. Renthal would help me out?"

"I don't know. He gives to the opera. He gives to the ballet. He gives to the museums. I don't know about disease. I especially don't know about that disease. He's still on the make. So far he only does the social-advancement charities."

"All I want, Gus, is an introduction to Mr. Renthal, and I can handle it from there," said Faye.

"Faye, you're a famous woman. You can get to anyone in the world you want to get to. You don't need me to meet Elias Renthal."

"He didn't return my call."

"I can't believe it."

"He didn't return my two calls."

"What did the secretary say?"

" 'Will he know what this is in reference to?' she asked."

Gus shook his head.

"I could do a fund-raiser," said Faye. "But it takes time. And time is not on our side."

"Elias Renthal's wife is the key," said Gus. "He does whatever she tells him to do. Her name is Ruby Renthal."

"I've seen her picture in the magazines. Pretty."

"Very pretty," said Gus. "And nice, too."

"Can you set it up for me to meet her?"

"I think so. She liked the piece I wrote on her. I'll set up a lunch."

"At Clarence's. I've always wanted to go to Clarence's."

"Okay, I hope."

"Thanks, Gus. Will you have time for dinner while you're in L.A.?"

"Probably not."

"You out on an article?"

"Family stuff," said Gus.

"Listen, Gus. I'm sorry about what happened to you and Peach. I mean, about your daughter."

Gus nodded.

"I was doing a picture in Italy at the time, or I would have written," she said.

Gus nodded.

"I don't know how you behaved so well under the circumstances. If that had happened to me, I would have shot the son of a bitch."

Gus nodded. It was the sort of thing that people said to him.

* * *

When Gus stepped into the dark bar after the bright sunlight of Studio City, he was temporarily blinded and waited for a minute at the entrance until he got his bearings. It was two o'clock in the afternoon, and the bar was empty except for a young woman sitting on a stool behind the bar adding up receipts at the cash register.

"Help you?" she asked, when Gus settled himself on a stool.

"Perrier," he said.

"Out of Perrier," she said, not moving from her stool.

"Coke?" he asked.

She rose, put her receipts on the cash register, picked up a beer mug, filled it with ice, and from a spigot filled the mug with the soft drink.

"It's Pepsi," she said, putting it in front of him. She was pretty, under thirty, Gus figured, and stared at him as if she knew the purpose of his visit was not to drink a Pepsi Cola at two o'clock in the afternoon. Her blouse was made of a thin material, through which the shoulder straps of her undergarments could be seen.

"Are you Marguerite?" Gus asked.

"What can I do for you?" she asked, without answering his question.

"I wanted to ask you a question."

"About what?"

"Is it true that you are engaged to marry Lefty Flint?"

"Who are you?"

"Is it?"

"What the hell is it to you?"

"The man is a killer. The man has taken a girl's life."

"Who the hell are you?"

"I am the father of the girl he murdered."

"He was drunk when he did that. Now he doesn't drink anymore. That was a one-time thing. He explained all that to me."

"You know then what he did?"

"Yes, I know."

"And you're still going to marry him?"

"You better get out of here, Mr. Bailey."

"Yes, you're right," said Gus. He was drained, white, shaken. For an instant their eyes met.

"Good-bye," he said.

"Good-bye," she answered.

"Look," said Gus.

"What?"

"Here's a telephone number and name. If you ever are in trouble of any sort, ring it."

"Whose number?"

"It's not mine. It's just if you're in trouble. Keep it."

"I'm not going to be in any trouble, Mr. Bailey."

"I hope not, Marguerite. With all my heart, I hope not."

He turned and walked out of the bar.

Marguerite picked up the card that Gus had dropped on the bar and read it. On it was the name and telephone number of Anthony Feliciano.

*   *   *

"May I go down into your storeroom?" asked Gus.

"For what?" asked Peach. Divorced, with her own house, which was not the house of their marriage, Peach sometimes objected to Gus's use of her home.

"I'm looking for something I might have left behind when I moved out," he answered.

"All your things were packed up and sent to New York," said Peach.

"There's something I can't find."

"What?"

"Some letters that my father sent me during the war," he answered.

"All right," she said.

Somewhere, not lost, but long out of sight and reach, in a box, or trunk, or drawer, was a black leatherette box, lined with satin, on which rested a medal and ribbon, commemorating an act of bravery in a war. With it was a Luger, taken off the body of a dead soldier.

In the gun shop, he waited until a customer had finished his business and the shop was empty before he ceased looking at the racks, as if he were planning on making a purchase.

"Help you?" asked the salesman.

"I have a German Luger from World War Two," said Gus. He opened his briefcase and took out the gun, which was still wrapped in a brown paper bag grown soft and greasy through the years.

The salesman watched as Gus unwrapped the paper on the glass counter and picked up the gun.

"A beauty," he said. "Worth a bit of money, you know. They don't make them like this anymore. Is it for sale?"

"No," replied Gus. "I wanted to get it put into working order. Could I get that done here?"

"How much of a hurry are you in?"

"I'm not in a great hurry," said Gus.

"A week? Ten days? It's a busy time here with hunting season underway."

"That's all right. I live in New York, not here, but I'll be back out in a month or so, and I can pick it up then."

"I'll need a deposit."

"How much?"

"Seventy-five."

"Okay." Gus reached in his pocket and brought out some money.

"Is it registered?"

"No."

"Name?"

"Mertens. Gene Mertens."

33

WITH THE invitations to the Renthals' ball in the mail, addressed by Mrs. Renthal's calligrapher, and supervised by Mrs. Renthal's social secretary, it quickly became the most highly anticipated party in New York in years. Ezzie Fenwick, who had taken upon himself the role of champion of Ruby Renthal, told certain people that he would be able to secure invitations for them, implying, not quite honestly, that he advised Ruby on her list. Those who had not been invited, and thought they should have been, planned earlier than usual migrations to their houses in Newport and Southampton, their ranches in Wyoming, their cottages on the coast of Maine, or elsewhere.

There was no one quite so distressed by his exclusion from the Renthals' list as Constantine de Rham, recovered now, nearly, from his gunshot wound, which he continued to insist was self-inflicted. In his own mind he felt the shooting had added a tragic melancholy to his persona, coming as it did so few years after the death of his wife Consuelo. He imagined, walking daily to his lunch table at Clarence's, first on a walker and then on a cane, usually led by Yvonne Lupescu, that people said of him, "Poor man. What a lot he has suffered."

When Elias Renthal was still married to his second wife, Gladyce, Constantine de Rham had made his house on Sutton Place available to Elias as a location for his assignations with Ruby Nolte. Had his affair with the airline stewardess been public knowledge, Elias would have had a more difficult and costly divorce from Gladyce than he already had. Constantine had been handsomely rewarded for his services, but he still felt entitled to an invitation and silently sulked every time he read something in the newspapers about the forthcoming party, even though his somewhat sullied reputation and his affair with Yvonne Lupescu had made further contact with the high-rising Renthals an impossibility.

But for a chance meeting in the fitting rooms of Sills, Lord Biedermeier's tailor, between Elias Renthal, who now ordered suits twenty at a time for each season, and Constantine de Rham, who, because of his extreme weight loss due to the bullet that had briefly lodged itself in his stomach, was having his own summer suits taken in by several inches, the matter might have gone unnoticed, for Constantine would never have shared with anyone, least of all Yvonne Lupescu, his extreme hurt at the social slight by the Renthals.

That day at Sills, only the lateness of Elias, due to a business emergency, caused the overlap of appointments between the one-time friends. Mr. Sills was a stickler for promptness among his fashionable clientele, but he dared not reprimand Elias Renthal for his tardiness, for who else these days, except Arabs, he once pointed out to Lord Biedermeier, ordered suits twenty at a time on a seasonal basis.

As Elias Renthal's time was limited, and Constantine de Rham's time hung heavily on his hands, Mr. Sills silently signaled to Sal, the fitter, to move from Mr. de Rham's mirrored cubicle to Mr. Renthal's, so that the busy tycoon could be dealt with instantly. De Rham, who had taken his snubs from people he once dined with on a nightly basis, was in no mood to take a snub from a fitter with pins in his mouth and moved outside his cubicle in order to complain loudly to Mr. Sills. It was then he saw Elias Renthal in his cubicle, with a large cigar in one hand, remove his trousers and put on the first of the twenty pairs he was to have fitted, beginning with the satin striped trousers that would have to be ready in time for the ball.

"What a handsome pair of legs you have, Elias," said Constantine, joking, with a recurrence of the Continental charm that had once worked magic for him.

"For heaven's sake, Constantine," said Elias, surprised. "What are you doing here?"

"The same thing you're doing here," said Constantine. "On a somewhat lesser scale."

Elias chuckled. He quite enjoyed references to his extravagances. He put his cigar in his mouth and puffed on it, ignoring the NO SMOKING IN THE DRESSING ROOM sign posted on the wall.

Constantine, following suit, took a cigarette from a leather case he removed from his jacket pocket. "Do you have a match?" he asked.

"Leather? In town?" asked Elias, touching Constantine's case, pretending astonishment. "What would Ezzie Fenwick say about that?"

They both chuckled. Elias reached into his suit pocket and handed a dark blue packet of matches to Constantine. It was not lost on Constantine that in discreet green letters were the words *The Butterfield*.

"Swell places you're going to these days, Elias," said Constantine. "Whose guest were you?"

"I'm a member," said Elias. "I want the break lower on those trousers, right above where the pump will be," he said to Sal on the floor, pinning the cuff.

"You're a member of the Butterfield?" asked Constantine.

"Why, yes."

"I thought they didn't take, uh—"

"You thought wrong."

"Consuelo once asked Herkie Saybrook to put me up for the Butterfield."

"What happened?"

"Herkie said you had to be born in New York."

"That's right."

"But you weren't born in New York either."

"I'm going to need this suit, with the tail coat, for next week, Sal," said Elias, cutting Constantine short. "Very important. You better get me Mr. Sills, so there's no misunderstanding about anything. The other stuff I don't care about until I leave for Europe on the sixteenth."

"I was wondering if there's been some mistake, Elias," said Constantine.

"Mistake? About what?"

"You know how social secretaries sometimes get things mixed up."

"Get what mixed up?" asked Elias. Like the deal maker he was, he gave no indication that he knew exactly what Constantine de Rham was hinting at, and he was determined to make de Rham spell out the words before he refused him.

"You don't know what I'm talking about?"

"I haven't a clue."

"Your ball for the Earl and Countess of Castoria."

"What about my ball?"

"I haven't been invited."

"A lot of people haven't been invited. There's just so many people the ballroom can hold. Ezzie Fenwick tells me Mrs. Astor could only have four hundred people to her ball because that's all her ballroom could hold."

"You're having four hundred, I hear," insisted Constantine.

"That's as many as my ballroom can hold, too."

"I see," said Constantine.

"How are we doing here?" asked Mr. Sills, as he walked into the fitting room. The air was blue with cigar and cigarette smoke, and he waved his hand to clear it.

"We're doing fine, but I'm running late," said Elias, wanting to get away from Constantine. "How about if you send Sal here up to the house about six, and we can finish the other ten suits up there."

The small room was now very crowded, with Elias, who was large and stout, and Constantine, who was large and slender, Mr. Sills, and Sal, who was still kneeling on the floor, pinning a cuff. Constantine, insufficiently bathed, as usual, increased the foulness of the air. He leaned against the back wall and caught Elias's eye in the mirror. Elias met his stare.

"Do you remember when you were fucking Miss Ruby Nolte in my house on Sutton Place, Elias?" he asked. "When you had no other place to go because your wife, Gladyce, was suspicious of you?"

Sal, the fitter, coughed in astonishment, and the pins in his mouth were spat out on the floor.

"Such language, gentlemen," said Mr. Sills, attempting to make a joke, but he realized that he had walked in at an inappropriate time. He signaled to Sal, and the two of them left the fitting room.

Elias, who understood when to give in on a business negotiation, merely answered, "I'll see that you get sent a card, de Rham."

"That's very kind, Elias," said Constantine, reverting to his charming self.

"But one thing."

"Yes, Elias."

"This invite is for you solo, not you and Mrs. Lupescu."

"Oh?"

"That's right."

"That will make things quite awkward for me."

"As we used to say in Cleveland, tough shit."

"But Yvonne will be so disappointed."

"No way that Ruby will let Yvonne into this party, after what she did at the Altemus wedding."

"The Altemus wedding?"

"She crashed the Altemus wedding. You must have known that."

Constantine looked at Elias. He had not known that Yvonne had crashed Justine Altemus's wedding.

"Not only crashed it. Caught the bride's bouquet," said Elias, imitating Yvonne with a derisive gesture.

Constantine blushed at his mistress's gall. Elias's derision of Yvonne was hurtful to Constantine, not for the pain that her exclusion from the ball would cause her, but for the aspersion that it cast on him that he should be allied with such a woman, who would crash a society wedding.

"Oh, yes," went on Elias. "Yvonne is not in good stead with Lil Altemus. Or Janet Van Degan. And they're both coming to the ball. So it's you alone, or not at all."

"Perhaps, Elias, rather than mail me an invitation to Sutton Place, you would leave it for me at your office with your secretary. That way no one will see it but me."

"Any way you wish," said Elias. Elias had dressed by now and was back in his business suit and ready to go. "Now let me tell you something, you foreign piece of shit," he said. Gone from his voice was any semblance of charm or bonhomie. "It was your dead wife's house I was using, not your house, and you, pimp that you are, were well paid for the use of your dead wife's house. So don't strong arm me again ever." He put his finger right in Constantine's face. "What I know about you could send you to jail."

Weak still from his wound, Constantine de Rham sank into a chair, his face white from Elias's attack.

"See you at the ball, Constantine," said Elias. "Oh, one more thing. Try to remember to take a bath that night, and use a little spray in those moist armpits of yours."

If Elias hoped, by insulting him, to dissuade Constantine from attending the ball, he was to be disappointed. Constantine, the very next morning, appeared at Elias's office and picked up his invitation, on which Ruby Renthal's calligrapher had written the word *Alone* at the top of the engraved ecru card to indicate, in case the point had not been made sufficiently clear in the fitting room at Mr. Sills's, that Yvonne Lupescu was not included.

It was on ladies' day at the Butterfield that Ruby Renthal was introduced for the first time to Ned Manchester, the estranged husband of her great friend, Loelia Manchester.

"Mrs. Renthal, may I present Mr. Manchester," said Laurance Van Degan, making the introduction.

Ned Manchester, whom Ruby had heard so much about, from Loelia and others, was not at all the way she had imagined that he would be. As fair-haired as Mickie was dark, as pink-complexioned as Mickie was olive, as lapis-lazuli–eyed as Mickie was black, as tall, as slender, but with the appearance of a life of sport and exercise rather than rigorous dieting, it was hard for her to imagine that Loelia could have fallen in love with two such different men.

"I know your children," said Ruby.

"I've heard," Ned answered, smiling at her. "They enjoyed visiting you in the country."

"That son of yours is the best-looking young man I've ever seen in my life, and Charlotte is to die she's so pretty," said Ruby.

"Thank you," Ned replied, smiling proudly over his children. Ruby Renthal, whom he had heard used to be a stewardess, was not at all how he expected her to be. In some ways she reminded him of Loelia, at least in the way she talked. "You may know my children, Mrs. Renthal, but I know your house. I used to go to Merry Hill when I was a child. The Grenvilles' son was a friend of mine when we were little."

"I think you probably wouldn't recognize the house," Ruby said.

"That's what I hear. Do you still have the indoor tennis court?"

"Oh, yes. Elias plays every day when we're in the country."

"That's where I learned how to play tennis, on that court."

"You must come and see the house."

"I'd like that, sometime."

"And play tennis. Elias is always looking for a fourth."

It was not a thing Ruby would ever mention to a soul, not even to Elias, but she wondered why her great friend Loelia would find Mickie Minardos more attractive than Ned Manchester. She loved all those people she met every night at dinner, like Ezzie Fenwick and Jamesey Crocus. There was no one more amusing in the city to sit next to at dinner. And the way Mickie Minardos could dance! She was forever telling him that he made her feel like Ginger to his Fred, but when it came to marriage, give her men every time, like Elias. And Ned. Even if they did have two left feet when it came to dancing.

34

G US, LATE, was stopped on the way out his door by the telephone.

"Feliciano here," said the voice on the other end when he answered.

"Oh, yes," said Gus.

"You were out here in L.A., I understand, and you didn't call."

"I was out on personal business," said Gus.

"To see a lady called Marguerite who runs a bar in Studio City," said Feliciano.

Gus paused. "Oh, yes, I did stop in there," said Gus.

"Not smart, Gus," said Feliciano.

"It was to warn her."

"That's not your job, Gus. That's only calling attention to yourself. When whatever happens is going to happen, I don't want you or your name to be involved in any way."

"Yes," replied Gus. He wondered if Mr. Feliciano knew about the gun he had left at the gun shop.

"Marguerite called me. You gave her my card evidently. She thought you were a nut," said Feliciano.

"Listen, I have to go," said Gus.

"It's Sunday morning. Where do you have to go on Sunday morning?"

"Mass," replied Gus.

Gus Bailey, a long lapsed Catholic, had lately, and quietly, returned to his faith. He himself could not understand his revived attachment to God, but attachment it was, even though he sometimes experienced comfort from imagining Lefty Flint dead.

He was surprised that Sunday to see Loelia Manchester sitting several rows ahead of him. She prayed with the intensity of a nonregular attendant at church, one who was there for solace and answers on a particular matter of distress rather than a commitment to religious ritual. Once, when Gus looked over at her, he saw her raise a handkerchief to her eyes and brush away what must have been a tear.

Only leaving, on the church steps outside, did she look and catch sight of him. Her eyes, which had appeared melancholy, sparkled back to attention, as if they had been caught out in an impropriety, and her face assumed the look he had often seen on her when she arrived at parties or when she smiled at photographers at the opera.

"Hellohoware?" she said.

"Good morning," Gus replied.

"Sweet, wasn't he, that little altar boy with the red hair and the Adidas sneakers under his cassock? Couldn't wait, absolutely couldn't wait, could he, to get to the park to play baseball? So sweet." Piety abandoned, she had reverted to her society-woman character.

"I didn't know you were a Catholic," said Gus.

"I'm not," she said. "I was out walking, and I heard the music, and I wandered in."

"They have good music at St. James's too," said Gus.

"True, but I know everyone there, and I didn't think I'd know anyone here. I only go to church when I have troubles."

"I take it you have troubles," said Gus.

Loelia looked at Gus, as if she wanted to say something and then decided against it. "I can't bear all that peace-be-with-you business and shaking hands with all these strange people you've never seen before," she said instead. "I just kept my head bowed, praying like mad all through that part. Is that awful?"

"I'm sure the Pope won't hear about it," said Gus. They both laughed. She opened her bag and took out a gold cigarette case, from which she removed a cigarette.

"I don't have a match," said Gus.

"I do," she said, lighting her cigarette with a lighter. She inhaled deeply.

"My mother used to say that no lady ever smoked a cigarette on the street. So much for early training, Mr. Bailey."

"Gus," he answered.

"Is it true that you had my husband to dinner in your apartment?"

"No, it's not true. I've never had anyone to dinner in my apartment. I don't know how to cook."

"But he came to your apartment."

"He came to my apartment for a drink."

"How did that come about?"

"It was the night I saw you and Mickie at Maisie Verdurin's."

"I know."

"A friend of mine brought him by for a drink."

"Was the friend of yours who brought my husband by for a drink Matilda Clarke?"

"Yes."

"She seems to have a thing for the men in my family. She once had an affair with my father, when her husband was in one of those alcohol places in Minnesota he was always being sent to."

Gus made no reply.

"After you left for Maisie Verdurin's party, did Matilda and my husband stay on in your apartment?"

"This is a conversation I don't think I want to be in," said Gus.

"I'm sorry. Of course you don't."

"Which way are you walking?"

"Up."

"I'm walking down."

"Gus. My friends all seem to know you, but I don't. I don't suppose I could talk you into coming to have tea with me one day this week. I live at the Rhinelander."

"Sure."

"How about tomorrow?"

"Sure."

Entering the suite in the Rhinelander Hotel that had been Loelia Manchester's home since she moved out of the apartment she shared with Ned Manchester and their children, Gus was aware of rooms that had been transformed, even for a transitory period, to the specific requirements of a woman long used to beauty and luxury. Loelia was standing, her back to him, as if looking out the window. As Gus walked farther into the room, she, without turning to greet him, raised her hand, which held a cigarette, to halt him. On the stereo Beethoven was playing; the Leonore Overture from *Fidelio*; Loelia remained transfixed until its grand conclusion. Then her back, so straight, collapsed. "Please forgive me, Gus. I cannot resist *Fidelio* when I hear it, especially the Leonore Overture."

"I feel that I have come at a wrong moment," said Gus.

"It's all right, Gus," said Loelia. Sitting, she lit another cigarette.

Loelia Manchester, he saw, was fastidious in everything but her cigarette habits. Her smoking was constant and slightly furtive, as if she had been told over and over again that smoking was bad for her, a filthy habit, and that statistics showed all sorts of dire consequences were in store if she did not stop, but she, powerless, could do nothing but continue, even in the face of constant disapproval. She only half stubbed out the butts into a green Meissen dish that served as an ashtray. A dozen or more butts already lay smoldering and smoking there, but she seemed not to notice. With a table lighter she used with two hands, she lit another cigarette.

"You didn't really want tea, did you?" she asked suddenly.

"No."

"Lil Altemus tells me you don't drink."

"That's right."

"How about a Coke? Will that do?"

"Perfect."

"I'll have one too. I drink about twenty Cokes a day. I seem to have all the noncriminal addictions, cigarettes and caffeine."

She rose and went into a small kitchenette to get the Coca-Colas. He could hear the sounds of a refrigerator door being opened and closed, of ice being removed from an ice tray, of glasses, of bottles being opened, of pouring. Looking around the room he thought, how alike they all are, these women. Bowls of roses, dozens of buds and blossoms, were on every table, all arranged, he knew by now, by Lorenza. Scented candles, needlepoint pillows, baskets for magazines, sofas covered in chintz, photographs in silver frames. Their houses were beautiful, and expensive, and interchangeable. When Loelia came back into the room, she carried a silver tray with the two glasses. She handed him a small linen napkin on which to place his glass, in which a thin slice of lemon had been placed. Her mind, he could see, had remained fixed on the cause of her distress during her bartending duties.

"I'm afraid you might laugh."

"I won't."

"The listener, they call you."

"Who calls me that?"

"Ezzie Fenwick. He says you're going to write about us all."

"Then don't tell me."

"But I have this urge to talk to you."

"Then I'm listening."

"It's not as if I am unaware of the consequences of falling in love with a man like Mickie Minardos. I am aware. I would have criticized any friend of mine who did what I did, but I can't help it. It is like another of my addictions. I cannot give him up. I absolutely adore him."

Gus did not reply.

"When I am not with him, I cannot stop thinking about him," she continued. "There's nothing about him I don't know, and I don't care. He's a snob. I know he's used me to make it socially in New York, but I don't care. He's bad-tempered at times. But when he's a good boy, and he's a good boy more than he's a bad boy, there is no one whom I've ever known I would rather be with. And the presents he gives me, to make up, are perfect, always perfect, exactly right."

Gus looked out the window.

"You see, he is frustrated by his enormous success because he wanted to be a success designing for the ballet and the opera, but he became a millionaire designing these damn shoes that he hates so much, and, in the meantime, all his creative energies are being wasted."

Gus, the confessor again, merely stared at Loelia.

"Mickie fell in love with my feet. Did you know that?"

"How would I know that?" asked Gus.

"He adores feet."

"I see."

"I, of course, had heard of people who admired feet, but I had never met anyone, nor ever expected to for that matter."

"Yes, of course."

"He likes me to wear shoes with very high heels, and black stockings, with seams up the back. Rather tartlike. Imagine! Me! He likes to watch me walk in them, back and forth across a room, his eyes riveted on my feet. He then likes to take off my shoes, very slowly, first one and then the other, the left one always first for some reason, touching, rather featherlike, the back of my legs and the bottom of my feet."

Gus, embarrassed, rose. "Would you mind if I got myself another Coke?" he asked.

Loelia nodded that she didn't mind and continued talking. "My own mother barely nodded to me when I saw her at Flora Spalding's memorial service. My brothers are tolerant but disapproving, and my sisters-in-law are, of course, siding with my mother. My daughter, Charlotte, played Roxanne in *Cyrano de Bergerac* at St. Cyprian's and didn't ask me to any of the three performances. I only found out she was in the play from Violet Bastedo, who has a daughter in the same school. Yesterday, before I saw you in church, my son, Bozzie, told me he wouldn't spend his summer vacation with me if Mickie was about. I know it's a terrible thing for a mother to say that she loves one child more than another, but it's true. It's always been rare and special between Bozzie and me, and now he doesn't want to have anything to do with me because of Mickie. But I can't give up Mickie, Gus. I can't. I just can't."

35

AS THE BALL drew near, Lorenza, the florist, and Mickie Minardos, the designer, fought bitterly for artistic supremacy, and each complained to Ruby Renthal about the other. Mickie called Lorenza a shop girl, and Lorenza called Mickie a prima donna. Lorenza thought her bowers for lilies and tulips and orchids were going to be overwhelmed by the weeping willow trees that Mickie thought were a necessity for the ten thousand live butterflies, in yellow and orange colors, that he planned to release at midnight on the night of the ball itself, and Mickie thought that Lorenza's bowers for lilies and tulips and orchids were no more than a backdrop to the fantasy of flora and fauna into which he was transforming the Renthal ballroom. Finally people had stopped referring to the apartment as Matilda Clarke's old apartment, or the Sweetzer Clarke apartment; it had become, if not forevermore, at least for now, the Elias Renthal apartment, and Matilda Clarke herself, who had lived in it for twenty-two years, could not recognize it as having been her own.

After midnight on the night before the ball, fifty flower arrangers and scene builders arrived at the Renthal triplex to begin the transformation of the first-floor rooms into sit-out rooms and the ballroom into a fairyland of flowers and twinkling lights for the ball. For Elias, who needed his sleep, the sounds of hammering and talking were too much, and he departed for the Rhinelander Hotel around the corner on Madison Avenue to secure his rest.

The weeping willow trees that Mickie Minardos insisted were absolutely essential to the décor of the Renthals' ballroom were too large by far to fit in the freight elevators of the building, and cranes were hired to raise the trees the sixteen floors from the street to the penthouse floor. Windows on that floor had to be removed for the trees to get into the apartment. When the crane stalled between the fifteenth and sixteenth floors, a workman, Julio Martinez, reached out to keep the weeping willow from swinging into the windows of the apartment below and fell to the ground. As if aware of the exclusiveness of the neighborhood he was working in at that hour, his fall to his death was unaccompanied by a scream.

Elias, asleep finally at the Rhinelander, was roused by a call from an hysterical Ruby. "Come back immediately, Elias," she said, crying. "Something terrible has happened."

In case the point was not made a police car arrived at the hotel to bring Elias the half block from the hotel to his apartment.

"This is a terrible thing," said Elias Renthal, and then repeated, "a terrible thing," all the time pacing back and forth on Fifth Avenue in front of his building, a fat cigar in his hand, waiting for the ambulance to arrive and put the mangled body of Julio Martinez in a body bag.

"We won't have to cancel the party, will we, Elias?" asked Ruby, nervously, when the policemen and foreman were out of hearing distance. She had pulled on a sweater over a pair of trousers.

Elias, without an answer for once, just looked at her.

"I know it sounds awful, Elias, but we have to be practical. The First Lady told me this evening when I was talking to the White House that she is ninety percent sure she's going to be here. She's opening a drug center or orphanage or something in Harlem. The Castorias have arrived from England and are staying at the Rhinelander. There are people from all over the world here for the party. We're going to look like fools."

"I don't know how I can keep this out of the papers, Ruby," said Elias.

"Bucks, Elias, bucks," said Ruby. "You once told me that there's nothing that bucks can't do."

"It ain't going to look good: father of four kids falls to his death raising weeping willow trees sixteen floors up to a forty-one-room apartment at two o'clock in the morning so the Elias Renthals can carry out a butterfly theme for their ball for four hundred guests from around the world."

"You sound like you used to work on a newspaper."

"Well, that's what it's going to be. Count on it."

"You can delay it being in the newspapers until after the party, Elias. Or at least have it buried in the back pages."

"How?"

"You're the country's success story, Elias. Figure it out."

"Help me, Ruby."

"What's the poor man's name?"

"Julio Martinez."

"He's got four kids?"

"And a widow."

"As soon as it's light, let's get in a car and go out to the house, in Queens or wherever he lives. Bring some lawyers with us. Set up educational trusts so that each kid's college education is paid for. Pay off the mortgage on their house so it's free and clear. Set up a trust fund for Mrs., uh, what's-her-name again?"

"Martinez," said Elias.

"For Mrs. Martinez, guaranteeing her an income for life that exceeds the yearly salary of her husband."

"That's a good idea, Ruby," said Elias, recovering himself.

"We'll go to the wake. We'll say the rosary. We'll send flowers like they never saw before and provide the limousines for the funeral."

"What about the papers?"

"Workmen are always falling off cranes. Just see that the address isn't given and our names aren't mentioned."

"You're a wonder, Ruby," said Elias.

"Are you carrying one of those big gangster rolls of bills in your pocket, Elias?" asked Ruby.

"Yeah, why?"

"Big tips to all the cops, all the doormen, and bonuses to every guy on the crane crew, after they get the last weeping willow tree up to the sixteenth floor."

Late in the afternoon on the same day, Bernard Slatkin telephoned his wife Justine at Bobo's hairdressing salon, where she was having her hair set with ribbons and rubrum lilies to match the new dress Nevel had designed for her to wear to the Renthals' ball that night.

"Just wait till you see me," said Justine to Bernie, looking at herself in the mirror while Bobo continued his work. "Bobo is so clever. He's taken the centers out of the rubrum lilies, the yucky part that gets all over your fingers and makes everything such a mess, and they look so beautiful. Why haven't I ever thought to do that? Now, don't tell me you're going to be late."

Justine's joyful attitude changed to one of dismay when Bernie told her to back out of the Renthals' party because there was something important that he wanted to talk to her about. Concerned with propriety, she wanted to plead that she couldn't, absolutely couldn't, upset Ruby Renthal's seating arrangement at the last minute like this, especially as they were two of only forty people who had been asked to dine first before the swarms of people came in after dinner for the dancing, but there was something in Bernie's voice and manner that forbade her from doing that. He was probably, she thought, calling from the control room at the studio and would hate to have to carry on that kind of conversation, about seating, with his buddies from the newsroom listening. "Justine's Crises," Bernie once told her his friends in the studio said about her kind of problems.

"Everyone will be there," said Justine wistfully, although she knew, even as she said those words, that they would not entice Bernie to change his mind, because, unlike most of the people she knew, missing a party where "everyone" would be was not a matter of great concern to him. What Justine feared more than anything else in the whole world was that Bernie was going to tell her that they were going to be transferred to Los Angeles and that he was going to have his own show as sole anchorman. Justine hated, absolutely hated, Los Angeles.

She didn't want to tell Bobo, after all his work, to take out the flowers and ribbons because she wasn't going to go to the ball at the Renthals' after all, so they were still in her hair when Bernie came home from the newscast. When she called Ruby to back out of the dinner, she was told that Ruby was attending a wake in Queens, which seemed odd to Justine, but that she would be back by seven, an hour before her dinner.

"Who is this speaking?" asked Justine, not recognizing the voice.

"This is Mrs. Renthal's calligrapher."

"Her what?" asked Justine.

"Her place-card writer."

"Oh," said Justine. "Just the right person. Will you tell Mrs. Renthal that an emergency has arisen, and Mr. and Mrs. Bernard Slatkin will have to cancel for this evening."

"Oh, dear," said the calligrapher.

When Elias and Ruby made their second call of the day on the family of Julio Martinez in Queens, this time at the Margetta Funeral Home, for the wake, they expected to stay only ten minutes. Neither realized that the arrival of Father Francis X. Mulcahey, from the Church of Our Lady of Perpetual Sorrow, whom they felt it was politic to meet before departing, signaled the saying of the rosary.

"It's a great pleasure to meet you," said Father Mulcahey. His gentle voice still bore the traces of his Irish birth. "Poor Teresa has told me of your generosity to the family during their great loss. Now, if you'll just sit here behind Teresa and the children, we'll be kneeling for the rosary. Are you Catholic, Mr. Renthal?"

"No, no, I'm not," said Elias.

"Mrs. Renthal?"

"Uh, no," said Ruby. She had been once, but wasn't anymore, and didn't want to get into the matter, at least at this time, with forty guests arriving for dinner in two hours, and four hundred for dancing thereafter.

"We'll be saying the Sorrowful Mysteries," said Father Mulcahey.

Elias and Ruby looked at each other, dismayed. The massive bouquets of lilies and roses that they had sent were displayed near Julio Martinez's closed casket, mingled with the carnation and stock sprays, with lavender ribbons and gold condolence lettering, that had been sent by family friends and relations, and the air in the un-air-conditioned room was oversweetened and close.

"I hate the smell of stock," whispered Ruby. She took a perfumed handkerchief from her bag and held it up to her nose. "How many of these Sorrowful Mysteries are there?"

"You're asking me?" Elias answered.

"The first Sorrowful Mystery. The Agony in the Garden," said Father Mulcahey. "Our Father, Who art in heaven, hallowed be Thy name, Thy kingdom come, Thy will be done,—"

"Bobo's coming to do my hair at six," whispered Ruby, pulling back the sleeve of her dark blue suit to steal a look at her oval-shaped Cartier watch with the Roman numerals that had once belonged to the Duchess of Windsor.

"He'll wait," whispered back Elias.

"Hail Mary, full of grace, the Lord is with thee," said Father Mulcahey, and the other mourners in the room prayed along with him.

"I still have to put out the place cards," whispered Ruby.

"Just don't seat me anywhere near Rochelle Prud'homme," whispered back Elias.

"The second Sorrowful Mystery," said Father Mulcahey. "The Scourging at the Pillars."

Dorisette, the youngest of Julio Martinez's children, began to cry. "Daddy, Daddy," she wailed, by the side of her father's casket, as Teresa Martinez held on to her, and her older brothers and sisters patted her head.

"Do you think I dare faint?" whispered Ruby.

Elias looked around him in the crowded room of the funeral parlor and considered the logistics of his wife's suggestion. If his chauffeur and his bodyguard had been in the room, he could have signaled them to pick up Ruby after her faint and carry her out, but he had asked them to remain in the limousine, so as not to appear conspicuous during what he had supposed would be a ten-minute call. He arrived at the conclusion that a faint would cause further delays with the upheaval that would certainly occur among the mourners. "No," he whispered.

"Then make a beeline for the door after the last Sorrowful Mystery," whispered Ruby.

That afternoon, in the prestigious law firm of Weldon & Stinchfield, a weeping young lawyer named Byron Macumber was arrested and handcuffed and taken out the rear entrance and down the service elevator, so as to attract a minimum of attention. It happened that Gus Bailey, still investigating the financial affairs of the late wife of Jorgie Sanchez-Julia for the article he was writing, was in the law firm at the time and witnessed the hasty exit.

"What happened?" Gus asked.

Beatriz Love, the young lawyer with whom he was meeting, simply shrugged her shoulders in a gesture that indicated she knew nothing of the matter at hand. She pushed her horn-rimmed spectacles up on her nose with her forefinger and returned her attention to the court papers in a manila file folder in front of her.

Gus Bailey knew when not to press, and he went on with his questions about the tangled estate of the crippled septuagenarian millionairess Geraldine Sanchez-Julia, establishing a friendly rapport with Beatriz Love at the same time. It was when he finished his questions and was ready to leave that he said, referring back to Byron Macumber, "Rather a dramatic exit for that poor fellow, wasn't it?"

"Hmm," answered Beatriz.

"Must have a wife and kids, a young man that age," said Gus.

"Two daughters," said Beatriz Love.

"Whatever could he have done?" Gus asked, in a rhetorical fashion, as if he didn't expect an answer. Gus had a way, even with lawyers, of having people tell him more than they planned, so he was not surprised when she added, "Something about an account in a Swiss bank in the Bahamas."

"Ah, the plot thickens," said Gus.

"Look for a very big head to roll," she said in a low voice, looking out the door of her glass cubicle to make sure that no one was watching.

"Here at Weldon and Stinchfield?" Gus asked.

"Oh, goodness no, not here."

Gus stared at her, knowing that more was to come. She mouthed but did not speak the two words, "Elias Renthal." If he had not been so stunned by the name she mouthed, he would have asked Beatriz Love if she knew Lil Altemus.

After he had said good-bye to her and thanked her for her help on the Jorgie Sanchez-Julia story, Gus, leaving, asked, "Does Elias Renthal know?" But Beatriz Love merely shrugged her shoulders. She had told him quite enough, far more than she intended, and she started putting Geraldine Sanchez-Julia's will back in the file folder.

"He's giving a ball this evening," said Gus.

"Oh, yes, I've read about the Renthals' ball in Dolly De Longpre's column," said Beatriz. "Didn't the Duchess of Richmond give a ball on the night before the Battle of Waterloo?"

All the way uptown in the subway Gus wondered if he should tell Ruby Renthal what he had heard. He felt very close to Ruby since the first night they met at Maisie Verdurin's party when she told him about her violent experience with Lefty Flint.

Late in the day he telephoned her.

"Oh, my God, Mr. Bailey. You're not backing out of dinner, are you?" asked the social secretary who answered the telephone. There was a note of hysteria in her voice. "Mr. and Mrs. Slatkin just backed out, and Mrs. Renthal is going to have a *fit* when she returns. It throws off the whole *placement*, and it's next to impossible to get anyone at this time of the day to fill in."

"Mrs. Renthal is not there?" asked Gus, surprised.

"No, the Renthals are attending a wake in Queens," said the secretary, in an exasperated voice that plainly said that she didn't understand what people like the Renthals were doing attending a wake in Queens, of all places, in the late afternoon of the evening of their ball when there were tables to be seated, decisions to be made, and a temperamental Mickie Minardos to be dealt with, not to mention Bobo, the hairdresser.

"Do you know what time they'll be back?" he asked.

"You're not backing out, are you?" she asked again, as if she could not deal with one more problem.

"No, no, I'm not backing out."

"Thank God."

"Would you have Mrs. Renthal call me when she returns? There's something rather important I must talk to her about," said Gus.

"Oh, Mr. Bailey, I really don't think it will be possible for her to call you when she returns. The calligrapher is going to have to do the new place cards when Mrs. Renthal finds someone to replace the Slatkins, and Mr. Minardos has a million problems for her to deal with, and, oh dear, Bobo, her hairdresser Bobo, is out of his mind with anxiety that she's not here, because he has to go from here to the Rhinelander to do the First Lady's hair. Oh, my God, I wasn't supposed to mention the First Lady. Forget I said that, will you, Mr. Bailey, so you see, it won't be possible for her to call you, but perhaps you can pull her aside during the evening and tell her whatever it is. Is that all right?"

"Sure," said Gus.

"I loved your article on the dictator's wife."

"Thanks."

When Ruby returned home at seven, she called Justine right away and said, "You can't. You can't do this to me, Justine. I'll never be able to replace you at this hour." Poor Justine, who wanted to go more than anything in the world, begged Ruby's forgiveness but said there was nothing she could do, absolutely nothing, and was, when Bernie arrived home, still smarting from the ice-cold freeze in Ruby's tone of voice when Ruby said good-bye to her. She thought of calling back and suggesting Nestor and Edwina Calder as replacements, but then remembered that they were going to Maisie Verdurin's dinner before the ball. Then she thought of the Trouts, everyone's favorite poor couple, the Trouts, who could always be counted upon to change their own plans and substitute when there was a *placement* emergency, like the one she had just created. But then Bernie arrived home, and it was not a problem that she felt she could inflict on Bernie, who never had understood the importance of things like that, which was one of the things she most loved about him.

For a while the inevitable conversation they were both dreading, for different reasons, was postponed as they decided at what restaurant they would have dinner. Bonita, their cook, was off, because Justine had thought they would be dining at the Renthals', but the cook was off most nights, as Bernie and Justine had never, in the ten months of their marriage, dined at home unless they were having guests. Justine hated Joe and Rose's, which was Bernie's kind of restaurant. Too meat-and-potatoes for her. And Bernie hated Harry's, which was Justine's kind of restaurant. Too "Hi, darling," for him. In the end Justine suggested Clarence's, even though she had had lunch at Clarence's. It was easy, she said. Nearby. And, of course, there was never a problem of getting a table, even if the place was packed, because Justine was a particular favorite of Chick Jacoby's, and room was always made for Justine Altemus, which Chick persisted in calling her, even after she became Justine Slatkin, with or without a reservation. Besides, she said, Clarence's would probably be empty tonight, because everyone, absolutely everyone, was going to be at the Renthals' ball in their new apartment.

For a long time, during the salad and the chicken paillard, Bernie talked about Reza Bulbenkian, an Iranian American who had made a fortune in oil tankers in the Persian Gulf, and had moved to New York after the death of the Shah, where he had increased his fortune by buying up small companies who were likely targets for takeovers, in much the same manner that Elias Renthal was doing. Justine realized that the conversation about Reza Bulbenkian, whom Bernie had interviewed on television earlier that evening, was a way of avoiding the conversation about whatever it was that was so damn important they had to miss the Renthals' ball, but each of them clung to it desperately, as if what Bernie was saying really mattered.

"I've seen him. He has an enormously fat wife," said Justine, feigning interest in the conversation, while she kept staring at Yvonne Lupescu and Constantine de Rham, who were dining together in silence farther back in the restaurant. Justine wanted to tell Bernie to turn around and look at the outfit Yvonne was wearing: a red turban, red blouse, and red knickers with red bows tied at her knees, but there was something about Bernie tonight that made her think it was wiser to listen to him talk about Reza Bulbenkian, in whom she had no interest whatsoever.

Once, when she thought the moment had come for the topic at hand, which she still assumed to be his transfer to Los Angeles to become sole anchorperson of his own news program, she delayed the conversation by describing to him the latest news on the wonders of the Renthals' ball, descriptions of the dresses that her friends would be wearing, and an account, as reported by Bobo, of the terrible fights that had occurred between Mickie Minardos and Lorenza, hoping that he might say, still, this late, "Oh, hell, let's go," but he didn't.

"I'm surprised to see the Slatkins here," said Yvonne Lupescu to Constantine de Rham. "Certainly they were invited."

Constantine, who had still not told Yvonne that he had been invited but she hadn't, postponed telling her, fearing her rage. Although he knew that she would never shoot him again, he feared that she would make a spectacle of herself, in her rejection, and do something untoward, like crashing the party, as she had crashed Justine's wedding. True to his word, Elias Renthal had left an invitation for Constantine with his secretary for Constantine to pick up. It was only for the ball. It had not been arranged for him to attend any of the ten big dinner parties that were being given before the ball, the two major ones being the Renthals' own dinner for forty in their dining room for the Earl and Countess of Castoria, their guests of honor, and Maisie Verdurin's dinner for sixty.

At home, his evening shirt was ready to be slipped into, the diamond-and-ruby studs and cuff links that Consuelo had given him for a wedding present in their proper holes. His white tie was even already tied and had only to be clipped on. His black silk stockings were in his black patent-leather evening pumps. Everything was in readiness. Only his fear of telling Yvonne that he was going off without her had to be dealt with.

"You've trimmed your beard, Constantine," said Yvonne, suddenly.

"Yes, yes, I have," answered Constantine.

"Have you had a manicure, too?"

"Yes, at the same time."

"Anyone would think you're going to the Renthals' ball."

"So likely," replied Constantine, nervously.

"I can't stand another evening of sitting home and watching television," said Yvonne, sulkily. Several times she had tried to get Justine's eye to wave at her, but Justine had not responded to her smiles.

"What do you have in mind?" asked Constantine.

"What about a movie?"

"Which?"

"I don't know which."

"Perhaps Chick Jacoby will have a newspaper," said Constantine, an idea beginning to form in his mind.

"Chick Jacoby is not here tonight," answered Yvonne, bitterly. "Chick Jacoby is at Maisie Verdurin's dinner before the Renthals' ball, at Maisie's table even, seated between Mrs. Frazier and Mrs. French."

"How in the world do you know all that?" asked Constantine.

"Maids," said Yvonne, wearily.

"There is a film on Fifty-eighth Street that I wouldn't mind seeing," said Constantine.

"Which?" asked Yvonne.

"I don't remember the name, but it's supposed to be terribly good." At last, he had figured out his plan.

During the grapefruit sorbet, Bernie told Justine that he wanted a divorce.

Justine, stunned, simply stared at her husband. She sat at the table for several minutes without saying a word and didn't even hear Michael, the waiter with the little ponytail whom she liked and regularly chatted with, when he asked her if she wanted regular coffee or decaffeinated. Instead, she stood up and walked through the restaurant, past the table where Constantine de Rham was paying his bill, to the ladies' room, where she threw up, rinsed out her mouth, reapplied her lipstick, removed and flushed down the toilet the seven rubrum lilies that Bobo had taken so long to set in her hair.

When she sat down again at her table, she said, quietly, "I haven't even written my thank-you notes yet."

"What thank-you notes?" asked Bernie.

"For the wedding presents."

"Oh."

"Is it Brenda Primrose?" asked Justine.

"Brenda Primrose?" replied Bernie, in a voice that stated the utter absurdity of the idea.

"Hubie told me he saw you dining with Brenda Primrose at an obscure restaurant in the Village."

"In the first place, Justine, how in the world would Hubie Altemus even know who Brenda Primrose was?"

"He didn't, by name. He recognized her from the wedding. He said she was beautiful with horn-rimmed spectacles. It was I who put the name to her. I told him she wrote your copy."

"She does not write my copy," said Bernie, annoyed. "I write my own copy. She does my research."

"Split hairs at this point. Is it Brenda Primrose?"

"It is not Brenda Primrose."

The waiter brought their decaffeinated coffee.

"Michael," said Justine, who had been raised to observe public appearance before all else. "Could you bring me some Sweet 'n Low?"

"Yes, Mrs. Slatkin," said Michael, taking a slightly moist packet from his shirt pocket.

"I never understand why Chick Jacoby is so stingy with the Sweet 'n Low," said Justine. Tears welled up in her eyes.

"Justine, your tears are falling in your grapefruit sorbet," said Bernie, glancing around to see if they were being observed.

Justine looked out the window of the restaurant until she was pulled together.

"It pains me if I have hurt you, Justine," said Bernie.

"Is your decision to leave me irrevocable?"

"Yes."

"Then let's not prolong this conversation."

"This is the movie that you wanted to see?" asked Yvonne. "I thought you despised this kind of movie."

"It's meant to be awfully good, I hear," replied Constantine.

"I love horror movies myself," said Yvonne.

"Would you like popcorn?" asked Constantine.

"A big box," said Yvonne.

When he returned to their seats with the box of popcorn, Yvonne was already immersed in the film and only nodded her thank you when he handed her the box.

"I'm going to go to the men's room," he whispered to her, after looking at the film for ten minutes.

She merely nodded again, her eyes glued to the screen.

The theater was only a five-minute walk from his house on Sutton Place. He raced there, as fast as he could race, recovering as he was from the bullet wound in his stomach. It took him only minutes to change from his blazer and slacks to his tail coat and trousers. He buttoned his ruby-and-diamond studs and cuff links, snapped on his white tie, combed through his beard, eyed himself admiringly in the mirror, and left his house. He wanted to be gone from there in the event that Yvonne missed him in the theater and returned to the house herself to look for him. He had at least an hour and a half still before the ball started, and the problem now was where to wait until the dinner parties that preceded the ball were over.

"I'm just not happy, Justine," said Bernie. They were sitting now in the living room of their apartment, one of the few times since their marriage began that they had been home, just the two of them. He talked about political aspirations that he had, saying, truthfully or not, that his alliance with a family as rich and powerful as the Van Degans would be inconsistent with his own liberal views and that now, before children, the marriage should be terminated. Home, away from public view, Justine sat on the arm of a sofa, her mouth hanging open, in a near catatonic state. How, she wondered, had she not suspected that she was losing her husband.

"I love you, Bernie," she said, finally, as the tears started to pour out of her wounded eyes. "I love you with all my heart and soul and mind and body. Please don't leave me, Bernie. Please."

"Don't cry, Justine," said Bernie, when he saw the tears welling up in her eyes. "Please don't cry."

Bernie felt helpless with tears. Anger he could have dealt with, but not tears. Many women had screamed at him and called him terrible names when he broke off relations with them, and it was like water on his back. For the sobbing woman in front of him, who was his wife, whose heart he was breaking, he felt compassion. He put his arms around her, patting her more than embracing her, a signal of the ebbing of love that she did not understand.

"I love you so much," she said over and over, putting her tear-stained face next to his, as if her declarations could revive his lost ardor.

"I wish I knew the right words to comfort you," he said. While he was talking, she stared down at his hands. What beautiful hands he has, she thought. She could remember when those strong hands had fondled her breasts and between her legs, with the gentleness of a feather. She longed to touch the hairs on the back of his wrist. Her desire for him was so great she felt as if she were going to swoon.

"Are you all right, Justine?" he asked.

"What?"

"You look ill."

"Fuck me, Bernie," she whispered.

"Justine," he said, amazed.

"Please, Bernie. Please. Just one more time. Please."

"Justine, it's not going to do any good. It's over."

"I know, Bernie. Please. Don't leave me in this state. Just once. Please."

She began kissing the backs of his hands. She put her own hands on his chest and started rubbing his nipples through his shirt. She brought her hands down to his trousers. She wanted to rip them open and get to the part of him that she had dreamed about for the weeks that he had been indifferent to her.

"Justine, for God's sake. Don't do this to yourself."

She slid to the floor and threw her arms around his legs, pushing her face into the fly of his trousers. She looked up at him, tears streaming down her face. He could not bear to see her in such a state and felt pity for her. Slowly, he reached down and lifted her up by placing his hands under her arms and carried her to the sofa.

He raised her dress up to her waist and slowly pulled her pantyhose down her legs to her shoes. When he placed his hand between her legs, she was wet with desire for him. He took off the jacket of his dark suit, unbuckled his belt, unzipped his fly, and let his trousers drop to the floor. As Justine stared at his legs, he kicked off his trousers and pulled down his undershorts, but he did not remove his shirt or tie, shoes or socks. Standing over her, he allowed her to bring his penis to erection with her hands and mouth, but he did not touch her breasts or kiss her lips. When he was ready, he lifted her legs and entered her, without speaking a word. He pushed in to the limit of himself and then he partially withdrew, and then he pushed himself in again, and again, and again, with long and even strokes. He did not rush her. Sex was a thing he understood, and he withheld his own climax until she had achieved hers, with gasps and muffled screams. When his climax followed, he did not pretend to not enjoy the feeling it brought, and Justine watched his face, his closed eyes, his slack mouth, as he quietly moaned and flooded her insides with the seed of a child. Finished, he did not immediately withdraw from her, but remained inside her as she ran her fingers over his buttocks and down between his legs.

She lay where she was as she watched him dress. She understood the finality of his lovemaking and did not beg him again not to leave her. Dressed, he talked briefly about his clothes, and possessions, and when they should be picked up.

"Good-bye, Justine," he said, finally.

"Good-bye, Bernie," she replied. She stared after him as he walked out of the living room, into the hall, and out the front door. She did not move from her position as she listened to him ring for the elevator. She heard the elevator arrive at their floor, heard the heavy door open, heard the night elevator man say "Good evening, Mr. Slatkin," heard Bernie reply, "Good evening, Willie," heard the elevator door close. Only then did she rise from the sofa. She walked to the window that looked down on Park Avenue, hid a bit behind the green drapery, and looked down to the street below. She watched him come out from under the canopy of the building, saw him turn to say good-night to the doorman and walk up Park Avenue to the corner. She dropped the curtain, raised the window, and leaned out as she watched him hail a cab, get in, and take off. She did not know where he was going to spend the night. She only knew that it was not going to be with her, that night, or ever again. "Good-bye, Bernie," she said again, this time to herself. Walking back to turn off the lights and puff up the cushions before Bonita, her maid, came in the morning, she saw the white stain, still wet, of Bernie's seed on the green damask of her sofa.

In the Presidential Suite at the Rhinelander, the First Lady, exhausted from a visit to an orphanage in Harlem, a home for teenage runaways in Bedford-Stuyvesant, the briefest, quickest lunch at Clarence's with Adele Harcourt, the *grande dame* of New York, an inspection of the AIDS ward at St. Vincent's Hospital, and an address before the New York Council on Alcoholism, was awakened from her rest by a call from a presidential adviser, telling her that it was inadvisable for her to attend the ball that evening, if that was her plan, of Elias and Ruby Renthal, as Mr. Renthal was the subject of a secret investigation by the Securities and Exchange Commission into illegal use of insiders' information.

Meanwhile, at the other end of New York, another dinner was about to take place, of a very different sort, but it was not without social overlaps. In the weeks past, since his Easter encounter with his mother, Hubie Altemus had absented himself from the world, seeing no one except for several visits from his increasingly worried sister, Justine. Juanito had taken over the management of the gallery in SoHo, irritating the regular staff with his newly acquired authority, but, for Hubie, the business was at least being seen to with his own interests at heart. He had stopped returning telephone calls or seeing friends.

On the night of the Renthals' ball, which he had declined, and which he would have declined even if he had not been afflicted, he felt a desire to see some friends and asked four gentlemen of similar inclinations to dine with him at his apartment over the gallery. Hubie was an excellent cook, and his little dinners were usually sought-after invitations, for, although he chose to disassociate himself from the upper-class world in which he had been raised, his china, his silver, his napery, the table at which his guests dined, and the Charles X chairs on which they sat bespoke another existence than the corner of Houston and Greene streets would usually evoke.

The idea of the dinner party was, he knew, a mistake, almost from the beginning of the evening. Juanito, who had been most solicitous of Hubie's welfare in the past weeks, seized upon the dinner party as an excuse for a much needed night off for himself, and, dressed in jeans and leather jacket, with his diamond earring screwed into his ear, he departed the loft before the arrival of the first guest, Boy Fessenden, whom Juanito loathed, referring to him always behind his back as Girl Fessenden. Boy Fessenden had been a roommate of Hubie's at one of the many schools he had been asked to leave, and their friendship had survived, despite Juanito.

Opening the door, Hubie was able to read in Boy's eyes the extent of the devastation of his own features. He had learned to pass mirrors without looking into them; even shaving, he could now concentrate on his stubble and razor without examining his whittled-down, almost indented, cheeks that, in healthier times, he had often sought to reduce by dieting. He knew later, when he was in the kitchen, where he declined culinary assistance, that Boy and the others were talking about him in whispered tones.

"Oh, my God," said Robert.

"He must have it," said Herbie. It was the thing they all most feared.

"That's just the way Sam looked," said Boy.

The meal itself, excellent as always, was, however, a dispirited affair because death was in the air. Boy Fessenden, breaking one of the silences, said, "How sensitively you've cooked the fish, Hubie," and, briefly, they talked about the proper way to roast red snapper. Then Boy, a raconteur, set out to save the evening and made everybody laugh by retelling the story, with embellishments, of Hubie's encounter with the lifeguard at Bailey's Beach when they were both teenagers staying with Hubie's mother in Newport.

"What an exaggerator you are, Boy," said Hubie, laughing, as he got up to clear the dishes. "That wasn't the way it happened at all. You were just lucky that you didn't get caught."

He carried the dishes over to a tray on the sideboard. Ted, a singer, who was Boy's companion, rose to help Hubie. "No, no, Ted," said Hubie. "I can do it. I have it all down to a system."

In the kitchen the chill began to come on him. He sat down for a few minutes, fearing that he might faint. Then he got up and left the kitchen. The others, listening to another of Boy's stories, about two men called Cecil, whom their friends called the two Ceciles, assumed that Hubie was going to the bathroom. In his bedroom, he lay down on the bed and wished that Juanito was there, instead of out tomcatting, which Hubie was sure he was.

"Where the hell is Hubie?" asked Boy fifteen minutes later, when he had not returned. On the kitchen table was a chocolate cake and a silver bowl filled with raspberries, blueberries, and strawberries.

"I thought he went to the bathroom," said Robert.

"I'll knock," said Boy.

The bedroom was dark when Boy went in.

"Hubie?" he asked. There was a note of fear in his voice at what he might find.

"I'm here on the bed," said Hubie.

"What's the matter?"

"Can you get me to Saint Vincent's Hospital, Boy?" asked Hubie.

"Taxi or ambulance?" asked Boy.

"A taxi's okay," said Hubie.

"Why didn't you tell me, Hubie?" asked Boy.

"What good would it have done?"

"What about your doctor?"

"There's her number there. I tried to dial her, but I was too faint. Dr. Alicia Montego," said Hubie.

"Dare I ask where Juanito is at a time like this?" asked Boy.

"Don't knock Juanito, Boy. He's been good to me lately. He needed a night off."

"Should I call your mother? Or Justine?"

"They're at the Renthals' ball. You'll never reach them."

As Mickie Minardos was tied up right until the ball itself with the last-minute preparations, Loelia Manchester was alone that evening. She had asked Gus Bailey to pick her up and take her to Ruby Renthal's dinner for forty before the ball, but Gus had already been asked for by Matilda Clarke and could not oblige Loelia. Dressed and ready, she was planning to walk around the corner to the Renthals' apartment when there was a knock on her door. A man, with a hearing contraption in his ear, whom she immediately recognized as a Secret Service agent, told her that the First Lady would like a word with her in the Presidential Suite on the floor above.

Inside the Presidential Suite, Loelia was surprised to find the First Lady still in her negligee and her hair not yet attended to.

"How pretty you look, Loelia," said the First Lady.

Loelia, complimented, smiled. "Thank you."

"I saw your mother today. Adele Harcourt had a little lunch this noon."

"Mother says unkind things about me these days," said Loelia.

"Not to me she didn't," said the First Lady.

"You're not dressed. Are you not going to the dinner first?"

"No. Nor the ball afterward."

"But why?"

"Oh, reasons."

"You mustn't miss this. You mustn't. Ruby will be crushed. At midnight, you know, ten thousand butterflies, live butterflies, just arrived today from Chile, all yellow and orange, are going to be released in the ballroom. It will be so divine. Please change your mind," pleaded Loelia.

"May I confide in you, Loelia?" asked the First Lady.

"But of course."

"I have heard there is a possibility that . . ." Alone, only the two of them in the room, she whispered in Loelia's ear what had been told to her earlier by the presidential adviser.

"Elias? Never!" cried Loelia, in total dismissal of the absurdity of the charge, as if the Pope himself in Rome had been accused of financial malfeasance.

"You're sure?"

"As sure of anything as I have ever been in my life," said Loelia. "I have never known a friend like Ruby Renthal. Not well born, perhaps, but a delight. She tells me everything, really the most extraordinary things, of extraordinary intimacy. If there were even a possibility of what you are suggesting, she would have told me."

"Perhaps she doesn't know. Perhaps Elias hasn't told her," suggested the First Lady.

"Oh, no, impossible. They have a marvelous marriage. Elias always says about Ruby, 'What a team we are,' and they are. They share everything."

The First Lady, who wanted to be convinced, was.

"I'm so happy to hear that. You know, she gave me those marvelous console tables, with the inlaid rams' heads, for the Green Room of the White House, and I have a special affection for her myself," said the First Lady.

"You'll reconsider then?" asked Loelia.

"Perhaps I'll go for an hour, to see the butterflies."

"I'll come back for you at eleven, if you'd like. It's only around the corner."

The Renthals hired the same red-and-white striped marquee, but covered on both sides, that Justine Altemus had used at her wedding at St. James's, so that their guests could pass into their building without the throngs who had gathered on Fifth Avenue to watch the arrivals of the fashionable folk being able to see the jewels that had been taken out of every vault for the party. It also shielded their guests' eyes from that part of the sidewalk where Julio Martinez had so few hours before fallen to his bloody death.

Whether the new apartment of the Elias Renthals was beautiful or not depended on the eye of the beholder, but it was deemed, by universal consent of the forty favored guests who were asked for the dinner preceding the ball, awesome and magnificent in size and contents. "Never have I seen such pictures," said Lil Altemus, who would have preferred to be in Rome visiting the Todescos, as she always was this time each year, but, alas, Laurance had requested that she postpone her trip until after the ball, and, always, all her life, she had accommodated her brother. Although Lil felt that her hostess had an excessive fondness for ancestral portraits of other people's ancestors—lords and ladies by Sargent, countesses and duchesses by Boldini, and an empress by Winterhalter that she had once seen in a museum—she could not help but be impressed.

"I'm surprised to see you here, Fernanda," said Lil to Fernanda Somerset, the mother of Loelia Manchester, who had only nodded to her daughter when they met in the elevator a few minutes earlier.

"I only came to see the furniture," answered Fernanda.

"How do you suppose these people collect so much in such a short time?" Lil said.

"When Mr. Duveen helped my grandfather collect, it took twenty years for the pictures alone," Fernanda Somerset replied. Then, holding her fingers in front of her mouth, she added, "Ezzie Fenwick tells me the curtains alone cost a million dollars."

"Imagine!" said Lil.

Everything had to move like clockwork that night. The dinner guests, asked for eight sharp, had to be in their seats in the dining room by eight forty, so they could be up and out, four courses later, before the first of the four hundred guests who would be arriving for the ball entered the apartment.

When dinner was announced, Lil looked about for Justine and Bernie, surprised that they were so late. She had heard from Bobo when he had come to her apartment to do her hair how pretty her daughter looked with the rubrum lilies in her hair, and she was eager to see herself how her daughter looked.

"I don't see Justine," said Lil to Ruby when Ruby came to tell them it was time to go into dinner.

"But she canceled at the last minute," said Ruby, surprised that Lil did not know.

"Justine? Canceled? I can't believe it," said Lil. "Bobo told me he set her hair only at five this afternoon."

"She canceled at six. I was at a wake at the time, someone who works for Elias, in Queens, and didn't hear until I got back. I've had such a hard time replacing them, but I finally got the nice Trouts to fill in."

Lil looked quizzical, wondering about Justine.

"Come along, Rochelle," said Ruby to Rochelle Prud'homme. "I'll show you where you're sitting." Although one of the dinner guests was still missing, Ruby, aware that precision was necessary to keep to the schedule of the evening, herded her guests to the dining room. Rochelle, feeling jealous of the magnificence of the Renthals' life-style, was already planning in her mind a party of her own that would rival the Renthals'.

Matilda Clarke, with Gus Bailey on her arm, wandered in silence through the rooms where she had once lived. It was a different kind of opulence than the opulence of Sweetzer Clarke's family, but even she would have to admit, if questioned, that it was an opulence to be reckoned with.

"How lovely you look, Matilda," said Ruby.

"A new dress for the occasion," said Matilda.

"I bought her that dress," whispered Rochelle to Ruby. "Otherwise she would have worn that damn black-and-white polka dot again. Terrible thing to go down the drain like the Clarkes did."

"Dinner for forty and everything matches," said Matilda to Gus, gazing around the dining room while looking for their seats, at the crystal and china and silver, all bearing the letter *R*.

Only a year before Ruby would have said, "I could have dinner for a hundred and everything would still match," referring to the Rothschild cache, but she had learned that Loelia Manchester would never have said such a thing, and now neither did she.

"You sit here, Rochelle," said Ruby, pulling out a chair for her.

Rochelle was concerned always as to where she would be seated, and an excellent seat at table could make her as ecstatic as a humble seat could make her miserable. Now her eyes darted around the dining room. Four tables of ten, she saw, with Lorenza's beautiful arrangements on each. She picked up the place card next to hers to see whom she was seated next to. Augustus Bailey, she read, written in a calligrapher's hand.

"Oh, no, no," she said to Ruby. "I don't want to sit next to a writer. They always want to do articles about me."

"You have the Honduran ambassador on the other side, Rochelle," answered Ruby. "You know Jaime."

"I feel a draft on my shoulders," said Rochelle. "I think I might be cold here from the air conditioning. Where's Elias sitting? I'll sit next to Elias. We're such old friends. I'll move Matilda over here where I was, next to the writer. She brought him anyway, didn't she? I'll sit next to Elias, and the ambassador's wife can go there."

"The Petite Dynamo has ruined my seating," said Ruby to Loelia. "Poor Elias. He begged me not to seat her next to him. Look, my God, the poor ambassador is now seated next to his own wife."

Although Ruby was desirous of becoming a member of only one set in New York, the set that she considered the best and most impenetrable, she, in turn, when she entertained her new intimate friends, always provided a celebrated person from the outside world to enhance the sociability of the evening. She liked hearing it said about her, "Last night I met the famous Dr. Priestly at Ruby Renthal's house." Her celebrated guest of that evening had, alas, not arrived.

Seated, finally, the thirty-nine of them, the waiters, in uniform and white gloves, began bringing in the caviar that made up the first course. Ruby engaged in animated conversation with her guest of honor Binkie Castoria on her right and, like the experienced hostess that she had become, signaled to a waiter to bring the Earl more caviar, for which she noticed he had an inordinate appetite, and, at the same time, with a gesture that indicated approval, let Maude Hoare know that her black dress, just arrived from Paris in time for the party, was perfection.

Arriving late, as she was famous for arriving late, entered the film star Faye Converse, ablaze with diamonds, and every eye in the dining room turned to stare at her. Faye, whose intimate circle of friends was of a more raucous variety than the refined friends of Elias and Ruby Renthal, played her role of movie star to the hilt, apologizing with the greatest charm to Ruby and Elias, both of whom had risen to greet her, as if they were the oldest friends, when, in fact, they were just meeting. A deal had been made, engineered by Gus Bailey, that Faye Converse would attend both the dinner and the ball afterward in exchange for a bountiful contribution toward the cure of the pestilence for which Faye worked so hard, although Elias was attributing to himself a nobility of purpose that was at odds with his true motive. Should his party be criticized in the press for its extravagance, he had in Faye the ready answer, that a contribution of enormous proportions had been made, as he intended to later point out in his speech, "toward a cure for the pestilence that is dwindling the ranks of the artistic community of the city."

Ruby took Faye's arm and led her to what was supposed to have been her place, on the left of Elias, but Rochelle Prud'homme, firmly entrenched in her usurped seat, showed no sign of surrendering it. Blocked by silence from Elias each time she attempted to engage him in conversation, Rochelle assumed that he was a nervous host, which was not the case, and she called across the table to Ezzie Fenwick, as if Ruby and Faye Converse were not standing there.

"The Duchess left me some gold plates," Rochelle called out. "What do you think I should do with them? Use them for ashtrays?"

"Or earrings," answered Ezzie, who had turned over his plate to examine the markings on the back. "China like this you only see today in the showcases of dukes' houses open to the public," he added.

"We've had a mixup with the place cards," whispered Ruby to Faye. "You were supposed to sit next to Elias, but someone, who shall be nameless, switched the cards."

"Sounds just like Hollywood," answered Faye, who couldn't have cared less. "That's what they do out there. Why don't you put me over there next to my friend Gus Bailey?"

When she was seated, Gus said to her, "It was to avoid sitting next to me that Mrs. Prud'homme switched the cards."

"How lucky for me," said Faye, as she picked up her napkin and looked around. When a waiter started to pour wine into one of the four glasses in front of her, she put her hand over the top of it to stop him and ordered a glass of water instead. "Who the hell are all these people, Gus?" she asked.

"To your right is Lord Biedermeier," said Gus.

"Oh, Lucien, how are you, darling? I didn't see you," she said with a laugh that indicated she had known Lucien way back when.

"Next to him is Janet Van Degan, as in Mrs. Laurance Van Degan, and next to her is Herkie Saybrook, and then—"

"Cute, Herkie Saybrook," said Faye. "My third husband looked sort of like Herkie Saybrook."

After the sorbets in assorted colors had been served, Elias rose and tapped a fork engraved with the letter R against a champagne glass engraved with the letter $R,$ and the room was silenced. He thanked the Earl and Countess of Castoria, whom he called Binkie and Antoinette, for the marvelous friendship they had shared with Ruby and him, although, in fact, the friendship was of less than a year's duration, and he told an anecdote about a visit they had made to Castle Castor the previous winter where Ruby got lost in the halls finding her way to dinner. Elias spoke charmingly and received laughter and applause. Then the Earl rose and made a similar toast to Elias and Ruby, thanking them for their friendship and this marvelous party, with the ball still to come, which was being given in their honor. No mention was made in either toast that the Earl of Castoria was a member of the board of directors of Miranda Industries.

Then Elias moved across the room to the table where Faye Converse sat, and spoke about the great star's marvelous career and the forty pictures she had made.

"Sixty, not forty," said Faye, correcting her host, and everyone laughed.

"Isn't she marvelous?" said Maude Hoare.

Elias went on with his toast and told about the good work that Faye Converse was doing with the private time of her life, working to raise funds "toward a cure for the pestilence that is dwindling the ranks of the artistic community." With that, he presented her with a check.

Faye rose to great applause and thanked Elias and Ruby for the wonderful evening that was just beginning and for the check, which she then opened. "My God!" she said, "two million dollars!"

Again the dining room rang out with applause.

"We are an army fighting an enemy that has no allies," said Faye, as she became serious and started to talk about her mission.

"What's she talking about?" asked Fernanda Somerset, who was hard of hearing.

"AIDS," said Lil, mouthing but not speaking the word.

"I thought she said something about an army," insisted Fernanda.

"Look at Aline Royceton's teeth," said Ezzie.

"Still looks pretty, doesn't she?" said Rochelle.

"Who, Aline, for God's sake?"

"No, Faye Converse."

"The speech is too long," said Ezzie.

"Shh," said Ruby.

"How old do you think she is?" asked Rochelle.

No one in the room clapped harder than Lil Altemus at the end of Faye Converse's speech. "So marvelous," she said. Lil, whose own son was at that very moment, a mere sixty blocks to the south of her, being checked into St. Vincent's Hospital by Boy Fessenden, repeated to the Honduran ambassador what she had repeated to her daughter a few weeks earlier. "Bobo, my hairdresser Bobo, says there won't be a man left in New York to hem a dress or hang a curtain," she said, shaking her head sadly for those poor souls, as if it were a thing far removed from her own door and the doors of her friends.

Binkie Castoria, getting drunk, turned to ask Ruby what was this pestilence that was dwindling the ranks of the artistic community, and Ruby turned her attention to him. A waiter named Chet, from the catering service, while nodding a greeting to Gus Bailey, whom he knew from A.A. meetings, inadvertently collided with the waving arms of Ezzie Fenwick, who was keeping his table in convulsions of laughter with an imitation of a model on the runway at the showing of Nevel's new collection the day before, and the bottle of red wine, Lafite-Rothschild, that the waiter was carrying flew from his gloved hand and spewed its ruby content all over the white satin dress of Ruby Renthal. There was a gasp from the Earl, who liked being on the board of directors of Miranda Industries, as well as the other guests at the table, for the ball would shortly be starting, and they all turned to look at the unfortunate waiter whose face turned crimson with embarrassment.

"Oh, Mrs. Renthal, I can't believe I did that," said the waiter, who expected to be fired on the spot.

"Don't be upset," said Ruby, looking down at her ruined dress. "White is such a boring color." Chet, the waiter, looked at her with adoration. With that Ruby left the dining room to change, after asking her guests to go to the drawing room for coffee.

"How marvelous Mrs. Renthal is," said the Earl. "A duchess couldn't have handled that better."

Patriotic since her elevated position as a frequent guest at the White House, Ruby had recently abandoned the French *couture,* "given up the French," she called it, for its American cousins, like Nevel. On the advice of Ezzie Fenwick, who had the ability to minutely observe a woman's dress, tell at a glance if it was from the *couture* or ready-made, identify the designer, quote the price, and remember its distinguishing details days later, Ruby had ordered three different dresses for her great night when she told Ezzie she couldn't decide what to wear. Changing, she also changed her jewelry, her pearls and diamonds making way for her emeralds and diamonds. She remembered a line from a movie she had loved: "If you got it, flaunt it," she said to herself in the mirror.

Returned, redressed, Ruby looked better than ever.

Elias, taking her in, leaned down and kissed her bare shoulder.

"Elias, how sweet," said Ruby.

"You look good enough to eat," he said.

"Watch your language, big boy," she said, in her Mae West accent.

"I love you, Ruby Renthal," said Elias.

Ruby blushed prettily. "Ditto," she said.

"Who woulda thought, the two of us?" whispered Elias.

"Who woulda thought?" Ruby repeated.

Ruby, with Elias by her side, stood in the receiving line, greeting, by name, her four hundred guests, including the French ambassador, the Spanish ambassador, the British ambassador, and various members of the deposed royal families of Yugoslavia, Bulgaria, and Rumania, who recognized certain of the pieces of marvelous furniture in the Renthal apartment as having come from palaces that had once been theirs. In the splendid crowd promenading from room to room, where gypsy violinists played, before descending to the ballroom, where a dance band played Cole Porter music, people who had seen each other as recently as lunch shrieked hellos like long-lost friends and exchanged kisses on each cheek. There were an abundance of social commentators, guaranteeing that the Renthal ball would be duly recorded for social posterity. Strobe lights flashed and the blinding lights of the television cameras went on and off as recognizable faces entered the marble front hall of the vast apartment. In addition to Dolly De Longpre, who was the only member of the press who had been invited to dinner, was young Florian Gray, as well as Mavis Jones, of the show-business columns, who usually did not attend the same parties as Dolly, nor Dolly the same parties as they, but the curiosity value of the Elias Renthals was such that all decided to overlook their differences and attend.

Ezzie Fenwick spoke to Ruby's maid, Candelaria, addressing her by name, establishing himself as a regular visitor to the household, known and smiled upon by its staff. Ezzie could hardly contain himself at the utter splendor of the Renthals' night. He made a rapid tour of inspection of the sit-out rooms, not knowing where to station himself to full advantage to witness the evening, before deciding on a position at the foot of the stairs leading into the ballroom, beneath a weeping willow tree, where he would not miss a single entrance. He was surrounded by women who clung to him to listen to his comments about everyone ("Just the nice Europeans, none of the trashy ones," he said) and compliment him on his pearl studs, as big as marbles, which all agreed, prompted by himself, stacked up to the pearls on any of the necks in the room. He greeted his particular friends, all women, with compliments on their dresses, and did not greet those he did not favor with his friendship. "Hello, Maude," he said. "Hello, Lil." "Hello, Dodo." "Hello, Rochelle." "Hello, Janet." "Hello, Matilda." "Hello, Maisie." "Hello, Adele. Marvelous, that dress." And they, in turn, all replied, "Hello, Ezzie," and kisses on each cheek followed.

"You know everyone, Ezzie," said Bijou McCord, the Texas millionairess who now sought New York recognition.

"Yes," replied Ezzie, beaming with pride and satisfaction for his high position.

Several times his brow furled with displeasure, as someone walked down the stairway whose presence on the invitation list had been unknown to him. The entrance of Constantine de Rham, about whose exclusion he had been particularly vocal to Ruby, came as a shock to him, and he instantly expressed the thought to his companions that de Rham had probably crashed, just the way Mrs. Lupescu, his companion, had crashed the wedding reception of Justine Altemus. "Elias will get rid of him, you mark my words," he said, but, at that moment, Elias, looking for Ruby, came upon Constantine and spoke a greeting to him, not a warm greeting, but the greeting of an important host to an unimportant guest.

Jamesey Crocus arrived with Adele Harcourt, whom everyone called charity herself, for all her good works for the city. Jamesey could always be pressed into service to escort Adele Harcourt, the *grande dame* of New York, and was inclined enough toward literature to have been asked to join Mrs. Harcourt's book club.

"My God, they got everybody," whispered Jamesey Crocus to Adele Harcourt, surveying the crowd through his spectacles, meaning that the *haut monde* had all turned out for the Renthals.

"*Tout* New York," whispered Mrs. Harcourt.

"What are you whispering about?" asked Ruby, walking by.

"I was just saying to Adele that we should read Trollope next in the book club, now that we've finished with the Russians," said Jamesey.

"I was saying what a marvelous job Mickie has done," said Adele Harcourt at exactly the same time.

Mickie Minardos's eyes were shining with the excitement of creativity fulfilled: a symphony composed, an epic written, a masterpiece painted. Compliments were being paid to him from everyone, even, he whispered to Loelia, who was bursting with pride for him, from Adele Harcourt herself. It was what he had always wanted, artistic recognition instead of shoe recognition. Modestly he brushed aside the compliments, without actually saying you-ain't-seen-nothing-yet, but thinking it, because, at midnight, during the waltzes, the spectacle would be enhanced when the ten thousand butterflies, yellow and orange, flown up from Chile only that day, were to be released to fly around the ballroom, in the bowers of flowers and in the weeping willow trees, as the final culmination of what he knew would be called forevermore the most beautiful party of the decade in New York.

"There can't be a yellow tulip left in all Holland!" cried Dodo Fitz Alyn Van Degan, looking at the ballroom.

"These people are spending a fortune to entertain us, and all they want in return is to be accepted by us," said old Ormonde Van Degan, who had been brought down on the freight elevator to see the ballroom before repairing upstairs, away from the music and the crowds, to enjoy a cigar with a few old friends he had spotted, while Dodo and Lil watched the spectacle and the dancing.

"It won't happen," said Lil to her father.

"Oh, yes, it will," said the old man. "It has happened."

Ruby and Elias then took to the dance floor, she with the Earl, he with the Countess, adhering to all the traditions, as if they had been giving grand balls all their adult years. People clapped, but no one clapped harder than Maisie Verdurin, her eyes glistening with tears of pride at the triumph of the Renthals, who had achieved business and social success without benefit of inheritance or heritage. "It's the American dream fulfilled," said Maisie, enthusiastically, to all around her as she continued to clap. Then Laurance Van Degan brought Faye Converse to the dance floor, and Jamesey Crocus followed with Adele Harcourt, and a Yugoslav prince with a Bulgarian princess, and then everyone was on the dance floor.

"Have you ever seen anything so beautiful?" asked Adele Harcourt.

"You've snowed us, Elias," said Janet Van Degan.

When Elias finally danced with Ruby, he thought that she had never looked more beautiful.

"We did it, kiddo," he whispered in her ear.

She smiled at him.

"We're a team," he whispered again.

"A team," she whispered back.

At that moment an ambassador cut in on Elias, but Ruby, before giving herself over to the ambassador, whispered again to Elias, "Don't forget, when the First Lady comes, you and I have to be at the front door to greet her and bring her in, and you have to have the first dance with her."

"I won't forget," said Elias.

"Don't go far. It's getting close," said Ruby.

It was only in retrospect, when the people who had not been invited read about the party in the *News* and the *Post*, and in this case, even the mighty *Times*, which did not usually cover private parties, that the Renthal ball began to develop as a legend that would make it stand out in peoples' minds for years to come. "I read you were at the Renthals' ball," people said. "Tell me everything."

Only the pool room, or the room with the pool table, had been declared off bounds, because the pool table, which had once belonged to Edward VII, still had its original felt, and Elias worried that people might place drinks on it. While Dodo and Lil watched the dancing, Ormonde elected to enjoy a cigar in the company of Lord Biedermeier in a small upstairs room, adjacent to the pool room, usually reserved for cigar smoking and poker playing, which Ruby didn't allow in her main salons.

Lord Biedermeier, whose mind was always on books, even during social occasions, would have liked nothing better than to publish a biography of the Van Degan family, whose roots in the city and the nation—politically, socially, and financially—could be matched by no other family, and it was in this little smoking room that he broached the subject to the octogenarian Ormonde Van Degan, knowing that his cooperation in such a project might entice his son,

Laurance, who was, on general principles, opposed to any form of publicity whatsoever, into agreeing to speak with the biographer he had in mind.

"You're looking particularly well since your marriage, Mr. Van Degan," said Lord Biedermeier, although, in fact, Ormonde Van Degan looked very much at that moment as if he were about to expire. The old man, who usually went to bed at eight, was exhausted by this late-night venture into society, which his son, Laurance, had asked him to attend, and his wife, Dodo, had begged him to attend.

"Who the hell are these people?" Ormonde Van Degan replied, his voice so faint as to barely be heard.

"What people?" asked Lord Biedermeier.

"Who are using my friend Sweetzer Clarke's apartment."

"Oh, I see," replied Lord Biedermeier, laughing. "Our hosts, you mean? Elias and Ruby Renthal. Elias Renthal is one of the richest men in the country."

"I miss Sweetzer. Damn fine sportsman. And a good shot, as he should have been; his mother was a Phelps. Gentleman, too. Something Mr. Renthal is not," gasped the old man.

Lord Biedermeier thought it best not to pursue this avenue of conversation and, instead, offered Mr. Van Degan a cigar, which had been the point of this visit to the smoking room in the first place. His cigars were from Cuba, by way of London, and he always felt proud when cigar smokers complimented him on their excellence.

"Cuba," he said, offering one to Ormonde Van Degan.

Ormonde Van Degan gestured to Lord Biedermeier to ready the cigar for him. When its tip was cut, he handed it to the old man, who placed it in his mouth.

"I've been thinking, sir," said Lord Biedermeier, as he lit a match and held it to Ormonde Van Degan's cigar for him to inhale on, "what a marvelous and distinguished family your family is and has always been in the history of this state."

"My father was the governor," whispered Ormonde.

"Exactly," said Lord Biedermeier.

"My uncle was the ambassador to France," he went on.

"My very point," continued Lord Biedermeier. "You must puff harder on the cigar, sir, for it to catch."

The old man inhaled the Cuban cigar.

"I thought that the time had come for a biography of your family, from the beginning, right up to the present," said Lord Biedermeier. "You see, Mr. Van Degan—"

As he coughed after inhaling so deeply, the old man's body was racked by a heart attack.

When Constantine de Rham asked Lil Altemus to dance, Lil, remembering Consuelo, her greatest friend, replied, simply, "No," with no reason or excuse, although she was not dancing at the time, nor did she seem to have any prospect of a dancing partner once her brother, Laurance Van Degan, had taken her around the floor. Loelia Manchester also declined Constantine's invitation to dance, as did Mary Finch. Ruby Renthal, who had been a party to using Constantine's house on Sutton Place during her affair with Elias when he was still married to Gladyce, said, when Constantine asked her to dance, "Not now," pleading hostess duties, but Constantine understood her answer to mean not later either.

Looking for a place to sit, Constantine saw Laurance Van Degan place his hand over the seat of an empty gold chair at his table to indicate that it was taken, although it remained empty for the next twenty minutes. Finally, he spotted, sitting alone, a discredited Wall Street financier, Max Luby, an early business associate of Elias's, who had briefly served time for forgery, and took his place there by him. When Elias invited Max Luby to the party, Max, who felt uncomfortable in society, had said to Elias, "I won't know what to say to all those people," and Elias had replied, "Don't worry, Max, no one will speak to you anyway." He might have been a foreigner unable to speak the language for all the attention anyone paid him. Presently Max Luby and Constantine de Rham, each happy to finally have someone to talk to, were joined briefly by Gus Bailey.

"Are you enjoying yourself, Mr. de Rham?" asked Gus.

"To be able to say tomorrow that one had been here is what matters," replied Constantine, who was not enjoying himself.

"Mrs. Lupescu is not with you?"

"Alas, Mrs. Lupescu had other plans for this evening."

In a lower voice, Gus said directly into de Rham's ear, "I saw your friend, Feliciano."

"Yes, yes, I know. He called to check on whether you were good for that much money."

"And what did you tell him?"

"I said that you dined at some of the best houses in New York."

"That, we both know, is no guarantee of solvency."

"True, true, but it satisfied Feliciano."

Just then Ruby walked past and spotted Gus.

"Gus Bailey, do you mean to say you're not going to ask me to dance?" she said.

"I'm a lousy dancer, Ruby," answered Gus. Throughout the evening Gus had tried to find a moment with Ruby to tell her about Byron Macumber, and here it was.

"I never believe men who say they're lousy dancers. Come on." Ruby took Gus by the hand and led him onto the floor. They danced for a time in silence.

"What do you mean you're a lousy dancer? You're not a lousy dancer at all."

"Look who my partner is," said Gus.

The music changed. The beat became slower. Gus put his arm tighter around Ruby's back, and she moved into him, putting her cheek next to his. "I hear you called me this afternoon."

"I did."

"What about?"

"Where are you going to be tomorrow, Ruby?" he asked.

"Right here. Can you imagine what this is going to be like, taking this party down?"

"I want to see you tomorrow, Ruby. Just for fifteen or twenty minutes. Alone," said Gus.

Ruby leaned her head back and looked at Gus. He looked back at her. His face was serious.

"This is not party talk, I take it?" she asked.

"No."

"Lefty Flint?"

"No, not Lefty Flint. There's something I think you should know about."

"Tell me."

"Tomorrow."

"Three o'clock. Here comes one of those Albanian princes to cut in on you. Give me a hint, Gus, quick. You've got me curious."

"Byron Macumber," said Gus.

She thought for a moment but could not place the name and indicated this to Gus with a gesture. The prince cut in on Gus. "Byron Macumber, Byron Macumber, it's twilight time," she sang to the tune of the song the orchestra was playing, and the prince twirled her around.

"I'm just a simple guy from the Midwest. Poor family. Worked my way through school all my life, but in the few years I've been here in New York, I've learned a lot about people like you," said Elias to Loelia Manchester, as he danced her around the floor of his ballroom. Unlike Mickie Minardos, who went to great lengths to conceal his humble origins, Elias Renthal had taken to exaggerating the hardships of his background, in order to greater emphasize his spectacular rise in the world to the very pinnacle of wealth and power. "Look how even here, with the *crème de la crème* of the city gathered in my house, everyone breaks up into their own little subgroups. Over there, for instance, all those has-been royals that Ruby's so mad about, all sitting together at one table. And over there, under that weeping willow tree, there's all the Old Guard of New York, all together, Lil Altemus, and all the Van Degans, and Cora Mandell, and old lady Somerset."

"Old lady Somerset is my mother, Elias," said Loelia.

"Oh, so she is, so she is. No offense meant, of course. Have I put my foot in my mouth?"

"Not this week, Elias. My mother is cutting me out of her will."

"Oh, she'll come round in time, Loelia. With people like you, blood is thicker than water. Now look over at that table. You have to say about me that I am loyal to my old friends," said Elias, observing the lonely duet of Constantine de Rham and Max Luby. "I don't drop them like everyone else does when they take the wrong turns in life. There is Constantine de Rham, whom people no longer invite. And poor Max Luby, recently released from prison for that stupid forgery thing they say he did, but I don't believe it for a minute. Very few hosts would have these people, but I do."

"Perhaps you should think about having them on a night when people like us aren't here," said Loelia.

"I take it you don't approve of my friends," said Elias.

"I don't wish to have to dance with them," said Loelia.

* * *

When Lord Biedermeier walked, his posture stooped slightly forward from the waist. Now, in haste to reach Elias with the news, his pince-nez, which he wore on a black string around his neck, fluttered in front of him as he loped across the ballroom, hitting his chest and flying about in all directions.

"Such haste!" said Lil Altemus, pulling in the satin skirt of her elaborate dress, as he brushed by her.

"Ah, Lil," he said, stopping. "Forgive me." For an instant he considered telling Lil that her father had had a heart attack in an upstairs room, but at that moment Elias came up to them to ask Lil to dance.

"How kind, Elias," said Lil, getting up and handing her bag to Dodo to hold for her.

"I must first have a word with Elias," said Lord Biedermeier, trying to forestall the dance so that he could tell Elias that one of his most important guests, the father of the woman he was about to dance with, was possibly dying upstairs.

"No, no, not until after this dance," said Elias, taking Lil to the floor.

"This is so gay, Elias," said Lil, beaming graciousness, as she danced backward, leading.

For an instant, Elias looked at her. "I don't think that's quite the right word anymore, Lil," he replied.

"Oh, no, it's a word I simply refuse to give up. My friends all know I mean it in the old-fashioned way," said Lil. As they danced by Laurance and Janet Van Degan, both couples smiled and waved, duty being properly adhered to on all sides.

It was only when Elias returned Lil to her seat next to Dodo that Lord Biedermeier was able to pull Elias aside and whisper to him that Ormonde Van Degan had had a heart attack.

"It'll ruin the fucking party," said Elias.

"Yes," agreed Lord Biedermeier.

"And the First Lady's about to arrive," whispered Elias into his ear. Elias had been awaiting the arrival of the First Lady with the same secrecy and suppressed excitement that a newly rich English financier might await the possible arrival of a member of the Royal Family under his roof.

"No!" said Lord Biedermeier, who had not heard that the Renthals were to be so honored.

"You didn't tell anyone, did you, about the old man?" asked Elias.

"Heavens, no. I almost told Lil and Dodo, but you came along."

As the two men rushed off together, Dodo Fitz Alyn Van Degan rose and said, "But it's my turn, Elias. You promised to dance with me after Lil."

Just then Gus Bailey walked by, and Elias grabbed him by the arm and delivered him in front of Dodo Fitz Alyn Van Degan, with an elaborate gesture of affability to indicate an introduction without introducing him with words, as if he had forgotten Gus's name, which he had. His mime went further to indicate that the two should dance together and then he turned and rushed off with Lord Biedermeier.

"We met at Lil's at Easter," said Dodo.

"I remember," said Gus. "I'm not much of a dancer."

"I don't care," said Dodo. "I'd hate to have to say that I went to the

Renthals' ball and hadn't once danced. We don't have to be Fred and Ginger, you know."

"That's true," said Gus, taking Dodo out to the dance floor.

Upstairs, outside the small room used for cigar smoking and poker playing, Elias and Lord Biedermeier looked in both directions to be sure they were not being observed before opening the door. Inside, Elias locked the door behind him.

"Where is he?" asked Elias.

"He was in that chair," said Lord Biedermeier.

"My God, he's on the floor," said Elias.

"He's dead," said Lord Biedermeier.

The two men looked at each other.

"It's going to ruin the party," said Elias.

"You already said that," said Lord Biedermeier.

"How about if we don't say a word until after the First Lady leaves, and then you come up and discover him, and we'll call an ambulance and get him down the freight elevator then," said Elias. "I mean, he's an old man, for Christ's sake. It's not like a big tragedy."

"Okay," said Lord Biedermeier.

"Jesus Christ," said Elias. "He took a shit in his pants."

"Apparently, they all do," said Lord Biedermeier.

"Gus, have you seen Elias?" asked Ruby, coming up to him and Dodo on the dance floor. Ruby had changed again, into her third dress of the evening, and she was bespangled with a new set of jewels, this time her rubies, in preparation for the imminent arrival of the First Lady.

"I saw him go upstairs with Lord Biedermeier," said Gus.

"I'm sure he went up to smoke one of his damn cigars," said Ruby. "Excuse me, will you, Dodo. I need to borrow Gus for a minute."

Ruby took Gus by the arm and walked with him toward the door.

"Go upstairs," she whispered in his ear. "Get him, will you, Gus? The First Lady has left the Rhinelander and we have to be at the door to meet her and bring her in."

"I didn't know the First Lady was coming," said Gus.

"Tell Elias to meet me at the front door."

Elias unlocked the door that connected the small room with the pool room beyond, and, together, the two middle-aged men carried the body of Ormonde Van Degan from one room to the other.

"Lift him up on the pool table," said Lord Biedermeier, sweating.

"That's an antique," said Elias. "That pool table belonged to Edward the Seventh."

"Put the carpet on the table, and we'll lay him on the carpet," said Lord Biedermeier. "And turn up the air conditioner."

"And lock the door," said Elias.

At that moment there was a knock on the door. The two men looked at each other, and Elias signaled to Lord Biedermeier not to reply.

Again there was a knock on the door.

"Elias," said Gus from the other side of the door. "Ruby wanted me to tell you that the First Lady is arriving and wants you to meet her at the front door."

"Holy shit," whispered Elias.

"We better get out of here," said Lord Biedermeier.

"Stinks in here," said Elias.

When Elias and Ruby Renthal reentered their ballroom with the First Lady between them, amid musical flourishes from the society dance band, their four hundred guests rose to applaud. What each knew, even those, like Lil Altemus, who found it difficult to accept any of the New People, was that he or she was at the most important party being given in the country, or possibly the world, that evening, and that each was a part of it. The Renthals, whom no one had even heard of only a short time ago, had pulled off the social feat of the decade.

When the orchestra played "The First Lady Waltz," which Ruby had had specially written for the occasion, Elias took the wife of the President to the dance floor.

"So pretty," said the First Lady, looking about as she danced, at the weeping willow trees, and the orchids and tulips and lilies that filled the room.

"Just wait," said Elias, as he twirled her around. "More to come."

Nearby Mickie Minardos danced with Loelia Manchester, and not a soul who saw them could deny that they were in love. Nowhere was Mickie more at home than on a dance floor, and Loelia seemed to float in the air as she followed every intricate step he led her through. Loelia had never seen Mickie happier, receiving compliments from every direction on the beauty of his artistic designs.

"Is everything ready with the butterflies?" Loelia whispered in his ear.

"At twelve sharp," whispered Mickie back.

"Where are they?" she asked.

"Hidden in the clouds," he said. She looked up and saw the billowing clouds made of tulle and silk that swung back and forth on wires from the ceiling.

"You're a genius, Mickie," said Loelia.

Just then Ezzie Fenwick cut in on the lovers, and Mickie excused himself to see that his team of workers were at their stations to carry off the job when the hour came.

Although he was stout, Ezzie Fenwick was a superb dancer, and his little feet, encased in black patent-leather pumps with black grosgrain ribbons, could pick up the rhythm of whatever kind of music was played and twirl the prettiest ladies in New York, and very few were as pretty as Loelia Manchester, around the dance floor. When Loelia whispered to Ezzie during their dance, and made him promise not to repeat it to anyone, that the First Lady had been warned not to attend the Renthals' ball because Elias was under investigation by the Securities and Exchange Commission for financial malfeasance, Ezzie, a consummate actor, hooted with laughter and pretended to consider the matter just as absurd as Loelia considered it. But, at the same time, he had to admit, while not missing a samba beat, that Elias Renthal had accumulated one of the greatest fortunes in America in record time, and the White House would not willy-nilly give the First Lady such a warning unless there were some cause for concern. Although he enjoyed a reputation as a secret keeper, Ezzie Fenwick had never, ever, in his whole life, been able to keep a secret.

"And you know, darling Ezzie, when Ruby asked Mickie to design her ball, Mickie's first thought was, you guessed it, butterflies, and he said—"

Ezzie's need to repeat the news that he had just sworn never to repeat was so strong that he ceased to hear Loelia, to whom he usually listened avidly, going on and on about Mickie's accomplishments, a subject on which she was becoming quite boring, Ezzie felt. His nimble feet, so alert to all the latest dance steps, felt suddenly clodlike, his need to escape the dance floor and repeat Loelia's news was so great, even though he knew, from firsthand experience on such matters, that the person he found to repeat it to would swear to him never to repeat it, just as he had sworn to Loelia never to repeat it, and then not be able to contain himself from telling just one person, and that person would tell just one other person, and soon everyone would know that Elias Renthal was under investigation by the Securities and Exchange Commission, even while they were supping on his lobster and sipping his champagne.

"What a dancer you are, Loelia!" he cried. "I'm exhausted!"

Loelia laughed, and they left the dance floor hand in hand.

"That conversation was just between us, Ezzie," said Loelia.

"Oh, darling, my lips are sealed," said Ezzie.

At that moment Dolly De Longpre walked by. "Hello, Ezzie, darling," said Dolly. "Isn't this all too magical?"

"It's De Lightful, it's De Licious, it's De Longpre," sang Ezzie, twirling Dolly around, at the same time wondering if Dolly, to whom he sometimes told bits of gossip for her column, should be the recipient of his news.

"Oh, Ezzie, you're mad!" screamed Dolly, thrilled with his attention. "Help me, Ezzie. You're so good at these things. Exactly what color would you call the First Lady's dress?"

"Magenta," answered Ezzie.

"Magenta. Absolutely. I couldn't think of the word. I'm counting on you to call me in the morning, Ezzie," she whispered to him. "You always remember what everyone wore and who sat next to whom."

"Say, Dolly," Ezzie said in a confiding voice, so ecstatic with the treasure trove within him that he couldn't wait until morning to fill her in. Just then he looked up and saw Florian Gray, Dolly's young rival. Ezzie realized that Florian Gray, still making his name, would run with such a rumor, while Dolly, dear Dolly, everybody's friend, would cry, "Nonsense!" and dismiss the ugly tale out of hand, or, worse, would first call the White House to check out the story, or even, horrors, ask the First Lady herself if it was true, in a good-hearted effort to show that it wasn't.

Dolly turned to see who Ezzie was looking at and saw Florian Gray retreating toward the men's room. With a dismissive shake of her head, she said, "I can't imagine why Elias and Ruby asked him."

"Oh, Dolly, he's not worthy to kiss the hem of your garment," said Ezzie.

Wishing to talk with Florian Gray, but not wishing to be seen talking to him, especially by Dolly, Ezzie spoke hurriedly to him in the men's room and arranged a rendezvous in a small room on the second floor that was used for cigar smoking and poker playing.

When he entered the room ten minutes later, Ezzie found Florian already there waiting for him.

"Stinks in here," said Florian.

"Cigars, probably," said Ezzie.

"Let me open this window."

"You mustn't say that you learned this from me," said Ezzie in a lowered voice, although there was no one but the two of them in the small room.

"Yes?" said Florian, eagerly. The sheer beauty of the notion that Ezzie Fenwick, the clandestine supplier of society news to Dolly De Longpre, should be giving him what could only be a hot story was not lost on the youthful professional gossipist.

And then, as if thinking better of his rash act, Ezzie hesitated, but Florian prompted him on.

"You don't mean about the workman who was killed raising up the weeping willow trees, do you?" asked Florian.

"No, no, I didn't know that," said Ezzie.

"What then?" persisted Florian.

"Oh, listen, the waltzes are starting," said Ezzie, again regretting that he was here with Florian. "I specifically asked Ruby to set aside twenty minutes for waltzing, and she remembered, with all she has to remember. Marvelous woman, isn't she? I'll arrange for us to meet later."

Florian understood that Ezzie was having second thoughts about revealing whatever it was he was going to reveal and knew that, once lost, the moment would never be reinstated.

"You mean about someone having a heart attack?" asked Florian.

"Someone had a heart attack? Here at the party? No, I didn't know that. Who?" asked Ezzie.

"I haven't found out yet," said Florian.

"I must get back, really. They're going to release the butterflies, thousands of them, all yellow and orange, on the stroke of midnight. They've been flown here from Chile. We can't miss that."

"Tell me, Ezzie," insisted Florian.

"They're going to indict Elias Renthal for trading on insider information," whispered Ezzie, drawing closer to Florian to indicate the confidentiality of his information.

"No!" said Florian, eyes wide, knowing a scoop, a scoop of scoops, was coming his way, more important by far than yellow and orange butterflies flown up that day from Chile, the kind of scoop that might be front-page news, superseding not only his own column but the financial page of his newspaper as well.

At that moment the door of the small room opened, and Lil Altemus walked in, with Dodo Fitz Alyn Van Degan, looking for Ormonde Van Degan, whom they both felt certain would want to see the release of the butterflies before they took him home to bed. As if caught out in something nefarious, Ezzie and Florian leaped back from each other, blushing.

"Oh, excuse me," said Lil, with great ceremony.

"Quite all right," said Ezzie. "I was just giving this young man the names of the out-of-town guests he doesn't know."

"Yes, of course," said Dodo, with a wink.

"You haven't seen my father, have you, Ezzie?" asked Lil.

"He came up here for a cigar over an hour ago, and we can't find him," said Dodo.

"I haven't seen him," said Ezzie.

"Nor I," said Florian.

"What's in that room?" asked Lil.

"Where the pool table is," said Ezzie. "Apparently it's off bounds tonight. Elias didn't want anyone putting drinks on it. Old felt, or something."

"It's locked," said Dodo, who was trying the door.

"He must be in there. There's not another room in the house we haven't checked," said Lil. "Look in the keyhole, Dodo."

Dodo knelt down on the floor and squinted one eye, while placing the other next to the keyhole.

"Look! He's asleep, right on the pool table. It's too sweet," she said, with musical intonations in her voice, like a bird cooing. "Look, Lil, at your father."

"I'm going down to see the butterflies," said Ezzie.

"Me too," said Florian.

"Let me look, Dodo," said Lil, kneeling down to peek through the keyhole.

By now all four hundred guests had heard about the ten thousand butterflies, yellow and orange, just arrived that day from Chile, that were going to be let loose at midnight during the waltzes to flutter about hither and yon in the bowers of flowers and weeping willow trees. Those nondancers who had been sitting out the evening in the drawing room and library in conversation, gossip, or cards, preferring the soothing strains of gypsy violins to the strident beat of society dance music, now descended the stairs into the ballroom, like New Year's Eve revelers awaiting the countdown until midnight.

Mickie Minardos, with Loelia Manchester by his side, issued last-minute instructions to his staff. Ruby and Elias, with the First Lady, the Earl and Countess of Castoria, and Faye Converse, grouped together in a trellised gazebo. Waiters in green jackets, designed by Mickie to blend with the flora, raced about replenishing champagne. Ezzie Fenwick was back on the dance floor, whirling Adele Harcourt about. Laurance Van Degan was dancing with Janet. The band played society music. Excitement was high.

The ballroom lights dimmed, and the partygoers gasped at the beauty as the regular lighting was replaced by pink-and-turquoise fluorescent light, giving the illusion of total fantasy. Then, with a pull of a golden rope, the clouds above burst open, and butterflies, thousands of butterflies, descended from the ceiling of the ballroom, fluttering here, fluttering there.

"Oh, heaven!"

"Divine!"

"Spectacular!"

"It's the most beautiful thing I've ever seen," cried Ruby Renthal. Ruby reached out and took hold of Elias's hand, and he, in turn, clasped his hand over hers. They looked at each other and knew that they had made it, as they always knew they would, but beyond their wildest dreams.

"Too marvelous for words," said the Countess of Castoria.

"Oh, look," said the First Lady, clapping her hands in delight.

Ezzie Fenwick, who knew beauty when he saw beauty, had tears in his eyes. "Divoon," he said.

People raced for the dance floor. Everyone wanted to dance. Abandon was the order of the night, as couples gave themselves over to the music and beauty of the Renthals' ball. The dance floor was full when the first scream came, from Rochelle Prud'homme, followed by screams from Matilda Clarke and Violet Bastedo, as the ten thousand butterflies, yellow and orange, flown up from Chile only that day, began dropping to their deaths, having been fried by the heat of the pink-and-turquoise fluorescent lights. Secret Service men rushed in past the dancers, who were now wiping dead butterflies from their hair and backs and shoulders, to rescue the First Lady before total pandemonium broke out.

"The *odor!*" cried Ezzie, waving his hand in front of his nose like a fan, as the dying butterflies kept descending.

"Turn out those fucking fluorescent lights!" screamed Elias.

"Don't say *fucking,* Elias," whispered an agitated Ruby into her husband's ear.

Mickie, nervous sweat pouring off his brow, pulled the switch that turned off the pink-and-turquoise fluorescent lights, and the ballroom was plunged into total darkness. Fernanda Somerset screamed. On the crowded stairway, an enormously fat Albanian princess fainted and, falling, knocked over several people.

"Turn on the ballroom lights!" screamed Elias.

"I can't find the switch!" screamed back Mickie Minardos.

"You ruined my party!" Ruby screamed at Mickie.

"How dare you yell like that at Mickie!" screamed back Loelia Manchester.

"Cobbler!"

"Twat!"

"Someone puked on my back," yelled Constantine de Rham.

"It was Binkie Castoria," said Jamesey Crocus.

"Adele Harcourt swallowed a dead butterfly!" cried Minnie Willoughby.

"Lights!"

"Lights!"

"Has someone called the police?"

"The phones are out!"

"Laurance, Father's dead on the pool table," screamed Lil Altemus.

"What do you mean, Father's dead on the pool table?"

"Let's get out of here!"

"The elevators don't work."

"The Greek shoemaker blew all the fuses in the building!"

"Who are these terrible people anyway?"

"I've only met them once before," said the Countess of Castoria.

"He's being investigated by the Securities and Exchange Commission."

"What do you expect from the kind of people who spend a million dollars on curtains?"

"Are those sirens I hear?"

"Is that police or fire?"

"Break the windows!"

"Not with that bergère chair, don't break the windows," cried Ruby.

By the time the police and firemen arrived, using the same cherry-picker crane that Julio Martinez had fallen to his death from the night before, the orchestra was playing "Nearer My God to Thee."

36

THE NEWSPAPERS reported, in addition to the death of Ormonde Van Degan, "whose roots in the city go back for generations," that there were two broken ankles, two broken arms, and a broken leg in the melee that had occurred when the power failed at the Elias Renthals' ball the night before, at which four hundred people, including the First Lady, had been present. The papers further reported that Adele Harcourt, the *grande dame* of New York, had very nearly choked to death on a dead butterfly but was resting comfortably in her room at Harcourt Pavilion of Manhattan Hospital.

"They've gone. They've flown the coop," said Ezzie Fenwick, over the telephone later that day.

"At least that saves us writing thank-you notes, or sending flowers, not that Ruby would ever want to see another flower again," said Matilda Clarke.

On the morning following the ball, the Elias Renthals left for Europe on their private plane, although no such plan had been in the making the day before. Later, people wondered if their flight was less for the embarrassment of the fiasco of their ball, which, knowing them, people like Ezzie Fenwick and Lil Altemus pointed out, they might have brazened out, than it was that Elias had heard the rumor at his own party of the investigation by the Securities and Exchange Commission of his financial dealings, and it was imperative for him to dispose of his extensive foreign holdings by transferring them to his wife's name before a freeze was put on his fortune.

"Today? We're going today?" Ruby had said, aghast, reported Candelaria, her maid, to Lourdes, Lil Altemus's maid. Ruby's eyes were still red and swollen from crying.

"Today," answered Elias. "In three hours, in fact."

"Elias," said Ruby, in a pleading tone. "I want to go. You know I want to go. I can't face anyone in this city, but I can't possibly be ready to go in three hours."

"Two hours and fifty-five minutes now," said Elias.

"But my clothes! My trunks! I can never get my things together for a two-month trip in that short a time," she said.

"Candelaria here," he said, pointing his thumb at the maid, "can pack up your stuff and ship it to you, and, in the meantime, buy new things there." Elias walked out of their bedroom and down the stairs. He was surprised in a minute when he heard Ruby following him.

"Is something going to happen, Elias?" asked Ruby.

"What do you mean?" asked Elias.

"Some sort of misfortune."

"Why do you ask that?"

"I feel it."

"Have you heard anything?"

"Look, Elias, don't play games with me. You told me we were a team, do you remember?"

"I remember, Ruby."

"A team means good times and bad times."

Elias walked into the drawing room and looked out the window onto Central Park. A weeping willow tree was being lowered on a crane outside his window from the ballroom above to the street below, as his party of the night before was being dismantled.

"Do you need money, Elias?" asked Ruby, following him into the room.

"God, no," he answered, with a laugh.

"I mean, I have all this jewelry," she said. She opened her black lizard jewelry cases, which she had brought downstairs with her and began taking out the pieces. "You can have all of this back, Elias. We can sell it. And there's all the money you signed over to me. It's yours."

"No, thanks, Ruby. I'm okay in the do-re-mi department, but I'll never forget what you offered."

"Tell me what's the matter, Elias. You're in trouble, aren't you?"

"Yes. Maybe."

"What did you do?"

"What a lot of other people have done before me, and a lot of other people will do after me."

"That's not an answer."

"I, uh, used, uh, insider information that I bought and paid for from young fellas in the brokerage offices who knew about mergers that were in the works."

"That's illegal?"

"Yeah."

"You knew it was illegal?"

"Yeah."

She breathed in deeply. "What do you want me to do, Elias?"

"Swear to my lies, if it comes to that."

It surprised Elias that Ruby's eyes filled with tears. The tears did not fill her eyes slowly, but sprang forth, as if he had slapped her. He understood that his wife's tears were not for his plight, which he knew she would see him through, but because he had asked her to lie for him. She walked away from him to one of the tall windows of their drawing room and looked out at Central Park across the street, where a bag lady began her preparations for the day on a bench on Fifth Avenue. Standing there, framed by the persimmon-colored damask curtains, with the fringe that had taken six weeks to be delivered from

France, Ruby Renthal wept. When Elias walked toward her, to comfort her, for he loved her, she raised her hand to halt him, without turning, having felt his footfall on her Aubusson carpet that she bought from Justine Altemus Slatkin, that Lil Altemus gave Justine for a wedding present, that had come from the Van Degan house in Newport and had once been a wedding gift from the Belgian court to the ill-fated Empress Carlotta of Mexico.

Elias Renthal was a nonconfidential man, and, as a result, he had few confidants. One of the few was Max Luby, his crony from Cleveland. Elias had sometime back taken the stand at Max's forgery trial as a character witness. "Nonsense. Utter nonsense!" he had said in the courtroom. "If a man's gonna steal, he don't steal for a lousy ten thousand dollars, which is all he wrote the check for. If he needed ten thousand bucks, there were any number of people, myself included, who would have given him the money in five minutes. What it was is, quite simply, a case of temporary aberration." Although his logic was thought to have carried weight with the jury, Max still had to serve six months, but he was known to be grateful that such a great financier as Elias Renthal had come to his rescue in court and even invited him to his ball.

"Listen, Max," Elias said, in a confidential tone on his private telephone, after having received Max's consolation on the failure of the ball. He was sitting in the little room Ruby had arranged for him to smoke his cigars, the same room where Ormonde Van Degan had died the night before. "Ruby and I are taking off. There's a little heat on me, if you understand what I'm saying."

"Right," replied Max, in his perfect second-in-command voice.

"There's a few things I'd like you to do for me, and then maybe you can meet up with me in Paris in a week or so. Check out for me, in a discreet way of course, the consequences of canceling my pledges to the museum and the opera. I think I pledged ten million to each, over a seven-year period. Just in case there's a temporary cash-flow problem, I'd hate to be shelling out that kind of moola to some nonsense like the opera and the museum. They got money coming out their kazoos, those people."

"What about the Julio Martinez fund?" asked Max.

"Who the fuck is Julio Martinez?" asked Elias.

"The workman who was killed hoisting the weeping willow tree for the ball."

"Christ, I forgot about him."

"It was only yesterday, Elias."

"Gimme a break. I got a lot on my mind. Better stick with that."

"Right."

"Oh, and one other thing, Max," he said, butting out his cigar in an ashtray where a dead butterfly lay. "You better stop payment on that check I gave to Faye Converse last night for AIDS."

Loelia Manchester wished with all her heart that Mickie Minardos had not called Ruby Renthal a twat the night before when Ruby screamed at him that he had ruined her party. She hated the word, had never used it herself, and knew that it must have caused pain to Ruby, who had worked so hard to put her background behind her. Loelia liked Ruby and had enjoyed their friendship, although she understood that Mickie had made a resumption of it impossible. Loelia had never seen Mickie cry until the night before, when they returned to the Rhinelander. He had held it in, all during the elevator ride up to the thirty-second floor, not only because of the elevator man, whom they both knew, but because the Earl and Countess of Castoria were in the same elevator, returning to their suite on the same floor. Wearing several Band-Aids and still drunk, the Earl had laughed hysterically for all thirty-two floors every time he looked at Mickie, and the Countess, who had a dead butterfly in her chignon that she was unaware of, held her ripped dress together in the front. On parting, the Earl had made a Latin American farewell by yelling, *"Buenas noches, amigos,"* as the Countess led him to his room. "He's not Mexican. He's Greek, Binkie," she could be heard saying as they went down the hall.

Mickie cried like a child. He was an artist, he told her, not an electrician. How was he supposed to understand about amps and wattage and voltage? Hadn't he created the most beautiful party ever given until those motherfucking, cuntlapping, cocksucking fuses blew and wiped out in an instant his months of work? He sobbed uncontrollably. Loelia wiped his brow with a linen towel she had dipped into her scented rosewater.

They both knew they had to leave town, before the newspapers started to call. Loelia suggested Greece. "Good God, not Greece," said Mickie. "My family. Think what my family will say," and he started to cry again, as new rushes of shame that he had not thought about yet came to him.

"But I have the most marvelous idea," said Loelia, finally. "No one will find us."

"Where?"

"A clinic in Germany. Bavaria, actually. On Lake Tergernsee."

"Tell me."

"They give shots. Live cell shots from the fetus of unborn sheep. And it's restorative. It will be marvelous. We will be brimming with health. And feeling as young as my children, and no one will know where to trace us, and by the time we get back, everyone will have forgotten about the ball. You go to bed, my darling—I'll handle everything."

Early on the morning following the ball, Lil Altemus called her daughter, Justine. At first she did not notice that there was lassitude in her daughter's voice.

"Have you heard?" Lil asked.

"Heard what?" Justine replied.

"Your grandfather's dead."

"Poor Grandfather," said Justine, although there was no tonal difference in the weariness of her voice.

"That's all you can say? 'Poor Grandfather.' Like 'poor dog' or 'poor cat,'" said Lil.

"He was eighty-five, Mother."

"Eighty-four."

"Well, in that case, I'm utterly shocked."

"You sound odd, Justine."

"I can sound odd if I want to, without accounting for it."

"If I didn't know you better, I'd think you were drunk."

"You want to know something, Mother?"

"What?"

"I am drunk."

"This is no time for jokes, Justine. You'd better get right over here. We have things to decide, about the funeral and all."

"I can't."

"Yes, you can. Uncle Laurance just called, and he thought it might be nice if the younger generation, like young Laurance and Hubie and Bernard, of course, were pallbearers. I think it's a marvelous idea, don't you?"

Justine had hoped to not have to tell her mother that Bernie had left her, at least for the time being, because she was certain her mother would say, "I told you so," but the news of her grandfather's death now made that impossible.

"Listen, Mother," said Justine, about to reveal her secret, but she couldn't bring herself to say the words without crying. "Listen, I'll be over. Have Lourdes make me some coffee. There's something I have to tell you."

"I expected to see you last night. The world was there, except you and Bernard," said Lil.

Justine hesitated, again tempted to get the task over with on the telephone, but she still couldn't bring herself to say the words. "Bernie had to work," she said finally.

"Bernie always has to work. That doesn't usually keep you home."

"Headache."

"Not pregnant, are you?"

"Oh, no. Thank God."

"I thought you wanted a baby. Don't wait too long, Justine. Look what happened to Muffie Windsor, and she was only thirty-six."

"How was the Renthals' party?"

"You mean you haven't heard? My dear, I know it's awful to laugh, with my poor father lying in a casket at Frank E. Campbell's, but wait until you hear. You won't believe what happened. Now, don't call Violet Bastedo. You just get over here, and I'll fill you in. And call Hubie. You better get him here as well."

It was a fact of Justine Altemus Slatkin's life that all the people she knew, and all the people her family and friends knew, lived within a thirty-block radius of each other in that part of the city known as the Upper East Side, and, just as in a small town, they were constantly running into each other in the streets and on the avenues in that small enclave.

Ezzie Fenwick happened to be in a taxicab going down Park Avenue at the moment Justine Altemus left her own apartment to walk the several blocks to her mother's apartment on Fifth Avenue and was witness to the fact that Justine took a swig from a can of beer she was holding. Later, describing the incident to a group of ladies he was lunching with, to rehash the events of the Renthal ball, Ezzie said that Justine's face looked like a fallen soufflé.

Justine, oblivious to everything around her, didn't see Ezzie leaning out the cab window, nor even notice Ned Manchester until he reached out and took her arm.

"Do you want to get a cup of coffee?" asked Ned.

"All right," answered Justine, listing a bit to the side.

Ned lifted the beer can out of Justine's hand and dropped it into a trash basket. They went into a coffee shop near the Whitney Museum.

"I know I look terrible," said Justine.

"Don't worry about it," said Ned.

"God, I hate beer. Bernie likes beer. I can't imagine why I drank it, let alone walked up Park Avenue with a can in my hand. You don't think I'm flipping out, do you?"

"What's the matter, Justine?" asked Ned.

When Justine looked over at Ned, she noticed that his hair was wet, as it always seemed to be wet when she saw him, and she assumed that he had probably just showered after playing squash at the Butterfield. "My dog died," she lied, without even caring whether or not he knew that she didn't have a dog.

"What's the matter, Justine?" he repeated.

"Bernie," she replied.

Ned nodded but did not reply.

"Bernie's not even in love with anyone else, like Loelia was," Justine continued. "Bernie just doesn't want to be married to me."

Ned lifted up the creamer and asked her with a gesture if she wanted cream in her coffee and poured it for her, did the same with the Sweet 'n Low, stirred it, and placed it in front of her. "It's a terrible time, I know," he said.

"The incredible thing was I thought we were happy," she said.

"Drink your coffee," he said. "You'll feel better."

"I never knew you were so nice, Ned," said Justine, drinking her coffee.

"I've been through what you're going through."

"It's awful to feel like this," said Justine.

"All the little things in life that make a marriage work, like going to the movies on Sunday afternoons, or playing tennis together, or having dinner at home, just the two of us, we ceased to do," said Ned, about his marriage. "And then, along came the cobbler."

"I only cooked dinner for him once the whole time we were married, and that was when Bonita, my cook Bonita, went back to Honduras for her mother's funeral, and even then Bernie told me the dinner was lousy, and we ended up ordering in from Food-to-Go on Lexington Avenue."

"Have you told Lil?"

"I was on my way to see my mother when you were kind enough to take the beer out of my hand. I'd better go. She's waiting for me."

"Sorry about your grandfather. Matilda called me."

"Thanks, Ned."

On the street, Justine continued to her mother's apartment.

"Would you like to sign a petition to save the porpoises?" a man on Madison Avenue asked Justine, offering her a clipboard and a pen.

She seemed not to have heard what he said, although she was aware that he had asked her something. "What?" she said.

"Would you like to sign a petition to save the porpoises?" he asked again.

"No, actually I wouldn't," she said slowly.

The walk, only a few blocks, seemed endless to her. Within her, she ached.

A television news crew was outside the building where the Renthals lived, shooting footage of the weeping willow trees being lowered from the sixteenth floor to the street. Justine watched the procedure for a moment before moving on.

"Justine, are you all right?" she heard someone ask her.

Turning, she saw that it was Brenda Primrose, with a reporter's notebook in hand, making notes on the dismantling of the ball.

"Justine?" Brenda said again, taking hold of Justine's arm. Justine, usually so perfectly groomed, looked to Brenda like she had slept in the clothes she was wearing. Her hair was uncombed. A button was missing from her blouse. She smelled of beer.

"I'm fine," said Justine.

"You poor thing," said Brenda. "Is it your grandfather? We had it on the news that he died."

"Yeah," said Justine. "That's it. My grandfather."

"Do you need help, Justine? Where are you heading for?"

"My mother's."

"Where's that?"

"Two buildings down from the Renthals."

"C'mon. I'll take you there. Be right back, Charlie."

They walked for half a block in silence. Brenda thought Justine was crying.

"You guys must have been pretty close, huh? You and your grandfather? He must have been some guy," said Brenda.

At the entrance of her mother's apartment building, Justine turned to Brenda and said for the first time the words she would be saying for the rest of her life. "Bernie left me." Before Brenda could react, Justine turned and walked into the building.

It was common knowledge that Lil Altemus thought her daughter had married beneath her, even though it was apparent, even to her, that Bernard Slatkin had not married Justine for her money. Nor could she ever say about Bernard that he had used her daughter for social advancement, because she knew that was not true. He had participated in Justine's social life in an agreeable and successful fashion, but her world held no particular fascination for him and his success in it was that he had remained a newscaster first and foremost.

However, when Justine informed her mother that the marriage was over, irreparably over, Lil, ever unpredictable, was enraged at the failure. Losing her son-in-law, she liked him better than she realized she had and felt sure she could reorchestrate the disastrous plans.

"Now, listen, please. What you're doing is overdramatizing an everyday marital situation. If anyone knows about these things, your old mother does. You've had a tiff, that's all. These things happen. It's a natural progression. The honeymoon is over. The marriage begins. He's simply flexing his muscles to show that he's the man in the family. He'll be back."

"No, Mother, he won't be back. I know him," said Justine.

The look on Justine's tear-stained face and the tone of Justine's heart-broken voice made Lil look at her.

"But what in the world has happened?" asked Lil.

"It was my fault. I tried to bring him into my life, which never really interested him, and I didn't make enough effort about all those news people."

"Oh, please," said Lil, dismissing her daughter's explanation. "Is there another woman?"

"I don't know."

"Matilda Clarke said he's a womanizer," said Lil. "Your Uncle Laurance even said he was a philanderer."

"Oh, please, Mother," said Justine, wounded by the thought.

"Where is that place his aunt and uncle live in New Jersey? Hackensack, is it?" Lil asked.

"Weehawken," replied Justine.

"Exactly," said Lil, reaching for her book.

"Mother, please don't call Mrs. Slatkin. Please."

"Of course, I'm going to call her. Hester will understand that this simply must not be. Young people all have problems. They just have to be worked out."

"Then let me leave. I can't bear to hear that conversation."

"Have you called Hubie to tell him about his grandfather?"

"No."

"Do that now, and tell him to come right up here."

After Justine left her mother's room, Lil Altemus picked up her telephone book, looked up a number, and called Hester Slatkin, whom she had not seen or spoken to since the day of the wedding. A divorce after several years she not only could have tolerated but might gladly have accepted, but a divorce after a year she felt had an unseemly quality.

"We can't allow this to happen, Hester. We simply can't."

"When Bernie makes up his mind about something, Lil, he never changes it," said Hester. The coolness of Hester's answer surprised Lil, who had assumed she would be a willing ally.

"I should have objected, you see, right from the beginning," said Lil. "I should have said that it was all wrong, that it couldn't work. Because, you see, it's what I actually felt. But then I would have been the heavy. They would have said I was anti-Semitic, because that's what it would have come down to, but that never had a damn thing to do with it. I thought they were wrong together."

"Good-bye, Lil," said Hester Slatkin, with a tone of finality in her voice that indicated it would be their last conversation.

"There's no answer at Hubie's, Mother," said Justine.

"Keep trying."

"There's no answer at the gallery either, and the machine's not on."

"I'll try," said Lil. She tapped the numbers out on her telephone.

"*Si?*" came the answer after several rings.

"You see?" she said to Justine. "There is someone there. This is Mrs. Altemus speaking. Is my son there?"

"*No está aquí,*" said the voice on the end.

"It's that damn maid," said Lil to Justine. "Tell him his mother called. His mother. His *madre*. Do you understand? *Cinco, ocho, ocho.* What's the word for six, Justine, quick?"

"I don't know."

"Oh, never mind," Lil screamed into the telephone and slammed down the receiver. "Don't you miss maids who speak English? Do you remember when you were a little girl, all those marvelous Irish maids we always had? Kathleen and Maeve?"

"Oh, Mother, please," said Justine. "Let's not talk about Kathleen and Maeve, for Christ's sake."

"Really, Justine. There is no reason for you to take the Lord's name in vain. None whatsoever," Lil replied to Justine's outburst. She looked at her daughter. "You look terrible. Do you know that? Simply terrible."

"I'm entitled to look terrible. My husband left me. My brother has AIDS."

"He does not have AIDS! And don't you dare say that to a living soul!"

"I'm going to call Juanito."

"Juanito, Juanito. Who the hell is this Juanito I'm always hearing the name of?"

"He's the man Hubie loves, Mother."

"I simply loathe that kind of talk, Justine. Now go and pull yourself together, and we'll meet Uncle Laurance at Frank E. Campbell's and go over the funeral plans."

Lourdes, Lil's maid, came in to tell Lil that there was a man on the telephone to speak to her called Boy Fessenden.

"Boy Fessenden?" said Lil. "There's a name from the past. I haven't seen Boy Fessenden since that summer when he visited us in Newport. Do you remember?" She picked up the extension. "Hello, this is Lil Altemus. Yes, of course, I remember you. How are you, Boy? What a long time it's been. How's your mother? Do give her my love. Now what can I do for you, Boy? I must be quick. We've had such a sadness in the family. My father died last night. Eighty-four. Thank you. You're so kind, Boy. How can I help you? Hubie? No, I can't reach Hubie on the telephone. Or in the gallery. I want him to get right up here because we have to make plans for the funeral. What? . . . When? . . . Where?"

"What is it, Mother?" asked Justine.

Lil, ashen, handed the telephone to Justine. "You'd better take this, Justine. Boy Fessenden took Hubie to the hospital last night."

That night, after calling hours at Frank E. Campbell's funeral home, where the mayor, the governor, the board of directors of the Van Degan Foundation, the entire membership of the Butterfield, and several hundred family and business friends came to pay their respects to Ormonde Van Degan, Lil Altemus refused her brother's invitation to join him and Janet and Dodo for a late dinner at their apartment and returned to her own, pleading exhaustion. At nine thirty the doorbell rang and she let Bernie Slatkin in, whom, unknown to Justine, she was expecting.

"I don't understand how you can do this to my daughter," Lil said, after they were seated in the library, allowing no time for amenities, not even a condolence message from Bernie to her on the death of her father. Nor had she offered him a drink.

"It was my understanding always that you did not care for the marriage in the first place, Mrs. Altemus," replied Bernie.

Bernie's addressing her as Mrs. Altemus, instead of Lil, which she had requested him to do after the wedding, and which he had been eager to do at the time, was not lost on Lil. When she spoke, she called him Bernard, as she had always refused to call him Bernie.

"That was then. This is now, Bernard," said Lil.

"The marriage is over," said Bernie.

"But why?"

"Feelings change."

"So quickly?"

"It's over, Mrs. Altemus," Bernie repeated, as if to bring the matter to an end. "I do not see any point in prolonging a situation that is going to fail in the long run."

"I have to be quite frank with you, Bernard," said Lil, as if she were paying him a compliment. "I did think in the beginning that you might be using Justine to further your career, or you were interested in her money, but I know now that that is not the case."

"Never was," he said.

"Stay married to my daughter for four more years and then divorce, and I will make it worth your while."

Bernie, who did not usually smoke, leaned forward and took a cigarette from a box on a table by his chair, lit it, inhaled deeply, and smiled as he exhaled, shaking his head at her at the same time. He stamped out the cigarette in a Meissen dish, threw the stub in the fireplace, and rose. "I never understood people like you, Mrs. Altemus. I never will," he said.

"And what does that mean?" asked Lil, aware that she was not going to convince him to change his mind, as she had not been able to convince him to live in Justine's apartment in the same building she lived in, or to use Cora Mandell to decorate the new apartment he had insisted he and Justine move to when they got married.

"Stay married for four more years and then divorce, is that it? A five-year marriage is less of a flop than a one-year marriage. It all has to do with face, doesn't it, how it looks? Your daughter is far too good for such an arrangement as that. Good-bye, Mrs. Altemus."

"I never liked you, Bernard," she said, wanting the last word.

"I never liked you either, Mrs. Altemus," said Bernie, getting the last word.

"You're a womanizer," she hissed at him.

"That's right. That's what my problem is," he answered, staring her down. Lil registered surprise that he had not denied the accusation. "And I don't want a wife who is a tragic figure. 'Poor Justine. Her husband cheats on her.' "

"Get out."

"Remember this. I came by summons, not by choice."

The word was out on Hubie Altemus's illness. The previous night, at Maisie Verdurin's, Ezzie Fenwick, who had heard that afternoon from Jamesey Crocus, who had heard from Juanito, whispered it to Maude Hoare, and Maude told Buster Dominguez, and Buster told Matilda Clarke, and Matilda told Gus Bailey, although there was no word on the matter from any of the members of the family.

The next day Gus was walking up Madison Avenue and passed Lil Altemus as she was coming out of the Wilton House Book Shop with a shopping bag in her hand. She looked as handsomely put together as always, but drawn.

"I'm sorry to hear about Hubie," said Gus.

Lil stiffened. It distressed her to think that people knew the news and were discussing it. A tear came to her eye. "I'm on my way to the hospital now," she said, indicating the bag of books she was carrying.

Their eyes met.

She mouthed but did not speak the word *lymphoma,* as if it were a release rather than a sentence. Gus understood that she was avoiding the subject that was so painful to her.

"How are you doing, Lil?" Gus asked.

"I'm all right," said Lil. "Really I am. I have been nipping a bit at the brandy and soda, but at least I'm no longer thinking of going out the window."

Gus, touched, reached out to take her arm.

"I couldn't figure out what to wear," she said, making a joke of it. "That's what saved me. Do you remember when poor old Mimi Chase wore a trench coat when she jumped, after they fired her from the magazine? I didn't want to wear a trench coat. I didn't ever have a goddamn trench coat, but I wouldn't have worn one if I had. Oh, Gus, it's been so awful. I don't know if I can live without him. No one understood it, I know, what we had, but I adored him. I absolutely adored him." She spoke of her son as if he were already dead.

In the several years they had been together, Juanito Perez had never been as kind to Hubie Altemus as he was in the months of Hubie's dying. Lying in bed at St. Vincent's Hospital, Hubie watched Juanito standing at the window looking out. Juanito was the only one now who could make Hubie laugh, telling his stories of the goings-on in the subterranean world that he still frequented, despite the dangers of the disease that was killing his lover. There were certain of their mutual acquaintances in the art world whom Juanito referred to with a gender switch, and it never failed to make Hubie laugh. That afternoon he was regaling Hubie with a tale concerning Jamesey Crocus, through whom he had met Hubie, and whom he always called Janie, or the furniture queen.

"So Miss Crocus kicks her train around and says, 'Those console tables are fakes, Ruby,' and walks out in a huff," finished Juanito.

By this time Hubie could only talk in a whisper. "You are awful, Juanito," he said, when he finished laughing.

As Juanito went on with his tales of the night before, Hubie watched him with affection. He wondered if Juanito's diligence in caring for him was because of the money he knew he was going to inherit, or because he really cared in return, but he decided not to allow it to occupy his mind for the time he had left, grateful that the caring existed at all, no matter what the reason. The only thing at that moment that bothered him was that his mother was coming to pay a visit, and he did not know if he had the strength to deal with his mother and Juanito in the room at the same time.

"Mother's on her way here," he said finally, hoping that Juanito would gather up his possessions and be off before her arrival.

"My mother-in-law here?" Juanito asked.

"Any minute," whispered Hubie.

"I've been dying to meet her."

"You're going to stay then?"

"Of course I'm going to stay."

"Juanito?"

"Don't ask me to go, Hubie."

"I'm not. When she's here, don't call Boy Fessenden Girl Fessenden, if his name comes up. Okay?"

"What do you think I am, from the slums?"

"Listen, one more thing."

"What?"

"Will you take off your earring before she arrives?"

"That's going to butch me up, is it, not wearing my earring?" asked Juanito, irritated, as he always was when Hubie acted embarrassed about him in relation to his family.

"No, that's not it," said Hubie.

"Then what? I like this diamond earring."

"That diamond was my mother's engagement ring from my father. She gave it to me when she thought I was going to marry Violet Bastedo."

Juanito and Hubie looked at each other, and both started to laugh. "That's the first good laugh I've had in weeks," said Juanito, unscrewing the diamond from his earlobe. He went over to Hubie and hugged him.

It was in this position that Lil Altemus saw them when she walked into the hospital room with her bagful of books. It was the first time Lil had seen Hubie since Easter night. He looked smaller to her, as if his face had shrunk. His teeth seemed bigger. His arms looked like the arms of an old man.

"Hello, my darling," said Lil, staring at him aghast.

"Mother, this is Juanito Perez. Juanito, this is my mother," said Hubie.

"Hellohowareyou?" said Lil, not looking at him.

"Ma'am," said Juanito.

"What a nice room, Hubie. My word, is that the World Trade Center out the window? Prettier from this angle than when you see it from Laurance's boat."

Neither of the young men answered her.

"Your grandfather's funeral was enormous, Hubie. You probably read about it in the *Times*. The governor. The mayor. All the Van Degans. The church was packed. Young Laurance gave the most lovely eulogy. We all went up to Laurance and Janet's afterward. Not the governor and the mayor. Just the family, I mean." Even to herself, she sounded rattled.

"How's Dodo taking it?" asked Juanito.

For the first time Lil looked at Juanito.

"Dodo?" she asked, raising her eyebrows in exaggerated surprise.

"She buys my paintings," said Juanito.

"Oh."

"How is she?"

"Mrs. Van Degan is coping well under the circumstances," said Lil.

Juanito looked over at Hubie. He could see that Hubie was suffering, although Hubie managed to make a slight wink of reassurance.

"I'm gonna split, Hubie," said Juanito. "I'm sure you and your mother have things to talk over."

"When will you come back?" asked Hubie.

"I'll stop by tonight. Good-bye, Mrs. Altemus."

Lil nodded, occupied now with her shopping bag of gifts. She realized, as he was leaving, that she wanted him to stay, so that she would not have to be alone with Hubie. She wished that Justine was with her. She knew that she didn't know what to say to her own son, whom she loved, so devastated was she by his appearance.

"Did you see Justine?" she asked when Juanito had left.

"She was here earlier."

"How was she?"

"Drunk, I felt."

"Drunk? Justine? Never!"

"I repeat, drunk."

"That son of a bitch has left her."

"I never heard you say son of a bitch before, Mother."

"I've never said it before," she replied. "It's all so embarrassing." Lil looked down at her bag. The word *all*, Hubie understood, included him as well as Justine.

"Justine feels hatred for Bernard now," said Lil.

"I didn't get that impression."

"Oh, yes, hatred without limits."

"You weren't very polite to Juanito, Mother."

"I've brought you some books, Hubie," said Lil, putting the shopping bag from Wilton House on his bed. "Arthur thought you'd like the new book on the Princesses of Monaco."

"Arthur couldn't have thought that," said Hubie.

"No, I thought it. Do you remember when your old mother thought you'd be perfect for one of those girls? Can you imagine?"

Hubie looked at his mother and smiled.

"And the new magazines are all in there too," she said. "Now, I'm off." She was out the door.

Hubie started to drift off to sleep.

When he woke, he looked out the window at the skyline of lower New York, watching a barge go slowly by. On the bed he saw the shopping bag from Wilton House that his mother had left earlier. Unable to sleep again, he took out the magazines and the new book on the Princesses of Monaco, about whom he had no interest. Inside, at the bottom of the bag, he saw a dark brown plastic container. He reached in and took it out. Inside there were fifty Seconal pills.

Hubie reached down and undid the drawstring of his pajamas. For a while his hand rested on his stomach. Then he allowed his fingers to slide down between his legs, resting in his pubic hair. He moved his fingers around, massaging himself lightly. When his penis was semierect, he made a fist around it and pounded himself. For the two minutes and thirty-four seconds that it took to complete the act of masturbation, Hubie Altemus forgot that he was going to die at twenty-seven.

Lil Altemus fainted when she left St. Vincent's Hospital. If her chauffeur, Joe, who had been with her for years, had not been there to rescue her, she might have been put into the same hospital where her son was a patient, but Joe understood her panicked look and delivered her back to her apartment on Fifth Avenue, where Lourdes cared for her, and Justine was sent for.

"I cannot bear it that that man is there," said Lil, resting in bed, about Juanito Perez.

"They're a couple, Mother," said Justine.

Lil shuddered.

"Under the circumstances, he has as much right to be there as we do," Justine continued.

When Lil was with her son, before his illness, and Hubie made what she thought was an inappropriate remark, such as Justine had just made to her, she would cover her ears and exclaim, "You know I can't *bear* that kind of talk!" Under the same circumstances, with Justine, Lil pretended not to have heard. It was a way she had of snubbing people who had gone too far.

"He makes Hubie laugh. He makes him forget that he's going to die," said Justine, who didn't care that she was being snubbed by her mother.

Hubert Altemus, the father of Justine and Hubie, always gave the impression, even in town, of a country gentleman. His tweed jacket fit too loosely on his lanky frame, but it was too loose by the mutual choice of its wearer and its wearer's tailor, and, to their refined tastes, altogether right. He had been summoned to town by his former wife, whom he had not seen since the day of Justine's wedding, to discuss the unraveling lives of their two children. Hubert did not enjoy going to Lil's apartment, where he had lived when he was married to her, nor did his present wife, Belinda, enjoy having him go there, so the lunch between the two was arranged for Clarence's, after he had visited Hubie in the hospital. They had, after desultory greetings, sat in silence until Hubert finished the first of the three martinis he intended to drink before they ordered lunch. As always, in the presence of her former husband, Lil, who rarely felt ill at ease, felt ill at ease and said to the waiter, Michael, with the small ponytail, who was always so nice to her daughter, "Will you take this thing away, please?" waving her hand over a vase of three pink carnations.

"Don't like flowers, Mrs. Altemus?" asked Michael, in his friendly way, obviously unaware that she had a dying son and a divorcing daughter.

"Yes, I do. I like flowers very much. I just don't happen to like those flowers," replied Lil.

With that Michael removed the offending vase.

"I cannot bear carnations," said Lil to Hubert, and Hubert nodded, knowing perfectly well that the carnations were not what was bothering her, that she was simply looking for something to find fault with to overcome her discomfort.

"Who was the guy with the diamond in his ear?" Hubert asked finally, not referring to Michael, who also wore a diamond in his ear, but to the man he had just seen in his son's room at the hospital, whose diamond earring was larger by far than Michael's.

"Pedro. Or Geraldo. Or some name like that," answered Lil, who often pretended not to know things she knew perfectly well, just as she now knew that her former husband was referring to their son's lover, Juanito Perez, or their son's catamite, as her brother Laurance, who was checking him out, referred to him.

"Who is he?"

"Justine says he is the man Hubie loves," answered Lil, looking away from Hubert as she said it.

"Jesus," said Hubert. He took a long drink from his martini and swallowed the olive at the same time. "If I didn't know better, I'd think that diamond in his ear was from the engagement ring I gave you when we got married."

"Oh, don't be silly," said Lil. At the same time she said the words, she realized that Hubert could be right, especially as she had given the ring to Hubie when she thought that he was going to marry Violet Bastedo, but that was not the subject that she wished to deal with now.

"When Hubie goes, Hubert, I hope you'll agree with me that there should be nothing in the obituaries about the cause of death," said Lil.

"Sure, Lil," said Hubert.

"Laurance can handle all that."

"I'm sure he can, Lil," said Hubert.

"It's Justine I really want to talk about, Hubert. What a crushed little creature she has become," said Lil, sipping a glass of white wine.

"She really loved that television announcer," said Hubert.

"I should never have allowed that marriage. Never. Nor should you have, for that matter," said Lil.

"Spilt milk," said Hubert, signaling the waiter for another martini.

"I don't particularly enjoy hearing that my daughter was seen walking down Park Avenue with a can of beer in her hand," said Lil.

"Do we know it's true?" replied Hubert Altemus.

"Of course, it's true. Ezzie Fenwick saw her himself."

"Of course it would be Ezzie who saw her," said Hubert, who had no patience for Ezzie Fenwick. "I'll talk to Justine."

"I want you to do more than talk to her," said Lil. "I want you to take her up to Bedford with you. Keep her there for a week or so. Make her ride and do all those things. She needs to get away from New York. She thinks everyone's talking about her. Everyone *is* talking about her."

"I'll talk to Belinda," said Hubert.

"Oh, we need permission from the former Miss O'Brien, do we?" asked Lil, who could never hear the name of Hubert's present wife without reacting adversely. She had once described Belinda O'Brien as the kind of woman who calls men at their offices.

"Ah, there's Belinda now," said Hubert, rising, with a look of pleasure on his face, and waving to his wife, who stood at the door of the restaurant.

"Belinda? Here?" asked Lil, gathering up her things.

"Yes, I asked her to meet me here." Belinda, waving back, smiled and made her way toward them through the crowded restaurant.

"I don't know how you could do this to me, Hubert," said Lil.

"Do what?"

"Ask that woman to come here to this table with everyone in the restaurant looking at us," said Lil.

"That woman has been my wife for twelve years," said Hubert, "and I don't see a single soul in this restaurant looking at us, except Chick Jacoby, who wants the table for Lord Biedermeier, who just arrived without a reservation, and, just to be perverse, I'm going to let Lord Biedermeier have a nice long wait."

"Hello, Lil," said Belinda, walking up to the table. Belinda Altemus, in her forties, was still pretty, although she had begun to put on what she herself called a few extra libs. Her face gave off a look of good humor, as if nothing bothered her. Her blond hair was what Lil Altemus called "touched up," and she wore what Lil called wet-looking lipstick.

"Hellohoware?" answered Lil, not looking up at her as she rose to leave. Hubert made no effort to detain her.

"You'll call me, Hubert, about the matter we discussed?" asked Lil.

"After I talk with Belinda," he answered.

Lil turned and walked out of the restaurant. Belinda and Hubert looked at each other. Hubert shrugged.

"I think she's still in love with you," said Belinda.

"Hardly likely," replied Hubert.

"Tell me something, Hubert. Did you ever love her?"

"Oh, I don't know. I probably thought so at the time. What it really was, I suppose, was the utter perfection of the union, smiled on by both sides." They both laughed. "Did I tell you today how beautiful you are?" he asked.

"Tell me that when you've had a few less of these," she said, tapping her very red fingernail against his empty martini glass.

Hubert smiled at her. "Want some lunch?"

"Sure," she replied, looking around the dining room. "How come we don't have any flowers on our table?"

Hubie clung stubbornly to a life that had brought him little happiness. Justine, back from Bedford, visited him daily.

"Beautiful," he said about the large bunch of white peonies that Justine had brought him. "My favorite flower."

"I remember," said Justine.

"There was this guy in my class at Simsbury. Bobby Vermont. Do you remember him? He was Mom's friend Teddy Vermont's son by his third marriage. A sad, lonely guy at school. I probably would have become good friends with him if I hadn't been kicked out."

"I remember Bobby Vermont," said Justine. "He threw up at my coming-out party."

"Funny you should remember that. It's the first thing he said to me. 'Has your sister ever forgiven me for throwing up at her coming-out party?' "

Justine laughed. "What about Bobby Vermont?"

"I ran into him here at the hospital the other day."

"What's he here for?"

"Same thing I am."

"Oh, I'm sorry. Poor Bobby, but at least you have a friend here then."

"Had a friend. He died yesterday."

"Oh, dear." Justine turned away from her brother and placed the white peonies in a vase. "Mummy sends her love."

"Send her mine."

"She'd come, Hubie, but she couldn't cope after her visit. She doesn't mean anything. It's just that it's too much for her."

"The way I look, huh?"

"Yes."

"Doesn't matter."

"Of course it matters, but that's the way she is."

"You're not trying to explain my mother to me, are you?"

They both laughed.

"What are you going to do about your money, Hubie?" asked Justine.

"Leaving it all to Juanito," said Hubie.

"Don't."

"I didn't think I'd hear that from you, Justine."

"Hubie, it's ten million dollars."

"So?"

"Leave him five hundred thousand dollars. A million even. But don't leave him the whole thing. You know what Uncle Laurance will do. He'll take it to court. He'll call it undue influence on the part of Juanito. He'll expose everything there is to expose about Juanito: the drugs, those terrible bars he goes to. He'll find a way to prove that Juanito is the one who gave you the AIDS."

"It's not undue influence, Justine. No one is forcing me to do this. It's what I want to do. That's why I went to Herkie Saybrook to make out my will, rather than some gay lawyer in the West Village. Our own kind, that's Herkie Saybrook. You don't need the money. Certainly Mother doesn't need the money. Who else am I going to leave it to?"

"You could do something marvelous with it, Hubie. Give it to medical research, or something like that."

"I know," said Hubie, looking off at the river outside, thinking about what his sister was saying. "There's something in me that makes me want to get even with Uncle Laurance and young shitface Laurance. All my life they made me feel like I was nothing."

"Think about it, Hubie," said Justine.

Hubie looked at Justine and held out his hand. She took it and squeezed it. "What's with the television announcer?" he asked.

"Flown off to wherever it is they fly off to these days for a quickie divorce."

"Did you see him before he went?"

"Yes."

"How'd it go?"

"We did not go down Memory Lane, if that's what you mean."

"You taking it okay?"

"I loved him, Hubie. I really loved him."

Hubie looked at his sister. "One of the nicest things about you, Justine, is that with a mother like ours, you didn't get tough."

Justine started to cry.

"We're a pair, aren't we?" continued Hubie. "The rich Altemus kids, they used to call us, like we were something special. What happened to us, Justine?"

"I'm going to miss you, Hubie," said Justine.

Still holding her hand, Hubie drifted off to sleep. When he awoke, Justine was still there.

"You were right about the money, you know," he said. He could speak only in a whisper. "Can you get Herkie Saybrook to come down here? I can still leave Juanito well cared for, but the bulk should go to a hospice for all these guys here who have no place to go and no one to take care of them."

"I'll call Herkie," said Justine.

"Better do it quick," said Hubie.

She nodded. "Guess what, Hubie?"

"What?"

"I'm pregnant."

Hubie, dying, was still interested enough in life to be amazed. "By Bernie?" he whispered.

"Who else?"

"Does he know?"

"No."

"You going to tell him?"

"No. I don't want him back like that."

"Does Mummy know?"

"No."

"Are you going to tell her?"

"Not yet."

"Are you going to keep the baby?"

"Oh, yes, and I'm going to be a wonderful mother."

Hubie, tired now from the excitement of the conversation, could only pat his sister's hand in admiration.

"Want to know what I'm going to name it if it's a boy?" asked Justine. She knew Hubie was not strong enough to answer her, so she continued without an answer from him. "Hubie. Hubie Altemus Slatkin."

Hubie nodded his head and signaled for his sister to come closer. She put her ear near to his mouth as he said, "Hubie Slatkin. It has a certain insouciant charm." He smiled.

Later, leaving, Justine stopped at the door of the hospital room and looked back at Hubie. When he looked up at her, she said, "I've loved being your sister, Hubie."

Hubie understood that it was Justine's way of saying good-bye. He raised his hand and waved good-bye.

Justine nodded and looked away to avert a tear that was forming.

"I'm so proud of you, Hubie," she said.

That night Hubie died. Herkie Saybrook never knew that Hubie wanted to make a new will. Only Juanito was with him at the end, holding on to his slight body. The last words Hubie heard were Juanito crying, "Don't die, Hubie."

37

D ESPITE THE prominence of the family, there was very little made in the
obituary columns, at the family's request, about the death of Hubert
Altemus, Jr., the son of Mrs. Van Degan Altemus of New York City and
Mr. Hubert Altemus of Bedford Village, New York, and the brother of Mrs.
Justine Altemus Slatkin. If it hadn't been for Ezzie Fenwick, who read the
obituary page before he read anything else in the newspaper, not just the
prominent names in the news stories of the dead, but the long columns of
names in the paid announcements, Hubie Altemus's passing might have gone
undetected, as the family wished, until after the funeral, by which time Lil
would have left for Europe.

Ezzie, a surprisingly early riser for one who spent every night dining out,
called Matilda Clarke with the news, and then Maude Hoare, and then, in lieu
of Loelia Manchester, who had still not returned from Europe, Loelia's
mother Fernanda Somerset, and Matilda and Maude and Fernanda all made
their six or eight calls, and by noon everyone who knew the Altemus and Van
Degan clans knew that Hubie Altemus had died of AIDS, although that was a
word not to be mentioned, under any circumstance, to family members, as the
official story was that poor Hubie, who really never had much of a life, Ezzie
commented over and over, had died of leukemia.

Leaving Lil Altemus's apartment after paying a condolence call, Ezzie
Fenwick ran into Cora Mandell in the lobby of Lil's building.

"Oh, Ezzie," said Cora. "I guess I'm going to the same place you're coming
from."

"Rather a sparcity of merriment in that household at the moment," said
Ezzie. "Not that it was ever a barrel of laughs at Lil's, or at any of the Van
Degans', now that I come to think of it."

"Who's up there?" asked Cora.

"All the predictables. Aunt Minnie Willoughby. Matilda. Janet and Laurance. Dodo, and poor Justine. Get the pic?"

"Evangeline wanted to come, but she was too drunk," said Cora.

"Just as well. Lil has enough to contend with, without Evangeline," said
Ezzie.

"How is poor Lil?" Cora repeated.

"Stoic. Absolutely stoic. Not a tear."

DOMINICK DUNNE

"Lil always does things so well," said Cora.
"I'm off to Sibila's cocktail party," said Ezzie.

Making her way down Madison Avenue to meet with Lorenza about flower arrangements for Hubie's funeral, Justine Altemus, who had decided to return to her maiden name, ran into Bernie Slatkin, who was on his way to interview Max Luby for a future television segment on Wall Street practices, although that subject did not come up in their brief exchange. If Justine had not been lost in thought and had seen the approaching Bernie before he saw her, she would have ducked into a shop in order to avoid the encounter, as it was the first time they had met since Bernie returned from his tropical-island divorce. In advance, she had agonized over how she would behave when that meeting came to pass. Seeing him, she dropped her eyes and hoped that he would do the same, until they had passed each other, but, alas, Bernie was not born for such subtleties of behavior.

"Justine," he said, reaching out to touch her arm.

"Oh, hellohoware?" she said, sounding more like her mother than herself, as she withdrew her arm from his touch.

"I'm so very sorry about Hubie," he said.

"Thank you," she replied. Her words were polite, but her tone was impatient, as if he were delaying her mission.

"I know what a wonderful sister you were to him," said Bernie.

"He was a wonderful brother to me," replied Justine. She made a gesture of moving on. Bernie looked at her, struck by the change in her. Gone was the lovesick attitude he had grown to despise. She had returned to the remote and distant heiress he had first spoken to in an elevator leaving one of Maisie Verdurin's parties. For an instant she looked beautiful to him again, and unattainable, or beautiful because she was unattainable. She met his eyes, as if understanding his thought.

There were things he wanted to know, even though he was no longer a member of her family: how had Lil taken Hubie's death, had Uncle Laurance been helpful, what had happened to Juanito? But he dared not ask the questions, and she, once so full of news for him on all the inner machinations of her family, provided no information. He knew that she had ceased to love him, that if he put out a hand to touch her, she, who had craved his touch to the point of humiliation, would reject him, first as a woman rejecting a lover, then as an upper-class woman rejecting an upstart.

Bernie Slatkin was a man who examined his feelings, right at the moment of experiencing them. Within him, he held on to a strange feeling that he did not recognize, not letting it escape until he understood it. What is this feeling, he thought? It was not a pleasant feeling. And then its meaning came to him. It was loss, he realized. He repeated the word to himself. Loss.

"Do you think in time we could be friends, Justine?" he asked.

"No," she replied.

"Why?"

"I wanted to stay married, and you didn't, so we didn't. Now you want to stay friends, and I don't, so we won't."

Bernie nodded. "You've gotten tough, Justine," he said.

"Don't you think it's about time?" she answered.

"When is Hubie's funeral?" he asked.

"Tomorrow."

"Where?"

"St. James's."

"Of course," he said. St. James's, where all the weddings, christenings, and funerals of the Van Degan family took place, and had always taken place. "What time?"

"It's private," said Justine. With that, she made her move and continued her way down Madison Avenue to Lorenza's small shop to discuss the flowers. Peonies, she thought. Just white peonies.

Uncle Laurance made the decision that it would be far better for all concerned if there were no eulogy or hymns at the service, just the simple prayers for the dead, to be followed by cremation. Young Laurance, who would have been the logical person to make the eulogy, having been born the same year as his first cousin, was relieved by his father's decision, because he and Hubie had never, for an instant, enjoyed each other's company. Hubie's father, Hubert, was offended that he was not consulted in any of the arrangements, although he would have arrived at the same decisions arrived at by the Van Degan family. He did, however, in a show of assertion, let it be known that he intended to have his wife, Belinda, by his side in the family pew.

Lil Altemus, in the front row next to Justine, looked up at the rose window that Alice Grenville had given the church in memory of her son, and fanned herself with a letter she took from her bag. In the extreme summer heat the black linen dresses and black straw hats that she, Justine, Dodo, Janet, and other female members of the family wore looked wilted, and perspiration scents could be detected through deodorants, bath oils, powder, and perfume. "Wouldn't you think they'd air-condition this church?"

"Yes, Mother," said Justine.

"The peonies are lovely," said Lil.

"Yes, Mother," said Justine.

"There's no one like Lorenza for flowers," said Lil.

"Yes, Mother," said Justine. She didn't tell her mother the idea for the white peonies had been hers.

"Wouldn't you know Belinda would wear white instead of black?" asked Lil.

"I think she looks very nice," said Justine.

"Make sure you ask Boy Fessenden back to the house afterward," said Lil.

"Yes, Mother," said Justine.

"And Gus Bailey. Didn't I see Gus Bailey? Sweet of Gus to come."

Juanito Perez walked up the center aisle to the front of the church where the small congregation of mourners were gathered in the front ten rows. He looked on both sides to see where to sit. Juanito nodded to Lil Altemus who took no notice of him, nor did Hubert Altemus, seated behind Lil and Justine with Belinda, when Juanito nodded to him. Juanito was not one for going unnoticed and genuflected, in the Catholic manner, and crossed himself in the abbreviated fashion of a former altar boy, a point of his forefinger to his brow, his chest, his left shoulder, and then his right. "Name of the Father, Son, Holy Ghost," he could be heard whispering. Lourdes Perez, Lil Altemus's ladies' maid and sometime confidante, had never until that moment laid eyes on the lover of Hubie Altemus, and was aghast to realize he was the runaway son of her brother, Duarte, in Puerto Rico. Lourdes dropped her eyes and concentrated on her rosary, although she was in an Episcopal church.

"Who is that man with the diamond in his ear?" asked Lil.

"That's Juanito, Mother," answered Justine.

"What's he doing here? Who asked him?"

"You don't have to be invited to a funeral, Mother. A church is a public place. And he has as much right to be here as we have."

Dodo Fitz Alyn Van Degan, who could be counted on to annoy everyone in the family, waved a little wave at Juanito and signaled him to sit next to her, while Laurance and young Laurance and their wives looked straight ahead as if they were unaware of his presence.

Behind them all, Ezzie Fenwick, who never missed a funeral, and enjoyed social drama above all else, nudged Matilda Clarke and Cora Mandell not to miss the family snub of Juanito Perez.

"I do not want that man back at my house afterward, Justine," said Lil, measuring her words.

"I'm not going to tell him that, Mother," answered Justine.

"Tell Uncle Laurance to handle it," said Lil. "One thing, we'll never have to hear from him again."

"That's what you think, Mother," said Justine.

"What do you mean by that?" asked Lil. The minister, the Reverend Doctor Harcourt, Adele Harcourt's nephew, came out onto the altar.

"Hubie left everything to Juanito, Mother," said Justine, quietly, picking up the book of psalms in front of her in the pew.

"What?" said Lil, in a voice loud enough that all the Van Degans heard her. Then she lowered her voice to a whisper. "You must be mad. Hubie wouldn't have done anything like that."

"Will you please rise?" asked Reverend Harcourt.

Justine lifted up the book of psalms and did not reply to her mother.

"The Lord is my shepherd," said Reverend Harcourt, and the small congregation read along with him. Lil Altemus acted out giving her full attention to the service, but she was only half listening.

"Did you know Hubie Altemus?" Ezzie Fenwick asked Babs Mallett at Baba Timson's party.

"Yes," said Babs. "They lived near us in the country growing up."

"He died, you know."

"Yes, I know. Poor Hubie. Sort of a lost soul, didn't you think?"

"He didn't leave a thing to his family. Not even a memento."

"Oh, dear."

"All that furniture, all those pictures, and the silver were all Van Degan things his mother gave him. They say Lil is furious, all that family furniture going to that friend of his, Juanito *quelquechose*. Wears an earring."

"Oh, dear."

"Now, this is what I call a perfect *crème brûlée*."

* * *

"I don't understand how Herkie Saybrook could have allowed this to happen," said Lil.

"Allowed what to happen, Mother?" asked Justine, who knew perfectly well what her mother was talking about.

"You know perfectly well what I'm talking about," snapped Lil. "Those Charles the Tenth chairs came from the Altemus side via Aunt Minnie Willoughby. Imagine that ghastly Juanito having them."

Justine had heard the conversation over and over again since the reading of the will in Uncle Laurance's office. She had pretended not to hear when Uncle Laurance called Juanito "your brother's catamite."

"I've known Herkie Saybrook all his life," Lil continued, with or without a reply from Justine. "His mother and I came out the same year. He should have told us that Hubie was going to leave everything to Juanito whateverhisnameis, and we could have done something about it."

"It's what's called client privilege, I believe. Hubie hired Herkie. Hubie paid Herkie."

"But Herkie Saybrook is one of us," said Lil.

"So was Hubie, Mother," replied Justine.

Lil turned away from her daughter.

"I'll never speak to Herkie again," she said, after a moment. "I think Uncle Laurance should talk to him about this will. I also think Uncle Laurance should have him put out of the Butterfield. I never liked him anyway. Arrogant."

"You wouldn't have minded if I'd married him at one time, I seem to remember," said Justine.

"Let's not get into whom you should and should not have married, if you please. I can only concentrate on one thing at a time."

"What are you concentrating on now, Mother?"

"I'm concentrating on that horrible man with the earring performing unspeakable acts in Grandmother Van Degan's bed from the house in Newport."

38

THE RENTHALS TOOK a cream-colored villa in Monte Carlo and chartered a yacht. They sailed to parties in St. Jean Cap Ferrat, and Beaulieu, and Villefranche, and Antibes. The kind of people they met had not heard of the impending investigation, or, if they had heard, didn't care, so pleasure-bent were they. Americans always took those things more seriously than they did. It was for the Renthals a period of calm before the storm.

At first Elias claimed to not take seriously the investigation by the Securities and Exchange Commission. He thought he was being persecuted by a self-righteous district attorney with political ambitions, hoping to bring him down simply because he was so rich. "I'm smarter than most of the people trading today," he said, "and all those SEC people can't stand that."

When Ruby read in the *Wall Street Journal* that Elias had been implicated by a young lawyer from Weldon & Stinchfield called Byron Macumber, she remembered the night of her ball when Gus Bailey had asked to meet with her the next day. "Give me a hint, Gus, quick. You've got me curious," she had said to him when the Albanian Prince had cut in on her. "Byron Macumber," Gus had replied. She knew now that Gus was trying to warn her. She also remembered that Byron Macumber had called once at the apartment when she was dressing for a party and Elias had acted strange when she told him, as if he didn't know who Byron Macumber was, when all the time they had been in cahoots.

Elias thought of himself as a member of the establishment. He pointed out his membership in the Butterfield. He pointed out his friendships with people like Laurance Van Degan. "People like that, you see, are not about to allow anything to happen to me," he explained to Ruby, pointing out that members of the establishment stood together. He pointed out the innumerable acts of charity he had performed in the past few years, all carefully recorded in the pages of the newspapers. "Maybe we should get that guy Bus Bailey to do another article on us, talking about all our charity work," he said, making a mental note to check on whether or not Max had stopped payment on the check to Faye Converse for AIDS.

"Gus," said Ruby.

"What?"

"It's Gus Bailey, not Bus Bailey," she said, quietly.

"Whatever. We could fly him over here in the plane."

"I don't think that's a good idea," said Ruby.

"Why not?"

"I don't think Gus Bailey's the kind of guy who's going to do a puff piece on us at this moment in time," she answered.

"What makes you say that?"

"Did you read this piece he wrote on Jorgie Sanchez-Julia?" She held up a magazine with a photograph of Jorgie Sanchez-Julia dancing with the club-footed Geraldine.

"Jorgie Sanchez-Julia was a fucking gigolo who stole an old lady's money, for Christ's sake," said Elias, as if Ruby's reasoning was flawed.

Ruby stared at Elias, without answering, but the words, "You're a fucking thief who stole a lot more money, for Christ's sake," were in her thoughts.

Elias looked away, as if he could read her thoughts. "I'm going to call Laurance Van Degan right now to let him know I'll be at the Paris apartment all next week. We'll get this all figured out."

Miss Wentworth said that Mr. Van Degan was in a meeting and not available. When Elias called an hour later, Mr. Van Degan was still in a meeting and still not available, Miss Wentworth said. Elias left his Paris telephone number with Miss Wentworth for Laurance to call him there. Mr. Van Degan was out of the office when Elias called from Paris the next day. No, he could not be reached at home either. Mr. Van Degan was at the Van Degans' fishing camp in the Adirondacks. No, there was no telephone there, Miss Wentworth said.

Ruby, who had grown quiet and withdrawn, went where Elias planned for them to go, but she no longer arranged their social life with the passion she once had, as her passion for it had diminished, and her participation in it was obligatory rather than exuberant. Within her, she felt shame about the things that were being said about her husband, but, since Loelia, she no longer had anyone to talk to or to confide in. It was now Elias who insisted on going everyplace, saying that it was important for them to be seen. Ruby was content to follow Elias rather than lead him. Her sense of social reluctance was favorably interpreted, especially by the grand ladies she met who thought she was impeccably mannered.

At the hairdressing salon in the Hotel de Paris in Monte Carlo, Ruby ran into Loelia Manchester. It was their first encounter since the night of the ball. They exchanged greetings, like old friends who had lost contact, but Ruby did not ask Loelia about Mickie, and Loelia did not ask Ruby about Elias.

"Are you all right?" asked Ruby.

"Oh, yes, I'm fine," answered Loelia, smiling, but the smile covered a sadness. "And you?"

Ruby shrugged. "Fine, too, I suppose," she answered.

The two friends looked at each other, longing to talk as they used to talk, to tell each other everything, but neither could make the suitable opening for such a conversation, at least in the hairdressing salon of the Hotel de Paris in Monte Carlo.

"We went to this marvelous place in Germany," said Loelia, retreating into social conversation, and not mentioning Mickie by name. "We had these wonderful shots. Live cells from unborn sheep. So marvelous. Halts the aging process, you know. Goes right to all the vital places, heart, liver, kidneys. Not that you would have to begin thinking of things like that at your age, Ruby."

Ruby watched her old friend and noticed how rapidly she was talking. She noticed that Loelia was wearing an excessive amount of makeup so early in the day. To an observer, who did not know either of them, it might appear that Ruby, in her expensive simplicity, was the more refined of the two elegant ladies. Then, surprising both herself and Loelia, Ruby placed her hand on Loelia's chin and lifted it, turning her head to the left a bit. In the same way that poor dead Hubie Altemus had once applied makeup to his face at his sister's wedding to cover the blemish of his first lesion, Ruby saw that Loelia Manchester had applied makeup to cover a black eye.

"I walked into a door at the Hotel du Cap," said Loelia, although, even beneath her excessive base, a flush could be seen in her face.

"Will I see you at the collections?" asked Loelia. She meant in Paris, at the *couture* showings, where the skirts were going higher and higher and higher.

"No," answered Ruby, shaking her head. Her passion for high fashion, like her passion for social life, had diminished. She knew she would have no place to wear the short, short skirts that had become all the rage, even though she had the right kind of legs to wear them, because she understood she would no longer be invited when they returned to New York.

When they parted, with regret, for they missed each other, they made no plans to meet again.

"I sold the plane," Ruby heard Elias say to Max Luby on board their chartered yacht, as they sailed to Antibes to lunch at a fashionable house. Max Luby came to visit them regularly. "No point in having anything they can seize. Whatever flies, floats, or fucks, rent, is my new policy."

"How do I fit into that, Elias?" Ruby asked from her lounge chair on the deck, putting aside the book she had been reading. "Does that mean I'm rented?"

Elias blushed. "Just a figure of speech, Ruby," he said. "I meant the plane. I meant the boat. I didn't mean you."

Ruby lifted her hand. She was wearing the enormous diamond that Elias had given her at the time of their rise, the same diamond that Ezzie Fenwick had remarked upon at Justine Altemus's wedding reception, "If that rock is fake, it's silly. If it's real, it's ridiculous." With her thumb, she flicked the ring off her finger, and the huge flawless diamond fell into the Mediterranean Sea.

"Ruby, for Christ's sake!" yelled Elias, jumping up and looking over the rail to the sea. "Do you know how much that's worth?"

"Six million, two," she answered quietly.

Elias, red-faced and infuriated, grabbed Ruby by the arm and pulled her up from her chair and stared at her with the kind of withering look that in times past brought tears to the eyes of employees who worked for him. Unflinching, Ruby held his gaze for what seemed an interminable time, at least to Max Luby, who witnessed it.

"If you are thinking of hitting me, Elias, don't," said Ruby, in a tone of voice that he had never heard from her before.

Elias dropped her arm.

"Seven years ago, when I was still a stewardess, a guy in L.A. beat me up. I said then, and I meant it, that if a man ever laid a hand on me again, ever, I'd kill him."

"Jesuschrist, Ruby, I would never hit you," said Elias, collapsing into a deck chair. "This whole thing is getting to me. I'm not myself. I mean, I'm under such a terrible strain."

He put his head into his hands. Max Luby coughed.

"Get lost, Max," Elias said, and Max Luby, who understood Elias, and had grown to love Ruby, gladly abandoned them to the conversation that both had avoided since their flight from New York. "What's with you lately, Ruby?" asked Elias.

"You don't know?"

"You're not going to be broke, if that's what's worrying you."

"How like you to interpret my distress for my marriage, my husband, and our lives as bucks, Elias."

"What then?"

"I feel like you cheated on me with another woman."

"I never have. I swear to God."

"It's the same kind of betrayal. The mistake I made was thinking you were brilliant, but you're just like a kid who cheated in school."

Elias flushed. Nothing Ruby said could have hurt him more. "I am brilliant. There's no one who understands how to make money like I do."

"You can tell that to the judge, Elias."

"Oh, Ruby, don't say that," said Elias, reaching for her hand.

She let him take her hand but did not return his squeeze.

"I'm not being a bitch, Elias," said Ruby. "I feel left out. You treated me like a mistress, not a wife. Buy her a new fur. Buy her a new jewel. If only you'd told me what was going on."

"And if you'd known?"

"I would have stopped you," she said. "It's as simple as that."

They looked at each other.

"Max explained it all to me," she said. "Something you haven't bothered to do, about the Swiss bank in Nassau, and the fake name on your account, my name, by the way, and paying off all those young cheats feeding you information, like Mr. Byron Macumber, and I could only think, why? What more did we need that we didn't already have? We'd run out of new things to buy, and we still had more money than anyone else, so for a lousy few more million bucks, we end up in disgrace."

"Who said we're in disgrace?"

"Oh, Elias, please," she said. "Let us face up to the reality of our situation. So we're sailing on a yacht to Lady Montagu's lunch at her villa in Antibes, but, back there, in New York City, they're going to come after you and probably put you in handcuffs, just the way they put Byron Macumber in handcuffs."

"No way," said Elias. "Laurance Van Degan wouldn't allow that to happen."

"Laurance Van Degan doesn't even answer your phone calls anymore, Elias."

"He's in the Adirondacks, and there's no telephone at the fishing camp."

"I don't believe that somehow," said Ruby.

"He's my friend."

"Do you really think Laurance and Janet are still going to ask us to sit in their box on the opening night of the opera?"

"Of course," said Elias, expansively. "Laurance is a businessman. He understands. How the hell do you think old Ormonde's grandfather started the Van Degan fortune in the first place?"

"Not this way, I'm sure," replied Ruby.

He knew Ruby was right. He had not told her that Laurance Van Degan had been quoted in the financial section of the *Times* as saying, "I feel that Elias Renthal is insensitive to his fiduciary responsibilities to his policy holders." But he felt that she knew all those things.

"What do you want to do, Ruby?" Elias asked, wearily.

"I want to go back home. Whatever's going to happen, I want to let happen. Surely you've sold everything there was to sell by now."

"I thought you liked this kind of life. Lunch with the princesses. Dinner with the duchesses."

"Not anymore," said Ruby. "Not anymore."

That night, back at the rented cream-colored villa in Monte Carlo, Elias said to Ruby, "You never told me a guy beat you up in L.A."

"It's something I don't talk about."

"What did he do to you?"

"He knocked out a couple of teeth. He blacked my eyes. He fractured my jaw. He threw me down the stairs," she said, quietly, reciting her injuries like a litany.

"Jesuschrist."

She nodded.

"Did they catch the guy?"

"Not then."

"What happened to him?"

"He killed Gus Bailey's daughter."

S INCE HIS separation from Justine Altemus, Bernard Slatkin had made no attempt to keep in touch with any of the people he had met during the period of his marriage, which was one more indication to the Van Degan family that he had not tried to use them in any way, although it was rather a disappointment to Lil, who would have liked nothing more than to have labeled Bernie as an opportunist who had badly used her child for self-advancement.

One night on Park Avenue, late, after visiting his former apartment to remove the rest of his clothes, Bernie ran into Gus Bailey, dressed in black tie, who was walking home from another New York dinner party. The two men greeted each other warmly.

"I was sorry to hear about your divorce," said Gus.

Bernie shrugged. "These things happen," he said.

"I know," said Gus. "I wasn't a great success in the husband department either."

Bernie nodded.

"Going away?" asked Gus, indicating the luggage that Bernie had put on the sidewalk.

"No. Just picking up the rest of my clothes and junk that I left behind. Justine has put the apartment up for sale and wanted me to get everything out."

"Where's Justine moving to?"

"Back to her old apartment in her mother's building. She's really a Fifth Avenue girl, you know, cabbage-rose chintz, that sort of thing."

"Oh, Bernie," said Gus, reprovingly. "That's really not fair, is it?"

"No, you're right. It's not fair," said Bernie, kicking one of the pieces of luggage. "I'm just feeling ornery, or maybe guilty. Justine didn't even ask me to stay for a drink just now. I told her the station was sending a car for me to move the stuff, and she asked me to wait down in the lobby."

"She's hurt," said Gus.

"I know," said Bernie quietly. "Justine's a wonderful girl. Justine tried to make it work. It was my fault, not hers. I'm a slut, as you've probably heard. It seems to me half of New York has heard, thanks to my ex-mother-in-law."

Gus had heard. "I'm surprised I haven't been reading about you in Mavis Jones's column, taking actresses to opening nights."

"I've gone into the low-profile business," said Bernie, touching Gus's black tie. "Who's party are you coming from?" he asked.

"Let me see," answered Gus, figuring out the relationship. "Your ex-step-grandmother-in-law's."

"Oh, Dodo," said Bernie. "I always liked Dodo. Lil and Laurance treated her like she was a maid in that family, and then she fooled the two of them by marrying their father. Did you know she used to jerk old Ormonde off after showing him dirty videos that Hubie's boyfriend got for her?"

The two men roared with laughter. "Of course, I didn't know that, but it's a bit of information I'll store up here," Gus said, pointing to his head.

"Ezzie Fenwick always tells people that you're going to write a book about the bunch of them."

"Oh, yeah, I've heard he says that about me."

"Is it true?"

"Who knows? If I ever get the time."

"Here's my car," Bernie said. "Hop in. I'll give you a ride home."

"I heard you had a nice place," said Bernie, after they had settled in to Gus's apartment. " 'Nifty,' somebody called it."

"Who'd you hear that from?" asked Gus, handing Bernie a drink.

"We have a mutual friend," replied Bernie.

"Who?"

"Ms. Myra."

"Ah," said Gus, nodding. "Nice lady."

The two men smiled at each other.

"And knows some nice ladies," answered Bernie. "Perfect for this interim period of my life."

"That's your low profile?"

Bernie nodded. "Ms. Myra told me you had a nifty place."

"On the other hand, Matilda Clarke says it's just the right degree of shabby," replied Gus.

"That's supposed to be a compliment, I guess," said Bernie.

"Absolutely. You're supposed to say thank you."

"I see." They both laughed.

"What a bunch they all are," said Gus.

"What a bunch."

Bernie got up and looked at the books in the bookcases. "Do you read all these books, Gus?"

"Most of them."

"I ran into Juanito Perez recently at a restaurant in the Village," said Bernie, picking up a book. "He's a rich guy now."

"According to Dodo, it kills Lil that Juanito got Hubie's money. She wanted to sue, but Uncle Laurance said the publicity would be terrible for the family."

"Did you go to Hubie's funeral?" asked Bernie.

"Yeah."

"I hear they didn't let Juanito come back to the house."

"True."

"Did you know that Lil brought fifty Seconals to Hubie on the one time she visited him in the hospital?"

"No, I didn't know that," said Gus.

"True. Left them in a bag of books from the Wilton House Book Shop. Juanito told me that. Juanito flushed them down the toilet."

"Jesus," said Gus. "Lil and Laurance still pretend Hubie didn't die of AIDS, and they expect you to believe them."

"The Van Degans are a tough bunch," said Bernie.

"They're all tough, those people," replied Gus.

"The Bradleys' cook jumped out a window on the day of my wedding, right around the corner from the Colony Club, and the Bradleys still came to the reception. Yvonne Lupescu shot Constantine de Rham in the stomach that day and crashed my wedding reception and caught Justine's bouquet." Bernie made a gesture that indicated madness.

"A workman fell out of a cherry picker raising a weeping willow tree up to the Renthals' apartment on the day of their ball, and the ball went on like nothing happened, after Elias paid off the workman's family," said Gus, carrying on Bernie's theme. "Ormonde Van Degan died at the ball, and they stashed his body on a pool table so as not to spoil the First Lady's entrance."

"There's a strong indifference to death around that group," said Bernie.

"There's a strong indifference to death everywhere, Bernie," said Gus.

"What's your story, Gus? There's more to you than this quiet guy whom everybody talks to. Some people say there's a mystery about you."

"There's no mystery about me, Bernie. It's just that no one ever asks me about me, and I don't volunteer."

"I'm asking you now."

"A creep came along and killed my daughter."

"I didn't know that."

"I don't go around broadcasting it, but it's why I moved here. To sit out the three years of the creep's sentence."

"And then what are you going to do?"

"I'm going to go back to where I came from."

"And do what?"

"I'm going to kill the guy who killed my daughter."

"Come on."

"I am."

Bernie looked at Gus, and Gus met his stare.

"I'm going to make me another one of these," said Bernie, holding up his whiskey glass.

"I'm going to call out his name. I'm going to say, 'Hey, Lefty,' " said Gus.

"I want him to be looking at me at the moment. I want him to know it was me who did it."

Bernie, in the door of the kitchen, stared at Gus, not knowing whether or not he was being serious. "And then what'll happen?"

"Prison, I suppose."

"Prison?"

"Maybe that's when I'll have the time to write that book Ezzie Fenwick tells people I'm going to write," said Gus.

Bernie walked over to where Gus was sitting. "Gus," he said.

"What?"

"You don't really mean any of this, do you?"

Gus looked at Bernie for a minute and then smiled. "No, of course not," he said.

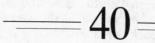

POOR HUBIE, people always said about Hubie Altemus, in remembrance, but his memory was already fading.

On several occasions Juanito Perez had tried to contact Lil after Hubie's funeral, once by telephone, on the butler's day off, when Lourdes had answered the telephone and hissed into the receiver in a torrent of Spanish that Juanito was not to call back at la Señora Altemus's house *ever,* or she, Lourdes, would tell her brother Duarte in Puerto Rico that his son was a *puto.* After that, Juanito wrote Lil on two occasions, but each time his letter to her was returned by Lil's lawyers, unopened.

"Isn't it marvelous the way Lil has handled the whole thing," people like Ezzie Fenwick and Matilda Clarke and Cora Mandell said about Lil Altemus, whenever anyone spoke about Hubie's death. They were referring to what her close friends called Lil's bravery in the face of tragedy. However, in the bosom of her family, those closest to Lil, like her daughter, Justine, her sister-in-law, Janet, her stepmother, Dodo, and her maid, Lourdes, knew that her grief, if grief it was, had taken on another form, an abiding hatred for Juanito Perez, whom she blamed for her son's death.

Sometimes in the night Lil would awaken from her sleep and remember family possessions she had given Hubie, that she hadn't thought about for years, that were now in the possession of Juanito Perez, and each time she would feel an anger so intense against Juanito that she began to have heart palpitations. She became obsessed over the set of twelve Charles X chairs from the house in Newport, that she had never cared for, that Aunt Minnie Willoughby had given Hubert and her when they were married, and that Lil had taken out of storage and given Hubie when he set up his own establishment. It mattered to her more than anything in the world that those twelve chairs be returned to the family, as though honor was at stake, although Justine didn't want them, and Lil had no room for them, even if she had cared for them.

Lil had not forgotten, although she had never mentioned it, that her stepmother Dodo had offered Juanito a seat in her pew at Hubie's funeral, nor that Juanito had asked about Dodo when she met him in the hospital at Hubie's bedside, so she asked Dodo to go to handle the task of retrieving the twelve Charles X chairs from the despicable Mr. Perez. Dodo, who had been left independently rich by Ormonde, no longer did the family's bidding, as she had done for years when she was a poor relation, and flatly refused the commission. "I wouldn't *dream* of doing such a thing," Dodo said, in one of her increasing shows of independence.

When her mother asked Justine to undertake the task she refused. Then she added that she would have nothing to do with such an unappealing task even if she were not pregnant. Lourdes, Lil's maid who listened to everything that went on in the family, had never told Mrs. Altemus that Juanito Perez was the son of her brother Duarte in Puerto Rico. She was glad she had not confessed to the relationship, as she knew that she would have been assigned the unpleasant task of getting back the chairs.

It was Ezzie Fenwick, whom Lil had taken into her confidence, over lunch at Clarence's, who suggested that the perfect person to arrange for the return of the chairs was Jamesey Crocus. As everyone knew, Jamesey Crocus was thought to know more about fine furniture than any man in New York and had lately served as private curator to Elias and Ruby Renthal during their period of acquisition. Jamesey, on his part, liked nothing better than to be sent on furniture forays for families like the Van Degans and the Altemuses, which always resulted in increased intimacies with the grand families and invitations to even their small dinner parties.

Jamesey Crocus, getting out of the cab in SoHo, looked in each direction before entering Juanito Perez's building, in the manner he often adopted late at night when, after he had returned a fashionable dowager to her uptown address, he entered a low haunt in a different part of town that he did not wish to be spotted going into, for fear of lascivious stories being circulated about him. Buzzed in by an intercom, he walked up three flights of stairs after a sign on the self-service elevator informed him it was out of commission. Juanito was standing in the open door of the loft that had once belonged to Hubie Altemus. Instantly, Jamesey, who had known Juanito before Hubie knew him, was struck by the change in his appearance. Although he was dressed casually, he was wearing a tweed jacket of excellent cut that Jamesey recognized as having been one of Hubie Altemus's and a blue shirt with a button-down collar open at the neck, in the manner that Hubie had always dressed. Jamesey looked at Juanito the way he had once looked at Ruby Renthal's console tables. Having money had eliminated from Juanito's face an expression that suggested furtiveness of character, a consequence of his extreme underprivilege, and replaced it with a look that brought out his good qualities. Only a cigarette hanging insolently from the corner of his mouth made him resemble the Juanito he had once known. For an instant they stared at each other.

"Very bad for you, smoking," said Jamesey, as a greeting.

"Don't see her for two years, and the first thing she says is, 'Very bad for you, smoking,'" replied Juanito, as if he were repeating this story to an audience. "Come in, Janie."

More than anything in the world, Jamesey Crocus, who moved in the finest circles, hated to be called Janie, but he said nothing. Inside, he looked around. The loft was, like Hubie, a combination of a life he left behind, but not completely, and a life he aspired to, but into which he never quite fit. A fire, going low, took the chill off the large room.

"How charming this is, Juanito," said Jamesey.

"I've kept everything just the same way Hubie had it," said Juanito.

"Oh, yes, of course," said Jamesey, who took this statement with a grain of salt. He had known Juanito to be promiscuous and notoriously unfaithful and doubted the sincerity of his maintenance of Hubie's home as a shrine. Jamesey expected Juanito to offer him a drink, so that time could be spent in friendly conversation before getting down to the purpose of the visit.

But Juanito did not offer him a drink. "To what do I owe the pleasure of this visit, Janie?" he asked.

"Mrs. Altemus, Lil, asked me if I would talk to you about some chairs that were left to you, a set of Charles the Tenth chairs," said Jamesey.

Juanito had not forgotten that his letters to Lil Altemus had been returned by her lawyers, unopened, a snub that still riled him. "Those, you mean?" he asked, pointing over to the dining-room area. Around the table were eight of the chairs. Two more were in a group of furniture by the fireplace. One was at a desk. The twelfth was by a telephone table.

Jamesey peered ecstatically through his owlish spectacles at the magnificent chairs. Clasping his hands before his stomach, he breathed heavily in the manner that he always breathed when he looked upon a rare and beautiful object. "Oh, my dear, how perfectly gorgeous," he whispered, breaking his own rule never to allow a possible seller to think that his wares were too valuable. "Charles the Tenth," he said, in his instructor's voice, as if he were giving a lecture on furniture at the museum, "was the younger brother of Louis the Sixteenth, who, as you know, was beheaded during the Revolution. During his reign—"

"Whatever it is you're up to, Janie, it's not in my favor. That much I know," said Juanito, interrupting a history lesson in which he had no interest.

"Don't call me Janie," said Jamesey, through clenched teeth.

"Too familiar? Is that it? Am I overstepping? Excuse me, Miss Crocus. Is that better?"

Jamesey decided to let it pass. The possibility of an association with the Altemus–Van Degan clans was too attractive for him to risk spoiling it by becoming irritated with a man he still considered to be no more than a hustler. "You see, Juanito," he said, in a friendly tone, "the chairs belonged to Aunt Minnie Willoughby, and she gave them to Lil, and Lil gave them to Hubie, but Aunt Minnie always wanted them to stay in the family, as heirlooms."

"Aunt Minnie Willoughby," said Juanito, in an exaggerated pose of pensiveness. "Wasn't she the dyke?"

"Oh, no, no, that was Aunt Grace Gardiner," said Jamesey.

"I never could get Hubie's family straight."

Jamesey, who understood the genealogy of all the best families in New York, said, "Aunt Minnie Willoughby was on the Altemus side, and Aunt Grace Gardiner, who indeed was a dyke, now that I come to think of it, was on the Van Degan side."

"I really don't give a shit," said Juanito. "Now, what are you here for?"

"Mrs. Altemus wondered—"

"You can call her Lil," said Juanito.

"Lil, of course. Lil wondered if you would give the chairs back to the family."

"Have you told Lil that you're the one who introduced me to Hubie?"

Jamesey paused. "No, no, I haven't."

"I wonder if she'd still send you as her emissary if she was aware of that fact."

"I'm sure that if money was the issue, Mrs. Altemus would buy the chairs back from you," said Jamesey, evading the turn the conversation was taking.

"You forget, Janie. I got more money than I could ever spend."

"It's quite chilly in here," said Jamesey.

"Hard to heat these big lofts in these old buildings. That's why I keep a fire going. Let me build up the fire," he said. Juanito walked over to the fireplace. "Remember the time you paid me by check, and it bounced?"

"I made that check good," said Jamesey, indignantly.

"Only after I threatened to black your eye on your way to Adele Harcourt's book club," said Juanito. "Shit, I'm all out of firewood." He picked up one of the Charles X chairs, turned it over, and broke off one of the legs.

"Juanito!" screamed Jamesey, as Juanito fed the chair leg into the fire and then broke off another leg.

"What's the matter? There's eleven left," he said.

"Those chairs are priceless. Were priceless, I mean."

"Now you tell Lil for me, when you report that you failed in your mission, that if she had bothered to speak civilly to me in the hospital when Hubie was dying, or if she had offered me a seat in the church at Hubie's funeral, or if she'd asked me back to the house after the funeral with all the other mourners, or if her fucking lawyers hadn't returned my letters to her unopened, in which I offered to return these family heirlooms which I inherited, I would have given them back to her, but now I won't. Get lost, Jamesey, and stay lost."

=== 41 ===

AT THE END of summer, the Elias Renthals returned to New York. Ever since details of Elias's corrupt stock-trading practices were revealed to his stunned colleagues in the financial world, as well as to the public at large, Renthal, a man once celebrated for his financial acumen, was now reviled by many as a symbol of Wall Street greed. Those who had not been invited to the Renthals' ball now let it be known that they had declined the invitation, as if they had advance knowledge of the financier's dubious behavior and chose, for ethical reasons, to absent themselves from what was now referred to as a vulgar spectacle. No one had a word to say in Elias Renthal's favor, or a doubt of his guilt.

At the museum there was a collective sigh of relief that the board of directors had stuck to its guns and not made Elias a member, even after his pledge of many millions of dollars for the construction of a new wing, and persuasive arguments on his behalf by some of its most conservative members like Laurance Van Degan and Addison Cheney. At the time an alternate proposal had been forwarded, before the financial scandal, of course, that Ruby Renthal join the board instead of Elias, as her elegance was thought to be more acceptable to the membership than the still-rough-around-the-edges Elias. That plan, too, had now been dropped.

To see Elias Renthal, however, in the weeks following his return, was not to see a crushed man. His business routines were followed the same as before, and, as was his practice, he continued to arrive at his office as early as six o'clock in the morning. He pored over financial publications, annual reports, and trade digests as avidly as ever, looking for investment ideas for his analysts to check out for him. His manner, which could be abrasive with subordinates who were not as quick as he in understanding market practices, remained as abrasive as ever. All of this was carried on with a sort of nonchalant attitude that belied the fact that investigators from the Securities and Exchange Commission were packing his files in cartons at the same time.

Nor was there any lessening of attentiveness in his manner of dress. He continued to order his suits, twenty at a time, from Mr. Sills, and his shirts and shoes from his shirtmaker and shoemaker in London, as if to show that all was right with his world, although there were those who wondered if he would not be in prison, in Allenwood, where his kind of felons were sent, by the time his suits and shirts and shoes, all of which took time, would be delivered to him.

It was not until after the taping incident, on a legally wired pay telephone in the office of the United States Attorney, that anyone made the connection between Byron Macumber's suicide the previous month and Elias Renthal. While Elias was still sailing the Mediterranean, an arrangement had been made between his lawyers and the office of the Attorney General to cooperate with their ongoing investigation by furnishing them with the names of his confreres in malfeasance.

When Elias walked into the Butterfield for the first time after his return from Europe, he did not notice that the usually affable Jasper, at the desk in the front hall where members signed in their guests, did not return his greeting. Walking up the curved marble stairway, which he had planned to copy for the new stairway at Merry Hill, he passed Sims Lord descending at the same time. At the moment of passing, Sims Lord gave no indication that he realized another person was within inches of him on the stairway. In the bar, where nearly every table was occupied with groups of two, three, and four, a pleasant buzz of conversation filled the air as members, recently returned from summer holidays, were happily greeting each other anew and ordering drinks and lunch from the excellent kitchen, which boasted of serving the best food of any club in the city. But, on the entrance of Elias Renthal into the lovely paneled room, a silence rose that was almost audible as each person looked up at the stout man standing in the doorway. There were many in the room whom he knew, from the club, from business, and from society. He had dined with many of them at their houses, both in town and in the country, and many he had entertained himself, some as recently as at his famous ball at the end of the spring season. No one rose to speak to him, and he was aware that he must bear their cold looks and silence without seeming to notice them.

He walked to an empty table, waving with a nonchalant air to Herkie Saybrook and young Laurance Van Degan, who were playing backgammon a few tables away, but neither raised his eyes from their game to return the wave. After sitting for several minutes, he rang the bell on his table for service, although Doddsie, who was usually so prompt in taking orders for drinks, was standing at the bar in quiet conversation with the bartender.

"An old-fashioned, please, Doddsie, easy on the bitters, but ample on the fruit," Elias said in a hearty voice. "And gimme one of your menus at the same time. I suppose you've got the chicken hash today."

"Every day," replied Doddsie. He was not rude. Nor was he friendly. Elias noticed the change in attitude.

"I'll have the chicken hash," he said, ordering, as if he were in a restaurant.

"If you would write it on the pad," said Doddsie. He did not add sir, and the omission was not lost on Elias.

"Oh, yes, yes, of course." He picked up the pad and small pencil and wrote his order, although he could feel the beginning of anger. If he were in a hotel, he thought to himself, and treated in this manner, he would buy the hotel, and fire Doddsie, and, now that he thought of it, fire Jasper at the entrance desk downstairs as well. With Sims Lord, he could understand. They had had a business difference, although Sims Lord's version of the hostile takeover of his company by Elias Renthal was described by him in stronger terms than a business difference. He looked over at Herkie Saybrook and young Laurance

Van Degan, still intent on their game of backgammon, and wondered if they had seen him or not.

He rose, old-fashioned glass in hand, and walked over to their table. When neither looked up, he stood next to young Laurance's side and watched the game for a bit.

"Hello, Laurance. Hello, Herkie," he said, when the game ended and Herkie was tallying the score.

"Mr. Renthal," Herkie and young Laurance said simultaneously.

"Mr. Renthal, indeed," said Elias, in an expansive manner, as if the young men were being formal with a respected elder. "You haven't forgotten, have you? It's Elias."

"We haven't forgotten, Mr. Renthal," said young Laurance. So saying, he banged on the bell on his table and called out, "Doddsie, I wonder if you could bring me the book with the rules of the club." While waiting, he continued to shake and roll his dice. When Doddsie arrived with the rule book, bound in blue, with green lettering, young Laurance said, in a voice heard throughout the room, "Will you look up and show me the page where it says that the Butterfield accepts members who wire themselves and entrap unsuspecting cohorts in order to lessen their prison sentences?"

Elias flushed scarlet.

Then young Laurance and Herkie rose and walked to the door leading to the dining room. "Are you ready for us, Doddsie?" Herkie asked.

"Indeed we are, Mr. Saybrook. Mr. Van Degan," answered Doddsie, back to his usual form. "There by the window."

Elias looked around the room and saw that the other members were staring over at the snub he had just received. When he caught their eye, they, in turn, held his for a moment and then looked away, except for Collier Stinchfield, of Weldon & Stinchfield, the old and respected law firm where Byron Macumber had been a junior partner. "Either that man leaves this club immediately, or I leave, and, if I leave, I will leave permanently," said Collier Stinchfield, his high aristocratic voice filling the room.

Elias placed his old-fashioned glass on the table where Herkie and young Laurance had been playing backgammon and walked toward the door where he had come in. By the entrance, he reached into a silver bowl and took out a handful of the Butterfield match books and stuffed them in his pocket. Walking down the marble stairway, he passed Laurance Van Degan coming up to have lunch with his son and Herkie Saybrook. Each met the other's eye, but neither spoke. In the downstairs hallway, Jasper did not look up as Elias Renthal walked by his desk and pretended not to hear the loud fart emitted by Elias at the front door as he walked out onto Fifth Avenue.

Instead of going back to his office, he decided to walk up Fifth Avenue to his apartment, have lunch there, and rest for an hour or so. On the marble-top table in the front hall, where the butler left the mail, he noticed an envelope from the Butterfield. Opening it, he saw that it was a letter from Laurance Van Degan, the president of the Butterfield, signed and dated two days before, requesting his resignation.

He needed Ruby. He needed to talk to her. He was tired of keeping up the front he had been keeping up for the last several months. He was hurt. He was ashamed. He needed solace. He went up the stairs. The door of her bedroom was closed. He tapped on it. It was his lovemaking tap, a light drumming of the fingertips against the panel of the door.

"No," replied Ruby from inside, recognizing the signal. "Leave me alone, Elias."

Renthal sings! said the headline in one tabloid paper. ELIAS (DON'T-CALL-ME-ELI) RENTHAL PLEADS GUILTY TO ONE COUNT! said another. Variations on this theme were echoed in every newspaper and magazine in the land.

"I always said, but no one ever listens to me," said Lil Altemus, dining at Clarence's in a family group, "that people like that are to be avoided at all costs."

"Oh, shut up, Lil," said Laurance Van Degan, who had himself been the recipient of numerous advance stock tips from Elias Renthal and lived in fear that his name would be brought into the investigation.

"Laurance!" said Lil, hurt, looking to her sister-in-law Janet for solace.

"We've all got trashy friends," said Janet, mediating between brother and sister, "but we should choose our trashy friends with more care."

"Oh, Ruby's not trashy," said Cora Mandell, quietly.

Ruby made no attempt to contact any of her friends. She remained mostly in her room reading or talking with her maid, Candelaria. She gave up Bobo as her hairdresser, not wanting to be the subject of gossip that Bobo could pass on to his other clients who knew her, and found another hairdresser, as yet undiscovered by the fashionable world, who came to her apartment. Lorenza no longer came to do the flowers two days a week, because there were no more guests and the doors to most of the rooms in the large apartment remained closed. At night Ruby went downstairs to dine with Elias, but she no longer shared a bedroom with him.

"It's Mr. Renthal's snoring," Ruby said to Candelaria in explanation of Elias's move to another bedroom. "I can't sleep with his snoring." But Candelaria understood what was happening.

One evening, early still, she crossed over to the park side of Fifth Avenue and sat on the bench opposite her own apartment, where each night she watched a bag lady make her home. She looked up at her own home and could see the soft pink light cast by the lamps on her persimmon damask curtains and walls. Above, the leaves of the trees on her terrace blew in the twilight wind. She thought of herself in the days of her grandeur, when the whole city, or at least that part of the city that interested her, came out to dance in her ballroom. It was several minutes before she realized that she had begun to think in the past tense.

"*Señora?*"

Ruby looked. Standing there was Candelaria.

Ruby had always wanted Candelaria to call her madam, the way Loelia Manchester's maid called her madam, instead of *señora,* but she had never had the nerve to tell that to Candelaria. Now she was glad she never had, for what did it matter? What did any of it matter now?

"Yes, Candelaria?" she said.

"*Hace mucho frío, señora,*" said Candelaria.

"You know I can't understand you when you don't speak English," said Ruby, who had learned to speak French but not Spanish.

"It's getting cold, *señora*. I brought you a shawl."

"You are sweet, Candelaria. Sit down."

"No, no, *gracias*."

"There's a woman who always sleeps here on this bench. I see her every night."

"*Si*."

"You know which one I mean?"

"*Si*."

"Later, when it's dark, I want you to bring her this," she said. She opened her bag and took out some money.

"Too much, *señora*," said Candelaria, looking at the two twenty-dollar bills Ruby handed her.

"No, it's not. Imagine what she must think looking up every night at where we live."

A jogger returning home from his run in the park walked rapidly by them. His face was pink from exercise, his hair wet, and his track clothes dripping. Had not Candelaria risen to leave at that same moment and collided with him, he might have gone on his way, not noticing Ruby Renthal, nor Ruby Renthal noticing him.

"I am sorry, *señor*," said Candelaria.

"No, no, it's my fault," he said, although it wasn't.

"Are you all right, Candelaria?" asked Ruby.

"*Si, si, señora*. Okay."

"Why, Mrs. Renthal, hello. We met at the Butterfield, on ladies' night. I'm Ned Manchester."

"Hello," said Ruby. "Of course. How are you?"

"Pardon my sweaty appearance."

"You look very fit and healthy to me."

"Do you often sit out here?"

"No. Never. I just had an urge to sit here and look up at my own house."

"Does it meet with your approval?"

"Too big, I've decided."

"Even the Clarkes used to get lost in that apartment, and they had the two boys," said Ned.

"I always wanted to have a child," said Ruby.

"And?"

"I guess it wasn't in the cards, even though I'm the mama type. When you're the third wife, the husbands already have their quota. How are your children?"

"They're well. Bozzie's going away to school. Charlotte says she wants to be an actress," said Ned.

"Oh, that should go over big with Grandmother Somerset," said Ruby, and they both laughed. Their eyes met. Ned liked the sound of Ruby's husky, fashionable voice. "You have a beautiful voice," he said.

"People say I sound like Loelia," Ruby answered. She spoke the name of his wife, for Loelia was still his wife, in a natural way, and he welcomed the openness of it, as everyone else he knew had gone to great lengths in the past year not to mention Loelia's name in front of him.

"You do," he said.

"When I first got to know Loelia, I used to imitate everything about her. Then it became natural. I'm what's called self-created." She laughed at herself and Ned joined in.

"Your looks are your own," he said.

"Had a little help there, too, my friend," she replied. "Oh, good heavens, the time," she said, looking at her watch. "I must go. Elias will be home."

"How is Mr. Renthal?"

"Let's just say he's been better," said Ruby. "We're in trouble. You've probably heard. I guess everyone's probably heard."

Ned nodded. "How have people been?" he asked.

"I don't know. I haven't seen anyone. I haven't called anyone."

"If you ever need anyone to talk to, I come by this way every night," he said.

"Thanks," she answered. She rose, shook hands good-bye, and left.

42

TIME WAS winding down for Gus Bailey. At some point along the way he stopped writing thank-you notes to his hostesses for the dinners he attended. Then he began declining invitations, first to one of Maisie Verdurin's dinners, and then to one at Violet Bastedo's, and then to Lil Altemus's. He had started to say, "I'll be away then," or, "I'm busy that night."

"They won't invite you anymore," said Matilda Clarke.

"I don't care," said Gus.

"Don't care?"

"I've seen enough."

Later, Matilda remembered that.

Bernie Slatkin ran into Gus Bailey at a restaurant in the Village and later told Brenda Primrose that he seemed distracted, as if his mind was on something other than what they were discussing.

Nestor and Edwina Calder came back from Hollywood, after shooting the mini-series of *Judas Was a Redhead*. Edwina and Nestor considered Gus one of their good friends, but, on the several times they called to invite him to dinner, he did not return their calls. People said Gus Bailey was spending more and more time by himself.

One night his telephone rang.

"Mr. Bailey?"

"Who is it?"

"You'll never remember me."

"Try."

"My name is Inez Peretti. We met once at—"

"At Ceil Somerset's. You're Ceil Somerset's psychic. Of course I remember you. Once I was going to call you, but I couldn't find the place card on which I wrote down your telephone number. I must have sent my dinner jacket to the cleaners, and they threw it out."

For a moment there was a silence.

"You're not surprised then to hear from me?" Inez asked.

"I'm not," said Gus.

"I got your number from Ceil."

"Fine."

"I feel like I'm always cautioning you."

"Yes."

"Last time I said you were going somewhere, and you said yes, you were going to Mary Finch's dance for Justine Altemus, and I said you were going somewhere before that, and not to go. Do you remember?"

"Yes."

"Did you go?"

"Yes."

"I feel that you are planning to do something."

"Yes."

"I feel revenge is in your heart."

"Yes."

"I wanted to warn you."

"Thank you, Inez."

"DO YOU HAVE any kind of religious affiliation?" asked Henry Caldwell, Elias Renthal's lawyer.

"Why?" replied Elias.

"I thought we might get you registered in some sort of theological school between now and the sentencing. We can get it planted in the papers. All that stuff really goes down with the judges," said Henry.

"Christ, I haven't been to church since God-knows-when, except for a Catholic wake I went to out in Queens a while back with the Sorrowful Mysteries, but that don't count as church. Besides, it wouldn't look good starting up religion now at this late date," said Elias.

"But there has to be something of that nature you can do, Elias. Like good works."

Elias was impressed with the idea. "Good works, right. How about if I work with the homeless? That's the big deal these days. Dish out soup or cut up carrots a couple of hours each day over at St. Bart's? And it's right near the office."

"Terrific," said the lawyer. "Mavis Jones will run that in her column for sure."

Deals had been arrived at, behind-the-scenes deals. For his cooperation in exposing other miscreants in the financial community with whom he had engaged in exchanging privileged information for personal gain, and paying a fine of $150 million, and divesting himself of his stock portfolio, Elias Renthal had had to plead guilty to only one criminal count, a single charge of stock fraud.

"I realize I've committed a very serious crime," said Elias Renthal, outside the courtroom, when the reporters asked him to make a statement. His lawyer tapped him on the arm to indicate that he had said enough, but Elias Renthal, even in adversity, was not one to be told when he had said enough. "I hope that by accepting responsibility for what I have done, I can make up for the anguish that I have caused my friends, my colleagues, and, most of all, my wife."

Looking at Elias, Ruby was unable to see his eyes. The lights of the television cameras reflected in the convex lenses of his gold-framed glasses and threw back the rays in iridescent circles. Elias had aged perceptibly in recent months. A blankness in his eyes and a permanent furrowing in his brows, and possibly his soul, bespoke shattered dreams and lost illusions.

"Poor Mrs. Renthal," said Bozzie Manchester, watching the evening news with his father. Ned looked over at his son and felt great affection for him, Yes, Ned thought, poor Mrs. Renthal.

It was impossible for any observer not to notice the change in Ruby Renthal's status, but Ruby was, everyone said, a model of rectitude, standing by Elias's side on the several times he had to appear in court before his sentencing, in a silent but supportive stance, dressed simply but expensively, her hair pulled back, her eyes not hidden by dark glasses. She never failed to hold her head up for all to see, assuming an attitude that could not be misconstrued as arrogant, which it was not, nor overly friendly, as if she were courting the press, which she did not.

The press had grown fond of her, and respectful. Even when they called her Ruby, which they did when they wanted to get her attention to pose for pictures or to ask her questions, they called her Ruby with affection, although she never answered any questions, nor ever stopped to pose. On her fingers she wore no more than her gold wedding ring. On her wrist she wore no more than her gold Cartier watch with the roman numerals that had once belonged to the Duchess of Windsor, but no one knew that except Ruby.

"My client is virtually penniless," Henry Caldwell had announced to the press over and over in the weeks preceding the sentencing, scoffing at reports that Elias had stashed hundreds of millions of dollars in Swiss bank accounts. Elias stood beside him, with a mournful expression on his face, but everyone knew that Elias Renthal was nowhere near penniless.

For propriety's sake, Elias, his lawyers, and his bodyguards squeezed into a Japanese compact car rather than his usual limousine to arrive at the court-house on the day of his sentencing, in the hopes of conveying the impression to the reporters and photographers that his circumstances were reduced. They drove downtown in silence, interrupted only by Elias, who shifted his position uncomfortably in the crowded backseat, saying to no one in particular, "I've been in roomier women."

On that morning the newspapers were filled with remarks by business leaders on the about-to-be-sentenced financier. Sims Lord, who had personal reasons for loathing Elias Renthal, said in the *Times*, "It is impossible for me to admire people who rape the system and then get nothing but a slap on the wrist because they have entrapped their fellow partners in crime. I hope the judge throws the book at him."

Elias looked neither left nor right as he walked up the steps to the court-house, flanked by his lawyers and bodyguards, ignoring the press as they yelled questions at him.

In the courtroom, there was not an empty seat. The sentencing of Elias Renthal was a media event, with press from around the world there to witness the great financier's downfall.

"Please rise," said the court clerk, as Judge Maurice McAuliff entered the courtroom.

Henry Caldwell pleaded that his client deserved leniency because he had exposed wrongdoing in ten major brokerage houses and had already paid a fine of $150 million. "A sentence in this type of case should not involve excessive incarceration," he said.

"It is unthinkable," argued the prosecutor, "that white-collar criminals can walk away by simply paying back what they have stolen in the first place."

Judge McAuliff, who was known to be lenient, listened to the arguments of both sides. "Your crimes, Mr. Renthal, are too serious to forgive and forget. It would be a terrible precedent for me to set in this court. The message must go out loud and clear that breaking the law is breaking the law," he said before passing sentence. "Criminal behavior such as yours cannot go unchecked."

Elias did not flinch when the judge sentenced him to five years in Al-lenwood, which meant, everyone knew, that, with good behavior, he would in all probability be released in two-and-a-half years. The judge was thought to have taken into consideration the work that Elias had done at a soup kitchen for the homeless at St. Bart's church during the time between his arrest and his sentencing.

If Byron Macumber had not committed suicide, and left two young daugh-ters, Kimberly and Sharon, Ruby might have been able to forgive Elias, but even after she had made an arrangement through her lawyers that would guarantee the education of the little girls from her own money, the suicide haunted her.

On the night before Elias was to check into Allenwood, Elias and Ruby dined alone, except for Max Luby, in their magnificent dining room, beneath ancestral portraits, on exquisite plates, and drank vintage wines from glasses embossed with *R*'s by a now dead Rothschild a hundred years before. Each was glad to have Max there because they no longer knew what to say to each other. Later, leaving, Max, good old Max, as he had become known to Ruby and Elias, embraced Elias, and the two old friends from Cleveland looked into each other's tear-filled eyes as they nodded farewell.

Later still, walking by Ruby's bedroom, on his way to the bedroom that had become his since they returned from Europe, Elias tapped with the tips of his fingers on Ruby's door, not for an invitation to enter, which he no longer expected, but as a way of saying good-night for the last time.

"Come in," came Ruby's voice from inside, to Elias's surprise.

"Really?" he said, entering.

"Really," Ruby answered, smiling, patting the side of the bed next to her for him to get in. Whatever had happened, Ruby knew that Elias Renthal had taken her out of one life and made another possible for her, and for that she was grateful.

They spent the night together, as if they were the young stewardess and the middle-aged millionaire they had been when they first met and had dreams, all of which had been realized.

"I'm not going to keep the apartment, Elias," Ruby said, in the back of their limousine as they drove to the prison in Pennsylvania for him to begin his term.

"Why not? There's still plenty of money," Elias answered. Even on his way to prison for illegal use of money, he still thought of everything in terms of money.

Ruby shook her head. "Too big," she said.

"The Rhinelander?" he asked. "Why don't you move to the Rhinelander, like Loelia did? That might be nice for you until you find a new apartment."

"I thought I'd leave the city for a while," she said.

"Leave the city?"

"I'm going to move to Merry Hill. Or, should I say, Not-So-Merry Hill."

"You'll miss your friends out there."

"No, I won't." She hadn't seen any of her friends since she returned from Europe.

When the limousine arrived at the gates of the prison, a swarm of television cameras and newspeople were gathered. Ruby touched Elias's face. "I'm not going to get out, Elias," she said, pulling back into her corner.

"No, of course not," he answered.

"I'll send books, and magazines, and things, and call and write."

"I'm sorry, Ruby," he said. "I don't know the right words to tell you how sorry I am that I put you through all this."

"I know, Elias," she answered.

"You know I love you, don't you?"

"Yes, I know," she said.

"You didn't hate being married to me, did you?"

"Only when you peed in my bidet," she replied.

They both laughed. "I'm going to miss you, Ruby," he said.

For a few moments they looked at each other.

"Kiss?" he asked.

"Sure," she replied. He leaned over and took her in his arms and kissed her warmly.

"Remember the good parts," he said.

"I'm trying," she answered.

"Bye."

"Bye."

Elias knocked on the window of the limousine, and the chauffeur opened the door. Immediately the buzz of the media could be heard as they swarmed around the door of the car.

"Listen, Elias," said Ruby.

"What?"

"You were swell to me. I'll never forget that."

LIL ALTEMUS, ever perplexing, cried unconsolably for Bobo, her hairdresser Bobo, when he died, in a way that she had never been able to cry for her son Hubie. Justine felt, as did Dodo and Janet and Matilda, that the tears she shed for Bobo were the tears she had not shed for Hubie. "So young," she kept saying. "So young," although Bobo was ten years older than Hubie had been.

It was when Bobo, whom Lil always claimed to have "discovered," was dying, in the same hospital where Hubie had died, that Justine, visiting him with armloads of his favorite rubrum lilies, the kind he had once used to adorn Justine's hair, decided to take hold of her life and do something useful so that she would not end up like her mother, serving on committees. "The Van Degan women have always had a sense of their responsibility to the city," Lil would say over and over to Justine, but Justine had other ideas about her responsibility than serving on her mother's committees.

After a gilded party chair collapsed under her weight during one of Maisie Verdurin's parties, Babette Bulbenkian, the immensely heavy wife of the billionaire Reza Bulbenkian, agreed to spend several months at a fat farm in Arizona. It was Yvonne Lupescu who had suggested the fat farm, which she called a diet farm, to Babette, telling her stories of wondrous weight reductions of friends who had gone there.

Returned, reduced, Babette pirouetted gracefully for her husband of thirty years, with the dainty mannerisms of a petite woman, to show off her weight loss of nine pounds and six ounces, a weight loss so insufficient to the amount she needed to lose that it was discernible only to someone as familiar with her body for as long a time as her husband was.

"Ah, yes, bravo, Babette," Reza said, clapping wearily for what Babette considered to be her triumph, and dreading the moments ahead of him. Reza had fallen hopelessly in love with Yvonne Lupescu, who had first caught his attention by complimenting him on the excellence of his toupee at another of Maisie's dinners, and, during his wife's absence at her fat farm, Reza had proposed marriage to her.

In prison, Elias Renthal had disturbing dreams that caused him to awaken covered with sweat, but he could never remember what it was he had dreamed. He missed the silk pajamas and linen sheets that the maids at his apartment in town and his house in the country had changed daily for him. He complained about the rough and scratchy toilet paper and wrote Ruby to send him a carton of the two-ply variety she ordered in England.

At first he was assigned to the laundry detail and later, after some string pulling, to the library, although he knew very little about books, other than books about finance and investments. He exercised every day and began to lose weight. On the advice of his lawyers, he attended church services on Sundays and agreed to be interviewed in prison by Gus Bailey, whom he called Gus, not Bus, wanting to be pictured in as favorable light as possible, as if the prison experience had transformed him and the greed that had enveloped his insides had evaporated. He talked to Gus of wanting to help other people when he got out, specifically the homeless of the city of New York.

He learned to play bridge, writing to Ruby that he was becoming a regular Ezzie Fenwick of the bridge table, and had a foursome with a former congressman, in for accepting bribes, a former head of a rock-and-roll record company, in for dealing cocaine, and the former head of a cement firm, in for illegal payoffs. He continued to read all the financial papers and magazines. Barred forever from trading on the stock exchange, he took to making imaginary investments. He found that even without insider information, he could have made himself a very rich man.

In the days of his business triumphs, Elias had disdained reading social columns as too frivolous or too time-wasting, but in prison he regularly read the columns of Dolly De Longpre, Florian Gray, and Mavis Jones and became consumed with curiosity about the social life of people he had once known. "We would have been there," he thought to himself, or told his bridge group, reading about Ezzie Fenwick's birthday party at Clarence's, or Adele Harcourt's small dinner for the First Lady, or Lil Altemus's reception at her Fifth Avenue apartment for Placido Domingo after his concert at the Metropolitan Opera House. Elias was envious of their freedom to come and go, and saddened to realize that, even after he had atoned for his sins of greed, those people who had once been his friends lived in a world that would never be available to him again.

45

A FTER GUS returned to California, he took to stopping in at Peach's house in the afternoons and sitting on the end of her bed. Sometimes she thought he wanted to tell her something, but he never engaged in anything more than desultory conversation.

One afternoon Gus thumbed through a magazine, casually reading an article he had written on Elias Renthal in prison, while Peach continued to look at her television set.

"Did you read this article I wrote about Elias Renthal in prison?" he asked.

"Not yet. I will," she answered.

Gus sometimes wondered if Peach ever read the articles he wrote. "As prisons go, that's the way to be in prison," he said. "I saw guys jogging with Walkmans in their ears. No high walls, or barbed wire. There's a painted white line, and the prisoners can't go beyond that, and none of them do, because if they do, they're shipped right out to a real prison, where the tough guys are, and there's no more jogging with Walkmans in their ears."

Peach nodded and went on looking at television.

"Did I tell you I put the apartment in New York up for sale?" he asked.

"I thought you liked that apartment," she said. "Doesn't it have a terrace? I think someone told me that."

"I did like it, but I wanted to get my things in order."

"Good heavens. You're not thinking of committing suicide, or anything, are you?"

"No."

"We've had enough to deal with in this family, you know."

"I know."

"Why did you come back to California, Gus?" asked Peach, turning off the television set.

Gus shrugged. "Why not?"

"I don't call that an answer, when I've asked you a question." They still talked like married people.

"I just decided that it was time to come back. I was gone for three years. I mean, this was home, wasn't it?"

"I thought you enjoyed New York. All those peculiar people you write about, like Elias Renthal and Jorgie Sanchez-Julia, and that ghastly dictator's ghastly mistress. I thought you liked all that."

"It was okay," Gus replied, not looking up from his magazine.

Peach looked at Gus. She was beginning not to understand her former husband, whom she had always understood so well.

Anthony Feliciano told Gus that Lefty Flint was being released from the Men's Correctional Institute in Vacaville, California, on the thirteenth of the month. His sister Agnes Flint and his fiancée Marguerite Hanrahan were planning to drive to Vacaville and bring him back to Los Angeles. He was going to work as a bartender in Marguerite's bar in Studio City.

"What was his record in Vacaville?" asked Gus.

"A model of decorum. Read his Bible every day. The warden's favorite," said Feliciano.

"Where's he going to be living?" asked Gus.

"In West Hollywood. On Reeves—1342¼ South Reeves. You can't see it from the street. It's a little apartment over the garage behind an apartment complex."

Gus took out his wallet and removed a blank check.

"I want to pay up," he said.

"I'll send you a bill at the end of the month, like always," said Feliciano.

"No, I want to settle," said Gus.

"You're not firing me, are you?"

"No, it's just the end of the line."

"This is the time to keep an eye on him, now that he's getting out."

"I'd like to settle up," repeated Gus.

"I thought you wanted his hands crushed in a vise."

Gus laughed. "That was only a figure of speech."

"Shit," said Feliciano.

"What?"

"I'd lined up a great guy for you."

"What kind of great guy? A hand crusher?"

"Something like that."

"No, no, thanks," said Gus. "That sort of thing is not up my alley." He moved toward the door. "Thanks very much for all your help."

"Listen, Gus," said Feliciano, stopping his exit.

Gus turned back to look at him.

"You don't mind my calling you Gus, do you?"

"Of course not."

"I read your article on Elias Renthal in prison."

Gus nodded.

"In case you're thinking of taking care of Lefty Flint yourself, the kind of place they'll send you to is nothing like the country-club prison that crook Renthal is in."

Gus looked at Anthony Feliciano for a moment, as if he was about to say something. Then he turned and left without saying anything.

At a red light on Sunset Boulevard, near the Beverly Hills Hotel, Gus looked into the light brown BMW in the next lane and saw Marv Pink behind the wheel. Marv Pink had been the defense lawyer who had managed to convince the jury that Lefty Flint had not committed murder, merely manslaughter, when he put his hands around Becky Bailey's neck for five minutes and strangled the life out of her. Marv Pink had on the same brown gabardine suit and brown tie with a single cream-colored stripe across the middle that he had worn during most of the trial. The feeling of revulsion that Gus always felt whenever anything to do with Lefty Flint intruded on his life came over him, but he continued to stare rather than look away, as if he were looking at a car wreck.

Aware suddenly that he was being stared at, Marv Pink turned and looked at Gus, whom he had not seen since Lefty Flint's sentencing three years earlier. The two men stared at each other from car to car. Marv Pink raised his hand in a gesture of greeting, and his iridescent cat's-eye pinky ring flashed in the California sunlight.

Gus Bailey did not give any indication of recognition.

46

WITHIN HOURS after Ruby Renthal put the vast apartment where she no longer wished to live on the market, the billionaire Reza Bulbenkian offered her twenty million dollars for it as a gift for his bride. Helene Whitbeck, the real-estate broker, said she had never had such an immediate reaction to an apartment in all her years in the business and thought that the famous ball of the Renthals had added to the cachet of the apartment.

After Bulbenkian divorced Babette, his wife of thirty years, at the same island resort where Bernie Slatkin had gotten his twenty-four-hour divorce, he immediately married Yvonne Lupescu, thirty years his junior, at a hastily improvised candlelit ceremony in the Lady Chapel of St. Patrick's Cathedral, which had been swathed in purple orchids and gardenias, Yvonne's favorite flowers, by Lorenza, for the occasion. Although the Cardinal did not officiate, because of all the divorces, he was present at the ceremony and at the small but lavish reception that followed at the Rhinelander Hotel.

Yvonne had hurried on the marital commitment, while Babette Bulbenkian was losing her nine pounds and six ounces at her fat farm in Arizona, following a confrontation scene between Reza and Constantine de Rham, who had burst in on the lovers in conjugal union in Constantine's house on Sutton Place.

Reza, in order to escape any unfavorable or even scandalous publicity, agreed to pay Constantine de Rham a sizable amount, after Constantine threatened to go to the police to tell them of Yvonne's part in his near fatal shooting.

Yvonne laughed and laughed. "It is simply this mad person's imagination, my darling," she said to Reza. "There is no truth whatever to what he says." However, she did not discourage her new fiancé from making his settlement on Constantine.

Reza's toupee was now gone. "I adore bald men," Yvonne told him. His teeth were now capped, also at the suggestion of his bride. Gone, too, were his black suits, replaced by smarter clothes made up in haste by Mr. Sills. Prodded by Yvonne, Reza made his offer for the Elias Renthal apartment, as soon as Ruby put it on the market, with a view to establishing himself and his new wife as top-flight social figures in the city.

"Look, Reza, we won't even have to change the drapes," said Yvonne, fingering the persimmon damask curtains of the drawing room, as if to prove to him early on that she was a woman who knew how to economize.

"Mrs. Renthal has marvelous taste," interjected Helene Whitbeck, the real-estate broker, who was showing the apartment.

Yvonne sniffed. "Ruby Renthal doesn't mean anything socially anymore," she replied.

The Bulbenkian purchase of the Renthal apartment came to naught however. The cooperative board of the exclusive building, embarrassed by the publicity brought on by Elias Renthal's financial disgrace, let it be known that the Bulbenkians would be turned down by the board if they should apply. Florian Gray printed in his column that the Bulbenkians had been turned down by the building.

"We'll sue," screamed Yvonne.

"Sue," replied Mrs. Sims Lord, who was the president of the co-op board and known to be fearless in her dealings with upstarts. It became known among the sort of real-estate brokers who dealt in dwellings for the very rich that the board wanted only people like themselves to live in that building from now on and had even voted to break up the enormous apartment into three smaller apartments, which people with lesser fortunes but more breeding than the Renthals and the Bulbenkians could afford. Or, as Mrs. Sims Lord said at a dinner that very night at Lil Altemus's, "We've had quite enough of the billionaires, thank you very much." To which Lil Altemus replied, "Hear, hear."

Undeterred by the rebuff, Bulbenkian purchased a house of embassy proportions that had long been shuttered on Park Avenue.

The crowds turned out in record number for the three-day viewing that preceded the auction of the four thousand lots that made up the contents of the Elias Renthals' forty-one-room apartment on three floors that they had purchased from the estate of the late social figure Sweetzer Clarke. So great was the public interest in the magnificent possessions of the convicted financier and his elegant wife that lines formed around the block of the auction house on York Avenue, and people waited for as long as three hours to simply march by the treasures, while guards admonished them to keep moving so everyone would have a turn before closing time. The *New York Times* said, in its front-page coverage of the event, "The Renthals collected it all in record time. Now they will dispose of it in even less time."

Antiques dealers, private curators and museum curators, and collectors of eighteenth-century French and English furniture arrived in New York from

London, Paris, and Tokyo for what had come to be known as the Renthal sale, in the way that their ball had come to be known as the Renthal ball. At night various charities took over the showrooms, and the rich of the city, unwilling to wait in line with the hoi polloi, paid hundreds of dollars each to view what the poor could see for free, with the certain knowledge that their admittance fee was going for a good cause. Ruby Renthal, who had become reclusive, declined to be present at any of the charity events.

"Oh, please, Ruby, come," begged Maude Hoare, who was chairperson for the evening benefiting the Hospital for Plastic Surgery.

"I can't. I'm sorry," said Ruby.

"You'd be an extra added attraction for the evening," said Violet Bastedo, who was chairperson for the evening benefiting Ballerina House, a home for indigent dancers.

"I'm sorry," said Ruby.

"Damn her," they both said later.

"Oh!" said Lil Altemus, covering her face with her catalogue, as she and Ezzie Fenwick jockeyed for position in front of Elias Renthal's pool table that had once belonged to Edward VII.

"What's the matter, Lil?" asked Ezzie.

"Daddy died on that pool table," Lil said, touching the faded green felt on which Ormonde Van Degan had expired on the night of the Renthal ball.

"Oh, right," answered Ezzie, whose eyes were eagerly scanning the crowd for people to wave to. He did not wish to be reminded that Lil and her stepmother Dodo had walked in on him passing information that Elias Renthal was under investigation by the Securities and Exchange Commission to the gossip columnist Florian Gray at almost the same moment that Lil had discovered her father dead on the pool table.

"Look, Ezzie, aren't those the console tables that Ruby gave to the White House?" asked Lil Altemus. "Over there. With the rams' heads."

"They were returned to the Renthals by the White House," answered Ezzie.

"Because of the scandal, you mean?"

"Because they were inauthentic."

"No!"

"Yes. Jamesey told me."

They exchanged looks, as if to say, "What can you expect, from people like that?"

At the last moment, the auction was canceled. Reza Bulbenkian made an offer for the entire contents of the vast apartment. At a hastily called meeting between the auction house and Ruby Renthal, the decision was made to accept Reza Bulbenkian's offer. The auction house felt that the enormous offer made by the financier could very well be in excess of the profits from an auction of the possessions of a disgraced figure, and Ruby Renthal felt that it would halt the avalanche of publicity connected with the sale that put her name and photograph in the newspapers every day.

"How did you manage to halt the auction?" a reporter asked Reza Bulbenkian, at the news conference set up by the auction house and Reza to announce that the sale had been canceled.

"You can buy anything you pay too much for," said Reza, nodding his head, like a wise sage of finance.

The antiques dealers who had traveled to New York from around the globe for the sale hissed and booed the decision.

"I am so happy with Reza," said Yvonne Lupescu at the news conference, linking her arm in his and smiling up at him, as if saving the day. Unlike Ruby Renthal, Yvonne had no desire whatsoever to shun the press. She waved to the cameras. On her finger was a diamond the size of the diamond that Ruby had dropped into the Mediterranean. "Reza is the man I have been waiting for all my life." They hoped, she said, to be able to start entertaining in their new home in two weeks.

To her hairdresser, in private, she added, "He's rich. He doesn't drink and, thank heaven, he doesn't want to be beaten."

I N PRISON, it hurt Elias Renthal when he heard that his apartment had been sold, even though Ruby had told him on the way to prison that she didn't want to live there anymore. The apartment represented everything that he had ever strived for in his life, and he had always enjoyed the astonished looks on the faces of even the most established and wealthy visitors when he showed them through it. It hurt him even more when he heard that it was being divided up into three smaller apartments, making it forever irretrievable and squashing the daydreams he sometimes indulged in of resuming his former life after his release from Allenwood, a better and wiser man.

It enraged him that Reza Bulbenkian and his new wife, the former Yvonne Lupescu, should have purchased all the furniture and paintings that he and Ruby had collected so lovingly and that they were already starting to entertain on a lavish scale in their new mansion on Park Avenue, rivaling the life-style that the Renthals had made famous. Elias loathed Reza Bulbenkian and told his three bridge companions of crooked things that he knew Reza had done in business and gotten away with. Then he added, "so far," meaning that his practices would eventually catch up with him, too. The congressman, the rock-and-roll executive, and the cement-company owner laughed. They loved hearing Elias's stories. Elias also told them that Yvonne Bulbenkian used to be one of Ms. Myra's girls, before she took up with Constantine de Rham, and carried her whips in a custom-made Vuitton case. "Imagine, a former hooker running New York society," he said.

Most of all Elias missed Ruby. More than anything in the world, he wanted to make it up to Ruby for the embarrassment and the ostracism that he had caused her. He never remembered her as she was when he first met her, a pretty stewardess with a sassy manner. He thought of her coming down the stairway of their apartment on the night of their ball, dressed in white and wearing all her diamonds, and marveled each time he thought of her as the great lady she had become.

"Max comes to visit," Elias said to Ruby one day when she drove up from Merry Hill to see him.

"Good old Max," said Ruby.

"Max saw Loelia Manchester at the opera."

"Max at the opera? What next?" replied Ruby.

"He said he thought Loelia was unhappy."

"Heavens," said Ruby.

From the time of her arrival, Elias knew there was something on Ruby's mind, all during the time they were talking of other things, like Max Luby and Loelia Manchester.

"Elias," said Ruby, finally. "There's something I have to tell you."

"What's that, Ruby darling? Anything you want. Anything."

Then Ruby asked Elias for a divorce. She brought with her the papers for him to sign. Elias was devastated by Ruby's request but was not totally surprised. The congressman's wife had divorced him. The wife of the head of the record company had divorced him. The head of the cement company was already divorced. His hand shaking, he signed the papers.

"At least you didn't break the news to me through a lawyer," he said.

"You know I'd never do that to you, Elias," she answered.

"My friend the congressman read about his wife's divorce in the newspaper."

"Or that."

"I'll miss you."

"I know."

"Don't remember me badly."

"I won't. Count on that." Ruby took out a handkerchief from her bag and wiped a tear from her eye. Then she began gathering up her things and put the papers he signed into her bag.

"Well, good-bye," she said, rising at the end of the visit.

"We're allowed to kiss," said Elias.

"Oh, yes, of course." She smiled. As he leaned toward her, she averted her face a fraction of an inch so that his kiss landed on the side of her mouth rather than full on her lips, like a son at boarding school saying good-bye to a departing mother. Elias understood. Each avoided the other's eye. For a few moments they simply stood there.

"I read in Dolly's column that Loelia married Mickie," said Elias, wanting to forestall her departure.

Ruby nodded. "I read that," she answered.

"What do they call her now, Loelia Minardos?"

"Apparently."

"Don't sound so snappy as Loelia Manchester."

"I suppose not."

"You don't see Loelia?"

"No."

Elias nodded. "I wonder if she paid Ned all that money he was asking."

"No," said Ruby.

"How come?"

"Ned would never have taken money from Loelia. It was just to keep her from marrying Mickie that he asked for all that money. Now he doesn't care."

"How do you know?"

"That's what I heard."

Lord Biedermeier visited Elias in prison and reported at a dinner party later that same evening, at Maisie Verdurin's house, that Elias had wept when he talked about the divorce. Feelings against Elias still ran high, and the consensus was that Ruby Renthal had done the correct thing.

"Ruby just dropped out of sight," said Maude Hoare. "I don't know a soul who sees her."

"Poor Ruby," said Aline Royceton.

"But why in the world did you go to visit Elias?" asked Maisie.

"Oh, I was always fond of Elias," replied Lord Biedermeier.

Lord Biedermeier did not say to the group at his table that he was hopeful of securing a second book from Elias, on the prison life of a billionaire, even promising him someone willing to make weekly visits to Allenwood to ghost-write it for him.

"A sort of *De Profundis*," Lord Biedermeier had said to Elias in the visitors' room, shifting his position to see him better through the mesh screening that separated them.

"A sort of what?" asked Elias.

"*De Profundis. De Profundis*," Lord Biedermeier said, clapping his hands in mock exasperation, as if everyone in prison would know about Oscar Wilde's final prose written during his incarceration. "Listen to this, Elias," he said, quoting, loosely, from Wilde's letter to Lord Alfred Douglas, that Lord Biedermeier had jotted down on the back of an envelope in the limousine on his way to the prison in Pennsylvania. " 'I have disgraced my name eternally.' " Lord Biedermeier gestured toward Elias to show that he, too, had disgraced his name eternally. " 'I have made it a low byword among low people. I have dragged it through the very mire, and turned it into a synonym for folly.' You see Elias, you could change folly to greed."

But Elias Renthal, whose name had indeed become a synonym for greed, could not think of *De Profundis* that day. Elias Renthal could only think that he had lost Ruby Renthal forever. He could only look blankly at Lord Biedermeier.

"Keep a journal, Elias. Write everything down, the day-to-day of what happens here. Get to know the most serious offenders. What a book it will make!" He clapped his hands, and his pince-nez fell off. "Start reading the Bible every day. You know the sort of thing, I-found-God-in-Allenwood. The public will eat it up, and everyone will be on your side by the time you get out. There's a whole great big life waiting for you out there. Oh, perhaps not with the Van Degans and that set, but there's other fish to fry in life than Laurance

Van Degan who, by the way, in case you hadn't heard, had to resign as president of the Butterfield."

Elias looked up. "Because of me?" he asked.

"Apparently," replied Lord Biedermeier.

"Holy shit."

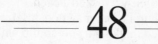

G US MOVED into a hotel in Hollywood. He read books he had always meant to read. He watched videos of films he had wanted to see, but missed. He called none of his friends from the years he had lived in Hollywood, when he worked in films, and he did not frequent any of the restaurants where he was likely to run into people he knew. Several times a day he drove by the apartment complex in West Hollywood that blocked 1342¼ South Reeves from view from the street, but he never got out of his car. Every day he stopped in to see Peach, usually late in the afternoon. Every few days he went to the cemetery where Becky was buried and lay a rose from Peach's garden on her grave. Peach watched her former husband and worried that he might be having a nervous breakdown.

"He's out," Gus said one day, when they were staring at one of the afternoon soap operas that Peach always watched. He had come into her room and sat on the edge of the bed for twenty minutes before he said a word.

Peach didn't say, "Who's out?" even though they had not mentioned Lefty Flint's name since Gus returned to California.

"How do you know?" she asked instead.

"I just know."

"Did your private detective tell you?"

"He wasn't a private detective."

"I know he wasn't a private detective."

"I fired him."

"Then how do you know? Vacaville doesn't send out announcements."

"I saw him."

"You saw Lefty?" she asked. Peach looked at the back of his head. She picked up the tuner and turned off the television set.

"Where?"

"Carrying groceries out of Stop and Shop."

"Did he see you?"

"No."

"Was he alone?"

"No. Marguerite what's-her-name was with him. The bartender."

"Don't make me pull it out of you line by line, Gus. Tell me everything."

"They were laughing. They were enjoying themselves. I can't stand it that he should be happy, after what he did."

"Where did they go?"

"He has an apartment at 1342¼ South Reeves in West Hollywood. They went there."

Peach picked up a magazine from the bed. "Of all the cities in this country, why did he have to come back here where it happened?"

"Sometimes I wonder why we were never searched all through the trial when we went into the courtroom," said Gus. "It would have been so easy."

"What would have been so easy?" asked Peach.

With his forefinger and thumb, he imagined his Luger in his hand. He pulled his trigger finger and fired, making a *pow* sound with his lips at the same time. In his mind, his bullet hit its target.

Peach stared at him. Then she leaned over and picked up the telephone. "I'm going to call Detective Johnston," she said.

"Why?"

"I know that son of a bitch is going to come here. I know it. I've known it ever since he wrote me that letter from prison. I want them to put a guard on my house."

"He won't come here, Peach. I guarantee you that."

By the end of the first week, Gus had gotten the movements of Lefty Flint down. He knew the time of day Lefty Flint rose. He knew the diner where he had breakfast. He knew the laundromat where he took his washing. He knew he marketed at the Stop and Shop for only one day's provisions at a time, as if he were a temporary visitor. After lunch he drove Marguerite to her bar in Studio City and left her there. Sometimes in the afternoon he went to a film. He stayed by himself most of the time. At seven he went to the bar again and took Marguerite out to an early dinner at a restaurant near the bar. After dinner, he went to work as night bartender and stayed on duty until closing time. Marguerite often left between ten and eleven, either taking a cab home or getting a lift from someone she knew, but it was usually about two, after the glasses were washed and the tables stacked and the trash put out and the waiters paid, before Lefty Flint locked up and left the bar by the back entrance. There was a space by the trash cans where he parked Marguerite's Nile-green Toyota. Gus had twice tried the doors of the car, but they were locked. He had tried hiding himself behind the trash cans, but once he accidentally knocked one over. Afraid that the sound would attract attention, he had retreated to the street and walked away as fast as he could.

On an early morning, before anyone in the area of bars and restaurants was around to open the businesses, he made an inspection of the alley behind the bar. He found a place to stand on the far side of the alley wall, where, at night, he could not be seen but where he could see perfectly the back door of the bar, the trash-can area, and the place where Flint parked Marguerite's Toyota. He held up his hand, as if he were holding up the German Luger, and imagined pulling the trigger. The gesture and the *pow* sound he made had become a habit.

* * *

On the morning of the day that Gus planned to kill Lefty Flint, he went to Mass at a church he had never been to before. He sat in a back pew throughout the service without participating in it, like a street person seeking temporary shelter, neither reciting the prayers nor taking communion.

"What the hell are you doing here, Gus?" asked a voice from behind him as he was leaving the church.

Gus, surprised, turned. It was Faye Converse.

"What the hell are *you* doing here?" he replied.

"They've got a hospice here for some of my people," said Faye. "I come to visit from time to time. Brucie is here. Remember Brucie? My secretary. You met her on the plane."

"Sure I remember Brucie. How is she?"

Faye shrugged the shrug that said not good, or good under the circumstances.

"Give her my love."

"You look strange, Gus."

"How strange?"

"Not yourself. Haunted, sort of."

"How's this?" he asked, assuming a happy stance.

"Better. Better. I read your piece on Elias Renthal in prison. The son of a bitch."

"Why son of a bitch?"

"Did you know he stopped payment on the two-million-dollar check he gave me at the ball?"

"I don't believe it!" replied Gus, amazed, although he did believe it. It was the first time in weeks he had been interested in anything but Lefty Flint.

"Ruby made the check good, though," said Faye. "I liked Ruby. Terrible position she's in now."

"She's a class act, Ruby," said Gus.

"You never let me know when you're out here. How long are you staying?"

"I'm not sure."

"I'm having a party tonight. Come."

"Can't tonight."

"Yes, you can. What are you doing that's more important than a movie-star party at Faye Converse's?"

"I'm going to kill a guy."

"Well, come after you kill the guy," she said.

They both laughed.

Later, on the evening of that day, Gus went to see Peach. He stood in the doorway of her bedroom most of the time, rather than sitting on the end of her bed, as he usually did.

"Did I ever tell you about this woman I know in New York called Ruby Renthal?" asked Gus.

"Whose husband is in prison for insider trading, that one?"

"That one."

"I don't know if you did or not. She gives parties and lives in that vast apartment. I've read all that."

"Her name used to be Ruby Nolte. She used to be an airline stewardess."

"Is there a punch to all this?"

"There is. About seven years ago, when she was still a stewardess, she got beaten up here in Los Angeles, by a man she was involved with at the time. The guy really bashed her face in."

Peach, interested now, looked at Gus.

"She was in the hospital for ten days. She wanted to press charges, but the guy warned her not to, and the guy had some tough friends, and so she didn't press charges."

"Yes?"

"The guy was Lefty Flint."

"Why did I know that was what you were going to say?"

"He's going to do it again. You know that, don't you?"

"Then call the police, Gus."

"The police can't do anything until after the damage is done."

They remained in silence for a few moments.

"I have to go," said Gus, finally, looking at his watch, as if he were on a schedule. He walked toward her bed. As usual, she was barricaded in it by her wheelchair and the long table covered with books and magazines. He undid the brake of her wheelchair and backed it out of his way, pushed the table to the side, and walked up to her. When he was by her side, he bent down and kissed her. In his gesture, she read farewell.

"S'long," he said.

"You sound like you're going on a trip," she replied.

"No."

"Are you all right, Gus?"

"Sure."

"You sound odd."

He looked at the woman he had been married to for so many years, and divorced from for so many years. Nearly bedridden, she had become accustomed to staring at a television set with picture but no sound when she did not wish to deal with the moment at hand in her life, but this time she returned her former husband's look. He felt a tremendous affection for her.

He turned and replaced the wheelchair in its correct position, braked it, put her table back in place, and walked out of her room, down her hallway to the front door. There, on a table, in a chipped porcelain bowl, was a bouquet of roses from Peach's garden, jammed together, in an arrangement that Lorenza, in the unlikely event she ever saw it, would disapprove of. Gus reached in and pulled out a yellow rose, open to almost full flower, and took it with him as he opened the front door and walked to his rented car parked in the driveway.

"Gus," called Peach after him, but he did not hear. In a louder voice, she called for her housekeeper. "Immaculata! Immaculata!" Next to her bed, on the overcrowded table, she found her bell and rang it and rang it again.

"Sí, señora?" said the older woman, shuffling into Peach's room in bedroom slippers.

"Stop him," cried Peach. "Outside. Mr. Bailey. Stop him."

Immaculata shuffled out of the room, unhurried, as always, down the hall to the front door, just as Gus's car was pulling out of the driveway. Alerted now to the emergency of the moment, she ran down the steps of the house, waving her dish towel in the air, but Gus did not see her.

His German Luger, cleaned and loaded, was in the glove compartment of his rented car. At eleven o'clock he drove to Studio City, being very careful to adhere to the posted speed limit, allowing other cars, going beyond the limit, to pass him. A car coming toward him in the opposite lane had on its bright lights, and he was momentarily blinded. He put his hand up to shield his eyes. As the two cars passed, he turned to curse the occupant, and his eyes locked for an instant with the driver's. He felt troubled, but he did not understand why.

He parked his car on a side street a block away from Marguerite's bar. He remained in the car until a quartet of noisy bar hoppers had turned the corner, and then he opened the glove compartment and took out the German Luger. He walked to the alley and took his place behind the wall. It was several moments before he realized that Marguerite's car was not parked in its usual place. An image of the car with bright lights flashed through his mind, and he wondered if he was now imagining that it had been Nile green. He walked out the alley to the street and turned the corner to where the entrance of the bar was. He had not been inside the bar since his brief encounter with Marguerite some months before. Entering, he turned away from the bar itself as if he were going to the men's room. Losing himself behind some patrons, he looked over at the bar. Lefty Flint was not tending bar.

"Help you?" asked a waiter with a tray of beer bottles.

"No, no, thanks," said Gus, making his way to the door.

Outside he ran the several blocks to his car. He drove to 1342¼ South Reeves. He parked his car on the street and walked down the driveway at the side of the complex, staying as close to the shrubbery as possible. Behind, the Nile-green Toyota was not in the parking place below the garage apartment. Upstairs, the venetian blinds were closed, but Gus could see light coming through the slats.

Frightened now, his heart beating fast, Gus mounted the rickety wooden stairway that led to the front door of the apartment. He looked but could not find a bell. He took the gun from his pocket and held it in one hand. With the other, he knocked on the door. There was no reply. He knocked again.

From within, he heard sounds. A shade covered the glass part of the door. He saw someone pull back the shade a crack and look out.

"Who is it?" came a woman's voice.

"I'm looking for Lefty," said Gus.

"You're too late," said the voice he recognized as Marguerite's. "Lefty's gone."

"It's Gus Bailey, Marguerite. We met once before," said Gus through the door.

She opened the door but left the chain on. "What do you want, Mr. Bailey?" she asked.

"Where's Lefty?"

"Gone. I should have listened to you, Mr. Bailey," she replied. "I guess you were trying to help me, but I didn't want to hear back then."

"Open the door, Marguerite. Let me in."

She took off the chain and opened the door. When Gus walked into the kitchen of her small apartment, he saw that her eye was closed, and her face had been beaten.

"Jesus," he said. "Come on with me. I'll take you to the emergency room at Cedars."

"I'm okay," she said. "I got off easy. It's not bad. I feel like such a god-damn fool. He just used me. I arranged for him to have a job when he got out, and a place to live, and he was all full of good intentions, and the parole officer thought he was all rehabilitated and on the straight and narrow, but working behind a bar was not exactly what he had in mind for himself. I thought the guy was in love with me, when I used to visit him in Vacaville, but the pickins are slim for guys in prison. They're not in great demand, if you know what I mean, and it's only some asshole like me, with my misguided sense of social con-sciousness, who would have thought that a man who strangled a woman and beat up other women was rehabilitated in three years."

"Where did he go, Marguerite?"

"You're just as big a fool as he is to go searching for him with a gun, Mr. Bailey," she answered.

"Tell me where he went," repeated Gus, insistently.

"Put your gun away, Mr. Bailey. He's gone. He's on a plane somewhere."

"Where?"

"He didn't confide in me. He just knocked me around a bit."

"Where do you think he went?"

"You weren't at the parole hearing, were you?"

"No. There was no point."

"There was some rich lady there who asked the parole board not to release him. He had a real grudge against that lady."

Gus stared at Marguerite. "What rich lady?"

"She's always in the magazines."

"You're not talking about Ruby Renthal, are you?"

"Ruby, that's right. Very high society."

Gus, listening, was stunned at what she said. "Ruby Renthal was at the parole hearing?"

"She asked the board not to release him."

"My God," said Gus.

$$=== 49 ===$$

ON THE DAY before she left New York for good, to take up permanent residence at Merry Hill, Ruby Renthal, in a nostalgic mood, paid a last visit to her apartment, which was shortly to be divided up into three smaller apartments. Wandering through the large empty rooms, she wondered if people would continue to refer to it as the Elias Renthal apartment, even after they were gone, in the way that people had continued to refer to it as the Sweetzer Clarke apartment for many months after she and Elias had purchased it, before it had become inalterably their own through its magnificent transformation by Cora Mandell, with the help of Maisie Verdurin and Jamesey Crocus. Only that day Ruby had seen a layout in the *Times Magazine* section showing Yvonne Bulbenkian lighting tapers for one of her parties in a pair of silver candlesticks that had only recently been her own, on a Chippendale dining table that had also been hers, beneath a portrait of King Boris of Bulgaria in hunting attire that had until their scandal hung in her own dining room. She felt no craving to own them again.

In her persimmon-lacquered drawing room, nineteen coats, or was it twenty, she wondered, the windows were bare, stripped of their elaborate hangings with the fringe from France that had taken weeks to come. She looked at the spot on the wall where her Monet of the water lilies, that she and Elias had purchased from Maisie Verdurin's wall on the night of her first party in New York, had hung, and the places on each side of the marble fireplace where her console tables with the inlaid rams' heads, from the Orromeo auction in London, had stood until she discovered they were fakes and donated them to the White House, which had returned them at the time of the auction, for reasons unknown.

In her ballroom, which she had not entered since the night of her ball, she stood at the top of the stairs, where she had received on that night, and remembered how it was in the magnificent hours before her world had begun to topple. She walked down the stairway and heard the music, the waltzes, and stood in the middle of the dance floor and closed her eyes as she remembered waltzing with Elias, with Mickie Minardos, with Gus Bailey, and her royal princes, from countries that no longer wanted them, who used to impress her so much. She looked up and could see the ten thousand butterflies, in the thirty seconds of their beauty, and hear the exclamations of joy from the mouths of her four hundred guests.

"Well, Ruby Nolte, as I live and breathe," came the voice that interrupted her reverie. She opened her eyes with a start.

Standing at the top of the short stairway leading to her ballroom was Lefty Flint. She watched him walk down the steps and across the dance floor to her.

"What are you doing here?" she asked, trying to keep the panic out of her voice.

"Paying a call," he replied. "You got yourself a gentleman caller, Ruby."

"How did you get in here?"

"I told them you were expecting me."

"But I don't live here anymore. How did you know I was here?"

"I got my ways." He looked around him, at the gold-and-white paneling of the room. "What do you call this room, Ruby? The ballroom? I didn't know people still had ballrooms. My, my. Imagine, having your own ballroom. You did good, didn't you, Ruby, for a stewardess? Look at you. Anyone who didn't know what I know about you would think you were one of the swells."

"Get out of here, Lefty, right now," she said.

"We've got a few things to go over, Ruby."

"No, we don't. We have nothing to go over."

"Oh, yes, we do. How fucking dare you come to my parole hearing and try to keep me in that place?"

"Obviously, it didn't have any effect."

"How could you do that to me?"

"I'd do it again."

"Listen, rich lady. I went to prison. I did my time. I have atoned."

"Only in your kind of circles, Lefty." Calm now, sure of herself, she met his eyes.

He looked at her. "You've changed," he said.

"You don't know how much," she answered. "If you have in mind to punch me out, I'd think again if I were you." She opened her bag and looked in it as if she were searching for her lipstick or compact. She lifted out her pistol and pointed it at him. "When my husband bought me this pistol, I thought it was the laugh of the year. He would say to me over and over, 'There are mad people out there, out to get people like us.' I never took him seriously about that, but now I see how right he was. I told you once. Now I'm telling you again. Get out, just the way you came in."

"Your husband in the slammer, that guy?" sneered Lefty.

"That guy," she answered, holding the pistol on him.

"Who stole all the money?"

"Who stole all the money," she replied.

"You're holding him up to me?"

"There's one big difference between you and my husband, Lefty. He didn't beat women or kill them. He can pay back the money. You can't give back the life you took. Wherever you go, people will say, 'He's the guy who strangled Becky Bailey.' You're a murderer."

Lefty said nothing. He moved toward Ruby.

"Get out of here, you son of a bitch," she screamed.

"Hold it, Lefty," came a voice from behind. Lefty turned quickly and faced Gus Bailey, standing on the stairs, his Luger drawn. During the split second before he fired, Gus remembered saying to Bernie Slatkin, "I want him to be looking at me at the moment. I want him to know it was me who did it."

Gus fired.

50

Men's Correctional Institute
Vacaville, California

Dear Peach:

My duties here, all manual so far, (although there is hope that a position in the library will open up soon, when Boyd Lonergan, who shot the jewelry salesman by mistake in the Tiffany's robbery, is released next month), have kept me so busy of late that exhaustion has kept me from writing sooner. Isn't it extraordinary that they should have sent me to the same place that they sent Lefty? Several of the inmates here remember him, and all of the guards. I'm pleased to say they remember him without affection. He told Boyd, with whom he shared a cell briefly, that he had beaten several women before he killed Becky.

For the first time in years, I feel calm. When I am washing clothes in the laundry, where I am currently assigned, or peeling potatoes in the kitchen, where I was assigned before, there is no longer a subtext of Lefty in my thoughts, as there has been for so many years. I keep thinking of all those nights in New York when I was talking about one thing and thinking about another.

How strange life is. If what happened had happened in the alley behind the bar in Studio City, the way I planned it, I would probably be here for twenty years. First degree, they would have called it. What ever possessed him to go to Ruby Renthal's house that day? How extraordinary that she was even there.

Do you know what I think, Peach? I think it's possible to be happy again. Even here.

With love,
Gus

51

EFFICIENT IN her duties, Justine Altemus walked through the rooms and
wards of St. Vincent's Hospital, as she walked through the rooms and
wards of St. Clair's Hospital and Bellevue Hospital, bringing magazines
and sweets to the victims of the disease that people called a pestilence, making
telephone calls or writing letters for those who were no longer able to do such
things for themselves. Steeled now, her duties before her emotions, she could
smile and banter with the boys. "Hi, Justine," they would call out to her. "Hi,
Billy," she'd call back. Or Phil. Or Christian. Or whomever. She knew all their
names, and most of them knew hers.

"Hi, Justine," she heard someone say in the same bed where Phil, her
favorite, had died a few days before.

"Hi," she called back brightly. She could see at once, whoever he was, that
he was beyond caring for reading material or Hershey bars with almonds.

"Would you like me to write a letter for you, or call anyone?" she asked.
He didn't answer. "I'd be happy to read to you. I have all the latest magazines."

"Don't recognize me, do you, Justine? Do I look that bad?" the patient
asked. "I used to be a good-looking guy."

She knew that he was young, even though he looked old. His arms were
like the handles of a broom. Then, on his earlobe, she noticed a diamond, the
diamond that her father had given her mother in an engagement ring, and that
her mother had given to Hubie when she had vain hopes that Hubie would
marry Violet Bastedo, and that Hubie had given to Juanito Perez.

"Oh, Juanito," she cried, sinking to her knees by the side of the bed. She
knew she would be asked to leave by the nurse in charge of the ward if she was
seen crying, but she could not help herself, burying her head in the bedclothes
to muffle the sounds. "I hadn't heard. I didn't know."

"Imagine, you crying for me, Justine," he said, with wonder in his faint
voice.

"I'm sorry."

"I heard about this volunteer lady called Justine, real classy, everybody
said, who comes here every afternoon, and I thought to myself, I bet that's
Justine Altemus they're talking about."

"That's me," said Justine.

"You had a baby, I heard."

Justine smiled and nodded her head. "I called him Hubie. He's beautiful,
Juanito."

"Got a picture?"

"Not here. Next time I'll bring you one," she said. They exchanged glances, each wondering if there would be a next time they would see each other.

"You're beautiful, Justine," said Juanito.

"Oh, no, I'm not," she replied. "Interesting looking. Almost pretty. Those are the adjectives that are applied to me, but it's sweet of you to pay me the compliment."

"Hubie always said you sold yourself short," said Juanito.

Justine smiled. "That's what Hubie used to say. You're right. I'd forgotten that."

"You seeing anybody since Bernie?"

"Not really. I'm turning into one of those women who call up men to take them places. I-have-two-tickets-for-the-theater-on-Tuesday-can-you-come?"

"One of these days you'll meet some nice doctor."

"You're different than I imagined you were going to be."

Juanito smiled. "I used to be a bum, but I classed up when I became a millionaire."

Justine smiled.

"There's a few things I want to tell you, Justine."

"What?"

"You know those chairs your mother wanted so bad?"

"It doesn't matter," said Justine.

"Charles-something chairs?" It was an effort for him to speak.

"Tenth. Charles the Tenth. Doesn't matter."

"No, you gotta hear this, Justine. Your Aunt Minnie Willoughby's chairs that your mother sent Jamesey Crocus to con me out of."

Justine nodded, knowing he spoke the truth.

"I left them out in the street one at a time, for those people who furnish their apartments with the discarded furniture they find on the sidewalk at night."

Justine started to laugh.

"Eleven poor people have got some pretty good chairs, if only they knew it," whispered Juanito.

"I think Hubie would have liked that, Juanito," said Justine.

"One more thing."

"Don't tire yourself, Juanito."

"About the money Hubie left me."

"Oh, I don't care about the money that Hubie left you. That was Hubie's money, and he wanted you to have it."

Juanito raised a hand to let him talk. "You have to know this. He wanted Herkie Saybrook to make a new will. He wanted the money to go to a hospice for guys without any money to die, to be able to die decent, but he died before Herkie could get here to make the change."

"It doesn't matter now, Juanito, really it doesn't, but you're nice to tell me that."

"But that's not it. I had Herkie Saybrook down to the loft before I got so sick they had to put me in here."

"Herkie? Why?"

"I know what you're thinking. I'm the first Puerto Rican Herkie Saybrook ever wrote out a will for."

She stared at him.

"I know you and your mother thought I was going to leave the money to a leather bar or something trashy, but I want to do with it what Hubie would have done if he'd lived a few days longer. It's all going, every cent of it, all those Van Degan bucks, to a hospice. Let me tell you something, Justine. Hubie and I may have had our problems, but he was the only person in my whole life who ever treated me nice."

"Oh, Juanito."

For a few minutes they remained in their positions, thinking their own thoughts. "Do you have any family you want me to get in touch with? That's one of the things I do."

"No," he said.

"Nobody?"

"There's an aunt, but she don't want to hear from me."

"A mother? A father?"

"My father kicked my mother in the stomach when I was a little kid, and she died. I grew up in a home for boys in San Juan. I don't even know if my father's alive or dead, and I don't care."

"Good lord," said Justine.

"That's the same thing Hubie said when I told him that story the first time. 'Good lord.' You swells all talk alike."

"Tell me more."

"I've led a dicey kind of life, Justine."

"What's dicey?"

"I used to hustle."

"That means doing it for money?"

"That's right. I knew from the time I was a teenager in that home that my looks were my only asset in life. There's not much I haven't done. Even porn, if you want to know the truth. After Hubie left me all that money, you don't know how proper I got. I mended my ways, and then I got sick. And here you find me."

"Oh, Juanito, I'm so sorry."

"I'm not afraid to die, Justine. I'm afraid of what happens between now and dying. I've watched some of these guys, what they go through. I don't know if I'm up to it. Hubie was a class act dying. I'm not a class act like Hubie," said Juanito.

"I think you're a class act, Juanito." She squeezed his hand.

Juanito squeezed hers back.

"Can I get you anything?" asked Justine finally.

"Just some water," he replied. "There's none left here."

"I'll fill the Thermos," she said.

When she returned a few minutes later, she poured him a paper cup of water and held it for him to drink. Then she puffed up the pillows behind his head. Juanito, sleepy now, smiled at her.

"I want you to have this, Justine," he said.

She looked at him. He reached out and took her hand. In it he placed the Altemus diamond.

                                    *   *   *

It wasn't until she read it on the front page of the *Times* that Lil Altemus learned that Juanito Perez, the lover of her late son, had left his entire ten-million-dollar inheritance to a hospice for AIDS victims to be known as the Hubert Altemus, Jr., Hospice.

52

AFTER GUS BAILEY went to prison, Ruby Renthal vanished from sight. The name Renthal was so well known and so associated with greed that even people in shops looked up and stared at her when she gave them her charge cards. She became altogether separated from the grand people who had once fought to sit at her table and to dance at her ball.

Ruby, however, in spite of the bad turns her charmed life had taken, was still the possessor of a large fortune, settled on her by Elias in their halcyon days. Her withdrawal from social life to a simpler existence in the country was from choice, not financial adversity, as many people thought. She enjoyed the quiet life, the country walks, and tending her garden. She saw a small group of country friends whose names never appeared in Dolly De Longpre's column, or Florian Gray's, and their sort of entertaining was of the last-minute variety, with dinner on trays in front of a fire, rather than with all the grandeur of her former life in New York society.

"The relief," she said to her maid, Candelaria, settling in to another quiet evening at home. She felt no yearning for the competitive life of charity events and nightly dinner parties and daily fittings that had consumed her for so long.

Ned Manchester, who lived nearby, taught her to play tennis and took her riding and eventually declared his love for her, but she resisted his attempts at love, although she was attracted to him. "I can't marry while Elias is in prison," she said to Ned. "I can't. He was too good to me. It would kill him."

Elias was still important to her, and she continued to visit him in prison, even after she divorced him. Their relationship, while not romantic, became as it had been in the beginning between them, before their financial and social fame.

Loelia Manchester, meanwhile, who had discovered that the object of her desire, Mickie Minardos, was not worthy of the sacrifices she had made for him, married him, at his insistence, although she no longer wanted to marry him. In the beginning, the romance of Loelia and Mickie had titillated New York society for about six months. They were pointed out wherever they went. Photographers fought to take their picture. They were asked everywhere.

Then, used to the sight of them, they ceased to fascinate. People began to wonder if Mickie wasn't a bit of a user, if Loelia wasn't drinking a bit too much, or if her last facelift hadn't been a ghastly mistake, with her popping-out eyes. On the rare occasions that Ned Manchester appeared in New York, at weddings, or funerals, or memorial services, people began to say how attractive he was, a gentleman to his fingertips, and hadn't Loelia been a fool to leave him for such an opportunist as the cobbler. Later they began calling her a damn fool, and then a goddamn fool. And then just poor Loelia.

Late in September of that year, Elias Renthal made several collect calls from Allenwood Federal Prison Camp in Pennsylvania. The first was to Max Luby. The second was to Laurance Van Degan. The third was to Ruby. Of the three, only Laurance Van Degan was haughty to him, although Laurance, like Max and Ruby, took the advice that Elias gave them from his confinement, for not one of them ever doubted that Elias was a financial genius. "Get out of the stock market," he told them. "There is going to be a crash."

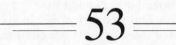

"**T**ALK LOUDER, Janet, or stop crying, or *something!* I can hardly hear you," Lil yelled over the transatlantic wires.

"It's Laurance," repeated Janet, for the third time.

"Oh, my God!" cried Lil.

The instant Lil Altemus heard of her brother's illness, from her tearful sister-in-law Janet Van Degan, she returned home from Rome, where she had been staying with her friends the Todescos, after what she always called her annual migration: Salzburg, for the music, Paris, for her fittings, and London, for the season.

In New York, she was met by Joe, her chauffeur, and a variety of officials from the Van Degan Foundation who had made arrangements to whisk her through customs without having to wait. She went straight from the airport to Manhattan Hospital, giving instructions to Joe as they drove to take her luggage on to the apartment on Fifth Avenue, to tell her maid Lourdes to unpack, to call Justine to join her for dinner, but not to bring the baby, and to return to pick her up at the hospital in an hour's time. It was not necessary for Lil to stop at the information counter to ask what room Laurance Van Degan was in. All the Van Degans, for as long as she could remember, during their illnesses, stayed in suite 690 of the Harcourt Pavilion of Manhattan Hospital.

When the elevator doors opened on the sixth floor, she was met by Miss Wentworth, Laurance's secretary, and even then, in her agitation and concern for her brother, Lil wondered anew why Miss Wentworth dyed her hair so very black.

"I hope your flight was satisfactory, Mrs. Altemus," said Miss Wentworth.

"Yes, yes, fine," replied Lil, walking down the corridor toward the room.

"And the customs?" asked Miss Wentworth, following, trying to keep in step.

"Yes, yes, fine. Right through. No wait. How is my brother, Irene?"

"Well," said Miss Wentworth, cautiously. "His mouth. You'll notice."

"These are pretty," said Lil in the sitting room of the suite as she entered, motioning to a large bouquet of roses. "There's no one like Lorenza for roses. Who are they from?"

"Mrs. Harcourt," replied Miss Wentworth.

"Sweet of Adele," said Lil. She took a deep breath, knocked on the door of the bedroom, and walked in at the same time. Laurance Van Degan was lying in the hospital bed. Laurance, so large, so imposing, so utterly aristocratic, looked small and frightened to her.

"Oh, Laurance," said Lil, as she bent down to kiss him.

"I've had a shitty little stroke, Lil," said Laurance.

Lil was startled. She had never heard Laurance say *shitty* before. His mouth, she noticed, had moved to the side of his face. He looked to her rather like their father, Ormonde, after his stroke.

"Oh, Laurance," she said again, and there was grief in her voice, for there was great affection between them. Her husband had failed her when he divorced her. Her father had failed her when he married Dodo and left her his fortune, even if it was only for her life use. Her daughter had failed her by making an inappropriate marriage, and then divorcing even more inappropriately. Her son, oh, dear, how her son had failed her. Only her brother Laurance had not failed her throughout their lives.

"Don't cry, Lil," said Laurance.

"It's so unfair, Laurance," said his sister.

"They say the mouth will go back in place in time," he said. His voice, coming as it was from a new position in his face, had a different quality, but its patrician intonations remained.

Lil watched him as he slowly lifted his left hand with his right hand and placed it on his stomach. When a nurse moved in to help, he waved her away with a slow shake of his head. "The left hand doesn't work too well," he said to Lil.

"It's that damn Elias Renthal who's responsible for this," said Lil. She could neither forget nor forgive that Elias Renthal's despicable financial manipulations had sullied the name of her brother, causing him to have to resign from the presidency of the Butterfield, which had broken his heart.

At that moment orderlies arrived.

"It's time, Mr. Van Degan," said the nurse.

"You caught me just as I'm on my way to therapy, Lil," said Laurance, slowly.

"Oh, of course, you're on your way to therapy. You know, Laurance, they do such marvelous things these days in therapy," Lil said, using the enthusiastic voice she used for invalids who couldn't move their arms. She didn't need to tell her own brother that she, as chairperson of the Ladies' League of

Manhattan Hospital, had raised a million dollars at the spring dance for the Harcourt Stroke Center.

"Lil," said Laurance.

"Yes, my darling," answered Lil.

"Get out of the market," he said.

"Get out of what?"

"The stock market, Lil."

"Don't you even *think* about the stock market, Laurance. You think about getting well."

"There's going to be a crash. Get hold of young Laurance as soon as possible. He'll know what to do."

With that, the orderlies wheeled the bed out of the room.

"Paris isn't what it used to be. Six hundred dollars a night for a room at the Ritz, a *room,* my dear, not even a suite, and if you could have *seen* the kind of people," said Lil Altemus, with a shudder. "All those ghastly common women with their horrid little clipped dogs having lunch at the Rélais Plaza. Arabs everywhere you look. And the clothes are a disaster this year. Skirts up to *here.* I saw Loelia in Paris wearing one of those new dresses. She looked ridiculous, at her age, and she's had something else done to her face. She can't even smile anymore, her face is so tight. She sort of purses her lips, like this, look."

Every year for as long as she could remember, Justine Altemus had been listening to her mother say how awful the people were in Paris, how expensive everything was, and what a disaster the clothes in the *couture* were that year. Justine only half listened, making an appropriate comment from time to time, waiting for the moment when she could tell her own news.

"I have some news for you, Mother," she said, finally.

Lil realized that Justine was not interested in hearing about her trip. She rang her silver bell. "Parker," she said, when her butler appeared.

"Yes, ma'am."

"Will you tell Gertie that the vinaigrette has too much oil?"

"Yes, ma'am."

"But the asparagus is delicious. Perfection, tell her."

"Yes, ma'am."

"My dear," she said, when the butler had disappeared, "the Todescos' chef could make a vinaigrette sauce like you never tasted before. Something about egg whites, I think."

"Oh, Mother, so what?" said Justine, impatiently, bursting to tell her news.

Lil looked at her daughter with surprise.

"You've changed," she said.

"You haven't," replied Justine, meeting her eye. She remembered that Hubie used to sing, "It seems to me I've heard this song before," when their mother went on and on about the same things year after year.

Lil thought about making a retort to her daughter's rudeness, or what appeared to her to be rudeness, but decided to let it pass. "Do you know that your Uncle Laurance, even in the hospital, even with his stroke, is thinking about his family? Do you know what he said to me today? 'Get out of the market,' he said. As they were wheeling him to the stroke center for his therapy, he said, 'Get out of the market.'"

Justine nodded. "Young Laurance called me about that today," she said.

"Do what he tells you. Your Uncle Laurance always knows. Have you been to the hospital to see him?" asked Lil.

"I sent a note, and flowers," said Justine. "And I stopped by the apartment to see Aunt Janet."

"Janet's fallen apart completely," said Lil, who was proud of her reputation in the family for holding steadfast in crises. People still remarked about how bravely she had dealt with Hubie's death.

"Herkie Saybrook said that young Laurance said that Uncle Laurance didn't really want to see anyone until he moves a bit better. Bad for the business or something if everyone knows his mouth is on the side of his face and his left hand just hangs there," said Justine.

"Still, you should have gone. You're not just anyone. You are his niece, after all."

"I will, when he can move better," replied Justine.

"In no time, he'll be as good as new. The Harcourt Stroke Center at the hospital is the best in New York, and I'm proud to say that I personally am responsible for raising a million dollars for it at the annual spring dance at the Rhinelander."

Parker cleared away the asparagus plates and reappeared with plates for the main course.

Lil placed her hand on her plate to see if it had been properly warmed.

"Herkie said—"

"Herkie, Herkie, Herkie. How many times are you going to tell me what Herkie Saybrook said?" Lil had still not forgiven Herkie Saybrook for writing Hubie's will. "The sole looks marvelous, Parker. Tell Gertie perfection."

"Yes, ma'am."

"Herkie's on the board of the hospice, and I see him at the meetings, and we talk."

Lil shook her head impatiently. The hospice. The Hubert Altemus, Jr., Hospice. She could not bear that her son's name was connected to it. She believed that the money should have been contributed anonymously, if it had to be contributed. She could not bear also that her daughter worked there with such passion.

"How long are you going to continue working there? Hasn't this Nurse Edith Cavell performance gone on long enough?"

Justine stared at her mother. "As long as they need me," she answered, evenly.

"What about your child?"

"My child, as you call him, has a name, Mother. He's called Hubie, after my brother, or your son. He's a year old and you've never called him by name once that I can recall. 'Your baby,' you say, or 'your child.' Never Hubie."

"That's not a very attractive tone of voice, Justine."

Justine did not reply.

"How is, uh, little Hubie?" Lil asked. The name pained her.

"He walks. He talks. Most grandmothers would be ecstatic to have such a divine creature, but, then, you're not most grandmothers," said Justine.

"What's that supposed to mean?"

"Oh, Mother, let's not fight. You're just back. Uncle Laurance is sick. I'm being cranky. And I have something important to tell you."

"You're not getting married again, are you?" she asked, excitedly. "If you want to make your old mother happy, that's what she wants to hear."

Justine shook her head. "No, I'm not getting married."

"Are you in love then? Oh, how marvelous, Justine. You have been holding out on me."

Justine shrugged. "I have what's called the occasional suitor. Herkie Saybrook takes me out to dinner, and would take me out more if I gave him a bit of encouragement, and there's a doctor I met at the hospital who's attractive, and I see him from time to time, but I'm not planning to get married, at least not right now. If it happens, it happens, but it's not my priority. I like the work I do at the hospital, and I'm good at it, and the patients like me and ask for me, and it has given me a great deal of satisfaction. And, Mother, I've been asked to be the executive head of the hospice."

"Is that what your news was?"

"Yes, Mother, that's what it was. I know it's not in the same league of importance as the Todescos' chef's recipe for vinaigrette sauce, or the length of Loelia's skirts."

"Please don't be sarcastic, Justine. If that's important to you, then it's very nice, but I would like to point out to you that all the Van Degan women have always felt a responsibility to the city of New York."

"Yes, that's what I feel, Mother."

"I'm not finished, Justine. I think that perhaps where you can be of greater service to the city is if you come on the boaad of the Van Degan Foundation. I'll talk to Uncle Laurance tomorrow when I go to the hospital."

"I don't want to be on the board of the Van Degan Foundation, Mother, and I am very much aware that the Van Degan Foundation does many good things for the city, but I have found something in my life that is really important to me."

"Hmm," said Lil.

"Mother, all my life I've been identified as Laurance Van Degan's niece, or Mrs. Van Degan Altemus's daughter, or, worse, the Van Degan heiress, as Dolly De Longpre always calls me in her column. Now I'm Justine Altemus, all by myself, without even the terrible word *socialite* in front of it, because no one knows I'm Uncle Laurance's niece, or if they know, it's not any more important to them than it is to me."

"I think we'll have coffee in the library, Parker," said Lil. "And bring some cookies for those naughty doggies, will you? And tell Gertie the eggplant soufflé was yummy."

For a moment after Lil sat in her regular seat in the library, Justine thought her mother was going to cry. Then she lifted her face and looked at her daughter. "Why don't they call it the Juanito whateverhisnamewas Hospice, rather than the Hubert Altemus, Junior, Hospice?" asked Lil.

"Good-bye, Mother," said Justine. "I'm going home to my baby."

"You're not staying for coffee?"

"No, I'm not staying for coffee."

Justine rose and walked out of the room and out of the apartment.

54

THE PREVIOUS day the stock market had fallen five hundred and eight points, exactly as Elias Renthal had told Ruby, and Max Luby, and Laurance Van Degan it was going to do, and exactly as Laurance Van Degan had told his sister, Lil Altemus, it was going to do, and a mild hysteria swept the lunch crowd at Clarence's where all the familiar faces were occupying all the best tables, and people were waiting three deep at the bar for the familiar faces to finish their chicken paillard and decaffeinated cappuccino and leave, but no one wanted to leave that day.

"How come Elias Renthal called Laurance Van Degan from prison with a tip to get out of the stock market?" asked Constantine de Rham. Everyone knew that Laurance Van Degan had felt that his sterling reputation had been tarnished in both the business and social community by his endorsement of Elias Renthal, especially at the Butterfield, and had publicly turned his back on Elias Renthal during the months of his disgrace.

"Listen, Constantine, Elias Renthal is first and foremost a businessman, and he probably wants to keep a finger in the pot. He'll be getting out of prison in a year or two," said Lord Biedermeier. He removed his pince-nez and cleaned the lenses with a napkin, so that he could survey the crowd at Clarence's. He noticed that despite the economic hardships that might be coming on the nation, the restaurant was filled to capacity. He noticed also that, because of his luncheon companion, Constantine de Rham, people who might ordinarily wave hellos to him, like Lil Altemus, chose not to cast their eyes in his direction.

"I thought he couldn't trade anymore. I thought he was barred for life," insisted Constantine, who enjoyed other people's ill fortune.

"You're right, he can't trade, and he is barred for life, but that's not to say he can't get someone else to trade for him. Max Luby, for instance. Max trades; Elias calls the shots."

"He won't be giving any more society balls," said Constantine, with grim satisfaction.

"No, he won't be giving any more society balls, and he won't ever get inside the front door of the Butterfield again, even as a lunch guest, but when he makes a new fortune, and he will, people will start seeing him again. Even Laurance Van Degan. They'll have lunch, at some obscure place, and pretty soon everyone will have forgotten. It's the way of the world."

Constantine wondered but did not say that no one had ever taken him up again. It was as if Lord Biedermeier read his thoughts. "Even you, Constantine. People will see you again. Write a book."

"About what?" asked de Rham.

"Playboys, my dear Constantine, are very fashionable this year. There is an enormous interest in Ali Khan and Rubirosa, and you are their heir. Look at the Monaco Princesses. The public can't get enough of them. That is why I thought that you perhaps would want to talk about the accident in Paris when that beautiful young girl lost her head. And all the rumors that have plagued your life," said Lord Biedermeier.

"But those rumors were utterly false," said Constantine, indignantly.

"It doesn't matter," replied Lord Biedermeier.

"They were never proved."

"It doesn't matter. People who haven't spoken to you in years will be all too glad to have you to dinner again if you have a hit book. All this happened years ago when you were very young. You didn't understand what you were getting into. Think about it. The public loves reformation."

"But I don't know how to write," said Constantine.

"The least of our worries. If you could read the marvelous manuscript Elias Renthal has just handed in about life in prison, and he didn't have to write a word of it. I simply sent an author to visit him once a week in Allenwood, and they talked and talked. It will guarantee him acceptance when he gets out of prison."

"Hmm," said Constantine.

Ruby Renthal was the first to say that only her dentist or her gynecologist could entice her to make the trip to town, for semiannual checkups, and it was the former who brought her to the city on the same day that Gus Bailey returned to New York. They met in the waiting room of Dr. Chase's office.

"Gus, my God!" said Ruby, surprised when Gus walked in.

"Hello, Ruby," replied Gus, as surprised as she. For an instant they looked at each other. When she held out her hand, he took it and leaned to kiss her on the cheek.

"I didn't know you were out."

"Just. The courts don't take your first shooting seriously these days," he said.

"Oh, Gus, don't joke."

"I'm not joking. It's the truth. I got less time than Elias."

"I wrote to you," she said.

"I know."

"You didn't answer."

"I thought I'd brought you enough notoriety already."

"Gus, for God's sake, you saved my life."

"I didn't really. You had a gun."

"Let me tell you something about that famous gun, Gus, and I don't mean that it used to belong to Queen Marie of Rumania. I always carried it because Elias wanted me to carry it, but what Elias never knew was that it was never loaded. I couldn't bear the idea of carrying a loaded gun."

Gus looked around him in the waiting room, aware that other patients were looking at them.

"Have you already been to the doctor, or are you going?" he asked.

"What do you have in mind?" she answered.

"A little lunch maybe?"

"You've got me."

"Let's get out of here."

Without a moment's hesitation, Ruby called into the receptionist's office and said, "Tell Dr. Chase I'll call back for another appointment."

"But he's ready for you, Mrs. Renthal," said the receptionist. "Mrs. Lord is just leaving."

"I'll call back," she repeated, taking her mink coat off the coat rack and following Gus out the door.

In the elevator, she said to him, "I watched you on television."

"A ghastly kind of fame, isn't it?"

"At least he didn't die."

Gus nodded. "Do you know what I think, Ruby?"

"What?"

"I think at that last second when my eyes met his, that Becky, from wherever she is, pushed my arm just enough to the side so I didn't kill him."

"Looking after her father, you mean?"

"Right, that wasn't the way. I realized it as I was pulling the trigger."

"You're not sorry it turned out this way, are you?"

"Not anymore. I was obsessed for three years with that man. Nothing mattered but that I kill him. That was all I could think of. That obsession has lifted, thank God."

"How much time did you serve?"

"I got a year. I served nine months."

"Do people talk to you?"

"I don't know. You're the first person I've seen. But I don't care if they don't. It's time for another beginning."

"Good for you, Gus. I'm a great believer in new beginnings."

They looked at each other.

"Do you see Elias?"

"Oh, sure. I go to visit."

"Do you see the old crowd?"

"Heavens, no."

They laughed.

"How about Clarence's for lunch?"

They laughed again. "Perfect."

"Laurance knew all this was going to happen," said Lil, who was lunching at the window table with her friends Matilda Clarke and Cora Mandell and Ezzie Fenwick, who had just told them about the fight over money at the Bulbenkians' house the night before. "Laurance has been saying for some time that the market was at an unsustainable high level." Lil Altemus quoted her brother more than any person in her life. She spoke with the ease of someone whose fortune would remain intact throughout any financial crisis. "Laurance got out of the market a week ago, and, of course, I did too, and so did Justine."

Ezzie, who had lost money, at least on paper, was testy that day and spoke of canceling a trip to Egypt that he had planned. When Michael, everyone's favorite waiter at Clarence's, placed his plate in front of him, Ezzie lifted his dark glasses and examined the plate with his good eye, which was not the eye that looked like a poached egg.

"I want tartar sauce with my crab cakes," said Ezzie, loudly. "That's not tartar sauce. That's mayonnaise."

"We're out of tartar sauce," replied Michael, with the courtesy and tact with which he was known to deal with difficult customers.

"Out of tartar sauce? How can you be out of tartar sauce?" asked Ezzie, raising his eyebrows in assumed exasperation.

"We are," said Michael.

"Then tell the chef to make some more, or send to the market and buy some more," ordered Ezzie.

"Yes, sir," said Michael, retreating to report to Chick Jacoby the latest incident from the quarrelsome Ezzie Fenwick.

"*Never* let them have the last word," said Ezzie, as if giving his friends a lesson in deportment, before resuming his account of the Bulbenkians' fight, which Lil had interrupted.

It was then that the reclusive Ruby Renthal, so long out of sight, and the just-released-from-prison Gus Bailey walked into Clarence's, without a reservation. "My dears, you will not *believe* who just walked into this restaurant," said Ezzie, all good humored again. Ezzie's companions, and everyone else in the front part of the restaurant, where all the good people, as Ezzie called them, sat, turned to look at the curious duet who stood quietly just inside the door waiting for Chick Jacoby to hurry forward to greet them.

"You watch," said Ezzie, in his nasal voice. "Chick will move Lord Biedermeier and Constantine de Rham over to his own table, as if he's giving them a big treat, and put Ruby and the jailbird there."

Of the three women with Ezzie, only old Cora Mandell, who had decorated the spectacular Renthal apartment, waved a greeting. Ruby smiled back but made no attempt to speak to the others, as she sat at the table just vacated by Lord Biedermeier and Constantine de Rham.

"Talk to me, Gus," Ruby said.

"About prison?"

"Make any friends there?"

"I wrote a book there."

"Ezzie Fenwick always said you were going to write a book."

"For once he was right."

At that moment Matilda Clarke appeared at their table.

"Gus Bailey!" she said.

"Hello, Matilda," said Gus, rising.

"Ages," she said.

"Ages," replied Gus. "You know Ruby."

"Hellohoware?"

"Well, Gus, tell me everything," said Matilda.

"I've been in prison."

"Oh, I know. I think you're a national hero."

"No, I'm not."

"Listen, Gus, Maisie Verdurin is having one of her dinners on Thursday, and it might be her last for a while, because no one's going to be buying paintings for a while, with the crash and all. Would you like me to arrange it so we can go together?"

"Can't on Thursday," said Gus.

"Then come to the country for the weekend. I've got Justine Altemus and Herkie Saybrook. They're an item, I hear, although Lil denies it vigorously. He's so much better for her than the TV announcer. Sweetzer always said, 'Stick with your own kind,' and he was right. You've simply got to come, Gus. We're going to Rochelle's on Saturday night."

"Can't this weekend," Gus replied.

"Not off on one of your mystery trips, are you?"

"No, my mystery trips ended with the bullet I put in Lefty Flint."

"Oh, I get it," said Matilda. "Branching out? New directions? That sort of thing?"

"Something like that," answered Gus.

"Well, all right," she said, shrugging her shoulders. "Us single ladies do what we can." She moved back to Ezzie's table.

Gus and Ruby looked at each other.

"You did that well, Gus," said Ruby.

"I can't get back into all that. I never fit in in the first place," said Gus. "It just kept my mind off what was going on in my life that I couldn't do a damn thing about at the time."

"What are you going to do now that you're back?" asked Ruby.

"I'm just here to sell my place, go to the dentist, close out a chapter. I'm moving on."

"Where?"

"Maybe just a block away. It doesn't matter. All that I know is that this ain't it."

Michael, the waiter who served the front part of the restaurant, came up to take their orders. "Welcome back, Mr. Bailey," he said.

"Thanks."

"Nice to see you, Mrs. Renthal," he said.

"Thank you, Michael."

"Let me tell you the specials for today."

Ruby and Gus looked at each other.

"Listen, Michael," said Gus.

"Yessir."

"We're not going to stay."

He looked over at Ruby. She was smiling at him.

"Why are you smiling?"

"That's just what I was going to say," she said.

Ruby rose from her seat. She looked over to Chick Jacoby at the bar and blew him a kiss. Then she walked out the door, followed by Gus.

For a while they walked down Lexington Avenue without speaking. At the corner of 72nd Street, Gus raised his hand and signaled a taxi. When the car stopped in front of him, he turned to Ruby and they looked at each other fondly.

"S'long, Ruby," he said.

"Bye, Gus," she answered.

"Will you be okay?"

"Oh, sure. And you?"
"Sure."
"Luck."
"Same."
As Gus got into the taxi, Ruby turned and walked across the street.

An Inconvenient Woman

For Griffin and Carey Dunne
with love

1

LATER HE WAS vilified and disgraced; Archbishop Cooning denounced him from the pulpit of Saint Vibiana's as a corruptor, and the archbishop's words spread throughout the land. But before the disgrace and the vilification Jules Mendelson was, seemingly at least, on top of the world: awesome in appearance, brilliantly married, and revered in the manner that the very rich are revered in America.

Clouds, the Mendelson estate, which looks down on Los Angeles from its lofty mountaintop, remains unlived in but cared for, although the massive iron gates that once fronted a ducal residence in Wiltshire have become dislocated, their hinges pried loose by vandals. The caretaker on duty has backed the gates with plywood boards to keep the curious from staring in; but, even if they could stare in, they would see nothing of the house and gardens, for a few hundred feet up the drive there is a sharp turn to the right. Pauline Mendelson's greenhouse, where she grew her orchids, has fallen into disrepair, but the kennels are kept up still, and a pack of police dogs patrols the grounds at night, as always.

There was a time when people said that the views from Clouds were the prettiest views in the city. Pauline Mendelson, mindful of this, had created one room to take best advantage of the sunrise over the downtown skyline, where she and Jules were meant to have breakfast together, but never did, except once; and another room for watching the sunset over the ocean, where, on most evenings, she and Jules did indeed meet to drink a glass of wine together and discuss the events of the day before dressing for dinner.

Probably no one ever conducted herself so well in a scandal as Pauline Mendelson. Everyone agrees on that. She held her head high and invited neither pity nor scorn. The city, or that part of the city that figured in the lives of these people, was beside itself with excitement. Nothing so thrilling had happened in years, except among the movie people, and no one they knew saw the movie people. Within a year of the events that riveted the city for so many months, Pauline became Lady St. Vincent and moved to England. She not only married quickly but also, being by birth one of the McAdoo sisters, the marrying McAdoos, as the papers often called them, married extremely well, even under the terrible circumstances. People say that all traces of her life as Mrs. Jules Mendelson have been totally obliterated, and in her new life she is not at home to people who knew her in Los Angeles, not even Rose Cliveden, and,

God knows, if anyone was a good friend to Pauline Mendelson, it was Rose Cliveden.

There were splendid times at Clouds for over twenty years. You had only to look at the signatures in the guest books when they came up for auction at Boothby's, along with the furniture, the personal effects, and, of course, the extraordinary art collection, to get an idea of Pauline Mendelson's voracious appetite for what she always called "interesting people." As to the pictures, or the auction of the pictures, there is still rage in the art world today. The Metropolitan Museum in New York said it had been promised the collection. The County Museum in Los Angeles said the same, as did the Kimball in Fort Worth. And there were other museums, with lesser claims. But that was typical of Jules Mendelson. He liked being called on by heads of museums—being courted by them, as he put it—and hearing them praise his magnificent collection. He enjoyed walking them through the halls and rooms of his house, spelling out the provenance of each picture, as well as the stage in the life of the artist at the time the picture was painted. He liked letting each one think it was his museum to which the collection would go, in time; and surely he meant to leave it to one, because he often said, even in interviews, that he never wanted the collection to be broken up, and that he was leaving money for the construction of a wing, the Jules Mendelson Wing, to house it. But the fact remained that he did not make such a provision, although he had intended to, just as he had intended to make a provision for Flo March. Or poor Flo, as she came to be known. It was Pauline who decided to break up the collection and auction it off along with the furniture and personal effects, minus van Gogh's *White Roses* and the bronze cast of Degas's fourteen-year-old ballerina, with the original pink ribbon in her hair, which, some people say, are already installed in Kilmartin Abbey in Wiltshire.

Pauline Mendelson was one of those people totally at home in the inner circles of several cities, although she seemed to belong to none. Even after twenty-two years of living in Los Angeles, and becoming a prominent citizen there, Pauline always seemed like a visitor rather than a resident. Her parties at Clouds were famous, and rightly so. She left nothing to chance in the planning of her evenings. It was through one such party that young Philip Quennell was brought into the orbit of the renowned couple. Pauline liked to ask writers and artists to her house to mix with her grand friends. Once Philip had seen her take communion at Andy Warhol's memorial service at Saint Patrick's Cathedral, and he had met her once before that, by accident, during the intermission of a play in New York. Pauline knew the stepmother of the woman he was with, and, after introductions, she and his companion chatted briefly while Philip stood by, simply watching her. She spoke in a fashionable contralto. "Awfully light, isn't it, but I'm being amused, aren't you?" she asked, about the play. They answered yes. "Dreadful about Rocky, isn't it?" she asked, about someone Philip didn't know, but his companion did, whose private plane had recently crashed. "Both his pilots were killed, but he'll be fine, in time," Pauline added. And then the bell rang, and it was time for the second act, and they didn't see her again. Given this minimal exposure to Pauline Mendelson, Philip Quennell was therefore surprised to find an invitation to her party, hand-delivered to his hotel by her chauffeur, on the very day he arrived in Los Angeles for what turned out to be a considerably longer visit than he could ever have anticipated. It was his birthday. He was twenty-nine, turning thirty that night, but of course that milestone, known only to himself, could have nothing whatever to do with the invitation from Mr. and Mrs. Jules Mendelson, as their names read in engraved script on the ecru-colored card.

He was late. The parking valet told him so. So did the maid who opened the door. Inside, on a hall console table where little envelopes with dining-table numbers inside had been alphabetically placed, there was only one left, his. The convivial sound of sixty voices, talking and laughing, could be heard from an interior room. Even late, however, with a butler hurrying him toward the voices—"They're about to sit down," he insisted—it was impossible for Philip to be oblivious to the grandeur of the interior of the Mendelson house. There were six ground-floor doors opening onto the front hallway. A curved staircase of superb proportions seemed to float upward on invisible pinions, its green moiré wall lined with six Monet paintings of water lilies, Philip's first glimpse of the Mendelson art collection; below, at its base, were masses of orchid plants in blue-and-white Chinese cachepots and bowls.

"Beautiful," said Philip, to no one in particular.

"It's Mrs. Mendelson's hobby," said an efficient, secretarial-looking woman.

"What?" asked Philip.

"The orchids. She grows them herself."

"Ah."

"Will you first sign the guest book, please," she said. She handed him a pen, and he wrote his name beneath the names of one of the former Presidents and his First Lady and that of the great film star Faye Converse, now in retirement. His eyes scanned the signatures. Although he knew no one, he recognized many of the illustrious names. It was not the sort of crowd that Philip Quennell was used to dining with.

Just then one of the six doors opened, and the party sounds increased in volume as Jules Mendelson entered the hall. He closed the door behind him again and strode across the marble floor with the purposefulness of a man who had been summoned to take an important telephone call. He was enormous, both in height and in girth, unhandsome and compelling at the same time, the possessor of an appearance that was likely to intimidate the fainthearted. His aura of power enveloped him like a strong scent. But people discovered on meeting him that he could be surprisingly gentle, and, more surprisingly still, a gentleman. When biographers of great men questioned him for his reminis-cences of their subjects, Jules invariably replied (if he could not get out of replying) with kindness and benevolence, even about great men he had disliked or done battle with, for he was always aware that his own biography loomed as a certainty at some future time.

Philip stared at him, fascinated, in a way that he would come to see many people stare at Jules Mendelson in time to come. Introduced by the secretary, Mendelson shook Philip's hand in passing, met his eye, and sized him up in an instant as one of Pauline's "interesting people," in whom he had very little interest. Political figures, senatorial and up; ambassadors; business tycoons, like himself; and heads of museums were the kinds of people who interested him. It was once written about Jules Mendelson in a magazine article that he had simplified the spelling of his family name from Mendelssohn to Mendelson because he figured he wasted seven and a half minutes each day correcting or explaining its spelling. His great-grandfather had been a second cousin of the Mendelssohns of Berlin, one of the most important families of the Jewish upper bourgeoisie and minor nobility before the war. Born in Chicago, Jules Mendelson had taken his inheritance and turned it into a vast fortune. All that was part of his public story.

"I'm sorry to be so late, sir," said Philip. "My plane got in from New York this afternoon, but one of my bags, the one with my dinner jacket in it, couldn't be found." Jules didn't care, nor did he want to be involved in such a drab story. He had a mission of his own on his mind.

"Go in, go in, Mr. Quennell," he said, directing him with a wave of his hand to a room on the right. "Pauline is in the drawing room. I must take a call and will join you then."

Last year, when Malcolm McKnight, who is writing the biography of Jules Mendelson, asked Philip Quennell what his impression of him was the first time they met, Philip remembered this moment and hesitated.

"What came into your mind?" Malcolm persisted.

Philip couldn't bring himself to tell McKnight that what came into his mind was how wonderfully cut Jules Mendelson's dinner jacket was, for such an enormous man. What he did say to Malcolm was, "I thought that this was a man that I would never like to cross," which had been his second thought.

For a newcomer without connections, Philip was extremely well seated that night, placed between Camilla Ebury, with whom he was to fall in love, and Rose Cliveden, a past-middle-age social celebrity of the area who would, inadvertently to be sure, cause havoc in the life of her great friend Pauline Mendelson. The reason for Philip Quennell's excellent *placement,* however, had nothing to do with his desirability as a guest. A man named Hector Paradiso had switched their place cards before dinner, for reasons known only to him, and had moved himself to what Rose Cliveden considered a more advantageous position at a table where the former First Lady was seated.

"Live by the place card, die by the place card," said Rose Cliveden to Philip's left. She was slightly tipsy and greatly miffed as she revealed Hector Paradiso's social disloyalty for the third or fourth time. Her neck had just the suspicion of a goiter, which moved up and down as she spoke in a voice deepened by years of heavy smoking. "Imagine Hector moving the place cards. He's gotten entirely too full of himself lately."

"Be careful what you say to Rose," said Camilla Ebury, to his right. "No matter how drunk she gets, she remembers everything. Total recall."

"Who is Rose Cliveden?" asked Philip.

"Old Los Angeles. Old money. Old friend of Pauline's. Married three times. Divorced three times. Once had an affair with Jack Kennedy. In the White House. In the Lincoln Bedroom. Or so she says. She's been known to exaggerate. What else do you want to know?"

"That's pretty good coverage," Philip replied. "You could be in my business."

"Your business is what?" she asked.

"I've only arrived here today, to write a documentary film. Quite honestly, I'm surprised to have been asked here tonight."

"Pauline collects people," replied Camilla Ebury. She was pretty in a quiet way that was not at first apparent to Philip. Her blond hair was parted in the middle and held back by two gold barrettes, a style he associated with the debutantes he used to watch at dances when he was at Princeton. She was, Philip found out in due course, a recent widow, although she was only a year or two older than he.

Like Pauline and all of Pauline's grand friends, Camilla's range of conversation was on a more elevated scale, at least economically, than his. "Don't ever die in a foreign country if you don't speak the language," she said, recounting her husband's sudden death on a street in Barcelona. "It's an absolute nightmare. The embassy was useless. Thank God for Jules Mendelson. He made a few calls and straightened everything out, and I was able to ship poor Orin home."

At that point, noticing that he was listening attentively, she picked up his place card and read his name, although she had already told it to her twice. "Philip Quennell. Why have you come out here to the Golden West?" she asked.

"To escape the heat," he said.

"What heat?"

"Something I wrote offended some very important people, and I thought it best if I left New York for a while."

"Oh, my lord! Are you the one who wrote that book that made everyone so angry in New York?" she asked.

He was. "Yes."

"No *wonder* Pauline invited you," said Camilla, smiling. "That's the sort of thing she adores." When she smiled, dimples mysteriously appeared in both cheeks and her eyes twinkled. Each of them looked at the other with more interest. "Didn't someone hit you? I think I read that."

He had indeed written a book, on a particular leveraged buyout, that had offended several important people in the New York business community. One well-known figure on Wall Street threatened to have his legs broken, and Philip did not think of his threat as simply a figure of speech, nor did his lawyer. The well-known figure was known to have "connections," as they are called. When Casper Stieglitz, a Hollywood producer, contacted him through his agent to see if he would be interested in writing a screenplay for a documentary based on the proliferation of drugs in the motion picture industry, he leapt at the opportunity, although he knew absolutely nothing about either the motion picture industry or the proliferation of drugs in it. He leapt at the opportunity because he thought a four- or five-month paid sojourn in Southern California might be just exactly what he needed in his present circumstances.

"This is a very swell party," said Philip, looking around the room.

Camilla, following his look, nodded. "It's always very swell at Pauline's," she said.

"Is there an occasion for an evening like this? I mean, is there a guest of honor, or is it a birthday or an anniversary, or something like that? Or do you people out here just have sixty for dinner with rare wines and a flown-in orchestra on a nightly basis?"

Camilla laughed. "You're right. It is quite special. I shouldn't act like I take it for granted, but I've been coming to parties here for so many years that I might have lost my sharp eye."

"You mustn't ever lose your sharp eye, Mrs. Ebury," said Philip. "Or ear, for that matter. You might miss something."

Camilla looked at Philip, interested. "Camilla," she said.

"I'm Philip," he answered.

"I know."

"What kind of people are these?" Philip asked, holding his hand out to indicate the guests. "Aside from the former President and the film star, I mean."

"Oh, the core, I suppose. My father used to describe them as the kind of people who can keep things out of the newspapers," said Camilla.

"What kind of things?"

"Oh, things."

"The woods are full of bodies, you mean?"

She laughed. "In a manner of speaking."

Philip looked around the room again. "This is all quite glamorous in a way. At least it is for me."

"I suppose it is when you're traveling like you are, staying a few days or a few weeks; but if you were to stay longer, you would begin to see that each evening is a variation on the same theme, except at the Mendelsons', where it's a little more extravagant, but then the Mendelsons aren't really Angelenos in the sense that the rest of us are who were born and brought up here. There are about two or three hundred of us who dine together in various combinations, and we rarely widen the circle, and you rarely read about us in the newspapers." She smiled almost apologetically and made a helpless gesture.

"Go on. I'm fascinated," said Philip.

"Well, we never mix with the movie crowd, and only sometimes with the people from Pasadena, except for civic evenings or certain charities, like the museums or the Music Center. I'm not saying it's right, but it's the way it is and the way it always has been. If you want to know the truth, I'd love to know a few movie stars."

Philip laughed. Camilla looked at Philip and saw that he gave her his full attention. She moved in closer to him and spoke in a lowered voice. "Now that you mention it, I think there was originally a point for this party. We all thought that an announcement was going to be made tonight that Jules was being sent by the President to Brussels to head up the American delegation at the statehood of Europe. It would have meant staying there for the whole of nineteen ninety-three, at least, and Pauline was looking forward to it enormously. She speaks perfect French, and I think she sometimes gets bored here."

"It's not to be?" asked Philip.

"Oh, yes, it is to be, but not to be announced as yet, apparently."

Philip nodded. "Good soup," he said.

"Marvelous."

A Mendelson party was, even for the initiated, a heady experience. The food was prepared by their own chef, a famed figure in gastronomic circles, and the wine, from Jules Mendelson's own cellar, was superb. There were orchids, and antiques, and priceless art on every wall in every room. In the library, which the Mendelsons used for a sitting room when they were alone, there were more French paintings, and English furniture, and armchairs and sofas covered in glazed chintz. There was a long table for photographs in silver frames, including several of Pauline and Jules with Presidents and First Ladies at White House dinners, as well as signed photographs from the monarchs of Spain and Great Britain. There was a matching table on the other side of the room for magazines, changed weekly or monthly, and newspapers, changed daily. Tall French windows, elaborately curtained and swagged, opened onto a terrace with umbrellaed tables, and a garden beyond, and a lawn beyond that. People who visited the Mendelsons always said about this room, "How marvelous!" So Philip Quennell, a newcomer to such grandeur, can be excused for gasping and exclaiming aloud when he wandered into this library, looking for a lavatory, and saw van Gogh's *White Roses,* which just happened to be his favorite picture, hanging over the fireplace.

"Good God," he said, walking over to it and staring upward. It was worth, he knew, forty million dollars at least, even in a depressed art market. He wanted to touch the thick vivid paint, and almost did, but resisted. Then he had a sense that he was not alone in the room. He turned, and there was Pauline Mendelson, sitting in a chair by the telephone, or, rather, perched on the edge of a chair by the telephone.

"That's my treasure," she said, about the painting. "It was my wedding present from Jules twenty-two years ago."

She looked, as she always looked in the photographs he had seen of her, resplendent, and was dressed, he was sure, from Paris, from the couture, black velvet cut in a classical fashion, having nothing to do with the trend of that season. She was more elegant than beautiful, although *beautiful* was always the word used to describe her in social columns and fashion magazines. She was tall and slender, and, even without the two strands of grape-sized pearls she was wearing, he would have noticed her astonishing neck. In a flash he remembered the Avedon photograph of her exquisite neck. It was no wonder that she was married to one of the country's most powerful men. It would have been unthinkable to imagine her in a lesser sort of union.

"I saw this picture at the van Gogh exhibit at the Met," he said.

"So you did," she replied.

It couldn't possibly be, he thought, that she had been crying, but there was a trace of moistness in her eyes and something about her face that was in disarray. She rose and walked over to a table over which hung a Chippendale mirror. From a box on the table she took out a compact and lipstick and expertly and quickly rearranged her face. He noticed that she seemed quite comfortable away from her sixty guests and in no hurry to be finished with him to return to them.

"I often wondered who owned it. I remember it said 'On Loan from a Private Collector.'"

"That was its first and last loan-out, believe me. I'll never let it go out of this house again. It was a nightmare. It seemed as though the whole mountain was blocked off when they took it out of the house to fly it east."

"Why?"

"Security. You wouldn't believe all the security, even police helicopters hovering above. They were terrified it was going to be hijacked, because of all the publicity. It's worth, they say, oh, I wouldn't even dream of telling you what they say it's worth, but it's ridiculous, I know, considering that poor Mr. van Gogh was never even able to sell it."

She spoke rapidly, barely stopping for commas and periods, in a low whispery voice, with that kind of accent that no one can really duplicate who hasn't had English nannies and French governesses and been educated at a school like Foxcroft. Philip understood why fashionable people were intrigued by her, quoted her, imitated her.

"Besides," she went on, "I missed it, all the time it was gone, hanging there over the fireplace. I find it such a comforting picture, and this room was forlorn without it. I kept trying other pictures there, but nothing looked right, after the *White Roses*. I'm mad about that color green in the background."

"Oh, yes," he replied, looking back at it.

"Is it true that Reza Bulbenkian threatened to break your legs?" Pauline asked, unexpectedly.

"Yes."

"Do you think he meant it?"

"I'm not sure."

"Hmmm," she said.

"Do you know Reza Bulbenkian?" asked Philip.

"Jules is on his board, and he's on Jules's board, and I sometimes have lunch with Yvonne Bulbenkian when I'm in New York."

"She's a piece of work."

"Isn't she?" Pauline agreed, smiling. "Hector says—have you met my friend Hector Paradiso? Terribly naughty, but very amusing. Hector says that Yvonne has calluses on her hands from social climbing." Pauline laughed. "She called her twins Oakley and Ogden, can you imagine, and speaks to them in French, poor little creatures. New York is so changed now. I've rather lost my taste for it, I'm afraid. It's not at all the way it was when I lived there." She walked over to a cymbidium plant and picked off a dying bud. "How long will you be staying in California?"

"Several months, if all goes well. I'm here to write a film."

"I heard that. For Casper Stieglitz."

"You do know everything."

"I don't know Casper Stieglitz. We don't see many of the movie people."

"Except Faye Converse."

"Faye's different. Faye belongs to the world, not just Hollywood. Faye talks about things, not just what's going on on the set, which is so boring, don't you think? Movie talk drives Jules mad."

"It was nice of you to ask me tonight, Mrs. Mendelson," Philip said.

"You're quite an addition, having been threatened by Reza Bulbenkian; and it's Pauline, not Mrs. Mendelson, and, of course, I'm going to call you Philip. You seem so young to have caused so much trouble. How old are you?"

"I'm twenty-nine until midnight, and then I'm thirty."

"Heavens, we must do something to celebrate."

"Oh, no, please," he said, meaning it. "I would hate that. I'm sure you don't remember, but we met once before."

"Indeed, I do. At the theater, at that silly play. You were with Mary Finch. Her stepmother was one of my bridesmaids, in my first wedding."

"How's Rocky, whose plane crashed and whose two pilots were killed?"

"What a memory you have! Rocky's completely recovered. Getting married again. Even bought a new plane."

"Atta boy, Rocky," said Philip.

"How are you getting on with Camilla?"

"She's very nice."

"Recent widow."

"She told me her husband dropped dead in Barcelona."

"He did. You know who she is, don't you?"

"No."

"Sam Worthington's daughter."

The name meant nothing to Philip. "Is that good?" he asked.

"Natural gas."

"I guess that's good," said Philip, and they both laughed.

Then Jules Mendelson came into the room. His massiveness filled the doorway. "Pauline, people are looking for you," he said.

"Yes, I'm coming, Jules," said Pauline, turning to him.

"I feel lost at these parties unless you're there," he said to her, as if Philip were not there.

"Oh, Jules, don't be silly."

"It's you they come to see, you know. Things slow down when you're not there."

"Isn't he sweet, this husband of mine?" asked Pauline, looking at Philip and indicating Jules with a wave of her hand.

"What are you doing in here?" asked Jules.

There was a pause, and she said, "Kippie called."

Jules looked at his wife. "Kippie? Called from France?"

"No, here. He's back."

"Here? In Los Angeles?"

"Yes."

"Is he coming over?"

"No."

"Where was he calling from?"

"I don't know, Jules. He wouldn't say."

"Everything all right?"

"No," she replied. For an instant they looked at each other.

Aware of Philip's presence, Jules persisted in the conversation, but in a lower voice, as if Philip could not hear.

"What did he want?"

"Money, what else?" answered Pauline, matching his lowered tone.

"I won't."

"I know, Jules. I told him that."

"We'll talk about it later, after the party. I'll wait up," he said, looking over at Philip.

"Yes," said Pauline. Philip was struck by the sadness in her voice.

"Your friend Hector changed the place cards," said Jules, in a chiding voice meant to distract his wife from her problem.

"I know he did. It's a long story. I didn't realize Hector and Rose aren't speaking at the moment," said Pauline. Philip noticed that Pauline was making an effort to shake off her sadness over whatever was troubling her and return to her hostess role. "But you know Hector, Jules. By tomorrow everything will have been straightened out between him and Rose, and he'll make a hilarious story out of it."

"My enthusiasm for Hector is more restrained than yours, I'm afraid," replied Jules.

"Not now, Jules. Have you met Philip Quennell?"

"How do you do, Mr. Quennell," he said, offering Philip a hand to shake. He seemed not to remember having met him an hour and a half earlier in his own hallway.

"Did you like the red wine?" Jules asked Pauline.

"Marvelous, Jules."

"From the Bresciani auction. Château Margaux."

"Oh, I know, darling. Everyone commented at my table."

"Did you notice the color? And the body? Jean-Pierre said it has all the characteristics of *une grande année.*"

"Superb. Everyone thought so," said Pauline.

"What did you think of the red wine?" Jules asked Philip.

"I'm afraid I'm one of those people who put their fingers over the rim of the glass when the waiter pours," answered Philip.

"Don't drink?"

"No."

"You must try this. It's exceptional. The quintessential 'eighty-five Bordeaux."

"No, thank you. I won't," said Philip.

There was an unmistakable look of disdain on Jules's face, as if to say his young guest was a fool to pass up such an opportunity to sip, for free, one of the great wines of France. "A problem?" asked Jules, in the direct manner he had of asking blunt questions.

"Far less dramatic," answered Philip. "Simply no taste for it."

Pauline, observing, quickly came to Philip's rescue. "As you can see, my husband is a wine enthusiast. Philip has come out to write a film for Casper Stieglitz," she explained.

Jules, disinterested, nodded.

Pauline was not deterred. "It was Philip Quennell's legs that Reza Bulbenkian threatened to break," she said.

Jules turned to him now, his interest captured. Suddenly his stern face broke into a wide grin, and the sternness evaporated. "So you wrote *Takeover.* I thought your name was familiar," he said. "Whoever told you all those things?"

Philip smiled but didn't reply.

"You were pretty damned accurate, I'll say that for you. You must know you're high on Reza's shit list," Jules continued.

"Oh, yes, I know."

"It's all talk, though. Reza Bulbenkian wouldn't hurt a fly. Or, have a fly hurt."

Philip wasn't so sure of that, but he replied, "I'm sure."

"It's inexpensive to have someone killed, but it's very expensive to have someone's arms or legs broken, because they can identify you," said Jules.

"What curious information to have at your fingertips, Jules," said Pauline.

"Reza, you know," continued Jules to Philip, "was the only one who didn't go to jail."

"Yes, I know," replied Philip. "He didn't go to jail because he testified against his former partners."

Jules looked at Philip. "Can't wait to tell Reza that you've been here to dinner," he said, chuckling at the thought.

"Will he be annoyed?"

"If he is, he won't say anything."

There was a moment's silence. Then Pauline said, "If you should move hotels, or take an apartment, Philip, make sure you let Miss Maple know."

"Miss Maple?"

"You met her when you came in, at the guest book. She's Jules's secretary. I'll want her to know where to reach you." Philip understood that he had passed inspection. He was going to be invited back.

"Pauline," said Jules again, giving a toss of his head toward the music to prompt her to return to her party. She put her hand beneath his arm.

"Tell the orchestra not to play too loud, Jules. It kills the conversation. Remember what happened at Rose's party? The music was so loud everyone went home by eleven, and they hadn't even wheeled out the birthday cake yet."

"That was because Rose was loaded and forgot to tell them to wheel it out," said Jules.

"Oh, darling, you shouldn't say that," said Pauline, giggling. "Poor Rose. She'd die if she heard you say that."

"You mustn't let her drive home tonight," said Jules. "She's in no condition to drive anywhere."

"I've already told Blondell to turn down the bed in the guest room," said Pauline.

Jules patted her hand in approval.

"Somebody's kissed you," said Pauline. She took his handkerchief from his breast pocket, touched her tongue to it, and wiped the lipstick off his cheek.

"Rose," he said, grimacing.

Pauline laughed and put the handkerchief back in his pocket. Jules smiled at her, and they returned to their party. Philip watched them. However rarefied their existence, he thought, they were married, a couple, committed, bonded in long wedlock. It was what he wanted for himself.

When Philip got back to his table, Camilla Ebury was not there. He looked out at the dance floor and saw her being whirled around by a tall, dark man, too tanned, who was almost too good a dancer, Philip thought, like an instructor in a tango palace. He moved too elegantly, too sleekly, his left shoulder assuming a slightly delicate twist as he steered Camilla through the dancers. Camilla was laughing in a carefree manner, and Philip, to his astonishment, felt a twinge of jealousy, although he scarcely knew Camilla Ebury.

On the other side of him, Rose Cliveden, drunk, was waving her arms as if she were leading the orchestra, and the red wine in her wineglass spilled onto her blue satin dress. Rose, Philip decided, was in her fifties, looked older, because of drink, and must have been very pretty at twenty, thirty, and forty.

As if understanding what he was thinking about her, Rose said, "A dim railway light is still becoming to me."

Philip, embarrassed, laughed.

"Out, out, goddamn spot," said Rose, dipping her napkin into her water glass and then vigorously rubbing her discolored blue satin dress with it.

"What did you spill?" asked Philip.

"Red wine," answered Rose.

"Awfully good red wine to spill," said Philip. "From the Bresciani auction. Château Margaux. The quintessential 'eighty-five Bordeaux. *Une grande année.*"

"A pain in the ass is what it is," said Rose. She had a cigarette hanging from the corner of her mouth. She removed it and stubbed it out in the brown sugar crystals, mistaking the silver bowl for an ashtray.

"Rose, look what you've done!" cried a lady from the other side of the table, but they were all used to Rose in their group and thought the things she did when she had too much to drink exceedingly funny.

Rose, oblivious, went on talking. "This dress cost me an arm and a leg, first time I ever wore it, bought it new for Pauline's party," she said. She unpinned and then repinned at an awkward angle a diamond brooch on her left bosom. She wore big-stoned old-fashioned jewelry, with settings never updated to the current fashion. "Heavens, why would I do that?" she would often say in a voice expressing astonishment at such a suggestion, and then relate that the piece being admired had been Granny's, or Mummy's, or left to her by Aunt Minnie MacComber, or Aunt Mildred Waymouth, and that took care of that.

"Who's Kippie?" asked Philip, suddenly.

"The difficult son. Used to have a kleptomania problem. All the shops in Westwood and Beverly Hills were alerted."

"I didn't know they had a son."

"They don't. Pauline does. Terribly good-looking. By her first marriage, to that fool Johnny Petworth."

"Never heard of John Petworth."

"Johnny, they call him. They keep Kippie stashed away in France somewhere, kicking drugs, I think. He got Madge White's daughter pregnant when they were both only fourteen. Oh, what a to-do there was about that!"

"He's here," said Philip.

"At this party?"

"No. In L.A."

"Kippie's here?" She seemed astonished.

At that moment Pauline walked past Rose and Philip, in the company of Faye Converse and the former First Lady.

"Pauline!" called out Rose.

"Oh, please," said Philip, quickly, not wanting Pauline to think he had been discussing her.

"I want to ask Pauline about Kippie," said Rose. She started to get up to follow Pauline.

"Would you care to dance, Mrs. Cliveden?" he asked, rising also, as if to take her to the dance floor.

"Can't dance, and I'm the best dancer you would have ever danced with," replied Rose.

"Then why can't you?"

"I have a broken toe. So why don't you stay right here and talk to me.

Camilla has been monopolizing you for the whole night. That son of a bitch Hector ditched me, did you know that? Changed the place cards."

"Yes, yes, you told me," said Philip, who had heard the account several times and did not want to hear it again.

"He's mad because the orchestra played so loud at the birthday party I gave for him last week, everybody went home before his birthday cake got wheeled out, and no one sang 'Happy Birthday' to him. He loves being the center of attention. That's why he's not speaking," said Rose.

"These are not what I think of as major life problems," said Philip.

Rose, surprised, looked at Philip for a bit. "Hand me that bottle of red wine, will you? If you wait for these waiters to pour it, you could be waiting for an hour. Now, as my problems are unimportant, you tell me, what kind of conversation do you want to have?" Looking about, she saw that Pauline was returning. "Oh, Pauline," she called out.

"Tell me, Mrs. Cliveden, what kind of a fuck was Jack Kennedy?" asked Philip, forestalling her from speaking to Pauline about Kippie.

"Oh, marvelous, simply marvelous," said Rose. She turned to him, giving him her full attention. "He was so good-looking. And so attentive. And *so* passionate. Until he came, and then he simply couldn't stand to be touched anymore, no affection whatsoever, just when a girl needs it most, when it's all over, the lust, I mean. I put my hand on his back when he was putting on his shoes, and he simply shrank from me. It's that Irish Catholic guilt. They all have it, those Irish people."

Suddenly, she looked at Philip and picked up his place card. "Who are you? Why are you asking me all these questions?"

"Here you are, delivered back to your table," said the dark man, pulling back Camilla Ebury's chair. "I've never cared much for purple flowers, but look how marvelously Pauline has arranged these, mixing them with the pink. It's perfect."

"You're a shit, Hector Paradiso," said Rose haughtily.

Hector elaborately ignored Rose.

"Hector, this is Philip Quennell, whom I've been telling you about. Hector Paradiso."

"Delighted," said Hector. "Oh, look, there's Pauline. I promised her this dance." He was off.

"I thought you were going to dance with me," said Camilla, taking hold of Philip's arm. "You don't mind if I borrow Mr. Quennell, do you, Rose? Come on, let's go." She almost pulled him from his seat and led him onto the dance floor. "I think Rose is going to be sick soon, so let's get out of the way so we don't have to help."

"I take it the Latino twirling you around was the place-card mover Hector Paradiso?" asked Philip, as he allowed himself to be led out to the dance floor.

"Yes, that's Hector. He's one of those men who's never off the dance floor," answered Camilla.

"All the ladies seem smitten with Hector," said Philip.

"Yes, in a way, I suppose," said Camilla. "He and Rose aren't speaking at the moment, but they're best friends at heart."

"I gather. She has a broken toe."

"Rose always has a broken something. She falls a lot."

"What do they all see in Hector?" Philip asked.

"He's really Pauline's pet. Pauline adores him. He makes her laugh and tells her all the gossip. They say Hector's in love with Pauline, but I don't see it like that. Just very close friends," said Camilla.

"Why do I think that under all that Latin charm and cha-cha-cha, he leads a very complicated life."

"I think it's only fair to tell you that Hector Paradiso is my uncle."

"Oh, God. That's the second time in fifteen minutes I've put my foot in it. Want me to take you back to the table?"

"No, but I wouldn't mind if you danced a little closer. There, that's better. I was supposed to go home with Rose, but I wouldn't dream of driving down the mountain with her in the condition she's in."

"Not to worry. She's staying here for the night. Blondell has already turned down the bed in the guest room."

"You certainly know a lot for a stranger in these parts."

"True."

"You're a pretty good dancer too," she said.

"Thanks."

"I asked my uncle Hector to drive me home, but he said he wanted to stay until the bitter end and talk over the party with Pauline," said Camilla.

"Just between us, I think Pauline and Jules are going to want to be alone when the party ends," said Philip. "Kippie is back in town."

"Kippie? He is? How in the world do you know that?"

"I just know."

Camilla nodded, looking at him, but did not miss a beat of her dance step. "Maybe Hector just had a late date and didn't want to tell me. It wouldn't be the first time. God knows where Hector ends up when the parties are over."

"Tell me about Kippie."

"Handsome. Hair too long, or was, the last time I saw him. Always in trouble. He got Madge White's daughter pregnant when they were both only fourteen. Oh, what a to-do about that! Takes drugs. Or did, I don't know about now. He's been in a rehab, somewhere in France," said Camilla.

It was the sort of answer Philip liked. "Succinct," he said.

"What?"

"Your answer."

"Thanks."

"How old?"

"Kippie?"

"Yes."

"I think he was three, or maybe four, when Pauline married Jules."

"So, twenty-five or twenty-six now," he said.

"Why this sudden fascination with Kippie?"

"You know what? I don't know," he said, and they both laughed.

They continued to dance. Behind them Jules and several friends were helping Rose, who was loudly singing the lyrics to "Camelot," to make as graceful an exit as possible. Blondell, Pauline's maid, stood waiting at the entrance of the room for her. Then Philip remembered that it was his birthday.

"What time is it?" he asked.

"Midnight," she answered. "Don't tell me you have jet lag, and it's really three o'clock in the morning your time, and you have to go home. I hate jet-lag stories."

Philip laughed. "I wasn't going to say that. I was going to say something entirely different."

"Like what?" asked Camilla.

"Like how about a club soda at your house?"

"Oh, the wickedness of it."

"Well?"

"I do need a ride home," she said, pulling back her head from his cheek and looking at him.

"I was hoping you'd say that," said Philip.

Flo's Tape #1

"*I was perfectly content to be his mistress. The guy had a wife. I understood that. I couldn't have done the things his wife did, all those parties, all that swank. He needed that kind of wife for his kind of life. But I could do things his wife couldn't do. I mean, the guy had a dick like a mule's. Not many girls could handle that. I could. I mean, you know, we're all good at something. That's what I'm good at.*"

2

JULES MENDELSON always arose at five o'clock to be shaved by a barber called Willi, who came to his home every morning at five-thirty, when it was still dark. It was a practice that Willi had been performing for Jules for twenty-five years, and for which he was handsomely recompensed with a small and very successful barber shop on Sunset Boulevard that was backed by Jules's money. It was understood that Willi would not speak unless spoken to, as Jules liked to think about the business affairs of the day ahead during that time, except on the mornings when a haircut took place as well as the shave, and then the two men exchanged baseball and football scores, for both were passionately interested in spectator sports.

Jules was in the habit of leaving Clouds for his office by six o'clock, in order to receive telephone calls from his associates in New York when the stock market opened and to talk with his partners in London. Invariably, with a private sign to Pauline, he slipped away from their parties at eleven, without saying good night to anyone, so as not to break up the evening, and Pauline carried on until the last guest left. The last guest was always Hector Paradiso. Hector liked to wander through the rooms with Pauline, helping her blow out candles and making sure the butler and maids had emptied all the ashtrays. Then it was their habit to settle down in the library with a last glass of champagne, beneath the van Gogh picture of the *White Roses,* and discuss every detail of the evening. It was a ritual they both enjoyed and looked forward to as the perfect denouement of the party. So it was a surprise to Hector, who had something urgent to say to Pauline, when Pauline, after she had blown out the candles, told him that she had a killing headache, "simply killing, darling," and was going directly to bed without their usual postparty chat and glass of champagne. She did not tell him that Kippie had returned to town.

Hector Paradiso loved Pauline Mendelson without ever having to play the role of lover, a relationship understood by them both, without its ever having been verbalized by either. Never was Hector happier than on those evenings, which had become increasingly frequent, when Jules was busy working, or away from the city, and he was pressed into service as Pauline's escort at a charity benefit, or a museum or ballet or opera opening. The photographers always went mad over Pauline Mendelson, who had achieved celebrity status in the social and fashion press, and Hector stood by her side smiling widely, sometimes even waving, as if the media acknowledgment were equally for him and his family's place in the history of the city.

Driving down the mountain from Clouds after the Mendelsons' party, Hector marveled at Pauline, at the utter perfection of her. Hector was a gossip. It was a thing about him everyone knew, and no one knew better than Pauline, but one of the people he never gossiped about was Pauline Mendelson. For Hector never to have mentioned to a single soul in the whole world what he knew about Jules Mendelson and Flo March was a measure of his utter devotion to Pauline.

Hector led a compartmentalized existence; people who were intimate with him in certain areas of his life knew nothing of the other areas, and it had always been so with him. Tall, dashing, bald, and fit, he looked younger than his forty-eight years. He was that rare sort of man whose looks had improved with the loss of his hair. Dancing, he always said, kept his waistline as slim, or almost as slim, as it had been at twenty-five, although tennis, which he played on Rose Cliveden's court every weekend, also helped. He was often described as being a descendant of one of the Spanish Land Grant families, like the Sepulvedas and the Figueroas, who had major boulevards named after them, in recognition of their involvement in the founding of the city; and he never did not enjoy the moment when a new person heard his surname, Paradiso, and asked, "As in Paradiso Boulevard, on the way to the airport?"

The fortune his family once possessed had long since evaporated, but he lived more than comfortably, for a person who didn't work, on a trust fund left by his sister, Thelma Worthington, the mother of Camilla Ebury, who had killed herself a dozen years ago after an unhappy love affair. His small but perfect house on Humming Bird Way, between Oriole and Thrush, in the Hollywood Hills, had been photographed for a house magazine and had been the scene for many a cocktail party through the years. He often said that his was one of the few houses where the many diversified groups of the city overlapped. They did, but not at the same time.

Anyone who wanted to know anything about Los Angeles society always called Hector. He knew the answers because he knew everyone, and those he didn't know, he knew about. "We may not all know each other, but we all know who each other is," he was fond of saying. He was able to interconnect the old families of the city for generations back. Like old Bronwyn Doheny, Caroline Phillips's mother, age ninety-one, whose funeral was to be held the next day at All Saints Episcopal Church in Beverly Hills. "Bronwyn was born a Parkhurst," he said to his friend, Cyril Rathbone, who wrote a social column for *Mulholland,* explaining it all in a nutshell. "She was Judge Parkhurst's second daughter. Her grandfather built that enormous French house on West Adams Boulevard, which is now the Center for the Church of the Heavenly Light. That whole neighborhood has gone black, you know. When I was just a child, I used to go to Caroline's birthday parties in that house before they moved to Hancock Park. Now, Bronwyn's first husband—who was *not,* I repeat not, Caroline's real father, that's another story entirely—was Monroe Whittier, and then when Monroe died, she married Justin Mulholland, who embezzled the money, do you remember that story? Now Justin Mulholland, who died in jail, was the first cousin of Rose Cliveden." When Hector Paradiso wasn't dancing, that was the sort of conversation he could carry on for hours, and did, when he was spending the evening with the kind of people he had grown up with, or, at least, the first part of the evenings, the part that preceded midnight. He was, furthermore, and had been for many years, the man who led the cotillion and taught the debutantes how to curtsy to the ground at the Las Madrinas Ball, where the daughters of the Los Angeles elite made their bow to society.

After midnight, Hector Paradiso's life took on a very different aspect, one that might have shocked some of his Angeleno friends. Even as sophisticated a couple as Pauline and Jules Mendelson could not have guessed the extent of his late-night adventures, looking for strangers to pay to kiss. Although they might have suspected there was another element to Hector's life—he had, after all, never married—it was not a subject ever voiced, even by people like Rose Cliveden, who often fought with Hector, but who fully intended to leave him the life use of one of her trust funds, should she die before him. Earlier, in his youth, there had been women in his life, like Astrid Vartan, the late ice skating star to whom he had once been engaged, and even, briefly, Rose Cliveden herself. Rose, who was never at a loss for words, reported that his equipment, as she called it, was minimal—"a rosebud, darling, no more"—but that he was marvelously adroit with his tongue. After midnight, Hector visited places that his friends in high society had never heard of, much less visited. One of these, more reputable than some he frequented, was Miss Garbo's.

Miss Garbo's was a late-night cabaret club located on a short street in West Hollywood called Astopovo, between Santa Monica Boulevard and Melrose Avenue. Hector, ever mindful of his own importance, even in an area where it was highly unlikely that he would run into any of the kind of people he knew from the main part of his life, pulled his small Mercedes into the rear of the parking lot himself, rather than give it to a parking boy in front of the club, so that, when he left, he would not have to stand in front of the club, possibly with a companion in questionable dress, and wait for his car to be brought around for him. A stickler for appearances, Hector always thought of things like that. He wished there were a rear door that he could enter, and it occurred to him to speak to Manning Einsdorf, the owner of Miss Garbo's, to put one in so that people like himself, who didn't like to be talked about, could enter and leave the club in complete anonymity, especially when wearing a dinner jacket like he was that night, having come directly down the mountain from the Mendelsons' party.

"Hi, Hector," a loud voice called out from the crowded bar, and he turned to see Joel Zircon, a Hollywood agent who was also a regular in the place, standing at the bar with a friend.

"Hello, Joel," replied Hector, not matching the familiar tone of Joel's voice.

"Say hi to Willard Parker," said Joel, introducing his friend. "Willard's Casper Stieglitz's butler."

"Hello, Hector," said Willard, putting out his hand. Willard already knew who Hector Paradiso was, and was anxious to make his acquaintance so as to be able to claim the social figure as a friend.

Hector nodded but did not take the hand that was offered. He had not come to Miss Garbo's to make conversation, especially with a movie producer's butler.

"What kind of night are they having here?" asked Hector.

"Not bad. Not bad," said Joel.

"Where's Manning Einsdorf tonight?" asked Hector.

"He'll be out in a few minutes. He's got a new singer opening in the next set," said Joel.

"I want to get in and out before the new singer goes on. I've heard enough of Manning Einsdorf's discoveries," said Hector.

"Well, you're looking pretty spiffy," said Manning Einsdorf, coming up to the bar. He was sixty, and his gray hair was combed upward and sprayed into place to cover his bald spot. He wore large rings on each hand. "You always add a touch of class to the place, Hector."

Hector, in his gleaming white shirtfront and black tie, preened a bit as he felt himself to be the center of attention of this admiring group, knowing that he was different from them, more important, better even. He nodded in acknowledgment, and turned to watch the action in the room.

"Been to one of your high society functions?" asked Manning.

Hector nodded yes. It was a game they played out together. He took a cigarette from a gold case in his pocket and lit it with a pack of matches labeled MISS GARBO's that Manning handed to him.

"Whose?" asked Manning. Like the outsider he was, Manning Einsdorf had an enormous curiosity about the social lives of his clientele, and Hector Paradiso, who greatly enjoyed his reputation as a social figure, could not resist impressing the impressionable Manning.

"Pauline Mendelson's," answered Hector, in a lowered voice, always aware of the impact of her society name.

"Oh, la de da," said Manning. "And how was Pauline dressed tonight?"

Pauline Mendelson would have been greatly surprised to know how frequently her name was invoked in the name of style and swank among the customers of bars like Miss Garbo's, as well as the hairdressers, and florists, and picture framers, and lampshade makers in the area of West Hollywood.

"Like Madame X herself. Black velvet. High neck. Low back. Very classical," answered Hector.

"And what jewels tonight? Lemme guess, the emeralds?" asked Manning.

Hector shook his head. "Two strands of her perfect pearls the size of grapes, and a plain diamond bracelet."

"Class, the woman has class," said Manning. "Have a drink on the house, Hector."

"I'll have a scotch and soda, Zane," said Hector to the bartender.

"Coming right up, Hector. How's it going?"

"Okay, Zane. You're looking pretty good for an old man."

Zane, who was forty, laughed. "You want to know the first time I made it with Hector, Manning? Nineteen sixty-eight. Right, Hector? Met him at Numbers up on the Strip."

"He was a hot number in those days," said Hector.

"Speaking of hot numbers, I got a couple of new hot numbers here tonight," said Manning.

"Start pointing them out. It's getting past my bedtime," said Hector. "And nothing Third World."

"Take a look at the far end of the bar, the one nursing the beer, with the leather jacket and the blond hair," said Manning.

Hector glanced down the bar. Sitting on a bar stool was a young man, aware that he was being looked at. He looked back and smiled. He was, in the dim light of the bar, very good-looking.

"Go no further. That'll do just fine," said Hector. "What's his name?" asked Hector.

"Lonny," answered Manning.

"Lonny what?"

"How the fuck do I know Lonny what? Lonny was what he told me," said Manning.

"You ought to get both names."

"For what? These guys aren't trying to get into the *Los Angeles Blue Book*. They have something else on their minds. Guys like that give you two names, nine times out of ten, the second name is a phony, so why waste time learning it?"

"What's Lonny's claim to fame?" asked Hector, staring at the young man.

"You're gonna love this one, Hector. This guy is supposed to have the rest of the missing manuscript of *Candles at Lunch*," said Manning. "Took it off Basil Plant one night when Basil was drunk and belligerent and wouldn't pay up. He thought Basil would come after him the next day and pay him a fortune for it, but Basil was so far gone on pills and booze he didn't even remember the incident, and a short time later he died. And Lonny's got three hundred and ninety-eight pages of a novel he's too stupid to read, but he brags about it a lot."

"That wasn't exactly what I meant when I asked what was his claim to fame," said Hector. "Let me put it this way: when I came here tonight, I didn't have in mind a night of literary pursuits. Let me be more succinct. Is he hung?"

"I have no personal experience in the matter. I've only seen his videos," said Manning.

"Well?"

"Extended, it rises two inches above his belly button. Is that what you want to know?" asked Manning.

"Yes, Manning, that's exactly what I want to know. Introduce me, and get the charges all set now, up front, so there's no misunderstanding later. I had a little trouble with that Puerto Rican number you set me up with last week."

"So I heard."

"I pay seventy-five, no more."

"It's a hundred-dollar market these days, Hector."

"Seventy-five," repeated Hector.

"And the pretty boy at the end of the bar that you've taken a fancy to is a hundred and a half, take it or leave it, no bargaining with him."

"How do you know?"

"He told me. He considers himself a video star."

"That is an outrageous amount of money," said Hector, with indignation in his voice.

"Let me put it in perspective for you, Hector," said Manning. Manning Einsdorf was an astute businessman and used to dealing with the penurious Hector. "A hundred and fifty bucks wouldn't pay for one centerpiece at Pauline Mendelson's party tonight, and you can't fuck a centerpiece."

Hector smiled. "I always said about you, Manning: you're a man with class."

"Do we have a deal?"

Hector turned to the bartender. "Zane, send another beer down to Lonny at the end of the bar. Compliments of Mr. Paradiso, tell him."

"I bet you five bucks he'll say, 'As in Paradiso Boulevard, on the way to the airport?' " said Zane.

"That's the point, Zane," said Hector. "They all say that. It worked with you in 'sixty-eight, and it's still working today."

Zane laughed and took a beer down to the end of the bar. Lonny accepted it, and raised it in a salute to Hector. Hector walked down to the end of the bar, and the two men shook hands.

There was a roll of the drums, and Manning's voice came out on the loudspeaker. "Lady and gentlemen, Miss Garbo's is proud to present the Los Angeles singing debut of Miss Marvene McQueen." The orange curtains parted to reveal a blond singer, in a black evening dress with thin shoulder straps, standing in the curve of a piano. She wore her long hair in the style of a forties movie star, like Veronica Lake, so that one eye and half of her face were obscured by it. As she began to sing "Moanin' Low," in what she hoped was the manner of Libby Holman, she threw back her head to get the hair out of her eyes. The customers turned to look and listen, but their interest in her musical efforts quickly waned, and the business of the bar went on.

"Is this a guy in drag?" asked Hector.

"Hector, please," said Manning. "She's a woman."

"Looks like a guy in drag."

"Well, she's not." Manning was annoyed. "Shhh," he went to some customers who were talking too loudly and not paying attention to his discovery.

"How much are you paying her?" asked Hector.

"Actually, she's paying me. This is her debut."

"Not so hot-looking for a nightclub singer."

"I think it's a very interesting face," replied Manning.

"Her family never heard of braces, I see."

"Braces?"

"She's got buckteeth."

"Well, they're not exactly buck. One of the two front teeth is in front of the other."

"Where I come from, that's buck. You're not going to tell me she makes a living at this?"

"Why?"

"Look around. Nobody's listening to your new discovery. How does she make a living?"

"She's the literary critic for *Mulholland,* but keep that under your lid. She don't want anyone to know."

"That's Hortense Madden?"

"Herself."

"Hey, Manning," said Zane, the bartender. "The singer's pissed off because you're talking during her number."

"Fuck the singer," said Hector.

"No, thanks. She's not my type," said Lonny, the video star, speaking his first words of the evening.

Hector looked at Lonny and laughed. "Let's get out of here," he said.

Lonny, smoking a joint, looked at all the photographs in silver frames that covered the tables in Hector Paradiso's living room. There were pictures of a great many grand people, as well as recognizable faces of film stars of past decades—Tyrone Power, Rosalind Russell, Dolores del Rio, Astrid Vartan— and they never failed to fascinate Hector's nocturnal visitors. Hector, his black tie off, his shirt open at the neck, sat in a chair with a strong drink of whiskey and watched the young man. In his arms was his dog, Astrid, a West Highland terrier. Astrid was used to the strangers her master brought home most nights of the week. Hector noticed for the first time that Lonny wore black jeans, a black Lacoste shirt, and black running shoes.

"A study in black," said Hector.

"What's that mean?"

"It seems as if all the interesting people dressed in black tonight."

Lonny nodded, disinterested. "Who's this?" he asked, picking up a picture.

"She's called Pauline Mendelson," said Hector.

"Movie star?"

"Oh, goodness, no. Just a friend."

"Looks high class."

"She is."

He picked up another picture, of a young bride, and stared at it. "I've never been to a wedding," he said.

"Never been to a wedding? Really?"

"I mean a real wedding like this, where the bride wears a white veil, and has bridesmaids, and walks up the aisle on the arm of her father. Hey, that's you in the picture? Is this your daughter?"

"No, no, my niece. My sister's daughter. Her father was dead, and I took her up the aisle."

"Wow." He took another toke from his joint. "This is good dope you got, Hector."

"Lots more where that comes from. And other treats, as well."

"How long ago was this wedding?"

"Nine years."

"Is it a happy marriage?"

"It isn't a marriage anymore."

"Divorced, huh?"

"No, the husband dropped dead on the street in Barcelona."

"No kidding? That's sad, really sad."

"What's your last name, Lonny?"

"Edge."

"Lonny Edge. Nice name. Is that your real name or hooker name?"

"It's my real name, and I don't like being called a hooker, Hector," said Lonny. There was a menacing note in his voice.

Hector recognized the note and looked at him. Beneath the cushion of his chair was the gun he always had at the ready for protection in case any sort of unpleasantness should break out with one of his night visitors.

"This is what I do for a living," said Lonny, explaining himself. "I have no problem with it."

"Oh, of course," said Hector, smiling nervously. "It was just a figure of speech. No offense, old man."

"I also happen to be a very big name in video," continued Lonny.

"Yes, yes, I think I may have seen some of your videos, now that I think of it. *Hard, Harder, Hardest*? Wasn't that you?"

"Yeah, man. That was me," said Lonny, pleased that he was recognized.

"Marvelous film. Why don't you come over here, Lonny," said Hector, getting down to the business of the evening. He placed the little dog on the floor and then lifted one foot, on which he was still wearing his black patent leather dancing pump, and pointed it at the crotch of Lonny Edge's black jeans. Hands on hips, ready for anything, Lonny watched the rich bachelor. Hector drank from his whiskey glass and slowly moved the toe of his black patent leather dancing pump up and down on the fly of Lonny's jeans, smiling at him at the same time.

"Let's see if what you've got in there is as good as Manning Einsdorf says it is, Lonny," said Hector.

The next morning, an hour before dawn, five shots rang out in the living room and library of 9221 Humming Bird Way. Hector Huberto Luis Paradiso y Gonsalvo, the last member of the great Paradiso family that had helped to found the city, turned and stared in disbelief into the mirror over his mantelpiece and saw the blood drain from his tanned face, leaving it a purplish gray color. Beyond in the mirror, his eyes met the eyes of his killer as that person looked back in haste before making for the front door. Astrid, his dog, barked furiously at the departing figure.

Leaning against the wall for support, Hector edged his way to the door of the library, trailing blood as he slowly moved toward the telephone. On his desk was a pile of blue stationery from Smythsons on Bond Street in London, with his name, Hector Paradiso, engraved across the top of each sheet. The stationery had been a favorite gift from Pauline Mendelson. "So personal, so thoughtful, so typical of Pauline," Hector had said at the time to Cyril Rathbone, to whom he sometimes flaunted his close friendship with the grand lady. As he leaned over the top sheet and wrote the name of the person who had fired the five shots that were causing his death, several drops of blood fell on the piece of paper, partially covering his childlike scrawl. The dog, Astrid, hugged his leg, crying.

Hector buzzed the intercom that connected with the room of his houseboy in the pool house across the lawn.

"*Si?*" came the sleepy voice of Raymundo.

"Police," Hector whispered into the phone. "Get the police."

"You all right, señor Hector?" asked Raymundo.

"Get the police." His voice was so weak it could scarcely be heard.

Raymundo, alert, hopped out of bed.

From the intercom came the last words of Hector Paradiso. "And get rid of all the porn before my niece gets here."

Flo's Tape #2

"There's something you've got to understand. I never for a moment expected Jules Mendelson to divorce his wife and marry me, and he never gave me any line like that either, in order to keep me hanging in there. If he had any complaints about his wife, he never talked about them to me. The thing is, the Mendelsons had an ideal marriage, like a great partnership, except that he was in love with me, as well as being in love with Mrs. Mendelson. He just loved us in different ways.

"Jules was a guy who'd had his own way all his life. And he thought he could have the two of us, and he could have as far as I was concerned, but it just didn't work out that way.

"You see, I had no intention of letting happen what happened between us. You've certainly seen enough pictures of Jules; he was never going to win any prizes in the looks department. And I'd never gone out with a guy that age before. There's something about power that's very sexy, you know, and what Jules lacked in the looks department, he more than made up for in the power department. When Jules walked into a room or a restaurant, people turned around. My friend, Glyceria, who was Faye Converse's maid, told me that in her time, women used to think Henry Kissinger was attractive. It's another version of the same thing, you know.

"And he was good to me. He wanted to improve me. He once said to me, 'You've got to start reading the newspapers, not just the gossip columns.' And then he started asking me about stuff in the news, like Gorbachev, and Bush, and the deficit, and stuff like that, and he could explain things to me so that I could understand. If you should happen to have any questions about the European currency after 1992, for instance, I'll probably be able to help you out, because he talked about that all the time. And he wanted me to wear nice clothes, and he began to buy me classy gifts, like this ring here with the sapphire and the diamonds, and these yellow diamond earrings. When I was seeing that putz Casper Stieglitz before I met Jules, all that he ever gave me was black satin underwear from Frederick's of Hollywood. And pretty soon, I started to fall in love with Jules."

3

THE NIGHT BEFORE, Philip Quennell and Camilla Ebury had made love for the first time, as well as the second and the third, each time experiencing increased acts of intimacy. Awakening later than Camilla, Philip lay in bed without moving and watched her as she brushed her hair, with a raised arm and long hard strokes, at the same time gazing into her dressing table mirror with an intent stare. The strap of her nightgown had fallen from her shoulder, and her concentration on her hairbrushing was complete.

"When I was a child, my nanny—Temple she was called, short for Temple-ton—made me brush my hair one hundred times each morning, no matter what. I used to hate it, but it became a habit, and now I find that my day is imperfect if I don't do it the first thing. Of course, I don't think about my hair when I brush it. It is for me a time for thinking," said Camilla.

"How did you know I was awake?" asked Philip.

"I could see you in the mirror," she said.

"Nice back," he said.

"Hmmm?"

"Nice back, I said."

"Thanks."

"It's a good look the way your strap has fallen off your shoulder."

"I'm experiencing shyness, if you can believe it."

He smiled at her.

"Do you always sleep with your pearls on?"

"Always. They belonged to my uncle."

"The place card changer, that uncle?"

She laughed. "Uncle Hector, although I never call him uncle. Hector Paradiso."

"As in Paradiso Boulevard, on the way to the airport?"

"Yes. The Paradisos were a Land Grant family. Hector's great-grandfa-ther, or great-great, I'm not sure, I never get it straight, was one of the found-ers of the city, way back when. My mother was his older sister."

"Now let me get this straight. On your father's side, according to Pauline Mendelson, you're natural gas, and on your mother's side, you're from a Land Grant family. Right?"

"Right."

"You're what's called well connected, where I come from."

"I cover all the bases, at least in Los Angeles."

"I know it's none of my business, but why did Uncle Hector have a pearl necklace?"

"It belonged to his mother, my grandmother, whom I never knew. When Hector was in the army, he wore it under his uniform. He claimed the pearls brought him luck. After the army, he gave them to my mother, and when Mummy died, they came to me. I almost never take them off, except when I bathe, of course, or go swimming—the chlorine in the pool is terrible for them —or when I wear Mummy's diamond necklace, which isn't often, because it's a bore to get it out of the bank and then back the next morning, because of the insurance."

Philip laughed.

She looked at him, confused. "What did I say that was funny?"

"Rich people stories always strike me funny," he said.

Her hundred strokes finished, she stood up and walked toward the bed and pulled the bedclothes off him. "Time to get up," she said. Looking down at him, she spoke again. "Oh, heavens!"

Philip, embarrassed, smiled bashfully.

"Is that because of me or because it's morning?" she asked.

"Both," replied Philip. He reached up and flicked off the second shoulder strap, and her nightgown slipped down to her waist. "Nice front, too," he said, quietly.

She folded her arms in front of her breasts but did not turn away.

"Don't do that," said Philip. He reached up and took down her protective arms and stared at her breasts. With his first finger he lightly touched the tip of her nipple and then moved his finger in a circular motion. "Perfect," he said. The night before, at the Mendelsons' party, he had thought she was attractive, but not quite beautiful. Now, seeing her, he revised his opinion.

"That's really nice," he said.

"What's really nice?" she asked.

"Your modesty."

"Listen, Philip, I don't want you to think I'm in the habit of picking up men at parties and bringing them home," said Camilla. "I'm not." She wanted to say, "This is the first time since my husband died," but she didn't, although it was true, because she knew it would sound like a protestation.

"That's not what I think at all," said Philip gently. For a moment they stared at each other. Then Philip reached out and took her hand and brought her down to the bed beside him.

"There's something I meant to tell you last night," she said.

"What?"

"I do think that's an awfully odd place down there for you to have a tattoo."

Later, Camilla went downstairs to make coffee and brought it back up to the room. She could hear Philip in her bathroom, with the water running. He was standing nude with his back to her, intent on shaving. Although she had spent the night with him, making love in endless variations, and repeated the process in the morning, she felt like an intruder on his privacy as she walked in on him in her bathroom.

"Oh, excuse me," she said.

He smiled. "It's all right."

"I need the Floris bath salts."

"Come in. It's your bathroom. I borrowed a razor."

"What are you using for shaving cream?"

"Just soap. It works all right."

Passing him, opening the cabinet, her body brushed against the front of him. Philip, always responsive to touch, responded. They both noticed. They both smiled.

The telephone rang in the bedroom.

"What? No extension in the bathroom?" joked Philip. "I thought this was the movie capital of the world."

"Not the group I'm in," said Camilla as she walked toward the ringing telephone. "We don't even speak to the people in the movie capital. It's probably Bunty. Did I tell you I had a daughter?"

"No."

"Age eight. She's spending the weekend at her friend Phyllis's family's ranch in Solvang. Otherwise, there'd be no way you would ever have spent the night here. Hello? Oh, good morning, Jules. What a marvelous party that was. I had such a good time. I was going to call Pauline to thank her, but I thought it was too early."

There was a long silence, and then Philip heard Camilla say, "No!" There was another silence, and again she said, "No! I simply can't believe it. How could this happen?"

Again there was a silence, and Camilla said, "Where are you calling from, Jules?"

Philip wrapped himself in a towel, walked into the bedroom, and stood by Camilla. He perceived at once from Camilla's face that something serious, possibly calamitous, had occurred.

"From Hector's house." He was able to hear Jules Mendelson's deep voice.

"I'll be right there," said Camilla.

"No, no, Camilla, don't come over," said Jules. He spoke hastily. "There's no point in that. It would only upset you terribly. I can handle everything here. What you should do is go up to Pauline's and stay with her, or I could tell Pauline to come to you, and I'll meet you in an hour or so."

Camilla was dissatisfied with this arrangement, but, as it was Jules Mendelson who was advising her, she capitulated to his wishes.

"Yes, of course, Jules. Have you told Pauline yet?"

"Yes, I called her," said Jules.

After she hung up, Philip asked, "What is it?"

"Hector's dead," answered Camilla.

"How?"

"Shot, apparently."

They looked at each other. He put his hand over her hand. "I'm sorry."

She nodded. "My father, my mother, my husband, now my uncle. What the hell's wrong with me?"

"Get dressed," said Philip. "I'll drive you there."

"Jules said not to come, that it would only upset me. He said for me to go up to Pauline's and that he would meet me there and fill me in."

"Is Jules Mendelson related to your uncle?"

"No."

"Was he his best friend or something?"

"No. Hector was Pauline's friend really. I never thought Jules liked him all that much. Why do you ask?"

"You are Hector's only living relation, aren't you?"

"Yes."

"How come Jules Mendelson knows your uncle is dead before you know it? Why would the police call him?"

Camilla looked at Philip. "I don't know, but it is so like Jules to handle things. Underneath that stern facade, he is an incredibly kind man, who would do anything for his friends. I told you how he helped me when Orin dropped dead in Barcelona."

"Yes, I understand all that," said Philip. "But I still don't understand why the police called him and not you."

"I suppose you're right," she said.

"Don't you think you should go to your uncle's house?"

"Jules said to go up to Pauline's."

"Somehow you don't strike me as the kind of woman who stays away just because someone tells her to stay away."

"I'm not."

"C'mon. I'll take you there."

Flo's Tape #3

"Once Jules told me he sometimes felt inadequate around Pauline's family. I couldn't imagine Jules ever feeling inadequate about anything, but he said he did. Pauline's father was a great sportsman, and Jules never participated in sports, except to watch football on television. What almost no one knew was that Jules had a little spindly leg, just about this big around. He was very sensitive about it. When he was a child in Chicago, he had one of the last known cases of polio. So he didn't play golf, or tennis, or any of the things that were important to Pauline's father.

"He also felt that Pauline never really lost her Eastern Seaboard background, even though she had become a fixture of the Los Angeles social scene. He said he thought of her as a permanent visitor. When her sisters came to visit her, as they did several times a year, he told me that he felt like an outsider among them, while they giggled and talked about people they had known whom he had never heard of. He said that sometimes they spoke in French together.

"Once he said that if anything ever happened to him, he was sure that Pauline would be gone from Los Angeles within the year."

4

TO HAVE THE NEWS of a misadventure before anyone else, even the media, was not an altogether new experience for Pauline Mendelson. In times past, because of the prominence and influence of her husband, she had known of certain minor misadventures involving her son and only child, Kippie Petworth, before anyone, even the police. Kippie's teenage kleptomania had long since come to a halt, but not without several highly embarrassing situations that had had to be covered for, atoned for, and hushed, all thanks to Jules, who was no more than the boy's stepfather. But, as everyone they knew knew, Kippie's real father, Johnny Petworth, was hopeless in any sort of crisis, except in cards and backgammon.

No amount of familiarity with misadventure, however, could have prepared Pauline for the shock of the early morning telephone call that aroused Jules and sent him flying out of their house at such an ungodly hour.

"But what is it, Jules?" she asked from their bed, seeing the haste with which he hung up the telephone, after an indecipherable conversation, and leapt from the bed and dressed, without either bathing or shaving. She feared, of course, for her son, who had returned unexpectedly the night before, having abandoned his clinic in France months before the time the doctors had prescribed as necessary for his treatment.

Standing at the door of their room, ready to go, Jules said to her, "It's Hector."

"Hector!" said Pauline, nearly collapsing with relief. "Oh, thank God. For a moment I thought it was Kippie again."

"He's dead," said Jules.

"Hector?" whispered Pauline, aghast. "How? What happened?"

"I don't know anything. I'll call you when I get there."

"Was it an automobile accident? What? How?" she asked.

"I don't know, Pauline," he replied again.

"Where are you going?"

"To his house."

"Oh, Jules, should I do anything about Camilla?"

"No."

"Of course, if they called you, they undoubtedly called her."

Jules nodded. "Do you have much on your agenda for today?"

"Whatever it is, I'll clear it."

"Good. Stand by."

Outside, a moment later, she could hear the frenzied barking of the police dogs that patrolled the grounds at night, as they rushed around Jules on his way across the courtyard to the garage. "Hi, boy, hi, boy, down, down," she could hear Jules say to the dogs. However fierce the dogs were to other people, they responded totally to the commands of Jules Mendelson. "Call them off, will you, Smitty. It's me."

"Anything wrong, Mr. Mendelson?" asked Smitty, the night guard, who had been with the Mendelsons for fifteen years.

"Apparently," answered Jules, without elaborating further. "I have to get up to Humming Bird Way. Remind me how to get there. I can't remember."

"Off the Strip, up Doheny, turn right on Oriole, and it turns into Humming Bird," said Smitty.

"I'll know it when I see it. I've been there a hundred times," said Jules.

"I hope everything's okay, Mr. M.," said Smitty.

Alone, Pauline turned on the All News radio station, but there was nothing on it that pertained to her life, or Hector's, as far as she knew: rapes, murders, gangs, drug deals gone awry, and a television star's divorce. Still stunned by the suddenness of the news, and the incompleteness of it, she could not yet cry, although she felt an ache of loneliness for her friend. In days to come, she would say over and over, dozens of times, "He was my first friend here when Jules and I moved to Los Angeles." She could only remember that Hector had wanted to stay on the night before after the other guests had left, as was their habit, and bring a bottle of champagne into the library to talk over the happenings of the party, especially his latest contretemps with Rose Cliveden, but she had said no. My God, she thought, perhaps if he had stayed, whatever has happened might not have happened. And then she remembered that Rose was sleeping down the hall in one of the guest rooms, having been too drunk to drive to Holmby Hills, let alone down the mountain from Clouds.

I'll wake up Rose, thought Pauline.

On Sunset Boulevard the traffic moved at a snail's pace and then stopped entirely. Philip Quennell and Camilla Ebury, en route from Camilla's house in Bel Air to Hector Paradiso's house in the Hollywood Hills, sat in impatient silence in the car.

"It's driving me mad, this sitting here," said Camilla, tapping her fingers on the dashboard. "The traffic usually moves on Sunset."

"There must be an accident, or something, up ahead," said Philip.

"More likely, some great event at the Beverly Hills Hotel. That's the holdup, I'm sure," said Camilla.

Philip pressed on the horn several times.

"Honking is not going to do any good, you know," she said.

"I know. I can't stand people who blow their horns, but I can feel how anxious you are."

"Perhaps if you turned left when we get to Roxbury, and got over on Lexington, we could go behind the hotel, and then come out again on Sunset," suggested Camilla.

"Did Hector keep great sums of money in his house, do you think?" asked Philip.

"I know he didn't. In the first place, he didn't have very much money."

"What do you mean, he didn't have much money?"

"I mean, people who don't have any money will think he had a lot of money, but people with money will say he didn't have any money."

"Money is a relative thing, is that what you're saying?" asked Philip, amused.

"Something like that. Jules explained that to me. And in the second place, Hector was extremely tight. Anyone who knew him will tell you that."

"Has Hector ever been married?" asked Philip.

"Engaged a few times, once to an actress, Astrid something, before my time, but he never married," said Camilla. She looked out the window.

"Why don't you cry?" asked Philip.

"I don't know you well enough to cry in front of you," she replied.

"Yes, you do."

"I only met you last night."

"We've come a long way in a short time, don't forget."

"I want you to know one thing."

"What's that?"

"I'm not in the habit of bringing men home from parties."

"You already told me that, and it wasn't necessary to say it the first time. I knew that."

She reached over and patted his hand on the steering wheel.

"Thanks for coming with me," she said.

"May I ask you a question?"

"Of course."

"About your marriage?"

"All right."

"Didn't you love your husband?" asked Philip.

"Why do you ask that?" replied Camilla, with surprise in her voice.

"You spoke of him very casually."

"How did I speak of him very casually? And when? I don't remember."

"Last night, at the Mendelsons'."

"What in the world did I say?"

"You said, 'Don't ever die in a country where you don't speak the language. It's a nightmare.' "

"But that's true."

"I'm sure it's true, but it's also a very casual way to talk about a husband who dropped dead on the street in Barcelona."

"Do you think I sound callous?"

"I don't know, but I'm curious."

She looked straight ahead, thinking before answering. "Oh, I suppose we would have gotten a divorce in time if Orin hadn't died. We weren't really happy, but Bunty adored him, and I wasn't desperately unhappy, just not terribly happy. Satisfied?"

"Honest answer."

"Now tell me something."

"Okay."

"Do you always remember everything people say?"

"Yes."

"I better be careful about what I say."

"Look, the line's moving," he answered.

"I'm sorry, ma'am, there's no one permitted to go in the house," said the policeman posted outside Hector Paradiso's house on Humming Bird Way. Already the driveway had been roped off with orange masking tape strung between trees. There were police cars lined up on both sides of the street, and a news van from one of the local television stations was driving up and down the street looking for a place to park. An ambulance, with its rear door open, was parked in the driveway, and the driver leaned against the fender smoking a cigarette. Across the street, neighbors, still in nightclothes, were huddled together, watching the scene.

"No one admitted here," said a policeman, holding up his hands, as Camilla Ebury and Philip Quennell walked up to the entrance of the house.

"I am Mr. Paradiso's niece," said Camilla.

"I'm sorry, ma'am, I can't let you in. Those are my orders," said the policeman.

"This is Camilla Ebury, officer," said Philip Quennell. "Mrs. Ebury is Hector Paradiso's only living relative."

"I'll go inside and ask, Mrs. Berry, but not at the moment," said the officer. "I'm really sorry for your trouble, but I'm just doing what I was told. The coroner's in there now."

"If you could just tell them inside that I'm here," said Camilla. "It's Ebury, not Berry. E-B-U-R-Y. My mother was Mr. Paradiso's sister. Mr. Jules Mendelson called me with the news."

Always, whenever it was mentioned, in any circumstance, the name of Jules Mendelson seemed to bring about a change in attitude. As the officer headed toward the front door, it opened, and two policemen came out with a young man between them, his hands in handcuffs behind his back. The television van had parked and unloaded, and the cameraman ran forward to get a picture of the trio. The handcuffed person in the middle shouted out, "Hey, man, don't photograph me," and bent his head down and turned it away from the camera. As he looked up from his bent-over position, his eyes locked with Camilla's.

"I didn't do this, Miss Camilla! I swear to God! I was asleep in my room in the pool house. Your uncle buzzed me on the intercom and said there was trouble, and by the time I got dressed he was dead, and whoever did it was gone. I swear to God, Miss Camilla."

"Oh, Raymundo," said Camilla, staring at him.

The policemen moved him on toward the police car. One opened the door, and the other pushed Raymundo into the car.

"Who's Raymundo?" asked Philip.

"He's my uncle's houseboy, has been for a couple of years," said Camilla.

From the front door, the policeman called out, "You can come in now, Mrs. Ebury, and your friend."

Walking toward the door, aware that they were being photographed by the cameraman, Camilla reached into her pocketbook and took out a pair of dark glasses and put them on.

"There was a blond man, looked like an off-duty marine, who ran out of the house," yelled a voice from behind some trees.

"Who's that?" asked Philip.

"The crazy lady next door," said Camilla. "She made Hector's life hell, spying on him all the time, imagining all these insane things."

They walked inside the house. There was a small central hallway. To the left was the dining room. To the right was the living room, and beyond that the library. The house was filled with police and medical people.

"This is the niece, Captain," said the police officer.

Philip took hold of Camilla's arm and walked her forward.

"Captain Mariano, Mrs. Ebury," said the captain, introducing himself.

Camilla nodded. "Mr. Quennell," she said, introducing Philip and looking around at the same time. The living room was in shambles. A shot had been fired into the mirror over the fireplace, and the glass top of the coffee table had also been shattered by a shot. There was blood on the blue upholstery of a sofa, and a trail of blood leading into the library. Camilla gasped when she saw the bare legs of her uncle's bare body in the room beyond.

"Will you be able to identify the body, Mrs. Ebury?" asked Captain Mariano.

She had turned pale. She looked as if she was going to faint. She looked at Philip.

"Didn't Mr. Mendelson identify him?" asked Philip.

"Mr. Mendelson didn't go in that room," answered Mariano.

"May I identify the body, Captain?" asked Philip.

"How well did you know the deceased?"

"Not at all well. Hardly at all, in fact, but we were at the same party last night, and I know what he looks like," said Philip.

"That all right with you, Mrs. Ebury?" asked the captain.

Camilla nodded. Philip walked into the library. Lying facedown on the floor, in a pool of blood, was Hector Paradiso, nude and dead. There appeared to be several shots in his torso, and red marks on the cheek that was visible to Philip, as well as on both his buttocks.

Philip nodded. "That's Hector Paradiso," he said. He thought of Hector last night, dancing so elaborately, his white teeth flashing in his tanned face. Too tanned, he remembered thinking at the time. Now the too-tanned face looked ghostly and white beneath the red welts on it.

"How many times was he shot?" asked Philip.

"There appear to be five shots fired in all," said the captain.

"What are those red welts on his backside?" he asked.

"The victim seems to have been slapped across the face and buttocks by his black patent leather dancing pumps," said the captain.

Philip nodded. From the other room he heard Camilla's voice. "I am stunned, simply stunned, that Raymundo could do such a thing," she said. "My uncle has been responsible for bringing Raymundo's family up here from Mexico and getting them green cards so they could work legally and sending them to schools where they could learn English."

"We're not at all sure that Raymundo is responsible, Mrs. Ebury," said a police officer.

"I saw him myself in handcuffs outside this house being put into a police car," she said.

"I'm not a bit convinced about Raymundo," said the captain. "Do you happen to know where your uncle was last night, Mrs. Ebury?"

"Yes, he was at Jules Mendelson's house," replied Camilla.

"I know that. We've talked to Mr. Mendelson. I meant, after Mr. Mendelson's."

Camilla looked at the police captain and understood what he meant. "No. I would have no way of knowing that."

Philip walked back into the room. "Where is Mr. Mendelson?" he asked.

"He left," said Captain Mariano.

"How long ago?"

"He only stayed a few minutes."

"Perhaps you should call him at home," said Philip to Camilla.

"Yes," she answered.

"I don't think he went home," said the captain. "I heard him telephone Sandy Pond and ask to see him immediately."

Camilla nodded.

"Who's Sandy Pond?" asked Philip.

"The publisher of the *Tribunal*," answered Camilla.

"Comin' through," called out a voice from the library.

"Step over here, will you, Mrs. Ebury, Mr. Quennell," said the captain.

Two stretcher-bearers made their way through the living room carrying the last remains of Hector Paradiso zipped into a black rubber body bag. In the silence that followed, the crying of a small animal could be heard.

"What's that?" asked Captain Mariano.

"What?" answered one of the policemen.

"Like crying?"

"Oh, my God," said Camilla. "Astrid."

"Who's Astrid?" asked Philip.

"Hector's dog," said Camilla. She called the dog several times. "Astrid. Astrid."

The sounds of crying became louder as Camilla went into the library. She knelt down on the floor and peered under the sofa. "Astrid, come out, you sweet thing," she said in a gentle voice. She reached under the sofa and pulled the small West Highland terrier out. The dog appeared terrified, and Camilla clutched it in her arms, kissed its head, and petted it. "Rose gave Hector this dog," she said to Philip. "I'm going to bring it back to Rose."

"That little dog knows who killed Hector Paradiso," said Philip.

"Too bad Astrid can't talk," said Captain Mariano.

"I don't give a shit if Mr. Einsdorf left strict orders he did not want to be disturbed until noon or not," yelled Joel Zircon into the telephone. "Wake him up!"

Several minutes later Manning Einsdorf, enraged that his sleep had been disturbed, came to the telephone. "This is outrageous, Joel. I need my rest. I didn't close the club last night until four."

"Have you heard about Hector Paradiso, Manning?" asked Joel.

"Oh, my God. AIDS?"

"No, Manning. Shot five times."

"What?"

"That's right."

"Dead?"

"Of course dead."

"Oh, my God. You don't think that Lonny . . . oh, my God. Is it on the news?"

"No, not a word so far."

"How'd you hear?"

"A sometime trick of mine was working on the ambulance. He called me."

"Oh, my God."

"You said 'oh, my God' three times now, Manning. You better get your ass in gear and get over to the place and destroy any records or phone numbers you have of hustlers and johns or you're going to be in deep shit."

"That fucking Lonny," said Manning Einsdorf.

"What was that lousy singer's name with the buckteeth?"

"Marvene McQueen."

"Tell Marvene she didn't see Hector Paradiso in your place last night. And Zane too."

"Don't worry about Zane," said Manning.

―――――――――――――

Flo's Tape #4

"Jules used to say that if you could visualize yourself as something, you could become it. I can't tell you how much that meant to me when he said it. You see, I always thought I would be famous, only I never could visualize what I would be famous at. He knew, he always knew, he told me, that he would become an important person, and he certainly did.

"When I visualized myself as famous, it wasn't this kind of fame."

5

ATER THAT DAY, Philip Quennell returned to the Chateau Marmont, an apartment hotel on that part of Sunset Boulevard known as the Strip that was frequented by the movie and art crowd. Casper Stieglitz's secretary, Bettye, had booked him a room, or, as Bettye described it, a junior suite. A junior suite, Philip discovered, was a bedroom and sitting room in one.

"Perfect for your writing," Bettye had told Philip when she called him in New York to confirm his reservation. "All the writers who come out from New York stay there." Philip, who was not a chatterer on the telephone, even with a full-time chatterer like Bettye, said the arrangement sounded fine, but Bettye sensed a dissatisfaction, where there was none, and added, as a further enhancement of the charms of his future lodging, "It's the place where John Belushi OD'd."

"Oh, right," Philip had added.

"But that was in one of the bungalows. Not the room where you will be."

"Right," said Philip.

The lost luggage had been returned by the airline to the hotel, and Philip showered again and changed the clothes he had worn since the morning before when he boarded the plane in New York, and had then worn to the Mendelsons' party the night before, and on the mission that morning to Humming Bird Way to identify the body of Hector Paradiso, and then back to Clouds at the top of the mountain to deliver Camilla Ebury into the comforting hands of Pauline Mendelson.

That time no butler or maid opened the door to receive them. Pauline herself was standing in the open door waiting for them when Philip drove his rented car into the courtyard. She walked to Camilla's side of the car and opened the door. When Camilla got out, the two women embraced.

"So awful," said Pauline.

"Poor Hector," answered Camilla. "What a good friend you were to Hector, Pauline. He adored you."

"And I him. I'm livid with myself that I didn't let him stay on last night after everyone left. He wanted to talk over the party, and I said no."

"Oh, Pauline, it's not your fault," said Camilla. "Anyway, I heard that Kippie was back, and of course you wanted to be with him."

Pauline smiled distantly in acknowledgment of the mention of her son's name, but did not reply.

Camilla continued. "How is he?"

"Oh, coming along," said Pauline. In the short silence that followed, the sound of a tennis ball being hit with great force against a backboard issued from an unseen court somewhere behind the house. Pauline was wearing a cashmere sweater over her shoulders, and she pulled it together in front of her as if she were chilly, although it was not cold. Instinctively, both Camilla and Philip realized that the player was probably Kippie. Turning, Pauline greeted Philip warmly. If she was surprised to see him in the company of Camilla, wearing the same clothes he had been wearing the night before, she gave no such indication.

"I don't see Jules's car," said Camilla.

"He went out very early this morning, as soon as he got the call, and he's not back yet," said Pauline.

"Who called him?" asked Camilla.

"I don't know. The police, I suppose."

Camilla and Philip looked at each other.

"Is Rose still here?" asked Camilla.

"Heavens, yes. On her second Bloody Mary already and her fortieth cigarette. I'm always afraid she's going to burn down my house," replied Pauline. She was back to being herself again, charming, and in charge.

"How's she taking the news?"

"In absolute despair, calling everyone. Blaming herself for everything. If only they'd been speaking, this never would have happened, that kind of talk."

"Like most lifelong friends, they were always not speaking," said Camilla, and both she and Pauline laughed.

From within the car, the dog started to whine.

"What in the world is that?" asked Pauline.

"Oh, my God, I forgot," said Camilla. "It's Astrid. We brought Astrid. I couldn't leave her in that house. Poor little thing, she was hiding under the sofa in the library. I thought Rose might want her back, as she gave her to Hector in the first place."

"That will be just what she needs," said Pauline. "She's planning the funeral already. High Mass at Good Shepherd in Beverly Hills. She wants Archbishop Cooning to officiate, can you imagine, and she's going to give a big lunch after the funeral at the Los Angeles Country Club. Are you going to mind that she's taken over completely?"

"Hell, no," said Camilla. "Rose is at her best when she's planning a party, and that's exactly what she'll turn this into."

"Now, come in, the two of you," said Pauline.

Philip, who had been watching Camilla and Pauline, said, "The papers are going to have a field day with this story. I'm surprised they're not buzzing your bell down at the gates now."

"Oh, no, I shouldn't think so," said Pauline.

"I mean, it has all the elements, doesn't it? Land Grant family. Prominent social figure. Millionaire, or at least one presumes. Uncle of Camilla Ebury. Close personal friend of Mrs. Jules Mendelson. It all sounds very front page to me."

"Oh, no. I shouldn't think it would be played up," repeated Pauline, shaking her head.

"But why not?" asked Philip.

"That's what Jules said when he called. He was at Sandy Pond's office at the *Tribunal*."

"But, Pauline, they took Raymundo away in handcuffs," said Camilla. "I saw him with my own eyes."

"They've let him go by now. A mix-up, apparently. Anyway, come in. Rose will be having an anxiety attack."

Philip, a newcomer and an outsider in the group, declined. Twenty-four hours earlier he had not known any of these people, and now he felt awkward among them in such personal moments. "I won't come in, Pauline. I'd better get back to the hotel and check on my luggage and call Casper Stieglitz to tell him I've arrived."

Pauline looked at him and smiled. "Happy birthday," she said.

Philip smiled back, touched that she had remembered.

"I didn't know it was your birthday, Philip," said Camilla.

"So much has happened since last night, I'd forgotten it myself," he said.

"How old are you?" she asked.

"Thirty," he answered.

"I'm thirty-two," she said.

"I like older women."

Camilla laughed. "I can't thank you enough for seating me next to this wonderful man last night, Pauline," she said. "I don't know what I'd have done without him."

Camilla and Philip looked at each other.

"I'll call you," he said.

As Philip was driving out of the courtyard, Jules Mendelson came up the driveway in his dark blue Bentley. He stopped the car by the front door and got out. Walking over to where Pauline and Camilla were standing, he put his arms around Camilla and hugged her. To Philip, leaving, he appeared weary.

When Philip Quennell told Jules Mendelson the night before, after refusing his Château Margaux wine from the Bresciani auction, that he did not have anything so dramatic as a drinking problem—"simply no taste for it"—he was not telling the truth, but it was an untruth with which he had long since come to terms. There had been in his past a problem, one with dire consequences, and as a result part of his life, a part that he never discussed with anyone, was spent in atonement. Twice each year he returned to the small town in Connecticut where he was born. He was the son of the town doctor, long dead, and had gone to good schools on scholarships. Across the causeway that separated Old Saybrook from Winthrop Point, an enclave for wealthy summer residents from Hartford and New Haven, was Sophie Bushnell, who had lived her life in a wheelchair since the accident that crippled her.

At seven o'clock on the morning following Hector Paradiso's death, Philip was seated in a small hall on Robertson Boulevard in West Hollywood, reading the *Los Angeles Tribunal* and drinking coffee from a cardboard container while waiting for the AA meeting to start. He tore through the paper looking for news of the violent event in which he had become involved. It surprised him that it was not mentioned on the first page, or in the first section. It surprised him more that it was not mentioned in the section known as the Metro section, which covered local news. Finally, on the obituary page, he found it in an inconspicuous position, quite easily missable, a small announcement of the death of Hector Paradiso. He folded the paper in half and then refolded it in quarters in order to read the item again to see if it bore some clue.

"Something fishy there," said a girl on a chair next to him, who was reading his newspaper over his shoulder.

"Hmmm?" said Philip.

The girl, who smelled of expensive bath oil and perfume, tapped a beautifully manicured fingernail on the story of Hector Paradiso's death.

"I said there's something fishy about that story," she repeated.

Philip turned to look at her. She was young and very pretty, with dark red hair and vividly blue eyes that met his with a look that hovered between flirtatious and humorous. Although she was fashionably dressed, her manner, her voice, and her way of sitting were at odds with her expensive clothes. She exuded sensuality rather than fashionableness and seemed to Philip a curious but dazzling presence at such an early hour in the drab surroundings of an AA meeting on Robertson Boulevard.

"I was thinking the same thing," he said.

"Want to know how I see it?" she asked.

"Sure."

"He went to Pauline Mendelson's party, right?"

"How do you know that?"

"He always goes to Pauline Mendelson's parties. He was her pet. You know how all those society ladies have their pets?"

Philip smiled. He liked her. "But how do you even know Pauline Mendelson had a party?"

"I read it in Cyril Rathbone's column in *Mulholland*," she answered, shrugging. "I always read the society columns."

"Go on."

"In my scenario, on the way home he stops at Miss Garbo's."

"What's Miss Garbo's?"

"You new in town, or something?"

"I am. Yes."

"It's a bar, with a cabaret. It's a place where well-to-do gentlemen of a certain persuasion go on their way home from fashionable places, like a Pauline Mendelson party, if you get my drift."

Philip, nodding, got her drift. "How do you know so much?" he asked.

"My last job. I used to know guys like that."

"Like Hector Paradiso?"

"Yeah. I even knew Hector."

"What was your last job?"

"We're talking about Hector, not me," she said.

"Of course. What's your name?"

"Flo."

"Flo what?"

"Flo M.," she replied, emphasizing the *M*.

"Oh, yes, sorry. I'm a little lax in the anonymity department sometimes," said Philip.

"You shouldn't be. I abide by the rules. No last names in AA."

"You're right. I'm sorry. I'm Philip Quennell."

"*K*," she corrected him. "You're Philip *K*."

"No, not K. Q," he said. "I'm Philip Q."

"Well, I was never much of a speller," said Flo, smiling. "Do you mind if I smoke?" she asked.

"No."

"Some of these people freak out. They've got so many no-smoking meetings now. This is the main reason I come to this one, at this ungodly hour of the morning—because I can smoke."

She opened a bag that hung from her shoulder on a gold chain and took out a gold cigarette case. Philip noticed that her name, Flo, was spelled out in sapphires on the top. "I'd give up smoking, but I love this cigarette case too much to put it in a drawer and never use it again." She lit her cigarette with a matching gold lighter.

"That's not a good enough reason," said Philip.

"For me it is," replied Flo. "I get a charge every time I open this pretty case. When I was still doing drugs, I used to carry joints in it."

Philip laughed. He was about to ask her another question, about Hector Paradiso, when the meeting started. Flo moved to a chair in the row behind him. Neither raised a hand to participate in the meeting, but each paid careful attention to the speaker and to the people who raised their hands to share.

At the end of the meeting, during the prayer, Philip looked around at Flo. She was saying the Lord's Prayer with her eyes closed, holding the hands of the person on each side of her, with a cigarette dangling from her lips.

"Will I see you at the Rodeo Drive meeting on Friday night?" he asked, as they were leaving the meeting.

"Oh, no, I never go to the Rodeo Drive meeting. Or the Cedars-Sinai meeting on Sunday mornings either. Too social for me. This is the meeting I like. You never see anyone you know."

Philip, puzzled, nodded. "You wouldn't want to have dinner one night, would you?"

Flo looked at him and smiled. "No, I'm spoken for," she said.

He nodded, understanding. "I wasn't coming on, if that's what you were thinking," he said.

"Oh, yeah?" said Flo, smiling, with a hand-on-hip gesture.

Philip laughed. "Is that what you thought?"

"The idea had crossed my mind," she answered. "You're not exactly hard to look at, you know."

"Neither are you," he said. "But that wasn't what I had in mind, really. I thought it would be nice to have a cup of coffee and talk."

"Oh, I see. We've moved down the scale from dinner to a cup of coffee, have we? To discuss sobriety, is that it? Hey, good line, Phil Q. I bet it works. Most of the time." She smiled at him and waved good-bye with a left-handed circular gesture and a toss of her red hair. He watched her as she walked away from him up Robertson Boulevard. There was a sway to her walk that he could not help but admire. Whether she meant it to be provocative or not, it was. Philip could imagine that she had been whistled at in her day. She turned into a parking place in front of an outdoor furniture shop that was not as yet open for business. She got into a red convertible Mercedes-Benz. He wondered where her money came from.

That day Philip Quennell was to have his first meeting with Casper Stieglitz, for whom he was to write a documentary on the proliferation of drugs in the film industry. Casper Stieglitz had an office at Colossus Pictures in the San Fernando Valley. Once a studio unto itself in Hollywood, Colossus now occupied part of the lot that used to be called the Warner Bros. Studios. Philip, unused to the freeways, and armed with a map provided by the Chateau Marmont, left an hour before his appointment for fear that he might get lost on the drive from West Hollywood to the San Fernando Valley. Much to his surprise, he found the studio with no difficulty at all, and was thirty-five minutes early for his appointment. Not wanting to inconvenience Casper Stieglitz, he decided to find a diner or coffee shop and have another cup of coffee rather than arrive too early. He pulled into the parking lot of a House of Pancakes. On the sidewalk in front of the restaurant, there were bins for the Hollywood trade papers, the *Reporter* and *Daily Variety,* as well as several city newspapers that Philip, being new to the city, had never heard of. Thus far, he had only seen or heard of the *Times* and the *Tribunal.* He put a quarter in one of the bins and took out a paper called the *Valley Sentinel.*

Sitting at the counter drinking a cup of coffee, he found an article on the third page of the first section that read, "Death of Millionaire Socialite." The facts in the piece were minimal. Hector Paradiso, descendant of a Spanish Land Grant family, had been found dead "under mysterious circumstances" in his Humming Bird Way house. Several shots had been fired. Cyril Rathbone, the social columnist for *Mulholland,* who described himself as Hector's closest friend, was quoted as saying about him, "He was like a Spanish don." Rose Cliveden, who was called a Los Angeles socialite, said by telephone from her home in Holmby Hills, "He was my lifelong friend. The world has lost a courtly gentleman." A Mexican houseboy, Raymundo Perez, who had been questioned by the police and released, was quoted as saying, "Mr. Paradiso was helping me get my green card. He was a very generous man."

"More coffee?" asked the waitress behind the counter.

Philip looked at his watch. It was getting close to the time of his appointment with Casper Stieglitz. "No, thank you," he said. He ripped the page out of the paper and put it in his pocket, grabbed the check, left a tip, and dropped the money on the counter of the cashier's desk.

Driving up to the gates of Colossus Pictures, he felt awed by the prospect of entering a Hollywood studio for the first time. At the guard's booth, he said, "I have an appointment with Casper Stieglitz. My name is Philip Quennell."

The guard was wearing dark glasses and did not reply. He picked up the telephone, consulted a list, and dialed an extension.

"I have a Mr. Quennell here to see Mr. Stieglitz," he said.

"Could I pull into that space over there?" asked Philip, pointing to an empty parking space.

"You do, and you'll be talking in a soprano voice," said the guard. "That's Marty Lesky's space."

"Oh, sorry," said Philip. Even Philip knew that Marty Lesky was the head of Colossus Pictures.

Philip could hear a person rattling on at the other end of the guard's telephone call to Casper Stieglitz's office. Bettye the chatterbox, probably, he thought. The guard hung up the telephone. "Bettye says to tell you Mr. Stieglitz had an unexpected appointment off the lot this morning and would like you to meet him instead at his house late this afternoon, for drinks."

"But I don't know where Mr. Stieglitz lives," said Philip.

"Bettye says call her when you get back to your hotel," said the guard.

Flo's Tape #5

"*I was going to live in Brussels when Jules went over there to head the American delegation during the year of the statehood of Europe. I'm sure you know all about that. There's going to be only one currency, like we have here in this country, no more French francs and Italian lire and German marks, and all that stuff. I can't remember what they're going to call the new money, but it's all going to be the same from one European country to the next.*

"*Jules had this apartment already picked out for me on the Avenue Hamoir, I think it was called. It was supposed to be a good address in a good neighborhood in Brussels. Of course, Jules and Mrs. Mendelson had taken a very swell house on the Avenue Prince d'Orange. I hope you notice my French accent on the Prince d'Orange. He sent me to French lessons at Berlitz.*

"*I mean, the guy really did a lot for me. I'll say that for him.*"

6

Rose Cliveden said it for everyone when she said, "Everyone adored Hector," to a reporter from the *Valley Sentinel* who quizzed her as she was going into Hector Paradiso's funeral. Rose, however, was never able to settle for anything so simple as a three-word answer to anything and added, quite unnecessarily under the circumstances, "He didn't have an enemy in the world."

"Except one," said the reporter.

Rose glared at him through her dark glasses, with what she meant to be a withering look.

The reporter, knowing he had gotten to her, pressed further. "It only takes one."

"Excuse me," said Rose grandly, and proceeded past the reporter up the steps of the Good Shepherd Church in Beverly Hills, trying to catch up with Pauline and Jules Mendelson, who had walked past the reporter without replying. Still using a cane, because of her broken toe, she stopped inside the vestibule to gaze about.

"Did you ever see such a crowd?" Rose said to Madge White at the holy water font, dipping in her white glove and making the sign of the cross in a single sweeping gesture. "There's Loretta Young. Doesn't she look marvelous? And Ricardo and Georgiana Montalban. Look, Cesar Romero. All the Catholic stars are here. They all loved Hector. Jane Wyman couldn't come. She's shooting her series, and you know Janie. Work, work, work. But she sent beautiful flowers. Yellow lilies, from Petra. Oh, there's Faye Converse." She waved hello to Faye Converse and one or two others, all the time maintaining a properly solemn face. "Poor Hector," she repeated over and over.

The church was filled beyond capacity. Those unable to obtain seats, or standing room, or space in the choir loft, remained outside on the church steps or on the lawn. Monsignor McMahon later said, at Rose Cliveden's lunch at the Los Angeles Country Club, that only at midnight Mass on Christmas Eve had the crowds been comparable. It was not that Hector Paradiso had been that great a man in life, or even that beloved. It was the bizarre circumstance of his death that created all the momentary excitement, far more than the death of a more important person would have caused, and people came who had only a passing acquaintance with Hector, or even none at all, and only wanted to stare at the grand or celebrated friends of the dead man.

All the ushers were old friends, but Rose decided to wait for Freddie Galavant, who looked so distinguished, she thought, in a gray suit that matched his hair, to take her up the aisle to her place. Freddie had been given an ambassadorship to a Latin American country during the previous administration, a reward for campaign funds raised, and his presence as an usher, together with Winthrop Soames, Sandy Pond, Sims Lord, and Ralph White, indicated the importance of Hector Paradiso in the community, although none of the men had been known to be particularly close to him. "Their wives were," Rose had said, when the plans were being drawn up. Jules Mendelson, stating that he was not a Catholic, had refused to give the eulogy. Jules said that Freddie Galavant, who still liked to be called Ambassador Galavant, would be far better in that capacity than he, although Freddie was not a Catholic either.

The person most put out by the choice of Ambassador Galavant as eulogist was Cyril Rathbone, the society columnist for *Mulholland*. Cyril Rathbone thought of himself as Hector Paradiso's closest friend and the natural choice to speak at the service. Cyril was known to be entranced with the sound of his own mellifluous English voice, and he imagined himself, from the moment he first heard of Hector's death, speaking beautiful thoughts from the altar of the Church of the Good Shepherd in the presence of the group he most admired in the city, particularly Pauline Mendelson, who had thus far resisted his charms. But his offer was declined by the funeral planners, Jules Mendelson in particular, when Sims Lord, Jules's lawyer, came up with the information that a morals charge was pending against Cyril. "A beating of some sadomasochistic variety," said Sims.

"That's all we need," said Jules, when he heard this news. "Freddie, you do it."

"But I hardly knew Hector," said Freddie Galavant.

"We'll fill you in," said Jules, ending the discussion and solving the problem. He was used to not having his decisions questioned, even by ambassadors.

Rose was seated, finally, in the row behind Camilla Ebury, next to Pauline and Jules. Although Philip Quennell had ridden to the church in a limousine with Camilla, he chose not to sit in the front row with her, feeling that he was too new a friend to take such a prominent position. Camilla understood, and Pauline, who observed the moment of Philip's removing himself to a seat farther back, admired the good taste of the young man. She leaned forward in her pew and whispered into Camilla's ear, "Be sure to bring Philip back to the house afterwards." Camilla smiled and patted Pauline's hand.

Rose whispered to Pauline, "Aren't the flowers lovely?" Pauline, praying, nodded her approval without involving herself in conversation, knowing that Rose enjoyed whispered conversations. Rose could not stand funeral wreaths and had instructed Petra von Kant, the florist her group all used—"She knows us all, she knows what we like"—to decorate the church with birch trees and great baskets of yellow and pink tulips and hyacinths, knowing that all the real friends of Hector would order their flowers through Petra. The others, the wreaths of gladiolus and carnations, with starched ribbons and gold lettering, the sort of flowers and arrangements that Rose and her friends abhorred, had been placed on the side altars, so as not to cause disharmony in the color scheme that Rose had worked out with Petra. Only the enormous spray of white phalaenopsis, which had come from Pauline Mendelson's greenhouse at

Clouds, broke with Petra's scheme; but, as everyone knew, Pauline knew more about orchids than anyone in the city, and Pauline had been the friend that Hector liked best. Her spray had been placed on top of Hector's mahogany coffin.

As far as Rose Cliveden was concerned, the single disappointing note of the otherwise perfect funeral was the absence of Archbishop Cooning, who had declined her persistent requests to officiate at the Requiem Mass, even though she had contributed handsomely to the redecoration of the archbishop's residence in Hancock Park. The archbishop, renowned for the fiery sermons on the decline of morality in the nation he delivered each Sunday from the pulpit of Saint Vibiana's, was not unaware of the secret life of Hector Paradiso, having heard his confession on more than one occasion, and he suspected that the circumstances of his death were other than were being reported. Mercifully, a conference at the Vatican called him from the city, and he was able to adhere to his standards without seriously offending Rose Cliveden.

Pauline was the person most devastated by Hector's death. She had fostered the story—without ever stating it—that Hector, had he been able to love women, would have loved her. When Hector kissed her, as he sometimes did, in moments of affection, after parties, his kiss and even his embrace were not the kiss and embrace of a lover. Pauline understood that even with encouragement from her, which, of course, was not forthcoming, the kiss and embrace would lead to nothing more. It was an arrangement they both enjoyed. And Hector had loved Pauline, in his way, so sincerely that even Jules, who had grown more sophisticated during the years of his marriage, had no objection to the "love match," and even found himself amused at times by Hector, who was funny and knew all the gossip about everyone, after an initial period of disliking him. "I have trouble with people who don't do anything," Jules said. On several occasions Hector had been their sailing companion when they chartered yachts and cruised the Dalmatian coast, or the Turkish coast, or the Greek isles. Pauline could not bear to think that Hector had died in sordid circumstances, and so had reluctantly accepted the suicide theory that Jules proposed when finally they were alone, after Camilla and Rose had departed.

"It's better this way," Jules had said.

"Why?" asked Pauline.

"It is a shabby and distasteful death," said Jules.

"How so? Tell me."

Jules blushed. "His sexual inclinations were, perhaps, pederastic," he said.

"How arch, Jules," said Pauline.

"You knew, then?"

"Of course I knew."

"And didn't care?"

"Oh, Jules, really. He was my friend."

"This sort of death, if the circumstances get out, will reflect badly on Hector, on his family, and on everyone concerned."

"His only family is Camilla, and she is only a niece, and his death is certainly not going to reflect badly on her."

"Well, his family that founded the city. It will reflect badly on the name Paradiso."

"And the 'everyone concerned' you speak about? Does that mean us, Jules?"

"The fact that he was here in our house until a few hours before it happened, and the fact that you are known to be his great friend will certainly involve us, yes. It is the sort of publicity that will be bad at this moment, with the appointment to the economic conference in Brussels coming up for nomination. There is bound to be fallout, and it is best that this be the solution."

"That he committed suicide?"

"Yes."

"But who would believe such a story, Jules? People are not such fools."

"That is a theory that I do not agree with at all."

"But *I* don't believe that story, Jules," said Pauline quietly.

"Believe it," he said.

"Are you ordering me to believe something I don't believe?"

"Yes." There was a harshness in his voice that she had never heard when he spoke to her. "Hector was ill, we will say, and Dr. James will confirm it. He was to have an operation, we will say. A bypass. I thought about saying he had AIDS, but this heart thing is better. More respectable. He was terrified of the operation, we will say, and terrified that he would be an invalid afterwards, and a burden to his friends. He had perhaps a few too many drinks, and he did this tragic thing."

"Jules, please. Dr. James was Hector's friend. He wasn't actually his doctor. Mickie Cox was his doctor."

"Only you know that, Pauline, and you've just forgotten it," said Jules. He leaned over and kissed her cheek.

"But, surely, Dr. James will deny such a story, about an operation and a heart problem."

"No, he won't," said Jules, quite emphatically, and Pauline understood that he meant that Dr. James would do as he said.

The suicide story began to be spread at the church, both before and after the Mass. "No, no, no," said Sims Lord, when he was asked if Hector's death had been a murder. "No, no, no," said Freddie Galavant to the same question. Both Sandy Pond and Ralph White replied in a similar manner, as did several other public figures of the city. Then the word *suicide* was mouthed. It was a disappointment to many that they were being deprived of the excitement of a murder, which some continued to believe was the case, although they would shortly cease to express that belief.

Philip Quennell, sitting toward the back of the church, was surprised to see the girl who had introduced herself as Flo M. at the AA meeting walk up the aisle and take a seat two rows in front of him. Her expensive bag was suspended from her shoulder on a gold chain, and she lifted it as she genuflected in the Catholic manner. Once seated, she knelt, made the sign of the cross, and bowed her head in prayer. Unlike most of the people present, she did not look around to see who was there, but a man with long hair swept upward to cover his bald spot, sitting directly in front of Philip, nudged his two companions and indicated the young woman. They smiled at one another in recognition. The men, unknown to Philip and to most of the mourners present, were Manning Einsdorf, the owner of Miss Garbo's, Joel Zircon, the agent, and Willard, Casper Stieglitz's butler, all of whom had talked with Hector shortly before his death.

During the Mass Pauline turned to Jules, who seemed deep in thought.

"What are you thinking about?" she whispered.

"I have a meeting with Myles Crocker from the State Department tomorrow," he whispered back. "About Brussels."

"You're thinking of that now?"

"Yes."

"Do you never pray?"

"No."

During the eulogy, the former ambassador spoke about Hector as a great friend to many people. "He cherished his friends," said Freddie Galavant, looking at Pauline and Camilla and Rose as he spoke. "He was a man of such great taste and sensitivity that he chose to spare those friends from certain aspects of his life, which can only account for this great tragedy. Good night, sweet prince. May flights of angels sing thee to thy rest."

Several sobs could be heard in the church, as well as a single chortle from Cyril Rathbone, who whispered to those around him that he would have done better. Ahead of him, Philip noticed that Flo M. was crying. He saw her open her bag to get a handkerchief and realized from her searching in the bag that she had forgotten to bring one. When she wiped her tears away with her fingers, Philip took his own handkerchief from his pocket. He leaned forward through Manning Einsdorf and Joel Zircon, tapped Flo's arm, and handed it to her. Flo nodded her head in thanks, but she did not turn to look at the person who gave her the handkerchief. She knew it was Phil Q. She had seen him out of the corner of her eye when she passed his pew looking for a seat.

During communion, the Catholics went to the altar, edging their way past the coffin to the rail where the monsignor, officiating at the Requiem Mass in the place of Archbishop Cooning, waited with lifted chalice. Among the communicants was Flo March.

Outside, after the Mass, on the steps of the church, Rose Cliveden raised her dark glasses and surveyed the crowd while the casket was being placed into the hearse by the pallbearers. "I was in floods the whole Mass," she said to Pauline, who was standing next to her. Her powdered cheeks were smeared with the tears she had shed during the eulogy, and she made no attempt to wipe them away. "Such a lot of strange people at this funeral," she continued, but Pauline was not in a chatting mood as she watched the proceedings. The unwelcome wreaths that Rose had so hated were being placed in a follow-up hearse, to be placed eventually on the gravesite at Holy Cross Cemetery, where the Paradiso family had a mausoleum.

Rose was undeterred by Pauline's lack of response. "I thought I knew all of Hector's friends. Who do you suppose these people are? Look at that amazing man with his gray hair swept up over his bald spot." She was staring at Manning Einsdorf, who was standing with Joel Zircon and his friend Willard, watching the people emerge from the church. "Did you ever see so much hair spray? He looks like Ann Miller. I can tell you for a fact that our Hector would never know anyone like him, or his friends there. I think these people are just sightseers looking for celebrities, don't you? Faye Converse, that's who they're looking for."

Out of the corner of her eye, she saw Jules talking with an unfamiliar young woman in the crowd.

The young woman spoke nervously when Jules Mendelson approached her. "Do you know what they call this church? Our Lady of the Cadillacs. The only poor people in this parish are the rich people's maids."

"What in the world are you doing here?" Jules asked. "I almost fell out of the pew when I saw you at the communion railing." He talked to her without looking at her, as if he were looking for someone else.

"I knew Mr. Paradiso," the young woman answered, defensively. "What do you think, I go to funerals of people I don't know?"

"Hector? You knew Hector?"

"Yes."

"Wherever from?"

"When I was a waitress at the Viceroy Coffee Shop, I used to serve him his coffee and croissant every morning," Flo said. "He was a cheap tipper, all the girls said so, but he told me good stories. I could tell you a couple of Hector Paradiso stories that would make your hair curl, about the kind of people he used to see after he left all the society parties. I don't buy this suicide story at all. I'll tell you what I think happened."

"I don't want to hear," Jules said brusquely, as if he were afraid she might start to tell him then and there. He signaled his chauffeur with a wave and indicated for him to bring the car around to the side street rather than wait behind the other limousines on Santa Monica Boulevard.

"Well, excuse me," she said, grandly.

"I have to go. There's my car."

"You're ashamed to be seen talking to me, aren't you, Jules?"

"No," he said quickly.

"Yes, I can see it. I can feel it."

"I'll be up later," said Jules quickly, and then he moved on.

Looking away, her eyes met the eyes of Philip Quennell, who was watching her. She nodded to him faintly and mouthed the words "Thanks for the handkerchief." He nodded back and smiled, but she did not go toward him, nor did he move toward her to speak.

"Look, Pauline, Jules is waving at you to go to the Bedford Drive side of the church," said Rose. "Are you going to the cemetery?"

"No, we're not," said Pauline.

"But you're coming to my lunch at the Club, aren't you?"

"Actually, we're not, Rose. You do understand, don't you?"

"Yes, of course, darling, but you're very foolish to feel like that about the Los Angeles Country Club."

"Call me later."

"Isn't it wonderful, Pauline, the way the Catholic church has relaxed its ban on burying suicides?"

Flo's Tape #6

"I never knew how terrible it was to be poor until I had money. All that I ever wanted to do about my childhood was forget it, never to even think about it. It was terrible. My mother burned to death in a fire in a welfare hotel. I never knew who my father was. She used to say he walked out on us when I was one year old, but the older I got I came to believe that she didn't actually know which one he was. It was like that."

$$\overline{\quad\quad} 7 \overline{\quad\quad}$$

W HEN, TWENTY-TWO YEARS EARLIER, it was suggested a week before their marriage, during a meeting at the law firm that represented Jules Mendelson's interests, that Pauline McAdoo sign a prenuptial agreement that would limit the amount of her settlement in the case of a divorce, Pauline read through the agreement without comment. When Marcus Stromm, Jules Mendelson's lawyer of many years, handed her a pen from a penholder on his desk to sign the prenuptial agreement, Pauline tossed the folder back at him with such force that the pen fell out of Marcus's hand and spattered black ink over the monogram on his custom-made white shirt. Then Pauline rose without looking at Jules, who had been seated at her side silently observing the scene, and left the office. No amount of protestations on Jules's part at the bank of elevators could dissuade Pauline from entering the first car that arrived, without answering him or looking in his direction as the doors closed behind her. For Pauline, from a distinguished New York and Northeast Harbor family, the affront of being asked to sign such an agreement, as if she were a groupie marrying a rock star, only confirmed the deep reservations that her sisters had expressed from the beginning when she had told them she was considering marrying Jules Mendelson as soon as her divorce from Johnny Petworth was final. Her marriage to Johnny Petworth, which read well in the social columns, had been a disappointment almost from the beginning, and she could not envision a life with a man who had no more ambition than to be the very best in squash, backgammon, and bridge at the smartest clubs in the smartest resorts.

"No, no, Pauline," her sisters had said to her, both separately and together, "I don't care how much money Mr. Mendelson has. He won't do. He won't do at all."

Her father, whom she revered, and who doted on her in return, said only this as a point of dissuasion to his daughter's proposed marriage: "Jules is very nice, Pauline, and certainly very rich, but he's not eligible for any of the clubs." She knew what that meant. It was a phrase she had heard all her life to distinguish people like themselves, the McAdoos, from the others. For their kind of life, clubs were very important. An early McAdoo had founded a dynasty that produced fortunes in shipping, trade, iron, railroads, land, and textiles, but those fortunes had evaporated over the century, and the present

McAdoo fortune was minimal by the current financial standards, although there was no lessening of McAdoo social standards.

"That would not bother me, Poppy," said Pauline.

"It will, in time," her father had answered.

Such familial disapproval had only increased her determination to go ahead with the marriage to Jules. What she felt most was that he would be an ideal stepfather to Kippie, who was then only three years old, and, as described by everyone, adorable, but badly in need of male supervision.

That night, following the incident with Marcus Stromm, Pauline left Los Angeles for New York. In her life there was still another man, whom she loved more than she loved Jules Mendelson, although his prospects were less, and it was to his side that she flew. Jules, fascinated by her independence and intimidated by her pedigree, followed, and placed on her finger a diamond ring larger by far than the diamond he would have placed on her finger a week earlier.

"My word," said Pauline, astonished by its size, wondering if it was perhaps too big, like the one owned by the actress Faye Converse. She knew that her sisters would scoff at it, but she also knew that they would say, finally, "Oh, Pauline, you're so tall you can get away with it."

"It's the de Lamballe," Jules said, as proud as he was the day before, when he had purchased van Gogh's *White Roses,* which was to be his wedding present to her.

"My word," said Pauline again, for she had heard of the de Lamballe diamond. He sketched its provenance: a French princess, a daughter of a German munitions maker, an American heiress, twenty years of oblivion before it resurfaced at an auction in Geneva. "It's too lovely," she said.

The following week Pauline and Jules were married in Paris, with only Sims Lord, who had replaced Marcus Stromm as Jules's lawyer, present. Although Jules could never stand to be away from the business of finance for more than a few days at a time, they went for their honeymoon to the Mamounia Hotel in Marrakech. One evening, sitting on the balcony of their suite at sunset, he said to her, "There's something I must tell you."

"What is that?"

"I got into a jam once when I was young. Please don't ask me about it. It happened. I can't undo it."

"Then why did you bring it up if you won't tell me?" asked Pauline.

"Please bear with me, Pauline."

"Do you have a police record?"

"No. One of the advantages of having rich parents," said Jules.

He looked so pained at that moment that Pauline did not pursue the subject. She felt that he would tell her in time.

"Oh, yes, I know all about that," she said, to cheer him up. "I had an uncle Harry. Harry Curtis. My mother's sister's husband. He was found dead in a seedy hotel on the West Side, and not a single one of the New York papers reported that he was in women's clothing. Poppy handled the whole thing."

"Harry Curtis? In women's clothes? I've heard a lot of things about Harry Curtis, but I never heard that," said Jules.

"Poor Aunt Maud. She's never been the same."

"Well, I wasn't in women's clothes," said Jules. "You can be sure of that."

Pauline laughed. The subject, whatever the subject was, was never mentioned again.

Jules would have lived anywhere Pauline wished. It was her idea to settle in Los Angeles and buy the old von Stern mansion on the top of a mountain and rebuild it into the famous estate that would become known as Clouds. The asking price was five million dollars, a sum considered outrageous and exorbitant at the time, but Jules Mendelson never quibbled over money when he wanted something, and he knew that his new wife wanted that particular property. He and Pauline arrived at the house for a final look, and then he handed a check for the full amount to the dumbfounded Helmut von Stern.

"I have been thinking, Mr. Mendelson," said von Stern, staring greedily at the check in his hand.

"Thinking what, Mr. von Stern?" asked Jules.

"Second thoughts."

"On selling your house, you mean?"

"On the price, actually. More like five point five million, I was thinking."

"I see," said Jules. He reached out, removed the check from von Stern's hand, and tore it in half. "Are you ready, darling?" he said to Pauline. "Goodbye, Mr. von Stern."

Jules took Pauline's arm, and they headed for the front door and the dilapidated courtyard.

Von Stern, aghast, saw the mistake he had made. The house had been on the market for three years and was in a deplorable state of repair. As the Mendelsons got into their car, von Stern called after them. "Come back, we must talk." There was an element of panic in his voice as he envisioned five million dollars driving out of his courtyard.

Jules, with Pauline behind him, followed von Stern back into the front hall of the house. "I have had second thoughts myself," he said.

"About what?"

"The price. My top price is now four point five. Take it or leave it," said Jules.

Pauline, fascinated, watched her new husband in a business transaction. That afternoon the Mendelsons purchased von Stern's estate and renamed it Clouds.

The clubs, which mattered so much to people like them in Southampton and Palm Beach and Northeast Harbor and Newport, did not matter so much in Los Angeles, and the problem of Jules's ineligibility to join them was less pressing. Both Rose Cliveden and Sims Lord had made an effort on Jules's behalf, but Freddie Galavant, who later became a friend, said to the admissions committee, "Look at it this way. If he weren't so rich, would you still want him to be a member?" No one answered, and the matter was never brought up again.

In the years since their marriage, Jules and Pauline had become a renowned couple in the world of wealth and power, and all earlier misgivings on the part of Pauline's family had long been forgotten. Pauline's sisters even took pride in their fascinating brother-in-law and entertained the Mendelsons in grand style several times each year. Jules had been a prominent background figure at all of the economic conferences under two Presidents, and, on at least two occasions, in Paris and in Toronto, had been photographed in the Presidential motorcade, in deep conversation with the Chief of State himself.

"Ask Jules," people would say, when matters of finance were under discussion. When Jules spoke, Pauline gave him her full attention, not only at parties when people asked him questions about the economy or the elections, but also at home, alone, with no one watching. Her ability to listen so intently to the man she loved was considered one of her most attractive traits. Only she, and not a single soul else, knew that she was sometimes able to plan the seating of a dinner party in her head at the same time. Their marriage was considered perfect. And it was, in its own way.

Jules had not wished to go to Rose Cliveden's lunch at the Los Angeles Country Club after Hector's funeral. Although there would be denials if such a claim were made in print, the club, a bastion of the old wealth of the city, had never taken more than a token member from the film industry or from certain religious and racial groups. In the case of the Mendelsons, it was felt that they were "perhaps too well known," an excuse delivered by Rose to Pauline that amused both Jules and Pauline. But it was not that he was ineligible to join the club that kept Jules from wishing to enter its white colonnaded portal after the funeral. He would have been quite welcome as a luncheon guest of Rose Cliveden. He knew, however, that there would be gossiping in every corner of the rooms, all to do with the prevalent excitement over the mysterious death of Hector Paradiso, and he did not wish to be questioned about the circumstances of the death, which, he knew for a fact, was about to be officially declared a suicide. He was abetted in his decision not to go by Pauline, who was truly grieving for her friend Hector and was afraid that the lunch, meant to be solemn, would take on a party atmosphere, as did all the events in Rose Cliveden's life.

Philip Quennell, accompanying Camilla, was pleased to be asked to lunch quietly with the Mendelsons at Clouds rather than attend Rose's lunch at the club, where there would be a lot of people he did not know and endless speculation about the demise of their beloved Hector, about which he knew a great deal more than they. He was pleased to be given a tour of the art in the house by Jules himself, while they were waiting for lunch to be served. It interested Philip to watch Jules gaze on each of his pictures as if he were looking at it for the first time. For every one he had a story about its provenance, or the state of mind of the painter at the time, or the subject matter, or even the price. They stopped beneath a Bonnard of Misia Sert sitting on a sofa in a drawing room. "That's only one of several pictures Bonnard painted of the old girl," he said. "Baron Thyssen has one in Lugano, and one of the Annenberg sisters has one in Palm Beach, but mine is the best by far. Look at her expression. I paid eight hundred thousand dollars for that picture only three, maybe four years ago, bought it at Boothby's at the Elias Renthal auction when he went to the slammer, and just last week I was offered fourteen million for it. Pauline hates it when I talk money in relation to the art, but you can't help not talking about it, when the prices are continuing to skyrocket the way they are. Of course, I wouldn't dream of selling it, or any of the other pictures for that matter, except to upgrade the collection, because I want to keep the collection together."

Philip nodded.

"This conversation is, of course, off the record," Jules continued.

"Of course," answered Philip.

"You are here as a guest of my wife, and with Camilla, who is an old family friend," Jules said, as if reminding Philip of the obligations of being a guest in such a grand household.

"Of course," repeated Philip, knowing that Jules was thinking of the book that he had written about Reza Bulbenkian.

"What kind of money do you earn?" asked Jules.

"Not enough to become seriously involved with a girl like Camilla Ebury, if that's what your train of thought is," replied Philip.

Jules chuckled at having been read through. He liked Philip's answer. Since Pauline had pointed out to him that Philip had written the book that so enraged Reza Bulbenkian, Jules had, surprisingly, taken a liking to him, even though Reza was a friend, or, at least, a business friend.

They passed through the open doors of the library out onto an awninged terrace. A Rodin sculpture of a naked woman stood at the top of the stone steps leading down to the lawn. Beyond, on the lawn and beneath the trees, was Jules Mendelson's sculpture garden.

"Good God," said Philip, looking out at the sight.

Jules, pleased by Philip's reaction, chuckled again. "It's amazing how many people don't notice this, you know, just think it's statues in a garden. Over there is my latest, the Miró. One of the few he ever made. Exquisite, isn't it? I'm not sure I have it placed correctly yet. I have them moved around several times until I finally decide. The Rodin here was my first piece of sculpture. Years ago it belonged to my grandfather, and then it went out of the family, and when I saw it in an auction catalog, I bought it back and started the sculpture garden with it. Then came the Henry Moores. If you're interested, walk over behind the orange tree and look at the rear of the Maillol. It's my favorite."

Philip walked behind the round and sensuous lady, amused that Jules had asked him to view the rear of her. From nearby came the sound of dogs barking and jumping against a fence.

"That's a fierce sound," said Philip.

"The watchdogs. Nothing to worry about. They're in the kennels. They're only let out at night to patrol the grounds," said Jules.

"They sound as if they would tear you apart," said Philip.

"They would, if you were the wrong person," said Jules, very matter-of-factly.

Behind them, Pauline came out onto the terrace. She had removed the hat she wore in church. "Jules, I want to borrow Philip, and Camilla wants to talk to you about Hector's will before lunch," she said. "She's in the library."

"That means Pauline wants to show you her garden," said Jules, smiling. As he went back up the steps to the terrace, he affectionately put his arm around Pauline's waist. "Did you like Freddie's eulogy?" he asked.

"Most of it," replied Pauline. "I could have done without flights of angels singing Hector to his rest. I didn't believe that for a minute."

Both Jules and Philip laughed.

"Scratch my back, will you, darling. I have an itch," said Jules, pointing over his shoulder to a spot on his upper back.

Pauline moved over to him and rubbed the area where he had pointed. "Here?" she asked.

"No, higher. A little to the left. That's it. Harder."

"Who was that girl you were talking to at the funeral, Jules?" Pauline asked, as she continued to rub.

"What girl?" asked Jules.

Philip, who was watching them in their marital moment, almost answered, "Flo. Flo M." But he didn't. He understood when to listen.

"When you were looking for the chauffeur," Pauline continued.

"I don't know, which one? I talked to a lot of people at the funeral," answered Jules.

"Quite pretty. Red hair. Rather vivacious, I thought," said Pauline. "I wondered who she was." She said "vivacious" in a way that only a very acute ear might have taken as a synonym for "common."

"Oh, yes, her. Some friend of Hector's, she said she was," said Jules. There was a vagueness about his answer, as if the person was not of sufficient consequence to spend time discussing.

"That was a very good-looking Chanel suit she was wearing. I almost ordered it myself," said Pauline. She was totally unaware that the girl she was talking about was her husband's mistress.

Neither Jules nor Philip responded, nor did they look at each other. Jules did not know that Philip knew Flo, but Philip, ever watchful, had the beginning of the idea that Jules might be somehow connected with the expensive red Mercedes that he had seen Flo drive.

"I don't remember her name," said Jules, shrugging, and went inside to Camilla.

"I'm rather touched by Jules's concern for Hector," said Pauline to Philip.

"How so?" asked Philip.

"In the beginning, Jules couldn't abide Hector. Jules never likes men who, as he puts it, talk about dresses, and parties, and who sat next to whom at dinner the night before, all that sort of thing, and he is absolutely intolerant of any man who doesn't work, so poor Hector had everything going against him, as far as Jules was concerned. But Hector was an awfully good friend to me when I first moved out here. Women like me need a Hector in our lives, to tell us we're still pretty, or look good that night, the sort of things our husbands are often too busy to remember to say."

Philip turned to look at Pauline. Her lovely face was momentarily sad. Seeing him look at her, she smiled and continued talking. "In time Jules, although he wouldn't admit it, grew rather fond of Hector. The fact is, Jules really adores hearing all the gossip about everybody; he just pretends he doesn't. Last summer, in Greece, Hector was really a godsend on the boat. He was so funny the whole time, kept us in stitches."

As she talked, Philip and Pauline walked across the lawn to the orangerie, which had trellised walls and espaliered trees. Through the orangerie was a cutting garden, in full bloom.

"This is very beautiful, Pauline," said Philip.

"What's a house without a garden? I always say. I brag about very few things, but I do brag about my garden and greenhouse. Look at my perennial border here. Roses, peonies, delphiniums, poppies, asters. Heavenly, isn't it?"

Philip nodded.

"Come see the greenhouse, and then we'll go back to lunch," said Pauline. "The cook says if we're not seated by one on the dot, the soufflé will fall. She is always full of dire predictions."

They walked inside. There were orchids everywhere. An older man in jeans and a sweater came up and nodded a greeting to Pauline.

"Hi, Mrs. Mendelson," he said.

"This is Jarvis. My treasure. People say about me that I am the most expert of orchid growers, but it's not true at all. It's Jarvis who does it all, and I get all the credit. This is Philip Quennell, Jarvis."

The two men shook hands.

"That's not true for a minute, Mrs. Mendelson," said Jarvis, smiling at Pauline. He turned to Philip. "Mrs. Mendelson knows more about orchids than anyone."

"Jarvis and I are perfecting a yellow phalaenopsis that we hope will startle the orchid world," said Pauline.

Philip nodded, but he was interested in people, not orchids.

"You see, Jarvis," said Pauline, laughing. "Mr. Quennell has no interest whatever in our botanical experiments."

Walking up the lawn to the house, Pauline turned to Philip and saw him smiling.

"Why are you smiling?" she asked.

"I suppose that less than one percent of the country lives the way you and Jules live, Pauline, and I'm just glad I got to look at it," said Philip.

"Do you think that's true?" she asked. "Less than one percent?"

"Certainly, I do."

"I never thought of that."

"It's just us," Pauline said when they entered the garden room for lunch, as if Philip might have been expecting a lunch party. It was a semicircular room, entirely enclosed in glass. "You come here by me. Camilla there. And Jules there."

They sat around a glass table on Regency bamboo chairs, looking out on the lawn. For a time Camilla and Pauline talked about the service: the eulogy, the music, the flowers, and the crowds of people. Dudley, the butler, passed the wine. Philip put his hand over his glass. Blondell, the maid, passed the poached salmon and cheese soufflé.

"It amazes me that the papers have not played up this case more," said Philip. No one replied, and he continued. "It has all the elements for front-page stuff." Again there was no reply. "Who do you think killed Hector, Mr. Mendelson?" asked Philip.

There was silence at the table.

"No one killed Hector," answered Jules, quietly. "Hector killed himself."

"Oh, but I don't believe that," said Philip, in a dismissive voice.

Jules was a man unused to having his statements challenged, let alone doubted. "The facts are incontrovertible," he said. There was a tightening of his neck muscles, and his voice was purposely measured. "There can be no reasonable doubt. I have checked this out with Detective McDaniels, who solved the shooting of poor Madge White's father two years ago in the garage of her house in Bel Air. You remember that, Pauline?"

Pauline, silent, nodded.

"Incontrovertible." Jules repeated the word. "It was the word Detective McDaniels himself used." He put stress on the word *detective,* as if that proved his point. "Suicide, he said. And the coroner agreed, a Japanese, I've forgotten his name. I was there. I heard."

"But certainly you don't believe that, do you, Mr. Mendelson?" asked Philip.

Jules looked at him without answering. It was a look that Philip remembered long afterward.

"I mean," continued Philip, persevering, "we've all seen enough movies to know that a single shot in the mouth or the temple would do the trick far more effectively than five shots in the torso, not to mention the fact that it is virtually impossible for a person to shoot himself five times in the torso."

There was silence again. Then Jules, red in the face now, threw his napkin on the table and slid back his bamboo chair on the marble floor with such force that the action produced a screeching sound. He stood up without speaking and headed toward the hall that separated the garden room from the house. Passing through, his massive body hit against the Degas sculpture of a fourteen-year-old ballerina, her feet in the fifth position, her hands held gracefully behind her back, with the original pink satin ribbon in her hair. It toppled from the marble pedestal on which it had stood in the Mendelsons' garden room for fourteen years.

"Jules, the Degas!" screamed Pauline, rising.

Turning, amazingly agile for such an enormous man, Jules reached and grabbed the head of the ballerina at almost the same instant that it hit the marble floor.

"Oh, marvelous, Jules," said Pauline. "Is she all right?"

He turned the piece of sculpture over in his arms as if it were a child he had pulled from a wreck or a fire and stared at it. When they were alone together, Jules and Pauline called the young dancer Clotilde. When he spoke, he spoke very quietly. "You were right, you know, Pauline, you always wanted me to have a Lucite case made for her, and I thought it spoiled her to be encased."

"Is she broken, Jules?" asked Pauline.

"Cracked," he said.

"Oh, Jules, how disappointing," she said, with a concern that was less for her devalued treasure than for her husband's concern for that treasure.

"Well, we can love her more, I suppose," he said. He spoke gently, in a father's voice.

"I'm very much afraid this is all my fault," said Philip. "I had no idea I was making you angry, sir."

Jules looked at Philip and left the room without replying, carrying the sculpture with him.

Philip looked to Camilla for confirmation of his position. She had been with him on Humming Bird Way. She had seen her uncle's body, the blood on the walls, the shots in the mirror and on the ceiling.

Camilla, silent until now, lowered her eyes. "Certainly if there were something awry, Philip, the coroner and the detective would not have both arrived at the conclusion they did," she said.

"I don't understand you people," said Philip, differentiating himself from the others. His voice had become perturbed. "A man has been murdered, and a cover-up is taking place, and you are all buying it, or participating in it."

"You must understand, Philip," said Camilla. "Jules believes it is for the best."

"But the best for whom?" persisted Philip.

"You must not misunderstand my husband, Philip," said Pauline. "There is no ulterior motive to what he has said. He is simply trying to protect the reputation of a great family. You heard him yourself say that the coroner said it was suicide."

Philip nodded his head. "There's something wrong," he said simply. He pushed back his chair. It was clear he was going to leave, but he had more to say. "Let me for a moment accept the theory that Hector's death was a suicide, which, of course, I do not believe. I was there. I saw the body. I saw the number of shots. Five. The suicide of a prominent man from a distinguished family who shot himself five times is a story in itself, and yet no such story is being written. It smacks to me of cover-up."

"I really don't understand why it should concern you so," said Pauline, quietly, as she moved a spoon back and forth over her linen place mat. She was torn in the conversation, knowing Philip was right, but unwilling to counter the position of her husband.

"I'll tell you why," replied Philip. "I do not believe that powerful people have the right to decide what the public should and should not know."

"Sometimes it's necessary," said Pauline.

"I don't think so."

"If it comes out, it could cause a great deal of grief."

"If it doesn't come out, that means I will be party to the same concealment tactics as you, and I can't do that."

Philip rose, aware that he was a guest who had overstepped a guest's boundaries, but still unwilling to make anything less than a dignified exit. "Of course, I will leave, and I am very sorry for the trouble I have caused you, Pauline, but I have to say before I leave that the reason it is so hard for me to say that it is all right for all of you to foster this bogus story is that a killer is being allowed to walk free. Remember that. I find that unconscionable. Goodbye."

He nodded to both Pauline and Camilla and walked out of the room. In the hallway by the garden room, he was momentarily confused as to whether to turn left or right to find the front hallway and door of the enormous house. The butler, Dudley, walked into the hall and anticipated his question. "This way, sir," he said, walking to the left toward the library, and then to the right toward the drawing room, and then to the left again to the hallway. There, on one of the console tables, Philip noticed that the Degas ballerina had been placed in a lying-down position facing upward. She looked forlorn, as if she were aware that she would no longer be desired by museums. Passing her, Philip did not stop to examine the crack.

The butler opened the door, and Philip nodded to him as he walked out.

Dudley, who always assumed the attitudes of his employer, did not return the nod. Philip's car was standing where he had left it earlier, but he noticed that Jules's dark blue Bentley was missing. Turning on the ignition, he backed the car around, wondering why he had taken such a stand in a house of strangers. As he headed for the entrance of the courtyard that led to the driveway, he heard his name called.

It was Camilla, running toward him. "I'll go with you," she called.

Philip lay in Camilla's bed, naked, with his hands clasped behind his head, staring at the ceiling.

Camilla, next to him, ran her hand over his chest lightly and then leaned over and kissed his nipple. "I've had such an incredible desire to do that," she said.

"Be my guest," he said. He watched her for a few moments as she kissed his chest, and then began to rub his hands over her head. When she looked up at him, he smiled at her and brought her up to him to kiss her on her lips.

Later, after their lovemaking, they lay in each other's arms. "You would have walked out of Pauline's house today and left me there, wouldn't you?" said Camilla.

"Yes. I meant what I said, you know," answered Philip.

"Oh, I know you did. You've made yourself an enemy. You must know that."

"Jules. I know."

"A severe enemy."

"I know. Imagine having antagonized Reza Bulbenkian and Jules Mendelson in the same year."

"Something could happen to you."

"It won't."

Later, when Philip was leaving, Camilla walked with him to his car.

"Beautiful night," said Philip.

She kissed him good night. "Pauline likes you, I know, and Jules worships her," said Camilla, as if she had been thinking about the problem.

"Yes, I think he does," agreed Philip, "but I think Pauline would prefer love to worship any day."

"What in the world does that mean?"

"Think about it."

Flo's Tape #7

"*I mean, Jules was a rich and famous man, and I was very flattered that he was devoting so much of his time to me. It was much more than a rich guy getting into my pants, believe me. I wouldn't have stayed with him so long if that's all it was. He taught me. He wanted me to better myself. Once he said to me, 'Don't say stoodent, say student.' At first, I thought he was putting me down, but then I found out he wanted me to do things right.*

"*Have you ever seen an older guy and a young girl in a restaurant together? And they're making forced conversation because they have absolutely nothing to say to each other once they aren't in the feathers? Well, Jules never wanted that to happen with us. That's why he was always teaching me things. And let me tell you something, I wanted to learn.*"

=== 8 ===

P HILIP QUENNELL was still unused to the streets of Beverly Hills, and he had difficulty finding the small cul-de-sac called Palm Circle where Casper Stieglitz, the film producer, lived. "Sunset to Hillcrest, right on Hillcrest to Mountain, left off Mountain to Palm Circle, the last drive on the left by the cul-de-sac," said Bettye, Casper's secretary, over the telephone to Philip, who wrote down the instructions on a Chateau Marmont scratch pad. Then Bettye added, as if it would simplify things for Philip, "It's the old Totie Fields house."

When he buzzed the intercom at the gate, a red light went on on the closed-circuit television. "Philip Quennell to see Mr. Stieglitz," he said, looking up into the camera.

"Proceed along the driveway past the tennis court to the front of the house and enter by the front door," said a voice, English in inflection, but not English.

The wooden gates, less grand by far than the gates at the Mendelsons' estate, opened slowly and laboriously, as if they needed a caretaker's attention. As Philip drove by the tennis court, he heard screams of laughter and saw two extremely pretty girls, one blond, one brunet, in extremely short shorts and angora sweaters, playing what appeared to be an extremely amateurish game of tennis.

"That shot was *not* in, Ina Rae, and you know it wasn't, you big cheater," said the blond girl.

"Fuck you, Darlene," said Ina Rae.

Ina Rae's language was greeted with more screams of laughter.

At the front of the house was a courtyard, with cobblestones, smaller by far than the Mendelsons' courtyard. He pulled his car around a center island with a birdbath and a great many geranium plants to the front of the house. Looking up, he could see that the house had once been Spanish, but the arches had been squared off, and a mansard roof replaced what had once been a red tile roof, giving the Spanish house a French look. The front door opened, and a butler, rather informally clad in dark trousers and a white shirt with the sleeves rolled up, stood in the doorway. He wiped his hands on a long green apron.

"Excuse my appearance, Mr. Quennell," he said, in an extremely friendly manner, "but I've been doing the silver. Messy job."

Philip nodded.

"If you'll follow me," said the butler. "My name is Willard, sir. Mr. Stieglitz is in the pool pavilion."

They crossed through a hall to the living room, which looked to Philip as if it had been decorated by a studio set dresser. Large paintings with white backgrounds and various colored dots lined the walls. Philip glanced at them.

"Mr. Stieglitz is quite the collector," said Willard.

"Yes," replied Philip.

They went out a pair of French doors to a terrace. He followed the butler around a swimming pool at the edge of the terrace to the pool pavilion, where the butler pulled back a long sliding glass door.

"Mr. Quennell is here, Mr. Stieglitz," he called in. He then stepped back so that Philip could enter first. Inside, the large room was in total darkness, except for the light let in by the open door and a small lamp at the far end of the room. Heavy curtains were drawn tight on all the windows. For a minute, the darkness blinded Philip after the bright sunlight outside, and he stood in the room, unsure which way to look.

"Could I get you a drink?" the butler asked.

"No, thank you," said Philip. "It's very dark in here. I can't see a thing."

"This is Mr. Stieglitz's projection room as well," he said. "He's been watching a rough cut. He keeps the blackout curtains drawn."

"I see."

A toilet flushed. "Mr. Stieglitz will be out directly," said the butler, with an English affectation. "Would you like coffee?"

"No, thank you."

"Perrier, Diet Coke, anything like that?"

"No, nothing, thank you."

"Sit down."

Philip sat in a deep chair. On a massive coffee table in front of him were bowls of gumdrops, small candy bars, chocolate pretzels, and a variety of nuts. There were also dozens of scripts in cardboard covers of varying colors.

The toilet flushed again. The door opened. Into the projection room walked Casper Stieglitz. He was dressed entirely in loose black velour, both shirt and trousers. On his head was a wide-brimmed plantation-type hat with a black ribbon around it, pulled down on his forehead to just over his eyebrows. His face was very tanned, as if he spent a great deal of time under a sunlamp rather than in the sun. He wore black-rimmed, thick-lensed dark glasses, through which it was impossible to see his eyes.

"Willard, tell those twats at the tennis court to keep their voices down. They're turning my place into a fucking slum with that filthy language," said Casper Stieglitz. He sneezed. "Don't they realize they're in Beverly Hills? Not wherever it is they come from." He spoke in a catarrhal voice, as if his nose were stuffed.

"Hello, Mr. Quennell. I'm Casper Stieglitz."

Stieglitz gave Philip his left hand to shake, at the same time sneezing again and speaking the word "Bursitis," in reference to his right hand, in a hoarse voice. Philip wondered why he wore a hat in the house.

"You seem to have a terrible cold," said Philip. He noticed that his nose was dripping.

"I do, yes, I do," said Casper. He reached into the pocket of his black velour trousers and pulled out a handkerchief and blew his nose, although the blowing seemed more noisy than nostril cleansing. "I liked your book on that Wall Street guy," he said.

"Thank you," said Philip.

"You get any flak from Reza Bulbenkian?"

"A bit, yes."

"He wanted to break your legs, right?" asked Casper.

"There was such a threat, yes," answered Philip.

Casper laughed. "I like the way you wrote it, kind of tough, a good style. I thought you'd be an older guy than you are. How old are you?"

"Thirty."

"Thirty, huh? Thought you'd be older. Now, uh, the picture I got in mind is quite a different proposition. We have this problem out here in the industry, you know, with drugs."

"Yes, that's what my agent told me you wanted to do this picture about."

"This is not a picture for the theaters, though. You understand that."

"Oh?" said Philip, surprised. "That's what I assumed."

"No."

"Television then?"

"No, not television."

"I'm confused."

Casper Stieglitz laughed again. Philip noticed that his bright gleaming teeth—too even, too large, too perfect—resembled Chiclets. In the minutes that followed, as his eyes became used to the dim room, it occurred to him that Casper's tight unlined skin was the result of a face-lift, a feeling that was confirmed when he saw the red scars of recent surgery behind his ears. Casper leaned over and put his hand into a bowl of nuts and started eating them as he talked, tossing them in his mouth one or two at a time. "You see, I was falsely arrested on a drug charge a few months ago. There was a shipment of drugs from Colombia that, uh, inadvertently got into the hands of an employee of mine who brought the package to this house under the impression that he was delivering film of some dailies of a picture I have been shooting in Central America." For a moment he seemed to lose his train of thought. "It's a long story."

Philip stared at Stieglitz. "I am at a loss to understand what my position is in all this," he said.

"That is what I am coming to," replied Casper, remembering where he was in his story. He sniffed and blew his nose again. "The judge in the case, realizing the terrible mistake that had been made, asked me to make a film on the proliferation of drugs in the film industry that could be shown to groups, like, uh, Cocaine Anonymous, and different places like that, rehabs, et cetera, where they are fighting this terrible battle against drugs."

"In return for which, no charges are to be brought against you, is that it?" asked Philip.

"It's ridiculous, the whole thing," said Casper. "I'm a total innocent bystander in this thing, and, uh, what we thought, my lawyers and I, that rather than have the terrible publicity that such a thing would entail, it would be easier to just go ahead and make the fucking film, and have a clean slate. Like

a, you know, a form of community service. At a very high level, you understand. Do you know about community service?"

"Yes, I know all about community service," said Philip quietly. "I really
don't know if I am interested in doing that, Mr. Stieglitz."

"Casper. Call me Casper, Phil. Listen, uh, would you like some nuts?"

"No."

"Cashews. No? You like candy?"

"No, thanks."

"Did the fagola offer you a drink?"

"Who?"

"Willard, the butler. Did he offer you a drink?"

"He did, thank you. I don't want anything."

"Beer?"

"No. We must talk about this," said Philip. "This is not what I thought it
was going to be. My agent told me this was to be a feature motion picture."

"Look, you get paid the same kind of bucks as if you were writing a
feature, for a first-time feature writer, that is, which you are. I mean, you never
wrote a picture before, and it's more money than you got for your leveraged
buyout book. What we have here is like a documentary, interviewing this law
enforcer, and that drug dealer, and so on, and arrangements can be made to
get you in on a drug bust, and include that in the picture. It will be a terrific
start for you in the industry."

Philip nodded.

"They'll show it to the various groups, you know, that deal with the drug
problem, and you'll have a showcase for yourself to show the other studios
what you've done. Will you excuse me for a second. I'll be right back. I've gotta
take a leak." As he rose, he sneezed again and the partially chewed cashew
nuts in his mouth flew all over Philip's face. "Oh, sorry, man, here," he said,
reaching into his pocket and bringing out his soiled handkerchief. Philip declined the handkerchief with a shake of his head. "I gotta take a leak," Casper
said again and disappeared into the bathroom. The sound of the door locking
behind him could be heard.

Philip looked at his sneezed-upon face in the mirror behind the liquor
bottles of the bar. Semimasticated nut particles stuck to his eyebrows and nose.
He turned on the water tap to wash his face but noticed there was no bar towel.
He went to the sliding glass door through which he had entered the projection
room and walked out into the bright sunlight. Retracing his steps around the
swimming pool onto the terrace, he reentered the house through the same
French door by which he had left it twenty minutes earlier. The butler was
nowhere in sight. He opened a door, looking for a bathroom, and found it was
another mirrored bar. He opened another door and found a hallway that led to
what turned out to be Casper Stieglitz's bedroom, its massive bed covered with
a spread of the prevailing color scheme of orange and brown. Through it were
his bathroom and dressing room.

Inside the bathroom, Philip turned on the gold-plated hot water fixture
and washed his face thoroughly with a bar of sandalwood soap from a gold-
plated soap dish in the shape of a shell. He then dried his face on a brown face
towel, elaborately monogrammed with the intertwined initials C.S. in white

satin, from a set of brown monogrammed towels on a heated towel stand. Still feeling soiled, he repeated the process.

When he finished, Philip looked at some of the dozens and dozens of framed photographs on the bathroom walls and the walls of the dressing room beyond. In almost every picture Casper Stieglitz, in younger times, was with a different beautiful girl, at awards ceremonies, or industry dinners, or premieres of films. In all the pictures he was laughing, happy, glamorous; they bespoke a life of fame and success. There were photographs showing him having a script conference by the side of his swimming pool and toasting a blond starlet with a glass of wine while lying on an inflated rubber raft in the middle of his swimming pool.

His clothes were arranged in cabinets, dozens of silk shirts hung on hangers, next to dozens of sport coats, next to dozens of suits, next to a variety of styles of tuxedos, in midnight blue, and maroon, and black. An open cabinet showed sweaters, all cable stitch, all cashmere, in the entire spectrum of colors, folded painstakingly one on top of the other. On the counter level there were bottles of aftershave lotions, gold-backed brushes, and a fitted leather case for dozens of pairs of cuff links, as well as an immense silver tray on which dozens of pairs of sunglasses were neatly arranged.

There was a knock on the bathroom door. "You in there, Phil?" asked Casper.

"Yes, I am," replied Philip. "I'm washing my face."

"The guest bathroom is off the front hall," called in Casper. There was an unmistakable tone in his voice that Philip was trespassing. "I'm not keen on people using my bathroom."

"I had no way of knowing that," called out Philip. At that moment his eye caught sight of some strange objects on the top of the clothes cabinets. At first they appeared to be hat stands, of the variety used in millinery shops, but then he saw that they were wig stands. He counted them. There were thirty-one, and on each was a full toupee, going from freshly cut hair to long hair in need of a haircut.

"I'll be out in a minute," said Philip.

Beyond the dressing room, he could hear the girlish laughter of Ina Rae and Darlene in an adjoining bedroom.

"Where's the dildos?" asked Ina Rae.

"I thought you brought them," answered Darlene.

"No, stupid, you were supposed to bring them. Casper's gonna be furious."

"How come you need a dildo, anyway?"

"The guy's got a dick like a Tampax," said Ina Rae.

Darlene shrieked with laughter.

Philip walked out of the bathroom. Casper was standing there. On his face was an anxious expression, and Philip understood that he was concerned that he might have seen his toupees.

"Interesting house you have, Mr. Stieglitz," said Philip.

"I did a total gut job when I bought the house. Got rid of all the Spanish shit and gave it this French look. Thelma Todd built the house," he said. "She was murdered. Remember that?"

"No," said Philip.

"Way before your time. Way before my time too, as a matter of fact. I was gonna make a picture about the case once. Faye Converse was gonna play Thelma, but it never got off the ground. Couldn't get all the elements together."

There was a silence.

"About this drug picture," said Casper.

"I think I'm not the right choice for this, Mr. Stieglitz," said Philip.

"Fifty thousand down. Fifty thousand when you turn in the first draft. Another fifty when we go into production. Not bad bucks for a young guy like you. You only got fifty for the whole fucking book you wrote on that chiseler Reza Bulbenkian."

Philip laughed. "I'm at the Chateau. Let me talk to my agent, and I'll call you."

"Call me when? I gotta let the guy from the community service know, or I'll be in violation."

"This evening. Tomorrow morning at the latest."

"Some guys would get down on their knees and kiss my hand at an offer like this."

"I'm sure," said Philip. "But I'm also sure that's not the kind of guy you want for a project like this."

He walked back through the living room and hall and opened the front door. Outside the sun was blinding. He covered his eyes with his hand. He would have to buy dark glasses, he decided, although he had an antipathy toward dark glasses. When he got into his car, he heard his name called. Turning, he saw Casper Stieglitz's butler standing at the front door. Philip rolled down the window, and the butler walked up to the car.

"Yes?" asked Philip. He couldn't remember the butler's name.

"Of course, it doesn't matter a bit," said the butler.

"What doesn't?"

"About the house."

"What about it?"

"It wasn't built by Thelma Todd at all. He always gets it wrong." He shook his head in exasperation. "Thelma lived, and died, bless her soul, on the Pacific Coast Highway in Santa Monica."

Philip stared at him.

"Mr. Stieglitz isn't really interested in the history of Hollywood. This house was built by Gloria Swanson, when she was married to the Marquis de la Falaise. After they were divorced, Mr. Hearst tried to buy it for Marion Davies, but Miss Swanson didn't want Marion Davies to have it for some reason, and she sold it instead to Constance Bennett. It was Miss Bennett who put on the mansard roof. To the best of my knowledge, Thelma Todd was never even in the house."

"I thought Totie Fields owned it," said Philip.

"Oh, later. That was much later," said Willard, dismissing Totie Fields's contribution to the house.

Philip felt that this was not the reason the butler had called him back.

"As I said, it doesn't matter a bit," said the butler.

"Interesting, though. I'm sorry, but I can't remember your name."

"Willard."

"Oh, right, Willard. Do you have to clean all those wigs when you're not cleaning the silver?"

Willard gasped. "You saw Mr. Stieglitz's toupees? He'll die, absolutely die. He thinks nobody knows he wears a rug."

"I won't tell."

"I saw you at Hector Paradiso's funeral."

"You do get around, Willard."

"Terrible thing."

"Was Hector a friend of yours?"

" 'Acquaintance' would be a better word."

"Suicide, they say it was," said Philip.

"You don't believe that, do you, Mr. Quennell?"

"That's what they say, even in the autopsy report," said Philip.

Willard looked back toward the house. "I better get back. Mr. Stieglitz will wonder what's happened to me."

"I think Ina Rae and Darlene are taking pretty good care of Mr. Stieglitz by now, although they forgot the dildos," said Philip.

"Aren't they the two cheapest?" asked Willard, shaking his head in disapproval.

Philip turned on the ignition. "I'll remember that about Gloria Swanson and Constance Bennett," he said.

Suddenly, Willard started to talk very rapidly. "Did you ever hear of a bar called Miss Garbo's?" he asked.

"No," replied Philip, although it was the same bar that Flo had mentioned to him at the AA meeting.

"On Astopovo, between Santa Monica and Melrose?"

Philip shook his head.

"Not exactly on your beat, I wouldn't imagine."

"What kind of a bar?"

"The kind of bar that after midnight caters to gentlemen of a certain age, looking for, uh, companionship, for, uh, a price."

"I see. Why are you telling me this?"

"Hector Paradiso was there on his way home from Pauline Mendelson's party."

"I thought Hector Paradiso was a great ladies' man," said Philip.

"Hector Paradiso was as gay as pink ink, Mr. Quennell," said Willard.

"How do you know he was at Miss Garbo's that night?" asked Philip.

"I was there myself that night," said Willard. "I saw him. I even talked to him. Joel Zircon, the Hollywood agent who works for Mona Berg, introduced me to him."

"How can you be sure it was the same night?"

"He was in a dinner jacket. He'd been to Pauline Mendelson's party. He said Pauline was wearing black velvet and pearls and looked like Madame X, in the Sargent picture."

"Hector said that?"

"Yes."

"To you?"

"To Manning Einsdorf."

"Who's Manning Einsdorf?"

"Owns the place. He was at the funeral too. Gray hair combed in an upsweep?"

"Willard!" came a voice from the house.

Willard, jumping to attention, turned and started back toward the house. Then he turned back to Philip and spoke very quickly. "Hector left with a blond about two in the morning. I saw him."

"A blond? Like Darlene?"

"A boy blond, called Lonny."

With the exception of some personal bequests, written by hand on blue stationery from Smythsons in London, Hector Paradiso had died intestate. "Typical," said Jules Mendelson, shaking his head in exasperation, when this information was passed on to him. Hector, everyone knew, was never one for business. In his personal bequests, which were neither notarized nor witnessed, he left his Paradiso family silver service to Camilla Ebury, his Flora Danica china to Pauline Mendelson, his dog, named Astrid, after the skating star he had once been engaged to, to Rose Cliveden, and a thousand dollars to Raymundo, his houseboy. "If that's not a fruit's will, I never saw one," said Jules to Sims Lord, the attorney who handled all of Jules's business affairs, as he tossed the blue notepaper on Sims's desk. It was Pauline who had suggested to Jules that it might be a nice gesture if Sims Lord would step in and handle the disposition of Hector's estate, such as it was, and expedite matters so that everything could be brought to a conclusion as soon as possible.

In the days that followed, Sims Lord had a telephone call from a woman named Mercedes Sandoval, who pronounced her first name Mer*the*des, in the Castilian manner. She had done part-time secretarial work for Hector for years, such as writing out his party invitations, paying his bills, and balancing his checkbook. Mercedes told Sims Lord that a check had come in written by Hector on the night of his death and cashed the next day. The check was made out to someone Mercedes had never heard of before called Lonny Edge.

"Should I send it over to the police?" asked Mercedes.

"Send it over to me," said Sims Lord. "I'll see that it gets to the police."

"Oh, thank you, Mr. Lord. I don't know what we would have done without you."

Flo's Tape #8

"I don't know if I actually thought of it at the time, but the more I think of it now, of everything that happened, Jules started to grow old right in front of my eyes. There were an awful lot of things that were coming down on him, all at the same time. But I didn't know that. I was bugging him too, about buying me a house, but I realize now he had other things on his mind. When Jules was young, he was in a big jam in Chicago in 1953, I think it was. I don't want to besmirch his memory, although I guess it's pretty besmirched anyway, because of the way he died, but it's an important part of the story. There was a girl he took to a hotel. It was the Roosevelt Hotel, I remember that. She wasn't a hooker or anything like that, but she was a kind of low-class girl he picked up in a bar. Like me, I suppose. What you have to understand about Jules is that he was a very sexually oriented man, even though he wasn't a sexy-looking man. The girl got frightened of him. He had a dick like a mule's. Have I told you that? I think I did. Anyway, the girl ran out on the balcony of the hotel, and he grabbed her by the arm to bring her back in and, somehow, her arm got broken, and somehow she went over the balcony. Everything was hushed up. Jules's family paid through the nose. The girl's family was taken care of. There was never any record of it. But Arnie Zwillman knew. And Arnie Zwillman blackmailed him."

9

WHEN CAMILLA EBURY asked Pauline Mendelson a few days later if Kippie would be available as a fourth for a few sets of mixed doubles— "I told Philip that Kippie has the best backhand ever," Camilla said— Pauline informed Camilla that Kippie had returned to France, to the drug rehab in Lyons that had been so highly recommended by the headmaster at Le Rosay, the school in Switzerland that had expelled Kippie twice, even after Jules Mendelson had offered to build a new library for it in Gstaad. Pauline seemed to be her old self again, less tense when Kippie's name was mentioned, and Camilla ventured to ask a few questions about him, between backgammon games.

"I thought perhaps he'd finished there, in Lyons," she said.

"Oh, no. He has to stay another three months, at least. It's part of the program," said Pauline.

"Why was he home then?" asked Camilla.

"To see the dentist. He dislodged a front tooth somehow. An altercation, I would think, but he was very noncommittal. You know what he's like. And he simply refused to go to one of those French dentists, especially in Lyons, and I don't blame him a bit. Dr. Shea saw him for a few appointments, implanted a new tooth, you could never tell. And then he went back."

"How was he?"

"Oh, you know Kippie. Utterly enchanting. Blondell spoils him rotten. The cook loves him, made him mashed potatoes and chicken hash, and all the kinds of things he could eat with a missing tooth. The butler couldn't do enough for him. Jules and he are forever at odds with each other. That's a given. And I try to be the peacemaker in the middle." For an instant she was silent, and then she added, "But he seems to be behaving. He even seemed quite anxious to get back to France, which came as a complete surprise."

"What will he do when he gets out of the rehab?" asked Camilla.

"He's thinking of opening a restaurant, can you imagine? At least, that's this week's scheme."

They went back to their backgammon.

A week before, on the night of the Mendelsons' party, Kippie Petworth had telephoned his mother to tell her he was back in Los Angeles. The news came as a complete surprise to her. Pauline was listening to the former

President, who was seated on her right, tell a long anecdote about a verbal altercation between his wife and the wife of the Soviet leader, which Pauline had heard several times before, when her butler, Dudley, came to fetch her. With both elbows on the table, she gracefully cupped her chin with one hand and gave her distinguished guest her full attention, as if she were hearing the tale for the first time, and smiled and laughed at the appropriate moments. She held her hand up to caution the butler not to interrupt until the former President had arrived at his punch line.

"It's really too funny," she said at the end of the story, laughing heartily with the other guests. The President's story caused the convivial laughter accorded to a distinguished man, although the same story, if told by a lesser individual, would have gone unremarked upon or unlaughed at. She then turned to Dudley to hear his message, expecting him to tell her of a crisis in the kitchen, or a problem with the band that had arrived to play for dancing.

"It's Kippie," said Dudley, whispering in her ear.

"Kippie?" she asked, turning to Dudley. There was astonishment in her voice, although even the person sitting on the other side of her, Sims Lord, her husband's lawyer, was not aware from her voice that a possible family crisis was at hand.

"On the telephone," whispered Dudley. "I told him you were having a party, but he insisted on speaking to you."

"Is he calling from France?"

"I don't think so. I think he's here," answered Dudley.

"Would you excuse me, Mr. President," said Pauline, placing her damask napkin on the table and rising. "There seems to be a slight soufflé problem in the kitchen."

"Woman's work is never done," said the President, and everyone laughed appreciatively at his joke.

"I'll send Rose Cliveden over here to keep my seat warm," said Pauline. With that, she was off. "I'll go into the library, Dudley. Will you stand outside the door and make sure no one comes in?" Several guests waylaid her on her way through the atrium to the library, and she returned each greeting or salute charmingly but never stopped moving. "What a marvelous dress that is," she said to Madge White, whose daughter her son had impregnated when they were both fourteen years old. "Thank you, Sandy. I'm glad you're having a good time," she said to Sandy Pond, whose family owned the *Los Angeles Tribunal.* "Faye, if there's a line for the powder room, use my bathroom upstairs. Blondell will let you in," she said to Faye Converse.

"Pauline, I must talk to you," said Hector Paradiso, grabbing her arm.

"Naughty you, moving the place cards, Hector," she said to him, still walking toward the library. "Why in the world did you do that? Jules will be furious."

"I felt wasted where you seated me," said Hector.

"I won't be angry if you promise to dance with Rose. I think you hurt her feelings."

"But Pauline, there's something I must tell you."

"Not now, Hector." She walked into the library and closed the door behind her, shooing him off when he tried to follow her into the room. As always, she looked up at the van Gogh painting of the *White Roses* over the mantelpiece, and it brought her a momentary sense of calm. She picked up the telephone. "Hello? Hello? Kippie, it's Mother."

Kippie had been calling from the house of Arnie Zwillman, although he did not tell his mother that. Even if he had, his mother might not have known who Arnie Zwillman was, although Jules Mendelson, Kippie's stepfather, certainly would have. Arnie Zwillman, in the eyes of people like the Mendelsons and their friends, was undesirable, which might have been part of his attraction for Kippie Petworth. Arnie had once owned a hotel in Las Vegas called the Vegas Seraglio, and the insurance money from the conflagration that razed the Vegas Seraglio was the basis of Arnie's original fortune. If someone wanted to incite Arnie's ire, which could be formidable, he had only to describe Arnie as the man who burned down the Vegas Seraglio for the insurance money. A lot of people had done that, and a lot of those same people were sorry that they had. On most other occasions, though, Arnie could be, as many of his friends claimed, "as nice a guy as you'd ever wanna meet."

Arnie always said, when a guest admired his house, that it was the old Charles Boyer mansion, although anyone who had ever seen the house when Charles Boyer lived in it would have been hard pressed to recognize any of the architectural elements, for sliding glass doors had replaced whole walls, and floor-to-ceiling mirrors had covered the French boiserie, and a steam room and spa were now where the old library had been. Turquoise, pink, and orange, the favorite colors of Gladyce Zwillman, who had been Arnie's fourth wife, dominated what Gladyce always called her decor. Now Gladyce was gone, and Adrienne Basquette had moved in and hoped she could retain Arnie's attention and affection until the legalities of Gladyce's severance could be worked out and she could become the fifth Mrs. Arnie Zwillman.

Adrienne heard the chimes and went to the door and turned on the outside lights. The door was bullet-proof glass, fifteen feet high, with a wrought iron design in front of the glass for privacy and safety. Through it, Adrienne could see a handsome young man with blond hair, and blood coming from his mouth. He's adorable, she thought to herself. Women always thought Kippie Petworth was adorable.

"Where's Gladyce?" he asked, when she opened the door.

"Where have *you* been?" asked Adrienne, in a tone of voice that let him know that Gladyce had been out of the picture for some time.

"France," he answered.

"Ooh, la la," said Adrienne. "Your mouth looks yucky."

"Feels yucky too," said Kippie. "Arnie in?"

"Who shall I say is calling?"

"Kippie," said Kippie.

"He's expecting you?"

"Ask him and find out." He smiled a smile he knew was beguiling, without opening his mouth. One of his front teeth was missing.

Adrienne closed the front door and left him standing there for a few minutes. He looked to see if anyone was watching and then spat a mouthful of blood into a terra cotta container holding a bonsai tree by the side of the front door. When Adrienne returned, she opened the door wide and indicated that he was to come in.

"Arnie will be out in a minute," she said. "He's taking a sauna. Can I get you anything?"

"A box of Kleenex," said Kippie.

"What happened?" she asked, pointing to her own mouth as a way of inquiring what was wrong with his.

"Could you get me some Kleenex and then we can chat?" asked Kippie, impatiently.

"You act like a spoiled brat," she said.

"I am a spoiled brat," he answered.

She went into a powder room off the hall and returned with a turquoise container holding pink Kleenex. "Don't drip on Arnie's carpet, for God's sake," said Adrienne. "Arnie will freak out."

Then Arnie Zwillman came into the room. He was deeply tanned, wore a terry cloth robe, and was slicking back his full head of wet silver hair with a comb. A diamond ring glistened on his pinkie finger. Kippie had once described him as handsome, in a Las Vegas sort of way. For an instant he stared at Kippie, taking him in.

"I couldn't imagine who was coming to call at ten o'clock at night," said Adrienne, breaking the silence.

"Get lost," Arnie said in a growl that sounded like "gedloss," with a toss of his head and a wave of his thumb, indicating for her to remove herself. Adrienne retreated to another room without a word. "Come on in the sauna," he said to Kippie. "We can talk there, and for chrissake, don't drip none of the blood on my white carpets." Moving ahead of Kippie, he straightened two Lucite picture frames and removed a speck of dust from a brass-and-glass end table on the way to the steam room.

"What kind of trouble are you in?" asked Arnie, when Kippie had undressed and followed him into the sauna.

"Who said I was in trouble?"

"Don't bullshit me, junior."

"What's it to you?"

"I can help you out of it, that's what it is to me."

"How?"

"You got Judge Quartz for your preliminary hearing, right?"

"Yes. How'd you know?"

"It's my business to know these things. I knew ten minutes after they busted you. Friend of mine came in on the same flight from Paris. They were looking for what he was carrying, and instead they found what you were carrying."

"I couldn't understand why they hit on me like that," said Kippie. "It was nothing, what I was carrying, a couple of joints, and they acted like I had a shipment from Colombia. You ought to see what they did to my luggage."

"Assholes picked the wrong guy, that's all," said Zwillman.

"My family's going to kill me."

"You lose a tooth?"

"Yes."

"How?"

"The cop hit me."

"Cops don't usually hit preppy boys like you. Did you pull your rich kid act on the cop?"

"Something like that."

"Called him a mick or a spic?"

Kippie nodded. "A mick."

They looked at each other and laughed. "I can read you like a book, Kippie."

"There were these two big cops the customs agent called. One held me under my armpit here, and the other held me under my other armpit, and they lifted me up so that my feet didn't touch the floor and carried me through the Pan Am waiting room. Not one of the great looks, you know. This is after they made me take my clothes off and shoved their finger up my ass looking for drugs. I was pissed off."

Over the intercom in the steam room came the sound of a woman's voice. "Ready for your massage, Mr. Zwillman," she said.

Arnie turned to the box and pushed a button. "Okay, Wanda. I'll be in in a minute. Get the table set up." He turned back to Kippie. "Wanna massage?"

"No thanks," said Kippie, who didn't want to be in the steam room either.

"This Wanda's good," said Arnie. "She'll bring you off if you get a hard-on."

Kippie shrugged. "Okay," he said.

"I take it you haven't contacted Jules and Pauline with your little adventure?" He said the names "Jules" and "Pauline" with an exaggerated pronunciation, in an outsider's allusion to their grandeur.

Kippie shook his head.

"You better call them from here," said Arnie. "Just don't tell them what happened. Don't tell no one, except your lawyer. I'll get you a lawyer. Gonna cost you ten grand up front."

"Are you going to lend me the ten grand?" asked Kippie.

"I bailed you out, sonny boy. There's a limit to my generosity."

"Where am I going to get ten grand?"

"Your rich mommy."

"She won't. I know it. She said so the last time."

"Be adorable, Kippie, like you know how to be, and she'll come through. Then when you go before Judge Quartz on Monday morning, the case will be dismissed. Count on it."

"What do you want for all this, Arnie? I can't think you're doing all this for me because you think I'm such a swell kid."

"Smart boy."

"What do you want?"

"An intro."

"Who the hell could I introduce you to?"

"Your father."

"My father? My father lives on Long Island, is now married to the former Sheila Beauchamp, and plays bridge all day every day in Southampton, or Palm Beach, or the Racquet Club in New York, or at Piping Rock, wherever he happens to be. What possible reason would you have to want to meet Johnny Petworth?"

"Don't get snotty with me, you spoiled brat. I'm talking about Jules Mendelson."

"He's not my father. He's my stepfather."

"All right, your stepfather. I want to meet your stepfather."

Kippie hesitated. He knew from past experience that he could not promise his stepfather. "My stepfather does not think highly of me," he said quietly.

"You want to get your case fixed without your family knowing about it, don't you?"

"Arnie, please, man. My stepfather will never come to your house. I know it."

"I know that, junior. What I want you to do is arrange for both your parents to have dinner and see a film at Casper Stieglitz's house. I'll be there too, but that's the part you don't tell them."

"Who's Casper Stieglitz?"

"The film producer."

"But my mother and stepfather don't mix with people like that. I'm not saying it's right. I'm just saying they don't."

"Arrange it, asshole. You don't want your name in the papers, do you, for getting busted on Pan Am flight number three from Paris? I don't think Jules and Pauline are going to care much for that, with the economic conference coming up in Brussels and all."

Kippie, abashed, only stared at Arnie Zwillman.

"What's Piping Rock?" asked Arnie.

"A club," answered Kippie.

"Where?"

"Long Island."

"What kind of club?"

"The kind that wouldn't let you in."

"As a member, you mean?"

"Not even as a guest of a member. Not even for lunch."

"How come?"

"You're not their type."

Arnie nodded. "Now, you better call your mama and tell her you're in dire need of ten thousand dollars. I'll take my massage first."

As a family, Jules and Pauline and Kippie had met only once during the days that followed. Although Hector Paradiso lay dead in an open casket at the Pierce Brothers Mortuary, life went on as usual in the city, despite the endless speculations as to the cause of his death. The Freddie Galavants decided not to cancel their dinner dance in honor of the visiting Brazilian ambassador. Polly Maxwell saw no reason not to go ahead with the fashion show luncheon at the Bel Air Hotel for the Los Angeles Orphanage Guild, even though Pauline Mendelson, Camilla Ebury, and Rose Cliveden had telephoned in their regrets. And Ralph White, despite Madge's protestations, refused to back out of a long-planned weekend of trout fishing on the Metolious River in Oregon, but did promise to be back for the funeral at the Church of the Good Shepherd.

It was a particularly busy time for Jules as well. The economic conference was coming up in Brussels, with all its attendant preparations. A group from the National Gallery in Washington had been promised lunch at Clouds and a tour of the collection, with him as their tour guide, and they could not be put off. And there were the arrangements for Hector's funeral going on concurrently, in which Jules seemed to have an inordinate interest. It surprised Pauline that he seemed so insistent on lining up former ambassadors and other prominent figures in the city to act as pallbearers, when none of them were known to have been more than acquaintances of Hector's.

Kippie was mostly silent during those days, saving his conversation for Blondell and Dudley, to whom he was not a disappointment, or hitting a tennis ball against the backboard on the tennis court for hours at a time, or going for several appointments to Dr. Shea to have a new front tooth implanted, or to Dr. Wright to have the forefinger of his right hand attended to, where Astrid, Hector Paradiso's dog, had bitten off the tip. When Kippie was alone with his mother and stepfather, he strummed on a guitar, which drove Jules mad, but Jules said nothing. There had been a time, before he wanted to become a restaurateur, when he wanted to become a guitarist.

Casper Stieglitz's secretary, Bettye, had telephoned Jules's secretary, Miss Maple, that day and invited Mr. and Mrs. Mendelson to a Sunday night dinner and screening of a film to be held at a date sufficiently in the future to ensure an acceptance.

"Tell him no," said Jules, when Miss Maple telephoned him at home to repeat the invitation. "We don't even know Casper Stieglitz."

Kippie looked up from his guitar playing and struck a chord sufficiently grating so that Jules looked up in annoyance from the telephone conversation.

"No, Jules, don't tell him no," said Kippie.

There was an authoritative tone in Kippie's voice that made Jules react to his stepson. He covered the mouthpiece of the telephone with his hand. "What are you talking about?" he asked.

"I'm telling you, accept that invitation."

"What do you know about this invitation?"

"Tell Miss Maple to say yes, Jules," said Kippie.

Jules and Kippie stared at each other. "Hold off on it, Miss Maple," said Jules, and hung up. "Your mother will never go to Casper Stieglitz's house."

"She will if you tell her she has to."

"There's a beat missing here for me," said Jules. "Do you know this Casper Stieglitz?"

"No."

"How do you know about this?"

"I just know."

"What's your connection?"

"Someone's going to be there who wants to meet you."

"Who?"

"I can't say."

"You better damn well say."

"Arnie Zwillman."

"Arnie Zwillman?" said Jules, in a shocked voice.

"Do you know him?" asked Kippie.

"Of course I don't know him. Do you?"

"Yes."

"How did you ever know such a person?"

"You sound like my mother," said Kippie. "She says things like 'How do you know such-a-person?' "

Jules ignored the remark. "This man is a gangster," he said. "He burned down the Vegas Seraglio for the insurance money."

"He's never been busted," said Kippie.

"And he cheats at cards. He has an electric surveillance system in the ceiling of his card room, and a man hides above the ceiling and sends him mild shocks telling him what's in the other players' hands."

"You know a lot about Arnie for not knowing him."

"Tell me, Kippie. What's your connection with him?"

At that moment Pauline came into the room, dressed in black. She had come from the calling hours at the funeral home where Hector Paradiso's body was on view.

"What was it like?" asked Jules.

"A nightmare," said Pauline. "Poor Hector. He would have hated it. Such sobbing. The Latins do cry so audibly. The rosary went on until I thought I'd die. And the flowers! You've never seen such awful flowers. Pink gladiolus. Orange lilies. Everything I hate. Tomorrow, the funeral will be better. Rose Cliveden and Camilla are handling everything, and Petra von Kant's doing the flowers herself." She turned to Kippie. "How are you, darling? How's the tooth? Let me see. Oh, look. He's doing such a good job, our Dr. Shea. How's the finger? Does it hurt terribly? I'm so glad that little dog is out of our house. Get me a glass of wine, will you, darling. Your mother's a wreck."

Kippie poured his mother a glass of wine. When he brought it over to her, she was lying back on a chaise, her feet up. "Thank you, darling. Isn't this nice, just the family, at my favorite time of day. It's been so long since we've been together like this."

She looked at her husband and son and smiled. Neither returned her enthusiasm, but both nodded. For a moment there was a silence.

"Casper Stieglitz has asked us to go there for dinner," said Jules.

"Casper Stieglitz? Whatever for?" asked Pauline, with a chuckle at the absurdity of such a notion.

"And a film," added Jules.

"Oh, heavens, all those people we don't know," said Pauline. As far as Pauline was concerned, there was no more to be said on the subject.

Jules turned to Kippie and shrugged, as if to point out that he had tried, and failed.

Kippie, looking at Jules, began to strum on his guitar again. "This is my latest composition," he said. "Kind of a catchy lyric." He began to sing in a low muffled voice.

> *"Flo is the name of my stepfather's mistress,*
> *She lives on a lane called Azelia.*
> *Each afternoon, at a quarter to four—"*

Jules, rarely stunned by the events of life, looked at Kippie, stunned.

"Whatever that is, it's lovely, darling, but I can't stand guitar music at the moment. I have such a terrible headache."

"Sorry, Mom," said Kippie, putting down his guitar. "Arnie Zwillman will be there too."

"And who, pray tell, is Arnie Zwillman?" asked Pauline. Pauline had a way of saying a name like "Arnie Zwillman" that left no doubt what her feeling was about such a person, without voicing a single derogatory word against him.

"You'll like him, Mom. Arnie Zwillman's from an old mob family. Old mob money. Listed in the Mafia Register. None of your new people stuff. You'll love him."

Pauline laughed. "Do you think my son is making fun of me, Jules?" she asked.

Jules did not reply.

"How do you know such a person?" she asked Kippie.

Kippie laughed. He dearly loved his mother. He was proud of her beauty. At all the schools he ever attended, the other boys and the teachers vied with each other for him to introduce them to her, and she was never not charming to them in return. He was always thoughtful to her on her birthdays and at Christmas. But he was also bewildered by her life in society, and he could not bear Jules Mendelson. He never confided in her, although he knew that his secrets would be safe in her keeping.

"I wish my son would spend more time in the company of the sort of people he was brought up with, instead of the marginal types he's constantly with," she said. "I simply don't understand how you get to know these people, Kippie."

"Look, Pauline," said Jules suddenly, rising from his chair at the same time. "I think we'd better go to Casper Stieglitz's. Just this one time."

"I never thought I'd hear that from you, Jules. I thought you couldn't stand all those movie people," said Pauline. " 'All they ever do is talk about movies.' Isn't that what you always say about them?"

"I think we'd better go," Jules repeated softly, looking at Pauline with a married look that indicated she should go along with his wishes.

"Suit yourself, Jules," said Pauline. "You go, but I have no intention of going. I don't know that man, and I don't know why I have to go there for dinner."

Jules looked at Kippie again and made a loose gesture that indicated he would talk Pauline into going when the time came.

Arnie Zwillman had been having his daily massage from Wanda when Kippie Petworth came to call. Kippie sat reading a magazine in another room until Wanda was finished.

"Wanna massage?" asked Arnie, when he came out of his workout room, tying the belt of his terry cloth robe.

"No, thanks," said Kippie.

"She'll bring you off if you get a hard-on," said Arnie.

"No, thanks," said Kippie.

"See you tomorrow, Wanda," said Arnie. He walked over to the bar and poured himself a glass of grapefruit juice. "This stuff's good for you."

Kippie nodded.

"What'd your stepfather say?" asked Arnie Zwillman.

"He'll go," answered Kippie.

"Good boy, Kippie. What about your mother?"

"My mother's iffy."

"Iffy, huh?"

" 'All those people we don't know' were her exact words," said Kippie.

"Very hoity-toity."

"That's my mom."

"You tell your mom—"

Kippie held up his hand in protest. "I can't tell my mother where to go. Only my stepfather can do that. He'll get her there."

Arnie Zwillman nodded. "What happened to your finger?"

"Dog bit me."

"You lost your finger?"

"Part of it."

"Yech. I hate blood," said Arnie. "What'd your old man say about me?"

"He's not my old man. I told you that."

"All right. What did your *step*father, Jules Mendelson, say about me?"

"He said you burned down the Vegas Seraglio for the insurance money," said Kippie.

Arnie Zwillman turned red and shook his head. "That fat dickhead."

"Hey, you're talking about my stepfather."

"What else did he say about me?"

"He said you cheated at cards."

"Big fucking deal. I don't know anybody who don't cheat at cards. That's part of the game to me. It's a case of cheating the cheaters."

"He said you had an electrical surveillance system in the ceiling of your card room."

"How the fuck did he know that?"

"Listen, Arnie, you're not hearing any criticism from me. I'm just the message carrier."

"Your arraignment's tomorrow. Judge Quartz will dismiss the case. Will your parents be going to the courtroom with you?"

"My parents don't even know. Besides, they'll be at a funeral."

"Come in here a moment, Kippie," Jules had said the next morning. He was standing in the door of the library, darkly dressed for Hector's funeral, holding a coffee cup in his hand, as Kippie made his way to the sunrise room for breakfast. "There's something we must discuss before your mother comes down."

Jules returned to his chair beneath van Gogh's *White Roses* and moved some newspapers aside. Kippie entered the room and closed the door behind him, but he did not sit down.

"I have called the rehab in Lyons," said Jules. "I talked to Father LaFlamme. They'll take you back. I think it's where you should be."

Kippie nodded.

"Miss Maple has booked your flight."

Kippie nodded again. "Much obliged," he said.

"Just get one thing straight. I did this for your mother. I didn't do it for you," said Jules.

"Much obliged, anyway," said Kippie.

Flo's Tape #9

*"They had me down on the books as a consultant, although God only knows what
I was a consultant for. I'll say this for Jules Mendelson, he was a very generous
man. Each month my check came addressed to F. Houlihan. Houlihan's my real
name, although I haven't used it for years. March is only a made-up name, in case
I became an actress or a model, none of which ever worked out, incidentally.
Sometimes, if Jules ever had to write me about anything, he always started out the
letter, 'Dear Red.' That was supposed to fool the secretary into thinking F. Houlihan was a guy instead of a girlfriend, and Miss Maple went along with the act.
Only you couldn't fool Miss Maple. She always knew who I was. One day she
called me up on the telephone and told me, in a very nice way, that she thought I
was spending too much money. Of course, Jules never knew she called me. If only
she'd said to me, 'Put some of that money in the bank and save it for a rainy day.'
But even if she had, knowing me, I probably wouldn't have listened. You see, the
big mistake I made was that I thought the merry-go-round was never going to
stop."*

10

HAD FLO MARCH known how unserious the conflagration was going to be, she would have reacted with less alarm than she did when someone, a woman, running, had screamed the word *"Fire!"* in an altogether hysterical voice in the corridor outside her suite in the Meurice Hotel in Paris at two o'clock in the morning. Later, she told the person most affected by her action that her mother had died in a fire in a welfare hotel in downtown Los Angeles. Had she reacted with less alarm, Flo's picture would not have appeared on the front page of *Figaro* and two other Paris newspapers, as well as the *International Herald Tribune,* with her lovely red hair in total disarray, wrapped in a blanket over her silver fox coat, and carrying a small Louis Vuitton case—its newness evident even in the photograph—that could only have contained jewels. Even that might have passed unnoticed, for Flo March was relatively unknown, as most mistresses are, but her benefactor and lover, dressed but tieless, was in the background of the same picture, another fleer from a four-alarm fire that turned out to be no more than a burned mattress caused by the dropped cigarette of an inebriated television star in an adjoining suite. And Flo March's benefactor and lover was extremely well known. He was so well known that it was known he was staying at the Ritz Hotel in the Place Vendôme several blocks from the Meurice and could only have been having a midnight rendezvous at that hotel, as Cyril Rathbone, the gossip columnist for the Los Angeles magazine called *Mulholland,* who happened to be in Paris at the same time, noted on the clippings that he sent back to his old friend Hector Paradiso in Los Angeles.

"Poor Pauline!" Cyril wrote in his spidery handwriting, on the border of the newspaper. Cyril Rathbone had never liked Pauline Mendelson, because she refused to allow him to cover her parties for his column, and no amount of persuasion, even on the part of her great friend Hector Paradiso, could make her change her mind. "Darling," Pauline had said to Hector at the time, "don't persist. We cannot have newspeople like Mr. Rathbone in our home. Jules hates that sort of social publicity. And besides, Mr. Rathbone seems to write a great deal about us *without* coming to our house." So, in Cyril Rathbone's code of behavior, the very grand Mrs. Mendelson was fair game.

On several occasions, as recently as at the Mendelsons' party on the night he died, Hector had tried to impart this information to Pauline, in order to save her from embarrassment should the photograph become public. Each time he approached his unpleasant task with reluctance, and each time he felt an inner gratitude that he had not been able to carry out his mission, because he knew how deeply hurt she would have been.

No man was more content with his marriage than Jules Mendelson. From the moment he first saw Pauline McAdoo Petworth twenty-three years earlier, at Laurance Van Degan's birthday dance at the Everglades Club in Palm Beach, he had known that it was she for whom he had been waiting. She was dancing that night with Johnny Petworth, whom she was also divorcing, and she epitomized everything to Jules that was proper and swell. Jules was not thought to be a great catch in those days. He was at the time ungainly and vaguely untidy, a large rumpled-looking sort of man who gave no thought to his appearance. And, moreover, word of his immense wealth and financial genius had not penetrated the world in which Pauline, as young as she was, was already a fixture.

Palm Beach people found him dull and difficult to seat. "Darling, do you mind terribly that I've put you next to Jules Mendelson?" hostesses said to their best friends. It was in that way that Pauline was seated next to Jules on the following night at the home of Rose Cliveden and immediately saw the possibilities of him. Once Mr. Forbes began publishing his annual list of the four hundred richest people in America, and Jules Mendelson was listed so near to the top, the very people who had found him dull in the beginning became the first to find him fascinating. "Lucky me, Jules, sitting next to you," the same ladies now said, but by then Pauline had been Mrs. Jules Mendelson for many years. No one who knew him then ever suspected that he would allow himself to be done over, as Pauline had done him over, in much the same way she had done over the old von Stern mansion in Beverly Hills that Jules had bought and Pauline had turned into a showplace. She totally redid his appearance. She instructed Willi, his barber, to raise the part in his hair and shorten the length of his sideburns. She picked out his ties and cuff links and studs. She took him to the tailor in London who had made her father's suits for years, as well as to her father's shirtmaker and shoemaker, and made his decisions for him until he understood the look of her kind of people. Everyone remarked on his greatly improved appearance, as well as his ability to carry on a conversation at a dinner party.

"Do you have a mistress, Jules?" Pauline had asked him once, more than a year before Cyril Rathbone had seen the picture of Flo March, with Jules in the background, in the Paris press. She waited until Dudley had set up the drinks tray and left the room before asking her surprising question, a question that surprised even her when she asked it. Although she was not an overly passionate woman, Pauline was feeling worshiped but untouched, and a certain feminine instinct brought forth the question more than any knowledge of such a fact. The conversation took place in the sunset room, where the Mendelsons met each twilight to have a glass of wine together and talk over the business of the day before they dressed for dinner.

"What does that mean?" asked Jules, astonished, turning away from the red and orange sunset to give her his full attention.

"Just asking," said Pauline, holding up her hands in a defensive gesture.

"But what does such a question mean?" Jules asked again.

"You keep repeating yourself, Jules. 'What does that mean? What does such a question mean?' Surely you can think up a better answer than that, you, a man used to handling hundreds of millions of dollars." For Pauline, usually so serene, she had become slightly shrill.

"Why are you being like this, Pauline?" he asked, with the attitude of a man who had nothing to hide.

"More questions. You answer me with questions. That might work in your business life, Jules—intimidation, putting people on the defensive—but it doesn't work with me. I'm probably one of the few people you've ever met who isn't afraid of you."

Jules smiled. "I know that, Pauline," he said. "I've always known that, from the time I saw you throw the prenuptial agreement at Marcus Stromm and splash black ink all over his shirt. That's one of the many things I love about you."

"You have a peculiar way of showing your love," she said.

"I can only answer you with a question again. What does that mean?"

"I am considered to be a beautiful woman. At least people tell me that I am beautiful, and magazines and newspapers write me up as a beautiful woman. I say this with no braggadocio. It is something I have been told about myself since I was a child. It is something I work on. It is the reason I swim forty laps in the pool every day, rain or shine. It is the reason I spend part of each day with Pooky for my hair and Blanchette for my nails. It is the reason I go to Paris twice a year for my clothes."

"I know all that," said Jules.

"Oh, yes, I know you do. I also know that you like to have me by your side when you enter those endless dinners you have to attend. I know you like and even need the way I am able to entertain and attract interesting people to your parties when you want to impress men you have business dealings with."

"Yes, that's true."

"It's not enough for me anymore, Jules. I might as well be married to Hector for all the love you show me."

"I do love you."

"You do understand that I am talking about love in the lovemaking sense of the word *love*. I am more than a mannequin. I am more than a hostess."

Of course, he understood. He worshiped his wife. He could not imagine life without her. His marriage was a contract as binding as any business contract he had ever signed. Forestalling further suspicion, he became attentive again to the obligations of his marriage, at least for a while, but a complication had set in, a sexual complication, that he had never imagined could happen to him.

Her name had been Houlihan, Fleurette Houlihan, and she could not bear the sound of it. "You don't think I look Irish enough, without having a name like Fleurette Houlihan?" she often asked, shaking her red hair at the same time. When she thought she might become an actress, and worked as a waitress at the Viceroy Coffee Shop on Sunset Strip, she renamed herself Rhonda March, after Rhonda Fleming, a red-haired film star her mother had admired. The Viceroy was said to serve the best coffee in West Hollywood, and that was where she had met Jules Mendelson, who was a coffee drinker, ten cups a day.

He had walked into the Viceroy Coffee Shop on a day when the coffee machine in his office was not working. She was wearing a nameplate with RHONDA on it.

Jules Mendelson was not the type of man who spoke to waitresses in coffee shops, but that day, for a reason he did not understand, he had said to the red-haired girl wearing the name tag with RHONDA on it, "I suppose they call you Red."

"No, they don't," she answered quite emphatically. She was a pretty girl who was used to dealing with lascivious older men. "I don't like being called Red, as a matter of fact."

"What do they call you?" he asked.

There was in his tone a genuine interest in her answer, and she felt she had mistaken him for lascivious. "Do you mean what is my name?"

"Yes."

"Rhonda," she said, tapping a red fingernail against her nameplate.

When he looked up from his *London Financial Times* and watched her wipe off the table with a turquoise-colored sponge, he said to her, "You don't look like a Rhonda."

"I was thinking of changing it to Rondelle," she said.

"Oh, no," he said, "not Rondelle."

"You want coffee?" she asked. "We got the best coffee in West Hollywood here."

"Yes."

When she put the cup down in front of him, he asked, "What was your name before you changed it?"

"You don't want to hear," she said.

"Yes, I do," he said.

"Fleurette Houlihan," she said, almost whispering. "It makes me cringe. Imagine that up on the screen."

He laughed.

"I kind of like the Fleurette part," said Jules.

"You don't!"

"Kind of."

"You're nuts." She liked talking about herself, though.

"How about Flossie?"

"Sounds cheaper than Fleurette."

"Flo?"

"Hmmm." She gave it some thought.

"I once knew a Flo," said Jules. He hadn't meant to get so deeply mired in such a conversation. "She was a very pretty girl too."

So she became Flo.

Flo March was then twenty-four years old, perhaps not the smartest girl in town but one of the nicest and, certainly, one of the prettiest, if red hair, blue eyes, and creamy-colored skin were an appealing combination for her beholder. She sometimes dated minor agents she poured coffee for in the morning, but they never took her to screenings or to dinners in restaurants, which were the sorts of things she yearned to do. They took her to dinner in other coffee shops and were after one thing and one thing only, and she usually gave it to them, because it was easier to say yes than to say no and have to deal with all that hassle. Hector Paradiso, who lived in the Hollywood Hills above the Viceroy, had breakfast there every morning, and often told Flo stories of where he had been the night before: at Faye Converse's party, or Rose Cliveden's, or, best of all, Pauline Mendelson's. Flo loved hearing about parties, especially Pauline Mendelson's parties. She read every word about Pauline Mendelson in the society columns and in the fashion magazines that Hector sometimes brought by for her after he had finished with them. Flo, no fool, knew all about the other part of Hector's life too, the part no one ever talked about. All the hustlers from the Strip came into the Viceroy too, and they told her about their adventures with the rich guys who stopped their Mercedes-Benzes and Rolls-Royces, made their deals, and took them to their houses.

Jules had returned to the Viceroy Coffee Shop every day since the first day, always carrying a financial newspaper, and sat at the same table, though the management frowned on a single person tying up a booth for four customers and only ordering coffee. But there was something about Jules—although the manager, whose name was Curly, had no idea who Jules was—that kept him from asking Jules to sit at the counter instead of the booth, especially after Rhonda, who now wanted to be called Flo, told the manager that the big man always left a ten-dollar tip, even though he only had coffee.

"I don't want you to think for a single instant that this is what I intend to do for the rest of my life," said Flo, a few days later, pouring Jules a second cup of coffee with one hand and wiping off the Formica top of the table with her turquoise-colored sponge with the other. *"This,"* continued Flo, referring to her job as a waitress in a coffee shop, "is only a means to an end."

"And the end, of course, is stardom," said Jules, watching her over the top of the *Wall Street Journal.*

"I'd settle for less than stardom," said Flo, quite seriously.

"What would you settle for?"

"I'd like to be the second lead in a TV series, best friend of the star, where the whole show wouldn't rest on my shoulders, and when it gets canceled after thirteen weeks, I wouldn't be blamed and would just go on to another series, again as a secondary lead. Or even just a running part would do."

Jules laughed.

Flo blushed. "What are you laughin' at? I'm serious," she said, defensively.

"It is a laugh of enchantment, not derision," he said.

"A laugh of enchantment, not derision," she repeated slowly, as if she were memorizing it so that she could repeat it in conversation. "Hey, that's really nice," she said.

"Are you doing anything about it?" asked Jules.

"What do you mean?"

"Studying, getting an agent, going on calls, or whatever it is actresses do to get ahead. You're not waiting to be discovered at the coffee counter, are you?"

"You have to have pictures," said Flo. "Or they don't want to see you."

"Then get pictures," said Jules, simply.

" 'Get pictures,' he says." She rolled her eyes, as if Jules Mendelson had said something stupid. "Do you have any idea what pictures cost?"

"You seem to be defeated without even starting," he said. "Let me tell you something. If you can visualize what you want to be, you'll make it, believe me."

She looked at him earnestly. It was not the sort of flirtatious conversation she was used to with her customers. "The thing is, I have this great desire to become famous, but I don't know whether I'm good enough at anything to become famous."

"You look very well today," Jules had said another day, noting the fresh pink uniform that she was wearing.

"My mother used to say that Maureen O'Hara was the first redhead in movies who had the courage to wear pink on the screen," said Flo.

Jules, bewildered, nodded. He didn't understand most of what Flo said, but he had grown to like listening to her talk. She had opinions on everything. His secretary, Miss Maple, whom he had had for years, couldn't understand why Jules left his office every morning around ten o'clock to go and have coffee at the Viceroy Coffee Shop, when Beth, her assistant, made perfectly good coffee right there in the office; but Jules said he liked to get the fresh air and to be able to read the *Wall Street Journal* and the *London Financial Times* in peace. Miss Maple didn't ask any more questions.

Flo looked out the window of the coffee shop. There, parked by the curb on Sunset Boulevard, was a dark blue Bentley.

"That your car out there?" she asked.

Jules looked out the window at the car, as if it were not his, and then looked back at her.

"Why would you think that was my car?" he asked.

Flo shrugged. "You kinda match each other," she said. Jules did not reply.

"And nobody else in this joint looks like they could afford a car like that. Do you have that on a lease, or do you own it?"

Jules, embarrassed, muttered, "It's mine." He wanted to terminate the subject.

"Sure, I'll go for a ride with you," she said, and then roared with laughter, blushing at the same time. "Hey, I'm only kidding. All my life I wanted to go for a ride in a Rolls-Royce."

"It's not a Rolls," said Jules.

"What is it?"

"A Bentley."

"A Bentley. What's a Bentley? Never heard of a Bentley." There was great disappointment in her voice.

"Well, it's like a Rolls, made by the same company," said Jules, as if defending his car. He knew it was an absurd conversation, unworthy of him.

"Like a cheaper model sort of thing?" Flo asked.

"Yes, I suppose it is, but not by much," he said. Looking at the next booth, he wondered if the people were listening, or if they knew who he was. He wanted to leave the orange Naugahyde booth where he was sitting. He visualized himself rising, leaving a large bill on the table to cover cost and tip, and walking out, but he did not. Instead, he pushed his coffee cup toward her to indicate that he wished another cup of coffee.

* * *

Like a moth drawn to a flame, Jules began to visit the Viceroy Coffee Shop more frequently. Outside the window of the booth where he always sat could be seen a tall building. The golden letters on the side of the building proclaimed it as the Jules Mendelson Building, which was where his office was, although so far no one in the Viceroy had connected him with that name, or that building.

One morning Flo kept him waiting while she joked with a young man at the counter, whom Jules recognized from previous visits. He saw that the young man was handsome, dressed in black jeans that were far too tight, and it surprised him how much anger and jealousy he felt. When, finally, Flo approached his table, he was cool and distant with her.

"Cat got your tongue?" she asked. She frequently used expressions that he could not bear.

"Who's that guy you're talking to at the counter?" he asked after she had brought him his coffee.

"What guy?"

"With the blond hair."

"Oh, him. That's Lonny." She made a thumbs-down gesture.

"You looked quite friendly with him."

"Oh, please!"

"What's he always hanging around for?"

"Drinking coffee, like you. Hey, you're not jealous of Lonny, are you?"

"Jealous. Of course not. Why should I be jealous? I just wanted to know who he is."

"Let me fill you in on Lonny. Lonny is *not,* repeat *not,* interested in pretty young girls, like me, believe me. Lonny is interested in rich old guys like you, who drive the kind of car you drive."

Jules reddened. He did not like to be described as an old guy. He was then fifty-three years old, and he did not think of himself as old. He had started to lose weight. He had started to eat only proper things—grilled sole and leaf spinach—and declined bread and dessert. Even Willi, his barber who shaved him every morning at five-thirty, had remarked only that morning that he was looking fit and years younger.

Flo realized she had insulted him. "I didn't mean *old,*" she said. "I meant *older.* Lonny was a friend of that famous writer who died. What was his name? I'm sure you've heard of him." She tapped her finger on her upper lip as she tried to remember the name. "Basil Plant, I think it was. Anyway, Lonny's supposed to have stolen the manuscript of his unfinished novel, or something like that. Somebody told me the story, but I hear so many stories here at the Viceroy that I can't keep them all straight."

Jules shook his head. He was disinterested in the young man's story.

"Curly thinks you've got a crush on me," said Flo, changing the subject.

"Who's Curly?"

"The manager. Over there, talking to Lonny. He says you'll only sit at my table when you come here and that you leave the biggest tips of anyone who comes into the place."

Jules did not answer. He lifted the *London Financial Times* higher, as if he had discovered something in the news that it was urgent for him to read, in order to hide the reddening of his face. The thing he most feared was to be talked about, although he was sure that Curly, or any of the people at the Viceroy, did not know he was Jules Mendelson. He wondered if he himself knew Jules Mendelson. The Jules Mendelson he knew would never be sitting each day for over an hour in an orange Naugahyde booth in a coffee shop on Sunset Boulevard in order to stare at a red-haired waitress called Flo March. That day he asked Flo March to go for a drive in his Bentley.

Her dress had been cheap and a bit showy. Jules felt that it did not suit her. He thought that the skirt was too short, even though she had beautiful legs. He was used to seeing her in her pink waitress uniform, which had a simple style to it, and he was at first disappointed in her appearance away from her job.

"You know what I like about you, Jules?" she asked.

"What?"

"You were awkward and clumsy about asking me out, like you weren't used to picking up girls like me. I was touched by that."

"I thought it was the car that got to you."

"That too," she said, and they both laughed. He noticed that she seemed to enjoy her own humor. If she said something funny, she laughed heartily along with her listener at her sometimes boisterous stories.

"You don't laugh enough, Jules. Did anyone ever tell you that?"

"I guess that's so."

"You want to know what else I like about you?"

"Sure."

"You didn't come on to me the minute we were alone in your car."

"That doesn't mean I didn't want to."

"I understand that, but still, you didn't come on. You acted like a gentleman, which is something I'm not used to with the kind of guys who ask me out.

"I don't even know your last name," Flo said to him, getting out of the Bentley in the parking lot behind the Viceroy, where her car was parked.

"What difference does it make?"

"No, c'mon, tell me."

"Mendelson," he said quietly.

She looked at him. Her mouth fell open. "Like in the Jules Mendelson Family Patient Wing at Cedars-Sinai Hospital?"

Jules nodded.

"That's you?"

Jules nodded.

"That's where my mother died. In the burn unit. She was burned in a hotel fire."

"I'm sorry."

Her high spirits had vanished. She had become quiet.

"G'night," she said. She stepped out of the car and slammed the door behind her. She started walking toward her own car and then turned back to look at him. He was sitting in the driver's seat, looking out at her. She opened the door of his car again and put her head inside.

"Does that mean you're married to Pauline Mendelson?" she asked.

He nodded his head in an almost imperceptible manner. He had heard that florists and hairdressers and people in shops called his wife by her first name, but it was the first time he had ever heard it himself.

"No wonder you didn't want anyone to know your name," said Flo. "You better get home. Your wife's probably having a party and is wondering where you are." She slammed the door again and got into her own car.

The next day Flo had been distant. After Jules was seated in his regular booth, she asked Belle to take her tables—her station, she called it—saying she was going to take her break early. Then she sat at the counter and joked with Joel Zircon, the Hollywood agent, and Manning Einsdorf, who owned Miss Garbo's, in a boisterous manner. Jules, furious, read his *Wall Street Journal.*

Out the window behind him, Flo noticed for the first time the gold lettering on the tall building that read THE JULES MENDELSON BUILDING. He stayed for only two cups of coffee, rose, and left Belle the same ten-dollar tip that he always left Flo. She did not get up from the counter when he left.

The next day he brought a gift with him, a small blue box from Tiffany tied with a white ribbon.

"For you," he said, sliding it toward her on the Formica table.

"Really?" There was a childlike look of joy on her face.

"Open it."

"Now?"

"Sure."

She untied the white ribbon carefully, as if she were going to save it. She smiled at him. Then she slowly opened the small blue box. Inside was tissue paper, which she tore aside. Beneath was a layer of white cotton. Under the cotton was Jules's gift. She picked it up. Disappointment registered on her face.

"Do me a favor, will ya, Mr. Big Bucks? Take your little silver trinket from the economy counter at Tiffany's, and shove it. My ex-boyfriend, Mikey, from the Mobil gas station over there, would have given me something better than a silver key chain with a heart charm hanging off it. What was it, a leftover from your office Christmas gifts? Save it for your receptionist's birthday. Hey, Belle, will you take my station? I'm gonna take my break."

Jules sat there, grim-faced. It was a cheap gift for the intention he had for it, and she had called him on it. She had also called it right; it had been a leftover from the office Christmas gifts, an accompaniment to the bonus that each of the girls on his staff received.

That night, as he was dressing for dinner, he telephoned her at her apartment to apologize. It was the first time he had ever called her, as well as the first time he had ever called another woman from his house. Her line was busy. He showered and then telephoned her again, and her line was still busy. He put his studs and cuff links in his dinner shirt and dialed again, but her line was still busy. He tied his black tie. The line was still busy. He put on his black patent leather shoes. Still busy. He put on his dinner jacket. Busy.

"Jules," called Pauline. "We're going to be late."

"Coming," he called back. One last time, he thought. He dialed again. Her telephone rang.

"Hello?"

"Your line was busy," he said. There was a tone of annoyance in his voice.

"Yes, it was," she said coolly.

"Who were you talking to?" He knew it was the wrong question to ask, even as he was asking it.

"None of your fucking business."

"What's the matter?"

"You're speaking to me in an annoyed voice, as if I have no right to talk on the telephone."

"I'm sorry. I'll tell you what. Call the telephone company tomorrow and have another line put in. I'll take care of it."

"You're some big gift giver, Bucks," she said.

There was a knock on the door of his dressing room, and then the door opened and Pauline walked in. "Jules! Please! We're going to be late! It's a surprise party for Madge, and Rose will be livid if we spoil it."

"I'll be right there, Pauline. I'm just finishing this call with Sims."

"My God, is that Pauline?" asked Flo, enchanted. "I can't believe it. Pauline Mendelson. 'Jules! Please! We're going to be late! It's a surprise party for Madge, and Rose will be *livid* if we spoil it.'" Flo spoke in an exact imitation of Pauline's upper-class voice.

"Jesus," said Jules, panicked. For him, familial domesticity of the highest order, such as he shared with Pauline, and love of the most sexual nature, such as he yearned for but had not yet shared with Flo March, were not incompatible, but it was unthinkable for him that the two could ever intermingle. "Look, I have to go."

"Bye," she said. Her indifference exasperated him.

"You still mad?" asked Jules.

"No."

"Who were you talking to before?" he asked.

"One of my lovers from Watts," she said, and hung up.

The next day Jules contacted a furrier in the San Fernando Valley that was not likely to be frequented by any of the people Pauline knew. He sent Flo a silver fox coat.

"Now we're talking," said Flo, after she tore open the box and pulled it out.

Even women who were jealous of Pauline Mendelson, for the silver platter that her life had been handed to her on, had to concede that she would be marvelous as the wife of the head of the American delegation in Brussels during the year of the statehood of Europe. Although Jules had not as yet been confirmed, the President had assured him that his confirmation was a foregone conclusion and preparations could be made. First the possibility of that high office, which Jules craved, and then the certainty of it, kept things on keel for him during the private torment of his obsession with Flo March.

On her twice-a-year trips to Paris to buy her clothes, Pauline had made several side excursions to Brussels and had secured for them a large house set in a verdant park on the Avenue Prince d'Orange, where it was expected she would entertain magnificently during the year of their stay. Mr. Jensen, the French decorator, had flown over from Paris with Pauline, and they had chosen the colors in which the rooms would be redone and had decided in what locations the paintings she intended to bring from Clouds, like van Gogh's

White Roses and the six Monets and the Degas and the Bonnard of Misia Sert, would be placed. Pauline, who was meticulous in all things, had over the years perfected her Foxcroft schoolgirl French so expertly that even her French friends, who were numerous, praised her on the faultlessness of her tenses and the elegance of her pronunciation. Jules, on the other hand, had no aptitude for languages other than his own. He spoke the kind of French that the French smile at, but no one ever smiled at Jules Mendelson in a condescending way, for he was too awesome in manner, posture, and wealth.

When Pauline had gone to China with her sister and brother-in-law, Louise and Lawford Ordano from Philadelphia, Jules took Flo to Paris, where he had business. They sat in different sections of the Concorde and never once spoke during the flight, because Jules knew several people on board. In Paris they stayed at different hotels. The Mendelsons always stayed at the Ritz on the Place Vendôme, and that is where Jules stayed. Flo stayed nearby at the Meurice. Jules lived in fear that one of Pauline's friends would see him with the young and beautiful redhead.

In the limousine leaving the Charles DeGaulle Airport for the city, Flo stared out the window of the car, overwhelmed to be in Paris. "Is that the Eiffel Tower?" she asked.

"No, that's the airport tower," Jules replied.

"Oh. It looks like the Eiffel Tower," she said.

"No, it doesn't," replied Jules. "It looks like the airport tower."

"To me, it does," insisted Flo.

He gave her a credit card to shop with and told her to go to any of the couturiers, except the one that Pauline went to, but he would not accompany her to the fashion showings, and she had no idea what clothes to order. A sympathetic vendeuse, sensing her confusion, advised her to try Chanel. "You can't go wrong at Chanel," she said. On the first day she went to Chanel, Flo ordered four outfits. On the second day, she ordered six more. When a fitter asked her questions about length and color, she turned to the vendeuse and said, "Just do whatever you think is right. I'm putting myself in your hands."

In two days she had spent nearly fifty thousand dollars. An accountant, who did not recognize her face or name, noticed the amount of her order and telephoned to check out her credit. He was told that there was a sufficient amount to cover whatever Miss March charged. He was told she had unlimited credit.

Each night they dined at her suite in the Meurice. It was there that Jules finally made love to Flo for the first time. He discovered that his sexual appetite was limitless. His requests for specific acts were not plebeian, and Flo denied him nothing. In the beautiful young woman who was once named Fleurette Houlihan, Jules Mendelson had found his perfect sexual partner.

If she was unhappy with the limited scope of her Parisian adventure, she did not let on. At that time in her life, just to have been in Paris at all was enough, even hidden from view. For her to be able to say, "When I was in Paris," when she was in conversation with her friends from the Viceroy Coffee Shop, or her hairdresser, Pooky, or even a stranger, thrilled her. Only the four-alarm fire that turned out to be no more than a burning mattress in the next suite brought the trip to a halt before its natural expiration.

For all his passion for Flo, Jules never once entertained the idea of a divorce from Pauline. Each was necessary to him, and it did not occur to him that he could not have both. He shut Flo out of every part of his life except his sex life and allowed her to have no life of her own that did not revolve around him. For this he paid her a great deal of money. If in the totally improbable event that the two women in Jules's life had ever met and compared notes, each would have found that the other woman had that part of Jules that she most wanted. The beautiful and elegant Pauline would have liked a more romantic relationship with her husband, instead of being kept on a pedestal by him, and the sexy and erotic Flo would have liked to receive guests and sit at the head of dinner tables full of famous and rich people.

Jules woke at three in the morning and could not go to sleep again. Pictures and thoughts of Flo March filled his mind. He yearned to be with her. He ached with desire for her. Turning, tossing, wanting to cry out her name, he pulled the bedclothes over him in such an abrupt fashion that he pulled them off Pauline, lying next to him.

"Jules, for heaven's sake, what is the matter with you?" asked Pauline, awakened now, and cold. She pulled the covers back.

"I'm sorry," he said. There was such a forlorn tone in his voice that it was impossible for Pauline to feel annoyance with him for ruining her sleep.

"Jules, is there something you want to discuss? Is it the conference? Has something gone wrong?"

"No, no. I'm sorry, Pauline. Go back to sleep. I'm all right. It's just—"

"Just what?"

"Nothing, really. Nothing." He began to snore lightly to show that he had fallen asleep again, which he had not. He had not meant to fall in love with Flo March. He had meant only to set her up and visit her when he felt like it, to give her gifts, to have her at his beck and call. It had never occurred to him that he might want to change his whole life and make her the dominant figure in it.

Flo's Tape #10

"*Jules once told me about this guy who had made him so mad he knocked over the statue of the Degas ballerina, which was one of the real treasures of his collection, but I never realized the guy he was talking about was Philip Quennell. If I had known that Jules had such a problem with him, I never would have gone to Philip's room at the Chateau Marmont on the night I decided to leave Jules, after he pretended he didn't know me when he ran into Madge White at that steak house in the Valley. I found out later that Philip had questioned Hector Paradiso's death right from the first day. After all, he was one of the few people who had actually seen the body and been in the house. He refused to accept Jules's suicide story, and then he called the publisher of the* Tribunal *to see why the paper hadn't covered the story, and that really pissed Jules off.*

"*Jules could be the nicest guy in the world, but he could be a bastard too. I actually never saw that side of him, but I know for a fact that it was Jules who got Philip Quennell fired off the picture he was writing for Casper Stieglitz.*"

11

"HOLLYWOOD IS VERY unforgiving of failure," said Casper Stieglitz, whose last four pictures had failed. He had taken to tutoring Philip Quennell in the thought process of the film industry. "It will forgive you, even overlook your forgeries, your embezzlements, and, occasionally, your murders, but it will not forgive you your failure."

Casper looked through his black-framed, dark-lensed glasses, which he never removed, and observed the restaurant quizzically. He shook his head and expressed disappointment with the noonday crowd. "I'm the biggest name here today," he said glumly. For a moment he wondered if Michel, the maître d', had put him into the wrong room, and he considered making a fuss and demanding a table in the rear room, where he had seen Marty Lesky, the head of Colossus Pictures, seated when he went to the men's room. Le Dôme, he had pointed out to Philip Quennell when he called to arrange the lunch date to discuss the progress of their project, catered to people in the film business and the music business, and it was a good place to be seen to get talk going about a new project.

Casper opened his large napkin with a flourish and placed it in his lap. Philip noticed that his toupee was in its mid-month phase, fifteen days from its last "haircut" and sixteen days away from its next, and he wore it that day in a ponytail, tied back with a rubber band. Ponytails tied back with rubber bands were the smart look of middle-aged producers and executives in the industry that season, and Casper, Philip noted, was always in the forefront of filmland fashion. His black velour Armani jacket was open over his T-shirt, on which was a reproduction of a section of Picasso's *Guernica*. Philip had to admit that the toupee was nearly undetectable. He wondered if Willard, the butler, who appeared to be fastidious, assisted in its placement on Casper's head each day and helped with the taping and gluing, or whatever had to be done.

Casper, still worried about his table, remained in a highly nervous state, constantly sneezing and blowing his nose. "I gotta take a leak," he said, and jumped up from the table. As he rose, he spotted Mona Berg. "Oh, look, Mona's here," he said to no one in particular, but his voice calmed considerably when he saw that someone as important as Mona Berg was in the same room that he was.

"Hi, Mona," he called over to her table.

"Hi, Casper," Mona Berg called back, making a gesture that indicated they should talk by telephone later in the day.

"Say hi to Philip Quennell," Casper said, as a way of introduction. "Mona Berg here is the top agent in this town."

Philip and Mona Berg called out hellos.

"And, Mona, Phil here wrote that hot hot hot book on Reza Bulbenkian, called *Takeover*. Did you read it?"

"I never have time to read anything but scripts, Casper. You know that," said Mona Berg. "But I'll make time to read your book, Phil. I promise. What did you think of my idea of Elliott Carver for the role of Bligh?" she asked.

Casper shook his head in an elaborate negative shake. "Elliott Carver has had six flops in a row. Elliott Carver is ready for a sitcom, on cable, not the lead in a Casper Stieglitz picture," he said.

"You're making a big mistake, Casper," insisted Mona, who was known to be relentless in the selling of her clients. "Marty Lesky ran the rough cut of *Career Girl* at his house last night, and said Elliott's fabulous. Even Sylvia Lesky thought he was great, and you know how hard to please Sylvia is."

"Excuse me a second. I gotta take a leak," said Casper.

"One of these days he's going to drop dead with all that stuff he's putting up his nose," said Mona.

Philip, who agreed, did not answer.

"I hear you're writing the drug documentary."

"Yes."

"Thankless task."

"I'm finding that out."

"If you don't go with actual cops, and do actors playing cops, which always works better, call me. I'd like you to meet Elliott Carver."

"Sure thing, but that will be up to Casper."

"Here's my lunch date, the putz. You almost kept me waiting, Joel," she said, looking at her watch. There was admonition in her voice.

"Sorry, Mona," said Joel, sitting down in the booth.

"I hate to be kept waiting, Joel."

"I said I was sorry, Mona. I got held up in traffic."

"What was your name?" she called over to Philip.

"Quennell. Philip Quennell."

"Joel Zircon, Philip Quennell."

"Didn't I see you at Hector Paradiso's funeral?" asked Joel. "You're the guy who gave his handkerchief to Flo March, right?"

"You gotta do something about the way you dress, Phil," said Casper Stieglitz, when he returned to the table. Philip had started to notice that each time Casper returned from one of his numerous trips to the bathroom, he had a new train of thought, about which he was momentarily passionate.

"What's wrong with the way I dress?" asked Philip.

"It's not the right look for out here," said Casper. "Blue blazer, gray flannels, Brooks shirt. Gimme a break. That look went out years ago. And you gotta lose the polka dot ties. You look like a history teacher, not a screenwriter. All you need is a fucking pipe to complete the picture. Especially for this kind of documentary we're doing. The narcs won't talk to you dressed like that."

"I thought you said you loved what I'd written so far."

"I do. I do."

"So the narcs *are* talking to me, blue blazer, gray flannels, Brooks shirt, polka dot tie, and all."

"I mean, the look is wrong for out here, that's all I'm saying."

"Look, Casper. I don't like the way *you* dress. Black velour was never very high on my list, but it's none of my business how you dress, so I don't mention it, just like it's none of your business how I dress. So you dress your way. I'll dress my way. Okay?"

"Okay, okay. Don't get hot under the collar. I'm just trying to explain California to you, that's all," said Casper.

"I'm just here in California temporarily," replied Philip.

Casper snapped his fingers. "Listen, you just gave me an idea. All of a sudden I like the way you dress. Including the polka dot ties. I got a favor to ask you."

"About the picture?"

"No, about coming to dinner a week from Sunday night."

"Oh, thanks, I can't. I'm going to be at my girlfriend's ranch outside of Solvang," said Philip.

"So? Come back early."

"Why?"

"I'm having some swells to dinner, and it occurred to me you'd fit in perfectly. I never know what to talk to people like that about."

"Who are you having?"

"Arnie Zwillman."

"Who's Arnie Zwillman?"

"He's the man who burned down the Vegas Seraglio for the insurance money."

"That's your idea of a swell?"

"No, he's no swell. The other people are swells."

"Who are the other people?"

"Jules and Pauline Mendelson."

"Jules and Pauline Mendelson are coming to your house for dinner?" asked Philip, not making any attempt to hide the astonishment in his voice.

"Do you know them?"

"Please tell me you're not planning on having Ina Rae and Darlene at the same dinner."

Casper laughed. "Did I tell you about the T-shirt Ina Rae was wearing last night?"

"No."

"It said 'Warning, I Scream When I Come.' Laugh, I thought I'd bust a gut. That girl is a riot."

"That should strike Pauline Mendelson as really funny," said Philip.

"I don't think Ina Rae's right for this group," said Casper, thinking over what Philip had said. "I could have her in for the movie later, but skip the dinner part. I'll need another girl to fill out the table. What about that girl you're seeing. What's her name?"

"Camilla Ebury."

"Actress, model, dancer, what?"

"None of the above."

"Bring her."

"Sunday nights she spends with her daughter. They have dinner together at the Los Angeles Country Club. A family ritual."

"Tell her I'm running a picture."

"She wouldn't care."

Casper snapped his fingers again. "Hortense Madden. That's who I'll get. She'll class it up."

"Who's Hortense Madden?"

"The literary critic for *Mulholland.*"

"For heaven's sake."

"You know her?"

"No, I don't know her. She panned my book on Reza Bulbenkian."

"That's Hortense for you. She pans everything that's popular."

"What is the point of this evening, Casper?" asked Philip.

"Arnie Zwillman wants to meet Jules Mendelson, that's all I know, and he asked me to set it up."

Philip thought for a moment. "Okay, I'll come," he said.

"That was sweet of you to take Bunty to the movies this afternoon," said Camilla.

"She's a great kid," said Philip.

"She adores you. She told me she thinks you're handsome," said Camilla.

"I don't suppose I could talk you into coming with me to Casper Stieglitz's house for dinner a week from Sunday," said Philip.

"Not unless I can bring Bunty," said Camilla.

"I somehow don't think Bunty is right for an evening at Casper's."

"That's what I figured," said Camilla. They both laughed. "Although I'd love to see his wig collection. Or Ina Rae. I don't know which fascinates me more."

"The Mendelsons are going."

"The Mendelsons are going to Casper Stieglitz's?" asked Camilla. "I don't believe that for a minute."

"That's what Casper said at lunch today."

"Must be some business something or other," said Camilla, shaking her head. "I'll make you a bet."

"What?"

"They'll back out at the last minute. I know Pauline."

After Paris, where they had become lovers, Jules Mendelson, in the throes of his passion, decided to lease a house for Flo to ensure their privacy. She stopped working at the Viceroy Coffee Shop, moved out of her apartment in the Silverlake district, and lived temporarily in the Sunset Marquis Hotel in West Hollywood. Jules's first intention was to take an apartment in a high-rise condominium on Sunset Boulevard, but when looking there, using an assumed name, he ran into Marty Lesky, the head of Colossus Pictures, in the elevator. The two well-known men nodded and chatted in a friendly manner. He later found out from the superintendent that Marty Lesky had an apartment in the building. Judging from Marty's nervous attitude in the elevator, and Jules's certain knowledge that Marty and Sylvia Lesky maintained one of the largest estates in Bel Air, he suspected that Marty kept a young lady there who was not his wife. Jules did not return.

"I saw a very nice house in Bel Air today," said Flo. It thrilled her to be looking at houses in what she referred to as the ritziest parts of town. House hunting was a new adventure that she enjoyed enormously. Jules leased her a bright red Mercedes, and she had taken to driving around for hours, discovering the expensive areas of Beverly Hills and Holmby Hills and Bel Air that she had never seen before, in the company of a real estate agent called Elaine, who used to be an actress and knew the history of every house. "That's where Lana Turner's daughter killed Johnny Stompanato," she said about one house. "Judy Garland took an overdose in that house," she said about another. Or, "Jack and Anjelica used to live there." Flo knew she meant Jack Nicholson and Anjelica Huston, and the information excited her.

"Where?" asked Jules.

"Up Stone Canyon, past the Bel Air Hotel. Elaine says it used to belong to one of Amos Swank's ex-wives."

"Bel Air? Oh, no, no," said Jules, shaking his head at the idea. "Not Bel Air."

Flo had come to know that whenever Jules said "Oh, no, no" to one of her requests, and shook his head at the same time, it meant that she had inadvertently encroached on his main life, the life that he shared with Pauline. For Jules, a house in Bel Air, where so many of the Mendelsons' friends lived, posed a danger in that he ran the risk of passing people he knew on the narrow roads of the exclusive enclave. Being ever protective of that part of his life, he could imagine one of Pauline's friends, specifically Rose Cliveden, saying to Pauline, "I saw Jules in Bel Air this afternoon." "This afternoon? I can't imagine what Jules could have been doing in Bel Air this afternoon," he imagined Pauline answering. "Up Stone Canyon, past the hotel," Rose, the informer, would continue. "For heaven's sake," Pauline would answer.

"I think it would be better if you looked off one of the main canyons, like Benedict or Coldwater," Jules said to Flo. Benedict and Coldwater canyons were areas where it was less likely that he would encounter the kind of people with whom he and his wife dined most evenings.

"That's a nice area," said Flo, agreeing. She reeled off the names of several television stars who had homes in the canyons.

Finally Flo found a perfect house, hidden from view by overgrown shrubbery, on a small street off Coldwater Canyon called Azelia Way. Elaine said that it was owned by Trent Muldoon, a television star whose series had been canceled and who had overextended himself in the four years of his semi-stardom. "Spend, spend, spend, and now he's broke, broke, broke," said Elaine. "Let it be a cautionary tale."

"This was Trent Muldoon's house, really?" asked Flo, delighted.

"His wife's taking him to the cleaners in the divorce, and he needs to get out from under," said Elaine.

Flo was ecstatic that she finally had a house of her own, with a swimming pool, as well as a Beverly Hills address and a 90210 zip code and a 274 prefix to her telephone number. She could hardly contain herself. When she confessed to Jules that she found Trent Muldoon's mounted cattle skulls and western furniture depressing, he allowed her to put most of Trent's furniture, which came with the lease, into storage and redecorate the house herself.

For a time she was never happier, but she was very lonely. Sometimes she felt herself to be no more than a receptacle for the fulfillment of his desires, and she drank a little wine in the afternoons, and very often she smoked marijuana cigarettes.

"Hello?"

"I'm on my way over."

"Now?"

"Be nude when you open the door."

As requested, she was nude when she opened the door.

"Drink?" she asked.

"No." He stared at her body hungrily and ripped off his tie and shirt. "Let's go in the bedroom."

There was an absence of endearments in his lovemaking. There was no fondling, and very little kissing. He wanted only to satisfy his imperious urge to be within her lovely body, and to stay within her as long as possible. His lust for her seemed insatiable. At that time he in no way feared that she would become an important person in his life. He thought of her as merely an outlet for his increasingly demanding sexual urges. For Jules, Flo was bracketed in that area of his life only. He was an art collector and an aficionado of splendid living, and her taste was too unrefined for him to experience feelings of love. There were things about her that drove him mad. She pronounced sandwich "samich," as if it rhymed with "damage." She moved her lips when she read. She drank soft drinks out of the can. She was uninformed on important matters.

He had never intended to play Pygmalion to her Galatea, but he discovered that when he did correct her, if something she did or said irritated him sufficiently, she was never offended. She even welcomed his corrections, and she never made the same mistake again. At first it amused him that she was so quick to act upon his corrections and suggestions. Then he began to do it in earnest. Her voice improved. Her carriage improved. Her walk improved. Within himself, he was aware that the beautiful young woman was wasted living such a hidden life, but he did not want to change that. A simple call to Marty Lesky at Colossus Pictures would have made it possible for Flo to get a small part in one of the many television series at the studio, or a reading for a film, or any of the things she might have done. And Marty Lesky would have complied. It was the sort of favor that rich men with mistresses did for each other, but he could not bring himself to make the call that might have satisfied Flo's yearnings to be somebody. He liked her there for him.

After their lovemaking, when he was spent and satisfied, he began talking to her in a way that he talked to very few people in his life: about his business, about the eventual disposition of his art collection, about an apartment in Brussels on the Avenue Hamoir that he had his eye on for her, when he would have to move there for a year during the statehood of Europe. The prospect of living in Brussels for a year thrilled her. Then, invariably, he would look at his watch and say, "I have to get out of here," and rush from her bed and dress and leave to get home in time to have his afternoon glass of wine with Pauline before they dressed for dinner and went out to whatever party they were attending that evening. Often, on the way home from her house, he would call her on the car telephone.

"What are you doing?"

"You mean since you came in me the third time eleven minutes ago?" she replied one day, exasperated. She knew he didn't like her to be vulgar, except when they were making love, and she used it in retaliation when she felt that he was overcrowding her. Hearing his disapproving silence, she relented. "I'm lying here on my brand-new sets of Porthault sheets that you bought me in Paris, exhausted from your lovemaking, Jules, drinking a glass of wine from the Bresciani auction that you brought over to my house. That's what I'm doing." She didn't tell him that she was also smoking a joint. She knew he wouldn't have approved of that. He told her once he had no patience with people who took drugs.

In time Flo became stultified by the persistency of Jules's demanding love in their relationship. He wanted her to be there always for him, in case he should drop in on her unexpectedly, or telephone her, which he sometimes did as often as ten times a day, or more. A busy telephone line could send him into a tantrum. He imagined that there were other men in her life, even though he knew there weren't. She drank more wine. She smoked more marijuana. Several times she threatened to pull away from him, but such threats did not unnerve Jules. There was no doubt in his mind that he was the most exciting thing that had ever happened in Flo March's life. He knew that Flo knew that too. He understood totally the power of money. How gorgeous it was. How easy it was to get used to. How terrifying it was to imagine life without it once one had become used to it.

Except in the evenings, when he drove Pauline to parties, Jules stopped driving his blue Bentley, because he felt that someone might recognize it when he drove each afternoon to Flo's house on Azelia Way. He leased himself an expensive but nondescript Cadillac with darkened windows that he could see out of but passers-by could not see into. One night when Pauline was in New York for a party, he drove Flo back to her old apartment in the obscure neighborhood—at least obscure to Jules Mendelson—known as the Silverlake district, where she had resided before the recent good fortune that had changed the economic circumstances of her life. She went to pick up some mail that her former landlady told her was there. When they stopped at a red light on Melrose Avenue, Flo looked out the window of Jules's car at a bag lady on the street, making her preparations for the night. Terror seized her.

"She reminds me of my mother," said Flo.

"Who?" asked Jules.

"Her." Flo pointed at the bag lady. "I bet that lady was pretty at one time, like my mother was."

Jules nodded.

"My mother died in a fire in a welfare hotel."

"You told me that in Paris," said Jules.

"You're going to take care of me, aren't you, Jules? I can't die poor like my mother. I just can't."

"I *am* taking care of you."

"No, I mean after."

"After what?"

"Nothing."

He knew what she meant, but he could not bear to think of what she meant. They drove on in silence.

Each morning without fail Philip Quennell went to the AA meeting at the log cabin on Robertson Boulevard. He sat reading the newspaper before the meeting started and rarely mixed in conversation with the other members of the fellowship.

A bright red fingernail tapped on the sports page of the *Los Angeles Tribunal* that he was reading one morning. "Think McEnroe will ever make a comeback?" asked Flo.

"Hi, Flo," he said.

"Hi, Phil," she answered. She opened her bag and took out the handkerchief he had handed to her at Hector Paradiso's funeral. It had been laundered and ironed. "Thanks for the loan," she said.

"That was some funeral," he said, taking it.

"Did you see Loretta Young?" she asked. "I hope I look that good when I'm her age."

Philip smiled.

"Who would have thought we would both be attending the same fashionable funeral so soon after meeting?" asked Flo. "I suppose you were at Rose Cliveden's lunch party at the Los Angeles Country Club afterwards."

"No, I wasn't."

"I read about it in Cyril Rathbone's column in *Mulholland*," said Flo. "Poor Rose."

"Why poor Rose?"

"You didn't hear? She fell down and broke her leg at her lunch party. She tripped over Hector's dog, Astrid."

"Did you read that in Cyril Rathbone's column too?"

"That's where I get all my information," said Flo.

After the meeting, when they were leaving, Philip said to Flo, "What was the name of that club you mentioned to me where Hector Paradiso went on the night he committed suicide?"

"I didn't hear you say Hector committed suicide, did I?"

"It seems to be the popular theory."

"I'm surprised you fell for that line, a smart guy like you. Miss Garbo's is the name of the club. Some of the guys who go there just call it Garbo's."

"Where is it?" asked Philip.

"On a street called Astopovo, between Santa Monica Boulevard and Melrose. Somehow I wouldn't have thought it was your kind of hangout."

"You wouldn't want to go there with me, would you? To Miss Garbo's? I'd like to find out who Hector left with that night."

"I'd like to, Phil, but I can't."

"Why not?"

"I told you I was spoken for."

"Listen, I'm not coming on to you, I swear. I meant as pals only. I didn't want to go there alone."

"But I've got a jealous fella. He calls me twenty times a day to keep tabs on me."

"A rejection, huh?"

"Sorry, Phil."

"Actually, it's Philip, not Phil. I really don't like to be called Phil."

"Oh, sorry. Philip. Sounds classier."

"You're sure you won't come?"

"Pretty girls like me they definitely do not want at Miss Garbo's after midnight. But I'll certainly want to hear what you find out. Ask for Manning Einsdorf. He's the one who makes the arrangements."

"So I hear."

"And Phil?"

Philip turned to look at her.

She snapped her fingers. "I mean Philip. A cute guy like you, you better put a padlock on your fly," said Flo.

That day Philip Quennell placed a call to Sandy Pond, the publisher of the *Los Angeles Tribunal.*

"Will Mr. Pond know what this is in reference to?" asked Sandy Pond's secretary after Philip had identified himself.

"Tell him I am the author of the book called *Takeover,* about Reza Bulbenkian," replied Philip.

"Would you care to tell me what it is you're calling Mr. Pond about?" asked the secretary.

"I wouldn't, no," replied Philip.

"It is customary for me to ask. Mr. Pond is extremely busy."

"I understand."

"Then you won't tell me?"

"No. You have only to ask him and to identify me. Then it's up to Mr. Pond to decide whether he will speak to me, isn't it?"

There was an icy silence. "Just a moment," she said.

In an instant Sandy Pond picked up the telephone. "I certainly enjoyed your book, Mr. Quennell," he said. "Is it true that Reza Bulbenkian threatened to break your legs? That's what we heard."

Philip laughed. "There was something like that, yes."

"I understand from my wife that you're seeing our great friend Camilla Ebury," said Sandy Pond.

"Yes." Philip did not elaborate.

"How can I help you?" asked Sandy Pond.

"I am very curious that your paper hasn't covered the murder of Hector Paradiso," said Philip.

There was a pause. "Murder? What murder?" replied Sandy Pond.

"Death, then," said Philip.

Sandy Pond did not speak.

"You did know Hector Paradiso, did you not?"

"I did, yes. I was a pallbearer at his funeral. A charming man. A great friend of my wife's. She always said he was the best dancer in Los Angeles. It's all so sad, so terribly sad."

"He was shot five times, Mr. Pond," said Philip. "I was there at the house a few hours afterwards, with Camilla Ebury. I identified his body for the police."

"But it was a suicide, Mr. Quennell. I have seen the autopsy report."

"Don't you find it odd that someone could shoot himself five times?" asked Philip.

"Apparently he was deeply depressed. The autopsy report goes on to say that he was a poor shot. I will be happy to have my secretary send a copy of it on to you," said Sandy Pond. His tone of voice indicated that he wished to terminate the conversation.

"But don't you think even that is a story worth covering, Mr. Pond?"

"Would you explain yourself?"

"A prominent man in the city, who moves in the highest social circles, dines and dances at the home of the Jules Mendelsons, and then commits suicide by shooting himself five times in the torso. Where I come from, that's a story. Add to that that he was a member of a Land Grant family and has a boulevard named after him, and that's a front-page story."

"Is that all, Mr. Quennell?"

"I believe that, for some reason I do not understand, there is a cover-up going on, and that your newspaper is a party to that cover-up."

"Ludicrous, and libelous," said Sandy Pond. All trace of pleasantness had vanished from his voice.

Philip, fearing that Sandy Pond would hang up on him, began to speak very quickly. "Isn't it a fact that Jules Mendelson went to see you on the morning that Hector Paradiso was murdered? I beg your pardon, on the morning that Hector Paradiso committed suicide."

"Good-bye, Mr. Quennell."

That evening at a dinner party at the home of Ralph and Madge White in Hancock Park, Sandy Pond motioned to Jules Mendelson to follow him onto the lanai after dinner, when the other guests were having coffee in the living room.

"Have you ever heard of someone called Philip Quennell?" he asked. "He wrote that book on your friend Bulbenkian."

"Yes, I have. He's seeing Camilla. Why?" asked Jules.

"I had a most upsetting call from him this afternoon."

That same night, in a different part of the city, Miss Garbo's was mobbed. Miss Garbo's was mobbed every night. Marvene McQueen, the chanteuse, was in the middle of her set.

"You are not my first love. I've known other men," she sang.

She stared straight up into the spotlight. Her lips puckered over her protruding teeth. Tears filled her eye-shadowed eyes as she moaned out her signature number. One of the shoulder straps of her black evening dress dropped down on her arm. She allowed her hair to fall over one eye, like a forties film star. It was a wasted performance. No one in the crowded bar paid the slightest bit of attention to her.

"Zane," called out Manning Einsdorf to the bartender. Manning sat on a high stool where he could survey the entire room. "Don't serve any more drinks to Mr. Coughlin and guest at table twenty-six. They've had enough. And tell the parking boy to call a cab and not let him drive home either. I'm not going to have the West Hollywood police closing down my place because of a couple of drunks."

"Calm down, calm down, Manning," said Zane. "It's all taken care of."

"Miss Einsdorf is very jumpy lately," said Joel Zircon, who was standing at the bar listening to the exchange.

"Miss Einsdorf has been very jumpy ever since you-know-who left here with you-know-who and ended up with five bullets in him. She bites my head off ten times a night," said Zane.

Philip Quennell walked into the club. For several minutes he was unnoticed in the packed and noisy room. Making his way through the crowd, he found himself a space at the bar by standing sideways. Joel Zircon, who had been introduced to Philip at Le Dôme by Mona Berg, looked down the bar at him in surprise and then stared at him through the blue mirrored wall behind the liquor bottles. Philip, waiting to be served, concentrated on Marvene McQueen's set.

"You better go now, because I like you much too much, you better go now," she sang.

"Beer?" asked Zane, when he found time to approach Philip.

"Soda water," answered Philip.

"Lemon? Lime?" asked Zane.

"Lemon."

Zane filled the glass from a rubber tube attached to a spigot and placed it in front of Philip.

"Who's the singer?" asked Philip.

"Marvene McSomebody," replied Zane.

"Drag queen?"

"No, real girl."

"Buckteeth."

"You can say that again."

"I'm looking for someone called Manning Einsdorf," said Philip. He leaned forward on the bar toward Zane so that he would not have to raise his voice.

Zane looked at Philip. "He's the fella sitting on the high stool at the end of the bar. He's pretty busy tonight. Is he expecting you?"

"No."

"Who shall I tell him wants to see him?"

"I'll tell him myself," said Philip. He pulled out from his position at the bar and walked down to where Manning Einsdorf was surveying the activity in his club.

"Zane!" hissed Joel Zircon. When Zane turned around, Joel signaled for him to come over to where he was standing at the bar. "What did that guy want?"

"Asked for Manning. Who is he? Doesn't look like our crowd, if you know what I mean," said Zane. "But you never know these days."

"No, no. Definitely not our crowd. He's writing a documentary for Casper Stieglitz so Casper won't have to go to jail for being caught with ten pounds of cocaine," said Joel. "Mona Berg told me all about it. What the fuck do you suppose he's doing here?"

"Who?" asked Manning Einsdorf, leaning down from his high stool and putting his hand to his ear.

Philip repeated the name. "Lonny."

"I never heard of such a person," said Manning.

"Blond, handsome, apparently."

"That could be any of a couple of hundred guys who come in here nightly."

"The name means nothing to you?"

"That's right."

"I see," said Philip. "Did you know Hector Paradiso?"

"I didn't, no," replied Manning Einsdorf. He turned away and called out to the bartender. "Zane, they need drinks at table twenty-two. And send Marvene a glass of champagne. Tell her she was terrific tonight. Tell her not to forget 'Moanin' Low' in the next set."

Philip, dismissed, remained. "You say you didn't know Hector Paradiso?" he asked.

"I already told you I didn't."

"But you went to his funeral."

"Who said I went to his funeral?"

"No one said."

"So, where did you get such an idea?"

"I sat in the row behind you. You were with Joel Zircon, the agent who works with Mona Berg, and Willard, Casper Stieglitz's butler."

Manning Einsdorf began to feel uncomfortable.

"Well, of course, I knew Hector slightly," said Manning. "I mean, everyone knew Hector Paradiso, God rest his soul, but he wasn't a close friend."

"I understand he was here in your club on the night he was murdered."

"He wasn't murdered."

"I beg your pardon. I understand he was here in your club on the night he committed suicide."

"No. I don't recall that he was."

"Think."

"Look around you. The place is packed like this every night. I can't remember everyone who comes in here. Miss Garbo's wasn't Hector's sort of place, you know. Hector was a high society sort of person."

Philip persisted. "He came here that night in a dinner jacket straight from a party at Pauline Mendelson's. People tell me he even described to you what Pauline was wearing that night."

"I don't remember any of that," said Manning.

"And you don't remember his leaving with a young blond man called Lonny?"

"How many times have I got to tell you that I never heard of anyone called Lonny, and I didn't see Hector in here that night?"

"Thanks."

"Stick around. My new singer's going to go on again."

"I heard enough of your singer."

In the parking lot, Philip Quennell handed the parking boy his ticket. "Beige Le Sabre," he said.

A back door of the club opened. Zane stuck his head out and, seeing Philip, whistled between his fingers. When Philip turned around to respond to the whistle, Zane signaled with his head for him to come over.

"I'm on a piss break. I gotta talk quick," he said.

"Your boss does not exactly dwell in the palace of truth," said Philip.

"No, no. Truth was never Manning's long suit," replied Zane.

"What's up?" asked Philip.

Zane looked behind him into the club before he spoke. "You're looking for Lonny?"

"Yes, I'm looking for Lonny, and I don't even know Lonny's last name."

"Edge. His name is Lonny Edge. Lives on Cahuenga Boulevard—7204¼ Cahuenga—near Ivar. I don't know the phone number, and he's unlisted, but he left here with Hector about two-thirty that night."

"What's your name?" asked Philip.

"Zane."

"Thanks, Zane. How come you're telling me this? Your boss could fire you."

"Hector Paradiso was a good guy to me, and I don't buy this suicide story. There was no way he was on his way to committing suicide the last night he was in here. No way. Someone's covering up his murder."

Philip nodded. "That's exactly what's happening. What's this Lonny Edge like?"

"You'll see for yourself. He's what's known in the trade as a famous fornicator. Men, women, you name it. He doesn't care if the price is right. Rich guys fly him to New York or Hawaii for the weekend. Like that. He does scenes, in groups, if you know what I mean. And he's a minor porn star in video. Listen, I gotta get back. Miss Einsdorf will have a shit fit. She's very jumpy lately."

"Thanks, Zane."

"You never talked to me, right?"

"Never saw you before, Zane."

As Philip got into his car, he noticed Marvene McQueen leaving the club by the same door that Zane had used. She was wearing dark glasses, as if she were a film star. She walked across the parking lot to an old Honda and got in.

Flo's Tape #11

"The trouble is, you can't talk to a Chanel suit. Except for Glyceria, who was Faye Converse's maid, and Pooky, who did my hair, and, I suppose, Nellie Potts, who was the decorator, I never had anybody to talk to. Sometimes I'd call up Curly, who was the manager of the Viceroy Coffee Shop, and we'd laugh a little like old times. Actually, I bought my grass from Curly, if the truth be known.

"One day I realized, between the grass and the white wine from the Bresciani auction that Jules insisted on my having on hand for him always, I was stoned almost every afternoon. When I was stoned, I didn't mind so much having no one to talk to. But my skin began looking not so hot, and, without bragging or anything, I happen to have beautiful skin. Everybody tells me that. So I just stopped both the wine and the grass. It was tough, though. Pooky, the hairdresser, who used to do a lot of coke, told me about AA. I mentioned it to Jules. He freaked out. He hated things like that. 'You can't be seen in there,' he said. Pooky told me about the early morning meeting in the log cabin on Robertson Boulevard at seven A.M. From my waitress days, I was used to getting up at that time anyway. That's where I met Philip Quennell."

12

S OMEHOW—NO ONE actually saw it happen, as it happened in the ladies'
room—Rose Cliveden fell down and broke her leg at the Los Angeles
Country Club during the luncheon she gave following Hector Paradiso's
funeral. Madge White swore Rose tripped over Astrid, Hector's little dog,
named after the ice skating star he had once been engaged to decades before.
He had left Astrid to Rose in his will, although she did not know the dog had
been left to her at the time it tripped her, if, indeed, it did trip her. With Rose,
when she had her many mishaps, nothing was ever quite crystal clear.

Rose, who loved dogs, would not have a word said against Astrid as the
cause of her fractured leg. Not only was the creature her final remembrance
from Hector, but, as Rose announced to one and all, she gave great sums each
year to the animal shelter. Rose blamed her fall on Clint, the bartender at the
Club, whom she claimed made the Bloody Marys entirely too strong, especially
for a funeral lunch. She told Madge White she intended doing something
about it, like making a complaint to the house committee about Clint. Rose
had had it in for Clint ever since it had been repeated to her that he had called
her Old Rosie, during a previous mishap, when she dislocated her shoulder,
and he had carried her to the ambulance.

When Madge White repeated the story to Pauline Mendelson, Pauline
asked, "Why in the world would Rose have had the dog at her lunch at the Los
Angeles Country Club in the first place?"

"Wearing a black mourning bow, if you please," said Madge. Pauline
laughed. Like all Rose Cliveden's friends, Pauline was both amused and exasperated by Rose's behavior.

"That Astrid is a mean little dog," said Pauline. "You wouldn't believe the
way she attacked Kippie after Camilla brought her up here to give to Rose
right after Hector died. None of us could believe it. She made a beeline for him
when he came up from the tennis court and bit off the tip of his forefinger,
right up to here. There was blood everywhere."

Then Pauline remembered that Madge White would have no sympathy for
Kippie, no matter how much of his forefinger Astrid had bitten off. Although
Madge was one of her best friends, she never mentioned Kippie to her, ever
since, years earlier, when they were both fourteen, Kippie had gotten Madge's
daughter, little Madgie, pregnant.

"Anyway," said Madge, changing the subject, "Rose gave the dog away already."

"No!"

"She gave it to Faye Converse. Faye always takes in stray dogs."

Pauline returned the conversation to Rose—poor Rose, as they had all started to call her—whose drinking had begun to worry all her friends. "She's getting worse and worse," said Pauline.

Of course, Rose was in deep mourning for her lifelong friend, but her friends knew that if Hector hadn't died, there would have been another reason for her to give as an excuse for her self-indulgence with spirits. Even before Hector died, Rose had said to Pauline, "Oh, what difference does it make if I smoke too much, or drink too much? I'm a sixty-year-old woman, and no gentleman wants to fuck me anymore."

"Oh, Rose," Pauline had said at the time, not knowing how to deal with the statement. Rose, who liked men, constantly bragged that she had once been to bed with President Kennedy, in the White House, in the Lincoln Bedroom, but some of her friends didn't believe her. She had been married three times and divorced three times. With Rose's husbands, one day they just weren't there anymore. There was never a scandal, and never a blow-up, at least publicly. "Where's Bakie?" "Where's Ozzie?" "Where's Fiske?" people had asked about her first, second, and third husbands, after she turned up at several parties alone, and she always answered, quite calmly, "Out of town." And then people would hear, not long after, that a quiet and quick divorce had taken place, usually in a Caribbean country. The things that made divorces long and drawn-out affairs, custody and alimony, never figured in Rose's divorces, because in each case the money was hers to begin with, and her only child, a daughter from her first marriage, whom some people say had had a lobotomy, was in what Rose always referred to as "a home."

She had taken to talking endlessly on the telephone, recounting every detail of every lunch and dinner party she attended, and it was impossible to get rid of her, no matter how hard her listener tried to hang up.

"There I was seated between two divine men. Of course, they were pansies, but at my age, what does it matter? *Such* good conversation! I mean, I'm certainly no intellectual, although I do like to read a good book and see a good play, and these two were divine, absolutely divine, so full of fun and mischief. Oh, how we laughed and laughed."

"I must go, Rose," said Pauline, on the other end of the line, but Rose seemed not to hear.

"Madge White was there," Rose continued. "Poor Madge, in that same dark blue polka dot dress. Don't you hate that dress? I think I can't look at it again. Do you think she'd be hurt if I sent her over some of my old clothes? She could have them let out. She's putting on weight, have you noticed?"

"Rose, darling, I must go, really. Jules has come home," said Pauline, but Rose seemed not to hear. Pauline blew a kiss to Jules, pointed to the telephone, mouthed the word "Rose," and rolled her eyes. Jules smiled. He walked to the bar table that had been set up by Dudley and poured two glasses of wine. It was their time of day to be together.

"Poor as church mice, the Whites," said Rose. "But Madge never lets on, that's what I like about her. Works like a slave in her real estate office and completely supports that husband of hers, who could never make a nickel. He's a big load of snow, Ralph White, if you ask me. The only deduction I could take on my income tax last year was on one of his stock tips. And that little Madgie's such a tramp, you know. Lives with who knows what. A Korean, or something."

"Rose, I'm going to hang up now," said Pauline. Jules placed Pauline's glass on the table beside her. "Jules is here. Yes, I will. I'll tell him. And he sends his love to you. Good-bye, Rose. Good-*bye,* Rose." She hung up. "Oh, God!" she said. "Spare me." She took Jules's hand and kissed it. The unmistakable aroma of another woman's most secret scent was on his fingers. Stunned, she looked up at her husband, as if he had slapped her.

Jules, unaware, asked, "How's old Rosie?"

"Oh, fine, drunk, same as ever," answered Pauline. "Let's not talk about Rose. I've had enough of Rose. She broke her leg at her lunch after Hector's funeral. Aren't you glad we didn't go?" She rose unsteadily from her chair, fearing that she was going to be sick, or faint.

"Look at the colors of the sunset, Pauline," said Jules.

"Fuck the sunset," said Pauline. Her wineglass dropped from her hand and smashed on the terrazzo floor of their sunset room. Jules, who had never heard Pauline use the word she had just used in the twenty-two years he had been married to her, stared at his wife, uncomprehending, as she ran out of the room.

When Philip Quennell told Camilla Ebury that he had been to a club called Miss Garbo's and learned the name of a young man with whom Hector Paradiso left the club on the night of his death, she became silent and aloof. They were sitting in the library of her house in Bel Air. She moved away from him on the sofa. Then she picked up the remote control and flicked off the television set that had been on in the background.

"How would you even know of a place called Miss Garbo's?" she asked, finally. "I've lived here all my life and never heard of it."

"Casper Stieglitz's butler told me," said Philip. "He was there the same night and saw Hector."

"Wouldn't you know it would be somebody's butler who would have a story like that," said Camilla.

"But it's true," said Philip.

"What kind of a place is Miss Garbo's?" she asked.

"Where rich older men meet young men for hire."

"I just do not believe such a story," said Camilla, shaking her head emphatically.

"You didn't exactly think your uncle Hector was girl crazy, did you?"

"That's not funny, Philip."

"What is it you're afraid of, Camilla? That they're not going to let your daughter come out at the Las Madrinas debutante ball in ten years because her great-uncle died in a gay murder?"

"What's that tacky expression I've heard you use? Smartass, is that it? Well, don't be a smartass with me, Philip," said Camilla.

"I'm not being a smartass, Camilla, and I'm sorry if that's the way I'm coming off, but let's be practical."

"All right, let's be practical. Why do you care so damn much?" she asked. "My uncle's death has nothing whatever to do with you. You didn't even know him."

"Why do you care so damn little?" replied Philip.

Philip could see that his question had made her angry. Her face turned red, and her voice, when she spoke again, had a harsh tone that he had never heard before. "I don't care so little," she said, measuring each word. "We have been through this and through this. My uncle committed suicide."

"No, he didn't."

Camilla looked at Philip for a long time before she spoke. "I understand you called Sandy Pond at the *Tribunal*. Sandy told Jules you'd called him. They seemed to think you were acting in my behalf, so they sent me over the autopsy report. I am satisfied. There is nothing mysterious to me about my uncle's death. Now I wish you would stop minding my business and mind your own damn business."

"One thing I've noticed about your group, when the chips are down you people all stick together."

Camilla, stung, rose from the sofa where she had been seated. "I think you should get out of my house," she said.

"Ah, the classic retort of the rich girl," replied Philip. "Agree with me or get out. Well, I am getting out, Mrs. Ebury."

Camilla was unused to people who were not awed by her wealth. From the beginning, Philip had been indifferent to her money, and it had been refreshing for her. She did not want him to leave, but she could not bring herself to say it. Orin, her late husband, who was the father of her child, always did everything she wanted him to do, like a bought-and-paid-for-husband should do, but Philip was different. She knew he would leave her if she did not stop him, because he was in no way dependent on her. But she remained silent and walked out of the library and started up the stairs to her bedroom above.

Philip followed her to the hall and looked up at her as she ascended the stairs. "Jules Mendelson is trying to tell us that black is white, and because he is so rich and apparently so powerful, most people—but not me—seem to be believing him, at least publicly. I just happen to be a nonbeliever in a social system where someone has the power to pick up a telephone and call a newspaper and say, 'Don't print this story,' and then call the police and say, 'Don't solve this murder.' I realize that the people in your set don't have a problem with that, but I do."

Camilla turned where she stood on a step near the top of the stairs, torn between the standards of her group and the strong feelings she had developed for the man who was walking out on her. "I am at heart a nonbeliever in those things too," she said.

"Good. Then act on them. So long, Camilla. You know my phone number."

"Don't you have things to pack?" she asked, wanting to detain him.

"One of the nice things about disposable razors is that there's nothing to pack when you break up with your girlfriend," he said. He walked out the front door and closed it behind him.

*   *   *

7204¼ Cahuenga Boulevard, the home of Lonny Edge, was not an easy place to find. Bettye, Casper Stieglitz's secretary, thinking the address on Cahuenga had something to do with the documentary Philip was writing for Casper on the proliferation of drugs in the film industry, typed out the instructions on how to find the place on one of Casper's memo pads. Philip drove up Highland Avenue near the Hollywood Bowl and turned right on a small street called Odin. He went under an overpass that led onto Cahuenga Boulevard, a main thoroughfare that had once been bulldozed through a mountain. In the background, from the Hollywood Bowl, could be heard a philharmonic orchestra rehearsing the theme from *Star Wars,* for a concert under the stars that was scheduled to take place that evening. On each side of Cahuenga Boulevard, bungalow dwellings and low-income housing, three- and four-story beige and pink apartment buildings built in the fifties, hugged the mountainsides above. The address numbers at street level for the dwellings above had been vandalized or backed into by vehicles. Occasionally, there was a number intact, in decals stuck on a board with an arrow pointing upward.

When Philip saw a board with a number in the high six thousands, he found a space, parked his car, and sought out Lonny Edge's address on foot. The sidewalk was cracked and littered with refuse—beer bottles, used syringes, used condoms—that homeless people had simply dropped when they searched the trash bins for refundable soda pop cans.

At 7200 Cahuenga Boulevard, there was a wooden stairway in rickety condition, wide enough for only one person to walk at a time. Fifty-five steps above, Philip came onto a courtyard around which were several dozen tiny bungalows of a regional style built in Hollywood in the thirties. Purple bougainvillea bloomed in great profusion, weedlike and untended, covering the roofs of most of the bungalows. In the center of the courtyard was a fountain, its sides cracked and broken, that appeared not to have been used for years. On the ledge lay a half-eaten grapefruit with a plastic spoon and a cardboard container of coffee that appeared to have been abandoned in haste, as if the late breakfaster had been called away to the telephone and forgotten to return.

The door of 7204¼ was open, but the screen door in front of it was closed. The music from the philharmonic rehearsal at the Hollywood Bowl faintly filled the air. A Strauss waltz now, it stopped in the middle of a passage and then started again, repeating the same passage. Philip found the doorbell, but it had been painted over and didn't work. "Hello," he called out, knocking on the frame of the screen door at the same time.

"Hey, you're early, Cyril," came the reply from inside.

Philip, confused, knocked again.

"Door's open," called out the voice again. "I'll take a quick shower. You're early, man. I wasn't expecting you until four, for chrissake."

Philip could hear the sound of the shower starting. He opened the screen door and walked into the small living room of the bungalow. It was sloppy but not dirty. Clothes were scattered on the floor. A black jockstrap hung on a wall light fixture. The furniture was the furniture of a furnished apartment of the period of the bungalow, serviceable but run-down. An open beer bottle had been placed on top of what appeared to be a manuscript in haphazard disarray on a painted wooden table.

"Make yourself comfortable, Cyril," called out the voice from the bathroom over the shower sounds. "The gin's in the kitchen and the ice is in the trays."

Philip, uncomfortable despite being told to make himself comfortable, sat on a kitchen chair that had been pulled up to the painted table. He had arrived without calling first, because Lonny Edge's telephone number was not listed, and he realized that Lonny was expecting a visitor. The telephone rang. It was picked up on the first ring by an answering machine.

"I can't come to the phone now. Leave your name and number, even if you think I already have it, and the time that you called, and I will get back to you as soon as possible. Wait for the beep."

"Hi, Lonny. It's Ina Rae. How they hangin', babe? Listen, I got us a gig, a four-way at my sugar daddy's on Sunday night, late. Big bucks. You, me, and Darlene. Remember Darlene? You met her at my place? Blond hair. Loves to rim. Bring your own condoms. Joke, Lonny. Gimme a call, doll. Love ya. And you know the fucking number. Bye."

Philip watched the answering machine as Ina Rae left her message. How many Ina Raes could there be? he wondered. She had to be the same Ina Rae who had forgotten her dildos at Casper Stieglitz's and worn the T-shirt that said "Warning, I Scream When I Come."

The open bottle emitted the strong aroma of beer, and Philip picked it up and moved it away from the area of his scent. From habit, he turned over the top page of the manuscript, wondering if Lonny Edge, the pornographic video star, might be penning his memoirs. The page was wet from the bottle of beer sitting on it. "Chapter Four" was typed at the top. He started casually to read. To his astonishment, the prose style was instantly familiar to him. He felt he knew who the author was, and it was certainly not Lonny Edge. Prior to the accident that had caused him to drop out of Princeton before his graduation, he had been writing his senior thesis on the work of the novelist Basil Plant, who had died in Los Angeles a few years earlier from an overdose of pills while drunk.

Basil Plant always claimed that *Candles at Lunch,* his long-anticipated novel, was finished, although his detractors, of whom there were many, said that his much-publicized writer's block was a permanent condition, brought on by drink and drugs, and that his writing career was over. Three chapters of *Candles at Lunch* were published in *Monsieur* magazine, causing a scandal that resulted in Basil's being ostracized by the very people he wrote about. The rest of the book was never forthcoming, although Basil always assured his publisher that the book was finished and would be turned in when he had completed the final refinements. When he died, the manuscript could never be found, and the first three chapters were ultimately published as a famous unfinished novel. Philip read:

"I'm looking for a Mr. Burns, a Mr. D. F. Burns? Am I speaking with that gentleman?"

"You could be and then again you could not be," answered Burnsie.

"That's you, Mr. Burns, I just know. I absolutely know."

"You're from the South, ma'am?" asked Burnsie.

"You are too, I just know."

"With whom am I speaking?" asked Burnsie.

"My friend Kate McDaniels tells me you are a scream, an absolute scream, and that we should meet."

"Mrs. McDaniels and I are not on good terms, ma'am. In fact, Mrs. McDaniels fired me from her employ sometime back and has left me in rather embarrassing straits, which is the reason you have tracked me down at such a down-at-the-heel residence as the Yucca Flats Arms in the wrong part of Hollywood. Now, who did you not tell me you are?"

"I'm your fairy godmother."

"Hmmmm," said Burnsie.

"What I have here in my hand for you, Mr. Burns, is an invitation from Kate McDaniels to meet her tonight at the Bel Air Hotel and take her to a party in the Upstairs Room at the Bistro in Beverly Hills."

So fascinated was Philip Quennell by what he was reading that he did not hear the shower in the bathroom turn off. He realized that Basil Plant's manuscript could never be found because it was sitting in the bungalow of a hustler and pornography star on Cahuenga Boulevard in Los Angeles, who had also gone home from Miss Garbo's with Hector Paradiso on the night he was murdered. He did not hear the sounds of Lonny Edge singing "Singin' in the Rain" as he dried himself off either. So he was totally unprepared when Lonny danced into the room, completely naked, and sang "Da-daaaa," in the manner of Gene Kelly.

The two young men looked at each other in astonishment.

"Holy fucking shit," said Lonny.

"Apparently I am not whom you were expecting," said Philip, at the same time.

"You can say that again," answered Lonny. "I thought you were Cyril Rathbone." He grabbed his wet towel from the hook on the bathroom door and wrapped it around his waist.

"I'm Philip Quennell," said Philip. He held out his hand. "I got your address from Zane, the bartender at Miss Garbo's. I would have called first, but he didn't give me your telephone number, and it's not listed."

Lonny looked at Philip appreciatively with wanton, slightly bloodshot eyes, and smiled. "Welcome. Any friend of Zane's, et cetera, et cetera. I mean, I wish I'd known in advance. I've got another trick at four, so we'll have to be quick, or we can set it for tomorrow. The thing is, Cyril's a regular, every Thursday at four, and a fussy one, very precise, gets kind of bitchy if I'm late, so I can't put him off, because it's like, you know, regular income."

Philip was at a loss for words. "Listen, why don't you get dressed so we can talk until your friend comes."

"I'm not cold," said Lonny. He retied the towel around his middle and walked over to the table where Philip had been reading to put the pages back in order.

For a moment, Philip's interest was divided between the manuscript and the reason he had come in the first place. "I suppose you think it's odd that I've come here," he said, trying to get into his subject.

"My God, how come you're paying for it, a good-looking guy like you?" asked Lonny, as he took Philip in. "Oh, I got it. I bet I have this one figured out right. You're married, right? And your wife's having a baby, right? And you're horny, right? Well, you've come to the right house, Cyril Rathbone or no Cyril Rathbone."

Philip spoke quietly. "No. I'm not here for what you think I'm here for, Lonny."

Lonny, suddenly suspicious, walked back to the bathroom and took a terry cloth robe off a hook on the bathroom door. He put it on. On the pocket of the robe was written in green THE BEVERLY HILLS HOTEL.

"What gives?" he asked. "What do you mean? How come you walked into my house like this? This is my private property."

"I wanted to ask you a couple of questions."

"You a cop?"

"No."

"A reporter?"

"No."

"What then?"

Philip did not reply. The questions were not unreasonable. What was he? he wondered. Not a cop. Or a reporter. He didn't know how to explain himself. Lonny Edge was not what he'd expected the killer of Hector Paradiso to be.

"I have curiosity about the death of Hector Paradiso," he said finally.

Lonny, frightened, swallowed. "What the fuck would I know about the death of Hector Paradiso?"

"You were with him when he left Miss Garbo's on the night he died," said Philip.

"Who says?"

"Several people. Zane among them."

"And what are you exactly to Hector Paradiso? Family? Lawyer? What?" asked Lonny.

Again Philip did not immediately answer. He was nothing to Hector Paradiso. He had seen him only twice in his life. Once at Pauline Mendelson's party, dancing the night away, without a care in the world, and a few hours later, lying dead in the library of his house with five bullets in him. He could not even answer, "I am the lover of Hector Paradiso's niece," because he was no longer the lover of Hector Paradiso's niece, and Hector Paradiso's niece seemed as willing as everyone else to believe the theory put forth by Jules Mendelson that he had died a suicide, despite all evidence to the contrary.

"I believe he was murdered," Philip said.

"And you think I did it?"

"I didn't say that."

"Then why are you here?"

"I don't know why I'm here," said Philip, quietly. "I just wanted to see what you looked like, and you're not at all what I thought you'd look like."

For a moment the two men stood in silence and appraised each other.

"What's your name again?" asked Lonny.

"Quennell. Philip Quennell."

"Look, I hit him a bit, because he wanted me to hit him a bit. I slapped him around with the soles of his black patent leather dancing pumps, because that's what he liked me to do to him, and that's how he got his rocks off. And I strapped him with a belt, but that's as far as it went. You know those rich guys? They've got everything in the world, but they hate themselves. And they like someone from the lower orders, like me, to tell them they're shit, and less. Do you know guys like that?"

Philip, who didn't know guys like that, nodded as if he did. "There was no fight, about money or anything?"

Lonny nodded his head. "Yeah, we had words about money. He paid me by check. I don't take checks. This is a strictly cash business, even with my regulars, like Cyril."

"So how did he pay you?"

Lonny shrugged. "By check. He said that was the arrangement he made with Manning Einsdorf. I didn't know he was dead until I got a call from Manning the next day. I swear to God."

"Did you fight over the gun?" asked Philip.

"There was no gun, I swear to God."

"The police didn't question you then?"

"No."

"Did someone called Jules Mendelson question you?"

Lonny stared at Philip. There were footsteps outside the screen door. "Hello-oo," came a voice from outside.

"Jesuschrist, it's Cyril," said Lonny.

"Hello-oo," said Cyril Rathbone again, knocking on the screen door at the same time.

"Come on in, Cyril," said Lonny.

"I brought you some cupcakes," said Cyril, walking into the room with a bakery box in his hand. He spoke in a frothy English voice. Cyril Rathbone was forty, dressed in a double-breasted seersucker suit, with a white shirt and pink tie. On his head was a stiff straw hat worn at a rakish angle.

"This is Cyril. Meet my friend, uh, Phil Quin," said Lonny, nervously making introductions.

Philip nodded to Cyril Rathbone, who turned away. He appeared troubled by an unwelcome stain he discovered on his pink tie.

"Damn," he said.

"What's the matter, Cyril?" asked Lonny.

He pointed to his tie. "Mayonnaise," he said. "Do you have any club soda?"

"I was just leaving," said Philip.

He walked to the door.

"The gin's in the kitchen, Cyril," said Lonny. "Ice is in the tray. Make yourself a drink."

Lonny followed Philip to the door, and the two men walked outside.

"This is my four o'clock appointment," said Lonny.

"I gather."

"Cyril doesn't know I was with Hector on the night he died. They were great friends. He wouldn't have liked it that I tricked with Hector. I don't want him to know."

"I'm not going to tell him," said Philip. "Was the houseboy there that night? Anyone like that?"

"Only that fucking little dog, Astrid," said Lonny.

"You didn't answer me about Jules Mendelson before," said Philip.

Lonny paused. "Jules who?"

A voice called out from another bungalow. "Hey, Lonny, you left your grapefruit and your coffee container on the fountain this morning, and the super's pissed off."

"All right, all right, I'll pick it up," Lonny called back.

"He says you're turning the place into a pigsty."

"Jesuschrist," said Lonny irritably. He walked over to the fountain and picked up the remnants of his breakfast. "I gotta go."

Philip nodded and started to walk off. Then he stopped and looked back. "How well did you know Basil Plant?"

"Basil Plant?" asked Lonny, surprised.

"Yes. How well did you know him?"

"I knew Basil pretty well," said Lonny.

"Where did you get that manuscript on your table?"

"That's a long story," said Lonny.

"I'd like to hear," said Philip.

"Stole it from him one night when he was drunk and belligerent. Why?"

"He didn't ever ask you about it later?"

"He didn't remember I took it. And then he died."

"And you never showed it to Cyril Rathbone?" asked Philip.

"Cyril comes here for one thing and one thing only. We don't talk much."

"That manuscript's worth a lot of money, if it's what I think it is," said Philip.

"Really?" He seemed interested.

"I'm at the Chateau Marmont, if you ever want to talk about it."

"Sure. Sorry you're straight. I wouldn't have charged you."

Philip laughed. "Oh," he said, snapping his fingers, as if remembering something.

"What?"

"Ina Rae called when you were in the shower. She wants you for a four-way on Sunday night, late."

Philip walked across the patio to the wooden stairway that led to the sidewalk below and started down.

"I'll tell you one thing," called out Lonny, from the top of the stairs to the retreating figure.

"What's that?" answered Philip.

"I wasn't the only gentleman caller on Hector Paradiso that night," said Lonny.

Philip stared up at him and then started to reclimb the stairs, but Lonny held up his hand. "Not now, fella. I got a customer waiting. My rent's due."

When Philip opened the door of his room at the Chateau Marmont, he was surprised to see the door to the balcony that looked down on Sunset Boulevard open. For a moment he thought he had been robbed, or was even in the process of being robbed. Slowly, without getting in the view of the balcony door, he edged his way along the wall toward it and, reaching it, slammed it shut and bolted it. Instantly a woman's face appeared on the other side. It was Camilla Ebury. They stared at each other through the glass for a moment. Then Philip unbolted the door and opened it. Camilla walked into the room.

"I thought it was about time I saw where you lived," she said. She looked at him shyly, as if she were unsure of how he would receive her.

He smiled at her. "Am I glad to see you," he said. "I thought you were a burglar."

"No. Just a lady looking for a guy she missed." She was embarrassed by her straightforwardness.

"I am deeply touched. I hated leaving your house like that."

"I couldn't bear it that you walked out on me," she said. "I didn't realize how incredibly fond of you I was. Oh, I mean I did realize it. I've realized it ever since we met, and I didn't want you to leave me." Camilla seemed close to tears.

Philip walked over to her and took her in his arms. "I'm glad you're here," he said. He held her very tight for several moments and then looked at her, touching her face before he kissed her. It was less a kiss of sexual desire than a kiss of the first stirrings of love.

"I have to tell you something, so there're no misunderstandings between us," said Philip. He stepped back from her and looked at her. "I went to see Lonny Edge."

"Who's Lonny Edge?"

"The guy from Miss Garbo's I heard went home with Hector."

She nodded. "I assumed that's where you went. Was he awful?"

"Not awful at all. A bit dim, perhaps. But not awful."

"Well, tell me. I came after you, didn't I? I want to hear. I want to know. Everything."

"He acts in porn videos and is apparently quite a star in that field."

"Good God. He didn't show you his videos, did he?"

"No."

"Did he leave Miss Garbo's with my uncle?"

"Yes."

"Well, what happened?"

"Something odd."

"What?"

"I don't think he's the one who killed your uncle."

―――――――――――

Flo's Tape #12

"*As you know, I always had aspirations to be an actress, but I'd never done much about it, except get my pictures taken for my portfolio. So, after I got my house on Azelia Way in order, I had nothing but time on my hands, and I thought now or never. I didn't know where to start even, and I certainly wasn't going to mention it to Jules because he would have come up with some reason for me not to. Oddly enough, Glyceria, of all people, had an important show business contact, and it wasn't Faye Converse. Her sister was the maid for a casting director at Colossus Pictures, and she arranged for me to meet the casting director, and the casting director sent me up for a reading for a leading part in a miniseries, in the event that they went with an unknown. The part was a wrong-side-of-the-tracks girl who marries into high society and then shoots her husband. The twist is that his mother, who hates her, stands behind her, but you don't need to know the damn plot.*

"*Well, I got all dolled up. Pooky did my hair, and Blanchette did my nails, and I walked into that office like I owned the world. I talked in my new fancy voice, like I'd once heard Pauline Mendelson talk, and Madge White, and Camilla Ebury. I was great in the meeting, being introduced to the producers and the director, chatting with them and making them laugh. They said incredible things about me, like I could be the new Maureen O'Hara, or Rhonda Fleming, or Arlene Dahl, because of the red hair. Everything was going great. And then they asked me to read. I panicked. I just clammed up. I couldn't do it. I stumbled over the lines, and even mispronounced some of the words. I know I turned beet red, and that kind of red and red hair don't match. I asked if I could start over again, and they said sure, but I knew by the way they said sure that I'd already lost the part.*

"*I never told Jules about it. The casting director that Glyceria's sister worked for said he'd call me the next time something came up, but I never heard from him again. Anyway, they gave the part to Ann-Margret. I guess they had to go with a name.*"

13

"WHO IS THIS WOMAN?" asked the interior decorator Nellie Potts about her latest client. Nellie was having lunch at the Ivy on Robertson Boulevard with the fashionable florist, Petra von Kant, whose shop was nearby.

"I have my suspicions," answered Petra, tapping her glass and indicating to the waiter that she would like another Bloody Mary.

"She's spending forty thousand dollars for new curtains in a rented house, not to mention knocking down a wall to have her dressing room and closets made bigger," said Nellie.

"All those Chanel suits," said Petra, who had started to arrange the flowers of the lady under discussion.

"But imagine spending all that money when she only has a three-year lease on that house."

"That's not your worry."

"She doesn't have the look of inherited money."

"Heavens, no."

"And yet she doesn't seem to work."

"Or do much of anything," said Petra. "She never stops talking. She wants to hear what parties I'm doing the flowers for and what flowers my clients have ordered, and even how much everything costs."

"She wants to know all about my clients too. She won't make a decision about anything until I tell her that someone very social she's read about in Cyril Rathbone's column has exactly the same sofa, or exactly the same fabric, and then she wants it. I kind of like her though."

"I do too."

"She must be kept by someone very very rich," said Nellie.

"For sure," replied Petra.

"Does she pay her bills?"

"On the dot. Doesn't even wait until the first of the month."

Without the blond wig, blue eye shadow, and blue contact lenses she wore in her secret nightclub life as Marvene McQueen, Hortense Madden, the much-feared literary critic of *Mulholland* magazine, reverted to her real life, heaping her contempt on commercial success. Her hair was pulled back in a spinster bun, and she wore glasses so thick they magnified her eyes. Her mouth was set in a puckered expression to conceal her protruding teeth, an expression that she did not relax even when chewing her omnipresent chlorophyll gum, which turned her tongue green.

There was that day a further deepening of the perpetual look of discontent on her face. Unhappiness oozed from her every pore. Not even the devastating review she had just completed of the latest work of a popular novelist—which would most certainly wound the author, as it was intended to do, so personal had she made it—could erase her troubled look, as her devastating reviews often did, or bring momentary surcease to her inner torments.

In her hand was a letter of rejection, made more painful by the fact that it was a form letter, from a disc jockey on an FM station, along with the tape of sad songs of lost love that she had so painstakingly recorded at her own expense. The disc jockey, who was named Derrick Lafferty, worshiped at the shrine of what he called "the long-gone enchantresses of the supper-club circuit," like Libby Holman, Mabel Mercer, Spivvy, and Bricktop, but he had found her tape unfit to be played on his program, even though she sang the same songs as the ladies he venerated. The rejection of her artistry was more painful than she could have imagined.

In the next office, through the paper-thin walls, she could hear Cyril Rathbone, the gossip columnist for *Mulholland,* laughing and chatting on the telephone, accepting invitations, getting tips for his column, and arranging lunch dates at fashionable restaurants. Hortense Madden loathed Cyril Rathbone, whom she considered a philistine.

Just as she was about to pick up her telephone and order a sandwich to be sent in for another lunch alone at her desk, her telephone rang. She allowed her bad mood to permeate her "Hello," which sounded like the bark of an angry dog.

"Hortense?" asked the voice on the other end.

"Who is it?" she replied, with no lessening of hostility.

"Casper Stieglitz."

"Oh, hello, Casper."

"What the hell's the matter with you?"

"Nothing is the matter with me."

"You scared the shit out of me."

Hortense hated that expression. "I'm working, that's all."

"Who are you crucifying today?"

She ignored his question. "Is there a purpose to this call, Casper?"

"I'm calling to invite you to dinner on Sunday night. A little party at my place."

Like everyone else in town, Hortense knew that Casper Stieglitz was on the skids and no longer held in high regard, and she was about to decline.

"Jules and Pauline Mendelson are coming, and a few others," said Casper, not waiting for her reply. There was no mistaking the note of elation in Casper's voice as he dropped the Mendelson names.

Hortense was stunned. She could not believe that she was being asked to a party where the Jules Mendelsons would be. In the next office she could hear the cackling laugh of Cyril Rathbone, as he received some bit of gossip about someone. She knew how Cyril longed to get to know Pauline Mendelson, and she knew that Pauline Mendelson resisted him and never invited him to cover her parties. The prospect of letting Cyril know of her invitation was so delicious to her that, for the first time since the mail had arrived with her letter of rejection from Derrick Lafferty, she felt lighthearted.

"Let me check my book, Casper," she said. She didn't have to check her book, because she had no plans whatsoever, except for her singing engagement at Miss Garbo's, but she allowed a sufficient time to go by before she said, "When is it?"

"Sunday," said Casper.

"I'll have to juggle, but I can," said Hortense.

"Eight o'clock. We'll be running a film after dinner."

"Marvelous, Casper."

Flo March lay on a brand-new lounge chair by her pool, part of a set of brand-new poolside furniture that Nellie Potts, her interior decorator, had told her was the same outdoor furniture that Pearl Silver had at her pool. Flo had taken the bra of her bathing suit off. She lay so that her back and shoulders would get the late afternoon rays, when the power of the sun had lessened a bit. On the table by her side was a timer set to ring after twenty minutes, which her trainer and aerobics teacher told her was the limit. There was also a white telephone on a long extension cord in case Jules called, which she knew he certainly would, as well as an ice bucket, several cans of Diet Coke, suntan lotion, a copy of the latest issue of *Mulholland* open to Cyril Rathbone's column, her gold cigarette case with FLO written on it in sapphires, her matching gold lighter, and her latest purchase, a pair of binoculars. Flo, who was more lonely than she would ever admit, had taken to watching her neighbors farther up the hills on Azelia Way.

She was somewhere between being asleep and awake when the sound of a small dog crying startled her. Opening her eyes, she removed her large dark glasses and saw staring up at her a white West Highland terrier.

"Why, he*llo*," Flo said to the dog. "What in the world are you doing here? Who do you belong to?" She clapped her hands, and the dog hopped up on the lounge chair with her. "What a sweet little doggie you are. Are you lost?" She sat up and put back on the bra of her bathing suit. "Are you thirsty? Do you want some water?" she asked. She got up and went over to the side of the house, where her new Mexican gardener had neatly rolled up a garden hose. She ran some water into the red clay saucer of one of the potted geranium plants that the gardener had placed around her terrace. "Here's some water," she called out to the dog. When the dog came over to where she was, Flo sat down on a chair and watched it while it drank. Finished, the dog jumped up on Flo's lap again, and she held it to her, as if it were a baby she was burping. "Oh, you sweet little thing," she said. She sat there with the dog, feeling content.

"Par'me, ma'am," came a voice through the tall hedges separating Flo's house from her neighbor's house. For a moment, Flo did not answer, never having been called ma'am before, although she listened.

"Ma'am?" The voice repeated the word.

"Are you calling me?" called out Flo, although she could not see anyone through the thick hedge.

"Have you seen our little dog?"

"Why, yes, she's here," said Flo.

"You mind if I come 'round by the front way and pick her up, ma'am? Miss Converse is going to be upset with me if she runs away again. Supposed to be my job to mind her, but I can't run this house for Miss Converse and keep my eye on that little Astrid at the same time."

"No, no, come around," said Flo. She rose from her chair and walked back to where she had been lying on the lounge chair and put on her terry cloth robe from Porthault, which matched her Porthault pool towels.

"There you are, you naughty little dog," said the maid from next door when she came around to the garden from the front of the house. "I'm sorry she's been botherin' you, ma'am."

"Oh, no, don't scold her. She hasn't been bothering me at all. She's a wonderful little dog, so friendly, aren't you, my darling? What did you say her name was?"

"Astrid," said the maid.

"What a strange name for a dog," said Flo.

"Named after some ice skating star, who died, something like that. I got enough on my mind without having to remember a dog's history. Anyway, Miss Converse, who's my boss, got her from Mrs. Rose Cliveden, the socialite, after Mrs. Cliveden broke her leg falling over Astrid at the funeral lunch, right after she inherited her from Hector Paradiso, who shot himself five times, although they say it was a suicide. Or something like that. I can't keep it all straight with those people." The maid shook her head in an exasperated fashion.

Flo looked at her, fascinated.

"Do you mean this was Hector Paradiso's dog?" she asked.

"Be careful of her, because she bit off some young man's finger too," said the maid. "I forgot his name."

"But she's the sweetest little dog I ever saw. I can't believe she'd ever bite anyone," said Flo. She held the dog in her arms. "What's your name?" she asked.

"Glyceria, ma'am. I'm sorry we're botherin' you like this."

"Oh, no, you're not bothering me," said Flo quickly. Flo had not spoken to anyone, except Jules, since Nellie Potts had been there two days earlier to supervise the hanging of the new forty-thousand-dollar curtains. "Could I get you a drink?" she asked Glyceria, not wanting her to leave.

"A drink? Oh, no, ma'am," said Glyceria.

"I didn't actually mean a *drink* drink. I meant, you know, a Diet Coke, or an ice tea, or something like that."

"Well, maybe an ice tea would be nice, only I won't be able to hear Miss Converse's telephone if it rings, and she won't like that," said Glyceria.

"Which Miss Converse is that?" asked Flo, cautiously.

"Why, Miss *Faye* Converse, of course," said Glyceria.

"Faye Converse?" cried out Flo. She could hardly contain herself. "The movie star? Faye Converse lives right next door to me beyond that hedge?"

"You didn't know that? You didn't notice the tour bus going by every day?"

"No. No, I didn't. I can't get over it. Faye Converse is my next-door neighbor. I can hardly believe it."

She rushed into the house, singing happily, to open a can of iced tea for

Faye Converse's maid. "You can leave little Astrid here any time," she called out. "I'll take care of her if you're busy. All my life I wanted to have a dog."

Jules Mendelson had seen Astrid for the first time when he went to Hector Paradiso's house after receiving the early morning telephone call telling him that Hector was dead. He did not share that information with Flo, nor did he share Flo's enthusiasm for Astrid, and the little dog, in turn, developed an instant antipathy to Jules. Although Astrid did not bite Jules, as she had bitten Kippie, she barked at him in such an angry fashion when he came to see Flo that Jules became enraged, in a way that Flo had never seen him before.

"I come up here to relax. What I do not need is that angry little shit barking at me like that," said Jules, staring at the dog and breathing heavily.

"She's Faye Converse's dog, Jules. She's just here visiting," said Flo, as if identifying its illustrious owner would lessen the anger of both her lover and the dog. Flo loved being able to use Faye Converse's name in her conversation, now that she had discovered that Faye was her next-door neighbor. It didn't matter to her that the great star wouldn't know who she was in return. "Come up here, you naughty dog, and stop all that barking," Flo said to Astrid, patting a place beside her on her newly upholstered sofa, which Nellie Potts told her was the same gray satin that Rose Cliveden used in her drawing room.

"Get her out of here," said Jules fiercely, pointing to little Astrid. "I don't want that dog around."

After that, as soon as Flo heard Jules's car in the driveway each afternoon, she sent Astrid back through the hole in the hedges, fearing that Jules would forbid her to see Astrid altogether. The little dog had become an important part of Flo's life. Each morning, after she came back from her AA meeting, she whistled what she called her Astrid whistle, and Astrid made her way through the hole in the hedges that separated her property from Faye Converse's property and came to call. The dog could not get enough loving, and Flo never tired of holding her, petting her, and talking to her. She purchased a dog's dish and bought all sorts of treats for her. She loved to break cookies in half and toss them in the air for Astrid to catch.

Often Glyceria came around by the front way to have a glass of iced tea or a cup of coffee, depending on the weather, and a little conversation. Flo, hungry for news of her celebrated neighbor, listened, rapt, to the tidbits of information that Glyceria told her about Faye Converse. Sometimes at night, when she was alone, Flo trained her binoculars on Faye Converse's house and watched the great star, when she was in the city, as she held forth with a constant stream of guests. Flo March longed to mix in the world of famous and fashionable people, but she came to understand that there was nowhere she fit in, except as Jules Mendelson's secret mistress.

Flo's Tape #13

"I also took up tennis. I didn't grow up in the kind of background where you play golf and tennis. But there was something about tennis that I always thought was kind of classy. And I liked the outfits, the short shorts and the hats with a visor. So I took lessons at the Beverly Hills Hotel three mornings a week. And guess what? I was pretty good. The pro at the hotel told me he never had a pupil who picked up the game as fast as I did.

"When Faye Converse went on location to make her comeback picture, Glyceria said she didn't think there would be any problem in my using Faye's court, as it was just sitting there. It would have been like having my own tennis court. The only problem was, I didn't have anybody to play with."

14

It would have been incomprehensible for Hector Paradiso ever to imagine that he had not been remembered, as he was in his time such a vivid figure, always present, always talked about, and both liked and disliked in more or less equal proportions. But it was a fact that he soon faded from memory after his expiration, leaving nothing behind to remind people of him: no heirs, as he had never married; no business, as he had never seriously worked; and no family except his niece.

Rose Cliveden, in bed, ill, never stopped talking on the telephone; it was impossible to get her off. Only the sounds of ice cubes against her wineglass competed with her monologues. "The other day someone said to me, 'Do you remember Hector Paradiso?' Good heavens! Imagine if darling Hector had ever heard anyone ask, 'Do you remember Hector Paradiso?' Are you listening, Camilla?"

"Yes, I'm listening, Rose," answered Camilla.

"Then say something."

"I'll repeat what I said five minutes ago, Rose. I have to hang up now."

Philip kissed Camilla good-bye.

"I wish I could go with you," said Camilla.

"Not a good idea," said Philip.

"I'd just like to see what a porn star looks like," said Camilla.

"My, my, how you've changed, Mrs. Ebury," said Philip.

When Lonny Edge agreed to meet Philip Quennell at the Viceroy Coffee Shop on Sunset Strip, he made only one request: he did not want to talk about Hector Paradiso, and Philip agreed. "It's that manuscript you have. Basil Plant's manuscript," said Philip. "Why don't you bring it along?"

"I'm not lettin' that manuscript outta my sight, man," said Lonny. Ever since Philip Quennell had given him the idea that it might be worth a lot of money, he had begun to look on the tattered pile of pages as a sort of nest egg. Famous fornicators in the age of AIDS were in less demand than before, and Lonny, approaching thirty, had begun to think of his future. He had removed the manuscript from the table in his front room, boxed it, and hidden it behind a stack of Lacoste shirts in the back of his closet.

Curly, who had managed the Viceroy when Flo worked there, nodded at Lonny when he entered. "Long time no see," he said.

Lonny nodded in return. "I'm lookin' for a Mr. Quennell," he said, scanning the premises with a practiced eye.

"He's waiting for you in booth number thirteen," said Curly.

"Flo's old booth," said Lonny.

"Right. I miss the redhead. She got rich, I hear."

When Lonny was seated at Philip's table, they both ordered coffee from the waitress. "Would you like some breakfast?" asked Philip.

Lonny, born poor, was not one to pass up an offer for anything free, even if he'd already eaten, which he had. "Sure," he answered. "Gimme some pancakes and eggs sunny-side up and bacon, crisp. That's all."

"You didn't bring it?"

"What?"

"The Basil Plant manuscript."

"I told you I wasn't letting it out of my sight."

"But I can't tell you if it's worth anything unless I read it," said Philip.

"I thought you read it in my house when I was taking a shower that day."

"I glanced at it for a minute and a half. I *think* it's what I think it is, a famous missing manuscript, but I have to be sure before I go out on a limb. Did you notice, are there any notations on any of the pages?"

"What's notations?"

"Notes? Insertions? Things like that. Like anything handwritten in the margins?"

Lonny shrugged. "I don't know. I never actually read the goddamn thing. What kind of money do you think it's worth if it does turn out to be what you think it is?"

"I can't tell you that. They published three chapters of it, and they could never find the rest after Basil died."

"Basil was a bad drunk. Turned mean. Rest of the time, he was the nicest guy in the world. Like approximately, what do you think it's worth?"

"I don't know. I could find out. It could be a lot, but I have to make sure it's not a hoax before I get involved."

As Philip started to explain to Lonny the complexities of identifying the missing manuscript, he looked up and saw Jules Mendelson walk into the Viceroy Coffee Shop, carrying a copy of the *Wall Street Journal.* Lonny, seated with his back to the entrance, did not see him. Philip watched Curly speak to Jules in a familiar but respectful manner and lead him to a table in the window. When he sat down, Jules spread the *Journal* out in front of him on the Formica-topped table and began to read. He did not look up to acknowledge the waitress who set a cup of coffee on the table in front of him.

"Excuse me," said Philip to Lonny when the waitress arrived with Lonny's breakfast. "I'll be right back."

"It's over there, with the orange door, by the cash register," said Lonny, pointing to the men's room.

Philip nodded and went to the men's room. When he came out a minute later, he walked over to Jules Mendelson's table.

"Mr. Mendelson," he said.

Jules looked up from his paper but did not acknowledge Philip.

"It's Philip Quennell," said Philip.

"Yes," he said, looking back at his paper in a dismissive manner. He had

taken a dislike to Philip Quennell since the day the statue of the Degas ballerina had been knocked over and cracked, and he blamed Philip for the accident although it was his own anger that had caused it.

As if reading his mind, Philip said, "I'm sorry about the accident with the
Degas ballerina. I wrote Mrs. Mendelson a note of apology."

"She told me," said Jules, not raising his eyes.

"This is not the sort of place I would expect to be seeing you having
breakfast," said Philip.

"I'm not having breakfast. I'm having a cup of coffee," said Jules. "I come
in here at this time to read my paper." He tapped the newspaper on the table
in a gesture meant to dissuade Philip from staying.

"Quite a clientele this place gets," said Philip. "See that guy over there,
scarfing down the hotcakes? Jeans, T-shirt, windbreaker?"

"What about him?"

"Hustler. Porn star."

Jules nodded, indicated disinterest, and looked back at his paper. "I didn't
realize that was your inclination," he said, chuckling.

Philip smiled and started to move on. "You know what they say about him,
don't you?"

"Of course I don't know what they say about him. I never laid eyes on the
man."

"They say he's the guy who killed Hector Paradiso."

Jules smiled wearily. "Oh, that old chestnut. Hector Paradiso was a suicide,
Mr. Quennell."

"No, he wasn't, Mr. Mendelson."

"You have only to check the police report."

"Hector went to a bar called Miss Garbo's after he left your party that
night. It's the kind of bar where rich johns make arrangements of a financial
nature to meet young companions. There are several witnesses who will tell
you that Hector left Miss Garbo's in the company of that young companion.
I've checked the police report. None of those facts are in it. Do you still want
to tell me that Hector Paradiso went straight home from your party that night
to shoot himself five times?"

"Playing sleuth may be the most important thing that ever happened in
your life, Quennell, but it's a matter of absolutely no importance to me," said
Jules. He slowly turned the page he was reading and continued to read the
story about the release from prison after five years of the Wall Street financier
Elias Renthal.

"This thing doesn't have one goddamn thing to do with my life," said
Philip. "Why the hell should it matter to me whether or not they catch the
killer? If I hadn't been at your house that night and gone home with Camilla
Ebury and been with her when you called to say that Hector was dead and then
gone with her to Hector's house to identify the body, I probably wouldn't give
it another thought, because it doesn't involve me. What *I'm* interested in is why
it is being covered up. Chances are it was what the supermarket tabloids refer
to as a gay murder. He picked up a trick at Miss Garbo's. He took home the
trick. He got into a fight with the trick, probably over money—they say he was
tight—and he got killed. Not a particularly uplifting scenario, but it is not a
particularly original one either. There was that big decorator in New York it

happened to last year. Bertie Lightfoot? Do you remember? I'm sure Pauline knew him. And in San Francisco. The gallery owner. What was his name? Ludovic Cato, wasn't it? Same story. Stabbed to death by a mysterious stranger, all trussed up. But why the cover-up here in Los Angeles? Do you think the people in your privileged group really didn't know Hector was gay? I don't think so. Your kind of group might not have talked about it, but they knew it. Who are you all trying to protect? He had no family who might be embarrassed by such a revelation. Only a niece, with whom I am involved, and she would now like to have it solved."

"Hey, Quennell," said Jules, looking up from his newspaper finally. His voice had turned harsh. He was not used to people who did not treat him with deference.

"Yes?"

"Read my lips, asshole. You don't know what the fuck you're talking about."

"Ah, the great art collector and philanthropist has spoken," said Philip. The two stared at each other, and Philip moved on.

Sometimes, after they finished making love, Jules—still nude, still in bed— would pick up the telephone and call his office to check with Miss Maple for his messages. Twice he spoke to the President, in the White House, while lying in Flo's bed, with the telephone sitting on his chest. Once Flo heard him say, "Best to Barbara," in a matter-of-fact way, as if, as she told it later to Glyceria, it was no big deal. On this day he signaled Flo with a drinking gesture to bring him something cool to drink, without interrupting his train of thought. Flo was fascinated by the way Jules was able to conduct business involving great sums of money over the telephone. Sell this. Buy that. She felt important just hearing such large sums discussed over her telephone in her house. She grew to know that Sims Lord was Jules's lawyer and closest associate, that Reza Bulbenkian was his contact in New York, and that Miss Maple, whom Jules sometimes called Syrup, was his secretary and had been his secretary for over twenty years. It was Miss Maple, whom Flo had never met, who paid all her bills and mailed her her allowance.

Flo handed Jules a can of iced tea. "I hate canned iced tea," said Jules. "In fact, I hate drinks out of cans, period."

"Oh." Flo always felt hurt if Jules criticized the way she did things.

"Look," said Jules, taking her hand. "What's the name of that decorator you're using?"

"Nellie Potts?" asked Flo.

"Right, Nellie Potts. Tell her to call Steuben in New York. Tell her to order some decent glasses for you. Twelve of each. Water goblets, highball, old-fashioned, the red wine, the white wine, the champagne. Drinks taste better out of good glasses."

"Wow," said Flo, impressed. "Should I get them monogrammed? You know, like FM? I read somewhere that Dom Belcanto has his glasses monogrammed."

"No, no, monograms are tacky," said Jules. "And they take too long. Just order the glasses. Have them sent out by Federal Express. They'll be here in a couple of days. And then you can serve me my drinks in some decent glasses."

"I'll call Nellie later," said Flo. She was delighted when she had projects to fill up her time.

"Speaking of Nellie Potts," said Jules, reaching out behind him in the bed and grabbing a handful of Flo's new curtains. "Have you any idea how much these curtains cost?"

"Yes, I do, Jules," answered Flo.

"That's a great deal of money, Flo, for some curtains. Did you inquire first about the cost?"

"Yes, I did, Jules."

"And you didn't question such an exorbitant amount?" he asked.

Flo raised her eyebrows. "You can afford it, Jules," she said.

"That's not the point."

"Then what is the point?"

"This is a rented house. To spend forty thousand dollars for curtains in a rented house doesn't make sense. You can't take them with you when you leave, and that has-been TV star you rent this place from reaps the benefits."

"You don't have to point out to me this is a rented house, Jules. And, by the way, the renovations of my closets are going to cost you that much again," said Flo.

"I don't believe this."

"Aren't I worth it, Jules? Any time you're dissatisfied with my services, I shall be happy to make other arrangements," said Flo, grandly.

"Now, let's not get into that kind of conversation, Flo. I'm tired. I have a lot of important things on my mind."

Flo got up from the bed where she had been lying next to Jules. She picked up her terry cloth robe and put it on. "I want you to buy this house for me, Jules," she said. "Trent Muldoon's business manager said he's ready to sell."

"This is not the time to be talking about buying houses," he said. "I just told you I'm tired and that I have things on my mind."

"You keep putting it off, Jules. No time is ever the right time for you. I want something in my own name. I live in a rented house. I drive a leased car. What's going to happen to me if something happens to you? I've gotten used to living like this."

"You are going to be taken care of. Sims Lord will be making the arrangements," said Jules.

"You know, Jules, I sit here all day waiting for you to come over. I have no friends, except the maid next door who works for Faye Converse. I have no job. You're afraid to be seen with me in public, so I almost never go out. I have thirty Chanel suits, and some forty-thousand-dollar curtains, and I'm about to have a couple of hundred Steuben glasses without a monogram on them, but it's not really a fulfilling kind of life. So, I repeat, I want something in my own name."

"All right, all right, I'll buy you the house," he said.

"Thank you, Jules, and I want the pink slip for the car too, in my own name."

"I better get dressed," he said, getting out of bed and reaching around for his clothes.

"Hey, Jules, you have to lose some of that lard around your middle," said

Flo. "Pauline's taking you to too many banquets. When you bend over to tie your shoelaces, your face gets all red and you get short of breath."

Jules was both annoyed and touched. He did not like to be reminded of his girth. He had recently been infuriated by a magazine article that described him as a man of ample proportions. But it struck him how different his relationship with Flo was from his relationship with Pauline. With Pauline, he dressed and undressed in his dressing room, as she dressed and undressed in her dressing room, and they did not present themselves to each other until they were ready to face the world or ready to go to bed.

Flo came over to him and put her arms around his neck. "Listen, it doesn't bother me. The way I look at it, there's more of you to love."

When Jules finished dressing, he walked into Flo's living room. She was seated on her newly upholstered sofa, reading Cyril Rathbone's gossip column in *Mulholland*. He was absurdly touched that she moved her lips when she read.

"Oh, la," said Flo, holding out her little finger in what she assumed to be a gesture of grandeur.

"What?" asked Jules.

" 'Pauline Mendelson is opening her orchid greenhouse for the Los Angeles Garden Club tour,' " she read. " 'Mrs. Mendelson, the elegant wife of Jules Mendelson, the zillionaire, has developed a rare yellow phalaenopsis orchid.' Is that how you pronounce that?"

Jules turned away. He could not deal with any overlapping of the segments of his life.

"You know, Flo, you mustn't move your lips when you read," he said.

"Did I do that?" she asked, slapping her hand over her mouth. "When I was in junior high at Blessed Sacrament, Sister Andretta, my home room teacher, used to say to me, 'Fleurette, you're moving your lips,' and all the kids in the class would laugh. I thought I got over that."

"Tomorrow I'm going to bring you over some books I think you ought to read instead of all those gossip columns."

"Not long ones, for God's sake. My lips will be exhausted."

Pauline Mendelson had not confronted Jules about the other woman's scent on his fingers after she had kissed his hand and smelled it. Instead, she began to observe him more carefully. There were no telltale signs, nothing so obvious as lipstick traces on handkerchiefs or collars. For the first time since they moved into Clouds twenty-two years before, their habit of meeting in the sunset room each twilight for a glass of wine before they dressed for dinner had been disrupted when Pauline failed to appear for several days following her outburst. When they drove together to and from parties, she had a sense that his mind was elsewhere, although, once having arrived at the house where they were dining, they both automatically fell into their roles of devoted husband and wife, with never a hint, to even the closest observer, of a masquerade being performed. Several times Pauline awoke at night and saw Jules lying beside her in their bed staring up at the ceiling, but she did not speak. She knew the time was at hand to go to see her father in Maine, but she made no mention of her plans.

She had grown used to her role as the wife of one of the country's most eminent figures, and she was not unmindful that there was a dearth of replacements for a man of her husband's importance, even for one of the marrying McAdoo sisters. Caution was the road she chose to follow. Jules, concerned, was aware from the attitude and the coolness of his wife that something was wrong. He even guessed that she may have heard of his involvement, although he had made every effort to keep the affair from being discussed. The very thought of dissolving such a marriage as he had with Pauline was unthinkable to Jules, even though he was in the grips of a grand passion with Flo March.

Under suspicion, facing the loss of a marriage he treasured, he still continued his afternoon visits to Azelia Way, as his ardor for Flo did not diminish for a second. His erotic longings intensified each day; he could not wait for the sight of her alert breasts and ample bush, which were more beautiful to him than her beautiful face. "Be nude," he would say to her on the car telephone so that not a moment of their time together would be wasted. He wanted more and more of her, and she always obliged. "Don't use those scents and unguents down there," he said one afternoon. "Your natural smells drive me mad." He begged her to talk dirty to him during their lovemaking, and she obliged. "Lower," he whispered in her ear once. She understood he did not mean the position of her hands on his testicles, but that he wanted her language to be even baser, and again she obliged. Afterward he said to her, "Where in the hell did you learn how to talk like that?"

She lay back in bed smoking a cigarette, looking up into space, and answered in a surprisingly harsh tone. "Don't go moral on me once you've come, Jules. It's what you begged for."

He looked at her. He knew she was right. The next day he brought her a jewel, a sapphire ring surrounded by diamonds. She was ecstatic. "Like Princess Di's," she said. "Only bigger. I used to think if I ever had a ring, a really good ring, I would love a sapphire. Did I ever tell you that, Jules? I didn't, did I? How did you know?"

"It's the color of your eyes," said Jules.

She was touched. "You are surprising, Jules. Sometimes you're so gruff and unsentimental. I didn't think you ever noticed the color of anything about me, other than my pubic hair."

Jules roared with laughter. He knew she was inferior to him, both in position and intellect, but he loved her. He loved her madly.

"I love you, Jules," she said simply.

"Really?" he asked.

She thought of what she had just said. She perhaps venerated him more than she loved him, but certainly love was present. "Really," she replied.

When he left that day, she walked him to his car. "I'm mad about this ring, Jules. I won't ever take it off. But you won't forget about the house, will you? I want to own this house."

A few days later the two women in Jules Mendelson's life met by accident in the parking lot of Pooky's salon. Pauline Mendelson rarely went to Pooky's to have her hair done. She was one of a few very special clients for whom Pooky happily adjusted his busy schedule, going up to Clouds to do her hair in her elaborately outfitted dressing room. But on the day before Casper Stieglitz's party, which Pauline never wanted to attend, Pooky was not able to accommodate her in their usual manner on such short notice, and she drove into Beverly Hills to have her hair done at his salon. As she was parking in the lot behind the shop, a red convertible Mercedes backed into the front of her car. It was Flo March, leaving the shop after her appointment.

"I'm so sorry," said Flo, hopping out of her car and running over to Pauline's. "That was my fault. But I'm insured. Don't worry. And it's not bad. Just a dent."

Looking in the window, she realized the person whose car she had hit was Pauline Mendelson. "Oh, my God, Mrs. Mendelson," she said. "Are you all right?"

"Yes, I'm fine. I hardly felt it," said Pauline. She got out of her car and went around to look at the dent. "Don't worry about it. It was an accident." The girl looked familiar to Pauline. "Do we know each other? Have we ever met?" she asked.

"No, no, we haven't," said Flo. She had become shy and spoke very quickly. "I just know who you are. I recognized you from seeing your picture in the papers and magazines all the time. You're sure you're all right?"

"I'm fine."

"Thank you, Mrs. Mendelson." She felt only fascination for the wife of her lover.

Pauline smiled. "I love your suit," she said.

"Oh, my gosh, coming from you," said Flo, thrilled with the compliment.

Then, looking at the Chanel suit, Pauline remembered. "I know where I saw you. At Hector Paradiso's funeral. Weren't you a friend of Hector's?"

Flo began to get nervous. "Yes, I knew Hector. I have to run. Thank you for being so nice, Mrs. Mendelson."

"Tell me your name. I'll tell Jules I saw you," said Pauline.

"Good-bye, Mrs. Mendelson." She ran back to her car and jumped in. She put her key in the ignition and the car leapt forward. She was bewildered. It had never occurred to Flo March that Pauline Mendelson would be nice.

Although Pauline was in no way the sort of wife who could be bought off with a trinket, no matter how expensive the trinket, Jules made arrangements for a gift for his wife that he felt might thaw the situation between them. He had heard from Pauline's great friend, Prince Friedrich of Hesse-Darmstadt, the head of the jewelry department at Boothby's auction house in London, that a certain pair of yellow diamond earrings were coming up for auction that week, and Jules had instructed the prince to bid on them for him.

On the Sunday of Casper Steiglitz's dinner, Willi, Jules's barber, who usually arrived before sunrise to shave him, came later in the afternoon to cut his hair. Only the day before had Pauline been reluctantly induced to accompany Jules to Casper's party. "It would mean a great deal to me, Pauline," he had said. She read into his voice a need that she did not often hear. She knew that was the moment to confront him about the other woman he was seeing, but she refrained, not wanting to approach that development of their lives in such a sideways fashion. "All right, Jules," she said, simply.

"Wait till I show you what I've bought Pauline," said Jules to the barber, in a rare moment of intimacy with the man who had been shaving him daily in his house for over twenty years. He reached into the top drawer of his dressing table and took out a small velvet box. Opening it, he held out a pair of yellow canary diamond earrings, surrounded by smaller diamonds.

"Look," he said proudly. "She has been looking for earrings to match her canary diamond necklace and bracelet, and I knew these were coming up at an auction at Boothby's in London last week and had my man there bid for me."

Willi, the barber, knew nothing of canary diamonds, but he saw they were large and knew they were expensive and made the appropriate exclamations of admiration. Just then, Pauline walked into Jules's dressing room, wearing a negligee and carrying two dresses on velvet-covered hangers.

"Which of these would be more appropriate for your friends, Mr. Stieglitz and Mr. Zwillman?" she asked, holding them up for his inspection. Jules, who knew better than anyone that his wife's taste in clothes was second to no one's, was not unaware of the slight sarcasm in her tone, but he ignored it. "Hello, Willi," she said to the barber.

"Hi, Miz Mendelson," said Willi. He continued his work of cutting and trimming, but he was aware at the same time that there was a change in the dynamics of the relationship of the couple he had come to know so well. Jules Mendelson was Willi's benefactor as well as client, having advanced him the money to buy the small shop on Sunset Boulevard where he cut the hair of the leading figures in the film industry.

"I would choose that one," said Jules, pointing to one of the two. "You know, Sunday night, not too dressy, don't you think?"

"I've never been to a gangster's party on Sunday night," said Pauline. "So I wouldn't know."

"Mr. Stieglitz is a film producer," he said.

"But Mr. Zwillman is a gangster, or so says Rose Cliveden," replied Pauline. "Rose suggested a corsage."

"I have a present for you," said Jules quickly, wanting to change the subject. "Here." He handed her the velvet box.

Pauline opened the box and looked at the canary diamond earrings. "Very pretty," she said, without the sort of enthusiasm that such an extravagant gift could be expected to engender. It appeared to Jules that she was about to say something else, and he waited, looking at her in the mirror while Willi continued to cut his hair. "I saw them in the Boothby catalog Friedrich sent me. They used to belong to a Mrs. Scorpios. What time are we due at Mr. Stieglitz's?"

Jules and the barber glanced at each other in the mirror. Jules, embarrassed, shrugged.

Pauline Mendelson was acknowledged to be one of the most gracious hostesses in society and one of the best conversationalists anywhere, but her skills in those areas applied only when she was with the sort of people she had always known, or with the creative people she mixed in with her own friends at her parties, or with the business, banking, museum, and government officials with whom Jules was involved in his myriad activities. The group of people she expected to encounter that Sunday evening at the home of Casper Stieglitz was not her kind of group at all, and she was prepared to make no effort whatsoever.

When the Mendelsons walked into Casper Stieglitz's living room, they found a larger party than they had been led to expect. At the request of Arnie

Zwillman, who exercised a control over Casper Stieglitz, Casper had enlarged his group so that it would be less conspicuous later in the evening when Arnie suggested a private conversation with Jules during the screening of the film. Pearl Silver, the widow of a prominent producer and a hostess of renown in the film colony, had been added only the day before. Ordinarily Pearl Silver would not have gone to Casper Stieglitz's house, but she agreed to come when she heard that Marty and Sylvia Lesky had also accepted. Marty Lesky, the head of Colossus Pictures, was considered by many to be the most powerful man in the film industry, and Sylvia Lesky, whose father had been the head of the studio that her husband was now the head of, was a woman who had been brought up in the film industry and was referred to as Hollywood royalty by such chroniclers as Cyril Rathbone. Marty Lesky was deeply opposed to drugs, and for that reason would not have gone to Casper Stieglitz's home ever, but he was told at a card game at the Hillcrest Country Club the afternoon before that the Jules Mendelsons were going to be there.

"You've got to be kidding," he said. "Jules Mendelson is going to Casper Stieglitz's house? And Pauline too? Will someone explain that one to me, please?"

Certainly Marty Lesky had no social ambitions, but, like many in the film industry, he had developed a great interest in collecting art and had recently been made a member of the board of directors of the Los Angeles County Art Museum. He explained to Sylvia, who didn't want to go to Casper Stieglitz's any more than Pauline Mendelson or Pearl Silver wanted to go, that he thought it would be advantageous to get to know Jules Mendelson better, in the hopes of getting his renowned art collection left to the Los Angeles County Museum, instead of to one of the other art museums that were vying for Jules's treasures.

Dom Belcanto, the famed ballad singer, who was said to have Mafia connections, and his fourth wife, Pepper, were also in the group. Dom was known to play cards every Friday night in Palm Springs with Arnie Zwillman, and it was Zwillman who had asked Dom and Pepper to come. The new additions to what had once been a small dinner were completed with Amos Swank, the late-night talk show host, who almost never went to parties and almost never spoke when he did go to parties, although he kept most of America in stitches five nights a week on his late-night talk show "After Midnight." Amos had just married his fourth wife, and it was she who had talked him into attending a party he would never have accepted otherwise.

Although they were not her friends, Pauline had served on committees with both Pearl Silver and Sylvia Lesky, and greeted them warmly, as they, in turn, greeted her. They all understood, without anyone's saying it, that they were there under duress. Pauline stood by herself, aloof, clasping her gold-and-diamond minaudiere in her hands, and pretended to be looking at Casper Stieglitz's paintings, all of which she hated. Then, in the disparate group, she saw Philip Quennell, whom she had not seen since he had so enraged Jules at lunch at Clouds following Hector Paradiso's funeral and, inadvertently, caused the toppling-over and cracking of their Degas sculpture of the fourteen-year-old ballerina with the original pink ribbon in her hair.

"Admiring the art?" asked Philip, when he made his way toward her.

Jules, standing nearby, acknowledged Philip with a brief nod but did not offer his hand.

"I hate this sort of thing, don't you, big white canvases with a blue dot in the center?" answered Pauline.

"It's not exactly van Gogh's *White Roses*," answered Philip.

Pauline smiled. "We've missed you," she said.

"I don't think Jules has missed me," said Philip.

"Well, I've missed you then."

"You seem different," said Philip.

"How?"

Philip thought for a moment and then said, "Sadder. Is that the right word?"

She smiled at him fondly. "You know, Philip, if I weren't a believer in conjugal vows, and if Camilla Ebury weren't one of my best friends, I'd make such a play for you, even if I am fifteen years older, or maybe it's sixteen, than you are."

Philip, pleased, blushed. "I can't remember when I've felt so flattered."

"This is certainly an unlikely place to have a reunion," said Pauline, indicating the room and the other guests.

"Yes, it is. I couldn't believe it when I heard you were coming."

"Neither could I," she said.

"How's the Degas ballerina?" asked Philip.

"Gone to Paris for repairs. Jules took her over on our plane. There's a marvelous man at the Louvre that Pierre Rosenberg told us about." She clutched her minaudiere to her and looked around the room. "Tell me, Philip. Is Mr. Stieglitz married?"

"He recently became single with a lot of drama, apparently," said Philip. "But they still go to award shows together. My informant is the butler, Willard."

Pauline laughed. "Tell me, who are all these other people? I know Pearl Silver slightly, and Sylvia Lesky and I were co-chairpersons of the Cedars-Sinai benefit, but the others. Who are they? Do you know them?"

"No, but I know who some of them are," said Philip. "I don't know Amos Swank, but he's the talk show host."

"Oh, of course," said Pauline.

"And I don't know Dom Belcanto."

"Oh, I know who Dom Belcanto is. He sang at one of my charities. But who are the others?" asked Pauline. "Who is the prim maiden with the buckteeth?"

"Hortense Madden, the book critic of *Mulholland*."

"And the lady talking movie business a mile a minute with Marty Lesky?"

"Mona Berg, a famous actors' agent, and the man with her is Joel Zircon, another agent."

Whereas the evening was no more than a disagreeable chore for the Mendelsons and the Leskys, it was a great step forward in the social life of Joel Zircon. He had been pressed into service at the last minute as the escort of Mona Berg, who did not wish to arrive alone. Joel had never heard of the Jules Mendelsons, but he was thrilled to be in the same room with the Marty Leskys and the Dom Belcantos and the Amos Swanks, and seemed not to mind that they did not include him in their conversations when he went to stand by them. When he spotted Willard, Casper Stieglitz's butler, with whom he often drank and cruised at Miss Garbo's, he pretended, for propriety's sake, that he had never seen him before.

"And which one is Arnie Zwillman?" asked Pauline. "He is one of those people one hears about, but I haven't a clue what he looks like."

"Deeply tanned, talking to Dom and Pepper Belcanto," answered Philip.

Pauline turned to stare at him. Arnie Zwillman never allowed himself to be photographed. When the *Los Angeles Tribunal* had done a special report on the Mafia infiltration of Las Vegas several years back, they were unable to illustrate their section on Arnie Zwillman with a picture, other than a flash photograph taken at a nightclub in London fifteen years earlier, when he was having a romance with a singer then performing at Talk of the Town.

"Who the hell is Arnie Zwillman anyway?" asked Pauline. "Can you explain him to me?"

"He's the man who burned down the Vegas Seraglio for the insurance money."

"That's all anyone ever says about him. It still doesn't explain him."

"His brother was shot to death in his swimming pool in Las Vegas. His previous wife was hospitalized at Cedars several times after having been beaten up by him, and no charges were ever brought against him. He has been connected with a number of gangland murders, and he has managed to elude the nets of the last six attorneys general. Does that explain him better?" asked Philip.

But Pauline had stopped listening. Entering the room was someone she did not wish to encounter. "Oh, heavens, a host of favorites," she said.

"Who do you see?" asked Philip.

"Mr. Cyril Rathbone," answered Pauline.

"The gossip columnist?" asked Philip. He looked over to where Pauline was looking and immediately recognized the man he had met in Lonny Edge's bungalow on the day he had gone to ask Lonny about Hector Paradiso's death.

"Yes. He drives me mad. He has a fixation on me. Never stops writing about me. I beg of you, don't leave me," said Pauline.

Unused to entertaining, Casper Stieglitz was not the kind of host who took each new arrival around the room to meet the other guests, but then, Cyril Rathbone was not the kind of guest who waited to be introduced. Seeing the famous Pauline Mendelson across the room, he abandoned Pepper Belcanto in midsentence and darted in her direction like a prancing fawn, his hand extended, crying out in his florid English voice, as if they were the greatest of friends, "Pauline! How marvelous!"

"Hellohowareyou?" replied Pauline, the four words becoming one. Pauline was sure that Cyril Rathbone intended to kiss her on both cheeks. While it was impossible not to take the hand that he offered her without creating a minor incident, she had no intention of allowing a man she disliked to do anything so intimate as kiss her. Seeing his face move toward hers, she stepped back away from him. "I have a cold," she said, shaking her head at the same time to forestall such an act.

Rathbone, rebuffed, became very red in the face. Cyril hated Pauline for her aristocratic high-handedness toward him, but he was, at the same time, grovelingly impressed with being in proximity to such grandeur as she represented to him. Had she so much as smiled in his direction, even once, or invited him to one of her famous parties, his hatred would have evaporated into nothingness, and he would have become her most adoring acolyte. But that was not to be.

"Do you know Philip Quennell? Cyril Rathbone," said Pauline.

Cyril looked at Philip, curious to know who the young man was who had been engaged in such deep conversation with Pauline when he entered the room. For an instant Philip looked familiar to him.

"What was your name?" he asked Philip.

"Quennell. Philip Quennell." He remembered that Lonny had not been able to remember his name that day and had called him Phil Quin when he introduced him to Cyril.

"Have we met?"

"I certainly would have remembered if we had," said Philip. If Philip had been standing next to anyone but Pauline, Cyril Rathbone would have instantly remembered the circumstances under which they did meet.

Cyril turned back to Pauline. "Even though you're here, and the Leskys, and Pearl, this is a B-group party," he said, as if he himself, along with the Mendelsons and Leskys and Pearl Silver, stood head and shoulders above the other guests. If he had expected that this comment would endear him to a lady who always resisted him, he was mistaken, as she neither laughed nor agreed with his statement.

"How is your yellow phalaenopsis coming along?" he asked, trying again. He was referring to the rare orchid she was developing in her greenhouse, which he had written in his column she was going to show to the Los Angeles Garden Club.

"Very well," she replied.

"I was thinking just today about our mutual friend Hector," he said, as a last resort for a conversational opening.

She nodded.

"Hardly a day goes by that something doesn't happen that I want to share with Hector," said Cyril. It was Cyril Rathbone who had sent Hector Paradiso the clipping from the Paris newspaper showing Flo March fleeing from a fire in the Meurice Hotel, with Jules Mendelson in the background. "We talked every day."

Pauline was unwilling to be drawn into a conversation about her great friend Hector with Cyril Rathbone. She looked downward. She had never understood why Hector found Cyril so entertaining, and she knew that any statement she made would be printed in his column, and not necessarily correctly. She observed during her downward look that Cyril Rathbone was wearing the tie of an English public school he had not attended and had little feet with highly polished shoes from Lobb on St. James's Street.

At that moment dinner was announced, and Pauline immediately seized the moment to distance herself from the man she found so disagreeable.

"Good heavens," she said, shuddering and wondering again what she and Jules were doing at such a house.

"You weren't very polite to Mr. Rathbone," said Philip.

"Cyril Rathbone is uninsultable," replied Pauline. "I hope you're seated next to me at dinner, Philip."

"If I'm not, I'll pull a Hector Paradiso and change the place cards," said Philip.   •

In another part of the room, Jules stood in a group with Marty Lesky and Dom Belcanto and their host. He pretended to admire the art on Casper Stieglitz's walls, which had been picked out for Casper by the studio art director who decorated his house for him. Actually, Jules, like his wife, hated the art on Casper Stieglitz's walls, but, as a great art collector, he was always courteous about other people's art, even if he found it inferior. His reputation on matters pertaining to art was so respected that his word was considered authoritarian, and Casper was delighted with Jules Mendelson's false admiration. He wished he could remember the name of the artist who stuck the broken dishes and coffee cups in the canvas when Dom Belcanto asked him, but he couldn't. He excused himself, whispering to Jules man-to-man that he had to take a leak and then check on the dinner. Casper was anxious that the dinner start on time so that the film afterward could start on time, as he was expecting Ina Rae and Darlene and a porn star called Lonny, whom Ina Rae insisted on bringing, for a four-way scene after the film, and he wanted all his fancy guests out of his house before they arrived. Arnie Zwillman seized the opportunity of Casper's disappearance to introduce himself and his about-to-be-wife, Adrienne Basquette, to Jules. Then dinner was announced.

Bettye, Casper's secretary, had done the place cards. Neither Jules nor Pauline mentioned to the person sitting next to them that their last name had been spelled incorrectly on the place cards, with two *d'* s instead of one in Mendelson, but the error seemed in keeping with the inappropriateness of the evening. Pauline minded that her difficult situation with her husband prevented her from catching his eye and smiling over the misspelling of their names, the sort of husband-wife togetherness that had marked the twenty-two years of their marriage. Or catching his eye and smiling across the table over the black napkins and black dishes. Jules knew how much Pauline hated black napkins and black dishes, but they could not exchange looks over that either, or over the several times the hired waiters from a catering service served the guests from the wrong side, or over the wine, an indifferent Italian Soave in long tapered bottles that had the price tag of $8.00 stamped on them, which Pauline knew would drive Jules mad. Jules was aware that there was a point to the evening and that the point had to do with Arnie Zwillman, and he waited for the other man to make the first move.

Almost everyone at the table deferred to Jules Mendelson in the forced conversation, even Marty Lesky, who was accustomed to dominating the conversation at the tables where he dined. Jules possessed a kind of power in his presence that made the ordinary conversation that people in the industry were used to talking about at dinner—films and grosses and casting and who was up and who was down in the studio hierarchy—seem trite, and he was asked questions about the presidency, about the economy, and, finally, about a senatorial confirmation hearing then going on in Washington for a presidential nominee for a vacancy on the Supreme Court, about whom embarrassing personal revelations concerning women and liquor had come to light.

"I have no firsthand knowledge, but apparently there are things in John's past," said Jules cautiously, not wanting to get into such a conversation with these people whom he did not know and who would certainly quote him the following day, especially the gossip columnist Cyril Rathbone. In fact, Jules knew a great deal about the confirmation hearing. He was not unmindful that certain aspects of the nominee's behavior mirrored his own and could be used against him when the time came for his own senatorial confirmation, should the news of his affair with Flo March leak out. A chill passed through him. He looked across the table at his beautiful and elegant wife and realized, not for the first time, what a necessary treasure she was to him. Jules, who never gulped wine, took a gulp of Casper Stieglitz's cheap wine and grimaced.

"But all public people have discreditable secrets," said Pearl Silver, who was known to be able to keep any conversation going. "Don't you think so, Jules? Even Roosevelt, in his wheelchair. He had that whatshername, Lucy *quelquechose,* who was supposed to be such a good friend of Eleanor's. I mean, they all have secrets."

"I suppose everyone has something in his past he doesn't want to come out," said Sylvia Lesky.

"Not me," said Casper Stieglitz, although almost everyone in the room knew that he had been secretly arrested for the possession of drugs while on a foreign location for a picture and that Marty Lesky, the head of his studio, had had to appeal to a Washington figure to keep him from being sent to jail in that country.

"You are an exception then, Casper," said Pearl Silver, catching Sylvia Lesky's eye while she said it.

There was a silence. Then Philip Quennell spoke up, although it was the custom that conversation at such parties was carried on by the important figures at the table, while the others listened. "I always figure if you've got something hidden in your past, it's going to come out at some time or other," he said. He looked across the table at Jules, but Jules turned to reply to a question asked him by Pepper Belcanto.

"You do?" asked Pauline. She too looked across the table at Jules.

Philip, having caught the attention of the table, continued. "But, believe me, Mrs. Mendelson, some way is always found for people in high places, and people close to people in high places, to beat the rap. As night follows day, this is the truth. It is part of the fabric of power."

There was an awkward silence in the room, and Philip could feel the dark look that was coming in his direction from Jules Mendelson.

"Who's this guy?" asked Arnie Zwillman, leaning over Adrienne Basquette to speak to Casper Stieglitz.

"He wrote a book," replied Casper, explaining Philip.

"Big fucking deal," said Arnie.

Then Casper excused himself and left the table. Philip could see that Casper's frequent trips to the bathroom were beginning to have their effect. He ate almost nothing, and he blew his nose frequently, feigning a cold. Joel Zircon, who had not spoken a word during the meal, followed Casper out of the room, hoping to be invited to participate in what he called a few lines.

Conversations of this type did not usually take place at Casper's house. There had been a time when he had been a popular figure in the social life of the film community, but it had been several years since he had produced a film that in any way approximated the films of his dazzling early successes, and movie people, aware of his questionable habits, had stopped asking him to their parties and had long since declined going to his. The kind of talk he had grown to prefer in the year since his divorce was the kind of talk he had with Ina Rae and the sort of people she brought to his house.

Throughout the meal Hortense Madden sat in angry silence. Her evening had been spoiled by the unexpected arrival of Cyril Rathbone, whom everyone seemed to know, while none of the guests knew who she was when she was introduced to them. Any dreams she had nurtured of being taken up by Pauline Mendelson, as one of the interesting people she invited to her parties, were squashed when Cyril monopolized Pauline before dinner and she did not get to meet her. Philip Quennell was seated next to Hortense, but he gave his full attention to Pauline Mendelson on his other side during most of the meal. On the several occasions she attempted to open a conversation with Arnie Zwillman, her table companion on her other side, he replied only with a yes or a no and then returned his attention to Adrienne Basquette on his other side. Arnie Zwillman never had time for girls who weren't pretty. After Casper left the table, the conversation became less general, and Philip turned to her.

"You're the literary critic for *Mulholland,* Casper tells me," he said.

"I am," she replied importantly. It was her first recognition of the evening.

"I was bruised by the review you wrote of my book," he said.

"Which book was that?" she asked, although she knew which book it was.

"*Takeover,* it was called," answered Philip. "About Reza Bulbenkian, the Wall Street financier."

"Oh, that, yes," she said dismissively. "Not my sort of book at all."

"I gathered as much," said Philip. Then he added, "But it was popular."

"As if that matters." She laughed a laugh that was nearly a snort. "That's all you people care about, isn't it?"

"And you don't care about recognition?"

"Of course not."

"Or applause?"

"No." She shook her head. There was something about her that was familiar to Philip.

She picked up his place card and looked at his name, as if she could not remember it. She squinted her eyes and pursed her lips over her protruding teeth as she read his name. "Do you make your living as a writer, Mr. Quennell?"

"I do, yes," he said.

"Hmmm," she replied. She nodded her head.

Philip watched her. "I know that you don't make your living as a nightclub singer," he said.

She looked at him in a startled way. "What in the world do you mean by that?"

"As Pearl Silver just observed to Jules Mendelson, all public people have discreditable secrets," said Philip.

"I don't have a clue what you're talking about," said Hortense.

Philip began to sing quietly in Hortense's direction, so quietly that even Pauline Mendelson, on the other side of him, could not hear.

"*You are not my first love, I've known other charms, but I've just been rehearsing, in those other arms,*" he sang.

Hortense looked at him, terrified of exposure.

"Marvene McQueen? The chanteuse? Of Miss Garbo's? Speaking of bad reviews, has your cohort Cyril Rathbone down the table reviewed your act yet? I'd be very interested in seeing that review," said Philip. He started to sing again, a little louder: "*You better go now, because I like you much too much, you better go now.*"

"What do you want?" she asked.

"I have a manuscript I want you to read."

"By you?"

"No, not by me."

"By whom?"

"That's what I'm not going to tell you. I want you to read it and tell me who you think wrote it."

"What is this, a game?"

The Marty Leskys left immediately after dinner, explaining that they had run the same film the night before at their house. Pearl Silver, pleading a headache, left with the Leskys. Dom Belcanto, his duty to Arnie Zwillman accomplished, also left, saying he and Pepper were driving back to Palm Springs that night. And Amos Swank and his new wife made a tiptoe-out-of-the-room departure, without giving any excuse at all, or even saying good-bye.

Fifteen minutes into the film in the darkened projection room, Arnie Zwillman tapped Jules on his knee and then rose and walked toward the door and left the room.

"If you're not crazy about this film, we can switch to another one," said Casper in the darkness.

"Oh, no, I'm enjoying it immensely," said Adrienne Basquette. "I love the costumes."

"Picture won't make a nickel," said Casper.

Several minutes after Arnie's withdrawal, Jules whispered into Pauline's ear. "I'll be back shortly. I have to make a call to Sims Lord."

He rose from his seat. For an instant he blocked the light ray from the projector in the booth, and his massive shadow nearly obliterated the screen.

"Down in front," came the voice of Hortense Madden, who was no longer impressed with the impressive Mendelsons, as neither had seemed to recognize her name and each had resisted conversation with her during coffee.

As Jules left the room by the same door that Arnie Zwillman had used, Pauline watched him. The evening had been an evening she had never understood since the idea had been introduced to her. She felt that the early departure of Arnie Zwillman from the darkened room had somehow triggered Jules's own departure. She could not understand the connection the two men could have together and hoped it did not have anything to do with Kippie.

"Isn't she divine?" whispered Cyril Rathbone, leaning forward from the seat behind Pauline's. Cyril Rathbone was not a man who gave up easily.

"Who?" asked Pauline.

Cyril named the actress on the screen, who was very beautiful. Pauline nodded agreement without turning. Although she never interfered in Jules's business, she had an urge to follow him.

"See this actor?" said Casper, talking about an actor in close-up on the screen. "He's had seven flops in a row. Nothing for him after this but a sitcom. He was sleeping with the director."

When Jules reentered Casper's house, he stood for a moment in the living room, not sure which way to go. The predinner drinks had been cleared away. From the kitchen he could hear the sounds of the caterers cleaning up the dinner dishes and running a vacuum cleaner in the dining room.

"Mr. Zwillman said to tell you he's in the den," said a voice behind him. Jules turned. The butler, Willard, was standing there.

"The den is where?" asked Jules.

"Through that hall. First door to the left," said Willard.

"Thank you," said Jules.

Jules felt uncomfortable with the situation he was in, but he proceeded to the den and opened the door. Arnie Zwillman was seated with a drink in his hand. The two men looked at each other.

"Shut the door behind you," said Zwillman.

Jules closed the door.

"Drink?" asked Zwillman.

"No, thank you," said Jules.

"Sure, have a drink. Clears the air."

"I never drink after dinner," said Jules.

"Except tonight," said Zwillman. He made up a scotch and soda from a drink table and handed it to Jules.

"Your wife always so quiet, or she didn't think the crowd was up to her usual standards?" asked Arnie.

"My wife is not feeling well tonight," said Jules.

"Does she know your grandfather was the bookkeeper for Al Capone and did time for income tax evasion?" asked Arnie.

"No, she doesn't," answered Jules, unperturbed. "But what happened fifty-five years ago is not of much concern to any of us today."

"Don't pull your upper-class bullshit on me, Julie," said Arnie.

"It's Jules, never Julie," said Jules.

"Oh, I beg your pardon. *Jules,*" said Arnie, with mock solemnity.

"Look, Zwillman, what is this? I don't need this aggravation from a two-bit arsonist and card cheat," said Jules. He made no attempt to conceal the derision in his voice.

Arnie Zwillman stared at Jules. When he spoke, he spoke quietly. "Does your society-lady wife know about the girl with the broken arm who went off the balcony of the Roosevelt Hotel in Chicago in nineteen fifty-three?" he asked.

Jules blanched.

Arnie Zwillman smiled. "Nor does your friend the President, who's going to appoint you to the economic conference in Brussels, I suppose."

Jules felt a tightness in his chest. His heart was pounding. He put his hand to it.

"That was an accident," he said in a voice barely above a whisper.

"Siddown," said Arnie. He spoke as if he were talking to hired help.

Jules, breathing heavily, lowered his large body into an Eames chair and stared at Arnie Zwillman.

"Over here," said Arnie, tapping the cushion next to where he was seated on a corduroy-upholstered sofa. "I got a polyp on my vocal cord, and I don't like to have to raise my voice."

Jules got up from the Eames chair and walked over to the sofa where Arnie Zwillman was seated and sat down slowly.

"You're carrying around a lot of lard there, fella," said Arnie. "How old are you, Jules?"

"Let's get down to what you wanted to see me about, Zwillman," said Jules.

"How old? Fifty-seven? Fifty-eight? Something like that? You gotta take better care of yourself. Look at me. I'm the same age you are. Look at this stomach. Flat as an ironing board. You know why? I eat vegetables. I eat fruit. I walk five miles a day, every day. I take a massage every day. I take steam and a sauna every day. It sweats the fucking pounds right off you. You gotta lose a little of that lard. Bad for your heart. What's your lady friend think about it? Does it bother her?"

"If Mrs. Mendelson has any complaints, she has not voiced them."

"I wasn't talking about Mrs. Mendelson, Jules."

Jules was silent for a moment. Then he asked, "What are we here for?"

"I'm a friend of your son, Kippie," said Arnie.

"*Step*son, not son," said Jules.

"Oh, right, *step*son. He kept saying the very same thing about you, *step*father, not father. A very naughty boy, your stepson, but charming, I'll say that for him, very charming. Ambition is not high on his priorities, but then with a rich stepdaddy like you, I suppose he has great expectations."

"No, no, he doesn't," said Jules, shaking his head emphatically.

"Perhaps not directly from you, but certainly indirectly through his mother, assuming that you cool first, which is not unlikely," said Arnie.

The idea of death was abhorrent to Jules Mendelson. As successful as he was, he still had plans for himself that would further expand his wealth and power. And there was the crowning achievement of his life so near at hand, his role as the head of the American economic delegation in Brussels during the year of the statehood of Europe.

"It was nice of Kippie to set up this meeting for me," said Arnie. "You're not an easy man to get on the telephone."

"I don't know how my stepson knows you," said Jules.

"Oh, Kippie gets in a little trouble from time to time, as I'm sure you know, and when he can't go to his famous stepdaddy or his society mama, he comes to see me for a little help," said Arnie. "One of these days he'll come to a bad end; you know that about him, don't you?"

Jules listened. It was not the first time he had heard such a prediction for his stepson. Headmasters at several very expensive schools had voiced more or less the same forecast for Kippie Petworth after expelling him.

"I think the preliminaries are over, Zwillman. What does my stepson have to do with this? Why am I sitting here talking to you in the house of this cocaine-sniffing man Stieglitz, whom I have never met before?" asked Jules.

"Not a goddamn thing. I'm not here to talk about Kippie. I'm here to talk about the laundry business, you being, or about to be, so involved in international banking in Brussels. How'd you like to go into the laundry business with me, Jules?"

"Pretty girl, isn't she?" said Pauline, in the darkened screening room, about the actress on the screen. She addressed her remark to Philip Quennell, but it was overheard by Casper Stieglitz, who, now very high, was returning from another trip to the bathroom.

"She's a big dyke," said Casper. He sat down in the row behind Pauline, in a chair next to the controls, where he could speak to the projectionist.

"Oh, no, I can't believe such a story," said Pauline, shaking her head.

"True," said Casper. "She's cleaned out half the muffs in California."

Pauline, shocked, sat in silence for several minutes. She ceased to look at the screen. She wondered where Jules was, and it occurred to her that he had gone home and left her there, as he was by nature too restless to enjoy looking at films or plays. She looked over at Philip. He smiled at her in the dark, realizing her discomfort with the unfortunate remark that Casper had just made. Pauline did not want to involve Philip, as she knew that he was working on a film for Casper Stieglitz. Finally, summoning her courage, she rose from her seat in the darkness. As Jules had before her, she blocked the light ray from the projection booth just behind her and cast a shadow on the screen.

"You looking for the toilet, Pauline?" asked Casper.

"Where is my husband?" replied Pauline.

"Talking to Arnie Zwillman in the house," said Casper.

"How do I get there?"

From the obscurity of the darkened room, Willard, the butler, appeared. "I'll take you back to the house, Mrs. Mendelson," he said.

"Don't you like the picture, Pauline?" asked Casper. He pressed the intercom and spoke in a loud voice to the projectionist. "What other pictures you got in there, Bernie?"

"*I* happen to be enjoying the picture, Casper," said Hortense Madden.

Pauline did not answer. Beside her, Philip Quennell rose. "Are you okay, Pauline?" he asked her.

"Fine, Philip, just sit down. I'm fine. I have to find Jules, that's all," whispered Pauline.

The butler reached out his hand to her, and she took it. He led her through the dark room to the sliding glass door, which he pulled back. "There's a step there," he said to her in a low voice.

Outside Pauline breathed in the fresh night air.

"Sorry, Mrs. Mendelson, for what Mr. Stieglitz said," said the butler.

"I have never in my life heard such an expression—" said Pauline, and then stopped.

"He gets a little hyper when he uses," said Willard.

Pauline looked at the butler, not sure if he meant what she thought he meant, but decided not to question him. She had been brought up with servants and understood what her father had always called the boundaries of communication. "Look at these roses," she said instead. "They need to be clipped. They need to be watered more. This garden is a disgrace."

"He's let the place go since his wife moved out," said Willard.

"He's let himself go too, I'd say," said Pauline.

"We'll go around this way by the pool," he said. "Careful here, some of the outdoor lights have gone out. One of Mr. Stieglitz's guests tripped last week."

"Heavens, I hope I don't trip," said Pauline, holding on to Willard's arm.

"I know your house, Mrs. Mendelson," said Willard.

"You do?"

"They used to call it the von Stern house before you bought it."

"Yes, they did call it that, years ago," said Pauline. "We bought it from Mr. von Stern."

"What most people don't know is that von Stern built it for Carole Lupescu, the silent film star. It's where she committed suicide."

"I didn't know that."

"Turned on the gas."

"Good heavens."

"In the garage, not the house, in a Dusenberg."

"Oh, I see."

"I'm a house freak, a movie star house freak. I know the history of every movie star's house in this town."

"Our house bears very little resemblance to the way it was when Mr. von Stern had it, I'm afraid."

"I know. I heard you did a total gut job on the house and doubled the square footage," he said.

"You know so much."

As they approached the terrace of the house, Willard said, very quickly, "Hector Paradiso was a friend of mine." If Hector Paradiso had been alive, Willard would not have called him a friend, merely an acquaintance; but dead, it was safe to secure the friendship without fear of detection. "I saw you at Hector's funeral at Good Shepherd."

"Such a sad thing it was," said Pauline. They were now on the terrace, and Pauline remembered the way. "Oh, yes, it's through here, isn't it, that we came out? I remember it now."

"Mrs. Mendelson, Hector didn't commit suicide. You know that, don't you?"

Pauline looked at Willard. "No, I don't know that. Suicide was the official finding in the autopsy report," she said, wondering why she felt obliged to explain that to Casper Stieglitz's butler, whom she probably would never see again. At the same time, she knew this man had been kind to her and realized he was sincere in what he was saying.

"Please listen," he said, with an urgency in his voice. "An undesirable called Lonny Edge was the guy who killed Hector. Believe me, Mrs. Mendelson. I only tell you this because I know what good friends you were with Hector."

Pauline did not know what to say. She had never understood Hector's death or her husband's insistence that it was a suicide. Her confusion was interrupted by loud laughter in the night air. Both she and Willard turned around to see where it was coming from. Three people, two young women and a man, all walking in an unsteady fashion, were coming around the side of the house to the pool area.

"And for God's sake, don't run your hands through his hair, because he wears a rug which he thinks we don't notice," said one of the young girls, and the three collapsed with laughter.

Willard recognized the voices but called out, "Who is that?"

"Hi, Willard. It's only us, Ina Rae and Darlene and Lonny," Ina Rae called back.

"Dear God," said Willard, looking at Pauline. "You're early, Ina Rae. Mr. Stieglitz is still running a film. Perhaps you should wait in his room until his guests leave. Go around by the kitchen entrance."

"Got any drinks, Willard?"

"Ask in the kitchen," he said. Then he turned back to Pauline, who had been staring at the young trio. "Next shift," he said simply, in explanation.

"Did she say that young man's name was Lonny?" asked Pauline.

"Yes."

"Is that the same Lonny you were speaking of just now?"

Willard nodded. He opened the door.

"This is a very active household," said Pauline. They stepped into the house. "Where do you suppose my husband is?"

"In the den with Mr. Zwillman."

"Will you show me the way?"

"Through there."

Pauline looked at Willard as if she wanted to remember his face and then opened the door of Casper Stieglitz's den without knocking. Inside, seated side by side in earnest conversation, were Jules and Arnie Zwillman. Both men held drinks in their hands, and the room was cloudy with blue cigar smoke. The men broke apart from their conversation, in surprise at the interruption.

Pauline wondered at the intensity of their involvement. It was the way she had seen Jules look when he talked with his friends from the financial world.

"Jules, I want to go home," said Pauline. She did not move from the door.

Jules looked at his watch. "Is the movie over?" he asked.

"For me it is."

"Is something the matter, Pauline?"

"I have a perfectly frightful headache, and I must leave immediately, with or without you."

"Did you meet Mr. Zwill—?"

"Yes, I did. Are you coming, Jules?" She turned and walked out of the room.

"Hey Willard," called out Ina Rae from Casper's bedroom, where she and Darlene and Lonny were smoking joints and drinking margaritas until the film was over and Casper's grand friends left and the orgy could start. "Come in here a minute, will ya?"

Willard was in the kitchen paying off the caterers and complaining bitterly to them that one of Mr. Stieglitz's black dinner plates had been broken.

"What is it, Ina Rae?" he asked, after he had completed what he was doing with the caterer. He wanted to make it perfectly clear that he did not drop everything and run when a person of the caliber of Ina Rae called him.

"My friend Lonny here has something he wants you to do," she said.

Willard looked at Lonny. He had taken off his jacket and jeans and was sitting on Casper's bed in a black jockstrap and T-shirt, with a joint hanging out of his mouth.

"You look familiar, Willard," said Lonny.

"I was at Miss Garbo's on the night you walked out of there with Hector Paradiso," answered Willard.

"The whole fucking world must have been at Miss Garbo's that night," said Lonny. "Poor Hector. Who woulda thought he'd have pumped all that lead into himself?"

For a moment the two men stared at each other. "You wanted something?"

"Yeah. Is Mr. Phil Quennell in the projection room watching the movie?"

"Yes, he is," said Willard, surprised.

"When he comes out, give him this, will you?" He picked up a large manila envelope. On it was written in a very simple handwriting, *Mr. P. Quinel. Personel.* Under it was written *Zerox copy.*

"You writing your memoirs, Lonny?" asked Willard. "You better learn how to spell first."

"Just give it to him, asshole, and don't give me any attitude. All right?" said Lonny. He reached over and put his hand on Darlene's knee and brought it all the way up the inside of her thigh, at the same time looking at Willard.

"Listen, you cheap hustler. Don't use any of Mr. Stieglitz's Porthault towels for cum rags. Got it?"

"I know the rules, Willard," said Ina Rae. "I know where he keeps the cheap towels. When's this movie going to be over, for God's sake? We may start without him. This boy's gettin' hot here."

Jules's Bentley was parked in the courtyard of Casper Stieglitz's house. He opened the door for Pauline to get in and then went around to the driver's side and got in himself. Both strapped on their seat belts without speaking. As he backed the car up, he crashed into the side of a small Honda.

"Good God," said Jules.

He opened the door of his car and looked out. "I should go in and tell the butler I hit that car," said Jules.

"No, you shouldn't, Jules," said Pauline.

"It might be Zwillman's."

"Zwillman wouldn't have a little car like that, believe me. At least you didn't hit the gold Rolls over there. That's probably Zwillman's. You can call tomorrow. It's just a dent."

"About a nine-hundred-dollar dent," said Jules.

"It's not as if you can't afford to pay for it. Let's go. I want to get away from this house," said Pauline. "I've never had a worse time anywhere."

He drove the car out of the driveway onto the cul-de-sac and made his way toward Mountain Drive, where he went through a stop sign.

"Are you drunk?" asked Pauline.

"I am a bit, yes," answered Jules.

"You're driving dangerously."

"Would you like to drive?"

"Yes, I would."

Jules pulled the Bentley over to the side of Mountain Drive and put the gearshift into neutral. He unstrapped his seat belt, opened the door of the car, and walked very slowly around to the other side. Pauline unstrapped her seat belt and slid across the leather seat to the driver's side. Then they both strapped their seat belts again. Pauline put the gearshift into drive and pulled out onto Mountain Drive, heading toward Sunset Boulevard.

"Mr. Zwillman," Jules said when the car stopped at the stoplight on Sunset Boulevard.

"What about him?"

"I never drink after dinner, ever, as you know, but he made me three drinks," said Jules.

"You didn't have to drink them."

"I know, but I did."

"Was Mr. Zwillman not the reason we went to that dreadful party in that dreadful house?" asked Pauline.

"Yes."

"At some time in the future, if someone asks you, the police or the grand jury, for instance, 'How did you get to know Arnie Zwillman?' you can now say, 'I was introduced to him at a party at the home of Casper Stieglitz, the film producer. My wife and I dined there. We saw a film there. Mr. Zwillman was also a guest, along with Marty and Sylvia Lesky, the head of Colossus Pictures, et cetera et cetera.' Is that it?"

"You're very perceptive, Pauline. Zwillman knew we wouldn't go to his house, and nobody else but a cocaine sniffer like Casper Stieglitz, who is himself no longer invited anywhere, would have him to theirs. He's a leper these days."

"And yet you bring me there, to the house of a cocaine-sniffing leper, while you meet up with a gangster," said Pauline. "It will all read wonderfully in Cyril Rathbone's column. I wonder if he'll include Ina Rae and Darlene and Lonny."

"Who?" asked Jules.

"The late shift was arriving as I was leaving."

"Jesus," said Jules.

"What did Mr. Zwillman want? Some nonpublic information for his stock portfolio?" asked Pauline.

"It had to do with the statehood of Europe in 1992," said Jules.

Pauline laughed. "What possible interest could Mr. Arnie Zwillman, who burned down the Vegas Seraglio for the insurance money, have in the statehood of Europe?"

"It is less the statehood of Europe than the role I am going to be playing in it, representing the United States," said Jules slowly.

"Don't make me pry this out of you, Jules, step by step. Keep talking until I get your point," said Pauline. She turned the Bentley off Sunset Boulevard onto Benedict Canyon and drove to Angelo Drive, where she turned left and proceeded up the winding hillside with the hairpin curves, which strangers in the city found too frightening to drive at night. It was a rare occurrence for Pauline to drive Jules, and he, although slightly drunk, was impressed with her ability.

"Mr. Zwillman is apparently involved in drug trafficking, and has at his disposal immense sums of money, immense beyond description, that he assumed I could facilitate his operation with by putting into circulation through the European Common Market," said Jules. He hiccuped.

"Why would he think you would be amenable to such a thing?"

"He threatened me."

"With what?"

Jules looked out the window of the Bentley and did not answer.

Pauline looked over at him. "What did you tell him?" she asked.

"To go fuck himself."

"It didn't appear to me when I walked into the room that you had just told Mr. Zwillman to go fuck himself," said Pauline. "That was not the impression I had at all."

Jules didn't reply.

"Are you going to report this to the police, or the FBI, or the CIA, or the President, or someone?" asked Pauline.

They looked at each other.

"No," said Jules quietly.

"Years ago, when we were first married, you told me that something had happened in your past, when you were young."

"I don't want to talk about that," said Jules quickly.

"You don't trust me, Jules, after twenty-two years of marriage?" asked Pauline.

"I trust you implicitly, Pauline, but I don't want to talk about that."

"Then just tell me one thing. Does Arnie Zwillman know about whatever it was that happened that you don't want to talk to me about?"

Jules stared out the window again.

"How do you know he wasn't wired?" asked Pauline.

"I don't," replied Jules. "I never thought of that."

They drove in silence for several minutes, as Pauline maneuvered a curve in the road. "Has it occurred to you that our lives, our so-called perfect lives, are unraveling, Jules?" she asked.

"Yes."

"Is it a matter of any concern to you?"

"Of course it is, Pauline. I don't want this to happen," said Jules. "What can we do?"

"I'm not the one who's having the affair," said Pauline. At the same moment she turned the Bentley sharply to the right, pulling up to the closed gates of Clouds. She pushed the button that lowered the window on the driver's side and reached out and pressed a seven-digit code on the calculator buttons of a computerized lock in the red brick wall adjoining the gates. Slowly, the impressive gates opened.

Jules, watching her, said, "You're an amazingly efficient woman, Pauline." Farther up the hill toward the house, the frenzied sound of the watchdogs' barking could be heard.

She looked at him. "I know," she said. The car started up the hill, and the gates swung closed behind them. As they pulled into the cobblestone courtyard, the police dogs, barking ferociously, surrounded the car.

Jules opened the car door. "Okay, boys, okay, now down, down, down. Smitty? Are you there, Smitty?"

"Over here, Mr. Mendelson," said the guard.

"Call the dogs off, will you?" said Jules.

"You boys calm down now, just calm down. I'll open the door for you, Mrs. Mendelson," said Smitty. "Hope you folks had a nice evening."

"Thank you, Smitty. We did indeed," said Pauline. Pauline's father had taught his three daughters that no matter what state their lives were in, it was important always to keep up appearances in front of the servants.

"You'll put the car away, Smitty?" said Jules.

"Sure thing."

Inside, in the hallway of their house, with the curved staircase and the six Monet paintings, Pauline started up the stairs with her hand on the railing.

Jules, following her into the house, reached out and covered her hand with his. "Perhaps we could have breakfast together in the morning," he said. The invitation was an unusual one, as Jules was always gone from their home for several hours by the time Pauline rang to have her breakfast tray brought up by Blondell. They had never once used Pauline's sunrise room for breakfast, as had been the plan when the sunrise and sunset rooms had been added on to the house.

"I had planned to sleep late," Pauline replied, withdrawing her hand from beneath Jules's hand on the banister. She continued up the stairs. The third of the six Monet paintings on the stairway wall appeared crooked to her, and she stopped to straighten it.

"Whenever you are available in the morning," replied Jules, watching her from below, "I will be here."

She turned halfway up the stairs and looked back at him. They both knew the time had come for them to talk. Then she said, quite arbitrarily, in the first of several arbitrary decisions she would make in the next year to assert her authority in her house, "I don't want to lend these Monets to the Carnegie Museum in Pittsburgh for their exhibit after all."

"But they've been promised," said Jules. "I'm sure their catalog has been printed by now."

"I don't care," she said. "I don't want to lend them. I want them here when the garden club comes."

"All right," said Jules, lifting his eyebrows. Her decision upset him, because he took his obligations in the art world very seriously, but he knew, being a dealmaker of renown, when to concede a point. While looking up at her, he made a mental note to think up an acceptable excuse before contacting the curator of the Carnegie Museum in the morning.

Looking back at him, Pauline thought, for the first time, that her husband had started to look old.

The few guests who had actually sat through the movie at Casper Stieglitz's house were leaving. Casper, glad to be rid of them, had not come to the parking area to see them off but, instead, had made straight for the bedroom where Ina Rae and Darlene and Lonny were waiting for him.

Philip Quennell opened the door of his rented car and was surprised to see a large manila envelope on the driver's seat. He picked it up, saw that his name was misspelled on the front, and knew immediately what it was and who it was from.

"Hey! Somebody put a dent in my car," screamed out Hortense Madden, as she went to open the door of her Honda. "I bet it was that ass-kissing Cyril Rathbone. As soon as Pauline Mendelson left the projection room, he lost all interest in the evening and took off in a snit. He's just the type who would back his car into yours and drive off into the night without leaving a note. I'm going to get that little prick tomorrow and make him pay through the nose."

Philip slammed the door of his car and went over to Hortense's, with the envelope in his hands. "Nasty dent," he said. "Will the door open?"

"Let me see," said Hortense. She tried her door and it opened.

"Could be worse," said Philip.

"That fucking Cyril Rathbone," said Hortense, seething with rage. " 'Pauline! How marvelous!' " she said, in an exact imitation of Cyril's florid voice.

"I don't blame you for being in a bad mood, and this is probably the wrong moment, but this is the manuscript I was talking to you about at dinner," he said.

"What do you want me to do with it?" she asked.

"Just read it," he said. "And tell me who you think wrote it. I'm at the Chateau Marmont."

Flo's Tape #14

"A lot of people think I went to Pooky, the hairdresser, just because he was the hairdresser to Pauline Mendelson, but that is not the case. That's not the kind of thing I would ever do. I knew Pooky from my days at the Viceroy Coffee Shop. He was a regular, every morning. Juice, whole wheat toast, tea. Never varied. One day he said to me, 'Rhonda'—I was still called Rhonda then, before I became Flo— 'you've got really beautiful hair, but you're wearing it in the wrong style. Come on in, and I'll do it for you.' I almost died. I mean, there were articles about Pooky in the paper, about all the famous ladies whose hair he did, like Faye Converse, Sylvia Lesky, and Pauline Mendelson. I said to him, 'Are you kidding? I could no more afford you.' He said, 'On me.'

"So, of course, I went. I've been wearing my hair this way ever since, and that was before I ever met Jules Mendelson. After I started seeing Jules, when I started wearing all the great clothes, and driving the Mercedes, and living in Beverly Hills, I began to pay the same price all the society ladies and the movie stars paid. I know he must have wondered where all the money was coming from, but he never asked any questions. I knew he was happy for me, though, that things had started to go my way.

"He always did Pauline Mendelson's hair at her house. I only saw that house once, and I never went upstairs, but I understand she had a whole, like, beauty shop of her own right off her dressing room, because she didn't like going into Pooky's shop. But one day when I was having my hair done, she walked in. I almost died. She was going back east to visit her father, unexpectedly I guess, and needed to get her hair done quickly. Wouldn't you know, I was sitting there reading about her in Cyril Rathbone's column at the time?

"That was the first time I ever thought Pooky might have suspected about me and Jules, because he quickly pulled the curtain behind me, as if he didn't want her to see me, and went outside the curtain to speak to her. When he came back in to finish me up, he never said a word."

15

"**D**UDLEY, please throw out the peonies on the upstairs hall table. There're petals everywhere," called Pauline the next morning from the top of the stairs.

"Yes, Mrs. Mendelson," replied Dudley, running up the stairs.

Dudley treasured his employment with the illustrious Mendelson family, and wished things to continue as they had always been. It was no secret among the help in the grander houses of the city that Dudley was recompensed for his services at a salary that far exceeded any of theirs, a knowledge that elevated him to a sort of celebrity status in domestic circles. On the numerous occasions throughout the years of the Mendelson parties, he knew that the guests attending were the greatest and grandest in the land, and it pleased him to be called by name by many of them, especially several of the former Presidents of the country who were regular visitors in the house. It was a measure of the high esteem with which Jules Mendelson held him that only he, and no one else, was allowed to dust van Gogh's painting of the *White Roses,* which was the most favored possession in the art-filled house.

When Pauline came down to meet Jules for breakfast, she was dressed for traveling in a tweed suit. Her mink coat, which she wore only in the east, had been placed on a gilded chair in the front hall. The size of her two bags, which had already been carried downstairs by Dudley, indicated that she planned only a brief trip. In her hand was a list of things to be attended to in her absence by her staff.

"And Dudley, I forgot to tell Blondell that the Kleenex in Mr. Mendelson's bathroom should be white, not pink ever. Make sure she changes it."

"Yes, Mrs. Mendelson," replied Dudley.

Jules, hearing Pauline descend the stairs, came out from the library, where he had been on the telephone with his various offices while waiting for her. In his hand he was carrying a coffee cup. "Where are you off to?" he asked, surprised, when he saw her bags and traveling clothes. He had expected to see her in one of her filmy negligees, which she favored for mornings in her house.

"I'm going back east for a few days to see my father," answered Pauline.

"Is he ill?"

"No more than he has been, but I haven't seen him for months, and I thought this would be a perfect time."

He had heard of no such plan the night before. "When did you decide this?"

"During the night."

He turned to go back to the library. "I'll make arrangements for you to take the plane," he said.

"No, no, don't bother. I've already made arrangements with Miss Maple," said Pauline. "The plane's going to fly me to Bangor and will turn around and fly right back so it can take you to Fort Worth for your meeting at the museum tonight."

"You're very efficient, Pauline," he said.

"You told me that last night, Jules."

"Have you had breakfast?"

"No, of course not. I thought we had a date for breakfast."

Her matter-of-factness bothered Jules. He was used to her in a different way, warm and compliant, and he was unsure of himself with her when her manner was so chilly. She preceded him down the hallway into their sunrise room, which they had never used together before for breakfast, as their morning hours had turned out to be so different. Pauline appraised the table and nodded. Her written instructions for Blondell the night before had been carried out exactly. The table was set with a Porthault cloth and napkins. Freshly cut roses from the garden were arranged in a low vase in the center of the table. Her favorite Minton breakfast china in the morning glory pattern was set at the two places. The morning papers from New York and Los Angeles were placed one on top of another on a side table. Even with a life in the beginning of turmoil, no detail in the running of her house was unworthy of her attention.

Jules watched her. "This looks very pretty," he said.

"It does, doesn't it?" she replied.

Dudley, whose instincts were keen, was aware of the unusualness of the breakfast. With proper solemnity, he entered the room with two silver pots on a tray and poured tea for Pauline and then coffee for Jules.

"Thank you, Dudley," said Pauline. "I will have only melon and one slice of toast. Tell Gertie to use the whole-grain bread. I'm sure you know what Mr. Mendelson will have."

"Yes, ma'am," said Dudley.

"Leave the coffee right here, Dudley," said Jules, rapping his knuckles on the table by his coffee cup. "I like to pour myself."

"Do you still drink six cups of coffee with breakfast?" asked Pauline.

"Something like that."

"Can't be good for your heart."

"My heart. All that I'm hearing these days is about my heart," said Jules.

"From whom else?" asked Pauline.

"Last night, from Arnie Zwillman."

"Oh," she said, in disgust, and waved her hands at the mention of Arnie Zwillman's name, as if a bad odor had suddenly permeated the room.

Dudley came into the room with Jules's scrambled eggs and bacon in a covered silver dish. Pauline lifted her delicate Minton cup with both hands and, elbows on the table, watched as Jules helped himself from the dish that Dudley held.

When Dudley retreated from the room again, she said, "I'm giving you back these yellow diamond earrings, Jules." She shook the diamonds in her hand as if they were dice and then shot them in his direction across the tablecloth.

Jules, surprised, took them. "You didn't like them?"

"Oh, yes, they're very beautiful, but I would never wear them."

"I thought you liked them last night."

"I didn't say I didn't like them. I said I wouldn't wear them."

"Why?"

"Because there is guilt attached to them. You bought them for me because you had been found out, as a sort of atonement. Rose always says the more unfaithful the husband, the greater the jewel collection," said Pauline.

"That sounds like something Rose would say," answered Jules. He put the earrings in his pocket. "I'll keep them. I'll put them in the safe. Maybe later."

"What do you mean? For Christmas? For my birthday? No, Jules. I don't want them. Send them back to Boothby's."

"All right," he said, quietly.

On the wall by her chair was a small painting of grapes and pears by Fantin-Latour. She stood up and straightened it by a fraction of an inch. "I've always loved this picture," she said.

"Do you remember when we bought it?" he asked.

"Of course." It seemed for a moment that she would recall the incident, but she chose not to. "Do you think we were ever happy, Jules, or was this all one big twenty-two-year show of a marriage?"

"Oh, Pauline, don't talk like that, please."

Dudley came in again, carrying the silver dish with the scrambled eggs and bacon, but Pauline waved him away, even though Jules would have taken more if they had been offered to him.

"Imagine dividing all this up," she said.

"All what?" he asked.

She made a gesture that indicated the whole of the contents of their house. "Everything," she said, looking at him.

A deeply troubled expression took over his face. At that instant his possessions and his position meant more to him than his obsession, and he was willing to abandon the latter.

"Don't even kid about something like that," he said.

"Oh, I'm not kidding, Jules. Not for an instant am I kidding." Pauline had no fear of meeting her husband's eye. She met it.

"No, of course you're not," he said.

"When you asked me to marry you all those years ago, my father advised me not to marry you, and now I'm going back to my father because I need to talk to someone I can trust to see whether I should stay married to you, or to end it."

"Listen to me, Pauline. I will do *anything* to keep from losing you."

"What about this woman with the red hair?"

"What woman with the red hair?"

"If you're not going to be honest with me, even now, there is no point whatever in continuing this conversation. Months ago I was sent a clipping, anonymously of course, from a Paris paper about a fire in the Meurice Hotel, with a photograph of you in the background, behind a young woman carrying a jewel case. I knew you were staying at the Ritz at the time. I chose to ignore it. I chose to forget it even. But subsequent signs have made it impossible to ignore and forget."

"Like what?"

"I smelled her on your fingers, Jules," said Pauline.

Jules's face turned scarlet. His expression was as clear as a signed confession. "All right, it's true, but it was nothing. It was meaningless. It will be over, I swear to you. I've never heard of anything so absurd in my whole life, that a marriage like ours must end because of an infidelity," he said.

"This hardly qualifies as an infidelity, Jules."

"It was an aberration, no more, I swear to you. I'm fifty-seven years old. Perhaps it was panic. I simply was carried away with an overwhelming feeling."

"Do you think I don't occasionally have feelings like that for other people, Jules?" asked Pauline.

Jules looked at her, as if the idea had never occurred to him.

"I do," she said. "Young Philip Quennell, for instance. I think he is very attractive. I even told him that last night at that terrible party."

At the mention of Philip Quennell's name, Jules winced. He could not bear Philip Quennell.

"I could visualize having an affair with him if I were the kind of woman who had affairs. But I *didn't* have an affair with him, Jules."

Jules was aghast at the thought of his wife even thinking of having an affair. "Because of Camilla?" he asked.

"That, yes. But also, Jules, because of you, because of our marriage, which is something I have taken very seriously."

"So have I."

"No. You want an ornamental wife, that's all, and that's not good enough for me."

There was a silence between them.

"Philip Quennell, by the way, has made no such offer to me, nor has he shown the slightest interest of that sort in me."

"I have taken a dislike to your friend Quennell," said Jules.

"He doesn't believe that Hector committed suicide," replied Pauline. "Neither did the butler at Mr. Stieglitz's last night."

Jules shook his head in impatience. "Who cares what people like that think?"

"I don't believe it either," she said.

"Believe it," he said.

"Are you ordering me to believe something I don't believe?"

"Yes." There was a harshness in his voice.

Puzzled, she looked at him.

There was a knock on the door, and Dudley entered with an attitude of anxiety, interrupting what he knew to be an important private meeting between the two people he had served for many years. "I'm sorry to interrupt," he said.

"That's all right," said Pauline.

"The car is here. The bags are in," he said.

"Yes, I'll be right there. Put these newspapers in the car, will you, Dudley?"

When Dudley left, Jules said, "I'll drive out to the airport with you."

"Oh, don't be silly, Jules." She took a final sip of her tea.

"You don't have to hurry, you know. Have another cup of tea. The nice thing about having your own plane is that it's not going to leave without you," said Jules.

Pauline shook her head. His remark was one she had heard often before. When she got to the door of the room, she turned back. "This room is really quite pretty, don't you think? Isn't it too bad we never used it?" She walked out.

Jules rose and followed Pauline out of the room, down the corridor to the hallway, and out the front door to the courtyard.

"Have you put Mrs. Mendelson's bags in the back?" he asked, even though he had just heard from Dudley that the bags were in the car already.

The chauffeur stood holding the door. As she was about to get in, Pauline turned to the butler and said, "Dudley, there's a crack in the windowpane of the lavatory off the library. Ask Joe to replace the pane, will you?" She stepped into the car. "Oh, and one more thing, Dudley. Will you check and see if one of the Flora Danica salad plates is missing? I counted only twenty-three yesterday."

Jules stepped up and nodded to the chauffeur that he would close the door. "Give my best to your father," he said.

"I will," replied Pauline.

"How long will you be gone?"

"I don't know exactly, Jules. Not long."

"When you're ready to return, let me know, and I'll arrange for the plane to fly to Bangor and pick you up," he said. He did not want her to leave.

Pauline pulled on her gloves. "Good-bye, Jules," she said.

"I'll miss you," he said.

Pauline nodded. "All right, Jim, let's go," she said to the chauffeur.

Jules stepped back and closed the rear door. As the car started to move forward, he raised his hand to wave to her. After the car pulled out of the courtyard and started down the driveway, Jules remained standing there, not moving.

In the upstairs hall, standing back from the window, Blondell watched the departure. She did not understand why she felt sadness. From the main hallway downstairs, Dudley also watched with a sense of foreboding.

It surprised Jules that he felt bereft. He had never acknowledged to himself that Pauline was necessary to him as a component part of his existence. Throughout his adult life and great worldly success, Jules had been much sought after to sit on the boards of directors of businesses and hospitals and museums. He had been asked to serve as pallbearer or eulogist at the funerals of a President of the United States, six senators, two governors, and numerous chief executive officers of banks and businesses. As the husband of Pauline Mendelson, he was considered a prize and a catch at social functions. And, yet, he knew deep inside him that he did not have a single intimate friend to whom he could turn in time of trouble. Except Pauline.

"Do you ever go to the doctor's, Jules?" asked Flo.

"For what?"

"Checkups? Anything?"

"No."

"You should, you know."

"I know. I know."

Flo bought Jules a treadmill, which she set up in her bedroom. She made him use it for twenty minutes each afternoon as a way to deal with his weight. When the canceled check came to Miss Maple, Jules was inordinately pleased to see how much money she had spent on him out of her allowance.

"Jules, honey, I don't understand what laundered money means," said Flo, sitting in a chair watching him.

Jules, hands on the rail, walked in place. His twenty minutes on the treadmill had become a talking time for them, and they both enjoyed it. "Look, let me explain," said Jules. He liked to discuss things with Flo. "Say I have a painting worth a million dollars. Arnie Zwillman buys that picture from me for that much money, but he pays for it in cash out of his briefcase. Then, with the art market the way it is, the value of the painting appreciates. That means it goes up in value, and he can then sell it on the open market, or at auction."

"Oh, I get it," said Flo. "So the dirty money becomes clean."

"Right," said Jules. "Only he wasn't talking about art."

"Honey, you can't get involved with that. You know that, don't you?" said Flo.

"I know."

"Then tell Arnie Zwillman to go fuck himself."

Jules nodded. He wished it were that simple. He turned the switch of his treadmill off. For a few moments he remained on the machine without speaking. Then he walked away from her toward the bathroom. At the bathroom door, he said quietly, "There's more to this than you know."

"What?"

"There're things about me that he knows that no one else knows."

"Not even Pauline?"

"Not even Pauline."

She stared at his back. "Like what?" she asked.

He turned around to look at her. She had never seen his face look so haunted. He opened his mouth to speak. Then he looked at his watch. "I'd better go. It's late. I have to meet Sims Lord for dinner."

"I want to hear," Flo persisted.

Jules was a keeper of secrets; he was not a person who confided in other people. Even Sims Lord, his trusted adviser, did not know everything there was to know about Jules. Sims only knew everything there was to know about Jules's business dealings. When Jules met with him later that evening, he planned to tell him about his extraordinary conversation with Arnie Zwillman, about the money-laundering proposition, but he would not be able to tell Sims the things that Arnie Zwillman knew about his life, about the girl who had gone off the balcony of the Roosevelt Hotel in Chicago in 1953. Or about Kippie. Sometimes he worried about his heart. It beat too fast when he thought about the things that were buried inside of him. He knew he should make an appointment to see Dr. Petrie, but he was always too busy, and he kept postponing it.

"Tell me," insisted Flo.

When, finally, he started to talk, he spoke slowly in a low voice, almost as if he were talking to himself, and Flo had to lean forward to hear him. She knew that if she interrupted him to ask him to speak louder, he would change his mind and not go on with his story. "When I was a young man, something horrible happened to me in Chicago, for which I bear the responsibility," he said.

In Northeast Harbor, Maine, it always amused Neville McAdoo when he heard himself described as Pauline Mendelson's father. It amused him even more when he heard himself described as Jules Mendelson's father-in-law. The previous summer he had celebrated his seventy-fifth birthday with a small dancing party under a green-and-white-striped marquee, given by his three daughters and their husbands. All his grandchildren came, even Kippie, who was known in the family as the California cousin. The men all wore blazers and white flannels, and the ladies, dressier than the men, were in silk prints or summer chiffons with a minimum amount of jewelry. No black tie for them. Among themselves, they chuckled at the pretensions and swank of Newport and Southampton social life, much preferring the simplicity of their own. "They have no denial of anything in those places," said Neville McAdoo. "They have no Northeast discipline." Northeast parties were never reported in the New York social column of Dolly De Longpre, who had been the recognized chronicler of society for three decades.

At that party Jules Mendelson had won the admiration of all the McAdoos when he made himself agreeable for several hours to Aunt Maud, who was known in the family as poor Aunt Maud. It was the late husband of poor Aunt Maud, Uncle Harry, who had been found dead in bed in a seedy West Side hotel in New York, dressed in women's clothing, and Aunt Maud had been a trial to everyone ever since. Kippie, who had been expelled from both St. Paul's and St. George's before going to finish up his preparatory years at Le Rosay in Switzerland, had a sort of mysterious glamour in the family. "So good-looking," the older ladies said about him. Or, "Such charm." His contemporaries had different opinions. It was at the party that Kippie had strangled a cat, as a prank, at the young people's table, to the horror and fascination of his eastern cousins. "I'll never speak to you again, Kippie Petworth," said his Philadelphia cousin, Louise Ordano, who was nearly in tears. "Lucky for you it wasn't one of Poppy's Abyssinians, that's all I can say." Cosimo and Cosima were their grandfather's Abyssinian cats, on whom he doted.

It was in keeping with Kippie's usual good luck that there had been very little commotion over the strangled cat, as it was an unknown cat that had wandered into the party tent, and it was not missed. Kippie, along with Bozzie Manchester, his New York cousin, had buried the unfortunate cat in the woods beyond his grandfather's property, and no more had been said about it.

"It's so lovely here, Poppy," said Pauline. "I always forget. I always mean to come back more often."

"The Van Degans want you for lunch," said Neville McAdoo.

"Oh, no, thanks, Poppy. I'll stay here with you," said Pauline. She dipped her napkin into a water glass and wiped away a stain on her father's white linen jacket where he had dripped carrot soup, without interrupting the flow of her conversation. "Lean closer to the table, Poppy, so you won't spill," she said. "And let me bring your napkin up higher. There. Now finish your soup. That nice girl from town made it especially for you. She said it was your favorite. What a treasure she is."

"Colleen," said old Mr. McAdoo. "Her name is Colleen. She's not a maid, you know, or a cook either. She comes in and takes care of me on vacations and weekends, when she's not at the university." Everything about Northeast Harbor fascinated her father. He took as much interest in the lives of the locals as he did in the summer people. "She's going to hotel school and wants to be the manager of the Asticou Inn one day."

"Marvelous," said Pauline. "The young today, they're so filled with ambition and purpose."

"How's Kippie?" asked her father.

"Well, sadly, Kippie doesn't fit into that pattern of ambition and purpose, but his charm continues unabated, I suppose. He's still in that rehab in France, for drugs."

Neville McAdoo patted his daughter's hand. Always slim, he had played tennis every day until a few years before his stroke. To shade his face from the sun he was wearing a white tennis hat that had been laundered so often it was soft and floppy. They were sitting on the veranda of his large cedar-shingle house, turned gray by fifty Maine winters, looking out on Somes Sound. It had been a blessing in disguise when the original McAdoo house in Bar Harbor, next to Northeast Harbor, had burned to the ground in the great fire of 1947. The once proud McAdoo fortune had diminished by that time, and the family could not have afforded to keep the place going for many more summers. With the insurance money, Neville McAdoo's father built a more practical house in Northeast Harbor, with only ten bedrooms rather than thirty, and it was there that Pauline and her sisters had spent all the summers of their lives until they were married.

"What's the matter, Pauline?" he asked.

"You always knew when something was the matter, didn't you, Poppy?" she said.

"You don't just appear out of the blue in Northeast in the spring before the season starts without something very important on your mind," he replied.

Pauline untied and then tied again the sleeves of a cashmere sweater that hung over her shoulders. She rose from her wicker chair and walked to the edge of the veranda and sat on the railing, facing her father. "I'm thinking of leaving Jules," she said.

Jules never discussed the whereabouts of his wife with his mistress, but his mistress religiously followed his wife's comings and goings in the society pages and gossip columns. Cyril Rathbone, in particular, continued to have an inordinate interest in the activities of Pauline Mendelson, although he had, fortunately, seemed not to have connected Jules Mendelson and Arnie Zwillman in his account of Casper Stieglitz's party. He simply named the Mendelsons as "surprise guests at a mixed-bag evening."

"Where's Northeast Harbor?" asked Flo.

"Maine," replied Jules cautiously. "Why?"

"Is it like Malibu?"

"Good heavens, no."

"Like Newport?"

"Are you referring to Newport, California, or Newport, Rhode Island?"

"I didn't know there were two."

"There are. It is not at all like Newport, California, and it is more under-stated than Newport, Rhode Island."

"Understated. Does that mean classier?"

"To some, I suppose."

"Like the quiet rich? That kind of thing?"

"I suppose. Why this great interest in Northeast Harbor?"

"I hear that Pauline is visiting her father there."

Jules was silent for a moment. "And where did you hear that?" he asked.

"I didn't exactly hear it. I read it."

"Where?"

"In Cyril Rathbone's column."

"I should have guessed that. You seem to rely on that swine for so much of your information."

"I'd die happy to have my name in Cyril Rathbone's column."

"Oh, please."

"I really would, Jules. I like to read about all those people and places he writes about. It's like another world to me. One day I'd like to go to all those places, like Newport and Southampton and Northeast Harbor," said Flo.

"I wouldn't mind another glass of wine," said Jules.

"With Pauline out of town, you don't have to go home tonight, do you?"

"Yes, I have to go home, but I don't have to go home right away. I was supposed to go out to dinner, but I canceled that. I thought we might have dinner here."

"How about taking me out to dinner, Jules?" asked Flo.

"Why not eat here?"

"Because I'm sick of eating here. Chinese takeout from Mr. Chow's, or pizzas sent in from Spago. That's what eating at home is for me. I know how to wait tables, but I don't know how to cook food. I want to go out." She stood up to show her impatience.

"It's not practical," said Jules, dismissing the notion with a shake of his head.

"And why not?" persisted Flo. She placed the forefinger of her left hand on the small finger of her right hand and moved it from finger to finger as she reiterated the immediate facts of Jules's life. "Pauline's out of town in North-east Harbor, Maine, visiting her old father. You don't have to go to one of Rose Cliveden's dinners because she's laid up in bed with a broken leg and a bottle of vodka, and besides you never go to those fancy dinners when Pauline is away. And the guy from the museum in Hartford who was coming to look at your paintings and try to get you to leave them to the Wadsworth Atheneum had to postpone because his mother-in-law committed suicide. And Sims Lord is at the bankers' convention in Chicago giving a speech in your place because you didn't want to go to Chicago. And the guy from the Louvre Museum in Paris who mended the crack in the Degas ballerina that you accidentally knocked off its pedestal because some guy got you mad at lunch after Hector Paradiso's funeral is not due in with the statue until tomorrow night. So you're free, and you're going to take me out to dinner."

Jules laughed. "Good God. How do you know all those things?" he asked.

"Because I'm a good listener, Jules. You lie here on my bed with the telephone on your stomach and make all those calls, and I just listen and remember."

He patted her hand. "Look, Flo, dear. It's not a good idea to go out to dinner," said Jules patiently. "Especially right now."

"I'm not asking you to take me to the Bistro Garden, or Chasen's. We don't have to go to a fancy place, where you're going to run into a lot of people you know."

Jules shook his head. He did not want to go out in public with Flo, but he could not bring himself to say that.

"There's even the goddamn Valley. You'll certainly never see anyone in the *Valley* who crosses over with your kind of life. Let's just have dinner together, like two normal people having an affair. Please, Jules. *Please.* I'm always all dressed up with no place to go. You don't know how lonely I get."

"Okay," he said quietly. He reached over and put his hand on her thigh and started to move it back and forth.

"Oh, no, none of that," she said, slapping his hand. "Don't get horny again. I know that trick. We'll start, and then you won't take me out to dinner. *After* dinner, I'll take care of your dick." She hopped out of bed and ran toward her closet. "A new Chanel suit came today. Black. Gold buttons. And a *very* short skirt, up to here."

"Where can we go where we aren't likely to see anyone?" asked Jules.

Twenty-two years earlier her father had advised Pauline not to marry Jules Mendelson. Neville McAdoo, who admired physical fitness and athletic prowess, had minded that Jules was overweight and never exercised almost as much as he minded that Jules was not eligible for any of the clubs that members of the McAdoo family had belonged to for generations. Clubs played a great part in their lives. But even Neville McAdoo could not ignore Jules's importance in the world of finance, and over the years he had come to like and respect his son-in-law.

And Jules, although he never would have admitted such a thing, was impressed with the lineage of his wife's family. He wondered in the beginning how a family that had received so much publicity through the brilliant marriages of the three sisters could have so little money. In the era of vast fortunes in which they were living, the McAdoo millions, which numbered less than five, were considered insignificant, at least in the circles in which Jules moved. It was Jules, the rich outsider, who had paid to put Poppy's old house in order again after his stroke, winterizing it, reroofing it, and adding on to the already ample veranda so that a ramp could more easily facilitate the wheelchair that had become a part of Poppy's life. Inside, the library, which Poppy always called the book room, had been made over into his bedroom, and the lavatory off the library had been enlarged to a full bathroom, with railings on the wall of his shower and tub. His greatest fear was falling and breaking a hip.

The telling of her tale was painful and difficult for Pauline. Normally so articulate and descriptive in her accounts of her life, she spoke now in a halting and disjointed fashion, looking away from her father so that he could not see the shame and pain that showed in her face. Jules was having an affair, she began. She had found out about it in the most shaming manner. "So hurtful,

Poppy. No, no, I won't tell you how I found out. He has a mistress. He is keeping this woman. He is besotted with her."

"Did he tell you he was besotted with her?"

"Several times I have awakened in the middle of the night, and he is lying there next to me, wide awake, staring at the ceiling."

If Pauline had expected her father to react with ungentlemanly glee, she was mistaken. And he would not indulge in any I-told-you-so type of conversation, for he loved his daughter and could see that she was deeply unhappy.

"Have you ever seen her?" her father asked, when Pauline had finished.

"Some anonymous person sent me a photograph of her from a Paris newspaper. He took her to Paris. Did I tell you that?"

"Is she younger than you?"

"Not quite young enough to be my daughter, but almost. And pretty. Slightly common, but pretty."

"Is she in your set out there?"

"Heavens, no."

"Are you likely to encounter her?"

"I shouldn't think so."

"Are your friends like Rose Cliveden and Camilla Ebury likely to encounter her?"

One of the Abyssinian cats strolled out onto the veranda. When it came to Neville McAdoo's chair, it raised its paw to scratch at his leg. "Oh, yes, here she is," he said, delighted. He leaned over and picked up the cat. "Or here *he* is, rather. I'm never quite sure which is which. Are you Cosima or Cosimo?" He raised the cat up and stared between its legs. "Cosima, of course. I knew you were Cosima all the time." He settled back with the cat in his arms. "Are you being gossiped about?" he asked, as if the cat had not interrupted.

"If we are, I am unaware of it," answered Pauline. "At least I have not noticed any change in attitude on the part of my friends."

"Does Jules want to leave you to marry her?"

"No. I don't think so. I feel just the opposite. I feel he doesn't want to leave me, or want me to leave him. He wants both."

"Perhaps it's that relentless social life you lead out there," said Poppy. "Jules was never much for social life when you met him. Maybe this woman is just a respite from all those parties."

Pauline felt stung. "The wives of brilliant men should be socially ambitious," she said defensively. "I have played an enormous part in Jules's success, and Jules is aware of that too, but our success together is built around Jules, make no mistake about that. He is an extraordinary man. That is a thing I have never doubted, from the moment I first met him that night in Palm Beach at Laurance Van Degan's dance."

"You sound like you love him still."

"I do," she said. "Remember, I had someone to compare him to, the socially perfect and totally ineffectual Johnny Petworth."

"Oh, Johnny," said Mr. McAdoo, shaking his head sadly. "I saw him at the Butterfield the last time I was in New York, in a perfect snit over a bid in a bridge game that Win Stebbins had called wrong."

"That's what I mean by totally ineffectual," said Pauline. "I knew that marriage was a mistake during the honeymoon, but if I hadn't met Jules, I might have remarried someone just like Johnny Petworth."

"Then stick it out, Pauline. Whatever he's having will pass. He's not the first man to have an affair, you know, and it's highly unlikely that you will be embarrassed by such a person, in the way you might have been if she was one of your own set."

Her father slowly raised his hand and pointed a bony finger out to Somes Sound.

"What is it, Poppy?" asked Pauline.

"Billy Twombley's new sailboat," answered her father.

"Yes, yes, isn't it lovely?" said Pauline. Her father, she knew, was finished with the subject of Jules Mendelson.

Flo and Jules drove to the San Fernando Valley to a steak house on Ventura Boulevard in Universal City. Listening as she did to everything that was said, Flo already knew that people in the group that the Mendelsons and their friends moved in considered the San Fernando Valley to be as remote as a different state.

"Do you have a reservation?" asked the maître d'.

"I don't," said Jules.

"I'm afraid there will be a wait of about twenty minutes," said the maître d', perusing his reservation list. "You may wait in the bar."

"I don't want to wait for twenty minutes," said Jules quietly.

"Look, there's a table over there in the corner," said Flo.

"I was about to seat a couple who have been waiting in the bar for that table," said the maître d', haughtily. He picked up two large menus to take to that couple when he fetched them.

Jules reached into his pocket and took out his money, which he carried in a loose wad, unencumbered by a clip or wallet. He peeled off a bill and handed it to the maître d'.

"Oh, no, sir. I'm afraid we don't accept tips for seating patrons out of turn." He looked down at the bill in his hand, and his expression changed. "Let me look to see if something has opened up in the John Wayne room."

"I don't want to sit in the John Wayne room," said Jules. "I want to sit at that table over there in that corner."

"Follow me," said the maître d'.

"How much did you tip him?" whispered Flo over her shoulder, as she followed the man to their table.

"Fifty," replied Jules.

"Wow," said Flo.

Seated, Jules ordered a martini and Flo ordered a Diet Coke. Out in public, Jules felt strange with Flo. In her house they could talk together for hours, but in the restaurant, even though it was highly unlikely that he would encounter anyone he knew, he found it difficult to keep up the conversation. He picked up the menu, which had a leather cover and a tassel, and glanced down it. "Let's see what they have," he said.

"Actually, Jules, I don't eat steak," said Flo.

"Why didn't you say that when I picked this place?"

"I was afraid you'd change your mind."

He looked down at the menu again. "They have lobster tails. Frozen, I'm sure. Does that appeal to you?"

"Oh, sure. I can't believe we're actually doing this, Jules."

She looked around her at the other tables. An expression of recognition came over her face.

"Do you see someone you know?" asked Jules.

"Trent Muldoon. The television actor who owns my house, that you keep telling me you're going to buy for me but never do."

"Don't say hello, for God's sake."

"I don't even know him to say hello to."

There was a moment of silence. "What did you do with yourself all day?" he asked finally.

"Read. I'm a great reader, you know," she answered.

"I didn't know, but I'm delighted to hear that. What sort of things do you read? Besides Cyril Rathbone, I mean."

"Biographies, mostly," she said, aware of the importance of the word.

"Biographies? Really? What sort?"

"Marilyn Monroe, mostly," she replied, quite unselfconsciously. "I think I've read everything that has ever been written on Marilyn Monroe."

Jules laughed.

"Oh, sure, go ahead, laugh. Typical, Jules," said Flo. She shook her head in dismissal of his attitude. "I happen to think that Marilyn was murdered. In fact, I know she was murdered. All the evidence points to it. She didn't die in her house, you know, like everybody thinks. She died in the ambulance, and they took her back to the house, where she was discovered dead."

Jules shook his own head in turn, but for a different reason. He was madly in love with a woman whose position in life was inappropriate for his position in life. This was not the sort of conversation he would ever have had with Pauline. Pauline understood world and economic affairs well enough to converse intelligently, and she could hold his interest when she discussed the events and personalities of the social world to which she had been born. No cockeyed Marilyn Monroe theories for her. "That whole story has always been absurd," said Jules.

"She was an inconvenient woman, you know," said Flo, ignoring him. She now nodded her head in a way to indicate to Jules that she wasn't telling half of what she knew about the case. "I used to hear things."

"Hear things where?" he asked.

"At the coffee shop. You'd be surprised at the things I used to hear there. And from Glyceria too. She knows things that Faye Converse told her. Faye was a friend of Marilyn's."

"What sort of things?"

"What do powerful people do with someone who's become inconvenient?" asked Flo.

"Tell me," said Jules.

"Don't you see?"

"No, I don't. What's to see?"

"You get rid of the person, and they got rid of Marilyn."

"Oh, for God's sake," said Jules impatiently. "You people with all those wacky theories."

"And you people who are always saying there are no conspiracies." There was a tone of harshness in her voice.

For a moment they stared at each other. "Is this a fight we're having?" asked Jules.

Flo smiled. "I'll back off," she said. "I don't want to blow my big night out on the town."

Pauline walked through a cluttered side hallway, past croquet mallets, tennis rackets, boots, and umbrellas, and entered a sitting room that had little to do with fashion but a great deal to do with taste. From the lower shelf of a table behind a sofa loosely covered in extremely worn chintz, she pulled out some photograph albums.

"Here they are," she said, returning to the veranda. "I knew I'd seen them somewhere."

Her father smiled at her. He took out his round gold-rimmed spectacles and put them on. She pulled up a chair next to his wheelchair and set the albums on a table in front of them. Slowly he started to turn the pages, and in a few minutes they were laughing together as they were reminded of other times. When they came to the latest album, the pictures of his birthday party the year before, he said, "What's happened to Justine Altemus?"

"You haven't heard? She married Herkie Saybrook."

Neville McAdoo nodded approvingly. It was the kind of match he believed in. "That must have pleased her mother," said Poppy.

"As much as Lil is ever pleased about anything, I suppose," said Pauline.

"Good croquet player, Herkie Saybrook. His grandfather and I were at Groton together." He turned a few more pages and made a few more comments about people. "You haven't told me everything that's bothering you, have you?"

"No."

"Well?"

"I don't know why I feel this, but I think he is being blackmailed by a gangster," said Pauline.

"Because he has a mistress?" asked Poppy. "Hardly likely these days, Pauline."

"That's not why, Poppy. Once he told me, when we were first married, that there had been trouble in his life years ago. He asked me not to ask him about it. I only said at the time, 'Were there consequences?' or something like that. He said, and I remember it distinctly, 'One of the advantages of having rich parents is that they keep you out of jams.' Then, not wanting to embarrass him about it, I told him the story of Aunt Maud's husband being found dead in a seedy West Side hotel in women's clothing."

"You didn't tell him that?"

"I did."

"We all promised never to refer to it."

"I know. But Jules never gossips, and he would never do anything to embarrass me, ever, that much I know."

"Except have a mistress."

Pauline looked away. "We never referred to what happened to Jules again; but, whatever it is, I think the gangster, Mr. Zwillman he's called—Arnie

Zwillman—I think he knows whatever it is that's in Jules's past. I used to think that perhaps he had gotten a girl pregnant when he was young, but now I think it is something more serious. Jules looked old to me for the first time, almost defeated, the other night after he saw Mr. Zwillman. Whatever it is, I think if it came to light, Jules's appointment to Brussels might be in jeopardy, and that appointment means everything to Jules."

Neville McAdoo closed the photograph album and removed his gold-rimmed spectacles before he spoke again. "All the more reason for you to stay with Jules, Pauline."

Jules took out his parking check and handed it to the parking boy.

"What kind of car, sir?" asked the boy.

"Bentley, dark blue," replied Jules.

Flo, who was always curious about other people, turned to look at a couple who were waiting for their car. "That's Trent Muldoon again," she said excitedly, tapping Jules on the arm to turn and look at the television star. "I think I'll go over and introduce myself while you're getting the car. I read in some column he's going to make a picture in Yugoslavia."

"No, no, don't," said Jules.

"Jules! Hello! Howareyou?"

Flo, without turning, immediately recognized the voice as the voice of a society woman. She wondered how they all learned to talk like that, with that slightly strident sound that announced their class and privilege. Later, alone, she would say to herself over and over again, "Jules! Hello! Howareyou?" until she had the voice imitated perfectly.

"Madge," she heard Jules say. She did not turn around, but she knew they were kissing on first one cheek and then the other, in the manner of society people. She would have liked to see Jules participate in that ritual, but she knew not to turn. "What*ever* are you doing all the way out here?" she heard the woman called Madge ask.

"A little business dinner with Sims Lord," she heard Jules answer. "And you? What are you doing out here?"

"We're on our way to the ranch for the weekend," answered Madge. "Ralph adores the food here, don't ask me why, all that awful red meat, so bad for you, every doctor says so. Where is Sims? I'd love to say hello. I haven't seen him for ages."

"I think he stopped in the men's room," said Jules.

"So did Ralph," said Madge. "How's Pauline's father?"

"Oh, fine," answered Jules. "A little stroke can't keep Neville McAdoo down."

"When is Pauline coming back?" asked Madge.

Jules's Bentley pulled up in front of the restaurant, and the parking boy hopped out. "Your car, sir," he called out to Jules. He went around to the passenger side and opened that door for Flo to get in.

Flo turned around and stood awkwardly in place, not sure what to do, and Madge White, whose daughter had become pregnant by Jules's stepson, Kippie Petworth, when they were both fourteen years old, sensed immediately that the pretty girl with red hair wearing a Chanel suit was there with Jules.

Jules, used to difficult moments in business, appeared unperturbed, as if he were in control during a complex moment in a negotiation. "Oh, may I introduce, uh, Miss, uh?—help me," he said to Flo, as if he hardly knew her himself. "I'm terrible with names."

"March," whispered Flo, embarrassed by Jules's attitude.

"Yes, yes, of course, Miss March, forgive me. I'm so terrible with names. This is Mrs. White. Miss March works with Sims."

"Hellohowareyou?" said Madge White, staring at the young woman.

Flo, confused, nodded but did not speak. Flo could see by the haughty look on Madge White's face that she understood the situation, and she shrank from the look.

A car horn honked at the delay caused by the Bentley's blocking the departure area. There were cars with impatient occupants backed up behind, waiting to be parked.

"Your car, sir," called out the parking boy again, but neither Jules nor Flo moved toward it.

A taxi pulled up next to the Bentley. As an arriving couple got out of the cab, Flo called out, "I'll take that cab," and ran toward it.

Jules, upset, called out after Flo, "I'll be happy to drop you off, Miss March." He wondered if Madge White noticed the concern in his voice.

Flo, in the cab, looked back at Jules. There were tears in her eyes. "No, no, I'm sure you and Mr. Lord have important things to talk over, Mr. Mendelson," she said. She turned to the driver. "Beat it. That Bentley is going to follow me, and I don't want to be followed."

"Where to, lady?" asked the driver. He was aware that the young lady was highly agitated, but he did not want to become involved in her drama.

"Please. Please. Move quickly," she pleaded. She gave her address on Azelia Way in Beverly Hills.

"Do you want to take Laurel Canyon or Coldwater Canyon?" asked the driver. He spoke with a heavy Middle Eastern accent.

Flo looked out the rear window of the cab and saw that Jules was shaking hands with Madge White and getting into his car. She knew immediately that he would go to Azelia Way to find her, and she did not want to be found by him. "No, listen, driver, I changed my mind. Take me to the Chateau Marmont on Sunset Strip," she said. "Take Laurel Canyon. You can go quicker on Laurel."

The Chateau Marmont was where Philip Quennell lived.

"On the afternoon of the day that Pauline left for Northeast Harbor to visit her father, Jules was, as always, in my house at the regular time, about a quarter to four. He didn't tell me she had gone away, by the way. I only knew that when I read it in Cyril Rathbone's column. Anyway, we'd done it a couple of times, and he was lying on my bed talking on the telephone, just like he always did, conducting a little business before we did it again. For a guy his age, he could go more times than most guys half his age.

"But that day he needed his little agenda book that he always carried with him, that told him where he had to be at what time, and listed the sixty or seventy telephone numbers that immediately affected his personal and business life. By the way, he had me in there under Red, as in red hair, in case Pauline or Miss Maple or someone was looking through it, I suppose. Anyway, that day he was talking to someone important, I forget who now, maybe Myles Crocker from the State Department, and he signaled to me without stopping his conversation to get him his agenda out of his suit jacket.

"Well, I got the little book out and, naturally, being curious, I started flicking through it to see what fancy dinner parties he was going to that week. And that was when I saw that he had several appointments with Dr. Petrie. Dr. Petrie, in case you never heard of him, was one of the eminent heart specialists of Los Angeles. I happened to know that because Jules had attended a testimonial in his honor. Kind of a cold chill went through me. I wondered if he was okay, healthwise.

"Later, I said to him, 'You okay, Jules?' He said, 'What are you talking about?' I said, 'Your ticker?' He said again, 'What are you talking about?' I said, 'I saw in your agenda you had some appointments with Dr. Petrie.' When Jules got mad, his face got red and he became very silent. That's what happened then. He got mad. He said it was because I shouldn't have pried into his book, that it was bad manners.

"You see, I always thought the merry-go-round was never going to stop, but I should have begun to see the signs that day."

16

ON THE AFTERNOON of the evening that Jules and Flo dined together at a restaurant in the San Fernando Valley, another encounter took place on a street in Beverly Hills that also caused a disruption in a relationship. Camilla Ebury, the rich and pretty young widow who was having an affair with Philip Quennell, had begun to experience feelings for him that she had never felt for her late husband, and thoughts of marriage were beginning to form, although she knew almost nothing of her lover's life before she met him at the Mendelsons' party. She only knew that he was not a fortune hunter. On his part, Philip was enjoying an extremely pleasant relationship, but, for reasons of his own, he did not think of it in terms of permanence. He was merely a transient figure in the city where Camilla was entrenched. It was his intention, as it had always been, to return to his home in New York when he finished the screenplay for the documentary he was writing for Casper Stieglitz. By that time, he felt sure that the furor that had been caused by the book he had written about Reza Bulbenkian would have died down.

As with many women of her position, much of Camilla Ebury's time was taken up with good works and cultural activities. She worked long hours for the fashionable charities of the city, the Los Angeles Orphanage Guild, the Colleagues, and the Blue Ribbon Four Hundred, and her name was often listed on the committees of charitable events. She felt that it was the obligation of people born with money to devote a portion of their time to helping those less fortunate. She was also a splendid tennis player and a first-rate golfer and was often involved in tournaments. She had her own tennis court at her home in Bel Air, and she and Philip often played early in the morning before he went back to his room at the Chateau Marmont, where he worked on his screenplay. Several times a week she played golf at the Los Angeles Country Club on Wilshire Boulevard.

"All you people look alike at this club," Philip had said one Sunday evening, looking around the dining room.

She knew what he meant. "Well, we all know each other," she said. She had belonged to the Club all her life, as her father and her late husband had before her, and she knew the names of most of the members and most of the help. Every Sunday evening she and her daughter, Bunty, went to the Club for the buffet supper, just as she had gone with her father when she was a child, and Philip had started to accompany them.

"No show folk."

"No."

"No ethnics."

"Mr. and Mrs. Watkins, remember."

"Tokens."

"Well, that's the way it is. That's the way it always has been," she said to Philip, with a shrug. She hated that kind of conversation. "They have clubs too that we can't get into. Don't forget that."

Philip laughed. It was not the first time he had heard her give this rationale.

"Even the Mendelsons couldn't get into the Los Angeles Country Club, and God knows, Pauline McAdoo comes from about as good a family as you get back east," said Camilla.

"I bet if you checked into it, you'd find the problem was Jules, not Pauline," replied Philip.

Camilla didn't reply. "Here comes Bunty. Don't continue this conversation in front of her."

Philip did not play golf, but on this particular day Camilla asked him to join her there for lunch in the Club grill, where all the golfers had lunch, after she had played. He liked the look of her in her visored cap and trim white shorts and pastel-colored sport shirts. Rose Cliveden made her first appearance at the Club since she broke her leg at the lunch she gave there following Hector Paradiso's funeral. Rose was one for dramatic entrances, and she had herself pushed into the grill in a wheelchair by a nurse, although she was able by that time to navigate by herself on crutches.

"I'm back," she yelled as she came in, and all her friends in the room rushed over to greet her, and Bloody Marys were ordered for all. As always, wherever Rose was, a party began. From the arm pocket of her wheelchair, she pulled forth several gifts, handsomely wrapped. One was for Clint, the bartender, whom she had accused of making the Bloody Marys too strong on the day she fell over Astrid, and the other was for her dear friend Camilla Ebury, who was that day thirty-three years old.

"You didn't tell me it was your birthday," said Philip, when he and Camilla had settled back at their own table.

Camilla blushed. "I never tell anyone it's my birthday. Trust Rose to make an announcement. She keeps one of those birthday books. I never know when anyone's birthday is."

"What are you doing when we finish lunch?" asked Philip.

"I have an Orphanage Guild meeting at four," she said.

"Between now and four?"

"Take a shower. Change clothes. Why?"

"You're coming with me," said Philip.

"Where?"

"To buy you a birthday present."

"You don't have to do that."

"I know I don't have to. But I want to."

A half hour later, Philip and Camilla walked hand in hand down Rodeo Drive looking in shop windows, both feeling carefree, as if they were playing hooky. Philip saw a very pretty young woman coming toward him from the other direction. He was surprised enough to stop in his tracks. The young woman, who had seen him before he saw her, was also surprised, and unnerved, by the unexpected meeting.

"Hello," said Philip.

"Hello," replied the young woman.

Camilla, watching the exchange, dropped hold of Philip's hand.

"What an incredible surprise," said Philip.

"For me, too," said the young woman.

"Do you live here?" he asked.

"No. Do you?"

"No. I'm here working for a few months. Where do you live?"

"I'm in San Francisco still. You're in New York?"

"Yes." There was an awkward pause.

Camilla said, "Philip, I think I'll go back to the car."

"Oh, I beg your pardon," said Philip. "This is Camilla Ebury. Terry—uh, what's your last name these days?"

The young woman laughed. "Still Sigourney," she said.

"Terry Sigourney, Camilla Ebury," he said.

The two women nodded to each other.

"I read your book on that Wall Street guy," said Terry to Philip.

He nodded. There was another awkward pause.

"Did he really break your legs? I read that."

"Oh, no. Only a threat that didn't happen."

"Philip, I'm going to get a taxi across the street at the Beverly Wilshire," said Camilla impatiently.

"No, no, wait," said Philip, reaching out for her hand.

Camilla pulled her hand away from him.

"Listen, I better be on my way," said Terry. She turned to Camilla. "Does he still have that cute little tattoo, down there?"

Camilla, angry, blushed.

Terry looked at Philip. "Good-bye, Philip," she said. "If you're ever in San Francisco, I have a gallery. Bird prints. It's in the book." She walked on past them.

Camilla and Philip looked at each other for an instant.

"You behaved like a bitch," said Philip.

"*I* behaved like a bitch? What about her? What about that tattoo crack?"

"You brought it on, you know."

"I was jealous."

"Well, where to next?" asked Philip. "Tiffany's is across the street there in the Beverly Wilshire Hotel, isn't it?"

"Why do I feel that Terry was something more than a casual acquaintance?" asked Camilla.

Philip didn't answer for a moment.

"Who was she?"

"A subplot," answered Philip.

"How sub?" asked Camilla.

Philip paused. "I was once married to her," he said.

Camilla stopped. "Married to her? You never told me you'd been married."

"Because I'd almost forgotten I was."

"How could a marriage slip your mind?"

"I was only eighteen at the time. An elopement to Mexico. There was always a question as to whether it was legal or not."

"Was it annulled?"

"No, we were divorced."

"How long were you married?"

"Under a year."

"Take me home, will you? I have the meeting at four, and I want to get my own car."

"I haven't bought you a present."

"I don't want a present."

They drove back to Camilla's house in Bel Air in silence. When he pulled into the driveway, she picked up her bag so that by the time the car pulled in front of the house, she had already opened the door. As she was about to step out of the car, he reached over and put his hand on her arm.

"Why are you being like this?" he asked.

"I've been sleeping with you for how long now? Since the night Hector was killed, and I just realized I don't know one damn thing about you. Nothing."

"I never thought credentials were required for a love affair," said Philip.

She ignored him. "I don't know if you have a mother, father, brother, sister, or a child even."

"No to all of the above."

"Now I find out for the first time that you've been married."

"So have you."

"It's not that you were married that I mind. It's that you simply neglected to tell me an important bit of information about yourself."

"It was twelve years ago. I was married for seven months. What's the big deal?"

"There is no big deal."

"Look, I was different in those days than I am now. Wilder. Rebellious. My parents sent me away to boarding school when I was only eleven, because they were getting a divorce, and I spent the next seven or eight years wanting to get even with them. What better way than to elope to Mexico? I think of it as a youthful error, no more than that."

"What's your secret, Philip?"

"What secret?"

"You have a secret. I feel it. I know it."

Philip looked away from her.

"And you're not going to tell me, are you?"

Philip didn't answer.

"I don't want to see you anymore, Philip."

"That's quite childish, don't you think?"

She shook her head. "Let me tell you what a fool I've been. I was thinking that perhaps you were going to ask me to marry you. I even went to see my lawyers, just in case. My life is run by lawyers, part of an arrangement my father made. If we were even to think of marriage, I was told, they would draw up a prenuptial agreement for you to sign."

Philip, astonished, laughed. "I wouldn't have signed it."

"They wouldn't have let me marry you then."

"But I didn't want to marry you."

Camilla, startled, blushed. "You didn't?"

"No. Men should never marry women who are richer than they are. It's bound to fail. So tell your lawyers to flush their prenuptial agreement."

"You don't have to be rude."

"I'm not being rude. I'm stating a fact. What's wrong with a love affair? Just a plain and simple love affair. This has been a very pleasant time between us. Don't just toss it out. I have never been one to believe every romance should end up in marriage."

"So long, Philip," she said. "When you're ready to tell me your secret, maybe we'll meet for lunch sometime." She stepped out of his car.

Philip looked at her back. "I caused a girl to be paralyzed when I was driving too fast with too many beers in me. It changed my life forever," he said. Without looking back at her, he drove out of her driveway.

Philip Quennell had not made many friends in Los Angeles during the time he was there. He had met Camilla Ebury at the Mendelsons' party on his first night in the city. The mysterious death of her uncle on that same night had intensified their love affair, and he had spent most of his free time with her since then, mixing in her life with her friends rather than creating a Los Angeles life of his own. The rupture that had been caused in that love affair by the unexpected appearance on the street of Terry Sigourney brought to an instant halt any further socializing with the people he had met through Camilla. He had no desire to call on Casper Stieglitz for companionship, as he had developed an intense dislike for the man. Nor did he have any desire to associate with Lonny Edge, even to gain further knowledge of Lonny's friendship with the great author Basil Plant, whom Philip revered. He wanted only to finish the writing assignment he had undertaken for Casper Stieglitz, so that he could return to his life in New York.

He was at work in his room at the Chateau Marmont that night, when there was a knock at his door. It was the policy of the hotel to announce all visitors, but no such announcement had been made. When he opened the door, he was surprised to see the pretty young woman he knew only as Flo M. standing there. She was dressed, as he had always seen her dressed, in a Chanel suit, but she appeared to be in an agitated state. The cool, withdrawn, and slightly mysterious manner that he had grown used to when he saw her most mornings at the AA meetings in the log cabin on Robertson Boulevard was not present.

"Aren't you going to ask me in?" she asked.

"Oh, sure," he said.

He opened the door wider, and she walked past him into the room. He closed the door.

"So this is where you live, huh?" she said. "I was never in here before. I used to be a waitress at the Viceroy Coffee Shop up the street on Sunset, and all the writers who stayed at the Chateau always came in for breakfast, so I was always hearing about the place. Nice, isn't it?"

"Why do I think that you haven't come here at half-past ten at night to discuss the writers who live and work at the Chateau Marmont?" asked Philip.

"Did I know you were a writer? You didn't tell me that, did you? I think I must have just felt it. I mean, you look like a writer." She walked around his room, looking at everything. His word processor was set up on a desk and his printer stood next to it on a card table. She leaned down and read the amber print on the monitor. "You're writing a movie, I see," she said.

"Are you in some kind of trouble?" asked Philip.

"Hell, no. Do you always work in a dressing gown? That's nice, that blue-and-white-striped dressing gown. What was that, a gift from your girlfriend, I bet."

"If I didn't know it wasn't so, I'd think you were on speed," said Philip. "You're talking a mile a minute."

She opened the doors to his balcony and walked outside. "God, look at all that traffic on Sunset," she called in.

He followed her out to the balcony. She was leaning on the rail, looking down. She had taken a cigarette from her gold cigarette case with the name FLO printed on it in sapphires. She lit it with her gold lighter, and inhaled deeply.

"What's the matter, Flo?" he asked. He took the cigarette out of her mouth and threw it over the balcony.

"You couldn't put me up for the night, could you, Phil?"

"Tight quarters here."

"I wouldn't mind that," she said.

They looked at each other.

"Are you still spoken for?" she asked.

He smiled sadly. "As a matter of fact, I'm not. Why?"

"I'm not spoken for anymore either."

When Ralph White came out of the men's room in the steak house in the San Fernando Valley and got into the car the parking boy had brought around, the first thing Madge White said to him was, "Did you see Sims Lord in the men's room?"

"Sims? No. There was no one in the men's room. It was empty except for me," said Ralph. "Why?"

"I can't wait to tell you what just happened to me," said Madge.

Jules Mendelson had already left. He had driven his Bentley out of the restaurant parking lot with such speed that Madge thought he would surely have been arrested had a policeman been present to witness his driving. He turned off Ventura Boulevard onto Coldwater Canyon and raced up the mountain, blowing his horn relentlessly at any car not driving at the speed that he was driving, until they pulled over to the side and allowed him to pass. When he reached the top of Coldwater, he slowed down his pace because the Beverly Hills side of the canyon was more closely patrolled than the Valley side. Halfway down Coldwater, he turned left onto the street that led into Azelia Way.

All the time he was driving, he planned what he would say to her. He had not wanted to go out in public. What he most feared had happened. The fault was hers, not his. He would make her see that. At the same time, he could not erase from his memory the sad and hurt look in her eyes when he had pretended he could not think of her name.

He pulled into the secluded driveway of the house that he rented for her.

He jumped from his car, leaving the car door open. He rang the bell. When there was no immediate answer, he took out his keys and opened the front door and walked in without closing the door behind him. The lights were on, as they had been left. The drinks that they'd had before going out were still on the coffee table.

"Flo!" he called out. "Flo! Where are you, Flo?" He went into her bedroom, her bathroom, out onto her patio. There was no sign of her. He walked frantically from room to room. He could not imagine where she could have gone. He knew she had no friends, except the maid next door, and he knew she would never go to Faye Converse's house to call on Faye's maid.

From behind the tall hedge that separated Flo's house from the house of Faye Converse, the dog Astrid, hearing activity, came over to call on Flo. She came in by the open front door, knowing she would be received with great whoops of joy, as she always was when Flo spotted her, and then be spoiled with doggy treats, as Flo always spoiled her.

Hearing the sounds of each other, each thought the other was Flo. Jules ran from the bedroom into the living room, where, instead, he encountered Astrid. They stared at each other, in the same way they had stared at each other in Hector Paradiso's house on the early morning Hector's body lay on the floor between them, with five bullets in it, and Jules removed the note that the dying Hector had left, before the police arrived. The little dog began to bark ferociously at Jules, as if she feared that harm had come to Flo as well.

"Get out of here, you little piece of shit," said Jules to the dog, menacingly.

Astrid held her ground, barking without stop and moving in on Jules.

From Flo's mantelpiece, Jules picked up one of the two brass candlesticks with dragons crawling up their sides that Nellie Potts had charged Flo several thousand dollars for, claiming that they were antiques from the childhood palace of the last emperor of China. Jules swung the candlestick as if it were a broom, and the little dog, terrified, retreated.

"Get out of here," Jules yelled, advancing on her until he had backed her out the front door, which he then slammed.

He went to Flo's bar. Her sets and sets of Steuben glasses were lined up on glass shelves. Taking a wineglass, he opened the small refrigerator under the bar and took out a bottle of white wine from the Bresciani auction and poured himself a glass. When he seated himself, finally, on Flo's sofa, he picked up the telephone and dialed a number.

"Dudley, this is Mr. Mendelson," he said to the butler at Clouds. "I'm very sorry to call you so late. Has there been a call from Mrs. Mendelson? I see. Dudley, I will not be coming home this evening. I am going to stay here in my office. I'm still working, and I have a very early meeting. What? No, no, thank you. That won't be necessary. There are clean shirts there, here rather, in the office, and linens. But that's awfully kind of you. Will you leave a note for Willi to come to my office in the morning to shave me there? No, I shouldn't think Mrs. Mendelson will call this evening. It must be after one in Maine now. I'll call in the morning, Dudley. Good night."

When Jules awoke on the sofa at five in the morning, his regular waking hour, he jumped up, furious that he had fallen asleep. He was sure that Flo had come home during the night and gone right into her room to sleep, not wanting to wake him. But she was not there. He went to his office, where he bathed and changed. Willi, who shaved him with a straight-edged razor, twice had to stop, for fear of cutting him, when Jules lurched in the chair. Every hour of the morning, he called her number. At lunchtime, he canceled an appointment and drove up to her house on Azelia Way. He had become frantic. He called the police department to see if there had been any accidents reported in a Valley cab. He called the emergency rooms of the hospitals to see if a Miss Flo March, or a Miss Fleurette Houlihan, had been admitted. He went to the Viceroy Coffee Shop. That night he went to Clouds and sat in his library alone, where he had dinner on a tray.

After two days, he called Sims Lord, his lawyer and friend. Sims Lord was not unfamiliar with the fact that Jules was having an affair. It was Sims who had purchased the sapphire-and-diamond ring for Jules to give to Flo, and the mink coat, and several other gifts that Jules did not want to have to purchase himself, for fear of talk. Sims, who was twice divorced, did not have the restrictions on his life that Jules had, and was happy to oblige. He was a Pasadenian by birth and an easterner by education. His clothes were of a cut and conservatism that appealed to Pauline's New England sensibilities. Handsome, he possessed what Pauline called a wintry look; his hair was prematurely white, and his eyes were very blue. He could be as personable as any man could choose to be, when he chose to be; and as cold as any man could choose to be, when he chose to be; both of these qualities endeared him to Jules. It was said of Sims Lord that he was a lawyer with one client—Jules Mendelson—which was an untrue statement in that he had many clients, but it was true in the sense that the affairs of Jules Mendelson had occupied 80 percent of his time for two decades.

What Sims did not know was the extent of the passion that Jules felt for the former waitress. He was shocked by Jules's appearance when he arrived at his office that morning.

"Flo has left me," said Jules. There were tears in his eyes. There was in his voice a pain that Sims Lord did not know Jules was capable of experiencing. The two men talked for hours. Jules told him everything about the affair.

"If she comes back, I want you to buy her the house, Sims. And the car. I want her to have everything in her own name. In case something happens to me, I don't want her left high and dry. Nor do I want to embarrass Pauline in any way. It is best to do these things in advance."

"Where do you suppose she is?" asked Sims, although they had asked the same question over and over.

"I don't know."

"Is there any family?"

"None."

"Listen, Jules. Now, don't jump on me."

"What?"

"There's no other guy, is there?"

"Good God." The idea of another man touching Flo was anathema to Jules.

"Have you ever thought about hiring a private detective?"

"Would it get out? I mean to the papers, or anything?" asked Jules. "There must be no publicity."

"No, no. I know just the right guy. Discretion himself. It'll cost you, but that's not a concern. His name is Trevor Dust."

When Philip Quennell went to Casper Stieglitz's house to deliver the first draft of the documentary on the proliferation of drugs in the film industry, Flo stayed in his room. They had scarcely left the Chateau Marmont since Flo's arrival, except to attend the early morning AA meetings at the log cabin on Robertson Boulevard, or to go out to dinner at Musso and Frank's on Hollywood Boulevard, a restaurant that Philip liked, where Jules Mendelson was unlikely ever to go.

There was a soft and tentative knock on the door. Flo was wearing Philip's blue-and-white-striped dressing gown, sitting on one of the two leather chairs in the room, reading Cyril Rathbone's column in *Mulholland* magazine. "Come in," she called out, thinking it was the maid.

When Camilla Ebury walked in, Flo March knew without being told who she was. For two days, she and Philip Quennell had told each other their stories.

"Oh, I beg your pardon," said Camilla. "I've come into the wrong room."

To Flo's eyes, everything about Camilla Ebury was perfect. Her blond hair was parted in the middle and held back by two gold barrettes. Her pearls were real. Her green-and-white-print dress was silk. Even her perfume had a refined odor. She looked to Flo as if she were on her way to a committee meeting at the Bistro Garden for a fashionable charity. Flo was certain she would say, under the right circumstance, "Hellohowareyou," the way Madge White had said it the other night.

Camilla backed out the door to look at the room number, although she immediately recognized the blue-and-white-striped dressing gown that the girl in the leather chair was wearing as belonging to Philip. She saw it was the right room. "I'm terribly confused," she said. "I seem to have made a mistake."

"No, you haven't. I'm Flo March," said Flo.

"Hellohowareyou."

Flo smiled. "You're Camilla, aren't you?"

"Yes. How did you know?"

Flo looked at her. Unlike her own pretty face, Camilla's pretty face revealed no struggle in life. Things had been placed there for her, in profusion. She had remained unspoiled with her privilege, but she also took it for granted.

Camilla said, "I think perhaps I'd better go. This was stupid of me to come here."

"Now, I bet you think that he and I have got something going between us, don't you? Well, you couldn't be more wrong," said Flo. "Phil's a friend of mine, that's all. No more than that. I needed a place to stay for a few nights, and he gave me one."

Camilla looked at Flo, not sure whether to believe her or not.

"It is possible for a man and a woman to be friends without having something going on between them, even for a cute guy like Phil. I didn't used to think that, but I do now. Besides, I'm spoken for, which I told him the first day we met, and he told me he was spoken for too, and I guess you're the one."

"He said that, that he was spoken for?" asked Camilla. There was surprise in her voice.

"Yeah," said Flo. "He did."

"I'm such a fool," said Camilla. "Twice now I've told him I didn't want to see him anymore, and I didn't want him to go either time."

"You sound like you're in love with the guy," said Flo.

"I am."

"Want my advice?"

"Yes."

"Hang out here for a while. He'll be back soon. I was just about to get dressed and get out of here."

She got up and opened the closet door. From inside, she took out her black-and-white Chanel suit. "He's gone to a meeting at Casper Stieglitz's to turn in the first draft on the documentary."

"Oh." Camilla watched Flo, fascinated. The suit was obviously for evening, not morning, but she saw the Paris label in the jacket as Flo dressed in front of her. The clothes and the woman did not match. She was pretty, very pretty, and there was humor and even kindness in her face, but there was a sound in her voice that bespoke a different background from Camilla's, and a harder kind of life.

"Are you an actress?" asked Camilla.

"I once had an audition for a miniseries. That was my total experience as an actress," said Flo. "Needless to say, I didn't get the part. Ann-Margret got it. They said they wanted a name."

"I was just wondering, that's all," said Camilla. "It's none of my business."

"I'm hard to get a bead on, I know," said Flo. "I don't seem to fall into any of the identifiable categories." She pulled on her jacket. She stepped into her shoes. She picked up her bag with the long gold chain and put it over her shoulder. "Well, I guess I'm all set. When you see Phil, tell him thanks. Okay?"

Camilla nodded.

"I bet he looks real cute in his Jockey shorts," said Flo.

"He doesn't wear Jockey shorts. He wears boxer shorts," said Camilla.

"You see how little I know the guy?" She went out the door.

Jules was sitting on one of Flo's gray satin sofas, in earnest conversation with Trevor Dust, the private detective who had been recommended by Sims Lord. There were photographs of Flo on the tabletop, the eight-by-ten glossies that she'd had taken when she was still working at the Viceroy Coffee Shop, as well as more recent snapshots taken by her pool. There were also several of her Chanel suits spread out on the sofa, to show the detective how she was dressed the last time she had been seen.

The detective took off his prescription sunglasses and replaced them with his reading glasses. From a back pocket, he took a spiral notebook and checked his notes. "The taxi driver was an Iranian, named Hussein Akhavi. He's okay. Checks out. Akhavi remembers a lady answering to Miss March's description getting into his cab outside the restaurant that night. Said she was excitable, and maybe crying. He was in mourning for the death of the Ayatollah and didn't want to get involved with this woman's problems. He said she gave him a Beverly Hills address first, presumably this address, but he couldn't remember, and then changed her mind and asked him to take her to a hotel on Sunset Boulevard called the Chateau Marmont. She paid him with a twenty and told him to keep the change. But there is no record of anyone by either of her names, March or Houlihan, who registered at the Chateau that night, or since then."

"Good job," said Jules, nodding his head. "Now, I'll tell you what I want you to do. Get me a printout of everyone who was registered at the Chateau Marmont that night, as well as every night since."

"Beat you to it," said Trevor Dust. He opened his briefcase and took out an envelope, which he handed to Jules. "Here's the printout for that night. I had to pay the night clerk for this. I'll have to get it for you for the subsequent nights."

Just then, a taxi pulled into the driveway, and Flo got out. She saw Jules's Bentley and another car of a nondescript variety in the driveway. She used her key and walked into the living room of her house.

"Hi," she said quietly when she walked into the living room.

"Flo!" cried Jules. "Where the hell have you been?"

"Thinking," answered Flo.

"But you came back."

"I got sick of wearing this same outfit," she said.

Jules rushed to her side and tried to embrace her, but her eyes had caught sight of the other person in the room.

"Who's your friend here? And what are my pictures doing out like that? And all my clothes? What are you, a cop? Or a private detective?"

"I have been frantic, Flo," said Jules. "I hired Mr. Dust to try to locate you."

"I am not having a personal discussion in front of him," said Flo, pointing to Trevor Dust with her thumb. "Lose the dick, and then we'll talk."

"Right. That will be all. Thank you, Mr. Dust. Send your bill to my office," said Jules.

When Jules walked the detective to the door, Flo went to her bar and took out a can of Diet Coke from the refrigerator. She opened it and started to drink it out of the can, but then she remembered her new Steuben glasses and poured the contents into a water goblet.

When Jules came back into the room, she pointed to her goblet and said to him, "Nice glasses you bought me."

"Who were you with?" he asked.

"A friend."

"What friend?"

"Just a friend."

"Male or female?"

"That's for me to know and you to find out."

Mad with jealousy, Jules grabbed her arm with such force that the Steuben glass flew from her hand and smashed as it hit the stone floor by her fireplace. She screamed with pain. Instantly, he released her arm.

"Oh, my God," he said. "Oh, Flo, I'm sorry. I didn't mean that."

She pulled back from him with fear on her face. "Is that what happened to the girl in Chicago who went off the balcony of the Roosevelt Hotel in nineteen fifty-three?" she asked. "Did you make her so frightened of you that she backed off the balcony?"

"Flo, forgive me," he begged. He knelt in front of her and put his arms around her thighs and hugged her to him. "Forgive me. I love you, Flo. I love you. Please forgive me."

Flo March had never seen Jules Mendelson cry before.

"Is Pauline still in Northeast Harbor?" asked Flo.

"Yes."

"Good. There's something I want to do."

"What?"

"I want to see Clouds."

"Oh, no, that wouldn't be wise."

"Why not?"

"You shouldn't have to ask that. It's Pauline's house."

"It's yours too. I just want to look, Jules. I just want to walk through the rooms. That's all."

"No."

"Why?"

"It could be disastrous."

"Who would know?"

"Dudley, for one. Blondell, for two. Smitty, for three."

"Who's Dudley and Blondell and Smitty?"

"The butler, the maid, and the guard. And there're people in the kitchen. The cook, Gertie, and the others—I don't always remember their names—but they're there."

Flo nodded. "Don't you sometimes have business meetings at Clouds?"

"Sometimes."

"How about if I'm a business meeting?"

"Oh, come on, Flo."

"No, listen. You go home. You say to Dudley, 'I'm expecting a Miss March for a meeting.' Then, at like eight or eight-thirty, I'll come up. I'll ring the doorbell. Dudley can let me in. He'll take me into the library where you'll be sitting, reading *Time* and *Newsweek*. He'll say, 'Miss March.' I'll shake hands like I'm meeting you for the first time, and then you can take me on a tour of the house and grounds. With all those people from all those museums going through the house looking at all your art all the time, one little person like me is not going to look suspicious. I want to see that picture with the white roses."

"I've had a postcard made of that picture," said Jules.

"Well, I'm not interested in the postcard. I want to see the original."

"It's too dangerous."

"Forty minutes later, I'll say good night, thank you very much, Mr. Mendelson, it was nice of you to make the time for me to see your beautiful collection, and I'll go back out the front door and get in my Mercedes and be off into the night."

"Why do you want to do this?"

"I'm interested in your life, Jules. Is that so strange? I see more of you than anyone else, but most of your life is closed off to me. You can't blame me for having curiosity about you."

"Okay," he said. "But no false moves. Dudley has eyes in the back of his head."

* * *

"Oh, my," said Flo, as she set foot in the hallway of Clouds, looking up, looking left, looking right. She was at a loss for words, and she was only in the hall of the magnificent house. The curved staircase seemed to float upward in front of her eyes, with six huge paintings on its green moiré walls. At its base, the great quantities of orchid plants in blue-and-white Chinese cachepots caught her attention. She's not even here, and the house is still filled with flowers, she thought to herself.

Flo's expectations of pleasure from her visit to Clouds were so high that she was bound to be disappointed. And she was. She could cope in her imagination with Pauline Mendelson's house, but the grandeur of the actuality was too much for her even to comment upon. She walked down the hallway behind Dudley, casting glances into rooms as she passed, each more perfect than the last. She had always thought of Pauline in terms of beautiful clothes and pearl necklaces and parties, the way she was presented in the newspapers and in magazines. She had not thought about tables and chairs that were not just tables and chairs, but tables and chairs of an exquisiteness that she, born without prospects to an unwed mother, could not even begin to comprehend. If ever, in the remote corners of her mind, she had entertained the idea that she might become the wife of Jules Mendelson, she knew at that moment that it would never be.

Jules waited for her in the library. She followed Dudley into the room. They went through the charade that she had planned. "Good evening, Miss March," he said, rising from an English chair and laying aside his magazine.

She looked into the eyes of the man whom she had made love to only three hours earlier, into whose ear she had whispered base things to incite his lust, whose body and desires she had grown to know intimately, and he appeared different to her in the surroundings of his home. She became shy.

"Good evening, Mr. Mendelson."

"Have you just arrived in Los Angeles?"

"Yes, today."

"Did you have a good flight?"

"Yes."

"I'll take you on a tour of the house and the pictures, if you'd like."

"Lovely."

"Would you care for a drink?"

"No, thank you."

"I'll ring, Dudley, if Miss March changes her mind. Will you put on the lights in the sculpture garden?"

"Yes, sir."

Alone, they were silent. She wished she had not come.

"This is van Gogh's *White Roses,*" Jules said, finally, pointing to the picture over the fireplace.

"Such thick paint," she said, looking up at the picture. "Didn't I read somewhere that that picture is worth about forty million dollars?"

"That's what that article said, yes."

"My, oh my," she said.

There was a silence again.

"This room we're in is the library. It is where we spend most of our time when we are alone," said Jules, who also felt the awkwardness of the situation.

He was used to giving tours of his house to the many museum people who visited Clouds, but he could not think of the appropriate descriptions and comments he usually made to say to Flo.

Flo looked around the room, without moving her position.

"Beautiful appointments," she said in a whispered voice.

Jules hated the word *appointments* when it was applied to the decorative arts, but he understood the extent of Flo's discomfort and, for once, did not correct her. Instead, he squeezed her hand and she was grateful.

"I guess I better be on my way," she said.

"On your way? You haven't seen anything yet."

"That's okay."

The lights went on in the garden outside. She turned to look through the windows toward the grounds. "You must see the sculpture garden, at least," said Jules. "It will look odd if you leave so soon."

The telephone rang. Jules made a move toward the instrument.

"I thought in swell houses like this the butler always answered the phone and said, 'The Mendelson residence,' " said Flo.

"He does, but that's my private line. It's Sims Lord, I'm sure. He was looking into something for me, about the house on Azelia Way," said Jules, looking at her to see if what he said had registered on her. He picked up the receiver. "Hello? Oh, Pauline. How are you? How is your father? What? No, no, there's no one here."

He looked up at Flo, and their eyes met. She opened the door to the terrace and walked out, as if to go to see the sculpture garden.

"What's that?" continued Jules, on the telephone. "You are? Oh, good. When? Yes, fine. I'll make arrangements for the plane to leave for Bangor in the morning. I've missed you."

When he finished the conversation with his wife, he rose and went out to the terrace, where Flo had gone. He passed the Rodin, which had once belonged to his grandfather. He passed the Henry Moore, running his hand over its smooth surface as he did so. He did not see Flo. He continued on to the Maillol, behind the orange tree. "Flo," he called out. "Flo!"

From behind him the terrace door opened and closed. He looked back and saw Dudley crossing the lawn to come toward him.

"Were you looking for Miss March, Mr. Mendelson?"

"Yes. She came wandering out here when I took a telephone call. I forgot to warn her about the dogs and didn't want her to be frightened."

"Miss March left, sir," said Dudley. "She said she had seen everything."

"Oh," said Jules.

Later that night, when Jules was undressing, he removed from the pockets of his suit jacket his wallet and change and handkerchief and keys and placed them on the top of a bureau in his dressing room. As he hung his jacket on a valet stand, he noticed an envelope in the inside pocket, which he had forgotten he had placed there. He took it out. On the top left-hand corner of the envelope was the name of the private detective, Trevor Dust. He tore it open and found inside the computer printout of the hotel guests at the Chateau Marmont on the night that the taxi driver from the Valley Cab Company told Trevor Dust he had dropped Flo March off at that address. He scanned the list.

Flo March was not registered. His eyes continued down the list. He was startled to find the name Philip Quennell. A blind, hot rage welled up within him.

At nine o'clock the next morning, Jules Mendelson had Miss Maple place a call to the office of Marty Lesky at Colossus Pictures. For several minutes the two busy men exchanged pleasantries, and then Jules got down to the purpose of his call, which had nothing whatever to do with the Los Angeles County Museum, as Marty Lesky had anticipated.

"There's a man working at your studio called Philip Quennell," said Jules.

"What's he do at my studio?" asked Marty.

"He is a writer, they tell me, who is writing a documentary film for Casper Stieglitz."

"Oh, right. I met him the other night. He was at Casper's for dinner. Wrote the book on Reza Bulbenkian. What about him, Jules?"

"Send him home."

"Where's home?"

"I don't know where home is, but wherever it is, send him there."

"A good writer's hard to find, Jules."

"No, he's not, Marty. You told me yourself once. 'You can always get another writer,' you said."

"I said that?"

"Yes, you did. I remember it distinctly. Send Mr. Quennell home."

"I gottahava reason, Jules. This is not Andover. He was not caught smoking a joint. This is a studio I'm running here. I don't just send guys home with no reason."

"When's your meeting for the new museum wing?"

"Tuesday. Your secretary phoned in your acceptance."

"I'm not going to be able to make it, Marty."

"Oh, come on, Jules."

"About my pledge to the museum, Marty."

"You can't welsh on a pledge, Jules. Even Jules Mendelson can't do that."

"Fuck my pledge, Marty. What do I care about a wing with your name on it?"

"What was this guy's name, Jules?"

"Quennell. Philip Quennell."

Flo's Tape #16

"Clouds. My God, what a house! I only saw it once, and I don't think I was even there for half an hour, but I saw enough. I mean, it was perfect. Every detail. Everything in its right place. Everything beautiful. When they make Hollywood movies about rich people, they never get the sets to look like Clouds looked.

"There are some of those ladies you read about in coffee table books, like Mrs. Paley, and Mrs. Guinness, and the Duchess of Windsor. They knew how to run those great houses for their husbands and for their friends. Well, I have to hand it to Mrs. Mendelson. She was right up there with those other ladies when it came to putting a house together and knowing how to run it in the grand style."

17

I T WAS BETTYE, Casper Stieglitz's secretary, who told Philip Quennell over the telephone, when he happened to call late in the afternoon to see what Casper's reaction had been to his first draft of the documentary film on the proliferation of drugs in the film industry, that Casper had decided to go with another writer.

"What does that mean, he has decided to go with another writer?" asked Philip.

"In other words, you're fired," said Bettye.

"I rather thought that was what you meant," said Philip. "No offense, Bettye, but I'd like to get fired by my boss, not my boss's secretary."

"I'm awfully sorry, Mr. Quennell, but Mr. Stieglitz is in an important conference," replied Bettye.

"Of course he is, that busy fellow," said Philip. "Will you ask him to call me?"

"How soon will you be vacating your junior suite at the Chateau Marmont?" asked Bettye.

"Who said I was vacating it?"

"I have informed the hotel that as of midnight tonight, the studio will no longer be picking up the charges for the room," said Bettye.

"What an active day you've had, Bettye," said Philip.

"I'm just doing my job, Mr. Quennell," replied Bettye.

It did not surprise Philip that the several telephone calls he made to Casper Stieglitz at his home were not returned. That evening he drove to Casper's house on Palm Circle, although he was sure he would be told by Willard, the butler, that Casper was not at home. When he buzzed the intercom at the gate, a red light went on on the closed circuit television. He heard Willard's voice. "Yes?"

"Willard, I'd like to talk to you for a moment," said Philip quickly, looking up into the camera.

"Mr. Stieglitz is not at home, Mr. Quennell," said Willard.

"It's you I wanted to see, Willard," said Philip. "I have learned some interesting information from Lonny Edge about Hector Paradiso's death, and I need some help from you in identifying someone."

Willard's voice became confidential. "Listen, Mr. Quennell. I'm not

supposed to let you in here if you come by. I don't know why, but I was told to
say that Mr. Stieglitz is not at home and not to let you in."

"I had the idea you were anxious to clarify the death of your friend Hector," said Philip.

"I am." There was uncertainty in his voice.

"I'll only stay a minute, Willard," said Philip.

"I'll open the gate. But, please, don't drive all the way up to the house. I'll
meet you in back of the pool pavilion," said Willard.

When the gates opened, Philip drove up the driveway, past the tennis
court. The night lights were on, and a game was in progress. He recognized the
girlish laughter of Ina Rae and Darlene. Coming down the driveway from the
house was Willard, wearing the long green apron he wore on silver-polishing
days. He waved frantically to Philip to stop his car. "No, no. Don't go up to the
house," he screamed. "I said to meet by the pool pavilion."

Philip nodded in a friendly fashion, as if he didn't understand, and continued up the driveway, leaving Willard behind. When he got to the courtyard, he
saw that Willard had left the front door open. With great haste, he hopped out
of his car and walked in the door, closing and locking it behind him so that
Willard would be delayed getting in when he ran back.

He walked through the living room to the door that opened on the terrace
and out to the projection room, where Casper spent most of his time. The
curtains were drawn, and it occurred to Philip that Casper was screening a film.

Slowly he pulled back the sliding glass door. As he stepped into the rear of
the semidarkened room, he saw Casper, wearing his dark glasses, rise unsteadily from his usual seat and go over to the bar. He was only half-dressed,
wearing a black velour shirt but neither trousers nor undershorts. The heady
scent of marijuana filled the air. It appeared to Philip that a session with the
ladies on the tennis court had recently been completed. Casper looked at
himself in the mirrored wall behind the shelves of bottles, as if he were admiring the remains of his good looks. Without removing his glasses, he turned his
face carefully, first to one side and then the other, assuming an expression that
erased the scowl line between his eyebrows. He held his mouth in such a way
that the sagging beneath his chin vanished. Finally, satisfied with his looks, he
lifted up his black velour shirt and began to urinate in the bar sink.

"That's class, Casper," said Philip Quennell, from behind. "And very sanitary, as well."

"Jesuschrist," said Casper, jumping. Through the mirror, he saw Philip
walking up behind him. "You scared me. You made me piss all over myself and
all over these glasses and bottles. What the hell are you doing here?"

"No, I won't have a drink, thank you," said Philip.

"Didn't Bettye call you?"

"Actually, I called Bettye, and she relayed your message. I had never heard
of being fired by a secretary before, and I said I wanted to hear it from your
own lips, but she said you were in an important conference, so I just came over
on my own."

"I'm going to fire that fagola, Willard. I told him not to open the gates,"
said Casper. He reached for a telephone.

"You mustn't fire poor Willard, Casper. I'm afraid I played a trick on him
to let me in. Good silver polishers are hard to find."

"What do you want, Quennell?"

"Oh, it's now Quennell, is it? I'll tell you what I want, Stieglitz. I want to know why you fired me."

"I just decided to go with another writer."

"Bettye's words exactly. Why is it I don't believe them?"

Casper looked at Philip and adopted a comradely approach. "You and me, Philip. We just ran out of gas. Don't take it personally. It happens all the time out here in Hollywood. Writers are an expendable breed. As Marty Lesky says, 'You can always get another writer.' Do you know how many writers I had on *Candles at Lunch,* for instance?"

"No, I don't, and I don't care."

Casper went back to where he had been sitting and pulled on his trousers.

"I want an answer, Casper."

Casper nervously picked up a handful of cashew nuts from the coffee table and began to throw them in his mouth, several at a time. "I was disappointed with your interview with the narcs. I didn't, uh, get a sense, uh, of the kind of obsession those guys have to catch the dealers in this war on drugs. Drugs, I don't have to tell you, are destroying the youth of this nation."

"Who do you think you're kidding, Casper?"

"What are you talking about?"

"You beat the rap for possession of ten pounds of cocaine by having some of your crooked lawyers and influential friends, like Arnie Zwillman, the gangster, come down on Judge Quartz to suspend your sentence in return for making an antidrug movie, and all the time you're taking drugs. I could blow the whistle on you, Casper, and, may I tell you, it wouldn't read well in the trade papers."

"I do not take drugs," said Casper indignantly. "I admit, in my past, I did try drugs several times, but I have not taken any drugs since the day of my arrest, which was, as everyone knows, a total miscarriage of justice, as well as a mix-up." His voice had become strident.

Philip walked over to the coffee table and picked up from the floor an amber-colored bottle of cocaine that Casper had dropped there. He carried it back to the bar and emptied the white powder into the sink in the bar. "It ought to be even better with your urine mixed in with it."

"Get out of here," said Casper, frightened.

Philip stared him down. "Did Ina Rae run her fingers through your hair?" he asked. "Your rug is crooked. Kind of at a tilt."

Casper, enraged, rushed at Philip. "Get out of my house!"

Philip leaned toward Casper and snatched his dark glasses off him, grabbing them by the bridge over his nose.

"What do you think you're doing?" asked Casper. "I can't see anything without my glasses."

"I knew that behind those shades you'd have darty little furtive eyes," said Philip.

Casper sneezed.

Philip held up his hands and stepped backward. "Oh, please. I can't handle another mouthful of your half-chewed cashews all over my face, Casper. I've already had that experience once."

"The studio isn't paying for the Chateau Marmont after tonight."

"Yes, yes, I know. Your Bettye told me that. Look, Casper, I don't mind being thrown off your picture, but I have a feeling it wasn't your idea, and I want to know whose idea it was."

Casper looked at Philip but didn't answer.

"Who told you to fire me? Or rather, who told you to tell your secretary to fire me?"

"Nobody, I swear to God," said Casper.

"Oh, sure," replied Philip. "You made this decision all on your own."

"Yes, I did. I just don't think you captured the interview with the narcs in the right way," said Casper.

"That's the same scene you told me you liked so much the day before yesterday, Casper," said Philip. "Who told you to fire me?"

Casper shook his head.

Philip dropped Casper's glasses on the floor and stepped on them. "Oops, I broke your glasses."

Casper went down on his hands and knees to retrieve his glasses.

Philip reached out and grabbed him by the neck of his black velour shirt. "You know, Casper, when I was at Princeton, I saw your film *A Mansion in Limbo* three times, because I thought it was so great. I used to want to meet you. And now I have, and you're nothing more than a pathetic drug addict with a face-lift and a wig. What happened to you, Casper?"

"Let me up," said Casper.

"Who told you to fire me?"

"No one, I swear."

"Either you tell me, or I'm going to rip this rug right off your head and call your girlfriends in here from the tennis court to see their little sugar daddy without his hair pasted on."

Casper, frightened, looked up at Philip. "Don't. I beg of you, Phil. Ina Rae doesn't know I wear a rug."

"Who told you to fire me, Casper?"

It was a surprise to Arnie Zwillman when he did not hear from Jules Mendelson after their initial meeting at Casper Stieglitz's party, so he telephoned him at his office to set up a second meeting to discuss further the proposition he had suggested to Jules. Miss Maple, Jules's secretary, was unfamiliar with the name Arnie Zwillman and asked him all the questions that an unfamiliar person is asked by an overly protective secretary.

"Will Mr. Mendelson know what this call is in reference to?" asked Miss Maple.

"Yes, he will," replied Arnie.

"Mr. Mendelson is in conference at the moment. May I have your number, and I will tell him that you called, Mr., uh, what did you say your last name was?"

"Zwillman. Arnie Zwillman. Ring through."

"What?"

"I said, ring through to his conference and tell him Arnie Zwillman is on the phone. He'll take the call, believe me, Miss, uh, what did you say your last name was?"

"I didn't."

"Just ring through, Miss I-Didn't." He chuckled at his joke.

When Miss Maple informed Jules that a very rude person called Mr. Zwillman was on the line and had insisted that she ring through, Jules turned to Sims Lord and said, "It's Zwillman."

"You better take it," said Sims. "You're going to have to talk to him sooner or later. I checked. All records of the Chicago situation in nineteen fifty-three were expunged at the time. It's as if what happened didn't happen."

Jules nodded. He pushed the button on his telephone. "Hello?"

"You really ought to fill your girl in on who I am, Jules," said Arnie. "It's not very good for my ego to be put through the third degree. 'Will Mr. Mendelson know what this is in reference to?' she asked."

"What is this in reference to?" asked Jules.

"I've been waiting to hear from you, Jules," said Arnie.

"Well, now you have me."

"I'm interested in getting together as soon as possible. Nineteen ninety-two is just around the corner, Jules," said Arnie. "There's a lotta crapola to be worked. What you people in your line of work call modus operandi."

"I don't want to meet with you, Zwillman. Now, or ever."

"You're kidding?"

"No, I'm not kidding. And don't call me again, or I'm going to call the FBI."

"Oh, you big dangerous man," said Arnie.

"So long, Arnie."

"You're making one big fat mistake, Mendelson."

"I don't think so, Zwillman."

"You were pretty cool, Jules," said Sims Lord, after Jules hung up the telephone.

"It was good to know those records were destroyed, Sims. I'm going out for a cup of coffee. I want to get a little air."

An hour later Arnie Zwillman informed the Secretary of State, through a highly placed intermediary, of the unfortunate event in the past of Jules Mendelson, the presidential designate for the head of the United States economic commission in Brussels during the year of European statehood, involving the 1953 death of a young woman who fell, or was pushed, from the balcony of the Roosevelt Hotel in Chicago during a romantic tryst.

The records of the death, which had been expunged by the mayor of the city at the request of the parents of Jules Mendelson, were in the hands of Mr. Zwillman and available to the Secretary of State, the highly placed intermediary was informed. The family of the dead girl had been handsomely recompensed for their loss at the time by the family of Mr. Mendelson.

That day at the Viceroy Coffee Shop Jules Mendelson did not read his financial newspapers, as he usually did. His mind was filled with other thoughts. The feeling of relief that he had anticipated when he told Arnie Zwillman that he would not meet with him again was less than he had expected it to be.

Perhaps it was the tone of voice Zwillman had used when he said to Jules, "You're making one big fat mistake, Mendelson." People simply did not call

Jules Mendelson, Mendelson. He was in deep thought, stirring his coffee, although there was neither cream nor sugar in it to stir, when Philip Quennell walked up to his booth and slid into the seat opposite him.

"Hello, Jules," said Philip.

"Get lost, Quennell," said Jules, in a snarling tone of voice. While he feared Arnie Zwillman, he in no way feared Philip Quennell, and he was relieved to be able to shift his focus from one man to the other. He disliked Philip Quennell and had disliked him from the first night they met, when he arrived at the Mendelson party late, the only guest without a dinner jacket, and declined the magnificent wine from the Bresciani auction of which Jules was so proud. Each episode he had spent with him since had only increased that feeling.

"I hear you got me fired from my documentary," said Philip.

Jules did not try to disguise the contempt that crept into his face. "I don't waste my time getting low-level people fired," he said. "Move on, will you?"

"Oh, no?" said Philip, very calmly, making no effort to move. "Casper Stieglitz, after I threatened to pull off his rug in front of a couple of his hookers, let it out that you had called Marty Lesky to, as he put it, send me back home, or you wouldn't follow through with your pledge to the Los Angeles County Museum, which would have been very embarrassing for Marty, who has recently embraced culture."

Jules stared at Philip.

"What I want to know is, did you have me fired because of the crack in the Degas ballerina statue? Or because I refuse to buy your suicide story and think you are involved in a cover-up of Hector Paradiso's death? Or, what is probably the reason, because we happen to share a mutual friend in the person of Miss Flo March?"

Jules could not stand to hear the name of Flo March come out of the mouth of the handsome, self-assured young man who sat opposite him. He hated Philip Quennell's youth. He hated his good looks. But what he hated most was to think that Flo, in her anger at him, had made love to Philip Quennell, had probably performed on him the same sexual intimacies that he had come to crave from her more than anything in his life. Enraged, his face very red, he rose in his seat and leaned across the coffee shop table and grabbed Philip.

Philip Quennell did not flinch for an instant. "If you're as smart as you're supposed to be, Jules, you will remove your hands from my body immediately," he said. "I don't care how old you are, how rich you are, how important you are, I will knock you down on your fat ass right here in this coffee shop, in front of all these customers who are staring at you."

Jules met Philip's eye and knew he meant what he said. He released his grip on the young man.

"Everything all right, Mr. Mendelson?" asked Curly, the manager of the coffee shop, who ran over to the table.

"Get this guy out of here, Curly," said Jules.

"No, no, Curly," said Philip, waving his forefinger back and forth. "You don't have to get me out of here." There was about him a menace that was felt by both Jules and Curly. If Curly had thought of touching Philip to prod him out of the coffee shop, he desisted. "I am about to walk out of here on my own.

I have just about finished with what I have to say to Mr. Jules Mendelson. But there is just one more thing, Jules."

"Come on, fella. Get movin'," said Curly.

Philip turned to Curly. "I am movin'. But first I'm finishin'." He turned back to Jules. Both men were standing, and people were watching. "Do not for an instant think that I will go gently into the night, Jules, despite your orders to send me home. I don't like you, any more than I liked your crooked pal, Reza Bulbenkian. I don't like people who can call up a newspaper and tell them not to print a story that the public has a right to know, or tell the police not to solve a crime, and allow a killer to walk free because you decided to dream up some cockamamie suicide story. You're covering up for somebody, Jules. And I'm not going back to New York until I find out who it is. For all I know, maybe you shot Hector Paradiso, Jules."

"Get lost," said Jules.

"I'm not going back to New York, Jules, despite your best efforts. I've decided to stay awhile. So long, Jules. So long, Curly."

Jules sank back into his seat in the orange Naugahyde booth as he watched Philip Quennell leave the Viceroy Coffee Shop. Within him, he knew that Philip, for all his youth and handsomeness, was not a romantic rival for Flo March's considerable favors. He also knew that his unreasonable jealousy of Quennell, caused by Flo's spending two nights in his room at the Chateau Marmont, had led him to make the sort of tactical error he would never have made in a business transaction.

Jules usually arrived at Flo's house on Azelia Way at a quarter of four every afternoon. As he had been in his office since six o'clock in the morning, it was not thought unreasonable by anyone that he should leave at exactly three-thirty, no matter what, and be unreachable until he called in for his messages an hour and a half later. What no one knew was that by then he had made love to Flo March as many as three times.

On the same day that he talked with Arnie Zwillman on the telephone and fought with Philip Quennell in the Viceroy Coffee Shop, he walked out of his office at exactly three-thirty, as was his custom. Miss Maple, who had been with him for years, was not unaware that he seemed dispirited. As he walked past her desk, she waved good-bye to him while she continued her telephone conversation.

"Mr. Mendelson is not available," Miss Maple said. "Oh, hello, Mr. Crocker. If you leave your number, I will be speaking with him in about an hour and a half and relay it to him. Oh, yes, Mr. Crocker. Oh, yes, I know the area code in Washington is two-oh-two. I should know it by now, shouldn't I, after all these calls between you and Mr. Mendelson."

Jules was at the main door of his office on the top floor of the Mendelson Building when he heard the name Crocker. He turned back to Miss Maple. "Is that Myles Crocker?" he asked.

"Would you hold on a moment, Mr. Crocker? My other phone is ringing," said Miss Maple. She pushed the hold button. "Yes, it is," she said to Jules. "Myles Crocker. State Department. Assistant to the Secretary of State."

"I know who he is," said Jules. He put down his briefcase on Miss Maple's desk and returned to his office.

Miss Maple was surprised at the break in his routine. She thought he had appeared older recently. He had seemed preoccupied since Pauline left for Northeast Harbor. He had seemed frantic for the several days he had been locked in with Sims Lord. He had seemed remote since he returned from the Viceroy Coffee Shop, reacting only to the information that a storm in Bangor, Maine, had delayed Mrs. Mendelson's departure for Los Angeles on the family plane by several hours.

Miss Maple said into the telephone, "Mr. Mendelson has just returned unexpectedly, Mr. Crocker, and will be picking up the telephone immediately."

"I've been asked to call you, Jules," said Myles Crocker. "The Secretary had been with the President all morning on the hostage crisis and couldn't make the call himself, but he will certainly be in touch with you when things calm down here."

"Yes," said Jules, quietly. He knew that he was about to hear distressing news.

"I'm afraid that I am the bearer of some bad news, Jules," said Myles Crocker.

"Yes?"

"The Secretary didn't want you to hear it from anyone else but him."

"Yes?"

"It is about your appointment to head the American delegation in Brussels."

"Yes?"

"Some information has come to the Secretary of a rather distressing nature."

"What sort of information?"

"A tragic event in a Chicago hotel room in nineteen fifty-three. There is no way that you would ever be ratified, if such a story became known, and it is thought best to simply withdraw the nomination."

Jules remained perfectly calm. "I have heard that vicious story myself. There is no truth to it. None whatever. When you are a man in my position, there are always going to be such stories spread about you. If there were anything to such a story, there would be records in Chicago, and no such records exist."

"The records were expunged at the time, Jules, but somehow, copies of them exist. At least *a* copy of them exists. A Mr. Arnie Zwillman, formerly of Chicago, has made that copy available by fax to the Secretary, and to the *Post*."

"Dear God."

"This is terribly embarrassing for me, Jules, to be the bearer of this news, after having been entertained so beautifully and so often by you and Pauline."

Jules did not reply.

"Are you there, Jules?"

"Yes, I'm here, Myles. Look, tell the Secretary he doesn't have to bother calling."

When he hung up the telephone, Jules Mendelson put his head down on the blotter of his desk and wept.

Flo's Tape #17

"*My mother used to say to me, 'Your father walked out on us when you were two.' I had romantic notions of what my father was like. I used to always think someday he'd come back and want to make life easier for us. I thought maybe he'd have curiosity about what I looked like.*

"*But when I grew older, I began to realize that my father hadn't ever married my mother. It sometimes even occurred to me that my mother wasn't even sure who my father was.*

"*Jules once said to me, 'Did you ever say that to your mother?' Of course not. Her life was hard enough as it was.*"

18

"YOU'RE LATE, Jules," said Flo. "I was beginning to think you weren't coming."

"Why are all those cars parked on Azelia Way?" Jules asked. "I could hardly get my car in the driveway. Somebody's Jaguar is blocking about half of it."

"I told those parking boys not to block my entrance," said Flo.

"What's going on?" The small street was usually silent, except for the several times a day the tour buses went by, and the voice of the tour guides could be heard announcing Faye Converse's house.

"Faye Converse is having a barbecue luncheon," Flo answered, breathlessly. She was beside herself with excitement at the activity in the next house. She had been watching the festivities through her binoculars, from her position of vantage in her bedroom window. "Look, Jules. Faye's parasol matches her caftan. She's got half the stars in Hollywood over there. Practically everyone you ever heard of. Oh, oh, my God. There's Dom Belcanto. Be still, my heart. And Pepper, the new wife. Glyceria said Dom sometimes sings at Faye's parties. Oh, look, Amos Swank, the talk show host. I just watched him last night, and there he is. And there's your favorite, Cyril Rathbone."

She handed Jules the binoculars, but he had no interest in looking at film stars cavorting at a lunch party that showed no signs of dwindling down at five o'clock. Screams of laughter could be heard.

"Don't you love the sounds of a party, Jules?" asked Flo, looking through the binoculars again. She reminded Jules of a courtesan in an opera box, enrapt with her first opera experience. "That hum of voices, and all that laughter? Wouldn't you love to know what they're all talking about down there? I may not fit in your world, but I could fit in with the movie crowd. I just know it."

Jules shook his head and walked out of Flo's bedroom into her living room. At the bar he took out a bottle of white wine from the refrigerator and poured himself a glass. He removed the jacket of his suit and threw it on the gray satin sofa. Then he sat down heavily and looked off into space. His mind was on the telephone call he had received from Myles Crocker. He imagined Myles reporting his reaction to the Secretary of State, and the Secretary of State reporting to the President, and he experienced the feeling of despair, a feeling unknown to him in his spectacularly successful life until that moment.

"Are you all right, Jules?" asked Flo, when she came in from her bedroom. She placed the binoculars on the bar.

"Fine, why?" he asked.

"You seem, I don't know, quiet, distant, something. Did I do something wrong? Are you mad at me? Because I was watching Faye's party through the binoculars? Is that it?"

Jules smiled at her. "No," he said.

"I suppose it is kind of cheap. I can't imagine Pauline doing anything like that," said Flo.

For once he did not turn away or turn red when she mentioned his wife's name. His eyes fixed on her, as if memorizing her face.

"Sometimes you look at me as if it's going to be for the last time," she said. "Are you sure you're all right, Jules?"

"I told you, I'm fine."

"I know how to cheer you up, baby." She began to sing. *"Gimme, gimme, gimme, what I cry for. You know you got the kind of kisses that I die for."*

Jules smiled.

"I knew I could cheer you up."

She kissed him and touched his face in a gentle fashion until he began to respond to her. When he made love to her, he had never been more passionate. He could not get enough of her. His tongue probed her mouth. He sucked in her saliva. He inhaled her breath. Over and over again he told her he loved her.

Afterward, when he phoned Miss Maple to check on his calls, he signaled to Flo that he needed the little agenda book that he always carried in the left-hand pocket of his suit jacket. He covered the mouthpiece and said to her, "It's on the sofa in the living room."

Because of the party going on next door, Flo slipped on a dressing gown and high-heeled satin slippers. As she went into the living room, she heard Jules say on the telephone, "Call the house. Tell Dudley to have Jim meet her plane. Tell him to be there half an hour ahead of time, so there's no possibility of a mix-up. And hold on, I'll have Friedrich Hesse-Darmstadt's telephone number for you in just a moment."

Flo realized from Jules's conversation with Miss Maple that Pauline was coming home from Northeast Harbor, and that as of tomorrow Jules would be resuming the heavy social schedule that he and Pauline customarily followed. As she sometimes did, she felt jealous that Pauline claimed more of Jules's life than she did. Outside, she could hear the guests from next door starting to leave the party, some in an inebriated state. "Bye, Faye," guest after guest could be heard saying.

Flo reached into the left-hand pocket of Jules's suit jacket and found his agenda book. Once he had said to her, "My whole life is in this little book. All the numbers I need. All the engagements I keep." As she took it out, her hand felt a small velvet box next to it. She took that out also. She went back into the bedroom and handed Jules his book. Then she opened the velvet box. Inside was the pair of yellow diamond earrings that Jules had given to Pauline and that Pauline had returned to him the next morning. He had meant to have Miss Maple send them back to Boothby's, the auction house, to be reauctioned, but he had forgotten to give them to her when he returned from the Viceroy Coffee Shop that morning.

Flo thought that Jules had bought them for her. Ecstatic, she let out a squeal of excitement and then covered her mouth with her hand to shut herself up, as he was still on the telephone and hated for her to talk when he was conducting his business. As soon as he hung up, she ran to him and threw her arms around his neck and kissed him.

"They're gorgeous, Jules," she said. "I never say anything so beautiful in my whole life."

"What?" asked Jules, confused by her outpouring.

" 'What,' he says." She fastened the earrings onto her ear lobes and pulled her hair back. *"This* is what."

Jules looked at her in a quizzical fashion. He was startled to see the earrings that he had bought for his wife, that his wife would not accept, on his mistress's ears. Flo's madly excited reaction to the beautiful jewels was what he had hoped Pauline's reaction would be when he gave them to her the week before. He did not have the heart to tell Flo that the earrings were not for her, or that he had just told Miss Maple to contact Prince Friedrich of Hesse-Darmstadt, the head of the jewelry department at Boothby's auction house in London, to inform him that he wanted to sell the earrings.

"Why are you looking at me in such a funny way?" she asked.

"I'm not looking at you in a funny way," said Jules. His voice sounded tired and weary. "I'm just feasting my eyes, that's all. They look beautiful on you."

"Do you think it's okay to wear the blue sapphire ring and the yellow diamond earrings at the same time?" she asked.

"I would think it's proper," said Jules.

Nothing put Flo in such a good mood as a beautiful gift. She turned the music up on the radio and slowly slipped out of her dressing gown. She began to dance around the room, wearing nothing but her high-heeled satin slippers. It was a look she knew Jules liked. He lay back on the bed watching her, as her erotic and exotic dance steps slowly began to arouse him again. He was mesmerized by her lovely young body, her beautiful creamy skin, her superb buttocks, her perfect breasts, and her ample red bush, which he could never become sated with, no matter how often he entered it, or kissed it, or breathed it, or rubbed his face in it. As she danced her way from the bedroom to the living room, he followed her. She reached behind her and took hold of his erection and led him to her newly upholstered gray satin sofa. Never losing the beat of the music she was dancing to, she perched on the back of the sofa and then allowed herself to fall backward, spreading her legs at the same time so that only her bush, open and ready to receive him, was visible to him. With one thrust he entered her and began to pump back and forth, without subtlety, a race to a mutual explosion that momentarily obliterated the great disappointment of his day.

The massive heart attack that followed was concurrent with his ejaculation, and Flo mistook the shudders of his body and the groans of pain from his lips for signs of passion. It was only when his spent penis slid out of her and he fell over backward onto her carpet that she realized what had happened. She pulled herself up off the sofa and ran to him. His face had turned gray. Drool was dripping from his mouth. She thought that he was dead.

The scream that came from Flo's lips was unlike any scream that she had ever screamed before. The sound traveled upward in the canyon, and people in houses higher up heard it, although they could not tell for sure from which house it was coming. The scream was also heard in the patio of Faye Converse's house next door.

All the guests from her barbecue lunch party had finally left, save one. Cyril Rathbone, the gossip columnist for *Mulholland*, who could not drag himself away from the great star, continued to engage her in poolside conversation, although Faye Converse was sick to death of him and his adoring chatter. He knew the plots of all fifty-seven of her films.

"How amazing you should remember *The Tower*, Cyril," said Faye politely, stifling a yawn at the same time. She could not think of anything she would like to discuss less than the plot of *The Tower*, one of her great flops, in which she had played Mary, Queen of Scots, against the advice of everyone. She wished she hadn't sent Glyceria out on an errand, for Glyceria always knew how to get rid of adoring guests who didn't know when the party was over.

It was then that Flo March's scream from the house beyond the tall hedge pierced the canyon air.

"What in the world is that?" asked Cyril. He jumped up from the lounge chair.

"Why don't you go check?" replied Faye, who intended to disappear as soon as Cyril had gone to investigate.

"Do you think it's a murder?" asked Cyril. He was wide-eyed with excitement.

"Oh, no, it didn't sound to me like a murder kind of scream at all," said Faye Converse.

"Who lives next door?" asked Cyril.

"I haven't the slightest idea," said Faye. "It belongs to Trent Muldoon, but he's rented it to someone."

"Perhaps I should call the police," said Cyril.

"You should go over and check first. It could be the television. I'd send Glyceria over—my maid, Glyceria—but she's out getting some disinfectant for the powder room for me."

"Is there an opening through the hedge?" asked Cyril.

"No, I don't think so. You have to go 'round, down my driveway, and then up that driveway," said Faye. Then she stood, expecting him to go. "It's been lovely having you here, Cyril. When you write up my party, don't mention that Pepper Belcanto drank too many tequila sours and got sick all over the walls of the powder room. All right? You know how Dom gets. Broken-kneecap time. Good-bye, Cyril."

"I'll come right back and tell you what happened next door," he said.

"Oh, no. That's not necessary."

Faye turned and walked into her house. Cyril had not expected to be dismissed in such a fashion, but his curiosity was such that he could not resist going to check on the source of the scream. He went down Faye Converse's driveway to Azelia Way. From the street the house next door was totally hidden from view by the overgrown shrubbery and trees in front of it. Cyril slowly went up the driveway of that house. Directly in front of the house was a dark blue Bentley, which blocked the garage in which was parked a red Mercedes convertible. From inside the house he could hear the hysterical crying of a woman. The front door was locked. He walked around the side of the house to the swimming pool area. There was no one in sight. Then he went up to the sliding glass doors and put his hands up to cover the sides of his eyes and peered in. There on the floor was an enormous man, totally naked. A beautiful young red-haired woman, also naked, was administering mouth-to-mouth re-suscitation.

Cyril slid open the door. "May I help?" he asked.

"Call an ambulance," screamed Flo, between breaths. Without lifting her face, she pointed to a telephone on the bar.

"What's the address here?" asked Cyril.

"Eight forty-four Azelia Way. Tell them it's next to Faye Converse's house," said Flo, between breaths.

Cyril dialed 911. In the moments before the telephone was answered, Cyril Rathbone noticed the great abundance of Steuben glasses on the bar shelves. His eyes wandered around the room, taking everything in. He noticed the gray satin upholstery on the living room sofas and recognized it as Nellie Potts's favorite fabric that season, ninety-five dollars a yard. He wondered whose house he was in.

"Oh, hello? Nine-one-one? Oh, yes, thank God. There is an emergency at number eight forty-four Azelia Way. Halfway up Coldwater Canyon. Turn right on Cherokee. It will be your second or third left, I'm not sure which. It's the house directly next to Faye Converse's house. There is a man who has suffered something or other, a stroke or a heart attack. I'm not sure if he's dead or not." He turned to Flo. "Is he dead?" asked Cyril.

Flo, not stopping her breathing, shook her head no.

"Hurry," said Cyril into the telephone. "He's not dead."

When he hung up the telephone, he moved closed to the life-and-death drama for a better look.

"They're sending an ambulance," he said.

The woman continued her resuscitation and nodded her head at the same time. Even in such a moment of crisis, Cyril did not fail to notice that the private parts of the besieged man rivaled Lonny Edge's in what he privately termed the equipment department. When the beautiful young woman raised her head to gasp for air, he saw for the first time the face of the man on the floor.

"Good God," he whispered, as he realized that the man was Jules Mendel-son, the billionaire, the art collector, the designate of the President of the United States to head the American delegation in Brussels during the year of the statehood of Europe, and the husband of the exquisite Pauline Mendelson. Only a little more than a week earlier, at Casper Stieglitz's ghastly little party, Jules Mendelson and his wife had both snubbed him.

"Good God," he whispered again. Within a second, he knew that the naked redhead trying to save Jules Mendelson's life was the same girl whose picture he had sent to Hector Paradiso from the Paris newspaper, fleeing the fire in the Meurice Hotel, with Jules in the background. Later, he had sent another, anonymously, to Pauline herself. "Good God," he said for the third time.

Cyril Rathbone was, after all, a member of the news media, and he knew that he was the first person present, aside from the principals, at what would undoubtedly be a major story, if he acted quickly, before powerful forces moved in to alter the facts of the story, as powerful forces had moved in to alter the facts of Hector Paradiso's death.

"Look, miss, I have called the ambulance, and it's on its way. I have to be off," said Cyril.

Flo continued her breathing into Jules's mouth. She lifted her head long enough to say, "Get me my robe, will you? On my bed. That way." As she resumed her breathing, she pointed in the direction of the bedroom. "And bring in his pants," she called.

When Cyril was in the bedroom, he quickly called the editor of *Mulholland* and asked for a photographer to be sent immediately to the emergency entrance of Cedars-Sinai Hospital. "Can't talk," he hissed into the mouthpiece. "But trust me."

For years Cyril Rathbone had dreamed of an opportunity that would catapult him from the gossip column of the magazine to a cover story that would be discussed across the nation. His time was at hand.

"You did the mouth-to-mouth resuscitation, lady?" asked one of the five attendants who had arrived in the ambulance. Another attendant was applying heavy pressure on Jules's heart by pumping his hands up and down. A third was trying to feel for a pulse.

"Yes," said Flo. She did not take her eyes off Jules. "Wasn't that what I was supposed to do?"

"You did exactly right. You did a good job. How'd you learn how to do that?" he asked. "Most people don't know how to do it right." He had his pad and pencil out and was preparing to ask her some questions, while two other attendants were setting up the dolly onto which the stretcher would be placed.

"Where I used to work. We had to learn how to do it, in case of a customer getting a heart attack or something. But this was the first time I ever put it to use," said Flo, distractedly, all the while watching what the other attendants were doing with Jules, lifting him onto the stretcher and strapping him on. She had managed to get his trousers pulled onto him before the ambulance arrived, although she had not had time to pull on his undershorts first, or his shirt afterward. As she heard the ambulance pull into her driveway, with its siren blaring, she had hastily pulled on the clothes she had been wearing when she was watching Faye Converse's party out the window of her bedroom.

"This your husband?" the attendant asked.

"No."

"Name?"

"Mine or his?"

"His."

"Jules Mendelson," she said.

He started to write the name. "Like in the Jules Mendelson Family Patient Wing at Cedars-Sinai?" he asked.

"Yes."

"Holy shit," he said, looking at her. "Age?"

"Fifty-six, I think, or, maybe, seven. I'm not sure."

"You are not Mrs. Mendelson, you said?"

"I am not Mrs. Mendelson. That's correct."

"This your house?"

"Yes."

"Is there a Mrs. Mendelson?"

"Yes."

"Has Mrs. Mendelson been informed?"

"Only you have been informed," said Flo. "It only happened twenty minutes ago, thirty minutes ago at most. He just keeled over. Some guy came in here from the party next door and called the ambulance. I didn't see who it was, because I was giving mouth-to-mouth at the time. Is he going to be okay?"

"Should I inform Mrs. Mendelson?"

"She's on a plane, their private plane, coming back from Northeast Harbor, Maine, due in sometime this evening. I asked you if he was going to be okay."

"We'll get him into the cardiac arrest unit as soon as we get him to Cedars," said the attendant.

The other attendants had wheeled Jules out the front door of the house and placed the stretcher in the ambulance. "Okay, Charlie," one of them called back.

"Do you want to ride with us in the ambulance? I can finish these questions on the way to the hospital," said Charlie.

"Okay," said Flo.

Charlie helped her in.

"What kind of car's that, Charlie?" asked the driver. "The blue one."

"Bentley 'ninety," said Charlie. "Beautiful, huh? That'll set you back about a hundred and fifty grand. Do you know who this guy is?"

"Who?"

"Jules Mendelson, the billionaire. Like in the Jules Mendelson Family Patient Wing at the hospital," said Charlie. "So make time, or we'll all be outta work."

"No kidding? That's Jules Mendelson? No wonder central said there's photographers at the hospital waiting for the ambulance. This is one narrow driveway, and steep. I can hardly back this around," said the ambulance driver.

"Did he say there's photographers at the hospital?" Flo asked Charlie, in an alarmed voice.

"That's what central just told him on the car phone."

"Listen, you have to stop and let me out," said Flo. "Please. It's very important."

"What's the matter?"

"Look, Charlie. Isn't that your name? Charlie? I'm the girlfriend, not the wife. Do you understand? I better follow in my own car," said Flo.

Charlie did not say, "I figured as much," but Flo could read that look on his face with absolute precision. As always with Flo, people liked her, and Charlie, the attendant, did too. "Hold it up, Pedro," he called out to the driver. "The lady's getting out."

The ambulance came to a halt at the bottom of Flo's driveway. Charlie opened the rear door of the ambulance for Flo to get down.

"Jules, honey," she said to Jules's inert body, leaning close to his face. His mouth had been covered with an oxygen mask. "I'm going to take my own car to the hospital. I'll be there with you in a few minutes. You're in good hands, Jules. I love you, baby."

"Do you know how to get to the emergency entrance of Cedars?" Charlie asked her.

"Yeah. My mother died at Cedars," she said.

In her haste to scramble out the back of the ambulance, she tripped and fell onto the driveway, tearing her skirt and skinning her knee. "Goddammit," she cried out.

"Are you okay?" called Charlie, from the back of the ambulance.

"I'm okay," Flo yelled back, waving the ambulance on. The siren started to blare, as the ambulance turned left down Azelia Way. When she tried to stand up on the steep driveway, she heard the sound of Astrid barking. She knew from Glyceria that the dog had been locked up in Faye Converse's bathroom during the whole of the party, as she had, since Hector Paradiso's death, developed a reputation for biting people, and Faye did not want to risk having one of her guests bitten.

The dog came running around from the back of the house. When she saw Flo trying to get up off the driveway, she ran to her and began licking her face, wanting to be picked up.

"No, no, Astrid, not now. I can't deal with you now," said Flo. "Go back home, honey. Go back through your hole in the hedge. You have to go home now, Astrid. You can't stay here. Go ahead. Glyceria's waiting for you. *Go home!*"

The confused dog, used to being loved by her, could not understand why Flo did not pick her up, as she always did, or why she spoke to her in such a harsh tone of voice. Flo, limping because of her cut knee, ran back up the driveway to get into her car. Then she realized that Jules's Bentley was blocking her car in the garage, and she could not get hers out.

"Oh, God," she screamed, in frustration. She felt the tears that she had held back for nearly an hour, but she refused to let them come. She ran to Jules's car and opened the door. "Thank God," she said when she saw that he had left his keys in the ignition. She jumped into the driver's seat and turned on the ignition before she closed her door. The radio came on to the news station that Jules always played in his car. Astrid tried to jump into the car after her. "No, no, out," she screamed, pushing her out of the car. For an instant they looked at each other. "I have to get to the hospital," she called out to the dog in explanation, as if the dog could understand her. But Astrid could not understand her. Rejected by the person she loved most, she ran forward down the driveway, heading toward Azelia Way.

Flo had never driven the Bentley before, and she was unprepared for its enormous power. As she applied her foot too hard to the gas pedal, the car shot forward. Halfway down the driveway, before she could apply the brake to slow down, she felt a thud, and heard a thud, and then a scream. The small white furry body of Astrid flew up in the air in front of the grille and landed with another thud on the hood of the car in front of the windshield. Flo screamed. The dog rolled over off the hood onto the driveway. Flo slammed on the brakes, put the car in park, and opened the door.

"Oh, no," she moaned, unable to accept the reality of what she had done. "Oh, no." She picked up the smashed creature from the driveway, and the tears that she had held back for nearly an hour came bursting forth from her eyes. "Oh, Astrid, my little darling Astrid, I love you so much. Don't die, Astrid, don't die, Astrid. Please. Please." She looked down into the dog's eyes, and the dog looked up at her. Their eyes met. She felt the dog relax, make a quiet sound, and die.

She held Astrid in her arms. From within the car, she heard the radio. "We interrupt this broadcast. The financier and billionaire Jules Mendelson has been rushed to Cedars-Sinai Hospital by ambulance, following a massive heart attack in the home of a friend in Beverly Hills. Mendelson's wife, the society figure, Pauline Mendelson, is thought to be en route in the family plane from Maine. Stay tuned."

Flo placed the little terrier by the side of the driveway, and kissed her. "I'll be back," she whispered to the dog. She got into the car again. Tears were rolling down her cheeks, and she made no effort to control her sobs. She raced the car down Azelia Way to Cherokee Lane to Coldwater Canyon. Without waiting for traffic, she pushed onto Coldwater, disregarding the cars that honked at her, and proceeded to Beverly Drive, passing cars all the way, until she came to Sunset Boulevard. She ignored the light at Sunset, crossed over and followed Beverly Drive again to Santa Monica Boulevard, blowing her horn at any car that wasn't driving fast enough. She turned left on Santa Monica Boulevard, again without stopping for the light, turned right on Beverly Boulevard, and followed it until she came to the Cedars-Sinai Medical Center. She slammed on the brakes, but there were no places on the street for her to park the car. She realized that she had brought no money with her and could not get into the garage for hospital visitors. At the parking lot reserved for the doctors and staff, she did not have the necessary plastic card to insert that would raise the gate to allow her car to enter. Desperate to reach Jules, she crashed his car through the wooden gate. A parking lot guard blew his whistle at her. At the same time, a police car that had been following her since she went through a stoplight at Beverly Drive and Santa Monica Boulevard pulled into the lot. She opened the door of the Bentley, oblivious to the havoc she had caused.

"Where's the emergency entrance?" she screamed to two nurses who were having a cigarette behind one of the parked cars. They pointed in the direction of emergency, and she ran toward it.

"Hold it!" called out the policeman to her.

"You hold it," she called back, and entered the hospital.

Rose Cliveden, who listened to the radio all day, heard the same news announcement about Jules's heart attack that Flo had heard on her car radio when Astrid was dying in her arms. Rose put down her glass and sprang into action. For a moment she couldn't decide whether to call Camilla Ebury, Miss Maple, or Dudley, the butler, first. She had spoken to Pauline several times since she left for Northeast Harbor, and knew she was returning that very day, but she also heard on the news that there were storms in Maine, and she thought the plane might not have taken off, or been delayed. Pauline had told Rose no more than that she was going to Northeast to visit her father, who was ailing.

Rose called Dudley.

"Is Mrs. Mendelson's plane in yet, Dudley?"

"It's due in at eight, Mrs. Cliveden."

"Do you think she knows?"

"I'm sorry?" Dudley did not understand Rose's question. He knew everything about the Mendelsons, he thought.

"Do you think she's heard the news?"

"What news? About the storms in Maine?"

"You mean you haven't heard?" asked Rose. She was full of importance with her knowledge.

"Heard what?"

"About Mr. Mendelson?"

"What's happened?" asked Dudley.

"He's had a heart attack. They've taken him to Cedars. I just heard it on the news."

"Oh, no." There was a silence for a minute. "I can't understand why Miss Maple wouldn't have called here," he said.

"Perhaps she doesn't know yet either."

"How could she not know?"

"It didn't happen in the office, apparently. The report said he was visiting a friend."

"Why?" asked Dudley.

"I don't know. They didn't say on the news. Who's going to meet Mrs. Mendelson's plane?"

"Jim, the chauffeur, is going out to the airport at seven. Mr. Mendelson wanted him to be there a half hour ahead of time," said Dudley.

Rose began to give orders, as if she were in charge. "Have Jim pick me up first, Dudley. I think I should be there when she lands. She should hear the news from a friend, and I suppose I'm her best friend. And I'll go on to the hospital with her."

"Yes, Mrs. Cliveden," said Dudley.

When Dudley hung up, he yelled upstairs for Blondell, Pauline's maid, to come downstairs, and for Gertie, the cook, to come out from the kitchen, and for Smitty, the guard, to come in from the kennels, where he was feeding the dogs, and for Jim, the chauffeur, to come in from the garage, where he was polishing the cars.

"Mr. M. has had a heart attack," Dudley said, when the servants were gathered together in the main hallway of Clouds. There was a feeling of silent dismay among them, as if their lives were being threatened. Dudley had been with the family longest, and was known to have a close relationship with Jules Mendelson. Blondell thought he was crying. Then the telephone rang. It was Miss Maple.

Miss Maple heard the news from her sister in Long Beach, who had heard it on her car radio and pulled in to a Mobil station to call her from a pay phone. She immediately called Clouds to tell Dudley, but Dudley said that he already knew and that he had been about to call her, as he had just heard the news from Mrs. Cliveden, who had heard it on the radio. Dudley told Miss Maple that Mrs. Cliveden was going to the airport with Jim and would break the news to Mrs. Mendelson.

"Just what she's not going to need at such a time is Rose Cliveden," said Miss Maple.

"That's what I was thinking," said Dudley.

"I wonder if I should call the pilot and tell him to tell Mrs. Mendelson," said Miss Maple.

"I'd wait," said Dudley. "There's nothing she can do while she's in the air."

While Rose was waiting for Pauline's chauffeur to pick her up, she called Camilla Ebury to tell her the news.

"I can't believe it," said Camilla.

"It's true, all right. It's on the news," said Rose.

"Poor Pauline," said Camilla.

"I can't stay on the phone talking," said Rose. She was full of purpose. "Pauline's chauffeur is going to pick me up and take me out to the airport so that I can break the news to her. She adores Jules."

Camilla called Philip Quennell at the Chateau Marmont.

"Where did it happen?" asked Philip.

"Rose said the news said it happened at a friend's house," said Camilla.

Philip knew immediately, without being told, that it had happened at Flo March's house, but he did not tell that to Camilla. He had not told Camilla that the girl she had met and liked in his room at the Chateau Marmont was the mistress of Jules Mendelson.

Philip called Flo, and got the answering machine. At first he was going to hang up. Then he said, without leaving his name, "Flo, I'm at the Chateau, if you need me."

Since the plane was late in arriving, Rose had several drinks at the bar in the lounge of the airport where the private planes landed. Jim, the chauffeur, twice stopped her from tripping over her crutches. By the time the plane finally arrived, an hour later than scheduled, she was sobbing incoherently over the news she had to break to her great and dear friend. When Pauline got off her plane and saw Rose in such a state, she knew that something dire had taken place. Her first thoughts were of Kippie. She was sure she was about to be told that Kippie was dead.

"Oh, my God," she said, "Kippie? Is it Kippie?"

"Not Kippie. *Jules,*" said Rose, throwing her arms around Pauline.

Pauline turned ashen. "Jules?" she asked. She had decided to take her father's advice and go back to Jules. During her last days at Northeast Harbor and on the plane ride home, she had further decided to wipe the slate clean and begin again with Jules. What husband had not had an indiscretion, she had reasoned. She thought of the many advantages of her life: her beautiful home, her flowers, her friends, the traveling she did, the thoughtfulness of her husband for all her comforts. She thought of the time ahead, when she would be spending a year in Brussels, and of all the entertaining that would entail. And, most important, she knew, despite his affair, that Jules needed her and even still loved her. She could not believe that he was dead.

Jim, the chauffeur, seeing the anguished look on Mrs. Mendelson's face, understood immediately that Mrs. Cliveden had made her think that Mr. Mendelson was dead. "No, no, Mrs. Mendelson," he said. "Mr. Mendelson has had a heart attack. It was on the news. He's in Cedars-Sinai, and I'm going to take you there right now."

"What is his condition?" asked Pauline.

"We don't know," said Jim.

"We don't know," repeated Rose, through her sobs.

At the hospital, Pauline would not allow Rose to come in with her. "Take Mrs. Cliveden home, Jim, and then come back, will you please."

"But I want to be with you, Pauline," said Rose. "You need me."

"No, Rose. You must understand. I want to be alone with my husband. You have been so marvelous, darling. Thank you. Thank you. I can never thank you enough."

"Do you need any of your bags, Mrs. Mendelson?" asked Jim.

"Just that small one, Jim. For God's sake, get her out of here, and don't let her talk you into bringing her back."

"Yes, ma'am. And Mrs. Mendelson?"

"Yes?"

"Tell Mr. M. we're all rooting for him."

"That's right, Pauline. Tell Jules we're all rooting for him," Rose called out of the window of the limousine.

The young red-haired woman with the ripped Chanel suit and the skinned and bleeding kneecaps raced into the emergency entrance of the Cedars-Sinai Medical Center in a highly agitated state. She made her way over to the admitting desk, followed by a policeman who was writing out a ticket while reeling off the charges of driving sixty-five miles an hour in a thirty-mile-an-hour zone, going through a red light, malicious damage to public property, and reckless endangerment. She turned to her pursuer and asked, angrily, "I didn't kill anybody, did I?"

The policeman continued to write his ticket.

"Or wound?" continued Flo.

"You could have," said the policeman.

"Then that ticket that you are writing out is *not* an emergency. And the reason I drove so fast *is* an emergency. So I will take your ticket, if you ever finish writing it up, and I will handle it in the proper way, and appear in the necessary court, and pay the designated fine, or go to jail if I have to, all at some time in the future, as well as pay for the gate that I knocked down outside. But now I am here on another matter, involving a life-and-death situation, and I'm telling you, in as courteous a way as I know how, not to detain me one instant longer."

"You tell him, sister," shouted a woman with two small children, whose lover had been taken up to the emergency room with multiple stab wounds, and others waiting on benches in the emergency entrance cheered.

The policeman looked at the beautiful young woman who had just read him off. She remained unflinching in her return of his gaze. Finally, he smiled at her and handed her the ticket.

"Listen, I can't tear this up, miss. I still gotta give it to you," he said.

"Sure," said Flo, calming down.

"I hope whoever's sick is going to be okay," he said.

"Thanks." She took the ticket and turned to the nurse on duty at the desk.

"Jules Mendelson," she said.

The nurse, whose name, Mimosa Perez, was on a nameplate on her uniform, had watched Flo handle the policeman. "You must be Mr. Mendelson's daughter, right?"

Flo looked surprised at the question. Jules would have hated it if anyone had mistaken her for his daughter. Then she remembered from the time her mother had been brought to this same emergency entrance, when she was burned in the fire in the welfare hotel, that only immediate family members were allowed upstairs to talk with the doctors.

"Have to ask," said the nurse, apologetically. "Hospital rules."

Flo, unsure how to answer, nodded.

"Only immediate families are allowed upstairs," said the nurse. "Some of these reporters will stoop to any kind of low trick to get into the ICU when there's a VIP or a celeb admitted to the hospital. You should have seen this place when Lucille Ball died. I mean, it was crawling with reporters."

Flo could not bring herself to say that she was Jules's daughter, and she would never have claimed to be his wife. The nurse, eager to help the distraught but expensively dressed young woman, said, "I'll buzz you in, Miss Mendelson. Down that corridor. Turn right by the water fountain to the elevators. Take the elevator to the sixth floor. They'll direct you from there."

Flo looked at her nameplate. "Thanks, Mimosa," she said.

Mimosa smiled. "You father's still in the operating room, but not in the Jules Mendelson Wing. I'll ring up and tell the nurse on duty that you're on your way."

On the bench next to the woman with two children whose lover was being operated on sat Cyril Rathbone, witnessing the arrival at the hospital of the mistress of Jules Mendelson. He was beside himself with excitement at the turn of events in his life that day. "Dressed in Chanel. Skirt torn. Pretended she was his daughter," he wrote about Flo March in his spiral notebook.

Every doctor and nurse in the intensive care unit was aware that Jules Mendelson had given the hospital wing that bore his name. On two occasions, Dr. Petrie, who was in charge of the case, sent out an intern to give Flo a progress report, assuming that she was an immediate member of Jules Mendelson's family.

"We are cautiously optimistic," said the intern.

"That's only telling me that he's still alive," said Flo.

"That is more than we had hoped for when he was first admitted," said the doctor.

"Can I see him?"

"Not yet."

"When?"

For several hours Flo waited in the lounge area outside the intensive care unit, drinking Diet Cokes from a vending machine and watching television. She tried to read magazines and newspapers that had been left there, but she found it impossible to fix her attention on anything other than the matter at hand. She felt the beginnings of fear, both for her and for Jules.

In the five years since Jules had walked into the Viceroy Coffee Shop and changed her life, Flo had often longed for a friend to confide in, over events of far lesser magnitude than the event that was now occurring around her. But never had she longed for a friend to be with more than she did in those hours she waited in the lounge of the intensive care unit to find out whether Jules Mendelson would live or die.

Since she had become so intimately involved with the billionaire, she had ceased to see Curly and Belle, her friends from the Viceroy, on his advice. "Mixing with people like that, it never works," he had said to her. Only Glyceria, the maid from next door, and Philip Quennell, whom she had met at an AA meeting at the log cabin on Robertson Boulevard, had offered her the kind of friendship she craved. But she had been afraid to confide too much in Glyceria, because she knew Jules disapproved of her friendship with Faye Converse's maid. She had told everything to Philip Quennell during the two days she had stayed with him at the Chateau Marmont, when she meant to break off her relationship with Jules for good, but she was aware that Jules despised the handsome young man who had been kind to her, and she knew she could not call on him for solace.

Her attention became diverted from her thoughts by a news bulletin from anchorman Bernard Slatkin on the NBC Evening News.

"Jules Mendelson, the Beverly Hills billionaire, banker, art collector and patron, and presidential designate to head the American delegation in Brussels during the statehood of Europe, suffered a massive heart attack at a private home in Beverly Hills this afternoon. He was found unconscious and in full cardiac arrest on the floor of the house. Medical aides who rushed to the house administered cardiopulmonary resuscitation to revive him before taking him to the Cedars-Sinai Medical Center in Los Angeles. A hospital spokesperson declined to comment on Mendelson's condition."

Flo continued to stare at the television set after Bernie Slatkin had gone on to another story. She was aware that "the private home in Beverly Hills" that he spoke about was her house on Azelia Way. A chill ran through her as she realized that if Jules died, she was only a step away from being in the news herself.

"You may go in now, but you can only stay ten minutes," said the intern. "Miss?"

"What?" asked Flo.

"I said you can go in now, but you can only stay for ten minutes."

"Is he conscious?"

"In and out. You must not excite him or tire him."

"Thank you."

Arnie Zwillman looked up from his gin game in the card room of his Holmby Hills mansion, which had once belonged to Charles Boyer, and listened to Bernard Slatkin, the anchorman on the NBC Evening News.

"I said to Jules only recently when we were dining together at the home of Casper Stieglitz, I said, 'Jules, you gotta lose some of that lard, or you're going to have a heart attack.' I swear to God, I said that. Hold on there, Dom, baby. It's my deal, not your deal."

"I'm Mrs. Mendelson," said Pauline to Mimosa Perez at the admissions desk of the emergency entrance.

"Oh, yes, Mrs. Mendelson," said Mimosa, transfixed by the elegance and serenity of the woman standing before her.

Cyril Rathbone knew better than to speak to Pauline Mendelson, or even allow himself to be seen by her. He leaned back on the bench where he was sitting and raised the *Los Angeles Tribunal* to cover his face as he listened to Mimosa Perez give instructions to Pauline on how to get to the intensive care unit. Cyril followed fashion each season and could identify with precision one Paris collection from another. He wrote in his spiral notebook that Pauline Mendelson was wearing a dark green traveling suit, with tattersall blouse, by Givenchy, when she arrived at Cedars-Sinai Medical Center by chauffeur-driven limousine, after having landed in her husband's sixteen-seat 727 from Bangor, Maine, where she had been visiting her ailing father, the sportsman Neville McAdoo. He also wrote that Rose Cliveden was sent home in the same limousine by Mrs. Mendelson.

When Pauline walked into her husband's room in the intensive care unit, Flo March was still there. Jules lay unconscious on the bed. She was sitting on the edge of his bed, rubbing his hand and whispering encouragement in his ear.

"Everything's going to be okay, Jules. Just think positive. You'll be up and around in no time. It's just the strain you've been under that caused this. With Arnie Zwillman, and the statehood of Europe, and everything."

Pauline stared at the scene before her. "I would like to be alone with my husband, please," she said.

Flo jumped, as if an electric shock had gone through her. She stared at Pauline, aghast, and put her hand to her mouth. Her face was wet with tears and running mascara and smeared lipstick. Her skirt was ripped. She had washed the blood off her knees, but she knew they looked scraped and ugly. "Oh, Mrs. Mendelson," she said. Her voice was weak and barely audible. She knew that this woman would never cry in public.

Pauline went to the other side of the bed. Taking the hand of her unconscious husband, she spoke as if Flo did not exist. "Hello, Jules," she said. "It's Pauline. The nurses all say outside that you can't hear when you're in a coma, but I've never believed that. My father said he could hear everything we said to him last year when he had his stroke. Do you remember? The plane was hours late. Terrible storms in Maine. Landing problems in Los Angeles. Father sends his love. Of course, he doesn't know what's happened. Rose came to the airport to break the news to me. She was so drunk. I'll tell you about it when you're better. It will make you laugh, I know. I've talked with Dr. Petrie outside. He's terribly nice, and I'm sure he's a good doctor. They're flying in Dr. Rosewald from New York, for a consultation. I insisted on that. In a few days, if all goes well, they're going to move you to the Mendelson Wing. What's the point of giving a wing if you can't use it. Right? You'll be more comfortable there. You're going to be all right, Jules. Dr. Petrie has great hope."

Flo was overwhelmed by the assurance of Pauline Mendelson. She had never seen a woman with such beautiful posture, with such a long neck, with such an aristocratic face, or heard a woman speak with such a deep contralto voice. Like a fired maid, Flo edged her way toward the door, listening to every word that Pauline said.

As she put her hand on the knob, the door opened, and a nurse came in.

"There can only be one person in here at a time," said the nurse, in an angry voice.

"I am just leaving," said Flo.

She turned to look back at Jules once more, and Pauline turned to look toward the door. The eyes of the two women met, but Pauline's eyes moved from Flo's eyes to her earlobes and became fixated on them. The large yellow diamond earrings that Jules had given to her on the night of Casper Stieglitz's party, and that she had returned to him the following morning when they had breakfasted together in the sunrise room of Clouds, were now on Flo March's ears. Pauline's coolness and reserve evaporated. Her face flushed with anger.

"You," said Pauline. "Now I remember you. I thought you looked familiar. You're the one who backed into my car. Why didn't I realize it was you? What a fool you must have thought me that day. I think I even complimented you on your suit."

"No, I didn't think you were a fool, Mrs. Mendelson," answered Flo.

"Did it strike you funny later? Did you laugh about it with my husband?"

"Never. Never. I swear to you," said Flo.

Staring at Flo, Pauline remembered the moment on her terrace after Hector Paradiso's funeral when she had asked Jules who the red-haired woman in the Chanel suit was he had been talking to outside the Church of the Good Shepherd, and he had pretended not to know her. Even then, she realized, she was being deceived.

"Get out of this room," she said, in a low and even voice.

"I said I was going," said Flo, frightened.

But Pauline had not said enough to assuage her anger. "You tramp," she added.

"I am not a tramp," said Flo. Tears came to her eyes. The word *tramp* hurt her deeply. Once she had heard a man call her mother a tramp.

"Call it what you will," said Pauline, turning back to Jules.

Flo's anger matched Pauline's. "You can afford to be so high and mighty, Mrs. Mendelson. For your whole life, you've had everything handed to you on a silver platter. You've never had to earn your living."

"Is being kept for sex what you call earning a living?" asked Pauline.

"Yes," snapped Flo, meeting her gaze. She did not say that she took care of needs that Pauline did not, or could not, or was disinclined to take care of, but Pauline understood her meaning and her gaze without having to hear the words.

Pauline looked away. "I won't ask for details," she said.

"No, better not," replied Flo. "I might tell you."

"I asked you to leave this room before this nurse asked you to leave. So please go," said Pauline.

From the bed Jules let out a moan.

The nurse, who had been watching, said, "Yes, miss, you must let your mother be here with your father. Only one person at a time."

"Her mother!" cried Pauline, in an outraged voice. "I am not this tramp's mother. Is that how she passed herself off?"

"Don't you call me a tramp again," said Flo. She walked out of the room.

The duty nurse could not believe the scene she had just witnessed. Within minutes she told the desk nurse outside, and the desk nurse told one of the interns, who told another of the interns. Before an hour had passed, the news had trickled down to the emergency entrance on the first floor, where Cyril Rathbone wrote in his spiral notebook, "Contretemps between wife and mistress in intensive care unit, as Jules Mendelson lay unconscious between them. 'Don't you call me a tramp,' cried Flo March."

Flo's Tape #18

"Cyril Rathbone says it's because of me that Jules didn't get to be the head of the American delegation to Brussels. That's not true, you know. Jules lost that appointment before the world ever heard of me. Not long before, but before. I happen to know why he lost it. I happen to be one of the few people who do know. Not even Pauline knew. Jules never told her. But he told me. Arnie Zwillman knew too. You know, the gangster? Arnie Zwillman was responsible for Jules not getting the appointment. Arnie Zwillman blew the whistle on Jules because Jules wouldn't play ball with Zwillman. Believe me, I know it. Jules knew it too. He told me that afternoon before he had his heart attack."

19

C YRIL RATHBONE once had higher literary aspirations than to be the gossip
columnist for *Mulholland.* At his English university, he had affected the
mannerisms, flamboyant dress, and speech patterns of a latter-day Oscar
Wilde, and his undergraduate plays, which were *hommages* to the great play-
wright, had attracted a certain youthful notoriety. However, his subsequent
postgraduate forays into the West End theater in London did not live up to his
early expectations. He had then arrived in Hollywood, a dozen years ago, as a
promising screenwriter. He let it be known that he was the illegitimate son of a
British aristocrat, an earl, who was, of course, dead. He let it be known that he
had come to seek his fortune because his father's legitimate heir, the present
earl, could not bear the sight of him and made his life in England impossible.
His story had a romantic quality that gave him an instant social entrée. Witty
and urbane, stylishly dressed in the English manner, and wickedly entertaining
in his storytelling, he was snapped up by the wives of producers and studio
heads as a new and amusing extra man.

People said about the hostess Pearl Silver that she must watch the airport,
because she always knew before anyone else when someone new arrived in
town. Pearl, who entertained at lunch and dinner several days a week, was
always on the lookout for interesting newcomers, and she became the first of
the movie crowd to ask Cyril Rathbone. Then Sylvia Lesky, who entertained
less frequently than Pearl but in a grander manner, and was considerably
harder to please, found Cyril an amusing addition at her parties. "He is a
breath of spring," she said about Cyril at the time. "We need new blood from
time to time. We see much too much of the same people."

Sylvia doted on Cyril for an entire season and was even instrumental in
having her husband, Marty Lesky, the head of Colossus Pictures, the same
studio that her father had once been the head of, sign him up as a staff writer.
But none of Cyril's three screenplays, for which he had been paid handsomely
by Marty Lesky, was ever produced. "Too fairyish," said Marty at the time.
Cyril's option was then dropped. Afterward, he was no longer invited to the
Leskys' house, where only the very successful were invited. Pearl Silver continued to have him, although more for lunch than for dinner, because he was, like
Hector Paradiso, who became his friend, one of the few men who could always
be counted on for lunch. Over the years, as success eluded him, Cyril changed
groups several times. Then a writing stint for the society page of the *Tribunal*

led to his column in the weekly magazine *Mulholland,* and the success that followed was sweet to him, although it was less than the success that he had always imagined would be his.

Some people did not believe his romantic story of being the illegitimate son of an earl. Pauline Mendelson was one of those people. To her observant eye, his excellent manners appeared to be manners learned by imitation, rather than manners acquired as a child from a parent or a nanny. He popped to his feet too fast when a lady entered the room, or held out a chair with too much flourish when a lady sat down to dine. And his accent, which was perfect to most ears, sounded altogether too florid to her well-tutored ears. Pauline was a student of English life. When she was young, her sisters thought she might marry Lord St. Vincent and live in Kilmartin Abbey in Wiltshire, but that had not come to pass. Neville McAdoo didn't possess the kind of fortune Lord St. Vincent needed to keep up his abbey, so he married one of the Van Degan heiresses instead, and Pauline married Johnny Petworth. It was Pauline who asked the present Earl Rathbone about his father's illegitimate son in Los Angeles. "An impostor, a total impostor," said the earl. "My father knew nothing of him."

Pauline was not the kind of woman who would repeat such a story, and did not. To her it was of no importance that Cyril had created such a background for himself. It was only after he became a celebrated social scribe and wanted, in that capacity, to be invited to the Mendelsons' parties at Clouds that she spoke up, when Hector Paradiso intervened in his friend's behalf.

"Do have him, Pauline," said Hector.

"Jules despises social publicity," said Pauline. "It's not good for his position in the administration."

"But Cyril is different," insisted Hector. "You know, of course, that he is the illegitimate son of the last Earl Rathbone. He's a gentleman."

"No, he's not," said Pauline.

"Not what? A gentleman?"

"That's for anyone to decide. He is not the illegitimate son of the last Earl Rathbone. It is an entirely bogus story."

"How do you know such a thing?" asked Hector.

"I asked."

"Asked who?"

"The present earl, the one who supposedly drove him out of England. He didn't drive him out of England. He never heard of Cyril Rathbone. You must never mention this, Hector."

"On my honor."

One of Hector Paradiso's lesser deficiencies was that he was utterly unable to keep a secret. When he passed on to Cyril Rathbone what Pauline Mendelson had told him, Cyril laughed in an altogether charming way. "But of course that's what Peregrin would say," said Cyril, referring to the present earl's denial of him. And he dropped the matter. But Cyril Rathbone remembered slights. He was in no hurry. He knew the time would come when he would get even.

Flo March's encounter with Pauline Mendelson at Jules Mendelson's bedside in the intensive care unit of the Cedars-Sinai Medical Center left her

shattered and shamed. When she returned to her home, the first thing she saw
in the glare of the Bentley's headlights, as she drove up her steep driveway, was
the body of little Astrid, in the place where she had left her five hours earlier,
in her haste to follow the ambulance to the hospital. It had never occurred to
Flo, who secretly cherished the dream of meeting her next-door neighbor, Faye
Converse, and being invited to her parties, that her introduction to the great
star would finally come when she rang her doorbell to tell her that she had
killed her dog.

Faye Converse, who was exhausted from her barbecue lunch party, rested
after Cyril Rathbone finally left her house to investigate the screams coming
from next door. She knew nothing of Jules Mendelson's heart attack, which
had taken place there. She had removed her makeup and hairpieces, put on a
caftan and a turban, and settled down with a goat cheese pizza, fetched by
Glyceria from Spago, to watch *The Tower,* her greatest flop, on the All-Movie
channel.

"You know, Jack Warner used to say to me, 'You don't have the right kind
of looks for costume epics, Faye. Leave those to Olivia de Havilland.' But I
insisted. I said, 'No, Jack. I want to play Mary, Queen of Scots, in *The Tower.*
It's a part I was born to play.' The son of a bitch turned out to be right, of
course. God, I hated Jack Warner."

"Yes, ma'am," said Glyceria.

"You know I sued him, don't you?"

"No, ma'am."

Then the doorbell rang.

"He said I was box-office poison."

The doorbell rang again.

"Whoever it is, I'm not home," said Faye to Glyceria.

"Yes, ma'am," said Glyceria.

"Imagine someone ringing the doorbell at this hour," said Faye.

"Yes, ma'am," said Glyceria.

"I really should have guards so this sort of thing can't happen," said Faye.
"Dom and Pepper Belcanto have guards now."

"Yes, ma'am," said Glyceria.

"And the Marty Leskys keep a police car parked in their driveway."

The doorbell rang again.

"Aren't you going to answer it?" asked Faye.

"I didn't know if you was finished talking, ma'am," said Glyceria.

When Glyceria opened the front door, she was astonished to see Flo
March, her friend from next door, standing there.

"Oh, thank God, Glyceria. I thought nobody was at home. I rang and
rang," said Flo.

"What are you doing here, Flo?" asked Glyceria. She looked behind her
into the house to see if Miss Converse was watching.

"I have to see Miss Converse," said Flo. "It's very important."

"She won't see nobody tonight," said Glyceria. She looked behind her
again. "She's watching herself on TV, and she don't like to be disturbed."

"It's very important, Glyceria," repeated Flo.

"You won't tell her I go over to your house and drink coffee, will you?"

"Of course not. Please, Glycie."

Glyceria looked at her friend. She thought she looked tired and drawn. Her usual ebullience, which Glyceria called bounce, was missing.

"You okay, Flo?" she asked.

"Please tell her I'm here, Glyceria."

"But she just told me she didn't want to be disturbed."

Flo cupped her mouth with her two hands. "Miss Converse," she called out in as loud a voice as she could muster, after the exhaustion she felt from the last five hours. "Miss Converse, please."

"I'm going to be in big trouble," said Glyceria.

Faye Converse entered the hall of her house. "What's going on here, Glyceria?" she asked.

"Miss Converse, this is Miss March from the house next door. She says she has to see you. She says it's real important," said Glyceria.

"I'm sorry to disturb you, Miss Converse," said Flo. "It's about Astrid."

"Oh, Astrid," said Faye Converse, throwing up her hands in the air. "That wretched little dog has run away again. She's been nothing but a problem from the beginning. She bit off Kippie Petworth's finger, and she tripped my great friend, Rose Cliveden, who broke her leg. And she runs away all the time. Have you found her?"

"I killed her," said Flo.

"You what?" asked Faye.

"I ran over her in my car. I didn't mean to. I was going down my driveway. Someone had a heart attack in my house and the ambulance came to take him to the hospital. And I was following in my car. And the little dog jumped in front of my wheels, and I ran over her," said Flo. She started to cry.

The telephone rang in the library.

"Whoever it is, I'm not home," said Faye to Glyceria.

"I loved that little dog," continued Flo. "You don't know how much I loved that little dog, Miss Converse. I wouldn't have hurt little Astrid for anything in the world. I'm sorry. I'm really sorry."

Glyceria looked from one woman to the other and then left to answer the telephone.

Faye Converse listened to the young woman. She noticed how pretty she was, even though her mascara had run and her lipstick was smeared. She noticed that her suit was a Chanel, even though it was ripped and had threads hanging off it. She noticed that her knees were scraped. She noticed that she wore large yellow diamond earrings, like the ones in the Boothby catalog that Prince Friedrich of Hesse-Darmstadt had sent her. "You poor darling," she said. She walked over to Flo and put her arms around her. "This is very nice of you to come and tell me yourself that you ran over my dog. That could not have been a pleasant chore for you. I can be frightful at times, which I'm sure you've heard."

"You're not mad?" asked Flo.

"Sad but not mad," said Faye. "She was a strange little dog. Did you ever hear of someone called Hector Paradiso?"

"I knew Hector," said Flo.

"Everyone seems to have known Hector. She was Hector's dog," said Faye.

"I know," said Flo. "Some people say she's the only one who knew who killed Hector."

"I thought Hector committed suicide," said Faye.

"Two schools of thought on that," said Flo.

Faye looked at Flo. "Is your house on that side or this side?"

"That side."

"Was that you who was screaming earlier?"

"Yes, I screamed. My friend had a heart attack."

"What a terrible day you've had. I hope your friend will be all right."

"Thank you."

"There's a call for you, Miss Converse," said Glyceria.

"Who is it?"

"Mr. Cyril Rathbone."

"Oh, God. The son of a bitch is probably calling to tell me *The Tower* is on the All-Movie channel."

"He says it's important."

"Would you excuse me?"

"I better get back to my own house."

"No, no. Stay a minute. You've been so kind. Come in and have a drink."

"Oh, no, thanks. I don't drink."

"Or some pizza. You must be exhausted. We have goat cheese pizza from Spago. Have you ever had pizza from Spago?"

"Yes."

"You'll stay?"

"All right. May I use your ladies' room?"

"Yes, in there. I hope it doesn't still stink. Pepper Belcanto threw up all over the walls this afternoon, and poor Glyceria had to clean it up."

The bathroom smelled of hyacinth air spray from Floris. Flo washed her face and combed her hair. She came out of the bathroom at the same time that Faye, aghast, hung up her telephone. Cyril Rathbone had just told her that Jules Mendelson had had a major heart attack in the house next door, which belonged to his mistress, whose name was Flo March, and that there had been a showdown between Flo March and Pauline Mendelson in the intensive care unit of Cedars-Sinai only a short time before. Faye did not tell Cyril that the very same Flo March had killed her dog, Astrid, and that she had just invited her to stay and share her goat cheese pizza from Spago.

Jules remained in the intensive care unit for three nights and two days before he was moved to the finest room in the Mendelson Wing of the hospital. There were nurses around the clock. Dr. Rosewald had flown out from New York for conferences with Dr. Petrie. Dr. Jeretsky had come down from San Francisco. Dr. de Milhau had come in from Houston on the Mendelson plane. The prognosis was not promising. On several occasions Flo March, wearing a nurse's uniform, had managed to get into the room and talk to the patient.

The weather was vile. It rained all day long. Persistent downpours, sometimes torrential, were interspersed with thick mists that obliterated the city below. Pauline nodded yes when Dudley asked her if she would like a fire in the library. Even the pink and lavender roses she had cut in her garden and carefully arranged in the blue-and-white Chinese cachepots the day before could not dispel the gloom of the day. She played Mahler on the compact disc, the Ninth, her favorite, and tried to read the seventy pages of the Princess de Guermantes's evening reception in *Remembrance of Things Past,* which was always her favorite passage, but she could not concentrate.

Pauline moved over to her desk and picked up a piece of her blue notepaper. She wrote to her father. "Jules very unwell. Doctors mystified. He has suffered a serious heart attack. He's brave but naturally extremely low. I'll keep you informed. It was lovely seeing you, Poppy. Thank you for still being the best father in the whole world. Love, Pauline."

Dudley came into the room to tell her that Sims Lord had arrived at the house.

"Oh, finally," said Pauline. Seeing Sims Lord was the point of her day. "Show him in."

When Sims walked in, Pauline was struck, as she always was, by how handsome he was.

"Hello, Pauline," he said.

"Are you soaked through?" she asked.

"A bit wet, yes," he said.

"You are good to come all the way up here to the top of the mountain on such a terrible day. Come over here and sit by the fire. What will you have? Can Dudley make you a drink, or bring you a cup of coffee, or tea?"

"No, thank you, Pauline. I was in Westwood at the Regency Club when you called, and I've just had lunch."

"Thank you, Dudley," said Pauline.

Pauline sat on a corner of the sofa opposite the chair on which Sims was seated.

"The fire feels so good," said Sims. "Look how your ring picks up the flames."

Pauline looked down at her engagement ring. "This ring and you came into my life the same week," she said. "Do you remember?"

Sims laughed. He had been retained as Jules's lawyer after Marcus Stromm had been fired, the same week that Jules gave Pauline the historic de Lamballe diamond, and the same week that he had married her in Paris, with Sims as their best man. In the years since, his successful career had been both enhanced and obscured by his proximity to the dominant presence of Jules Mendelson. "I certainly do."

"I've grown to hate this ring," she said.

"Hate it?"

"For years I've enjoyed watching people react to it. It is quite blinding. Now it seems fake to me. Like my marriage."

"Oh, Pauline," said Sims.

"It's true. Don't pretend it's not, Sims. I understand your loyalty to Jules, but I know you must be aware of all that has been going on with Miss Flo March, as she seems to be called."

Pauline stood up. She took the ring off her finger. "I don't intend to wear this anymore," she said. For an instant Sims thought she was going to throw it into the fire, but she placed it in a silver box beneath the painting of van Gogh's *White Roses.*

"Someone could pick that up there," said Sims.

"I'll put it in the safe later," she said, dismissing it. "But, of course, I didn't ask you to come up here on this hurricane-like day to talk about the de Lamballe diamond, Sims. I know all about the affair. I have met this woman."

"You have?"

"She was in his room in intensive care when I arrived. She had passed herself off as his daughter. She was whispering in his ear when I walked into the room. That woman is interested in one thing and one thing only, and that is Jules's money. Imagine, with a man as ill as Jules is, possibly dying, that she should be in there grubbing for money. It's disgusting, but not surprising. I understand that she has been there on two occasions since I asked her to leave. I understand she dressed herself as a nurse and was able to get herself into his room."

Sims did not tell Pauline that Jules had told him that he must see that Flo March was taken care of, that the house on Azelia Way must be bought and put in her name, with no further haggling about price, and that a trust should be set up for her that need not be in the will, so as not to embarrass Pauline.

Pauline continued. "There is something that I want you to handle for me, Sims. I want to bring Jules home from the hospital, and I want you to tough it out with the doctors to agree. They never will with me. We all know how tough you can be. Jules always said about you that he was glad you were on his side."

"Do you think that's wise, Pauline? Jules is a very sick man. He is not out of the woods yet, not by a long shot," said Sims.

"I'll have round-the-clock nurses, male nurses, who can lift him and get him to the bathroom and wash him, and I'll have the doctors call here twice a day. I want him home."

"This will all be very expensive," said Sims.

"Oh, for God's sake, Sims. This picture alone," she said, pointing to the *White Roses,* "is worth forty million dollars, at least. Let's not waste any time on what something is going to cost."

"When do you want to do this?"

"As soon as possible."

Lucia Borsodi, the editor of *Mulholland,* never removed her harlequin-shaped dark glasses, even in darkness. She was credited by everyone in the magazine business for saving, "absolutely saving," the floundering magazine and turning it into the enormous success that it had become. "She not only has an extraordinary story sense," a cover piece in the arts-and-leisure section of the *Sunday Tribunal* said about her, "but she has an uncanny sense of timing as well." It was Lucia, as his editor, who told Cyril Rathbone, to his consternation, that he must hold back on his story about Jules Mendelson.

"It's too early, Cyril. Don't jump the gun," said Lucia.

"But, Lucia," exclaimed Cyril, almost in tears.

"No, no, Cyril, trust me. It's the gossip columnist in you that is rushing this story, but it's a much bigger story than that, as you yourself have pointed out. You simply want revenge on Pauline Mendelson because she has always snubbed you."

Cyril blushed. If there was any doubt about his motive, the reddening of his face belied it.

"Don't you understand," Lucia said gently to the man she had just embarrassed. She understood writers and knew how to handle them. "What you have here is a story unfolding. This is not a complete story yet. You have the inside track. You were there. You saw the heart attack. You saw the girl breathing life into her lover's mouth. You have the photographs taken at the hospital. You interviewed the policeman who gave Flo March the ticket. You saw Pauline Mendelson arrive. You heard from the admitting nurse that the two ladies had hot words over Jules Mendelson's dying body."

"All that," said Cyril, like a miser gloating over his gold. "It will be the story of my career."

"But you have nothing from any of the principals. You must interview Flo March. If you get an interview with Flo March, I will give you the cover," said Lucia.

"The cover," gasped Cyril. It was beyond his wildest dreams.

"In the meantime, start planting things in your column, little hints. That will build up your audience for the story when we're ready to go with it."

SQUIB from Cyril Rathbone's column in *Mulholland:*

> The cafés are buzzing. . . . Who was the gorgeous redhead who rode in the ambulance with billionaire Jules Mendelson after he suffered his massive heart attack at a secluded house off Coldwater Canyon last Friday?

Madge White, who was loyalty itself when it came to her friends, did tell Rose Cliveden, in strictest confidence, that she had actually met the girl—"so common, you wouldn't believe it"—at a steak house on Ventura Boulevard.

"No!" gasped Rose. Although Pauline Mendelson was Rose Cliveden's very best friend in all the world, as Rose frequently told anyone who would listen, Rose was not averse to hearing just the slightest little bit of gossip that just might put a chink in the armor of Pauline's perfection.

"Jules pretended he couldn't remember her name, and he told me the most awful lie about Sims Lord being in the men's room, and that the girl was actually with Sims, but, you see, my Ralph really *was* in the men's room and he would have known whether Sims Lord was in the men's room or not, and he wasn't."

Rose didn't want to hear about Ralph White in the men's room of a steak house in the Valley. "It's too sad," said Rose. "Poor Pauline. Do you think I should say something to her?"

"Heavens no, Rose. You mustn't."

"But she's my very best friend in all the world," said Rose.

"She'd die. She'd simply die, if you brought it up," said Madge.

"I suppose you're right," said Rose.

"We must keep this to ourselves, Rose. Not a word to anyone."

"Oh, darling, my lips are sealed."

When Rose hung up on Madge, she called Camilla Ebury and told her, in the strictest confidence—"No one knows but us, darling, so not a word to anyone"—that Jules had his heart attack at the home of a common prostitute. "And guess what?"

"What?"

"Madge actually saw her."

That night Camilla Ebury dined with Philip Quennell at Morton's Restaurant. Because of Camilla's great friendship with the Mendelsons, Philip had not told her that Jules Mendelson had been instrumental in having him fired off his documentary film. Camilla seemed unusually quiet throughout the meal, as if her mind was on something else.

"Is anything the matter?" asked Philip.

"No." She looked around her at the restaurant. "I never know who any of these celebrities are they make such a fuss over. Do you know any of them?"

"That's Barbra Streisand you're staring at. You certainly have to know her," said Philip. It always annoyed him that the social Angelenos he met through Camilla took such pride in distancing themselves from the film people.

"Why do you suppose she does her hair in that awful frizzy way? It's so unbecoming," said Camilla. "She should go to Pooky."

"You're changing the subject. I asked you if anything was the matter. And there is. I can tell. When you're silent like this, there is always something troubling you."

"Rose told me something today that is so upsetting I can't stop thinking about it."

"What's that?"

"I promised I wouldn't tell."

"All right."

"But I want to tell."

"Then tell."

"It's about Jules and Pauline."

Philip looked at her. "What about them?"

"Do you know where he had the heart attack?" asked Camilla.

"No," replied Philip, although he was pretty sure he did know.

"At the home of a prostitute."

Philip, understanding, nodded slowly. "She's not a prostitute," he said. "She's a mistress. It's a very different thing."

"Jules has a mistress?" asked Camilla.

"Yes. For quite a few years."

Camilla stared at Philip in disbelief. "How could you possibly know such a thing?"

"Because I know her."

"You constantly amaze me, Philip."

"You know her too."

"I do?"

"You met her. Flo March."

"You mean that pretty red-haired girl wearing an evening Chanel suit in the morning, who was sitting in your room at the Chateau Marmont?"

"Yes."

"She said she bet you looked cute in Jockey shorts."

Philip smiled.

"At least she didn't mention your tattoo, down there."

Philip laughed.

"Do you know something, Philip?"

"What?"

"I kind of liked her."

SQUIB from Cyril Rathbone's column in *Mulholland:*

> The cafés are buzzing. . . . Who was the gorgeous redhead comforting billionaire Jules Mendelson in the intensive care unit when his wife, the elegant best-dressed Pauline, walked in?

"Hello?"

"Miss March?"

"Yes?"

"This is Cyril Rathbone."

"Oh, my God."

"I hope I haven't caught you in the middle of a suicide attempt."

"What's that supposed to mean?"

Cyril chuckled. "Just a little joke, Miss March."

"You've got some sense of humor, Mr. Rathbone."

"Well, you sounded so, what shall I say, so desperate. Is that the right word? Desperate?"

"What can I do for you?"

"I'd like to see you, Miss March."

"Oh, no."

"I would like to do an interview with you."

"Oh, no."

"Why?"

"No."

"You are being credited with saving his life, Miss March."

"I am?"

"The mouth-to-mouth resuscitation you did on Mr. Mendelson that you learned when you were a waitress at the Viceroy Coffee Shop."

"How did you know that?"

"I was in your house."

"You were? When?"

"I was the one who called the ambulance for you."

"That was you? The guy in my house was Cyril Rathbone, the columnist? That was you?"

"Exactly."

"Listen, Mr. Rathbone."

"I'm listening."

"I always thought I'd die happy if I could be written up in your column, just once even, but now I don't want to be written up in it anymore, even though you don't use my name."

"I think we should meet."

"No."

"Why?"

"I'm afraid I have to hang up now, Mr. Rathbone."

SQUIB from Cyril Rathbone's column:

> The cafés are buzzing. . . . Is the reason billionaire Jules Mendelson is being secretly moved from the VIP section of the Jules Mendelson Wing

at Cedars-Sinai Medical Center to his hilltop estate, Clouds, on Friday afternoon that a certain gorgeous redhead has managed to get into his room by disguising herself as a nurse?

Outside the hospital and then again outside the gates of Clouds, Pauline stayed by Jules's side the whole time, holding his arm and maintaining a pleasant countenance as the photographers took their picture what seemed like a hundred times, or two hundred times, strobe flash after strobe flash.

Inside the gates, the Bentley, moving slowly, appeared at the turn in the drive and then came forward into the courtyard. The chauffeur, Jim, jumped from the car and opened the rear door. First Pauline got out. Then Jim reached in and pulled Jules out of the car. Dudley, the butler, ran forward from the house pushing an empty wheelchair. For a moment Jules stood leaning on a cane, until the wheelchair reached him. The staff who watched him out of the various windows of the house were not prepared for the drastic change in his appearance. He looked shrunken. He had become an old man, although he was not yet sixty.

Inside the house, finally, with the door closed behind them, Pauline maintained the same composure in front of Dudley. "I would like some tea, Dudley," she said, anxious to be rid of him before he said anything sympathetic, which she felt he was going to do. "And a drink. I'm sure Mr. Mendelson would like a drink, wouldn't you, Jules?"

"Yes, yes, fine, a scotch, Dudley, and a little Pellegrino water," said Jules. His complexion was pale, and he had lost a great deal of weight. When he spoke, his voice was barely above a whisper.

"But make it quite light for Mr. Mendelson, Dudley," said Pauline. "I forgot to ask Dr. Petrie if it was all right."

"In the library?" asked Dudley.

"Fine, yes, fine," they both said together.

Alone, still in their splendid front hall, their staircase floating upward, their six Monet paintings of water lilies lining its wall, their blue-and-white Chinese cachepots filled with orchid plants from their greenhouse amassed at its base, Jules and Pauline Mendelson looked at each other.

"I have to rest here for a while, Pauline," he said. "I can't make those stairs."

"Of course. Sit here. Olaf will be arriving any minute, and he can carry you up the stairs," she said.

"Imagine me being carried," Jules said, shaking his head. "I don't want you to watch me when he does lift me."

"But you didn't want to leave the hospital on a stretcher, Jules."

He nodded. "I wanted to walk out of that hospital under my own steam, no matter what. All my life I've avoided the press, and I wasn't about to allow those sons of bitches to photograph me being carried out on a stretcher. It would make me look sicker than I really am."

Their eyes met for a moment. Each knew he was far more ill than described in the optimistic propaganda about his condition that was being carefully circulated in business circles by Sims Lord and other associates. Jules sank onto the caned seat of a gilded chair, one of a set of six, which he had never sat on before in the twenty-two years that he had lived in the house.

"Did Dr. Petrie give you the pills?" he asked.

"Yes," answered Pauline.

"May I have one?"

"He said one every four hours, Jules. It's only slightly more than an hour since the last."

"I'm weary from the drive. I want one now."

She opened her bag and took out an amber plastic container. He took the pill she handed him and swallowed it.

"Is this what our life is going to be like, Jules?" asked Pauline. "Photographers lying in wait for us outside the gates of our own house? Reporters screaming rude questions at us? There is a limit, Jules, to the obligations of the marriage vows, and I think I can honestly say that I have reached that limit."

He weakly nodded his head in recognition of the truth of what Pauline had just said. Pauline again noted how old Jules looked.

"I am not the first woman whose husband has had a mistress," she continued. "I might not like it, but I could have learned to deal with it, if it was a thing that never encroached on my life; but this way—no, never. This common little strumpet has made a mockery of my marriage."

"Don't think of her as a bad girl, Pauline. She's not a bad girl. I may be a bad man, but she's not a bad girl. If you only knew her, you'd agree."

"Knowing Miss March is a life experience that I intend to deprive myself of, Jules," said Pauline. "I don't know which I dread more, having everyone I know, and tens of thousands of people I don't know, gossip about me. Or pity me. To the best of my knowledge, I have never been gossiped about in my life, and, in certainty, I have never been pitied."

Jules, drained, could only stare at Pauline. "Don't leave me, Pauline," he said.

"No, of course, I won't leave you, not now, not with you so weak and sick." She started to say more, but stopped herself. Instead she walked over to the foot of the stairs and broke a yellowed leaf off an orchid plant.

Jules nodded his head, understanding.

"How terrible, Jules, to end such a distinguished life in a cheap sex scandal. That is what people will remember about us," said Pauline.

Jules nodded again. He knew what she said was true, but he could think of no reply. "I've never sat in one of these gold chairs before," he said.

"They were a wedding present from Laurance and Janet Van Degan. Absolutely authentic, of the period. Whatshername at the Getty Museum verified them, Gillian somebody, but you didn't like them. You said you hated gold furniture. Too spindly, you said. So I put them here in the hall where they wouldn't be sat upon too often."

Jules nodded. "Thank you, Laurance and Janet Van Degan," he whispered. From the courtyard came the sound of cars and voices. He rose slowly from his seat and looked out of the window. "What are all those cars coming into the courtyard?" he asked.

"Cars?" asked Pauline.

"Three, four, six of them, eight of them, with a lot of ladies in flowered hats getting out. What is this?"

"Oh, my God," said Pauline. "I forgot."

"What?"

"It's the Los Angeles Garden Club. I agreed weeks ago, months ago, to give them a tour of the gardens and the greenhouse. They heard about the yellow phalaenopsis that Jarvis and I have developed, and I promised."

"I'll tell Dudley to tell them you're not well and can't come out. They can come another day," said Jules.

"You can't do that, Jules," said Pauline.

"Then let Jarvis take them on the tour."

"No, Jules, no. They've paid fifty dollars each for the tour. Let's face it, it's me they want to see as much as the yellow phalaenopsis, not poor Jarvis, who did all the work."

"I was only thinking of you."

"I know."

They looked at each other.

"We're acting as though we're still very married, aren't we?" said Pauline. She touched his shoulder.

Dudley entered the hall, making a coughing sound to announce his entrance. "There are people arriving who say they are expected."

"Dudley, I completely forgot that this is the day that the garden club was coming to see my yellow phalaenopsis, and the ladies are outside in the courtyard. I'll go out and take them around. Tell Gertie in the kitchen to make tea for I don't know how many, and some cucumber sandwiches, and to use those lemon cookies she made yesterday. We'll have tea in the library. They'll love the *White Roses,* the perfect group for that."

"Yes."

"But first, help Mr. Mendelson up the stairs, and then ask Blondell to turn down his bed. Mr. Mendelson will be in the room where Mrs. Cliveden usually stays. And, Dudley, there will be a nurse arriving soon. Miss Toomey, she is called, Mae Toomey. Have the red room next to where Mr. Mendelson will be staying made up for her, and, Dudley, tell Gertie that Miss Toomey's meals will be served on trays in the upstairs sitting room, and make sure there's a television set in her room, and magazines, any of the ones that I've finished reading."

She walked over to the Chippendale mirror over the gilded console table and pinched color into her cheeks, reapplied her lipstick, and combed her hair. "There will be two male orderlies arriving tomorrow to lift Mr. Mendelson, and take him to the doctor when he's feeling better, and whatever else. They can sleep in the pool house. Have beds brought down from the third floor and put there. This dress is all right, isn't it?" Without waiting for an answer, she opened the front door and walked out into the courtyard.

"Hello, Blanche. Hello, Mavis. Welcome to Clouds."

Flo's Tape #19

"*I've heard myself called trash and tramp, and other words in that same category, and they hurt. So I want to make something absolutely clear. Except for once, only once—I mean only with one guy, not one time—was I ever unfaithful to Jules, and that was during the time I broke up with him, briefly broke up with him, after he pretended he didn't know what my name was when we ran into that snobby Madge White at the steak house in the Valley. I guess there's no protocol for a situation like that, where a guy is having dinner with his girlfriend and runs into his wife's best friend. Like, should he introduce her, or not? That's one for Dear Abby or Dr. Joyce Brothers.*

"*Anyway, there was this guy who took me in for a few days, after I ran away from Jules that night. He's called, uh—No, I'm not going to give his name, because he's back with the girl he had just broken up with, and I made it sound to her like nothing had gone on between us. But it did. I'd be lying to you if I said it was just a grudge fuck against Jules. This guy was really a cute guy. I originally met him at an AA meeting, and that night he was lonely and I was lonely, and we told each other all our secrets, and we did it during those days he let me hide out in his place. This guy had a tattoo in the damnedest place you ever saw. I could never get over that.*

"*Then I met his girlfriend. I'm not going to give her name either, because I liked her, and later she did me a good turn. Right away I could see that they really belonged together. After that I went back to Jules.*"

20

"Mr. Mendelson's office."

"Miss Maple?"

"Yes."

"This is, uh." Flo stopped, afraid to use her own name. "My name is, uh—"

"I know who you are," said Miss Maple, recognizing the voice of Flo March from the one telephone call she had had with her, when she told her she was spending too much money.

"Red Houlihan," said Flo at the same time, blurting out the name finally that Jules sometimes used as a disguise.

"Yes, yes, I know."

"I haven't received my check."

"I know."

"For two weeks."

"I know."

"Where is it?"

"There's a problem."

"What sort of problem? I was to be taken care of for life."

"I think you had better contact Sims Lord."

"There's bills here at the house. There's men working on the new closets. Nellie Potts said they're union workers and have to be paid on time."

"Look," said Miss Maple. "I think what you should do first is tell those men to stop working on your closets. And tell Nellie Potts that you're not going to have anything more done on your house. Then call Sims Lord. Do you know Sims Lord?"

"Yes. Kind of. I've never actually met him."

"I'll give you his number."

"I have his number. Jules left his book here."

"So that's where the book is. We've been looking everywhere for it. I'll send someone to pick it up."

"No, don't. I won't give it to you."

"Look, Flo. You have to understand. I only work here. I'm just doing what I have been told to do."

"Is it her? It is her, isn't it?"

"Who?"

"You know damn well who. Pauline."

"You must understand, I can't talk," said Miss Maple. "You have to call Sims Lord. He's the closest person to the situation."

Flo could hear kindness in Miss Maple's voice.

"Listen, Miss Maple?"

"I really have to go."

"Do you go up to the house to see him?"

"Yes."

"Tell him. Please. Tell him she's cut off my money. He wouldn't want that to happen."

It was not that Miss Maple was unsympathetic to the plea of Flo March that kept her from relaying Flo's message to Jules Mendelson. Each afternoon she was picked up by Jim, the Mendelsons' chauffeur, and driven up to Clouds, where she stayed with Jules for only fifteen minutes, which was thought by Dr. Petrie and Miss Toomey to be all the time that he was able to concentrate before he became exhausted and had to rest. During that brief time Miss Maple kept him abreast of the business transactions of the office, the stock market closings, and the enormous numbers of calls from well-wishers in the business and banking community. Mostly Jules only nodded in agreement, or shook his head in disagreement, although sometimes he managed to smile in recognition of the name of a business associate who had called to wish him good health. When he did speak, he spoke in a voice that was barely above a whisper, and the effort tired him. Miss Maple was shocked at the physical wasting-away of the enormous and vital man she had served for so many years. She knew that he would go into a rage if he were aware that Flo March's weekly check had not been paid for two weeks, and she was aware that such a rage might terminate his life.

In her day Faye Converse had had her share of love affairs with married men. So she was sympathetic to the plight of her beautiful young neighbor, who was so distraught over the condition of her married lover, Jules Mendelson.

"Did I ever tell you about Senator Platt of Wyoming?" Faye asked Glyceria.

"No ma'am," said Glyceria.

"Jack Warner threatened me with suspension if I didn't break that one off, after Mrs. Platt claimed she was going to spill the beans to Dorothy Kilgallen. That was when *Rittenhouse Square* was about to open, and Jack was not about to jeopardize his investment. 'Break it off, Faye, or else,' he said. That was Jack all over. God, I hated Jack Warner."

"Yes, ma'am," said Glyceria.

"And then there was Harry O'Dell. I was making a picture with Cagney, and he introduced me to Harry. Harry had millions. Did I tell you about what Edith O'Dell did?"

"No, ma'am," said Glyceria.

But Faye Converse was in an extremely awkward position in that Pauline Mendelson was a close friend of hers and she was a frequent guest at Clouds. And Jules had advised her on several investments that had made her future secure. She felt it best to distance herself from her neighbor, whom she liked. She felt also that Cyril Rathbone, who seemed to be up-to-date on every aspect of the affair, might be planning to write about it in a more serious way than in his gossip column.

The last time she saw Flo, she said to her, "Whatever you do, Flo, don't talk to Cyril Rathbone. He's trouble."

Glyceria continued to make her late morning visits to the next house, however. She noticed that Flo March sometimes didn't get dressed up anymore, the way she used to. She just pulled on her terry cloth robe in the morning and stayed in it all day. She also noticed that Flo didn't drink Diet Cokes all day, the way she used to. Sometimes she opened a bottle of white wine and drank a glass or two.

"No more hammerin'," said Glyceria one day.

"The workmen stopped," said Flo.

"How come?"

"I can't pay them. I haven't gotten a check for three weeks."

"I didn't know your gentleman was Mr. Jules Mendelson," said Glyceria.

"You didn't?"

"You never told me his name," said Glyceria. "You just always said, 'Don't come by in the afternoon after three-thirty.' I didn't know the gentleman was Mr. Mendelson."

She said "Mr. Mendelson" in such a way that Flo looked at her.

"Do you know Jules Mendelson?" she asked.

"Yes, ma'am."

"How?"

"My brother is his barber."

"Willi? Willi, who's shaved Jules every morning for twenty-five years, is your brother?"

"Yes, ma'am. Do you know Willi?"

"No, but I hear of him."

"Mr. Mendelson gave Willi the money to start his own shop on Sunset Boulevard," said Glyceria.

Flo stared at her friend.

"Tell me something, Glyceria."

"Yes, ma'am?"

"Does Willi still go up to Clouds every morning to shave him?"

"Yes, ma'am."

"Even now, when he's so sick?"

"Yes, ma'am."

When Marty Lesky, the head of Colossus Pictures, walked into Willi's Barber Shop on Sunset Boulevard without an appointment, as was his habit, it was not thought remarkable that Joel Zircon, the agent, who did have an appointment, but was considered to be no more than up-and-coming in the business, was asked to remove himself from Willi's chair and give his place to Marty. Joel Zircon was only too happy to inconvenience himself in order to accommodate Marty Lesky. The brief exchange of conversation between them was considered, from Joel's point of view, to be advantageous to his career.

"We met at Casper Stieglitz's dinner, Mr. Lesky," he said.

"Right, right," said Marty, who didn't remember and didn't want to get into a conversation with an agent on the make.

"At the party where Pauline and Jules Mendelson were," continued Joel.

"Right, right," said Marty.

"And Arnie Zwillman, and Amos Swank," said Joel, wanting to prolong his moments with the studio head as long as possible.

"Right. You ready for me, Willi?" Marty called out, and disappeared into the private room where Willi dyed the hair of his famous clients.

While Joel was waiting for Willi to finish dyeing Marty's hair, he used the time to schmooze, as he put it, with Lupe, the receptionist, and then to read the trade papers. His attention was momentarily taken up by an announcement that Hortense Madden, the literary critic of *Mulholland,* "may have discovered the lost manuscript of Basil Plant's *Candles at Lunch,* his famous unfinished novel." But Joel Zircon's attention span was brief, and he wearied of the story before he finished reading it.

The brass-studded leather entrance door of the shop opened, and a young woman entered. She hesitated inside the door, as if she felt out of place. Then she approached the appointment desk.

"May I speak to Willi, please?" She spoke quietly.

"Do you have an appointment?"

"No."

"He doesn't do women's hair."

"I didn't come to see him about my hair."

"Your name, please?"

"My name will mean nothing to him."

"He's in with a customer."

"Would you ask him if he could step outside for a minute?"

"He's in with Marty Lesky, the head of Colossus Pictures," said Lupe importantly. "I can't ask him to come outside."

"I'll wait." Flo March took a seat opposite Joel Zircon.

Lupe watched her from her appointment desk and noticed from the style that her hair had been done by Pooky, that her suit was couture, and that her bag and shoes were very expensive. She got up from her desk and went to the back of the shop.

"Flo?" said Joel Zircon. "Is that you?"

Flo looked at Joel Zircon and smiled. "Hello."

"It's Joel Zircon. Remember me? From the Viceroy Coffee Shop? You used to wait on me every morning."

"Two over easy, toasted bagel, lox, and coffee," said Flo.

Joel laughed. "You remembered."

"You can take the girl out of the coffee shop, et cetera, et cetera."

"You look like a million dollars, Flo. Ten million dollars," said Joel. "I bet you don't know where I saw you last."

"No."

"At Hector Paradiso's funeral."

"For goodness' sake."

"You cried, right? And this guy sitting behind me at Good Shepherd, Philip Quennell, who was writing a picture for Casper Stieglitz, before he got fired, he handed you his handkerchief, right?"

"Did you say that Philip Quennell got fired?" asked Flo.

"You didn't hear? What a story!"

"What happened?"

"Did you ever hear of this billionaire called Jules Mendelson? Lives in some big estate up on top of a mountain here?"

Flo swallowed. Before Joel told her what he was going to tell her, she knew what he was going to say.

"This guy Mendelson hates Philip Quennell. Why, I don't know. But he calls Marty Lesky and says get rid of Quennell." When he said the name Marty Lesky, he lowered his voice, and pointed toward the room where Marty was having his hair dyed to indicate that the studio head was on the premises. *"Or— get this—or* I won't honor my five-million-dollar pledge for your new wing at the Los Angeles County Museum, which is a very big deal to Marty. So Marty calls Casper and says lose him. Casper told me."

Flo stared at Joel Zircon and said nothing. Slowly she rose, as if to leave.

"But I haven't gotten to the punch line," continued Joel. "That very same day, Jules Mendelson has a massive heart attack at the home of some broad he's schtuppin' up off Coldwater, and now he's just hanging on by a twat hair. Is that poetic justice, or what do you want to call it?"

Flo began to walk toward the door. As she opened it to leave, a voice from behind her said, "Miss? You wanted to see me?"

Flo turned and faced Willi. She looked over at Joel Zircon and saw that he was watching.

"Is there a place I could talk to you in private for just a minute?" asked Flo.

"Come in here," said Willi. "My customer's in the dye room in back. Be with you in ten more minutes, Joel. Maybe fifteen."

"I'm a friend of your sister," said Flo.

Willi looked at Flo. "I didn't know Glycie had such ritzy friends," he said.

Flo opened the bag that hung from her shoulder on a gold chain and took out a letter.

"My name is Flo March," she said. "I am a very special friend of Jules Mendelson. I know you shave him every morning, even since the heart attack. Would you give him this letter, please? It's very important. Very. He will be very grateful to you for giving it to him, I promise you."

Willi looked down at the letter. Only the word *Jules* was written on the front of the envelope. "I take it this is confidential?" he asked.

Flo nodded.

"No one else should see it?"

"Oh, no. Only Jules. No one else," said Flo.

"Hey, Willi! How the fuck long are you gonna keep me waiting back here?" yelled Marty Lesky from the dye room.

Willi put the letter in his back pocket and patted it. He smiled at Flo, then turned around and went back to Marty Lesky.

That night at dinner at Morton's, Joel Zircon was able to say to Mona Berg, "I was talking to Marty Lesky today."

"You were what?" asked Mona, instantly jealous.

"I said I was talking to Marty," repeated Joel, thrilled with the effect the impressive name had made. "I bet you didn't know he dyes his hair."

"Of course I knew," said Mona.

Later that same night at Miss Garbo's, after he dropped Mona Berg off home, Joel said to Manning Einsdorf, "I saw Flo March today. Remember her? The waitress. She behaved very strangely."

The following night the chimes in Flo March's house rang. She was sitting in front of her television set watching one of Faye Converse's old movies, drinking white wine from a Steuben wineglass. Expecting no one, she got up and peered through the closed curtains out to the front of her house. Although she could see the lights of a car, she could not see the car. She went to the front hall.

"Who is it?" she called through her front door.

"Olaf."

"I don't know an Olaf."

"I'm one of the orderlies for Mr. Mendelson. I have a message for you, Miss March."

Flo pulled open the door. Olaf was a very large young man dressed in a white T-shirt and white trousers.

"Come in," said Flo.

"I just got off my shift, Miss March. He got your note from Willi this morning. I don't know what it said, but he was very upset. Missus watches him like a hawk, you know, and also that Miss Toomey, the nurse in charge."

"Yes?"

"I'm the only one who's big enough to lift him to the bathroom, so I spend a lot of time alone with him. I have to take him on Friday to the doctor for a CAT scan, which they can't do at the house. He's going to stop here at lunchtime. He said to tell you that Mr. Lord is going to be here too. He said for you not to worry about anything."

Flo's eyes filled with tears. "Thanks, Olaf. When? What time?"

"Friday. Twelve. Twelve-thirty. One. I don't know. Depends on how long the scan takes."

"Should I have lunch for him?" asked Flo, eagerly.

"Something simple."

"Oh, how wonderful. I'll get all the things he likes. And you? And Sims Lord? You'll have lunch here too?"

"You don't have to have anything for me."

"Oh, no. I would like to. I will. Oh, thank you, Olaf. I've been so worried about him."

"I know all about you. He told me. We've gotten very close, and I don't think he likes that Miss Toomey too much."

"Come in. Would you like a drink? I have a bottle of wine open."

"No thanks, Miss March. I have to get back up the mountain. I have the Bentley outside. He wants me to get used to driving it, because he doesn't want Jim to drive when he comes here on Friday."

Flo's Tape #20

"I often wondered why Jules never had children. It always seemed to me that he would have liked a junior, a little Jules, to leave all that money to. He hated to be written about in the newspapers, but he sure liked to have his name on buildings and wings of buildings, and what better monument could there be than a kid to perpetuate your name? I once asked him about it. I thought maybe it was Pauline who didn't want children, but Jules said no, it was he. Maybe it had something to do with what happened in Chicago, with that girl in the Roosevelt Hotel. Maybe he thought it was in the genes.

"I would have loved to have had his kid. He never knew this, but for the last year I was with him, I wasn't taking precautions."

21

THE WEEKS OF ILLNESS wore on, and the household revolved around the sickroom, the nurse, the orderlies, and the daily visits of the doctors. Since Jules's heart attack, Pauline had behaved in an admirable fashion that was favorably commented upon by her many friends. Despite the frequent allusions in Cyril Rathbone's column to a "redhead" who had figured in the scene of her husband's heart attack, Pauline acted as if she were totally unaware of such a story, although she was certain that everyone she knew must have been reading the same columns, or been apprised of them. She confided in no one. To anyone who called, whether it was her father, or one of her sisters, or a close friend like Camilla Ebury or Rose Cliveden, or even a museum curator who had been entertained in her home, or a high official in public office, she gave minute details of her husband's condition, as well as assurances that he was doing well. "Yes, yes, he's home from the hospital already. Isn't it marvelous? You know, Jules is as strong as an ox. The whole thing was a terrible scare for both of us. And a great warning. He has to lose weight, and now he will. I'll tell him you called. He will be so pleased. And thank you. We both so appreciate hearing from you." Callers who had heard rumors of problems in the long marriage ceased to believe them.

After Jules was brought back to Clouds to recuperate, much to the consternation of the doctors in charge of his case, Pauline began to go out to small parties in the evenings again. "No, no, of course I'll come, Rose. I'd love to come. Jules wants me to go out again. I think he loves to hear all the gossip I tell him the next day. In a few weeks he'll be up and around again himself. Long dress or short?"

When Prince Friedrich of Hesse-Darmstadt, the head of the jewelry department of Boothby's auction house, called Pauline from London to inquire about Jules, he told her that he intended to be in Los Angeles in two weeks' time, after first attending a billionaire's party in Tangier.

"I'll give a dinner for you, Friedrich," said Pauline. She was very fond of the prince.

"No, no, Pauline. I wouldn't think of letting you, not with Jules so ill," replied the prince.

"But you wouldn't believe how well he's doing," said Pauline. "I didn't mean anything large. Just ten or twelve."

"It would be marvelous, Pauline."

"Is there anyone you'd particularly like to see?"

"I long to see Faye Converse."

"Perfect. Faye just sent Jules the loveliest flowers."

Flo, lying in bed that afternoon, listened to the telephone ring several times. She thought of letting the machine pick up, but then it occurred to her that it might be Jules calling, and she grabbed the instrument. She worried that Pauline might have heard of their plan for Friday lunch.

"Hello?" Her voice was tentative.

"Flo?"

"Yes."

"It's Philip Quennell."

"Oh, Philip." Flo's voice relaxed.

"I haven't seen you at the morning meetings for quite some time," said Philip.

"I know."

"Are you all right?"

"Oh, yes. Things have happened, Philip. You must have heard. It's been on the news."

"I have, of course. I understand he's already gone home from the hospital."

"Yes. But it was much too early for him to be moved. He wasn't ready to go back to Clouds yet."

"Then why did they move him?"

"Can't you guess, Philip?" asked Flo.

"No, I can't," replied Philip.

"It was Pauline. She heard I went into his room dressed in a nurse's uniform, and wanted to fire the whole nursing staff. That was why she had him brought home."

"But how do you know that?"

"Mimosa Perez, one of the nurses, told me. The doctors were furious that he was taken home."

"But certainly he's being treated at home?"

"Yes."

"I assume you're not being allowed to see him."

"Correct."

"This must be a very difficult period for you, Flo."

"Yes."

There was a long silence.

"Flo?"

"Yes."

"You're not drinking, are you?"

"No!" She knew that she had answered too quickly and too emphatically. She knew that he knew too.

"I'm here, you know, if you want to talk," said Philip.

"You are sweet, Philip."

"Even in the middle of the night."

"Thanks. I won't forget your offer. And I hope that society girlfriend of yours knows what she's got," said Flo.

Philip laughed. "Would you like me to pick you up in the morning and take you to the meeting?"

"No. I'll be back real soon, Philip. Really."

"Okay."

She started to hang up, and then she stopped. "Listen, Philip?"

"Yes."

"Is it true that Jules got you fired from your documentary?"

"Did he tell you that?"

"God, no. Some jerk called Joel Zircon told me."

"Well, don't worry about it."

"I feel terrible about that. I want you to know I didn't tell him I was with you those days."

"I know you didn't, Flo."

"He had a private dick trying to locate me."

"I'm sure."

"I feel terrible about that. I feel responsible. You didn't ask me to go to your room. I just burst in on you that night."

"Jules had it in for me ever since he knocked over his Degas statue of the ballerina."

"Pauline's asked us for dinner on Friday night," said Camilla.

"I can't believe she asked me," replied Philip.

"Indeed she has. She's very fond of you. She asked specifically for me to bring you."

"Is it a party?"

"Small. Quite small. Only twelve or fourteen, I think. Because of Jules being ill and all."

"Is Jules up then? Is he about?"

"Heavens, no. Not yet."

"Odd time for Pauline to be giving a party then, don't you think?"

"Pauline says he's almost well again. It was just a terrible scare. She said he's on his way to a complete recovery."

"How is Pauline handling all this?"

"A model of good behavior. Everyone thinks so. Class, you know. I've always hated the word *class,* but it does say it, doesn't it? Apparently, that ghastly Cyril Rathbone has been writing such awful things in his column about the red-haired woman I met in your room. Of course, I didn't breathe a word to a soul that I had met her, and I never read Cyril Rathbone's column, but I hear about it from everyone. Mainly Rose Cliveden."

"But why is Pauline giving a party at this time?"

"For Prince Friedrich of Hesse-Darmstadt."

Philip laughed. "And who the hell is Prince Friedrich of Hesse-Darmstadt?"

"The head of the jewelry department at Boothby's auction house in London."

Philip laughed again. "Of course he is."

"Why is that funny?" she asked.

"It just is, Camilla."

"Sometimes I don't understand you, Philip," said Camilla.

"Sometimes I don't understand you, Camilla," said Philip.

On Friday morning, the day of Jules Mendelson's CAT scan in the Jules Mendelson Family Patient Wing of Cedars-Sinai Medical Center, as well as the day of Pauline Mendelson's small dinner party for Prince Friedrich of Hesse-Darmstadt, Flo March arose early to prepare for her lunch party for Jules and his lawyer, Sims Lord, whom she had never met. She went at seven, the time she usually went to her AA meeting at the log cabin on Robertson Boulevard, which she had not gone to for weeks, to have her hair done by Pooky and her nails done by Blanchette. Pooky said later to Blanchette that he had never seen Flo so nervous, or so unresponsive to the gossip about the fashionable clientele of the salon, which she usually enjoyed listening to. Because Pooky liked Flo so much, he did not ask her if she was the redhead everyone was talking about in the blind items in Cyril Rathbone's column.

Flo had never learned how to cook well enough even to attempt the cheese soufflés she planned to serve, but she did know how to set her table in the grandest style. Months earlier, she had cut out of a magazine a picture of a table setting that Pauline Mendelson had arranged for a lunch party at Clouds for a visiting ambassador, and using her new Steuben glasses and her new china and silverware from Tiffany and her new tablecloth and napkins from Porthault, she copied the photograph of Pauline's table exactly. Petra von Kant, the favored florist of the moment, arrived early to arrange the flowers for the centerpiece. The out-of-season tulips she had ordered from Holland were not sufficiently open to please Flo. "They're too tight, they're too tight," she wailed. "I wanted them to look as if I picked them in my own garden. You promised me they'd be open." Petra, used to tantrums from her society clients, borrowed Flo's hair dryer and blew hot air on the tulips until they were open to their fullest. Later Petra told Nellie Potts, Flo's decorator, that she had never seen a hostess who worried more about the height of the flowers in the center of her table. Petra had no way of knowing that, according to the same magazine article, it was a rule of Pauline Mendelson's that the flowers in her centerpieces never be so high as to be a deterrent to conversation, and Flo March, in her first outing as a hostess, adhered wholeheartedly to her lover's wife's philosophy. "I want people to be able to talk," she said, as if she were entertaining forty instead of four. She longed to use place cards with names written in calligraphy, but a look she caught in Petra's eye convinced her, without any words being spoken, that place cards for four would not exactly be Pauline's way of doing things.

The Bistro Garden, where she sometimes lunched with Nellie Potts and stared at the society ladies she knew were friends of Jules and Pauline, prepared her cheese soufflés with suitable instructions as to how many minutes they should be in the oven. "Thirty minutes at three-fifty," said Kurt, when she picked them up, and she repeated and then wrote down his instructions. Kurt also told her that the vinaigrette dressing should be added to the crisp endive-and-lettuce salad they had also prepared "just minutes before sitting down," and even told her how long the rolls should be heated. She wrote down everything he said, as if she were taking a course from him. She chilled the white wine from the Bresciani auction. She drove to the bakery at the Farmers

Market to pick up the mocha cake, which was Jules's favorite, that she had ordered for dessert.

In the hour before Jules was scheduled to arrive at her house, she changed her clothes three times. More than anything, she wanted Jules to be proud of her that day in front of Sims Lord. She could always tell from the look in Jules's eye whether she was overdressed or perfect. She decided against wearing her yellow diamond earrings, as being too elaborate for daytime. She decided against wearing one of her Chanel suits, as being too dressy for lunch in her own house. She decided against wearing black, as being too downbeat for what she hoped would be a happy occasion for Jules. On her third try she knew she had found the right look for her that day. She wore beige slacks and a beige cashmere sweater and a gold chain belt, and only her sapphire-and-diamond ring, which she told Jules when he gave it to her that she would never take off, except when she bathed.

When she heard the Bentley come up her driveway, she rushed to the front door and opened it wide. Olaf, dressed in his white T-shirt and white trousers, was driving. Sims Lord, upright and aristocratic-looking, was seated in the backseat and stared out at her. She felt a momentary chill. If she had known the word *imperious,* she would have used it to describe him. Jules was slumped down in the backseat next to Sims Lord, his head barely showing. Flo saw him raise his hand weakly and wave to her.

Olaf greeted Flo, hopped out of the car, and went around to open the rear door. He reached in and placed one strong arm under Jules's legs and another behind his back and picked him up and carried him across the driveway to the house. Flo, instantly aware that Jules was embarrassed for her to see him being carried, turned back into her house. She was unprepared for the sight of her lover. His shirt collar looked several sizes too large for his neck. His face was drawn and gray-looking, with dark circles under his eyes. He appeared to her to be thirty or forty pounds lighter than when she had last seen him in the hospital, but she knew it was not the kind of weight loss that she should compliment him upon.

"Is there a particular chair where you want him to sit?" asked Olaf, still carrying Jules.

She had not thought about a particular chair for Jules to sit in until that moment, but she acted as if it had been one of her main concerns of the morning. "Yes, there, on the sofa, I thought," she said. "On the corner where he can lean on the arm, or even lie back if he wants to. Let me place this pillow behind him first. Is that all right, Jules?"

Jules nodded his head. After Olaf placed him in that location and arranged him so that he was comfortable, Jules looked over at Flo and smiled at her. For an instant he looked like his old self, as his broad smile eradicated the weariness of his face. Both Sims Lord and Olaf noticed it and looked over at Flo. Jules's eyes traveled around the room and rested on Flo's luncheon table. He smiled again and nodded in appreciation at the work she had done, which he knew she had done just for him.

"Oh, Jules, it's so good to see you again," said Flo. She moved over to where he was seated and knelt by him. "I've missed you so. You have no idea how much. I didn't realize myself how used I had gotten to you."

"I've missed you too," said Jules. His voice caught. He sounded as if he was going to cry, but he stopped himself.

"Sometimes it drove me mad how often you telephoned me each day, twenty times, or however much it was, but you know, I miss all those calls."

He smiled at her again. "You know Olaf?"

"Oh, yes, I know Olaf," said Flo. "He was so kind when he came here the other night. But, of course, I don't know Mr. Lord. Hello, Mr. Lord." She rose from her kneeling position and put out her hand to Sims. Although he was handsome and appeared to be friendly, he seemed chilly to her. She noticed his ice-blue eyes and his prematurely white hair. She noticed his splendidly cut gray suit and his blue English shirt with his initials on the breast pocket.

"Please call me Sims, Flo," said Sims Lord, shaking her hand. The picture that Sims had in his mind of Flo March was different from what Flo March turned out to be. He had imagined her to be pretty, but common. He had imagined her to be interested only in Jules's money. He was unprepared for her to be beautiful, and beautifully dressed. He was unprepared for her to be living in such an elegant manner. Mostly, he was unprepared to find the relationship between Jules and Flo was so affectionate.

"Quite honestly, I didn't know if you were going to be friendly toward me or not," said Flo.

"Friendly," said Jules, answering for Sims. There was no question that orders had been given in advance. When Jules spoke, his voice was barely above a whisper, but he was still in charge.

"That makes me very happy," said Flo. She smiled at Sims. "I have some marvelous white wine in the fridge. From the Bresciani auction."

Both Jules and Sims laughed.

"Jules? Will you have some?" asked Flo.

Jules looked at Olaf, as if asking for permission, and then nodded yes.

"Sims?"

"Fine."

"I have everything, if you'd like something different."

"No, white wine is fine. Especially that white wine."

"Olaf?"

"I won't, Flo. But thank you."

She went to the bar and uncorked the wine and poured it into three glasses.

Jules looked at Flo, surprised. "Are you having some wine?" he asked. "I thought you didn't drink anything except Diet Coke."

"Oh, just this once," said Flo. "This is the most wonderful celebration, after all. Welcome home, Jules." She raised her glass in a toast, and the others followed suit. "I just want to put the soufflés in the oven, and then we can talk."

"She's perfectly charming, Jules," said Sims, when Flo had left the room, but there was in the tone of voice of his compliment the slightest trace of condescension, which was not lost on Jules.

Jules, annoyed, nodded. He signaled with a wave of his hand for Sims to open his briefcase. Sims understood and did so, bringing forth the papers that he knew Jules was impatient to see.

When Flo returned to the room, there were papers and pens on the top of her beveled-glass coffee table.

"Lunch will be just a few minutes," she said.

"Something smells awfully good, Flo," said Olaf.

"My cheese soufflés," she said. "What are all those papers?"

"Read them," said Jules.

Flo took up one of the papers. It was an official-looking document, with Jules's name across the top, and the address of his office. Then, in the right-hand corner, was her name, Miss Flo March, 844 Azelia Way, Beverly Hills, California 90210. Flo looked over at Jules and then at Sims Lord. Both men were looking at her.

"Read it," said Jules.

" 'Dear Flo,' " read Flo out loud. " 'I agree to pay you twenty thousand dollars a month for five years, commencing immediately. This money will be paid to you by the thirteenth day of each month from the proceeds of my profit from the Santucci shopping centers in Santa Ana, San Jose, and Santa Cruz. Sims Lord, my attorney and executor, has been authorized to do this. Regards, Jules Mendelson. Witness Olaf Pederson, Margaret Maple.' "

Flo looked up from the letter at Jules and burst into tears.

"That's just over a million bucks," said Jules, smiling. "You're an heiress."

"Oh, Jules," she said. She knelt in front of him again and put her head in his lap. "I knew. I always knew you'd take care of me."

Jules lay his hand on her head. "There's more," he whispered. Again he signaled to Sims Lord, and Sims passed him another paper. Flo looked up and Jules handed her the paper.

"This house is yours," he said.

"Almost yours," corrected Sims, holding up his hand in caution. "The actor who owns this house is in Yugoslavia on a film, and the papers have not been returned, but everything has been tentatively agreed upon."

"Oh, Jules. I don't know what to say." She put her arms around his neck and kissed him on the cheek. He turned to look at her.

"I think your soufflé is burning, Flo," said Olaf.

"Oh, my God!" she cried. She jumped up and ran into the kitchen. "Shit!" she yelled from the kitchen.

When she reentered the room in a few minutes, she carried one of the burned soufflés in her hand. "I just want to show you what it would have looked like," she said.

Jules, delighted with her, laughed, and Sims followed suit.

"There's still salad, and hot rolls, and your favorite mocha cake from the bakery at the Farmers Market," she said.

"Sounds good to me," said Jules.

Olaf picked up Jules and carried him to the table.

"Jules, sit here by me," said Flo, tapping the top of the chair to her right, as if she were used to giving lunch parties. "There's no place cards. Olaf, you there, next to Jules. And Sims, here, on my left. I'm so pleased to meet you finally, Sims. Jules talks of you constantly."

Sims pulled out Flo's chair, and she sat down, pleased with her performance, knowing she was doing a good job.

"Your table looks beautiful, Flo," said Jules, when he was seated. He knew how much it meant to Flo to be having guests in her house. He reached over and touched the out-of-season tulips in the centerpiece. "Pauline always said that there's no flower that dies as gracefully as a tulip." The strange remark met with silence, and then Jules said, "I can't think what made me remember that bit of esoteric information at this time."

At first, after Jules's compliments on Flo's table and flowers, conversation lagged. The weakness of Jules's condition did not allow him to dominate the small party in the way that he usually dominated the conversation at any table where he was seated, with his extraordinary knowledge of international affairs and his very high-level inside information from the business and art worlds. Olaf, who was unused to social life, keenly felt that he was merely an employee asked to sit at the table because of the unusual circumstances, and thought it inappropriate to enter the conversation. And Sims Lord was a reluctant guest, whose chilliness of manner might have made the lunch party a failure, but for the force of Flo's personality as a hostess. To entertain Jules's friends in an elegant manner that he could be proud of was a thing that she deeply desired, and she was not about to allow her first chance at it to be unsuccessful, despite her burned soufflés. In a very short time, her self-deprecating account of the events of her morning preparing for her first party had her three guests roaring with laughter. Sims Lord, who greatly liked the ladies, especially ladies who were married to other people in the social groups in which he moved, wondered to himself why none of the ones with whom he engaged in amorous escapades were as entertaining as Jules's mistress.

Jules, exhausted, could only nod with pleasure at her stories. When Flo rose from her seat to clear the table, she said, "Wait until you see this cake." When she was in the kitchen, Olaf was the first to notice that Jules had slumped over in his seat. "You all right, boss?" he asked.

Jules's head had fallen forward. He shook it slowly. Both Olaf and Sims jumped to their feet.

"Jules, what's the matter?" cried Flo, when she came back into the room, holding the cake, and saw the two men kneeling in front of Jules.

"It's all this excitement of coming here," said Sims to Olaf in a low voice, although Flo could hear. "I think we better get him back up the mountain."

Olaf, ignoring Sims, was on his feet. He picked up Jules and carried him over to the sofa, where he laid him down and began massaging his chest. Both Sims and Flo stood by and watched. In a few minutes color began to come back into Jules's face.

"Olaf, I really think we should get him home," said Sims again. Sims had become edgy and nervous. "We can't let him collapse in this house again. She'll have a fit." The "she" he referred to needed no identification.

Jules, hearing, nodded. "It would be bad for Flo," he said to Olaf. Olaf picked him up again and carried him toward the door. As Jules passed by Flo in Olaf's arms, she took hold of his hand and went with them to the car. She opened the rear door of the Bentley, and Olaf put him in the backseat.

"Good-bye, Jules," said Flo, holding on to his hand.

Jules looked at Flo. His mouth had started to hang open. He looked exhausted. He touched her hand and lifted it to his mouth to kiss, not taking his eyes off her.

"Flo, we have to go," said Sims.

"Yes, yes, I know. Good-bye, Jules," she said again. "Please call me later, somebody. I want to know how he is."

Olaf, seated behind the wheel, nodded to Flo and pointed to himself to indicate that he would call. He turned on the ignition.

"Please, Flo, we have to go," repeated Sims. There was a note of impatience in his voice now.

Flo pulled back from the car and closed the door. She and Jules continued to look at each other as Olaf backed the car around until it faced downhill. Then she ran down the steep driveway next to the car until it reached Azelia Way. The car passed her. She watched it until it disappeared onto Coldwater Canyon. She knew that she would never see Jules Mendelson again.

"No one can give a party quite like Pauline," said Prince Friedrich of Hesse-Darmstadt, in a voice brimming with enthusiasm. The prince was in a position to know, because he was entertained by all the great hostesses everywhere, all of whom fussed shamelessly over him because of his splendid title. Rose Cliveden, who secretly longed for a monarchy, even dropped a deep curtsy to him, although no member of the prince's family had been near a throne for seventy-two years, and the principality that had borne his name had ceased to exist in the last century. It mattered not a whit to any of the ladies who fussed over him that he hadn't a cent to his name and needed his job as the head of the jewelry department at Boothby's auction house in London, if for no other reason than to pay the cleaning and laundry bills on his three dinner jackets and nine pleated evening shirts, which were the mainstay of his life. In social circles, he was considered to be a great asset to any party anywhere, because he knew all the international news that people in society loved to hear, and he had the good sense to leave his wife, whose lineage was equally splendid but who was stout and boring and thought to be difficult to seat, back in London. He had promised Pauline that he wouldn't say a single word about the billionaire's party in Tangier that he had just attended until all her guests were there, as everyone wanted to hear.

"But where is your de Lamballe diamond?" he asked Pauline, even before he inquired about the state of Jules's health, as he bent over to kiss her hand on arriving in her house and saw that it was missing from her finger. She was wearing diamonds at her neck and diamonds on her wrists, but she had put away forever her magnificent engagement diamond. No one cared more about jewelry than Friedrich of Hesse-Darmstadt, and there were few stones he admired as much as the de Lamballe diamond that Pauline Mendelson had worn for twenty-two years as a symbol of her brilliant marriage. He did not need to peer through a jeweler's eye to tell exactly how many carats a great stone had, and he could hold a prospective buyer enthralled as he recounted the provenance of an important piece, who had worn it, owner by owner, and what had become of each.

Pauline looked down at her bare finger. She could not bring herself to tell Friedrich what she had told Sims Lord, that the ring seemed to her to be as false as her marriage. "Oh," she said. "I must have forgotten it."

There were only fourteen guests that night, which, for a Mendelson party, was quite small, but every detail was planned to perfection, as only Pauline could plan such details, and each guest remarked on that perfection. It was a warm night, and there was to be a full moon. Pauline's flower gardens had never looked more beautiful, and Jules's sculpture garden had never been shown to better advantage. There were drinks in the pavilion by the pool, and the air was filled with the scent of orange blossoms from the orangerie. There was Rose Cliveden, drinking far too much, but amusing, everyone thought, at least before dinner. And Faye Converse. And Camilla Ebury, with her boyfriend, Philip Quennell. And Madge and Ralph White. And Freddie and Betty-Ann Galavant. And Sandy and Eve Pond. Except for Philip Quennell and Faye Converse, there were none of Pauline's usual arty crowd, just the group that Hector Paradiso used to say were "old Los Angeles."

Everyone asked for Jules. "He's so much improved. The doctors are thrilled," Pauline said over and over, or a variation on that statement, even though she had seen him when Olaf brought him home from his CAT scan at three-thirty that afternoon, in an alarming state. All the servants in the house were watching out the windows. Dudley had rushed into the courtyard with a wheelchair to assist, but Olaf had pushed it aside and simply picked up Jules, as if he were a child, and carried him in his arms into the house and up the stairway. It had occurred to Pauline then, as Jules passed her at the top of the stairs, unable even to speak to her, to cancel her party that evening, but later, after he seemed to revive somewhat in his bed, he insisted she go ahead with it.

Miss Toomey, the nurse in charge of his case, said over and over again that she could not understand why they had been gone for such a long time. "It's not as if Mr. Mendelson has to wait at the hospital," she said. "He did give the wing, after all. His name is on it. They should have given him priority." Miss Toomey had started to adopt a bit of the grandiosity of the family with whom she had come to live. Olaf, busy with his orderly duties, did not respond to Miss Toomey.

"Jules is simply furious that Dr. Petrie is keeping him upstairs tonight, but he sends you all his love," said Pauline.

"His sculpture garden is breathtaking," said Prince Friedrich. "I would love to run upstairs and peek in and tell him. I've never seen it lit up at night before."

"Perhaps later," said Pauline quickly. "Look, Dudley's calling us up to dinner." She put her arm in his, and they walked across the lawns to the terrace of the house.

"I was sorry you didn't like the yellow diamond earrings, Pauline," said the prince. "I thought they were exactly what you were looking for."

The image of the earrings on Flo March's ears in Jules's hospital room on the night of his heart attack flashed through Pauline's mind again. She suppressed the anger she still felt at the thought that Jules had given them to his mistress.

"Why do you say that?" she asked.

"Jules's secretary called to say he was returning them. He wanted them put up for auction again."

"He did?"

"You didn't know that?"

"When was that, Friedrich?" She tried to keep a conversational tone in her voice.

"On the very day of his heart attack. Miss Maple called me to say they would be returned, and that same night I heard from Yvonne Bulbenkian that Jules had had his heart attack."

"I see," said Pauline evenly. She stared in front of her as she continued to walk toward her house. Flo March, she thought, must have stolen the earrings after Jules collapsed in her house. She shuddered. In her mind, Flo March had become an evil woman.

"Have I said something to upset you, Pauline?" asked the prince.

"Oh, no, no," said Pauline.

Because of the warm night, Pauline had arranged for dinner in the atrium instead of the dining room. Jarvis, her head gardener, had filled the atrium with pot after pot of her yellow phalaenopsis. "It's too beautiful, Pauline," said one guest after another as they stood by the long table and admired the sight.

"You're next to me, Friedrich," said Pauline. "I've put Faye Converse on your other side."

"All my favorites," said the prince, clapping his hands.

"You must tell us about the party in Tangier."

"A nightmare. An absolute nightmare. Tangier in August! You wouldn't believe the heat. All those people. And the *smells*! And no air-conditioning. And long lines for everything. And long faces everywhere. And the *placement* was a disaster. People like us seated next to people they never heard of and didn't want to hear of. If you could have seen the look on Lil Altemus's face when she saw the hotel where Cyrus put us. It was worth the whole trip." He made a face of haughty disdain, and everyone laughed. "And then she moved out and stayed on Reza Bulbenkian's yacht. Frightfully amusing, really. I wouldn't have missed it for the world."

Philip Quennell, seated on the other side of Faye Converse, watched Pauline. He had no interest in the party in Tangier, as he did not know any of the people they were talking about, and he had ceased to listen. Instead, he noticed how elegantly Pauline sat at the head of her table, her elbow on the table, her hand cupping her chin in the most graceful fashion, paying her utmost attention to her guest of honor as he recounted anecdote after anecdote about a society party, which seemed of great interest to them all. It occurred to Philip that Pauline was going through the motions of listening, but that her thoughts were elsewhere.

Dudley also watched Pauline, as he went about his duties. He noticed the tenseness beneath her calm exterior. When she charmingly excused herself from the table to attend to a hostess duty, she entered the kitchen and complained to Dudley because one of the maids was chewing gum while serving her guests.

"I wasn't chewing it, Dudley," said the maid when Pauline returned to the table. "It was in my mouth, yes, but I wasn't chewing. How in hell did she know?"

Miss Mae Toomey, the nurse in charge of Jules Mendelson's welfare, walked into the kitchen in a stormy fashion. "I am at a loss as to understand how there could be a party going on in this house on one floor while a man is dying upstairs," she said.

Dudley, ever loyal to the household he had served for so many years, had no wish to engage in a subversive conversation with the efficient nurse, and he had no authority over her to request her silence in front of the other servants working in the kitchen. He looked up and exchanged a glance with Blondell, who was helping Gertie, the cook, arrange green mints on silver dishes for the drawing room after dinner. With Blondell, who had been with the Mendelsons nearly as long as he had, he could engage in such a conversation, but he would not with Miss Toomey. Instead, he moved to the pantry, out of their earshot, and she followed him. Although he did not disagree with what she had said, he went about his chores without as much as a nod to indicate his own feelings.

When he had finished arranging demitasse cups and spoons on a tray, he looked at Miss Toomey and said, "Is Mr. Mendelson worse?"

"He will not live through the night," she said. "The man belongs in a hospital. I want to call Dr. Petrie and have him readmitted."

Sounds of laughter came from the atrium, at the completion of one of the prince's anecdotes, followed by the ringing of the table bell.

"She's calling me," Dudley said, excusing himself from the angry woman.

"More seconds for the fat prince, no doubt," said Miss Toomey. She followed Dudley toward the door. "Tell her I must speak to her. Tell her it is urgent."

As Dudley opened the door to return to the atrium, another great burst of laughter could be heard. During dessert, Dudley tried to interrupt Pauline to whisper that the nurse had to speak to her on the intercom, but she held up her hand for him not to speak until the prince had arrived at his punch line. Then, after more laughter and appreciative comments, she turned to Dudley to hear his message.

"Miss Toomey," he whispered in her ear.

"I'll call her after dessert," said Pauline. "Tell Gertie the grapefruit sorbet is divine. Perhaps you should pass it around again, and the blueberries also. Such a good combination. I don't know why we haven't tried that before."

Dudley persisted in his mission. He mouthed but did not speak the word, "Urgent."

Pauline lifted her damask napkin to her lips and then pushed her chair out. "There's a call I have to take," she said to the prince, but she did not leave the table without first seeing to his welfare while she was gone. "Friedrich, have you read Philip Quennell's book on Reza Bulbenkian? So marvelous. What's the first line, Philip? Jules was always so amused by that."

Philip, who did not enjoy being the center of attention, said, "I can't remember exactly. It goes something like this: 'Reza Bulbenkian made one of the great American fortunes by knowing all the right wrong people.'"

"Frightfully funny," said the prince, who then pulled the attention back to himself by starting on a long story about the social-climbing exploits of Yvonne Bulbenkian, and the fortune she was spending. With her guests in rapt attention, Pauline left the atrium and walked into the house and down the hallway to the library. She crossed to the telephone and pushed the intercom button.

"Yes, Miss Toomey. Forgive me for taking so long, but I assumed you knew I have guests. Is this something that can't wait?" asked Pauline.

"I'm sorry, Mrs. Mendelson, but I think you should come upstairs immediately," replied Miss Toomey. The adoring tone that Miss Toomey had previously had in her voice whenever she spoke to Pauline was missing. She was serious and businesslike and made no attempt to underplay the urgency she was communicating.

Pauline heard and understood the nurse's tone. "I'll be right up," she said. She hung up the telephone and walked out of the library. She was surprised to see that Dudley was standing outside the door in the hallway.

"Is everything all right, Mrs. Mendelson?" he asked. There was concern in his face.

"Yes, yes, of course. Go back to the party, Dudley," she said. "Perhaps serve coffee at the table rather than inside, don't you think? They all seem quite comfortable. It would be a shame to interrupt the mood."

Dudley realized that Pauline was afraid to go up the stairs and was postponing what she had to do.

"Should I call Dr. Petrie?" Dudley asked.

"No. Miss Toomey should be the one to do that, and I'm sure that's not necessary," said Pauline.

"I could ask the guests to leave, Mrs. Mendelson. I'm sure they'd all understand."

"Oh, no. Please don't. You're being an alarmist, Dudley. Mr. Mendelson is going to be fine. Now I must go up. Remember, coffee in the atrium."

She walked up the stairway, holding on to the red velvet banister. On the way up, she noticed that the third Monet painting of the water lilies was crooked again, and she straightened it as she passed, without stopping. At the top of the stairs she turned right and walked down the hall to Jules's room. She stood outside his door for a second, breathed in deeply, and opened the door.

At first Pauline could not see Jules. Olaf was on the far side of the bed, leaning over him, and Miss Toomey was on the near side with her back to the door. Hearing the door, they both turned to her.

"He is very bad, Mrs. Mendelson," said Miss Toomey. There was a censorious tone in her voice for the lateness of the arrival of the about-to-be widow. "I don't think he has long."

Pauline, frightened, stared at the nurse for a moment and then walked over to the bed. Jules lay with closed eyes. His head was turned to the side, and his mouth hung open. He was breathing in an erratic fashion, with gasping noises.

"I would like to be alone with my husband," she said.

"I'll call Dr. Petrie," said Miss Toomey.

"Not yet," said Pauline. "Not until you hear from me."

"Would you like me to stay, Mrs. Mendelson?" asked Olaf.

"Come back in a bit. I would like to talk to my husband in privacy. Can he hear me, Miss Toomey?"

"Ask him," said Miss Toomey.

"Jules. Can you hear me, Jules? It's Pauline."

Jules opened his eyes and looked at his wife. His hand moved feebly along the blanket cover, as if he were reaching for her. Pauline turned and looked as both Miss Toomey and Olaf left the room and closed the door behind them.

"Did you ever think you'd hear me say I'm scared, Pauline?" he asked. His grave illness had weakened the resonance of his voice.

"No, I didn't," she replied.

"You look very swell," he whispered. "How's your party going?"

"I should have canceled this damn party this afternoon when you came back from the hospital."

"If they criticize you, tell them I insisted you go ahead with it."

"Oh, Jules," she said, looking at him. "I feel so helpless. If you were a religious man, I would call for a priest, or a rabbi, or even Rufus Browning from All Saints."

"No, no. No last sacraments for me. I'm dying, Pauline."

She looked at him but did not reply.

"No tears, I see," said Jules, in a voice barely above a whisper.

"I've shed all my tears, Jules," said Pauline.

He blinked his eyes.

"For whatever it's worth to you, Pauline, flights of angels are not singing me to my rest."

"If you're thinking I want you to suffer, Jules, you're wrong. I don't," said Pauline, looking away from him. She held her elbows in front of her, as if she were cold, although the room was not cold.

"I remember that night in Palm Beach years ago, when I first saw you at the Van Degans' dance. You were everything I ever wanted. I'm sorry, Pauline. I really am."

She shook her head. "Oh, Jules, please, please, let's not go down memory lane."

"Listen, Pauline." There was an urgency to his weak voice. "She's not a bad girl."

"I'm not interested in hearing about her virtues."

"Take care of her, Pauline."

"You must be mad. How could you ask me such a thing?"

"I'm giving you good advice."

"No. I don't have to take care of her."

"It will be terrible for you if you don't, Pauline. There are things I know about in life. Money is one of them. Trust me in this."

The exertion of talking had exhausted him. His head rolled back and fell to the side. Pauline looked to the door. She wanted to leave the room, but an instinct told her not to. She knew that he was about to die. She moved to the bell on his bedside table to call for Miss Toomey. She noticed from the light on the instrument that one of the telephone lines was being used. She wondered if Miss Toomey was calling Dr. Petrie.

"Don't ring for Miss Toomey," said Jules. "I don't want another reprieve."

She picked up the receiver and listened in. She heard Olaf's voice, speaking rapidly. "I'm sorry, Flo. He can't talk to you. Missus is in there with him. It's almost at the end. I think Toomey suspects we were at your house today." Pauline slammed down the telephone.

"There's something you should know, Pauline," said Jules.

She could not bear to hear one more word about Flo March. She had never hated anyone before in her life, but she hated Flo March. When she spoke, she sounded weary. "No. There's nothing more I need to know, Jules. I know everything, about everything, and so does everyone we know."

"Kippie killed Hector," he said, in a voice so low as to be almost inaudible.

Pauline, stunned, gasped. Their eyes met. "No, no," she whispered, shaking her head in denial at what her husband had told her, although she knew that what he said was true.

"Open the safe in the library," he said. "There is a sealed manila envelope. Hector's note is inside."

"Where did you get it?"

"I took it from Hector's house before the police got there."

"What did it say?"

"He wrote down the name of his killer."

Pauline began to cry, as things fell into place in her mind. Kippie. Kippie did it. Kippie needed money that night, and she had refused him. And Kippie had gone to Hector. And the suicide story that she had never understood was a cover-up by Jules to protect her from knowing that her son had killed her best friend.

Pauline knelt by Jules's side, weeping. "Oh, Jules, I'm sorry. Oh, my God, Jules. You did this for me. Oh, Jules, I'm sorry. I'm sorry."

She took hold of his hand and leaned over to kiss it. She felt a resurgence of love for him, but the feeling became overwhelmed by a dark thought that leapt into her mind. "Jules? Does anyone else know what you just told me? Please tell me. Does anyone else know what you just told me?"

Jules's eyes had started to glaze over in preparation for death, but he was able to forestall that by-now-welcome event for the moment it took to meet Pauline's gaze. He saw the panic in her eyes, and he could not bring himself to tell her that it was at Flo March's house on Azelia Way that he had hidden Kippie for the six hours it took until all the arrangements had been made that changed Hector Paradiso's death from a murder to a suicide. He could not, out of respect for his wife, have the last words he uttered be the name of his mistress.

"Who, Jules? Please tell me," begged Pauline.

But Jules Mendelson was dead. Pauline, born Episcopalian, could be devoutly Episcopalian when she felt inclined toward religion, and at that moment she felt so inclined. Still kneeling by Jules's side, with her face in her hands, she said the prayers of her youth for her husband, the same prayers she had said for her mother when she knelt at her deathbed so many years before. Then she rose, still in the final stages of the Lord's Prayer, as the overwhelming thoughts of what she had to do pushed the prayers from her mind. "For thine is the kingdom, the power, and the glory, forever and ever," she said in a churchlike whisper, but she was thinking of the obligations of her life. She caught sight of herself in the mirror over Jules's fireplace. She wished she were not covered in jewels, which she had only worn for the benefit of Prince Friedrich of Hesse-Darmstadt, and which were too glittering by far for the circumstances at hand. But she could not remove them, as she had to return to her guests downstairs, and they would notice and tell afterward, after the story became public that Jules had died while she was giving a party for a prince who was no more than a jewelry salesman.

When she buzzed for Miss Toomey, the door opened immediately, as if she had been standing outside, and Miss Toomey entered and ran to the side of the bed.

"He's gone," said Pauline quietly.

"My God," said Miss Toomey. "Why didn't you call me?" She was distressed not to have been present at the moment of death.

"It was very peaceful," said Pauline. "One moment he was here, and the next he was gone. I wasn't even aware immediately that it had happened."

"I'll call Dr. Petrie," said Miss Toomey.

"I don't want anyone to know yet," said Pauline.

"But I must call the doctor."

"There's not much the doctor can do now," said Pauline. And then she repeated, with emphasis, "I don't want anyone to know, Miss Toomey. Do you understand?"

"Until when, Mrs. Mendelson?"

"Until I get rid of my guests downstairs. A half hour at most. I don't want them to know that my husband is dead. It is urgent that the press not find out. Urgent. Just stay here with him until I come back upstairs." She started toward the door.

"I'll call Olaf," said Miss Toomey.

Pauline stopped at the mention of Olaf's name. The tone of her voice hardened. "No, don't call Olaf. I don't want Olaf in this house another minute. I do not wish him to see my husband's body. I blame him for my husband's death. Get rid of him."

Miss Toomey, startled, looked at Pauline. "Yes, Mrs. Mendelson."

Pauline walked out of the room where her husband lay dead and up the hallway to the stairs. She stopped to look in a mirror hanging over a chest in the upstairs hall and checked her appearance in the manner she had of looking at herself in the mirror of her dressing table, her face to the left and then her face to the right. Extremely pale, she pinched her cheeks very hard to bring color to them. She opened a drawer and took out a lipstick that Blondell always placed there for her and applied it to her lips. Then she adjusted her hair with her hands.

Grasping the red velvet banister, she walked down the stairs. She could hear that her guests had moved inside from the atrium to the drawing room. She could tell from the conversational voices that Rose Cliveden was now very drunk and that Friedrich of Hesse-Darmstadt was annoyed by her constant interruptions of his anecdotes. The rest of her guests seemed not to be talking at all. Being a born hostess, she knew that she had been gone from her party for too long a time, and was needed to restore the room to harmony, but when she reached the bottom of the stairs, she turned in the direction of her library rather than her drawing room. She entered the library and closed the door behind her. For an instant it occurred to her that she should lock the door, but she thought it might look suspicious to Dudley if he came looking for her.

She went quickly over to van Gogh's *White Roses,* hanging over the fireplace mantel. Taking hold of the famous treasure by its frame, she unlatched a hook behind the picture and swung it outward to reveal a wall safe behind. She pulled up a footstool, stood on it, and leaned closely into the combination lock. With great dexterity she turned the lock to the left, then to the right, then to the left again, then around twice, ending up at zero. The door lifted back. Within was a small light which she switched on. Inside were all her velvet and leather jewelry boxes for her necklaces and bracelets and rings. She shifted through some papers and envelopes in the back of the safe and brought forth a five-inch-by-seven-inch manila envelope. It was taped shut. On it, in Jules's handwriting, was written the word *Private.*

Still standing on the footstool, she tore open the manila envelope. From inside, she pulled out a sheet of blue stationery, which she recognized as the stationery from Smythsons on Bond Street in London that she had given Hector Paradiso for Christmas the year before, with his name engraved in a darker blue across the top of each page. It was folded in half. With shaking hands, she opened the sheet of paper. There were stains of dried blood on the page. In blue ink, running downhill, in the shaky penmanship of a dying man, each letter becoming more indecipherable, were written the words "Kippie Petworth did this."

Pauline felt weak and dizzy. She covered her mouth with her hand and breathed great heaving sounds, as if she were going to be sick. Overlapping thoughts of Jules and Hector and Kippie filled her mind.

The library door opened, and Philip Quennell walked in. They looked at each other.

"Pauline, I'm sorry. I didn't realize you were in here," he said.

She was standing on the stool. Hector's stationery was in her hand. With extraordinary calmness, she said, "Yes, I was looking for my ring, Philip. I forgot to take it out of the safe tonight before the party, and, wouldn't you know, Friedrich would notice I wasn't wearing it the first thing when he came into the house." She turned back to the safe, pushed the piece of paper inside, and took out a leather ring box, which she opened. She put the de Lamballe diamond on her finger, shut the door of the safe, swung around the dial, and closed the painting of van Gogh's *White Roses* over it, latching it in the back. She stepped down off the footstool. "Now you know where the safe is," she said.

Philip, fascinated, watched her. "I came in to use the men's room," he said.

"It's there," said Pauline.

"I know," he answered. "I feel like we've played this scene before."

"We did," she replied. "The first night you ever came here." As she said the words to him, she remembered that she had been on the telephone with Kippie at the time. He had called asking for money. She had not known then that the call was the beginning of her life falling apart.

"Oh, I remember. Are you all right, Pauline?"

"Of course. Why do you ask?"

"You've been gone such a long time."

"There was a long-distance call I had to take. My father has not been well in Maine. The party's moved inside. I could hear the voices. Or rather, I could hear Rose's voice annoying poor Friedrich."

Philip did not want to get into a social conversation. "Is Jules all right, Pauline?"

"Yes. Fine. Why?"

"Would you like me to get rid of your guests?"

"Heavens, no. I must get back to the party. Poor Friedrich will think I've deserted him."

When Philip returned to the drawing room, he looked around for Pauline. She had rejoined the group and was seated on a sofa between Camilla and Madge White. She sat silently, smiling, looking very beautiful, but content to listen while Rose Cliveden talked and talked, repeating the same story. Philip felt that Pauline had abdicated her authority, that her mind was elsewhere, that although she knew her guests were bored with Rose, she was making no attempt to salvage her failed party. When she smiled or laughed, he noticed that there was no merriment in her eyes to match the laughter on her lips. He thought she might not even know what she was laughing at.

Finally, when the hall clock struck ten-thirty, Faye Converse said, "This movie star has got to go home."

"Oh, I'm so sorry," said Pauline, jumping to her feet. "Let me ring for Dudley to get your coat. Darling, could you take Rose home? I don't think it's safe for her to drive down the mountain."

It was apparent to all that she wanted them to leave, but would not have asked them to if Faye Converse had not made the first move. She stood in the hallway, taking the furs from Dudley as he took them off hangers in the closet. "This is yours, isn't it, Madge?"

Outside, in the courtyard, Ralph White said to Madge, "Do you think Pauline was rushing us out?"

Flo's Tape #21

"I got the sexual part of Jules, but I never had the feeling of living together with him. I never saw him shave, for instance. The kind of things that wives see. I never had his shoes in my closet. I like to see a man's shoes in my closet.

"I don't want you to think I'm conceited, or anything, but I can tell you for a fact that Jules really loved me. But, believe me, that had never been his intent. At first, it was like an infatuation. I think he thought that after we'd done it for a while, like the trip to Paris, for instance, that the spell would be broken, and he'd unload me with a nice gift, like a jewel or a fur coat, and probably a little cash, the way rich guys do when they unload their superfluous women. And it would be terminated with grace. And I'd go back to the coffee shop, and he'd go back to Pauline.

"I thought that was what was going to happen too. I expected him to unload me. But he didn't. After the first year, I knew it was the real thing."

22

When all her guests had finally gone, Pauline went back to the library of her house. First she took off all her jewelry and placed it in the safe. At the same time, she removed Hector's final note from the safe and put it in her bag. Then she picked up the intercom and buzzed Jules's room.

"Yes?" answered Miss Toomey.

"Call Dr. Petrie, Miss Toomey, and inform him of my husband's death," said Pauline. She spoke in the same authoritative tone of voice she used when she was giving her instructions for the day to her maid or her butler or her cook.

"Yes, Mrs. Mendelson."

Then Pauline buzzed for Dudley.

"Yes?"

"Could you come in the library, please, Dudley?"

"Yes, Mrs. Mendelson."

When Dudley came in a few moments later, she said, "Mr. Mendelson has just died, Dudley."

"Oh, Mrs. Mendelson," said Dudley. "I am so sorry."

"Thank you, Dudley. And thank you for these past weeks since he came home from the hospital. You have practically run this house yourself, and my husband was very appreciative and so am I. Now, there is a great deal to be done, and I very much need your help."

"Yes, Mrs. Mendelson." Dudley turned away from Pauline so that she could not see his face. She understood that he was crying. It had always fascinated Pauline that the people who worked for Jules—his butler, his guard, his chauffeur, his secretary, his barber, his lawyer—had always cared deeply about him and stayed on with him year after year. She knew he had private dealings with them all, buying them houses, or businesses, or paying their hospital expenses, or helping educate their children.

"Will you tell the staff, Dudley?" asked Pauline. "Except Blondell. I'll tell Blondell. Tell Jim, and Smitty, and Gertie in the kitchen, and that little maid, whatshername, the one I became upset with tonight?"

"Carmen."

"Yes, of course, Carmen. Ask her not to be angry with me about the gum chewing. I was upset. I was worried about Mr. Mendelson the whole evening. I so regretted that I had not canceled the party this afternoon when he came home from his CAT scan."

"We all understand."

"Has Olaf left the house?"

"Yes."

"With all his things?"

"Yes. He said you fired him."

"I did. He deserved to be fired."

"May I know what he did?"

"Yes, but not now. Nurse Toomey has called Dr. Petrie. He should be here shortly. Alert Smitty outside that he will be arriving. Dr. Petrie is terrified of the dogs. They jumped all over him the last time. There will probably be an ambulance also. Or a hearse. I don't know what they use. Will you call Miss Maple and ask her to call the mortuary and alert them? We use Pierce Brothers, of course. Will you ask Miss Maple to be here in the morning as early as possible? Will you also get me my telephone book in my office? I have to call Sims Lord tonight and tell him, and I can't remember his home number."

"Yes, Mrs. Mendelson," said Dudley. He went to the desk and jotted down the things she had asked him to do. It did not surprise him that, even in grief and sorrow, Pauline Mendelson remained calm and organized.

"Oh, and Dudley?"

"Yes, Mrs. Mendelson?"

"Please tell the staff, and Miss Maple as well, that no one, and I mean *no one,* is to repeat this information outside the house. I do not want the press to know of my husband's death until after the funeral."

"When will the funeral be?"

"If possible, tomorrow. And it will be private."

Alone, after Dudley went about his chores, she looked at her clock. It was fifteen minutes past eleven. She counted on her fingers the time it would be in Paris. Fifteen minutes past eight o'clock in the morning. Hubert, she knew, was always up and about at seven to do his calisthenics before leaving for his atelier. She had always called her Paris couturier by his first name. He had made her clothes for twenty-five years, and she knew him well. "Hubert," she said, when he answered the telephone in his apartment. She pronounced his name *Hubair.* She told him what had happened.

"I'm so sorry, Pauline," he answered.

"Thank you, Hubert," she replied. She wanted to get right down to business. She did not want to receive sympathy. "Can you make up some things, black and gray, and maybe some white, it's so hot here, to wear for the next few months. I leave it all up to you. Nothing above the knee. Whatever you think is right, but I'm going to need a couple of black dresses immediately. I'll send the plane. Oh, and Hubert? I want one of those black veils. A total cover, don't you think?"

Olaf Pederson, fired by Miss Toomey, drove down the hill from Clouds. Miss Toomey, who did not like him because he had grown so close to Jules and she had not, did not know why she was firing him, and told him that. She would have liked him to stay to assist in what had to be done when Dr. Petrie arrived. Olaf realized that it must have been Pauline Mendelson who had picked up the telephone and heard him talking to Flo March on the extension and then slammed down the receiver. He had become very fond of Jules Mendelson in the weeks he had spent with him at Clouds, and he understood the deep complications of the man's life. Olaf Pederson was a decent man. He was sorry that he had upset Mrs. Mendelson, but he had promised Flo that afternoon that he would call and let her know how Jules was. His home was in the Silverlake district, but on the way he drove up Coldwater Canyon until he reached Azelia Way. There he told Flo March that her lover was dead.

When the ambulance arrived to take away Jules's body, Pauline waited in the library with Dudley and Blondell until the attendants had zipped his corpse into the body bag. Then, alerted by Miss Toomey that the body was being removed from the house, the three went into the front hall to watch the attendants bring Jules Mendelson down his winding stairway for the last time. As they rounded the curve by the third of the six Monet paintings of water lilies, the shoulder of one of the attendants hit against the gilded frame of the famous picture and knocked it askew. "Be careful!" called out Pauline from below. It was unclear to the attendant whether her concern was for the welfare of the body or the painting of the water lilies.

The Reverend Doctor Rufus Browning of the All Saints Episcopal Church in Beverly Hills was contacted to conduct the private service. Dr. Browning assured the widow that the secrecy she desired would be scrupulously kept.

"But Jules was not Episcopalian," said Sims Lord, when he was made aware of this arrangement.

"Nor was he anything else," replied Pauline. Then she added, "It was not necessary for you to point that out to me, Sims. After all, I was married to Jules for twenty-two years, or twenty-three, whatever it was. I know perfectly well he wasn't Episcopalian, but he was always very fond of Rufus Browning, whenever Rufus came up to the house, and he was very generous to All Saints. Rufus will do something quick and quiet. I want this all over with before that horrible woman finds out. I do not wish the funeral to turn into a circus."

"You could always have him cremated," said Sims. "That way there's no coffin to contend with to attract attention."

"Cremated, yes. That's what should be done. He should be cremated," said Pauline, seizing on the idea.

"Oh, no, Mrs. Mendelson," said Miss Maple, looking up from her notes. "He hated cremation. He always said so. He wanted to be buried in Westwood. He has the plots, for both you and him, right next to Armand Hammer's mausoleum. Isn't that right, Mr. Lord? Isn't that in Mr. Mendelson's will?"

Sims Lord nodded.

"Well, he's not going to be buried in Westwood," said Pauline. "He's going to be cremated. Otherwise, that woman will have photographers taking her picture throwing herself on top of the grave. I know that type, believe me."

Miss Maple looked over at Sims Lord, but Sims did not look back at her. It was not lost on either of them that Pauline had become irrational on the subject of Flo March.

"Do you suppose people will say about me, 'She is the widow of a man who loved another woman'?" asked Pauline.

"No, they won't say that, Pauline," replied Sims. "Jules loved you. I know that."

She didn't hear what Sims said. She continued with her own thoughts. "Or, 'Her husband died in the arms of his mistress'?" she asked.

"He didn't die in the arms of his mistress, Pauline," said Sims Lord. "He died here in your house."

"To all intents and purposes he did. He had a heart attack in her arms. And he went to see her yesterday after his CAT scan. That duplicitous Olaf took him to her house. Did you know that, Sims?"

Sims Lord knew how to control the reddening of his face. He shook his head no in answer to Pauline's question. The day before, knowing that Jules was at the end of his life, he had gotten out of the Bentley when Olaf passed the Beverly Hills Hotel, as he did not want to be in the car when it returned to Clouds. It was important to him that Pauline not find out he had been party to the deception.

Pauline, unaware, continued. "I firmly believe that if my husband had not gone to that woman's house yesterday, he would still be alive. Dr. Petrie said that the CAT scan proved how well he was doing."

Dudley opened the door and came into the library.

"If it's a telephone call for me, Dudley, I'm not home to anyone except my father or my sisters," said Pauline. "Or, of course, the White House, but they couldn't know yet."

"It's Kippie," said Dudley.

"Kippie?" She stared at Dudley. "From France?"

"Yes."

"Does he know?"

"Yes."

"Who told him?"

"I assumed you would want him to know, Mrs. Mendelson."

"Yes, yes, of course, Dudley."

"Would you like us to leave the room, Pauline?" asked Sims.

"I would, yes," said Pauline.

"The staff would like to go to the funeral, Mrs. Mendelson," said Dudley, as he was leaving the room.

"Oh," said Pauline. She had moved to the telephone but had not picked it up. "But only you, and Blondell, and Gertie, Dudley. I want to keep this very small. As little attention as possible."

"Yes, ma'am, but Smitty and Jim have been with Mr. M. for years too," said Dudley.

"Yes, of course. Smitty and Jim too. I'm just not thinking," said Pauline. She turned to Sims Lord. "I suppose I have to ask Camilla Ebury too. I'll call her. But not Rose. I can't deal with Rose. And she'll tell someone. She tells everything."

"What about Camilla Ebury's boyfriend?" asked Sims.

"Philip Quennell? No, not Philip. He wasn't a friend of Jules. Just Camilla. Jules adored Camilla. No one else."

When she was alone, she picked up the receiver. "Hello?"

"*Mère*? It's Kippie."

There was a long pause, as Pauline stared at the telephone and did not reply.

"*Mère*? Are you there?"

"Yes, I'm here," she said, finally.

"Look, I'm awfully sorry, *Mère*. I know Jules and I never got along, and it was probably my fault, but I am sorry."

"Yes."

"I'll come for the service. I'm booked on the Concorde tomorrow."

"No. Don't," said Pauline.

"Don't?" he repeated, surprised.

"Don't come. The service will have already taken place. And he will already have been cremated."

"But to see you. I want to be there with you."

"No, don't." She spoke in a low voice.

"Mom, what's the matter? I mean, I'm clean this time. I'm not on drugs anymore. I've licked it. I won't embarrass you. I promise."

Pauline did not reply.

"Mom, can you hear me? Is this a bad connection?"

"I know, Kippie. Jules told me. I know everything," she said.

Kippie was not sure what she meant. "About Flo March, you mean?"

"Yes, about Flo March, among other things."

"What other things?"

"About you."

"Me?"

"And Hector."

"What about Hector?"

"That it was you who did it."

There was a long silence. Pauline could hear her son breathing heavily, and then she spoke again in a hollow voice. "Why? Why? Hector Paradiso was my friend."

"But it's not true," said Kippie. He began to speak very quickly. "There was some hustler there, some blond trick he picked up in a gay bar called Miss Garbo's. Your great pal Hector was not the old sweetheart you always thought he was, *Mère*. He had a very complicated private life, and people who lead that kind of complicated private life get into that kind of trouble with those kind of people they cavort with in the small hours of the night. You're not so isolated up there at Clouds that you're not aware of things like that."

"Oh, don't con me, Kippie. Just don't. I'm in no mood for being conned. Jules Mendelson would not have gone through this complicated suicide story for a hustler from a gay bar, believe me. And it will come out, sometime. You know it will."

"Mom. Don't you understand?"

"What is there to understand?"

"I couldn't have done it. I couldn't have shot Hector five times. It's impossible."

"Oh, Kippie, please don't lie to me. Hector left a note. There was blood on the paper, and your name."

"But, Mom, listen to me. That little dog, that mean little dog of Hector's, what was that dog's name?"

"Astrid?"

"Yes, Astrid. Astrid bit off my trigger finger. Don't you remember? You can't shoot somebody five times if you don't have a trigger finger, *Mère*."

"Oh, Kippie, don't treat me like a fool. That was afterwards. He bit off your finger the next day here at Clouds."

"But only you know that, *Mère,* and you just forgot it," said Kippie.

There was a silence, as she realized her son had just said to her the same line her husband had once said. "Good-bye, Kippie," she said. "Don't come home. Not now. Not ever. I'm going to hang up now. I have a great deal to do."

"Mom, please. Please, Mom," cried Kippie.

But Pauline had hung up. She opened her bag and took out Hector's note. Then she picked up a package of matches from an ashtray and lit one. Holding the note in the fireplace, she lit the piece of paper and watched it burn until she had to drop the scorched end. Then she walked over to a sofa and lay on it, facedown. She hugged a pillow to her, as first the tears came and then the sobs, great heaving, uncontrollable sobs. When Sims Lord, Miss Maple, and Dudley returned to the library to continue with the plans for the funeral, they were touched that grief for Jules's death had finally penetrated the stoic calm of Pauline Mendelson.

"Jules is dead," said Camilla, when she hung up the telephone.

"When?" asked Philip.

"Last night, apparently."

"How come it's not on the news?"

"Look, Philip. It's a secret. No one knows. Pauline doesn't want anyone to know until after the service."

"When's the service?"

"At four."

Philip nodded. "Do you know something, Camilla?"

"What?"

"I think he died last night when we were there at dinner."

"Don't be silly, Philip."

"Do you remember when Pauline got up from the table and was gone for so long? I think that's when he died."

"That couldn't be. She came back."

"Pauline's a cool customer."

Nothing remains a total secret, no matter how well planned the strategy is for maintaining total secrecy. In the ambulance that removed the body of Jules Mendelson to the Pierce Brothers Mortuary for its subsequent cremation was the same attendant, Faustino, who had been in the ambulance that removed Hector Paradiso's body to another mortuary ten months earlier, and who had reported the fact of that death to Joel Zircon, the Hollywood agent, who had been drinking and cruising at Miss Garbo's the same time as Hector Paradiso the evening before.

Jules Mendelson's death, like the death of all rich and famous people, fascinated Joel Zircon, and he pressed Faustino for each and every detail to pass on to Cyril Rathbone and his other friends. He especially delighted in Faustino's story of carrying the famous financier's body down the winding stairway and hitting his shoulder against a painting of water lilies and knocking it askew, much to the consternation of the widow, Pauline Mendelson, who had screamed, "Be careful!" Faustino felt sure her concern was more for the picture of the water lilies than for his bruised shoulder, or the body he was carrying.

At breakfast the next morning at the Viceroy Coffee Shop on Sunset Boulevard, Joel Zircon had Curly, the manager, in hysterics, doing an imitation of Pauline Mendelson screaming over her painting almost falling off the wall, as Faustino carried the stretcher with Jules Mendelson down the winding stairway, on its way to the Pierce Brothers Mortuary. "She's a regular Harriet Craig, that one," said Joel about Pauline.

Pooky, the hairdresser, wondered at the hilarity at the counter between Joel Zircon and Curly, and the story was repeated to him. He could only think of Flo, whose hair he had done the previous day for her lunch party, and he wondered if she knew. Cyril Rathbone, who never spoke to anyone until he'd had his third cup of coffee, sat at his booth reading the Hollywood trade papers, and asked, irritably, what the big joke was at the counter, and couldn't they hold down the noise, *puleeze,* as some people wanted to read their papers, and then Joel went through his story for the third time, adding embellishments to his portrait of Pauline Mendelson with each retelling.

Cyril Rathbone rushed to the pay telephone near the men's room and called Lucia Borsodi, the editor of *Mulholland,* waking her up, and told her the latest development in the Mendelson saga. Lucia knew a story when she heard it. "Get a photographer," she said to Cyril. "Let's see if we can get a picture of Flo March being turned away at the gates of Clouds."

When Pooky called to tell Flo the sad news, she had already heard it from Olaf Pederson the night before. What she didn't know was where they had taken Jules's body, and Pooky told her he was at Pierce Brothers Mortuary in Westwood. Flo knew that Pauline would never allow her to see Jules, so she decided to go to the mortuary and ask to look at him once more. Jules had come through on all his promises to take care of her, and she had the papers in her possession to prove that.

"Do you think they'd let me in, Pooky?" she asked.

"Act like you belong. Act like a society lady. They'll let you in. It's too early for them to call the house and check."

It was as she was leaving her house twenty minutes later, dressed in a black Chanel suit, and carrying the centerpiece of tulips from Holland that Petra von Kant had arranged for her final lunch with Jules, that the telephone rang again. It was Cyril Rathbone.

"I'm very much afraid that I am the bearer of sad news, Miss March," he said. His florid English voice was very dour, as he prepared to tell her of the death of her lover. His pencil and paper were propped to record her reaction.

"I already know what you're going to tell me, Mr. Rathbone," said Flo.

"Oh?" He was distressed not to be the first to have reached her with the sad news, and he wondered how many other people knew. "Who told you?" he asked.

Flo did not reply.

"I wondered if I could stop by, to tell you personally how very sorry I am," he said. "I feel a very special interest because of having been in your house at the time of the heart attack last month."

"I'm sorry, Mr. Rathbone," said Flo. "I'm on my way out."

"To Clouds?" he asked, excitedly. "Are you going up to Clouds?"

"No, Mr. Rathbone."

"I could make you famous, Miss March."

"I don't want to be famous, Mr. Rathbone."

"Just one shot for my magazine. You at the gates of Clouds, waiting for news. Just one shot. It would flash around the world."

"Good-bye, Mr. Rathbone."

Flo hung up the telephone.

Cyril, rebuffed, wondered where she could be going at that hour of the morning, still before eight. On an off chance, he called the photographer that Lucia Borsodi had assigned to him for the day and asked him to "rush, rush, rush," to the Pierce Brothers Mortuary in Westwood. "Out Wilshire. Turn left at the AVCO Theater," he said impatiently, when the photographer said he didn't know where the Pierce Brothers Mortuary was. "They did Marilyn Monroe, Natalie Wood, Peter Lawford, the Zanucks, *everybody,*" said Cyril. He could not abide people who had no understanding of the things that he considered to be important.

"Did? Did what?" asked the photographer.

"Laid out. Embalmed, idiot," said Cyril. "Get over there quick."

"You want me to photograph a dead body?"

"No. I only want a picture of a beautiful red-haired woman, about thirty, who will probably be wearing a Chanel suit, either going into or coming out of the mortuary."

The private and unannounced funeral service for Jules Mendelson at All Saints Episcopal Church in Beverly Hills was in great contrast to the elaborate service that had been held for Hector Paradiso at the Good Shepherd Catholic Church, only two blocks to the west on Santa Monica Boulevard, which had been attended by the social and power elite of the city. Outside on Camden Drive there were no limousines that might attract the attention of the curious. Jim, the Mendelson chauffeur, dropped off the heavily veiled Pauline Mendelson five minutes before the scheduled time, at a side entrance. She ran into the church, looking neither left nor right. There were no flower arrangements and there was no music. The service was attended only by members of the household and office staff who had been in the Mendelson employ for over ten years, as well as Miss Maple, Jules's secretary, Willi Torres, Jules's barber, and Sims Lord, Jules's lawyer and closest adviser. The only outsider present was Camilla Ebury, who was Pauline's great friend. Rose Cliveden, who could not bear to be left out of anything, felt certain that Pauline meant to invite her and had forgotten to in all the haste, so she arrived uninvited and knelt unobtrusively in the last pew of the near-empty church. She bowed her head in prayer, as the Reverend Doctor Rufus Browning read the prayers.

"I am the resurrection and the life, saith the Lord; he that believeth in me, though he were dead, yet shall he live; and whoever liveth and believeth in me shall never die."

While her head was bowed, a second uninvited figure quietly entered the church. It was Flo March, who had heard at the funeral home that there was to be a religious service at the same time that her lover's body was being cremated. Flo meant only to drop in to say a prayer and then leave before she was seen. She had never been in an Episcopal church before, and was unsure of how different the rituals were from those of the Catholic Church. She hastily genuflected in the Catholic manner that she had learned in her parochial school as a child and made the sign of the cross, touching her forehead, her breast, her left shoulder, and then her right, whispering as she did so, "In the name of the Father, the Son, and the Holy Ghost." She rose from her genuflection and entered the last pew. It shocked her that the church was so empty. She found it inappropriate that there would be fewer than a dozen people huddled together in the first few rows for the funeral service of such a famous man. It amazed her that there were no flowers on the altar, no music playing. She looked behind her up at the choir loft. It was in darkness. The organ was closed and covered. She listened as the minister read prayers from his prayerbook.

"Blessed are the dead who die in the Lord; even so saith the Spirit, for they rest from their labors."

All her life Flo had whispered her prayers, and it was her whispering that disturbed the Protestant worship of Rose Cliveden, kneeling in the last pew opposite hers. Although Rose was uninvited herself, she knew that she was at least a friend of the family and would be more welcome at such a private occasion than would the strange woman across the aisle from her, whom she took to be a reporter. Rose cleared her throat in a loud and theatrical way that was meant to attract the attention of the mourners in the front rows and to warn them that there was an impostor in their midst. No one turned. She got up from her seat and walked up the aisle.

Pauline sat alone in the front row. Her back remained ramrod straight, while the others leaned forward to pray. Her face was covered by the black veil her couturier had sent from Paris, along with the black dress she was wearing. Behind her sat Camilla and Blondell. Next to Blondell was Dudley, and then Sims Lord. Rose leaned in and said in a loud whisper to Camilla, "Tell Pauline that there's a reporter in the back of the church."

Rose's whisper carried, and was heard by Miss Maple, seated behind Camilla, who turned back to look. At just that moment, Flo raised her head from her prayer and saw that several faces in the front pews were looking back at her. Miss Maple leaned across Blondell and tapped Sims Lord on the shoulder. Sims looked up from his prayer.

"Flo March is in the rear of the church," whispered Miss Maple.

"Shit," said Sims, under his breath.

He too turned back to look at Flo. Recognizing her, he leaned forward and whispered to Pauline about the interloper, "It's that Flo March," as if he hardly knew her.

For Pauline Mendelson, the presence of Flo March at her husband's funeral was more than she could stand. The composure that had been so much a part of her demeanor during the months of Jules's illness abandoned her at the news that Flo March was in the church at the private service, planned in secret, so that exactly what was happening would not happen. Enraged, she rose from her seat and turned to look back at Flo. Seeing her, meeting her gaze, she brought her hand up to her veiled face, aghast at the woman's brazen behavior.

The de Lamballe diamond on her engagement finger picked up the light from the rays of the afternoon sun that filtered through the stained-glass rose window above her.

"No, no. Sit down, Pauline. I'll get rid of her," whispered Sims, standing up.

Pauline disregarded Sims Lord's offer. She left her seat and walked past him down the aisle to the rear of the church with purposeful strides. The heels of her shoes echoed her anger throughout the apse. Only Dr. Browning's prayer continued as if nothing were amiss.

"Grant to all who mourn a sure confidence in thy fatherly care, that, casting all their grief on thee, they may know the consolation of thy love. Amen."

The attention of the household servants and the employees of the office was diverted from the prayers for the dead to the more fascinating drama that was being played in front of them.

"How dare you come in here?" asked Pauline. "This is a private service."

Flo, terrified, looked at Pauline. She could not make out her face through the black veil.

"I want you to leave this church *immediately.*" Her voice had risen to a scream.

"I'm sorry. I'm really sorry, Mrs. Mendelson. I didn't know this was private," said Flo. "I really didn't. They told me at Pierce Brothers that there was a service here. I just wanted to say a prayer."

"Get out!" screamed Pauline.

No one who knew Pauline Mendelson had ever seen her behave in such a manner. Camilla rushed down the aisle after her and placed her hand gently on her back.

"Darling, Pauline. Come back so Rufus can finish the service," she said. The prayers from the altar continued.

"Give courage and faith to those who are bereaved, that they may have the strength to meet the days ahead in the comfort of a reasonable and holy hope, in the joyful expectation of eternal life with those they love. Amen."

"Someone get this *tramp* out of here," said Pauline.

Tears streamed down Flo's face as she shook her head in denial of the word *tramp.* "I'm sorry," whispered Flo again. She felt so humiliated she could not move.

Camilla looked at the two women staring at each other. She leaned over and took hold of Flo March. "Come on, Miss March," she said gently. She put one arm behind her back and held her hand with the other as she led her from the church.

From the altar the Reverend Doctor Rufus Browning began the Lord's Prayer. Sims Lord led Pauline back to her seat. The servants from the house and the employees from the office all looked down, as if they had not witnessed what they had just witnessed.

On the steps outside, Flo began to cry. "I feel so ashamed," she said. "I shouldn't have come."

"No, you shouldn't," said Camilla quietly, but there was no reprimand in her voice.

"I thought it was a funeral, like Hector's," said Flo.

"No," said Camilla.

"I better go," said Flo.

"Yes," said Camilla.

"Listen, Camilla, before I go, I want to tell you something. Please listen."

"Of course."

"It's important for me that you know this."

Camilla nodded, waiting to hear what Flo had to say.

"I don't blame her for hating me so much, but I want you to know something. I really loved the guy. It wasn't the bucks, I swear. I really loved him," said Flo.

Camilla looked at her helplessly, divided in her sympathies and loyalties.

"And Jules used to tell me he loved me. Really. At the end he even said I was his reason for living," said Flo.

Camilla stepped forward and hugged Flo. Then she turned and ran back into the church.

The death of the Beverly Hills billionaire and art collector Jules Mendelson was announced the day after his funeral. The *Los Angeles Tribunal,* the *Los Angeles Times,* the *New York Times,* and the *Wall Street Journal* carried the story on the front page. Bernie Slatkin, the anchorman of the NBC Nightly News, had a special segment on his newscast, with a film montage of events from the great financier's life, including shots of him in intimate conversations with Presidents of the United States and other world leaders at various economic conferences. Several of the weekly magazines, including *Time* and *Newsweek,* paid homage to his distinguished career.

Hortense Madden had worked for weeks on her story of the discovery of the lost manuscript of Basil Plant, the author who had died in drunken and drugged disgrace, without turning in the book that he considered to be his masterpiece, a novel about the smart set with whom he had been spending his time. The book, if it existed, could never be found after his death. Hortense credited Philip Quennell with some small part in the recovery of the long-missing manuscript, but in her story in *Mulholland,* for which she had been promised the cover by Lucia Borsodi, she herself was the heroine, who knew in an instant that the manuscript was the one Basil Plant's publishers had long since despaired of recovering. It was she, according to her story, who had sought out the mysterious young man called Lonny Edge, in whose Hollywood bungalow the manuscript had been located. There was a hint that perhaps, just perhaps, Mr. Edge had starred in a few pornographic films, and advertised his wares in prurient magazines, to heighten the interest in her story and suggest an unsavory relationship between the two, but as she was a literary critic, and a member of the intellectual establishment of the city, she did not dwell on the sensational. Lonny Edge, however, was reluctant to be interviewed, even though he was unaware that the mousy Hortense Madden and the blond Marvene McQueen, who was singing at Miss Garbo's on the night he went home with Hector Paradiso, and thereby became permanently persona non grata at that nightclub, were the same person.

Hortense Madden's rage knew no bounds when Lucia Borsodi called her into her office to tell her that her story had been bumped—"Just temporarily,

Hortense, calm down"—in favor of Cyril Rathbone's story on the former coffee shop waitress, Flo March, who had become the mistress of one of America's richest men, Jules Mendelson, and lived in splendor in Beverly Hills,
where she was credited by the doctors with saving his life after he had a
massive heart attack in her house.

The picture on the cover of that week's issue showed Flo March carrying a
centerpiece of dying tulips to the Pierce Brothers Mortuary in Westwood.
Inside was the long-forgotten photograph of Flo March escaping from the fire
in the Meurice Hotel in Paris, carrying her jewel box, with Jules Mendelson in
the background.

On the Sunday that followed, Archbishop Cooning, whose mission was
morality, preached from the pulpit of Saint Vibiana's Cathedral on the disgrace of a man who used his vast wealth to corrupt the morals of a girl young
enough to be his daughter.

When Dudley removed the biodegradable plastic cover from the new issue
of *Mulholland,* Pauline, watching, noticed that he reacted to the photograph of
Flo March on the cover.

"Did you ever know her, Dudley?" asked Pauline.

"No, no, I didn't," said Dudley, but his face flushed with embarrassment at
the same time. He turned away to attend to a chore; some petals from a flower
arrangement sent by the White House—"Darling Pauline, Our love and
thoughts are with you, George and Barbara," the card read—had fallen onto a
tabletop, and with one hand he swept the petals into the palm of his other
hand, a task usually attended to by a maid.

"Dudley," said Pauline.

"Yes, Mrs. Mendelson." He was emptying the petals from his palm into a
wastebasket.

"Turn around."

"Yes, ma'am."

"Was that woman ever in this house?" There was a long silence. "Answer
me truthfully, Dudley."

"Yes, Mrs. Mendelson."

If Pauline Mendelson were to live her life over again, she would not have
made the decision she made that day, a decision that she knew at some deep
level was a wrong decision even as she was making it. But her pride overtook
her senses, and she made the decision that no amount of persuasion on the
part of people who had her best interests at heart could dissuade her from
making. She decided to cut off Flo March without a cent, even though she
knew it had been Jules's intention to provide handsomely for her.

Her decision had nothing to do with money, for there was ample money.
Only three days before, the day after Jules's funeral, there had been a discreet
inquiry from Titus Fairholm in Melbourne, Australia, who had always admired
van Gogh's *White Roses,* to see if the estate wished to sell it, at the proper time,
for forty-five million dollars. Pauline knew it would probably fetch even more
at auction at Boothby's. Money did not figure in Pauline Mendelson's decision.

She could not bring herself to provide for a woman she regarded as little more than a whore, a whore who had destroyed the final years of what had appeared to be a perfect marriage.

"That woman was here in my house," said Pauline. "When I was in Northeast Harbor visiting my father, she came here into my home. What kind of a person would do a thing like that?"

"Pauline, as your husband's adviser, I must caution you against this. He made arrangements. She has papers. They are signed by Jules. And by me. And they are witnessed by Miss Maple and Olaf Pederson, who was the orderly with Jules."

"I know perfectly well who Olaf Pederson is. Olaf Pederson was in cahoots with Flo March. They were only after Jules's money. I heard him talking on the telephone to her at almost the moment that Jules was dying. 'She's in there with him,' he said. The 'she' he was talking about was me, Jules's wife. I happen to know for a fact that she stole some yellow diamond earrings out of Jules's pocket on the day of his heart attack. Friedrich Hesse-Darmstadt told me himself that he had spoken with Jules only a short time before the heart attack, and that the earrings were being sent back to him in London."

"I don't know anything about yellow diamond earrings, Pauline, or about her and Olaf. What I do know is that the papers she has in her possession are legal. I can vouch for that," said Sims. Sims Lord had had a career both enhanced and obscured by his proximity to the dominant presence of Jules Mendelson. Now, emerging from the shadows of that dominance, he sought to use patience in dealing with the widow.

"Are these things written in the will?" asked Pauline.

"They aren't in the will, but the papers were already executed."

"When?"

"Last week."

"Only last week? And when did Miss March receive those papers?"

"On Friday."

"Friday? The very day Jules died, you mean? The day of the CAT scan, when Olaf, old loyal Olaf, dropped him off at her house on the way home from the hospital?"

"Yes," said Sims.

"In anticipation of death then?"

"It could be so construed, I suppose."

"I'll take her to court. This constitutes undue influence on a sick man. Remember, there are witnesses who saw her sneak into his room in intensive care at Cedars-Sinai, dressed in a stolen nurse's uniform, and passing herself off as his daughter. Remember all this, Sims."

To Sims Lord, the elegant and refined Pauline Mendelson had become a different woman since Jules's death, maddened by hatred of Flo March, but he was struck by her power. "Pauline, next to you, I was probably the person closest to Jules. This was what he wanted," said Sims patiently.

Pauline's voice rose. She had become quick to anger of late. "Whose side are you on, Sims?" she asked. "We'd better get that straightened out right here and now."

"Of course, I am on your side, Pauline," said Sims, in a placating tone. "That is a thing you never have to question. But there could be consequences, very unpleasant consequences, to what you are suggesting."

"How much does it come to, what she wants?" asked Pauline.

"Over a million. Under two, I suppose. I suggest you pay her, and be done with it," said Sims.

"Pay her over a million dollars! Are you mad?"

"That's what that ring cost that's on your finger. It's a sixth of what that Sisley picture costs behind your head," said Sims, holding out his hands in exasperation to indicate the absurdity of her concern for a million dollars. "What the hell difference does it make? Pay her."

"Never!" Pauline spat out the word. "If she is so broke, tell her to sell the yellow diamond earrings she stole out of my husband's suit pocket on the day he had his heart attack in her house."

Sims shook his head. "I'm terribly afraid you're going to be sorry, Pauline."

Pauline wondered, looking out her library windows at the lawn and sculpture garden, and beyond at the pool and pavilion, if she and Jules had ever been happy, or if Clouds was no more than a magnificent set for the performance of a marriage.

Flo's Tape #22

"I ordered my new sofas, and I picked out the gray satin fabric for ninety-five bucks a yard. Jules used to say it was an outrageous amount to spend, but I didn't care. He had the money. If Pauline had said she spent ninety-five bucks a yard, or even a hundred and ninety-five bucks a yard, he wouldn't have thought anything of it.

"Let me tell you about these sofas, because they're important to the story, especially since Kippie Petworth dripped blood all over one of them. Nellie Potts, my high-class decorator, said they were copied from a design of Coco Chanel from her apartment in the Ritz Hotel in Paris. I liked the sound of that. I waited and waited for them, in anticipation. They took forever to make. And then finally they came. And I arranged them where they should be, and there was great excitement, and for a few days I could think of nothing else but my new gray satin sofas, and I'd sit on different places on the sofas, until I found just the right place for me to use as my regular place to sit down. And then I got used to them. And it was back to plain life again, waiting for Jules to come at a quarter to four each afternoon. Or playing with Astrid. Or drinking ice tea with Glyceria, the maid from next door. The sofas, they were nice, but they weren't it. Do you know what I mean? IT. They weren't it. They were just sofas. And I was just a mistress again."

23

F LO MARCH. Flo March. Flo March. Since her picture appeared on the cover of *Mulholland,* Flo March had become notorious. People discussed her everywhere. The discredited mistress of a disgraced billionaire, the magazine called her. "Have you heard? She crashed Jules's funeral, and there was such a scene you wouldn't believe it, darling, between Pauline and this ghastly woman." Her name became as well known at fashionable dinner parties as it was at the Viceroy Coffee Shop, where she used to work, and where all the customers wanted to hear about her. Curly and Belle, who defended her, became important for having known her. At the bar at Miss Garbo's, Manning Einsdorf and Joel Zircon had stories to tell about her. Women who had sat next to her under the hairdryer at Pooky's Salon and not noticed her, or not spoken to her, now claimed to have been acquainted with her. Even those closest to Pauline Mendelson could not resist, among themselves, supplying each other with every bit of information about the woman in whose house Jules Mendelson had suffered the heart attack that eventually killed him. "She went to communion at Hector Paradiso's funeral. Pushed her way right past the casket." Or, "Of course you've seen her. She has her hair done at Pooky's. Very pretty, in a cheap sort of way, all tarted up in Chanel." Or, "Madge White actually met her, at a steak house in the Valley, having dinner with Jules." Or, "She ran over Faye Converse's dog. Killed it. That sweet little Astrid, that used to belong to Hector."

During the two-week period that her picture was on the cover of *Mulholland* magazine, Flo March, shamed by the controversy she was causing, shrank from contact with everyone she had ever known. She stopped answering her telephone and did not check her message machine. Friends came to her house and rang her bell, but she did not answer her door. Pooky left message after message on her machine that he would be happy to come to her house before he opened his shop in the morning to take care of her hair, but she did not reply to his messages. Even Glyceria, Faye Converse's maid, was not able to get into the house on Azelia Way, although she came by each day and brought things to eat, which she left by the sliding door that opened onto the swimming pool. On some days Flo never rose from her bed. She had started to drink wine all day long and take Valium.

It became Sims Lord's duty to inform Flo that the financial arrangements made in her favor by Jules on the day of his death were going to be contested

by the estate. He came to her house to tell her personally, at the behest of
Pauline Mendelson, after she did not return several of his telephone calls.

"What exactly does that mean?" asked Flo, stunned by his announcement.

"There won't be anything for you, Flo. Other than what Jules had already
given you."

"But why?" asked Flo.

"The estate feels that undue pressure was placed on Jules at a time when
he was too ill to realize what he was signing," replied Sims.

"Pressure by whom?" asked Flo.

Sims did not answer.

"By me? Is that what you mean?" asked Flo again.

"I am merely the messenger here, Flo," said Sims.

"No, Sims. You are not the messenger at all. You are a participant in this
matter. Your name is on those documents as a witness."

"I am acting for the estate, of which I am an executor," he said.

"The estate is who exactly, Sims? Pauline? Is it Pauline who feels that
undue pressure was placed on Jules? You know that's not true, don't you?"

Flo was sitting on her gray satin sofa. A feeling of panic overtook her. She
rose from her seat so that it would not be apparent to him that her hands were
shaking. She walked by him on her way to the bar, where she reached up for a
glass and then poured herself some white wine from an open bottle she removed from the refrigerator. He liked the way she was dressed, in pants and a
sweater. He liked the whiff of Fracas perfume that preceded and trailed her.
He liked the way her beautiful red hair was tied back in a ribbon. He liked that
she was wearing no makeup. He realized that he was very attracted to her.

As she passed Sims on her way back to the sofa, he took hold of her arm
and stopped her. "You didn't offer me a glass of wine," he said, smiling at her.
She understood his smile. She had seen that same smile on the faces of older
men who desired her since she was fifteen years old. She pointed to the bar
with her head and with her thumb at the same time. "Help yourself," she said.

He pulled her to him and began to kiss her. She stood there as he kissed
her, but did not respond. He began to breathe heavily and pushed himself
against her. She pulled back from his embrace.

"No, Sims. That's not what I'm all about," she said, waving her hand in
front of her.

He continued to hold her. "Listen to me, Flo. I could take care of you. You
could stay on in this house. I'd set you up."

She pulled away from him. "You've come here to tell me I'm being deprived of my rightful inheritance, and you want to knock off a quick piece of
ass at the same time? Is that it?" she asked. "How did I make the mistake in
my mind that you were supposed to have class?"

"Come on, Flo. You've really got me going. Feel how hard I am," said
Sims. He took the glass of wine out of her hand and placed her hand on his fly.

"I'm pretty sure that your great friend Jules didn't lead you to believe that
I'm that easy, Sims," she said, shaking her head.

Sims had unzipped his fly. He reached in and pulled out his penis and held
it out to her, as if the sight of it, erect and strong, would send her into fits of
passion and lust.

Her glance, filled with contempt, ignored his offering. "Do I really look that cheap, Sims, that you think it's all right to just pull out your dick in front of me? I don't think you'd do that with Pauline, up there in the library at Clouds. Put it away. Or jerk it off. White pubic hair never turned me on."

She sat down on the sofa and picked up a magazine, which she leafed through, while Sims Lord, red with rage, reinserted his diminished penis into his trousers and zipped himself up. Arranged, he moved toward the front door, thin-lipped now and distant. He opened her door and left without a farewell.

One day Philip Quennell came to her house and rang and rang her bell, but she did not answer. He could see that her car was in the garage and knew that she was inside. As he was about to leave, he tried the door and, to his surprise, found that it was open. He walked in.

"Flo?" he called, when he was in the hall.

Although it was bright daylight outside, the curtains were drawn, and the living room was in near darkness. When his eyes adjusted to the light, he saw that Flo was sitting in the corner of one of the large sofas. In front of her on the glass coffee table were a bottle of white wine and a water goblet from her set of Steuben glasses.

"Not safe to leave your door open these days," said Philip, taking in the scene. "There's all kinds of nuts out there."

"What difference does it make?" asked Flo, looking up at him.

"What are you doing?" he asked.

"I'm on what's known in the program as a little slip," she replied.

Philip picked up the bottle.

"Frightfully good, you know, from the Bresciani auction," she said, in an exact imitation of Jules Mendelson's voice.

"This is not going to help," said Philip.

Flo shrugged. "He hated my cheap wine that I used to buy at Hughes Market, so he sent over a few cases of his best for when he came to call. He hated my cheap glasses too, so he had me order a dozen of every conceivable size glass from Steuben in New York. He also hated my cheap sheets, so he ordered sets and sets from Porthault when he was in Paris. The only thing he liked cheap was me."

"You're not cheap, Flo," said Philip.

"Thanks, Phil Q. That's sweet of you to say, but you don't know some of the things I did with him."

"I don't want to know either."

"You're sounding priggish, Phil Q."

Philip took the bottle of wine into the lavatory off the living room and poured the remains of the bottle down the toilet.

"You sound like an elephant pissing," she called out to him.

Philip laughed. He returned to the living room and put the empty bottle in the wastebasket.

Flo watched him. "Lots more where that comes from," she said.

"Do you want me to take you to a meeting?" he asked.

"Hell, no. I'm not about to stand up in some hall and reveal all my troubles to the world. I can deal with this myself," said Flo.

"This is dealing? Lying in a darkened room with a bottle of wine?"

"Don't blow my low, Phil." She lit a cigarette and let it dangle from her lips. He sat down in the darkened room and watched her.

"Do you want me to turn on the lights?" he asked.

"No," she said. She inhaled and exhaled her cigarette without touching it with her fingers. She started to cry. "I'm scared, Phil. I'm just so damn scared."

She got up from her sofa and walked over to the bar in a weaving fashion. She reached into her refrigerator and took out another bottle of wine. She put a corkscrew into the cork, but her hand slipped, and the corkscrew cut her finger. "Do this for me, will you?" she said, holding out the bottle and the corkscrew to him.

"No," he answered.

"There's something you don't understand, Philip," she said. "I've gotten used to living like this. I didn't have a pot to pee in or a window to throw it out of until I met Jules. I was with the guy for five years. It was more than the clothes and the jewels and the car and the house. He protected me. He paid my taxes. He paid my medical insurance. He covered my overdrafts. He was good to me. I couldn't go back. I couldn't. They're going to take everything away from me."

"Who is?"

"Pauline and Sims."

"But what did you think was going to happen?"

"I thought the merry-go-round was never going to end. That's what I thought. I thought Jules Mendelson was immortal. That's what I thought. Oh, for God's sake, open this fucking bottle for me, Philip. I need a drink."

"Look, I can't deal with you when you're drunk," said Philip. "I have no patience with people who are drunk. I feel no sympathy for them. I have come here to help you, but you are too drunk to understand what I am telling you. If you should pull yourself together, call me. Otherwise, I won't bother you again."

He walked toward the front door.

"How's Camilla?" called out Flo.

"Fine."

"Tell her Flo says thanks."

Philip stopped and turned back to Flo. "Thanks for what?"

"She'll know."

"I want to know."

"She was nice to me at Jules's funeral."

"She never told me that."

"The girl's got class, Philip."

When she ran out of things she needed, like frozen dinners and sanitary napkins, she started to shop at all-night grocery and drug stores. She would leave her house at two o'clock in the morning, when she knew she would run into no one she knew or who would know her. She wrapped her hair in a scarf and wore wraparound dark glasses and drove to the Hughes Market at the intersection of Beverly Boulevard and Doheny Drive. It was when she was pushing her cart through the aisles, past the magazine rack holding the magazine on which her picture was on the cover, that she came upon Lonny Edge, whom she had not seen since her days as a waitress at the Viceroy Coffee Shop.

He was dressed in black, as always, leaning against a counter, reading the article about her in *Mulholland*. To avoid him, she quickly reversed her course, but in turning, her cart accidentally bumped Lonny, and he looked up from the magazine. He recognized her immediately, even though she thought she was unrecognizable.

"Flo! What a coincidence! I was just reading about you," said Lonny.

"Hold it down, will you, Lonny?" said Flo, looking around to make sure no one heard him, even though it was after two in the morning and there was hardly a soul in the market.

"You're a full-fledged celeb," said Lonny.

"That's not the kind of celeb I ever wanted to be, Lonny," said Flo.

"You're out late," said Lonny.

"So are you."

"You know my kind of life, Flo. Normal hours were never part of my trade."

"Are you still making those dirty videos?"

Lonny smiled and shrugged. "They keep telling me I've got star quality."

Flo laughed. "I remember hearing about your star quality."

"Good to see you laugh, Flo. Want a cup of coffee? Or a drink, or something?"

"No, I have to get back," said Flo.

"Sure."

"Good seeing you, Lonny."

"Listen, Flo. I didn't know Jules Mendelson was your, you know, whatever, boyfriend? Until I heard about this piece in *Mulholland.*"

"No reason why you should have known," said Flo. "Not many people did." She turned to go.

"Did you ever meet his son?" Lonny asked her retreating figure.

"His son?" asked Flo, stopping. "Jules Mendelson didn't have a son. I think you've got the wrong guy, Lonny."

"*Step*son, I mean," said Lonny.

"I don't think he had a stepson, either," replied Flo. "I mean, it's the sort of thing I would have known. I was with the guy for five years."

"Spoiled kid. Snotty kid. Named Bippie, or Kippie, or some name like that?"

Flo, hearing the name Kippie, stopped again and looked at Lonny.

"A lot of people thought I was the one who killed Hector Paradiso that night, including that dickhead Manning Einsdorf, because I left Miss Garbo's with Hector. I went home with him, sure. I balled him, sure. I even hit him around a little, because that was what he wanted. But I wasn't the last one to see him that night. The Mendelson stepkid came there before I left, looking for money, a lot of money, and Hector wanted me out of there quick."

Flo stared at Lonny. "Kippie Petworth? Was that his name?"

"Yeah, Kippie Petworth. Snobby little prick."

Thoughts began racing through her head. She remembered the boy called Kippie. Jules had arrived at her house before the sun was up, and woken her. "There is a young man here with me," Jules had said. "Let him sleep on your sofa for a couple of hours. I'll be back to get him."

"But who is he, Jules?" Flo had asked.

"He's the son of some friends of mine."

"Is he in some sort of trouble?" asked Flo.

"Nothing serious. Some kid stuff."

Flo pushed her shopping cart back to where Lonny was standing. "Are you trying to tell me that Kippie Petworth killed Hector Paradiso?" asked Flo, looking about her at the same time and speaking in a low voice, although there were no other customers in the aisle of the market at the time.

"Somebody did. And it wasn't me. And it certainly wasn't suicide, like your friend Jules Mendelson wanted everyone to believe," said Lonny. "You can't shoot yourself five times. Any asshole knows that."

Flo nodded. "I often wondered about that myself. Listen, I have to be off, Lonny. How do I get hold of you if I have to?"

Lonny took out a ballpoint pen from his jacket and wrote a telephone number on the cover of *Mulholland* magazine and then tore the corner off and gave it to Flo. Then he repositioned the magazine back into the rack, putting another issue in front of it so that the torn corner wouldn't show.

On the way back to Azelia Way, Flo thought back on the early morning that Jules had brought the young man called Kippie to her house. Until minutes before, when she met Lonny Edge at the all-night market, she had not thought of him again.

"I can't remember your name," the young man had said the next noon after he had awakened and she came into the living room. She had wanted to go to an AA meeting early that morning, but she wouldn't leave her house with the young stranger in it.

"Flo. Flo March," she had answered.

"Right. Flo March," the young man repeated.

"And I'm not sure I got yours. Kippie? Was that it?"

"Kippie. Right."

"Kippie what?"

"Petworth."

Flo laughed. "That's what I call a pretty fancy name. It's not a name you hear much in the Silverlake district."

"No, no. It's strictly Blue Book," he said and laughed.

When he laughed, it was the first time she had noticed that one of his front teeth was missing.

"I'm afraid I dripped some blood on your sofa," he said.

"Oh, my God," she said, rushing over to pick up one of the cushions of her gray satin sofa. It was covered with blood. "This is a brand-new sofa. It was only delivered yesterday. Do you have any idea how much this fabric cost? It cost ninety-five dollars a yard."

"Just have to have it recovered, I guess," he said. "Jules will pay for it."

"But I've only had it one day," she repeated. "It's brand-new."

"In the meantime, you just turn it over like this, with the blood side down, and nobody will notice the difference." He turned over the cushion and patted the clean unspotted side. "See? Only you and your decorator can tell the difference."

"Yeah," she answered, shaking her head. She was crestfallen that her beautiful new sofa was marred. She was annoyed with Jules that he had brought this careless stranger to her house, especially as he seemed unconcerned with the damage he had done, as if he were used to having things taken care of for him.

"Look, it's pointless to spend time worrying about something so unimportant as the cushion of a sofa," Kippie said, when he realized that she was truly upset over the stains he had made.

She had to admit he had charm and style, the kind of charm and style that is not acquired but innate. She tried to think of a word to describe him. "Adorable" was the word that came to mind. She wondered what he was doing in her house. She wondered why Jules had delivered him to her at six o'clock in the morning and said, "Keep him here until I come back for him. Don't ask any questions."

"Mind if I smoke a joint?" Kippie had asked, taking a joint from his pocket. He reached for a package of matches without waiting for an answer.

"Yes, I do mind," she had answered. "I don't want you to smoke a joint in my house."

He looked at her, surprise on his face. "Isn't that funny? I wouldn't have taken you for a lady who would object," he said.

"There was a time when I wouldn't have, but I do now," Flo said.

"Because I rooked your new sofa?"

"No, because I don't want any dope smoked in my house."

He shrugged and put the joint back in his pocket. "Have you got any orange juice then?"

"I'll squeeze some."

"And coffee?"

"I'll put some on. But don't talk to me like I'm the maid. This is my house you're in, and I'm apparently doing you some kind of favor by letting you stay here," said Flo.

"Did I sound like that? I'm sorry." He covered his mouth with his hand and smiled at her. She could see that he was used to getting his own way, especially with women.

She poured him coffee at the kitchen table, where he seized the *Los Angeles Tribunal* that she had read earlier and left on the table. He seemed inordinately interested in the morning paper. He turned the pages very quickly, scanning each one as if he were looking for something specific. Finally, he pushed the paper away and drank his coffee.

"What are you to Jules Mendelson?" Flo asked.

Kippie Petworth looked at Flo March, but he didn't answer her question. He realized that Jules had told her nothing.

"I asked you a question," said Flo.

"What are *you* to Jules Mendelson?" he asked in return.

Each stared at the other. Neither replied to the other's question. Kippie Petworth had a pretty good idea who Flo March was, but Flo March had no idea who Kippie Petworth was.

Later Jules picked him up, and they left together without exchanging a word between them. Jules never brought up his name. Neither did she. Then, in the excitement of the death of Hector Paradiso, which consumed everyone's conversation for days afterward, she forgot about the young man called Kippie Petworth who had spent six hours in her house, and she never, for even an instant, formed a connection in her mind between him and the death of Hector.

When she had called Nellie Potts to tell her that she needed more of the gray satin fabric to recover one of her cushions on the new sofa, Nellie told her that the fabric company was temporarily out of stock, but she would let her know when it became available again.

The next morning Flo checked her date book. The day that Jules had brought Kippie to her house at six o'clock in the morning was, indeed, the same day that Hector Paradiso was found dead. She remembered also that Jules had been annoyed with her for attending Hector's funeral. She realized that if she had not gone to the all-night market and run into Lonny Edge, whom she had tried to avoid, she might never have realized that it was Pauline Mendelson's son by a previous marriage who was hidden in her house while Jules made the arrangement to cover up the murder he had committed. She remembered the young man's charm and style, the kind of charm and style he could only have inherited from his mother. The knowledge was comforting to her.

"There's something I want you to do for me, Sims," said Flo, when she called Sims Lord later in the day.

"What's that?" asked Sims. The tone of his voice was chilly.

"I want to meet with Pauline Mendelson," she said.

"Oh, come on, Flo. Be practical. Pauline Mendelson will never meet with you," said Sims.

"Perhaps you should tell her that I have some information that might be of great interest to her," said Flo.

"Forget about Pauline. That's a hopeless cause. She thinks you ruined her life. She'll never let up on you."

"Tell the great lady she's going to be very very sorry if she doesn't come and see me, Sims." When he did not reply, she added, "Tell her it has to do with Kippie."

"What about Kippie?" he asked. In the years he had been the lawyer and confidant of Jules Mendelson, he had been involved in getting Kippie Petworth out of a great many scrapes.

"I'm not talking to you anymore, Sims. She's the one I want to talk to."

"Never. Never, never, never," said Pauline. "There is no way I would meet with her. With people like that, it's blackmail. It's all about money."

"She said—" said Sims.

"I don't care what she said," said Pauline.

"She said it had to do with Kippie," continued Sims.

There was a silence. "With Kippie?" she replied. Pauline Mendelson was not the type of woman who perspired, but she felt moisture in her armpits when she heard her son's name, as having come from the lips of Flo March. She remembered the last thing she had said to Jules before he died. "Does anyone else know, Jules?" she had asked, but he had died without answering her. She remembered Kippie's telephone call after Jules had died. "I know everything," she had said to him. "About Flo March?" Kippie had answered.

That afternoon the Reverend Doctor Rufus Browning, of the All Saints

Episcopal Church in Beverly Hills, came to have tea with Pauline in the library at Clouds. She could not bring herself to tell anyone what she knew about her son, not even her father, whom she trusted implicitly, or either of her sisters, or Camilla Ebury, and certainly not Rose Cliveden. Rufus Browning was a great admirer of Pauline Mendelson's, and relished his role as her spiritual adviser. On those occasions during the year when she attended his Sunday services, she always called him Dr. Browning when they spoke on the steps of the church after the service, but in her library, on those occasions when he came for tea, she always called him Rufus. It was not lost on either Blondell or Dudley that Mrs. Mendelson had been crying during the hour and a half that she remained behind closed doors in the library with Dr. Browning. Afterward, she telephoned Sims Lord at his office.

"I'll see her," said Pauline. "But not in my house. I do not want her here. And I will most certainly not go to her house."

"We can meet in Jules's office," said Sims.

"I will go to court, Mrs. Mendelson," said Flo. "I have these papers that Jules signed. You will notice on these photocopies that they were witnessed by Olaf Pederson and Margaret Maple, and Sims Lord's name is right here in the letter."

"Those papers were delivered within hours of my husband's death and will not stand up in court. I have been assured of that by some of the finest legal minds in the country," replied Pauline. The words she said were the words Sims Lord had coached her to say, but even she could hear that the force and power she had acquired since Jules's death were missing from her tone. "My husband was coerced by you into signing those papers. You insinuated your way into the hospital, first pretending to be his daughter, and then dressing yourself up as a nurse. There are ample witnesses at the hospital who will testify to that. I hold you responsible for my husband's death."

Flo nodded, calmly. The two women whom Jules had loved stared at each other. Flo realized that she had the upper hand. "Jules's health had been failing for more than a year, Mrs. Mendelson," said Flo. "And you know that to be true as well as I do. So don't blame me for his death. In case you're interested, which I'm sure you're not, the ambulance attendants will tell you I saved his life. And if you're looking for someone to blame, blame Arnie Zwillman for telling Myles Crocker about the girl who went off the balcony in Chicago in nineteen fifty-three, and blame Myles Crocker for telling Jules that the Brussels appointment was off, about two hours before his heart attack."

Pauline remained silent, devastated that Flo knew more about her husband than she did.

Flo rose, as if she were about to leave. "I know a great deal about Jules, Mrs. Mendelson," she said to Pauline.

"Ignore her, Pauline," said Sims. His tone of voice was icy. "This is a woman who was paid handsomely for sexual favors and is looking for a free ride for life."

"I'm not talking to you, Sims," said Flo. She made no effort to hide the contempt in her voice. "I'm on to you. I've been on to you ever since you pulled out your dick after Jules died, and thought I was the kind of girl who'd drop to my knees."

Sims turned to Pauline. "You must understand the kind of person this is, Pauline. She would stoop to anything."

Pauline was not unaware of a controlled reddening of Sims Lord's face. She nodded.

"I don't believe that Miss March knows anything," continued Sims.

"Miss March knows who killed Hector Paradiso, for one thing," said Flo. She ignored Sims Lord and directed what she was about to say to Pauline. "Miss March knows because Mr. Mendelson brought the killer to her house to hide out for six hours on the early morning of the murder, while he went about the business of covering up the murder and making it appear to be a suicide."

Pauline turned pale but remained silent.

"No one would ever believe such a thing," said Sims.

"They would if they tested the blood samples on one of the cushions of my gray satin sofa, caused by dripping blood from a missing front tooth," said Flo. Her eyes never left Pauline's as she spoke. Pauline dropped her eyes and looked away.

"I'm not asking for much, Mrs. Mendelson. I'm just asking for what Jules wanted me to have. The house on Azelia Way and an income from one of his investments to continue to live in the style in which he wanted me to live. That's all. Not one cent more. With your kind of bucks, that's not much. Think it over. And should you ever wish to talk privately with me, without Sims hovering, Miss Maple will give you my number."

She opened the door of Jules's conference room and walked out.

Sims and Pauline sat in silence for a few moments.

"Pay her off, Sims. Give her what she wants. God knows, I can afford it," said Pauline.

"It never ends, once you start, you know," said Sims, finally.

"Pay her," repeated Pauline.

"It is a mistake, Pauline," said Sims.

"What do you mean?" asked Pauline. She was shaken by her encounter with Flo.

"You agree to this now, next year she'll come back for more. It's a form of blackmail. I've seen cases like this before. What was that she was talking about? The missing tooth? The blood on the cushion? I didn't understand that."

Pauline shook her head. "I don't know," she said.

"I've concluded that not only is she a liar, but she's delusional, money-hungry, and a danger to you and the memory of Jules," said Sims.

"Are you saying we shouldn't pay her?" asked Pauline.

"Isn't that what you wanted?" asked Sims in turn.

"But I thought you were in favor of honoring the agreements Jules made," said Pauline.

"Not anymore," replied Sims, flatly.

Pauline, troubled, nodded. She was afraid to pursue the subject for fear of having Kippie's name come up. She gathered her bag and rose. At the door of Jules's office, she turned back to Sims.

"What will happen to her, do you suppose?" she asked.

"She'll fall into oblivion, never to be heard from again, no doubt."

Flo's Tape #23

"*Jules always separated his married life from his life with me. He didn't like to talk about Pauline with me, and I respected that in him, but I picked up a lot about her over the five years I was Jules's mistress, in bits and pieces, and put them all together. You talk about a privileged life. She had a privileged life, all her life. When she was sixteen, for instance, she was at this fancy girls' school in Virginia, I can't remember the name, where all the girls rode horses, and she was such a good rider and jumper that she entered the horse show at Madison Square Garden in New York and got a blue ribbon or whatever they give for the first prize. Stuff like that. She seemed to do everything just right. The only mistake she ever made was marrying that first husband of hers, because she was destined for bigger things than him.*

"*Listen, I have to be practical. She was the perfect wife for Jules. It's too bad we couldn't have worked out some kind of arrangement between the three of us, like they do in those European marriages. I would have settled for that in a minute. Everyone always said what a wonderful woman she was. I guess she was, until she heard about me. I suppose if I were in her shoes, I would have hated me too.*"

24

IN A SHORT TIME, the news of the financial plight of Flo March reached the
ears of Cyril Rathbone. Other people's plights—divorce, job loss, cancer,
AIDS, bankruptcy, arrests, suicide, adultery, and perversion—were Cyril
Rathbone's fortune, and while he listened to these tales of woe, as reported to
him by informants, he always said such concerned things as, "Oh, dear, how
sad, how frightfully sad," but his mind was working at the same time on the
manner in which he would report the news in his column. As he once said to
his great friend Hector Paradiso, "What is the point of a secret if it is kept a
secret?" Such sadnesses were the mainstay of his column, far more than his
reportage of parties and openings and social doings. They were the very reason
people tore to his page of the magazine first.

In the case of Flo March, however, his plans were more grandiose, going
far beyond mere mentions in his column, because the names in her plight,
Pauline and Jules Mendelson and the glittering group of greats and near-greats
with whom they moved, were so celebrated. The girl, poor silly creature, was
sitting on a gold mine and couldn't be made to realize it. Although Flo had not
been a waitress for five years, Cyril never could resist referring to her as "the
former waitress Flo March," as if that explained her inability to understand the
power of her position. A book deal and a miniseries flashed through his mind.
He even visualized her appearing on "After Midnight," the late-night Amos
Swank show, all done up in one of her Chanel suits, telling about the mean
Pauline Mendelson, who was doing her out of her rightful inheritance. Such an
appearance, he knew, would guarantee that her book, if she could be induced
to participate in one, would soar to the top of the best-seller lists across the
country. The possibilities for promotion were staggering.

It was the great star Faye Converse, who cared about Flo, her neighbor,
but didn't want to get involved in her situation—"After all, I hardly know her,
poor thing, I only met her on that night she killed my dog"—who told Cyril
that Flo rarely rose from her bed, and that unopened bills were piling up in
great stacks on the floor of the front hall. "I don't think she can afford to stay
on in that house much longer."

"But how do you know such things?" asked Cyril, disguising his delight
over the report with a somber tone.

"Glyceria, my maid Glyceria, is devoted to her," said Faye about her
neighbor. Faye Converse, who always told interviewers she didn't like gossip,

lowered her voice to a whisper and looked about her, although she was alone at the time, in her own house, and whispered into the telephone, "I think she drinks." Then she looked about her again and said, "She is positively catatonic, poor thing."

Later that day, Cyril called Flo March and left a message on her answering machine saying that it was a matter of utmost importance that she call him. He felt sure that he would hear from Flo. But she did not return his call.

Instead, in a stroke of luck that he took to be a sign from above, as he called it, he ran into her. Cyril Rathbone put a great deal of stock in signs from above. "It was meant to be," he often said, in psychic tones. Or, "There are no accidents." Early the very next morning Flo walked into the Viceroy Coffee Shop, where he happened to be having breakfast. She stood timidly inside the door, unsure where to sit. She was, she thought, incognito, wearing large dark glasses, with her red hair completely covered by a scarf, but Cyril picked her out right away, encompassed as she was in an air of melancholy.

"Is Curly here?" she asked the cashier.

"Curly? I don't know no Curly," said the cashier.

"Belle? Where's Belle's station?" asked Flo.

"Belle don't work here no more," said the cashier.

Flo had not been to the Viceroy since she walked out of it five years before, when Jules Mendelson took her to Paris, and their love affair started. He had not wanted her to go back there, and she hadn't, although for a while she kept in touch with Curly and Belle. She stood, undecided whether to stay or leave, and then moved to a stool at the counter and ordered a cup of coffee. The waitress who took her order was new since she had worked there and did not know her. Cyril noticed that her hand shook when she raised the cup of coffee to her lips. She put it down and took out a cigarette from her gold case with the name FLO written on it in sapphires, and her hand shook again when she attempted to light the cigarette with her matching gold lighter. He knew the time had come.

Without a word to Joel Zircon, with whom he was having breakfast, Cyril picked up his cup of coffee and crossed from the booth around the counter to where she was sitting. "Good morning, Miss March," he said. "What an early hour for you to be up and about. I always imagined you were one of those ladies of leisure who sleeps late and has breakfast in bed on a tray with Porthault place mats."

She looked up at Cyril Rathbone but did not reply.

He seated himself on the stool next to her. "I heard you ask for Curly," he said.

"Yes, I did," she answered.

"Dead, poor fellow."

"Dead?" She gasped and covered her mouth with her hand.

"Oh, yes. AIDS. Terribly sad. He took pills toward the end. What's that new sleeping pill everyone's taking? Halcion, isn't it? That's what he took. A marvelous decision of Curly's, don't you think?" asked Cyril.

"No, no. I don't think that at all," answered Flo.

"It's very important to know when not to exceed one's span. Curly understood that. All his friends were with him when he did it. I understand it was a glorious experience."

Flo looked at Cyril Rathbone and shook her head in disagreement. "I hadn't heard any of that. I'd kind of lost touch. I didn't even know he was sick. Poor Curly. What about Belle?"

"She went over to Nibblers Coffee Shop on Wilshire Boulevard," said Cyril. "She didn't want to stay here after Curly died. They were great friends."

"I know."

"This is West Hollywood, after all, Miss March. People come. People go. Nothing lasts."

"I suppose." She signaled to the waitress. "Check, please."

The waitress handed her the check for the coffee.

"Stay, stay. Have another cup of coffee," he said.

"Thank you, but I can't. I have things to do," she said.

"No, you don't," he replied. When she looked sharply at him, he smiled at her. She didn't have anything to do. "Please pour Miss March another cup of coffee, will you, Maureen?" He picked up the check that the waitress had left on the counter. "I know you're broke," he said.

"Not that broke," replied Flo, taking the check back from him with an abrupt gesture.

"It occurred to me that perhaps you had come here at this very early hour to try to get your old job back."

"Wrong," she replied. She opened her bag and took out a dollar tip to leave the waitress, as if that proved she was not broke.

"Pretty ring," he said, pointing to the sapphire-and-diamond ring that Jules had given her. "That should keep the wolf from the door for quite a few months."

"Oh, no. I'll never sell this ring," said Flo, looking at her ring. "No matter what. When I die, this ring is still going to be on my finger."

"A lovely young woman like you shouldn't talk about dying, Miss March. You have an extraordinary life ahead of you, if you play your cards right," said Cyril. Their eyes met. He lifted her hand and gazed at the ring. "A gift from Jules Mendelson, I assume?" he asked.

Flo did not reply. She inhaled deeply on her cigarette and stubbed it out in an ashtray.

"Very bad for you, smoking," he said.

She stood up, preparing to leave.

"Your plight has been made known to me," he said, wanting to detain her.

"My plight?"

"Your financial problems."

"Oh, I see. By whom?"

"Oh, heavens, Miss March," said Cyril. He spoke in his acquired upper-class English voice that he knew intimidated some people. "A good journalist never reveals his sources. Anyway, it doesn't matter. What matters is that it seems so appropriate that we should meet like this, by accident, here at the Viceroy Coffee Shop, where your great romance began. Of course, as we both know, there are no accidents. It was meant to be, that you should walk in here like this. Don't you agree?"

Flo, confused, stared at Cyril Rathbone, not knowing whether to stay and listen or get up and leave. "I guess so," she replied to his question, not sure whether she agreed or not.

"You are holding so many trump cards, it is a shame for you to fall apart the way you are apparently doing. I have a plan to suggest to you."

"What sort of plan?"

"Sit down, Flo. I assume I may call you Flo? It seems so formal to call you Miss March." He stood up and indicated with a flourish of his hand for her to reseat herself. After a moment, she sat down. "Why don't you take off your dark glasses so I can see your eyes?"

"My eyes are puffy," she said.

He nodded his head in a concerned fashion. "I heard you were drinking," he said.

She was frightened of him. She made no reply.

"All that fine wine from the Bresciani auction," he said. "Rare stuff, I've heard."

"I've run out of all that fine wine from the Bresciani auction," she replied.

"My, you have been drinking. Those gallon bottles of Soave from the Hughes Market must have a bitter taste after the delights of Jules Mendelson's cellar."

"What is it you want from me, Mr. Rathbone?"

"So formal, Flo. It's Cyril, please."

"What is it you want?"

"What you need first is a good lawyer," he said. "And not a Waspy frigid-type like Sims Lord. He's no friend of yours, as you may have discovered by now. He is, in fact, the leader of the opposition. Am I correct?"

Flo, riveted, nodded.

"Next, you need a good agent. And then you need a good writer. I, of course, am your writer. Your Boswell, if you will, your poet laureate. My friend Joel Zircon, over there in the booth by the window, with his head buried in the Hollywood trade papers, scarfing down the bagel and lox and slurping his coffee, can be your agent. You must remember Joel? From your waitress days? He certainly remembers you. Ghastly table manners, to be sure. Eats like a pig. But terribly clever in his chosen career. Mona Berg, the queen of Hollywood agents, increasingly relies on him. He is a young man on the way up. Joel probably even knows exactly the right lawyer for you."

"But what do I need a lawyer, an agent, and a writer for?" Flo asked.

"For your book, and your miniseries, which I am going to write in your name," said Cyril.

"What book?"

"*Jules's Mistress.* You see, I already have your title, Flo. All those bills that are piling up in your front hall, stacks of them, I hear. Now you'll be able to pay them."

Flo stared at Cyril.

Rose Cliveden had become habitually intemperate. Among themselves, her friends complained and murmured that something simply had to be done, but no one had the nerve to speak up, as Rose could not bear criticism. Instead, certain of her friends stopped inviting her. Madge White, for one, said Rose spilled red wine all over her Aubusson carpet that had been left to her by her grandmother, and ruined it, absolutely ruined it, and she would never, ever, have Rose in her house again. And Millicent Pond, Sandy Pond's mother, the matriarch of the newspaper family, complained bitterly that Rose constantly interrupted one of the former Presidents at a dinner at her house when he was trying to explain the present administration's policy in Nicaragua, and she wasn't going to have Rose back, even though she'd known her all her life. And Faye Converse, who was tolerant of everyone, was furious with Rose because she dropped and smashed two Baccarat glasses on the marble floor of her lanai, and Faye's maid, Glyceria, who vacuumed barefoot, cut her toe badly on a piece of broken glass and threatened to quit if Rose came to the house again.

When she dropped a cigarette in her bed and caused a fire in her bedroom, as well as minor burns to her arms and legs, after having drunk ten vodkas at a charity ball, Pauline and Camilla and even Madge, who relented, decided that the time had come for them to intervene in Rose's life and send her to a clinic in Palm Springs to deal with her addiction to alcohol. Rose claimed that she had no such problem. When the moment came to intervene, all of them became silent and were afraid to say to Rose what they had said about her behind her back.

"I've been dying to do that room over, anyway," said Rose to her friends, not daring to admit how frightening the experience had been for her. "I was so sick of those damn purple violets in the wallpaper and the curtains. No more chintz for me. I've had it with chintz."

"I think we're getting off the subject here, Rose," said Pauline. "I called the people at Betty Ford. They're booked ahead for months, but they will make an exception and take you immediately."

Rose was horrified at the suggestion. "All those movie stars, with their drugs, telling those terrible stories. I read about them in the *Enquirer*. That's not for me, thank you very much. Making your own bed. Mopping your own floor. Sharing a room with God-knows-who, from God-knows-where. Puleeze!"

"Either you go there, Rose, or we, who are the only friends you have left, are going to abandon you, too. Your life is out of control," said Pauline.

"No, no, I'll just stop. It's as simple as that. I mean, I stop every Lent."

Pauline, exasperated, turned to Camilla. Camilla smiled but said nothing. "Fine then. Stop. But leave me alone until you do. Don't call me. I don't want to hear from you, Rose," said Pauline. They were at the Los Angeles Country Club. She got up from the table and left, pleading an appointment with Sims Lord.

Rose was shocked by the harshness of Pauline's tone. Her great friend had never spoken to her in such a manner before.

"She's not herself. She hasn't been herself for weeks," said Camilla, in defense of her friend.

"Pauline's become bitter," Rose said, as a way of avoiding the issue about herself. "All that business about that whore Jules was involved with."

"She's not a whore," said Camilla. The picture of the husband-grabbing hussy that Pauline's friends perpetuated when discussing Flo was in conflict with Camilla's remembrance of the pretty young woman she had met in Philip's room at the Chateau Marmont and had later hugged at Jules's funeral.

"Pauline's changed," continued Rose. "Don't you feel it? She's gotten terribly tough."

"You're only changing the subject again, Rose," Camilla said shyly. "Pauline is right. She's the only one of us who had the guts to say what she said. Madge wouldn't. Even Archbishop Cooning wouldn't. You simply have to do something, Rose. You'll be dead if you don't. None of us can remember when you haven't had an arm in a sling, or been on crutches, or a walker, or a cane, all from falls when you were loaded. This time you could have burned to death. Thank God your fire-alarm system was working."

Rose, unexpectedly, started to cry.

"You should talk to Philip," suggested Camilla.

"Philip? Your Philip? That good-looking young man? I'm always happy to talk to Philip. But why?"

"Are you going to be home at six?"

"I think so. Why?"

"I'm going to send Philip over. Just talk to him, Rose. Listen to what he has to say. And don't interrupt him, the way you always interrupt everybody, like the former President. I hear the President's wife was furious with you. Please. Do it for me."

In the beginning the arrangement between Flo and Cyril was felicitous. Joel Zircon approached several publishers and related back to Flo and Cyril that there was immense interest in *Jules's Mistress*.

"What they want is an opening chapter and an outline for the rest of the book," Joel reported. "After that, we make the deal."

"What kind of money are they talking?" asked Cyril.

"In the six figures, at least," said Joel.

That was also what Flo wanted to know but couldn't bring herself to ask. Her pool man had left her a note that morning, saying that he wouldn't be able to come anymore, as he hadn't been paid for his services. She feared that other services she had long taken for granted were going to be cut off. Whenever she thought of her financial situation, a feeling of desolation and hopelessness came over her. She had begun to realize that her only salvation was with Cyril Rathbone.

"I could always go back to modeling," she said to Cyril one day, as if she had other alternatives in her life to the one that he was offering her.

"You were never *in* modeling, Flo," answered Cyril. "This is a time for you to be practical about your future. Jules is not here anymore to take care of you. You have to think of taking care of yourself."

They met late each afternoon after Cyril finished his column for *Mulholland*. He came to her house for two hours with his tape recorder, before he went home to dress for whatever dinner or screening he was going to attend that evening. He asked her questions. At first she was guarded in her answers, always protective of Jules. She was critical about herself. "I was stupid about money. Jules was very generous with me. I spent, spent, spent," she said. "If I had saved something each week, when that enormous check came, I wouldn't be in the jam I'm in now."

"Allow me to play devil's advocate for a moment, Flo," said Cyril.

Flo wasn't exactly sure what devil's advocate meant, but she nodded in agreement for Cyril to play it.

"Did it ever occur to you that that was the way Jules liked it?" he asked.

"What do you mean?"

"As long as you didn't have any real money, you wouldn't ever leave him. After all, Jules's money was limitless. Your weekly spending sprees were nothing to him. So your curtains cost forty thousand dollars. So your new closet cost forty thousand more. So this gray satin fabric cost ninety-five dollars a yard. So what? That was peanuts for Jules. So were all your Chanel suits. Did he ever buy you a valuable picture that you could sell? No. He didn't give you any equity, Flo. Think about it."

"But he wanted to take care of me," insisted Flo.

"But he didn't, did he?"

"Yes, yes, I have these papers. Look."

"Delivered on the day of his death, Flo. Wise up. Jules was a very brilliant man. He had to know that Pauline could do what she's doing and every court in the land would agree with her. He had five years to do what he waited until the last day of his life to do."

Flo's eyes filled with tears. She could not bear to think that Jules deprived her in order to hang onto her. "I blame everything on Sims Lord," she said.

"Sims Lord is just a very high-priced hired hand, Flo. He's only doing what first Jules told him to do and now what Pauline is telling him to do," said Cyril.

"He wanted to set me up and I turned him down," replied Flo.

"Set you up how?"

"As his lady friend."

Cyril remained perfectly still. He had learned never to exclaim with pleasure when someone he was interviewing began to reveal something that the person had no intention of revealing. He merely nodded, as if what she was saying was of no more interest to him than anything else she was saying.

"Right here, on this same sofa," said Flo. She patted the cushion next to her, the same cushion with Kippie Petworth's blood on the reverse side, about which she had not told Cyril yet. "About a month after Jules died. He came here to tell me the estate wasn't going to honor the agreements Jules made for me."

"And he came on to you at the same time, did you say?"

"Oh, yes."

"Held your hand, or something?"

"Held my hand, Cyril? He put my hand on his dick. And he was supposed to be Jules's best friend. And Jules was only dead a month."

"And what did you do?"

"Took it away, of course."

"And what did he do?"

"Took it out."

"Took what out?"

"His dick."

"No!"

"Yes! Like I was supposed to go into raptures over it."

Cyril was beside himself.

"Let me tell you something about Jules," said Flo. "He was a gentleman with me. I knew he had the hots for me from the day we met in the coffee shop, but he never laid a hand on me until he took me to Paris. That was the first time."

"Yes, yes, you've already told me that. Let's get back to Sims Lord for a moment."

In time, as orchestrated by Cyril Rathbone and Joel Zircon, the word was about that Flo March, the one-time waitress who had become the mistress of Jules Mendelson, was writing her memoirs, to be entitled *Jules's Mistress*. By design, Cyril's name was never mentioned as her collaborator. It was reported that Flo was dictating her remembrances into microcassettes, and that already there were forty hours recorded.

"Flo March is prepared to tell all," wrote Army Archerd in *Daily Variety*. "Her story promises to be hot, hot, hot," wrote George Christy in the *Hollywood Reporter*. Cyril Rathbone, echoing both of the above in his column in *Mulholland,* could not resist adding, "Arnie Zwillman, are you listening?"

"But why did you say that about Arnie Zwillman?" cried Flo, after she read Cyril's column.

"It's called creating a market," answered Cyril, in a patient tone of voice. He spoke to Flo as if he were a great teacher and she a backward pupil.

"But Arnie Zwillman is a very dangerous man," said Flo. There was an element of fear in her voice. "I know for a fact what he did to Jules. He destroyed his chances of going to Brussels, just like that, overnight. You can't fool around with a man like Arnie Zwillman."

"Believe me, you have nothing to worry about, Flo," said Cyril.

"I wouldn't be too sure about that, Cyril."

"Joel Zircon says his phones are ringing off the hook. Publishers can't wait to get their hands on the outline."

"What's taking you so long to write the first chapter and the outline? I've done forty hours of tapes. How much do you need?"

"Patience, Flo. Patience," said Cyril.

That night, late, a car drove up the driveway of Flo's house on Azelia Way. She was alone, as she was always alone those nights, and could hear the sound of the tires on the gravel of her driveway. She couldn't imagine who would be coming to call at such an hour. She could hear the sound of the engine running. Waiting, she expected her doorbell to ring, but it didn't. Her curtains were drawn, and she opened them just enough to peek outside. A car, which she at first thought was Jules's Bentley, was sitting there, idling, with the headlights on and the engine running. Then she realized it was a different color than Jules's car, a color that looked like gold. She saw also from the grille that it was not a Bentley but a Rolls-Royce. In the front seat sat two men who were looking at her house. A feeling of panic gripped her. She quickly closed the curtains. On tiptoe, she went to the front door and double-bolted it. She went through her whole house, closing curtains and making sure doors and windows were locked. After twenty-five minutes, she heard the car turn around in her driveway and pull out.

She waited for fifteen minutes more and then peered out of the curtains again. The car was gone. Everything appeared normal. She went to the front door and listened. There was no sound. Very quietly she unbolted the lock and, with the chain still on, opened the door a crack to look outside. Everything was quiet. As she closed the door again, she saw a white box that had been left on her doormat. She opened the door just wide enough to grab the package and then slammed the door again and bolted it.

In her living room, she opened the box. There was a card in an envelope, which she opened. "It's loaded," the card read. "Put it in your mouth and fire it." The note, typed, was unsigned. She removed the pale pink tissue paper. There, nestled, was a small gun. For a long time she stared at it. Then she picked it up. She could not believe that it was loaded, but she did not know enough about guns to know how to open it to check. Using both hands, she pointed the gun at the sliding glass window that opened onto her terrace and swimming pool. After several moments of indecision, she pulled the trigger, and the gun fired. The noise was deafening. The plate-glass window splintered in all directions.

She could not move from her place on the sofa. Her body was soaked with perspiration. Her breathing was heavy. She felt a different sort of fear than the fear she had felt from having no money. For reasons which she could not explain to herself at that moment, she thought of Marilyn Monroe. "They got rid of Marilyn," she remembered saying to Jules at the steak house in the Valley.

The next morning, still shaken from her experience of the night before, Flo went back to the AA meeting in the log cabin on Robertson Boulevard. She had not been there for several months, but she knew that she had to begin to put her life in order again. She wore her huge dark glasses and her hair was wrapped in a scarf. She sat away from the other people, drank a cup of coffee, smoked a cigarette, and looked around for Philip Quennell, but she did not see him. At first she was disappointed that he was not there, because she had parted from him so badly the last time he went to her house to try to help her, but then she was relieved. If he had been there, she might not have been able to do what she decided to do.

She had never raised her hand to share at a meeting before, but that morning she felt the need to speak. She raised her hand in such a tentative fashion that the speaker did not notice her at first and called on several other people. Then, when she decided that she would not raise her hand again, the speaker called on her. "The lady with the dark glasses and head scarf," he said, pointing at her.

Flo knew that she could not use her own name, even her first name, because she had become notorious. "My name is, uh, Fleurette," she said. She had always hated her real name. Even before she learned about the ways of elegant life from Jules Mendelson, she thought her real name sounded cheap, and she spoke it in a muffled voice, as she did the next words, "I am an alcoholic and chemically dependent." She looked about her, still wearing her impenetrable dark glasses, frightened. The room was silent. "I had almost a year in the program, and then I had a slip. This is my first day back."

There was applause from the group, who were celebrated for their tolerance of the transgressions of their members. Encouraged by their friendliness, Flo began to talk. She said that she had been a kept woman. "I am a mistress. Or, rather, I was a mistress. I hate that word, but it's what I am. I have been kept by a very rich man for five years. When I first met Mr. So and So, I didn't have a pot to pee in, or a window to throw it out of."

She said that she knew his business secrets and the deals she had heard when he made telephone calls from her bed during the afternoons after they made love. She discussed his heart attack and his death. She said that she had lived the life of a princess for five years but that now she was broke and about to lose the house that she thought had been put in her name. She said she knew about a covered-up murder and who the murderer was. She could not stop talking.

In a corner of the room, also disguised with dark glasses and a head scarf, was Rose Cliveden. Her hands were still bandaged from the burns she had suffered when her bed caught on fire. She had refused to go to the clinic in Palm Springs, as suggested by her friends, but, after meeting with Philip Quennell, she had agreed to go to AA meetings for two or three weeks. On this particular morning, he had promised to meet her there at the log cabin, as he guaranteed that she was unlikely to see anyone she knew, as she might at one of the more fashionable meetings in Beverly Hills, but, to her annoyance, he had not appeared. She could not relate to any of the stories told by any of the people who had shared their experiences. "I have nothing in common with any of these people," she thought to herself, as she gathered her bag and prepared to leave.

It was then, while she was slowly walking out of the frightful little room, as she later described it, that the woman called Fleurette began to speak. Rose was already at the door, tiptoeing out, when it suddenly dawned on her, when she heard the words *gangster* and *President of the United States,* that Fleurette, with the dark glasses and the good-looking suit, was none other than the infamous and notorious Flo March, who had brought such unhappiness to the life of Pauline Mendelson. Riveted, she stared at her.

"My God," thought Rose. "That's the same woman I saw outside the church talking to Jules at Hector Paradiso's funeral last year. And the one from Jules's funeral." As if she were in a theater at a play, where the second act suddenly began to show more promise than the first act had, she tiptoed back to the seat that she had abandoned and sat, rapt, throughout Flo March's sharing.

Philip Quennell, who regularly attended the early-morning meetings at the log cabin on Robertson Boulevard, arrived very late that morning. An unexpected telephone call from Lonny Edge, complaining bitterly about a description of himself that had appeared in Hortense Madden's account in *Mulholland* of his possession of the manuscript of Basil Plant's supposedly unfinished novel, had caused the owners of the bungalow where he lived on Cahuenga Boulevard to serve notice that he must vacate the premises by the first of the month.

"On what grounds?" Philip asked.

"They said the article insinuated that I was using my apartment for purposes of prostitution. I mean, I only turn a couple of tricks a week in my apartment. Most of my work I do elsewhere, in my clients' homes. But I don't exactly want to go to court over it, if you know what I mean," said Lonny.

"Listen, Lonny. I have to be somewhere. I can't talk now. I'll call you back later," said Philip.

"You giving me the runaround, Philip? You're the one who got me into all this about that fucking manuscript that was just sitting on my table peaceably for three years, until you came along and began stirring things up."

"No, I'm not giving you the runaround, Lonny. I just promised somebody I'd be somewhere. I'll call you later."

Philip arrived at the meeting as it was breaking up.

"I'm so sorry, Rose," he said, when he saw her. Knowing how spoiled she was, he expected her either to have left or to be in a foul mood with him for suggesting that she meet him on Robertson Boulevard at seven o'clock in the morning and then not showing up. "I had a sort of emergency telephone call that I had to attend to. How did the meeting go? At least you stayed to the end."

"Darling, it was fascinating, absolutely fascinating!" said Rose. He had never seen her so animated, except when she was drunk. "You have no idea what you missed. You won't *believe* who spoke."

"Who?" asked Philip, confused by her enthusiasm.

"Flo March!" she said.

Philip, surprised, looked at her.

"She's the one who was Jules Mendelson's mistress," said Rose, in explanation. "My dear, the things she said! I'm *sick* you weren't here."

"Rose, would you like to go out for a cup of coffee with me," said Philip. "We have to talk."

"Oh, no, I can't, darling. I have things to do," she said. "But I'll be back tomorrow. Every morning. It's fascinating. Better than the movies. Why didn't you tell me it's so fascinating?"

"Listen, Rose. You do know, don't you, that what you hear in these rooms must never leave these rooms," said Philip.

"What does that mean?" asked Rose.

"It means that you mustn't discuss what you've heard here, or tell the names of any of the people you might have seen here. That's why it's called Anonymous."

"Oh, darling, my lips are sealed," said Rose. She could not take her eyes off Flo and squinted to better take her in. "Pretty little thing, isn't she? You'd never know she was only a waitress, would you? See you tomorrow, darling. Love to Camilla. Big hug." She blew Philip a kiss and ran off.

Flo was surrounded by people. Unused to such friendliness, she smiled nervously as she accepted their thanks for her sharing with them. Several people offered to give her their telephone numbers. When she looked up, she was glad to see Philip standing there.

"Oh, Philip," she said, breaking away.

"Hello, Flo," he said.

"Are you still mad at me?"

"Of course, I'm not mad at you."

"You were the last time I saw you. I was afraid you'd given up on me."

"Never," he said, smiling at her. "I'm delighted you came back."

"I looked for you earlier, but I didn't see you."

"I just got here. I was very late."

"Philip, I raised my hand," she said, proudly. "I actually spoke up at a meeting for the first time."

"I heard. I'm sorry I missed you. How do you feel?"

"Wonderful. Everyone was so nice."

"What made you come back today? What made you speak up for the first time?"

"Something happened," she said. She looked up at him. Although he could not see her eyes through her dark glasses, he felt that something was wrong.

"Would you want to go out for a cup of coffee and talk?"

"Sure," she said. "But I'd rather you came up to my house for a cup of coffee. I want to show you something."

Inside her house, she showed him the note, the gun, and the splintered plate glass window.

"Good God," he said. "Did you get a look at the car?"

"I think it was a Rolls-Royce. I peeked out those curtains at it. It was eerie. Two men sat in the front seat with the motor running and the lights on and just stared at the house. I think the car was gold, or some shade of yellow," she said.

"I'll tell you who has a gold Rolls-Royce," said Philip.

"Who?"

"Arnie Zwillman. I saw it one night at Casper Stieglitz's house, when Jules and Pauline were there."

Flo shivered. "Arnie Zwillman?"

"Do you know him?"

"He tried to get Jules to launder money," she said. "When Jules turned him down, he called the State Department and told them something about Jules that had happened years ago in Chicago that I can't tell you about, and the State Department told Jules, just an hour before his heart attack here, that he wasn't going to get the job as head of the American commission to Brussels."

"Were you planning to put all that in your book?" asked Philip.

Flo, embarrassed, nodded. "That's the kind of stuff my collaborator is interested in."

"You're playing with fire, Flo. You must know that. Arnie Zwillman is not a swell guy."

"I'm broke, Philip. I need bucks. My pool man quit. The telephone company is dunning me. That third-rate actor who owns this house wants me out. I don't have any choice."

"And Pauline won't help?"

"You must be kidding."

"Let me ask you a question, Flo. If you had the money that Jules wanted to leave you, would you still be writing this book?"

"Of course not," said Flo.

"That's what I wanted to hear you say," said Philip. "You wouldn't mind if I interfered a little bit in my own private way, would you?"

"How?"

"I can't tell you that yet. Trust me."

As Philip was leaving, Flo followed him to the door. "You wouldn't want to move in here with me, would you, Philip? No strings attached. Not like it was between us at the Chateau Marmont. You in that room. Me in here."

"Somehow I don't think that would go over very well with Camilla," said Philip, smiling.

Flo laughed. "No, I suppose not."

"It's nice to see you laugh, Flo."

"Before I used to be afraid because there was no money anymore. Now I'm just afraid."

At the same time that Philip was with Flo, Rose Cliveden called Pauline Mendelson, whom she hadn't spoken to since her outburst over lunch at the Los Angeles Country Club. "My dear, I have the most riveting thing to tell you," she said. "You won't believe who spoke at an AA meeting this morning."

Late that night, Flo couldn't sleep. She got up and drove to the Hughes Market on Beverly Boulevard. As she pushed her shopping cart through the aisles, she stopped to stare at the gallon bottles of Soave wine, but she kept moving and bought twelve cans of Diet Coke instead. Ahead of her, standing at the magazine counter, was Lonny Edge. When he looked up from the magazine he was reading and saw her, he grinned his wide grin, the grin that buyers of his pornographic videos found so beguiling.

"Hi, Flo," he said.

"Hi," she answered.

"We have to stop meeting like this," Lonny said.

Flo smiled.

Lonny waved the magazine in her direction. "Last time I saw you here, you were on the cover of *Mulholland,* and now I'm *in* the magazine. Have you read this about me?"

"No."

"I'll treat you to a copy. They're trying to kick me out of my building because of this article."

"Really? What's the article about?"

"This manuscript I have that turns out to be the lost manuscript of Basil Plant. That famous writer who cooled a couple of years ago?"

"I always heard you had his manuscript, way back in the Viceroy Coffee Shop days. Curly told me that. Why would they kick you out of your apartment because of that?"

"The dame who wrote it makes it sound as if I turn tricks there, and the manager of the building has been dying to get rid of me for a long time, and he's using this magazine for an excuse. Like I'm giving his dump of a building a bad name."

"Do you?"

"Do I what?"

"Turn tricks in your apartment?"

"Hell, no, I don't. Just a couple of my regulars. Otherwise, I go out. Anyway, I want to get out of that kind of business. I'm over thirty now. Time to get serious about my life."

"Well, we've all got our problems, Lonny," said Flo, moving her shopping cart past him.

"I don't know where the hell I'm going to move to. I've lived in that bungalow ever since I came to this town."

Flo stopped and looked back at him. An idea came into her head, which she then rejected. "Good luck in finding a place," she said.

"After Jules died, when Cyril Rathbone's article in Mulholland *magazine came out about me, with my picture on the cover—oh God!—Archbishop Cooning started to give these sermons every Sunday from the pulpit of Saint Vibiana's. Oh, my, the things that he said about him! Poor Jules. He said Jules corrupted my morals. When I was a kid back in parochial school, we used to hear about Archbishop Cooning, only he was just Bishop Cooning then. He was always carrying on about virginity and stuff like that, saving yourself for marriage, ha ha ha. We were all scared of him, but the nuns thought he was great, especially Sister Andretta.*

"Which brings me to Cyril. I always knew he was vile. Jules hated him. And Pauline did too. And yet, I put my fate in his hands. That was a mistake, one of my many mistakes. Any vestige of sympathy I might have received from Pauline over Jules's estate, I lost when I said that Cyril Rathbone was going to write my book. I mean, just from that article he wrote about me in Mulholland, *I should have known. When facts failed, he just embellished his accounts with whatever came into his head.*

"I didn't tell him everything. Some of it I held back. The part about Kippie Petworth, for instance. For about five minutes I had the upper hand in the situation, with the information about Kippie that I had learned from Lonny, that he was the one who killed Hector Paradiso. But when I met with Pauline, I saw the look of terror in her eyes when I approached the subject of Kippie. I mean, terror. And I backed down. I didn't press my advantage. Like I felt sorry for Pauline Mendelson, this rich lady who'd had every whim of her whole life attended to.

"I'd like to have had that out with Jules, about Kippie. That he hid the kid out in my house, and I was there squeezing orange juice for him. I don't think Jules should have done that to me. But people like that, Jules and Pauline and their whole crowd, they really didn't think the rules applied to them."

25

T HE DEATH OF Jules Mendelson was a great sorrow to Dudley. He felt that never again would he be able to serve so great or so kind an employer. He had been generously provided for in Jules's will, and had also received a handwritten letter from Jules, delivered after his death by Sims Lord, asking him to stay on with Mrs. Mendelson at Clouds, for which there would be a substantial added remuneration for each year he remained in her employ. The muffled scandal of Jules Mendelson's love affair was a thing that Dudley chose to overlook, as if it had not happened. When pejorative remarks about the great man's behavior came to his ears, and a great many had, he faced his informer with a look of such hauteur that it silenced further discourse on the subject and caused the informer to retreat in shame. It was, he felt, up to him to see that there was no lessening of the established standards of the house.

When Philip Quennell, a half hour after leaving Flo March's house, rang the buzzer at the gates of Clouds and asked over the closed circuit television system if Mrs. Mendelson was at home, Dudley was quite put out. Although he knew that Mrs. Mendelson was fond of the young man who had become the boyfriend of Camilla Ebury, he felt that it was an impertinence for him to arrive at the gates of such a house as Clouds and ask to see her, without having called first to make an appointment. Dudley was not unaware that Jules Mendelson had despised Philip Quennell, and he joined his late employer in blaming Philip for causing the crack in the statue of the Degas ballerina.

"Is Mrs. Mendelson expecting you?" asked Dudley over the closed circuit system.

"She is not, no," replied Philip, looking up into the television camera.

"I really don't think it is convenient for her to see you, Mr. Quennell," said Dudley, taking upon himself the task of speaking for the lady of the house. Although he was in no way impolite, he allowed a mild note of annoyance to creep into the tone of his voice. "Perhaps you should telephone Mrs. Mendelson later today and try to make an appointment to see her."

Philip was not to be dissuaded so easily. "I realize I have come without calling first, Dudley, but could you please ask Mrs. Mendelson if she could see me for a few moments," said Philip, in an insistent voice.

Dudley, annoyed now, made no reply. He turned off the system and called Pauline on the intercom to tell her that Philip Quennell had arrived at the house without an appointment and wished to see her.

"Heavens," said Pauline over the intercom.

Although Dudley could not see Pauline, he imagined that there was a look of surprise on her face. "I've asked him to call you later to make an appointment," said Dudley.

"No, no, I'll see him, Dudley," said Pauline. "It's just that I have things to do. I have to meet with Jarvis in the greenhouse first, and then I'll be up. Have Mr. Quennell wait in the library."

Dudley, without saying anything welcoming to Philip, pushed the button that opened the gates, and Philip proceeded up the long driveway to the house. When his car pulled into the courtyard, Dudley opened the front door.

"Mrs. Mendelson has asked that you wait in the library, Mr. Quennell," said Dudley. He walked in that direction with Philip following him. "Mrs. Mendelson is with Jarvis in the greenhouse and will be up shortly."

He opened the door of the library and Philip went inside. As always, when he entered that room, Philip walked over to the fireplace and looked up at the painting of van Gogh's *White Roses*.

"Is there anything you'd like? Tea? Coffee? Drink?" asked Dudley, as he turned away and put into alignment a row of magazines on the fireplace bench.

"No, thank you. I'm fine," replied Philip, as if he were unaware of the butler's lack of civility.

After ten minutes, Pauline walked into the room through one of the French doors that opened onto the terrace. She was carrying a basket of roses that she had just cut in her garden. "Hello, Philip," she said.

Philip hopped to his feet. "Pauline, I know this is inexcusable, to drop in on you without calling first. I think I have upset your butler."

"Oh, don't worry about it," she said. "I hope you won't mind if I put these flowers in a vase while we talk." Without waiting for an answer, she took a blue-and-white Chinese vase and carried it into the lavatory, where she filled it with water. "I'm having a guest for lunch. I'm afraid I can't ask you to join us."

"Oh, I wouldn't dream of staying. It's extremely kind of you to see me. I'll only be a few minutes." He was beginning to feel nervous about his mission.

Pauline came out of the lavatory and took a pair of clippers from her basket and began to strip the roses and cut off the ends at an angle. "You haven't fought with Camilla again, have you? That's what I imagined," she said.

Philip smiled. "No."

Then she started to arrange the flowers in the vase, with the expertise of a person who had spent a lifetime arranging flowers in rare Chinese vases.

"It's not unlike your painting," said Philip, pointing to her arrangement.

"Mr. van Gogh's picture always influences me, but certainly you didn't come here to talk about flower arrangements," she said.

"No." He shook his head. "I came here to talk about Flo March."

Pauline's body stiffened at the mention of the woman's name. She put down her clippers for a moment, breathed heavily, and then picked them up again and went on with her arranging.

"Have you become her spokesperson?" she asked. The expression on her face had changed, as had the tone of her voice. "If so, please contact my lawyer, Sims Lord. I have no wish to hear any message from her."

"No, Pauline. I am not her spokesperson. Nor am I bringing you a message from her. Nor am I speaking in her defense. There is something I think you should know. Please listen to me."

"Does Camilla know you've come here, Philip?"

"No, she doesn't."

"What do you think she'd say if she knew?"

"She'd say that it was none of my business."

"She'd be right."

"She would be right, I know, just as you are right to be annoyed with me because I am interfering, but I anticipate a catastrophe if you don't listen to some reason, and it is worth your disapproval."

Pauline continued with her work. "I've always liked you, Philip. You must know that. I've been a good friend to you. But I think you have overstepped the bounds, and I would like you to leave my house and not come back."

Philip nodded. He walked toward the door of the library. As he opened it to leave, he turned back. "There are things she knows, Pauline."

"Please go," she said.

He continued to talk as if she had not spoken. "She is a desperate woman, and desperate women do desperate things. She is being manipulated by an unscrupulous man who despises you."

"And who is that?"

"Cyril Rathbone."

"Oh, puleeze," she said, laughing dismissively. "A ridiculous man. An imposter. He holds a grudge against me because I would never invite him to my house."

"You must understand that that makes him dangerous. He is writing a book in Flo March's name, called *Jules's Mistress*. Did you know that?"

Pauline's silence told that she had not known. "A whore's trick," she said, finally.

"Cyril Rathbone has taped her for forty hours," said Philip. "She has told him things that could be embarrassing to you."

Pauline wanted Philip to go, but she wanted him to stay also. "What sort of things?" she asked. In order not to show the interest she had in what he was saying, she continued to arrange the roses in the Chinese vase.

"I don't know. I haven't heard the tapes. I must ask you something, Pauline. And you don't have to answer me. In fact, don't answer me, because it is none of my business. But I'm still going to ask you. Does she know something about you? Or Hector? Or something about your son that no one else knows?"

"Is that what she said?"

"Alluded to, but didn't say."

Ashen-faced, Pauline turned away from Philip. "The woman is a liar. She would say anything."

"You're wrong, Pauline," said Philip. "That is just not so. She would prefer not to write this book. I can tell you that for a fact. She has told me that within the hour, but she is desperate. Put yourself in her place."

"Once you start paying off a blackmailer, it never ends. Anyone will tell you that," said Pauline.

"It's only what Jules promised her. It's less than what that ring on your finger is worth."

Without looking at her finger, she lifted up her left hand and pulled the ring back and forth with her right. Since Jules's death, Pauline had begun to wear his ring again, the huge de Lamballe diamond. When people commented on it, as they invariably did, she had taken to looking at it and smiling and then telling the story of how Jules had given it to her in Paris on the week she married him. The story was told with affection for the husband she had been married to for twenty-two years. People remarked later that there was no trace of bitterness in her toward Jules for the humiliation he had caused her. "It's so typical of Pauline. She's a lady through and through. After all, she is a Mc-Adoo," her friends said.

"Good-bye, Philip," said Pauline.

"Good-bye, Pauline."

He knew that he had failed in his mission and lost the friendship of Pauline at the same time. Dismissed, he walked down the hallway toward the front hall. At the instant he arrived there, Dudley entered the hall from another of the six doors that opened onto it and went straight to open the front door. But he had not opened it for Philip's exit from the house, as Philip thought, but for the arrival of another guest who was standing there.

"Mrs. Mendelson is expecting me," said the man. He spoke with an English accent.

"Indeed, Lord St. Vincent," said Dudley.

Philip Quennell and Lord St. Vincent looked at each other as they passed. Dudley did not introduce them.

"I can't understand it," said Flo. "People are interested, very interested in my book. There is great excitement. And then, suddenly, those very same people are no longer interested. We're never going to sell my book."

"You are entirely too quick to be defeated. You don't seem to understand how strong a position you are in, Flo," replied Cyril.

She shook her head. "I'm not in a strong position. There are forces working that have nothing to do with us."

"You dramatize."

"They're no longer interested because the person to whom they have to present the idea has already been gotten to by someone," said Flo.

"Oh, come on. Who has such power?"

"Friends of Pauline."

"What sort of friends?"

"One of the former Presidents who has dinner in her house."

"I don't believe that."

"Oh, yes."

The initial enthusiasm in publishing circles that Joel Zircon reported for Flo March's book, *Jules's Mistress,* seemed to abate overnight. Publishing companies that as recently as a week earlier had claimed they were ready to make a deal, once the first chapter and the outline were turned in—which they assured Joel was only a formality—were now difficult to get on the telephone.

"It's been a long fucking time since someone didn't return *my* telephone calls," complained Joel Zircon to Mona Berg, when they were having lunch. Joel had been given a promotion in the Berg Agency. "I can't understand it."

Mona, ever practical, had an instant solution. "Go the miniseries route," she suggested.

"Meaning?"

"You take your first chapter, and your outline, and you go to the networks, and say, 'I have here the first chapter and the outline of *Jules's Mistress,* Miss Flo March's book, which all the publishing companies are snapping at my heels for, but I have decided to skip that step and come straight to you while the story is still hot, hot, hot.' "

"Yeah?"

"Then you start teasing them a little. Drop the big names. Jules Mendelson. Pauline Mendelson. All those Washington people. And bank presidents. And cabinet ministers. You'll have them eating right out of your hand."

"*Former* cabinet ministers."

"All right, all right. *Former* cabinet ministers. Don't get picky with me when I'm doing your creative work for you."

"Sorry. Go on."

"Use words like billionaire, and high society, and mansion when you describe it. They always like that."

"Great idea, Mona. You're the best in the business."

"I know," said Mona.

"Something's gone off," said Joel.

"Meaning?"

"They're not going to do the miniseries."

"I thought you said they were going to buy it."

"They changed their mind."

"Why?"

"They said mistress stories are not commercial."

Flo pulled the covers up over her and turned toward the wall. "Somebody got to them," she said.

"What do you mean?"

"Just what I said. Somebody got to them."

"Oh, come on."

"You don't know these people the way I do."

Joel tried the other two networks. There was enthusiasm at the lower echelons, followed by rejection when the idea was presented at the highest levels of programming.

"I must be losing my touch," said Joel to Cyril. "I thought if anything was sure-fire, this was it. I mean, it has all the elements."

"I have an idea," said Cyril.

"What's that?"

"Get Flo an appearance on the Amos Swank show. Have her tell her story to late-night America. Beautiful young girl with a story to tell can't get it published because the powerful of the country are conspiring against her."

"I'd stay up late to look at that."

"So would most of the country."

"Is Flo up to that?"

"What do you mean?"

"She don't look so steady to me."

"What do you mean?"

"She's falling apart again."

"Don't worry about Flo. I'll get her in shape."

There was great excitement when the date was set for Flo to appear on "After Midnight," the Amos Swank show. She began to pull herself together again. She went each morning to the log cabin to attend the AA meetings. On the advice of Philip Quennell, she did not raise her hand and discuss her life anymore at the meetings.

"People know who you are now. They talk about you. They're not supposed to, but some of them do," said Philip. He did not tell her he suspected that Rose Cliveden had repeated everything she had said to either Pauline or Sims Lord. He only said, "Don't go out for coffee with Rose C."

"Why not?"

"She's a talker."

"But she was so nice to me."

She went to a gym and began to work out. She went back to Pooky to get her hair done, and to Blanchette to get her nails done. She brought Pooky back to her house with her to help her decide what she should wear on the night of her appearance. She had not been able to afford new clothes since Jules died, but Pooky assured her that the Chanels in her wardrobe were classics and timeless. He took the one they picked out for her to wear on the Amos Swank show to a dressmaker friend of his in the San Fernando Valley and had it shortened to the latest length. "Wear the sapphire-and-diamond ring," he said. "That's all. Don't wear the canary diamond earrings."

"You're a pal, Pooky," she said.

Cyril took on the job of coaching her. He brought her video tapes of Amos Swank interviewing other celebrities to study. "Sit like this," he would say. Or, "Don't use that expression." Or, "If you talk about Lonny Edge, make sure you say porn star."

"I'm not going to talk about Lonny Edge, Cyril."

Flo was frightened.

A call to Mona Berg from Freddie Galavant, who had once been an ambassador and was a close friend of people in high places, warned her that if her agency represented the book or miniseries of the whore Flo March, the IRS would never give her a moment's peace again. Mona called Joel Zircon into her office and said, "Drop it."

"But I almost have a deal."

"Drop it," repeated Mona.

Joel dropped it.

Because Dom Belcanto, the ballad singer, was the main guest on the Amos Swank show that night, Arnie Zwillman gave up his nightly card game to stay home with Adrienne Basquette and watch his great friend. "I never miss one of Dom's appearances," he said to Adrienne. It was not until the opening credits, when all the guests were billboarded, that he realized that Flo March, "the girl who wrote the book that everyone is afraid to publish," as Amos Swank himself described her, was to be the final guest on the show, after Dom Belcanto, who was plugging his new album, *My Cigarette Burns Me.*

"That fucking broad's a loose cannon," said Arnie to Adrienne.

Pauline Mendelson, who led a busy life, almost never watched television, except for the news, and certainly never watched the Amos Swank show. "I never know who any of those people are," she used to say to Jules, about the roster of guests on the show, who were mostly the leads in television series she had never seen, or comics from Las Vegas, where she had never been. But she was to be the chairperson of a benefit for the Blind Children's Home of Los Angeles, which she agreed to do before Jules's death, and Dom Belcanto, who did "marvelous things" for charity, as his publicist was quick to point out, had agreed to sing at the dinner at the Century Plaza. So that night she watched, as she had to meet Dom the next day to discuss the benefit.

Flo had met that afternoon with the researcher from the Amos Swank show, who had been most sympathetic with her story and assured her that her segment, although it was to be the last one of the show, could be the most popular, except for Dom Belcanto's.

"You mean that I won't get to talk with Amos Swank until we go on the air?" asked Flo. "Even get to meet him?"

"That's right," said Laurette. "Amos feels it's better for the spontaneity of the show when you meet on the air for the first time."

"How will he know what to ask me if we don't talk first?"

"That's what I'm here for," said Laurette. "I've read Cyril Rathbone's piece in *Mulholland,* and I've read your first chapter, and the outline. Dynamite. Really dynamite. We talk through your story, you and I, and then I go and talk it through with Amos, and decide what parts are the most interesting, and then I write the questions, and they're put on the teleprompter," said Laurette.

"That's how they do it? Really?"

"And there'll be a large audience tonight because of Dom Belcanto. The whole country will be watching, believe me. What a draw that guy is," she said.

"I don't want to talk about Mr. Mendelson's stepson," said Flo.

"No, no, no, not to worry," said the researcher.

"Do me a favor, Cyril. Wait outside somewhere. You make me nervous," said Flo. She was in the chair in the makeup room.

"I just wanted to stress about the letter that Jules wrote you leaving you the million dollars," said Cyril. "Did you give them the Xerox of it, so they can show it on the monitor?"

"Please, Cyril. I went through everything with Laurette this afternoon. She has the letter."

The makeup artist, Jess, placed Kleenex all around the collar of her Chanel blouse so that the pancake wouldn't come off and cause a stain. The makeup artist admired her hair. "I never saw such beautiful hair," he said.

"Thank you," said Flo. "Everyone's so nice here. I can't get over it."

"We've been together a long time here on the show. It's really like a family," said Jess.

"Do you think I should kiss Amos on both cheeks when I make my entrance?" Flo asked.

"How well do you know Amos?"

"I've never met him," said Flo.

"No, I wouldn't kiss him then."

"That's what I thought. I saw Roseanne kiss him when she went on, so I thought I'd ask," said Flo.

Flo was very nervous as the time approached, but she was also very excited. She had always wanted to be in show business. She loved being in the makeup room, having Jess work on her. She loved sitting in the green room talking with the other guests who were going to be on the show. She wished she had pursued her career in show business. She used to want to be no more than the second lead in a situation comedy, but she felt now that she could do more important roles. It occurred to her that maybe this appearance could lead to some acting jobs. She thought about getting new pictures taken. And an agent. She would need an agent. Maybe Joel Zircon would handle her as an actress as well as an author.

"Miss March?"

"Yes?" She looked up to see a page in a dark blue uniform. "Is it time to go on the set? I'm so nervous."

"Would you come with me, Miss March?" said the page.

"Thank you."

"Mr. Marcuzzi would like to see you in his office," said the page.

"Who?"

"Mr. Marcuzzi. The executive producer."

"Oh, my," said Flo.

"He's in the West Building. On the fifteenth floor."

"Is there enough time before I go on?"

"There must be. He runs the show."

She followed the page through the corridors leading from the studios in the East Building to the executive offices in the West Building. The page stepped aside as she got into the elevator and then pushed the button for the fifteenth floor.

When the elevator doors opened, Flo got out. Cyril Rathbone was standing there. He stared at her.

"Cyril, are you supposed to see Mr. Marcuzzi too?" asked Flo.

"They canceled the segment," said Cyril.

"What?" she gasped.

"You heard me."

"I don't believe it. Laurette spent two hours at my house this afternoon. We went over everything. They just did my makeup."

"And then they canceled you," said Cyril.

"But Mr. Marcuzzi wants to see me."

"He wants to see you to tell you you're not going on, that's why he wants to see you. Do you know what he said? He said, 'Amos don't like guests who write books. He don't read books. He likes big stars, like Dom Belcanto, or girls with big tits, like Roseanne, or animal acts.' You don't need to hear it twice," said Cyril. The annoyance in his voice was with her for her failure rather than the failure of the Amos Swank show.

Flo felt faint. Beneath her theatrical makeup, she had become ashen-faced. She felt that if she couldn't sit down, she was going to fall down. Opposite the elevator bank were three windows with deep sills. She walked over to one of the windows and leaned against the sill. "Somebody made a call again," she said. She spoke more to herself than to him. She stared out the window. Her face revealed an awareness of the hopelessness of her situation. She was deep in thought at what had just befallen her, but there was no aid from Cyril for her distress. To Cyril, she had become an unimportant person, and therefore her thoughts were unimportant thoughts.

She looked down, out the open window. Fifteen floors below, the traffic on Ventura Boulevard raced by. She leaned slightly out the window and stared down. Thoughts of her mother filled her head, moving from welfare hotel to welfare hotel with all her worldly possessions in torn shopping bags.

In that instant Cyril saw the possibilities of the thought that was forming in Flo's mind. He resisted his initial impulse to reach out and grab her. "I was there. I tried to stop her," he would say to the police. "I screamed, 'Don't, Flo! Don't!' But she eluded me.''

"Jump," said Cyril behind her, in a low voice. "Go ahead, Flo. Do it."

Flo slowly turned her head to him, and their eyes met. He looked eager and excited, and was breathing heavily. "It's all over for you," he said, talking rapidly, in a low but urgent voice. "You have nothing to live for. Jules is gone. In the long run, he forgot about you. You're broke. You're never going to have any money again. No one wants to see you. No one wants to know you. Do it. Jump, Flo. It'll be all over the papers. It will be a sensation. People will remember you for years, Flo. Death can be a beautiful experience. Go on, Flo. Go on."

Flo stared at him, transfixed. He nodded at her. She looked back at the street below and knelt on the windowsill with one leg, still looking down. She then raised her other leg to the sill. Perched now, she stared down. The traffic on Ventura Boulevard raced below her, the headlights and taillights mesmerizing her. She leaned out farther on the ledge.

"Go on," whispered Cyril, from behind her. "Do it." He repeated and repeated the words as if he were arriving at an orgasm, and she, his submissive accomplice, obliged in the act as she moved farther and farther out on the ledge. She raised her arms.

At that moment the elevator stopped on their floor, announced by a bell and the opening of the door. "Going down," called out a passenger from inside.

The spell was broken. Flo leapt backward onto the floor. Pale, almost fainting, she stared up at Cyril Rathbone and slowly pulled herself away from him, with fear in her eyes, like a dog that had been whipped by its master. Tears streamed down her cheeks. She tried to raise herself from the floor, but her legs were too weak to rise.

"Going down," called out the voice from the elevator again, and the door started to close.

"*Hold it!*" screamed Flo. She half rose to her feet and ran into the elevator. Cyril followed her. Inside, a janitor with a trolley of cleaning utensils nodded to them. Flo held on to the railing of the elevator for balance. Cyril began to speak to Flo, but she turned away from him. With shaking hands, she wiped the tears from her face and, in an automatic gesture, unscrewed her lip gloss and ran the stick over her lips without looking into a mirror. The elevator descended in silence.

"I'll get the car," said Cyril when they got out.

Flo shook her head. "Never mind. I'll get a taxi," she replied.

"No, no, darling Flo. Don't be silly." His voice had returned to its florid tonality, as if what had just happened between them had not happened.

"Yes." She leaned against the wall, exhausted.

"Would you like me to get you a glass of water?" he asked, nervously.

"Why did you do that to me?" She barked out the sentence at him, as if it were one word.

"It was a joke, Flo. I was kidding. You know I didn't mean it."

She stared at him. "That's some joke, Cyril. That's really funny. Amos Swank could have gotten a lot of mileage out of that bit of comic business." She walked away from him.

"Flo," he called after her.

She stopped and turned toward him. "Stay away from me, Cyril," she said. She pointed her finger at him for emphasis, and repeated, "Stay away."

The Iranian taxi driver from Valley Cab kept looking at her in his rearview mirror. She looked familiar to him. He thought she might be a television star from one of the series at the studio where he had picked her up, but he couldn't remember which one. She gave him her address on Azelia Way off Coldwater Canyon, in Beverly Hills. The address had a familiar ring to him. He looked at her in the mirror again, but she was deep in thought. He watched her as she opened her bag and took out her wallet. She kept looking at the meter and then looking down at the money in her hands, probably counting to see if she had enough.

"Driver," she said, "when you get to Sunset and Coldwater, you can let me out. I'll walk the rest of the way."

"You can't walk, Miss. It's pitch dark, and it's almost two miles up Coldwater to the Azelia Way turnoff."

"Listen, driver. I don't have enough money with me to go any farther. I didn't realize that when I got into the cab. I'm very sorry. I was supposed to get a ride home with the person who brought me to the studio, but something came up and I had to take a cab, and I didn't realize I didn't have enough money with me."

The driver snapped his fingers. "The Chateau Marmont, on Sunset Boulevard. That's it, right?"

"What?"

"Didn't I drive you once from a steak house in the Valley to the Chateau Marmont? You were crying and upset about something?"

Flo smiled. "And you're the same driver? You seem to catch me on my peak nights."

"You tipped me ten bucks that night. I never forgot that. Most people, it's fifteen percent of the fare, if that, no more. You didn't even think about it. You paid, and then you handed me ten bucks. I thought, this lady has class. I'm not letting you out on the street, lady. I'm taking you all the way home." He turned off the meter. "This ride's on me."

"That's very nice of you," said Flo.

"Some private detective came after me a few days later. Did you know that? Wanted to know where I took you. I had it all on my call sheet. This address on Azelia Way, where you first told me to take you, and then that was crossed off, and the Chateau Marmont was written in."

Flo looked at the driver's permit in the cab and saw his name. "Hussein? Is that right?"

"Hussein. That's my name."

"I want you to know I really appreciate this, Hussein. Not too many classy guys around these days."

When the cab turned right off Coldwater Canyon to Azelia Way, a car came down toward them. As it passed, Flo looked out the window and saw that it was a gold Rolls-Royce. Two men were seated in the front seat. They did not look in her direction. A chill went through her. As the cab proceeded up the hill toward her driveway, Flo looked out the back window toward the Rolls.

"You wouldn't do me a favor, would you, Hussein?" she asked, as the cab pulled into her driveway.

"What's that?"

"Would you just wait here until I get in my house?"

"I'll go to the door with you," he said. He got out and opened her door, as if he were a chauffeur rather than a cabdriver.

At the front door, as Flo took out her keys to unlock the door, she saw that the door was pulled to, but open.

"Maybe you forgot to close your door when you went out," said Hussein.

"Maybe," said Flo. She pushed it open.

"Want me to go first?" asked Hussein.

"Would you mind?"

Inside the house, Flo looked around her. Everything seemed to be in order. She looked in her kitchen, in her unused maid's room, and finally in her bedroom. She opened one of the drawers of the wardrobe in her dressing room and felt behind some boxes for the Louis Vuitton jewel case that she was photographed carrying out of the Meurice Hotel in Paris during the fire. When she opened it, she was relieved to see that her yellow diamond earrings, which she considered to be her last gift from Jules Mendelson, were still there.

"Everything okay?" asked Hussein.

"Seems to be," said Flo.

"Are you going to call the police?" he asked.

"No, nothing seems to be missing. I want to thank you a lot. I really appreciate this. If you give me your address, I'll send you the money after I go to the bank tomorrow."

"This was on me," said Hussein. "Good luck to you. You seem to have a lot of difficulties in your life for such a young lady."

Flo smiled. "Good luck to you, Hussein."

When she was alone, she put the chain lock and dead bolt on the front door. She walked through her house and pulled down the shades and blinds and closed all the curtains. She turned on every light. In her bedroom, she began to undress, taking off the Chanel suit that Pooky had thought was the right one for her to wear on the Amos Swank show. She sat down at her dressing table and rubbed cold cream on her face to remove the television makeup that Jess had been putting on her when the page asked her to go up to Mr. Marcuzzi's office. As the thought of what she had almost done on the fifteenth floor of the West Building in the Valley Studios went through her mind, she felt faint again. She went into the bar and looked for a long time at the gallon bottle of Soave from the Hughes Market. She pulled out the cork and then emptied the wine in the sink, turning her head away so that she would not be attracted by the heady aroma. Then she reached into the refrigerator and took out a can of Diet Coke. She opened the tab on the top and started to drink it from the can. Looking at herself in the mirrored wall of the bar, she remembered how Jules had hated her to drink from the can and poured the liquid into one of her Steuben glasses. "I'm still trying to do things your way, Jules," she said into the mirror. "And it's getting me absolutely nowhere."

As she turned to walk back into the living room, her stockinged foot stepped on a hard object. Looking down, she noticed Cyril's tape recorder on the floor of the bar. She leaned down and picked it up. It had been smashed with a hammer. The microcassette that had been in it was gone.

She could not sleep. She brought the pillows from her bed into the living room and lay on her gray satin sofa, with a package of cigarettes and a few magazines. Every time she heard a car go up Azelia Way, she stopped to listen until she was sure it had passed her driveway.

She picked up *Mulholland*. There was Hortense Madden's article about the missing manuscript of the late writer Basil Plant, which had been located, possibly, at the bungalow on Cahuenga Boulevard of Lonny Edge, the pornography star.

She looked at her watch. It was two o'clock in the morning. She knew it wasn't too late to call. She wondered if he would even be home yet. She dialed the number.

"It's Lonny. I can't come to the phone now. Leave your name and number, even if you think I already have it, and the time you called, and I will get back to you as soon as possible. Wait for the beep."

She did not wish to leave her name on his machine. Just as she started to hang up, she heard Lonny's voice. "Hello? Hello?"

"Lonny?" she said.

"Ina Rae?" asked Lonny.

"No, it's Flo."

"Flo?" She could tell that he did not recognize her.

"From the Viceroy. From the newsstand at the Hughes Market."

"Flo, my God. How are you? I was expecting someone else."

"I gather. Ina Rae. Who's Ina Rae?"

"Oh, don't ask."

There was a silence.

"Are you all right, Flo?" asked Lonny.

"Sure."

"What's up? It's two o'clock in the morning."

"Are you still looking for a place to live?"

"Yeah. I sure am. They're kicking me out of here. I was gonna move in with this friend of mine, Ina Rae, but it's not gonna work out. Why?"

"How much are you prepared to pay?"

"Six, seven hundred a month. Why?"

"You can't get much for six or seven hundred a month these days, Lonny. Can you swing a thousand?"

"Maybe. Why? Do you know a place?"

"I have a maid's room in my house you could move into, as a temporary measure," she said.

"Really? You mean at your house in Beverly Hills?" There was excitement in his voice. "That would be great."

"Now, listen. No monkey business between us. No turning tricks in my house. No dirty videos. Strictly a roommate proposition. And two months' rent paid in advance."

"Why would you want a guy with a reputation like mine living in your house for, Flo? Are you that broke?"

"Yes. I'm that broke, Lonny. They're about to turn off my telephone."

"Why do I think there's more to this two A.M. call than that you're broke," said Lonny.

"Because I'm scared, Lonny. I'm scared to be alone here."

Flo's Tape #25

"*I was like a feather in the breeze. Except for Phil, this friend of mine from AA, I didn't know who to believe. I really had nowhere to turn. I suppose that's how I ended up with Lonny for a housemate. Lonny Edge, imagine. The thing is about Lonny, he's actually a nice guy, but he's in a line of work that most people don't have much truck with, at least publicly. My God, the stories he used to tell me about some of those famous people he visited in Bel Air and Holmby Hills, the kind of people you'd read about in the papers as being oh-so-proper. Lonny told me everything about Kippie and what happened that night at Hector's. It was all about money again. Kippie needed money, and his mother wouldn't give it to him, and neither would Jules, apparently. So he went to Hector's and surprised him with Lonny. I mean, what are those people hanging on to all that money for? Is it worth it, to cause all the trouble they cause, just to hang on to all the money?*

"*Probably the only smart thing I ever did was to go to the Wells Fargo Bank the morning after Cyril tried to talk me into jumping out the window of the Valley Studios and get the tapes and bring them back here to the house.*"

26

C YRIL RATHBONE, awakening, remembered with regret what he had said and done the night before. He knew only too well that the impulse that had driven him to seize the moment of Flo March's despair and urge her to jump out of the window on the fifteenth floor of the administration building of the Valley Studios—which seemed logical to him at the time, promising him personal headlines as well as a spectacular finish for his book—had severed forever her association with him. He was not able to erase from his mind the combined look of fear and hatred on her face when she had told him to stay away from her. Even so, he tried to reach her by telephone and then by a Federal Express letter, explaining his act, in a revised version of the facts and thoughts that had flashed through his mind at the time; but there were no replies, and he knew there never would be. He was history, as far as Flo March was concerned.

The thirty-nine hours of microcassette tapes that she had recorded were in a safety deposit box at the Wells Fargo Bank in Beverly Hills, for which they both had keys. When he went to the bank several days after the evening of her dismissal from the Amos Swank show, he found that the safety deposit box was empty. Without Flo, his dreams of expanding his career from social columnist to book writer were dashed.

In his column, Cyril Rathbone began writing of the widowed Pauline as Pauline, Mrs. Mendelson, the sort of style used for dowager peeresses of the realm. Pauline had started to go out again in the city, appearing at small dinners of close friends and at cultural events, but at all times she avoided the cameras of the social and fashion press, which had followed her for so many years. "Pauline, Mrs. Mendelson, arrived for the opening of the ballet after the curtain had gone up. These days she guards her privacy," wrote Cyril in one column.

Although it appeared to be an accidental meeting, it was no accident that Cyril Rathbone should happen to pass Pauline Mendelson on Bedford Drive at the precise moment she left Pooky's salon, after having had her hair done and nails manicured, beauty chores that were usually performed at her home. That morning at breakfast at the Viceroy Coffee Shop, Pooky had told Blanchette, the manicurist, that Mrs. Mendelson would be coming into the shop at eleven and, no matter what, she must not be kept waiting, even if it meant canceling the previous appointment, as she had to leave the salon by eleven-fifty in order to be back at Clouds for a lunch she was giving for a visiting ambassador. Pauline Mendelson was the kind of customer for whom such adjustments were made. Cyril, in the booth behind the hair stylist, could not help but perk up his ears.

At eleven forty-five Pauline's chauffeur, Jim, parked the Bentley directly in front of the entrance of Pooky's salon and stood holding the car door open for her. Exactly at eleven-fifty the doorman opened the red lacquer door of the hairdressing salon, and Pauline emerged, in the rushed manner of a celebrity. Her hair was covered with a scarf, and she walked with rapid strides across the sidewalk, looking neither left nor right, hugging her bag to her, as both the doorman and the chauffeur tipped their hats. Cyril, carrying a briefcase in one hand, affected a rapid walk himself, looking neither left nor right, as if he were on his way from one important meeting to another and time was of the essence. Midway in the sidewalk they collided, and both almost lost their balance. Pauline's bag fell to the ground. Cyril's briefcase fell to the ground.

"Good God," he said, with a trace of annoyance in his florid English voice, as if the fault were not his own. He picked up his briefcase.

Jim, the chauffeur, rushed forward and grabbed Pauline's arm to keep her from falling, and then reached down to pick up her bag. "Are you all right, Mrs. M.?" he asked.

"Yes, Jim, fine. The thing is, I wasn't looking where I was going." She turned to apologize to the man. "I'm terribly sorry," she said. "I'm afraid it was my fault."

"No, no, please," said Cyril. "Forgive me. My mind was a hundred miles away. Did I hurt you? Oh, my word, Pauline. I didn't realize it was you."

Startled, she nodded in a distant manner when she realized that the man she had collided with was Cyril Rathbone.

"This is too extraordinary," he said. His voice took on its psychic tone of wonderment. "I have been thinking of you. But then, as I'm sure you know, there are no accidents, even though we seem to have had a minor collision." He smiled, as if he had made a joke.

Pauline did not wait for him to continue. She proceeded over to her car and entered the backseat. As Jim was about to close the door, Cyril stepped over, held it open, and leaned into the car. No such proximity to her would come his way again, and he knew it. "It is urgent that I speak with you, Pauline. Urgent."

"I'm afraid that I am terribly late," she said, retreating into the far corner of the Bentley.

He wanted to say, "Yes, I know, the ambassador is coming for lunch," but he didn't. Instead he said, "You will be very grateful to me for what I have to tell you. It is of the utmost importance to you."

She looked at him, without replying.

"It concerns Miss March. I have heard her tapes," he said.

Pauline shook her head, not wanting to listen. Jim, the chauffeur, moved around the driver's side of the car and opened the front door. Pauline did not want Jim to hear what Cyril Rathbone was about to say.

"I'm in a frightful hurry," she said, holding up her hand at the same time to forestall any further conversation.

"So am I," he replied. "I'm late for an appointment." He patted his brief-case, as if it contained state secrets. "But you must hear me out."

"We'll go straight home, Jim," she said to her chauffeur.

"Please, Pauline," insisted Cyril.

She spoke without looking at him. "Call Miss Maple, my husband's secretary. Ask her to set up an appointment."

For nearly three decades Arnie Zwillman, about whom there was much media speculation, had managed to elude the photographers, journalists, and investigative reporters of the *New York Times,* the *Wall Street Journal,* the *Los Angeles Times,* and the *Los Angeles Tribunal.* As story after story appeared over the years on mob activities in trucking, in Las Vegas, in the record business, in the motion picture industry, in drugs, in prostitution, in pornography, in everything, his name came up time and time again, but always as a mysterious figure, an éminence grise, rarely seen, never photographed, inaccessible in the extreme, except for occasional forays to the Friars Club for cards, which were his passion. His social life was limited to his current wife, whom, with the diminishment of desire, he changed with regularity every seven years, and to the company of such celebrated cronies as Dom Belcanto, the ballad singer, and Amos Swank, the late-night talk show host, and their current wives.

It was to Amos Swank that Arnie Zwillman had made the call the night before, after his program was on the air, during the first commercial, to request that his last guest of the evening, Flo March, be dropped from the lineup.

"Dump the cunt," he said.

"Roseanne? Dump Roseanne?" replied Amos, horrified by the thought.

"Not Roseanne. Flo March."

"That puts me in a real bind, Arnie," said Amos. "We're on the air. I can't get a replacement."

"Tell Dom I said to sing a few more numbers," answered Arnie. "The public's tuning in to see him, not the March broad."

Later, when Arnie listened to the only tape that had been found in Flo March's house, his face was a study in displeasure. The encounter that had taken place between Jules Mendelson and him in the den of Casper Stieglitz's house, while the rest of the party was watching a movie, was recounted in detail, as told to Flo by Jules himself. The words "laundering money" appeared frequently, as well as the methods for doing so during Jules's tenure in Brussels, as suggested by Arnie to Jules.

It was Arnie's firm belief that only the unexpected interruption of Pauline Mendelson, who had been offended by a lesbian reference made by the drugged Casper Stieglitz, had prevented the deal from being solidified, there and then.

"Christ, this March dame should have been a secretary. She must have taken down everything Jules told her in shorthand while she was taking down his pants to blow him," said Arnie. His remark caused loud laughter in the room, but Arnie Zwillman was in no mood for laughter. He raised his hand and the laughter curdled. "Where's the rest of the tapes? There's supposed to be forty hours. This is only an hour. I want to hear the rest of the Kippie stuff."

"That's all we could find," said Jo Jo, his aide.

"They're probably in some safety deposit box. Get that fruitcake, Cyril Rathbone. Scare the shit out of him," said Arnie.

"It's Mr. Rathbone. I am expected," said Cyril, sounding more English than ever, as he peered up into the camera of the closed circuit television at the gates of Clouds. Dudley, looking back at him in the monitor in the butler's pantry, was not kindly disposed toward the writer from *Mulholland* magazine, after what he considered to be the shameful and traitorous article he had written about Jules Mendelson and the woman called Flo March, an article that he knew had caused mirthful glances and suppressed laughter in the butlers' pantries of the other important houses of the city. Dudley went so far as to express disapproval to the lady of the house when she had told him that Cyril Rathbone was expected, but Pauline Mendelson had merely shrugged and not replied, as if it were an occasion over which she had no control.

As Cyril drove up the long driveway of the Mendelson estate, turning right to enter the magical part that could not be viewed through the gates at the entrance, his heart beat faster. It had always been a disappointment to his editor, Lucia Borsodi, that he did not have access to the great house. It had not mattered to her that no other social columnist in the city had access either, or that the late Jules Mendelson loathed social publicity. Lucia Borsodi told him over and over that in New York, Dolly De Longpre, the famed doyenne of the breed, had access to all the best houses of both the old and new society, and even, when she visited Los Angeles, as she did once a year, was invited to dine at the Mendelsons', which was an annual rebuff to Cyril. But, finally, he had arrived at the private and exclusive estate that for years had been his dream to enter.

As he drove his car into the courtyard, he gazed ahead with joy. The vast house before him was everything he had imagined it was going to be. The front door opened before he reached it, and he walked into the hallway, without even looking at Dudley, drawn to the sight of the sweeping stairway and the six Monet paintings ascending upward, as if it were a magnet.

"Oh, marvelous, marvelous," he said, looking up, looking left, looking right, at the treasures everywhere, forming sentences in his mind of the descriptions he would write. Catching sight of himself in a Chippendale mirror over a console table, he was pleased with his smart appearance, in his well-cut seersucker suit, blue shirt, and pink tie.

Dudley, who refrained from offering a greeting, led him down the corridor into the cool shadows of the library. Outside it was very hot, but blue-and-white-striped awnings kept the sun from the beautiful room. Immediately responding to the luxury, Cyril felt comfortable. To the right, over the mantel, was van Gogh's *White Roses*. He wanted to stop and look, but the butler opened the doors to the terrace and went outside. "Mrs. Mendelson is cutting roses in the garden," he said. He raised a hand and pointed toward a large sculpture of a sleeping woman. "Beyond the Henry Moore, to the left, is the rose garden." He then turned and reentered the house.

Cyril felt disappointment. He loathed the sun. His fair skin was of the variety that burned and blistered. He would have much preferred to have his meeting with Pauline in the cool library, sitting on fine chairs beneath fine paintings, holding cool drinks in fine glasses. He would have liked a tour, room by room, antique by antique, painting by painting, as he had so often heard from Hector Paradiso honored guests were sometimes treated to, if they expressed interest in the treasures of the house.

The outdoor locale had been Pauline's idea. Whatever the disagreeable man had to say to her, she wished it to be out of the earshot of Dudley and the other servants. As Cyril walked across the acre of lawn, he wished he had brought his straw hat to protect his sensitive skin from the strong rays of the sun. At the same time, he noticed and memorized the extraordinary pieces of sculpture that Jules Mendelson had collected. "Beyond the Henry Moore," the butler had said. He wanted to remember that.

Pauline's back was to him when he saw her. She was leaning over to clip an enormous pink rose, which she then held to her nose for an instant. She wore gardening gloves and a large straw hat. On the lawn beside her was a basket in which were several dozen roses of different hues of red and pink. He watched her as she waved away a wasp that buzzed too closely to her. Even unobserved, he noticed that she retained her elegance, and the picture of her was pleasing to his eye.

"Pauline," he called out, excitedly, as if he were a guest at a garden party approaching his hostess, rather than the almost author of a salacious book about Pauline's late husband and her late husband's mistress. Although he knew she must have heard him, as the distance between them was not excessive, she did not turn around immediately, and he called out again, "Pauline."

Pauline had not turned around because she could not bear it when the feline old Etonian, who never actually went to Eton, called her by her first name. She felt the intimacy to be an impertinence, but she did not correct him. Instead, she called him Mr. Rathbone.

"Hello, Mr. Rathbone," she said, bestowing on him the overly gracious smile that people like her reserved for underlings who had overstepped the bounds. He recognized her look and refrained from requesting her to call him Cyril. Nor did he attempt to kiss her on the cheek, as he had at Casper Stieglitz's party when she pulled back from him and said she had a cold. There were garden chairs by the pavilion, and she indicated with a gesture that they would sit there.

"This is all very beautiful, Pauline," he said, looking around at the house and grounds.

"Thank you," she replied.

"The Maillol sculpture is to die for," he said.

She nodded at the mention of the sculpture that had been her husband's favorite, but she made no attempt to apprise him of the fact that it had been her husband's favorite, nor did she attempt to engage in hostess talk, as it had been he who insisted he had urgent information to impart to her. To indicate to him that the moments between them were to be brief, she neither removed her gardening gloves nor settled back in her chair.

Although such signals as she gave him caused him to be nervous in her presence, he adopted a languid posture when he seated himself, as if he were used to such afternoon tête-à-têtes in the rose garden at Clouds.

"Such a hot day," he said. With his hand, he shielded his eyes from the sun and wished there were an umbrella to pull up for shade.

"Yes," she agreed.

"I long to see your famous yellow phalaenopsis orchid plant," he said.

"Mr. Rathbone, please," she replied, closing her eyes and waving her hand. "No garden club tours today. You spoke on the street of a matter of urgency. Let us deal with that matter and forget about my yellow phalaenopsis."

Even then, holding all the aces as he did, he would have tossed them aside to become her acolyte, the way Hector Paradiso had been, but he realized she was not to be won over by his compliments or charm. Rebuffed, he smiled in defeat. "As I often write in my column, Pauline, there is no one tougher than a tough society lady," he said.

"True," she agreed.

"You've never liked me, have you, Pauline?" he asked.

"With very good reason, Mr. Rathbone. But, again, let us get to this matter of urgency." She pulled back her glove and consulted her watch, with no attempt to disguise the gesture.

He ignored her request. "In a moment. There's something I would like to straighten out first. Was it because you didn't like me that I was not asked to deliver the eulogy at Hector's funeral last year?"

"Oh, for God's sake," she replied impatiently.

"You know, don't you, that it should have been I who gave the eulogy." He tapped his forefinger on his chest to indicate himself. "After all, I was his best friend."

Pauline did not respond, but she had the ability to speak without uttering a word, merely raising her eyebrows, and make her meaning very plain.

"After you, I mean," Cyril said quickly, correcting himself. "That ambassador who gave the eulogy hardly knew him. I always felt it was you who prevented me from giving the eulogy."

"Was there not a morals charge pending against you at the time, involving a beating, or something?" asked Pauline.

Cyril, surprised, blushed deeply and said nothing.

Pauline continued. "I seem to remember that my husband was informed of that fact. Archbishop Cooning was already of two minds as to whether or not he should officiate at the funeral Mass, despite the fact that Rose Cliveden had contributed a hundred thousand dollars to the refurbishing of the archbishop's residence in Hancock Park. Under those circumstances, your candidacy as eulogist was considered by the planners of the funeral, of which I was not one, to be, uh, unseemly. I think that was the word that was used at the time. Unseemly."

Cyril's silence continued.

"There is a bee on your shoulder," he said, finally.

"It's not a bee. It's a wasp," she said, brushing it off her shoulder with her gloved hand.

"Pesky creatures," said Cyril, waving his hand frantically to discourage the wasp from coming in his direction. He did not like to say, for fear of appearing unmasculine, that he was terrified of wasps. "Should we not go inside?" he asked.

"It's gone," she said, unconcerned. "Tell me, Mr. Rathbone. As we seem to be playing the truth game, were you the one who sent me, anonymously, the photograph of my husband and Miss March fleeing the fire in the Meurice Hotel from the Paris newspaper?"

"Yes, I thought you should know," he said.

"Oh, I see. You did it out of kindness, you mean?" she asked. "Your reputation for duplicity clings to you, Mr. Rathbone." Reserve, propriety, and good manners were born within her, but she made no attempt to disguise the disdain in her voice.

"I felt you should know," he repeated.

"Of course, you did," she said, with no lessening of the edge in her tone.

"Hector saw the picture. I sent it to him, but he didn't have the nerve to show it to you," said Cyril.

"Hector was a gentleman. One of the many differences between you and that fine man," she replied.

Smarting now from her contempt, he no longer tried to be winning. "There is a book being written about you and your husband, as I am sure you have heard," he said.

"It would be hard not to hear about it, as you have covered it extensively in your column," she replied.

"I have heard the tapes that Miss March has recorded," he said. "There are forty hours recorded thus far."

Pauline folded her gloved hands.

He began to pour out to her the story of her husband's long affair with the former waitress, sparing nothing, feeling no constraint. He knew now he could never make her his friend, so there was no longer any point in constraint. He leaned forward toward her and hissed out her husband's history, truths and untruths intermingled, wanting only to wound.

"When Jules left all the parties early, right after dinner, leaving Hector to bring you home, because he had to be up so early in the morning to take his calls from his offices in Europe, he really got up so early because he wanted to see Flo, because he needed to knock off a quick piece on the way to work, to hold him over until his regular visit in the afternoon. His sexual appetite was insatiable. He reappeared on her doorstep every afternoon at a quarter to four, without fail, no matter what the business crisis, first things first. In the several hours he spent with her each afternoon, before returning home to you for his glass of wine in your sunset room, to discuss the events of the day, before you dressed for dinner to attend whatever the party of the evening was, he came three and sometimes four times, each time varying the position. He could not get enough of the woman. It's all on the tapes, Pauline."

Pauline sank back in the wrought iron chair.

"There is more," said Cyril.

She looked at him. "How much more?"

"Much more."

"Are you going to make me pull this out of you, sentence by sentence, Mr. Rathbone? Or are you going to tell me? After all, that was what you came here for, was it not?"

"It is simply that it is indelicate," he said. The insincerity in his voice was so apparent that he heard it himself.

"Then be indelicate. I'm sure it will not be your first indelicacy."

"You see, I have the forty hours of microcassettes. Actually, I mean that I have thirty-nine of the forty hours. There was one cassette left in my tape recorder which is still in Miss March's house. She seemed very private about it.

Something about our mutual friend Hector's death. Even to me, she would not reveal the entire contents."

Beneath the wide brim of her straw hat, Pauline closed her eyes. She was determined not to allow Cyril Rathbone to witness a tear escaping.

"For a price, I would be able to turn everything over to you," he said.

"So that's what this matter of urgency is about," she said. "I should have known. Blackmail."

"Your son, your bad-boy son, Kippie, isn't that his name? It has something to do with your son," said Cyril.

Pauline raised her eyebrows in an arch of displeasure meant to disguise the fear that she felt, but she did not trust herself to speak, as that fear might have become apparent. Another wasp buzzed near her. She looked down at her shoulder and, with her gloved hand, flicked it off her in a nervous fashion that had nothing to do with the wasp but everything to do with the words that were coming out of the mouth of Cyril Rathbone.

He leaned forward toward her again, aware that finally he had succeeded in reaching her vulnerable point. A smile twisted his lips as he continued elaborating on the details. "Apparently—this is all according to Flo March, of course—your son, while on temporary leave from his drug rehabilitation center in France, was arrested in the Los Angeles airport for carrying drugs. He needed ten thousand dollars immediately. You refused him, apparently. As did the gangster Arnie Zwillman, with whom your son enjoys a peculiar sort of friendship. And so he went late that night to visit your best friend, Hector, catching poor Hector, apparently, in the middle of a sexual act of a deviant nature with a well-known video star of the pornographic variety named Lonny Edge, whom Hector picked up in a gay bar in West Hollywood called Miss Garbo's on the way home from a very swanky party in your house that you declined to let me cover for my column. Incidentally, of no moment here, Mr. Lonny Edge has subsequently become the housemate of Flo March, to help cover the destitute woman's living expenses, since you saw fit to cancel the bequests made to her by your husband. At any rate, your son, Kippie, was so hard-pressed for the ten thousand dollars that you would not give him that he offered himself sexually to your friend, Hector, although that sort of thing was not remotely his inclination. When Hector refused, there was a bit of a scuffle, apparently, and Hector produced a gun, and—"

The wasp that Pauline had flicked off her shoulder flew into Cyril Rathbone's mouth and stung his tongue. In an agony of pain, he could not even scream as his tongue swelled with the poison of the sting. His eyes rolled in his head, imploring Pauline for help.

Pauline stared at the spectacle of the writhing man in front of her. Sweat broke out on his face and body. His shirt became soaked, and the sweat seeped through to his seersucker suit. He tried to stand and then fell to his knees in front of her. She picked up the basket that held the roses she had been cutting.

Pauline drew out her clippers and started to work on her roses. "You must always clear away any foliage that will be beneath the water level in the vase," she said, bringing her gloved hand down the stem and pulling off the leaves. "And then, when you cut off the bottom of the stem, make sure always that you do it at an angle, like this, do you see? Now, these roses from my garden have particularly thick stems, which makes it difficult for the water to penetrate, so I always suggest, when I talk to the newcomers at the garden club, to peel away half the stem, like this."

Cyril Rathbone twisted and turned. With his mouth wide open, she saw that his tongue was hugely inflated and vividly red. Saliva dripped out of his mouth and rolled down his chin. He began to choke, holding his hands to his throat, and terrible noises emanated from his mouth.

"I hope it hurts terribly, Cyril," she said calmly.

Finally, she had called him by his first name, but he was by then beyond caring. Cyril Rathbone fell over, dead.

Pauline walked across the lawn and into the house through the French doors in the library, carrying her basket of roses. As she did so, Dudley passed in the hallway beyond.

"Dudley," called out Pauline.

"Yes, Mrs. Mendelson?" he said, entering the room.

"That man from *Mulholland* magazine?"

"Mr. Rathbone?" he replied.

"He seemed to be in some sort of distress. A coughing fit, choking or something. Perhaps Smitty or Jim should go down and check on him."

"Yes, Mrs. Mendelson. I'll buzz Smitty in the kennels."

Pauline deposited her roses on the table and continued on to the hallway and up the stairs. Midway up, she turned. "And, Dudley," she called.

"Yes, Mrs. Mendelson."

"I think you should call an ambulance." She continued up the stairs. "And the police."

Flo's Tape #26

"It often surprised me that Jules didn't have a bodyguard, or bodyguards. So many of the film stars went around surrounded by them, as did many of the millionaires in the city who were nowhere near as rich as Jules. Of course, there were guards at Clouds and attack dogs, and they kept a fake police car in the driveway to scare off the curious, but he never went out in public with guards. He thought they attracted too much attention. And he said if anybody was going to get him, they'd get him anyway. He didn't think it looked right for a presidential designate, which he was, to go around with guards just because he was rich.

"One time when I was in the Bentley with him, driving back to my old neighborhood in Silverlake to pick up some mail, he opened the glove compartment and took out a gun that he held in his lap while we drove. I hated that. But he said there were people out there, mad people, who were out to get people like him."

27

B Y THE TIME Pauline had bathed and changed, both the ambulance and the police had arrived and parked their vehicles in the courtyard. She sent word down to Dudley by Blondell not to allow the attendants to carry Cyril Rathbone's body through her house to get to the ambulance, but to carry it around by the side of the house behind the kennels. From her bedroom, where the windows were open, she could hear one of the attendants say, in a Hispanic accent, as he was lifting the remains of Cyril Rathbone into the ambulance, "They're dropping like flies in this house. This is my second time here. Last time I accidentally hit the picture on the stairs, and you should have heard the lady squawk."

Pauline waited until the ambulance had departed before she came downstairs to meet with Captain Nelson and Officer Whitbeck of the Beverly Hills Police Department.

In the library where they were waiting, the two policemen wandered around the magnificent room, silently looking at objects on tables and the pictures on the walls. Officer Whitbeck occasionally cleared his throat to get the attention of Captain Nelson, and then pointed to a treasure he thought the captain might have missed in his perusal of the room.

"Do you think it's okay to sit?" asked Officer Whitbeck, eyeing the green leather English chair that had been Jules Mendelson's favorite, wanting to lounge in it.

Captain Nelson shook his head. "We better stand," he said.

The library door opened and Pauline entered the room. Wafts of expensive perfume preceded and trailed her. "I hope you've been offered a drink, or something, Captain," she said, going toward him and shaking his hand. "I'm Pauline Mendelson." They had heard and read about the beautiful and very rich widow.

"No, thank you, Mrs. Mendelson," said Captain Nelson. "This is Officer Whitbeck."

Pauline smiled at Officer Whitbeck. "Please, for heaven's sake. Don't stand. Take a seat. Sit there, Officer Whitbeck. That was my husband's favorite chair. You must forgive me for keeping you waiting. I stayed upstairs until the ambulance attendants had removed Mr. Rathbone's body. It brought back such sad memories. My husband recently died."

"Yes, yes, of course," said Captain Nelson, unable to take his eyes off her.

The sheer social power of her overwhelmed the room. Although neither policeman knew anything about fashion or style, each was aware that Pauline Mendelson was wonderfully dressed, in printed silk and quiet gold jewelry, as if she were on her way to a tea. She sat perfectly and with a gesture turned the meeting over to them, as if she were in their power; but they knew, as she did, that they were in hers.

"I'm so sorry, ma'am," said Officer Whitbeck. "But we have to ask you a few questions."

"Of course," she said.

"About your guest, Mr. Rathbone," continued Officer Whitbeck.

"But I barely knew Mr. Rathbone, Officer Whitbeck. He wasn't a guest, in the sense that he had been invited here by me. It was such a strange thing. He is a writer of some sort for *Mulholland* magazine. He had taken a great interest in a yellow phalaenopsis that my head gardener and I have developed, and asked that he be allowed to visit my greenhouse."

"A yellow what?" asked Officer Whitbeck, who was taking notes. "Can you spell that?"

"It's a breed of orchid," said Pauline. "Usually white, but Jarvis, my gardener, and I were able to develop a yellow variety, which I'm proud to say has caused quite a stir in horticultural circles. My garden is my passion. The Los Angeles Garden Club has been here to see it, and it's been photographed for several of the gardening magazines. Mr. Rathbone wanted to see my phalaenopsis, for something he was writing, I suppose. I was cutting roses in my garden when he arrived. There they are there." She pointed to the basket of red and pink roses that she had left on the library table. "I must put them in water before they die. Do you mind? It's terrible for them to just lie there in this heat. We can talk at the same time."

"No, no. Go right ahead, Mrs. Mendelson," said Captain Nelson.

"The next thing I knew he had started to cough and choke, and I asked Dudley, my butler, to send the men down to see if he was all right," called out Pauline from the lavatory, as she ran water for the flowers.

"Do you know his age, Mrs. Mendelson?"

"You'll have to call his magazine. I really didn't know him. Was it a heart attack?" she asked, as she came back into the room with the roses in a vase. "I'll arrange these later."

"He was stung in his mouth by a wasp," said Captain Nelson.

"Good heavens," she said.

When they were gone, she picked up the telephone and dialed. "This is Mrs. Jules Mendelson. I would like to speak to Mr. Pond. . . . I see. . . . Well, ask him anyway. I'm sure if you buzz in, he'll take my call. . . . Sandy, darling, it's Pauline," she said when the publisher came on the telephone. "Such a strange thing has happened. I need your help. This awful man who keeps writing these terrible things about Jules and that woman. What? . . . Yes, yes. That's his name. . . . Rathbone . . . I'll tell you what-about-him. He just died in my house."

Much was made in the press of the bizarre death of Cyril Rathbone, the controversial columnist for *Mulholland* magazine, who had "choked to death after having been stung on the tongue by a wasp in the sculpture garden of the mountaintop estate of Mrs. Jules Mendelson." The only other mention of Pauline Mendelson's name in the account in the *Los Angeles Tribunal,* however, was to say that she had not been home at the time. Exactly what Cyril Rathbone was doing sitting alone in Pauline Mendelson's sculpture garden, where his body was discovered by the butler, was a mystery that caused much speculation, as it was a known fact in social circles that the lady of the house despised him and had never invited him to her home.

No one contributed more to the speculation than Hortense Madden, the literary critic of *Mulholland,* who had also, for quite different reasons, despised Cyril. She reveled in each grotesque detail of his demise, as reported to her by the ambulance attendant, Faustino, whom she managed to track down, as well as by the undertaker, who had both embalmed Cyril and laid him out in the closed coffin. Their descriptions of the size and the color of Cyril's tongue fascinated her, and she made them repeat certain particulars, which she wrote in a notebook, like a reporter at the scene of a crime. She even begged to have the coffin opened for a final look at Cyril, but the undertaker refused her request, on professional grounds, as she was not a member of his family.

"My dear, the tongue was swollen to four times its size, ready to burst, apparently. Bright red, turning black," Hortense breathlessly reported to Lucia Borsodi. "Imagine what he must have been saying to Pauline at the time to have God pick that moment and that manner to take him."

God was not someone who regularly appeared in Hortense's conversation or thoughts, and Lucia, for propriety's sake, drew a halt to the conversation. "But Pauline Mendelson wasn't even there, Hortense," she said. "He went there to see her yellow phalaenopsis."

"I don't believe that story for a single moment," said Hortense with a dismissive gesture. "You mark my words, Pauline hotfooted it out of there as fast as she could, as soon as Cyril choked out his last breath."

"Well, I must write a eulogy," said Lucia. "I haven't a clue what to say."

"Say that in whatever corner of hell Cyril is residing, he is most certainly bragging to the other devils that he managed to die in Pauline, Mrs. Mendelson's, sculpture garden," said Hortense.

On the advice of Sandy Pond, Pauline left Clouds as soon as she had finished speaking with him. "Reporters will be calling. It's just as well not to be there," he said. "You've had enough publicity since Jules's death."

Fortunately, Jules's Bentley was parked in the courtyard, with the keys in the ignition, and she hopped into it and drove down the mountain to Camilla Ebury's house, without a word to Jim, her chauffeur, who was in the kitchen with Gertie, the cook, getting the grocery order, which had to be picked up at Jurgensen's Market.

When Camilla looked up from her serve and saw her unexpected guest coming toward the court, she halted her second serve and waved to Pauline. Camilla said something to Philip, and he turned to look at Pauline. Both knew that Pauline was not the sort of person to drop in on people, even on a friend as close as Camilla Ebury was, and Camilla suspected that there was something wrong.

"Keep playing, keep playing," said Pauline. "I don't want to interrupt your game."

"Is everything all right?" asked Camilla.

"Of course. I was just passing, and I thought I hadn't seen you for a bit and that I'd stop in for a glass of iced tea. But I don't want to stop your game. Hello, Philip."

"Hello, Pauline," he replied, in a polite but guarded fashion, remembering the unpleasant conclusion to their previous encounter.

Pauline smiled at Philip in a friendly way. "I've never seen you in shorts, Philip. What marvelous legs you have. No wonder Camilla is so mad about you."

"Pauline!" said Camilla, blushing and laughing.

Philip was surprised by Pauline, as her friendliness belied their last leave-taking, when it had seemed that they would never see each other again.

"I'll ring for some iced tea," said Camilla.

"No, no. Finish your set," said Pauline. "I'll watch."

Camilla could never picture Pauline spending a leisurely sort of afternoon, or even a leisurely hour, lying back on a chaise watching a tennis game. She was always so frenetically busy, in her garden, or with her correspondence, or her charities, or her guest lists, or her seating charts, or her flower arranging. But she sat back on Camilla's chaise in a totally relaxed fashion and watched the completion of the set with total concentration, even occasionally making the appropriate remark on a good serve, or lob, or backhand.

When the set was completed, they returned to the house and talked for over an hour on matters of no consequence, in the sort of conversation that Pauline was usually contemptuous of as a waste of valuable time.

"Am I in the way?" asked Philip, thinking there was a point to the visit that his presence was delaying. "Would you two ladies like to talk alone?"

"No, no," cried Pauline. "Tell me, what is it you're writing now? I hope you're not still involved with Casper Stieglitz. Will you ever forget that night? Wasn't it a nightmare?"

"Philip's moving back to New York," said Camilla.

"When?"

"Next week."

"Next week? Philip, why?"

"I've finished here. I came for a few months, and I've stayed almost a year. It's time."

Pauline looked at Camilla, who appeared downcast at Philip's decision.

"And here I am interrupting one of your last days together," said Pauline, getting up to leave.

As they stood in the driveway and watched the Bentley pull out onto Copa de Oro Road, Camilla remarked to Philip, whose arm was around her waist, that she hadn't seen Pauline in such good humor since before Jules's death.

When Philip read in the *Tribunal* the next morning that Mrs. Mendelson had not been at home at the time of Cyril Rathbone's death, he understood.

"There goes my Thursday-afternoon income," said Lonny Edge, tossing the *Tribunal* aside.

Flo March was too young even to think of reading the obituary pages of the newspaper, unless the death announced was of sufficient news value to rate headlines, like Rock Hudson's, or Lucille Ball's, and she did not know that Cyril Rathbone had died until her new housemate happened to mention it, over their morning coffee.

"Cyril Rathbone is dead?" asked Flo, shocked. "How?"

"Got stung on his tongue by a wasp."

Flo thought for a moment. "Not inappropriate," she said.

"What does that mean?"

"The guy had a tongue like a viper. Where did this happen?"

"At Pauline Mendelson's house."

"At Pauline Mendelson's? You have to be kidding!"

"That's what the paper says," said Lonny.

"Let me see that," said Flo. She took the paper and read the account. "I wonder what he was doing at Pauline's."

Lonny shook his head.

"He hated Pauline. And Pauline didn't like him. Jules used to tell me that. I bet I know what he was doing up there at Clouds," said Flo.

"He was a regular of mine. Every Thursday afternoon at four. Rain or shine. Always brought doughnuts."

"You get fat eating doughnuts, Lonny. You were beginning to get a gut," said Flo.

"Hey, I didn't think you ever noticed me, Flo."

"Don't get any ideas."

Lonny laughed. "He was kind of a snazzy dresser. He always wore seersucker suits and a pink tie. Not my kind of taste. Kinda English. I'll miss the guy."

"I won't."

"No?"

"He wanted me to jump out a fifteenth-story window."

Lonny stared at her. "You got any more cigarettes? I'm out."

Jo Jo had reported back to Arnie Zwillman that he had not been able to locate Cyril Rathbone, either at his office at *Mulholland* magazine or at his condominium in the Wilshire district.

"Not like you to let me down, Jo Jo," said Arnie, from the telephone in his steam room.

When Arnie read about Cyril's death in the *Tribunal* the next morning, he understood and called Jo Jo immediately. "This means that the dame is the only one who has the tapes, so they're either in her safety deposit box or her house."

"That's what I was thinkin'," said Jo Jo.

"I wonder what the fruitcake was doing up at Pauline's house," said Arnie.

The funeral service, which was held in the tiny chapel of a mortuary near the Paramount Studio, was sparsely attended, as might be expected for the funeral service of a man who was unloved. According to Hortense Madden's count, there were only fifty seats in the chapel, and not all of those were occupied. Most of those present were employees of the magazine, whom Lucia Borsodi had given orders to attend, even including the man who ran the photocopying machine. In the back, by a spray of pink gladiolus that would have offended Cyril's eye, sat Lonny Edge, the pornography star. Hortense Madden, who had a fertile imagination, was quick to figure out the connection.

Neither of the two ladies in whose lives Cyril had become intertwined at a literary level in the months before his death, Pauline Mendelson and Flo March, was present, although Pauline, to avoid criticism, as Cyril had died in her garden, sent flowers. The flowers she sent were not from her own garden or greenhouse, which was her usual habit, or from the fashionable florist Petra von Kant. Instead she dispatched her maid, Blondell, to send them, and Blondell, with no instructions from the mountaintop as to choice, chose the pink gladiolus, which Lucia Borsodi relegated to the back of the chapel.

"You were my husband's friend, Sims," said Pauline.

"Yes."

"You knew him better than anyone."

"Perhaps."

"There are tapes that Miss March has recorded. Did you know that?"

"No."

"Forty hours, so far. Apparently, there are revelations on those tapes, if I am to believe what that frightful Cyril Rathbone told me, that could prove embarrassing. Business revelations. Personal revelations."

"Did you believe him? Half of what he writes is bullshit. Everyone says so."

"I did believe him, yes."

"Did he say more?"

"That was when the wasp flew into his mouth and stung his tongue."

There was a brief silence. Sims asked, "Are you crying?"

"A bit. Yes. Something has to be done, Sims. These tapes, if they do exist, must be stolen."

"Easier said than done. I wouldn't know how to go about such a thing."

"I have an idea," said Pauline. "Did you ever hear of someone called Arnie Zwillman?"

"The guy who burned down the Vegas Seraglio for the insurance money?"

"Yes. Ghastly man. I met him once. He has that sort of extra-clean look that gangsters sometimes have. I think they bathe more often than other people."

"What about Arnie Zwillman? He tried to shake down Jules. He was responsible for Jules not getting the appointment to Brussels."

"He's on the tapes too, apparently. All that business about Brussels and the laundered money."

"I'm missing a beat here, Pauline."

"It seems to me that Mr. Arnie Zwillman would know a thing or two about breaking into Miss March's house and stealing the tapes," said Pauline. "I mean, isn't that the sort of thing those people do?"

Flo's Tape #27

"Last night, when I couldn't sleep, I watched Laura *on television. There was this character called Waldo Lydecker played by an old movie star, probably long dead now, named Clifton Webb. I kept thinking to myself, 'Who does this guy remind me of?' and then I realized it was Cyril Rathbone, and not just because the two of them were gossip columnists. They even dressed alike, and they talked alike.*

"I heard from the lady at the Wells Fargo Bank in Beverly Hills that Cyril had a fit when he found that I had taken the tapes out of the safety deposit vault. We both had keys. I bet the reason he was up at Clouds to see Pauline had something to do with these tapes. Knowing Cyril like I came to, he was probably trying to blackmail her with what was on the tapes.

"I'm surprised he didn't come up here and try to get them away from me."

28

A T FIRST, after Jules's death, when the money stopped coming, Flo
March's economies had been relatively painless. She stopped renewing
her magazine subscriptions when they came due and purchased cheaper
brands of bottled water. Then she gave up her daily excursions to the boutiques
on Rodeo Drive and began marketing at Hughes in West Hollywood instead of
at Jurgenson's in Beverly Hills. The man who regularly cleaned her swimming
pool stayed on as long as he could without getting paid, because he liked Flo
and realized she was in trouble, but he eventually left. In his absence, the water
in the pool developed a scumlike surface, and the drain became clogged by
leaves. Then Flo let her gardener go, when Lonny Edge suggested that he
could do just as good a job as "the little Jap" was doing, but Lonny soon tired
of the chore and forgot to turn on the sprinklers, and kept postponing mowing
the lawn or tending the garden, so the grass became long and brown, and the
garden was choked by weeds, sights that would not please any landlord's eye,
and they were certainly displeasing to the eye of Trent Muldoon, the television
star, when he returned to look at his home on Azelia Way after a long absence.

He pushed the front doorbell and could hear pretty chimes ring inside the
house. The chimes were but one of the many improvements his tenant had put
into the house. There was no answer, but he could see that there were two cars
in the garage. After several minutes, he rang again. This time the door was
opened by a sleepy Lonny Edge, dressed only in a towel wrapped around his
middle, who had been awakened from his late-morning siesta by the pool by
the sound of the chimes.

"Yeah?" he asked.

"I would like to see Miss March," said Trent.

"She's asleep. She don't get up till noon."

"Would you tell her Trent Muldoon is here."

"Trent Muldoon," said Lonny, breaking into a wide smile as the television
star's face came into focus. For a moment he could not remember the name of
Trent Muldoon's canceled series, which he used to watch, but he was still
delighted to be in his presence. "I thought I recognized you."

"Would you wake her up, please?"

"Sure thing. Come in, Trent. Wait here in the living room. You can sit right
there on her gray satin sofa. I'll get Flo."

It was then, when he was alone in the room, that Trent Muldoon saw how the plate glass window had been shattered by the gunshot that Flo had fired in the room. She had not replaced the glass in the window, because the cheapest estimate had been eighteen hundred dollars, which she could not afford. She had taken her canary diamond earrings to a dealer in antique jewels in Beverly Hills. The extent of her financial plight was so well known that the manager of the shop took advantage of her immediate need for money and offered her a sum of less than half of their worth. At the last moment, she could not bear to part with them, as they had been Jules's last gift to her, so she sold the jeweler only one of the earrings for the value of the canary diamond. It had been Flo's intention to replace the smashed window, but she used the money to pay off her most pressing bills, and then there was nothing left.

Trent Muldoon was standing by the window, running his fingers over the shattered plate glass, when Flo walked into the room, followed by Lonny. She was barefoot, wearing only a terry cloth robe and dark glasses, and her hair was uncombed.

In her years of being tutored by Jules Mendelson, she had developed an eye for style and an understanding of manners and good taste. Even with her head and heart pounding, even without looking in the mirror of her bar for verification, she knew exactly how she appeared to Trent Muldoon at that instant, as he looked up at her from the shattered window. She knew that she presented a picture without style or taste, and that Lonny Edge, the porn star, standing behind her with only a towel wrapped around his middle, detracted even further from her diminished image. She put her hands to her head in a vain attempt to bring some kind of order to her hair.

"I can explain that," she said, about the window, before he had a chance to speak. "This box was delivered to me, in the middle of the night. Like a corsage box. And I opened it, and there was a lot of wrapping paper inside, you know, like pink tissue paper, and at the bottom of the box was this gun, and there was a note, and the note said, 'Put it in your mouth and fire it,' I swear to God. In my whole life, I'd never held a gun in my hand, and I didn't know what to do with it, so I aimed it out there to the door and fired it, just to see if it was loaded; and as you can see, it was, and the door got shattered. Now, it's being fixed. I can assure you of that. There is a new plate glass window on order."

She looked at him. She knew how she sounded. She looked at Lonny. She knew how he looked. She wished she had never asked Lonny to come to share her house with her.

"I'm very sorry about this, Miss March, but I'm afraid that I have to instruct my business manager to go ahead with eviction proceedings," said Trent. "It's been four months since you paid the rent, and my house has been not only neglected, but destroyed."

"Hey, please, Trent. Or, Mr. Muldoon, I mean. Give me a break, will you. Don't make me move. I love this house," she said, trying not to cry. "If I'd known you were coming, I'd have had it looking all spick-and-span, the way it's always been. I've been going through some bad times. I'm getting straightened out. You'll get your rent, and the plate glass window will be fixed. I swear to God."

Trent moved across the living room without answering and walked out of the house.

"Hey, Trent." She ran after him, calling out, "Listen, please. Look at all the money I put into this house. You have to see the closet space. It was designed by Nellie Potts. She's the best decorator in Beverly Hills. It cost thousands. And the wet bar. I put in the wet bar and the mirrored walls."

She stood at her front door and continued to talk to him as he got into his Ferrari and closed the door and started the motor and backed out of her driveway, which was not going to be her driveway much longer. "How can you kick me out of here, Trent, when I've increased the value of your house? Please. Just give me three months. I need three months to get my book finished. Please. Please. I spent a fortune on your lousy house."

Trent Muldoon was not hard-hearted. He knew what it was to go through a bad spell, and he felt sorry for Flo March. But an instinct told him that she was not going to have a comeback, as he was, if the picture he'd just completed in Yugoslavia turned out to be the hit the Italian producer told him it was going to be. He knew panic and desperation when he saw it, and Flo March was panicky and desperate.

When the eviction notice was served, Flo became too paralyzed with fear of what was ahead of her to be able to find a place to move. She had thirty days to vacate the premises, but it was only at the end of three weeks that she began to look for a new place.

"Don't mention my name, Lonny, when we look. Nobody wants to touch me with a ten-foot pole," said Flo.

She disliked every apartment or condo she saw, when she compared it to what she had on Azelia Way. "If I have to live in a dump, at least I'd like to live in a dump in a better neighborhood," she said about each one she saw.

Each day she cursed herself for spending so much money when she had money. Driving with Lonny Edge in his car to look at places that she could not afford and would not have liked to live in if she had been able to afford them, she repeated over and over again the litany of her expenses. "The curtains alone cost me forty thousand dollars, and the closet with all the built-ins, that was another forty. Right there, there's eighty thousand. Do you want to know what I spent on mirrors?"

"Hey, hey, hey. You're sounding like a broken record, Flo. You've told me all this a hundred times. I'm sick of hearing it," said Lonny.

"I know. I know. Listen, Lonny," said Flo.

"Yeah?"

"Can you get me some Valium? My nerves are jangled. I need to calm down."

"I thought you couldn't have any pills in AA."

Flo ignored what he said. "Could you get me some, Lonny? After the move, I'll calm down again."

"Sure."

They had started to argue. They were mismatched and tired of each other. She didn't want to be seen with him in public and was afraid that he would leave her. She had stopped going to the AA meetings in the early mornings again. She could not bear to see Philip Quennell. She did not want him to know what dire circumstances she was in, or that Lonny Edge was living in her house. She had heard through an AA acquaintance she ran into at the Hughes Market that he was moving back to New York. She tried to call him at the

Chateau Marmont to say good-bye, but he had checked out. The forwarding number was at Camilla Ebury's house.

"Hello?"

"Is that you, Camilla?"

"Yes."

"This is Flo March."

"Oh. Hello."

Flo spoke very quickly, as if she was afraid of being cut off. "Listen, Camilla. I know you're Pauline's friend, and I don't want to put you in a spot talking to me, so just let me talk quick, and you don't have to say anything. First, thanks for being so nice to me at Jules's funeral. You didn't have to do that, and I was very touched, and, second, I need to talk to Philip. I heard from someone he's moving back to New York, and I have to speak to him before he goes. I think my phone's tapped, so he better not call me here. Ask him if he'll be at the meeting on Thursday. We can talk there. Okay?"

"Of course. I'll tell him," said Camilla.

"You know I'm not after him, don't you, Camilla?"

"I know that."

"It's just a business thing I want to discuss."

"I'll tell him. And Flo?"

"Yes?"

"Good luck to you."

Lonny Edge was very vain about his body and took great pains to keep in shape. Each afternoon since he had moved into Azelia Way, he drove down Coldwater Canyon to Beverly Park and ran around the track for three miles. Several days in a row, he noticed a gold Rolls-Royce parked in the alley near the completion of the run. Lonny always stared at expensive cars and had curiosity about the people in them. After the second day, he noticed that the two men in the front seat were looking at him. After the third day, he responded when they nodded to him. On the fourth day he did not think it amiss when they asked him if he needed a ride. He didn't need a ride, but he got in the backseat of the Rolls anyway. He was used to being picked up, and he missed the adventures of the streets in the expensive neighborhood where he now lived.

The adventure was of a different sort than he expected. But it involved wealth, more money than he had ever imagined would be his. He had only to unlock a door.

"What do you mean, unlock a door?"

"Just that. Leave the door unlocked. Very simple."

"And then, you do what?"

"Pay a visit. That's all. There's some tapes in that house I want."

"Tapes? You mean, my videos? You don't have to break in for that. You can buy them at the all-night bookshop on the corner of Santa Monica and Havenhurst for thirty-nine ninety-five."

"No. Not your videos, Lonny. Audiotapes. Forty hours of audiotapes. Microcassettes. Those little ones."

"I don't know anything about that," said Lonny.

"They're there. They used to be in a safety deposit box at the Wells Fargo Bank in Beverly Hills, but they're in that house now."

"And Flo?" asked Lonny.

"What about Miss March?" asked Arnie.

"Nothing would happen to Flo, would it?"

"Heavens, no. I have no interest in her whatever. It's just the tapes I want." They dropped Lonny back at Beverly Park.

Later, back at the old Charles Boyer house, Arnie Zwillman telephoned Sims Lord. "I saw him. I took him for a ride."

"And?"

"Lonny Edge has an IQ that hovers around room temperature."

In the background, Jo Jo, listening, laughed, but Arnie raised a disapproving hand, and the laughter curdled.

It was Lonny who came up with the housing solution. He reported to Flo that he had run into his old landlord from his bungalow on Cahuenga Boulevard. The new tenant had caused a small fire, and the landlord said that Lonny would be welcome back.

"But I thought the landlord and you parted on very bad terms," said Flo.

"We did."

"I thought he accused you of turning tricks in your bungalow," she said.

"He did."

"Why would he welcome you back then?"

"I told him I'd given up all that. I told him I'd turned over a new leaf." Flo nodded. It seemed to her that there was a beat missing in his story.

"Also, if they go ahead with publishing Basil Plant's book, I'll be in the news for having discovered this long-lost masterpiece, and he liked that," said Lonny.

"But I thought you said it was just a tiny little place with hardly enough room for you," said Flo.

"It is."

"Then why would you want me to move in with you?"

"You did me a favor when I needed a place. I'm just returning the favor." She missed Jules more and more. She missed having him make decisions for her.

"Listen, it could be just a stopgap for you, Flo," said Lonny. "You could put your furniture in storage, rather than rush into some place you don't like. Then, when you find something, you can move on. It might be just the thing for you, to drop out for a while, and you certainly won't run into anyone you know from Beverly Hills over in my old neighborhood."

"Okay," she said. She had no other choices.

For one whole day Flo and Glyceria stood on a ladder and unhooked all her curtains.

"They'll never fit anyplace else," said Glyceria.

"I don't care. I don't want Trent Muldoon to have them," she answered.

"What are you going to do with them?" asked Glyceria.

"Do you want them, Glycie?" asked Flo.

"Hell, no. I've only got three little tiny windows in my place," said Glyceria.

"Then I'll put them in storage. I think I'll break the mirrors in the bar before I leave," said Flo.

"No, don't break them. He could cause you trouble. I'll take them off the walls for you," said Glyceria.

On the last night she spent in her house, the front hall was lined with cartons and packing cases going into storage, and with shopping bags filled with things she was taking with her to the bungalow on Cahuenga Boulevard. Her gray satin sofas and her other upholstered furniture were tagged for the warehouse, as were her Chinese brass candlesticks with the dragons climbing up the sides. Glyceria helped her wrap her Steuben glasses in newspaper, and her Tiffany plates and silverware in the boxes and bags they arrived in. The moving vans were coming the next morning at ten. She had only to pack her clothes. All her Louis Vuitton bags were out and open, but she had not yet taken her Chanel suits off their satin hangers, or emptied the many drawers and shelves in her dressing room cupboards of her blouses and sweaters and nightgowns and underwear and stockings.

Hidden away behind the lingerie that she had ordered from Paris, from the same shop on the Rue de Rivoli where Pauline Mendelson had her lingerie made, was the small brown bag with the thirty-nine hours of microcassette tapes that she had removed from the safety deposit box at the Wells Fargo Bank in Beverly Hills on the morning after Cyril Rathbone had tried to talk her into jumping out the fifteenth-story window of the Valley Studios.

"Here's your key to my place," said Lonny. She was relieved that Lonny Edge had, as he put it, "things to do" that evening, and absented himself from Azelia Way. She thought that perhaps he had returned to the nocturnal habits he had said were a part of his past. Men called him at the house, and he had spent several evenings and afternoons away, without explanation, since the decision was made to move into his old bungalow on Cahuenga Boulevard. She noticed that he had a great deal more cash on hand than he usually had, and he exhibited a show of generosity toward her that she was unused to from him. He stopped bickering with her over inconsequential financial matters. When she asked him to go to the Hughes Market to get her things, he went without complaining and paid for even her personal items, like sanitary napkins and nail polish, without insisting on being reimbursed. Sometimes he brought home pizzas and made her eat.

"I don't think you should stay here tonight, with the house all upside down like this," said Lonny. "Too depressing. Go over to my place. I'll be there after midnight. I'll bring you back here in the morning before the movers come."

"Okay, Lonny. Give me that address once again on Cahuenga."

"Seventy-two-oh-four and a quarter. Up Highland Avenue to Odin. Turn right under the bridge to get to Cahuenga," said Lonny patiently. It was the third time he had told her the address.

"Right. Right. I'll remember. I just want to stay here for a while by myself. You know. Memories. There were good times in this house, believe it or not."

"Sure, Flo," said Lonny. He leaned over and kissed her on the cheek.

She wanted to be alone on her last night on Azelia Way. Over and over again, she walked through the rooms of the small and elegant house where so much had happened to her. It was not a house with happy memories, but she loved it because it had been hers, or almost hers, and in her mind she relived the joys and sadnesses she had experienced there. She wondered to herself if she would ever again live in the manner that she had lived there. Finally, late, she lay down on her gray satin sofa. She picked up the cushion with Kippie Petworth's blood, now faded to a dark stain, on the reverse side and placed it behind her head. She meant just to lie there for a bit and rest, to think of her life with Jules Mendelson, as well as the life that was ahead of her. Her sole asset was her tapes. She felt sure that she could get someone to help her put them into book form. The someone she wanted to help her was Philip Quennell. She knew that he would understand both the shortcomings and the greatness of Jules Mendelson. She knew that he was not seeking revenge, the way Cyril Rathbone had been seeking revenge on Pauline Mendelson. The prospect of working with Philip Quennell was pleasing to her. She dwelt on the pleasing thought. She had not meant to fall asleep when there was so much work still to be done, but she did.

She was awakened by a sound. She knew there was someone in her house. At first she thought it might be Lonny, returning for her when he discovered she wasn't at the bungalow on Cahuenga Boulevard, as she had promised him she would be. But the sounds she heard were not the Lonny sounds she had become accustomed to during the month they had been living together on Azelia Way, the sounds of slammed refrigerator doors, belches, and the television set turned on far too loud. She lay where she was on the gray satin sofa without moving, as if she were still asleep. From behind her she heard a breathing sound and realized that the person in her house was in the same room, by the fireplace. Very slowly she sat up on her sofa and turned her head to see the figure of a man rifling through the packing boxes on the floor. The definition of his face was obliterated by a woman's stocking pulled over it.

"Lonny, is that you?" she asked, even though she knew it wasn't Lonny. Her voice was tinny and high-pitched. She could feel the frightened beating of her heart pounding against her chest. Her fingers stiffened. Her lips, her nose, even the follicles of her hair began to tingle with fear. "What are you doing in my house? Why are you ripping those cartons and bags apart? Who are you? What are you looking for?"

The man did not reply. Very quietly, he stood up. She saw in his hand one of the brass candlesticks from China with the dragon crawling up the side, and a red tag on it to identify it as one of the pieces to go into the moving van for storage the next morning.

"That's Chinese," said Flo. She was breathing very heavily. "That's an antique. One of the dynasties, Jules told me. Ming, maybe. I could never get it straight. What are you doing with it? Why are you coming toward me like that? Please. Don't. Is it the tapes? Is that what you want? Those damn tapes. Is that it? Take the tapes. They're in the other room. Oh, no."

She watched the brass candlestick descend to bash in the side of her head. "Oh, dear God," she said. She raised her hands to cover her face. "No, not my face. Please don't hit me in the face, please, mister. Not my face, please." The sapphire in the diamond-and-sapphire ring that Jules had given her, which she told Cyril Rathbone would be on her finger when she died, smashed from the force of the next blow. Her lipsticked lips moved again, but her attacker knew that she was only saying a prayer. "Oh, dear God, help me, help me" were her last audible words. The sounds that came from her mouth through the next eight blows were prayers, "HailMaryfullofgracethelordiswiththee," indecipherable to her attacker, asking God to forgive her sins, asking her mother for help, asking Jules to let her die before she was hit again, because she knew, before the first blow landed, that there was no rescue for her.

"*I know I should be thinking about this damn book, but all that I can think of these days is what's going to happen to me. It's a terrible feeling to think that the best things that have happened to me have already happened, and everything else is going to be downhill from here. But no matter how hard I try to visualize what my life will be like from here on, I can't seem to come up with a picture. What the hell does that mean?*"

"PHILIP. Once you said to me that you had caused a girl to be paralyzed and that it had changed your life forever," said Camilla.

Philip Quennell's romance with Camilla Ebury had lasted the better part of a year. During that time she had given thoughts to marriage, but he consistently made it clear that he resisted permanence in love. In his past there was a nameless girl whose life he had thwarted, for whom he felt a responsibility that precluded such thoughts, and Camilla learned to accept what she had for as long as it lasted. They had loved and fought and parted and made up and loved again, and the arrangement, finally understood by each of them, brought pleasure to both.

On their last night together before Philip returned to New York, they dined alone in Camilla's house and then made love with the same ferocity and frequency as they had on their first night, following their meeting at Jules and Pauline Mendelson's party on the evening of his arrival in the city.

Philip got up from the bed. Camilla watched him as he opened the door of her closet and took out his blue-and-white-striped dressing gown and put it on. He walked over to her dressing table and pulled the chair from its place so that the back of it was facing the bed. Then he straddled it and looked at her as he started to speak.

"Her name was Sophie Bushnell. Her name *is* Sophie Bushnell, I should say. She is alive, but alive in a wheelchair because of me."

"I want to hear, Philip," said Camilla.

With his finger he traced the design on the back of the chair as he talked, looking at it. "We were in her car, but I was driving, too fast, over a causeway that separated the part of town where she lived from the part of town where I lived. We had been drinking. I hit an abutment. She broke her neck."

He raised his eyes and looked at Camilla.

"Is there more?"

"Yes."

"What?"

"I was trouserless at the time." He rose from his seat and walked into her bathroom.

"Is that why you're so afraid to commit?" she asked when he came out.

"Pretty good reason, don't you think?"

* * *

"I'll miss you," she said later, laying her head against his chest.

"Me too," he answered. He placed both his arms around her.

"You've turned me into a wanton woman."

"It's what you were born to be."

"It won't really be over, will it?"

"You know it won't."

"There'll be other times."

"Of course."

"You'll come out?"

"Sure."

Philip could not bear leave-takings. It was arranged between them that there would be no morning farewells. When he kissed her good night, he told her he would be gone before she awoke in the morning. Philip was always up before six to attend his AA meeting at the log cabin on Robertson Boulevard, and Camilla, more often than not, slept late; so the morning of his leaving was no different from their usual routine, except that she did get up and make him a cup of coffee while he was shaving and showering. Their last kiss was just a peck, as if he were off to the office for the day or, with his packed bags, off on a business trip, although he would not have honked his horn twice at the end of the driveway if he were just off for the day or for a business trip.

He planned to see Flo March at the meeting and take her out for a cup of coffee afterward, before he left for the airport.

"You don't have to worry about me," Flo had said to him at the meeting the day before, when they made their coffee date.

"I do worry. You're the most fragile tough girl I ever knew," he answered.

"Is that good?" she asked.

"I don't know." He had an urge to kiss her.

"How's Camilla?" she asked, understanding his urge.

He laughed.

"You don't think my life is complicated enough?" she asked. "I'll give you a nice AA hug, though."

They both laughed.

"Listen, there's something I want to talk to you about before you go," she said. "Of a business nature."

Driving toward West Hollywood, he imagined that what she wanted to talk about had to do with the book that she had been writing with Cyril Rathbone before his death. His plan was to advise her to leave Los Angeles and start anew someplace else, where her name was less well known.

He saved a seat for her by putting his car keys on the chair next to his, but Flo March did not appear at the meeting. When the room became crowded, and there were not enough seats for all, he picked up the keys and relinquished the chair. Every time a latecomer entered the room, he looked anxiously toward the door. A feeling of unrest came over him. He tried to focus his attention on the talk being given by a former surgeon who told of operating on a patient while he was drunk, but he could not concentrate on the man's pain. Halfway through the talk, he rose and went outside. There was a public telephone on the corner of the street. He dialed Flo's number. The ring had a peculiar tone, and then the recorded voice of an operator came on and said that the number he was dialing was no longer in service. He wondered if the telephone company had disconnected her phone for nonpayment of her bill, or if she had ordered it to be disconnected because she was moving. His feelings of unease about Flo returned.

When he got into his car, he found that it was blocked by the cars in front of him and behind him, both of which had parked too closely, and he could not get out. He knew he would have to wait for the end of the meeting for the occupants to come and move their vehicles. Just then a yellow cab turned the corner to drop off a latecomer in front of the log cabin. Philip recognized that it was Rose Cliveden, hiding behind dark glasses and a head scarf that were meant to disguise her, although no one at the meeting would have known who she was, even if she announced her name and bank balance.

He ducked down into his car, not wanting to be waylaid by Rose. In her sobriety, she talked as much as she had talked when she was drinking. Turning, she saw him and waved as she approached his car.

"I need your advice, Philip," she said. "I'm scheduled to speak tomorrow on my three-month anniversary, and I have the most awful confession to make."

"Rose, I'm in rather a hurry this morning," answered Philip.

"You see, I never heard the word grandiosity until I came into the program, and I'm afraid I've been very guilty of it," she said, as if Philip had not spoken. "For years, almost thirty, I've always told people I had an affair with Jack Kennedy, in the Lincoln Bedroom in the White House. I think I even discussed it with you on the first night we met. Do you remember? You said to me, 'What kind of a fuck was Jack Kennedy?' And I told you he was a marvelous lover until he came, and then he couldn't stand to be touched, because of all that Irish Catholic guilt. Do you remember all that?"

"Yes, Rose, I remember, but—"

"Well, I just made it all up."

"Rose, please, I must go," he said, but there was no getting rid of Rose Cliveden when Rose was discussing herself.

"It wasn't true. I never went to bed with Jack Kennedy. But I told it so many times I began to believe it. I thought it made me a more interesting woman. How do you think that would sound when I speak on my anniversary tomorrow? Is that the sort of thing they like to hear?"

Philip looked outside the car as the taxi that Rose had gotten out of began backing up in order to turn around. He began to talk very quickly. "That's not really the point, Rose, whether they would like to hear it or not. You see, it's not an entertainment when you speak. You only have to say that you made up stories to enhance your importance during the years you were drinking," said Philip. "But I really must go, Rose. I have to be somewhere."

"Do you think I should write Jackie and apologize for telling that awful story?"

"No. Good-bye, Rose. I'm going to try and grab your taxi. I can't get my car out of here."

As Rose disappeared inside the log cabin, he opened the door of his car and ran after the cab, waving his arms to attract the attention of the driver.

"Please," he said, when he got to the cab. "Can you take me to Azelia Way? It's halfway up Coldwater Canyon."

"Can't, fella. I'm a Beverly Hills cab in West Hollywood. I'm not supposed to pick up customers off the streets out of my own district, or I could get a fine. Sorry."

"This is important," said Philip. He didn't understand why he felt a sense of urgency. He took a twenty-dollar bill from his pocket and handed it to the driver. "Nobody's looking. Nobody's going to report you. It's only twenty minutes past seven. The streets are still empty."

"Does the fare come out of the twenty?"

"No. The twenty's on top of the fare."

"Hop in."

When they turned off Coldwater Canyon onto Azelia Way, the taxi driver said, "Oh, Azelia Way. That's where Faye Converse lives."

"The house I'm going to is the first house past Faye Converse's house," said Philip.

"I know her maid," said the driver.

"Uh-huh," said Philip.

"Glyceria."

"What?"

"Her maid's name is Glyceria. I drive her to the bus station every night. Faye pays."

"It's right here," said Philip. "Turn here."

"Oh, no, fella. That driveway's too steep. I'll never be able to turn around up there. You can get out here."

Philip paid the driver. He hopped out of the cab and ran up the hill. The grass had turned brown and had not been cut. The shrubbery along the path to the front door looked ragged, in need of clipping. When he got to the door, he rang the bell. There was no answer. Then he rang again. He tried the front door, and it was unlocked. When he opened it, he called out, "Flo?" He waited a moment. Then he called again. "Flo? Are you here, Flo? It's Philip. Can I come in?"

There was no answer. He peered inside. There were cartons and packing cases and shopping bags along the walls of the hallway, in preparation for moving, but they had been torn apart, and the contents were scattered. He wondered if there had been a robbery, or if vandals had gotten into the house. As he walked in, he saw that the living room was in shambles. He walked down the hallway to the bedroom. The bed had not been slept in, and there were half-packed bags on it. The door to the elaborate dressing room that Flo had had built was open. All the drawers were pulled out, and blouses and sweaters and stockings and belts and lingerie were hanging out of them, as if the place had been ransacked.

"Flo?" he called out again.

Slowly he walked out of her bedroom back into the living room. The back of the gray satin sofa was facing toward him. There was a pair of her shoes on the floor, one halfway under the sofa, the other by a chair. A brass candlestick with a dragon crawling up the side had been dropped on the floor, its bloody base staining the white carpet. He leaned down and picked it up. There were pieces of red hair mixed in with the blood. He rose and walked very slowly over to the sofa and, with dread, looked down at the body of Flo March. Her red hair was matted with blood. Her hands covered her face, as if to protect it, and the sapphire in her ring was smashed, as was the finger on which it was worn. There were contusions on her forearm.

All the blood drained from Philip's face as he looked down at his beautiful friend. "Oh, Flo," he breathed out. On the bar was a telephone. When he picked it up, there was no dial tone, and he remembered that it had been disconnected. He ran out of the house. In order to get to Faye Converse's house next door, he had to run down the long steep driveway to Azelia Way and then run up the driveway next door. He rang and rang the bell, but there was no answer. He called out her name, "Miss Converse!" and then called out the name of Glyceria, the maid, but the house was closed up. Faye Converse had gone to New York to promote her new perfume, and Glyceria had not arrived yet for work.

He ran down to Azelia Way and then up to Flo's house again, hoping that the keys to her car would be in it, but they were not. Again he ran down the driveway and then down Azelia Way to Coldwater Canyon. He was sweating from all the running. The heavy morning traffic down the canyon had started. He tried to hail a ride, but the cars passed him by without stopping. He began to run frantically. A passing motorist dialed the Beverly Hills police on his cellular telephone.

"There's a crazy guy running up and down Coldwater Canyon," he said.

Blondell, Pauline Mendelson's maid, who had been with Pauline for over twenty years, tapped on the door of her bedroom and entered without waiting for a reply. She was carrying a small tray with a cup of tea, which she placed on a table by Pauline's bed. She went over to the curtains and pulled them back to let in the morning light.

"For heaven's sake. What are you doing, Blondell? What time is it?"

"Early. Are you awake?" asked Blondell.

"Just slightly," said Pauline. "Come back in an hour. I'm going to try to sleep some more."

"I thought you would want to know—"

"I've had a terribly sleepless night again."

"—that that woman who was in the church at Mr. Mendelson's funeral—"

"Oh, puleeze. I don't want to be awakened to hear anything about her," said Pauline.

"She's dead, Mrs. Mendelson."

"What?" Pauline sat up in bed.

"Murdered," replied Blondell.

"What?" Pauline said again.

"It's on the news."

"How?"

"Beaten in the face and head with a brass candlestick."

"Good God. Do they know who did it?"

"They've arrested a man who was running wildly away from the house down Coldwater Canyon."

"Do they know who it is?"

"They didn't give his name."

* * *

In the old Charles Boyer house, Arnie Zwillman was doing laps on his treadmill when he watched the same newscast that Blondell had seen. He was not bewildered by the reports of the death of Flo March, that troublesome creature—or fucking cunt, as he was more likely to call her—but he was utterly bewildered by the reports of an unidentified man running wildly away from the scene of the crime. It bothered him enough to turn off the treadmill and go to the telephone in his workout room.

"What the fuck is going on?" he asked when the person whom he dialed answered.

"They arrested the wrong guy," was the answer he received.

Philip Quennell, in custody in the Beverly Hills police station, remained totally calm as he was fingerprinted and booked. His attitude and demeanor were a source of immense annoyance to the policeman, Officer Whitbeck, who had picked him up on Coldwater Canyon and arrested him fleeing from the scene of the crime.

"You're in deep shit, fella," he said more than once.

"No, I'm not," replied Philip. He knew that in time it would be ascertained that Flo March had been dead for several hours by the time he arrived at her house. He knew that Camilla Ebury would give evidence that he had spent the night at her house. At least fifty people would remember that they had seen him at the early morning AA meeting on Robertson Boulevard. Rose Cliveden would swear that she had talked to him on Robertson Boulevard at seven-twenty. His car would be discovered parked on Robertson Boulevard, and the taxi driver of the Beverly Hills cab would be located and have on his log the hour that he had driven Philip to the house on Azelia Way.

"I think it's highly unlikely that I would have suggested taking Officer Whitbeck back to the house on Azelia Way if it had been I who crashed in her head," Philip said to the captain.

"Get yourself a lawyer and tell him your story," said Captain Nelson.

On the television news, a detective from homicide determined the cause of Flo March's death as multiple skull fractures and intercerebral hemorrhage due to blunt force trauma. He said it was not simply a blow that had killed Miss March, but blows, many blows. He estimated nine. Pauline Mendelson watched on the television set in her library. The detective described the blows as gaping blunt lacerations of the scalp. More than one of the blows, possibly as many as four, would have been sufficient to kill, although it was believed that the fatal blow was one to the left side of the head, over the ear. The face of the young woman was, by contrast, relatively unmarked. Robbery was immediately ruled out as a motive, as a yellow diamond earring, thought to be of considerable value, remained in one ear lobe, and a sapphire ring, smashed by the murder weapon, remained on the victim's ring finger. There were multiple lacerations on both hands, as well as fractures of the fingers of both hands.

"They have arrested Philip Quennell," said Sims Lord, later.

"Philip Quennell! No, that couldn't be true," said Pauline, in disbelief.

"It's true. They found him running down Coldwater Canyon away from the house."

"That doesn't mean he killed her."

"People do not speak well of him."

"What sort of people?"

"Casper Stieglitz, the producer, for one. Marty Lesky, the head of Colossus Pictures, for another. And Jules, you must know, despised him."

"That doesn't mean he killed her," repeated Pauline. "I don't believe it." She rose and walked around the library. "Oh, my God. How could this happen? Do you know something, Sims? If I had paid Flo March the lousy million dollars she wanted, none of this would have happened." She went to the telephone.

"Who are you calling?"

"Camilla Ebury."

In the weeks of his residence there, Lonny Edge had never felt comfortable in Beverly Hills. Even in the privacy of the secluded house on Azelia Way, people in such lowly capacities as the man who cleaned the swimming pool had looked askance at him when he paraded nude by the pool, and Trent Muldoon, the television star, had given him the same kind of disapproving look when he answered the door with only a towel wrapped around his middle. Lonny Edge was not used to indifference when he showed his disrobed body. He felt slighted when he did not observe desire in the eye of his beholder.

"They're a big bunch of snobs in Beverly Hills," he complained during that time to his friends at the Viceroy Coffee Shop. "Even the cops in Beverly Hills have attitude."

When the cops from Beverly Hills knocked on the door and identified themselves at 7204¼ Cahuenga Boulevard, accompanied by their fellow officers from the station house on La Brea, Lonny Edge was nervous at first, thinking that his immoral past had caught up with him.

"Just a moment," he yelled out, tearing down from the wall the poster from his best-known video, *Hard, Harder, Hardest,* in which his jeans were revealingly dropped to his pubic hair.

"Yes?" he said, when he opened the door.

"May we come in?" asked Captain Nelson.

"Yeah. What's the matter?"

"We wanted to ask you some questions."

"About what?"

"Flo March."

His relief knew no bounds. "Oh, Flo. Sure, I know Flo. She's my roommate. Not exactly roommate, per se. Housemate is a better word for it. Why?"

"When did you see her last?"

"Last night I saw her. Why? I've been living there in her house on Azelia Way. But we were moving out today. I better get over there. The movers were coming by ten. She was supposed to be here last night. I don't know why she didn't come, and the phone is out of order, or disconnected, or something, I don't know what. I didn't want her to stay alone there last night, because she was depressed and all. What's this all about? You know who Flo March is, don't you?" He said her name as if it were the name of a movie star that they should recognize. "She's been in all the papers. She was the mistress of Jules Mendelson. You know, the billionaire? With all the art? A close personal friend of a lot of the Presidents. Lived up on top of the mountain, at the estate called Clouds? You know of Pauline Mendelson? The socialite?"

The police officers stared at Lonny. Finally, Captain Nelson spoke. "Would you come with us, please, Mr. Edge?"

"Where?"

"To the Beverly Hills police station."

"Hey, what the fuck is this, man?"

"Just routine questioning," said Officer Whitbeck.

"You can't routine question here? What are my neighbors going to say, me going out of here with a whole posse of cops?"

As the two policemen approached him, Lonny made a dash for the front door. One of the two leapt after Lonny in a pantherlike motion and made a lunge for him, grasping him around the chest from behind.

"What's going on here?" screamed Lonny, fighting off the assault.

When he was subdued, the officers jerked his hands behind his back and clamped handcuffs on his wrists. Another knelt on the floor and clamped shackles on his feet.

"How come you killed your girlfriend, Lonny?" asked Officer Whitbeck.

"Flo? Flo's dead? Oh, no. Oh, Flo. Oh, no. You're not going to pin this on me. No way. I know too much about all these people. Pauline Mendelson's son killed Hector Paradiso. Kippie Petworth, that's his name," he screamed. With one officer on each side of him, they pulled him out the door and across the courtyard to the stairs that went down to Cahuenga Boulevard. "I saw him. I was there. Kippie Petworth, Pauline Mendelson's son, shot Hector five times, and Jules Mendelson covered it up and told the world it was a suicide. That's why they killed Flo March. She knew. She knew too much."

"The guy's nuts," said Officer Whitbeck to Captain Nelson.

When Glyceria, Flo's friend, who had helped her pack to move, showed up for work at Faye Converse's house, she was immediately made aware of the dire happenings in the house next door. By that time Flo's body had been removed to the morgue, and the news of her death was in every newspaper and newscast. Two men in two separate jails had been booked for the murder. The driveway in front of Flo's house was filled with reporters, some of whom peeked in the windows.

Avoiding them, Glyceria made her way to the back of the house, to the swimming pool area where she used to sit with Flo in the early days of their friendship, when little Astrid brought them together. It surprised her that the sliding glass door with the smashed window was ajar. She wondered why there was not a police guard on duty, or why a house where a murder had taken place was not sealed.

For a six-hour period, two men in two separate jails were booked for the same murder. When finally Philip Quennell was released from the Beverly Hills jail, with abject apologies for having been wrongfully booked, he emerged into a glare of television lights and strobe cameras. His money and credit cards and watch and cuff links were still in the sealed manila envelope that the arresting officer had handed back to him as he was discharged. His tie had been lost. He felt soiled and looked weary as the reporters crowded around him.

"Flo March was my friend," he said. "I am heartbroken that her life has ended in this terrible way."

"Are you bitter that you were falsely arrested?"

"No."

"Are you going to sue?"

"No."

"What was it like to discover her body?" asked a reporter.

Philip sheltered his eyes from the bright lights of the television camera. As he looked past the crowd of media people surrounding him, he saw Camilla sitting quietly on a bench watching him.

"Excuse me," said Philip as he pushed through the reporters and made his way to where Camilla was. "Am I glad to see you."

"Oh, Philip. Are you all right?"

"Let's get out of here," he said.

"They towed your car, but I was able to get your bags."

On the steps outside, he said, "I'm really glad you were there. I can't tell you how much it means to me. I want to hug you and kiss you, but I don't want to have them take our picture at the same time. Do you know what I feel like?"

"Crying?"

"That's right. How'd you know that?"

"Because I love you. Come on. My car's in the lot," said Camilla.

He took hold of her hand and they headed for the parking lot. "There's something I must ask you," he said.

"What?"

"When you heard I had been arrested."

"Yes?"

"Did you think it was true? That I killed her?"

"No. Not for an instant."

Flo's Tape #29

"Lonny's expecting me over at his little bungalow on Cahuenga, but I really want to spend my last night here in this house. God, how I love this house. What memories, including the lousy ones, but that's what makes a house a home. I wanted to think about Jules in private, because after tomorrow, when the moving men come, everything's going to be different for me. Sure, he had a lot of faults, but he was good to me. If I had it all to do over again, knowing what I know now, would I still have gone with Jules? I think about that a lot, and I've finally come to an answer. Yeah, I would."

====== 30 ======

N OT A SINGLE SOUL, except for Philip Quennell, who made the arrangements, knew that Camilla Ebury paid for the cost of Flo March's cremation and burial in the Westwood cemetery.

Ina Rae attended every day of Lonny Edge's three-week trial. She was
distressed that he was so pale and thin and listless, but she reported to Darlene
that he was as handsome as ever and always seemed pleased to see her in the
courtroom. Throughout the trial, Archbishop Cooning, who was militant on
morality, preached from the pulpit of Saint Vibiana's on the tragic life of Flo
March. The archbishop did not blame her alleged killer, Lonny Edge. The
archbishop laid the blame directly on the late billionaire who had corrupted
the young woman and led her into a life of luxury and entrapment. Poor Jules,
his friends said in private. It was a good thing he was dead, so he didn't have to
hear what the archbishop had to say. He always hated to have his name in the
newspapers.

It was as if Lonny Edge's life mattered less because he had been involved
in what was considered an unacceptable style of existence. He now resides in
San Quentin, and will remain there, in all probability, for the rest of his life,
which is not expected to be a long time. There have been rumors that he has a
fatal disease. It has been reported that he looks more than twice his age and
weighs but a fraction of what he weighed when he appeared in his pornographic videos, and that lesions cover his once-handsome face.

Nothing has gone right for Lonny. The lawyers for the publisher of Basil
Plant's lost manuscript of *Candles at Lunch* argued successfully in court that
the manuscript had been stolen before Basil Plant's death, and that Lonny was
due no payment whatever. This was particularly distressing to Marv Pink, the
lawyer who agreed to represent him on the condition that 50 percent of the
proceeds from the sale of the manuscript be turned over to him. The book will
finally be published in the spring. There is great interest in it from both the
book clubs and the movies.

Philip Quennell has visited Lonny in San Quentin several times. Philip is
one of many who do not believe that Lonny killed Flo March, but that he
merely left the door to her house open that night in order to allow unnamed

people to enter and search for her tapes, believing that she would be in his apartment on Cahuenga Boulevard at the time.

"Lonny's fingerprints were not on the murder weapon," he said over and over to no avail. It was not a point that was stressed in the courtroom. He could never understand why so little was made of the fact that the drawers and packing cases in Flo's house had been ransacked. Lonny Edge had lived in the house, and wouldn't have needed to ransack anything. One of the many things Philip could not figure out was why one of the cushions of Flo March's gray satin sofa was missing. The tapes, if they existed, and Philip Quennell believes they did exist, have never been found.

Kippie Petworth has not come to the bad end that Arnie Zwillman and the headmasters at several fashionable schools predicted he would. At least, as yet. He has become the young lover of Mrs. Reza Bulbenkian, who dotes on him completely and keeps him in very smart style in an apartment on Beekman Place in New York. Yvonne pays a publicist to keep her name in the papers, praising her parties and her clothes, and to keep Kippie's name out. Her husband, Reza, of course, is totally unaware of the arrangement.

Kippie's mother, Pauline Mendelson, became Lady St. Vincent, and lives at Kilmartin Abbey in Wiltshire. There is no contact between mother and son. She brought with her very few reminders of her past life, other than the vast Mendelson fortune, which was now hers, and two artworks that she did not sell. She tried to hang van Gogh's *White Roses* in several locations of her new home, but it seemed inappropriate among the Canalettos in the drawing room, and out of place among the Raphael drawings that lined the walls of the library. The insurance company disallowed it to be hung in any of the hallways, for security reasons, or in any of the rooms that the public was allowed to wander through on visiting days. Finally, Lord St. Vincent suggested to Pauline that she hang it on the wall of her morning room, where she attended to her correspondence, menus, and invitations each day, but she found the picture too overpowering for the small room, as her attention was constantly drawn to it for the memories it evoked of the twenty-two years it had hung over the fireplace in the library at Clouds. She did not wish to sell it, because of the attention it would cause on the international art market, and donating it to one of the many museums that had craved its possession would also have attracted the kind of media coverage that would resurrect the history of her previous marriage and the brutal death of Flo March. Finally, she had it wrapped in blankets and tied with twine. It has been placed in one of the storage rooms of the abbey, along with the great silver pieces that have not been brought out since the wedding of Lord St. Vincent's daughter nine years ago.

The last time Philip Quennell saw Pauline St. Vincent, she was seated in the backseat of a Daimler in Beauchamp Place in London, staring straight ahead. He was sure that she saw him, but she gave no sign.

Clouds was sold to a Japanese who had lately become involved in the motion picture industry, having purchased Marty Lesky's Colossus Pictures. Mr. Ishiguro's plans for the beautiful house were more grandiose by far than anything the Mendelsons had ever dreamed. An indoor ice skating rink and a bowling alley were but two of the planned additions. In time Mr. Ishiguro came to feel that it would be less expensive to tear down the house and build again on the same site. The house has now been leveled, although the kennels and the greenhouses remain. Construction on the new house is expected to be completed in three years.

About the Author

In addition to the three novels in this collections, all of which were *New York Times* bestsellers, DOMINICK DUNNE is the author of *Season in Purgatory*, *The Winners*, and *Mansions in Limbo* and *Fatal Charms*, two collections of his essays from *Vanity Fair*, where he is a contributing editor.

Mr. Dunne also produced the films *The Panic in Needle Park*, *Ash Wednesday*, *Play It As It Lays*, and *The Boys in the Band*. Mr. Dunne lives in New York City.